SOUTHERN MAN

ALSO BY GREG ILES

SOUTHERN MAN

A Novel

GREG ILES

WM
WILLIAM MORROW
An Imprint of HarperCollins*Publishers*

SOUTHERN MAN. Copyright © 2024 by Greg Iles. All rights reserved. Printed in the United States of America. No part of this book may be used or reproduced in any manner whatsoever without written permission except in the case of brief quotations embodied in critical articles and reviews. For information, address HarperCollins Publishers, 195 Broadway, New York, NY 10007.

HarperCollins books may be purchased for educational, business, or sales promotional use. For information, please email the Special Markets Department at SPsales@harpercollins.com.

FIRST EDITION

Designed by Leah Carlson-Stanisic
Illustration by Matt Gibson/Shutterstock, Inc.

Library of Congress Cataloging-in-Publication Data has been applied for.

ISBN 978-0-06-282469-1 (hardcover)
ISBN 978-0-06-282486-8 (international edition)

24 25 26 27 28 LBC 5 4 3 2 1

For
Elliot Hungerford Iles
Our own personal Transformer

They were the sort of people that lynch negroes, that mistake hoodlumism for wit, and cunning for intelligence, that attend revivals and fight and fornicate in the bushes afterwards. They were undiluted Anglo-Saxons. They were the sovereign voter. It was so horrible it seemed unreal.

WILLIAM ALEXANDER PERCY
LANTERNS ON THE LEVEE, 1941

In this world goodness is destined to be defeated. But a man must go down fighting. That is the victory. To do anything less is to be less than a man.

WALKER PERCY
THE MOVIEGOER, 1961

SOUTHERN MAN

Thursday

CHAPTER 1

THE HIGHEST-PAID POLITICAL consultant in America disembarked from his Cessna Citation at Medgar Evers Field in Jackson, Mississippi, and slid into a limo that shuttled him toward the white-flight ring of the capital. Rafael Carrera—"Tio" to his clients—savored the irony that he had to remind himself not to drink the public water when visiting the capital city in an American state.

"Mississippi," he muttered. "*Que barrio cochambrosa.*"

Tio Carrera's olive-skinned face had the hard, knowing look of a career gambler's. In his late seventies, his belly now had twice the girth of his shoulders, but he'd been in the game since Nixon in '68, and he had seen everything, forgotten nothing. Tio knew where actual bodies were buried. Cuban by birth, he had been first a Kennedy-lover, then a Kennedy-hater, until he'd given up all conviction and worked for whoever paid best—which was usually Republicans. But woe betide the WASPs who saw him merely as a Florida specialist. Insiders loved telling a story about Tio taking Karl Rove for five figures by bluffing at poker on a late-night plane ride during the Bush-Gore litigation. A few claimed that Tio had been present at the actual Bay of Pigs as a teenager, and nobody was sure if he'd been on the beach or in the boats. In any case, he'd been credited with some of the most devastating negative attacks in the history of American politics, and one thing was sure: if you paid for his opinion, you got it without Vaseline.

Today Tio was flying from Washington, D.C., to Brasilia, Brazil, to advise during the special presidential election, but he'd agreed to touch down in Jackson for sixty minutes to give the two men waiting at Magnolia Star Studios a thumbs-up or -down on a single political ad. He wouldn't normally have bothered with something so small, but the potential candidate in this case intrigued him.

The kid in question—a forty-two-year-old conservative radio host named Robert E. Lee White—had literally come out of nowhere, exploding into the national consciousness after a book by a disgraced Delta Force operator revealed that "Bobby" White had personally killed Abu Nasir El Sherif—second-in-command to Abu Musab al-Zarqawi—during the famous 2008 raid in Afghanistan. White had also lost an arm while doing this. His pitching arm, as it turned out, when America learned that Bobby White—in the tradition of Pat Tillman—had after 9/11 walked away from a Division I baseball scholarship at Ole Miss to enlist in the army and fight Al Qaeda. Better still, the killer of Abu Nasir turned out to be the son of Big Ed White, the Hall of Fame left-hander for the Astros in the 1980s. It was a story an old baseball fanatic like Tio couldn't resist.

As Bobby's biography took shape on social media, mainstream America began to learn what the conservative radio audience already knew: that saving a brief dip when he condemned Trump on January 6, Bobby White had virtually *owned* the Center in conservative morning radio. Media experts believed it was only his refusal to deny the 2020 election results or condemn all abortions that had kept him from taking the number-one spot. White's record as a special ops soldier had always been public, but the Abu Nasir revelation changed everything. His audience had rocketed from eight million to nearly twelve million in the interval since, which put him within spitting distance of Sean Hannity. By the time the GOP donor class learned that he had a law degree from Vanderbilt and had authored two respected nonfiction books on the South and the Lost Cause, they were talking Bobby White up as a national candidate.

But it was TikTok that had truly sparked his meteoric rise, to the point that oddsmakers in Vegas were now giving three-to-one that the kid would announce a third-party presidential run by next week. What made this anything but juvenile fantasy was the army of young foot soldiers who had been relentlessly gathering names to register the war hero by petition on the presidential ballot in every state in the union. Rumor had it that the nascent White campaign had already gathered nearly enough signatures to put their candidate on every ballot in the country in January 2024. What drove those kids Tio didn't know. Bobby White was Hollywood handsome—anyone could see that. But beyond this, all Tio had seen were stunt videos, in which White used jaw-dropping special operations skills to execute extreme physical feats while calmly dissecting issues like bookbanning or the lunacy of arming teachers in grade schools. Tio didn't really get it. But then, he was too old to live by the pulses of his cell phone.

He would see Bobby White in the flesh soon enough.

Tio was a little taken aback by the modest studio that hosted White's radio show, but he'd seen gifted men shake the souls of millions from tiny cubicles before. And the idea that one of the most consequential campaigns of the twenty-first century might go airborne from a small corner of Mississippi was no less likely than it had been in 1980, when Ronald Reagan gave the dog whistle of all time from the Neshoba County Fair. Tio had been there on the day, on that goddamn harness-racing track, forty feet from the candidate, sweating like a pig though he'd been fifty pounds lighter. And who the hell was Reagan then? A former governor. An out-of-work actor.

Wiping his face on his jacket sleeve, Tio walked into the Magnolia Star studio and surveyed the two men who stood waiting in the small reception area. The candidate made an impression up close. Six feet two inches tall, Robert E. Lee White possessed a craggy handsomeness to which no photograph did justice, and his photos were *good*. This kid was what Tio's staff kids called an "American archetype." To a modern audience, the retired master sergeant probably landed somewhere between Matthew McConaughey and George Clooney. But his masculinity quotient was off the charts, with the gravitas of an earlier era, suggesting a young Gregory Peck or even Clark Gable. But Bobby White was no actor; he was the man those actors were *hired to play*. It wasn't hard to see why he'd taken off on the damn TikTok, or whatever it was.

Tio stuck out his pudgy hand—his left, because Sergeant White was missing his right arm from the shoulder down, and he wore no prosthetic. Despite his weight and age, Tio still had considerable strength, but in the grip of the one-armed special forces vet he sensed a power that could have crushed his own, even in his prime.

"War hero cleans up good in person," Tio said, withdrawing his hand with a throb of refilling blood vessels. "That's good. Ben Affleck's got nothing on you, Sergeant."

"Call me Bobby," said his host with an easy smile. White leaned to his left, toward another well-conditioned man of six feet who, if not quite as intimidating, was equally handsome. "This is Corey Evers, my literal right hand, no pun intended."

Tio nodded to the staff man, but Corey's name was already forgotten. "Nice," Tio remarked, touching his own right shoulder. "Pinning your coat sleeve to the shoulder like you do? Reminds me of old Bob Dole. Connects you to that whole generation. And they all vote."

White didn't acknowledge the observation. He knew well the effect the coat sleeve had. He cultivated it.

Tio looked around as though he actually gave a shit about their surroundings. "What a country we live in, right, Sergeant? Two months ago I didn't know your name. Now Vegas is taking three to one you'll announce by the middle of next week. Like you're Ross Perot already. They say you've already met the ballot by petition requirement in thirty-nine states. You've got fanatical ground troops, like none anybody's ever seen. Most kids under twenty-four. But what do I know about this TikTok shit? I saw the video you call 'Don't Be Afraid of History.' Filmed upside down over the damn Grand Canyon, they told me. This crazy country moves faster every hour. So, show me this ad you got. Ads, I understand."

Tio signaled his driver to wait, then followed White and his staff man to a video room, where a stool had been placed before a thirty-two-inch monitor. Tio sat and waited with a neutral expression. He'd seen thousands of political ads, and he had a wise farmer's gift for separating wheat from chaff.

Corey touched a remote, then waited in tense equipoise just one step behind Carrera. On the screen, incandescent light rose over a night street in a rural town—Bruce Springsteen's America. Then the camera tracked in as Bobby White walked through the gleaming doors of the Dixie Grand Theater in Bienville, Mississippi, his old hometown. Though north of forty by the calendar, Bobby still wore his high school baseball jersey with ease, and he cupped a worn Rawlings in his left hand as he smiled through the lens with a born actor's intimacy. He wore no glove on his right hand, because he'd left his pitching arm in a cave in Afghanistan, and by now everybody knew it.

"I like the baseball," Tio murmured. "I saw your old man pitch against the Braves during his final season. He was tough. Lost some money on him."

At this moment Bobby's father lay in the cardiac recovery unit at University Medical Center a few miles away, but he was already enshrined in Cooperstown, his legacy assured. And men like Tio Carrera did not forget.

"It seemed like the natural angle," Corey said.

Tio held up his hand for silence.

"Friday night in a small town," Bobby said to the camera. "Maybe there's an early game. Afterward, you hook up with your friends, drink some beers, hang at the fast food joint, maybe go to the movies. At the theater you pair off, couples go their separate ways. Ritual old as time."

Through some video magic, Bobby strolled through a montage of small-town imagery, his feet crunching on gravel. Soon he stood beside a line of eighties-vintage cars parked on a dark slope beside a river.

"But eventually you all end up down at the same place—the lake or the river. Coziest places in the world, some of those cars."

Bobby tossed the baseball up and down, then turned into the camera and lowered his voice with conspiratorial candor. Behind him at least one of the cars was gently rocking.

"Found out who we were in those cars, didn't we? Sometimes . . . we even got lucky." Bobby grinned. "But sometimes we *didn't* get so lucky.

Sometimes we got in a bind. In *trouble*. And when that happened . . . who paid the price? You and your boys? Nope. If you lived in the kind of town I did—or you lived in my mom and pop's time, especially—it was the *girls* who paid the price. The *girls* who got stuck in these tired old towns, becoming worn-out housewives at nineteen, when they could've been doctors or lawyers or God knows what else."

A car door opened, and a young woman climbed out with an infant wrapped tightly at her breast. She walked dejectedly off along the road as though looking for a ride.

Bobby stopped tossing the baseball. "Too many men in Washington have got the wrong end of the stick on this problem, folks. We all know it. Hell, they don't know what they want themselves, other than a fundraising issue. But I know one thing about women: *They deserve the same chance we get in this life. No more, no less.*"

More car doors opened, and trim young women in white medical coats and business suits climbed out and walked up toward the road reading charts or holding cell phones to their ears.

Bobby stepped closer to the camera as though winding up for a hard throw. "It's time to leave all the Sunday school stuff in church, fellas. Because any society that tries to hold half its members in domestic servitude has only got one future in my book:

"Lights *out*."

With a *whoosh* like a catapult, Bobby White fired his left arm into the darkness, and 150 feet away a streetlight exploded into a shower of sparks worthy of a Hollywood feature film. Tio jerked on the stool, but it was impossible to read his reaction from behind as the screen went black. Good or bad, it had been visceral.

A production team could have faked the exploding light shot, of course, but they hadn't. Even if they had, Bobby knew how the American male thought. Any one-armed vet who could HALO jump onto the roof of a Mississippi Delta hospital to dramatize its imminent closure due to lack of Medicaid expansion—or make fifteen-hundred-meter sniper shots to check off his to-do list—as Bobby had done on YouTube and TikTok— could sure as hell bust out a streetlight with a baseball.

"Well?" Corey asked anxiously.

The feared consultant's voice came back hard and flat. "You crazy bastards aren't thinking about asking for revocation of the Second Amendment in your next ad, are you?"

"We hadn't planned on it," Bobby replied.

"Good. Because I thought you were Republicans. Baby steps, okay? Even for crazy bastards who want to start a revolution. *Dios mio . . .*"

"So, what do you think?" Corey prodded.

"*Esta volado.*" Tio Carrera spun slowly on the stool and looked at Bobby with something like admiration—which appeared to be a rare emotion for him. "Sergeant White, if I were thirty years younger and a woman, I'd fuck you myself."

"Is that what we're going for here?" Bobby asked.

"It never hurts, my friend."

"So . . . you think we run with it?"

Tio folded his arms and mulled over the question like a man who didn't have a would-be dictator waiting for him in South America. "How old are you boys? Forty? Forty-five?"

They nodded in unison.

"Do you remember Edwin Edwards? Democratic governor across the river? Colorful guy, old school."

"I remember him," Bobby said. "He came out to the house once. My dad knew him."

Tio chuckled fondly. "Edwin used to fly his campaign plane to Las Vegas with a briefcase full of cash and hooch. Some flights maybe a pistol or two. And the women? *Tremenda manguita.* Ask James Carville, he can tell you stories. Anyway . . . after Edwin got his ass in hot water in Korea and elsewhere, he ran for a third term. And he had a saying."

"'Unless they catch me in bed with a dead girl or a live boy,'" Corey said, "'I'm going to win again.'"

Tio looked at Corey with fresh eyes. "I'm gonna give you boys my gut, as crazy as it sounds. Looking at Sergeant White here, and knowing his record, I feel like an old atheist tasting his first breeze of faith in a generation—maybe the last before he dies. A hell of a wave is building under you. And the field is weak this time out. Trump clones, wannabe Nazis, QAnon conspiracy nuts, brownshirt governors, a token *prieto* . . . and Trump's liable to burn down the whole party, if they give him half a reason. Bobby here is the only candidate who never took a lick of shit off Donald. You called the son of a bitch a traitor on January 6 and you never wavered. Never gave an inch, so far as my staff can find."

Tio licked his lips as though working the plan out in front of them. "In '92 Perot proved a third-party run is viable—even a last-minute one. And in 2016 Donald proved *anything* is possible. With this TikTok insanity my interns and media staff keep telling me about—they say you're breaking all kinds of records—those stunt videos of yours are turning you into some kind of combination of Elvis and the Beatles."

Corey grinned at the dated references.

Tio shrugged. "I'm old, I get it." He clapped Bobby on his shoulder, squeezing the thick pad of muscle. "But *you*, my friend, seem to be that rara avis—the full package. Military service always gives candidates a halo, though it's never enough by itself. Carrying a rifle can't get Buttigieg over the queer hump, and we've already had two draft dodgers win the goddamn Oval. Right? But *you*, Sergeant? You crept into the heart of darkness, mano-a-mano, and killed the beast. And *you never even claimed credit*. That's the kicker. That's the John Wayne center of it all. You're an old-school hero. You've got *humility*. Vanishing breed." Tio leaned back and fixed Bobby with a basilisk stare. "So long as you don't have an Edwin Edwards problem."

"You don't think we're going too far, coming out pro-choice like this?" Bobby asked.

"You don't . . . do you?" Tio pressed. The consultant's glassy eyes seemed almost lidless as they peered into Bobby's. "Have that kind of problem?"

"No dead girls or live boys," Bobby said with an easy laugh.

Tio nodded as though only half-convinced. Clearly he'd been burned before. "Just making sure. Best to know early, I've found."

"What about Bobby's ad?" Corey asked. "How big a slice of the Right do we lose by going at the issue this hard?"

Tio shrugged. "Two schools of thought. One, Dobbs lost us the midterms. You don't give women something for fifty years, then snatch it back. This ad here buys you back a *lot* of goodwill."

"And the other school?" Corey asked.

Tio laughed like a Cuban Santa Claus. "What the hell do you care? Third-party run, your odds of winning are shit anyway, so why not campaign on what you really think?"

Bobby grinned. "That's a strategy I understand. Fastballs right down the middle."

"Only one glaring negative I see," Tio said with a look of displeasure. "You gotta know it, right?"

Corey shrugged.

"No Jackie O."

"And no kids," Bobby said.

Tio nodded. "What's the story? I can't believe there's not at least one rice-strewn ex–homecoming queen in your past. All-American stud like you? I read your CV three times on the plane to be sure I hadn't missed an early divorce."

Bobby shrugged. "I saw a lot of guys make mistakes early on. Didn't want to do the same."

Tio tilted his round head. "Not sure how I feel about that. Part of the country won't be, either. They like stability."

"In your experience," Corey interjected, "does marriage provide stability?"

Tio gave him a withering glare. "It's still America, kid. They like tradition. Perception is everything." The consultant returned his focus to Bobby. "So, I only got one other question. And given what I've seen today, it's a killer. How the *hell* are you going to bring the QAnon crazies into this third-party tent of yours long enough to get them to vote for you? You may nail every suburban GOP housewife in America with this ad. You've got the Center Right from your radio audience. But a hard fifty-one percent are stone-cold MAGA rats who'll vote for Donald for president in an orange jumpsuit in solitary confinement—how you gonna get them, Sergeant? Because you're going to need every one of 'em to win."

Bobby felt the heavy burden of expectation shift onto him. "I'm not worried about Trump."

Tio mocked a look of being impressed. "No? Your war hero bit goes a long way with that crowd, but not far enough. Not when you're spouting pro-choice from their TVs and calling January 6 straight-up treason."

"Have you ever been to a Trump rally, Tio? I mean, out in the heartland?"

"No."

"I have. You know what Trumpers love more than anything? What really gets their motors spinning? *Violence.* Trump, too, or so he thinks. Well, unlike Diaper Don, I'm an expert on that subject. I am intimately acquainted with violence, from every side. And that makes me a viable substitute candidate for him—the *only one*, in fact, for those voters. Trump knows it. And that's why I terrify him."

Tio stared at the young candidate with new appreciation. "You know what I know, don't you, Sergeant? Even the dumbest Republican advisers have figured out the skinny on the next election. There's only one way they win. *White panic.* Because if white America doesn't vote as a block this time out, the GOP *can't* win. Not without stealing it."

Bobby shared an uncomfortable look with Corey. He'd figured this out some time ago. "Agreed. So what are you telling us?"

"Accept that as fact, then forget it. Because *somebody's* going to find a way to provide that fear. A summer of chaos. Riots from Baltimore to Watts. Who knows over what? The next George Floyd. Who cares? Look at that shooting in Memphis last week. Second time this year up there. Protests spreading across the country as we speak. That's just a taste of what's coming. The background of the next election."

"Are you that sure?" Corey asked.

Tio looked at him like the original sucker. "The white elite in America *needs* riots, sonny. Looting-level chaos is the only hot glue that can bind the winning block I mentioned. And given recent history, I doubt anyone will even have to manipulate the Blacks into it. The cops in some city will screw up by default. You're too young to remember the summer of '67. The Long, Hot Summer. A hundred and fifty race riots, cities on fire from coast to coast. Eighty-three dead by September. Detroit and Newark were battle zones. I think that's coming down the pike again. Maybe bigger this time. Take it from me. There's no critical mass like white anger plus white panic."

Bobby's eyes shone the way they did when his team had been planning ops in the TOC back in the Sandbox. "I'm with you. Go on."

"Not before you tell me a secret, Sergeant. What are these white people so angry about?"

Bobby grinned. "Hard to figure for you, I'll bet. But to me it's plain as piss on a dress boot. They're being forced to face the fact that no one ever had it easier than their people. They were raised to believe nobody ever worked harder for success than their grandpaw or memaw, or their fourth ancestor up the line who came over from God-knows-where and fought for every scrap they got. But the truth is, they had it better than any immigrants anywhere ever did. *Everybody* else had it tougher. Except the Melania Trumps of the world. The refusal to let go of that myth. . . . That's the root of white privilege, and of the threat to democracy. The irrational hell we're living through now."

The old Cuban nodded with both approbation and worry. "You're not going to win any new white voters with that pitch."

"We'll see. I know those people. I came from them. Unlike their orange Ozymandias."

Tio got up from the stool, which didn't raise his height by much, but this did nothing to diminish his personal intensity. "Well, here's *my* take on what's coming. You've been to war, Sergeant. Anybody with a match can start a fire. But it's not *starting* fires that gets you the White House this time out. It's *putting them out*. Every GOP candidate will compete to exploit the coming battle. The role you need to be ready to step into is that of another vanishing breed—a possibly extinct specimen."

"Which is?"

Tio smiled with genuine pleasure. "*Statesman*. Don't just be the law-and-order man. Be the law-and-order man with a *vision*."

"Law and order's good enough for most white people," Corey observed.

"Order's enough for most," Tio conceded. "That's the root of Donald's appeal. But people like to feel good about themselves, too. Figure a way to help them do that, you might even pick up a few Black votes along the way."

"I plan to," Bobby asserted. "Wait till you see my plan to transform the Mississippi Delta into the Imperial Valley of the east."

Policy plans went right past Tio Carrera. "You've *got* some Black friends, I assume? Real ones? Army buddies?"

"Sure. My catcher on our state championship baseball team was Black. He's one of my best friends."

Tio gave Bobby a hard look. "Just make sure that's the last time you call him *my* catcher. I hate to piss on your party, boys, but you're gonna have to start paying attention to the little things from now on."

"What about money?" Bobby asked.

Tio waved his hand as though he had brought up popcorn concessions. "Don't worry about that right now. If you're really the man of the moment, the golden boy, the dollars will flow to you. You just need seed money to start. A hundred million. Two hundred's better." Tio checked his watch, then glanced at the door for his driver. "You got a source for that?"

"Yeah." Bobby looked uncomfortably at Corey. "I think so."

"Good. Well . . . *Me voy*. I've got a date with the Concrete Christ."

"You advise down there a lot, huh?" Corey commented.

"Less and less, thank God. But every time I try to beg off, they up my fee. Things are getting crazy down there. I don't know about global warming, but if that rain forest they got is really the oxygen factory for the planet, we're in trouble. I see less of it from the window every time I fly down."

"Maybe you ought to support some different candidates," Corey suggested.

Tio snorted. "I live on Jupiter Island, sonny. Just down the road from Tiger Woods. They don't give that sand away."

The consultant walked to the door, turned the knob, then looked back over his shoulder. "So . . . have you boys already gathered the signatures to register as an independent on the ballots in all fifty states? Because if you have, and I knew that, I could make a hell of a killing."

"I'm going to make coffee now," Corey said, using an English version of the Cuban hint that it was time for a guest to leave.

Carrera's face darkened for a moment, but then he smiled. "You sons of bitches. I think you've already got the names. I think this TikTok thing is bigger than I've got my head around."

"Could be," Corey teased.

"I'm glad I came today. You boys give me that old tingle on the back of my neck." The old man dropped his hand from the doorknob. "You know, I was with Reagan in '80 when he spoke at the Neshoba County Fair, not two hours east of here. He started the Republican Revolution right here. That nervy bastard talked states' rights not ten miles from where the Ku Klux Klan buried those three civil rights workers in the dam. And from that moment on, he had the right wing with him."

Tio held up two thick fingers. "Two lessons there. *One*, you gotta have some big balls to play this game. And *two* . . . one way or another, you gotta bring the Right with you." Tio jabbed his finger at Bobby's chest. "*That's* your job now, Sergeant."

"How about you get some of your Miami buddies to bump some of Trump's free coverage off Univision? Then maybe we can do some business."

Tio Carrera smiled like an old wizard. "Alas, my powers are great, but they have limits. *Chao pescao!*"

And with that, he vanished from their lives, leaving only an astounding bill as evidence that he had ever been there.

"Jupiter Island," Corey said, staring at the door. "He'd clear-cut the rain forest so he can keep living on Jupiter Island."

"Next to Tiger Woods," Bobby said with a grin. "What a character, though. Huh?"

"He did have one tough question. How are you going to bring the QAnon crazies into our camp long enough to get them to vote for you?"

Bobby nodded.

"You sounded like you're reconciled to the kind of street warfare he's predicting."

"You and I can't stop that, Cor."

Corey had hoped for more, but he didn't press it. "Oh, I got a text from your mom while Carrera was here. Some more enzyme tests came back on your dad's heart. He's still stable, but they want to keep him in the unit another night."

Bobby clucked his tongue. "Okay."

"She also said to tell you Penn Cage's mother is sinking fast. She had a stroke on top of her cancer treatment, and she's unconscious. I don't know why Frances thinks you'd be interested in that, as busy as you are."

"Small towns, Natchez and Bienville. Penn went to school with my dad, and he had a big career as a prosecutor and author. He was mayor of Natchez, too."

"He also just won a record-breaking verdict in that environmental suit against Triton Chemical. But I didn't know your families were that close."

"It's the South, Cor. People being born, marrying, cheating, dying . . . that's what we talk about. I hate to hear that about Mrs. Cage, though. She's a classy lady, and her husband was old school. Dr. Cage stitched up my ankle once during a game after a guy cleated me. Right in the dugout. You think these doctors now would risk that? Too afraid of being sued."

"I'll send them something."

"Don't. I'll speak to Penn after she passes."

Corey looked surprised. "And the ad video?"

Bobby made a fist and pumped it. "We're going with it. Every GOP senator who ever paid for an abortion is going to wish he'd made it first. Also—call the Belle Rose Country Club people. They can put me down for the PGA pro-am in Bienville next week. I'm committing. I'll do those commentary pieces for the Golf Channel, too, straight through the weekend."

"Are you serious?"

Bobby smiled, and his eyes glinted. "Southern presidents have hometowns, Corey. Plains . . . Hope. It's time I pressed a little flesh."

Corey's eyes narrowed. "When Tio asked you if you could get a hundred million dollars, and you told him yes, I nearly shat myself."

Bobby chuckled. "You need some time in the bathroom?"

"What the hell were you talking about? Who's your source for that kind of bread?"

Bobby didn't reply.

Corey's face showed exasperation, but then his eyes went wide. "You're thinking about Charles Dufort, aren't you? You're thinking about the Poker Club. That's why you want to visit Bienville."

Bobby's smile let Corey know he was on the right track. "We'll talk about it. Let's sketch out tomorrow's show and get out of here."

Corey shook his head. "You liked Tio, didn't you?"

"'They don't give that sand away,'" Bobby repeated, laughing. "I'll bet he *was* at the Bay of Pigs. That SOB has got the look. You know?"

Corey gave a reluctant nod. A veteran of military intelligence himself, he knew the look Bobby was talking about. The world-weary expression of men who had seen the elephant. "I didn't like what he said about the riots. Summer of chaos? Cities on fire? He sounded pretty damned sure."

"He knows his business. And I don't think he's wrong. We've got six months to plan for a desperate summer—the last spasm of white America before the demographics turn against us forever. That's when the election will be decided. Most people warning about a second Civil War don't know shit about the first one. But it's going to get rough. I feel that in my bones."

Saturday

CHAPTER 2

NOTHING IS STILL but the dead.

The wind, the earth, the sun and stars, the twitch of the nerve, the whispering rush of blood through the vein, the snake coiled on the sand, the hibernating bear, all are in motion, save those settling toward death, as is the woman on the bed before me, my mother, eighty-six now but soon to be no more, and I . . . I must follow her sooner than she knew, and by the same route, the same dread affliction.

But first . . .

THE CHAOS THAT Tio Carrera predicted in Bobby White's studio arrived much sooner than promised. Only five days after the consultant flew on to Brazil, a historic antebellum mansion in Natchez, Mississippi, called Tranquility exploded into flame and burned to the ground, leaving only haunting columns smoldering in the dusk. Later that night, a second mansion went up, and that time a graphic note claiming responsibility for both fires was nailed to the dewy courthouse door. Drawn on the inside of a vintage LP jacket—Tupac Shakur's *Strictly 4 My N.I.G.G.A.Z.*—was a Black fist bearing a broken shackle on its wrist. Below the fist someone had stapled a printed note declaring the arsons to be but the first in a series of retributive strikes for both police misconduct and centuries of oppression. The note was signed: *The Bastard Sons of the Confederacy.* Under this signature appeared a long list of names, which turned out to be those of locally lynched Black men that dated back to 1861. (More than fifty of these had died less than two miles from the house I grew up in as a boy—something I didn't learn until I was past fifty—but that's a matter for later in these pages.)

For America, this was a new crime under the sun: domestic terror clothed in the garb of historical retribution. The scale and effect of the blow were shattering. News of the "Bastard Sons" and their Black fist swept through the Magnolia State like a storm, spurring condemnation from the governor down to local mayors, and out into the digital hinterlands of social media. White supremacist militias in all eighty-two counties issued warnings of apocalyptic revenge, and when the Bastard Sons made good on their threat of additional strikes, the militias began pushing Natchez and nearby Bienville inexorably toward war in the streets. The very night

Tranquility burned, a sheriff's deputy torched a Black country church as payback, and that was only the start of what was to come.

The Bastard Sons had chosen their first target well.

Unlike so many of Natchez's antebellum mansions, which had long ago been sold to out-of-towners, Tranquility remained the ancestral home of perhaps the richest man in the state—the attorney, energy speculator, and well-known GOP donor Charles Dufort. Dufort's most famous ancestor had helped Natchez survive the Civil War intact, by supporting Abraham Lincoln and opposing secession. (He'd also enslaved more than a thousand Africans on his five plantations, but that astonishing irony is also best dealt with later.) Charles Dufort represented for many the last in an unbroken line of educated "Southern gentlemen" who still existed with honor under the long shadow of the Civil War. Thus, for many whites across the country, the intentional burning of Tranquility represented an attack on History Itself, and on the unspoken hierarchy that defined their sense of place in America.

But the Tranquility fire didn't happen in a vacuum. Three days before Dufort's mansion lit up the Natchez skyline, the deadliest local tragedy since the Rhythm Club fire of 1940 had sent the Black community reeling, leaving twenty-one dead and the Tenisaw County Sheriff's Department buried in civil litigation. This incident—now dubbed the Mission Hill massacre—also touched my family in the most destructive way, and still shrouds us in mourning as we wait to watch my mother pass. It was probably naïve for the white community to think such a terrible slaughter could occur without some retaliatory consequence, especially in the post–George Floyd world. Yet I was present at Mission Hill when the fusillade of bullets did their damage, and I didn't imagine anything like the Tranquility fire as a possible result.

If the nation's attention had not been focused on Memphis—the eye of America's most recent racial hurricane—some of the resulting violence might have been averted. But the national lens was aimed upriver, and consequently civil order in southwest Mississippi unspooled at a rate that made almost any atrocity possible. In the shotgun shacks of the Black quarters where some fathers still rode horses to work in 2023, and in the mobile homes where the white trash cooked the meth, old folks began muttering that it felt more like 1965 than the twenty-first century. Tio Carrera would have told them that where race in America was concerned, the twenty-first century might soon make 1965 look like a warm-up bout for the main event.

Unknown to anyone, the man Tio had made his prophecy to—retired sergeant Bobby White, the hero who dreamed of saving America from itself—was already on his way to our little corner of the republic, the corner from which he had sprung forty-two years earlier. His public arrival—the baseball star who blew out the brains of Abu Nasir—would forever alter the course of history in the two counties and the Louisiana parish in which I not so long ago fought the murderous legacy forces of the KKK and the Double Eagle group, losing loved ones and family members in the process.

Until 2016, I had believed that battle mostly done.

Then the patients took over the asylum.

I watched in disbelief as businessmen voted for a repeat bankrupt, laborers for a boss infamous for stiffing his workers, evangelicals for a serial adulterer, women for an admitted sexual assaulter, patriots for a draft dodger who would sell his country's secrets for trivial gain, educated men for an ignoramus. But they did so with fierce gladness in their hearts. Because what their chosen one had done was open Pandora's box—yes, the old one, filled with the ancient calamities of race hatred and rage and cruelty and bloodlust and infinite greed—and tell them that these things were the remedy for all their grievances, that all their anger was justified, and most important: *None of what ailed them was their own fault—or ever had been.*

They took to that like infants to a honeyed tit.

The problem, as any midwife can tell you, is that honey can kill babies under a year old. It carries botulism spores, lethal to those without antibodies. The gospel of Trump is just as lethal, and unlike poisoned honey, highly contagious. Worst of all, it demands an adversary . . . as all great stories do.

The Other.

Once you accept this equation of fault and blame, the road to war is a short one. And somewhere an enthusiastic engineer is designing new prisons, and the ovens that will wait at the end of the tracks.

Forgive me if I'm screwing up the sequence of events, or not making sense at all. I've been having trouble with time lately. I haven't really slept for days, except for brief naps in the chair beside my mother's rented hospital bed. Losing your first parent is a stunning blow, jarring to the soul. But losing your last truly orphans you, unmooring you from the past, destabilizing your sense of self.

I am and remain Penn Cage. I can keep that much in my head, even after swallowing two oxycodone pills from my mother's hospice supply. But I'm not the man you remember, the man I once was—if I ever was. I'm no longer the mayor of Natchez, Mississippi. I no longer even live in Natchez, but in Bienville, forty miles to the north. (Had it been solely up to me, I'd have left the South altogether—at least for a while—but my grieving daughter didn't want to get too far from her grandparents, who were going through hell at the time I resigned the mayoralty.) Seventeen years have passed since I put the last of the Knox clan under the ground, the same since my father sent himself to Parchman Prison for the murder of a Black woman whom he did not kill, but in fact loved as much as he ever did my mother. My daughter, Annie, who was eleven when a motorcycle gang member nearly ran her over with a van in front of my old Natchez house (and my father's best friend gave his life to save her), is now twenty-nine and a civil rights lawyer in Jackson, Mississippi, practicing with the widow of my querulous and involuntary mentor Quentin Avery.

After my mother passes, only Annie and I will remain to carry on the Cage name, and Annie's not even dating anyone, much less close to marrying. There's a reason this concerns me. I carry a lot of scars that I didn't fifteen years ago. I also carry a secret that I did carry back then, one held so closely that only my father knew about it, and it weighed on him like a tumor. My mother eventually learned of my private burden, but she never revealed it to Annie, and she will carry it to the grave soon enough.

But nature now, it seems, has her own ideas about outing me.

It's probably best that I stake my narrative into the earth somewhere, tie us to a place and time, some fixed point from which to view what came before and after, for only by so doing will we make sense of the horrifying truths that the Bastard Sons' arsons and the resulting violence eventually revealed. Were this only a story of politics, I wouldn't waste the time to write it down. But as I have so often found in the South, mysteries that date back more than 150 years retain the power to wreck families and destroy fortunes, even today, when almost every vice is permitted. In so doing, they teach us things we desperately need to learn.

This is one of those tales.

IT'S SATURDAY.

This past Monday my mother suffered the first of several strokes, likely brought on by one of the harsher chemotherapy agents she recently began taking as the milder ones failed one by one. She's been fighting blood cancer for five years, and the toll on her body and spirit has been relentless. Three days ago she lost consciousness and began taking on the look of a cadaver. Her oncologist told me she's unlikely to wake again. At this point that's a blessing, though I've spent hours pondering questions I should have asked about our family history before losing the chance forever.

Mom had already signed a DNR order when she fell unconscious, and she'd also told me she wants to die in Edelweiss, the residence she's been living in since 2008. The most unique house in Natchez (other than the octagonal, unfinished Longwood), Edelweiss stands on the bluff's edge, two hundred feet above the Mississippi River, looking out over the seemingly endless plain of the Louisiana Delta, where my mother was raised. The 1883 chalet was the dream house of my fiancée, who was murdered in 2007. When I announced that I intended to sell it rather than live with traumatic memories, my mother confessed that Edelweiss had always been her favorite as well, and asked if she might live out her days there. I agreed. Now—fifteen years later—she will die here, fifty miles and a world away from the poor parish where she was born.

She lies supine on the stained sheet, breathing with interminable slowness, so shallowly that I almost can't feel the air move when I cup my hand over her mouth. And yet . . . I do. The sigh of a long, slow respiration animates her pale lips, and I listen for even the semblance of a word.

There is none.

Through the brick walls of the ground floor, I hear the low chanting of a hundred Black people protesting the police shooting in Memphis that happened ten days ago. Like some human timekeeping device, they march out an endless, weary oval with signs in their hands, high above the copper-colored river. They march in solidarity with thousands of protesters three hundred miles upstream, where two cops committed yet another case of egregious misconduct. Their signs demand to know whether Black lives matter, when, sadly, the nation has answered that question many times over. They might as well ask their question of the river.

Maybe they are.

The killing they're protesting is the kind of story where, if you're white, you want to switch off the TV set or scroll down your Twitter feed before you see the body-cam footage, because you know it's going to be worse than you feared. But sitting by my mother's deathbed, I've had little to distract me since her last stroke. The facts are depressingly simple: a twelve-year-old mentally challenged Black boy was attending a birthday party in a white Memphis neighborhood, and running between houses carrying one of the few realistic-looking toy guns still for sale in America as he played some anachronistic variant of *Star Wars*. Despite his age, this teddy bear of a boy was nearly six feet tall and reported by a neighbor as a "prowler."

When he didn't respond to police warnings, he was shot seven times by a white cop.

Protests immediately broke out in a dozen major cities across the country, and two or three more joined in every day. The bluff city of Elvis and Dr. King still shudders under ever-increasing pressure, but after ten days, the chanting downstream in Natchez has a more perfunctory timbre than it did in the beginning. The marchers have grown tired of dedicated action with no response. Fox News began by predicting that this would be the next "George Floyd phase" of American politics, but despite the ever-expanding demonstrations, a prevailing sense has already settled over the nation that not even mass slaughter will spur anything more than a few days' outrage plus "thoughts and prayers" for the victims' parents.

What fools we are.

Sometime after the cop shot that boy, one of the three fates must have turned to her sister and said, "Hold my beer." For what lay in store for me, my family, and those I love would soon make the Memphis tragedy seem inconsequential by comparison. But I did not know. So I sat in the little sickroom atop the bluff in my own hometown and held my mother's hand while she settled toward the final stillness, while chaos worked beneath the ground, and the buildings, and in the hearts and minds of those who long ago gave themselves over to anger and hatred. Worst of all, like termites that never sleep, it worked also in the mind of one who cared nothing for others, and only for himself.

It is those people who harry us all down the road to hell.

EVERY SON BELIEVES his mother beautiful, but God, mine truly is. Here at the end, after the yearslong struggle, her luminous loveliness has finally risen through the ravages of both poison and cure. The pain and regret for so long etched into her features has somehow relaxed, so that her papery skin—lately transparent as the wrapping of a summer roll—has taken on the supple smoothness of youth, like a memory come to life. Perhaps the most recent IV hydrated her at last, or maybe it's the fentanyl patch (yes, fentanyl can be a blessing—I tasted its mercy when I lost my lower right leg in a car crash more than a decade ago). But whatever the reason, her face has taken on an aura of gentle radiance, as though giving off its own light.

Marveling at this change, my gaze falls upon the coarse white fabric serving partly as a coverlet, and which even in her coma Mom clenches in her right hand. It's a "cotton sack," and by this I mean cotton-*picking* sack—ten feet long and two feet wide—that Mom herself likely dragged behind her as a child, on the subsistence farm she grew up on in Louisiana. There, like her four siblings, she began picking cotton at the age of three— yes, *three*—and did not stop until eighteen, when she left home as the first in her brood to attend any college, to ultimately graduate first in her class. She brought this particular sack back from a journey over the river to Quitman Parish during her recent researches into her family's past. In that desperately rural parish, near a town called Heronville, she picked her own family's cotton, then other people's for fifty cents per hundred pounds—same as the Black pickers working at her shoulder. Now she cannot even lift the cloth. But Lord, she traveled far before she faltered. How does a woman of such humble origins look *regal* at the end?

The vibration of my cell phone startles me from my reverie. Reluctantly checking the screen, I see an incoming FaceTime from my daughter, Annie. Pressing the answer button, I wait for the flickering image to stabilize into the features that somehow meld the comeliness of the wife I lost at thirty-six with the earthy beauty of the woman on the bed before me. The pounding of powerful subwoofers thumps through my phone, and the whoops and cries of an amped-up crowd override whatever vocal is being chanted over the bass-driven hip-hop music. The first clear image I see is a message on Annie's silk-screen T-shirt: JUST BECAUSE IT DIDN'T HAPPEN TO YOU, DOESN'T MEAN IT DIDN'T HAPPEN.

Next I see the café au lait face of Martine Boucher, the fortysomething French-Dominican filmmaker I befriended fifteen years ago, during the worst weekend of my life. Martine has been filming a documentary in "Cancer Alley," between Baton Rouge and New Orleans, one featuring General Russel Honoré, but she brought a skeleton crew north for the weekend to film an all-day hip-hop concert being staged on a former cotton plantation called Mission Hill, a few miles south of Bienville. The outdoor festival is being held in solidarity with all protesters against the Memphis police shooting. While the Mission Hill event has proved controversial, even among local Black politicians (primarily because its organizers are notorious former felons), in the end the festival came off, drawing considerable talent from across the South. Our local mayor—a close friend for whom I reluctantly serve as city attorney—asked that I make an appearance if I can possibly get away from Mom's sickbed.

"How's Gram doing?" Annie asks, trying to hide the excitement in her eyes.

"No change."

"Aww. I'm sorry. Well . . . is Althea still coming to relieve you at four thirty?"

Althea Foster is my mother's favorite sitter. "She's supposed to be."

"Are you still planning to make it out here?"

In truth I never promised to attend the concert, and Annie knows this. "Hasn't it been raining on and off all day?"

"Oui!" Martine cries with exuberance. "But the temperature's wonderful, so it's no problem. The music is *fantastique*! And the crowd is so young and wild. You must come out, Penn! You'll enjoy yourself, I promise."

The prospect of stumbling across muddy, uneven ground with my prosthetic leg while being jostled by a crowd of rap fans fills me with dread, but Annie and Martine already know this. Yet still they're asking me to come. They must figure I really need the break.

"I just talked to Mayor Berry," Annie says. "He *really* wants you out here."

Ezra "Doc" Berry is a retired physician whom I helped elect mayor in Bienville's last election by largely running his campaign. After a rocky start, we closed out that battle in the history books, after Doc—a married Black man known to be homosexual—beat his white opponent by taking 94 percent of the vote in the general election. I don't know whether Doc's victory says more about his long history as a beloved physician, his distinguished record as a Vietnam medic, or Bienville's character as a progressive Mississippi town, but his tenure as mayor—barring a highly contentious Covid year—has been relatively smooth and successful.

"Doc wants a white face in the social media photos," I say wryly.

"Wouldn't hurt," Annie concedes. "But you won't be the only one."

"Who else is out there? A few old blues freaks?"

"How about Master Sergeant Bobby White?" A note of challenge puts an edge on Annie's voice.

"*What?*"

"I shit you not, Dad. Bobby effing White has been all over this bluff, shaking hands with Black politicians and talking smack with guys he used to play baseball with."

"Is anybody with him?"

"Nope. No bodyguards, no staff people, and most important, no camera crew. I figured he might be out here to film one of his TikTok videos. One with some Black faces in it, right? But no. And people are treating him like he's the goddamn Second Coming! *Black voters*, you hear me?"

"What the hell is Bobby White doing at a local rap concert when he's trying to put together a third-party run for the White House by next week? He *must* be there to film something."

"They say he's playing in that PGA pro-am at Belle Rose next Wednesday. And the rumor is that if his TikTok army gets enough names to register him third-party in every state, he's going to announce from Bienville, since it's his hometown."

"I saw that on Twitter. I'll be damned. I mean . . ."

"You seriously need to get out here, Dad. Bobby White may be running third party, but everybody knows he's a Republican. You need to fly the flag for our side!"

"Well, at least Bobby's pro-choice. I saw that ad he did on my cell phone. I liked it."

"*Daaa-ad*," she whines with real irritation.

"Boo, seriously, my stump is giving me hell today."

"What if you don't have to drive? What if Doc sends Ray to get you?"

Ray Ransom is a former Parchman convict who, after serving thirty-five years, runs a program in Bienville for wayward youth. A close friend of Doc's, he also handles a dozen different jobs, from political adviser to bodyguard. "Doc needs Ray there a lot more than he needs me. And I'd still have to walk that uneven ground."

"Ray has a golf cart! He can come get you in the parking lot and ferry you to the VIP bleachers where Doc and the Black aldermen are sitting. You won't have to do any serious walking."

She's not going to relent.

"Penn, *please*," Martine pleads, tilting her head in an inviting way she knows I can't resist. "Give yourself two hours! The headline act is coming up. They're flying in this young female rapper from New Orleans. 'Octa' is her name, short for Octoroon. She's the hottest new thing in the country. It's going to be *wild*. Come dance with us!"

Despite considerable pain in my leg and elsewhere—sharp enough to penetrate the cushion of oxycodone—I feel my resistance crumbling.

"Okay . . . I'll text you guys when I'm nearing the parking lot. Have Doc send Ray with his golf cart. I'll watch this Octa girl long enough for Doc to get some photos with me there."

"Awesome!" Annie darts out of frame as two young Black kids dance in front of her. "We'll see you when you get here!"

Martine touches blue-painted fingernails to her lips and blows me a kiss, and then the screen goes blank.

Looking down at my mother's placid face, I already regret giving in. If only they understood what I'm actually going through . . . they'd give me the space I need to deal with something that no one can be prepared for—

Imminent mortality.

As difficult as it is for any child to watch their parent die, for me it's harder still. For my mother is dying of the same disease that will someday kill me—likely sooner rather than later. I am, in fact, watching a preview of my own passing, as I have been for the past five years, though only a handful of people know it. I realize I'm outing myself here—after decades of secrecy—but I can't fully tell this story without doing so, and beyond that . . . two things occurred over the past week that let me know I'll soon have no choice about public knowledge of my condition. The first was simple yet terrifying in the most visceral way imaginable. Lying half-asleep in bed, I rolled over my iPad and snapped a rib clean in two. I've dreaded such an event for more than twenty years, and nothing made it any less terrifying or painful when it finally happened.

The second event—which took place yesterday morning—was almost too surreal to believe. Having left Edelweiss to meet a photographer dispatched by *Southern Living* for an absurd photo spread on porches, I found myself facing a six-hundred-pound black bear standing on its hind legs outside the Parsonage, the antebellum home across the street.

The *Ursus americanus luteolus* stood with one enormous claw resting on the wrought-iron fence, as though considering purchasing the mansion within.

I was in my motorized wheelchair—something I use at times to rest the stump of my right leg—and thus could not flee. With a single swipe he could have decapitated me. Yet, strangely, I felt no fear. Or perhaps my helplessness was so complete that I'd simply passed into a state beyond terror. I felt rather a conviction that the great shaggy creature—like dogs that can smell certain tumors—somehow understood my plight, and most important . . . that my time is near.

Searching the bottomless brown eyes for a clue, all I could see was ineffable sadness, something akin in scale and kind to grief. The standoff continued without him closing the distance dividing us, our eyes locked like those of any two beings separated by lack of common language.

I realized I might be deluding myself by searching for meaning. I might be nothing more than a meal on wheels to this beast that had stepped out of Faulkner's Mississippi and into mine.

He had scars, I realized, one raking slash from ear to yellow snout, and another at his belly, a pale cicatrix that transected his ribs and ended in an ugly hump, most likely a spent bullet. This told me that the bear lived under ever-present threat of death, and more important, he knew it.

Our communion was broken by the squeal of motorcycle brakes and a uniformed cop shouting at me to back away from "the animal" as slowly as I could. As the officer drew his pistol, the bear broke eye contact to gauge the threat and I felt myself touch the joystick that put the wheelchair into reverse. With a click and hum I began to recede from him—or him from me—and even as the cop shouted uselessly, and sirens sounded in the distance, the bear dropped onto all fours and crossed Broadway, paused at Silver Street as though considering a visit to Natchez Under-the-Hill, then changed his mind and loped south toward Fort Rosalie with almost equine speed and vanished over the rim of the bluff. What I saw as a suicidal leap, he saw as safety. Two hundred feet of kudzu-covered loess soil with just enough slope to offer escape from men and guns.

The wildlife people had their explanation, of course, but I could have demolished that in three minutes. The thing I couldn't put out of my mind was how, when at least a hundred marchers occupied the green space just across Broadway from Edelweiss, that old bear found his way to me alone, and others would only see him later, as more police and hunters were called in to try to run him to earth.

As a squad car screamed onto Broadway, the brief rumble of a turning cycle startled me from behind.

"Hey, mayor. You okay? You need help with that wheelchair?"

"No, I'm good. Thanks."

"You look pale. You all right?"

For once, I actually considered this question: "No . . . No, I don't think I am."

CHAPTER 3

WHEN I WAS thirty-eight years old, I began living a nightmare universally feared by most Americans. Feeling in perfect health, and possessing no symptoms of any kind, I walked into a tiny cubicle where an uncomfortable physician (in this case one of my father's younger partners) nervously informed me that I had one of those diseases for which medical science can do nothing, and which would in an unknown but surely brief time remove me from the mortal plane.

It sounds like fiction, I know. A movie setup.

It wasn't.

Having just published my third legal thriller as a Houston prosecutor, I found myself unexpectedly flush with money and flirting with fame. On the advice of my brother-in-law, an accountant with Arthur Andersen, I applied for two million dollars in life insurance, to protect the security of my four-year-old daughter. (Having lost Annie's mother to cancer six months earlier, it seemed only prudent.) I went in for the insurance physical without a thought, and when my total protein came back a tenth of a point above normal, I didn't worry. My father even told me not to worry. The only dangerous illness that my abnormal number might indicate was "an old people's cancer"—multiple myeloma.

Ten days later, after a battery of further tests, I got the diagnosis: Myeloma.

When you read that unfamiliar word, imagine a cobra wrapped around your bare leg, its hood flared, fangs bared, and slit eyes locked on yours. Imagine you are hours away from medical care, and that no antivenin exists, even should you reach a hospital. I'll spare you the numbness, shock, confusion. The Kübler-Ross stages of grief: you'll go through them all soon enough. (For your sake, I hope, much later in life.) But to understand how hopeless my verdict was in those days, one need only know that this obscure blood cancer had just killed the Arkansas billionaire Sam Walton—founder of Walmart—and that Walton had endowed a massive research center in Little Rock to try to discover a cure. I soon learned that myeloma wasn't so rare after all, that Geraldine Ferraro suffered from it, in fact. Like all diseases, mine had its celebrity patients. But celebrity protects no one from such a deadly foe.

Because my father was a doctor, we were given access to an early experimental treatment in Little Rock, but side effects from the infusions nearly killed me, and after months of being monitored like a guinea pig waiting to be given its death date (all done in secret), I suddenly and quite irrationally walked away from all treatment, including Walton's own physician.

Then . . . a strange thing happened.

I didn't die.

Everyone else in my boat did, I'm sorry to say. But through some rare dispensation of fate or chance, I found myself in the luckiest one-hundredth of one percent of patients—those who live years beyond the normal prognosis, thanks to what doctors call a "smoldering" form of the mutation that would soon take the lives of Roy Scheider, Susannah York, Norm McDonald, Colin Powell, and many less famous people I knew from Mississippi and Texas. As those worthies fell, and their obit photos flickered across my TV screen, I would sit numb with my unknowing daughter, not quite believing I carried the same malignant proteins they did. I lived in terror of the inevitable moment that I would roll over in bed and snap a brittle bone, or find that my organs were failing after being choked with runaway immunoglobulins. . . .

And yet—

That didn't happen, either.

Despite possessing the deadly daughter cells that had bored lesions into my spine and skull (and created an agglomeration of cancerous plasma cells, called a plasmacytoma, in my pelvis), my smoldering variant of the cancer gave me what even Sam Walton had not gotten: the option of suffering in secret.

This was a precious gift, but also a curse.

Why?

Because it's a desolate way to exist.

At first I lived in constant fear of exposure, a man walking in existential shadow, the hawk of mortality hovering over my shoulder. But my secret was so hopeless that eventually I learned to keep it not only from the world, but also from myself. You can do that, though you might not believe me. It requires a perpetually exhausting exercise of will, a supreme act of denial, but it's a viable path, and perhaps a peculiarly male one. To reveal terminal vulnerability—the mark of doom, the black spot—to those who see you every day, to those who *employ* you, is more than a sobering prospect. It's a submission, a surrender. I'd known people in that era to lose promotions, even careers, after being diagnosed with cancer. In response, I withdrew from doctors and science and began living a lie to protect my career, and thus my family. I believe profoundly in science, but the instinct to protect one's child runs marrow deep, and the compulsion to huddle in the dark at the back of the cave lives deeper still. Confronted by a fatal disease for which no effective treatment exists, one either accepts death or turns away and perseveres in hopes of . . .

What?

A miracle? A reprieve? Granted by whom? The gods? Fate? Whatever that alternative is, I chose it. I simply went on with life, secretly knowing I lived under sentence of death. After all, doesn't everyone live that way? They simply comfort themselves that their expiration date waits much further in the future. To my amazement, the road I chose not only led to an unprecedented period of survival, but to the absurd reality of watching my mother perish from the same disease—which she would not even be diagnosed with until two decades after fate condemned me to the same scaffold.

Things have changed profoundly since Sam Walton died. In the two decades of life my miracle has given me, tens of thousands have been treated with revolutionary new drugs and much-improved bone marrow transplants. Some have survived a considerable number of years. In the end, of course, they've all died. But today's prognosis is better than it once was. If I'm correct about my present plight—that my smoldering cancer has finally "switched on"—then I'm likely to be hurried into a transplant regimen (something my mother was too frail to qualify for), which will offer me the best chance at long-term remission. That's the future I've been trying to come to terms with for the past week: one in which I enter the Kubrickian isolation of a transplant room, where a sterile team obliterates my living marrow—the spongy cradle of all human existence—putting me into a terminally compromised state, during which they will seed my barren marrow chambers with stem cells previously harvested from the reservoirs in my pelvis, sternum, and spine . . .

Am I really ready for that?

In truth, I have no choice. The broken rib informed me of that, and yesterday the bear confirmed the none-too-subtle message (which I might have found a way to ignore). *And if I ignore the message of the bear? What will nature send me next? A third warning? Or will Annie find me lying in my bed, having perished from organ failure, or anemia so severe that I die without even being aware the serpent was at my throat—*

"Mr. Cage?" calls an alto female voice. "Mr. Penn? Hey! Mayor Cage! Are you all right?"

Someone is gently but persistently shaking my shoulder.

Starting in my chair, I look up and back, into the warm brown face of Althea Foster. The nurse and sitter is staring down with concern. "I knocked, but nobody answered," she informs me. "I saw your car outside, so I figured you must be in here. And it's four twenty now."

"Althea," I manage, rubbing my face. "I'm so glad to see you."

"I'll bet you is. You look terrible, if I say so myself. You need sleep *bad*."

"Yeah . . ."

"How Mrs. Peggy doin'? Looks the same to me."

"No change, I'm afraid."

"I figured."

I straighten up in my chair. "You didn't want to go to the concert at Mission Hill?"

"*Lord*, no. I got no use for that hip-hop stuff. I'm an R&B girl from way back. Still got my daddy's vinyl record collection."

"I'm with you, 'Thea."

"Besides, I hear it's a mess out there with this rain. And that's not all. My niece told me they had some food poisoning earlier, off a barbecue truck. And they've had so many kids just walk in up the bluff that they don't have near enough toilets. They're charging ten dollars for bottles of water out there. It's still hot for October."

"Wow. Well, I have to run out there for at least a few minutes."

"Oh, no!"

"Mayor Berry asked me to, and Annie won't let me out of it. Just tell me one thing before I go."

"What's that?"

"If I leave for two hours, is Mom likely to pass while I'm gone?"

Althea steps closer to the bed, reaches down and touches Mom's cheek with her experienced fingers. "I don't believe she will. Too well hydrated. Look at that color in her skin. Better than yesterday. I'm not saying she couldn't have another stroke, now. That happens, I can't take responsibility."

"I understand. But she's not just going to fade out like this?"

Althea touches my arm with empathy. "I'll call you if I sense any change."

"Thank you."

Before I can go, the nurse lifts her hand and touches my cheek with the same fingers she used on Mom's face. "How are *you* feeling?" She takes hold of my fingers and examines my nail beds. "You look mighty pale to me."

"I'm just tired. Exhausted, really."

"I think you ought to go by Dr. Shaw's and get stuck for a chem panel. Not my business, of course, but caretakers have to look out for themselves."

"You're right," I say, wanting to get away before she can examine me more thoroughly. "I'll check into it."

She gives me the chiding look of one of my old grade-school teachers. "I wish Dr. Cage was still around to take care of Mrs. Peggy. You, too. I only worked with him two years before that damned trial, but Lord, he was one of a kind. Best family doctor I ever saw."

"Mom would have had a completely different experience if he'd been here to take care of her."

The nurse shrugs philosophically. "You know what they say . . . we ain't put here to stay."

She takes out a book and her smartphone, then settles into the recliner still warm from my body heat. "You be careful at that concert. Liable to be some rough types out there. All this gang trouble we been having . . . all that dope. You look out. You're not young as you was, Mayor."

"I'll be careful."

FOURTEEN MILES FROM the Mission Hill concert ground, Corey Evers pulled Bobby White's gray Range Rover into the driveway of Belle Rose, the "big house" of one of the largest cotton plantations in Mississippi prior to the Civil War. Ten years ago, two thirds of the land had been sold to develop the Belle Rose golf community and country club. Next week, the club would host a PGA tournament it had been trying to attract for most of the decade. The board had finally succeeded, thanks to the economic boom brought on by the construction of the Azure Dragon paper mill, a two-billion-dollar Chinese manufacturing facility sited on the Mississippi River.

Charles Dufort, the eighty-four-year-old attorney and oil speculator who sold the board the land for the club, had retained a third of the original plantation for himself, as well as Belle Rose itself, an Italianate mansion of palatial scale and renowned design. He'd also kept three of the original six plantations his ancestors had owned before the war, which included two sugar plantations in South Louisiana and Tranquility in Natchez, a spectacular "suburban villa" in a city famous for them.

"Look at this palace!" Corey breathed with undisguised awe. "If it was anywhere but Mississippi, it would cost fifty million dollars."

"That's why we're here," Bobby said, as Corey put the Rover in park.

Corey nodded. "Didn't Dufort tell you he wants you to evaluate a family letter? One suggesting that one of his ancestors played a heroic role in helping the Union navy run the Confederate guns at Vicksburg, prior to the siege?"

Bobby chuckled. "He did. It's a decent pretext for this meeting, you have to admit. But if he has such a letter, it's almost certainly a lie, if not an outright forgery. A typical attempt at reputational rehab in our PC era. The Dufort family actually looks pretty good from our age, despite being slaveholders prior to the war. They both resisted secession and supported Lincoln. But I used to play in Charles's study when I was a boy, with his youngest son. He had some weird shit in there. Framed sugarcane machetes from various centuries. Stuffed pit vipers that the cane cutters had to contend with on the daily. Canebrake rattlers, copperheads . . . it was creepy, man."

"The more I hear, the more Dufort sounds like a Harlan Crow–type billionaire. Just how well do you know that old man?"

"I know the son a lot better. As you know."

Corey sighed with several degrees of frustration.

"I'll tell you this much," Bobby added. "I'm the son that old bastard wishes he'd had. He literally told me that when I was home on leave at nineteen."

"That's so pitiful." Corey thought of what he knew of Bobby's history with the family. "I can't believe you're even trying this."

"Look, Charles called *me*. After getting calls from the biggest GOP donors from around the country. Something's happening at the major donor level. But if we're going to get access to that money, it has to go through Charles. I don't really have a choice."

"Don't you? What about the Poker Club?"

"Ahh," Bobby sighed. "If only . . ."

The Bienville Poker Club was a largely hereditary private club that dated back to the Civil War in Bienville, when some bankers and planters had banded together to resist the occupying Yankee forces in every way possible. Using a combination of business smarts, ruthlessness, and courage, they exploited the black market in cotton, thwarted and even cheated Union officers at every turn, and afterward—during Reconstruction—conned carpetbagging businessmen out of most of the legal profits they'd tried to extract from Tenisaw County.

Today some heirs of those men still possessed considerable fortunes, but on the Mississippi scale. In the Magnolia State, an oil magnate like Blake Donnelly might be worth eighty or ninety million dollars, and that bought a lot of respect. But in Massachusetts or California, such money wouldn't even get you a seat at the VIP table. Men of such meager millions couldn't help Bobby in his present situation. For that he needed *real* money, and the only man he knew personally who possessed it was the father of one of his most intimate friends from childhood.

In 1850, the original Dufort ancestor had been among "the nabobs of Natchez," those cotton planters whose fortunes were so large, and spread so liberally among family and friends, that the Natchez District contained more millionaires than any city in America except New York. But unlike most of those other families' descendants, the Dufort children down the generations had inherited sufficient business acumen (and luck) to maintain their fortunes through all the lean years that followed the war, even through the Great Depression.

"How do you ask somebody for a hundred million dollars?" Corey wondered aloud.

"Start at two hundred?" Bobby suggested with a laugh.

Corey put one hand over his eyes and sighed with bitter humor as his phone pinged with a text. He checked it without hesitation. "Boom! We just hit forty-five thousand signatures in Indiana. That's forty-three states, Bobby. This is getting real."

The candidate grinned and pumped his fist. "Boo-ya! That's a good omen going into this meeting."

Corey made a fist with his left hand and gnawed at his forefinger. "Bobby . . . your history with this family's too damned complicated to risk the kind of entanglement you're about to get into with this old man. The risk is potentially catastrophic."

"What alternative do you suggest? Seriously."

"Something *cleaner*. Where there's only a present and future, not a past filled with land mines."

Bobby sighed with exasperation. "It's the South, Corey. Every road leads back through the past."

"Jesus. Let's get this over with."

Bobby yanked the Rover's door handle and marched across travertine pavers to an entrance that dwarfed him. The man who lived behind that door could make or break his presidential campaign, and he was about as right-wing as they came, short of being a conspiracy nut. Bobby hoped this invitation had nothing to do with any historical letter about the Vicksburg campaign. Old people often became obsessed with genealogical pig trails like that, and he had no time to waste. And Corey was right to worry about the personal risk of dealing with the Duforts, of course. Bobby knew things about the family that would likely make the patriarch expend millions to destroy rather than anoint him. But

Charles Dufort didn't know he possessed such knowledge, and Bobby wasn't about to walk away from this chance. As he listened to the heels of an efficient maid clacking over the floor inside, Bobby heard Tio Carrera's parting words in his head: *You gotta have some big balls to play this game . . .*

CHAPTER 4

MISSION HILL PLANTATION is one of a string of former cotton plantations that line the Mississippi River between Natchez and Bienville, forty miles to the north. Most of these beautiful and accursed tracts still exist, and I've owned one for the past year, though I put it in my mother's name during her lifetime, at her request. Bobby White keeps a hunting retreat on one near mine (Canaan Plantation, purchased by his father during his Major League Baseball career). I can take Highway 61 most of the way to Mission Hill, then turn off onto a gravel road that follows the bluff's edge north past the gates of these properties, a road likely to be hell after a day of intermittent rain.

About seven miles south of Bienville proper, the old rolling fields of Mission Hill are still mostly treeless. The "big house" burned in the early twentieth century, and the land is now owned by a widow from New York, who inherited it more than two decades ago and rents it out as pasture to a local farmer. When the promoters of the rap concert—the Burrell brothers—found themselves unable to secure a Bienville site for their "Black Woodstock" (as they were calling the show then), the liberal Yankee widow stepped in to offer Mission Hill. The complex optics of a racial protest concert being held on the grounds of a former cotton plantation seemed to escape the Burrell brothers, and despite a complete lack of resources such as electricity or plumbing, they began planning the concert there. Had they been paying attention, they might have realized they were setting themselves up not for a "Black Woodstock," but a second Altamont.

As my Audi rolls north up 61, the cushion of oxycodone combines with the drone of my tires to induce a road hypnosis, and in this state my thoughts run to my final exchange with Althea Foster. How she remembered my father, and wished he were still here to manage the care of our family. No one has longed for that more than I, except of course my mother, who is beyond wishing now. But I know how badly she missed him. It seems strange that I'm about to see Martine Boucher, the last person to see my father alive on earth—except the person who likely murdered him.

I met Martine for the first time only thirty-six hours after Dad died, having taken a call from her while trying to arrange his funeral (not an easy task when a man dies as a convict in a prison riot). I accepted the call because Martine had been held hostage in Parchman for nine hours during that riot, and I had been told that Dad gave his life in order to save hers. I'd seen her several times on TV that day. The filmmaker spoke English well, albeit with a French accent, and she seemed cool and self-possessed, despite surely being in shock. From several reports I knew that her hours as a hostage had been more harrowing than the battle tours of many combat veterans. I knew from my police contacts, for example, that she'd suffered at least one sexual assault. And when a woman who has endured that kind of hell tells you only hours later that she needs to talk to you . . . you go. Beyond this, Boucher informed me that before they were separated, Dad had entrusted her with two messages for me. She wouldn't pass them to me over the phone, and instead arranged for me to meet her at the bar of the Grand Hotel in downtown Natchez at 10:00 p.m., after she'd driven down from the Delta.

Piloting my Audi through fierce, nearly horizontal rain to the Grand, I used my iPhone to replay the interview footage of Martine Boucher after the Mississippi Highway Patrol SWAT team stormed the prison in the wake of her miraculous escape. The closer I studied the screen, the more she looked and sounded like a woman trying to cover severe shock.

I parked at the curb near the hotel's side entrance, then hurried inside and found the filmmaker waiting at a table in the small, crowded bar off the lobby. A dark-haired woman in her early thirties, Martine was in the process of blowing off a drunk businessman, something a traveling professional with her mixed-race beauty probably spent a lot of time doing. The guy was persistent, and given what Boucher had endured in the prison, I didn't figure she had the resources to waste on that kind of crap. Approaching the table, I said, "The lady isn't interested, and I'm not in the mood to be nice. Go back to the bar."

"You her husband?" asked the drunk in a challenging tone. "Don't see no ring on her finger."

I removed my coat and hung it on the back of the empty chair, then looked him full in the face. "I'm not her husband. But I am the mayor of this town, and I'm very friendly with the local cops. Understood? Goodbye."

He contemplated escalating the situation, then thought better of it. Once he was ten steps away, I sat down and looked into the grateful eyes of the woman my father had supposedly died to save.

"Sorry about the redneck. Local hazard. Especially in places like this."

"It's not just the rednecks," she said in a weary French accent. "That man at the bar just told me I look like a cross between Jessica Alba and Sade."

Glancing left, I saw a Black personal injury attorney I know well from the Natchez and Bienville courthouses.

"I'm not sure how to begin," Boucher said, trying to get a read on me.

"Say whatever you need to. God knows we're past small talk, though we've never met. I can't believe you're even here."

I saw something inscrutable in her eyes. "I had to come. If it weren't for your father, I'd be in a casket in the belly of a plane bound for Paris. But more than that . . . I want to understand why Tom did what he did."

I nodded silently.

"You, too?" she asked softly.

"I'm not clear on exactly what happened or how, but Dad sacrificing himself didn't surprise me at all. I would like to know about his last hours on earth, though."

Boucher jumped at a rebel yell from the corner, from a table where a group of men were watching football highlights on a glowing TV. "Is this too public a place?" she asked. "We can go to the lobby, or to my room."

"I'm fine here. Actually, I could use a drink."

"Of course. Have you scheduled Tom's funeral, by the way? I must return to Paris in three days."

"That should work out. I'm flying in a pathologist for a private autopsy before the burial, but he should be done in time. The forensic delays in Mississippi are absurd. Unless you tell me something to change my mind tonight."

She shrugged. "Your father was alive when I left him. But I think that's a good idea."

"Can you give me the messages you spoke of now?"

She leaned forward and spoke in a softer voice. "The first, yes. The second . . . makes me uncomfortable, to be honest."

"How so?"

"I'm a pacifist. I feel quite conflicted about it."

"I see. What's the first message?"

"There's a man on death row in Parchman. His name is Carl Hardin. Your father believes he's innocent. He told me to tell you to do all in your power to free him."

I sagged a little in my chair, trying not to show my disappointment. "I see. Is the second message like that?"

"No. Much more personal. Why don't we deal with our other questions first? Then we'll see."

I felt an unexpected quickening in my blood. "All right. Do you have any questions for me?"

"I do. I haven't been able to sleep since the riot. No surprise, I guess. I napped a little during the drive tonight. My cameraman drove me down. But I spent this afternoon reading everything I could find about the case that put your father behind those prison walls. It was plain to me that he didn't belong there. As a journalist, it was also plain that you left a great deal out of the public accounts you gave of the events around you, your father, that Texas Ranger, and the journalist Henry Sexton pursuing the KKK offshoot group, the Double Eagles."

The filmmaker was right, of course. "Some things can't be put to paper. Not for public consumption. I plan to write some more about Henry over the next year. But very carefully."

She nodded. "I've had to do much the same in my own work. You know . . . your father's story is quite unique. A war hero, a beloved physician, yet he essentially put himself into that awful place. Clearly he must have felt a great deal of guilt over something. But having read all I could, I don't understand what it was. I'm tempted to make a film of his life story alone."

She waited, but I didn't comment.

Martine Boucher closed her eyes, and for a moment I thought she was weeping. Then she said, "For nine hours, the gangs controlled that prison. Scores were settled, guards tortured. Right in front of me. Yet the whole time, your father worked tirelessly to keep the wounded alive. Guards or inmates, it made no difference. He was a physician, nothing else. To me, he looked like a white-haired angel laboring in the underworld. I don't exaggerate. Were it not for him . . . my fate doesn't bear thinking about."

"Was Dad aware of what you were going through? The assault?"

She nodded. "He treated me after the first couple of hours. He told the gang leader—Xavier Smalls—that if they didn't stop, I would die. Smalls stopped it. I think he wanted me for himself. But he'd been stabbed in the initial struggle, and things were too chaotic for him to follow through. He worried the FBI would storm the prison at any moment. Your father did a good job of working him, psychologically speaking."

None of this surprised me. "That's who Dad was. The men he served with in Korea could tell you that."

"But I want to know more. Here's what I've discovered so far: Tom fell in love with his Negro nurse in the 1960s—Viola Turner. But after the nurse's brother and his friend were murdered by the KKK, she moved to Chicago, carrying a child your father never knew he'd sired. Yes? So . . . forty years passed, then the nurse returned to Mississippi to die with her family. Cancer. Her plan was euthanasia. And because of this, your father ended up charged with her murder by a Black district attorney, mainly for political reasons?"

"That's the shortest summary I've ever heard."

Boucher smiled. "Film writing forces one to be concise. The curious thing is, everyone involved in the trial seemed to believe Tom and his nurse were planning the euthanasia together, to spare her pain. But in the end he refused to go through with it."

"Everyone but the district attorney."

"*Oui*. But you and Henry Sexton went a long way toward proving former Klansmen murdered the nurse to keep her quiet about events that had happened back in the sixties. The same men who'd murdered her brother in 1967."

"Too late, I'm afraid."

"Yes, but here's what I don't understand: *Why* did your father change his plea to guilty during his trial? Such a drastic decision, and all twelve jury members—both Black and white—later stated that they would have voted to acquit him."

Martine Boucher had put her finger on the central riddle of my father's life. Should I reveal my version of the answer to her? People tell stories for different reasons, and writers are no different. Some we give to the world for money. Others we save for those closest to us. And some we keep for ourselves. In this case, I felt that Boucher had earned the truth—at least as I knew it.

"After a very bumpy prosecution, the DA in that trial—Shadrach Johnson, the Black candidate I'd beaten for mayor—delivered what might be the most brilliant closing statement I've ever heard. Even Quentin Avery admits that, and Quentin is a master of the form."

"What was so special about it?"

"Shad delivered the story of Viola's life and death as a fictional biblical parable. And Dad, hearing his own history with Viola retold in that context, began to see his relationship with her in a profoundly different way. There was no question that the sex had been consensual. My God, he loved her more than my mother in some ways—though I'll deny I ever said that."

Boucher waved away my worry.

"And her love for him was beyond question. It was a very near thing that he didn't leave us for her in the early years after she went to Chicago. But looking back on it as an older man, he began to wonder how much chance Viola had really had to *not* get involved with him. Becoming his mistress must have seemed a better option than any other she'd had at that time, as a young Black war widow in Mississippi."

"Vietnam?" Martine said, and I saw an old fatigue in her eyes. She probably had some familial connection to the French period of the Vietnam War.

I nodded. "Viola's husband was killed after only five months in-country. And the way Viola's life went after reaching Chicago—raising the son Dad never knew he had, with very little money—let's just say that all that triggered a complex guilt reaction in him. An irresistible one, as it turned out. So he took an Alford plea. That's not admitting guilt, only stating that it's reasonable to believe that a jury might find you guilty. Never mind what the jury really thought. On that day, *Dad felt compelled to punish himself.* So he did. Knowing that he would likely never walk out of that prison under his own power. And neither I nor his lawyer could talk him out of it."

Martine shook her head in amazement. "How did you feel about that?"

"Enraged, to tell you the truth. By doing that, he destroyed what remained of our family. Deprived his wife of a husband, his granddaughter of a loving mentor she worshipped, and . . ."

"A loving son of his father?"

"I suppose so, yes."

Infinite sadness filled the filmmaker's eyes. She reached across the table and squeezed my hand. "Let's change the subject for a bit. Tell me about Monsieur Daniel Kelly. I would very much like to know more about him as well."

"You and every other reporter in the country."

Boucher acknowledged this with a tight smile. "Most seem to think he's some sort of federal agent, but no one's discovered anything confirmable. The FBI refuses to comment."

Thank God, I said silently, praying that Kelly was somewhere safe.

"I gather that he was posing as a prison guard. And that he was there for your father, in one way or another?"

After gauging the character I could discern in her eyes, I said, "Off the record?"

"*Oui. Naturellement.*"

"Kelly was there for me."

A curious light entered her eyes. "As what? A *mercenaire*?"

"You could say that. He's a close friend. Kelly and I go back a long way."

Boucher's eyes remained unsatisfied, but she seemed content to proceed gently. "I've been in some tight places in my time, with some very hard men, but I've never seen such a survivor as that one. I think you could toss him into a pit of mambas overnight, and in the morning he would still be alive."

I nodded. "That's why I chose him."

"But what did he hope to accomplish in that awful place?"

"Look what he did accomplish. He saved your life, didn't he?" I hesitated for a few moments, then decided to trust her with more. "Initially he went in there undercover to check on Dad's well-being. In the end, we decided Kelly would have to break Dad out. It was the only way to ensure his safety. Dad was in grave danger in Parchman, from more than one source."

"Get him *out*? You're a famous attorney and author, and you couldn't get your father out. What could Kelly hope to do?"

"Kelly's a retired soldier, but not a conventional one. He was in the First Special Forces Detachment. They call them 'operators.'"

The filmmaker's eyes narrowed. "Ahh. Like our GIGN commandos."

"Close enough."

"Can you tell me anything about that part of the story? I shall never reveal it, unless you both give me written permission. But I must know the circumstances that led to my survival."

I'm not sure why I trusted her that night, but twenty subsequent years of intimate friendship have validated my decision. "When that riot broke out, Kelly was twenty minutes from walking Dad away from a work-release job, with no intention of ever taking him back to Parchman. I was two miles away, waiting at a motel filled with convict wives and kids. I had everything I needed to take Dad into hiding until I could speak to the FBI about the danger he was in. If you don't know, Parchman is one of the most corrupt prisons in the country, and the rot runs all the way to the state capital. But when I heard that siren go off, I knew something terrible had gone wrong."

Martine's eyes were wide. "You were willing to risk prison yourself to break your father out of that place? Kelly, too?"

"We'd exhausted every other possibility. It was the only way."

"Surely—"

"You don't know the danger he was in."

Martine shook her head in confusion. "Will you please explain this?"

"I need that drink if I'm going to do that."

She nodded. "I also."

"PENN? PENN CAGE! WAKE UP, MAN!"

Someone is knocking on my car window, hard enough that it hurts my left ear. Blinking awake, I find myself staring into the fearful face of Ray Ransom, Mayor Berry's longtime friend and factotum. Though he's older than seventy now, decades of pumping iron behind bars kept Ray built like an NFL safety, and with his clean-shaven head, he looks more than a little like the great Pittsburgh Steeler Mel Blount.

Ray churns his right hand in a circle, indicating that I should roll down my window. I seem to be sitting in an endless line of vehicles stalled on the gravel road leading to Mission Hill Plantation. I don't know how I got here. I must have driven to the gravel turn on autopilot, then fallen asleep as I inched forward toward the concert site. I need to think twice before driving again on oxycodone. After rubbing my eyes hard, I obey.

"Get out and climb in my golf cart!" he orders. "Jimmy can park your car for you."

A Black kid of about eighteen leaps off the back of the cart and comes to my door. Ray opens it and helps me out, then guides me up onto the seat and climbs behind the wheel. From the direction of the Mississippi River, I hear a pounding hip-hop beat. Then the door to my Audi slams, and its motor revs.

"You look wiped, bro," Ray observes. "How's your mama doin'?"

"Same."

"Well, I'm glad you came. Doc's waiting for you in the stands. Not many white faces out here today. So much for solidarity."

"How many Black faces do you see at a Brad Paisley concert? Let's do it. I've got to get some sleep soon."

Ray puts the cart into forward. "You will, you will. I'll have you back to your car in an hour."

"Thanks, Ray. Hey, is it true that Bobby White's been out here?"

"Sho 'nuff, man. Or was."

"Doing what?"

The cart eases forward along the line of cars as Ray searches for an opening to cross onto the grass, where a steady line of new arrivals trudges along on foot. "Pressing the flesh. Hanging out. Amazed me, man. All these kids out here know him from that TikTok shit. He's a bigger celebrity than most of the rappers performing today. Kids are begging him to do sniper shots or jump from the bluff in a parachute."

"What a world," I mutter. "That guy could be our next president?"

Ray laughs heartily. "Better than a couple of others I could think of." He floors the cart pedal, and we shoot through a gap between a pickup and an old Cutlass Supreme, hurtling onto the worn grass with a spray of flying gravel.

CHAPTER 5

WITHOUT RAY RANSOM'S golf cart, I'd never have made it across the Mission Hill concert grounds. To describe the scene as "controlled chaos" would be a misnomer. It was pandemonium. Mission Hill made the Delta Blues Festival in Clarksdale look like a geriatric retreat. More than four thousand people had bought tickets, and Ray estimated that another twenty-five hundred had simply walked onto the property by hiking along the bluff from points north or south. Most of the crashers appeared to be kids—underage by the liquor laws, for sure, and some as young as twelve or thirteen. Ninety-nine percent of the crowd was Black, and Ray told me people had come from as far away as Texas and Arkansas to see the acts that the Burrell brothers had secured on the bill.

The logistical setup was simple, and appeared to be patterned on the annual Natchez Balloon Festival. An elevated main stage had been set up at a right angle to the bluff, about 150 yards from the edge with its stunning view of the Mississippi River. A line of blue Porta Potties functioned as a dangerously porous barrier between the audience and the two-hundred-foot drop where the sheer bluff ended. Opposite these—forming a giant U with the stage as the anchoring link—a long line of food trailers and merchandise booths ran back toward the ticketing/entrance area, where a carnival had been set up with inflatable bouncy houses and carnival rides for toddlers. Between the Porta Potties and the booths was a mostly flat meadow covered with folding chairs, ice chests, families on blankets, and thousands of younger fans pressed hard against the stage. Last, a single unit of VIP bleachers had been erected in front of the Porta Potties, about fifty yards from the stage, and it was there that Ray pointed the golf cart.

"I hear there was some food poisoning out here this morning," I tell him, as we trundle over the uneven ground. "That true?"

"Oh, hell yeah," he says bitterly. "People puking all over the place. Some ass from Jena brought over a barbecue truck, and his pork was bad. Liable to be lawsuits behind that."

"Guy's probably not worth suing."

"The Burrell brothers might be. I hear they're still in the pharmaceutical business, if you know what I mean. They might have some cash stashed somewhere."

I point at a group of young teens swaggering in front of us, most of the boys wearing fanny packs at the pit of their flat bellies. A cloud of weed smoke envelops us as we pass. "Looks like a pretty young crowd," I observe. "And I don't like the look of those fanny packs."

"You know they got handguns in there. But what you gonna do? The Burrells hired off-duty city cops as security. They start trying to take weapons off these kids, we're gonna have shooting out here. You think it's worth it?"

I see his point. "Probably not. But the potential for disaster looks pretty serious to me."

"Piss-poor planning, counselor. There's not a single metal detector out here. Not even wands. But Doc's been on the phone with Chief Morgan all day, and the best they've come up with is to try to keep the temperature cool. Laissez-faire enforcement, Doc calls it."

"Any sign of Sheriff Tarlton or his deputies? It's really their jurisdiction."

Ray laughs with derision. "I think they look at this as a Black event, and therefore *outside their purview*."

"You're probably right."

Ray parks the golf cart beside the bleachers, and a dozen people seated on the incline of bench seats shout greetings or wave to me. They're dressed more formally than the rest of the festival crowd, since most hold political or corporate positions in the community. Ray gets out and helps me onto the bottom landing of the stands, then starts me up the steps to where Mayor Berry sits with his two new progressive aldermen, Robert Gaines and Elijah Keyes. Along with Doc's triumph in the special election, the unexpected victories of these two younger men helped put the Bienville city board—historically dominated by whites since the 1700s—under Black control for the first time in more than three hundred years.

Though born and raised in Mississippi, Doc radiates more of a James Clyburn energy than that of a Bennie Thompson. He's always been quick to laugh, and his eyes are wise and deep behind large black square glasses, like those of a storybook owl, and his baritone voice carries a fine articulation and reassurance that feels paternal even to me.

"Mayor *Cage*!" Doc cries, using my old title half in jest, as he always does. "Glad to see you. How's Peggy doing?"

"Still unconscious," I say quietly.

The retired physician gives me a sober look of empathy. "I expect she'll stay that way. But I'm gonna get by there for a visit anyway. Slide over, Elijah. Let me have a word with my city attorney."

Alderman Elijah Keyes doesn't look overjoyed at being asked to move aside for the token white audience member, but he reluctantly accedes to his mayor's order. I feel a comforting familiarity as I squeeze in next to Doc. Our relationship goes all the way back to my tenth-grade year, when Doc lived in our house while doing his family practice rotation under my father as a Tulane medical student. Practically fresh out of Vietnam, Ezra Berry befriended me then, and our closeness has lasted ever since, to the point that when he asked me to run his mayoral campaign, I couldn't even consider declining.

"I hear Bobby White's been out here today," I say softly. "What's the story there?"

Doc raises his eyebrows to let me know he has no idea, but that he's intrigued. "White's got a hell of a pitch for Black voters, Penn. He's talking about using the USDA to transform the Mississippi Delta from a hundred-dollar-per-acre-per-year profit monoculture crop to twice-a-year California vegetables—with profits of five thousand dollars per acre. Bobby's a clever boy, which is not something you generally see in athletes of his caliber."

"He got those brains from his mother," I murmur. "His daddy was no dummy, but his mama's as sharp as a roofing nail. They called her and her sister the Trophy Twins, because they were both looking to marry up. Anyway, Bobby cruised through Ole Miss and Vanderbilt Law after he got back from overseas. Graduated third in his law school class."

"I'm reading that book he wrote on the Lost Cause. It's damned insightful, and I told him so about an hour ago."

"Still. The idea that he could be running for *president*, having never held a public office of any kind—"

"That's the new paradigm!" Doc cuts in, only half joking again. "Unless he screws up some way, I think he has a real shot at taking out the major parties. The scale of this TikTok thing is just hard to believe. When you add in Instagram and YouTube and the rest. . . ."

"So why is he wasting time here? This is his hometown."

Doc shakes his head. "All will be revealed. Isn't that what the Good Book says? Luke, I believe?"

From the bench below us, Alderman Gaines says, "You know your Bible, Mayor. 'Nothing is covered up that will not be revealed, or hidden that will not be known.' Chapter twelve, verse two."

Doc nods with satisfaction.

"Have you seen Annie in the past hour?" I ask.

"I have indeed. With that French filmmaker, Martine whoever. Man, she's a lovely creature. She has that *island thing* going."

Doc may be gay, but he appreciates natural beauty. "Martine Boucher. She's French-Dominican."

"Well, I'm pretty sure she and Annie are in the VIP area backstage, filming interviews with the performers."

"Where's that?"

Doc points toward a giant plastic banner that flares out from the left side of the stage like an interstate billboard. Thirty feet tall and a hundred feet long, it advertises 19 Crimes' "Cali Red" Wine, and features Snoop Dogg wearing dreadlocks. It must shield the backstage trailers and generators that make the spectacle on the stage possible. The whole setup is surprisingly professional, with massive lighting trusses over the performing platform, which is elevated at least twelve feet above the ground. The right side of the stage anchors a second banner, this one showing a massive photo of the smiling twelve-year-old who lost his life in Memphis ten days ago.

As I consider texting Annie, an insistent hip-hop beat fades into the general background noise of the festival. Then a familiar voice begins rapping over a drum loop, and a light-skinned Black man in his late twenties marches proudly to the center of the stage. Stripped to the waist, he wears "slave chains" in an X across his muscular chest. Rusted reddish brown, the chains look to weigh at least fifty pounds, but his bulging arms and rippling six-pack make you think he could carry that burden all day if necessary.

"Is that the kid who gives tours downtown?" I ask.

Doc nods with a grin. "Kendrick Washington. He looks like a high-school football player, but he's in his late twenties. He's an army combat vet, but now he devotes his time to educating tourists about the slave experience. He also attends Jackson State at least part-time. Majoring in history. I suspect he may have some service-related traumatic brain injury, but he's sure committed to his calling. I didn't know he was a rapper, though. Let's see what he does!"

As the hip-hop beat rises in volume, buffeting the residual air in my lungs, the crowd before the stage sways forward and back. Then, in a surprisingly powerful voice, Kendrick Washington begins reciting a literary passage, one I'm sure I've heard before.

"That sounds familiar," Doc whispers. "Who's he quoting? Maya Angelou?"

Doc is wide of the mark, I think. "Sounds more like . . . James Baldwin to me. *The Fire Next Time*, maybe?"

"I'll be damned. I like that! Shows some respect for the past."

"The backing track is Tupac," offers Robert Gaines from the bench seat below us.

"Tupac meets James Baldwin!" Doc marvels, rocking with the beat. "What a combination."

Just as my attention drifts, the music drops away, leaving only the drum loop, pounding incessantly. Kendrick ducks down, then pops up with an acoustic guitar and rips off a lightning sequence of blues licks that brings a gasp of awe from the crowd. A barrage of notes conjures a huge seventh chord over the field, and then suddenly Washington's strumming a minor and singing in a rich, edgy voice that reminds me of a young Lenny Kravitz, though the melody and lyrics come right out of my own youth.

"What's that he's singing now?" Doc asks. "Elijah?"

"I don't know. Something he wrote, maybe?"

"No," I tell them. "That's Neil Young. 'Southern Man.' People think that's the song 'Sweet Home Alabama' was written in response to it, but that was actually 'Alabama,' also by Young."

"I think I heard this in 'Nam," Ray says from where he stands beside the bleachers. "Or maybe in L.A. after I got back. I think I heard a sister do it, though."

"Neil Young sang it pretty high. Although . . . now that you mention it, I think Merry Clayton covered it. The background singer on 'Gimme Shelter'?"

"Oh, *hell* yeah! Sounds like Kendrick's changin' the words, though. Am I right?"

Focusing on the young singer, I let my mind drift back to the adolescent trance when I listened endlessly to the *After the Gold Rush* album. The warm yet incisive baritone filling the concert ground sings lyrics that sound similar to those I remember, but Ray is right; they've been altered considerably:

> *Mississippi brothers, free your minds*
> *Northern justice was never blind*
> *Push that change till it comes at last*
> *Judgment's flames come to cleanse the past*

After this call to action comes a personalized rewrite of Young's verse about an interracial relationship and KKK reprisal.

As the young man's cry for reparations reaches a passionate crescendo, the *whup-whup* of a distant helicopter enters the mix, then grows in amplitude. After a minute passes—during which Kendrick Washington astonishes the crowd with more blazing riffs played over a hip-hop beat and looper pedal—I watch a familiar Robinson R44 drop out of the sky and flare toward an open area behind the right side of the stage.

"Is that Dr. Ford's chopper?"

"Sure is," Doc confirms. "Dwight flew down to New Orleans to bring the headliner up in style. That Octa girl."

"I'll be damned. Doc Ford doing his part for the people?"

A close friend of mine, Dwight Ford is a radiation oncologist who travels the state providing services to medically underserved communities. He's no medical charity; he does very well for himself. But it's rare for poor Mississippi Delta residents to see a Black medical specialist of his caliber, and he likes giving their children someone to look up to as a life example.

The R44 touches down behind the stage, and a girl wearing hot pants and so much glitter I can see it sparkling from my seat climbs down and runs out of sight, one hand clapped over her piled-up blue hair.

"*Octoroon!*" the crowd screams as one. "*Octa! Octa! Octa!*"

"I guess they booked the right headliner," Doc reflects. "That girl's barely nineteen. Streaming millions of songs."

Dwight Ford's R44 revs loudly, then lifts into the sky, nose dipping as the chopper heads out over the river, where it turns north toward Bienville and climbs into the clouds. Taking out my iPhone, I text Dwight: *You've hit the big time now! As a chauffeur driver anyway!*

Thirty seconds later, my friend's reply comes through: *Air taxi, baby. Don't tell me you're down in that chaos!*

For as little time as possible. Let's get a drink this week.

Dwight texts me a thumbs-up in reply.

As I look up from my phone, the pounding drumbeat fades in the PA, and I see Kendrick Washington march off the stage with the dignity of a royal African soldier. His muscular back—crisscrossed by the heavy chains—leaves an indelible impression in the mind.

"Octa comes on in ten minutes," Elijah Keyes says excitedly. "This crowd's going to go crazy!"

"It's *been* crazy," Doc says worriedly. "I'll be glad when this is over and these folks head home. With all the gang trouble we been having, I feel like we've dodged a bullet today."

"Keep your fingers crossed," says Gaines. "We've still got another hour before they call a halt."

As we watch the crowd ebb and flow over the grounds during the break, I text Annie and ask where she is.

"What the hell?" says Alderman Keyes, pointing south. "Are those Tenisaw County sheriff's deputies?"

Like Doc, I squint across the heads of the crowd to where two men wearing dark brown uniforms and Stetson hats stand pointing at the vending area. "Sure looks like Buck Tarlton's men," Doc agrees. "In fact, I recognize one. Johnny Tackett. I delivered that boy when he was born. Emergency C-section. I don't think he's ever got over being delivered by a Black doctor."

"They're not the only ones out here," says Keyes. "Look."

He points to the right, and my eyes follow. I see at least three more white deputies moving deliberately through the crowd, almost as if fanning out to cover the audience from behind. As a text reply comes in from Annie, I watch the Stetsons move slowly forward, the surprised Black concertgoers making way for the deputies beneath them.

"Damn it," Doc mutters, reading a text from his phone. "Apparently neighboring property owners have been calling in complaints about the noise and the traffic. That's why these deputies have shown up. Tarlton must be considering trying to shut the concert down."

"He can't do that!" Keyes protests. "This is the country. There's no enforceable noise laws."

"Maybe not," I allow. "But there are drug and weapons laws, and any of those deputies could find ten violations within yards of where they're standing now."

"I hope they don't try it," Doc says, almost like a prayer. "I don't dare think what the result might be."

My phone pings again with Annie's reply. Looking down, I see: *Hey Dad! We're backstage in the VIP section. It's so awesome! Martine just interviewed Octa! It's crazy. Octa just got offered a role in the new Angie Thomas movie!*

Angie Thomas is the young writing phenomenon from Mississippi, author of *The Hate U Give* and *On the Come Up*. Like so many successful Mississippians, she recently migrated to Atlanta, but Mississippi is still proud of her. *Great*, I reply. *Just be careful. Things feel tense in this crowd.*

Annie replies with the speed of young fingers: *Don't worry about us! It's totally cool backstage. Come back if you can. Martine has the promoters wrapped around her finger! She'll get you back.*

Shaking my head, I type: *I'm fine where I am,* then add a wry smiley face.

A few moments pass. Then an incoming text reads: *Look at the left side of the stage, by the Snoop banner. Martine and I are waving at the bleachers!*

Sure enough, on the right edge of the huge advertising banner, in a narrow opening between it and the stage, I see my daughter, tall and willowy and pale, her auburn hair like a flag in the filtered sun, and beside her Martine's more compact body dressed in red capri pants and a white T-shirt. Both are waving wildly, like actors pulling aside a theater curtain to greet friends in an audience.

I raise my right hand high and wave back, though I doubt they can see me. Then, just as the pounding kick drum of a hip-hop beat cranks up, someone switches on a mic and the speakers squeal with feedback. I'm jerking my hands to my ears when five quick pops echo through the crowd.

A moment of stunned silence follows, revealing just how loud the background noise of the audience had been. Then panicked screams erupt with ear-piercing volume. As one, the fans near the stage surge backward, like beachgoers trying to escape an approaching tsunami. In so doing they create a human tidal wave, and from the VIP bleachers I see people being trampled as the mass of humanity tries to escape whatever made the popping sounds.

I've lived through enough gunfights to know already.

Getting to my feet, I flatten my hand over my eyes, trying to make out the action near the stage. When enough bodies clear the ground before the platform, I see a young man standing with a pistol in his outstretched hand, pointing it at a body lying prone on the ground before him. Then the body moves, and the boy fires twice more.

A thousand voices shriek as one, and Doc cries, "Don't do it!"

While we stare in horror and disbelief, at least four deputies open fire on the shooter with their service weapons, emptying their clips as police are wont to do. The hail of bullets knocks the gunman to the ground beside his victim.

Even as the deputies fire, I realize that mass disaster is unfolding before us. From my elevation, I can see that at least some of the officers—being on the ground, and positioned to the right of the boys—probably perceived what they believed to be a clear field of fire at the threat. But that was an illusion. For behind the gunman was only the wine banner—a sheet of plastic a few mils thick. It wouldn't stop the projectiles from a pellet gun, much less .40-caliber bullets. And behind the banner is the VIP area.

The potential scale of the carnage is hard to take in.

The next wave of screams sounds more like a chorus of despair and shock than fear, and it's coming from behind the banner, which now half-hangs from the wires that supported it only moments ago. God knows how many people have been shot behind that deceptive barrier.

But that's not the most immediate crisis. The deputies don't seem to realize what they've done. As the screams rise in volume and the crowd mills around the field in panic, at least fifty people stampede the bulging banner from behind, unknowingly running toward the source of the shots. The right side of the banner gives way, and a phalanx of bloody kids comes tearing out from behind it, running directly at the Tenisaw County deputies, who have racked and aimed their weapons as though in preparation for a second volley. This insanity I don't understand, unless the violent action has driven them into a hyper-aroused state, producing tunnel vision.

At last the kids fleeing the VIP area recognize the threat and skid to a stop on the muddy ground, resulting in a standoff that looks like nothing so much as the documentary film footage from the Kent State shooting in 1970. I fear the deputies will open fire out of reflex, killing dozens more. But in this awful, suspended moment, a newly familiar figure separates itself from the crowd and walks right into the gulf dividing the bloody kids from the deputies. It's Kendrick Washington, the rapper who left the stage only minutes ago, after reciting James Baldwin to the music of Tupac Shakur. Still shirtless and wearing the iron slave chains in which he appeared onstage, Washington in this moment looks like a Black Moses entering the chasm in the Red Sea.

Raising his muscular arms, palms open to the sky, the young veteran walks directly toward the officer commanding the line of armed men. The chief deputy aims his service pistol at Washington's chest, but the young vet doesn't stop. He walks forward with what I can only describe as religious conviction, calling out in a calm voice: *"Don't shoot, brothers! We mean you no harm!"*

The rattled deputy brandishes his pistol and orders Washington to the ground, but the soldier-turned-tour-guide-turned-rapper keeps moving steadily toward him, repeating, *"Peace, brother! Stand down. We mean you no harm!"*

While the deputy roars orders back at him, Washington turns to the panicked crowd behind him and cries: *"If you want to live, lie down! Like you're going to sleep! Only then will you rise again. Do it now, brothers and sisters. Don't give these men an excuse to hurt you! Remember Jackson State . . . remember Kent State. Lie down like lambs!"*

The power radiating from Kendrick Washington must be akin to that experienced by those who saw Joan of Arc in battle. Whatever its source and nature, its intensity is such that the deputies *do not fire*. Rather, they stare in amazement as the young man's voice somehow short-circuits the panic around the stage, and the people behind him begin kneeling, then lying prone in the mud. Repeating his words like a mantra, Washington in less than a minute somehow gets the whole crowd between him and the now-empty stage to obey him.

Staring in wonder, I realize that the PA system has gone silent, and in the resulting vacuum I hear sobs of joy and relief. Moans of pain and horror still come from the area behind the banner, but in the crowded space immediately before and around me a kind of awe has taken hold. The sight is indeed overwhelming, but before anything further can happen, I scramble down to the ground and start stumbling toward the torn banner.

The mud sucks at my prosthetic foot every time it smacks into the ground, forcing me to restart my journey every few seconds. The milling crowd buffets me again and again, like human waves, and it's all I can do to keep my feet. Yet fear drives me on. Halfway across the open ground, I trip over someone's ankle and crash into the muck. Pumping knees collide with my back and side as I try to struggle to my feet, sending paralyzing arcs of pain out from my fractured rib, and I'm about to collapse when someone jams his head under my right shoulder and lifts me almost effortlessly to my feet.

It's Bobby White.

"*Bobby?* What the hell are you doing?"

"Trying to keep you from being trampled to death!" he answers, his jaw clenched tight.

"Annie was behind that banner! I think there are casualties back there."

"That's where we're heading!"

"Go on! I'll catch up. Do whatever you can!"

He stops hauling me forward. "Are you sure?"

"*Go!*"

Bobby stands me up like a department store mannequin, then sprints toward the fallen Snoop banner. In four seconds he vanishes from my sight. Once again, I begin my clumsy trek toward the chaos. It's easier now, because most of the main audience has dispersed to some other part of the field. Two minutes of struggle takes me nearly to the stage, and all the way I ask myself if those might be Annie's last two minutes on earth.

Swatting the torn plastic of the banner out of my way, I see a scene unlike any I've ever witnessed. Only the documentary footage of the Las Vegas shooting compares to the carnage before me. Even though the deputies fired only a single volley, the opaque banner and the large number of people concealed behind it caused almost every round to hit a human being. The people on the ground look like extras in a graphic war film, like the first five minutes of *Saving Private Ryan*.

Within ten yards of the banner I see at least three open head wounds, clearly fatal, on what appear to be teenagers. Beyond these victims, people wounded in the legs and torso roll in agony on the ground. A few un-wounded people are trying to render first aid, but clearly no one has tools adequate to handle such trauma. I see a single ambulance forty yards away, near the tree line behind the stage, but only two paramedics, and they're working on a single victim.

"*Daddy!*" cries Annie's voice. "*Oh my God! Over here!*"

Whirling, I see an arm waving near ground level, almost beneath the stage-access steps. Following this hand downward, I see Bobby White crouched over my daughter. He seems to be working feverishly at the left side of Annie's chest, beneath her arm.

"Is she hit, Bobby?" I call, stumbling toward them.

"Twice," he answers in a taut voice. "Left hand, through and through. Second shot only grazed her side, thank God, but it's deep, and she's got a tension pneumothorax. I'm trying to reinflate it now."

My daughter has a collapsed lung. But Bobby White—veteran of Delta Force, like my friend Daniel Kelly—seems to have the training to deal with such an emergency, even with only one hand. A wave of gratitude floods through me for Bobby's presence. Dropping to my knees, I grip Annie's hand and squeeze with assurance. "You're going to be okay, boo. We've got you. Bobby's fixing you up."

"*They shot Martine!*" she wails, sobbing. "I think she's dead, Daddy . . . she's right over there."

Annie's meaning doesn't fully register at first, so great is my concern for my daughter alone. But then it hits me: Martine should be with her.

"Is that who she means?" Bobby asks, tossing his head to the left as he works.

Looking left, I see a limp body lying face up on the ground, but this woman looks as though she's been snatched up by a giant and tossed like a rag doll. Her face is several shades lighter than Martine's, her eyes open but flat and lifeless, and there's a hole punched through the center of her sternum. But then I notice the capri pants . . . and the blue fingernails.

It *is* Martine.

The woman my father died to save in Parchman penitentiary fifteen years ago now lies dead on the ground beside my daughter—*at a fucking concert*. It seems impossible, like something I read as a boy in *Ripley's Believe It or Not!* Yet there's no denying the stillness of the corpse lying in the mud beside us.

"How's she doing?" I ask Bobby as though from miles away.

"I've just about got the lung handled. But we need to get her to a hospital. Everybody back here needs a trauma surgeon."

"How the hell can we manage that?" I jab my hand toward the makeshift access road the crew used backstage. It's blocked by so many parked, stalled, and even wrecked vehicles that I can't imagine us getting out. Besides, we have no transportation.

"Do you have a car?" I ask Bobby.

"It's all the way back at the lot. Look! Her lung's filling."

Annie's chest rises suddenly, and her face colors in a way that fills me with hope.

"Stay with her!" Bobby orders.

"Where are you going?" I ask, feeling twinges of panic.

"To get us a vehicle!"

He's gone before I can reply. Looking around, I realize that between fifty and a hundred people have come backstage to try to help, or else to find friends and relatives. Even a few white deputies from Tarlton's department are trying to render aid, while others call for medevac choppers and ambulances on their radios.

"Martine's gone, isn't she?" Annie whimpers, blinking tears as she looks up in obvious pain.

"She is, boo. I'm sorry. She didn't have a chance. I think it was instantaneous."

"Ohhh, my God, my God. No—"

"Don't think about it now. Focus on breathing. Bobby and I are going to get you to a hospital."

She nods, her eyes showing trust. "Am I hit bad?"

"No. Your hand's got a hole in it, but that's no big deal. And it looks like Bobby fixed your side up. Just hang tight. You're tough, girl."

She nods bravely, as she always did when trauma came her way—which was more often than it did for the children of fathers who didn't pick fights with former Klansmen.

"Time to move!" Bobby says, sliding to a stop behind me and giving my shoulder a hard punch.

"You think we two cripples can move her?" I ask, nodding at his missing arm.

"Goddamn right we can. That's your kid, man."

Reddening with shame, I struggle to my feet. "Where are we going?"

Bobby points at an old Ford Bronco parked at the edge of the crush of vehicles. "I already cranked it."

He kneels at Annie's left shoulder. "Okay, Annie, we're each getting under one arm." He turns her head so that they are eye to eye. "You're about to walk forty yards, and we're going to help you."

"I don't know if I can do it."

"Oh, you're doing it. Get under that arm, Penn!"

Bobby's gift for leadership is so innate that I find myself obeying without question. After he gives a three-count, we heave Annie to her feet by main strength. The pain in my stump shoots up my thigh, then vanishes by some alchemy of adrenaline.

As we march Annie awkwardly toward the Bronco, it strikes me that she was the only white person backstage when the bullets struck. The only one I saw, anyway. If we take her alone to the hospital, she'll likely live while others who might have survived will die.

"Bobby, we can't take just Annie. You know?"

He winces, making what must be political calculations, then looks back over his shoulder. Doing the same, I see Ray assisting Doc Berry as he treats a pair of wounded kids.

"*Ray Ransom!*" Bobby shouts. "We're making a hospital run! Give me two wounded with a chance of making it! Three if they're kids."

"*Coming up, Sergeant!*" Ray shouts back. "Don't leave without them!"

"You know Ray?" I ask, surprised that Bobby would even be aware of such a low-level figure in Doc's campaign.

"I know everybody in Bienville," Bobby grunts, humping the greater share of Annie's weight over the rolling earth. "Every vet, anyway. Ray served in 'Nam before he went to prison."

By the time we get Annie laid out on the Bronco's back seat, Ray has appeared with a wounded teenage girl in his bulging arms. She's unconscious but obviously breathing. He stretches her out on the rough metal floor of the rear compartment. "I'm bringing one more, then get this thing moving. These kids are bleeding out! Those goddamn deputies fired hollow-points. I could kill them myself."

"Understood," Bobby acknowledges, climbing behind the wheel.

The Bronco sags a little when Ray deposits his next victim. Then he slams the rear door and smacks the roof twice, hard. Through some military code, Bobby knows this means *Go*, and he throws the Bronco into gear.

To my surprise, he floors the gas pedal and begins charging straight up a forty-five-degree incline so thick with volunteer trees that we almost can't pass through them. Ten seconds later he smashes over a stand of saplings, jouncing us so hard that the top of my head slams the cabin roof.

"Can we make it this way?" I ask in a juddering voice.

"You never seen a Delta operator drive?" Bobby asks, his eyes flashing as he wrenches the wheel left with his single hand. "Strap in, old man! You'll never be the same."

The four-wheel-drive vehicle fishtails in the mud, then catches a grip, lunges forward, and leaps over the crest of the hill. Below us I see the gravel road that at its end joins the legendary Blues Highway.

"God have mercy on anybody between us and 61," Bobby says, flooring the pedal for real. "Because I won't."

CHAPTER 6

I MAY BE politically liberal, but at this moment I'm sitting at my daughter's bedside with a loaded Rock River Arms AR-15 across my lap. The overwhelmed trauma docs at UMC gave me the option of bringing Annie home after they treated her in the ER, and I took it. With the help of Nurse Althea Foster, I installed her one room down from my mother's sickroom, on the ground floor of Edelweiss in Natchez. Then I took two of the four Ring security cameras that surround the house and placed one in each sickroom. This way I can keep an eye on them both, even without a sitter helping. Pain pills have kept Annie half-sedated, and for that I'm thankful. She'll be shattered when the full weight of Martine's death hits her, without the cushion of narcotics to deaden the pain.

I know what it's done to me already.

The exhaustion that caused me to slip into a near-narcoleptic state today has vanished—blown from my brain by the gore and terror I witnessed backstage at Mission Hill. Outside, on the bluff, the demonstration that felt perfunctory this afternoon has multiplied tenfold, and the steady chants, mournful hymns, and enraged yells from the crowd make it plain that they want explanations for the concert shooting, and probably more: many want retribution. I wouldn't normally fear a Black crowd in this county, but twenty-six people were shot by the white deputies at Mission Hill—most under twenty years old. Fourteen were declared dead at the scene, six died on their way to hospitals, and another died in the hospital earlier tonight, bringing the death toll to twenty-one. (My daughter was literally one of the luckiest five people on the scene, but a lot of people outside may not know we share in their suffering to the extent we do.) There are surely distraught relatives among the protesters who wouldn't be blamed for taking out their anger and grief on the nearest available target. For this reason, I stopped by my Bienville town house and got my rifle from the safe in my closet.

I bought the AR when I lived on sixty acres with a feral hog problem, but my real motive was my violent history with white supremacists. It dated from my years as an assistant DA in Houston and ran through my time as mayor of Natchez, when I killed or imprisoned enough of the bastards to make me a target for the rest of my life. Besides, the house where I raised Annie from age eleven to eighteen had a half-hour response time from the local constabulary. I am all for commonsense gun control, but I bought the AR specifically *because* it will kill a large number of humans quickly.

I spent a good hour disassembling and cleaning the rifle earlier this evening. The bananas-and-gasoline smell of Hoppe's No. 9 gun oil still hangs in the air. The solvent's unique tang will always remind me of my father, a pacifist at heart, although he fought the Chinese in Korea and died behind bars. But the scent also reminds me of my mother, who for decades folded mashed overripe bananas into a secret mixture that by some alchemy produced the best muffins in Mississippi. Until tonight, I hadn't smelled the Hoppe's for longer than I could remember. But once Annie settled into drug-induced sleep, I laid a quilt over Mom's worktable, got out the yellow-labeled Hoppe's jar and a bottle of Hendrick's gin, and cleaned the carbine the way my father taught me to clean all guns as a boy—carefully.

A Texas wind as bleak as Townes Van Zandt's "Waitin' Around to Die" slammed steadily into the bluff and rattled the eaves as it deflected skyward, but I remained bent to my task, trying to shut out the worst images from the concert ground. Levon Helm carried me through with his plaintive yet hopeful wail, and after I finished, I loaded two thirty-round magazines, then gaffe-taped them together jungle style, the way my uncle did in Vietnam. An extreme reaction, maybe, but I can't get the sight of Martine's lifeless eyes out of my mind. Especially when earlier, during the drive up from Natchez, I'd been reliving my memory of that first night we met, after the Parchman riot. It's hard to get my mind around the fact that Martine had so much luck on that violent night in the Delta, and then today none at all. But then it wasn't really luck that saved her at Parchman; it was Daniel Kelly's courage, and my father's selfless sacrifice.

SITTING BESIDE ANNIE'S bed, my hand gently holding her unbandaged one, I remember how fascinated Martine was in the hotel bar when I revealed the nature of the threat against my dad in Parchman. Even after working on documentaries in some of America's toughest prisons, the Frenchwoman seemed to find the pervasiveness of Parchman corruption hard to accept. I can still see her magnetic eyes across the bar table, pulling the story from me with almost physical power.

"Within a month of Dad being remanded to Parchman," I told her, "my mother moved up to the Delta to be close to him. She attended every possible visiting session, and they made it a nightmare of delay and harassment—every time. Within two months, she'd lost twenty pounds she couldn't afford. After four months, she was literally wasting away. Nothing I said could persuade her to care for herself. One month later I found out why."

A waitress finally appeared at our table.

"Pernod for me," Boucher told her. Confusion clouded the server's face. "Umm . . . I don't think we have that."

"They won't have Ricard, either," I told her.

Martine frowned. "They serve it in some New Orleans bars."

"French city."

"Wasn't Bienville also founded by France?"

"So was Natchez. But the bars don't serve Pernod."

"Remy-Martin?"

"There you go. Stella for me."

The waitress smiled in relief and walked away with a backward glance at Martine. "So?" the filmmaker prompted. "Please continue."

An image of my mother's emaciated face returned. "It was then that Mom appeared at my house in Bienville and asked for a hundred thousand dollars."

"*Mon dieu!*"

"I know. I was stunned, but I tried not to show it. I asked what she needed the money for. She told me she couldn't answer. I gently reminded her that she had four hundred thousand dollars in retirement money, and would have three times that after Dad died. At this she broke down, began to sob, and told me that those accounts were empty. All of them. She was stone broke."

"What?"

"Long story short, one of the gangs in Parchman had started extorting her less than a month after Dad went inside. That's one of the prison gang rackets, and Mom was the perfect mark. They made her pay a certain amount every week to keep Dad from being abused. Once they saw how terrified she was, they steadily upped the payments until they'd squeezed her dry."

Martine shook her head. "She never told you what they were doing?"

I shook my head. "She knew I'd try to find some way to stop it, and they'd kill him before we could get him protection. She didn't tell Dad, either. She worried that if he knew what they were doing, he'd commit suicide to take away their leverage over her."

Martine drew back in horror. "Do you think she was right?"

"Absolutely—on both counts. Even if I'd gotten the FBI Hostage Rescue Team to the gate to rescue Dad, the warden or gang leader could have had him killed and some fish confessing by the time the HRT got to him."

Boucher took all this in. "So you sent Kelly inside to find out the lay of the land?"

"Exactly. But first I paid fifty grand to buy the time for Kelly to scope things out. His decision? The only way to get Dad out safely was to break him out."

"How the hell did you get Kelly in?"

"You've been in Parchman. You don't even have to have a high school diploma to get hired as a guard. Back then they'd hire anybody with two weeks' training."

Martine shook her head in disbelief.

"After two weeks, Kelly not only knew the gangs ran the prison, but that the corruption went all the way to Jackson. It's Shawshank in that place. Daniel actually brought some photos out to use as leverage if we needed it later. And I think we might."

"What a movie this would make," Martine whispered.

"Anyway, as I told you, Kelly was waiting to walk Dad away from that work-release gig when Xavier Smalls's gang killed that first guard in D-block. If they'd done it just twenty minutes later, my father would be a free man now."

Martine's eyes welled with tears. "I'm so sorry, Penn."

"Do you know why they killed that guard when they did?"

"I don't."

The waitress arrived with our drinks, and Martine took a swallow of cognac. "Terrible," she whispered. "So. As so often happens, chance determined our fates. It trapped Tom behind those walls, just as it trapped me."

I took a slow sip of beer and thought about that. "I wondered whether maybe it was the presence of you and your cameraman that triggered the riot. Given that it would focus a much bigger lens on the event, and even provide interior footage afterward."

Martine didn't argue the premise. "I'm sure a few of them felt that way. You know, I've seen third-world prisons where conditions are better than Parchman. But there was nothing noble about that riot. Once they started, it was the law of the jungle in there. Hobbes was right, I'm afraid—not Rousseau."

The Frenchwoman's remarkable composure while discussing a nightmare in which she'd been personally victimized had struck me from the beginning. "I hesitate to be so personal, but . . . should you really be here? After what you went through?"

She tilted her head slightly, considering the question. "The physical trauma was terrible, of course. The emotional trauma is . . . a different thing. But I'm no stranger to either, I'm afraid. I made a film in a failed state in Africa. I was assaulted by two teenage soldiers during one of those shoots."

I blinked at her candidness. "God. I'm sorry."

"That's one of those experiences I left out of a project. But this time my assault will be part of the story. It must be. In all honesty, it's the STDs I have to worry about now. I won't know about those for some days. From what I've learned about the prison, the odds of a bad outcome on that front are significant."

"I'm so sorry, Ms. Boucher."

"Martine, please. Well . . . I'm alive. And for that I owe your father. And Daniel Kelly. I've thanked Monsieur Kelly profusely, but I hope you'll pass on my condolences to your mother. I understand she's not doing well."

"She took Dad's death hard." I glanced at my watch. "I do need to get back to her."

"Of course. Is there . . . anything I can tell you? Something you'd like to ask before we part?"

"You know the answer to that. The second message. What was the other thing Dad wanted me to know?"

Martine looked down at the scarred tabletop, the napkins with printed steamboats on them. Then she turned to the bar, where the personal injury attorney still watched us with a mix of jealousy and resentment.

"He gave you that message in case he died," I pressed. "Well . . . he did die. And if you don't tell me what it was, then the man who saved your life will take those words to his grave."

She held up her hands in surrender. "I understand. I've wrestled with this all day."

"I'm sorry to push you."

"Do you know a man named Leo Marston? A former *magistrat*?"

"Of course. Judge Marston. I dated his daughter in high school. I basically sent Leo to Parchman for murder twenty years later. He's been serving that sentence since 1998."

"Well . . . your father told me to tell you that Marston wants revenge for what your family did to his."

"That's no secret. I worried from the beginning that he'd have Dad killed as soon as he got into Parchman. But the gang extorting Mom kept Marston off him, so they could take her last dollar. After that, I'm sure they'd have let Leo murder him. That was the other part of the threat to Dad's safety."

"Whatever the case," Martine said, "your father said to tell you that if Judge Marston ever reached out to you in any way . . . you should have him killed. However hard that might be, you should find a way. 'Don't hesitate,' Tom said."

I took a swallow of beer and processed this. For some reason, her unblinking stare was hard to endure. The directness of Dad's instruction surprised me, as did the nature of it. "So you think he meant . . . that even though he's dead now, the threat hasn't passed?"

"Yes."

"That means my daughter's in danger."

"That's why I'm relaying the message, despite my misgivings."

The grim reality settled into me like a poison. "*Merci.*"

The filmmaker didn't look relieved by the fulfillment of my father's second charge. "I've got to say," she murmured, "America overall is a violent country, but the South seems a particularly brutal and vindictive place."

"It can be."

Martine looked like she was about to take her leave. I closed my hand around hers, and she did not pull away. "If you don't mind, I'd like to know a little about Dad's final minutes. Before Kelly took you out of there. I've heard Daniel's version, of course. But you were in there with him while Kelly was positioning the motorcycle—"

"Of course." She seemed to gather herself. "Well . . . it's straightforward enough. Your father was working to keep his patients alive—both guards and inmates, as I said. Kelly had discovered the motorcycle in the guards' parking area. He knew how to start it without a key. He'd already procured a ballistic vest for your father, and magazines and duct tape to protect his legs. He expected to take gunfire when they made their run for the gate. The inmates were manning the towers with the guards' rifles."

"Why did the gangs allow Kelly so much freedom of movement?"

Admiration showed in her eyes. "Somehow Daniel had made himself the go-between for all parties. Between the authorities outside and the gangs, as you know. But also as a messenger between rival gangs in the prison."

Nothing about this surprised me. Kelly could talk a stripper into a free lap dance. "Where were you during the final minutes?"

"On a hospital bed in the infirmary. Partly sedated by a drug your father had given me. To deaden my terror as much as my pain, I think."

"And then?"

"I witnessed the last conversation between Kelly and your father. The inmates had panicked, because someone in a tower reported the arrival of two more SWAT vans. It was then that Tom told Kelly he wouldn't abandon the wounded, and insisted that Kelly take me out instead. Kelly argued, but your father held firm. The whole exchange lasted no more than a minute. During an argument between the gang leaders. While that situation worsened, Kelly asked if I was capable of getting out of bed under my own power and going through a certain door. I wasn't sure, but I knew if I stayed where I was, I would die. They'd never let me testify about what they'd done in there. So I told Kelly I could make it."

"I don't blame you."

"I did manage the walk. Kelly had set a makeshift incendiary explosive in an adjacent building as a diversion, and that was the signal to go. The moment I went through that door, he threw the vest on me and duct-taped magazines to my thighs and upper arms. I asked what he was doing, and he said, 'Protecting your arteries.' I knew then he was some kind of professional. The rest . . . you saw on television."

I thought of the now viral footage, Kelly roaring across the prison parking lot like Steve McQueen in *The Great Escape*, not stopping even as one bullet slammed into his shoulder and another hit a magazine shielding his left thigh.

I squeezed her hand again. "I'm glad you made it out, Martine."

The first tears finally spilled from her eyes. "That can't be easy for you to say."

"How old are you?" I asked.

"Thirty-six."

"Dad was seventy-three. He had congestive heart failure, diabetes, and a half dozen other ailments. For him that wasn't even a decision. He was like Alfred Vanderbilt on the *Lusitania*. He'd have given up his life jacket and loaded women and children until the ship went under before he ever got into a boat himself."

"He did," Martine said. "Kelly was his life jacket." She wiped her bloodshot eyes with the napkin. "He taught you the same, didn't he?"

"I hope so." I hated to push her further, but one question remained. "I know now you didn't see Dad die. And the authorities haven't given me a cause of death yet. But I've gotten some private hints that he might have been murdered. By guards or by a fellow prisoner. Do you have any idea how that might have happened?"

She looked back at me with what felt like bottomless empathy. "I'm afraid I don't. And it breaks my heart to even imagine what you say." She reached out with her other hand and squeezed my free one, so that we sat linked across the table. Two survivors with no idea what to do next.

"I'm glad you came, Penn. I appreciate you driving out here in this storm."

"I am, too." With nothing substantive left to say, I wrote my email address on the damp napkin and gave it to her. "Please contact me, if you ever feel the need. Maybe we can help each other get to the final truth."

She smiled. "I will, my friend. *Merci.*"

We stood, and she came around the table and embraced me. After a few moments, she kissed me on the cheek. "*Au revoir*, Penn Cage," she said into my ear. "*Je suis de tout coeur avec vous.*"

"*Merci*," I said, not quite sure of her final meaning, but certain that her words expressed heartfelt emotion.

I waited for Martine to leave the bar, to be sure that neither the drunk redneck nor the resentful lawyer hassled her further. Then I exited the hotel by the side door, which was closer to my car than the main entrance.

The night chill sliced through me before I reached my Audi, and I cranked the engine as quickly as I could. Glancing at my side mirror, I saw Martine emerge from the same door and embrace a man who looked like the camera tech I'd seen interviewed with her on TV. Wondering if their relationship was purely professional, I pulled out of my space and made a tight turn in the wide boulevard, which pointed me toward Canal Street.

The traffic light was red, but I could see yellow backscatter glowing in the rain on the side facing Canal. I'd have a green in seconds. An image of my father working over wounded men bloomed in my mind. Drifting slowly toward the intersection, I looked back once more and saw the cameraman kiss Martine's forehead. As I stared, the blast of a horn hit my left eardrum like a swordpoint, and I whirled toward the pain. Headlights the size of full moons filled my vision, then wiped out all shadow in an acrid explosion—

I felt no impact.

BLACK WATER SURROUNDS me. I kick my feet as hard as I can, sure that the surface must be within reach. My air is running out, my muscles burn, and I kick and kick but see no light. And yet . . . I hear something.

Voices.

My eyes burn. Defying instinct, I struggle until they open.

A blurred world appears, seen through a lens rubbed with Vaseline.

Then a voice I know better than any other says: *"Are his eyes open? My God, he's waking up!"*

My mother's voice quickens my pulse, fills me with hope. *I can't see*, I try to say, but only a croak escapes my parched throat.

"Give him the eye drops!" says a familiar male voice.

Cold wetness hits my cheeks, then blessed moisture washes the sand-grit burn from my eyes. My mother's face, wracked with fear, fills my field of vision. "Do you know me?" she whispers.

"Mom," I croak.

Tears flood down her cheeks. "He's back! Dear God, he's come back!"

"What's your name?" asks the male voice. Then its owner moves into the frame with my mother. Blond hair, blue eyes, weathered skin. The hair he usually wears shoulder-length, but it's still cut close from his role as a prison guard.

"Kelly . . . you SOB."

"Not *my* name, asshole." He grins. "But that's good enough for me."

"What . . . ?" is all I can manage.

"What's the last thing you remember?" he asks.

I try to answer, but I'm blank. "I don't know. A hotel?"

Kelly glances at Mom. "What hotel? Where?"

"The Delta Dawn? Up by Parchman?"

Fear clouds my mother's eyes.

"Where's Annie?" I ask worriedly. "Where's Dad?"

Mom turns away in a vain attempt to hide what looks like despair. Kelly leans over the bed and squeezes my upper arm the way my father once did before stitching up a bad laceration on my jaw.

"Listen, bubba," he says in his soldier's voice. "I'm going to give it to you straight, the way I'd want it. The way we've always been together. You ready?"

I nod, bracing myself against whatever might come.

"Tom's gone. He was killed in the prison riot. Your daddy gave his life to save the female hostage, which was the only way that stubborn son of a bitch was ever going out. You know what he did in Korea. He was a born hero."

I hear my mother sob.

"As for you—you got T-boned by an electrical utility truck near the Grand Hotel in Natchez. You've been in a medically induced coma for nearly a week. You're mostly intact, but your right leg's gone from the knee down. That ain't great, but I've got a lot of buds with that injury, and you can handle it. You've also got about twenty other broken bones, but that's just carpentry."

Realizing Kelly is nodding at my right arm, I look down and see it encased in a cast from above the elbow down. A tent of some kind also covers my right leg, lighted from within by what feels like a heat lamp. Fear caroms through me, then settles somewhere between my diaphragm and where my balls should be.

"Skin graft under that tent," he explains. "No big deal. The critical thing is your heart. The crash impact tore your aorta, and fewer than five percent of people survive your particular injury. Luckily, Drew Elliot was in the Natchez hospital when they brought you in, and he insisted on treating you. Drew noticed a bulge on the X-rays and got you onto a chopper up to University Med in Jackson. The trauma surgeon floated in a stent just before your aorta came apart. Kevlar and chicken wire, baby. So . . . that brings you up to now. You're not vertical yet, but you will be eventually, and that's all that matters."

"Was it an accident?" I ask softly.

Kelly nods. "Spoke to the driver myself. His crew was working overtime on downed lines on the north end of town. He tried to make the yellow light but ran the red. While you, in all probability, were daydreaming about whatever Martine Boucher told you in the hotel bar."

"Who?"

My friend's eyes narrow. "Don't worry about it now."

"Where are we?"

"Still University Medical Center in Jackson."

All this is simply too much to process. "You're saying I'll walk again? For sure?"

"Damn right you will. By the way, your male equipment is all intact and in working order. You've still got a catheter in, though. You want me to yank it out and wake you up good?"

"Jesus . . ." Relief floods through me. "I feel like I'm underwater."

"That's the fentanyl. A hundred times more potent than morphine. If you want to feel better, I'll tell you what the nurse who's been taking care of you at night said, even though you couldn't hear her."

"What's that?"

"She studied your chart for a couple of minutes, then looked at you and said, 'Well, Mr. Penn Cage, *the Lord obviously ain't through with you yet.*'"

"Oh, my God," says my daughter's quavering voice. "Is Daddy awake?"

"He is," Kelly informs her, backing away after giving my arm one more goose.

My thirteen-year-old runs to the bed, looks into my eyes to make sure I'm really there, then carefully puts her arms on my shoulder and leans down until her head rests on my chest. The sound of relief in Annie's voice as she shudders against me nearly unmans me.

"Papa's gone," she whimpers. "Do you remember that? Did they tell you?"

"They did." I gently rub my left hand through her silken hair. "But it sounds like he went out the way he would have wanted to."

"He was so brave, Daddy."

My eyes fill with tears, and then the room begins to fade. I try to call out to Kelly, but my vocal cords don't seem to be working. I squeeze Annie's neck with my left hand.

"What's happening?" she asks, her head popping up. "What the matter with him?"

"He's just exhausted," Kelly explains. "I've seen this a hundred times. It's relief, more than anything. He's realized he's alive again."

"Can we stay?" Annie asks. "I'm not leaving him again!"

"We ain't going nowhere, baby girl." Kelly leans down and peers into my eyes. All I can see in the gathering darkness is the confidence in his familiar face. "I'm here, brother," he assures me. "And we'll still be here when you wake up. All of us. Rest easy till the next watch."

And then he vanishes.

THE SOUND OF sharp knocking at the ground-floor door of Edelweiss brings me from a deep sleep at my daughter's bedside. It's past midnight, but outside the protests have continued without abating. I'm reluctant to answer the door, even with my AR-15. There are four glass panes in the door's upper half, and it would be easy for someone to smash their way inside, or to simply shoot me through one of them. But after I sit in silence for a full minute, the knocking starts again. Then I hear a voice that sounds somehow familiar speak urgently through the door:

"It's okay, Penn. I'm a friend. I'm here to check on Annie."

"Who are you?"

"Don't want to say. Too many people out here. Reporters."

Could that be Kelly? I wonder, getting to my feet. So far as I know, my buddy and sometime protector is somewhere in the Crimea or the Donbas, advising Ukrainian troops for either a private security company or the U.S. government. After racking the slide on the AR, I tiptoe to the curtained door, aim through it at the target I visualize on the other side, then move forward and peer through the tiny gap between the curtain over the glass and the wooden door frame.

Bobby White stands outside, tall and impatient and looking like the most competent son of a bitch I've seen since Walt Garrity and my father teamed up against the Double Eagles. Instantly I flash on my memory of Bobby on his knees beside Annie in the blood and mud, working to reinflate her lung. With a deep sigh of relief I unbolt and open the door.

Bobby smiles. "How's our girl doing, Mayor? How are *you* doing?"

A wave of emotion so strong that it obliterates my capacity for speech rolls through my chest. Without hesitation or shame, I lunge forward and clench the son of my high school friend in a hug that might crush an average man beyond breathing. But Bobby just wraps his sole arm around me and returns the embrace.

"Take it easy, brother. It was a tough day. Especially for a civilian."

The lump in my throat feels as big as a golf ball, and it aches. "I can't . . . can't ever repay you for what you did today."

"You don't have to. I just did what she needed me to do."

"Jesus, Bobby . . . you'll understand someday, after you have a kid."

"Maybe I will. I hope so."

Drawing away from him, I shake my head at the memory of his commanding self-possession as he worked to save Annie in the midst of lethal chaos, then drove us twenty-five miles to the hospital through panicked traffic without stopping once.

"Come inside and take a look at the angel you saved," I tell him. "I'll fix you a drink."

He looks at his watch. "I don't have much time. I'm doing the Sunday shows in D.C. in the morning. But I could use that drink."

"How the hell are you getting to D.C. in time to do the morning shows?"

He laughs wearily. "At great cost, my friend. I missed my commercial flight because of Mission Hill, but we've got a charter sitting out at the Natchez airport. I can spare twenty minutes for a drink, though."

"I'm paying for that flight, Bobby. Your charter, I mean. Don't even think about it."

"No need for that. I got to spend some time visiting my father at UMC once the doctors started working on Annie."

"I'm glad, but that's bullshit. You saved my daughter's life. I'm paying your charter. And I'll tell you this: if you really run for president, you've got my vote."

Bobby laughs. "I don't know about all that. We'll see."

"Whiskey?"

He points to the rifle in my hands. "Penn, let me have that before you hurt somebody."

I pass him the AR without hesitation. He expertly ejects the banana clips and clears the chamber.

"Vodka," he says. "Cold."

"Coming up, Sergeant."

The man they're calling the TikTok candidate leans my AR-15 in a corner, then slaps me on the shoulder and follows me upstairs to the kitchen.

"I'll tell you who the hero of Mission Hill is," comes his voice from behind me. "Kendrick Washington. That guy's gone from twenty-two thousand followers before the shooting to nearly three million. In half a day!"

"Three *million*? Wow."

"That's the world we live in. But still . . . that rate of increase is breaking almost every record, from what I understand. It's unprecedented."

If I didn't know better, I'd swear I heard jealousy in Bobby's voice. But this is a man whose exploitation of social media has been so perfect that he's being talked about as a serious presidential candidate. How could he be jealous of a nearly penniless tour guide's numbers?

"That teenage rap singer, Octa, caught some shrapnel from a ricochet, and that blew the story up bigger than it might have been. She may have some facial scarring. More than twenty dead, and watching the news you'd think she's the lead story."

"Celebrity's the currency of our age, Bobby. You know that."

"I need that vodka is what I know."

As I pour him a double shot of Stoli from the freezer, I realize I haven't looked in on Mom for too long. "I'm overdue checking on my mother. Let me run down there while you finish that first one. I'll be right back."

"Take your time. I'll look in on Annie. I want to see what luck looks like. Maybe pick up a little by osmosis. The gods were smiling on her today."

"Luck, maybe. Gods, my ass. You saved her, buddy, end of story."

Bobby holds up the shot glass and grins. "Nothing like a win, Penn."

I nod, but deep in my gut a sour acid rush makes me clench my belly.

"What is it?" he asks.

"A lot of people lost today. Lost everything."

He nods soberly. "Bad times coming, no doubt. But don't question your own good fortune. That's asking for trouble."

"Maybe. But this family was due some good luck."

Bobby's eyebrows go up. "How you figure?"

I pour myself a Hendrick's and Fever Tree tonic, and then I tell him.

Monday

CHAPTER 7

ONLY THIRTY-SIX HOURS had elapsed since Bobby White left Penn Cage in the chalet atop the Natchez bluff, but his life had changed profoundly. He'd easily made the call times for the political shows the previous morning, including a particularly tight crosstown commute to the CBS broadcast studios for *Face the Nation*. But there a figure out of his past had resurrected himself to threaten everything that had broken Bobby's way during the past few months.

As Bobby passed through the crowded lobby of the building housing the CBS studios, he'd felt someone shake his hand as though in congratulations. When he looked up, he saw the face of Paul Beckley, an army general he'd served with in Afghanistan, when Beckley was only a captain in intelligence and Bobby's unit—Task Force Coral—had been hunting high-value targets like Abu Musab al-Zarqawi and Abu Nasir El Sherif across the globe with almost no regard for national boundaries. Rather than release Bobby's hand, as anyone without an ulterior motive would have done, Beckley had steered him out of the general flow and guided him to a pair of empty chairs near a granite column.

"What the hell's this?" Bobby asked quietly.

"I just need a brief word," Beckley told him. "Surely you've got time for an old comrade in arms. Even a man as busy as you are these days."

If Bobby's memory served him, Major General Paul Beckley ought to be nearing retirement after spending the remainder of his career in Europe, specializing in theoretical battles with the forces of the former Soviet Union. A stultifyingly redundant specialty until Putin's invasion of Ukraine turned him into an in-demand expert on the "new old battlefield." Overnight, Beckley had gone from frustrated two-star headed toward anonymous retirement to well-compensated pundit for the cable networks.

In his mid-fifties, the general was more than a decade older than Bobby, but he still ran ten miles a day, as he humblebragged while nervously trying to make small talk. Sadly, constant exercise had not preserved what had been a striking handsomeness twenty years before. Beckley's youthful face had fallen, giving him pronounced jowls for a man of his age. Comparing him to memory was like looking at Julia Ormond in *Sabrina*—at thirty a beauty so stunning she'd been cast to replace Audrey Hepburn—and then seeing her in films at fifty and not recognizing her for several minutes.

"How about you get to the real reason you're here?" Bobby said in the first gap after making his initial assessment of the man's affect.

Beckley drew himself up and spoke with dignity, like a gentleman imparting information out of a sense of honor. But as his sentences piled clumsily upon themselves, Bobby sensed the shame of a self-deluded hustler working his way through the process of blackmail. Beckley had little talent for the crime. Bobby, on the other hand, had gained some experience with blackmail over the past year, and it struck him how similar his old comrade's body language was to that of the other thorn in his side. The general was like a nervous mugger pulling back a coat to reveal a knife—one he didn't realize had two sharp edges. The gist of his pitch was simple:

Last month I was offered a book deal. An autobiography. Because of the Ukraine angle, the publisher wants to rush it out. They're also interested in the famous people I've worked with. Naturally, you number among those. Thanks to recent developments, you're right at the top, in fact. Now, Bobby . . . I know you, ah, in a way that . . . well, a way you've chosen to keep secret for the past twenty years. And if you remain a private citizen—despite your success in law and entertainment—that's your business. But if you really decide to run for president, it becomes difficult to defend that position to myself. Second, as regards your killing of Abu Nasir, we both know that didn't happen in a vacuum, which is the conventional understanding. Ten days of intensive operations preceded that hit. I think I'm the only person outside your unit who knows what took place in the Nasir house in Iraq. What led you to know he was hiding in Afghanistan. I've never spoken or written of it outside the initial debrief. But if you're lining up to run for commander in chief of all U.S. forces, then I think most people would say that's information the voters need.

Beckley made this sound so noble—almost a civic obligation. But the reality? He was a parasite, prodded to hunger by Bobby's sudden fame. Tio Carrera would have warned Bobby to expect just this kind of threat, had they maintained contact. As Beckley spoke, Bobby thought back to Afghanistan, when they'd shared two nights in a hooch that the captain assured him no one with any military connection would enter between dusk and dawn. Seven hours after the death of Abu Nasir, they'd each swallowed cups of *bhangawa* tea, letting it bring them down from the hyperactive state that often followed successful combat operations. After the tea, they'd smoked some *shirac*, the potent Afghan hashish that one of the interpreters frequently used. Then—and only then—did they allow themselves to enjoy the kind of release that Bobby, at least, had spent most of his life, before and since, denying himself.

Bobby regarded the anxious officer in conflicted silence for half a minute, then calmly asked, "Are you threatening to *out* me, Paul? On multiple levels?"

"Of course not," Beckley hissed in a tone of offense. "I'm only doing what any good officer would do. Giving you fair warning. If you mean to run for president—and part of me hopes you will—I believe the public deserves to know all that can be known about who you are and how you make decisions. And *you* deserve to know that you'll likely be required to explain those things."

Bobby pursed his lips and leaned forward. "I'll *likely* have to? Or *will* have to?"

When Beckley didn't answer, Bobby laid it out starkly. "I'll ask you three questions. One, would you reveal this information to a reporter today for free? Two, do you intend to keep quiet, put it in your book, and get paid for it down the line? Or three, are you asking for compensation not to reveal it at all?"

Beckley colored at this final question, and it was then Bobby knew that—one way or another—his old intel officer would act to maximize his financial gain for what he knew, regardless of his answer. This realization gave Bobby a chill of foreboding, because Paul Beckley absolutely possessed information that would destroy any chance he had of becoming president.

Now, thirty hours later, Bobby understood it had been right there, in the CBS lobby, that he'd made the decision to kill Beckley. He didn't want to do it. He hadn't even *chosen* to do it. Beckley had called the play. And he ought to have known better. Any man who threatened to destroy another's life or livelihood by blackmail ought to realize he was forcing retaliation from his victim. After all, there were only two choices for the subject being pressured: cave and pay, or strike back. And if you paid . . . the demands would never stop.

Beckley had to know that. Crazier still, how did he think a special forces operator would react to an existential threat? Maybe he figured Bobby had grown soft over the years, as he had. On the other hand, maybe Beckley had never been a very good intel officer. After all, yesterday he'd passed on what was essentially self-targeting information during the first two minutes of their conversation.

Bobby knew a dozen ways to kill a man in seconds. He'd been trained by the best, and he'd been forced to use more than a few of those methods during his career. But it was Beckley's boast about his running regimen that had prompted him to go to an internet bar and begin seining the general's social media history. It had taken all of ten minutes to find GPS maps of some of Beckley's favorite running and biking routes. The most common threaded through a downtown cemetery called Mount Olivet, which offered surprising isolation in the midst of urban D.C. Seeing those maps, Bobby had felt a powerful enough premonition to plan what was essentially a lightning strike against a man who had made himself the ultimate HVT.

Whatever method Bobby chose, speed mattered most. Now that Beckley had confronted his mark, he'd begin second-guessing everything he'd done up till then. He might even suspect the danger he'd put himself in, and as a result confide what he'd done to a friend, or even make some record on his phone or computer. The fastest way to minimize this threat would be to ambush Beckley on the street, then rob and kill him, making it look like a mugging gone bad. But there were countless cameras in the nation's capital, and while Bobby was an expert at disguise, a more exotic method struck him as the smart way to handle this problem.

He worried that his chosen method might require a side trip to Virginia Beach or North Carolina, where so many former operators lived. But D.C., too, offered a lot of opportunity for specialized veterans, especially in personal protection, and Bobby knew more than a few of those guys. Most important, he knew a couple who weren't above working on the wrong side of the law. By visiting the right residence when its owner was away (another skill Delta had trained him for), he could obtain a lethal weapon that would point so far away that he'd never have to worry about suspicion falling on him.

While carrying out the necessary burglary last night, he'd reflected on his greatest piece of luck, which was that Corey Evers had remained at the hotel while Bobby did the Sunday morning shows. With their announcement deadline fast approaching, Corey had felt his time would be better spent in the makeshift "war room" he'd set up in their suite. From there—while Bobby took questions from the networks' various D.C. anchors—Corey had gone down the list of TikTok connections running the national effort to sign petition names. Corey had no idea that Bobby had run into Paul Beckley (whom Corey would remember from Afghanistan) at one of the studios. Thus, when he eventually heard of Beckley's death, Corey wouldn't connect it to his employer in any way.

THIS MORNING, WHILE supposedly doing an exercise run (and while Corey worked the East Coast organizers via Zoom and Skype), Bobby

had sat alone on a wood-and-steel park bench facing one of the main asphalt lanes in Washington's Mount Olivet Cemetery. He wore running
clothes and a blue Nationals cap. An umbrella lay on the bench beside
him. Thanks to his Delta training, Bobby looked nothing like the man
that millions watched on TikTok and YouTube every day. His careful
makeup job and the prosthetic left arm he wore almost guaranteed that no
one looking at camera footage caught by chance would suspect they were
seeing one of the leading candidates for president of the United States.
In fact, had his mother walked within twenty feet of him, she would not
have recognized him. Bobby looked like a fortysomething Arab who had
stopped to rest in the middle of a recreational jog.

As he waited for Paul Beckley to appear, Bobby thought about a
Natchez alderman who at Mission Hill had asked him whether Washington, D.C., should be considered a Northern or Southern city. To answer
that, the alderman need only have traveled from Mississippi to the capital
in October, as Bobby had done. For while Mississippi was still green, au-
tumn had already splashed the trees of Mount Olivet with red and orange,
bringing a bite to the air that demanded he wear a windbreaker. Bobby
had been glad for the pretext to cover up with the jacket and hat.

The cemetery was deserted, his pulse slow and steady. K Street's lobby-
ing firms lay three miles to the west, Beckley's condo a little farther on.
Bobby's hotel was about half that distance, and his cell phone was safely
back in his room. This was the longest he'd gone in the two days since
Mission Hill without checking the fallout on social media. The wounded-
versus-dead count was still changing (the old KIA/WIA/MIA of the
Sandbox), and it was freaky to follow such numbers in the USA, especially
with the kill ratio so high. The setup of the musical stage and the huge
wine banner had created a situation where nearly every bullet fired from
the deputies' guns had struck a human, and their hollow-point rounds had
done horrific damage. When Bobby abandoned his phone at his hotel this
morning the number of dead had been twenty-two, with four critically
wounded survivors, but there was concern that another teenage girl might
die by nightfall.

The concert shooting had greatly magnified the number and intensity
of national marches that had begun as a reaction to the Memphis incident,
but Bobby had kept a tight focus on his hometown. The most remarkable
development of what was now being called the "Mission Hill massacre"
was the emergence of Kendrick Washington as a national social media
figure. Because so many cell phones had recorded his courageous confrontation with the deputies during the height of the standoff, the young

military vet who'd worn slave chains during his musical appearance had become a sort of quasi-religious civil rights leader with more than thirty million followers on various social media platforms.

Thirty million.

Bobby had never seen anyone gain that kind of traction in the public consciousness so fast. There was surely something to be learned from this. For two days he'd sensed the deepest part of his mind working on the concept. While his own social media numbers had been considered astounding, they were based on what were essentially contrived videos. But Kendrick Washington's actions had been an authentic response to an actual crisis unfolding in front of five thousand cell phone cameras, at least a hundred of which had recorded the entire event. They were *real*. There was absolutely nothing artificial about what Kendrick had done. It was as though a cameraman had been present in the moment that fifteen-year-old Aitzaz Hasan tackled the suicide bomber outside the gate of his school in Pakistan in 2014, giving his life to save hundreds of his classmates.

Kendrick Washington hadn't been killed during his heroic act, but the risk of death was indelibly burned into every frame of the videos that recorded his march toward the line of armed deputies at Mission Hill. And the result? The young man had in less than three days achieved a global fame that made Bobby's seem trivial by comparison. That was the key to his massive number of followers—global resonance. The image of an unarmed young Black man fearlessly facing armed white deputies triggered something visceral in the masses of Brazil, Nigeria, and India, where smartphone penetration was pervasive. India alone had more than eight hundred million smartphone users. Because of this, even Kendrick's rewritten performance of "Southern Man," a fifty-three-year-old Neil Young song, had 19.6 million views on YouTube, far more than most videos by Young himself.

Frustrated by having no internet-connected device to check, Bobby studied the makeup he'd applied to his wrists and hands as carefully as he had to his face. Putting on his old "Arab face" had reminded him of his operational years in Iraq. The ease and speed with which he'd accomplished it had surprised him, but here in the U.S. it was easy to find the peach foundation that was the secret to getting a good olive skin tone. Paul Beckley had surely known that trick at one time, but he probably hadn't thought about it for years, having been transferred to the European theater shortly after El Sherif's death.

Bobby glanced right, where the empty asphalt lane ran along a ditch lined with drying kudzu, still green but on its way to its dormant fall state. Back in Mississippi, the kudzu was still climbing 120-foot hardwoods, strangling them like Burmese pythons killing Florida deer—

A trim figure had appeared in the distance. It grew steadily larger. It looked like Beckley, but Bobby couldn't be sure. He squeezed the handle of the mini-umbrella on the bench beside him and counted silently from one to twenty in Arabic. It was an old trick of his from the field, to remain calm.

Nerves had never been a problem for him, even on hit missions. But something about the geometry of this setup rattled him. Lying in wait for an unsuspecting target with a handheld weapon . . . it threw him right back to the first murder he'd ever seen, which was his grandfather's.

Marked Tree, Arkansas . . .

A parched nothing of a town in the Arkansas Delta, forty dusty miles northwest of Memphis. The dead hours between morning and evening church in that part of the country. They should've been fishing in the shade somewhere, or sleeping off Sunday dinner at the Goodloes' house, which was where they'd been sleeping for the previous week. But Grandpa Corbin had insisted on preaching a sermon outside the little movie theater they had there. The cashbox was low, and he figured a good fire-and-brimstone holler outside an R-rated movie would fill it back up. *Chained Heat II* provided just the pretext he needed, and Brigitte Nielsen's picture on the poster had given Bobby plenty to think about while he did his best to round up a crowd of rubes. He was nearly eleven then, though, and people were more skeptical of him than they'd once been.

Grandpa Corbin waited until he had eight or nine grown-ups, plus a baby carriage and a handful of teens who looked ready to make fun of him. Then he started in on St. John's Revelation. Bobby cut his eyes at the *Chained Heat* poster and thought about his father, who was pitching in St. Louis that day, just 240 miles up the river. His mother would be sitting in the stands with the richer wives and pretending to care about the game rather than protecting her investment, which was why she was really there. Bobby sat on a concrete wall and forced himself to look away from what his mother called a "scantily clad female" and Grandpa called a "Whore of Babylon," but he'd heard the sermon so many times he was nearly asleep when the first scream pierced his eardrums.

Bobby opened his eyes just as Dr. Raymond Goodloe, their host, closed the last two feet between himself and Grandpa and plunged what the local boys called an "Arkansas toothpick" into his sternum. Grandpa stared at his killer in disbelief, then grabbed for the hilt sticking out of his chest. Dr. Goodloe, the local dentist, removed the blade for him and plunged it in once more, this time farther to the left, and with greater deliberation. Grandpa staggered, tried to keep his feet, then dropped to his knees as blood poured from his mouth. He whipped his head right and left like he was looking for somebody, but then another scream rent the air, this one from a woman who'd found the object of Grandpa's search—

Dorothy Goodloe lay dead in the front seat of her husband's car, having died there shortly after confessing to adultery with "Pastor Corbin." As three or four onlookers ran to the Buick to see her with their own eyes, Dr. Goodloe must have decided the jig was up, for he yanked the frog-sticker from Grandpa's chest and slashed his own throat with it, while several of his patients looked on aghast. A couple of husbands covered their wives' eyes while bright blood spurted into the dust and the family dentist sagged to his knees exactly as Grandpa had, then died next to the man he'd come to kill.

Grandpa outlived Dr. Goodloe by about ten minutes, likely because, having survived thousands of Germans trying to kill him at the Bulge, he was hell-bent on surviving a dirty Arkansas street. But all the anger and lust he'd carried for all those years since the war couldn't keep him alive until the town's solitary ambulance got there. The attendants arrived to find a bloody old sheet thrown over him, one provided, oddly enough, by the owner of the theater whose movie Grandpa had chosen to rail against.

Bobby supposed he'd been in shock for the rest of that day, but the truth was, over the previous summer he'd figured out that Grandpa Corbin didn't give two shits about God, if he believed in him at all. His whole "career" was a racket meant to keep him flush with cash and fixed for pussy in whatever town he landed. He was railing the moms in most of the houses they stayed in on his "preachin' circuit" (and some of the older daughters, too, which Bobby wouldn't have believed if he hadn't seen it now and then with his own eyes, or heard it in the night). It was practically foreordained that he'd die as he did, given the way men settled disputes in Delta country. In any case, his murder had put an end to Bobby's summers on the road, and took him back to Bienville, where the rich kids' fathers put him on a traveling baseball team—fought over him, in fact, which was nice after five years of being treated as chief-cook-and-bottle-washer of a one-man traveling revival—

The sound of panting pulled Bobby's gaze to the right.

The runner was definitely Paul Beckley, and he was scarcely fifty yards away. Bobby's pulse quickened as he wondered whether he'd have to rise when his target passed. Did Beckley have conventional habits that would make him stand at the farthest urinal from the next man? Put the most space between himself and another rider in an elevator? Or did he choose his own path regardless of others? On his present track, the general would pass within three feet of Bobby—an easy reach from the bench.

He found the trigger on the umbrella handle and waited, staring in the opposite direction, as if oblivious to the approaching runner. Even with the olive skin, he didn't dare offer Beckley a profile—not after the general had seen him up close the previous morning. Even marginally intelligent humans had an uncanny ability to recognize familiar facial features. Bobby panned his eyes across the cemetery but saw no other visitors. Mount Olivet wasn't a big tourist draw. Mostly what it offered was what he needed from it today—solitude. A sanctuary for meditation.

Or murder.

He focused on the regular *clap-clap-clap* of Beckley's running shoes hitting the asphalt. His training told him just how far away the man was, and how soon he would pass Bobby's position. Time slowed . . .

Three seconds . . . two—

Bobby lifted the umbrella and turned in the same moment, targeting Beckley like a striking snake. The tip hit Beckley in the left mid-chest, its embedded needle springing forward to inject a lethal toxin that would eventually be identified by gas chromatography in the nearby FBI lab. And since General Beckley had earned his most recent money not as a pundit but as a consultant to American companies supporting the Ukrainian struggle against Moscow, the Bureau would assume he'd been murdered by the FSB, Putin's intelligence service, who favored exotic assassination methods. Certainly not by a former acquaintance from the U.S. Army, and not in anyone's wildest fantasy by a man considering a run for the White House.

Beckley backpedaled away from Bobby in surprise, then called him a "haji motherfucker" and ran on. Thirty yards past the bench, he began slapping his chest like a man being stung by a bee. Then he swayed on his feet and collapsed, falling onto his back. Bobby jumped up like a concerned bystander, then hurried down the lane and knelt over his old intel officer.

Beckley stared up in confusion, mouth moving but producing no sound. The man was wearing AirPods. Bobby looked around again, then removed the earbuds and pocketed them. He found Beckley's iPhone in an elastic strap on his upper arm beneath his jacket. He quickly stripped this and pocketed it as well.

"Wha . . . why?" Beckley croaked.

"Do you recognize me?" Bobby leaned close over the blanching face. At first he saw only more confusion, infinite fear. Then awareness dawned.

"Oh, God," Beckley croaked. "Can't believe . . . you did this."

"You left me no choice, Paul. You put yourself between this country and its future."

The frightened eyes grew even wider. "You're insane."

"Furthest thing from it," Bobby corrected.

Beckley's head rolled back and forth on the asphalt. "I think I knew it back then . . . the night after the Abu Nasir raid. When we were alone."

"But you never told anyone?"

Beckley shuddered like a Victorian TB patient. He tried to raise his arms but couldn't. "My hands are numb . . ."

Bobby nodded and prepared to rise.

"Tell me you didn't use thallium," Beckley pleaded. "Or polonium twenty."

Now Bobby understood his old comrade's deepest terror. "No. You'll be gone in ten minutes, not ten weeks."

"Thank God."

Relief flowed into the general's eyes. The unknown was always hardest to face. And at least his impending death had a logic behind it, a motive he understood. Bobby would have preferred to remain until he was sure Beckley had departed this world, but the risk of someone simply driving up in a car was too great. The risk of leaving the scene was negligible. Given the toxicity of the compound he'd stolen, even if an ambulance showed up in the next minute, its paramedics would be unable to revive Beckley. Would the general be able to speak or write Bobby's name? It was possible, in theory. But Beckley would likely be dead before Bobby even lost sight of him.

"I'm leaving, Paul. Sorry it had to be this way. But as I said, you made the choice."

Beckley's eyes cleared for a moment. "You're crazy, Bobby . . . whether you know it or not. And I pray you never get to be president. I pray it's killing me that stops you."

Bobby smiled strangely. "No more TV lights for you, General. No best-seller list, either. I already stole your laptop and manuscript notes from your apartment. While you ran your first two miles this morning."

As Beckley's eyes went wide, Bobby smiled and got to his feet, then began walking away. Soon he was jogging in the opposite direction of his hotel. He'd ditch Beckley's SIM card in a city drain, his cell phone elsewhere. Then he'd head back to his room, retrieve his own phone, wash off the makeup, and head for the airport with Corey. Tonight they'd be in New York for Bobby's guest spot on *The Last Word*. Tuesday morning he'd balance the MSNBC appearance with *Fox & Friends*, then stick around for an interview with old friend Shepard Smith in the New Jersey studios of the well-funded upstart Apogee News. Finally—in a very tight connection—he'd fly back to Mississippi on the Donnelly Oil jet, landing just in time for the VIP dinner party preceding Wednesday's PGA pro-am. And if Corey had kept their volunteers on track, on Friday—the second day of official tournament play—he would walk to the center of the amphitheater stage above the Mississippi River in his old hometown and announce that his "TikTok Army" had succeeded in gaining enough signatures to place his name on every state ballot in America in early 2024—which would make his third-party run a reality.

Bobby saw no other humans in the cemetery as he left. Trotting up the deserted exit road, feeling the unfamiliar weight of the prosthetic arm, he tried to keep his motion natural. *Long time since I've felt that*, he thought, watching his olive-colored hands pump forward and back.

Despite his success with Beckley, the nerves were still with him. But he wasn't thinking of his grandfather now. He was recalling the forty minutes he'd spent with Penn Cage before flying out of Natchez on Saturday night, after the slaughter at Mission Hill. During their surprising conversation over glasses of Stoli and Hendrick's, the former Natchez mayor had been struck by a confessional mood. In an awed voice he'd told Bobby about a strange encounter he'd had with a Louisiana black bear outside his mother's house on the morning before the day of the concert. Though this human-bear meeting had actually taken place in the world (Bobby had verified it by checking the Bienville *Watchman* online), Cage had interpreted it as some sort of preternatural experience, a message or vision from the afterworld, or perhaps from nature itself. As an avowed atheist, the former mayor and author had expressed surprise and puzzlement at his own conclusion. Then, when Bobby questioned him further, Cage had unexpectedly confided that he was suffering from incurable cancer—

The same type that was killing his mother in the bed downstairs.

Stunned, Bobby had felt nearly overcome by this revelation. He'd always admired Cage, mostly for the relentless conviction with which he'd pursued the old Double Eagle group, who were not intellectual white supremacists, but redneck psychopaths who'd found the Klan and their offshoot gang a convenient vehicle for their particular brand of sadism. But beyond this, he and Cage shared several things in common: they'd both lost limbs through trauma; they were both attorneys; they were both published authors; and while Cage had spent years as a politician, Bobby was now entering the world of politics, at the highest possible level. Cage was also losing his mother, while Bobby might lose his father any day now (if Big Ed suffered another heart attack, which the doctors deemed likely). Finally, unknown to Cage, they had both recently experienced visions that felt like messages from fate.

Bobby had said nothing about his recurring vision to Cage, of course. Presidential candidates couldn't go around talking about near-religious premonitions of destiny. But Bobby felt a kinship with the former Natchez mayor that he couldn't explain in any other way. He felt the same way about Charles Dufort, though in a much darker sense. As if their destinies were somehow linked. One thing Bobby knew for certain, though: Penn Cage would never kill a man to ensure the continuation of his political career. At that level, they were diametric opposites. In killing Paul Beckley, Bobby had acted with the ruthless cynicism and dispatch of a Tio Carrera. But Penn was like his father, an idealist, even a martyr at heart.

As Bobby left Mount Olivet, the brisk scents of the National Arboretum to the south reached his nostrils, even as ugly concrete buildings rose around him. He ditched the SIM card and phone over the next two blocks, then reversed course, back toward his hotel. When the shadows and odors of the urban reality enveloped him, he felt his own vision returning again, but today he resisted. It wasn't always within his power to stop the process, but today his system had endured a double shock: first, the nearly tangible memory of seeing his grandfather murdered before his eyes; and second, practically playing the role of the man who'd killed him, in the way he had ambushed General Beckley and finished him off.

Beckley called the play, he told himself again. *He left me no option.*

Anyway, the thing was done. He supposed he felt a sort of Shakespearean conviction about the rightness of his actions on this day. For if a man wasn't willing to kill to be king . . .

He had no business on the throne.

Tuesday

CHAPTER 8

TO MY AMAZEMENT, Natchez and Bienville held themselves together for almost seventy-two hours before they started coming apart. By that time, a false sense of security had fallen over the simmering towns, to the point that, against my advice, Mayor Berry had accepted an invitation from a Black congressman to fly to Washington, D.C., and testify before the House Select Committee on Police Misconduct. Thus, when another of the critically wounded teenagers from the Mission Hill shooting died on Tuesday at UMC (thirteen-year-old Esther Griffin), and her grief-stricken father tried to retaliate against the white sheriff of Tenisaw County, Doc was a thousand miles from where he needed to be.

I'd spent the past three days sleepwalking between the sickbeds of my mother and daughter, Mom grimly hanging on while her failing blood vessels tried to finish her off, Annie lying in the room farther up the hall, a ragged hole from a reckless deputy's .40-caliber service weapon in her hand and the graze wound showing signs of infection. The only evidence I'd slept at all were those moments when I startled myself awake to the Spotify mix of Mom's favorite songs—Jim Croce, James Taylor, Emmylou Harris, Willis Alan Ramsey—and believed it was 1970, or maybe '73.

I would not have left "my girls" for anything short of civil disorder, but the desperate act of Esther Griffin's father threatened just that. So when the panicked call came in from Ray Ransom, I called him back. Ray told me that two hours after his daughter died, Johnny Griffin had stumbled into the Tenisaw County Sheriff's Department building with a pistol in his hand. Had a visiting city cop named Donte Harris not noticed the sidearm hanging at the distraught father's side, and subsequently tackled him, Griffin would likely have shot Sheriff Buck Tarlton, who was sitting in his office less than forty feet away at the time. Mr. Griffin claimed that he'd come only to force the sheriff to make a public apology, but nobody believed him.

According to Ray, Tarlton was ready to arrest Griffin for attempted murder in spite of the sensitive circumstances (which would surely push Black Bienville over the brink), and I might be the only person who could maintain the fragile peace. Even so, I resisted, until Ransom said, "Penn, I know your mama's sick, but with Doc gone to Washington, you're the only one who can get in front of this sheriff. That son of a bitch ain't gonna listen to a Black man now. Not to preachers, not anybody. We're past all that. You gotta come, man."

This was exactly what I'd feared since Saturday's shooting: an escalation so racially charged that it would function like a nuclear trigger for the populations not only of Bienville and Natchez, but also for the nearby counties, which are divided roughly fifty-fifty between Black and white. If Johnny Griffin had killed Sheriff Tarlton, no power short of the National Guard could have prevented the clash of the angriest Blacks and whites in southwest Mississippi. I'm no white savior, but I am Doc's city attorney, so I hurried out of Edelweiss and pointed my Audi north toward Bienville.

The irony of my race to TCSD headquarters was that I never even saw the sheriff. Buck Tarlton is a redneck show pony in his mid-forties, a poster boy for the far-right sovereign sheriff movement. Leave it to an asshole like that to keep me pacing in his waiting room while his county unraveled around him. Though I fumed at being forced to endure delay by a fool playing power games, I'd wasted enough time as mayor of Natchez to not be surprised. I did my best to keep up with Ray's frantic texts (he'd finally gotten Johnny Griffin under the care of his two sisters and his mother-in-law)—but then my cell phone rang with worse news. Althea Foster was calling to tell me that Mom appeared to have suffered yet another stroke. Her face was almost completely paralyzed, her breathing labored, and in the nurse's judgment she was likely to "pass" in the next twenty or thirty minutes.

At that point I lost my temper. I could drive back to Natchez in an hour at normal speed (maybe as little as forty minutes if I risked my life), but under the existing DNR, I'd still be unlikely to reach Mom before she died. In that moment I pretty much wished Johnny Griffin had shot the sheriff during his earlier visit. After shouting *You insufferable bastard!* at Buck Tarlton's door, I hobbled from his waiting room to my car and left six feet of smoking rubber at a dumbstruck deputy's feet.

Before I made it two blocks, my cell phone rang again. The caller was Dwight Ford, my doctor friend who had delivered Octa to the Mission Hill stage in his helicopter. It turned out that Althea Foster had broken about a dozen rules to call Dwight and explain my situation. Being a true friend, Dwight didn't offer to help me; he'd already started. After postponing his final two patients in Vicksburg, he'd raced for the slab where he parks his Robinson R44 while working that town. He told me to get my ass to the Bienville hospital helipad, and he'd be landing by the time I got there. As soon as I was on board, he'd ferry me to Fort Rosalie on the Natchez bluff, which is only a hundred yards from the front door of Edelweiss.

You'd think his offer would have filled me with relief. The problem is, the car accident that took off my right leg forever altered my psychological relationship to small machines. While I can still tolerate flying in a jetliner big enough to convince me I'm riding in an airborne building, the prospect of riding in a chopper that feels like an overgrown dragonfly made me react to Dwight's offer with a cold sweat. But then the existential reality of my plight hit me—

Your mother is dying.

I thanked Dwight and told him I'd be at the pad as fast as the Audi could get me there. A few blurry minutes later I spied his gray Robinson Raven sitting on the Bienville hospital concrete, rotor slowly turning on its tall mast. When I parked but hesitated to get out, Dwight opened the Raven's door and waved me forward, beckoning me from my paralyzed position. My cell phone began to ring again.

"*Move your ass, man!*" he ordered. "We're gonna be cutting this damn close, if we make it at all!"

CHAPTER 9

TO A SATELLITE orbiting the earth, Dr. Dwight Ford and I flying down the Mississippi River in his helicopter must look like a dragonfly following the track of a sidewinder rattlesnake. To see us, the satellite would have to use cloud-penetrating technology, because a Louisiana Delta thunderstorm has roared across the endless fields and ramped over the great bluff that bounds Mississippi on the west here, where the river towns perch on it like china settings on a shelf's edge. The dark sky looms low, as though it will press us into the copper-colored river, and I see tension in my friend's forearms as he pilots his frighteningly light ship. In truth, the Raven feels like it has about the same mass and strength as a butterfly in a hurricane.

"How dangerous is this weather?" I ask the little boom mic at my lips. "I don't see any other aircraft in the sky."

"The danger is poor visibility," Dwight answers over the headset. "I'm going to stay below the cloud ceiling, west of the bluff, and hopefully above the water. Long as I'm over that river, I'll know where we are. It'll feel like flying through a tunnel, but I'll still get you to your mama's bedside in twenty minutes, barring mishap."

Mishap. The word sounds almost benign. Trivial, even. Like a sprained ankle. Frozen in the R44's shuddering cockpit, I grip my seat arms as though I could somehow save myself if we were to crash into the river, but I know that's bullshit. This chopper has been splashed all over the internet for killing people, though Dwight assures me the problem is inexperienced pilots. Above me, the six-cylinder piston engine rumbles like a lawn mower that could sputter out any second, but I give Dwight a thumbs-up and say: "Do whatever you have to! I trust you!"

I don't fool him for a second.

"You look green, man. Still haunted by your wreck, huh. Just sit back and hit that coffee, like I told you." He jinks his elbow at my prosthetic leg. "You'll have one foot on the ground again in no time."

He looks pleased with his little anatomical joke.

I'm lucky to have Dwight at the controls. He's practiced his emergency auto-rotations with the same meticulous care he brings to implanting radioactive pellets in prostate glands. But fear knows no logic. My right hand trembles as I lift the chilled Starbucks bottle and take a long, bracing drink, then gulp again. When the caffeine hits my bloodstream, I pull my right pant leg up over my carbon-fiber socket and pop a hidden silver button, releasing negative pressure with a hiss like air brakes. The relief in my stump is instantaneous.

"That's it," Dwight says. "Just chill. And hey . . . I'm really sorry about your mom. I figured Peggy had another six months to a year, for sure."

I blink in dull shock, even shame. Fear temporarily blotted my mother from my mind. "Do you think these strokes are separate from her cancer?"

He considers the question, or perhaps how frank he should be. "Peggy's been taking increasingly toxic rounds of chemo for years. That takes a toll no one can measure. Especially at your mother's age. Peggy's tough, but . . . I think her vascular system has just played out."

I nod in grateful silence. This is the simplest and truest-feeling explanation I've heard since the first bleed felled my mother eight days ago.

"You know, it's ironic," I say, "but I think it was her cancer that snapped her out of a depressive slide she'd been in for a long time. Over the past decade, she'd gone from being an open-minded, gregarious woman to a self-isolating, Fox-addicted pod person. Wrapped in shells of xenophobia, even paranoia."

"I see that in so many of my elderly patients. Those cable channels feed them a steady diet of fear, and it really amps up their neurotransmitter metabolism. They start to need those fight-or-flight chemicals like a drug, every day. It's almost criminal, in my book."

A thousand feet below our skids, the river rolls toward Baton Rouge and New Orleans without awareness of my fear, or even my existence. A string of barges a half mile long plows upstream as silently as one of the ship models on the Rhine my father painted on the plywood base of the electric train set he brought back from military service in Germany. But the silver raindrops slapping the acrylic bubble in front of my face snap loud enough to penetrate the acoustic padding of the big headset over my ears.

"Look," Dwight says, angling his head left, past my chest. "Mission Hill Plantation. Christ, what a bad idea that was."

To my surprise, the stage and lighting trusses are still in place on the bluff, bounded by hundreds of yards of yellow crime-scene tape. I wish I could close my eyes for the duration of this flight, but even a few seconds of isolation threatens to bring up the contents of my stomach. Yet opening them gives me the feeling of standing on a mountain cliff, with the forward momentum of the engine pushing me ever forward into empty space.

"You know," Dwight says, "when I was landing that girl rapper, Octa, I had a bad feeling in the pit of my stomach. It just looked like chaos down there. Like a disaster waiting to happen."

"It was. You know, 'Octoroon' sure seems like a problematic name for the era we're living in."

"No shit. But there's a young female rapper in Atlanta who went by 'Mulatto' before she shortened it to 'Latto,' and she's bigger than Octa right now. At least she was until Mission Hill."

"How's Octa doing, by the way?"

"She's already started plastic surgery at Ochsner. Keeping me updated via text. She was damn lucky, Penn. Had aluminum stair rail fragments embedded in her cheekbone. Any of those could have hit an artery, blinded her, God knows what. Those damned Burrell brothers." Dwight's hand grips the cyclic control. "Whoa!" he cries, whipping his head back as Mission Hill drifts past. "I just saw the Tenisaw County helicopter sitting behind the stage. And a couple of cruisers parked alongside it. What you think they're doing?"

"Nothing good. I've seen a draft of Sheriff Tarlton's internal investigation—don't ask me how—and it's a total whitewash."

"How can he even try that? Most of what happened is on video."

"Tarlton knows the governor and the legislature will go shields-up to take his side. They'd like nothing better than to dominate the news cycle by defying federal authority for a few weeks during an election year."

"They're not afraid of the Black reaction?"

I actually laugh. "Tell me you didn't ask that. Your people have been getting the shit-end of the stick in this state since Eli Whitney invented the cotton gin. And except for the 1960s, I've seen damn little protest around here. Surely not enough to stop the governor and the legislature from giving Tarlton a pass."

Dwight shakes his head. "This feels different, Penn. I've only lived here fifteen years, but I've never seen the Black community this upset. We've got twenty-three dead"—he's included Martine in that number—"one survivor with a GSW to the head, and two more with critical wounds. The only non-critical wounds were your daughter and a nationally famous rapper. Never mind the psychological trauma on that crowd. If the Black folks of southwest Mississippi don't see some officers suspended—or even arrested—pretty damn soon, I think Bienville is going to self-destruct."

I hold up my left hand, a silent plea that he not begin gaming out the nightmare that could await us.

"I never thought I'd say that in this town," he goes on, "but that's where we're at. People have had *enough*."

"I hear you. I've been scared shitless since Saturday. I even got out my AR-15. The problem is, with the triggering event being a Black gang shooting, Tarlton knows he's got his political base on his side. Same with the governor and the legislature. They won't admit wrongdoing. It'll be like those L.A. cops who shot the Latina girl through the dressing-room wall—no accountability."

Dwight doesn't usually talk politics with me, but I can see he's upset. "Gang shooting or not . . . do you think those deputies would have opened fire in the middle of a damn George Strait concert?"

"Hell, no."

"You're damn right, no. And I can't say I don't understand Johnny Griffin flipping out like he did. His daughter was only *thirteen*."

"Even so, Tarlton will find a way to weasel out of what happened. You watch. Didn't Griffin do some jail time a while back?"

"For passing bad checks."

"You know how it works in this state. You haven't been flying this chopper so long that you've forgotten your *Tales from the Mississippi Highway*, have you?"

Dwight shakes his head dispiritedly. "*Tales*, my ass. It's all one tale. Happened again two weeks ago. I got held up fifteen minutes in Athens Point, Mississippi. It's always local badges, 'cause the Highway Patrol boys know my Mercedes now. Especially with my Gators bumper sticker. But it's never enough for the yokels. Until they get hold of my wallet and confirm I'm a physician, I'm just another nigger who boosted a Benz."

What must such experiences feel like to a man who owns a helicopter? Might that even be the reason he bought *the helicopter?* Strangest of all, over the years, Dwight has confronted more than one of those cops on his clinic table, as they sought treatment for prostate cancer. How do those men—who felt so superior to him out on the state asphalt—feel when they come to him in the desperate hope that he can prolong their lives with his knowledge and skill?

He nods past me toward the eastern shore of the river. "Hey, that house we're passing now, up on the brow of the bluff? That's Black Oak, right? The Barlow plantation?"

"That's it. Hell on earth for your tribe. Only place I know of in the Natchez District where they burned a slave to intimidate the rest."

Dwight nods thoughtfully. "I've heard that story. And back to the north of it? That's the place you bought last year? Pencarrow Plantation? Five hundred acres?"

"Closer to seven hundred. It was over a thousand back in the day."

"And you bought it because your mother asked you to? No other reason?"

I shrug. "She was on a quest to find out something about her family history. Spent the whole last year of her life pursuing it. If it meant enough that she asked me to spend that kind of money, I wasn't about to say no."

My friend nods slowly. "What did she end up finding out?"

"I don't know. She's written a lot about it, privately, but we don't talk about it."

Dwight looks confused. "Wait a minute. Peggy's writing about all this—your family history—and her son is a published author with a string of books behind him. But y'all don't *talk* about it?"

I shrug. "That's the deal we made. I'd actually started researching a book about the mass lynchings in Natchez and Bienville in 1861 when Mom asked me to hold off while she finished her research. Apparently, her work had somehow led her into that same historical nightmare. Anyway, I stopped. All I've done for the past year is litigate suits over Bienville's Covid-19 enforcement in 2020, and battle the Triton Chemical Company."

Dwight chuckles low in my headset. "Well, we know which of those two pursuits proved the more lucrative."

Though I haven't practiced law in any regular sense for more than twenty years, one week ago I won a punitive award in federal court that made headlines across the country. It was an environmental case, with local victims, one I only took as a favor to a man my father treated for four decades—a man named Julius Dunphy.

"Twenty million dollars," Dwight says. "That's the number I saw reported. Is that for real?"

"The punitive damages, yeah."

"And you get forty percent of that payout?"

I tilt my right hand back and forth. "Eventually. Maybe. There's many a slip 'twixt the cup and the lip."

"Son of a *bitch*. After thirty years of lawyers trying to nail those bastards, you did it in two?"

"Closer to three. But I had the evidence. They didn't."

"An old Black man with a guilty conscience? Who came to you because he'd always thought the world of your daddy?"

"Not exactly. He came to me because of his dying brother. His brother Joe was his conscience. He felt like he'd murdered his brother. Cain and Abel, man. But Julius was dying, too. What broke the logjam was a jug of the same sludge he'd secretly dumped for the company for thirty years. He'd kept it in a paint can, in a shed right behind his house."

"I'll be damned." Dwight shrugs. "Families, man. Nature versus nurture. Makes you wonder."

"In all honesty . . . that award money doesn't mean shit to me. And you're one of the few people on earth who know why."

Dwight closes his eyes. "Don't remind me, man. For what it's worth, my wife thinks you're a hero for what you're doing with Pencarrow." A glow of pleasure lights his face in the shadowy cockpit. "A thirty-year-old Black academic in charge of a former slave plantation? I love it. How's that young brother coming with his restoration, or whatever he calls it?"

"It's amazing, Dwight, at least what I've seen so far. It was John Cummings, a Louisiana trial lawyer, who first tried this on the large scale, with the Whitney Plantation near New Orleans. That was a sugar plantation, unlike Pencarrow. They've done some powerful work down there, especially with sculpture, to portray how slavery affected children. It'll take your breath away. People have no clue what slavery truly was in this country. Andrew McKinney has his own creative strategies, of course. We'll see what happens after he gets finished transforming Pencarrow. Maybe we'll change the world just a tiny bit. Mississippi, anyway. I know he's pissing off some people. To tell the truth, I haven't been out there in a while. I just sign the checks. Annie goes out a lot, though."

"Who's Andrew pissing off?"

"Shotwell Barlow, mostly. That militia cocksucker's about to shit a peach pit at the prospect of having what he calls 'the museum for jungle bunnies' going up across from his ancestors' plantation."

Dwight's laughter reverberates through the cockpit bubble. "*Screw* that Klan bastard! There aren't many people I'd turn away from my office door, but I'd turn him away from the ER if he was bleeding to death."

"I'd help you," I tell him, lifting the coffee bottle and taking another long pull from its wide mouth. "Hey, Nona doesn't know about . . . my situation?"

My friend's face hardens. "Hell, no. Give me some credit, bro."

I nod in appreciation of him honoring his medical confidentiality. I know a lot of doctors who don't.

Flying downriver from Bienville to Natchez is like a journey through my past, and that of America. Not far behind us lies New Carthage, the spot where General Grant met Admiral David Porter's ironclads after they ran the gun batteries at Vicksburg, which ultimately divided the Confederacy and saved the nation. Back over Dwight's shoulder lies the antediluvian Davis Island, ancestral home of Jefferson Davis, president of that seditious government. Today his home plantation lies underwater, shrineless and neglected, his eldest brother's body not far away, while the man himself lies in Virginia under a polished stone that calls him a martyr. But his ideas live on like an unkillable virus in the American bloodstream. I know this because downriver, nearer Natchez, wait Rodney, the Jericho Hole, and Lake Concordia: all landmarks from my war against the Double Eagle group. All are places of gruesome death that still come to me in my dreams—along with the faces of Henry Sexton, Brody Royal . . . Frank and Snake Knox.

As if to remind me I'm not sliding physically back in time, the five-hundred-foot cooling tower of the Grand Gulf nuclear station looms out of the kudzu-choked forest to our left. I'm staring in momentary confusion when the floor drops away and my harness yanks me toward the earth. Fifty feet closer to the earth, the Raven's rotor blades catch lifesaving air, and the seat bucks me like rodeo bronco.

"Windshear!" Dwight cries. "We're good now! Take it easy!"

My heart's beating so wildly it feels like a baby rattle. I focus on the dials in front of me and force myself to breathe with a steady rhythm. My pilot watches me from the corner of his eye, making sure I'm past the point of panic.

"You know, I never met your daddy," he says. "But the man intrigues me. He died in prison more than a decade ago, but every week I still have patients telling me he was a damn saint. I only hope I have a handful talking about my ass a year after I'm gone."

"Dad was no saint," I say, still feeling like I'm teetering on a ladder top. It strikes me that Dwight has been more talkative during this flight than I can ever recall him being on the ground. Then I get it—he's talking to distract me from fear. He's probably worried I'll have a real panic attack and bump the controls or something.

"You must have some idea what Peggy's been working on this past year," he presses.

"What's got you so interested in my mother?"

"She's the reason I canceled those patients to haul you back to Natchez, boy. This ain't no *Driving Miss Daisy* gig."

Dwight's Chris Rock–ish delivery brings a smile to my lips. "Well . . . I did hear that the woman who got Mom started on her genealogy kick— Deborah Fannin—paid for a lot of people around here to take DNA tests. Fannin was a mixed-race professor who moved down from Minnesota to research her own roots. Did you have any contact with her?"

"Oh, I met Deborah. Nona and I had her out to the house for dinner when they first got here. She had an older white husband. Man, was she obsessed with race. Then the husband tried to clear a pecan limb from the Pencarrow entrance during a storm and got the rest of the tree across his back. Lucky he survived."

I nod. "That guy was too old to be messing with a chain saw. Anyway, I gathered Mrs. Fannin's quest didn't end the way she'd hoped, and she sold me Pencarrow and headed back to Minneapolis with her husband in a wheelchair."

Dwight's silent nod says, *Typical Mississippi story.* Then he says, "I heard more than a few people got surprises from those DNA tests she paid for."

"Black families finding white blood?"

"Oh, yeah. No real surprise there, of course. Not in this corner of Mississippi. But I heard a few tests went the other way, too. Soul brothers in the woodpile. Which some white folks are fine with, I'm hearing. Others, not so much."

Hearing Dwight put such complex situations into simple terms makes me wonder if his views are shared by the larger community. "I suspect that's what started Mom down the road she's been on all year. She resisted getting a DNA test at first. But after Fannin's husband was paralyzed, she agreed. But she never mentioned it to me after that, and I didn't ask."

"What did that tell you?"

I shrug. "Could have meant either thing. But given all the research she's done since, I figure she got a surprise. Because we had a detailed family history going back to the Civil War on one side and the Revolutionary War on the other. Lily white all the way back. DAR, the works. Something must have upset that perfect picture."

Dwight clucks his tongue as he considers my theory. "But she hasn't discussed any of this with you?"

"Nope. I think she's been building up to it. She probably figured she had another six months to get her ducks in a row . . . based on her prognosis. These strokes came out of nowhere."

Dwight surprises me with an amused look. "So . . . it's gonna turn out that my token white buddy's been part brother from the beginning? No wonder we always got along."

I jab his left side with my elbow, and the chopper bucks again. He laughs when I grab my seat for purchase.

"Learned your lesson, didn't you?"

"Get your own DNA test, motherfucker. We'll see what you're carrying around in your double helix."

"Hey, I *know* I'm gumbo!" he laughs. "But it doesn't matter when you're my color. People just see Black. It's whitebreads like you that gotta *adjust*. You're lucky this country's past the one-drop rule!"

I wave my hand in dismissal.

"Seriously, though," he goes on, "your mama's one in a thousand, no matter what's in her veins."

"You think so?"

"Shit. To be born on the flat side of this river, in a shack with no plumbing or electricity, and start dragging a cotton sack when you're three years old? She told me she read a hundred library books to get ready for college. Then she became a teacher, just like my mother. To get from that to where you're at today? In one generation? That ain't *just* white privilege. That was a single-minded woman who lived for her kids, brother. That woman *worked*."

Dwight is right. And now the lady who so impressed him is about to pass from this earth—perhaps without me at her side. He's silent for a couple of minutes, his eyes tracking the river as he flies us down it with expert skill. His comparison to flying through a tunnel comes back to me, and for some reason I think of the Great Natchez Tornado of 1840, which blew up the river from the south, killing more people than any other in American history. Meteorology books record that twister as the *second*-deadliest in history, but only because in 1840 the dead slaves lining both banks for miles were not counted as fatalities.

As we press southward, I turn and look west, over Louisiana, where my mother's people came from. "Forty miles that way," I tell him, pointing a little behind us. "Quitman Parish, past the good cotton soil, is hardscrabble dirt. I think about Mom dragging that burlap sack with bleeding fingers, like some bad country song. Then I think about writing a check for Pencarrow Plantation eighty-five years later, just because she asked me to. Sometimes I can't get my head around that."

Dr. Ford's expression tells me he's familiar with this kind of class disorientation. "Don't ever feel conflicted about that. You wrote those novels, and you won those legal cases. Ain't nobody's business whether you donate the money to the Cancer Society or blow it in a goddamn strip club. If it helps your mama figure out who she was, or find some peace before she passes, then you put it to good use." He turns and looks hard into my eyes. "You *owed* her, boy. Same way I owe my mama. If she asked me to buy her the Taj Mahal, I'd spend my last dollar to try to get it for her."

I have seen Dwight with his mother. "I know you would. I also know she'd never ask."

He rolls his head slowly on his shoulders, like a wrestler. "But she *can*. And she knows it."

As the little chopper buffets through the wind and rain, I'm nearly overcome by anticipatory grief. I'm thinking of calling Althea Foster and telling her to wake Annie when we hit another column of wind shearing earthward, and the Raven drops like a stone once more. This time, though, I simply grip my seat edge with my right hand and wait for the rotor to catch the calmer air, like a swimmer escaping a rip tide.

"Hey . . ." I say with a dizzy sort of relief.

"Hey, what?" Dwight asks. "We're good."

"The last time that happened I nearly pissed myself. Now . . ." My fear, I realize, is more cerebral than visceral. "Did you put something in my coffee?"

Dwight looks at me like I'm crazy, clearly meaning to deny it, but then a grin breaks through his mask. "Versed. Short-acting benzodiazepine. Call it compassionate use. Compassion for myself."

"You unethical son of a bitch! I'm gonna sue."

He laughs with genuine mirth. "You're thanking God I gave you that dose! Admit it."

He's right, of course.

For the first time, my friend seems content to let silence reign. He must be confident that the midazolam he slipped me is doing sufficient duty in my brain. Soon I realize he's begun flying directly over the river bends. Is he worried that even a couple of minutes' delay might make us too late? Whatever the case, I have no power to affect the outcome. For me, the toughest part of this journey will be covering the final hundred yards from the landing field at Rosalie to my mother's front door. As I think of calling Althea again, my phone shakes with the coded ringtone that only sounds for my daughter.

"That's Annie," I say, answering. "Can you hear me, boo? What's going on?"

"Where are you, Dad? Althea said you had to go to Bienville?"

She's breathing hard. "Never mind that now. I'm in Dr. Ford's chopper, and I'm nearly home. He's going to land me at Fort Rosalie."

"Oh, thank God!"

"*Five minutes!*" Dwight says loudly.

"I heard him!" Annie tells us. "Dwight, you're so great, thank you!"

"How's Mom doing?"

My daughter is not easily upset, but she sounds close to hyperventilating. "Gram's breathing, but . . . it's like forever between breaths. I think this is really the end. So does Althea. I can tell."

"We knew this was coming. I know that doesn't make it easier."

I have trouble hearing her reply, so I switch to speaker and max the volume.

"... I'm squeezing her hand while I talk to you," Annie goes on. "I was rubbing her forehead. I know she can't hear me, but maybe she can feel my touch. Oh, Dad . . . she's so cold."

Hot tears squeeze from the corners of my eyes. "You don't know she can't hear you. Don't let go. Keep talking to her. I'll be there before you know it."

"Hurry! I don't think we have long."

"I won't hang up. We're still a family, even if . . . you know."

"I want Gram to hear your voice before she passes. And tell Dwight—"

"I hear you!" Dwight breaks in. "And I think Rosalie's gonna take too long with this one-legged daddy of yours. Imma put his ass down at the top of Silver Street! If the cops have a problem with that, we'll let our former mayor use whatever pull he's got left to deal with it."

"Thank you so much!"

"Ain't no thing, girl."

"What happened in Bienville, Daddy? I know you wouldn't have left if it weren't something bad."

"Close call, that's all. Everything's okay. You focus on Gram. I'll—"

Dwight grips my arm and thrusts his finger forward, pointing southeast. In the distance, on the high bluff where I'm almost certain Natchez stands, a thick column of dark smoke rises into the clouds.

"Annie, listen," I say, squinting into the rain as acid floods my stomach. "We're getting close. I'm going to hang up so I can help Dwight watch for power lines when he lands. You focus on Gram. Play her that Jim Croce song she loves. Maybe she'll smile one last time."

"I think she's past that now. But I'll try it."

"You'll hear our rotors any minute. I love you."

It takes a supreme act of will, but I hang up, my gaze locked onto the disturbing sight ahead. More unsettling still, Edelweiss lies on a direct line between us and that smoke. "What are we looking at, Dwight?"

"Natchez burning again, buddy."

In spite of the Versed my anxiety spikes. "Don't even say that, man."

"If it weren't for this rain, you'd see it like a movie. We're only four miles out."

"Is all that smoke coming from one building?"

"No way to know, unless we fly over it. And you don't have time for that."

He's right. "Maybe if you get a little altitude during our approach, we can pinpoint the fire."

Dwight nudges the cyclic, and the Raven climbs toward the cloud ceiling. Within thirty seconds I make out most of the landmarks of Natchez's skyline: Jewish Hill at the cemetery; the Victorian homes lining the bluff on Clifton Avenue; St. Mary's Cathedral; the Eola Hotel; the old train depot; and then my own Edelweiss, crowning Silver Street above Natchez Under-the-Hill. My eyes track the thick gray pillar down from the clouds. It seems to be rising from a stand of woods between Highway 425 and Highway 61. As I peer through the rain, an eerie certainty fills my gut. Unless a fuel truck exploded in the woods, only one thing could be feeding that fire . . .

"That's Tranquility," I think aloud. "The old Dufort mansion!"

Dwight gives a piercing whistle in my headset. "Jewel in the antebellum crown . . . holy shit. That's real money burning, there."

The premonitory itch of impending danger at the back of my neck hurls me back in time. In the dimness of the chopper's bubble, we share a gaze that reassures neither of us. "Dwight . . . you don't think—"

"That this fire could have something to do with Mission Hill?"

"Fuck. Don't say it out loud."

"Shit, you're thinking it. Tell me you're not."

For a few seconds of fearful concentration, I consider asking him to land at Tranquility, but as though reading my mind, my friend shakes his head and starts a wide turn back toward the bluff.

"You haven't thought far enough ahead yet," he says quietly.

"What do you mean?"

"Fires are like air crashes. Investigations can take months. Perception is everything. Given where things are now"—he looks into my eyes once more, his face filled with foreboding—"does the truth even matter?"

CHAPTER 10

Belle Rose Plantation

AT EIGHTY-SIX YEARS old, Charles F. Dufort was still six feet three inches tall and could shoot a dove on the wing with a motion as smooth and swift as a martin turning in the air. Dufort had kept his silver mane of hair, and more. He had that rugged patrician handsomeness, the aura of strength and hard-won wisdom that made even people who knew better think maybe it *did* make sense that old white guys like him had run the world for as long as they had. In almost any situation, strangers assumed Charles Dufort was the man in charge. In boardrooms, the CEO. On a ship, the captain—or the owner, which would have been more accurate. For Charles Dufort was the richest man in Mississippi's eighty-two counties, as his original American ancestor had once dreamed of being, and had come within a couple of million dollars of becoming during the Reconstruction era.

A Southern power broker since his early forties, Dufort always surprised people when he revealed that he, like so many of his ancestors, had attended both Penn and Harvard Law School. It wasn't his legal training, however, but his business instincts that had exponentially increased the holdings he'd inherited from those ancestors. In 1939, Dufort's father had been ideally positioned to exploit the oil boom that blessed their corner of southwest Mississippi. Even so, Charles—unlike his Mississippi peers—had diversified during the 1970s, and that had not only saved him during the oil bust of the Reagan years, but also set him up for breathtaking gains later on in far-flung regions of the world—like California.

These days Dufort mostly stayed around his home place, which was what remained of Belle Rose Plantation. He'd sold off a big chunk to some local boys who wanted to build a world-class golf course, but he'd kept a sufficient buffer around his house so that he could walk outside and piss without fear of anyone complaining except his housekeeper—and nothing surprised or upset Ruby Brooks. Except for nights like tonight, when the country club brought in a band to play for a to-do worthy of the old days, Charles had the peace he craved.

Actually, those same boys had invited him over tonight for some kind of VIP event, one preceding the PGA tournament they'd spent the last decade luring to Bienville. Dufort still remembered the night they'd come over seeking an audience—the little delegation of four—to tell him they needed to break the covenant they'd made with him never to integrate their club. "If we don't let *any* Black folks in," they said, hanging their heads like shamed toddlers, "we'll never get a top tournament to come in here. Not the way the world is these days, Charles." They'd sworn they'd limit Black membership to doctors, if they could, or maybe the retired NFL receiver who called Bienville home. Dufort had merely waved his hand and given them his tacit permission. You couldn't fight that kind of battle any longer—not in public, not even with the legal paper on your side.

The world had changed too much.

He looked up from the mahogany desk that sat like a great island at the center of his study. He might be old, but he could still hear Ruby's light footsteps as she approached his door. Five seconds later, the big slab of cherry floated open, and Ruby entered in her white uniform.

Not many people in Bienville still had Black maids, and he knew of none who wore uniforms, but Ruby did, and she'd never asked to discontinue the practice. She was only seventy, but she still had a figure, unlike the big Black servants he'd mostly grown up with, and also a wise, handsome face. More than that, she pretty much governed his life these days. She had a quicker mind than a lot of men running companies out in the world, and Belle Rose was his world now. Ruby was his sole companion, but for his memories and his driver, Amadu, who never said much of anything. Dufort had his children, of course. His elder daughter, Sophie, anyway. His true heir—Philippe, the son of his first wife—had died young, at thirty-six, like Payne Stewart, flying into the void of eternity on a depressurized plane. Charles's younger crop of kids were about worthless. His youngest daughter, Pia, lived in California and almost never returned to the South. And his surviving son . . .

"What's going on?" Dufort asked, looking at his watch. "There's still the best part of an hour till my tea."

"Your baby boy has called here three times in the last five minutes."

Dufort scowled and looked away. "Why would you bother me with that?"

Exasperation showed on Ruby's face. "This doesn't seem like the other times. I think you'd best listen to whatever he's got to say. Charlot sounds pretty desperate."

"Charlot" (pronounced with intimate softness: Shar-*loe*) was a French diminutive of "Charles," and it had stuck like honey to his beautiful boy the moment anyone heard it. Charlot Dufort had melted the hearts of women from six to ninety-six since he was a toddler. Which wasn't the problem. He'd done the same to a lot of men, too.

"That's exactly how he sounded all the other times," Dufort said.

Ruby shook her head and gave her employer no relief from her hard gaze.

The old man sighed and rubbed his temples. "Gambling, drugs, apology, begging . . . then the whole show all over again. Leave me in peace, Ruby."

Dufort picked up the newspaper on his desk and shook it. "Hell of a story in the *Watchman* this morning. There's a bear running loose in Bienville. Maybe two or three. One got within a couple feet of Penn Cage in a wheelchair. Could have ripped his head right off if he'd felt like it." Dufort gestured at the big bearskin rug on his study floor. "And I can tell you, that close to a bear isn't where you want to be without a heavy-caliber rifle."

Ruby blew out an angry rush of air. "Mr. Charles, Charlot sounded *really* upset. The way he did when he was a little boy. Like that time he lost your war medals in the catfish pond playing army."

An unfamiliar tug in his chest made Dufort sit up and look at the old South Central Bell telephone he kept on his desk. "It's dope or cards," he muttered. "Can't be anything else. He's probably gambled himself into a hole Elon Musk couldn't climb out of."

"So, what then?" Ruby demanded. "You gonna let them loan sharks cut him up for bait in some alley? Boy don't deserve that."

Dufort looked up sharply. "Everyone who ever loved him has tried to help him. And he's bled them dry. What does he deserve, Ruby? Have you gotten what you deserve?"

The maid sighed heavily. "I'd have to say *hell* no to that."

"And me . . . ?"

A different look came into her eyes then, a knowing one. "I'd say nobody knows that but you, Mr. Charles. You figure you've got what you deserve?"

Dufort rubbed a callused hand over his white-stubbled chin and looked down at the open newspaper. As a lifelong hunter, he'd always been fascinated by the habits of large predators. He'd read and reread the statements of every witness who'd come into contact with the bear. "Let me tell you a secret, Ruby. Not many of us get what we deserve. And truth be told, not many of us want that. You understand me?"

She looked back at him with rare candor. "I reckon I prob'ly do, Mr. Charles. I reckon I do."

As they stared at each other, the cell phone in Ruby's pocket chirped.

Dufort scowled, but she risked his wrath to take out the device and check it.

"Sophie," she told him, referring to his daughter by his first wife, which made Sophie Charlot's half sister. "I'm answering this."

Charles waved his hand as she turned away and put the phone to her ear. The patriarch was on relatively good terms with his elder daughter—who shared the beauty of her mother and half brother but had more good sense—even if on matters political they had less in common than a Marxist and a tsar.

"Sophie needs to talk to you," Ruby said, walking forward with the cell phone. "She sounds upset, too."

Sophie was sixty-four now, and had a level head for a liberal. "What the hell's going on?" Charles growled. "Has the stock market crashed or something?"

"From the sound of her voice, I'd say worse."

"Well, is somebody dead? Who's left?" Before he could ponder an answer to his own question, Ruby shoved her phone into his hand.

"What the Sam Hill is going on?" he demanded.

"Forgive my using a cliché, Daddy," Sophie said, "but are you sitting down?"

"Goddamn, *what's happened*?"

"Tranquility's burning."

Dufort felt the floor shift beneath his feet. He didn't ask her to repeat herself. He'd heard her clearly, and he knew Sophie wouldn't have called him over something trivial like a burned outbuilding or kitchen fire.

"How bad? Tell me!"

"They think it's going to burn to the ground."

"*Who* thinks that?"

"The Natchez fire chief. I just got off the phone with him."

Dufort sat in the roaring vacuum produced by his daughter's news. Tranquility wasn't just another suburban villa built by a Natchez nabob, one that decayed into a shell after the war, only to be repainted as a tourist attraction for *Gone with the Wind* fans in the 1930s. Tranquility had been the nerve center of an empire that lasted two hundred years, one built on sugar and cotton, then rebuilt on crude oil and cell phones and even things you couldn't see—pulses of energy moving through silicon chips and wires, and even the air. Dufort himself had lived at Tranquility until 1977, when his first wife died and he'd sensed the fortunes of Natchez waning. It was then that he'd moved upriver to Belle Rose, the second-most-admired plantation among his family's holdings.

"Goddamn it," he whispered. "How is this possible? Tranquility's not a half mile from the main fire station."

"I don't know," Sophie said helplessly. "The caretaker was running an errand. The fire apparently started quickly and spread faster."

An itch of anxiety made Dufort shift in his chair, but there was something deeper troubling him than that. "Do they have any idea how it started? I mean . . . I know you don't, but—"

"Daddy, I don't know *anything*. But this is a crazy week, and news like this seems just about predictable."

Sudden suspicion transformed to conviction in his chest. "Don't tell me Charlot started this fire! Don't you tell me that boy was squatting in our ancestral home and set it on fire. Goddamn *barn burner*!"

"What?" Sophie cried through the phone. "Daddy, no! That's not it at all."

"It better not be." With violence that made Ruby jump, the old man shoved his chair back from the desk and barked, "Tell Amadu to get the car ready! We're going to Natchez."

"Why?" Ruby and Sophie asked at the same time. Then Sophie said, "It'll be an hour at least before we could make it. You want to watch the last embers crumble into ashes?"

"You're goddamn right I do! There's probably a crowd of rubberneckers out there gawking and drinking in the schadenfreude. Sons of *bitches*!"

"I think it's a bad idea," Sophie told him. "It's like going to an open-casket funeral. Once I see somebody as a painted corpse, I can't ever remember them as they were in life. Not unless I dream them."

"Amadu!" Charles shouted. "Get the Rolls!"

"Daddy, you're going to give yourself a stroke. I'll be pulling up outside in one minute, and I'll drive you to Natchez if you really want a final look before it's gone."

"Heard you holler, Mr. Charles," Amadu said in his resonant bass voice, having appeared at the glass doors of the garden that Dufort called his rosarium. The bearded Black driver stood about five feet six, and though his hair was white, he was built as solidly as a Southern live oak and wore an expression of eternal resolve. But to what end? None could tell.

"I want to be rolling toward Natchez in three minutes," Charles said in a voice of grim command.

"I'll bring the Rolls around." Amadu turned and vanished.

Ruby was staring at her employer as if he'd gone mad. What did she understand about the real situation? he wondered. How much had she been aware of as a teenager, when they'd all lived together at Tranquility? Not

as much as her mother, surely, who'd worked for Charles's father, as well as
Charles himself for some years. How good was Ruby's memory? Too good,
in his experience. She surely knew that estates as old as Tranquility—
whether they stood in the North or the South—always held secrets.

"I'm taking the Rolls, Sophie," Charles said into the phone. "You can
ride with me or not."

"I'm coming."

Charles hung up and looked at Ruby, who was shaking her head in apparent disbelief. "Tranquility?" she echoed. "Is that what I heard? Tranquility's burning up?"

"That's right. And I owe it to my ancestors to watch it die." He sagged
in his chair. "I can't believe it."

"I can't, neither," his maid said softly, her dark eyes misting with memory. "That big old place. I can still see it when I was a little girl. Like a
castle, it seemed. Lord, that's hard to picture."

"You can ride with us, if you like. Sounds like we'll never get another
chance to see it."

Ruby tilted her head as though listening to distant music. "I reckon I
will, Mr. Charles. A body ain't likely to see the like of that but once."

"It's like the pyramids coming down," Dufort whispered.

She looked at him over the mahogany slab with inscrutable intensity. If
he'd looked up, he might have read her gaze as one of empathy.

It wasn't.

"You know," she mused at length. "It's *exactly* like that. Lord, what a
thing to live to see."

CHAPTER 11

AS DWIGHT FORD'S helicopter descends toward the crest of Silver Street, atop the Natchez bluff, Annie waves from the wraparound gallery of Edelweiss. Tall and still thin at twenty-nine, she looks so much like her mother that the resemblance sometimes takes my breath away. The bandage on her hand makes my stomach clench, but she's better off than most people who took rounds at Mission Hill.

Looking north along Broadway, I see a large crowd of Black protesters watching us, their hands raised to their eyes. The mass of marchers standing vigil in the little park has doubled since I left for Bienville. I figure there were maybe a hundred then, mostly family relations of victims shot at Mission Hill. But something has rapidly increased their number—

"*Keep your eyes on those damned power lines!*" Dwight warns me.

With the asphalt circle and power poles rising toward my feet, the chopper stops feeling small and insectlike and starts feeling like a Chinook gunship attempting to land on an aircraft carrier.

"I don't know enough to call a landing!" I shout, even though we're connected by headsets. "You're clear of the power lines I can see, but it's *tight.*"

"It just looks tight," Dwight replies, working the controls with careful confidence. "Implanting radioactive seeds in a prostate gland is tight. All I need is forty feet for my rotor . . . and there's gotta be seventy down there."

"I was going to say, 'It's your funeral,' but it'll be mine, too, if you snag something."

Dwight works the collective with a surgeon's care, and we descend another twenty feet into the closely bound landing zone. The crowd from the vigil surges toward our intended landing site. They obviously recognize Dr. Ford's helicopter. They're probably worried that he's making a forced landing.

"You're drawing a crowd!" I tell Dwight. "They think you're in trouble."

"Wave 'em off!"

I try my best, but without opening the door, I'm not going to persuade anybody.

"I can't hang around after we're down," Dwight tells me. "Soon as I touch down, get your crippled ass out and I'm gone."

"Understood." I continue to wave my arms as broadly as I can in the bubble. "What about afterward? You gonna stick around and see whether things stay under control?"

"I am *not*. I'm gonna tell Nona to pack a bag, and we're gonna fly charter to my time-share in Dominica for a week."

His answer stuns me. "Seriously?"

Dwight gives me a quick look, and I see defensiveness in his face. "Does that surprise you? Did I just stop being a hero?"

"Uhh . . . not to me. But what about John Lewis? 'Good trouble'? All that?"

His focus is already back on the asphalt LZ. "Makes a great eulogy. But I'm fifty-one, not twenty-one. I've still got two daughters in college. I've seen those militia knuckleheads knocking around Bienville ever since Obama got elected. It won't serve any purpose for me to get down in those streets and fight them. I don't listen to Bob Dylan, but my older brother played me a song once about staying in Mississippi too long."

I've never heard Dwight sing, but he can certainly speak with heartfelt conviction. "I hear you, man."

He leans to his right, eyeing the apron of rain-soaked asphalt beneath us. "Come down to Dominica with us. We got plenty of room. Tell Annie I said she needs to come thank me in person."

"She won't leave. We damn near came to blows last night arguing about it."

"That was last night. Things are about to change, aren't they? Now you can tell her it's what her grandmother would have wanted."

Again, Dwight is one step ahead of me. "That might just work."

"Hang on—here's the ground!"

I jerk in my seat, having lost my spatial awareness. But Dwight's Raven settles the final few feet as lightly as a feather, and we only kiss the wet pavement.

"Go!" he cries. "There's the handle! Right there!"

Grabbing clumsily at a lever, I finally get the door of the bubble open and scramble out onto the black surface. Turning back to the open cockpit, I find myself at a loss.

"Give me your keys," he says.

"What?"

"Your car keys! I know a nurse's aide who'll drive it down here for you. His brother can follow and take him back."

Nearly overcome with gratitude, I dig in my pocket and pass over my Audi's remote. "Dwight—"

"Go hug your mother while you can! I hope we made it in time."

He slaps my outstretched hand.

I shut the bubble's door and run through the rotor blast toward the crowd gathered beyond it, which now fills half of Broadway. The people are clearly confused. Many regard me with suspicion, and some look outright hostile. A few recognize me, but even they look less congenial than I remember. As their voices rise with questions, Dwight's engine revs, then roars, and the little chopper lifts once more into the sky. Within seconds, my aerial ferryman is back over the river, headed north toward Bienville and home.

"Is Doc Ford okay?" asks a voice out of the chaos. "How come he landed in the *road*?"

"He's fine," I assure them. "He's good! He was helping me out. I need to get into that house over there!"

Several heads turn and look at the nineteenth-century chalet towering over the street. Then they look back at me, far from certain about the situation.

"My mother's sick," I tell them.

At first there's only silence. Then a woman a couple of rows back snaps, "Don't just stand there! Let the man pass! His *mama's* sick."

The last sentence slowly works its magic, and the crowd begins to part.

"That's Mayor Cage," says another voice. "Ain't seen him in a long time."

"He's been up here every day for a week," says another. "His daughter got shot at Mission Hill."

"Oh, Lord! Let the man through, y'all. *Damn*."

ANNIE AWAITS ME beneath the elevated gallery of Edelweiss. The Betadine- and bloodstained gauze on her wounded hand makes it hard to focus anywhere else. As she pulls me into the central hall of the elevated basement, the shuddering thump of "bro country" rocks the buildings along Broadway. Looking back over my shoulder, I see the crowd that just gave me safe passage surge back toward the bandstand area of the park atop the bluff. "Go back to Mom," I tell Annie. "I'll be right there."

"No. Come with me. Where are you going?"

"I'm worried."

"About bad country music?"

I hesitate to tell her, but I can't find any way to delay it. "As Dwight and I were flying in, we saw a fire."

Annie goes still. "What fire? Where?"

"I'm pretty sure it was Tranquility."

"The Dufort mansion?"

I nod.

"In the middle of all this other insanity? That's . . ."

"Worrisome. And there was a close call at the sheriff's office in Bienville. A grieving father." The bass decibels have risen by at least 30 percent farther along the street. "Let me check on this situation. I don't want a confrontation between whoever's playing that music and those people standing vigil. I'm just going to stand with them until the vehicle passes."

"I'll go with you. I don't want you getting beat up trying to stop a brawl."

"No, you stick with Mom. I'll be right back."

"Dad, I'm coming. I'm not twelve anymore. And I can outrun you, if it comes to that."

I can't argue this point any longer.

By the time we reach the middle of the broad avenue that fronts the Natchez bluff, confrontation seems imminent. The vehicle producing the redneck roar is what I expected: a massive red dually pickup, its double wheels clinging to the pavement like the fat legs of some saurian giant as it rolls slowly in our direction. Even from eighty yards away, I can make out two big banners flying from masts behind its cab. On the driver's side waves the familiar scarlet-and-blue banner of Lee's Army of Northern Virginia. The passenger's-side flag shares similar colors, but I can't quite make out its design. The truck's big engine—with old-school glass-pack mufflers—shakes the ground, and its exhaust rumble echoes off the faces of the buildings that look across the water toward Louisiana.

The dually slows when it comes abreast of the crowd, and four Black men in their early twenties separate from the larger mass, walking forward and staring into the bed. Annie and I walk farther up the street, instinctively grasping each other's hands. Getting closer, I realize there are three white men standing in the truck's bed, and I see at least one AR-style rifle worn over a shoulder, military style.

The truck is still rolling in our direction, but at no more than three miles per hour. The walking crowd easily keeps pace. An angry murmur slowly rises to a pitch that competes with the deeper rumble of the engine. As this group comes within forty yards of us, a man in the truck bed yells something at them. An older man behind them yells, "*You ain't right, boy! Show some respect!*" Then two young marchers charge forward.

The truck's driver lays on his horn and cranks up his hi-fi system.

As Annie and I stare, my phone vibrates with a call, which tuns out to be from Marshall McEwan, the publisher of the Bienville *Watchman*. There aren't many calls I would answer in this situation, but given the events of the afternoon, I feel I must.

"Don't tell me Sheriff Tarlton has arrested Johnny Griffin," I say into the phone.

"Not yet," Marshall replies. "I'm calling about Natchez news, actually. And I only have a second. This is huge, Penn, something you can't talk about. Do you know about the Tranquility fire?"

"Yes, go," I say, watching the big dually roll nearer the Black crowd beside it. "I only have a second."

"I just got a call claiming that fire was a purposeful attack, carried out in retaliation for the Mission Hill massacre."

Nausea instantly flips my stomach. "What?"

"The caller claimed to be a member of the group who started the fire. He told me their name is 'The Bastard Sons of the Confederacy.' And he said that attack is only the first. More fires will follow. He also said the incendiary device they find will be built from high-intensity military flares."

"Jesus, that's specific."

"I know. I think the call was for real. We've got a major nightmare in progress here, buddy."

"Shit's about to hit the fan down on the bluff, I'll tell you that. What did he sound like? Did he sound Black or white to you?"

"Black. I'm ninety-nine percent sure."

"Damn it! Marshall . . ."

"I know. So . . . I'm calling to ask you something I'd almost never ask anyone."

"Should you publish this to the Internet?"

"Yeah. I'm afraid we're one straw from breaking the camel's back. War in the streets. We publish this to our website, it could put us there."

"Buddy . . . I'm watching what looks like Barlow militia and some Black marchers about to go at it on Broadway. I'd put a close hold on this until you're sure. Or at least get more confirmation. Because Natchez or Bienville could explode by dark."

"That's what I wanted to know. Your gut."

"Now you have it. I've gotta go."

As I stare in disbelief, one young marcher reaches behind his back with what looks like lethal purpose. I've read too many headlines in the past six months about juvenile homicides in the Black community to wait to see what he means to show the guys in that truck bed. When one of the militia guys shouts something I can't make out, I snap, "That's it! Back to the house."

"Dad, he's got—"

"We can't help! My rifle's back at Edelweiss."

Annie plants her feet as though nothing will move her. "This is insane! We have to do something!"

Down by the truck, the young marcher decides not to pull whatever he was reaching for, and instead sprints forward like a track star, leaps onto the dually's rear bumper, then vaults into the midst of the rednecks, swinging both fists. A shout goes up from the crowd, which surges toward the truck, the women crying out in fear, the men in anger.

Taking Annie by the arm, I turn and drag her back along the road toward Edelweiss. I look over my shoulder as I run, terrified for the boy who jumped into the truck. Sure enough, from the blur of flying fists and twisting torsos his body comes sailing—headfirst over the side of the truck—to crash half on the cement and half on his friends. After a stunned moment, he scrambles to his feet, and I know he's alive. But the roar that bursts from the crowd carries unadulterated rage. The men in the truck recognize that sound. To survive, they must either retreat or open fire. The dually's engine bellows, and its tires burn while the big vehicle fishtails through the crowd.

"*Run!*" I shout.

Ignoring the pain in my stump, I catch Annie's shoulder and run as close to full speed as I have since Mission Hill. Ten yards before we reach Edelweiss, the dually catches up to us. But instead of passing, the driver brakes, and the big engine settles into a clattering growl at our sides. I turn just as we reach the double staircase that leads up to the wraparound gallery, for beneath it lies the safety of the door to the fenced ground floor.

Annie turns with me.

This close, I see the red dually is basically a monster truck, customized for competitions in rodeo rings and sports domes. I also recognize the second flag now. It's the war banner of the Tenisaw Rifles, a Bienville regiment raised in 1861 by Shotwell Barlow: ancestor of the Shot Barlow who's now technically a neighbor of mine near Pencarrow, the plantation I bought for my mother. He occupies the same land his forebears did, and he shares their antebellum politics. After Barack Obama was elected to a second term, *this* Barlow reorganized the Tenisaw Rifles as a modern-day militia and began arming them with technology that eclipses that possessed by local law enforcement. And while I don't recognize the guys in the truck bed today, I know they're forty miles from their Bienville home, which tells me they're not just killing time. They're making an intimidation run, and probably doing recon on Natchez, to keep tabs on the Black community's response to Mission Hill.

The driver leers as he idles past at the speed of a strolling dog. But it's the riflemen in back who hold my attention. A couple look soft: overweight men with graying goatees and spotless tactical gear. But a third guy is younger, gaunt as a rail, with hollow eyes as hard and merciless as those a doomed Yankee infantryman might have seen sighting a musket over the wall at Fredericksburg. A fourth militiaman sitting on a stool just behind the cab glares at me as they pass. Bearded chin set in his hand, he slowly raises his middle finger over his cheek. The eyes behind his orange Oakley shooting glasses tell me he knows damn well who I am. From reflex, I start to flip him off in return, but then I notice an AK-47 leaning against the cab behind his back. Edelweiss is built primarily of wood. If they were to circle the block and rip off even one thirty-round clip, both Annie and I—not to mention the nurse and my mother—could be chewed into hamburger by the Russian gun's heavy rounds.

While my right hand closes into a frustrated fist at my side, the guys in the truck suddenly howl with laughter, confusing me for a few seconds. Then I turn and see that choosing discretion was pointless. Behind me, my daughter stands with both hands turned up, her middle fingers jutting upward with obscene stiffness.

"I know those fuckers from Pencarrow," she explains. "Every one ought to be in the county lockup. Half of them have been, at one time or another."

The big dually slows nearly to a stop once it's past us, and I'm worried they mean to hassle Annie. As I step toward them, though, I notice one of the most revealing accessories ever added to any truck, a chrome-plated pair of testicles hanging below the trailer hitch, like a bull's balls. Some guys call these "truck nuts," but whatever you call them, I doubt anything could better demonstrate male insecurity or lack of concern for decency than hanging a pair of balls from your vehicle. As a style point, they scream "I'm a short-dicked moron!"

I'm about to break my own rule and yell an insult when the clouds overhead unleash a hail of rain, spattering us all. The chubbiest rifleman slaps the cab roof, and the driver hits the gas as though called to some emergency. My chest loosens with relief as the truck squeals away.

"Boo, you can't play games with trash like that."

"Oh, I can," Annie replies. "It's our *duty*."

"You can until you can't. Because on the wrong day, they'll shoot you."

"How about that flag of theirs? Real Army of Jesus stuff. And those chrome balls? Woohoo!"

Seething with frustration and fear, I watch the receding truck. Even its tailgate has been custom-painted with the 162-year-old banner of Barlow's

Tenisaw Rifles: a Christian cross of white stars emblazoned over a navy blue canton, while the field displays three stripes: blood red, white, and red again. The regiment's name adorns the top stripe, and the Barlow family motto appears on the bottom: *ready in faith.*

"Ready for what, I wonder?" Annie muses.

"A week like this one. That's the problem. Let's get inside."

"Mayor Cage?" says a hesitant voice behind me.

I've asked Althea to call me Penn a hundred times, but only rarely has she done so. Turning toward the house, I find her standing in the shadows cast by the deep gallery above us.

"I didn't know where you were," she says, her eyes filled with sadness.

"I'm sorry. We got distracted." I realize I'm bracing myself as though for a blow.

She gives me a forgiving nod. "I'm afraid your mama stopped breathing a couple of minutes ago."

"Oh, God," Annie whispers, her eyes welling. "Oh, no."

"Go on," I tell her, "I'm right behind you."

She rushes into the hall, headed for my mother's sickroom.

The nurse gives me a glance that asks, *Should I go with her?* Althea's worked here long enough to realize that a young woman with the nerve to face down white militiamen might still be reduced to helplessness by the death of someone who has been more mother to her than grandmother.

"Is it agonal breathing?" I ask. "A DNR situation? Or is she really gone?"

"She's passed, Mayor. I'm sorry."

I shake my head. "Let's let Annie deal with it, then."

Althea nods with empathy and understanding.

Turning instinctively to my right, I look down the sidewalk in the direction that the Barlow truck vanished only moments ago. But the big dually is not the beast I'm thinking of. I'm thinking of the bear that appeared to me last Friday morning, at the wrought-iron fence of the Parsonage next door. His face is as clear to me now as it was then: scarred and questioning, yet also burdened by some knowledge he wished to impart. At once both mystical and mortal, he carried more than anything an aura of death. *Did my mother just fulfill his silent prophecy?*

As wrong as it seems, I hope that she did.

But standing on the empty street, where the exhaust of the big dually blends with that left by Dwight's helicopter, I sense there is more death to come, and that my friend Dwight's instinct to flee the state—even the country—might be the sanest of all.

CHAPTER 12

I'M STANDING IN the central hallway of Edelweiss's elevated basement, which Mom decorated as a foyer, with a double-length workroom to the left and two bedrooms to the right, the first of which became her sickroom at the end. Annie's with her now, but I can't bring myself to face the terrible stillness of death again. Not yet. Through the ceiling I hear the heels of Althea Foster as the hospice nurse gathers her things from the main floor and calls to tell her family she'll be coming home early.

The first time I really understood the stillness of death was when I lost Annie's mother to cancer, twenty-six years ago. Annie was only three then, but she instantly understood the change in her mother. Whatever spirit had animated that loving form had abandoned it. Forever. One desolate year later, I left Houston to take my little girl back to Natchez for a comforting visit with her grandparents, and that became a nine-year residency. Ever since that move, my mother has been the primary female figure in Annie's life. Only once in the years after losing Sarah did I come close to marrying again. The woman I chose was the one I bought this house for, but she was murdered a month before the ceremony. Annie was eleven then. In the end, my mother stepped into the maternal role with heroic dedication that lasted until today.

Her death will be the most wrenching blow in Annie's life.

ANNIE DIDN'T MITIGATE the danger of her own existence by her career choice. She practices civil rights law in Jackson, Mississippi, and she's more liberal than I will ever be. She works for the widow of the legendary Black civil rights lawyer Quentin Avery. Even after cradling Martine in her arms while she choked to death on her own blood (something that happened just before Kelly found her), Annie has been urging restraint and pleading with people to work through the legal system to try to remedy the fallout from Mission Hill.

I wish I could do the same. But my daughter is young, and still has her illusions. I am not, and I don't. Life taught me long ago how thin the veneer of civilization really is, how quickly society can devolve into chaos. I saw it as mayor after Hurricane Katrina, and over the past three days, I've felt inchoate anger and fear rising in this corner of southwest Mississippi like floodwater from the river seeping into the cotton towns in 1927. Like a divine punishment, it snaked through the fetid bottomlands, curled into gullies, pressed ever harder against the old levees, heralding the coming deluge. Anger and panic are doing the same now, and they will not be stopped.

Yesterday, I did all I could to try to persuade Annie to leave the state for a few days, or barring that, to at least remain in Jackson while she works on the cases of those who came to them after Mission Hill. But all my effort was for naught. The downside of having an adult child—especially a head-strong attorney whose intellect and passion surpass your own—is that you can't control them any longer. Annie heard me out, then informed me that she was scheduled to begin interviewing victims and witnesses before the end of the week.

I should have quit while I was behind, but fear made me push her. After I'd said my piece, she looked me squarely in the eyes and, speaking with quiet conviction, cut me to the bone. "Dad, all my life you've been my hero. For a lot of other people, too. I'm not exaggerating. You've never let bad odds intimidate you, much less stop you. You were just like Papa was. I only pray I can accomplish half of what you have before I'm done. But now you want to *run*?"

"Yes," I confessed. "And I'm asking you to run with me. Begging you, really."

In that moment I saw something I'd never endured before: true diminishment of my reflection in my daughter's eyes.

If Annie knew all the sins that had been committed over the years to bring her alive and safe to adulthood, she might not presume to lecture me about danger. But she doesn't, and she never will. It's not that she's led a sheltered life, nor is she a stranger to loss. She knows that when she was an infant, I shot a convict in Houston who tried to take her from our house as revenge for the execution of his brother. When she was thirteen, she was kidnapped from her school parking lot by members of a prison gang, and what she endured in the course of being rescued by my friend Daniel Kelly is more than most people will ever face. But she does *not* know that what made that rescue possible was my mother, who committed an act so ruthless it shocked even Kelly, a soldier who later declared it proof that in the last analysis, the female is the more pragmatic of the human species.

"Dad?" Annie calls from Mom's sickroom. "Can you hear me?"

Closing my eyes against the sting of tears, I settle my weight fully onto my stump and hobble into the room where my mother took her final breath.

Annie sits beside the bed where Mom lies, her good hand resting on the pale forehead. I wonder if she remembers her own mother's stillness, as I do. Touching a family member from whom one has only ever felt warmth and words and respiration—all the quiet rhythms of life—only to feel a waxlike surface shedding heat like the last ashes of a fire leaves you disoriented, even repulsed. Yet love holds you where you are, wishing for the impossible.

"I feel so bad that we missed her final moments," Annie says in a hushed voice. She looks back at me, her hazel eyes inflamed. "And just because of those *Barlow* assholes."

Looking past her, I realize I'm thankful Mom has been unconscious for the past three days. We said our goodbyes before that, after a fashion. Now the last battle is done. Some people don't like the use of war metaphors to describe a terminal disease process; it seems to blame a patient for losing a struggle they had no real chance of winning. But like my physician father, I'm old school. And given my mother's approach to survival, I won't insult her by calling it anything else.

Peggy Cage died a warrior.

"Don't torture yourself," I say softly. "We spent almost every minute with her after that first stroke, and God knows you were there for her during this past year. She never could have kept up her work without you."

Annie's face collapses inward, and she covers it with her hands.

I step forward and pull her up to me, squeezing her as tight as I dare. She shudders, and the emotion I feel within her is a fearful thing. I have known much grief in my life, and I've worked hard to spare my daughter the same. But holding her now, I realize I may not have succeeded to the degree I'd hoped.

"Boo, listen. Earlier today, the father of Esther Griffin took a gun into the sheriff's office. He's claiming he went in to force him to make a public apology. But he might have gone in to kill him."

Annie draws back, looking at me in confusion. "I haven't heard anything about that."

"Almost no one knows yet. But they will. Now . . . I know you think we've settled this, but things have changed with Mom's passing."

"Oh, God, Dad. Do *not* ask me to leave town again."

"I want you to think about what would be happening now if Johnny Griffin had killed the sheriff."

She blinks, nonplussed. "What do you want me to say? It would be bad, sure. But we'd have to deal with it."

"With a riot? With war in the street? Because that's a reasonable prediction of what could happen." After a few moments' hesitation, I say, "Marshall McEwan just informed me that a Black radical group has claimed the Tranquility fire as intentional retaliation for the Mission Hill shooting."

Annie slowly blinks as she processes this revelation.

"Marshall's not going to reveal it yet, so you can't tell a soul. Not even anyone at your firm. Not even Doris. But I want you to factor it into your decision. Because it's going to get out soon."

She shakes her head slowly. "We can't fight a riot alone, obviously. But that's what the government exists for, right? City, county, state. Even the feds, if that's what it takes."

"Annie, you know Bienville is a jurisdictional nightmare, and Natchez is nearly the same. Legally, because of the special charters. Two separate governments in each city: one white-dominated, one Black. Two law-enforcement agencies in each county: one white, one Black. But the real authority rests with the whites. The Tenisaw sheriff is a true believer in the sovereign sheriff movement, which is a whole other kind of crazy, and the state government—"

"I know. White Republican governor and legislature."

"Exactly. Hoping for a good outcome in those circumstances is like hoping for a chorus of 'We Shall Overcome' at a KKK meeting."

"And *yet*—" Annie wipes her face and stands a little more erect. "The voters of Bienville, Mississippi, elected a *gay Black man* as their mayor in a massive landslide."

"They elected a war hero who's still technically married to his high school sweetheart."

Annie waves her hand. "Everybody knows Doc's gay."

I take hold of her left wrist and hold up her wounded hand. "You could be lying on a drain table at the funeral home as easily as Esther Griffin. And I could *not* deal with that. Do you understand?"

She nods. "As much as I can without being a parent. But it *wasn't* me, okay? I literally just dodged a bullet." She holds up her bandage. "Well, not quite. I dodged a *fatal* bullet. And I'm going to make damn sure Martine didn't die for nothing, okay? That none of them did. I'm the one whose job is to get Mr. Griffin and the other victims the closest thing there is to justice. I have to do all I can, *without fear.*"

"You don't have to be in Natchez or Bienville to do that."

"Of course I do! I'm going to be taking depositions, filing the—"

"Annie!"

She pulls her hand free and takes a step back. "I've been thinking about all you said last night. If things really break the way you think they will—if we get a race riot that spreads from city to city—where exactly do you think we could go that would be safe?"

"Dwight Ford is flying to Dominica to get away from this."

"*What?*" She looks at me in disbelief, but then her expression changes. She doesn't even try to hide her disgust. "So . . . it's people with *money*, then. Things go to shit, and the folks who can afford to bug out, leaving families like the Griffins to swallow whatever bullshit the state forces them to."

"Annie—"

"What about the people who can't afford to go kitesurfing while Sheriff Tarlton's goons make the streets safe for MAGA-world again?"

I shake my head with something close to exhaustion. "You're not going to change anything by fighting in the streets."

"At least I'll be able to live with myself."

Suppressing my frustration, I close my eyes and search for a line of argument that might affect her. But nothing comes. Then I feel my daughter's hand cover mine.

"Dad, what's going on with you? Gram was seriously worried about you, but she wouldn't tell me why. She didn't want you *burdened* with anything, that's what she kept saying. But you've said almost nothing about Martine getting killed, and I know that had to hit you hard. And losing Gram . . . that's beyond words. Now all this talk of leaving . . . I know you'd never walk out on Mayor Berry in the middle of a crisis. Not if things were okay. Doc will need you now more than he ever has."

"I promised Doc eighteen months as city attorney. I've been doing it nearly four years."

"Mask mandates and lockdowns? Please. This is like war footing. That's not Doc's skill set. He was a medic in Vietnam, not an officer."

"Then he's got infinitely more experience with war than I do. A dozen Bienville lawyers will step up to replace me. Doc's got friends who are excellent attorneys."

"Doc didn't ask his buddies to fill that post. He asked you. Beyond that . . . come on. Are you going to make me say it?"

"What?"

"Papa was Doc's mentor. And I know what Papa would tell you to do if he were here."

She's bringing out the heavy guns. The girl is as ruthless as her grandmother.

"You know I'm right," Annie presses. "Doc went to Washington to try to prevent exactly what you're afraid of. And to recruit some heavyweight help in case things really go sideways."

Maddened by her easy optimism, I drop all pretense of patience. "They're *going* sideways, Annie. I've never felt more certain of anything."

With this voicing of irrational certainty, our argument ends. Annie touches my hand and smiles sadly but says nothing, and instead sits down beside my mother's body and gently takes her dead hand. I suppose I've surrendered, but in truth it's like yielding to a younger incarnation of myself, before life shook the last of my naïveté from my soul.

A soft knocking breaks the silence, and Althea, our hospice nurse, leans into the room with her huge purse slung over her shoulder. "Sorry if I interrupted," she says, but I know she's been out there waiting for a moment's pause to make her exit. "I need to tell you something."

"What's that, Althea?" I ask.

"Mrs. Peggy wanted me to give y'all something after she passed. She told me a few days ago."

The nurse reaches into her purse and takes out a James Lee Burke novel with a bright red cover. The big jacket type reads: *Burning Angel*. I squint in puzzlement, but then she says, "There's a letter in here. Mrs. Peggy wrote about half of it, but I had to finish it. She couldn't really write after that second stroke."

"A letter for me?"

"For both of you," says the nurse, holding out the book. "You'll see."

Walking forward, I take the novel and nod thanks. "We really appreciate everything you did these past weeks, Althea. All the nurses were good, but you were Mom's favorite."

"Well." She starts to take her leave, then pauses. "I was glad to be able to take care of her. I work with lots of old folks, and they can get pretty hard on you. Prickly. Especially old white ladies. They kind of revert back to when they was young, you know? They call you the N-word ten times a day, and you see things . . ."

"What things?" Annie asks from the bedside.

"Oh, child. I tended one lady who had two little Black lynching dolls in her bathroom with ropes around their necks."

"*What?*"

"For real. Like they were meant to be cute. I left that house quick. But . . . that's not what I wanted to tell you. Tending to Mrs. Peggy was special. That's what I wanted to say. She had a kind soul. She really cared about people. I mean everybody. Y'all were lucky to have her."

"We appreciate that."

"By the way . . . the last of her drugs are in a box in that dresser over there. I can take them if you want, make sure they're disposed of. Or I can leave 'em here, so long as you take responsibility. She's still got oxy in there. Those fentanyl patches can be dangerous. There's liquid Xanax, too."

"We'll take care of that," I say, suddenly conscious of my myeloma pain, but hoping Althea figures I want something in the house in case of unexpected dental pain at 3:00 a.m. "There are no children around here."

Althea nods with understanding. "All right, then."

Annie waves a somber farewell, and then we're alone together once more.

"Well?" she says with an expectant gaze. "Aren't you going to read the letter?"

Opening the Burke novel with some reluctance, I find an envelope marked in my mother's hand, rendered barely recognizable by the first strokes. It reads *Penn/Annie*. I move to the chair I've used for the past week, lay the book on an end table, then sit and pop the pressure release on my prosthetic leg. My stump aches badly, and for all I know, it's turning purple within the carbon-fiber socket. Annie watches me, her grandmother's hand tight in her own.

The first two paragraphs are much like the writing on the envelope; the remainder is written in a clearer but blockier script, which must be Althea's hand. But the moment I begin to read, Mom's voice rises from the paper as clearly as when she spoke aloud as a woman in her prime.

"'Dear Penn and Annie,

"'If you're reading this, I'm likely gone, and without finding the answers to those last stubborn riddles that confounded me. I thought I'd have a little more time on earth, but this second stroke feels like a bad sign. If it is . . . then Penn, I want you to pick up my lamp and finish my quest. You owe it to yourself, not to me. You can't know who you are until you know who and where you came from. Even at your age. You'll need Annie's help to get started, and maybe at your side going through this.

"'There's another serious matter to be dealt with. Until now, there are things Annie has kept from you at my request, and I now release her to tell you what she will, when she's ready. I've also held—'"

I stop there, but too late for Annie not to realize something is up.

"Don't you dare leave anything out," my daughter warns.

Sighing heavily, and with more than a little dread, I go on.

"'I've also held something back from her at your request, as you know. A wish I mostly agreed with. But like most children, she's grown up far more than we knew. Now that I'm gone, you need to share that burden with her. It's too much to carry alone. I know that better than anyone.

"'As for practicalities, I want you to bury me beneath the Duel Oak at Pencarrow. Call me crazy, but I don't want a big funeral, or even to be embalmed. Put me in the ground in a wooden casket and let me be. (You can do it. I've checked the law.) During winter, when the kudzu's down, you can stand under that tree and see the bluff drop all the way down to the river—the old "unappeasable God" that Will Percy wrote about in *Lanterns on the Levee*. That's the land that bore me, and you too. A tree surgeon once told me that old oak has been standing since 1800, so it was mature when Robert Pencarrow married his first wife. It was watching when he turned away from her, back toward Calliope, and later when he fought that fateful duel in the shadow of his own death. It was probably 40 feet tall when Duncan Pencarrow was wounded at the Mule Shoe, and Petersburg. That tree was waiting for us all those years, Penn. It wanted us to know what it knew. I sat beneath it when Deborah Fannin first told me about her search for her white ancestor. Fair warning: that old oak has seen darker doings than any you've experienced in your life, and I know that's saying something. I've been forever changed by what I've learned, for better and worse. But I suppose that's what we're sent here for, after all.

"'If digging my grave will damage the roots of that tree, then move me outside the drip line. I won't be needing shade, and you can sit under the leaves when you visit me. Put a bench there and tell me what you uncover. Don't worry about your father lying alone in the Natchez Cemetery. Tom never believed in an afterlife. (Remember his mantra? "When you die, you're dead. Anything you want to do or say, best do it here, and soon.") But if Tom can see us, he of all people would understand my decision. My spirit will be with his, that I trust.

"'As for my writing: I've tried to organize what's in my satchel, but my mind isn't as sharp as it was. "Chemo brain" is a real thing, I'm afraid. A kind of neurological fog. Fair warning. I hope you can make sense of my prose, son. Annie can help with the chronology. That girl is smarter than you and me put together.

"'You still have time to live, my boy. Annie may be grown, but she needs you. Please give yourself the gift of another good woman. They're still out there, and there's no point in being alone. Not even to spare another pain. Love is all there is, and you've been by yourself too long.

(I like the Sullivan girl myself. Martine Boucher is a fine person, but she's French and leads a dangerous life. Nadine Sullivan is younger than you, but she comes from good stock and she's got her feet well beneath her. She gave up lawyering to open a bookstore, and she's smart enough to make money at it. Could there be a more perfect mate for you than that? I'll stop now. Your choice, not mine.) —*Mom*

"'P.S. I still hate that you lost your leg, but there are worse things you can lose. I know you know that. Be happy! I die in peace because you are your father's son. Protect your family, as Tom did. That's what a man is put on earth to do. Never shy from duty, Penn. Never.'"

I feel about twelve years old when I read these words. Then I look up into my daughter's welling eyes.

"What do you think?" she asks, wiping away tears.

"About which part? The burial stuff? It's hard to go against this letter, obviously. But let's wait until we've had some sleep to decide."

"That's not the part I meant. I meant coming clean with each other."

Something goes tight in my chest. But before I can put up my defenses, she says, "This isn't anything Gram asked me to keep from you, but I'm tired of hiding it from you."

"What's that?"

"I know about you and Nadine. I mean, I know you guys used to be a thing."

This truly surprises me. "How long have you known?"

"I suspected when I was in college. I drove home in the middle of the night once without telling you I was coming, and when I got to the house, I found her car parked at our house. I decided to stay over with a friend."

A needle of guilt goes through me.

"But I've known for sure for a couple of years. I ran into Nadine at a wedding neither of us had really wanted to go to. We were both buzzed, and sitting in a hotel bar. We got to talking, and I told her about that night. She said she figured I was grown up enough to know the truth, and she didn't want to lie. So she told me a little. Not big details. I don't know why you guys didn't end up together. I don't think she understands, either. But I just . . . I feel better not having to hide that I know."

"How do you feel about Nadine?"

"I think she's great. Smart as hell. Gram obviously liked her, too."

Annie looks like she's about to go on when a strange ring comes from the cell phone in her pocket, and her face goes slack with surprise.

"What's that?"

"A coded ring from Doris. She only uses it for really important firm business."

"Answer it, then. It might be about Esther's father. I'm afraid Sheriff Tarlton wants to arrest him."

"Christ, what a prick."

Now her phone pings, and she reads a long text message. "Oh . . . I see. Bobby White's scheduled to appear on a news special with Shepard Smith in a few minutes, to do some kind of legal commentary on that composite video of Mission Hill. Doris wants to know if I can watch."

Cortisol floods through me with sickening intensity. Apart from my personal distress over Saturday's shooting, the hundreds of video recordings uploaded by concertgoers now exist as a real-time movie depicting the negligence and violence of the actual mass slaughter. It was put together by a gifted editor at Tyler Perry's Atlanta studios. Judging by reported viewing numbers, white deputies firing into a Black rap concert crowd has proved to be more irresistible than TikTok dances and kittens playing with otters.

"Dad . . . ?"

"I'm fine with you watching it, I just . . . I don't want to see that ever again."

Annie glances at her grandmother's body. "I'll run up to the kitchen then. Unless you're ready to do what Gram asked us to do in her letter. I'll blow it off to exchange these damned secrets."

"I'm sorry, boo. I just—"

"Hey, no . . . I get it." She bends and kisses Mom's forehead, then straightens up and lays her good hand on my shoulder. "I need to call Doris before it comes on, and you need some time alone with Gram."

I nod and motion for her to go ahead, but she hangs back, looking worried. "Are you okay? Seriously?"

"Absolutely. I'm going to sit here with her. Say goodbye." When I take Mom's hand, darkly bruised from her last IV, Annie visibly relaxes. Then she waves and says, "I'll be back as soon as the segment's over."

Seconds after she leaves the room, a profound sense of aloneness empties my heart. My mother effectively left this frail shell days ago. Without her spirit animating it, her desiccated face looks as empty as this house will be without her keeping it alive and open to the world.

Looking along her body and the crocheted coverlet, my eyes are drawn to the window near the foot of her bed. It's set in the southern wall of the house, and faces the Parsonage, where I encountered the bear Friday morning. Staring at the closed blinds, a certainty seizes me that once again the bear stands outside, waiting beside the wrought-iron fence. *Delusion?* Perhaps, but based in a real event. I know because the newspaper published a story about it.

Rather than struggle in a recursive loop of anxiety, I go to the window and turn the long handle that opens the blinds. Dusk is deep now, or seems to be from within this lighted room. But looking across Washington Street, I can see that the cracked sidewalk where I came face-to-face with the great creature is empty. Filled with relief, I drop my hand and turn back to the sickroom.

The bear stands six feet away, his triangular head level with mine, his yellow snout and bottomless black eyes pointed at me. I know him by the scar running from nose to jaw. This time I hear no grunt, but his eyes burn into mine, and the stink of him is as real as the sharp ache of my bladder as I struggle not to piss myself.

"Not here," I whisper, terrified to be sucked back to a point in my life that I thought I'd safely navigated. "Not now . . ."

The bear tosses his great head, and again I sense the enormous mass of him, the power of death in his curved black claws. Closing my eyes, I count silently to ten. Then I open them.

He's gone.

Not since the car crash that took my leg and tore my aorta have I experienced hallucinations. After being trapped for days in the intensive care unit, awaiting repeated surgeries, I developed what's known as ICU psychosis. There's nothing unique about that. The question is why I should experience it again fifteen years later.

Moving to the dresser that Althea Foster pointed to a few minutes ago, I open the drawer containing Mom's hospice drugs. My shivering fingers lift the bottle of oxycodone, unscrew the cap, and shake a fat white tablet into my left hand. My heart lightens at the sight of it. Bitterness floods my mouth as I crush the tab between my back teeth, and the taste hurls me back to the period during which I had to learn to walk again.

An inch of water from an old Dasani bottle helps me wash down the fragments, but then I remember the Hendrick's gin and Fever Tree tonic I drank with Bobby after cleaning my gun after the Mission Hill shooting.

And I walk across the hall.

CHAPTER 13

ROBERT E. LEE White stood before a mirror in the greenroom of CBAC's Apogee News show and checked his empty coat sleeve, which was pinned to his right shoulder. Cursing the jacket again, he shifted the stump of his right arm, but it did no good. In the radio business, details like jacket sleeves didn't matter, but in TV everything did. "Still doesn't look right," he said to the empty room, raising first one shoulder, then the other, to check the blazer's balance and movement. "*Crap.*"

Bobby was speaking to himself because his executive assistant had migrated to the hall to get better Wi-Fi reception. A media source back in Mississippi was trying to send Corey a digital file "borrowed" from a TV producer at AXS TV in Dallas. Out in the hall, a big sign bearing the words *SHEPARD SMITH GUEST EP* had been taped to the greenroom door. Bobby's friendship with the former CNBC anchor had led to this interview, which Apogee saw as a chance to take a shot at both Fox and Newsmax during prime ratings slots.

The hall door opened, and Corey Evers entered waving his iPad in triumph. His excited eyes and handsome, angular face made it plain that he'd gotten exactly what Bobby asked for—an advance look at the Dan Rather–helmed profile and interview that would run nationally one night before the possible announcement of his presidential run.

"Good news or bad?" Bobby prompted.

"Better than good," Corey replied, his eyes flashing. "Damn near hagiography."

Bobby felt a jet of adrenaline. "I want to see it before this interview. And I need you to fix my damned sleeve."

Corey was getting accustomed to this task, which fell more under the purview of valet than executive assistant, but satisfying his boss's obsessive-compulsive tendencies was part of the gig. "They'll be coming to take you to the set any minute. We can either fix the sleeve or you can watch the intro."

"Shepard's a Mississippi boy," Bobby reminded him. "He knows I'll be out there on time. Gimme that iPad. We're gonna multitask."

Corey sighed in resignation, then handed over the tablet. "Hold your shoulders as level as you can. Screw that mirror. Turn and face me." Corey removed a single AirPod from his ear and jammed it into Bobby's right. "I should demand a raise," he said, sounding half-serious. "Stand still!"

Bobby laughed. "If it's as good as you say, I'll give you a bonus."

A sharp rapping rattled the door, which opened to reveal a harried female production assistant. "Three minutes, guys."

"We may need longer," Bobby said, nodding at his empty sleeve. "What's the outside limit?"

The young woman sighed irritably. "Five minutes, but we'll have to run."

Bobby gave her a curt nod, then focused on the iPad again while the door closed.

After Corey unpinned the jacket sleeve and stuck the safety pin between his teeth, Bobby went into data-absorption mode and stared at the iPad screen.

Corey rolled his eyes, then hit PLAY on the screen. Bobby judged Dan Rather's vocal delivery while his eyes took in the set, the graphics, the relationship between himself and the old anchor in the wide shot.

"Our profile subject tonight is Robert E. Lee White, who—it seems to many Americans—has appeared out of nowhere to mount the first credible third-party run at the White House since H. Ross Perot went on Larry King in February 1992 and dared King's viewers to put him on the presidential ballot in every state. Mr. Perot's fans took up that challenge, and the rest, as we know, may soon be very interesting history.

"A remarkable forty-one years later, rumor has it that Bobby White has nearly accomplished the same feat, but in a fraction of the time and in updated style. Ingeniously exploiting platforms like Instagram, Z, and most notably TikTok, the former special forces soldier, lawyer, author, and radio host has in a stunningly short window of time put himself—if rumor can be believed—within a few states of having the signatures to register on all fifty state ballots well in advance of next year's deadlines. If he makes it by Friday, he'll have accomplished this in one tenth of the time it took Perot's supporters three decades ago."

"I'm still miles in the dust behind Kendrick Washington," Bobby muttered. "That kid's got over thirty-two million combined followers at this point, and he's still exploding."

"More than three quarters of those are outside the country," Corey pointed out. "You've got to let that go. It's the ultimate black swan event."

Bobby grunted as Dan Rather said, "What made this extraordinary run possible? Perhaps the most unique biography in American politics for half a century, including a grandfather who was a hero in the Battle of the Bulge and a father who's already enshrined in the Major League Baseball

Hall of Fame. Even so, experts will tell you that Bobby White's real secret is a small but first-rate team of former military intel experts, and political instincts second to none. Using these assets, this unlikely candidate has managed to do what no potential Republicans candidate has done since Donald J. Trump walked down those stairs in 2015—and more. White has seized the center of the old GOP voting block and—perhaps more important—tapped a big chunk of the youth vote—at least the *white* youth vote.

"Experts agree he did this by issuing the following on-air statement on January 6, 2021—one that initially triggered a nearly terminal fall in listeners for the popular radio host. But his early and persistent stand against Donald Trump's effort to illegally cling to power would eventually help bring Bobby White to where he stands today: the cusp of a historic run for the presidency."

The screen showed a car radio, and then Bobby's voice said: "My fellow Americans, it is with a heavy heart that I tell you that your president has aided and abetted treason against the country he swore to protect and serve. Before his political career ends, Donald John Trump will either be going to prison or to a nonextradition country—and he deserves the former fate."

"Nearly three years later," Rather went on, "Trump—while still the putative GOP nominee—stands indicted for multiple felonies, while the party that sought to marginalize Bobby White has become a chaotic parody of its former self. Held hostage by its most extreme elements, embattled over many of its points of departure with Bobby White, today's GOP brings to mind one of White's viral TikTok videos, which includes the following words: 'Any political party that seeks to ban books or rewrite history is too damn chickenshit to govern anybody. They're doomed to the ashbin of history, and deserve that fate.'"

"What's taking so long with the sleeve?" Bobby asked irritably.

"Finish the damned profile."

As Bobby focused on the tablet screen, a text message popped up from a friend in Natchez, Mississippi, forty miles from his childhood hometown.

"What's Cal Herrin want with you?" Corey asked. "Probably something about that damned PGA tournament."

With practiced fluidity, Bobby tapped the screen with his nose.

A moment later, the image of a burning mansion opened over half the screen, dark smoke billowing skyward into the clouds. A hollow feeling entered his belly as he recognized the house. "That's the Dufort mansion," he said softly. "Tranquility."

"My *God*," Corey breathed. "I remember seeing that place a couple of years ago. What a loss. That's unbelievable."

Bobby had seen a lot of buildings hit by incendiaries during his combat service, and he could tell Tranquility was going to burn to its foundation. He wanted to return to the Rather program, but his mind was whirling at lightspeed. The image of a burning antebellum mansion—especially an icon so familiar from his youth—had triggered something deep within him. As he stared, he realized it wasn't merely the fire, but the proximity in time to Mission Hill that had ignited his interest, and even his suspicion.

"What are you thinking?" Corey asked. "I can hear your brain spinning."

"That house has stood there damn near two hundred years. Maybe longer. *Now* it's burning? The little man inside is telling me something, Cor."

"Oh, shit. Like what?"

Bobby shook his head, feeling a sudden tingle along his back and sides. "Opportunity's tapping my shoulder."

"Oh, man. You don't have time for this. You'll see Herrin tonight at the VIP dinner for the PGA thing."

"If we make it. Have you got the Donnelly Oil jet confirmed?"

"I've given Dixie Donnelly all our details. That's all I can do." Corey shook his head and kept working at the sleeve.

Bobby returned his attention to the iPad. Dragging the scroll bar forward, he picked up the narrative a little further along. ". . . most provocative part of the story, when White walked away from his sophomore All-American season at Ole Miss and a certain MLB career to enlist as a private in the army and wind up in special forces, where four years later he would lose his arm while killing Al Qaeda's successor to Abu Musab al-Zarqawi—Abu Nasir.

"Remarkably, none of us would ever have known this but for a dispute that erupted into public view when a loose-lipped Delta operator tried to claim personal credit for that kill in a book. Eventually, angry comrades present on that HVT raid corrected the record by crediting the kill to their disabled fellow operator, Bobby White. It was then that Bobby White exploded into the global consciousness as worldwide media picked up the story of the humble hero.

"A graduate of Vanderbilt Law School, White has written two Southern histories. Listen to the judgment of historian Jon Meacham."

The screen cut to Meacham.

"For someone considered to be a right-wing radio host, Mr. White's two nonfiction works show remarkable insight into the psychology of the

South, and how the Lost Cause myth was facilitated by writers and scholars in the North—as well as Hollywood—all to the detriment of Black Americans freed from slavery. That didn't initially earn White a lot of fans below the Mason-Dixon Line, but modern scholars agree that his histories give a more accurate view of the deep dynamics of the war than fellow Mississippian Shelby Foote's—especially as regards what White himself calls 'the Karo syrup–smeared lenses of old Shelby's vision.'" Meacham grinned. "I'm sorry, I can't help but smile at that."

Dan Rather laughed and then said, "As most people have become aware in recent weeks, Bobby White is anything but disabled. The veteran has rehabilitated his surviving arm to the point that he competes nationally as a pistol shot, as well as in golf, fencing, and some other sports. In recent weeks Bobby White has actually become something of a sex symbol for the middle-aged demographic. Of the candidate, Ann Coulter tweeted: 'Bobby White is the George Clooney of the Right. He makes Ron DeSantis look like a constipated Pillsbury Doughboy.'"

Rather grinned. "As we head toward Friday night's possible announcement, Bobby White remains employed as a talk-radio host whose audience has grown from seven million one year ago to twelve million last week, making him second to only Sean Hannity in the national ratings. That leaves a backlog of literally millions of words for enemies to dig through in search of weapons, but Bobby White seems refreshingly unconcerned by his verbal record."

Bobby heard himself speak in voiceover: *"Anything I ever said, I'm willing to stand by or live with."*

"The only remaining question as we march into the circus of this coming election year," Rather went on, "is whether Bobby White can pull in enough of the disgruntled fifty million or so voters who still claim loyalty to MAGA and Trumpism to make victory possible? Can he become the first candidate to make a third-party run a viable path to victory?

"If you want to gauge Bobby White's chances of reaching the average voter on the street, and get a sense of what drives people's connection to him, listen to this veteran who went through boot camp with him at Fort Benning."

"I busted my hump to become a good soldier, but Bobby went all the way to Delta, man. He killed Abu Nasir, for God's sake, right before that bastard clacked off an S-vest. None of these tin soldiers in Congress have seen action like that. No disrespect to anybody who wore the uniform. But Bobby's record is a whole different thing. He could twist off Vladimir Putin's head with that one arm he's got left. You know, Bobby is the one who pressed for Task Force

Coral in the first place. He sensed that the Taliban and Al Qaeda were work-ing in unison to protect some of their most hunted High-Value Targets. Coral followed them between Iraq and Afghanistan like it was nothing. And that's how they got Abu Nasir in the end. You ask me, that's what we need in the White House. Direct action types like Bobby. Not these soft-ass billionaires or mealy-mouthed, throw-the-fools-red-meat politicians. And sure as hell not these rainbow-assed, kumbaya, I don't-know-what-gender-I-am numb-nuts from the Left . . . Jesus Christ, what's happened to America?"

"This is practically a campaign ad," Bobby exulted, closing his eyes and lowering the iPad. "You get your bonus, Cor."

"Which will be . . . ?"

"Think about it while I—" Bobby stopped and tapped the phone call that popped up on his iPad. The caller was his personal contact at the Bienville *Watchman*—a lower-level employee who had access to the news-paper's computers and good contacts with the reporters at Bobby's old hometown paper.

"What's up, Dale?" he asked the earpiece.

"Something big. You gotta keep this quiet, man."

Bobby stiffened as Corey worked at the sleeve. "Sure, like always."

"This is different. You keep it quiet unless . . ."

"What?"

"Unless you want to really make it worth my while."

This was unusual. "Jesus. How big is it?"

"Big. And it's only gonna get bigger. It's time sensitive, too."

"Fire away."

Corey grunted in concern, but Bobby shook his head, meaning he should stay out of it.

"Somebody just called in a claim for that fire. The Tranquility mansion. That was no accident, Bobby. It was *arson*. Retaliation for Mission Hill. *Black* retaliation."

Bobby swallowed at this confirmation of his instinct. "Holy Christ."

"Uh-huh."

"You have any details?"

"Just the name of the group. The radical group. 'The Bastard Sons of the Confederacy.' That's what they call themselves."

Bobby whistled and glanced at his watch. "Is that all you have?"

"No. The caller said there would be more burnings. More attacks."

"Oh, *man*. Did the caller sound Black or white?"

"I heard Marshall say he sounded Black. Black for sure."

A hard knock rattled the greenroom.

"I've gotta go, Dale. Keep me posted, you hear?" Bobby used his nose to disconnect.

Corey leaned back once more, then nodded with satisfaction. "You're parade ready, Sergeant."

"Thanks. I need to make a call before that schedule Nazi gets back—"

The door banged open, and the production assistant waved her hand. "We're on commercial now. Let's get you in your chair, Mr. White."

"Lead on," Bobby said with a grin.

They moved up the bright corridor at double time.

"By the way, how's Annie Cage doing?" Bobby asked.

"Same, I hear," Corey said. "Hands are tricky."

"Beats the hell out of a vital organ. We might run into Penn at the PGA tourney this week. Make sure I give him my best Bill Clinton."

Corey smiled and drawled, "*I feel your pain, bubba.*' His daughter will be repping victims in the Mission Hill lawsuits. She works civil rights cases with Doris Avery."

Bobby whistled with respect. "I figured Ben Crump would be all over that action."

"I think Crump refers some Mississippi stuff to Avery. He worked with Quentin some before he died."

Bobby absorbed all this with interest. "I wonder whether Penn's been rethinking his politics since the shooting?"

"Not likely. Cage is a yellow-dog Democrat, just like Grisham."

"He was pretty upset Saturday night. He had an AR-15 in his lap, locked and loaded. An injured kid can change a father from John Lennon into John Wick in about three seconds."

"Shepard told me you're never late," said the assistant, looking back. "But you're cutting it close this time."

"He knows I'd never embarrass him."

"How do you know him?"

Bobby's smile widened. "Mississippi's like one big family. Everybody knows everybody."

Corey leaned toward Bobby and whispered: "What was that call from Dale Dawson? Anything serious?"

Bobby leaned into Corey's ear. "Only a tip that the Tranquility fire was an intentional arson attack. Retaliation for Mission Hill."

Corey went pale. "Bobby . . . you can't say that on air."

"I know, I know. I hear you. But I'm sick of simply analyzing that Mission Hill composite video while Kendrick Washington goes on the news and talks civil rights and philosophy."

Corey rolled his eyes. "I know you, Bobby. You've taken your centrist position as far as you can. At some point you have to pivot right, as Rather said. You lost ground in that effort by going on Lawrence O'Donnell. If you did it tonight, though—really pivoted right—your radio audience could equal Hannity's by Thursday. Maybe even surpass it. That would make a hell of a headline going into our announcement. But you can't use *this* to do it. Not without more proof than you have. Use the massacre if you have to."

Bobby glared and answered in a whisper: "You just lost your bonus. We don't use the word 'massacre.' Ever. It's the Mission Hill *shooting*, now and for all time."

"Damn it," Corey muttered.

"And I'm not wild about pivoting further right to get those MAGA votes. I don't want to be beholden to those sons of bitches for the next four years. They all think they're victims, even if they're rich." They'd reached the huge black door that led to the studio. The production assistant paused to send a text. Bobby lifted his phone and called up the image of Charles Dufort's burning mansion. His heart began to pound with excitement. He shook his head, eyes glinting with confidence.

"This fire is big, Cor. And it's *Dufort's* ancestral place. You never know when or how fate is going to give you a gift . . . but that's the moment you seal your destiny."

"Bobby, I'm begging you. Don't say a word about Tranquility."

"Right in my hometown. And *this* week? It's almost too perfect."

A shadow passed over Corey's face. "Remember you said that."

Corey tapped the assistant's shoulder. "We're going to have a jet waiting at Teterboro before he's out of the chair. Can you make sure we're out to our car service the second Shepard's done with him?"

"No problem," she said, not even looking back.

The assistant hit a button, and the big door opened to a cavern of blackness with a brilliant white island of light at its heart. Supercooled air rushed out and enveloped them.

"Just like a ride at Disney World," Bobby said. "God, I love this shit!"

CHAPTER 14

AS SHEPARD SMITH began his intro of Bobby White, Annie could feel the composite video of the massacre being cued at the Apogee studio, and she felt an urge to pop another Vicodin. It was disorienting to watch a multi-angle film of a fatal event you'd witnessed from the inside. Her father had told her many military veterans experienced battles in this fractured way. Their memories were primarily gut level, chemically imprinted, up close and overwhelming, while their sense of the larger conflict was often completely mistaken.

Annie went still as Bobby walked out and seated himself at the news desk. He moved with an athlete's grace, and there was no denying his good looks. The man who had saved her life only three days ago was clearly wearing tailored clothes, and the pinned-up coat sleeve served as a substitute for the Silver Star that everyone knew he'd earned in combat but never wore in public. It gave him a gravitas that most men his age simply did not possess.

"Bobby," Shepard began, "I want to thank you for appearing in person today. You've been pretty circumspect about the Mission Hill shooting up to now. And your legal background and military experience give you a unique perspective to comment on what happened before your eyes in what—until very recently—was your own hometown."

"It always will be in some ways, Shep. That's how Mississippi is, as you know."

Smith smiled. "As you requested, we're not going to run an endless loop of the shooting and the grisly chaos following, as so many networks have. We'll run it once, with your commentary. So why don't we set the stage first? What mistakes, if any, do you feel were made in the lead-up to this concert?"

"Before I comment on that, I should tell you . . . I've just gotten word from Mississippi that this story may have leaped ahead of where we thought it was. Only ninety minutes ago, one of the most significant antebellum mansions in Natchez, Mississippi, started burning. And while arson has not yet been proved at this time, contacts in law enforcement there have informed me that they have a high index of suspicion. If that's the case, then we have to consider that we could be looking at a retaliatory strike for the Mission Hill shooting. That would constitute an escalation of a type we've never before seen in this nation. Something that would go far beyond, for example, the looting of commercial businesses."

From what Annie could tell, Shepard Smith hadn't had any idea that Bobby was going to do what he'd just done, which amounted to breaking an explosive story that had not yet been verified as news.

"Well . . . that's a shocking thing to hear, Bobby. I'm sure our staff will be following those developments as we move through the Mission Hill tape. Perhaps we can revisit the topic after the break, after we get some verification on what you've learned so far."

Annie's heartbeat accelerated as Bobby gave the host a taut smile. "Understood, Shep."

Smith's production team rolled the tape, and Bobby brought his hand to his chin with casual grace. "Speaking as an attorney, when I watch this video, I feel as I do when studying tragedies like airline crashes. They almost invariably result from a string of small mishaps and bad judgments that cascade to produce a disaster that, once initiated, can't be stopped without something close to divine intervention."

"Would you elaborate on that?"

"Let's consider the obvious." White began ticking off points using the fingers of his one hand, but as he did, Annie saw the concentration in his eyes waver. She knew before it happened that Bobby was about to deviate from his intended points yet again.

"Shepard, forgive me, I've got to tell you something else I just can't keep to myself. Just before walking on set, I got a reliable tip that the fire I mentioned in Natchez *has now been claimed as arson* by a radical group as retaliation for the police shootings—or rather the sheriff's department shooting—at Mission Hill this past Saturday."

Smith had gone pale.

"The self-proclaimed name of the group in question is—forgive me— 'The Bastard Sons of the Confederacy.' The best guess at this time is that they are an African American activist group. The man who received the claim of responsibility identified the caller as a Black male."

The anchor's mouth hung halfway open, and his eyes looked like those of a shell-shocked soldier in a minefield, unsure of which way to step.

"Whoa," Annie breathed.

She leaped to her feet but found it difficult to pull herself away from the television. As Shepard tried to steer Bobby back onto Mission Hill, she whirled toward the stairs, then rushed back down toward the first floor.

"*DAD?*" CRIES A voice from behind me. "Are you awake?"

"What?" I start in my chair, realizing I've dropped my mother's hand. "Yeah."

"I don't think you were. That's the third time I've said your name."

"I must have drifted off."

"You made a gin and tonic, I see."

I look down and find ice more than half melted in an empty glass. "I needed something to take the edge off."

"No criticism from me. Alcohol's never been your problem."

Annie's face looks paler than it did when she rose from her sickbed. "So what did Bobby White have to say about Mission Hill? Another right-wing defense of our noble sheriff's constabulary?"

"Far from it." She walks around the chair until she's looking down at me. "Dad, Bobby just broke the claim of responsibility for Tranquility on Shepard Smith's show."

My heart thumps in my chest. "You can't be serious."

"Shep nearly fainted when he did it. I could tell."

"Did Bobby have the name of the group responsible?"

"He had exactly what you had. The Bastard Sons of the Confederacy."

"Jesus Christ. Bobby White? There's no way Marshall called him with that news."

"I wouldn't think so. But are you one hundred percent sure?"

I set down my drink. "Positive. Shit, I was already worried that the more extreme whites wouldn't wait to find out whether it was arson or not."

Annie sits on the edge of her chair by Mom's bed. After half a minute, she says, "Have you thought about Gram's letter at all?"

"Not in depth, no. We obviously need to deal with the burial issue right away. But as far as the other things, I'd rather we get some rest and handle them in a few days."

She looks far from happy with this. "How *do* you feel about her burial preference?"

I shrug. "It bothers me a little. The idea that after all these years, she doesn't want to rest beside Dad in the plot where she'd already paid for her headstone? A plot she's visited for years? But I don't know the details of the genealogy work she's been doing this past year. You do, I assume. If you believe it's the right thing, then I'll abide by your decision."

Annie looks as surprised as I've ever seen her. "You really want me to make that choice? On my own?"

"It's probably best. I'm not about to start digging into that satchel of hers. I'm not ready. I only want you to tell me this: If I spent the next three days reading all that, would I believe she was right to bury herself away from Dad on that old plantation?"

Annie looks at the floor, then slowly nods. When she looks up, her hazel eyes carry not the slightest doubt. "Absolutely. The day will come when you'll know it was one of the most fitting things you ever did."

Inexplicable relief lifts a weight from my heart. "All right, then. That's one decision made."

A smile breaks out on Annie's face, and she wipes her eyes. "You know, seeing those images of Tranquility has turned my mind to Charles Dufort. He was part of Gram's research."

"Really?"

"The Dufort family has a well-known history of Union sympathies, and being pro-Lincoln during the war. Shouldn't that make their house one of the least likely targets for an attack like this? Especially by a radical group that knows any history?"

I nod thoughtfully. "The Duforts were still major slaveholders. They owned more than five hundred human beings." This paradox has always left me puzzled. "How were the Duforts tied to Mom's research?"

"I wish I could give you a better answer. You remember Gram asking you to set your lynching book aside while she finished her work?"

I shift in my seat, discomfited to be reminded of one of the most difficult things I've had to do in the past few years. "I'm not likely to forget that."

"She kept a lot of this to herself, but I think she suspected that the Duforts of that era were somehow involved in the Natchez lynchings at Second Creek. Those, and also the lynchings up near Bienville. On the Barlow place. I'm not sure *how*, though. It was sort of her private obsession."

"What makes you so sure?"

"It was one area where she was concerned with getting documentary proof of whatever her private suspicion was."

"But you don't know the nature of that suspicion?"

"Well . . . those tortures and lynchings were supposedly the result of a planned servile rebellion in the Natchez District in 1861. One that ultimately didn't happen. Why didn't it? Because the supposed ringleaders were executed—extrajudicially—by the planters of these über-wealthy communities. Now, there was a spate of lynchings across the South in 1860 and '61, for the same reasons. Paranoia about slaves revolting as the white males rode off to war. But here . . . Gram was convinced something else had gone on. And I think she believed the Dufort ancestor was somehow tied up in it."

"She never said anything to me about this."

"She was really obsessed with the idea of protecting you from all of it, somehow. I never understood her attitude about the whole thing. Like she was the rock, and you're the sensitive one. It made no sense to me."

Here we're on delicate soil, because I *do* understand what drove Mom to shield me as she did, even if her reasoning was flawed.

Annie nods. "I know some things that might shed a little light on the lynchings. But—if we get into that, we'd be getting into the other matters she refers to in the letter. And you just said you didn't want to do that."

My daughter wants to manipulate me into getting all the way into this story—with its implied exchange of withheld information. "Let me make one guess about what started all this. Did Gram's DNA test come back with some sort of indication of African American descent? 'Black blood,' as people around here say?"

Annie's eyes widen. "She told you?"

"She didn't have to. Once I heard that Deborah Fannin was paying for tests for Black people all over town, I figured it had to be something like that. Nothing else would have started Mom on such an intensive quest. She never cared that much about genealogy before."

"So, how would you feel about that?"

"What was the percentage?"

"One point seven percent, basically."

I wave my hand in dismissal. "It wouldn't matter if it were ten times that. We grew up the way we did, as white people, and that's determined how we're seen and how we feel. Who we are. Anything else is just conversation. Fifty years ago, that would have been different, with the old one-drop rule. But there was no DNA testing back then, of course."

"Luckily for a lot of whites around here," Annie says with obvious snark. "But Dad, what really messed with me about her DNA test isn't that it proved we have some Black blood. It's something else."

"What?"

With that question, Annie gets the permission she's craved. She leans forward in her chair, her eyes glittering. "As Deborah Fannin's raft of DNA tests came back, several patterns emerged. One of the most interesting—and shocking—was the number of Black families around here that are at least partly descended from the Barlow family."

"Shotwell Barlow? The ancestor of the militia guy?"

Annie nods. "And his brother, at least until the duel. The one our ancestor fought under that tree where Gram's going to be buried."

"What explanation did Mom come up with for that?"

"Barlow and his brother owned more than a hundred and fifty slaves between them. They were probably the most violent slaveholders in this area, notorious for their cruelty. And it seems they raped their female slaves as a matter of course. They saw that as a way to increase their human holdings without paying out further cash."

"Common practice at the time."

"These guys made a real industry of it. One of the worst things is that when the Tenisaw Rifles finally went into the field, to harass Grant's troops during the engineering operations prior to the Vicksburg siege, they took a group of young female slaves with them to keep camp and provide recreation at night."

"I can't say I'm surprised by anything those assholes might have done. But I sense you haven't given me your big revelation. What is it about the Barlows and the DNA, Annie? Out with it."

She leans back a little and puts her right forefinger to her lips. "I'm actually afraid to tell you."

"Well, now you have to. Just get it out."

She nods in silence. "Dad, we are *related* to the Barlow family."

A deep sense of unreality settles over me. Maybe it's the narcotics hitting me, or the gin, since I felt the first comforting warmth of the oxycodone several minutes ago.

"I don't understand," I tell her. "We're related to the Barlows through this unknown Black ancestor? Is that what you mean?"

"I'm not saying that. But think about it. Black Oak Plantation and Pencarrow Plantation were contiguous to each other back then. They still are for a long way, except for the boundary of River Road. Only a narrow carriage lane separated them back then. In some places only a horse trail. Constant contact was inevitable. That's what makes it such a pain for Andrew out there, working the place. Being so close to those bastards." I can see Annie struggling with some internal dilemma. "But Dad . . . I've told you about all I can about what Gram found, without you having the historical context you need to really understand it. And the only way you can get that is to do what Gram asked. Take her satchel and read her work."

"Are you serious?" I ask, incredulous. "You're gonna stop here?"

"If you read two pages, you won't stop until you finish. Gram gave the last part of her life to that writing. I'll tell you this much: the story that answers the question you just asked—our connection to the Barlows—is the worst thing I've ever read. I hate to leave you hanging like that, but I'm going to. Because you owe it to Gram to read what she's done. As she told you in the letter: until you know who and where you came from, you can't know who you are."

I dispute this notion, but I've already lost one argument with Annie today. I'm too high, drunk, and tired to fight another one.

"I guess I'll go upstairs and make up a bed," I tell her. "I'll make some calls about the burial in the morning. That's not going to be as easy as Mom thinks. Funeral homes are a powerful lobby in this state. Burial laws are a pain in the ass, but I'll get it done."

Annie stands and lays her hand on my arm. "It's not that bad. I've already checked the law. Why don't you let me take care of those details?"

I sigh wearily. "It may take pull more than legal maneuvering."

Annie smiles and shakes her head. "Dad, it's no sweat. The next few days are going to be a nightmare for you. Everybody's going to want your help. I think you should drive back to Bienville and sleep at home. You can make your most important callbacks on your way, then turn off your phone and get ten hours."

I can't imagine anything that would give me more relief, but the odds of my getting to sleep through this night are minuscule. "I'm not going to leave you here alone with Gram's body while armed rednecks ride the streets, threatening the Black protesters on the bluff. You've already been shot twice."

"I'll be fine," Annie assures me.

After pondering the likely course of this night, and honestly gauging my fatigue, I say, "I tell you what. If you let me hire a cop to stand guard outside and a nurse to spend one more night in the house with you, then I'll go home. If you're really serious."

She gives a weary sigh. "I'm fine with the cop, but I don't need a nurse. Gram's spirit hovering here is better than any nurse."

I guess I'll have to be satisfied with this. I lean forward to stand, but pain arcs up my right leg, stabs my lower back.

"You've been limping since I saw you," Annie says. "Is your stump hurting bad?"

"It's not good. But I can make it."

Catching hold of my hands, she counts to three, then pulls me to my feet.

With a smile of gratitude, I hug her tight. "Dwight was going to have a nurse's aide drive my car down here from Bienville. I wonder if he made it?"

She smiles. "Yep, it's parked out front. I already saw it."

"Dwight really saved my ass today. I guess they left the keys inside? Or on the tire?"

"I'll bet they dropped them in the mailbox."

"I'll go up and get my suitcase."

She pushes me back. "Don't even think about it. I'll get your stuff. But it's not quite time for that."

"What do you mean?"

My daughter regards me with unalloyed suspicion. "Oh, come on. I already fulfilled my half of what Gram's letter told us to do. At least in broad strokes. But you haven't even started."

A wave of heat passes over my face. Everything she's said and done so far was to manipulate me to this end. She wants to know what her grandmother and I have been keeping from her. The problem is, she can't imagine the magnitude of the secret. It will make even revelations about DNA connections to white supremacists seem trivial. But I see no way to avoid it now, other than outright refusal, which will leave her bitter and furious until the hour I finally relent. I look over at the James Lee Burke novel on the end table, the envelope on top of it—

"Don't even think about stonewalling me," Annie warns.

Every instinct I possess tells me to deny her what she thinks she wants. What parent willingly burdens their child with terrible foreknowledge? But . . . didn't my mother write that Annie is far more mature than either of us have understood? And that I should keep this from her no longer? That's what brought us to this point.

"All right," I say softly. "I don't agree that this is the right thing to do. But since it was Mom's last request, I will do it."

Without being asked, Annie backs up and takes her chair again. In a perfect physical echo of her mother, she folds her hands on her lap and waits with what looks like infinite patience.

"Your grandmother and I," I begin, "had something in common that we wished we didn't."

Annie slowly takes this in. "Okay. I'm listening."

When I don't continue immediately, she says, "What was it?"

"Her diagnosis," I answer softly, but to me the words fall like hammer blows in the room.

"What do you mean?" Annie asks. "You don't mean . . . her blood cancer? Her myeloma?"

I nod once. "That's exactly what I mean."

My daughter shakes her head in disbelief. "But . . . how is that possible? When were you diagnosed?"

"Twenty years before Mom was."

She blinks in disbelief. "Twenty *years*? But you're not sick. Are you?"

"Yes and no. Not like she was. I do have the disease, but I turned out to be in the tiny percentage with extremely slow progression. In fact, most oncologists would put me into the luckiest one tenth of one percent."

Annie is still shaking her head, either in disbelief or protest against this new reality. "I don't understand. Myeloma's not even a genetic cancer."

"They don't know if it is or not. There's no simple explanation for any of this. But it's the truth. I have bone lesions. Plasmacytomas. Elevated proteins. All of it. But for now, I'm all right. I could live for ten more years, or—"

"Or you could die by Christmas?"

"Unlikely," I assure her. "Highly."

"You don't know that."

"No. But the treatments are much better than they were when I was diagnosed. So let's not start planning a second funeral, okay?"

Annie's cheeks puff out like Dizzy Gillespie's as she exhales. "I don't know what to say. I feel like I'm dreaming."

"Well, I wish you didn't have to think about it."

"Oh my God, don't even *go* there." Her eyes gleam with moisture. "Wow. I get it now. What can it have been like for you to watch Gram die from this? It's like watching a foretelling of your own—"

"Don't," I tell her. "Really. There's no point thinking about all that."

"*Now* I see why she didn't want to burden you with anything."

I nod slowly. "It hasn't been any worse for me than for you. Sometimes I just had to get away from it. That's all. I'm sorry about that."

"Don't be absurd! God, I see it *all* now. Why you took the Triton Chemical case, even. You couldn't cure Gram, you couldn't help yourself, so you took on the case of some cancer victims you *could* help."

"Maybe," I concede. "I didn't know what else to do."

Tears are flowing from the corners of her eyes. I see the bravery she has always possessed, but my revelation has clearly shaken her to the core.

"You're not telling me everything. I know it."

Her penetrating gaze spears me like a primitive weapon.

"Dad, what's happened? Are you having new symptoms? What?"

After a deep breath and a long, rattling sigh, I tell her I broke a rib last week by simply rolling over in bed. She's well enough acquainted with Mom's disease to know what this means. Annie makes a tight fist, brings it up to her mouth. She tries to smile behind it, but then her composure breaks, and she sobs from deep within.

"You can't leave me, Daddy," she says in a child's hoarse whisper. "Not now. Not yet."

"I'm not going anywhere," I promise, though I have no power to honor that commitment.

"You don't know that. Nobody does." She looks up into my face, tears flowing. "You'll qualify for transplant, right? I mean, you're still young and strong compared to Gram—"

"I will. That's probably where we're headed soon." Getting to my feet with a stifled groan, I move behind her chair and lay my hands on her shoulders. "I'm not going anywhere, boo."

After several seconds of crying softly, Annie nods once, then again, like someone using all their reserves to summon faith. "I'm going to think about what you said."

"What do you mean?"

"About the danger. I'll consider working the Mission Hill cases out of our Jackson office."

Nothing she could have said would have surprised me more.

"You don't have to do that. Not because of this. You're not a child any-more, and it's time I faced that. I just worry about you."

Still facing forward, she reaches up and takes hold of my hand, squeezes hard. "I guess that's going to work both ways now, huh? God, life sucks."

In the wake of her words, I look over at my mother's body on the bed. Outside, the grief and anger of hundreds makes itself felt as a low and steady chant that rolls across the bluff like dark water. "Sometimes it does, yeah."

CHAPTER 15

DRIVING SOUTH DOWN the curving road cut into the bluff to access the Mississippi River bridges, I shut my mind to the memory of my daughter's face when I left her. From this night forward, she will carry the fear of losing me decades before she should. I can only hope my mother was right in her belief that this was something Annie needs, or maybe deserves, to know.

I didn't tell my daughter my real plans for the remainder of the night. After the double shock of dealing with her grandmother's death and my diagnosis, she didn't need to worry about me running the roads with the current unrest. God knows I should be in a bed somewhere after nine days without sleep—not to mention the gin and oxy—but before returning to Bienville, I want to see what remains of Charles Dufort's Tranquility.

A blanket of familiarity descends over me as I turn inland at the bridges and drive east along the bypass toward the Dufort estate. I could drive these roads with my eyes closed, and that familiarity is both comforting and melancholy. Beyond a cluster of businesses that includes a Subway, a yogurt shop, and the small Trailways bus depot, the road is lined only with trees, which means I'm already riding parallel to the forested acreage that surrounds Tranquility. Up ahead, across the median, I see orange cones and striped sawhorses, the faint flash of distant red and blue lights. In Natchez red means fire trucks, blue police. Adams County has sheriff's cruisers with red lights, but they generally only use them outside the city limits. Two hundred yards farther along, I make a U-turn, then join a line of rubberneckers idling toward the Tranquility gate.

I soon realize people aren't being allowed into the estate proper. Cops are routing them off the highway, turning them in a small gravel circle outside the Tranquility gates, then sending them back onto the highway. I should probably head on back to Bienville, but something keeps me in the line, despite fatigue and little chance of seeing anything meaningful.

Thirty years ago, I watched another antebellum mansion burn to the ground in Natchez, and the atmosphere felt more like a Kentucky Derby cocktail party than a tragedy. Spectators gathered at the gate, passing around bottles and flasks to the sound of tinkling ice cubes. While the fire department struggled in vain against the blaze, the crowd swelled, and some older ladies went back to their houses for wine and cheese. Then we all stood out by the road watching the Greek Revival palace burn like some *Gone with the Wind* set piece that ended up on the cutting-room floor.

Has the destruction of Tranquility been the same?

Historic buildings are surprisingly permanent in towns like Natchez. The tear-down-to-build-anew rhythm of cities is foreign to much of the South, and Natchez, missed by the interstate, has aged like a diorama in the back of some off-the-beaten-track museum. Thus, the landmarks of my youth disappeared rarely. Tranquility was among the oldest of the survivors, dating to at least 1815. I still remember sneaking back to the mansion after a Gatsby-like party to meet the daughter of the house, a girl one year my senior. Sophie Dufort was without question the most beautiful girl in our school, as well as the richest. She was also intimidatingly remote, and almost always with older guys. She and her cousins started drinking as children, and experimenting with drugs before anyone else I knew. And yet . . . at times, when I caught sight of her walking alone outside the school, or downtown somewhere, she seemed an incarnation of untouchable purity—a perfect canvas upon which to project the fantasies of a high school boy.

The night of that party, Sophie and I watched a cleanup crew gather empty glasses and bottles as a jazz band packed their cases and equipment into a U-Haul. I can still hear their singer, Cassandra Wilson, who would later become internationally famous, crooning Harold Arlen and Johnny Mercer's "Blues in the Night" among the Chinese lanterns, reeling off an unusual list of Southern towns that included my own humble Natchez, along with Mobile, Memphis, and St. Joe. Never had a moment seemed more pregnant with romantic possibility. I was shivering simply from being alone with Sophie, and my heart nearly seized when she kissed me in those bushes. After the last lights went dark, she led me down to the pool, where we shed our clothes and slipped into the barely cool water. Soon afterward, one of the primary rites of adolescence passed between us—at least for me. For her, I imagine it was just another Saturday night. And tonight the fire department probably used that swimming pool as a last-ditch reservoir for their hose truck.

"Yo, Mayor!" says a voice that sounds familiar from my earlier incarnation in Natchez. "I thought I recognized that Audi!"

A short but powerfully built policeman materializes in my headlight beams and raps on my fender with the flat of his hand, sending my heart into high gear. "*Shit*," I mutter, dreading a Breathalyzer test.

The cop signals that I should roll down my window. In these situations, it's always the luck of the draw. Tonight the lady is on my side. The face that leans down into my window is dominated by bright teeth and coffee-colored skin. A familiar gold crown flashes near his lower left incisor.

"Mayor *Cage*," said Sergeant Gabriel Davis, a veteran cop who guarded me from danger on several occasions when I was threatened while in office. "It's been a minute, ain't it?"

"Hello, Gabriel," I say, directing my breath toward the floor. "I saw the fire from Dr. Ford's helicopter a while ago. Looked like a bad one. Anybody hurt?"

"No, praise Jesus. Caretaker was gone to the hardware store. Ms. Sophie stays in the remodeled slave quarters now and then, but she wasn't here. And the quarters escaped the fire, so far, anyway."

"Any idea how it started?"

Davis shakes his head. "You know how these things go. It can take weeks for the state and the insurance company to finish their investigations."

"Hell, the state crime lab can take a year for homicide evidence, much less arson."

Davis laughs ruefully. "How you been makin' out? I heard your mama's been down. I sure hate that. They prayed for her at my church. Made me miss old Dr. Cage."

I can't quite bring myself to tell him that she's died. "Cancer's a tough road."

"Oh, Lord. It takes somebody from my neighborhood every week. How's that little girl of yours? I heard she took a bullet at Mission Hill."

"She was lucky. And she's grown now, Gabe. Practicing law up in Jackson with Doris Avery. She's liable to sue Buck Tarlton into poverty over that shooting."

"Good! Following in old Quentin's footsteps, huh?"

"Big shoes to fill, but she's trying."

"That's all we can do, ain't it?" He grins, but his eyes linger on mine.

A horn honks impatiently behind me.

Gabriel curses and starts to go back there, but then he stops and says, "We're not supposed to let anybody in, but . . . do you need to get back there?"

"Tense times, brother. Doc Berry's still up in Washington. I'm trying to do what I can to hold the peace."

"If I let you in, can you promise not to start any shit back there? Just take a good look and get out?"

"You have my word."

He gives me a long, appraising look. "Aiight, then. I want to see you back here in twenty minutes."

Smiling thanks, I drive slowly past him, then through the tall wrought-iron gates onto the long asphalt drive that makes me think I've entered a *Downton Abbey* set. By the time I get to a point where I should be able to see Tranquility through its screen of magnolia trees, all I can make out are six scorched columns and a spire of gray smoke rising from the pile of glowing rubble behind them. It looks like the kind of place where you could stumble onto the ghost of Tennessee Williams picking through family secrets before they disintegrate among the soaked ashes.

Two fire engines stand parked in front of the slender Tuscan columns, while a third waits back by the servants' quarters and outdoor kitchen, which seem to have survived the blaze. A line of SUVs stands off from the columns. Most look official, while another half dozen cars dot the great lawn around the house. I slow beside an archipelago of azaleas, trying to decide where to park for a good view.

I've about decided to park where I am and walk when a constellation of portable video lights clicks on, and to my horror I see Shot Barlow and several of his militia crew standing at the painted tailgate of the red dually truck with the rebel flags and chromed scrotum. They're about to be interviewed by a female TV reporter. Barlow leans aggressively forward, his barrel chest puffed out, his thick salt-and-pepper beard giving him the look of a veteran woodsman. The idea that I could be biologically related to this fascist son of a bitch is beyond my comprehension. I'm going to reject the idea until I see proof, and in that case I might just have to skim my mother's research.

Touching the accelerator with my left foot, I roll forward to the edge of the shrubs, then shut off the engine and get out, walking slowly toward the little gathering, trusting the lights to blind the Barlow militia to my presence. The big man is already talking, of course, loud and proud, filled with historical grievance, presenting it as righteous indignation.

"You see what it's come to, don't you?" he demands. "They're literally destroying history here. *History itself.* If they can't twist the past into some woke script the way they want to, then they try to erase it! But here's the thing, hon. You *cain't erase history.* History is history! You hear what I'm sayin'?"

"Damn right," says one of the armed men flanking him.

"History *don't care* what you think about it!" Barlow exults. "See? You go to Russia, they'll tell you a Russian invented the radio, the telegraph, the airplane, and the goddamn moon rocket. A shot of vodka and they'll

claim a Russian invented apple pie. You listen to some of these Black Studies professors, they'll tell you their version of the same shit. Whatever
great thing's been done, some African did it first. Well, I'll give 'em this
much ... they're the first ones since General W. T. Sherman to set fire to a
living monument of the South."

"Are you saying this was arson?" the reporter cuts in. "And that you
know who's responsible?"

Shot Barlow responds with a smug look. "You're damn right I am!"

"And who is that?"

"Well ... I'm not gonna use the word I'd like to, because then you won't
run this on the TV."

"Are you referring to what's called the 'N-word'?"

Again the grin. "Let's use the *M*-word tonight, hon, so we'll be sure not
to offend anybody. Let's say the Martians done this, okay? You hear me?"

The reporter stands shaking her head. "I believe I do."

"Well. Those Martians would do well to remember it was General Sherman who said 'War is hell, and you cannot refine it.' And that's what they
got comin' now, hon. They have sown the wind."

"Amen," says a gaunt young man in the shadows behind Barlow. One
of those I saw earlier in the bed of the dually. The one with the infantry
sniper's eyes. "Now they reap the whirlwind."

My eyes have adjusted enough for me to see that the interviewer is a
pretty white reporter in her late twenties, one I've seen on the Jackson
television station. Her cameraman is Black and looks about twenty-two.

"Why don't you guys just keep your mouths shut?" suggests a voice out
of the darkness to my right.

The video lights whirl, illuminating a man I recognize from the
Natchez branch of Alcorn University, a Mississippi HBCU. Dr. Dave
Egan is a white history professor with a dogged manner and an almost religious reverence for accuracy. I've appeared on more than one panel with
him at the Natchez Literary Festival, and I learned a lot each time. Beside
him stands his wife, looking fearful but also accustomed to this kind of
confrontation.

"All you're doing," Egan goes on, "is confirming people's worst stereo-
types about Mississippi. They'll think we're all like you, and we're not."

"Mind your own business, professor!" calls Barlow. "We *mass-
communicatin'* this evenin'."

Barlow's crew laughs at this quote from *O Brother, Where Art Thou?*

The TV reporter has turned to Professor Egan and his wife. "You have
a different opinion about the fire?"

"About *all* of this," he says, like a man who's been waiting a decade to speak. "About these grand houses in general. They shouldn't be held up like they are, enshrined as icons of some lost golden age. These mansions were built by enslaved human beings, for people who owned their bodies. For people who held the power of life and death over them and their children, like Pharoah in the Bible. These mansions are testament to the fact that beauty can be built on ugliness, that dreams can flourish on the scaffolding of nightmare."

"Would you *listen* to this asshole?" croaks a heavy man wearing a camouflage T-shirt. He looks like a volunteer offensive line coach at a rural Louisiana high school.

"Shut that fool up," Barlow mutters.

Camo Guy crosses Tranquility's drive and stands towering over the wiry academic. "If you don't like the South, man, get the fuck *out*. Move to Oregon or some other lib hellhole. We don't need you. And we don't *want* you."

With that, he pushes one huge hand into the professor's chest, driving him six feet back into the azalea bushes behind him.

The professor's wife screams, and even the reporter jumps back, worried that the violence isn't over. As Egan scrambles out of the bushes, her cameraman steps forward as though to protect him, but Barlow's paramilitary sidekick doesn't hesitate to assault him too, shoving the Black technician into the recovering professor. This tangles their legs, and they fall back among the flowered branches.

While Barlow and his crew guffaw like extras in *Road House*, the reporter shakes her head, probably furious that she didn't get the assault on camera. Taking out her cell phone, she starts to film Barlow and his men with it.

"Put that away, bitch," warns the wiry guy behind Barlow. "If you don't want the same treatment."

"What treatment's that, asshole?" she shoots back.

"You saw," comes an eerily reedy voice.

When the owner of the voice steps out of the crowd, I see that he's wearing a Ted Nugent T-shirt. "On the other hand . . . we might come up with something special for your sassy ass."

"Yeah?" snaps the girl, obviously no rookie with hostile subjects. "You want to poke me with your two-inch dick?"

Ted Nugent blanches.

The young reporter reminds me of my daughter, with her reflexive sense of fight. But she's crossed a line that she shouldn't have—not here. Scanning the grounds in the vain hope of finding a cop, I wonder where her father is. Probably Jackson. Without even wanting to, I find myself walking forward on my throbbing stump, balling my right fist in anticipation of defending her.

Catching sight of my approach, Shot Barlow's eyes take on a sheen of excitement. He'd like nothing more than to draw me into a brawl in which his militia could kick my ass with justification that might keep them out of jail. Before we come together, though, a new vehicle rolls up the driveway with a low, thoroughbred rumble. Turning, I recognize a black-and-silver Rolls-Royce Phantom that can only mean one thing:

Charles Dufort has arrived.

Built in 2003, Dufort's Rolls is one of the finest automobiles ever made. I know because I rode in it once, during a period when I agreed to assist the old man with a legal matter he'd pitched as a minor inconvenience. He also gave me a five-minute lecture on the car. I wasn't a lawyer for hire at the time, but I was seeing his daughter (we were both single parents with kids in the same class), and if I'm honest, being asked by a Harvard Law alum to handle a case for him both flattered and intrigued me.

I should have known better.

Dufort was merely renting my reputation for integrity, and using my recent intimacy with his daughter to do it. By the time I navigated the "small matter" involving a construction company he owned (and which was awarded a job in spite of submitting the *high* bid out of three), I was more than half-certain that Dufort had committed at least one felony. When I confronted him about it over dinner at his palatial Bienville mansion, he lied to my face. Since my work was nearly done, and since some measure of doubt remained, I extricated both of us from the mess and moved on down the road—leaving his daughter behind as well.

But I never got the bad taste out of my mouth. Most disturbing, I think, was the paradoxical *seediness* of the whole thing. Dufort couldn't have earned more than $150,000 by making the illegal move he did—sofa change for a man of his wealth. So *why did he do it*? It's like a man who screws his friend's wife not because he wants her, but simply because he can. It made me think Charles Dufort had gone through life grabbing everything within reach, and that maybe his ancestors had done the same. That's why Annie's revelation about the Charles Dufort who lived during the Civil War not being the man history would have us believe intrigued me. Truly wealthy men generally don't become that way by virtuous methods.

The low-slung Rolls stops fifteen yards from Barlow's red dually pickup.

As the cameraman climbs up out of the bushes and Barlow's thug moves toward him again, Barlow gives a quick whistle, and Camo Guy holds his ground. The Rolls glides forward another five yards, then turns broadside to Barlow and his men. There's too much tint on the windows for me to see inside the vehicle, but moving left a little, I notice the rear passenger window on the driver's side sinking into the heavy door.

A white male hand beckons for Barlow to approach.

The militia leader walks forward. He peers into the Rolls, then puts his hands on his knees and crouches to listen. I hear only a muffled voice, and I can't make out distinct words. It only speaks for about twenty seconds, but its effect is immediate. Shotwell Barlow stands erect, then walks back to his men.

"Pack your shit," he growls. "We're headin' back to Black Oak."

"Who's in that car?" the reporter asks him.

Barlow ignores her.

"If you don't know that," says the guy who shoved the cameraman, "you don't know shit from shoe polish."

"Charles F. Dufort," Professor Egan tells her. "A modern-day Natchez nabob. Heir to one of the originals. He owns this estate."

Signaling her camera operator to follow, the reporter makes her way to the Rolls. As she does, the driver's door opens, and Dufort's chauffeur, a blue-black man named Amadu, gets out and blocks her way. As he stands silent and immovable, Sophie Dufort climbs out of the backseat wearing a white linen dress with a royal-blue wrap against the chance of further rain. Though she's thirty years older than the TV reporter—who was obviously chosen for her looks as well as her skill—Sophie moves with regal grace, and she looks like the daughter of an emperor passing a shopgirl as she walks to the edge of the drive and stares at the glowing ruin of her family's ancestral home in the falling dark.

One of the puzzles of my recent life has been figuring out why a woman this wealthy decided to get herself elected to Bienville's board of aldermen. Despite her father's politics, Sophie has always been a committed liberal— with a few Libertarian tendencies—but I'd never have believed she had the patience to deal with local politics and the people who get involved in them. Thankfully, she has proved me wrong.

Sophie turns away from the columns, but instead of going back to the car, she crosses the drive and steps onto the wet grass, making her way over to me. She must have spied me through the tinted windows. Her hair still looks rich and dark, and hangs loose below her shoulders, fram-ing the flawless bone structure that has made her one of the area's most noted beauties for decades. "Just like her mother," matrons have always said, knowing that a whispered echo always follows: *But you know what happened to her.*

I stand as straight as I can on my prosthetic, then hold out my hand. Sophie gives a light squeeze, perfectly judging the etiquette for two people who once shared a bed for a few months.

"How's your mother doing?" she asks with genuine concern. "No more strokes, I hope?"

"Actually . . . she just died, Soph. About an hour ago. Annie and I were with her."

Sophie blinks in astonishment. "Oh, my God. I so hate to hear that. Peggy was such a lady. Always so kind."

"I appreciate that, Soph. Really."

We stand in the awkward but increasingly familiar silence of shared grief. These days, more and more people in our peer group have succumbed to various illnesses, and parents of those we attended school with die almost weekly.

"I hate to see this fire," I tell her. "Another piece of the old town gone. A big piece. I can't believe it, really."

"I still remember the night of the jazz party," she says. "The night Cassandra sang."

My face colors. "Me, too, as I drove up. God, that was a long time ago. You don't look much different than you did then."

She cuts her eyes at me. "You're a damn liar. But I'll take the compliment." Her smile is like a lamp coming on in the dark.

"Any idea how the fire started?" I ask.

"Well, I was going to ask you. I just got a text from a friend saying Bobby White just went on Shepard Smith's show saying this fire was arson, and it's been claimed by a group called the Bastard Sons of the Confederacy."

"I know about that."

"So it's true?"

"It's true that someone called Marshall McEwan and claimed that. Now, whether it was really arson is another thing altogether. Have y'all had any physical plant issues out here? Electrical? Gas? I know nobody's lived here regularly for years."

"That's true, but we've kept it on tour for Pilgrimage, and that means keeping it up to the mark. Also, I stay out here now and then, painting in the old quarters."

Five years ago, she would have said "slave quarters," but time has changed even the most entitled families.

"We have a great security and fire system, too. So this is more than a bit of a mystery."

"One I don't like."

"What does our esteemed mayor say about all this?"

"I haven't spoken to Doc yet. He's still up in D.C. Won't be back until tomorrow night, at the earliest."

"That's not good."

"I warned him not to go."

"The House Select Committee on Police Misconduct," Sophie says with precise diction. "Sounds so important, doesn't it?"

"You know they're not going to do anything in time to help us."

"Nobody can help those Mission Hill kids. Except surgeons. What was that asshat Barlow saying to the reporter as we drove up?"

"The usual white supremacist bullshit. History is history. Blood and soil."

"Jesus, spare us."

"I tell you . . . if a significant part of the white community decides to see this the way the whack jobs spin it—or even if they simply believe the claim by the 'Bastard Sons'—then God only knows what could happen next. You ought to hire at least one guard to patrol out here tonight. To keep looters from picking over the ruins."

"I think Amadu's going to stay out in the quarters."

Hearing the name of Charles Dufort's spooky driver spoken aloud gives me a chill. "That ought to keep even the most brazen looters away."

As we watch the last embers fade behind the columns, I feel her take my hand and squeeze again, this time harder. "I'm really sorry about your mom," she murmurs. "It's been years since I lost mine, but I remember the pain like it happened yesterday."

Sophie's mother died when she was a freshman at Tulane. Drowned in her own bathtub. In that era, the story was short on details, and it stayed that way. But everyone knew Lily Dufort had had a serious drinking problem for decades, and that she'd made at least two suicidal gestures in the past. Recalling this, I'm reminded of Sophie's half brother, Charles—Charlot to those who know him well—the child of her father's second wife. After making a good start as a lawyer in Bienville, he reportedly slipped into a downward spiral of drug and alcohol dependence that's cost him his marriage and most of his real property.

"Can I ask you something personal?" I say quietly. "How's Charlot doing?"

She sighs with a sound of exhaustion and disgust. "Between you and me? Worse than ever. Why do you ask?"

"Well . . . I heard he lost his house."

"Not quite yet. The bank repossesses tomorrow, I think."

"Shit. I'm sorry. I also heard he might be disbarred. Even prosecuted. Some kind of escrow irregularities? Embezzlement?"

"All true, I'm afraid. Between you and me, Charlot's got a terrible gambling problem. Also substance abuse. It's a bad situation." Sophie leans far enough left to bump me with her muscular shoulder. "I know you, Penn. What are you thinking?"

"I'm just wondering whether Charlot has a key to this place. Or if he might be desperate enough to break in here for shelter. A guy in his state of mind might easily start a fire by accident. Especially if he was trying to cook. And forgive me . . . but that scenario beats the hell out of the 'Bastard Sons' angle."

"Charlot knows not to come out here. Daddy's made sure he knows he's not welcome." Sophie drops my hand and looks into my eyes. "Do you think this really could be retaliation for Mission Hill?"

I shrug. "Dwight Ford doesn't think the idea is crazy."

She considers the premise for nearly half a minute, then nods slowly. "I can see it, I guess. But I've never heard of anything like that happening before. Angry Black people usually burn their own neighborhoods."

"Not really. Not residences. They burn businesses in their neighborhoods. But after the death toll at Mission Hill, you couldn't blame them for lashing out in anger . . ."

"I know. I can't imagine doing anything else."

Looking back at the Rolls, I see Ruby Brooks, the Duforts' longtime housekeeper, a slender woman with intelligent eyes, standing beside the car in her maid's uniform. She's watching the smoldering ruin with an expression I can't interpret. "Ruby is still with y'all, huh?"

"Are you kidding? Daddy couldn't make it through a day without her. Ruby's *mother* is still alive, if you can believe it. She's ninety-five, and still gets around well."

This, I believe. "Do you mind if I have a brief word with your father?"

A shadow of suspicion crosses Sophie's face. "If it's about Charlot, I'd rather you didn't. Daddy gets pretty upset on that subject. And his blood pressure's a real problem."

"It's not about Charlot. It's business."

Her suspicion doesn't diminish. "I didn't know you two had any business in common."

"Old business."

She hesitates, looking stiff.

"Sophie, I'm going to have to speak to him."

I feel her focusing her irritation to push back, but then her gaze floats off to my left, and her eyes betray sudden disinterest in me.

"Do whatever you want. I want to walk over and see if anything of my old room survived."

I give her a half wave of farewell, but she's already picking her way back toward the smoking ruins.

I turn toward the Rolls, smile at Ruby Brooks (whom I know on a first-name basis), and prepare to interrogate the richest man in the state.

CHAPTER 16

RUBY NODS KINDLY as I come within earshot. "Evenin', Mayor."

"Evening, Ruby. You keeping Charles on the straight and narrow?"

"Ha. A bulldozer couldn't do that. Thankfully, he's a little slower than he used to be."

"I'm glad, for your sake."

She glances over toward the ruins. "This is sure a sight to see, ain't it?"

"Two hundred years, then gone with the wind."

"More like the whirlwind," she corrects me.

Her eyes seem freighted with more emotion than her words, but I know it would be pointless to question her further. Here, anyway. "I'm going to have a word with Charles in the Rolls. I won't be a minute."

"Take all the time you want. He needs a burr under his saddle now and then, and you're one of the few around here with the nerve to be one."

I can't help but smile again.

Making my way to the far side of the vehicle, I tap on the passenger-side window, then get into the back seat without waiting to be invited. The silver-haired billionaire gives me a put-upon look as I collapse on the butter-soft seat. "You lost more than a step when you lost your leg, didn't you?" he observes.

The cabin smells of damp but fine leather. Thankfully, a large console separates our bodies.

"To what do I owe the pleasure?" Charles asks with open sarcasm.

Our honeymoon is long over. I called this man a liar under his own roof, and I was sleeping with his daughter at the time. That doesn't foster comity. Had I not been involved with Sophie, I would have reported him to the sheriff. The coldness in his blue-gray eyes tonight tells me he's known this since our quiet confrontation.

"I've only got two questions," I tell him. "You won't like them, but I have to ask. I'm worried about this fire."

"Barlow thinks the colored started it. And Bobby White says he has a source who knows a Black terrorist group already claimed they started this fire."

"I'd sooner believe Barlow started it himself, to stir up anger at the Blacks."

Dufort chuckles dryly. "False-flag operation? That's probably worth exploring. But do you seriously not believe Black radicals have come to the point where they might do something like this? After the past two or three years of marches and media frenzy? Mission Hill got them stirred up like a hive of hornets."

"If Blacks were going to hit an antebellum home, it wouldn't be yours. Would it? Thanks to Sophie in this generation, and your Unionist ancestors, you've got a reputation in these parts as a friend to the Black man."

The haughty head pulls back slightly, and he makes a sound of derision. "I'm not sure the national fringe groups are up on local history. What's your question?"

"Simple. You're a businessman. And I, for one, happen to know you don't always play the game according to Hoyle. Given that, I'm wondering whether this fire might be some sort of retaliation by somebody who feels like you screwed them on something totally unrelated."

Genuine humor lights his face. "You think this is *The Godfather*, Cage? Horse heads in the bed?"

"For all I know, you got the horse head last week. Maybe this week they burn your house. I really don't give a shit, but the civil peace could be at stake."

"Let's not get the vapors over one little fire. Places like this have been burning in our area since the late 1700s. One burned to the ground right across the river just four years ago. Frogmore Plantation. And then there was Hope Farm in March of this year."

He's right. I'd already forgotten about Frogmore.

"I read that piece in the paper about the bear sightings," he says, his eyes avid with interest. "It said you were the first to see it. Or one of the first. You came the closest to him, anyway."

"I did see a bear. I don't think it's the one they printed a picture of."

"Why's that?"

"The bear I saw wasn't a juvenile searching for new territory. He weighed a good six hundred pounds, and he had multiple scars. One on the snout, and a bullet track on the abdomen that was clear as day."

Dufort leans slightly forward, and his eyes glint. "What color was his snout?"

"Yellow."

Now the old man looks really interested. "Some experts claim there *is* no distinct Louisiana black. *Ursus americanus luteolus*. I'd love to get a shot at him, prove those schoolboy sons of bitches wrong once and for all."

"They're protected, aren't they?"

Dufort looks back at me like some kid who thinks you're a coward because you won't shoplift something with him, or jump a speeding freight train.

"What is it with guys like you?" I ask. "You gotta kill something to feel like you really saw it?"

Dufort shrugs. "That depends."

"On what?"

"The animal. Shit, Cage, you sound like my younger son. Let me ask *you* something. Do you feel like you really know a woman if you've never fucked her?"

After a few silent seconds, I realize I'm actually trying to answer his question. "Of course."

"Well, stop kidding yourself. And that bear's the same. They're mostly shy and secretive, but if a male gets a chance to eat you for dinner, he won't hesitate. He'd like a chubby toddler better, of course. So if I get a chance to draw a bead on him, I'll blow out his brains, skin him for a rug, and eat him for dinner."

"Just like you'll nail whatever woman is willing to give it to you."

Dufort purses his lips, considering. "In my prime, that was my rule. Hell, don't try to kid me. You weren't playing tiddlywinks with my daughter the year you were with her."

"No. Touché."

He turns up his hands as though he just won our argument.

Our earlier conversation comes back to me. "Have you got your insurance all paid up on this place, Charles?"

His eyes narrow in suspicion. "Do you really think I'd leave an asset this expensive uninsured?"

"Full replacement cost? That's got to be millions. Good source of quick cash, if you needed some."

The rugged old man snorts with contempt. "Cage, I could rebuild this place with the crumbs from one of my grandkids' trust funds. I'd never even feel it."

This must be true. *And yet . . .* "Says the man who falsified a construction bid to make an extra hundred thousand on a county project."

Dufort's cheeks go red. "Get the hell out of my car."

I lay my fingers on the handle, look back at the affronted face. "Charles—"

"If you ever get it in your mind to talk about that case in public," he warns, "you'll find it sticking to you as stubbornly and unflatteringly as to me."

This threat doesn't sound empty coming from his mouth. Shaking my head, I pull the handle, but to my surprise, he touches my shoulder in a surprisingly paternal way.

"I hope your mother's doing all right," he says.

For a moment I think he already knows she's dead, and is really trying to goad me. But then I sense I'm wrong. "Don't go there, Charles."

"Why not? Peggy's a real lady, even if you and I don't exactly jibe like Amos 'n' Andy."

Jesus, this guy. "If you want to know . . . Mom died an hour ago."

A shadow like physical pain darkens the old man's face. "Christ, I hate to hear that. I mean it. All the good ones . . . going so fast."

"Too fast."

"And your little girl? She took a bullet at that jungle festival, I heard. She healing up all right?"

"She'll be okay after a couple of surgeries."

Dufort gives me a helpless look, as though wishing he could somehow make me see the world as he does. "Don't take this the wrong way, son. But I don't know what you're thinking sometimes. All the time you spend helping these Blacks try to run things their way around here? Then you let your little girl go out to a zoo like that. Sooner or later something bad's *bound* to happen. Life just doesn't mean to them what it does to us."

"Charles—"

"That's how your daddy got himself in trouble! Remember? He was a damn fine doctor. Spent his whole career treating half his patients for free . . . then he got tangled up with that colored nurse and her radical brother."

I start to argue, but it's pointless. "And what's your parental advice, Charles? I hear Charlot's about one step from prison, or the hospital."

At the mention of his younger son—the forty-two-year-old offspring of his second wife, and not Philippe, the Dufort scion I attended school with—the old man closes his eyes and waves me out. I feel small for hitting him back like that, but he should have left my family out of it.

"Do you remember Philippe?" asks the old man.

"Sure," I admit, but I offer nothing further, knowing my memory will not give the old man the comfort he craves. Philippe and I were in the same class all the way through school, and there were a couple of periods where we spent a lot of time together. (Neither of us played basketball, so we rode to the out-of-town games together.) But I never really let myself get close to him. He was the personification of white privilege, and during his second year of college, he hit a pedestrian (a Hispanic housekeeper) while blind drunk in his car and crippled her for life. Anyone else would have gone to jail, but after Charles Dufort's attorney got through spreading cash and threats around, Philippe walked free with only a misdemeanor conviction. When he died in the aviation accident a decade later, I felt only a mild sense of regret, no true sense of loss.

"What about Charlot?" I ask. "Could he have started this fire? By accident?"

"To tell you the truth, that was my first thought. If Bobby White hadn't broken that Bastard Sons story, I might still be leaning toward Charlot. But I don't think he's even in town anymore. He's got the casino collectors after him."

"Jesus, Charles. They could kill him, if the debt is high enough. How much does he owe?"

The old man sighs. "More than you'd believe."

"Try me."

"Seven figures."

"*Jesus.*"

Dufort nods. "He also does that sports betting from his phone, no limit. You can get in trouble in a hurry that way. Then he did some goddamn day-trading with the money he embezzled from his clients, trying to get himself out of the hole. Buying on the margin, the damn fool. Penn, he could owe as much as three million, all told. And he hasn't got a thousand dollars to his name."

"Charles . . . you can't leave him hanging."

"The hell I can't! I've given that boy enough money to start five companies over the years. He's a bottomless hole. A hopeless case. He *never* learns."

Charlot is twenty years my junior, but I remember him as a star student who frequently made the newspapers for acing national tests and winning national science fair competitions. He even began his legal career with some big victories in notable cases. I've never understood what started his downward spiral, but my best guess is that it had something to do with being the son of one of the biggest sons of bitches in the state.

"How will you feel if he turns up dead? Or paralyzed?"

With a shake of his head, Dufort waves me out of the Rolls.

Pushing open the heavy door, I climb out into the smoky air and find the grounds mostly deserted but for a few firemen still working in the distance. I see no sign of Sophie, or Ruby Brooks, but after scanning the dark lawn, I spy the housekeeper sitting cross-legged on a stump about sixty yards from the scorched columns still sending up smoke and sparks into the night. I wave farewell to Ruby, but I'm not going to wait around to say good night to Sophie. As she predicted, I'll likely see her soon at an emergency meeting of the city board.

Climbing into my Audi, I carefully execute a three-point turn, but as I brake and shift into drive, sudden movement to my left draws my attention. Near the old slave quarters, two figures stand facing each other, gesticulating with violent emotion. One is several inches taller than the other. Squinting into the dark, I realize one figure is Sophie. The other I can't make out, but he appears to be male. As I stare, two powerful headlight beams switch on and sweep across the yard. They belong to the fire truck parked behind the ruins of the mansion. When the headlights rake over the two silhouettes, then return, I recognize Charlot Dufort, Sophie's half brother. Handsome as any male model, he's dressed in khakis and a white shirt, and one sleeve appears to be soaked in blood. When the light fixes him like an insect against a black board, Charlot throws up his other arm to shield his face. Whoever's driving the fire truck leaves the beams on the pair until Charlot flings his arm out in obvious fury, ordering them to get the lights off him.

I don't know what the hell the half siblings are arguing about, but I do know two things: one, Charles Dufort has no idea that his son is here; and two, Sophie may have known Charlot was within shouting distance when we were talking earlier, and lied to me about it. *Why would she do that?* Whatever the reason, Charlot's mere presence makes him a suspect in this arson. Any man as desperate as he is (and with his history of substance abuse) could accidentally start a fire. And a "child" with the kind of history Charlot has with his abusive father might well burn the place simply out of hatred. Sophie surely understands that. Could she know that her brother is guilty, but mean to protect him from any legal consequence?

I never had any intention of acting as a detective on this case, but who else has the requisite knowledge to place these developments in the appropriate context and unravel the underlying truth? Were this merely an expensive working out of the Dufort family's dysfunctional secrets, I wouldn't waste five minutes on it. But the local funeral homes are filled with bodies tonight; the hospitals bulge with wounded. And this arson, I sense, is somehow tied to those casualties. Before pulling back onto the highway, I arrange for Officer Gabriel Davis, who's going off the clock in half an hour, to stand watch over Edelweiss until dawn.

CHAPTER 17

Teterboro Airport, New Jersey

BOBBY WHITE AND Corey Evers were sipping drinks in the Meridian private aviation terminal when the Donnelly Oil Citation touched down at Teterboro, just eight miles from the CBAC studios. They slipped on windbreakers and walked outside as the sleek jet taxied over to the boarding area.

"'Bastard Sons of the Confederacy' is now trending on Twitter," Corey said, peering at his cell phone screen as he walked toward the approaching plane. "All thanks to you."

"That's a good thing," Bobby said. "Puts me at the center of the story."

"I'm not sure that's where you want to be. Not this week."

"It's exactly where I want to be." Bobby stopped and bent his head against the sprinkling rain as the Citation slowed and turned toward them.

"Whoa," Corey said, his tone surprised as he scrolled his phone. "Here's a story about Paul Beckley. Remember him? He apparently died of a heart attack while running in a D.C. cemetery yesterday. Mount Olivet. The FBI suspects Russian involvement. The FSB."

"Paul Beckley from intel in Afghanistan?"

"That's the one. He was killed with some exotic poison, delivered by a contact needle. Classic FSB tactics."

"Why the hell would Putin want Beckley dead?"

"He'd apparently been doing some consulting with the Ukrainian army."

"Still. That's weird."

The Citation slowed its taxi, but the noise of its engines increased with proximity.

"I can't believe they're making us double up with Birdie Blake!" Corey complained.

Robin "Birdie" Blake was a Mississippi-born actress who, after ten years of playing background roles in Hollywood, had broken out playing a Nashville funeral home makeup artist in a streaming comedy on Netflix.

Bobby knew her from charity events in both Mississippi and New Orleans, and he'd enjoyed her irreverent sense of humor both times.

"If I were paying the fuel and pilot costs for this ride," Bobby said, "I'd make people double up, too. Anyway, Birdie's probably saying the same thing about us. She was on Fallon last night, for God's sake. Where were we? But this jet seats nine, so there's room to spread out, if you want to be antisocial."

Corey grunted with displeasure.

"You really don't like Birdie?" Bobby asked. "I think she's a riot."

His assistant made a sour face. "I only know her from her TV show. Her laugh annoys me."

Bobby shook his head in amazement. "Well . . . I'm sure you can handle it for"—he glanced at his watch—"the two hours and twenty minutes it'll take us to get to Bienville. Or would you rather fly multiple commercial legs through Atlanta on rattletrap 727s?"

Corey held his silence. Flying commercial hadn't even been an option. Bobby appearing at the pre-tournament donor party wouldn't have been possible without a private jet to get them there. Not doing Shepard Smith's show beforehand. Even with the jet, Bobby would almost surely miss the dinner that would open the VIP party.

The Citation stopped when its forward door came even with them. Bobby glanced appreciatively at the big blue DO legend on the tail, with its oil derrick separating the bold letters. He'd ridden a few private jets in his day, but he still considered them a luxury, and he knew that Blake Donnelly's wife, Dixie—who was thirty years younger than her oil magnate husband—would have the interior of this aircraft in top shape.

The door opened with a hiss, then descended with a hydraulic hum, so that the staircase lining its interior face inverted, then stopped a few inches off the concrete. Bobby was mounting the bottom tread when a shapely young woman in a tight-fitting blue skirt uniform slid dramatically into the open doorway like a Broadway dancer.

"Good evening, gentlemen! Are you ready to fly the *really* friendly skies? Coffee, tea, or Purple Kush?"

Birdie Blake had a gamine face, bright eyes, and just enough curves to fill out the old-school stew's fitted skirt and jacket she was wearing. She'd done her best to hide her trademark red hair under the tilted cap, but that had proved impossible.

"I figure an Afghanistan vet knows his weed," she added in a stage whisper.

"Where the hell did you find that outfit?" Bobby asked with a grin.

"You look like you stepped out of a snapshot from the glory days of my dad's baseball career."

"Stowed in a closet of this flying time capsule! I couldn't resist. My great-aunt was a stew for Southern Airways. This is what the Donnelly Oil FAs actually *wear*. It's still the *awl* business, Bobby boy."

Bobby turned to Corey, daring him to pretend he wasn't enjoying this. Corey gave the actress a smile, but he couldn't hide the tightness in it. That triggered real irritation in Bobby, and then he felt time slip, and he was riding in back of the mildewed old Caprice Classic wagon while his grandfather rambled on about a crazy army buddy who'd ended up flying for Southern Airways when they were starting up in what he called the barnstorming days. Shaking off the memory, Bobby turned back to Birdie and held up his hands in supplication. "May we come in out of the rain, ma'am?"

"But of course! *Bienvenue! Wilkommen! Cead mile failte!*"

"What the hell was that last one?"

"Irish for 'A hundred thousand welcomes!'" Birdie lowered her voice. "And I'm serious about the weed. It's been a shit day. Do you think the pilots will care?"

"Maybe you ought to text Dixie Donnelly and ask."

"What do you have?" Corey asked. "Flower, drops, or gummies?"

Birdie looked at him as though deep in thought. Then her eyes widened, and she snapped her fingers. "I have a few gummies in the bottom of my jewelry bag! Emergency rations. Thanks, ah . . . ?"

"Corey."

"Right. Dixie told me. Well, let's get this crate back in the air. The PGA VIP party starts in ninety minutes in Mississippi, and that's enough initials to make me curious. I heard Faith Hill and Tim McGraw might bring some of the cast from *Yellowstone*. We're gonna be late as it is. Gentlemen?"

She slid out of the doorway and motioned them forward. Bobby elbowed Corey in the ribs and laughed as he boarded.

CHAPTER 18

CHARLOT DUFORT NEEDED money, and not the kind most people in Bienville, Mississippi, had. He knew only two people in the world who might be able to pay off his debts—and by so doing save his life—and one had long ago disowned him. The other was his childhood friend Bobby White. Charlot had known Bobby since they were four years old, and they hadn't just been close. They'd been tight enough that when Bobby's nerdy first cousin Martyn was nineteen, and came up with a plan to approach record companies with a way to combat Napster, which for two years had been destroying their profits, Charlot had invested the whole hundred-thousand-dollar "nest egg" his father had given him in the tenth grade. Martyn and Bobby had had no money to contribute, of course. They'd invested only "sweat equity" in the company Charlot named "Three Amigos Music." Martyn's combination MP3 player and royalty distribution software was good enough that it attracted the notice (and investment) of a successful venture capitalist in Silicon Valley, and as juniors in high school, Charlot and Bobby had never known such excitement. It lasted all of five months—until the record companies proved unwilling to compromise with each other to battle their common enemy. Three Amigos immediately went broke.

That was the last money Charlot's father gave him outright before the age of thirty-seven, outside of tuition and room and board for college and law school. And Charles Sr. never ceased reminding Charlot that Philippe, the son of his first marriage, had parlayed his hundred grand into a million dollars in three years, by sagacious investment in the stock market. Philippe was long dead now, of course. If he weren't, Charlot might have been pulling up to his house in a "borrowed" car to ask for money. As it was, he was left with a poor substitute: he was visiting Martyn Black, Bobby's cousin, in the hope of discovering whether Bobby could afford to pay off the debts that hung over him like a sword of Damocles. Because he was going to have to ask Bobby for the money.

Charlot eased the blue Prius forward, under a great weeping willow that hung over the driveway of the bungalow that Martyn rented for the Chinese girl he helped to live illegally in Mississippi. Charlot hadn't warned Martyn to expect him. With casino thugs hunting him, he was terrified of making calls, even on his burner phone. His right shirt sleeve was stained with sticky blood, from a slash wound they'd given him around noon in his own driveway. But their pursuit wasn't the only reason he'd arrived without warning. Long before he'd become human prey, Charlot had joined that class of friend that no one wanted to find on his doorstep.

Yesterday he'd borrowed the Prius from his niece, for example, after forgetting to ask her permission. (He'd also found five Adderall tabs in her glove box, which had put him in an unexpectedly optimistic mood.) Charlot didn't feel bad putting Martyn on the spot, though. It was Martyn's brainstorm that had wasted every dollar of his trust account before he'd gotten old enough to know its value. (Never mind that Steve Jobs would change the world with the same idea three years later, and that Martyn had simply been ahead of his time.) Charlot was now penniless, and Martyn worked for the city of Bienville, doing its IT work for a pittance, and only made his monthly nut by playing competitive video games professionally on the side.

Charlot sniffed his left armpit as the tiny car rolled up to the house, and a sour reek bit his nostrils. He wondered whether Martyn might lend him his shower, or even a clean shirt. He probably would, if the damned Chinese girl wasn't here. But what were the chances of that? She hardly ever went out. Martyn had chosen this neighborhood because it was cheap, and the residents sketchy enough that they asked no questions of anyone.

He parked the Prius alongside Martyn's Accord, shut off the engine, then got out and edged up to the side door. A doorbell camera covered the front door, which was what had sent him this way. But now he saw a second camera mounted beside this door as well. (Probably to warn of the arrival of people like him.)

Exhausted, and weakened by pain, Charlot walked into full view of the camera and depressed the bell on the wall. There was no immediate response, but he sensed the occupants looking at him. The girl (Lanying was her name) would be dreading whatever complication Charlot had brought to her house. Wishing her boyfriend had the guts to deny him entry. But Martyn wouldn't do that. They not only shared the Three Amigos disaster, but they had been through AA together—for a while, anyway. More than that, though, they had shared secrets.

"What are you doing here, Charles?" Martyn asked through the tinny speaker in the digital bell.

"I need to ask you something. Won't take any time."

"Ask me."

"Face-to-face. Come on."

Silence. "I can see you fine from where I am. You look terrible."

Charlot felt like kicking the door open, but that wasn't his style.

"Martyn . . . you know these doorbells are made by Amazon, right? I don't want Alexa recording this shit, and you don't, either."

"Then don't say 'Alexa,' man."

A female voice released a rush of angry Mandarin behind the door, which Charlot couldn't begin to follow. He wondered if Martyn had picked up enough to be able to understand her.

"Charles," Martyn said with obvious discomfort. "You look like you're bleeding. What the hell is going on?"

Charlot's dry mouth worked nervously around his teeth. "I'm in a tight spot, bro. Some guys are looking for me. Hunting me, actually."

"What guys? Cops?"

"No. These are money guys. *Collection* guys. From the casino."

"Tommy Russo's guys? Jesus, I don't have any money to give you. You know that."

"I don't want money. Not from you. I need information. Please, can't we get away from this damn door? Just give me two minutes. Tell Lanying to go watch *Real Housewives* or something."

Another furious blast of Mandarin rattled the speaker. Charlot regretted his choice of TV shows. Lanying was more likely to watch reruns of *Cosmos* than a reality show.

"I'm coming out," Martyn said reluctantly. "Back away from the door. I can give you two minutes. After that . . . I can't be responsible for what happens."

This was a veiled threat to call the police, but it had no teeth. Neither Martyn nor Lanying could risk contacting the authorities, because she had no green card. "Jesus, Martyn, why you gonna be that way?"

The muffled Mandarin harping was becoming almost comical.

"It's that or nothing, Charles."

Charlot sighed, then backed away from the door.

Thirty seconds later, Martyn cracked the door and slid through wearing jeans and an R.E.M. T-shirt from the Reconstruction III tour. His hair was uncombed and hung to his shoulders, his skin as pale and blotchy as it had been in junior high. They stood together under the willow, not far from the door. Martyn had a funny smell about him, but Charlot couldn't place it, and he was lucky to smell anything, his BO was so bad.

"What do you need?" Martyn asked.

"Why the rush, man? Has somebody been here looking for me?"

"Who would even know that you know me?"

Charlot shrugged. "Shit. People we went to school with? Anybody in the AA group?"

"School was twenty years ago! Look, I'm sorry . . . but this is like the worst day you could have picked to come here."

"Why?"

Martyn shook his head. "Lanying, man. She'll be fine for a while, but then she freaks out, like out of nowhere."

"About what?"

"The citizenship thing. What else?"

"You haven't got her papers yet?"

"Jesus, you think it's easy?"

Charlot looked at Martyn with growing clarity. "It's not *that* hard. Not given what I know about her situation."

Martyn's head snapped up. "What do you know about immigration?"

"A lot, nimrod. I'm a lawyer, remember?"

Martyn cursed and looked cowed. "I know, you're right. You know the deal, man. She and I just have this weird codependency thing."

Charlot hadn't spent much time around Lanying, but he was pretty sure he understood the nature of their relationship. The girl was five feet nothing and beautiful enough that, when people saw her with Martyn, they immediately wondered whether he'd bought her from some skeezy broker in Thailand or Russia. It wasn't that Martyn was ugly, exactly, but he wasn't in Lanying's class. She tipped about an eight on the local scale, whereas Martyn was a four, at best. The differential was enough that Charlot had often wondered what kept her with him. Now he sensed he knew: Martyn had been gaslighting her about the difficulty of getting asylum status in the U.S. This was surprising, since the girl was supposedly a whiz with computers. But Martyn was no dummy. He'd probably invented some credible lie that had kept her in his thrall, at least up to this point.

"Okay, listen," Charlot said, trying to focus. "There's a PGA tournament starting at Belle Rose tomorrow. Bobby's supposedly coming to town to play in the pro-am event."

Martyn blinked at him, then shrugged. "I heard about that. But I didn't know Bobby was playing."

"You're his cousin, for God's sake!"

"So? I haven't talked to him since his dad's heart attack last week. If he's in town, and you need to see him, drive out to Canaan and press the button on his gate."

Canaan was the plantation Bobby's father had bought in the 1980s, and which now served as a hunting camp and retreat.

"Better yet," Martyn said, "go out to Belle Rose and find him. Didn't you used to be on the board out there?"

"In another life," Charlot said softly.

"Well, they're having a VIP party out there tonight, for the celebrity players. I think the Mannings were scheduled to come, until Tranquility burned and those Bastard Sons claimed to have done it." Martyn snapped his fingers. "Shit. I forgot. Your family's Natchez mansion burned down tonight! What the hell happened?"

"I've got no idea. But the house is gone. Nothing left but the slave quarters and kitchen."

"That's crazy, dude."

Charlot clenched his pounding temples between the thumb and fingers of his left hand. "You don't understand, Martyn. Tommy Russo belongs to Belle Rose. For a VIP event, he'll be out there for sure. And if Tommy sees me, he'll sic his gorillas on me in about two seconds."

"Christ, Charlot . . . I can't believe you've done this to yourself." The gamer made a sound like a marathon runner giving up and leaving a course. "I want you to listen to me for once. You and I are different, you understand? You're like, one of the beautiful people. Blessed."

Charlot gaped at his friend. "You're kidding, right?"

"No! Your father is probably the richest man in this state. He may be an asshole, but a lot of sons have that problem. You're the handsomest guy I've ever met. My girlfriend despises you, but she'd still probably do you if she was drunk. You get breaks a guy like me could never even hope for! You're like a goddamn cat with nineteen lives."

"Martyn—"

"Listen! What I'm saying is, you've pushed your luck to the point that you've used up your eighteenth life." Martyn stepped closer and looked hard into Charlot's eyes. "If Tommy Russo means to kill you, then *get out of town*."

The urgency in his voice rattled Charlot, magnifying his fear. "You can't run from these people. They never stop looking."

"Well, what is it you want here?" Martyn demanded. "You think *I* can help? Come on, your time's up already."

Charlot forced himself to focus. "Two weeks ago, Bobby renegotiated his deal with his radio satellite company. Did you know that?"

"His mother said something about it at the hospital."

Charlot felt a ray of hope. "Did she say how much the new deal was for? I can't find out how much he got."

Martyn stared back in disbelief. "Are you kidding? *That's* what you came here to ask?"

"I've tried every other way I know to find out. Nobody knows the number."

"Well, it was a shitload, bank on that. Doing a deal in the middle of all this TikTok frenzy? This talk about him running for president? Talk about smart, or lucky on timing. I guarantee you, he bent them over a barrel. But I have no idea how much he got paid."

"Can you find out?"

Martyn shook his head helplessly. "Not tonight. I mean . . . under certain circumstances Bobby might tell me. But not if I went to him specifically for that. I'd have to ask him in the course of some normal interaction. And I almost never see him. Lanying might be able to hack into his agent's computer or something. There'd likely be email negotiations. But she's not about to do that to help you."

"What has she got against me, man?"

Martyn rolled his eyes. "Oh, let me think . . . Are you serious? Trouble follows you like a toxic shadow. Lanying doesn't want you anywhere around us."

"I need to know that number, Martyn. Tonight. I'm deep in debt, man. Deep enough that they'll kill me over it. They almost got me today."

Martyn's Adam's apple bobbed. "I'm sorry, but . . . I can't help you. I wish I could."

"Just get me a ballpark figure! Did he *double* his last contract? Triple it?"

"Charles . . . how much do you owe, man? A hundred grand? More?"

Charlot shook his head with an almost frantic motion. "It's real money, Martyn. Not pocket change. Seven figures, man."

The gamer blanched. "Jesus. You gotta get out of town. Out of the state. People *will* kill you over that kind of money."

"I know that! That's why I'm trying to figure out whether Bobby can really help me or not. Can he afford to save my life, even if he wants to?"

Martyn looked back at his door. "You're scaring me, dude."

Charlot laid a hand on the gamer's arm. "There's no danger for you or Lanying. I promise."

Martyn initially recoiled at the touch, but in the end he kept his arm in place. "Charles . . . you've made promises before. Remember? Even if Bobby has three times the money you thought he did, you think he'd give it to you?"

"You don't understand. He's already been helping me. For most of a year now."

Martyn froze. "What? I can't believe that."

"He cares about me, man. He's like the last person who does. Even my sister has cut me off."

Martyn stared back, gauging his truthfulness. "If Bobby's been helping you, why haven't you used the money to pay off your debts?"

"The money he's been giving me wouldn't begin to do that. He's just keeping me from starving or having my house repossessed." Charlot looked angrily away. "Besides . . . in the end I always go back to the tables. To try to get caught up. I nearly did once, with sports betting. But in the end, fate hammered my ass again."

"Why did Russo let you get so far underwater? Because of who your father is, I suppose?"

Charlot nodded. "Why else?"

"And the old man has cut you off for real? Jesus, Charlot, why don't you reconcile with him? Do whatever he asks you to. Be whatever he wants you to be! Your dad could buy that damned casino ten times over."

Corrosive acid rose into Charlot's throat. "But he *won't*. Reconciling isn't an option. He's written me off for good."

"I see. Tough love, finally?"

"Bullshit. There's no love in that man. Except for himself."

Martyn glanced at the door behind him like an animal looking for an escape hole. The screech of crickets rose to an annoying pitch.

"You know how far back Bobby and I go," Charlot said finally. "And you know how close we are."

"This is what I know," Martyn said. "No matter how close you think you are, or how well you think you know him . . . I know him better. And here's the bottom line. If Bobby's been paying you money for a year . . . you've already crossed into dangerous territory."

This gave Charlot pause. "Why?"

"Blackmail. Don't even try to deny it, man. I know you know things about him that other people don't. Things that might have value, given his celebrity. But if I'm right . . . you're an idiot. Because Bobby doesn't play, man. You know that, right? He's a survivor. If he's been giving you money, it's only because he sees you as a minor irritant. A slow leak he can endure as part of his normal burn rate. But if you make yourself a real threat to him?" Martyn shook his head. "*I* wouldn't want to be in that position."

Charlot stared at Martyn with something like defiance. "Bobby would never hurt me. No more than he would you."

Martyn's face had taken on the expression it wore when he played against top competitors across the globe. As Charlot tried to read his features, he recalled the surreal night that they'd shared a ride home after an

AA meeting downtown, a fateful journey that had ended at a liquor store across the river, in Ferriday, Louisiana. After three hours of heavy drinking, Charlot had scored some coke from a sound assistant on a local film crew. By five they were down to meth, and it was then that he and Martyn had started talking about the most famous person they knew.

As it turned out, among all the men and women in Bobby White's past, Charlot Dufort and Martyn Black possessed secret knowledge about him. And while the secrets they knew were unconnected, each had the power to destroy the life Bobby had built for himself. Somehow, during those moments of shared confession in the predawn light, their confidences had felt almost sacred. But later, each would realize that what he had felt was the delicious vanity of possessing shocking knowledge about a celebrity who guarded his privacy with almost religious care. Each had wanted to impress the other, and each had done so. But later, in the sober wake of their revelations, they had felt only shame.

Charlot shuddered when Martyn reached out and took hold of his upper arms. He felt more strength in the hands than he'd expected, and he started to shiver like a man dumped from a car during a blizzard. There was concern in Martyn's touch, something Charlot hadn't felt for longer than he could remember.

"*Please* listen," Martyn implored. "If things are as bad as you say . . . just tell Bobby what you need. How much money you owe, or that you need him to intervene with somebody. Because if he's going to help you for any reason, it'll be honest need. He won't care that you fucked up. He's generous that way. But whatever you do, Charlot . . . *don't threaten him.*"

"I would never—"

"Shut up! You don't know what you'll do! You're not thinking straight. You haven't been for a long time. Just don't do anything to make Bobby perceive you as dangerous. That's all I'm going to say. Now, get going, man."

A fresh note of fear in Martyn's voice sent a chill racing along Charlot's back and arms. He'd lived with so much anxiety over the past couple of weeks that he'd developed a numbness to it, like a kid who's ridden the same roller coaster enough times for it to become routine. It was only today, when he'd caught sight of two muscled-up thugs exiting his house in broad daylight—the house that only two months ago he'd shared with his wife and children—that he'd felt the animal terror that reawakened him to his true plight.

Charlot felt himself entering the psychological state that the French called *presque vu*—the sense of being on the verge of a great epiphany— when the side door burst open, and Lanying began chattering furiously at them. Seeing abject fear behind the anger in the diminutive woman's eyes, Charlot knew his time was up. He'd hoped to use Martyn's shower, but Lanying would never let that happen now. He backed farther away from the door, holding up both hands in apology.

"I'm sorry, man," Martyn said. "But you've gotta split. Take care, okay?"

"Can you throw out some soap?" Charlot asked quickly. "I need to wash up. At least get the blood off. I'll use the garden hose."

Martyn looked as though Charlot had asked for a seven-course meal, and Lanying's voice rose higher in pitch. But just before Martyn shut the side door, he nodded assent.

Charlot stood staring at the blank wood, savoring the last of the Adderall buzz until the door opened wide enough for a tiny female hand to toss out a bottle of Ivory Liquid. Just before the door closed, he heard her voice, constricted with anger but speaking perfect English.

"*Don't come back here*," it said. "Not ever. You have *mogwai* on your shoulder."

"What?"

"A demon," she translated. "Don't come back."

CHAPTER 19

I WAS HALFWAY from Natchez to Bienville when Ray Ransom called and told me he'd finally located Doc Berry, our mayor, in Washington, D.C., but my relief changed to worry as he related the circumstances.

"I spent the last three hours calling hospitals and police precincts," Ray told me. Trying to obtain help from overworked cops in a distant city could not have been fun for a convicted felon. "I finally found him at Howard University Hospital. A John Doe with no ID, but an ER nurse remembered him from my description. Doc still has his unit tattoo from Vietnam. Looks a lot different from the ink they usually see these days."

"A John Doe?" I asked, fearing the worst.

"He was unconscious when they brought him in. It was early afternoon. He'd been attacked at a metro station. Three teenagers stole his iPhone and his wallet, and beat the hell out of him while they were doing it. That's why we haven't been able to reach him. A cop who worked the scene told me that if a bystander hadn't intervened, they'd probably have killed him."

"In the middle of the day?"

"They get about fifteen attacks a month on the metro up there, but lately muggings are getting more frequent. And more savage."

"Jesus, Ray. What kind of bystander intervenes in that kind of trouble?"

"Another military vet, about fifty years old. I haven't spoken to him yet, but he apparently had some close-quarters combat experience. Punks ran off after they got a taste of that."

"Thank God they didn't shoot him. Or Doc."

"No shit."

I could hardly process this news. "This timing's pretty suspicious, Ray. On the day we need Doc more than we have in years, he nearly gets killed in a daylight attack in the nation's capital?"

"I know. The teenagers were Black, though. You'd figure anybody in Mississippi trying to hit Doc while he's up there would use somebody from . . . you know, *their side*."

"They could hire somebody Black, couldn't they?"

"I guess. With the right contacts."

"What about the Good Samaritan?"

"He was Black, too. Told the cops Doc reminded him of his daddy, so he couldn't walk away."

"Sounds like Superman. Or Ray Ransom."

"Oh, I would like a piece of those boys," Ray says softly. "I'd teach 'em the price of that kind of bullshit quick."

"What's Doc's prognosis? He must have a concussion if he's still out."

"No serious bleed they could see, but he's seventy-four years old. Not in shape to take blows to the head."

I wince at the thought.

"They're gonna call me as soon as he's conscious."

"Call me as soon as you hear. I don't care what time it is."

"Will do. But this is bad, Penn. Who's gonna run the city without Doc here? The board? Every vote will be tied three to three, Black against white."

"Except the ones where Sophie Dufort votes progressive. And she's been pretty good about that this year."

"But the mayor pro tem is that goddamn MAGA nut, Vivian Paine. And with a paralyzed city board, the county board will run things by default. And Sheriff Tarlton."

"Oh, man. That's a nightmare."

"You got that right. Goddamn it. I'll call you as soon as Doc's awake."

I hang up and push the Audi to eighty-five on the asphalt of 61, hoping no state trooper is lying in wait among the trees that grow thick along the highway. Alone with the low whine of my motor for a few minutes, the weight of my mother's death falls full upon me. I'm lucky to have my daughter to ease my grief, but losing your mother means losing a kind of unconditional love that no one can replace. The eye you were the apple of has gone out. Whether you acknowledged it or not, that love served as emotional bedrock for all the years you had it. But when it's truly gone . . . you understand.

On a straight stretch of road, I look down at Mom's work satchel, which Annie strapped onto my front seat before I left Edelweiss. The leather case is stuffed so full of papers and photographs that the zip closure at the top can't be closed. Jutting from the case is a manila folder with PENN: START HERE, written on it in black Sharpie. The writing looks more like my mother's than my daughter's. And Annie would almost certainly have written DAD: START HERE. I have almost no desire to wade through the pounds of paper that Mom's genealogical research produced, even though Annie has promised it will change my life. Her revelations about our family having a small percentage of African DNA doesn't make me more curious. I was more startled to discover that we're somehow related to the Barlow family, whom I know to be white trash, despite their having a couple of oil wells on Black Oak, their antebellum plantation. But Annie made a good point: Black Oak is contiguous to Pencarrow, the place I bought for my mother so that she could work on the ground where "her people" lived before and during the Civil War. That made close contact between the two families unavoidable, and intimate contact quite possible. And beyond this . . .

The START HERE keeps tickling my brain, the way the DRINK ME note on the bottle did to Alice before she embarked on her adventures in Wonderland. Maybe when I get home, I'll have a gin and tonic and read whatever awaits me in that first envelope. I surely owe Mom that much.

As the Audi eats up the rolling hills atop the loess bluff that lines the eastern bank of the river, I remember the day Mom asked whether I would mind laying down the manuscript I was working on for a while. I didn't want to do it, but given the state of her health, we both knew that wouldn't mean an infinite pause, so I agreed. Now that she's gone, I realize I'm free to turn my attention back to the mysterious mass lynchings that occurred within a few miles of my childhood home in Natchez (fifty-plus slaves tortured and hanged in 1861 alone), and the second spate that happened on Black Oak Plantation a month later. Maybe that's what awaits me in the manila folder: a passing of that torch back to my hand, so that I might continue the quest for what I have always suspected must be a terrible truth.

I wonder if I still have the stamina—or even the desire—to do that kind of work. I spent much of my life as a prosecutor, writer, and mayor: all jobs that led me to delve into some of the darkest annals of human behavior. That kind of labor exacts a mental, physical, and even spiritual cost from those who take it on. I've lost too many friends to forget that. And now—at my age, and with my wounds and scars—the temptation to try to find some peace is powerful.

When you have a terminal illness, even one without obvious symptoms, you mourn your life far in advance of your death. I clearly remember standing over my young daughter's bed in the dark and begging a God I didn't believe in to spare me until she graduated from high school. Then, I promised the empty darkness, I could go in peace. No doctor believed I would live that long . . . but I did, and more.

Yet now that my illness has "switched on," I face a different situation, one that offers at least one road that might lead to further remission. That's undoubtedly what I should be focused on. Yet from habit, my mind keeps tracking onto the old crutches of distraction and denial. *Work.* Historical research into cold cases (and what case could be colder than a 162-year-old mass lynching?). Trained and even celebrated historians have taken on those crimes, and either gotten them wrong or fallen short of the complete truth. And if my mother was correct, I might actually have a blood connection to those murders. But on which side? The Barlows, who surely did much of the hanging? Or the slaves themselves?

This question piques my curiosity.

Shaking off these morbid ruminations, I focus on the green-and-white TENISAW COUNTY sign as it flashes past on my right. Since Tenisaw is the smallest county in Mississippi, in only a few miles I'll pass the BIENVILLE, MS, FOUNDED 1818 sign. The great river runs only a mile out to my left, beyond the dense hardwoods at their darkest green before the colors of fall appear. The Mississippi runs like a great blood vessel linking the towns and cities of the delta—the largest vein in the nation—and its powerful current has always drawn and comforted me, as it did T. S. Eliot (who grew up in St. Louis) and every other writer who came of age in the thrall of the river's unique gravitational pull.

My phone pings, and I check my car's LCD in the hope of seeing news about Doc. Instead, the screen identifies the sender as Nadine Sullivan.

Nadine.

Those letters instantly burn through my highway reverie. Nadine Sullivan (whom my mother mentioned in her final note to me) is texting me on the night my mother died? Can this be by chance? Not too many years ago, Nadine and I carried on a secret but deeply intimate relationship for two and a half years. And unlike my mostly physical dalliance with Sophie Dufort long before, this one might have ended in matrimony had I not ultimately walked away from the relationship. In the time since, Nadine and I have been civil and even friendly to each other—after all, she owns the local bookstore, and brings many of my author friends to Bienville for signings or even more unique events. During this period, she got into a long relationship with Marshall McEwan, the publisher of the *Watchman*, one I was certain would end in marriage. But about two years ago they broke up, surprising everyone, and I have little idea about her romantic life beyond that. Nadine isn't the type to volunteer personal information.

The only intimate contact we've had in those years occurred about seven weeks ago, at an authors' protest organized by Pulitzer Prize finalist Jerry Mitchell, formerly of the *Clarion-Ledger* and now of *Mississippi Today*. With the help of Mississippi's revered indie bookstore owners, Jerry brought together a sparkling coterie of Mississippi writers and indie bookstore founders to protest the banning of books at a library in one of the white-flight communities outside Jackson. The event was a great success in terms of generating publicity, and included tragically funny moments, such as when some condescending Karens showed up and got into altercations with famous writers whose books they loved, but whom they did not recognize until long after they had embarrassed themselves with self-righteous condemnations. Afterward, the authors retired to more hospitable environs to enjoy an adult beverage, as writers are wont to do. After that establishment closed, a much smaller group of us discovered we were staying at the same hotel. At about 1:00 a.m.—after some of the best conversations I'd taken part in for years—Nadine and I found ourselves in a scene worthy of a 1940s rom-com, when she ran to make the elevator without any idea that I was the person holding open the door.

A couple of minutes later, we got off on the same floor, had a brief conversation in the hall, then spent the night in the same room. Neither of us had planned this contact, and in the days afterward, we went through some awkward moments. We'd both experienced a powerful resurgence of our old feelings, but we kept a cautious distance from each other, and after some halting phone conversations, we went back to our previous lives of walking on eggshells.

Just friends.

It's been at least three weeks since we had any contact at all, so tonight's text surprises me. She's not the type to text out of loneliness, so I suspect something unusual must be happening. Maybe she's heard my mother died. Mom was one of her best customers, and as the postmortem note revealed, she obviously liked Nadine a lot.

Picking up my iPhone, I touch the screen, and a photograph blooms above the brief text message. The image looks like a nightmare from an old Stephen King novel: a giant columned mansion with flames lighting every window from within. Below the image appear the following words:

Arcadia's burning! Have you heard? WTF? Are you at your town house? Go to your bedroom window!

"Arcadia's burning?" I say aloud. "Dear Lord."

Bienville isn't really my town. Natchez will always hold that distinction. But my heart begins racing as I press the Audi's accelerator to the floor. As impressive as Tranquility once was to even European tourists, Arcadia is a landmark of another order. Built in 1848 by one of the richest planters in Mississippi, the massive mansion still dominates the southern quarter of Bienville proper. After General Sherman famously remarked upon its majesty in 1863, Arcadia survived as a private home until the late

1980s, when it began operating as a commercial event venue and high-end restaurant. It thrived until very recently, when two successive blows knocked its owner into financial ruin. The first fell in 2019, when wedding magazines ceased covering all ceremonies and receptions held on ante-bellum plantations. The second was the pandemic. Since the summer of 2020, a Sotheby's sign has hung on Arcadia's twelve-foot gates, throwing its future into doubt. Yet because Arcadia served as a location for several notable Hollywood films (plus innumerable weddings), it possesses a kind of immortality in the local imagination. The idea that someone set it on fire while I was driving away from the ruins of Tranquility leaves me short of breath. If Arcadia is really burning, then the "Bastard Sons of the Confederacy" have already fulfilled the threat they made to Marshall on the phone. And if that's true . . .

Then God help us all.

CHAPTER 20

THE BURNING OF Arcadia is like no fire I've ever seen.

The mansion is three times the size of the one I watched burn in Natchez decades ago. Even from a mile outside the city, I could tell something was happening on a titanic scale. The usual night skyline of Bienville includes a domelike penumbra to the south, a deep black void amid the general scatter of background light. Beneath that dome sits the one hundred acres of Arcadia, a mostly wooded parcel of an original British land grant. But tonight I see what looks like a CinemaScope film about London during the Blitz—a deep-red glow lighting the underside of the clouds southeast of the Mississippi River. Where the black void should be glows a dome of orange light, with a vertical black smudge severing it in two. That smudge, I realize, is a towering column of smoke, spreading outward as it climbs toward the cloud ceiling. Staring at the otherworldly scene, I know that anyone in sight of that glowing dome will hurry toward it, to witness the destruction beneath. It's a compulsion as instinctive as the urge to fuck or to sleep. A similar limbic signal must have prompted Nadine to text me after such a long silence.

As I eat up the final mile into town, I feel the itchy premonition thrown off when the past unexpectedly abrades the present, opening a channel to futures thought impossible only moments before. Closing my eyes, I smell Nadine's scent in the car, as vivid as if she just climbed into the passenger seat on a spring evening. I cut my eyes right, half expecting to see her sitting beside me. Of course the seat is empty. Looking forward again, I see the spectral glow of the fire, seemingly larger than it was only moments ago. *What in God's name is going on?* I wonder. *Who is really doing this? And why?*

From two blocks away, the blaze consuming Arcadia lights up the night like a stick of bombs dropped from a B-52. The fearsome red clouds look like some special effect from a horror movie, black smoke billowing upward to stain them like a harbinger of apocalypse. The spectacle has already drawn such a crowd that I have to park a hundred yards from the gate. Jogging painfully up the congested road, I struggle to draw enough breath to grunt in pain. Mixed with the familiar scent of wood smoke, I smell burning paint, vaporizing varnish, melting tar, scorched metal, exploding sap, seared shingles. A caustic reek I can't identify underlies all that, and above the trees I see a column of smoking debris hurtling up through what appear to be living clouds of sparks.

I recognize a few faces as I pick a path through the crowd thronging the gate. All are gazing at the disaster unfolding sixty yards beyond the tall wrought-iron fence. The scale of the blaze is breathtaking from this close. Arcadia is a fully colonnaded mansion, its colossal Doric columns wrapping around the galleries on all sides, each as thick as a 150-year-old oak. Yet even from where I stand, I can see the fire is devouring it faster than the men and trucks silhouetted against the flames can ever hope to counter. Hose crews blast water through its double-height jib windows, but they're not making any headway. The fire has already breached the roof in one place, and the widow's walk on the roof has begun spouting flame.

My phone vibrates as another text comes in. I half-expect a follow-up from Nadine, but the message is from Annie. It reads: *Somebody texted me Arcadia's on fire. I saw a pic on Instagram but I don't know if it's real.*

It's real, I reply. *I'm watching it burn. Just got here. U still at Edelweiss?*

Yes. I can't believe this is happening after the fire in Natchez! Any chance of saving the mansion?

I study the steaming company of men and machines beyond the fence. *I don't think so. It almost looks like a bomb blew up inside it. You're not going to try to drive up here are you? It's insane. Massive crowd.*

Annie doesn't answer immediately. *I'd like to, honestly. But I'm not going to leave Gram's body alone.*

I'm glad to hear this. Officer Gabriel Davis will be guarding Edelweiss, but that's not the same as a family member watching over the body in the old way.

I'm glad you feel that way, boo. I'll update you. I promise.

Thanks, Dad.

Pocketing my phone, I work my way closer to the gate, like a teenager trying to reach the front row of a concert. With my prosthetic it takes longer than it should. You don't know what a miracle an articulating ankle is until you lose one of those God gave you. I smell alcohol as I near my goal, then see the people closest to the iron bars holding glasses and bottles. *Did*

*these drinkers wander across the street from the B-and-B on the hill opposite
Arcadia?* I wonder. *Or did they migrate from one of the downtown bars?*

When only two dense rows of humanity separate me from the gate,
I feel a furnace blast of heat, and hear the fire's peristaltic roar. A living
monster, it devours wood and metal, burps toxic gas, and splits great
beams with cracks like pistol shots. How could it feel to stand twenty feet
from that inferno? Bracing my prosthetic foot, I make a quick sweep of the
people around me. I don't recognize the faces here. Not at first.

Then I see Ray Ransom to my left, standing with one muscular arm
against the Sotheby's sign on the gate. Ray is hard to miss, and his presence
comforts me a little. Ray's prison sentence overlapped my father's in the
lethal pressure cooker of Parchman, and he once confided to me that he'd
gotten to know Dad a little, just before his death. Five years after I met
Ray, I was stunned to learn that he was descended from an enslaved man
on Black Oak Plantation (the Barlow place), and that his ancestor had
been involved in the planned slave revolt I'd begun researching.

Since his release from prison, Ray has repaired small engines for a living, but his real calling is working with young Black men, from gang-
bangers and cons to military vets, to keep them from falling back through
the cracks in the system. I met him through Doc, who gives free medical
care to the boys in Ray's program. Both Doc and Ray served in Vietnam,
but Ray also spent some years as a Black Panther in California and New
Orleans before being remanded to Parchman. That background makes
him uniquely suited for his "scared straight" approach to troubled youth.

"Yo, Penn!" he calls, picking up my gaze. "Ain't this some shit?"

"Hard to believe, man."

He lowers his arm and moves closer, saying, "Hard to believe it's an
accident, you mean. I'd say those Bastard Sons mean business."

A couple of onlookers in front of me turn to see who said this, but Ray's
glare spins them forward again.

"You hear anything specific?" I ask.

Ray puckers his lips, looking hesitant. "Not exactly. But during the
George Floyd protests last year, a Natchez rapper mentioned burning
some antebellum homes on Facebook. Some bangers was talkin' 'bout setting the mall on fire, and the kid said they'd be fools to burn their own
hangout. Told 'em these homes were like the concentration camps of the
nineteenth century."

"My daughter told me about that."

Ray nods. "The kids know everything first. A rapper up here in Bienville picked up that same line and amplified it. And I think Kendrick

Washington has said the same stuff during some of his heritage tours of Bienville."

That pulls my gaze away from the fire. Kendrick Washington is no simple tour guide any longer. He's a globally famous hero of the Mission Hill shooting. "It's a hard thesis to argue with," I admit. "But now that you mention it, he sang something about the 'fires of judgment' in the lyrics he wrote to that Neil Young song."

Ray gives me a sober nod. "Kendrick wouldn't do anything like this, though. Take my word. It ain't in him. I'm just saying it's in the wind. The FBI will hear some of these things sooner or later. But that's not my point. This was bound to happen eventually. These houses are the next step up from Confederate monuments, right? They're where slavery actually happened."

I think about that. "Actually, not so much. These mansions were suburban villas, not working plantations. Just showplaces for the owners. Status symbols."

Ray looks skeptical. "Showplaces for the slave masters, right?"

"Well, sure."

"Slaves cooking the food, brushing the horses, carrying out the slop jars in the morning?"

"I get your point. I just meant that the working plantations—the cotton farms with hundreds of slaves—were mostly across the river."

Ray gives me a tight smile. "That's a mighty fine hair you trying to split, counselor. That's like saying Hitler's retreat at the Berghof was different from Dachau, or Goering's Karinhall was different from Luftwaffe HQ. It's all the part of the same horror show."

"You're absolutely right. Still . . . it's hard to see somebody local burning this place down. As an act of protest? Targeted attacks like that haven't happened anywhere in this country yet. Not by Black groups. Usually it's retail stores in the path of riots. A Wendy's or a Walgreen's. A police station. This could be something new, I admit, but your theory seems like a bridge too far to me."

"I hope so. But my gut says it's a protest." Ray's eyes find mine in the fire's glow. "One a long time comin'."

"If you're right . . . the government will call it straight-up terrorism."

Ray bows his head and mouths some words I can't hear. After he looks up, we watch the fire lick the eaves of the roof, then race across the shingles toward the widow's walk at its apex, which is already burning from within.

As I stare in stubborn disbelief, I hear Nadine Sullivan speak my name. After my hallucination in the car, I recognize her voice as though I hear it every day. Turning right, I catch sight of corn-silk blonde hair weaving left and right behind several men in the crowd. I'm not generally a fan of blondes, but Nadine is an exception.

"Penn!" she calls again, smiling and waving.

Then I see her face, her eyes as bright and filled with life force as they always were. I wave back, giving her a smile of encouragement.

She turns to speak to someone, then works her way toward me along the fence. The sight of her stirs something in my chest, and I feel a sudden anxiety. Though I spent more than two years sleeping with this woman, almost no one knew that. We didn't keep our relationship secret because of any illicit component. I was simply living like a hermit at the time, and Nadine didn't want anyone in Bienville knowing her private business. Born and raised here, she left at eighteen and built a successful career as an attorney in North Carolina. She only returned to take care of her mother, who would die at the same age I am now. A slower-than-expected decline led to Nadine starting a book club for her mother, and that's where I came to know her, as a guest author. After her mother's eventual death (she outlived her prognosis by two years), Nadine opened Constant Reader and turned it into the first thriving bookstore in Bienville since the 1970s.

"You believe this?" she asks, squeezing between two women to my right. "It's fucking awful."

"I can't, really. Especially after Tranquility."

"No shit." In a low voice she says, "Marshall's right behind me."

Maybe this is the source of my anxiety. Marshall McEwan is another Bienville prodigal, and I like him a lot, though he isn't a close friend. He might have been, had Nadine not gotten intimate with him soon after he moved back here from Washington, D.C. But the fact that Marshall knows nothing of our previous intimacy has enforced a certain careful distance on my part.

"Does he know you texted me?" I ask.

Nadine shakes her head.

"Got it."

A flicker of relief crosses her face. "How's your mom doing after the stroke?"

For a second I consider keeping quiet about today, but what's the point? "Mom passed away a couple of hours ago, actually."

Nadine's face appears to collapse inward. Dropping all pretense of distance, she hugs me tight and presses her face into my chest. "I'm so sorry," she whispers. "I loved Peggy. She was the real deal."

I look over her shoulder and see Marshall, who is about my height but considerably more handsome, moving sideways along the fence, his cell phone pressed hard against his ear. He isn't smiling. After ten years working as a network journalist in Washington, D.C., Marshall now owns and publishes his family newspaper, the Bienville *Watchman*, which was founded the year the Civil War ended. Following in the footsteps of his father—who won a Pulitzer for writing about Klan violence in the 1960s—he's brought a fresh dose of liberalism to Mississippi that would have made Hodding Carter proud.

Pulling back from Nadine and pretending to focus on Arcadia, I whisper, "Is Marshall up to speed on our history now?"

"Nope. Everything's the same."

Define "same," I think. "Okay. Just getting oriented."

She gives my left wrist a quick squeeze, and the intimacy of it sends a hot tingle racing up my arm.

"Does anybody have any idea how this thing started?" I ask loudly. "Has anybody been living in the house? A caretaker or something?"

She shakes her head. "The owners say no."

"Maybe some kids broke in and did something stupid," I suggest, though I don't believe it. "Like they did down at the Eola Hotel in Natchez."

"Or a homeless person," Nadine says. "We've had some squatters downtown over the past few months, staying in abandoned buildings. Sometimes they build fires to cook."

"I didn't know that."

"How could you, living the way you do? Has isolation been good for your book, at least?"

"No. But it helped me win the Dunphy lawsuit."

"Oh, yeah. Congratulations on that verdict. I thought I'd won some impressive judgments, but that's real money." Nadine leans in and sniffs. "You smell like gin. Did I interrupt a party with my text?"

"Marshall!" I call, reaching over another woman's shoulder to shake his hand.

The publisher holds up a finger while he finishes his call. Just as I turn back to Nadine, he clicks off, leans in close, and whispers, "*The same group just claimed this fire, too.*"

His words silence us. I'm not sure I understood him correctly. Or maybe I know I did and want to pretend I didn't. "What do you mean?" I ask. "Like a terrorist act?"

"An act of protest."

"The Bastard Sons again?"

Marshall nods, and Nadine's lack of surprise tells me he already revealed the earlier phone call to her.

"I knew it," she whispers. "What the actual fuck is going on?"

Nadine was never a prude, but when she and I were together, she didn't punctuate every sentence with an f-bomb. "How'd they claim it?" I ask. "Another phone call? Social media?"

Marshall shakes his head. "They nailed some kind of weird note to the courthouse door. Then they let off a pack of firecrackers to draw sheriff's deputies from down the street."

"Analog," I think aloud. "Smart. Any security cameras there?"

"Inside, plenty. But not covering that door from the outside. Whoever left that note knows this town."

"What did the note say?" Nadine asks. "Exactly?"

Marshall calls up a photograph on his cell phone and zooms in. The "note" appears to have been written on a very large sheet of paper. Then he holds his screen so that we can read the handwritten words: "*The Mission Hill Massacre happened because of places like Arcadia and Tranquility. George Floyd died for the same reason. It's time you people stopped revering concentration camps. These antebellum 'homes' are the root of the poisoned myth. A whitewashed façade for hell on earth. That myth must be destroyed, root and branch. It will be destroyed. This is only the beginning.*"

Even with the heat of the fire in my face, I feel a chill. "Is it signed?"

Marshall scrolls down, and I see the words *Bastard Sons of the Confederacy.*

"What the hell?" I breathe. "I've never *heard* of any such group. Have you?"

"Never," says Marshall. "And my people have been searching all afternoon."

"What kind of paper is that?" asks Nadine.

"An album cover, ripped inside out."

"What album?"

"Tupac Shakur. *Strictly 4 My N.I.G.G.A.Z.* Released in 1993."

"Oh, I know it well. I was thirteen when that came out. The boys in my class used to listen to it in the halls, and it drove the teachers *crazy.*"

"Could a white group be behind this?" I ask quietly. "False-flag operation?"

"Sure," Marshall concedes. "But something makes me doubt it." He scrolls up a little more. Below the signature are the words *Black Lives will Matter one day!*

I groan. "Whoever's behind this, that note is a fuse connected to a different kind of bomb."

Marshall straightens up. "It definitely connects the Tranquility fire to this one, and it makes plain that they're both retaliation for Mission Hill." He shakes his head, then flings his right arm wide to take in the crowd. "Look at them. They're acting like it's a goddamn party! They don't know it's likely the first attack in a civil—"

"Don't say it," I warn him. "Just stay cool."

"This can't be happening," Nadine insists, watching the almost uniformly Caucasian crowd surge and shout like drunk spring-breakers in Destin. "Unless the cops nail the arsonist by tomorrow afternoon, this is Pearl Harbor. Race war by tomorrow night."

"Sooner, if that note leaks," I point out. "Riots, anyway. Some sort of white retaliation is the next act, guaranteed."

"These fires are a gift to white extremists," Marshall says. "Which makes me think maybe you're right. False flag. But who could be behind it?"

"How about the Barlow militia?" I suggest. "The Tenisaw Rifles."

"*Hey, hey, what do you say?*" sings a deep voice I recognize as Ray Ransom's. He leans his big bald head between the three of us. "Let's not scare the squares, huh?"

Recognizing Ray, Marshall nods in frustration.

"How 'bout we move this convo away from the crowd?" Ray suggests.

The four of us back away from the gate, triggering curses as we negotiate a course through the bunched bodies. Some high school asshat starts playing a song by Arcade Fire as we pass, and Nadine takes his arm, snaps something in his ear. To my surprise, the song dies behind us.

"That could be a superpower," Ray says.

"I know his mama," Nadine says in a taut voice.

"Something just hit me," I tell them, my background as a prosecutor coming to the fore. "Has anybody spoken to Chief Morgan?"

"I saw him earlier," Ray says over his shoulder, stepping in front of Nadine to clear a path through a stubborn knot of people. "But I think he's behind Arcadia now, with the fire chief."

"What about Doc?" I ask. "Any word?"

"The mayor appears to be incommunicado," Marshall says from behind me. "Not a good look on this particular night."

"No word," Ray says quickly, which tells me he doesn't want the newspaper publisher breaking the story that Doc was beaten to within an inch of his life up in Washington. "What should we do here? Any productive ideas?"

We've reached the ragged edge of the crowd, which is still growing. Looking up, I see a handful of people standing on the front porch of

Colfax House, the B-and-B sited on a steep hill opposite Arcadia. It's too dark under the porch roof to distinguish faces, or even to discern gender. Though the crowd is thinner here at the edge, I motion for the others to lean in like a basketball huddle.

"In cases like this," I say, "the arsonist is almost always present at the fire scene. They feel compelled to watch their fantasy play out. Cops in a big city would know that, but Chief Morgan may have his hands full."

"I've got a staff photographer here," Marshall says. "I'll get her to start shooting the crowd."

Ray is nodding. "I'll start mug-shotting these motherfuckers with my cell phone."

"Getting everybody could be tough in a crowd this size," I point out. "It's a big site. The arsonist could be on a rooftop, in the trees behind the mansion, or even up there—" I flick my head to indicate the B-and-B atop the hill.

Marshall nods. "Let's start with the main crowd. I'll get my shooter to take group shots from every angle. She can get inside the fence, too."

I turn to Ray to ask him to shoot the people on the porch of the B-and-B, but he's already walked away, shooting as he goes. When I turn back, Marshall is on his cell phone again.

Seeing him engrossed, Nadine leans closer. "I don't know why I texted you about the fire, okay? No ulterior motive. I just figured that with your yearslong plunge into all the related history, and your mother's recent work . . . you'd want to see it. I guess that makes no sense."

She and I were no longer together when my mother began her genealogical quest, but Nadine seems to know about it—maybe through owning the bookstore. "No harm, no foul," I tell her.

She looks unconvinced.

Marshall still seems preoccupied, so I turn my back to him and speak very softly. "Are you and he dating again?"

She shakes her head. "Just friends."

Friends. The deadliest post-romance description of all. Before I can think further down that track, Nadine says, "Do you think there's any way that note could be held back for a while? Twenty-four hours? Even twelve?"

"If it were just Chief Morgan out here responding, maybe."

"A Black chief with a mostly Black department," Nadine thinks aloud.

"Too late for that," Marshall says, stepping up behind me. "Too many people know about it already. Sheriff Tarlton will take great satisfaction in spreading this news. It will set the hair of his base on fire. Fits his political narrative to a T."

Dread fills me as I realize how right Marshall is. "I haven't seen his Stetson yet, but Tarlton's got to be here. I passed two sheriff's department cruisers as I ran up. And Buck won't wait for a press conference. He'll leak that note to a major outlet before you can say Alex Jones. Then it's game on. *Rappers burning down antebellum homes!* We're about to become the center of the media universe." I look at Marshall and give him a sympathetic smile. "At least you've been there before."

"I haven't missed it a bit. You've been at the center of some media insanity yourself."

"Thankfully, I'm not part of this story."

"Keep dreaming," Nadine says. "After a relatively peaceful few years, Mississippi finally says, 'Hold my beer, we do race war better than anybody.'" She pokes me in the chest. "And *you* are one public face of this state."

Marshall is turning in a slow circle. "Have you noticed this crowd is ninety-eight percent white?"

I quickly text Ray Ransom: *Sorry, but shoot the brothers first.*

He hits me back in seconds: *Already figured that out.*

Another siren wails farther up the street, bouncing off of every possible surface. When Marshall rotates back toward me, I say, "Both Tranquility and Arcadia have absentee owners. Whoever chose those targets either went to some trouble to learn that, or they already knew."

"If it's the latter," Marshall reasons, "the perp's more likely white, right?"

I shrug. "Not necessarily."

"Hang on," he says, reading his phone again. "The fire chief." He mashes his cell phone hard against his ear. Before I can turn back to Nadine, the blood drains from the publisher's face. "Thanks, I won't," he says, then slips the phone back into his pocket.

Nadine watches him with foreboding. She knows Marshall well enough to sense that something terrible has happened.

"What is it?" I ask.

He looks right at Nadine. "The firemen just found a six-year-old girl hiding out back, crying her eyes out. She and her father were apparently squatting in an annex on the back side of the house. The father didn't make it out."

A numbness like general anesthesia spreads outward from my heart. "This isn't arson anymore. It's murder."

"I may *know* that girl," Nadine murmurs, looking dazed. "If I'm right, she and her dad were squatting in a building near my bookstore a couple months back. I used to take her treats sometimes."

Marshall slowly shakes his head. "Looks like smoke inhalation got the father. The girl tried to wake him up but couldn't. Fire chief says he smelled like cheap wine from ten feet away. The girl finally roused him, but he couldn't get his leg on quick enough. He told her to run for it. Thank God she finally did."

"His leg?" I ask dully.

"The father was diabetic," Nadine explains, looking bereft. "He had a prosthetic leg. A piece of junk."

The numbness I felt earlier reaches my extremities.

"Who's with the little girl now?" Nadine asks.

Marshall doesn't know. "Firemen, I guess. Till they can get somebody from the state children's services over from Jackson."

I blink in horror, thinking of the dead man. I had nightmares exactly like that during the first year after my accident, especially when sleeping above the first floor in any building.

"Were they white or Black?" I ask. "The squatters."

"Does that matter?" asked Nadine.

"In this context?" Marshall says. "It probably will."

"White," Nadine says. "Take me to that girl, Marshall. Somebody get me in there. She's got to be terrified."

"I'll get you in," Ray Ransom says from behind us. "I'm tight with the fire chief."

Ray reappeared without making a sound. He offers Nadine his arm and leads her away. After they've gone only twenty yards, she turns her head and looks back at us. There's something new in her eyes, something fleeting and hard to decipher. She seems to be pleading for understanding, or maybe apologizing. Whatever her intent, her face shows deep regret. But with Marshall standing beside me, I don't know how to react, so I turn back to him without responding. After all, Nadine created this awkward triangle where ignorance rules.

"Murder," I say quietly. "That's what this is now."

"Terrorism," Marshall says. "That's what they'll call it."

He starts humming a song in the face of the inferno, but the tune seems too inappropriate for me to believe I've guessed right. "What are you humming?"

"Remember the old AC/DC song? 'Highway to Hell'?"

"I thought that's what that was."

He shrugs as if to ask the point of self-deception. "We're on it, buddy, and we ain't got no brakes. Mission Hill just became yesterday's news."

CHAPTER 21

BY THE TIME Bobby White and Birdie Blake landed at the Bienville airport and got shuttled to the Belle Rose Country Club, the pre-tourney VIP dinner party had been underway for two hours. The club's president had tried to limit the guest list to board members, big donors, and the celebrities and pros who would be playing in the pro-am the next day. But as Bobby walked through the soaring clubhouse lobby, he realized that like most plans, that one hadn't survived the first ten minutes. In a small town like Bienville, the presence of celebrities had drawn at least forty club members who'd used every pretense they could contrive to crash the party.

The ballroom crowd stretched to the back wall, where a tuxedo-clad swing band played before glass picture windows that looked out over the eighteenth green. The club members wore a mix of sportswear, expensive suits, and glittering cocktail dresses, and many openly gawked at Birdie as Bobby escorted her into the room. (Ten minutes before the Donnelly jet landed, the actress had changed into a jade-green dress cut just below the knee. It set off her fiery red hair, which sparkled with green glitter and emerald earrings.) Her beauty was a cut above that of most women in the room, though when Sophie Dufort walked through wearing a floor-length white column dress, she drew stares from both women and men, especially the pro athletes gathered around the casino gambling tables set up for their entertainment.

Birdie got stopped for selfies a half dozen times as she and Bobby made their way to the bar, and Bobby had to pose with her or risk coming off like an asshole in his hometown. Both handled the attention with better humor than they might have, having eaten two gummies apiece on the flight down from Teterboro, both more potent than Bobby was accustomed to. Corey had glared at him over Birdie's shoulder, warning him not to overimbibe, but Bobby had ignored him, figuring the risks of being stoned down here were limited. Now Corey was working alone in Bobby's cabin on Canaan Plantation while his employer got to enjoy the night with the actress of the moment.

After quenching their thirst with vodka, Birdie and Bobby began dancing through the whirling mass of partygoers. Even with only one arm, Bobby moved with fluid grace, and Birdie's eyes flashed with pleasure.

"I'm surprised you dance so well!" she said breathlessly.

"At all, you mean?" Bobby replied with a wink.

"Well . . . to music from this era, anyway."

"It's one of the perks of being raised in Bienville. It's like growing up in a charm school. Have you been gone so long you forgot that? Dancing's one of those things they teach you early. Even the boys."

Birdie laughed. "I know Bienville and Natchez are two of the smallest towns in America where owning a tux is de rigueur."

The band paused, then struck up an interesting version of Gershwin's "Summertime."

"I love DuBose Heyward's lyrics," Bobby said, cradling Birdie in his arm for a risky dip. "Especially this song. Sondheim thought he was a genius."

"Yikes!" Birdie yelped as she brushed the floor during a dip, but Bobby brought her back to her feet with impressive control. "Someone told me the Manning boys backed out of the tournament. Not Archie, but Peyton and Eli."

"Probably good PR advice," Bobby said. "They don't want to be within five hundred miles of these fires. Maybe you should have checked with your agent before you got off the jet."

"Screw the PR. I'm ready to party." Birdie glanced around, avoiding the eyes of the fans staring at her. "If only the club could replace some of these celebrities with any Mississippi ones they wanted."

"What do you mean? Who do they not have?"

She lowered her voice slightly. "I mean, like, remove the death limit. You do that, Mississippi has the top people in almost any field of art. We're impoverished in so many ways, but not that one."

"Name your 'best-of' list."

"Faulkner. Elvis. Tennessee Williams, Eudora Welty. Robert Johnson. Howlin' Wolf and B. B. King. Leontyne Price. Tammy Wynette, Charley Pride. Jimmie Rodgers, the father of country music—"

Bobby was surprised at her depth of knowledge. "Okay, okay, modern."

"Oprah, John Grisham, Morgan Freeman, James Earl Jones, Donna Tartt, Jimmy Buffett—"

"With that talent pool, we could definitely come up with more interesting pairs for tomorrow's pro-am."

Birdie squealed with joy as Bobby twirled her beneath his arm. "I'd pair them for maximum friction, to goose the entertainment value."

"Give me an example," he said, as her eyes flashed.

"Uhh . . . Thomas Harris and Cat Cora."

"*Who?*"

"Hannibal Lecter meets the Iron Chef. Imagine the buffet—"

"Okay . . ." Bobby tried to think outside the box. "Ahh, Brett Favre and Tennessee Williams. They could trade dick pics."

"Ouch!" Birdie cried.

"Oprah and Ike Turner! Faulkner and Britney Spears!"

Her eyes flashed gamely. "Name another pair!"

"We need more gummies!"

As the liquor flowed, more dancers stopped to ask for selfies. People saw them as two local kids who'd gotten out and made a name for themselves, and not much makes small-town folks feel better than that. It proves they're as good as anybody. By the time Bobby got Birdie clear of the main circus (by spinning away to "September" by Earth, Wind & Fire), he could tell she was in the mood for more than dancing. But just as she began breathing into his ear, Wyatt Cash, a local multimillionaire a few years older than Bobby, leaned in and said, "Some Poker Club members would like to speak to you in the card room when you get a minute."

Bobby nodded without looking at him. "Let's do it now, before I get too much vodka in me."

Cash patted his shoulder, then smiled at Birdie and walked confidently off through the crowd.

"Do you know Wyatt?" Bobby asked.

She rolled her eyes. "Earlier today he asked me about doing some modeling for his company."

"Prime Shot Outfitters?"

Her laugh was filled with gleeful malice. "Can you imagine me in camo?"

"AI-designed camo! What did you tell him?"

"I'm vegan." She burst out laughing.

"Are you really?"

"God, no! But I have to diet so much that I feel like I am. Where do you have to go?"

"Some of their little club want to talk to me. About politics, I suspect."

"What club? The country club?"

"No. The *Poker* Club. Ever heard of them?"

Birdie rolled her eyes. "I grew up here, didn't I? The richest bastards in town—going all the way back to the war—and their bitchy wives."

"That's them. Though some of the wives are pretty good sports."

Birdie peered into his eyes and slowly shook her head. "Isn't it funny that whenever you say 'the war' around here, people know you're talking about the *Civil* War? Even today? It's unbelievable."

"Not if you grew up in Mississippi."

She sighed. "I'll hit the bar and the ladies' while you're gone. Don't take all night, lover."

Bobby gave her waist a squeeze, and she winked as she spun away through the crowd.

THE BELLE ROSE card room was tucked into the north end of the club-house's second floor. The club president had given Bobby a tour the Friday before Mission Hill, and he'd taken care to point out that the soft cypress floors and fireplace mantel had been salvaged from a Louisiana sugar plantation owned by Charles Dufort, who still owned the original Belle Rose, which stood less than a mile from the clubhouse. That wasn't something they mentioned in "mixed" company, the president told him with a wink, but it meant a lot to some of the members.

Bobby knocked once at the door, which was answered by Wyatt Cash, who led him to a chair that faced a long table with five people seated behind it like a tribunal. Bobby had always heard the Bienville Poker Club had twelve members, a tradition handed down since 1863, with new ones inducted only upon deaths of the old. Blue-blooded heredity was the prime membership criterion, though wealth alone sometimes proved sufficient. Tommy Russo, the lean, fortyish Italian-American who owned the Sun King casino down on the river, was a prime example. But all the others present tonight were from old Southern families. Claude Buckman, Junior, represented the Bienville Southern Bank, whose founder, Claude Senior, rarely left home anymore. Wyatt Cash had revived the flagging fortunes of his family by founding a modern outdoor equipment and apparel company. Seated at the right end of the table was Arthur Pine, a gray-templed former city attorney who'd served as fixer and consigliere for the Poker Club for the past forty years.

The lone woman at the table was Dixie Donnelly, second wife of Blake Donnelly, an immensely wealthy oilman of eighty-four, who sat at the left end of the table, in a comfortable chair suited to his age. Dixie was closer to fifty, a classic big-haired ex–pageant queen with an acid tongue and a surprisingly quick mind, as many had learned to their detriment. Dixie ran GOP fundraising in southern Mississippi, and it was said she could suck blood from a stone. Bobby knew Dixie better than anyone else at the table; last week she had tipped him that a meeting like this might happen over the tournament weekend.

"Glad you could tear yourself away from our new Emmy winner," Wyatt Cash began. "We won't keep you long." He pointed to what appeared to be a hand-carved wet bar. "What you drinking, Bobby?"

Bobby demurred with a wave of his hand. "I like to keep my wits about me in meetings like this one."

"Good practice, Sergeant," Arthur Pine commented.

"Please, call me Bobby. I've met you all at one point or other."

"Well, Bobby," said Claude Buckman, Junior, who looked like a pale copy of his father, who had built the Bienville Southern Bank into a regional powerhouse. "We're not going to beat around the bush. You grew up in this town, so I'm sure you know something about us. Rumors, mostly, I'd guess. But I won't waste time on history. Let's talk about you. And Mississippi."

Buckman paused to light a cigar, then began an impressively succinct summary of his subject. "As you know, our state economy has been shrinking for decades. It's one of only two Southern states that lost population in 2020, and the drain has been constant. Especially the brain drain. But while the rest of the state has shrunk, Bienville has grown. After a brief period of stasis during the Covid pandemic, damn near every available house in town has sold. Every commercial building, too. Even retail is growing by double digits here. The engine of all that is the Chinese paper mill, of course, Azure Dragon, whose recruitment we won in 2018."

Bobby had heard rumors about how Bienville beat out the other Southern cities contending for the two-billion-dollar mill—larger river towns in Alabama and Arkansas—but he saw nothing to be gained by bringing that up now.

"Within the confines of this room," Buckman went on, "I'll concede that we didn't accomplish all this playing by the rules. We've done whatever was necessary, whenever necessary, to outpace every competitor. Our forebears began that practice after the Yankee occupation in 1863."

"Understood. What is it you want from me?"

Buckman smiled like a man unaccustomed to doing so. "Why do you assume we want something?"

Bobby smiled easily. "Because meetings like this always end with an ask. What's the ask, Mr. Buckman?"

"Claude, please. This isn't like other meetings you've been to, Bobby. No, we want to give *you* something. First, congratulations on your unprecedented transformation into a potential presidential candidate. I believe you're about to outpace old Ross Perot, whom I met several times, and on a much shorter time scale. The thing is, your chances of *winning* a general presidential election as a third-party candidate are almost nil."

Buckman held up his hand to keep Bobby silent a bit longer. "You'd probably outperform Perot—although he did better than people remember—but you'd certainly lose. Now, if you were to run as a *Republican*, you'd be a damn walk-in for the nomination. I'm not talking about this cycle, of course. Not unless Trump implodes beyond what most of us think is possible."

"Think Trinity test–level implosion," groused Arthur Pine. "That's what I'm hoping for."

"If he were to do that," Buckman went on, "I think you'd find the national party coalescing around you in record time. They could make you the nominee by acclamation as late as the convention. The upside of you being nominated should be obvious."

Buckman clearly meant to go on, but Bobby held up his hand as signaling surrender. "Gentlemen—and lady—let me spare you some breath. Have you called me up here to ask me not to run for president?"

Arthur Pine cut his eyes at Buckman, then Donnelly. "In a way, we have."

"If we thought you could win this cycle," Buckman clarified, "we'd say go for it. But Trump has poisoned the well, Bobby. For all other Republicans. We've got a different idea for you."

Bobby nodded slowly, trying to guess what that might be. "Before you expend any more energy, let me say something. I've been a Republican all my adult life. But since 2016, I've watched the party destroy itself beyond repair. Beyond resurrection, even. Hell, Stuart Stevens wrote the obituary. The party as it exists today contains no real leaders. No guts. No honor. It surrendered to Trump at every turn, even past the point of treason. It's a cult that denies reality. It has no policies, no guiding principles, and in fact has betrayed those that formed its sacred core through the latter half of the twentieth century. Christ, its primary activity is voter suppression."

Dixie Donnelly was nodding.

"We were afraid you would say that," Buckman admitted. "But we had to ask. Now that we have, can I get to my real point?"

"All right."

"At the risk of pissing you off, I'm going to restate my thesis: you're not going to win the presidency as a third-party candidate. And down deep, you must know that. If you don't, youth and ambition are clouding your judgment."

"So what is it you want, Claude? Excuse me, what is it you want to give me?"

"The governorship of this state."

Bobby leaned back in genuine surprise. "That election is less than a month away."

Buckman smiled expansively. "And yet—here we are."

"I don't understand."

"You're about to. You're familiar with the TANF welfare scandal, I'm sure? The one that's swept up Brett Favre and former governor Bryant, et cetera?"

"It's only the biggest welfare scandal in history."

"We think it's about to get bigger. A couple of our sources claim to have new info, and it's staggering. If what I'm told is true, the present governor won't survive the firestorm. If he has to pull out of the race, the only person we believe capable of stepping in and winning at this point—over a

Democratic cousin of Elvis Presley, mind you—is *you*, with the phenomenal fame you've racked up these past few months."

Bobby blinked in silence as he took in the scale of their scheme.

"That said," Buckman went on, "let me add that the backward-looking,
Confederate-flag-hugging, country club frat boy model hasn't been working
in this state for a long time now. Mississippi has been fiftieth in nearly every
measure of quality of life for so long that we're now the benchmark of shit.
Hell, we trail *Puerto Rico* in education. Medicaid expansion alone would have
brought more than a billion dollars into this state, and saved countless lives.
But still the clowns in the legislature vote against it. If you ask me, they're trying to kill as many Black voters as they can. If we keep going down this road,
Mississippi will become a national pariah. Forget losing contracts to build
navy ships on the coast. NCAA teams will start refusing to cross the state line
to play Ole Miss or State in football. Our recruiting will go straight to hell."

"And we can't have that," muttered Blake Donnelly, who had played for
Ole Miss back in the sixties. "We need a centrist Republican running this
state, Sergeant. A Ronald Reagan or George Bush. And we think you're him."

Bobby found himself amused by their assumptions, but more by their
proposition. It really was the last thing he'd expected to hear. He started to
demur, but the banker held up his hand again. "Before you say no, Bobby,
please humor me. You've got the White House in your sights, but you're
only forty-two years old. You could serve four years as governor, then use
that as a springboard for the presidency. Even if you served two terms,
you'd still only be fifty when you ran for president."

Bobby didn't want to insult these men. They had millions to offer him
down the road. But neither did he wish to encourage a fool's errand. And
he'd learned long ago that when you have to eat a turd, you don't take
small bites. "Claude, I'm going to pay you the compliment of being honest. I don't want 'governor of Mississippi' on my résumé. I can't afford
it. As you said, people hear that title and think of the Confederate flag,
backward whites, hungry Blacks, the worst infant mortality in the nation,
and a capital city without drinkable water. They think of Pappy O'Daniel
from *O Brother, Where Art Thou?* If I didn't turn this state around in four
years, it'd be an anvil hanging around my neck for the rest of my life."

"But you *can* turn it around!" Buckman insisted. "We can help you."

"I'm happy to hear your enthusiasm. But you can't come close to guar-
anteeing that outcome."

"It's the White House or nothing, isn't it?" Dixie said in a husky Ava
Gardner drawl. "Trump showed you what was possible, didn't he? He
whetted your appetite."

Bobby shrugged but did not deny it. "That may be partly true. But I'm not worried about Trump. Put me on a debate stage with him, I'll do what nobody ever has."

"What's that?" asked Donnelly.

"Shame him. I'll tear strips of hide off him from the get-go. I'll expose him as one of the stupidest men ever to run for president. A disloyal coward. And when he leaves his podium and comes into my space like he did with Hillary—which he'll try, because he's about an inch taller than I am in his high heels, and he'll want to draw that comparison—I'll give him one warning. Then I'll make him touch me."

"How will you do that?" asked Pine. "And why?"

Bobby smiled with absolute confidence. "Psych training. Experience. And after he touches me, I will bitch-slap that draft-dodging piece of shit to the floor. They'll have to call an ambulance, because he won't be able to get up. But I'll take an assault charge in exchange for the White House."

Dixie's cheeks went red, and she squirmed on her chair. Her reaction didn't escape the other men in the room.

"Jesus," growled Blake Donnelly. "You sound ready to rumble."

"It sounds personal to me," Pine said.

Bobby grimaced with long-suppressed rage. "You ever hear of Belleau Wood, Mr. Pine?"

"The name's vaguely familiar."

"It's where the Marine Corps made its bones in World War One."

"I remember," said Blake Donnelly. "That's where a marine captain yelled, 'Retreat, hell! We just got here!' when the French came tearing through our lines, urging us to run."

"That's the battle," Bobby said quietly.

"Trump would've run with the Frenchies," Dixie said with a smirk.

"When it came time to charge into German machine-gun fire," Bobby went on, as though he had been there himself, "Sergeant Dan Daly—who had two Medals of Honor—turned to his men and said, 'Come on, you sons of bitches! Do you want to live forever?'"

"By God, that's a man," Blake Donnelly murmured.

"A thousand marines went down that day," Bobby told them. "And those are the men that Donald Trump refused to visit when he was in Paris. First he lied and said his chopper wouldn't fly in the rain. But his real worry was that the rain would mess up his hair. Then he told witnesses that the men who'd died at Belleau were suckers. Later, at Arlington, he asked John Kelly what his son had died for. What was in it for him? he asked. So . . . you want to know if this election's personal for me?"

"I think we know the answer to that," Pine said thoughtfully.

Bobby nodded. "I mean to take that SOB apart, if a D.A. doesn't get him first."

Claude Buckman looked impressed. "I hate to see you drive the last nail into the GOP, Bobby. But after these past couple of years, and the circus in the House—which has more kooks and crooks than the Mississippi legislature—I can see why you're hungry to roll the dice."

Bobby got up and poured himself a straight vodka while they discussed him as though he weren't there—as though he would consider acting on anything they might have to say. The only thing that kept him in the room was the prospect of money down the road. Big money.

"Let's save all this chatter for later," Dixie said. "Bobby's way ahead of us. He has been all along. Aren't you, Bobby?"

"I might be, in this case."

"You already know you're going to have the signatures to make the ballots in every state, don't you?"

His eyebrows slowly arched. "I might."

From his club chair, Blake Donnelly leaned forward, and with his aging bulldog's mien said, "The damn thing of it is, son, whatever you do, you're going to have to pivot right, and soon, if you're going to pick up the hardcore Trump voters you need to win the presidency."

"He knows that, too," Dixie said.

"Pivot, my ass," said Wyatt Cash. "He needs to *veer* right, like Dale Earnhardt making a move at Watkins Glen."

A sudden sharp knocking came from the card room door.

"That might be Birdie," Bobby said. "She doesn't like waiting."

"Can't blame the girl," Dixie remarked. "Bring that little fireball in here."

Wyatt Cash got up and went to the door and opened it just enough for Bobby to see that the visitor wasn't Birdie Blake, but a thin clerk type he didn't recognize. "Sorry to interrupt, Mr. Cash," the bespectacled man murmured. "But I texted Mr. Buckman and got no reply."

"I told you to leave us undisturbed. The damned clubhouse better be on fire."

"It's not the clubhouse, sir. But Arcadia's burning."

Every face in the room registered shock. Even Bobby felt a wave of portentous dread. But he also felt a fillip of excitement. Because the old cliché was true: *Every crisis is also an opportunity.*

"What do you mean?" Cash asked. "Like a kitchen fire?"

"No, sir. They think this fire will take down the whole mansion. It's mostly gone now."

Claude Buckman turned in his chair and gaped at the newcomer.

"You know what this means?" said Tommy Russo. "That claim by the so-called Bastard Sons of the Confederacy wasn't bullshit. It was real."

Arthur Pine shook his head slowly. "Someone has crossed the Rubicon, folks."

"It's a new world, all right," Bobby said, a strange smile on his lips. "Wow."

"I just don't believe it," said Buckman. "You really think Blacks around here have got the balls to burn down our mansions?"

"The arsonists may not be from here," Bobby pointed out. "But I think the answer is yes. It's a generational thing. The George Floyd protests changed everything. The whole world. And you haven't changed with it. That's why Doc Berry and those two progressive Black aldermen were able to whip you in a city election. You never saw them coming."

"If Blacks *are* behind these arsons," said Russo, "they're dumber than I thought they were."

"You're both right," Dixie said, her eyes twinkling with possibility. "The ground just shifted beneath our feet. And in our favor. This could trigger *exactly* the kind of outrage you could base your pivot on, Bobby. Mission Hill put us on the defensive. But these two arsons—and any that follow—will unite the white community regardless of petty differences."

All eyes turned to Bobby, but he gave them nothing. He was thinking about Tio Carrera, who had predicted all this only five days ago.

"Dixie's right," Pine said quietly. "As usual."

The old pageant queen preened under the approbation.

"I need to get back to Birdie," Bobby said, getting to his feet again. "I appreciate the faith y'all have shown in me. And I hope you'll think about joining my run for the White House."

"Oh, you can count on that," Buckman said, getting up and shaking Bobby's hand. "In fact, to show you what a good sport I am, I'll pledge you a million dollars of PAC money to start, right here and now." The banker grinned, pleased at having surprised Bobby. "That ought to help you sleep a little easier tonight."

Bobby squeezed the banker's soft hand. "Thank you, Claude."

"You mentioned the city elections, Bobby," Arthur Pine said in a more fraternal tone. "We should probably address that before you go. Fact is, we were surprised to have the Blacks take over the board. You see, Bienville has never quite been a democracy. We control the governing boards behind the scenes, and we make decisions based on enlightened self-interest. Our club has never hesitated to co-opt Black leaders or even to buy the Black vote outright, from the preachers. Though that's proven more difficult in recent years—"

"They all have big agendas now," muttered Tommy Russo.

"We knew Doc Berry had a chance," said Cash. "People love the old guy. He's a war hero, like you. But he won more than ninety percent of the vote! *That* surprised us. That means he got huge numbers of whites. And we weren't ready for that."

"Blame Penn Cage for that," Arthur Pine groused.

"Why?" Bobby asked, genuinely interested.

"Doc was still practicing medicine when he decided to run. His campaign was haphazard, his speeches disorganized and uninspiring. Penn convinced him that if he was serious about being mayor, he'd have to close his medical practice. So Doc retired. Then Penn started writing speeches for him, or editing them, and before you know it, Doc had a juggernaut going."

"Penn's no rookie," Bobby said. "He's ghostwritten speeches for some senators."

"Well, we could live with Doc alone, but when the Blacks flipped those other two seats," said Pine, "they got absolute control of the board. Which we cannot tolerate. It's already costing both us and the town."

"How's that?"

"There's a lot of vindictiveness. They've canceled long-standing contracts for insurance, engineering, and maintenance with companies we own, and awarded them to Black companies based thousands of miles away."

"They're sticking it to us," muttered Buckman. "They want their turn at the trough. Naturally."

"They're selectively reassessing properties owned by wealthy whites to beef up the city's revenues," Pine explained. "Then they route that money over to Bucktown on the north side, for massive drainage and recreation projects."

Bobby didn't comment. He knew the white-controlled board had spent as little as possible on the north side for unconscionable decades.

"Not to mention forcing their left-wing politics into education," said Dixie. "They want full-on CRT in the new public school, all that bullshit. The blue-collar white parents have been up in arms for months."

"I see. And what do you plan to do about all this?"

Buckman's sly smile appeared again. "We're going to re-balance the power dynamic on the board. It's well in hand. We only mention it now because I sense that these arsons may offer us the opportunity we've been waiting for, and since you're going to be in town all week . . . we don't want you blindsided by the media or anything."

Bobby didn't like the sound of this. "Exactly what are you planning to do?"

Buckman waved his hand. "You don't want to get into the weeds of all that."

"How on earth can you re-balance the board with its present racial makeup, and Doc Berry in the tiebreaking position?"

"We've got a Trojan horse on our side," Cash offered with a grin.

"And we're old hands at changing the minds of stubborn people," Donnelly said. "Especially idealists."

Bobby didn't feel reassured. "Just remember the blowback the Tennessee legislature got for expelling those two Black representatives. The two Justins."

Dixie chuckled. "Those Tennessee boys are about as subtle as a fleet of cement trucks. We know what lube is for, hon."

Bobby sighed heavily. "Just tell me this: Do you intend to remain fully within the law throughout this action of yours?"

Arthur Pine smiled. "Thanks to Senator John Stennis, God rest his soul, we've got the law on our side. Or very nearly so. A law tailor-made for just this purpose, local and private legislation drafted in 1972. It could only be valid in three counties, due to special city charters, and we're one of them."

Bobby didn't want to press the issue now. "I'm going to give Birdie a couple more twirls around the dance floor. Let me know if you learn anything else about these fires, but not via text. No digital record about any of this from now on. And don't take this conversation any wider in your club. I don't care if you've taken blood oaths."

"Understood," Dixie acknowledged. "This bunch knows how to be discreet."

Bobby knew his skepticism was showing.

"Go play with your firecracker," said Pine. "We're going to stay here and talk about Case Green."

"Case Green?"

"Weren't you a history major?" the attorney asked.

Bobby ransacked his memory. "The only Case Green I know about was the German plan to seize Czechoslovakia at the beginning of World War II. A false-flag operation."

Pine acknowledged this with a single nod. "You get a star from teacher."

Bobby was continually surprised by the stupidity of his nominal allies. "Arthur . . . you might not want to get into the habit of code-naming plans after Nazi actions."

Pine colored. "The comparison seemed apt at the time. I was watching the History Channel."

"We'll change the name," Buckman said easily. "Best of luck getting your petition names, Bobby. But something tells me you won't need it."

Bobby forced a smile, but he was thinking how he was going to have to spend a lot of hours in rooms like this over the next year, trying to wheedle contributions out of men and women he wouldn't normally spend five minutes with. That was why Charles Dufort was so important. When you had men like Dufort on your side, you didn't need to go begging.

CHAPTER 22

MARSHALL AND I stand like a pair of stoned teenagers before Arcadia, which now burns like a target beacon for an armada of bombers. Around us the crowd has entered a sort of muted, drunken awe, like a New York crowd at Manhattanhenge, feeling at one with the living specter of a massive fire.

"Why would a Black protest group do this?" Marshall asks the night. "There's no way this ends well for Black people."

I think about all I've learned working civil rights cold cases. About the descendants of people enslaved here, and the destructive fallout that poisoned the lives of the generations born after the actual crimes.

"Maybe they just don't give a damn anymore. Maybe to them it's worth the hell that's coming, to force white America to reconsider these places. This blood-drenched history that's held up to be admired."

Marshall tilts his head from side to side, not quite able to accept this. His phone pings, but after checking the screen he puts it back into his pocket. "I don't see local Blacks doing this, Penn. They may not be happy, but they're focused on incremental change. For the first time since Reconstruction they control the city board. And Doc isn't merely the mayor elected by Blacks and whites, but also the true leader of the Black community."

"He's still got enemies. More Black than white, to be honest."

"Reverend Doucy?" Marshall asks, his eyes still on the blaze. "Doucy's motivated by money and power. He's not going to risk all he's accumulated to this point to commit felonies like this. And I can't think of any other politically minded Blacks who would do this on their own hook."

Looking back at the publisher, I'm reminded of a tragic incident that led him into a recent conflict with the Reverend Willie Doucy. During last spring's high water, the river rose to the point that it threatened the Matheson Lumber mill below the bluff. As happens every two or three years, volunteers gathered to bolster the company's protective levee by adding a few extra feet of sandbags. As dusk fell on the second night, a barge rumbled past above the flood speed limit, sending a set of waves to batter the Matheson levee. Thirty seconds later, a portion of the earthen berm slid into the roiling current, taking two members of the Bienville High School football team with it.

While a dozen men gaped in horror, Marshall McEwan tore off his boots and leaped into the dark river. He'd been a champion swimmer in high school, but his older brother had drowned in the Mississippi at seventeen during an ill-advised dawn race, and despite being present, Marshall had proved unable to save him. The caving levee seemed to offer even less chance of success. In seconds Marshall was swept out of sight, and no one had seen the boys surface after the initial collapse. But twenty minutes later, the publisher staggered up the downstream bank carrying Kevin Matheson—the son of the company's owner—over his shoulder and alive.

Marshall's triumph triggered an astonished cheer, and word of his miraculous rescue began flashing across town through cell phones. But he quickly told the crowd of diggers that he'd never even seen the other boy in the water. As chance would have it, the other football player was Black. It also soon emerged that the missing boy did not know how to swim, and so might have sunk instantly. Marshall pointed out that even if the boy had managed to float for a while, a brown face or arm in that muddy river at dusk would have been nearly impossible to see.

Most of the town praised Marshall's act as selfless heroism. But Reverend Willie Doucy began spreading a rumor that the newspaper publisher had chosen to save the rich white boy—Matheson—over the Black kid who'd only been brought into their circle to play football. This accusation didn't get much traction, not even in the Black community, but the fact that the drowned boy had never learned to swim escaped no one. A city pool had been stalled in the planning stage for years, perpetuating a dangerous inequality that lingered from the Jim Crow era. Interestingly, it was Marshall McEwan, and not Reverend Doucy, who made completion of that project a personal mission. He not only led a private fundraising effort, beginning with the Bienville Poker Club, but also devoted dozens of columns of space in his newspaper to accomplishing the goal. As a result, the completed pool is scheduled to open in less than thirty days.

"Why burn Tranquility in Natchez?" Marshall asks, still watching the fire. "I understand Arcadia. The planter who built this place was a Confederate fire-eater, and he owned thousands of slaves. As a symbolic target, Arcadia's hard to beat. But Tranquility? Weren't the Duforts Unionists? Even supporters of Lincoln?"

"Maybe. But they still owned hundreds of slaves. And they owned a sugar plantation in South Louisiana. Those places were hell. I'm no expert on that period of history. Even though Natchez has close to a hundred antebellum homes, we never heard about the dark side of these houses growing up there. We'd go to parties in them, get married in them, but you never once thought about their actual pasts. I knew more history than most of my contemporaries—and I knew the Dufort family fairly well—but I never thought deeply about it until my thirties."

Marshall considers this. "Can you think of anything about Tranquility that would make it a target?"

Reflecting on the unique city in which I was raised, I hear Annie telling me that Mom suspected the Duforts might not have been the noble Unionists that our public history always painted them as.

"Natchez had a lot of Anglophilic planters who opposed secession. Many were born and raised in the North. But that was no guarantee of leniency with slaves. God only knows what horrors could have happened at Tranquility before the war. Or during it. The authors of that note on the Tupac album sound literate. They might know a lot of history we don't. Hell, they could be descended from people enslaved at Tranquility, like Ray is descended from a slave at Black Oak."

Marshall's head snaps toward me. "Is he really?"

"Damn straight. A hero, by any stretch of the definition. His ancestor, I mean. A slave named Doby."

This strikes a resonant note in Marshall. "We have to assume that ninety-five percent of the history of Bienville and Natchez was never recorded anywhere. But that doesn't mean it wasn't passed down orally among the Black community."

"I think my mother discovered that before she died. The Blacks around here passed down a lot of knowledge that was never written down, much less published."

Another rending crack splits the night, its echoes bouncing off Colfax House and reverberating back over the crowd. People scream, then gasp as half the Arcadia roof collapses into the square of columns that has supported it since the early 1800s. After an explosion of sparks and debris, two columns topple into the wrecked mass like the temple pillars in Cecil B. DeMille's *Samson and Delilah*. Only tonight Samson is out of the frame. *Who is he?* I ask the night. Is he a spiritual descendant of the actual Samson, enslaved by the Philistines, who means to bring down the old temples of white supremacy no matter what the consequences? Or is he a white extremist bent on triggering anti-Black rage? I feel a sense of inevitable tragedy, not from the loss of the structure, but because of what will soon be lost to this town. Not innocence, which is long gone, but the partially earned peace in which most present-day residents have believed that racial reconciliation is genuinely possible.

"Hey, look over there," I say, catching sight of a group of men walking between the big fence and the burning mansion. Half are uniformed deputies, but the rest appear to be civilians wearing tactical paramilitary equipment. "They look like Barlow militia guys to me." I suddenly spy Shot Barlow himself—the burly frame and thick black beard make him easy to spot—walking beside Sheriff Buck Tarlton.

Marshall nods. "What the hell are *they* doing back there?"

"You don't think Tarlton deputized them."

The publisher blinks in disbelief. "I'll bet he did."

As the militiamen disappear from sight, Marshall seems only marginally aware that I'm still here. Scanning the darkening property, I see no sign of Nadine, and a hollow ache in my chest manifests itself with surprising force. Unlike with the Natchez fire I watched thirty years ago, I have no desire to see what remains of Arcadia implode like some Southern Gothic House of Usher.

"I'm going to head home," I tell Marshall, still trying to banish visions of the one-legged homeless father who failed to escape this blazing nightmare.

"Nadine was right about your reputation," Marshall says, still watching the fire. "You're gonna get national reporters wanting comment on this. Are you open to that?"

"Don't want any part of it."

"You don't want to try to pour oil on the waters?"

He's right to ask. A media hurricane is about to hit this town. I'm like some nineteenth-century Cajun fisherman trying to hold it back by turning away from it. No matter what I do next, the great whirling disk will keep barreling toward us with all the destructive power of national obsession, destroying lives and property for however long it lasts, until the monster gets its fill or something worse happens elsewhere.

"I wouldn't know how," I say finally. "I've prayed we could avoid this kind of reckoning. One this violent, I mean. And I don't pray."

With strange solemnity, Marshall offers me his hand. "I think we're going to remember this night for the rest of our lives."

"I wish we had some whiskey. A drink before the war?"

The publisher smiles sadly. "Good luck to you, Penn."

"You too, buddy. Keep a close eye on Nadine, if you can. I think she's pretty upset."

His eyes glint, but I see no suspicion in them. "Will do."

I shake his hand, we part, and I walk slowly back to my car, the raucous, drunken revelry drowning out any expressions of communal loss amid the buildings that line Tensas Avenue. Within hours, the ignorance of the partiers behind me will turn to rage or fear depending upon each person's experience, education, and constitution. I wonder whether my father felt the same dread back in the 1960s, when the White Knights and United Klans began their ascendancy. Back then, the situation deteriorated until the governor had no choice but to order in the National Guard, which managed to halt the descent into chaos. But as traumatic as that era was, the destruction of Tranquility and Arcadia might bring worse. The South—even the nation—is already primed for an explosion. Memphis and Mission Hill saw to that. These arsons (and the bold note claiming them as justified actions) might provide the critical mass required for detonation. But what frightens me most is something less tangible. The common fealty to American ideals—a living principle that survived even the traumatic sixties and seventies—has withered to nothing during the brief span of years since my daughter left home for college. The social contract has frayed to a ragged relic, and no remedy seems sufficient to repair it.

Driving back toward the bluff, I feel depressingly sober. Confused fragments of Yeats and Arnold spin through my head, disjointed yet apocalyptic. Alarms of struggle and flight, the falcon deaf to the falconer. The best lacking all conviction, the worst being filled with passionate intensity. And of course, ignorant armies clashing by night. I remind myself that no one can help matters if they lack all conviction, but in truth, my tank is empty. The last two weeks have drained me. They ended with the death of my mother and the awakening of my own deadly affliction. I've never been prone to depression, but if that's not what I'm feeling now, then it must be utter exhaustion.

As I near Battery Row on the bluff, my phone pings with yet another text. This message is from Earl Bell, a friend at the Southern Poverty Law Center. Half an hour ago I called him to try to find out whether he'd ever heard of the Bastard Sons of the Confederacy, but I only got his voice mail. I left a message and told him he'd understand soon enough why I wanted to know. His texted reply reads:

Got your message. In case you don't know, that "Bastard Sons" claim note was published on Joseph Francis Farah's blog and website six minutes ago. Dan Bongino amplified it almost immediately, and he posted video. As for the "Bastard Sons of the Confederacy" name, I've found no record of any modern activist group with that appellation. If you really need to talk now, I will, but I'd prefer to wait until morning. I know you understand the danger of this escalation, but you'd better prepare for unprecedented scale. The right-wing hate groups and militia will go to a war footing after this. It will end in riots at a MINIMUM, and I don't look for your governor to de-escalate things. I'm praying for Mississippi tonight, Penn. Stay safe until tomorrow.

Shaken to have my worst fears confirmed by a man I deeply respect, I turn onto Battery Row and coast slowly along the broad avenue that lines the bluff where the Mission Hill protesters have been keeping vigil since Saturday. My town house stands just across from Confederate Park, with its memorial fountain and the famous seacoast guns that still command a long stretch of the river. A group of tents has been set up near those cannons, and I see Black families huddled around cookstoves to keep warm (since making wood fires on the bluff is illegal).

I can't wait to get my prosthetic off. After the overexertion at Arcadia, my stump throbs with every beat of my heart. It hasn't escaped me that Ray hasn't called with news of Doc waking from his coma. I should probably check social media to see what the wingnuts have posted about Arcadia, and how fast the story is metastasizing, but I don't need numbers to convince me of clear and present danger. Earl Bell understands what Marshall and I realized at Arcadia: today's arsons will begin an unstoppable train of events that no one will have the power to slow, much less stop or derail. If Doc can get back to Bienville, he might minimize the risk to some innocents, but Sheriff Tarlton will follow his own agenda, and ultimately the governor will dictate events.

That's the most frightening thing of all. The extremist Republicans have already shown us what they mean to do with the power they have left. In states like Mississippi (with Republican supermajorities in the legislature), they will ruthlessly destroy anyone they perceive as an enemy— democracy and public safety be damned. Given sufficient excuse, they will publicly embrace fascism and call it "law and order." And under that catchall, there's almost nothing they won't do. Their first step will likely be to suspend the rule of law in favor of "martial law," which in a single step would obliterate democracy at the local or even state level.

I've seen the fearsome visage of the beast slouching toward Bienville to be born. The American public only glimpsed it in the fevered mob of rioters who savagely beat cops on the steps of the U.S. Capitol. But tonight's fires will change that. A friend once told me that we're never more than seventy-two hours from Armageddon. He wasn't referring to nuclear war. Since 2016, we've all been living through a great unraveling of the America in which we came of age, and the final act of that process is not an empty stage littered with thread from a betrayed flag. It's the "blood-dimmed tide" that Yeats predicted a hundred years ago.

Only a few hours ago, I pondered the ten steps that could take us from normalcy to race war in twenty-four hours. I first identified them shortly after 9/11, when the Pentagon hired a group of writers to predict unconventional lines of attack by international terrorists. Unlike my fellow authors, I focused on internal danger, believing, as Lincoln did, that *"If destruction be our lot, we must ourselves be its author and finisher. As a nation of freemen, we must live through all time, or die by suicide."*

What disturbs me tonight is that my 2001 thought experiment was predicated on a simple police shooting gone wrong—like what happened in Memphis thirteen days ago. Today's arsons dwarf that familiar tragedy by orders of magnitude. More than half the nation will view Arcadia as domestic terrorism, similar to the Oklahoma City bombing. But Arcadia was no sterile federal building. It was a cultural symbol, whether publicly acknowledged as one or not. And I can't escape the feeling that sometime in the future, when historians debate which spark set off the war I've felt coming since 2016, it may well be the fire that destroyed Arcadia. In the end, I suppose it makes no difference. All that matters is that, after tonight, no one will be able to contain the most dangerous force in this country—

White panic.

CHAPTER 23

AT THE BELLE ROSE COUNTRY CLUB, Bobby had kept dancing despite Birdie Blake's hints that they leave together. But when the band broke into a dentist-office's version of a Bee Gees medley, he started devising an escape strategy. Just as he was about to try a solo exit, Dixie Donnelly tapped Birdie on the shoulder and said, "Sweetie, do you mind if I borrow him for one more song? I have some news."

"News?" Birdie echoed, looking irritated. "It's after work hours."

"I just need to put a bug in his ear."

Birdie nodded suspiciously. "Just make sure you confine your attentions to his ear."

Dixie laughed. "I can do a lot with an ear. But don't worry, this is business."

Birdie looked ready to sting the older woman, but Bobby gave her a little squeeze and said, "I won't be long. How about you grab us a vodka-tonic for the road?"

Birdie perked right up at the prospect of leaving together.

"Don't worry, hon," Dixie said to the younger woman. "You've got dibs."

The actress swept off toward the bar, sashaying like Vivien Leigh lost in a bipolar fantasy.

"That girl knows what she wants," Dixie said, sliding into Birdie's place and gliding around the floor with more practiced grace than the young actress possessed. Bobby noticed Dixie's perfume, too, which he didn't recognize but knew had cost a lot, the way his fingers knew expensive fabric.

"She may be disappointed," Bobby said.

"Cruel world," Dixie drawled with a wink. The slur in her voice told him she'd had at least a couple of drinks since he'd seen her upstairs.

"So what's your news?"

Dixie smiled to herself. "Hold on to that sculpted ass of yours, Bobby boy. The Bastard Sons just claimed the burning of Arcadia. In writing. They mentioned Tranquility in this note, too. They said both fires are retaliation for Mission Hill, as well as for some lynchings back during the Civil War."

Bobby couldn't hide the hitch in his step, or his excitement. "There was a physical note this time?"

Dixie nodded, a smile threatening to break out on her lips as well.

"Written on the inside of some old rap record cover. Or CD cover maybe, I don't know. There was also a hand-drawn picture of a Black fist with a broken manacle on it."

"I'm starting to believe there's a real Black group behind this."

"Let's pray you're right."

Bobby knew then that Dixie might be the cleverest person in the Poker Club, even if she'd only been brought in as a trophy wife.

"By the way," she went on, "the Arcadia fire also killed a homeless man who'd been squatting inside with his daughter. The girl got out, but the father died of smoke inhalation."

At this news Bobby went still. "Collateral damage. But that still makes it murder. Black or white victims?"

"White." Dixie clucked her tongue like a cashier ringing up a sale. "This is a gift from the political gods, Bobby. If you're ever going to pivot right, this is your moment. If you don't do it now, you never will."

He gave her nothing. "Has this hit the internet yet?"

"God, no. We just got it from Sheriff Tarlton. They're not telling anybody. We could have riots by midnight if they did."

Bobby's thoughts raced as he tried to assess the implications of all this. Then, to his consternation, through the faces whirling around him, the harried eyes and visage of Charlot Dufort appeared, vanished, and appeared again, tracking him as he led Dixie through the sweating sparkling bodies. Bobby shook his head to dispel the illusion, but once more the hauntingly familiar face flashed past. The whirring in his ears grew to a ringing whine.

"What is it?" Dixie asked. "Hey . . ." She touched his chin with her fingernail. "Did you see a ghost?"

"Sort of. I think Charlot Dufort's over there. I roomed with him at Ole Miss twenty years ago. I'm not sure what's going on in his life now, but he's been trying to reach me. He was a friend at one time, but . . . he sounds desperate."

"Oh, hell," Dixie said, obviously annoyed. "A year ago he was a sad story—now he's a walking disaster." She looked over a few heads, then between bodies. When she found what she was looking for, she nodded toward Charlot, who stood wobbling at the edge of the dance floor. Bobby drained his vodka as though to quench a thirst, then set his glass on a nearby trolley. Twenty seconds later, two burly men in suits took Charlot by the elbows and escorted him toward the clubhouse exit.

His heart pounding, Bobby spoke as casually as he could. "What's the story with Charlot now? Do you know him? Surely you must."

"Only from the club. Charlot was actually president of Belle Rose a few years ago. But if his father weren't who he is, the son wouldn't be allowed within a mile of this building now. How long since you were close to him?"

"Vanderbilt, fifteen years ago. I'd heard he was doing well as a lawyer."

"He was, actually. For a while. Sexual confusion's his problem. He married a girl from Crystal Springs, but that was just a cover. Years of painful melodrama at home. His daddy's a classic Southern homophobe. A few years back Charlot got into drugs, which eventually led to money trouble. Or maybe it was vice versa. Who knows these days? The story's so common. He started gambling to try to solve his money problems. Then he emptied clients' escrow accounts to pay his gambling debts. I think he even embezzled from his *partner's* clients. Charles finally cut him off. He's circling the drain, Bobby. Best not to think about it. And you certainly don't want to be seen talking to him."

"Man, I hate to hear that. He looks bad. Physically, I mean."

Dixie looked up into Bobby's eyes with surprising frankness. "Let's get back to the main subject. I have one question for you. How far are you willing to go to nail down those right-wing votes you need? Because so far you've spent your time and capital courting the Center—and, some might argue, the Left."

"If you'd been at my side in Afghanistan, you wouldn't have any doubts."

Dixie's laugh touched the border of patronizing. "That's boys with guns, sweetie. I'm talking about real blood sport. Who rules this country."

The glint in her eye told him she knew as much as he did about ruthless combat.

"We're on the same page," Bobby said. "But playing in that league takes more money than the Poker Club can raise. A lot more."

"On their own, maybe. But we have friends. Half a mile up the road is a man who can pay full freight from here to the White House."

Bobby thought about her words. "You mean Charlot's father?"

"That's right, hon. Charles Dufort is the original Big Daddy."

"Oh, I know that."

"I've got history with Charles if you'd like me to call him. Set up an introduction."

Bobby could imagine what kind of history Dixie Donnelly shared with Charles Dufort. "That's all right. I got to know him pretty well during high school. Took some golf lessons from his older son, the one who died like Payne Stewart. I know Charles well enough to call him."

"Then don't waste a day." With a saucy twinkle in her eye, Dixie said,

"Now I've got one question about that miracle arm of yours, before Birdie gets back."

"Why don't I wear a prosthetic?" That was what everyone asked him, once they got up the nerve.

"Oh, no. I meant the arm you have *left*. How are you at one-armed push-ups?"

The levity evaporated from her face, and he knew she'd have left the party with him then without a backward glance.

Bobby granted her a playful smile. "If one-armed push-ups were a sport, I could turn pro tomorrow."

She gave his upper arm a squeeze. "Oh, hell, there's Birdie, making her way back. You call me if you need a training partner while you're in town." She slipped a card into his front trouser pocket, and didn't remove her hand until she'd given his upper thigh a powerful squeeze. "And if Miss Fire-Crotch doesn't get the job done tonight, text me later."

Dixie broke away with a little wave to Birdie, vanishing before she had to endure another exchange with the younger woman.

The actress handed Bobby a sweating glass and slid into his arms as the band transitioned to "Ac-Cent-Tchu-Ate the Positive."

"Did the big-haired Mrs. Robinson make a play for you?" Birdie asked.

He laughed. "She puts it right up front, all right. I imagine Blake's too old to do his due diligence in the bedroom."

"For a gold digger, she made a good choice. I hear Donnelly's worth at least a hundred million, the old dinosaur. I can't believe he lets her run loose at these things."

"He's upstairs in the card room."

Birdie pursed her lips in thought. "You're not going to tell me what they wanted with you?"

"Not worth talking about."

"She tell you anything else about the Arcadia fire? Everybody in the bathroom's talking about it."

"No."

Birdie sighed in disappointment, then looked around at the flagging crowd. "Are we getting out of here or what?"

Since hearing about the Arcadia note, Bobby had hoped to leave alone again, but the prospect of running into Charlot Dufort outside didn't excite him. "Let's do it."

He took hold of her wrist and led her through the dancers. As they neared the door, Wyatt Cash appeared in their path. "Headed out, Bobby?"

"Afraid so. We're looking for a little privacy."

"Of course. But you'll be here for tomorrow's Golf Channel commentary, right?"

"Absolutely."

"You doing your radio show remotely from Bienville?"

"After these fires, I've gotten several requests to do early-morning drive-time interviews on some big shows. I might drive over to my Flowood studio, but I'll get back on time. Corey's got it worked out to the minute."

Wyatt gave Birdie an air kiss and spoke over his shoulder as he walked away. "Red State America would love to see Birdie Blake wearing Prime Shot!"

Birdie grinned, but before she'd taken four steps she said, "I wouldn't wipe my butt with his Malaysian-sweatshop crap. Get me out of here."

Thankfully, quite a few couples had chosen this time to make their exits, so Bobby led Birdie among them under the porte cochere. He'd hoped this would prevent any approach by Charlot, but it didn't. He saw the young Dufort angling in from some potted shrubs to his right. Mercifully, someone took Bobby's arm and leaned in to speak, and Charlot froze in his tracks. Bobby looked at the face that owned the hand on his arm: it was Tommy Russo, owner of the Sun King casino.

"I need a minute," Tommy said. "Can you spare it?"

"Love to," Bobby said with a grateful smile. "Birdie, rest on that bench for a second. I need to speak to Mr. Russo."

Birdie looked annoyed, but she seemed to respect Russo enough not to make a crack. Sitting on the bench, she took a cigarette and lighter from her purse.

Tommy led Bobby along the line of columns that fronted the plantation-style clubhouse and ducked behind one, out of public view. In the dim light of a sconce, his face looked alarmingly serious.

"What's up?" Bobby asked.

"Charlot Dufort," said the casino owner. "He says you and him go way back. Childhood buddies. That true?"

Bobby worked to keep his face impassive. "True enough. Why?"

"He's into me pretty deep, bro."

Bobby recalled what Dixie had told him. "Gambling debts?"

"What else?"

"Drugs, I hear. How bad is he into you?"

"Worse than most. Seven figures."

"How? Were you fronting him money to play?"

Russo shrugged. "You know who his daddy is. I figured he was a decent risk. Reputable attorney, good client list. But it turns out he's a doper. Bad.

As you obviously know. He's gonna lose his house, and he might even be disbarred. The thing is, this last week he tried to dig himself out of the hole with one bet, and he went to someone else to do it. He's so far underwater now he'll never get the money to pay me back. And now I hear his father and he are not only estranged, but practically mortal enemies."

"What does this have to do with me, Tommy?"

Russo turns up his hands like *Come on, man*. "If Charlot has the friends he says he has . . . that's the only reason he's still ambulatory."

There was no mistaking the meaning in Russo's words. "I see."

"Charlot says you'd never let him go down like that. Says you've been helping him to stay afloat for most of a year now."

Goddamn it, Bobby thought. "He's not lying about that. But we're talking small numbers. Sane numbers."

Exaggerated concern tightened Russo's brow. "Is he wrong to count on you as his white knight?"

Bobby felt cornered. He wasn't sure himself.

"I know this is a hassle for you," Russo went on, "given your present political reality. But I've let this go too long already. And if Charlot is shining me on about you . . . then his clock has run out."

"You know you're talking to an attorney, right?" Bobby said.

Russo's eyes twinkled. "I know exactly who I'm talking to."

Bobby was surprised by the casino owner's directness. "Look . . . don't do anything until I speak to him. Okay?"

"Easy enough. He's stalking you right now."

"Not tonight. I've got somewhere to be."

Russo grinned at last. "Yeah, I saw the fireball. I can always make an exception for pussy. But don't let tomorrow go by without getting back to me. Capisce?"

"I hear you, Tommy. Look . . . can you keep Charlot off me till I get out of here with Birdie?"

Russo chuckled. "You saw him see me, didn't you? He's probably a mile from the clubhouse by now, running hard." The casino owner slapped Bobby's back. "You enjoy yourself tonight, but get a little sleep. Tomorrow I want to see what kind of golf a one-armed man can play."

"I'll play you any day, buddy. A thousand bucks a hole?"

Russo laughed as Bobby walked back to the porte cochere and gave Birdie his arm, then led her to his Range Rover. Panning his eyes around the lot, Bobby saw that Russo was wrong. Charlot was *still* stalking him, this time from another stand of shrubs opposite the clubhouse. He looked wild-eyed, but he was also clearly watching for Russo or club security.

Bobby unlocked the Rover with his remote, then helped Birdie into the passenger seat. Charlot quickened his pace, then froze again. Bobby didn't look over his shoulder to see what had frightened his old friend. With a quick wave at Charlot, he climbed into the driver's seat and whisked the Rover away from the man he'd been paying extortion money to for ten months.

"What's the hurry all of a sudden?" Birdie asked. "Not that I'm complaining. We should have left that nursing home an hour ago."

"I saw somebody I didn't want to have to talk to."

"In that whole crowd, I only met three people I actually wanted to talk to."

"Where are we going?" Bobby asked.

Birdie pressed her dress flat and began massaging her thighs. "I don't care, so long as we can get horizontal. My feet are blasted, and my calves are cramping."

Bobby pointed the Rover down the long curving access road that led back to the highway. To the west, he saw the grand silhouette of Belle Rose, Charles Dufort's closest surviving antebellum estate. He was remembering the recent visit he and Corey had made there, but Birdie startled him by reaching over the console and running a fingernail from his knee up to his groin.

"Can I ask you a question?" she said softly.

"Sure."

She withdrew the nail, then ran its edge along his neck and jawline. "Why don't you wear a prosthetic arm? Seriously. Is it vanity?"

Bobby felt himself go cold inside, not with anger, only boredom. This was going to be heavier lifting than he'd thought.

CHAPTER 24

I DIDN'T MAKE it home from the Arcadia fire before my phone started ringing. The first call was from Jerry Mitchell, the Mississippi reporter who in 1994 helped convict Byron De La Beckwith for murdering Medgar Evers. Jerry already knew that two antebellum homes were burning in southwest Mississippi, and he'd somehow caught wind that a Black activist group might have claimed credit. I told him I couldn't confirm, but that he should stay after the Tenisaw County Sheriff's Department, because they might leak critical info at any moment and CNN was liable to be in town by morning.

Ten seconds after I clicked off with Jerry, Annie called back to remind me that I'd promised to update her. She gasped when I told her about the homeless man who died, and his orphaned daughter.

"I've never heard of any activist group called the Bastard Sons of the Confederacy," she said with the irritation of a veteran researcher. "Especially not a Black one. Wait, here's a rockabilly band called just the Bastard Sons, but they're white."

"That's not what we're looking for. Leave them to the FBI."

"Does that mean you're looking?" she asked hopefully.

"Figure of speech." I pressed the garage remote and turned into my short driveway, then waited for the door to rise.

"Wait, *wait*," Annie said. "Oh . . . never mind. This is an article about actual biological sons of Confederate veterans."

"Annie, we're not thinking clearly," I told her, pulling into the small cubicle. "At least I'm not."

"Why would you be? You lost your mother today."

"We both did, honestly."

"I know. But Dad, the world isn't going to wait until you and I feel better. Tourists from every continent have traveled to Natchez and Bienville since the Pilgrimage started in 1932. When this hits the news, they're all going to remember that. And because of your history with cold Klan murders, and your books, people are going to be looking to you for perspective, background, analysis."

Climbing out of the car, I slung Mom's heavy satchel over my shoulder and limped to the pantry door as my garage door closed behind me. "They can look elsewhere."

"You haven't heard from Doc yet, have you? Dad, you've got to hold the fort until he gets back from D.C."

"I forgot to tell you. Ray found him in a D.C. hospital."

"*What?*"

Pausing by my pantry door, I quickly summarized Doc's medical status. "I haven't told anyone yet. Until he regains consciousness, I'm honestly not sure what my next move should be."

"That's a no-brainer! Hold the city board together until Doc gets back, so the county doesn't drive the narrative for the next critical hours. The law-enforcement reaction is everything now."

The clarity of her assessment cut through the jumble swirling through my mind. "You're right. But I'm not the mayor pro tem. I'll start working the phones when I get upstairs."

"Pound some coffee! You don't have the luxury of avoiding this. Not even out of grief."

"I hear you." My door opened with a welcome click, and the smell of stored coffee hit me like a blessing.

"Well, you turned out to be right after all," Annie said. "I guess Mission Hill *is* going to lead to fighting in the streets."

QED. I closed my eyes and strained to hear my inner voice. "There may still be some chance to avoid that. I love you, punk. We'll talk tomorrow. Unless the balloon goes up tonight."

"What the hell does that expression really mean?"

"Google it. First World War."

She groaned in frustration. "Night, Dad."

"You're not going down to Arcadia to watch the fire, right? It's over."

"Several people are livestreaming it now anyway."

"Jesus wept. Good night."

Walking into the kitchen, I pour myself a tall Hendrick's and tonic, take a long swallow, then shift the strap of Mom's case on my shoulder and climb the stairs to the second floor of my town house. Moving through my bedroom, I open the door to my terrace, which overlooks the Bienville bluff and the Mississippi River.

The stink of Arcadia's destruction is strong even here, but I hope the west wind racing up the bluff will eventually drive it away. With a groan of relief I set Mom's satchel on the wrought-iron table and sit, taking the weight off my stump. Cell calls keep coming in every few seconds, but instead of handling them, as Annie advised, I put my phone on silent and leave the screen in view to make sure I don't miss a call from Ray or Doc. Then I lift my left foot onto the empty chair next to me to prevent blood from pooling in my reconstructed ankle. Trying to decode the white noise of competing thoughts and fears in my head, I watch a string of barges ply southward toward Baton Rouge and New Orleans, and sip my Hendrick's as medicinal therapy.

The Bienville bluff seems blessedly quiet, given all that's happened. From this elevation I can see another fifty or so protesters lying on the stone benches of the amphitheater a couple hundred yards to the north. But even as I wonder at the serenity of this edge of the city, the illusion of peace is shattered. First a jacked-up pickup tears along Battery Row, then another screeches out of one of the east-west running streets that open onto the avenue. Young men ride in the open truck beds, like my friends and I did as boys in the sixties and seventies. They're drinking beer and shouting, as we often did, but several are also brandishing rifles. I start to call 911, but no one has yet fired any rounds, so in the end I don't. The last thing I want to do is kick off a high-speed chase that ends up killing teenagers or cops. With luck the bedlam will die down on its own. If it doesn't, some of the Mission Hill mourners standing vigil on the bluff will surely report them, if they haven't already.

The Arcadia fire has triggered something in the town. A babel of music begins blaring as the trucks roar past, every heavy pulse putting me further on edge. It begins with modern country, the kind Tom Petty called "shitty rock music with a fiddle." The rest is "bro country," a hybrid that Steve Earle christened "hip-hop for people who are afraid of Black people." Then a new sound builds beneath the ersatz country: actual hip-hop that shakes the foundation of my building as it blasts from overpowered amps in the trunk of a low-slung ride making a slow pass up the Row. If I had the option, I'd drop a blanket over all of it and focus on the reassuring thrum of the big pushboats driving barges up and down the river. But not even that could dull my awareness that the vehicles running our streets right now carry weapons as well as people.

After more than seventy missed calls from various officials—including four out of six members of Bienville's board of aldermen—Doc Berry's name still hasn't appeared on my iPhone. I'm starting to worry. I fear for his health, of course, even his survival. But I'm also depressed that he's not huddled in a Senate office somewhere, laying the groundwork to authorize rapid federal intervention should our situation deteriorate. I doubt the White House will have time for him, given the larger crisis centered in Memphis—which is reported to be expanding—but surely the Congressional Black Caucus will do all they can to help him? Given what we're liable to be facing now, the African American Mayors Association isn't going to cut it.

As I sit here ignoring calls, the Tenisaw County sheriff, president, and board are undoubtedly making plans to exploit the arsons to their advantage. Until tonight, their goal was to minimize the fallout from Mission Hill. But today someone has given them two gifts that will keep on giving. Thanks to the white fear and fury that will result from the fires, the sheriff and his cronies can now be confident of escaping the blame for Mission Hill. They'll now enjoy the full support of Mississippi's governor and the GOP-controlled statehouse. That is bedrock fact: here in the Blackest state in the Union, nearly all meaningful power still rests with white men.

I've just about caved to the necessity to start calling aldermen back when Doc Berry finally telephones from Washington. His call is preceded by a text message from a number I don't recognize. It reads: *This is Doc. I'm about to call from a cash cell phone. Answer no matter what you're doing.*

After a deep breath, I gulp down the remnants of my gin, then answer Doc's call with "It's about goddamn time! I told you not to go up there. How are you doing?"

"My head's pounding like a bass drum in the Alcorn marching band." Doc's familiar baritone is only a sonic shadow of itself. "What the hell's going on down there? The whole city on fire?"

Doc is rattled, I can tell. "Who have you talked to? Ray?"

"I just got off the phone with him. *He* sounds scared to me, and it takes a lot to scare Ray Ransom."

"Tell me this, Doc. Did you get to do any good up there before you were attacked? Did you recruit any help for this kind of situation?"

"Man, I didn't even get to testify before the committee. I spoke to a few congressmen, and they gave me moral support—the equivalent of 'thoughts and prayers.' But Memphis is sucking up all the available oxygen. I've heard some demonstrators were caught trying to break into the Shiloh Military Park earlier tonight, hoping to pull down the Defeated Victory monument. That's where the media's focused, which means the politicians, too. Everybody's spooked, Penn. Everybody sees a big conflict coming between federal and state authority, and it's Memphis that's going to dictate the D.C. response."

"Even after the Arcadia fire?"

"They're only just beginning to process that here. And the claim of Black responsibility hasn't yet gone public."

"It's happening now. At least that's what Earl Bell told me. The right-wing internet's got it now. By morning they'll be calling for a second civil war."

Doc sighs heavily. "If we don't do just the right things, we could have one. You know that. You've predicted it."

"How soon do you think you can get back down here?"

"Shit. My doctors don't want me leaving this bed for forty-eight hours."

A cold wave of foreboding washes through me.

"One of those punks put the boots to my skull, Penn. If that Good Samaritan hadn't stepped in and shielded me, I wouldn't be here to tell you about it."

"That's what Ray told me. Listen . . . do you think that attack was random?"

He doesn't answer right away. "It almost had to be, didn't it? On the other hand . . . it was broad daylight in a station that was far from deserted."

"I'm worried, Doc. I wish to God you could get back tomorrow."

"Well, I've got my secretary checking flights. I'll get there by day after tomorrow for sure. I know that's not much help to you now."

"There's a lot of time for chaos to erupt between now and then."

Doc groans as though in pain. "Damn it, I forgot to call you about Peggy. I'm so sorry I wasn't there when she passed."

"You were here when it mattered. The hospice nurses you recommended were plenty good, and Mom was out of it by the time you left for D.C."

"That makes me feel a little less wretched."

"We'll have our own memorial someday. After whatever's coming. Now, I've only got one other question tonight. Do you believe, in your gut, that a Black activist group could really be behind these fires?"

When Doc answers, I hear the confident old physician, not a rattled pol. "I'm very reluctant to accept that, Penn. I've never heard of any Bastard Sons of the Confederacy. And nothing like this has happened anywhere else in this country. You know? Why here? Why now?"

"Mission Hill, obviously."

Doc curses under his breath. "That's what people will say. But to me this feels more like the kind of thing those boogaloos were doing during the George Floyd marches, to discredit Black Lives Matter and gin up riots. Like the Nazis dressing up as Polish troops and destroying their own radio stations at the outset of World War II. Black folks are angry, sure, but they don't want a war. Not a real one. We're not *fools*."

"But if this is a false-flag attack, why pick a name like 'The Bastard Sons of the Confederacy'? Why not just sign the note 'Black Lives Matter'?"

"BLM was in the note, according to Ray. And it won't matter anyway. Not to the average white person. We're going to see panic and rage like we haven't seen for decades. I hate that the right-wing media got hold of the story first."

"I think Jerry Mitchell got wind of it before they did, so there's some hope."

"I hope they have Jerry on the major networks tomorrow. God help us . . . we're going to need curfews, probably even the National Guard."

"The governor will likely have the Guard deployed before noon tomorrow. Buys him points with his base. The law-and-order man."

"I'm going to form a task force tomorrow, Penn, even if I'm stuck here. And you're gonna be in charge of it."

"Doc—"

"Don't even *try* to beg off. I know you've already given me more years than you promised, but this is a special case. Vivian Paine will fight me, since she's the mayor pro tem, but you've got the experience for this kind of crisis. And I'm still the mayor, goddamn it."

"I'll serve on your task force, Ezra. But I won't run it. That's your job."

"We'll see. Lord, I feel whipped. I'm leaving this phone on, and the nurses will make sure I get the message if you call while I'm asleep."

"You get well, boss."

"I mean to."

As I set my phone on the table, despair blows through my chest like a winter wind. The number of people standing vigil on the bluff has grown appreciably during my time up here. I see cars pulling into the city amphitheater parking lot up the bluff. Whatever's going to happen next has already started. I hope those people don't remain in that parking lot overnight. By tomorrow Battery Row is likely to be closed to all traffic.

Feeling humanity swelling and moving around me in the dark, I realize the futility of hope for any quick resolution. For there is no ready source of aid. Who can come? What meaningful help can they bring? The fault lines that underlie this civic breach are vast and deep. As a boy growing up on this river, I should have known what they fed me at school was tripe. Just outside my town was born Richard Wright, the original Black Boy. (No one told me that, of course.) I was raised in a little tract house one mile from the site of the second-largest slave market in the South, where not even a sign stood to mark the place. Yet all around me, Greek Revival mansions built by cotton barons were toured like a Dixie Disneyland, with enraptured blue-hairs writing endless articles about the wonderful azaleas and the "happy darkies" working there. Slaves actually built the mansions that sustained my town, yet scarcely a trace of them or the "peculiar institution" seemed to exist.

Here in the land of Faulkner, I walked to my clean little school, filled with only white faces until I turned nine, and learned the comic book tale of the founding of America: intrepid Columbus followed by the scrubbed-clean Pilgrims in their sturdy *Mayflower*, who landed at Plymouth Rock carrying God's Word with the Purest Intentions, who shared Tom Turkey with Squanto and then Settled the West according to the Divinely Inspired law of Manifest Destiny, Christianizing the Wayward Heathen as they went. Hollywood helped me along this simpleminded path, with formulaic westerns that left no doubt about heroes and villains, or the symbolism of white versus red, white versus Black, or white versus any other color.

But even in the fog of that controlled culture—in the coddling arms of Papa Walt Disney and the United Daughters of the Confederacy—I wasn't physically blind. I lived in Mississippi, ground zero for what would soon become known as the Movement. And slowly I came to realize that the slavery I had always wondered about, the evidence of this great historic crime that people had begun to murmur about—and then speak openly, bitterly about—was all around me. All I had to do was look. Half the people in my town were Black. They lived among us, yet apart. They reared us, fed us, bathed us, taught us. And all the while, they performed their great trick of survival, which was to be simultaneously visible and invisible. Present but nonthreatening. And yet . . .

One unguarded look by either party could reveal so much.

I almost can't bear to think about it now. I know the faces of people doing all they can to make do without in a land of plenty. People trying to find good work where none is on offer, at least not to them. People trying to overcome being ignorant and uneducated, while knowing it was government policy to keep them so. I know the faces of mothers who would have given everything to be with their children, but who raised the children of others so as to be able to feed their own. A woman like that helped to raise me. And if I'm right about something I will never know for sure, the greatest tragedy of all this is that in spite of these pressures, Ruby Flowers gave unselfishly of herself to me all her life, and I tried to do the same in return. I learned that from my parents, in their treatment of Ruby. And there I find some cause for hope. For it is that capacity that just might save us in the coming days, if anything can. The capacity of human beings to rise above the worst in the world around them, and even in themselves.

I can't see the faces of the Black people camping in Confederate Memorial Park tonight. But I know this: they are the descendants of enslaved

Mississippians. We are well into the twenty-first century, and they're standing vigil over dead and wounded children. After the Arcadia fire, I can't imagine what is likely to be hurled at them. All the sound and fury of a white nation coming to grips with the realization that the comic book myth the world allowed it to believe about itself is finished, and that a new national self-image must take its place. With that new image must come a new nation, one that lives up to its founding philosophy. And I know only one thing about the birth of nations: they don't happen quietly, under anesthesia. Nations are born—or reborn—in blood and fire.

My phone pings again. This time the text is from Robert Gaines, one of the young progressive Black aldermen. The message reads: *I'm told Sheriff Tarlton is meeting with the county board right now. The county attorney is with them, and they have a quorum. I don't know what kind of moves they're discussing, but it won't be good. You're the city attorney, Penn. What do we do? We need Doc, but Ray tells me he won't be back for two days at the earliest. That QAnon bitch Vivian Paine is mayor pro tem, so . . . what the hell do we do?*

I wish Gaines would remember that his texts are legally a matter of public record. The same law that could implicate Sheriff Tarlton for misconduct at Mission Hill could reveal every word Gaines texts about Vivian Paine and her fellow fanatics.

Before another thought can enter my head, the red dually pickup that threatened Annie and me this afternoon comes blasting along Battery Row, stirring the mourners in the little tent city to their feet. I'm cursing the Barlow group's rudeness when someone standing in the bed rips off thirty rounds of .223. Orange and blue flames spurt from the barrel of the offending rifle, mercifully revealing the direction of fire, which is skyward. Screams of terror and panic echo across the Row, and I see at least twenty people jamming cell phones to their ears to call 911. I do the same, but not to call an overwhelmed dispatcher. Watching the big pickup tear away—the chrome-plated balls hanging from its hitch confirming it's the Barlow truck—I call the number Doc Berry called me from. Thankfully, he answers himself.

"Who is this?" he asks.

"It's Penn, Doc. Thank God you're still awake."

"I was just about to drift off. But I was on the phone with Reverend Baldwin, who's down on the bluff, and I heard gunfire."

"Some idiot just ripped off a whole AR clip at the clouds. We've got no time cushion to work with, Doc. We need you back here *yesterday*. The sheriff's meeting with the county board as we speak."

"Damn it! I told you: they've been itching to use that Stennis Institute statute to try to merge the city into the county, effectively dissolving the city government. This is their chance."

I don't share Doc's anxiety over this unlikely scenario, but I don't want to wait two days in the political vacuum that will exist until he returns. "What if I told you I'll send a private jet up there to pick you up and bring you home?"

He doesn't answer for several seconds. Then he says, "I'd say praise the Lord, son. You feeling rich?"

"Weren't you telling me two days ago that you could think of a lot of good uses for the Dunphy judgment money?"

"You haven't got that money yet. And these doctors up here aren't gonna want to let me go. I guess I could sign myself out against medical advice, but . . . I can't pretend there's no risk."

"What if I put a doctor on the plane to fly back with you? You get in trouble, they can land and get you to an ER."

"How the hell you gonna do that? Your daddy would have come for me, but Tom's been dead for a dog's age now."

"One of his partners, Drew Elliot, owes me a favor for keeping him out of jail. He'll come get you if I ask him to."

"Well . . . if Drew will do that, then I'll check myself out."

This promise is the first news in hours to lift my heart. "Get what rest you can, Doc. You're going to have to project strength when you get here. Act like you've got half of Congress behind you. Like we're at the top of the call list at the Russell and Dirksen buildings. The White House, too."

"Who should I call first? Our folks? Or the opposition?"

"Neither. Call Marshall McEwan. Don't let Sheriff Tarlton or the county president control the narrative. Make a statement that you're in transit home and you'll be announcing a task force first thing in the morning. From city hall."

"I'll do that right now. And send that jet on. I want coffee on your terrace tomorrow morning with Ray. The way we did it during the campaign."

"Campaign headquarters," I say softly, pleased to focus on good memories. Memories of victory. "We kicked ass then, didn't we? But this is a different kind of battle coming."

"We can handle it."

"I'll have my daughter take care of all the arrangements for the flight—car service, all that. Annie will get you everything you need."

"For the first time tonight, I feel a little better."

"Don't lose your perspective, Doc. That jet's just bringing you to the eye of the storm faster."

He chuckles. "I've ridden out some storms in my time."

"I know. I'll see you soon."

As I text Annie my intentions, the flashing blue lights of two police cars hit me. They're pulling up before Confederate Memorial Park to check the reports of shots fired.

THANK GOD! Annie texts me back. *I'll handle everything. But will Drew really fly up there in the middle of the night?*

Her question triggers an epiphany. After replying *Hold on*, I speed-dial Dwight Ford, the doctor who flew me downriver from Vicksburg earlier today. Dwight answers in a resentful voice, like a man angry to be pulled away from a ball game, or maybe more intimate recreation.

"Dwight, are you in Dominica, like you said you'd be? Or are you still in the U.S.?"

"Man, I'm still in *Bienville*. We're scheduled to fly out tomorrow morning. But we should have left today. A patient just called and told me somebody fired an assault rifle down on the bluff."

"I saw it happen. But if that's what you're thinking, you won't like the reason I called you."

"Oh, shit. What now?"

I give him a quick summary of Doc's situation—during which Dwight does nothing but groan at the appropriate points. Then I explain my plan of an airborne medical relief mission to D.C.

"That's some damn concierge care you're asking for," he mutters. "A lot different than that little river hop we made today."

"It's not for me, Dwight. It's for Doc. And your adopted hometown."

The radiation oncologist snorts with something like contempt, and my heart sinks. But then he says, "Hell . . . I guess we'll be as safe on a private jet as we would be in the Caribbean. Nona was a nurse before she turned to teaching Pilates, you know."

My pulse begins to pound. "Are you serious? You'll do it?"

"Shit. You know I can't leave Doc hanging. That man was fighting the 'Cong and pumping plasma into marines when I was still wetting diapers."

A surge of emotion goes through me. "Thank you, Dwight! Annie's going to set everything up. How early can you fly?"

"How quick can you charter the jet? Lemme talk to Cheryl. Tell Annie to call me in ten minutes. I've got reservations to cancel."

"Expect her call!"

This time, after I set down the phone, my heartbeat has slowed a little. And as much as I feel duty bound to stay up and do what I can to prevent further violence, I simply don't have the energy.

As I rise stiffly to go to bed, I hear a muffled knocking from inside the town house. My thoughts go to the pistol in my bedside table, but before I can get it, my iPhone lights up with a text message. The Sender field reads *Nadine Sullivan* yet again. When I touch the message, I see these words:

I saw you sitting on your terrace. This was a shitty night and it's been a long time. You want to talk for a minute?

CHAPTER 25

BOBBY WHITE AND Shot Barlow stood together in a recessed pit surrounding the circular hatchway that led down to the Tenisaw Rifles' underground bunker complex. Bobby crouched to remain out of sight of the men gathered around the campfires about fifty meters east.

"You stink," Bobby said.

The black-bearded militia leader laughed. "I was in the middle of that fire at the end. You should have seen it. Talk about some good propaganda film."

"I'm not sure about going down here. I've been awake since four a.m., and I still have a lot to do tonight. I only have one question for you, and I can ask it right here."

"You'll be a lot less exposed in the bunker. And seeing the kid I told you about won't take more than ten minutes. Did anybody see you pull up?"

"I don't think so. But my Range Rover doesn't exactly fit the rest of your motor pool."

Barlow chuckled. "Agreed. There's nobody below right now, though. Let's get down-hatch."

Barlow bent over the wheel and rotated it, a task that flexed his bulging forearms. A belch of positive pressure sounded when the hatch's seal broke, and then the two men went down the ladder: Bobby first, with the practiced ease of an operator accustomed to fast-roping out of choppers; then Barlow, more slowly, as befitted his age and girth.

The interior of the bunker complex reminded Bobby of hooches he'd crashed in, only the décor suggested a neo-Confederate unit rather than the U.S. Army of the twenty-first century. Also, the walls were concrete rather than plywood, with the eternal odor of mildew. Barlow's end-of-the-world sanctuary had the stunted-puberty stink of a junior-college men's athletic dorm.

Barlow squeezed past Bobby in the first bunker and moved down the tight corridor like an oversize submariner. Three compartments along, he indicated a stool, and Bobby sat with his back against a heavily stocked shelf of provisions.

"So what's your question?" Barlow asked, squatting on a stool facing him.

"Did you or any of your men have anything to do with these fires today? Tranquility or Arcadia?"

Barlow looked incredulous. "Are you serious? Hell, no! I wish we had. Now that I see how it's triggered everybody. Shit, this town's gonna be at war within forty-eight hours. Maybe half that."

Bobby wasn't convinced. "Don't bullshit me, Shot. A lot's going to be riding on what happens over the next couple of days. I need to know if you came up with that Bastard Sons of the Confederacy crap."

"Hey, you're out of line. I told you, *we didn't do it.*"

"I also know you've got some kind of grudge against the Cage family. You have some long-running feud, you've hassled his mother and that Black guy he's paying to make a slavery museum out of Pencarrow Plantation across the road."

Barlow laughed. "The temple of white guilt, you mean?"

"Whatever you call it. I need you to stand down for a while, unless we agree on a mission that'll further both our goals. I don't want you trying to take petty revenge on Cage while I'm playing high-stakes chess here this week."

A malicious light began to glow in Barlow's eyes. Bobby feared he had guessed right. But the first words out of Barlow's mouth were a strong denial.

"Listen, when I heard about Tranquility, we rode out there to see for ourselves. And I'll admit it: I was sorely tempted to go out and do some copycat ops, once I saw how freaked everybody was. Man, I've got a guy in my group that I damn near had to chain down to stop. But *we didn't do nothing.* Hell, Charles Dufort himself showed up at Tranquility and practically ran us off."

"The old man?"

"Him and that fine-ass daughter of his, and his maid. Oh, and that African motherfucker who drives Dufort around. The Leopard Man."

"Leopard Man?" Bobby echoed.

"Yeah. Name's *Amadoo*, or something like that."

"Why do you call him a Leopard Man?"

"He told a yardman I know he used to be one. Part of some secret society in one of them African countries. Liberia? Nigeria?"

"Sierra Leone," said Bobby. "That's where the Leopard Society began. But it's a real thing. They carried out a campaign of anti–Colonial protest actions. Lethal."

"I figured it was something like that. I'm not the jumpy type, but that spooky sumbitch is as quiet as a cigar-store Indian. Gives off a vibe like he could cut out your guts as easy as say hello to you."

"He probably could. The Leopard Society wore leopard skins and carried claws and teeth during missions. They used them to simulate leopard attacks whenever they murdered an official."

Barlow was staring intently at Bobby. "I heard they were cannibals. Any truth to that?"

Bobby nodded. "They practiced ritual cannibalism. Ingested parts of their victims when celebrating successful attacks. I don't know how Dufort hooked up with a guy like that. I've read all that faded out in the mid-twentieth century."

"Maybe that's why that spearchucker needed a job," Barlow suggested with a snort of laughter.

Barlow pulled open a dorm-room refrigerator and popped the top on a Schaefer, sucked down half the can, then used his sleeve to wipe the foam off his beard. "There's something really different about that Dufort, man. I ain't scared of much, but that old bastard . . . he's like an apex predator, you know? Like we're wolves on the ice cap, but he's a fuckin' polar bear. Him having that leopard guy driving him around makes perfect sense to me."

With a grunt of satisfaction, Barlow took out a tin of Skoal and tucked a pinch under his bottom lip. While he did, Bobby surveyed the space he was in for the first time. Rebel flags from different Confederate regiments had been taped to the walls, and a Charlie Daniels Band poster from the seventies declared: THE SOUTH'S GONNA DO IT AGAIN! A glossy ad torn from a 1977 magazine touted the Harley-Davidson Confederate Edition motorcycle. Mixed in with this memorabilia were much older talismans: Civil War pistols and bayonets mounted on the walls and lying in cubbies. And loose on almost every surface were ultramodern handguns and high-tech accessories for assault rifles. No question these men were deadly serious about their intentions. Bobby heard from guys like this now and then on his show, when they managed to slip through Corey's call-screening protocol.

"Oh, I saw Penn Cage out at Tranquility, too," Barlow announced. "That libtard son of a bitch."

Bobby sat up straight. "What the hell was he doing out there?"

Barlow shrugged. "Who knows? Poking around, I guess. But he got in the Rolls with Dufort for a while."

Bobby shook his head in confusion. "Is that all you know?"

"Uh-huh. And I almost missed that. If I remember right, didn't Cage used to screw that daughter of Dufort's? For a while anyway?"

If this was true, Bobby hadn't known about it. "He doesn't seem like her type to me. Or vice versa. Penn likes the wholesome type."

"Apparently not all the time." Barlow leered as though Bobby ought to get his meaning easily enough.

Bobby looked into his host's eyes again. "I've asked what I came to ask, Shot. You said you wanted me to talk to this kid of yours. Evaluate him. Do you really think it's worth the risk to me?"

Barlow nodded soberly. "I don't believe in ESP. But every instinct I have tells me this kid is headed toward some kind of large-scale lone-wolf action. And he ain't exactly a kid."

"Who the hell is he?"

"Donahue Kilmer. Goes by Donny. Got a complicated history. His people lived in Pennsylvania before the Civil War, but they split over a contested will. Half the extended family moved down to Mississippi, but Donny's half stayed up north, working in an iron foundry. Didn't even enlist for the Union, most of 'em. The Southern half fought, of course. One died during Pickett's Charge at Gettysburg, not sixty miles from where he'd been born."

"Damn."

Barlow's teeth showed yellow in his beard. "Ain't history something? For example, Donny didn't move down here till 1991, yet he's got more true Southern feelin' than guys I know whose people been here eight, nine generations. That's what this Trump thing has done, man—shown that the true white tribe's got nothing to do with geography. Not really. It's a blood thing. Always has been."

"If this kid makes you nervous, Shot, just what kind of action is he contemplating? Driving a car through a crowd of marchers or something?"

"Well . . . he might do something like that, if the law was chasing him. But he's more the mass-shooter type. Like Vegas. Or maybe an IED op or something, you know? Like the Boston Marathon. I'm talking *scale*, Bobby. This kid wouldn't lose a minute's sleep if he killed five hundred people."

This frank assessment intrigued Bobby. "I see. He's talked about doing stuff like that?"

"All the goddamn time! He lines out plans when he's drunk, and you can tell he's given it a lot of thought. It's all logistics. Talks about how easy this or that would be, or how the niggers are always askin' for it. You want to see somebody lose his shit? Turn on MSNBC with all the colored commentators they got on there. Hell, sometimes I can't believe Al Sharpton's still alive. When the Ferguson marches were going on, Donny started getting obsessed. And when the George Floyd stuff went down . . . that sent him right over the top. I thought he was gonna drive to D.C. or Atlanta and do something major for sure."

"But he didn't?"

"Mostly because I kept him busy 'round here, working on the bunkers and such. He's a good welder, good at most everything, really. He spent a lot of years working the oil fields before the last contraction. Self-starter type. And he's gettin' to the end of his rope. Obsessed with conspiracy theories. Nothing unique about that these days, of course. Difference is, he's got the skills to succeed where others would fail. If he decides to act, nothing's gonna stop him. He's got *no* fear. And with the next election coming, he's gettin' high-strung. But with a guy like you? A vet he feels hero worship for? You might be able to channel him into something useful, or even critical, when H-hour comes."

As Barlow expounded, Bobby felt a sense of rightness to his presence here. As though he'd been brought here for a purpose, and that purpose was to meet Donny Kilmer. He wouldn't know until he'd seen the kid up close, of course. Coming out to Barlow's place had been risky, but after years of being sealed up in his studio, insulated by a phone desk and a delay circuit, he needed to get a look at a sample of those millions who seethed with anger day and night, and tuned to his voice like a beacon in the darkness.

"Bring him down, then," Bobby decided. "No phone, no camera, no recorder. Nothing."

Barlow got up with an arthritic creak of his knees. "Understood."

WHEN BARLOW BROUGHT Donny Kilmer down the ladder, Bobby White saw a walking stereotype from his youth. A rail-thin creature of sinew and bone, Kilmer had the pasty skin of the Appalachian hillbilly, but one whose people had headed south to the Louisiana oil fields in their quest for higher hourly wages. Though in his thirties, Kilmer still had acne that made him look like a teenager. And while "the kid" probably had only the barest formal education, his pale blue eyes hinted at a native cleverness that would make him a dangerous petty criminal, and a survivor in prison. In this militia outfit whose members favored 5.11 Tactical and Prime Shot Outfitters gear, he wore ripped Levi's and a stained Ted Nugent concert T-shirt.

Barlow made the introduction, then moved off to a distant part of the bunker complex. Bobby was only six or seven years older than Kilmer, but he felt twenty years ahead of him on the maturity curve. The kid spoke mostly in a monotone, his reedy voice rising and falling in amplitude depending on his intensity level. He made only occasional eye contact, staring into the middle distance in the close air of the bunker. When he did, Bobby sensed the heat of a long-banked fire, stoked by traumas he couldn't even begin to guess at.

"I'm not going to waste your time, Sergeant," Kilmer began. "I know you got a lot going on. I just want to say I admire everything you done over there, kickin' ass like you did, even after they shot your arm off. I read them books you wrote about the Civil War, and philosophy, too, and I can't say I agree with it all. But I ain't much of a reader. To me, what a man does matters more than what he says. In fact, I got a feeling maybe you been playin' people along, so that when you finally make your move, you'll take 'em off balance."

Bobby saw a flicker of admiration in his eyes. "Could be," he said, as though Kilmer had made a prescient guess. "How about you tell me a little about yourself? Maybe where you see yourself fitting into what's coming at us now."

Donny continued without hesitation. "Shit, I'm just a hand from a family of roughnecks. I'm a derrick man, 'cause I got no fear of heights, see? Past coupla years I been working for Mr. Barlow. But I don't like the way the country's been goin'. And I mean to do somethin' about it when I can."

Bobby was thankful for the kid's brevity. He'd expected a flood of oral diarrhea, all too common among the callers on his radio show. When Bobby leaned close, he caught a musty smell coming from the stringy white flesh under the Ted Nugent T-shirt, but he forced himself not to pull away.

"Shot tells me you've got some ideas. Solo plans. How about you give me a clue as to what those might be? Then I'll decide if I can make use of you going forward."

Kilmer hesitated only moments. "I want to be clear about one thing, okay? So you don't think I'm crazy. I understand that Mr. Trump is the most important historical figure born in this century, at least since World War II. I get that. But things didn't go right at the end of his term—thanks to the dumbasses running that Capitol assault. Those Oath Keepers, man . . . what a pack of pussies. So, now the timing of everything is messed up. All these Soros-driven prosecutions . . . the odds are really stacking up against him. I'm also worried Mr. Trump's got some kind of medical issue going on, either naturally or because the people around him have sabotaged him some way. That's why when I heard you turn away from him after January 6, I hung with you. I figured you must have seen it too. That diaper, man . . . it gives me the willies. Nothing against old folks, you know. But we're talking about the commander in chief. You think George Washington was wearing a diaper when he crossed the goddamn Delaware?"

"Not likely." *But Roosevelt was in a wheelchair when he won World War II.* Bobby gestured with his hand, encouraging the kid to go on.

"My original plan was just to make the most dramatic mass-casualty attack I could. Just hit the enemy hard and make my statement. Bigger than the Vegas shooting, I'm talkin'. But then I got to thinking . . . how many people really care if a bunch of niggers get killed all at once? SWAT eventually nails you, and ten days later it's all forgotten. Right? But *targeted attacks*. I mean, if I traveled up through Atlanta and D.C. and New York, slowly taking out the people who most deserve it? That would shake up the whole country. I got an album of targets here on my phone. Nothing suspicious. Just photos I've taken of my TV screen, when certain people expose themselves for what they are."

"Mind if I take a look?" Bobby held out his hand.

"Nah. Look all you want." Donny took out an Android phone and called up a photo album, then laid it in Bobby's callused palm.

Scrolling right-to-left with phenomenal dexterity, Bobby watched a gallery of familiar faces flash past: *Nancy Pelosi, Bennie Thompson, Fani Willis, Chuck Schumer, Al Sharpton, Maxine Waters, Alvin Bragg . . . David Hogg, Cecile Richards, Maya Wiley . . . Caitlyn Jenner, Michael Cohen, Rachel Maddow, Chokwe Lumumba . . . Eric Swalwell, Jack Smith, Jamie Raskin, Stacey Abrams, Tim Miller, Liz Cheney, Justin Pearson, Adam Schiff—*

"Long list," Bobby observed.

Donny nodded but said nothing. Bobby wondered how long these faces had been marinating in the kid's head. Kilmer certainly didn't lack for ambition. And was such a target list as unrealistic as it seemed? The D.C. sniper had avoided capture for a month back in 2002. Given "permission" to carry on a private war, a resourceful roughneck like Donny Kilmer might take out a third of these people before the FBI stopped him. Excepting the president and VP, almost no U.S. officials had adequate security protection. It might be like January 6. Until that day, most Americans had assumed the Capitol was heavily protected by an invisible but impenetrable ring of U.S. security forces and high-tech weapons systems. It had stunned the nation to watch a bunch of yahoos break into the seat of government without advanced technology and smear shit on the walls like a bunch of juvie escapees.

"I've also been thinkin' about a truck bomb for one of these trials," Kilmer added. "Just take the whole goddamn building down, you know? That's how you teach people a lesson. Tim McVeigh style."

"No doubt." *Nothing like wiping out a day care for toddlers—*

"The thing is," Kilmer went on, "this Trump situation has changed my mind about a lot of stuff. I been thinkin' that, if there's a candidate like you in the race, and if Mr. Trump is attacking you—you know, even from jail—then in one stroke I could do something that could put you right on top. I mean guarantee a win."

"What's that?" Bobby asked, more than a little intrigued.

"Take him out," Donny said flatly, his eyes suddenly locked onto Bobby's. "Make a martyr of him. At that point all his voters would be like . . . *free agents*. You could grab up as many as you could bring to your side, like scoopin' up fish after dropping dynamite in a pond."

Donny's pale blue irises burned with his vision of the future. "What you think, Sergeant?"

Bobby's ears were ringing. He'd come down this hole to peer into the hot forge where the limitless anger he'd heard so often was born. But what he'd found was something different. He sensed, in fact, that without any intent whatsoever, he might have stumbled into the presence of his life's destiny, or at least the mechanism of attaining it. He did not know how or why, but rather than turn away, Bobby leaned back against the damp bunker wall, took a couple of breaths, and let his instinct guide him.

"Donny . . . I'm gobsmacked, son. That's some serious strategic planning. But it's also a high-risk mission. One you're unlikely to survive. All former presidents have Secret Service protection, you know."

Kilmer dismissed this with a wave of his hand. "I don't care about that. I been waitin' my whole life for somethin' like this. I'm a soldier. I'll make whatever sacrifice is required."

While Bobby stared, deep in thought, Donny began to rock back and forth on his stool, unable to contain his nervous energy. Men like Donny existed all over the world, men who would throw away their futures— even life itself—for a fever dream. And this one had come under Bobby's influence at the precise moment when Bobby could exploit his obsession to the fullest possible benefit.

"So what you think I should do?" Donny asked. "Just say the word, Sergeant. Mass attack? Targeted hit? Or the Man himself—"

"First," Bobby interjected, "don't breathe a word of this to *anybody*. Not even Barlow. I'm gonna give you a burner phone before I leave. Don't use it to speak to anyone else." Bobby leaned even closer, so that they were nearly nose to nose. "I'm going to let you in on something, Donny. While I admire the scale of your vision, you're not the only operator considering big moves like that. Other groups with far more money and logistical resources are working on it. You'd be much more effective here on your native ground, where things are already starting to break down into open conflict. And I've got something cooking that you might be perfect for. Yes, sir."

Before Donny could vent his disappointment, Bobby stood and squeezed him on the shoulder. "I'm going to tell Shot I think you're in fine shape."

Donny ducked his head like a proud puppy. "I 'preciate that."

"Meanwhile, I'd like you to do something for me. Civil order's going to break down quickly in the wake of these fires. What nobody can know is how fast it will happen. I'd like you to go down to the bluff tonight and keep an eye on things for me. Till, oh, four a.m. If things get too far out of control, call me on the burner. If I don't hear from you, I'll call you about four and give you instructions for tomorrow. That sit all right with you?"

"Yes, sir. Absolutely."

"Just promise you won't make any sort of attack without clearing it with me first. We're playing chess, not checkers. The eyes of the world are on us, Donny. There are a lot of government agents in town, and more coming. I don't want you carrying out a suicide mission. You're too valuable for that."

Some color came into the pale face at last.

A question popped into Bobby's mind fully formed. "Tell me this . . . if I asked you to take out somebody local, would you have any problem with that?"

"Hell, no! Just name the target. I been sittin' on go so long with this outfit I'm ready for whatever."

Bobby nodded thoughtfully. "What if the target is white?"

Donny shrugged at what he clearly considered a pointless question. "You're command and control, Sergeant. I just follow orders. Tip of the spear."

As comical as it sounded, the kid was right. "How about Kendrick Washington?"

Kilmer's eyes widened. "The nigger who wears them slave chains?"

"That's the one."

"*Shee-it.* Just say the word."

Bobby knew then that Donny Kilmer didn't look at such a mission as a duty, but rather as enjoyment.

"Hey, Sergeant," Donny said in a deferential voice. "Can I ask you something?"

"Sure."

"When you killed that Abu Nasir guy, El Sherif or whatever . . ."

"Yeah?"

"Where'd you shoot him? Center mass?"

Bobby had been asked this hundreds of times, usually by overweight civilians who'd never been within a thousand miles of a war zone. Donny might never have tasted battle, but he was a born killer. In an advanced industrial economy they were next to useless, except as common laborers. But on a battlefield they were worth a hundred conscripted soldiers. Donny was the archetypal infantryman. His grandfather had talked about them when Bobby was a boy. The Donny Kilmers of the world stormed the beaches and seized the hills riddled with tunnels and ringed with machine gun nests. They didn't dive on grenades to save their buddies; they snatched them up and hurled them back to their throwers, taking out a half dozen enemy for lagniappe.

"Right here," Bobby said, tapping the point of his chin.

"First shot?"

"Yep."

"You double-tap him?"

"Nope. Even with all my training—having indelible muscle memory of delivering thousands of double-taps in the shoot house—I just popped him once in the face. It was dark in that cave, and I fired from the hip."

"One freakin' shot, huh? Damn."

"Blew out his cervical spine. Brainstem, too. The rest of my unit opened up after my muzzle flash lit him up. We had a lot of dead batteries, so no night vision. That asshole who claimed the kill in his book probably did hit him second. But Nasir was dead the instant I shot him. I saw a cell phone pic of the wound."

Donny nodded solemnly. "I've killed a lot of whitetail with my AR. Some were spine shots. I know what thirty-five hundred feet per second does to bone."

"Thirty-five hundred? Muzzle velocity of a standard AR-15 is thirty-two fifty fps."

Kilmer gave him a crafty smile. "I use the hot rod .224 varmint cartridge. Not .223."

Bobby felt himself slipping into a meditative state, a nearly narcotic state of divine intervention. What were the odds that chance would place a man with this particular skill set in his path during this fateful week? Donny Kilmer was ready to play Patroclus to his Achilles, or even Oswald to his David Ferrie. The kid was practically a born assassin. An archetypal lone wolf. One thing Bobby knew for sure: he didn't intend to squander the opportunity this afforded him. All he had to do was give the kid a target, and that person would cease to exist within whatever time frame Bobby specified. Like pressing a remote control The only question was who he would kill . . . and when.

SITTING IN SILENCE with the eager militiaman, Bobby considered the staggering possibility that someone so anonymous and plebeian might be a critical cog in the wheel of history. A fulcrum of the future.

"Did they make you read *Julius Caesar* in school?" Bobby asked in a distant voice.

The kid's eyes went dull, like centuries-old Wedgwood china.

"It's a Shakespeare play," Bobby said softly. "'Friends, Romans, country-men, lend me your ears . . .' No?"

"I ain't much of a reader, Sergeant."

"I get that. You're a man of action. I was just thinking of some lines from it."

"Yeah? I write down movie quotes sometimes."

"Do you? From what?"

"Just the quality stuff, you know. Like *Outlaw Josey Wales*."

"That's a good one," Bobby said, to foster camaraderie. *"Dyin' ain't much of a livin', boy."*

Donny's face shone with puerile delight. "Best line in the movie. Any movie ever. What about that Julius Caesar, though? He conquered the world, didn't he?"

"Not really. But he *changed* the world."

Kilmer's eyes narrowed with genuine interest. "How so?"

"He changed Rome from a republic to a dictatorship."

"Oh . . . cool. What lines were you thinking about?"

Bobby didn't want to jinx anything. But he felt compelled to speak the ageless words aloud: "'There is a tide in the affairs of men. Which, taken at the flood, leads on to fortune . . .'"

Donny shook his head in confusion. "What does that mean?"

"Seize the moment, Donny. Seize the motherfucking moment."

"Ohhh. Well . . . yeah." The kid stood and rolled his shoulders like a private getting ready for a long march. "Guess I better get movin', huh? No telling what them jigs is up to on the bluff by now."

Bobby smacked Kilmer's bony shoulder. "You go ahead. I'll clear every-thing with Shot before I leave."

Donny saluted, then turned and headed for the hatchway ladder.

Something thrummed in Bobby's chest, exactly the way it did when he leaped out of a C-17 high above the Kindu Kush. Despite his fatigue, he knew that this trip had been worthwhile. It might well prove to be historic, something he would look back on decades from now as a moment filled with Jungian import. But as he walked back toward the main bunker in a half crouch, an image of Penn Cage and Charles Dufort sitting in the back of Dufort's big Rolls filled his mind. Then he saw Cage mounted atop Sophie Dufort, Sophie panting and sweating beneath him. Bobby remembered having her when he was eighteen, in the pool house at Belle Rose. She'd been twenty years older than he, and coming out of a bad relationship with some local loser and his drug of choice, but God had she been beautiful. Call him confused, but he could *still* see that jet-black hair whipping across her muscular back, the deep V over her spine flexing as she strained against him. What could possibly tie her to Penn Cage? More important, could it endanger Bobby's future political and financial relationship with the old man? Bobby couldn't see how it would, not at this point. He couldn't imagine two men less alike than Penn Cage and Charles Dufort. But he would have to find out more . . .

And soon.

CHAPTER 26

NADINE LOOKS ROUGH when I answer the door. Running mascara, bloodshot eyes, puffy bags beneath them. I pull her inside and walk her to the kitchen, where I make two mugs of coffee. All I have is K-cups, which is embarrassing, since she runs a gourmet coffee shop inside her bookstore.

"Sorry about the quality," I say, setting a mug before her.

She takes a scalding sip. "Couldn't fucking care less."

"I notice you say fuck a lot more than you used to."

A sarcastic laugh escapes her lips. "It's that kind of night."

"What did I miss?"

"The fire wasn't bad enough?" Her face flares with a false smile. Then the smile cracks. "I'm kidding. I just spent an hour alone with that orphaned girl. I waited with her while the fire department called the Department of Human Services, which in Mississippi is a criminally underfunded agency without the resources to handle a six-year-old girl who just lost her father in a house fire."

"Let me guess. No family."

Nadine shakes her head.

"So where does she sleep tonight?"

"Temporary foster home."

"And . . . ?"

"I saw the family. Spoke to the mother." Nadine swallows to keep from choking up. "Not great."

This is the least surprising statement of the night. "I know you would have liked to take her."

Nadine's facial muscles flex, and her chin begins to quiver. "Ohh, you have no idea. I nearly fought them for her."

I sip my coffee and wait. She stares at the kitchen table, running her forefinger over its surface, following the wood grain with a clear-coated nail. Three years past forty, she's one of the most self-possessed women I've ever met. Before she opened Constant Reader, Nadine was a plaintiff's attorney in North Carolina, with a reputation as a killer in the courtroom (which is hard to imagine for people who only know her more recent incarnation). She's one of those humans who have a kind of lamp burning inside them. On most days they radiate a positivity that few of us can summon for even a few hours. She truly wishes the best for everyone. If I'd been ten years younger when we met, and healthy . . . I'd have married her, no question. But therein lay our problems.

"Kids," she says in a flat voice. "It was kids that broke us up. Right?"

Only now do I remember her gift for reading my thoughts. I'm not sure how to respond to such a blunt statement. She continues without looking up from the table.

"You knew I was ready to have a family, and you already had Annie. You'd lost your first wife, and then you lost Caitlin. One to cancer, one to murder. That would wreck anybody, okay? I get it."

I hold my silence. She's heading somewhere.

"It's been a long time since Caitlin," she says. "Fifteen years."

She's made no mention of the night of the book-banning protest seven weeks ago, when we slept together. Before she can push on with a surgically incisive question, I decide to push back. "Since you're diagnosing relationships, what about you and Marshall? I thought you guys were headed for the altar."

She takes a deep breath, exhales slowly. "So did everyone else. But our situation was the reverse of you and me. Ironic, isn't it? He'd only been divorced three years when we got together. He was ready to start over. Too ready, I realized. At least for me."

"It seems like he was just what you were looking for."

A wistful smile. "Maybe. But there's the rub. The person matters. I like Marshall a lot. I respect him. I love him, in a lot of ways."

"But?"

At last she looks up, directly into my eyes. The intensity in hers sets me back a bit. "But it wasn't like us. You know?"

Looking at her here, densely real, alive in a way few people I've ever known are, I do know.

"I think Marshall was trying to fill the void his son left behind," she says softly. "That's my feeling, anyway."

I've known for some time that McEwan and I have profound loss in common, though we've never spoken of it. He lost his toddler son in a swimming pool accident when he lived in Georgetown, something that ultimately drove him and his wife apart. While I lost a wife and a fiancée . . .

Nadine sits in silence for a couple of minutes, her gaze mostly in her coffee cup. Then without guile or even softness she says, "I know you want me. Same as after the book-banning protest."

While I search for the right response, she adds, "And yet . . . I know you're going to deny yourself. And me. Without even knowing why. Not really."

In this moment I'm not so sure she's right. Part of me wants to repeat everything we did in that hotel north of Jackson. But part of me is more aware than I've ever been that, even with a best-case outcome, my time on this planet is very short compared to hers.

"Let me point out one thing," I say, knowing I need to give her something to blame our failure on. "I was born the year JFK was elected."

Her eyes flare with old anger, and her cheeks darken with blood. "Oh, do *not* give me that shit. Reagan was president when I was born, and his scandal was Iran-Contra, not the Bay of Pigs. Who cares? I want to puke when people look at couples with an age difference and say, 'What do they find to *talk* about?' As though married couples sit around discussing what top forty records were big their senior years, or who shot JR, or whether you liked Rachel or Monica. Human beings talk about their families, their jobs, and what's happening in the world in which they're living. *That's* what life is. The rest is judgmental bullshit."

Seeing her filled with angry passion, all I can think is that her logic feels ironclad, as it always did when we were together.

She takes another deep breath, then blows out the air in an obvious effort to calm herself. "I had no intention of having this kind of talk when I texted you about the fire. It was hearing about that little girl, and then trying to comfort her, that pushed me to come." Her eyes find mine again. "Because life is going by, Penn. On nights like tonight, I feel like it's running in fast-forward. You know?"

"I do."

"Did you get hold of Doc at least?"

"I did."

"Why's he been out of contact?"

"He was attacked in a D.C. metro station. Savagely. He's in a hospital up there."

"Oh, no. How bad is he?"

"His doctors don't want him to move, but I'm flying him back on a charter jet tonight. Dwight Ford's flying up to ride shotgun."

"Wow. Thank God for the Dunphy verdict, right?"

"Joe Dunphy would definitely have approved this expenditure. He loved Doc. And he loved stickin' it to the Man."

A true note of pleasure animates Nadine's laugh.

I sip my coffee and wonder what will happen next. Nadine doesn't seem concerned with my response to her soliloquy on our May-December romance. She looks more like she simply needed to get it off her chest, and now she has. If I'm too stupid to respond appropriately, that's my problem, not hers.

"You're only half-right about why I ended our relationship," I tell her, surprising myself.

Her eyes narrow. "How so?"

"I had a secret then. I still do."

She blinks, and I feel her reaching back in time for some clue to what I might be talking about. "Are you going to tell me?"

Why am I doing this? What unlocked the interior cell in which I've held this secret so long? "I told Annie this tonight, and I'd kept it from her just as long. Mom left a letter telling me it was time. She also mentioned you. She was a big fan of yours, by the way."

Rays of deep emotion shine from Nadine's eyes. "You know that went both ways. So. What's this secret?"

"I have the same cancer Mom did."

Nadine doesn't blink for several seconds.

"I was diagnosed with it twenty years before she was. But utterly by accident, I proved to be one of the luckiest few patients on the planet."

Nadine's face hasn't changed, but her phenomenal perception is working in overdrive. I feel it like heat from an oven. "Yours is terminal, too?"

"Every case is terminal. I knew that when you and I were together. It's just . . . the course of my illness was so slow then that I didn't have to think about it much. But around the time we began getting really serious, I experienced a few things that made me afraid the cancer was switching on. Turning truly malignant. That's what made me pull away. It wasn't fair to have you start up a marriage that might end in a year or two—much less have a child, which I knew you wanted."

She's staring at me with disconcerting intensity. "You son of a bitch. You could have told me that. I spent nearly five years wondering what I did wrong!"

"I'm sorry. But I hadn't told anyone at that point. Only my father knew. The young partner of his that diagnosed me had already died of asthma himself, at forty-three. Talk about irony. Bottom line, I didn't want you carrying that weight once we were apart."

She's clearly unconvinced. "And *now*? You've lived five years since we split up. Five years we could have been together! What's your status now?"

I look away for a moment. "I honestly don't know. I haven't had my proteins checked in a long time. But I've experienced . . . some changes recently. The other night I rolled over in bed and broke a rib. That's a bad sign."

"How bad?"

"I'm going to need treatment soon. Right away. Probably a stem cell transplant."

She shrugs after a few seconds. "I know women who've had those. And they're doing *great*."

"Some people do. It's conceivable I could live another five years. Or, if I remain among the luckiest patients, seven, or even ten."

"Christ. It's time to get you to a hematologist. Or oncologist, or whoever you need to see."

"I know."

She gets to her feet and begins pacing out the space from kitchen to den and back. "I literally cannot believe this."

"I'm sorry I kept it from you. But watching my mother die from this has been tough. Knowing I was headed down the same road. I didn't want you walking it with me if you didn't have to."

She stops at the edge of the kitchen floor. "Well, mister, I have my own secret. One I had no intention of telling you, at least for a while."

"What are you talking about?"

"Our little one-night stand a few weeks ago?"

"Of course."

"Well, it produced a result."

"What do you mean?" I ask, afraid she's about to tell me she just got an abortion.

"Just what I said. What's the usual result of sex, when there is a result?"

I slowly shake my head. "Ahh . . . there are several answers to that question. STDs. Any number of things."

She sighs at the universal stupidity of men. "I'm *pregnant*," she snaps. "Is that clear enough for you? And before you freak out, let me just say this: I expect nothing from you. I have my own money, and I'm quite capable of raising a child on my own. You can tell me how you feel about it, but nothing you say is going to affect my decision to keep it. *I'm having this baby.* I want it, and I'm *having* it."

I feel as though she just bent down, took hold of the floor, and jerked it out from under me. How can I respond to this new reality? I'm not even sure how I feel about it. The only other time I was in this situation, I was decades younger. The girl came to me in panic and we both tried to work out how to remedy what was a crisis for both of us. But Nadine has presented me with a fait accompli.

"So you're seven weeks along?" I ask.

"No, nine. You count from your last period before conception."

"I didn't know that."

"I hope you're not trying to work out trimesters and the law, et cetera."

"No, no. I'm just trying to get it straight in my head."

She nods slowly, watching me with preternatural sensitivity. "In seven months, I'm going to have a baby. *Your* baby. That's pretty straightforward."

"So you're ready to raise this child without me?"

"Absolutely." Her face softens, almost against her will. "Although I'd be quite all right raising it *with* you. You know . . . in case you're wondering."

We've spent so much time apart, yet here we sit, discussing a possible future together. "Even knowing what I just told you?"

She turns her palms upward. "What's the effing difference? This baby's coming. We can have zero years with you, or maybe five or ten. Given the choice, I'll take the five or ten."

"Nadine—"

"You know that saying, you can't time the stock market? Well, you can't time fate, either. The doctor who diagnosed you died of asthma at forty-three. You think he knew that was coming? By making the decision you did in 2018, you cheated us of every year since. You're *really* going to have to work to make that up to me. Okay?"

I hardly know how to respond.

"But I'm going to give you a chance," she goes on. "If you're sick for some of it, well . . . we'll deal with that when it comes. But we're not going to make big life decisions based on that. You lost your wife and mother to cancer, and I lost my mother. *Fuck* cancer. Okay? *Fuck it.*"

"Nadine—"

"No!" she says sharply, holding up her hands. "Forget whatever you were about to say. Short-circuit your cerebral cortex and tell me what you're really feeling right now. What do you *really want*?"

I remember my mother telling me recently that I've been grieving for twenty-five years, and doubly grieving for eighteen. I also remember what she wrote in her last letter: *Please give yourself the gift of another good woman.*

"Where are you sleeping tonight?" I ask.

Nadine goes still for about ten seconds, then focuses all her attention on the floor between us. Just when I've decided I went too far, she looks up and says, "I have options?"

I don't want to plumb the subtext of any of this, so I simply raise my right forefinger and point to the ceiling.

She closes her eyes and breathes calmly. "This isn't what I expected. None of it. But it's what I need. I've been pretty stressed for a while."

"I'll bet."

Her eyes open, and the light in them seems to have changed. "Let's go up. Your AC's too damned cold."

The memory of her sensitivity to cold comes back in a pleasing rush, and I smile. She takes my hand, but I break away to pick up my mother's leather satchel from the sofa.

"What's that?"

"The last year of Mom's life. Annie gave it to me tonight, and I've been keeping it close ever since. Can't risk losing it until I've read it."

Nadine nods approvingly, then takes my hand and leads me to the staircase. After climbing the first step, she turns back to hug me with our height difference canceled out.

"Familiar, isn't it?" she says in my ear. Then she draws back and looks into my face.

"Thanks for being brave enough to knock," I tell her.

"One of us had to do it."

I squeeze her close again. "The timing literally couldn't be worse. We could wake up in a war tomorrow."

She winces in a way that tells me she fully comprehends the danger. But after looking away for a few seconds, she touches my cheek and says, "You've forgotten how tough I am. Haven't you?"

"I haven't forgotten a damned thing."

"No?" One arched eyebrow goes up. "I guess we're about to find out."

The glint in her eyes in the dim stairwell brings back the night we spent together after the book protest. But life is never that simple, not past a certain age anyway.

"You probably don't know this," I say hesitantly. "But one of the first drugs they put you on when you have myeloma is called Revlimid. It's derived from thalidomide."

At first there's no reaction. Then I feel her tense in my arms. "Birth defects," she says softly. "I remember the photos from a law school class."

A shudder goes through me. "Right. Most of the defects caused by thalidomide happened around the year I was born, but I remember the *Life* magazine photos from when I was a boy."

Nadine looks into my eyes with a depth of perception I've rarely experienced. "That case had a lot to do with subsequent regulation of the pharmaceutical industry," she says. "Have you ... taken any of this drug yet?"

"No. Never even touched it."

She blinks in uncertainty, but then relief shines in her eyes. Relief like that of someone learning their biopsy is benign.

"But once you start taking Revlimid," I go on, "life gets complicated. You shouldn't have any more children, or even unprotected sex."

"God."

"Yeah. Mom's favorite sitter actually had to stop taking care of her, because she was trying to get pregnant and she didn't want to risk any proximity to that drug."

I don't know how much time passes before Nadine speaks again. But just when I think she's about to pull away, she squeezes me tighter and speaks in a soft voice filled with conviction.

"Penn, I'm forty-three years old. I love sex, but I've had my share, and I want this baby more. And I want him to have his father, for as long as he can. So how about we do what we were about to start doing before you told me that? Living one day at a time. You haven't started the drug, which means tonight is ours. Once you start . . . we'll follow the rules and do what we have to do." She raises her left hand and brushes some hair out of my right eye. "How does that sound?"

My throat has gone so tight it hurts. "I don't . . . don't know what to—"

"Lucky for you, no words required from this point forward."

"Nadine, listen—"

"I did." She wipes a tear from her eye, then smiles with the ineffable joy and sadness of life. "Plenty of time for talk tomorrow."

CHAPTER 27

BOBBY WHITE'S BIENVILLE refuge was an eighty-acre hunting camp carved out of the old Canaan Plantation, contiguous to the southern boundary of Shot Barlow's Black Oak. Bobby had bought the land from his mother after a Thanksgiving ten years earlier, when staying at his parents' house had proved too frustrating to contemplate suffering through again. After building a $450,000 log cabin with world-class air-conditioning and a priceless view of the river, he'd figured he was set for the next holiday season. To his surprise, though, the isolation that his "New Canaan" offered proved irresistible, and he'd used it far more than originally planned. If he was honest with himself, its very existence had changed the way he lived his life.

It was well after midnight when he hit the remote to his security gate and drove through, his mind filled with the unexpected possibilities this night had offered. The Bienville Poker Club's pitch had been merely a curiosity, but learning that they planned to move against the Black city board could help him protect himself during this public-facing week. Of course this was trivial compared to learning that an actual Black activist group might have carried out two arsons of such polarizing symbolic power that they could shake the nation. But none of that could compare to the appearance of Donny Kilmer. Sitting below ground with the aspiring assassin had given Bobby a sense of stepping a thousand years into the past—a place where modern calculations of morality meant nothing. He recalled the pale gleam in the eyes of the lone wolf, who'd been simmering his brain in the slow cooker of MAGA madness for so long that containing himself was becoming impossible. And that made anything possible. So many disparate elements coming together in the same week—in the same place—made Bobby wonder about his last-minute impulse to accept the invitation to play in the PGA tourney. He'd once thought it was Tio Carrera's visit that pushed him over the edge, but now . . . it felt more like fate.

The driveway of New Canaan was nearly half a mile long, curving gracefully around to the cabin, which sat on a slight elevation on the Bienville bluff, a safe sixty meters back from the eroding edge. Even in the dark you could see the kudzu invading the treetops below, steadily covering them like suffocating blankets. Bobby pulled the Rover up to his front door, got out, and punched a code into his iPhone. The door lock opened with a snick. Once inside the cabin, he walked through the dim great room by the light of the open kitchen's undercounter fixtures and entered the master suite.

Corey Evers lay shirtless in the bed, propped on a stack of pillows and reading his iPad.

"I worried you might be all night," he said without looking up.

"I could have been," Bobby said, tossing his wallet onto a chair, then sitting to remove his shoes.

"As aggressive as that damned Birdie was, I worried you might have to fuck her."

Bobby chuckled. "Oh, I did. She didn't give me much choice."

Corey looked up, revealing a combination of surprise, disappointment, and resignation. "You son of a bitch. I should have gone to sleep."

"The lengths I go to protect us," Bobby deadpanned. "Don't worry, I faked my nut."

Corey threw a pillow at him.

Bobby laughed and looked back at his lover with a fondness he hadn't felt so keenly in a long time. Then he slipped off the rest of his clothes and moved from the chair to the foot of the bed, where he rubbed Corey's left foot. He'd made no mention of his visit to the Barlow bunker, and the more he thought about it, the more certain he became that he would not. He and Corey made such a natural visual couple, if only one knew the secret dynamic of their highly controlled life. While Corey took care to mask it, he had a pop-star prettiness that teenage girls found irresistible. He might live in Mississippi, but most people assumed he was from California or New York. By contrast, Bobby possessed the rugged masculinity of a native capable of exporting his looks to a national stage, the way the Mississippi-born actor Dana Andrews had done in the 1940s. Bobby remembered being glued to the screen watching Andrews with Gene Tierney in *Laura* as a boy of twelve. Then later being moved to tears seeing him as a combat vet with PTSD in *The Best Years of Our Lives*. The father-son bedtime scene with real-life double amputee Harold Russell could still shatter him.

"This is a big night for us, Cor," he said with unfeigned sincerity. "You just don't know it yet."

"Big how?"

"Did you see the news about the Arcadia fire?"

"I did. So terrible about that homeless guy and his daughter." A note of suspicion had entered Corey's voice. "But what's that got to do with us, other than needing to come up with a suitable comment?"

Bobby shook his head, wishing he could somehow tamp down the excitement building within him. "I'll tell you later. Opportunity's knocking."

Corey sighed and looked away. "I hate you when you're like this. You're like a toddler with a new toy. Tell me now."

"I'm not sure I fully understand things myself yet. In other news, the esteemed Bienville Poker Club would like me to run for governor of Mississippi."

Corey's perfect mouth fell open. "How precious. My God, such small ambitions. When do they want you to do this? Four years from now?"

"Next month."

Corey blanched. "*What?*"

"Apparently, the guv may have to drop out of the race. The welfare scandal is going nuclear, or so says the Poker Club."

"Holy hell. I can't believe . . . I mean, you know what? I absolutely can believe that."

"They also say I can't win the White House running third party. Not next year."

"Well, that proves they're stupid."

Bobby waved his hand in dismissal. "Not the point. Those old bastards have real money. Buckman and Donnelly, especially."

"Well. String them along as needed."

"Obviously. But that's just prologue. Dixie Donnelly is the Lady Macbeth of that operation, by the way. Sharp and ruthless."

"Interesting." Corey set his iPad on the duvet and spoke with feigned disinterest. "So. How was our Emmy winner in the sack?"

"Energetic."

"And how did you get out of staying the night with her?"

"I told her I promised a couple of the golfers' caddies they could come fishing out here early in the morning. Birdie's a late riser."

Corey laughed. "She bought that?"

"My man, I'm a better actor than Birdie Blake ever dreamed of being on her most ambitious day." Bobby grinned again. "Get those covers off."

"You take a goddamned shower first."

Bobby laughed. "Are you sure?"

"God knows who else has plowed that ginger field. I googled her earlier, and even the public list is long. Must be something about redheads."

"Can't hold that against the girl."

"I can tonight."

Bobby stood and headed for the master bath. "Hey, I know we canceled the show so I could focus on the tournament tomorrow, but I've gotten strafed with texts asking me to do morning drive-time interviews tomorrow. Everybody from Glenn Beck and Mike Gallagher to Hugh freaking Hewitt."

Corey made a sound like he was choking on something awful. "You also got asked to do a couple of TV hits."

Bobby looked up sharply. "Really?"

"*Fox & Friends* and *Morning Joe*, believe it or not. If only you hadn't been banging Birdie, you might have said yes in time."

Bobby smiled to himself. He didn't know if those requests were real, but he did know Corey hadn't texted him about them. Jealousy was a poisonous emotion. "Let's let the tension build before we do any TV this week. But given what's happened with the fires—the Bastard Sons' written claim of responsibility—I ought to do at least one radio show. Or maybe all of them, except Hewitt. Christ, we haven't sunk that low. We could run over to the studio and knock them all out before tee-off."

Corey picked up his iPad and started making notes. "So, early to Flowood tomorrow. Then back here for the first Golf Channel appearance *before* tee-off. We'll be cutting it close."

"That's your specialty."

Corey sighed wearily, but compliments always made him glow. "Hit the shower, for God's sake. I'm tired."

"You can forget sleep. History's on the march. And right in our backyard."

Corey sighed and flopped his head on the pillow.

Bobby grinned and went into the bathroom.

AN HOUR LATER, Bobby sat naked at the kitchen table, waiting for an espresso to finish brewing on La Marzocco. Corey stood by the machine in his boxers, poised to work the paddle. Bobby steadily tapped Corey's iPad, repeatedly updating the Bienville *Watchman*'s online edition. Marshall McEwan, the publisher, had been steadily posting updates on the Arcadia fire, but so far he hadn't broken the news that Bobby was waiting for. Bobby was almost grateful, because his true preoccupation was the image of Donny Kilmer's pale blue eyes in the stinking belly of Barlow's bunker: the eyes of a soldier volunteering to carry out the will of his commander, whatever his order might be. It was the nature of that order that was working in Bobby's subconscious, an inhumanly bloody plan laboring to be born into a world where only a very few things retained the power to shock—

But this would be one of them.

"I can't look at another damned pop-up ad," Bobby complained.

"What are you waiting for?" Corey asked irritably.

"I leaked the Bastard Sons' claim note," Bobby announced. "I got a photo of it from a deputy I used to play baseball with. Marshall McEwan can't keep it under wraps much longer. He must be worried about the white reaction."

"With good reason," Corey said, turning from the espresso machine. "What if people find out you leaked it?"

"I practically announced the Tranquility claim on Shepard's show. As for the vintage Tupac cover note and the names, I'll say the public has a right to know about anything that threatens civil order."

Corey ran his hands through his hair, trying to wake himself up. "I've been thinking about the seed money. If Charles Dufort and his friends really give you a hundred million dollars, there are going to be strings attached, no matter what he tells you now. Dufort's in the seduction phase, but he's going to want to say how everything goes."

Bobby didn't want to engage in this discussion. Not tonight. For the past few weeks, they'd engaged in an on-again, off-again conversation with so much subtext that the spoken words could hardly support the weight of it. What terrified Corey wasn't merely the risk of exposure that a campaign would bring, but the changes it would demand in their hidden life. He knew better than anyone how careful Bobby had been to conceal his true orientation, but Corey had paid the highest price for that long-running deception. So many public events Bobby attended alone. He got to shine, or to let himself go as he had at the PGA party tonight: acting the role of heterosexual "player" while Corey sat at home streaming cable series or working on the next day's radio show. And it was always Bobby's prerogative. Bobby could have taken Corey to the Belle Rose party, of course, but they'd learned early that the pretense of an "executive assistant" at certain functions caused tangible awkwardness more times than not. Corey could have taken his own beard to the party, of course, and sometimes he did. But that got tiresome, too, as he had to select them for their dullness, so that they wouldn't detect the electric intimacy between Corey and his employer. In truth, the central labor of their lives had been learning to become skilled actors, as Bobby had joked earlier.

"If it gets out that you leaked that note," Corey said carefully, "there's no going back. Terrible things could happen as the result of these arsons, and fast. Street violence, Bobby. And that could blow back onto you. Don't think it can't. White nationalists are going to lose their minds over those fires. It's already happening."

Bobby shrugged. "That's what us white folks do best."

Corey compressed the Marzocco's paddle with his expert hand, and the kitchen filled with the bracing aroma of espresso. He carefully set the small cup on the table. Bobby was lifting it to his lips when his iPhone gave out a harsh squawk—an alert from the cabin's security system. He assumed it was a deer triggering a motion sensor at the gate, but then Corey said, "Oh, no!" and dropped his own cup with an ear-piercing clatter as the wall intercom rang.

"What is it?" Bobby asked, clicking his composite view of the security camera feeds.

"Charlot Dufort's at our gate!"

A shiver raced up Bobby's back.

The composite feed came up on his phone, and he touched the gate cam to expand it to full screen. Charlot was peering into the camera from one foot away, his distorted visage like something from a serial killer movie, a pervert trying to see through a peephole in a hotel door. The puffy, wrecked face pushed closer until a single bulging eye filled the screen . . .

"Gross!" Corey snapped. "That man is *cuckoo*."

Bobby went still. The word *cuckoo* had lodged in him like an arrow. It was simultaneously the key to and confirmation of his plan. He hadn't quite experienced the full epiphany yet, but he was standing at the verge. He knew it was coming, the way he'd known Abu Nasir had been waiting for him in the dark beyond the mouth of a particular cave. Data and intelligence could only take you so far. At some point, you had to trust instinct. And the premonition he felt coming now was as electric as any he'd ever experienced . . .

Brood parasite, he thought, watching Charlot make faces into the camera. *The cuckoo is a brood parasite, delivering its eggs in the nests of other birds. Tricking or forcing other species to raise its young. Yesterday Kendrick Washington had more than twenty-five million followers, and now he's over thirty-two million. I can't catch him by imitating him. He's the first person ever to do that so fast. I need to replace him. To become him . . .*

"I don't see a car," Corey said, as the intercom rang again. "You don't think he *walked* out here? We're four miles from the city limit sign."

Charlot grinned and waved at the camera from three feet away, as though his appearance might be anything but a nightmare for whomever he chose to visit.

"He's still handsome, you know," Corey said with a hint of jealousy. "Beautiful, really. He reminds me of someone. An actor. But I can't think of who."

"Alain Delon."

Corey clucked his tongue once. "That's it. *Purple Noon.*"

"Delon beat the hell out of Matt Damon as Ripley," Bobby said, "decent as Damon was. There was a time Charlot was a dead ringer for that French bastard."

At last Charlot pulled back and pressed the call button.

Bobby shook his head, feeling a strange excitement. "He always was persistent. But Belle Rose sits almost on the eastern county line. He either drove or hitched."

"Jesus, this is bad. What do we do?"

Bobby thought fast as the bell pinged again. "He's here now. Better to bring him in than leave him at the gate where anybody driving past can see him."

Corey growled in frustration. "I guess you want me to go get him?"

"Indeed I do, sugarplum. Quick as you can."

Corey cursed and went into the bedroom for his clothes.

Bobby remained at the table, wondering what was driving Charlot to such desperate actions. His debts alone? As huge as they were, his father could pay them off without breaking a sweat. Maybe the old man had truly run out of patience at last. He never had been the forgiving type. Maybe it was simple terror of Tommy Russo's leg-breakers. Whatever the case, Charlot was clearly decompensating now. And after a year of low-level hassle, the timing of his psychological crisis couldn't be worse.

Maybe I can turn this visit to my advantage, Bobby thought, recalling the casino owner's hard face at Belle Rose. He forced himself to stop thinking that way. Maybe Charlot wasn't in as bad a shape as everyone seemed to believe. After all . . . he was still one of the smartest people Bobby had ever known.

And no one knew Charlot the way he did.

CHAPTER 28

BOBBY WAS FULLY dressed and sitting on the leather love seat in the great room when Corey led Charlot Dufort through the cabin's front door. With great effort Bobby had wiped Donny Kilmer and Kendrick Washington from his mind.

The smell alone told him that his old lover hadn't bathed for days. More worrisome, Charlot's eyes looked as hollow as any he had seen, even on the battlefield. In the light of the great room, Charlot looked ten years older than Bobby, when in fact they were the same age.

"Hello, Robert." Charlot's cultured voice was still intact, at least. "Thanks for letting me in. I'm persona non grata at most of my old haunts these days."

The use of his Christian name hurled Bobby back to his college days. "How'd you get here from Belle Rose?"

"I hitched. Ann Hadley drove me into town, for old times' sake. Then some kind old farmer drove me to the head of River Road. Don't know his name. I walked the rest of the way."

Bobby offered Charlot his hand as he passed. Charlot squeezed it lightly, as though he weren't desperate for any human touch, then backed away and took a seat on the larger sofa opposite Bobby, nearer the door.

"Did the farmer know you?" Bobby asked.

"I don't think so. Said he lives out this way. Worked most of his life at the Masonite plant."

"Did you tell him you were coming here?"

The question clearly annoyed Charlot. "Bobby, what's the problem? Do you think I'm trying to screw you over somehow?"

Bobby tried to decide how frank to be about his suspicions. "Well, I don't know. You've been blackmailing me for nearly a year."

The swollen face betrayed genuine hurt. "*Blackmail?* Where did that come from? You offered to help me out of a jam, as I recall."

Corey walked over to the kitchen counter and began working at his iPad. With the open plan of the cabin, he still had a direct line of sight to Charlot.

"I did offer to help," Bobby conceded. "But your pitch was the Mario Puzo version, wasn't it? One I couldn't really refuse."

Charlot blinked as though in surprise. "I don't remember it that way."

"It held an implicit threat."

"I would never hurt you, Bobby. You know that. I'm just—I'm in trouble. *Real* trouble this time."

"Tommy Russo told me his side of your trouble tonight. And it's a lot different than what you've been telling me these past months."

Charlot's face twisted with something close to hatred. "That wop son of a bitch. Don't let him close to you, Bobby. He's bad news. A monster, deep down."

"How's that?"

"He comes on like a friend, but he encourages whatever your weakness is, and lulls you till he gets you in as deep as he can."

"Deep into what?"

"Every dirty game there is. Then he sends his thugs around to collect. And if you don't pay—and I mean sell your house, empty your retirement, whatever—they hurt you. That's why I need to talk to you so badly. They slashed my arm today. They might have killed me if I hadn't managed to get out into the street where neighbors could see me. I'd have been dead a week ago if I hadn't mentioned your name."

Bobby's internal radar went on high alert. "Russo pretty much told me that tonight."

An uncomfortable silence descended.

"Can I make you an espresso, Charlot?" Corey called from the kitchen.

Tears welled in Charlot's eyes at this simple kindness. "Oh my God, yes. I'm *so* tired. I couldn't risk staying at my house last night. I slept in Abbott Park. The mosquitoes ate me *alive*."

Bobby sighed. "I'm sorry about that."

Corey began loading the espresso machine.

"How did we get here, Bobby?" Charlot asked in a cracked voice. "Two years ago I had my house, my practice, my reputation . . . all of it. I even had somebody special. It's all gone now. Or very nearly."

"Are you really losing your house?" Bobby already knew the answer, but he wanted to stall for time while he worked out how best to handle Charlot's unexpected arrival.

Charlot nodded. "Tomorrow I have to be out permanently. But the date doesn't matter. I can't go back there ever again. Russo's gorillas have it staked out."

"What about your law practice? Russo intimated that you might be disbarred. Penn Cage told me the same thing last Saturday night."

Charlot closed his eyes, but Bobby knew him well enough to read the shame in his face. "I moved some money out of a client escrow account. I was going to put it right back, but . . . you know how that goes."

Bobby did. It was the oldest story in the world for lawyers crossing the line. Charlot kept talking, moving backward in time, trying to explain how he'd gotten into desperate straits through no fault of his own. He barely paused to nod thanks when Corey brought him the espresso, and the blast of caffeine only made him more voluble. Corey sat on the arm of a club chair and listened with apparent sympathy, but Charlot didn't flag as he went on. In fact, his intensity grew.

As the once-persuasive courtroom baritone droned on, Bobby's mind reeled back into the past. Though they'd been born at opposite ends of the economic spectrum, Charlot, like Bobby, came from a Southern family that didn't have a tolerant attitude toward homosexuality. But Charlot Dufort was no average Southern boy. He was half brother to the scion of a family whose wealth had been multiplying for generations. And since the son of his father's first marriage had died in his early forties, Charlot was expected to take over the primary role of heir and eventual patriarch. But while he was stunningly handsome and blessed with a superior intellect, those gifts were insufficient to guarantee his father's love and support. Because no "fairy boy" was going to assume the mantle of power in the Dufort family empire.

Bobby's family situation was different. His father had been raised in the most modest of circumstances, but pro baseball had made him a local hero, and he'd saved enough money to keep the family comfortable after his retirement from the major leagues. While the allowable gender roles in the White home were as binary as those in the Dufort mansion, anybody paying attention knew that when it came to big decisions, it was Mama Frances who wore the pants in the family. Pops could buy himself a seven-thousand-dollar ATV if it caught his eye at the Honda dealership, but if he started cruising ClassicCars.com and lusting after a '65 Corvette, Frances brought the hammer down. The retired pitcher understood that without his wife riding shotgun on his "pile," their money would drain away like sand through a sieve.

Back in Bobby's high school days, so long as Charlot kept his grades up, a classic sports car like the ones Bobby's father craved had been his for the asking. Bobby often wondered why Charlot had been so willing to risk his father's wrath by revealing his true sexual identity on his eighteenth birthday, when the risks had been so obvious. But that was the plan he'd made, the defiance he'd insisted on. Part of it grew from the fact that Natchez and Bienville had always been havens for gays, a rare thing in Mississippi. But Charlot had possessed an unbelievable confidence back then, bordering on hubris. He saw himself as a young Gore Vidal, with a sparkling future that would soon take him to Rome, Berlin, Morocco, Copenhagen, the Pacific islands. Conditioned by the townspeople of Bienville, Charlot thought of himself as a Southern prince in waiting. Bobby, too, was looked at that way by much of the town, despite his lack of wealth. His athletic gifts were such that by the tenth grade, coaches, teachers, and his fellow students had lifted him up as the rising star in their midst—a golden boy destined for fame. After the two princes crossed certain secret boundaries together, Charlot had convinced himself that Bobby wanted the same thing he did: to reveal his "true nature" to the narrow-minded community into which they'd been born, and then go out into the world to taste all it had to offer.

The problem was that Bobby—at that time, anyway—was far from certain that he was gay. He saw himself more as what people now refer to as "sexually fluid." He was content to take life as it came, and he didn't question his impulses. He was also far more prudent than Charlot about expressing those impulses in public. But nothing he said could convince Charlot of his hesitancy, and when his occasional lover's eighteenth birthday arrived, calamity ensued.

The explosion that followed Charlot's coming out to his parents was the most traumatic experience of his life. Thankfully he'd left Bobby's name out of his confessional script. But before the dust settled, his father had restructured his businesses and rewritten his will. His mother became clinically depressed. His younger sister Pia was so self-obsessed that she only felt anger, and even his older half sister Sophie had shown little understanding in those early years. Worse yet, while Charlot received academic scholarships to most of the Ivy League universities, his father had insisted that Ole Miss was "good enough for a gay boy."

That decision had made Bobby's first year at Ole Miss problematic. He'd lived in the athletic dorm, of course, while Charlot—despite having a dorm room in Kincannon Hall—somehow managed to rent a house on Buchanan Avenue, and he and Bobby occasionally met there (Bobby almost always being drunk during these visits). And though Bobby hadn't realized it then, when he decided to walk away from his scholarship and enlist after 9/11, part of his motive had been to get away from Charlot and their explosive situation.

After Bobby received his discharge in 2008, and entered Vanderbilt as an undergrad, he learned that Charlot had quietly transferred to Vanderbilt for his final year of law school, which put them right back in dangerous proximity. But because almost no one in Nashville knew either of them, that year became a more intimate one than their freshman year at Ole Miss. For a while Bobby had been content to go along with this. He was struggling with depression after losing his arm, and Charlot was good at keeping up his spirits. But as the months passed, he felt Charlot doing what he always did—pushing things toward some outward expression of the tie that bound them in secret. Looking back, Bobby realized how lucky he'd been to escape the consequences that would have ensued had Charlot not agreed to leave Nashville after graduating from law school. Where was that independence now? he wondered. What had killed it? What had led Charlot to ultimately marry a Bienville girl, have two children, and enter the world of playacted heterosexuality after so many years of undisguised gay life?

Whatever it was, the result had become a nightmare.

Charlot was droning on about his mother's death now, which had happened three years ago. Her loss had shattered him, because she'd "forgiven his sins" during her final year of life. Pretending to focus on Charlot's endless tale of woe, Bobby admitted one thing to himself: Dixie Donnelly's diagnosis had been correct. Charlot was circling the drain. He wouldn't come back from this, no matter how much money Bobby might give him. For nearly a year Bobby had been writing Charlot a check for thirty-five hundred dollars per month, enough to pay his kids' prep school tuition and some of his insurance bills. But if Charlot really lost his law license, he'd have no way of earning a basic living—

"Bobby?" Charlot said, and waited.

It took Bobby a second to realize that the endless flow of words had stopped, like a long rain that had ceased in silence.

"Bobby . . . what do you think?"

Bobby blinked and sat up on the love seat. "Oh . . . I'm sorry. I lost track for a minute. I'm sort of jet-lagged, Char."

Corey jumped in to save the moment. "Charlot was asking if you might be able to front him enough cash to keep Russo's men off his back for two weeks. He's going to try to talk his father into paying off his total debt."

You might as well ask the Easter Bunny to leave a million dollars under your pillow—

"I know it sounds unlikely," Charlot almost whimpered. "In most ways Dad still hates me. But I don't think he wants me to die in a ditch somewhere. I really don't."

Bobby wasn't so sure. He shifted on the love seat. "Russo told me you're seven figures in debt. And to multiple entities. How did you get yourself into such a deep hole?"

A wistful smile came over Charlot's face. "Remember Hemingway's line from *The Sun Also Rises*? Someone asks Lady Brett's fiancé how he went bankrupt, and he answers: 'Two ways. Gradually, then suddenly.' That pretty much covers my situation."

"Not for me. Did you really blow that much money in Russo's casino?"

"God, no. It was trying to dig myself out of debt to him that really got me in trouble. First I started doing sports betting over my phone."

"You don't know shit about sports!"

Charlot turned red. "I did all right at first. But once the hole got deeper, I tried the markets as a way out. I did well there, too . . . at first. And that encouraged me to buy on margin, hoping to hit a big lick."

Bobby sighed and looked at the floor. "We both know your father. The idea that Charles is going to pay off a couple of million dollars of debt for you . . . that's just fantasy, isn't it?"

Charlot winced like a fearful child. "Not even to save my life?"

Bobby shrugged. "I wish I could say different."

All remnants of humor left Charlot's face. "Then let me be frank. When I first approach him, I'm going to ask him to help me out of mercy. Paternal love, even duty." Charlot's face hardened to a surprising degree. "But if he refuses . . . I'm going to take a different approach."

A worm of unease turned in Bobby's gut. "Which is . . . ?"

"My father's a cruel man, Bobby. You know that. But he's done things in his life you know nothing about. I know about some of them. Others who are close to him know things, too."

Bobby leaned forward. He wondered if the old man knew about this vulnerability. "Such as? I mean, who are we talking about?"

"Ruby, our maid, for one. And Ruby's mother, Pearl. *She's* the one who really knows things."

"I thought you were going to say Amadu."

Charlot winced. "That blue-gum son of a bitch is an accomplice to some of the worst of it. He's the kind of Black man who'd have bought his own slaves if he'd been freed during the war. But Ruby and her mother? They're haunted by what they know."

"You're talking about blackmailing your own father," Bobby said quietly.

"A father who's willing to let his son die. A father who denied his son love and support all his life—"

Bobby held up his hand. "You're right. I just think it's a dangerous play."

"I don't have a choice, Bobby! Unless you want to give me a couple of million bucks."

Bobby shook his head. "I'm afraid I don't have that kind of money to give."

Charlot stared at him for a while. "There's one other alternative. But it's the most desperate and dangerous of all."

"Which is?"

Charlot's voice took on a disconnected coldness. "If Charles were to die . . . even if he truly disowned me back when he claims he did, on paper . . . you have to figure Sophie would inherit most of his estate. Right? And Sophie has always been good about helping me when I'm in real trouble."

A chill raced over Bobby's skin. "Jesus, man. Are you talking about *killing* your father?"

Charlot didn't answer.

Bobby looked over at Corey, who had gone motionless at the turn the conversation had taken.

"What if it's him or me?" Charlot asked softly. "What would you choose, if you were in my position?"

Bobby laid his hand flat on his muscular thigh. "I'm not going to have this discussion. I want to do what I can to help you. Part of that means stopping you from doing crazy things. How much do you figure it would take to keep Russo at bay for two weeks?"

Charlot shook his head helplessly. "Just the vig might do it. A hundred grand, maybe? If you ask Russo to cut me some slack when you give it to him, I think that would do it."

Bobby tried to imagine the exchange. Was it an accident that Charlot was asking for the same amount he'd lost in the "Three Amigos" Silicon Valley debacle during high school, over which he could make a credible claim of Bobby being partly to blame? "I can probably front you a hundred, Charlot. But I won't give it to Russo myself. I can't give him that kind of leverage over me."

"No, no!" Charlot said, his face coloring as relief flooded through him. "I understand. I can get it to him. And look, when Dad finally pays, I'll get all your money back to you."

Bobby nodded as though this were anything but a pathetic fiction.

Charlot looked at Corey with gratitude, then picked up the espresso cup with his forefinger and drank the remnants of his second serving. As Bobby watched, he felt something within him go cold. A glacial freeze that started at his heart and radiated out through his circulatory system.

He'd first experienced this in Afghanistan, before his third combat engagement. He'd come to think of this phenomenon as Absolute Zero. It wasn't numbness exactly, but a sort of internal armor against all feeling, including pain, both mental and physical. As the icy armor spread through him, he heard his own thoughts the way an eavesdropper would.

What if no one really knows Charlot came out here? He was seen at the country club, acting erratically. He was kicked out by security. So some old man dropped him a few miles from here . . . It's common knowledge that he's a drug addict, and probably that he's deep in debt to Russo and the casino. If he were to disappear . . . what would people think? What would the police assume? If his body were never found, even the cops would figure Russo had probably disappeared him—as a warning to other welshers. The question is . . . does anybody know he's here? On the other hand, even if they don't . . . what are the odds that Charlot has reached the age of forty-two without telling someone he's been intimate with Bobby White—local war hero and new icon of the conservative movement?

Pretty much zero. . . .

As his brain spun out these lines of probability, Bobby realized Corey was watching him. And what he saw in Corey's eyes was fear. Corey knew his lover well enough to read what was happening inside him. Bobby had told him about Absolute Zero. Corey had even seen him enter the mode once or twice. Before Bobby could break eye contact, Corey almost imperceptibly shook his head.

"I need to hit the rack, Charlot," Bobby said, suddenly getting to his feet. "I'm sorry, but I've got several drive-time shows to do tomorrow, and also some commitments to the PGA tournament."

Charlot looked confused and disappointed. Then a pleading, childlike look came into his eyes. "I was . . . kind of hoping I could crash here, just for tonight. I wouldn't get in you guys' way. I could sleep on this sofa right here." He patted the cushion beside him and grinned weakly. "Curl up like an old coon hound."

He sounded like a frightened little boy searching for any pretext not to spend the night alone.

"That's not a good idea," Bobby said firmly.

"Bobby . . . Russo's guys are cruising the streets for me."

"I don't think so. I told Tommy I was going to speak to you. He's waiting to hear from me before he does anything else."

Hope flashed in the hunted eyes. "Really?"

"Yes. Look, Corey will take you to a hotel in town and give you enough cash to check in for tonight."

Corey winced at this offer.

"Actually," Bobby decided, "he'd probably better just drop you down-town with the money. You can walk a couple of blocks to a hotel, can't you?"

Charlot looked at Bobby with infinite sadness. "Sure, Bobby. Yeah. I can do that."

Bobby forced down all memory of the distant past, taking refuge in the cold within him. "All right. Let me talk to Corey alone for a sec. I'll probably see you tomorrow afternoon or evening, after we get something worked out with Russo."

Charlot's face worked through several stages of emotion, a couple of which threatened to descend into tears. But then he gathered himself and said with quiet dignity: "Thank you, Robert."

"Happy to do it. You get some sleep tonight, okay? You really need it."

Charlot got up and stood awkwardly in front of Bobby. Bobby didn't rise to embrace him, or even shake his hand. Instead, he rolled off the sofa and walked back to the bedroom to get some cash from a small stash he kept in a wall safe there. He heard Corey speaking softly, and then Corey appeared in the bedroom.

"We can talk for a second. He's in the front bathroom."

Bobby nodded. "He's out of control. He's a threat to everything we've built, everything we're hoping to achieve."

Corey looked like he might argue the "we," but he didn't. Instead, he said, "I saw what was in your eyes."

Bobby looked away. "What did you see?"

Corey shook his head. "Terminal thinking. That's no answer to this problem. There's no telling who Charlot's told about you and him."

"I realize that." Bobby looked back at Corey. "But he's talking about killing his father, for God's sake. Our political bank. The richest man in the goddamn state. I don't know what I can do about that except—"

"Nothing! That's what you can do. If this gets strung along much lon-ger, Tommy Russo might make the whole question moot anyway."

Bobby hesitated, then acknowledged his agreement with a slight incli-nation of his head. "I think you're right."

Corey shivered, then hugged himself. "No way Russo could know about you and Charlot, right?"

"If he does, he'll own my ass from the outset of the campaign." Bobby heard the front bathroom door open. "You'd better get going. Don't let anybody see you with him."

"I'll try not to. Christ, Bobby. Do you think he'd really kill his father?"

"He might. He's terrified. Let's just thank the gods he knows nothing about my financial relationship with Charles."

"And pray it stays that way. Does Sophie know about it?"

Bobby shrugged. "I hope not. But she's smart, and I really have no idea."

Corey lifted Bobby's hand and kissed the back of it. "Are you all right? You seem preoccupied, even with this going on."

"Sorry," Bobby intoned. "We'll talk about it when you get back."

After a couple of seconds, Corey nodded, then hurried back to the great room. Behind him, Bobby felt his internal temperature sink still further.

CHAPTER 29

THE SENSE OF falling brings me out of sleep with a hypnic jerk. A yellow vertical line marks the edge of the bathroom door, steam floating through it. *Nadine's taking a shower*, I remember. *I must have dozed off.*

If I lie in bed another minute, I'll pass out for good. Naked, and cold from my sweat evaporating in the air-conditioning, I reach down to the floor for my jeans and pull them on. Then I sit up and grab my prosthetic, cursing in anticipation of the pain in my bruised stump.

First, I roll my thick neoprene liner from the tip of my severed bone up over my knee, then pull a white cotton sock over the liner. Next I slip the distal end of my leg down into the carbon-fiber socket. Using the bed as a fulcrum, I lever my body up and jam the stump downward to seat it in the vacuum socket. Because of bad habits, I'll have to stand here thirty seconds with my leg pounding while my circulatory system labors to shrink my tissues to fit the socket. Most amputees would have been wearing an elastic "shrinker" to keep their "residual limb" tight and ready for insertion, but when Nadine and I removed each other's clothes, I didn't feel like wearing the damned thing to bed.

Flexing what remains of my truncated calf muscles, I shiver as I recall what it was like to make love with Nadine in a completely different mental state than we've ever experienced together. The act bore almost no relation to being with Sophie Dufort, or even Martine, back when we were intimate for most of one summer. With Nadine aware of my illness (and me aware of her pregnancy), the unspoken understanding between us surpassed anything I've known, and the resulting release of tension dropped me almost instantly into sleep.

At last my stump settles into the bottom of the socket, which allows me to roll the exterior neoprene cover up the outside of my thigh. After fighting to work the right leg of my jeans down over the bulbous combination, I roll the cuff down to my ankle, then pull on my left shoe, stand, and speak through the crack in the door.

"I dozed off a minute. I'm going down to get something to eat. I haven't had anything in a while. You want something?"

"It's too late for me to eat," she calls from behind the curtain. "Thanks. I'll see you when you get back."

"Take your time."

"Oh, I am. I don't think that fire smoke is ever going to come off."

She's right, I think, smelling my own hair. Rounding the bed, I lean over and extract the PENN: START HERE folder from the top of Mom's satchel. Then I carefully make my way down the main staircase to the kitchen.

Since I spent the past week and a half watching over Mom in Natchez, there's not much edible left in this fridge. An omelet looks like the best choice. After taking out the eggs and setting a pan on the gas flame, I open Mom's folder and take out the papers inside. On top is what appears to be a handwritten note to me, while the rest seems to be a brief chapter titled THE DUEL. Realizing I'm hungrier than I thought, I crack three eggs into the pan and begin reading my dead mother's words.

Dear Penn,

Here is one of my first attempts at writing that truly reflects the results of my research. The style of the first chapters is far too close to yours, which I hope you'll take as a compliment and not plagiarism. My style changed significantly as I gained more experience and lost some of my anxiety. I think my greatest fear, given the subject matter, was committing a literary crime on the scale of William Styron's *The Confessions of Nat Turner*, which in my view is no less than the rape of a great man after he was long dead. It's scary to think that a white liberal did such a terrible injustice by projecting his own pathetically weak neuroses onto a militant Black leader, while a known racist— Thomas Ruffin Gray—gave us a far more honest portrayal. I remember you telling me you'd met Styron in Willie Morris's class at Ole Miss, and that you were more impressed by his wife, Rose. Having read *Nat Turner* twice—and the published responses by ten Black writers—I can believe it. The fact that Styron became a literary darling—and that *that* book won a Pulitzer!—pretty much damns all of us white folks and our mossy old literary institutions, to a degree. Nothing but elite and racist "gentlemen's clubs" in the end.

Anyway, to business. When I first saw my DNA report, it hit me hard. Even the tiny percentage of West African DNA shown there I felt must be a mistake. But as the days passed, it began to absorb all my attention, like a tiny root growing through a crack in a neat masonry wall. Before long, I took hold of that root and gave it a gentle tug. As more fibrous bark emerged, dirt and water came with it. After that, there was no sealing the hole, nor any way to sever the root. And what waited behind that wall of bricks . . . was a flood.

Withstanding that flood without being drowned by it took a year of intense investigation—exhausting legwork as well as hundreds of hours of library research—all punctuated by manic efforts to begin a writing career in my eighties. I spent the past few weeks trying to pummel those efforts into something like a book, but I simply didn't have the strength. I'd never empathized so deeply with you and your career until then. Still, the resulting manuscript was unlike anything I'd produced to that point. I hadn't been completely fearless when I wrote it, but I think I went further than most white Southern women would in exposing the secret history of their families. (Certainly any of my generation.) Even so, I held back from some things I'd wanted badly to do, like write from the point of view of enslaved people. I know you've done that in your lynching project, and decently, I think, at least by my lights as a judge, though I certainly can't claim to be an authority. (I sneakily read a few chapters without telling you. My sin, I know.) But as my cancer numbers worsened, I realized that I regretted my choice. So without telling even Annie, I set about trying to rectify that. I didn't know whether I could do it well or not, but the words felt much closer to the 1861 I'd uncovered than anything else I'd committed to paper. And I was no longer thinking in terms of publishing a book— not in my lifetime. I just wanted to charge forward, and to hell with the consequences.

I'm no judge of what's acceptable today, but I've observed one thing. While in Mississippi the "one-drop rule" remains more than a memory (as it does elsewhere in America, truth be told), we've come a long way since its darkest days. Far enough that it's "almost fashionable"—as a female friend recently told me—to go to the coffee shop to visit with your newly discovered Black cousins, even though you all know they exist because your ancestors raped theirs somewhere back in the fog of history.

Please don't think I'm blind to the underlying horrors. I've already uncovered moral inversions that knocked the breath out of me. They set my internal compass spinning, and it has yet to stabilize. I've also discovered heroism and self-sacrifice that did the same. So many times I've come back to Lord Acton's old saw: "Absolute power corrupts absolutely." For that is the nub of it. Slavery is absolute power. A personal dictatorship for every major landowner. Tyranny over body and soul, and it corrupted both enslaver and enslaved in ways that most people haven't even begun to grasp. (Some freed slaves in Bienville and Natchez enslaved others themselves and treated them as badly as white owners did.) Yet less than a mile from Pencarrow, a twenty-year-old

Black father of a newborn son killed himself to keep from betraying his fellow rebels.

Don't open my notebooks lightly, Penn. For they are not separate from you. They lead directly to you. Through me. And in this world we came from, treason was seen as honor, slavery as God's plan. Rape was leisure activity. Yet some white men in that world loved women they owned more than their white wives. They freed them, married them, and left them all their property. But, as with Thomas Jefferson, not in our family. What happened in our family is, to me, the worst story that I know.

This assertion hits me hard enough to break my reverie and make me realize my omelet is burning. But as soon as I slide the skillet off the fire, I pick up the pages again.

I tried to keep all this from Annie in the beginning. But you can't fool someone that intuitive for long. When my granddaughter finally wheedled the truth out of me, she punished me with days of justly deserved coldness. I'd kept her in the dark for two reasons: first, I didn't want her burdened with "such knowledge" until I knew the shape and size of the underlying truth. Second, I never really understood that for millennials, race isn't the bogeyman it is for us older folks. Even so, if I hadn't changed profoundly as I did this work, I would have carried my discoveries to the grave. But I *did* change. And now I believe the story should be told. The only question is how. I hope you will pick up the baton that death is forcing me to lay down too soon. If you read what I've done so far, I don't think you'll be able to think about anything else until you go to the finish line. These are your people, Penn.

Please remember, I'm just a beginning writer. As you and your friends used to say in high school: "Cut me some slack."

Mom

SETTING THE NOTE aside, I scrape the burned omelet onto a plate, lightly salt it, then pour a glass of orange juice and carry the food and pages to the Eames lounge chair in the corner of the den. As I sit carefully, lifting my legs onto the ottoman, my phone pings. The lateness of the hour surprises me, but the message is only a summary of charter flight arrangements from Annie. A quick glance tells me that Dr. Dwight Ford and his wife will be leaving Bienville airport on a Cessna Citation jet operated by Nicholas Air at 3:00 a.m. A ground ambulance will be waiting at Reagan National (DCA) to take them to Howard University Hospital, then bring them back with their passenger, Dr. Ezra Berry. The price for the trip, Annie tells me with a grin emoji, could buy a decent house in Bienville, Mississippi, for cash.

Thanks, boo, I text back. *Are you okay in Edelweiss with Mom's body? It's weird even typing that, but I feel bad that I abandoned you.*

I'm fine, she texts back. *I wouldn't want her lying anywhere alone. I've heard too many freaky stories about funeral homes. Even in Natchez.*

Get some rest, if you can. Tomorrow's going to be a tough day.

I will. Love you.

U2.

With that I set my phone aside, click on my reading lamp, and open my mother's first "submission" to me. The first line gives me the unsettling feeling that I'm reading something I wrote myself but somehow forgot, which is enough to pull me forward with nervous expectation.

CHAPTER 30

IN THE FINAL hour of daylight, Captain Robert Pencarrow climbed unsteadily down from the trap buggy and staggered into the shade of the silver oak to await the man who would shortly arrive to kill him. Behind Captain Pencarrow walked his butler, Cadmus Nelson, who was acting as his second on this day. By the code duello, Cadmus's participation was a violation, as seconds were required to be of equal social rank with the principals. But since dueling had been outlawed two decades earlier, and since Captain Pencarrow considered the Barlow brothers to be trash, he felt that using his immaculately dressed slave as a second sent the proper message to his opponent.

Cadmus carried a polished box containing two pistols bequeathed to the captain by his commanding officer during the Seminole Wars in the Everglades. Pencarrow hadn't fired the antiques for years, favoring instead the small revolver given him by General John Quitman during the Mexican War. But pistols were the least of Pencarrow's worries as the sun began to sink toward the Mississippi River. He shivered in the grip of what the doctors called National Hotel disease, an affliction he'd acquired while attending President Buchanan's inauguration dinner in Washington with General Quitman. Quitman had already died from a relapse, and after several similar episodes, Pencarrow feared that he too was soon for the grave. But he did not intend to sleep there tonight.

Behind him, his four children dismounted. His white offspring, Duncan and Evelyn, eighteen and seventeen, had ridden in the trap buggy. His Black children, Romulus and Niobe, seventeen and fifteen, had brought the market wagon, pulled by Hercules, the big gray. Their mother, Calliope, rode her roan, and kept her distance from Evelyn. Evelyn's mother had died eleven years before, and her daughter fiercely guarded her legacy. She lived in a state of perpetual fury, refusing even to look at the enslaved woman upon whom Pencarrow had sired her half siblings. That made life difficult enough, but this evening all the children's faces wore the shadow of fear.

While Robert Pencarrow steadied himself against the oak's silver trunk, Cadmus set down the box and carefully marked out two squares upon the ground, thirty-six feet apart. It had been years since men settled a matter of honor by the old code in these parts, but many locals still recalled the melee that had made Jim Bowie famous. Fought on a sandbar just south of Natchez, it began with a duel settled peacefully by the seconds, with no shots fired.

But due to hard feelings on both sides, the premature peace quickly devolved into a brawl that killed or wounded several of the party that had traveled there to watch. Pencarrow prayed that today's affaire d'honneur *would end with a single shot, and himself the victor. If it did not, God alone knew what might happen to his children, particularly his darker ones.*

The chain of incident that had led to this single combat was as simple as it was unusual. It had begun with the rape of a slave. Not just any slave, but Pencarrow's beloved daughter Niobe. Two months ago, the plantation's long-time overseer had died of a heartstorm. Forced to hurriedly find a replacement, Pencarrow had reluctantly hired a scoundrel named Gilmer Book, a relative of both the sheriff and the neighbor he was now waiting to fight. Despite clear warnings about the peculiarities of life on Pencarrow, Overseer Book had failed to appreciate the captain's seriousness on the matter of rules. After only three weeks, he'd followed Niobe into a corn-drying shed and forced himself upon her. Hearing screams, another female slave had run for Romulus, who at seventeen was strong enough to whip any man on the place. A minute later, Romulus entered the shed and saw his sister being violated. Where most slaves would have willed themselves blind and left, Romulus picked up the nearest tool to hand and brained the overseer with it. He happened to choose an iron froe used for ripping shingles from blocks of raw wood, and his single stroke peeled off the back of Book's skull, killing him outright.

In that moment, Romulus condemned himself to death. On any other plantation in the district, a slave who killed a white overseer wouldn't have reached the gate alive, much less jail. But on Pencarrow, the first white man into the shack was Romulus's half brother, Duncan. Taking in all at a glance, Duncan Pencarrow wrenched the froe from Book's bloody neck, carried it into the big house, and told his father that he'd killed the overseer himself, in the act of raping Niobe. This "confession" stunned Captain Pencarrow, who'd always worried that his eldest son was too soft for plantation life. He didn't believe Duncan had killed the overseer, but he respected his son's willingness to risk prison to shield his half brother from execution. Duncan's confession also presented Pencarrow with a dilemma. Every human being on the plantation knew Niobe to be his favorite child, color be damned, and that if he'd caught Book raping her, the captain would have killed the man himself. Punishing his own son for doing what he would have done would be the act of a hypocrite. After taking a night to consider the possible repercussions, Pencarrow summoned the county sheriff and told him that he'd caught Gilmer Book embezzling building materials. Confronted with his crime, Book had attacked his employer. Only the timely intervention of Pencarrow's son—his white son—had saved his life. To support this story, a half dozen Pencarrow slaves claimed to be eyewitnesses and confirmed the captain's account.

The sheriff didn't believe a word of this lie, but he could do nothing about it. On that stretch of the Mississippi, no sheriff could contradict a plantation owner and hope to retain his office. Should he do so, he would find the nabobs closing ranks against him, which amounted to earning the disfavor of the gods. But not even near-divine status could prevent personal grudges. The dead overseer's most influential relatives—two "second planters" called the Barlow brothers—lived just across the river road, on Black Oak Plantation. And the Barlows quickly made it clear that they meant to exact revenge for the death of their cousin. A pattern of harassment began, mostly directed at Pencarrow's slaves, who were treated far better than those on Black Oak, where the whip governed every waking hour. This campaign culminated with the brutal flogging of two elderly slaves caught retrieving a cow that had broken through a Pencarrow fence and made it to the road that divided the plantations. Claiming that the Pencarrow slaves had been insubordinate, Frank Barlow tied both the man and the woman to trees and administered forty lashes apiece.

Upon being informed of this outrage, Captain Pencarrow dragged himself from his sickbed and ordered Romulus to drive him into town, where he filed a complaint at the sheriff's office. After this futile act, he mounted the courthouse steps and "posted" his grievances on the door, in a notice proclaiming Frank and Shotwell Barlow to be brigands and cowards, men who willfully and recklessly damaged other man's property. This posting soon produced its desired result. A messenger appeared at Pencarrow and verbally delivered Frank Barlow's challenge. Having resigned himself to a duel, Captain Pencarrow abandoned all pretense of seeking/offering an amende honorable. He proposed the oak tree inside his gate as the dueling ground and named pistols as his weapon of choice. Had he been healthy, he'd have offered swords as an option, but in his present condition he could barely stand.

Now the fateful moment had come.

The rattle of tack from the direction of the gate alerted him. Then came the abrasive, hollow ring of alcohol-spurred laughter—something he knew well from his war years. Last he heard hoofbeats on the hardened mud of his driveway.

Everyone looked up to watch the Barlow party arrive.

First came the brothers themselves: Frank, aged thirty-five, and his brother, who was forty. They wore work clothes. With them was their brutal overseer, Seth McCutcheon, a man who'd killed more slaves than anyone in

Tenisaw County. He'd whipped or beaten many more during his moonlight job of pateroller, hunting down runaways for bounty. Behind the brothers, in a painted carriage, rode Betsy Dufort, the concubine of Frank Barlow. A dark-haired Natchez beauty, and the daughter of one of the richest men in the district, Betsy made a great pretense of being a lady, spending great sums on the latest fashions from New Orleans. Yet she looked more like a painted whore from the French Quarter than any Natchez quality. The anticipatory glee in her face made it plain she'd come to watch the haughty war hero bleed out the last of his life upon the ground.

She just might get her wish today, Pencarrow thought, pushing himself away from the oak and forcing his body erect. God damn mortal frailty. He'd seen dysentery fell more soldiers than cannon fire or musket balls ever had. And now—on a day when everything he'd built or loved would come down to a single shot—a mysterious variant of that disease had closed its cold fingers around his belly. Every rib ached, every cough burned his throat. His roiling bowels might betray him at any moment. He fought through the fits by pretending he was standing in line for inspection on a parade ground. He might not be able to stop shivering, but at least he could stand straight for whatever the fates had in store.

TEN FEET FROM his principal and master, Cadmus Nelson stood rigid as a carved angel on a tomb. He knew what to expect from the trash who owned Black Oak Plantation: curses and contempt. He'd endured it from better men for years, and he could give as good as he got without uttering a word. Such was the lot of men forced into bondage.

Cadmus watched the Barlow brothers approach, and his blood quickened at the realization that they'd been drinking. Brandy, by the smell of it. Still, he tempered his optimism. Whatever these men were, they were not fools. Their father had carved Black Oak out of raw woodland, and through sheer cruelty the sons had turned a profit for years, both here and on their second plantation across the river in Louisiana. But the notorious brothers were committing an error by underestimating the captain. Word had likely reached them of Pencarrow's relapses, and how unsteady he'd been on the courthouse steps as he condemned them. This, they surely figured, was their chance to do away with a neighbor whose politics they hated and whose land they'd long coveted. But Cadmus knew the captain in ways they never would. He'd watched the precocious boy grow until forced to assume the mantle of his older brother, who along with his mother had been felled by yellow fever in '41. Cadmus had twice watched Robert go off to war, each time returning with more pain and wisdom in his eyes.

More relevant today, however, were his nerve and skill with weapons. One drunken evening, after returning from the second Seminole War, he'd asked Cadmus to tack a playing card to a sapling behind the big house. Cadmus then watched in amazement as Robert rode wild circles around the tree, firing balls through the face of a red queen from his heaving saddle. Twenty years had passed since that day, but Cadmus knew that the wreck the Barlows saw when they looked at the captain was not the man he was—or at least the man Cadmus hoped he still was. For if Robert Pencarrow lay dead when the sun set over the river, God alone knew the fate of all those who lived under his care.

"Who's your second?" called Shotwell Barlow. "Your son? Your white son, I mean."

"I am the captain's second," Cadmus declared.

"The hell you say!" Shot Barlow glared at Pencarrow. "You can't have no goddamn slave as a second. That's an insult!"

"It might be to a gentleman," Pencarrow replied.

Shot Barlow went red.

"He's got a slave for a wife," said Frank. "Least he treats her like a wife." The younger Barlow waved his hand at Calliope, Romulus, and Niobe. "Got the whole Black half of his family right here to watch him die."

Cadmus watched the captain's face for signs of temper. He saw none. Unlike most men, Pencarrow responded to insults and danger by getting colder and more phlegmatic.

Frank Barlow raised his voice: "I said—"

"I heard you," Pencarrow said. "Let's get this business done. Choose your pistol."

Cadmus opened the polished box before Frank Barlow. He steeled himself against provocation, silently vowing not to respond, not even to a blow. The younger Barlow acted as though being this close to a Black man offended his sensibilities. As always, Cadmus wore clean black breeches and a spotless velvet coat, with a rice-starched shirt and cravat beneath. Beside him, Frank Barlow looked like a muleskinner fresh off the Natchez Trace, and he stank like one, too. He appeared to be on the verge of saying something to test Cadmus, but instead he removed one pistol from the baize-lined box and checked its balance, then its action. After sighting once along the barrel, he took a lead ball and ramrod from the box and loaded the weapon with easy familiarity.

"It's customary for your second to load your pistol," Cadmus said.

Frank laughed and continued loading. "It's also customary to have a doctor on hand for these little dos, but I don't see one here. Besides, in matters of life and death, I trust my hands and nobody else's. Not even my brother's."

Shot Barlow laughed. "Words of wisdom."

"That is your square," Cadmus said, pointing to the chalk mark nearest them on the ground.

As he'd expected, Frank Barlow defied his "order" by walking to the far square. This placed him where the setting sun would be directly in his eyes. Thankfully, clouds obscured this advantage for the moment, but with luck the sun would drop a little at an opportune moment. Cadmus would try to time his count accordingly.

As he walked toward the captain with the box, Pencarrow held up one hand and said, "Load for me, if you will."

Cadmus removed the remaining pistol and loaded it with proficiency that equaled that of Frank Barlow. When the captain reached for his outstretched weapon, nothing could hide the shaking of his hand. Pencarrow looked like an old man crippled by palsy, not a war veteran in his prime. Laughter from the Dufort slut reinforced Cadmus's fear, but he could do little now to help his master. The captain's life rested on his skill with the notoriously inaccurate smoothbore pistols used by all gentlemen to settle disputes only a few decades ago.

Pencarrow shambled to his square, then stood as straight as he could. Coming at last to some semblance of stillness, he opened his jacket as if to let the air in. The curved butt of his deadly revolver showed in its holster. As Cadmus reflected on its presence, the sun flashed on the turquoise set in the captain's silver Mexican belt buckle, and Frank Barlow blinked. With the sun beginning to clear the clouds, Cadmus wanted to delay further, but his fear that the captain might collapse overrode his hope of stealing further advantage.

"I will now count to ten," he announced. "After I reach ten, either man may fire. If neither party draws blood, we will reload the pistols and continue, unless an amende honorable is reached. Then the parties will shake hands and leave the field as friends."

"Like hell," said Barlow. "Only one of us leaves this ground tonight."

"Count it off," Pencarrow ordered.

Cadmus began.

Fear etched every face in the Pencarrow party. As Cadmus counted, he saw the fear rise into panic. How would the children react if their father were shot dead before their eyes? And Calliope? Her whole life—all her special treatment—existed because of the favor bestowed upon her by Robert Pencarrow. What would Evelyn, the white fury, do if that protection were removed? And without her father there to shield the Black children he'd sired upon the slave woman, she could take her revenge at last—

". . . six . . . seven . . ."

Barlow raised his pistol and aimed with absolute assurance across the twelve yards separating him from the man he hated. His pistol did not waver. But when the captain raised his weapon, the sun danced on its polished barrel, which bobbed as if held by a child of two or a man of eighty.

"...eight...nine..."

Barlow's face had become a mask of hatred. Nothing else showed in his eyes. The captain's face looked ghostly—pale, anemic, sweating, yet somehow cold. Only in his eyes did the warmth of life burn, all the hope that still lived within him. Hope of protecting—maybe even saving—those under his care from the war that had already broken out in South Carolina.

"...ten."

In the final second, Pencarrow's hand steadied like that of an elderly craftsman whose fingers shook day and night—except in those moments that he turned them to his trade, whether repairing watches or mending nets.

Frank Barlow fired.

His ball winged the captain, violently knocking Pencarrow's left arm back. Blood spurted from the wound, and the captain staggered, but somehow he kept his feet. Pencarrow let a second pass, then another, while Frank Barlow pondered the terrible void of mortality.

Then the captain shot him through the heart.

Cadmus felt the shock in his legs when Barlow's body hit the ground. He'd always fancied himself a hard man, but his palms began to sweat. The dolled-up hussy in the Barlow carriage let out a yelp, and from Shot Barlow came a cry of shock as he dropped to his knees and took his sibling by the shoulders. He shook the dead man several times, then bellowed with rage and got to his feet.

Captain Pencarrow swayed on his feet, but he retained enough sense to recognize danger. As Shot Barlow yanked a derringer from his pocket, Pencarrow drew his revolver from its holster, then extended it. The surviving Barlow was already aiming at his chest from a distance of thirty feet.

"The duel is done!" Cadmus cried. "By the law of the code, honor has been satisfied. The vanquished party will leave the field!"

But Shot Barlow had no intention of retiring. Cadmus expected him to fire any second. Seth McCutcheon, the Barlow overseer, drew a Bowie knife from his coat. To Cadmus's left, Romulus eased forward, ready to charge the brutal overseer if necessary.

"Get that big buck back!" Shot Barlow shouted.

"You're violating the code!" Cadmus insisted, raising his voice.

"Damn your paper rules! None of this is legal anyway!"

"Go home, Barlow," Pencarrow ordered over the shaking revolver in his outstretched hand. *"You don't want to die the same day as your brother, do you? Haven't you got a regiment to take to war?"*

Shot Barlow's eyes blazed. "I ain't dying today, you son of a bitch. You are."

Pencarrow held his aim, but he shuddered like a sentry braving a winter storm.

Barlow grinned. "I can hold my bead a hell of a lot longer than you can, Cap'n. So you'd better take your shot. The second you let that gun hand fall, you're a dead man."

Cadmus wondered whether his master oughtn't to go ahead and fire. What would be the result if he did? Legal complications. He'd likely have to kill the overseer, too. That would mean another visit by the sheriff. Maybe a crack in the usually solid wall of plantation owners. That was why the captain hadn't fired again. But Shot Barlow had no such fear. He'd sensed that the peculiarities of life on Pencarrow made the captain vulnerable in ways he hadn't quite appreciated before.

"That gun looks heavy," Barlow teased, grinning with confidence. "Take a rest, Cap'n. Let that tired old arm down."

Cadmus surveyed the scene once more—the corpse on the ground at Shot Barlow's feet, the captain's terrified children. Then he drew a pistol from beneath his velvet coat and aimed it at the surviving brother.

"Mr. Barlow?" he said. "I can hold my aim until the sun comes up tomorrow. So you'd best get on back to your place now."

While Barlow gaped at the spectacle of an armed slave, McCutcheon stumped sullenly forward with his Bowie knife, likely to get within throwing range. Romulus quickly cut him off, blocking his path like an obsidian statue. The overseer paused. He knew a lot about slaves, and he didn't like what he saw in the eyes of Romulus Pencarrow—or rather what he did not see:

Fear of white men.

Pencarrow clenched his belly in a way that told Cadmus his bowels were about to let go. Another sixty seconds and the captain's trousers would be soaked with excrement. Panic bloomed in Cadmus's chest.

Succumbing to exhaustion, Pencarrow finally dropped his gun arm, then lurched toward the carriage. Cadmus kept his aim on Shot Barlow, his heart hammering. If Barlow meant to shoot, he'd do it now. Cadmus didn't dare fire first. If the captain wanted Barlow dead, he'd have fired himself.

To Cadmus's left, Duncan Pencarrow got under his father's good arm and helped him into the back of the market wagon. Barlow watched this without firing. Calliope leapt off her horse and climbed into the wagon to treat the arm wound.

"You men get home now!" Cadmus pleaded, waving his heavy pistol. "I'd

hate to have to shoot you, Mr. Barlow. But I'll do it. As God is my witness, I will."

Duncan had taken possession of his father's revolver, and now he walked directly toward Barlow. "I'd love to kill you, you bastard," he said, pointing the revolver at the dead Barlow on the ground. "Get that trash off our land."

"I'll need some slaves to help lift him," Shot Barlow said finally.

"If you and McCutcheon can't get him into your carriage, tie a rope to his feet and drag him home. He's meat for the buzzards anyway. Isn't that what McCutcheon always says about dead slaves?"

Hatred glowed like banked fire from the overseer's eyes.

Cadmus winced at the sound of bodily functions from the wagon. Five seconds later the stench hit him.

"Back to the house!" Calliope called to Romulus.

Cadmus looked over at the market wagon. Captain Pencarrow's good arm floated in the air, signaling that he should be driven home.

"You'd better hope he lives," Barlow warned. "All y'all." He jabbed his derringer toward Cadmus and Romulus. "But especially you two. If Pencarrow dies, I'll buy every slave on this place for pennies on the dollar and start burning you one at a time. Not branding you. Burning you."

This was no empty threat. A month ago, Seth McCutcheon had burned a serial runaway in front of the assembled Barlow slaves. While the Barlow brothers stood by in their Sunday clothes, six hundred eyes had watched a fellow slave scream out his last breath while his legs roasted.

Cadmus stole a glance at Evelyn Pencarrow. In the white daughter's eyes, he saw a fierce joy at Barlow's savage threat. That frightened him more than Barlow's words. War was coming to Mississippi, likely sooner rather than later. And in war, it was every man for himself. Of all the captain's children, only Evelyn seemed to understand that. She wouldn't hesitate to sell every slave she hated to Shot Barlow—into the bottomless hell of Black Oak Plantation. And if the captain died, Cadmus would have no choice but to work with Evelyn, not against her. He wasn't ready for that. Not quite yet. He needed the captain to live a little longer.

A few days, anyway.

"PENN, ARE YOU downstairs?" Nadine calls from the head of the staircase. "Penn! Did you fall asleep?"

"Nearly! I'll be up in a second."

With a groan of pain, I force myself to my feet. My plate is empty, so at some point while reading I ate the omelet, though I don't remember doing so. I still feel hungry. "Are you sure you don't want some eggs?"

"I'll take a piece of toast if you have one!"

Toast sounds good to me, too. "Butter or jelly?"

"Both!"

Slipping Mom's pages back into the manila folder, I lay the folder on the counter and start fixing Nadine her toast (plus an extra piece for myself). Mom was right about her writing echoing my own, at least in this particular chapter. But the immediacy of her style impressed me, as well as her inclusion of accurate historical detail. Most surprising of all was her entry into the mind of Cadmus, the enslaved butler. She'd clearly pored deeply over the man's published diary, and used all that was known about him to create a multi-dimensional human being. Nevertheless, I wonder whether she could possibly have achieved a similar level of verisimilitude if she'd dared to try to penetrate the mind of Calliope, who spent most of her life in an intimate relationship with Robert Pencarrow, a man whose father had owned her almost from birth. This was the essence of the challenge that had made me so wary of novelizing my research into the Second Creek lynchings, and those that followed near Bienville soon after. I didn't want to commit the literary crime that William Styron had, either, one born primarily from the sins of narcissism and hubris. And yet . . .

The story of these people—the Barlows and the Duforts, and the human beings they enslaved (some so clearly related to their descendants, whom I have known intimately)—has never let me go. If Mom is to be believed, I carry both Pencarrow and Barlow blood. But how, I wonder, is that possible? Since the Shotwell Barlow who walks the earth today would like nothing better than to avenge his ancestor's death upon me, I'd love to know the answer. I wonder if Barlow knows himself? All I know for certain is this: if the city devolves into bloody chaos over the next few hours or days . . .

Shot Barlow might get his chance for revenge.

CHAPTER 31

THE DAUGHTERS OF Egypt Church lay in the bottomland in the
northwest corner of Tenisaw County, tucked into the last stand of hardwoods before everything went to cottonwood and bamboo cane at the
river's edge. A gravel road offered the only access, dropping from where
the asphalt petered out a hundred feet above, in the kudzu-choked forest. The bluff here was slashed deep by erosion, leaving ugly cuts through
which torrents of rain and mud poured down behind the church in the
spring. Back in the 1950s, a great mudslide had knocked the whole church
down one night, but mercifully the building had been empty, and the congregation soon rebuilt it better than before. The present building had decent plumbing, good insulation, a proud steeple, and a shining steel cross.

But Daughters of Egypt was not empty tonight. Two sober deacons, one
young, the other old, had stretched out sleeping bags on the carpeted floor
of the sanctuary and spent the early hours of the night on the church steps.
Each had brought a sack supper and a firearm from his home. Smoking on
the steps, Duncan Gardner, the older man, told his younger comrade tales
of what it had been like to stand watch back in the 1960s, when he'd been
a member of the Deacons for Defense. He'd guarded many a civil rights
meeting, and sometimes things had turned violent. He'd listened to Medgar Evers recruit for the NAACP from the very steps they sat on now, and
watched him forced to leave in a big damn hurry.

"I heard you was a member of the Black Dot Club back in the day,"
said Kemontrae Woods. "They say you guys used to protect the civil rights
workers coming in and out of the area when the Klan was after them."

Duncan smiled with modest pride. "We done what we could. My boys
and I used to race cars, you know. Stock cars. We used what skills we had
on these old back roads."

"Ol' Miz Ables tol' me you once saved John Lewis on these old roads."

"We did. The Klan was after him bad, but we got him in and out both."
Gardner gave a deep chuckle. "Good trouble, man. And he never forgot.
He tol' a buddy of mine to thank me twenty years later."

"That's fire, man." Kemontrae lit another Kool. "You figure they'll mess
with us down here tonight?"

Duncan figured that with forty-three churches in Tenisaw County—

more than half of them Black—the odds of Daughters of Egypt being hit were low. "Nah. We way off the beaten path these days."

Nevertheless, the two men kept sipping coffee from the thermos Duncan Gardner had carried to the old Triton battery plant for decades. They kept two lights burning in the church behind them, plus the security lamp overhead, to let night riders know the place was guarded.

"What's that smell?" asked the younger man. "Sweet, like honeysuckle, but different."

The older man drew in heavily perfumed air. "Confederate jasmine, the white folks call it. They think that refers to the Old South, but it's Chinese, some way. Just plain jessamine, my granny called it. Or star jessamine. Best scent in the world, you ask me."

"It's strong here."

"The Lord smilin' on us, boy. Life's little gifts."

Around one a.m., a large group of does gathered to feed at the edge of the hardwoods just south of the church. The men watched in silence, sharing an occasional glance. Shortly after three, Duncan went inside to take a catnap in his sleeping bag while Kemontrae stood post on the steps. To Gardner's surprise, he dozed quickly, which was rare now that he suffered from most of the afflictions common to Black men in their early eighties. He kept his rifle close by on the floor, and said a half-conscious prayer that the boy would remain awake until it was time to relieve him.

Barely an hour later, a gunshot shattered his sleep.

As Duncan struggled to his feet in the dim light, the front door burst open. Kemontrae staggered in, his eyes wide and unfocused. A red flower the size of a soup bowl bloomed from his upper left chest. The roaring engine of a big pickup sounded from outside, driving a fast circuit of the church as someone riddled the walls with bullets. Duncan grabbed his rifle and ran to a stained-glass window to return fire, but before he reached it, a Molotov cocktail shattered the pane and skittered under a church pew.

The truck engine roared, country music pounding from its hi-fi. Gardner whirled and chased down the bottle, following the pungent tang of gasoline. He knew well the risk he was taking, but he'd come to defend his church, and he didn't hesitate. Bending low among the pews, he grabbed for the bottleneck and the satanic blue flame of the wick—

Got it!

Jerking up the bottle, he hurled it back at the smashed window.

His aim was unlucky. The heavy chunk of glass struck the leaded frame and bounced back onto the floor, where it spun under the pews once more, right past Gardner's shoes. This time it exploded into a horizontal sheet of flame that spread outward like a lake of fire. When the flames ignited his trouser legs, Duncan rolled onto the wooden floor of the aisle in a vain attempt to smother them. As he struggled, a second window shattered on the opposite side of the church, and another flaming bottle landed among the pews.

"*Kemontrae!*" he screamed. "*Help me, brother!*"

But Kemontrae was down.

The dry floor caught flame like fatwood kindling, and by the time the roar of the truck had faded among the cottonwoods, half the building was gone, and two men lay dead among the pews.

Outside, the river rolled past as it had for millennia, and nothing ever changed.

CHAPTER 32

BOBBY WHITE STOOD ALONE on the cypress deck behind his cabin, listening to the birds run riot in the trees, even in the pit of night. It was still full dark at 4:00 a.m., but he couldn't bear to be inside with Corey and think about what he meant to do tomorrow. His partner possessed an internal seismograph of phenomenal sensitivity, and he would sense Bobby was pondering something beyond the pale. And while Corey might believe—for a while—that this thing had to do with Charlot Dufort and the threat he posed, before long he would detect something deeper, and he'd begin to probe for it.

That was why Bobby had pretended to be asleep after Corey returned from dropping Charlot downtown. Thankfully, Corey had passed out within minutes of climbing into bed, and after two fitful hours, Bobby had carefully rolled over and crept out to the deck, where he could give his dark epiphany the space it deserved.

The boundless bowl of sky over the Mississippi River gave him a sense of continental scale. This vast alluvial plain, and not the Rocky Mountains, had always been to him the true Continental Divide. The great delta, which ran from Arkansas down into both Louisiana and Mississippi, might seem a backwater to some, but they were blind to the deepest truths that underlay the establishment of the United States. For the last few years, the echoes of those truths had been rising implacably to the surface, their power shifting the tectonic plates upon which American society had been standing with such a convincing illusion of solidity.

Bobby could still smell the ashes of Arcadia on the air, like an after-action wind in Afghanistan. It quickened his blood, tuning him to the tide of opportunity. Unlike the Mission Hill massacre—which had simply been a law-enforcement fuck-up of historic proportion—the burning of Tranquility and Arcadia represented something new, a profound escalation by . . . someone. Blacks, maybe, or perhaps right-wing whites hellbent on open conflict. Whoever set the fires, they appeared to be acts of economic terrorism and historical revenge, which made them eminently exploitable. They would drive white supremacist groups to retaliatory violence, without question. Even a local political conniver like Dixie Donnelly could see the political potential.

But Bobby's mind had spun infinitely further ahead than that. For he had looked into the eyes of Donny Kilmer and seen the future. His future, and that of the nation. At first, he'd misread the pale lone wolf in Barlow's bunker. He'd seen an ignorant hillbilly ready to play Patroclus to his Achilles. But the more he thought about all Kilmer had said while they were "down-hatch"—particularly his fantasies of mass-casualty attacks—the better Bobby understood that Donahue Kilmer was his personal Lee Harvey Oswald, a mixed-up young man whirling in a tornado of political confusion, searching for a mission to validate his life. Bobby didn't know who had given the order to kill John Kennedy, but he now knew how they must have felt when they looked into young Lee's eyes back in New Orleans in the early sixties.

The plan for tomorrow had bloomed in his mind when Corey said the word "cuckoo," and now any other course appeared foolish by comparison. Trying to create a circumstance in which Bobby could emulate Kendrick Washington's selfless action at Mission Hill was a million-to-one shot. Even if he somehow managed it, he might die attempting its execution. After all, risk was what validated the heroic act, whatever it might be. Kendrick had already achieved global fame by his act of peaceful resistance, saving God-knew how many lives, and the only way for Bobby to fully exploit that in the short term was to leverage Kendrick's fame and take it for his own—as a young cuckoo would do after being planted in the nest of another bird.

There was precedent in the political world. Benjamin Netanyahu surely owed some of his political lives to the heroism of his brother Yonni, the only Israeli casualty of the daring hostage rescue from Entebbe in 1976. If Donny Kilmer did what Bobby would ask of him tomorrow—and Bobby provided the public climax, for all the cameras to see—then Bobby would link himself forever with Kendrick in the public mind, and ultimately replace him. Possibly within as little as twenty-four hours.

All that stood between him and Kendrick's ever-expanding universe of social media followers was the willingness to sacrifice a certain number of lives. How many, Bobby could not know. Thirty or forty innocents seemed likely, but two or three hundred wasn't beyond possibility. Bobby was a visual thinker, and the likely sequence of events seemed simple enough. At some point tomorrow, Kendrick—in Doc Berry's absence—would take it upon himself to address the African American crowd that had taken possession of the bluff. And when he did . . .

He would make himself a perfect target.

Bobby saw Donny Kilmer assassinating the young leader from some high perch near the bluff, a church steeple or a water tower. Something quintessentially American. The first result would be panic, as the thousands listening to Washington went into paroxysms of grief. But what would Donny do when he found himself high above the streets, having slaughtered the lamb who foolishly dreamed of becoming a lion? Of leading his people to true equality after decades of failure by greater men?

Donny wasn't the type to run.

Nor was he the kind to kill himself out of remorse. *Because he'll feel no remorse,* Bobby thought. *He will, in fact, be in a state of bliss. He'll feel triumph. And he'll keep shooting. He'll have packed dozens of clips with him, hundreds of rounds. Maybe thousands. He'll be going for the record . . .*

Donny will switch his AR-15 to full auto and start spraying bullets into the grieving crowd, like any red-blooded militiaman worth his salt. Dozens will die in seconds, before any cops on the scene can even locate the source of the shots. In Las Vegas it had taken ten minutes to isolate the shooter to a single hotel, and they only found him then because he'd shot a security guard who reported his location. Even with that information, more than an hour passed before SWAT breached the shooter's room and found him dead.

So—

Kendrick will be down, shot in the head or chest . . .

Donny will be firing nonstop into a hunkered-down mass of humanity, his mind awash in adrenaline and oxytocin. Juvenile ecstasy. Racking up kills like it's Call of Duty IV. *The wounds will be worse than the kills. Every bullet creates a nightmare for a trauma surgeon somewhere down the line, and Mississippi has only one level I trauma center within its borders. Then, even as the police and the sheriff's department and the National Guard prove their incompetence in the face of such an event, and some brave reporter crouches amid the tracers to film the unfolding carnage—*

Robert E. Lee White will rise from the crouching mass, draw his competition pistol from his ankle holster, take aim at some deadly shadow no one else has discerned . . .

And blow Donny Kilmer's heart out.

This single act—the simultaneous punishment of Kendrick Washington's assassin and the saving of countless Black lives—would make Bobby as great a hero to the Left as he was now to those in the other parts of the fractured nation. Even the fame he enjoyed as the executioner of Abu Nasir would pale in light of viral footage of him taking down a wild-eyed redneck with an AR-15 machine-gunning Black families in Mississippi. By killing a MAGA lone wolf in the midst of carrying out the deadliest mass shooting in U.S. history, Bobby would all but guarantee his ascent to the White House in the next election.

Who could stand against him after that?

The Black votes that surge his way will cripple the Democrats, and the constant pressure to pivot hard right and suck MAGA voters away from Trump will also diminish, because they'll be drifting toward him anyway. The racial dynamics of tomorrow's action might not suit their tastes to a T, but MAGAs love nothing better than decisive action—especially a "good guy with a gun" scenario—and what else could a hero do when he found himself in the midst of mass slaughter?

Knock down the bad guy—no matter what color he is.

Of course, even as Bobby was lifted onto the collective shoulders of the country, he would bear the weight of the unparalleled sin that had placed him there. Sending Donny on that mission—even with the intent of killing him seconds after he began firing—was a mortal sin by any standard. Not merely against God (though Bobby could hear his grandfather thundering about the Sixth Commandment in some airless Louisiana tavern whose floor was still sticky with the lifeblood of some farmer knifed to death the previous night). Slaughtering innocents by the dozen, or even the hundred, was a sin against nature, too, like killing a doe carrying a calf. Also against humanity itself, even if all the dead were Black. For Bobby knew, just like every white supremacist who walked the earth, that Blacks were as human as anybody else, and their deaths counted equally in whatever karmic calculus swayed the unfolding events of the world.

All this he had taken into account, lying in the dark as Corey lightly snored beside him, and he had come to terms with it. Tomorrow's action was what had brought him back to his hometown, even if he hadn't known it at the time he made his decision. Winning the PGA tourney meant nothing. Charles Dufort's millions, while critical to his electoral effort, could have been bargained for some other way. But this—the exponential and almost instantaneous magnification of his presence in the national consciousness—could not be obtained by any other means.

Were he doing it for no better reason than Trump or the GOP—simply to attain power—Bobby knew it would mean the end of him. But he was not like those men. His motive was as noble as that of any patriot in the history of the nation. For he knew, by means of the recurring vision he'd kept from Penn Cage on the night the writer confided his terminal illness, that he *had* to win the next presidential election. Unbeknownst to anyone but him, history was narrowing to an inflection point in which the very existence of the United States would be thrown into doubt. During this crisis, a decision would fall upon the president that could result in the loss of millions of lives.

Millions of lives.

And any man who made that decision using the old moral reasoning that had guided American leaders in the past would likely doom the nation to destruction. This dilemma would require a man capable of fully seeing the three sides of all future conflict—the political, the racial, and the religious—and more important, of acting without regard for old alliances. As best Bobby could determine, the likely crisis year was 2027.

Which meant he had to win the Presidency in 2024.

The 2027 date he had determined in two ways: first by a clue in the vision itself, one it had taken him months to notice. The second involved a numerical system he'd observed during his study of American history, a mathematical cycle based on the number **82. For the United States, the initial year was 1781. After that came 1863. Then 1945. Next would be 2027. Bobby knew a hundred history professors who would laugh at his "theory," and compare him to the morons who'd sat waiting for the world to end by the Mayan calendar. But he also knew a dozen Navy SEALs who'd laughed when he told them Abu Nasir was hiding not in Iraq, where they'd finally run down and vaporized al Zarqawi, but in Afghanistan, under the protection of the Taliban.

Yet it was Bobby who had nailed his hide to the wall.

Again he saw tomorrow unfolding in his mind, the unbridled chaos of people being shot to pieces in the public square—a thing he'd witnessed more than once during his service in the special forces. Americans were simply unprepared to deal with such realities. They could scarcely absorb the deaths of thirty children in a school shooting. How could they grasp the incineration of a half million infants? Three million families. Such carnage was possible, of course, and in the same time frame that existed during the hottest phases of the Cold War. Thirty minutes from any given point in time, a Russian MIRV could be dropping warheads on multiple American cities. In six minutes a Chinese submarine could be delivering them to Washington, D.C., via cruise missile.

And yet as realistic as these nightmares were, they were not the substance of Bobby's vision.

In Bobby's vision, the end of the world began in the only place it was ever meant to end—

The Holy Land.

He felt the vision coming upon him once more, the sickening sensation of the elevator dropping swiftly into the earth beneath Cheyenne Mountain, and he pushed back against it, hard. He focused instead on the subsonic drone of diesel engines pushing barges upriver, traveling to him through the water and the ground. Feeling their power, he caught another whiff of scorched wood and paint on the wind. For a moment he wondered again who was behind the fires that had destroyed Tranquility and Arcadia, but in truth he didn't care. If tomorrow unspooled the way he believed it would, then the burned mansions would only be remembered as prologue to the greater drama of assassination and justice that would play itself out before day's end.

As he stared out toward the bluff's edge, a deep snort came out of the darkness.

For a moment Bobby wondered if it might be a whitetail buck, but the timbre was wrong. Squinting into the blackness, he slowly realized what was in front of him. Fifty feet away, faint moonlight limned the outline of a huge figure standing between the cabin and the bluff's edge. He saw a great head, tall rounded ears, and the yellow-red glint of eyes in the void.

A bear.

Penn Cage's bear? he wondered, trying to estimate mass. The creature weighed five hundred pounds, if he weighed fifty. Maybe six hundred, as Penn had described the one he'd come face-to-face with in Natchez.

The great creature snorted again, then pawed the earth.

He was looking straight at Bobby.

Bobby bent at the waist and drew his pistol from his ankle holster, the very one he would use against Donny Kilmer tomorrow. He seldom went anywhere without it these days, and tonight was no exception. As he straightened up, the bear dropped onto all fours and began lumbering toward him, swaying from side to side with a momentum that made Bobby's stomach roll.

He raised his pistol.

Bobby felt no fear. From this distance he could put a bullet through either eye, even in the moonlight. Yet he felt no inclination to do so. Monday he'd killed a man who threatened to ruin him, but this creature had not revealed any malicious intent—not even to take Bobby as a meal. Bobby was more curious than anything else. In fact, he realized, as the bear stopped just ten feet away and rose onto his hind legs once more . . .

What he felt was awe.

Which was exactly what Penn had described. A sense of standing face-to-face with the universe itself, of contemplating its will through the face of the bear. From such close proximity, it came home to Bobby how helpless he would be without the pistol. A bear that size could tear down the cabin with his paws. He *was* the universe made manifest in flesh and claw and bone. Bobby suspected this experience was something like swimming with a whale, only on land.

Again the bear snorted, and this time Bobby caught the carrion stink of his breath. He'd killed and eaten something recently. In the silver light, Bobby saw Black blood on his snout, and on the fur of his chest. *What have you come to tell me?* he asked silently. *Is this a confession? Who or what have you killed?*

Of course it's no confession, he thought. *You cannot sin. You can only be sinned against . . .*

While I—

I have eaten from the Tree of Knowledge. I remember all those I have killed. I understand all I've taken from them, and from theirs. I send Donny Kilmer out to take a man's life tomorrow, knowing he will take a hundred others with him . . . I do it in full knowledge of my crime.

The glowing eyes stared into Bobby's with as penetrating an intelligence as he'd sensed in any human for some time. As they stood in silent communion, an impulse pushed Bobby to set his pistol on the deck railing, then slowly shove the weapon along the wood until it was out of easy reach. He shuddered as he straightened up, for the balance of power had changed.

Now they stood equal, each before the other. Or at least, more equal than they had been. All Bobby's training told him that reaching the weapon might not be possible if the bear lunged with lethal intent.

And that's the point, he thought, addressing the universe. *I'm giving you a chance to stop me. If you want Kendrick Washington to live . . . if you want the one or two hundred innocents that Donny will tack onto the bill before I nail him to survive . . .*

Then kill me now.

Because tomorrow I mean to let Donny run amok long enough to justify my slaying him. I can't be elected bearing blood guilt. I'll be wearing blood as triumph, as a flag of justice. Soldier's blood.

While the bear stared in confusion, Bobby held out his left arm and tilted his head back. Then he closed his eyes. The moonlight beaming through the clouds was too faint to penetrate his eyelids. He was floating in blackness, the sound of the bear's breathing like a great pump compared to his own feeble respirations. The birds had ceased their chatter. He heard the big diesels out on the river again, but far away now. Then he heard the bear breathe again, impossibly close and alive. The deck boards transmitted the vibration of great weight moving. Nearby. Had the bear moved forward, sensing advantage? Was it preparing to swipe at him, to take off his head with one swing?

Bobby was about to open his eyes when a wavering light like a torch bloomed yellow over his lids, moving so quickly that he wondered if Corey had come out and waved a flashlight over his face.

Opening his eyes, he saw a flaming orange fireball rocket over his shoulder, cross the river, and traverse the flat wastes of Louisiana and Texas in about six seconds. His mouth fell open. This was no tiny meteorite skipping off the atmosphere, but a boiling ball of orange flame, utterly soundless, flying low and fast like a phosphorus shell fired between artillery positions in the Afghan mountains. As he gasped, a great flash lit the sky to the west, and he wondered if the damn thing had crashed into the Sangre de Cristo Mountains in New Mexico, or splashed down in the far Pacific. It seemed to fly so slowly compared to other objects he'd seen, but Bobby understood enough science to know it had likely been moving at close to sixty thousand miles per hour. Trying to imagine such velocity was like trying to imagine thirty million deaths. . . .

Dropping his eyes, he realized the bear still stood opposite him, fully erect, maybe seven feet away, and not at all interested in the flaming rock. The bear hadn't even turned to follow the light with his eyes.

You are that rock, Bobby thought. *And I . . . have my answer.*

If God or the universe wanted to prevent what was almost certain to happen tomorrow, it could have used the bear to stop him during the last twenty seconds. Bobby couldn't possibly have gotten to his pistol and dropped the bear under those circumstances. He would be bleeding out at this moment, while the bear prepared to devour him at leisure.

And yet . . .

Something in the animal's expression seemed to chide him now. Something in its eyes. Something accusatory, judgmental . . . something that said, *It's not up to me to stop you, Sergeant. You must stop yourself.*

With a slow, deliberate movement, Bobby took out his burner phone and called Donny Kilmer. The kid answered on the second ring.

"Yes, sir?"

"How's it looking out on the bluff?"

"Things got a little crazy around one thirty. Some white teenagers came down in trucks, hollering shit at those tents. But nothing came of it. Nobody fired. It's mostly quiet now. A few colored marching up and down the Row with signs, but that's it. They look wore out, Sergeant."

"Okay. There's a Confederate cemetery near the eastern edge of the county. Not far from Belle Rose. You know it?"

"Sure. I got people buried there."

"I should have known. Be there at ten a.m. If I can get there, I'll meet you with orders. If I can't get away, I'll call. Either way, I suspect you'll have a target by noon. You good with that?"

"I'll be there. Loaded for bear."

This expression threw Bobby for a second. But of course it had just been coincidence. "Good man. Out."

Without really forming intent, in a fluid motion Bobby pocketed his phone, picked up his pistol, and shot the big bear through its left eye. The giant staggered once, like a drunk man trying to keep his feet, then collapsed with an impact that shook the ground beneath the deck.

As Bobby laid his pistol back on the rail, the glass patio door behind him slid open. He turned to see Corey rush out onto the deck, the duvet from the master bedroom pulled tight around his naked body.

"Are you okay?" Corey asked worriedly. "I heard a shot!"

"I'm fine, Cor, that was me. A bear walked up on me before I knew what was going on. He got close enough to take my head off, same as happened to Penn Cage."

"My God."

"I just reacted out of instinct, drew from my ankle holster, and fired."

Corey came to the rail and peered down into the dark. The bear's carcass lay like a hillock of earth, but darker than any dirt Bobby had seen for years.

"It's so sad," Corey said. "I mean, I'm glad you're all right, of course. It just seems . . . sad."

"Yeah," Bobby said, as though in agreement, although he felt nothing.

Corey watched him in silence. "Are you really all right?"

Bobby nodded slowly.

"I was already awake when I heard the shot. I thought you had turned on the light, but when I opened my eyes it was dark again, and you weren't there."

Bobby thought about the surreal sequence of events: the bear's silent appearance, the silent fireball. Last night he would have described it all to Corey in wonder.

Tonight he offered nothing.

"I checked my mail," Corey said awkwardly. "We've got the names to take another state ballot. North Carolina. Seventy thousand, six hundred sixty-six signatures. Jamie wanted to verify the total commitments before he passed them on to us."

"Good deal," Bobby said without enthusiasm. "That's great, Cor."

"You're not excited?"

"Sure. Hell. I don't know."

Corey took a couple of steps closer and leaned forward until his head rested on Bobby's pectoral muscle. "I'm scared, Bobby."

"I know."

Bobby understood what was happening. While Corey had been an integral part of this campaign ever since running became a remote possibility, the truth was, neither of them had really believed Bobby had a chance of winning. But during the past week—after old Tio Carrera's visit—that had changed. The possibility of victory hung in the air like a fragrant promise, of love or redemption. And the unspoken truth they'd begun to absorb was that victory would, by definition, mean the end of their relationship.

Their intimate relationship, anyway.

Despite Bobby's celebrity, they'd lived a comparatively small life up to now, only safe because it was so tightly controlled. The nature of the radio industry had offered them that option. For them, their world was Bobby's home, the studio, a few restaurants. A vacation villa on South Caicos provided a haven of real freedom. But if Bobby stepped out of that cocoon to run for president . . . there would be no sanctuary. He would be climbing onto a high wire in front of millions. And if you climbed onto a high wire where the audience could throw rocks . . . you were a hell of a lot safer alone.

For a brief period they'd flirted with the idea that four years wasn't that long to endure sexual separation—not if it meant a chance to change the world for the better. But the more real the prospect of occupying the White House became, the more they were forced to acknowledge that taking that job aged everyone faster than normal. Surviving four years of intense pressure without the outlet of intimacy was a fool's fantasy. And the possibility of carrying on in secret was ridiculous. In that world, Secret Service agents would move in and out of their personal space as required, making secrecy impossible.

And there's one more thing, Bobby remembered. *Tio's objection. Which might be what Corey's thinking of now . . . "No Jackie O."*

To reach the pinnacle of power in America, you almost had to be married.

To a woman.

What a thought, Bobby mused silently. *At this point in my life*. It wasn't like young ladies wouldn't line up for the position, but in all seriousness, who could he possibly marry and live with? And if he did go that far, would they be *in* on the deception? Or would Bobby have to pretend to be sincere for the duration?

Four years of acting . . . ?

For some reason an image of Sophie Dufort rose into his mind. Her long neck and patrician face . . . the cool intellect behind those eyes. The idea was ridiculous, of course. Sophie was twenty years older than he, and time had slid twenty years forward since their brief and shallow encounter as he'd entered college. Yet her beauty and breeding were still beyond question. And when Charles died . . . Sophie would be *truly* wealthy—

"You don't have to be scared," Bobby said, stroking Corey's hair.

He could see that Corey didn't believe him. Bobby put his arms around his partner's shoulders, which were shivering. "Let's go back inside."

Corey didn't move. He stood with his head on Bobby's chest, crying softly, desolately in the dark.

CHAPTER 33

CHARLOT DUFORT ROLLED over in the Hampton Inn queen bed and reached blindly for his burner phone, enjoying the deepest sleep he'd managed over the past ten days. He couldn't imagine who would be calling this late—the bedside clock showed 3:52 a.m.—but he knew he had to answer.

"Hello?" he said, praying that Russo's collection gorillas had not somehow located him.

"Do you recognize my voice?" asked Martyn Black.

"Uh . . . yeah. I saw you earlier tonight."

"Right. Are you awake? I don't want to have to repeat this."

"I'm awake."

"So my girlfriend hacked into a certain agent's office computer system for you. I got the numbers on our friend BW's latest radio deal."

Charlot snapped to full alertness. "Wait . . . Lanying did this?"

"*No names, goddamn it.* But yeah. She didn't want to, but she did. In the hope that you'll leave us alone from now on. Her words. Anyway, you're not going to like what she found."

"What's the number?" Charlot asked. "How much did he get?"

"Before I tell you, you've got to swear you won't tell you-know-who where you got the information. You hear me?"

"Of course. Christ, absolutely not."

"He doesn't let things slide. You must know that by now. You make him suffer, you will suffer."

"I've got it, man. Now, what's the number? It's millions, isn't it?"

Martyn paused. "Yeah."

"Three million?"

"No."

"More?"

"More."

Charlot could scarcely believe it. "Four? Four fucking million?"

"More."

"*More?* Not five."

"You're not even close. It's twelve million, Charlot."

The extended silence made Martyn think he'd lost the connection. "Charlot? Are you still there?"

"Twelve per *year*?"

"Uh-huh."

"I can't even . . ."

"I know."

"That *lying bastard*. He could pay off my whole debt and never even *feel* it!"

"Charles . . . it's *your* debt, dude."

"I know, but . . . goddamn, it's my *life*, too. And you guys blew every bit of my trust fund in high school. All of it! Bobby could erase my whole nut with less than twenty percent of a single year's salary!"

"Listen, Char . . . I'm out of this, okay? I have no opinion. But I'm begging you. Think long and hard before you tell Bobby that he somehow *owes* you two or three million dollars. For your own sake. Do you hear me?"

"That *lying motherfucker.*"

"I'm hanging up now. Please . . . be careful, man. You're on dangerous ground."

"I'm not the only one."

"I'm out of this, bro. I mean it." Martyn hung up.

Charlot lay awake for a long time afterward. His father's indifference to his fate, perhaps even to his premature death—however unnatural such callousness might be—was something so familiar that Charlot could almost accept it. But to discover that the man who had once been the love of his life held in his hands the power to save him, yet chose not to . . . was a soul-searing wound that stung more than the blade of the killers Russo had sent to his home earlier that day. And from this pain was born an anger of such exquisite intensity that Charlot had never before tasted it. Try as he might, lying in the rented darkness, he could not force his exhausted eyes to close.

CHAPTER 34

NADINE SAT AT Penn's desk in the spill of moonlight from his open blackout curtains, looking back at the bed where he lay sleeping. After the release of sex, followed by his downstairs meal, he'd fallen into deep slumber, but she'd been unable to stop the torrent of thoughts racing through her brain. Penn's revelation of his medical diagnosis had profoundly altered her perception of their parting, and of the years since. His reaction to her revelation of the pregnancy had pleased her, but almost as swiftly had come his confession about the harsh realities of cancer treatment. And despite their age difference, at least one *Life* magazine photograph of the "thalidomide babies" of the 1960s had burned itself into her brain at UNC law school, a heart-wrenching image of a mother bathing her deformed infant. At age twenty-four, it had pierced her more deeply than even the "napalmed girl" photo from the Vietnam War. And yet . . .

She had told him the truth on the stairs. In her heart she felt no doubt about what meant most to her in life now. She studied the V-shaped stump of Penn's right leg, fully exposed since he hadn't pulled up the bedcovers before passing out. The amputation and suture scars remained livid even after fifteen years, and the thigh muscle above his knee had clearly atrophied compared to the one on his left leg. His intact leg, though it appeared normal, had also been shattered in the accident, and was filled with metal pins and bolts from hip to ankle. Penn had had those injuries the first time she saw him naked, of course, back in 2016, but he'd seemed stronger and more vital then. In the seven years since their first coupling, he had aged a lot. Yet not in the obvious ways. Not as a still photograph that differed from her older memory, but at a level deeper than sight. In his blood and glands, hormonally, at the level of bone density, and suppleness of skin. There was a clock ticking in him now, a metabolic chronograph, the gnomon of mortality. The same was true for every human being, of course, but in Penn that process had somehow become audible, if not readily visible.

Confronted by this new frailty—and finally aware that he'd been struggling with the possibility of imminent death—she understood why he'd resisted the prospect of marrying her. And of course there *was* the age difference. But she'd been around the marital track once with a man her own age, and by the time she secured her divorce, she'd learned what mattered in a marriage, and it wasn't your birth year. She wondered what her mother would have made of her romantic dilemma. Marshall McEwan was ten years closer to her in age, and in every way a desirable match by the old Southern standards. Handsome, smart, a good provider, and divorced through no particular fault of his own.

And yet . . .

The years she'd spent with Penn were the most contented she'd ever known. She'd asked the night why many times, and the answer that most often echoed back was simple: he possessed something that most men of her generation did not. For lack of a better word, she thought of it as *gravitas*. A quiet, sober rectitude that hailed from an older time. His father had possessed it also—might in fact have been the font of it—and it had made Tom Cage beloved in Natchez, in both the white and Black communities. Despite Penn's keen intelligence, he never resorted to sarcasm for humor, as the men she'd grown up with so often did. He always fought for the underdog, no matter the odds, and while he was more a cerebral observer than a man of action, when backed into a corner he had defended his family to the death. He'd even killed in defense of those he loved. It worried Nadine a little that she saw this as a positive trait, but she did. To know that a man would lay down his life to protect others—as Dr. Cage had done at the end of his life, and for a woman he'd known only a few hours—was reassuring at a level deeper than language. It got at the evolutionary imperative that lived within us all. And when Penn moved inside her, as he had done only an hour ago, his entire being focused upon and within her . . . the rest of the world went dark.

Sitting in the dim light of the bedroom, the air conditioner humming softly, she remembered something a gay male friend from Asheville had said when she tried to explain her dilemma. "*It's not complicated, girl. You don't want Ryan Reynolds or even Brad Pitt. You want Gregory Peck. You don't want Will Smith. You want Harry Belafonte. You were just born too late for those guys.*"

She turned away from the bed and looked down at the desk. A MacBook Air lay there, lid closed. She nearly opened it, but she didn't want to wake Penn simply to doom-scroll Twitter. The desk itself posed something of a riddle. There wasn't enough room between it and the low footboard to fit a chair in the space. But then she understood. She recalled Penn waking countless times in the middle of the night when they'd been together, to scribble thoughts on whatever scrap of paper might be close before he forgot them. Sometimes he'd even written on his arm or hand. With his setup he could write at a desk without having to put on his prosthetic. He could simply slide to the end of the bed and hang his one leg off it while he worked.

Nadine knew she was right when she saw his father's old Montblanc jammed into a crowded coffee mug that served as his pen holder. She fished out the fountain pen and looked at its engraved script: *Capt. Thomas Cage, M.D.* A gift from his commanding officer in Korea. She did some quick math in her head. That pen had probably written a half million prescriptions during the fifty years Dr. Cage had practiced medicine. It had "heard" and "seen" things that altered the lives of countless patients, and ultimately enriched the novels of his son. She pulled off the cap and tested the nib on the back of an envelope.

It still delivered a clean, unbroken line.

Feeling a little guilty, she put down the pen and slid open the center dresser drawer. When she saw what lay there, she caught her breath. A stack of handwritten pages in longhand script, maybe two inches thick. The first read: *White Man's Burden: Sin and Darkness. Penn Cage.* Beneath this was an epigraph: four lines taken from Kipling's controversial ode to paternalism.

> *By all ye cry or whisper,*
> *By all ye leave or do,*
> *The silent, sullen peoples*
> *Shall weigh your gods and you.*

She wasn't breathing. She'd never heard Penn speak of this project. Unless it was part of his work on the lynchings of 1861. Was this nonfiction? Another novel? Gently, she fanned through the stack, trying to intuit its essence not only from the prose, but from the authority of the hand that had set down the sentences. Most pages had lines slashed through strings of words, and some bore balloons with separate notes in them. These comments were often block-printed, though she recognized the hand as Penn's as well. The second page was laser printed, and began with an adage often attributed to Winston Churchill or Hermann Goering, but which Nadine knew preceded their use of it by at least a century.

> *"History is written by the victors." So they always say, anyway. But where I was reared, in the Old South, history was written by the losers. And with the help of the white North, and Hollywood, and ten thousand other unexpected allies, this carefully tended myth spread through the American psyche like a poison vine, an unkillable virus*

infecting the body politic, transcending all sectional boundaries, obscuring the ugliest truths. (Think of clematis growing over an unfilled grave.) Now, in the winter of white rule, we begin to see what lies beneath. And soon we'll reap the foul harvest. Make no mistake: white fear and rage are the atavistic impulses behind the AR-15s, the billions of stockpiled rounds, the Barrett rifles. And before the scales of democracy tip from white to brown forever . . .

War is coming.

Beneath this passage, a green felt-tip note in parentheses read: *(Mixed metaphors/choose.)* Sliding this aside, Nadine realized the pages weren't necessarily connected by theme. The one beneath showed a series of handwritten questions obviously related to the lynchings in Bienville and Natchez, many of which had been left unanswered—or answered wrongly—in the "definitive" account by award-winning historian Winthrop Jordan.

Why did the Vigilance Committee act extrajudicially? Slave rebellion was a capital felony, and the circuit court was very much functioning during this period. Why not prosecute and hang the rebels under the law?

They hanged ten slaves the first day in Natchez. Why such a rush? How did they choose those ten? Was someone trying to silence a Black man ASAP? If so . . . what did he know?

Was a real slave rebellion ever planned at Second Creek?

Discussion by slaves of the war in progress would have been natural, their curiosity avid, esp. about Union victories and proximity

Talk of running away would have been common

White fear was extreme with combat-age males far away fighting

White anxiety about the cotton crops would also have been high

Why did planters tolerate the murder/lynching of their slaves? Economic loss significant. (Fear of peers during wartime?)

How did the "Vigilance Committee" organize so quickly? (Refer to "Death of an Overseer.")

List of "first planters" present at Pharsalia Racetrack during torture
incomplete. (Stephen Minor later revealed to be present throughout, with
bullwhip.) Who else was present or being reported to?

Who were the white men who painted themselves as Indians? Disguise
seems improbable, ineffectual. Unlikely.

Where did the inciting slave "Jupiter" come from? Where did he disappear
to? What was his real intent? Could he have been a spy for the planters?

How did the lynchings at Natchez (Second Creek) and Bienville (Black
Oak) differ? How regular (and easy) was contact between enslaved
teamsters from the two cities? Initial sources suggest very.

List slave-owning families whose descendants I went to school with. Which
were involved in the Second Creek lynchings? Did any—other than the
Duforts—also own plantations or homes near Bienville in 1861?

Nadine looked back at Penn's sleeping form, listened to his heavy, regular breathing. An image of Sophie Dufort materialized in her mind, gleaming pearls over dark skin with jet-black hair cascading over her regal neck. The temptation to continue reading was strong. Yet Nadine resisted.

Turning back, her gaze fell upon the leather satchel Penn had carried up from the kitchen. The cumulative results of Peggy Cage's final research and writing efforts, about which Nadine knew more than she'd admitted, since she'd helped Peggy to order special genealogical resources through her bookstore. Peggy had actually solicited her opinion on certain handwritten passages during rainy afternoons at Constant Reader. For this reason, Nadine didn't feel she would be breaking the same taboo to relieve her insomnia by peeking into this cache of work. Besides, she'd always wondered whether Penn's literary ability had sprung from his mother or his father. Here was a chance to find out. Very quietly, she removed a bound stack of laser-printed pages near the top of the satchel and laid them on the desk.

It only took a few seconds to realize she was reading a letter from Penn to his mother, written sometime after Peggy had asked him to set aside the novel he was researching—and apparently drafting—about the mass lynching of enslaved men in Natchez and Bienville in 1861. It read:

Mom, I've hit Pause on my Second Creek/Black Oak lynching book project until you tell me it's okay to continue. I haven't done even a fraction of the research you have into the Pencarrow family, but I know a fair amount about Romulus, and a bit about Captain Pencarrow. I also read all I could find on the slave called Doby, from Black Oak Plantation. I figured I might as well let you see my early attempts to write from their POV, and also my chapters in what I call "close third person," where in third person you enter the minds of characters so intimately that it feels like first. (Thomas Harris is a master at this.) I hope this helps you in some way. But feel free to ignore it. This is sensitive and problematic material these days, and I have a long way to go. But I feel the story is too important to ignore. There's something dark at the bottom of these lynchings, and I don't think it was "servile rebellion." I'm glad you're working on it. Good luck!

Very quietly, Nadine slid out the stack of laser-printed pages beneath Penn's letter. The first was labeled "Chapter 3 (Romulus)."

CHAPTER 35

Black Oak Plantation, 1861

ROMULUS PENCARROW RACED *through the tall wet grass, his shoes clutched to his side in the falling darkness. Behind him, under the Osage orange trees that divided the cotton fields, sixteen slaves swung from their necks by horsehair ropes, four to a limb. The Vigilance Committee had tried to hang one set from a pecan tree, but the chosen branch snapped when the sheriff's men smacked the horses' flanks, braining one slave, and the whole grotesque tableau had to be repeated. "No more goddamn pecans!" Shot Barlow had shouted. "You could hang a horse from an Osage orange, and it wouldn't break! That's the hardest damn wood in the country. That's why the Indians make their bows from 'em."*

Romulus tried to shut out the bulging eyes and gaping mouths in the lantern light behind him. He'd known most of the dead men since he was no bigger than a cypress knee. He was nineteen now, long past boyhood, strong enough to whip two men in a fight, smart enough to do his sums and read English and a little Latin and Greek. Those things made him different, he knew—a black unicorn, his father called him once—and if he ever got away from Mississippi, they would be advantages. But right now they were liabilities. The captain had told him so. So had old Cadmus, the butler who practically ran things at Pencarrow. For the time being Romulus had to keep his head down and pray no chatterbox fool had tied him to the planned revolt before a noose choked off the last of his life. If they had, he'd be stretching hemp himself soon enough.

He shot out of the grass into waist-high cotton, casting a moon shadow on the white bolls. Romulus thanked the fates for the earlier rain, which deadened the sound of his bare legs swishing through the long green blades. A wild whoop burst out of the darkness behind him, and from habit he almost stopped running. In Romulus's experience, hanging was serious business, but the white men at Black Oak were treating it like a party. Maybe you could expect no better from men who'd used whatever dodge they could to avoid military service. Most were the kind of trash the captain wouldn't allow past the gate of Pencarrow, except for the sheriff who'd come out the morning af-

ter Romulus killed the overseer. The memory tightened his chest like an iron band around a barrel.

Willing his mind away from terrors past and present, he thought about the fates. Three pretty ladies spinning out the mother thread of your life. That picture beat the hell out of white-bearded old Jehovah that Captain Pencarrow's wife used to harp about in the little cabin she used as a schoolhouse for slaves who showed interest. Since Sunday attendance brought an extra ration of food, the cabin had always been full. But even after reading the whole Bible, Romulus had never accepted the Christian god. Jehovah was too damn fickle, smiting thousands in one book, then sending his son to whimper about forgiveness a few books later. Creating man to sin, then damning him for doing what came natural. Didn't seem fair. Not that fair had anything to do with it. Pious Ruth Pencarrow had been struck down by a fever at thirty-two, while Romulus had grown up strong and proud. If a just or even vengeful God really ruled the world, Romulus would be hanging back there under the Osage trees instead of running like he had the Furies behind him. But he wasn't. And neither was Doby, his best friend on Black Oak, and the brother of Selah, his woman.

Romulus didn't know how the Vigilance Committee had missed Doby—not unless his friend had run for his life. If Doby had bolted, he was as good as dead. The Barlows would have their hounds out at dawn to run him down, and almost no one ever escaped them. There was another possibility, of course. The Committee had Doby staked down to the ground somewhere, torturing him like they had the others. If they did, then Romulus's life too hung in the balance. But he had faith in Doby. That boy could stand serious punishment. He'd proved it countless times on Black Oak. At twenty, his body already bore an ugly web of scars, of the type the captain called "keloid."

Arrowing down a cotton row, parting the white sea faster than any plow ever had, Romulus summoned a memory of the captain reading to him from the Iliad, *his deep voice filling the library during their stolen hours. The Trojan War had spurred Romulus to improve his reading, and the* Odyssey *had been his reward. He envied Odysseus's craftiness, and he felt in his own blood the king's longing to return to Ithaca. Strange, because he had been born on Pencarrow and rarely spent a night off it. How could you be homesick for a place you'd never known? Of course, right now he'd be grateful just to get his hide back onto Pencarrow land, where only his master could punish him.*

It disappointed the captain that Romulus didn't feel kinship with the Greek poets, as he did. But Romulus had good reason. The Greeks were like the pharaohs in the Bible, who saw slavery as the way of the world, part of the divine order. The Romans, too, whose city founders Romulus and his brother had been named after, believed people could be property. Remus didn't belong to any man now, but only because he was dead. Gone fifteen years now, another entry in the account book Romulus kept in his head for the Day of Reckoning. That long-dreamed-of day was not so far off as it once had been, if the rumors from South Carolina could be believed. A teamster from the Surget Plantation had told him word had come in to the telegraph office at Natchez and caused a hell of a stir: a Yankee army might be only days away, with its general promising to eat his breakfast in New Orleans.

Captain Pencarrow told Romulus that a telegram didn't make a rumor any more true than a tavern whisper, and he was usually right. But if that rumor turned out to be wrong, Romulus meant to run himself. Far better to try swimming out to a Yankee gunboat than to revolt and try to hold a bunch of plantations until a liberating army arrived—even if most of the young white men had gone north to the war long ago. Plus, unlike most slaves, Romulus was a strong swimmer. He'd never braved the Mississippi . . . but he'd try it if he had to. He worried more about the cold than the fearsome current.

Besides, he thought with a shiver, revolting on Pencarrow might mean exposing the captain and his own white siblings to slaughter. And even if the slaves did revolt, success wasn't guaranteed. Every servile rebellion Romulus knew about had failed, to be followed by murderous reprisals against any Black folks within reach. A single whisper had doomed the men hanging from the trees behind him. What bloody revenge would an actual slave rebellion unleash?

Romulus had done all he could to keep the boys' excitement tamped down. He'd managed to hold them in check for nearly a month. But in the end, that had made no difference. Somebody had talked, and to the wrong person. He didn't know who, and it didn't matter. In Natchez, whispers and gossip had been enough to execute two dozen innocent men so far, with no end in sight. No arrests, no trials, just white men galloping from place to place and taking up slaves for "questioning." Which meant the whip. A rain of rawhide, with a doctor standing by to decide how much punishment a man could stand, and to revive those who collapsed.

Romulus felt a sudden beating in the ground. Skidding to the earth between the cotton plants, he cupped the shell of his left ear against the damp loess dirt. Hoofbeats for sure, but moving away, not toward him. He gave the riders half a minute to get clear, then scrambled to his feet and raced on. Soon he was galloping like the black stallion he'd won two bits on at the Pharsalia Racetrack in Natchez. He thought of the day he'd sneaked whiskey at the far rail with the other teamsters, his money riding on that big black horse. Now the Vigilance Committee was hanging slaves in the middle of the track, after a charade of a trial that fooled no one, not even the white women.

Scenting the creek that marked the western boundary of Pencarrow, he said a prayer of thanks. It might be a sin to pray to a god you didn't believe in, but some things stuck with you—especially what they stuffed into you as a child. Romulus heard the silky gurgle, then his legs splashed into water. He pulled down his pants to relieve the tension that had been coiling in him since he saw the bastards loop the nooses around his friends' necks. What would the captain say when he heard they'd started hanging slaves in Tenisaw County? He'd be angry. But powerful as he was, even Captain Pencarrow couldn't stop the Vigilance Committee. Not while he was sick, anyway. Even in his prime, the captain might not have been able to stop this madness. War was in the wind, and war was bigger than any man. It made them crazy, like the moon did women. The captain had seen war up close, and more than once. In the Everglades, fighting the Seminoles, he'd vowed never to kill again. Then Governor John Quitman had begged him to go down to Mexico, pleaded for his aid. The captain had gone, reluctantly, and he'd come back even more disgusted than when he left, claiming men weren't fit to rule the earth.

Romulus had known this since he was a tot. He just wanted to get his mama and sister someplace where you had a chance to live as you saw fit. Like white folks did. He'd heard there were places in the North like that. He'd also heard that such tales were abolitionist lies. Romulus had seen enough of the world to know that every man was ruled by another in some fashion. He could live with that. He just didn't want any man to own him outright. Even with a master as kind as Jesus Christ, a slave was a slave—damned like the snake to crawl on his belly for eternity.

Even if his master was his own father.

Romulus pulled up his pants and climbed out of the creek onto Pencarrow dirt. Then he hightailed it through Pencarrow cotton, making for the big house. No stopping in the quarters on the way, even though he smelled sizzling fat and cornmeal in the skillets. Venison, too. The captain would want to know about the hanged men right away. Like as not, after offering Romulus a coin, he would sit up most of the night, nursing his Scotch and smoking a cigar, trying to plan his way through a war he had publicly stated would mean the end of the world. The world they knew, anyway. Though he was only forty-three by the calendar, Captain Pencarrow already had a head full of gray. Smoking at his library desk, his eyes on the dark window that faced the river, he put Romulus in mind of old King Priam waiting for the Greeks to land on his shore.

Romulus couldn't wait.

CHAPTER 36

NADINE ENDED PENN'S chapter hungry to read on. Skimming ahead, she saw pages written to dramatize events surrounding the lynchings that had occurred in the Natchez District during the fall of 1861—the lethal panic triggered in part by a false report that maps of Adams County had been discovered in the saddlebags of John Brown after the Harper's Ferry raid. As rumors of incipient revolt circulated, the death toll in Natchez rose to sixty slaves tortured and lynched before the panic spent itself. By then the Bienville lynchings had come and gone.

Nadine knew Penn had spent months researching these events before his mother asked him to stop, and from even her cursory reading it seemed plain that Romulus Pencarrow had been involved in the discussions of revolt in the Bienville area. In particular, he'd had contact with some of the mysterious "instigators" who had always haunted the rebellion narrative: a huge slave named Jupiter, who'd been described by almost every man "taken up for questioning," plus two white men who painted themselves as Indians to avoid being identified later.

Settling in to read again, Nadine realized that the next chapter began differently, with Romulus as dutiful son awaiting the arrival of his father in the library. When the captain did appear, Penn portrayed him as a fundamentally gentle man of deep contradictions, a younger son thrust into the running of his crippled father's and dead brother's plantation, a man with no greed for money and little taste for expansion. A war hero who'd never wanted to go to war, an agnostic weary of wanton evil committed under flags and crosses. And while the mental and moral inversion required to view the world this way while operating a plantation built upon the ownership of human beings seemed absurd to the modern eye, Robert had stated publicly that he was open to transitioning to a wage-based cotton economy. The problem was, those planters who agreed with him (much wealthier men with holdings in the North) had left Mississippi for safer environs the previous year, leaving Pencarrow surrounded by neighbors who would fight and die to defend the status quo. Worst of all, Robert's father—who never left his upstairs sickroom, yet stubbornly clung to life year after year—shared the neighbors' views.

The captain had made it known during the run-up to war that he didn't support secession. His objections were practical as well as political. In

Mexico, he'd fought alongside the officers who would become the most famous generals of the Civil War: Robert E. Lee, Thomas "Stonewall" Jackson, James Longstreet, William T. Sherman, George Meade, Ulysses Grant. He'd known most of them personally, and well enough to expect any war in which they contended to be long and bitterly fought—not quick and glorious, as so many local planters had predicted over the summer. Nadine wondered how a man so out of step with his neighbors had managed to remain a part of Southern society, but Penn's portrait soon answered her questions.

Robert Pencarrow was that rare soldier both beloved by his men and respected by his superiors. For this reason he'd been invited to become a founding member of the Aztec Club, those elite officers, "gentlemen," and adventurers credited with the taking of Mexico City. They'd formed the Aztec in an eighteenth-century palace, and it had endured as the most exclusive sort of military society, sanctified by foreign conquest. Pencarrow cared little about this kind of "honor," but it meant everything to his white daughter, Evelyn, who cherished her father's reputation as a gentleman of distinction in the Natchez District. And it had done much to preserve his social position, even as he eroded it by taking unpopular political stances.

Penn humanized Pencarrow with small details, but what made his second chapter live was the relationship between the captain and his enslaved son. Mutual respect clearly obtained between the two, and the captain implicitly trusted young Romulus's assessment of the Black Oak lynchings. He questioned his son about possible rebellion, but not so directly as to pin him down on anything that might incriminate him. Based on Romulus's account, the captain decided to confine all Pencarrow slaves to the plantation, out of fear that some, including Romulus, might be "taken up" or worse. He clearly understood that his son might be involved in a possible revolt, or at least have guilty knowledge. As a teamster, Romulus enjoyed the freedom to move between plantations and even towns without constraint, and men on the Vigilance Committee suspected that plans for rebellion were being carried by men of that trade. As counterintuitive as it might seem, Robert Pencarrow's primary goal seemed to be to protect his Black son, regardless of any potential slave rebellion.

Into this haven of father and son came the butler, Cadmus, a stone-faced but preternaturally attentive and efficient house servant. An educated man, trusted by the captain to keep accounts and perform managerial functions (and even to deal with visitors from outside the plantation), Cadmus warned the captain that his white daughter Evelyn was pacing angrily in the hall and might soon breach the library.

This she did, after loudly advancing up the hallway. Furious at Romulus being admitted to her father's inner sanctum while she was relegated to the rest of the house, she started to vent her anger, but the captain let his temper flare and banished her. When Romulus finally left the library, Evelyn glared at him like a vengeful ghost, and Nadine heard echoes of Eugene O'Neill. Evelyn Pencarrow seemed to live a frigid New England life in the midst of the South, going through her stark daily round in the shadow of some mythic injury, animated by cold envy and bitterness, underneath which lay a burning, murderous rage. Penn ended that chapter with a brief exchange between Cadmus and Romulus, a warning by the butler that if the captain were to die from his chronic illness, Evelyn would make life hell for them all. Nadine got the sense that Cadmus remained oddly opaque to Romulus, and might well be inscrutable to all who lived on the plantation, whether enslaved or free. As a result, Romulus did not quite trust the man.

The third chapter opened in the slave quarters, where Romulus waited in the dark for word of his friend Doby. Deep in the night, not only Doby, but also his sister Selah appeared, whom Romulus loved intensely. Brother and sister had suffered the nightmare of being bought onto Black Oak, where the whip ruled every hour and life was cheap. During the panic of this lynching day, Doby had bolted from the plantation and hidden in the woods, somehow managing to evade the most skillful riders of the Vigilance Committee. Romulus used all his powers of persuasion to try to get Doby to return to Black Oak and pretend he'd simply fled in terror during the day's confusion. With luck, the bloodlust would have abated after the hangings, and they'd let him off with a few stripes.

But Doby wouldn't listen to sense. His prime concern was the figure who called himself Jupiter, who'd simply walked out of the woods one day as Romulus and Doby sat fishing. He'd presented himself as an escaped slave, but Doby now blamed Jupiter for the murder of a young cousin beloved by both Doby and Romulus. Eli was a simple boy, only nine years old, and he'd been present when Jupiter told them in sickening detail about the ongoing torture and hangings in Natchez. According to Jupiter, the lynchings had begun after a white boy who'd overheard two slaves talking innocently about "freedom coming" repeated part of that conversation to his parents.

The morning of the Black Oak lynchings, Jupiter had appeared and warned Doby that he'd heard "Master Barlow" might be onto their plans. He suggested that Eli was likely the source of any betrayal, and if not, the boy still represented a lethal danger. Doby warned the big outsider that nothing should be done to the boy and told Jupiter to get clear of the district as fast as he could. But before sundown, Eli was found dead in a pond not far from the creek where the first fishing conversation had taken place.

Doby vowed to cut Jupiter's throat if he saw him again, but Romulus figured the mysterious instigator was long gone. Doby, on the other hand, seemed to believe Jupiter might be hiding in the bottomland where Pencarrow Plantation abutted the river. He'd heard that safe ground had been marked down there with colored rags, and that boats might be passing that could carry slaves fleeing the Committees to a different stretch of river, at the very least.

After making his best effort to persuade Doby to return to Black Oak, Romulus hugged Selah close, then sent her back into the dark with her brother. Selah he trusted to return home. She had the nerve to brazen her way through anything. But Doby possessed a defiant streak of pride, and having so many friends hanged had driven him to the point of reckless rage.

Turning the final page of the chapter, Nadine felt a quickening in her blood. She'd felt sure that the next chapter would carry her through the bedroom door of Pencarrow, or else into the private room in the slave quarters where the captain often spent his nights. From these rooms Robert Pencarrow and the mother of his Black children had worked to keep the little world they ruled as safe as it could be as the tides of war rolled toward it. But while Nadine turned the page in hope, she saw not more printed prose, but another handwritten letter to Penn.

Dear Penn,
I deleted the chapter I wrote in which I went inside the mind of Calliope, the enslaved woman whom I believe lived as common-law wife to Robert Pencarrow, and from whom I believe we are descended. I may be an old woman, but I'm not blind or deaf to the racial reckoning we've been living through, with its attendant changes in how we view everything from daily life to art. I've heard you and Annie discussing "cultural appropriation" and the question of who can legitimately write about whom. One rainy afternoon at Constant Reader, Nadine Sullivan told me about the controversy over the novel <u>American Dirt</u>, which was written from the point of view of a Hispanic woman but authored by a white woman. This apparently ignited a firestorm of criticism and changed some of the unwritten rules of publishing. I've also seen debates on television in which gay actors argued that straight actors should not play gay roles, while other gay actors argued the opposite.

I don't consider the small percentage of African DNA in my blood to be a "ticket" to write about the Black experience. I was raised white and consider myself to be white. That said, I emphatically refuse to believe that one must be the same race or sexuality or religion as (or suffer the existential plight of) any character one writes about to be "allowed" to do so. The closest analogy I can think of is my illness. I'm dying of cancer. I could easily argue that no writer who is not dying of cancer can possibly know what it means to endure this process. However, I would never argue that a writer not dying of cancer should be forbidden from writing about a character in that situation. (One might argue: "That's not the same as being Black, or being Jewish, or being gay, et cetera." Well, maybe not. But to that I say, "Wait until you're dying of cancer.")

For me the question is simple: if a writer somehow "gets it," and writes about the plight of a terminally ill person in a way that resonates with people who are dying, then he or she has succeeded. One of the Black writers who wrote an essay in the published response to Styron's Nat Turner discussed this issue, and mentioned a book written by a white author (John Clellon Holmes, a Beat author) who succeeded in portraying Black jazz musicians with such authenticity that he himself wished he'd written it.

I wouldn't feel too uncomfortable writing from the point of view of Romulus Pencarrow, as you did, because I have access to some of his actual words, set down by his grandson in 1936, the year Gone with the Wind was published, as well as the WPA interview he gave in 1932. Similarly, Cadmus Nelson, Pencarrow's butler, left behind his business and personal papers, some of which were published as a "diary" in the 1970s. These give great insight into the workings of his mind, while knowledge of his actions allows us to make certain deductions about his less noble ambitions.

However, after reviewing the scenes I wrote between Captain Pencarrow and Calliope, I decided I had gone "a bridge too far." The tragic truth is that no firsthand writing by Calliope survived to the present day (though I know she could both read and write, and so hold out hope). Similarly, no writing by her daughter Niobe is known to have survived. The only contemporaneous writing that mentions Calliope was written by Reverend Henry Calvert, the priest who lived for a time on Pencarrow. Calvert made several trenchant observations about Calliope, and also about the unique living conditions on Pencarrow, but in the end he didn't provide enough insight or detail to create an authentic literary character. Rev. Calvert himself was white, of course, and thus likely blind to many of the contradictions that played out right in front of him.

To authentically portray the thoughts and feelings of an enslaved woman who lived as wife to a white man whose father legally owned her is surely impossible without being able to speak to that woman, or to read her personal diary. Some would argue that even this would be insufficient. Others would assert that every act of physical intimacy between those two would be rape, regardless of the opinion of Calliope herself, basically considering her to be "brainwashed" by the plight in which she found herself, and thus unable to consent or to act in her own best interests.

To this I say only that I've learned of quite a few voluntary long-term relationships between enslaved women and white men during the antebellum era, and they occurred across all social classes. In some cases there were marriages, in others not. In some cases the white man ultimately freed the woman and bequeathed her all his property. In others he did not. Knowing all that I do now, my sense is that, as James Baldwin said, "People are trapped in history, and history is trapped in them." Human beings are born into a particular epoch, and they try to make the best of the plight in which they find themselves. I've found no accounts of slave owners—whether born in the South or the North—who simply freed all their slaves and went north as paupers because they knew slavery was morally wrong. That's not the way human nature works.

Consider freed slaves like Cadmus Nelson or William Johnson, the "Barber of Natchez," who upon attaining freedom immediately bought slaves of their own and began behaving exactly like white slave owners. Obviously, they'd been deeply corrupted by the system in which they lived. So—if a Black man at that time could be so psychologically trapped that he behaved thus, then how much more trapped was a white son born into that system, after being told all his life—and after reading in the Bible, and the classics—that slavery was simply "the way of the world"?

Some will claim that I portray Robert Pencarrow too sympathetically, and that this amounts to a literary crime. Any slaveowner, they will argue, was de facto evil, and must be shown to be so. They argue this because of the historical Lost Cause apologia: "In general, slavery and slave owners were benign. It was just a few bad apples who gave the practice a bad name." God knows I would never assert that lie. Slavery is the very definition of evil. But no one can deny that some slave owners had to be better or worse than others, just as some Nazis were better or worse than others. Yes, they all served the same machine. But that doesn't erase human differences, or degrees of guilt as regards those who had absolute power over other human beings. We can choose either to face and examine this reality or not. I choose to portray Robert Pencarrow, Cadmus, and Romulus to the best of my ability, and hope for the best. Whereas when I come to Calliope . . . I must lay down my pen and "see" her only from the outside. What lies behind those eyes is impenetrable, and beyond my power to divine.

I hope that if I die before I discover any clues to the interior lives of Calliope and Niobe, you will persist until you find whatever might exist. For without their courage and indomitable spirits, neither you nor I, nor Annie, would ever have existed. Also, I feel quite guilty over asking you to pause your work on the lynching book, and never more so than when I read the brief chapter about the fate of Doby, one of the young ringleaders of the planned revolt on Black Oak. His bravery was of the rarest kind, and no one who reads his story can fail to understand how fundamentally criminal something "legal" can be.

Nothing could ever make up for this.

Thanks for everything,
Mom
WUI (writing under the influence of chemo and high-dose steroids)

NADINE'S STOMACH FLIPPED when she read the first line of the final chapter in the little stack of pages. So filled with dread was she that she almost didn't read what remained. But that, of course, was the obligation that this kind of story placed upon you. You had a duty to not look away, but directly into the flame, or into the darkness at the heart of the flame—a truth you wanted no part of but *were* part of, by nature of your country's history and your genetic descent. In a few brief pages Penn revealed the system of slavery with all its false trappings stripped away. What remained was the raw essence of the practice that had turned the Deep South into a factory for white gold, a factory in which the threat of lethal force lay behind every word and deed, regardless of how gently a white man spoke or how kindly he might treat his "servants."

What it cost those involved was as plain as a corpse in a ditch.

The utter negation of their humanity.

CHAPTER 37

Pencarrow Plantation, 1861

THE SLAVE CATCHER trapped Doby by penning him against the river.

Now the runaway sat on the middle seat of the little rowboat as it recrossed the swamp south of Pencarrow, his wrists chained, his face bloodied, his dark eyes fixed upon the muddy water sloshing around his lacerated feet.

Only a few slaves had bolted during the past few weeks, even after the Natchez hangings, and Baldry's dogs had run them all down. Not one had stayed free for a full day. Doby had done better than the rest of the fugitives, striking out through the sloughs between Pencarrow Plantation and the Mississippi River, which was brave for a man who couldn't swim, but in the end he'd been doomed like the others. Baldry found rope loops and fresh paint marks on the cottonwoods, just as he'd been told he might, marking a path through the muck where the water ran deep. Which meant somebody had helped Doby to escape. But not even a fast human could outrun good hounds. And once this slave hit the big river, his only choice had been surrender or death.

Baldry wondered why there hadn't been a boat waiting for him. If there had been, this boy might have got away clean, at least for a while. He could have floated down to Natchez and mixed in with the free niggers who worked day labor and slept in abandoned buildings at night. But there had been no boat. So now, like the others, he was bound for the noose.

At eighteen, Doby was young to be part of the bunch planning rebellion, but he looked smarter than the general run. His skin was darker than the water in the boat's bottom, but a long way from true black. Might have some white blood in him. Not a lot, but enough to leaven the stubbornness of his kind.

"You got some talking to do," Baldry said, looking over his shoulder to gauge the distance to the swamp's eastern shore. Above the water's edge, the loess bluff rose sharply more than two hundred feet to the plantations of Canaan and Black Oak and Pencarrow, like the wall of a great green fortress.

When Baldry looked back around, the slave was still staring into the boat's bottom. He hadn't even grunted in response. Behind him, Jasper Smith, the white fool doing the paddling, shook his head in amazement, expecting Baldry to knock a divot in the buck's head. The slave catcher wasn't accustomed to being ignored, but this evening he had time to be more patient than usual.

"I'm talking to you," Baldry said, nudging Doby with the toe of his boot. "And you know it."

He telegraphed the next blow through his boot toe, but the slave didn't seem concerned. This one had taken more than his share of whippings at Black Oak; Baldry had seen the scars from the overseer's cat. The odd blow wouldn't faze this boy at all. Baldry wished he'd brought one of his dogs along. That would have got the nigger talking. But panic was never a good thing over water.

"Massa Barlow and the sheriff gonna hang some more of your gang tonight," Baldry went on. "They got a half dozen or so corralled up at Black Oak, staked to the ground. Got 'em spaced far enough apart so they can't hear each other, and they're questioning every one. Hard. What I'm wondering is why you ran. Your friends didn't, but you did. That tells me you're the one knows what Massa wants to know. Which is who organized this plot y'all got goin'. Some of them Natchez slaves said they's white men mixed up in this. White men who paint their skin like Injuns. And some big nigger named Jupiter."

Baldry might as well have been talking to the cypress trees. He thought about breaking the buck's nose, but he figured that would be about like hitting a tree. Maybe even a rock.

"Am I right?" he went on, carrying on a conversation with himself. "You know this Jupiter? If you do, you could save yourself some hell and get me a bonus, too. I'd offer to split it, but let's face facts, you're dead already. Revolt don't go over in a place like this. You prob'ly don't know it, but in this little corner of Mississippi, colored outnumber white ten to one. And that was before the war started. The rich folks left up on that bluff are scared silly. So . . . you got something to tell, you'd best tell it, and I'll make the end as painless as I can for you."

Doby looked up at last. Baldry couldn't read anything in the blank gaze. All he saw was hatred, flat and limitless.

"Tell me about this Jupiter," he said in a friendly voice. "Ain't no local slaves 'round here called by that name. And these outside white men? You don't give a damn what happens to them. And one more thing: Massa Barlow wants to know if any slaves off of Pencarrow Plantation is involved in this uprising."

Something shifted in Doby's eyes when Baldry mentioned Pencarrow. A flick of something, way down deep.

"Sooo," he said. "Pencarrow slaves *are* in on this. Well, that's something. Massa Barlow don't care much for Cap'n Pencarrow. Says the captain puts on airs and goes too easy on his niggers." Baldry leaned forward. "Listen now, buck . . . you gon' talk afore this thing's done. Before sundown, for sure. Make it easy on yourself, why don't you? Up on that bluff, all your friends is rattin' on each other fast as they can bang their gums together."

There was life in the black eyes now. Baldry decided to play his hole card. He'd hesitated, because you never knew how slaves felt about their offspring. What could you expect a buck to feel about a cub born out of some breeding house? On the other hand, he'd seen slaves strong enough to wrestle an alligator sob like women when their kids were sold away.

"They tell me you got a little boy back on Black Oak," Baldry said in a softer voice. "Name of Justus, like in the Bible. I don't know how you feel about Justus, but you know the sheriff ain't gonna hold back usin' him to make you spill. Why not tell me what you can? Do that, and I'll see to it he don't bring your boy into it."

This threat struck Doby like an arrow through the lung.

"Is he cryin'?" Jasper asked from the stern seat. He peered at Baldry from behind Doby's head, his Adam's apple bobbing. "Looks like he's cryin' to me."

Tears had indeed formed at the corners of Doby's eyes. The young slave stared with such intense hatred that Baldry drew back, as he would from a wintry blast through an open window. There wasn't much the slave catcher hadn't seen in his day; he'd doled out suffering and death to men of all colors and creeds. But the icy rage in Doby's eyes discomfited him. It was akin to the wild light in the eyes of trapped animals, cornered beasts that would rip out your throat given a moment's chance. In fact, he realized, the slave appeared to be making some sort of decision at that moment.

"Don't do nothin' stupid, now," Baldry warned, shifting on his seat and murmuring as to a spooked horse. He drew his long-barreled pistol from its holster and aimed it at Doby's face. "I'll plow a furrow right through your skull."

Jasper Smith scooted left, out of the bullet's likely path. He'd seen Baldry kill men from that close before. Even bound men, as Doby was.

Baldry cursed himself for not chaining the slave's feet. Just as he turned to see how far they remained from shore, the boat lifted and skated sideways. Jasper gasped, and Baldry heard a splash, heavy and somehow final. When he turned back, he saw Jasper Smith sitting alone in the stern.

Doby was gone.

"He jumped!" Smith shouted, pointing at the rippling black water. "I didn't do nothing! I swear! He done escaped!"

Baldry laid his heavy pistol on the gunwale and waited, his gaze moving among the cypress trunks. The black water was too opaque to see more than a couple of inches down. He was ready to shoot Doby the second his black face broke the surface, even though it wouldn't serve his ends to do so.

But Doby's face did not appear.

Jasper grew impatient, but Baldry never ceased scanning the surface for any sign of nostrils or open mouth, the way he hunted beaver. To avoid a killing shot, a wounded beaver would remain perfectly still in the water even as it bled to death.

Surely a desperate man could do the same.

"He's gotta come up for air," Jasper insisted, squinting at the water.

Baldry slowly holstered his pistol.

"Stay ready, boss!" Smith pleaded. "Any second now."

"He ain't comin' up."

"He's got to!"

Baldry spat into the water. "No, he don't."

"What if he's swimming away right now?" Jasper cupped his hands over his eyes, blocking the afternoon glare to search farther from the boat.

"Field hands can't swim," Baldry said with a shiver. "But he jumped in anyway. With *chains* on him."

Jasper Smith was a living sketch of confusion. "You mean . . ."

"I mean he killed hisself so he wouldn't have to tell those Barlow sons of bitches what he knows."

Smith's mouth formed an incredulous O.

"He knew they'd break him," Baldry figured aloud, "no matter how hard he fought. So he done the only thing he could do to hold his silence."

"Well," Jasper said, perplexed. "I'll be goddamned."

Baldry shook his head, a strange feeling in his belly. "We met our match today, son."

"What you mean, boss?"

The slave catcher took out some tobacco, pinched off a plug, and stuffed it between his cheek and his hard back teeth. "I don't believe these planters know what they're up against."

"How so?"

"You can't whup a buck like that. One who'll kill hisself to keep from sellin' out his friends? That's trouble. A man like that can't abide bein' a slave. No wonder he's mixed up in this revolt. And with all the white boys goin' off to war, the whole South'll be full of niggers like the one drowning under us right now. There's thousands more between here to South Carolina. And fewer white men every damn day."

Jasper pooched out his lower lip as he thought about this. He looked like a squirrel trying to learn arithmetic. Baldry cursed the world that made him work with men no smarter than animals. The slave Doby had twice the brains of a lump like Jasper Smith. Any honest man could see it.

"Take us back," Baldry ordered. "Quit gawpin' and git movin'. They're gonna hang more slaves tonight, and they'll want to know about this one."

Smith reluctantly gave up his thoughts and resumed paddling.

Baldry let his eyes play over the dark water. There was a man down there somewhere. Dead by now. A Black man, but a man all the same. Baldry had hunted slaves long enough to know what he was hunting. He'd apprehended hundreds of runaways. Few resisted at the end, and only one had done anything like what he'd just witnessed. He wondered if it was a fraction of white blood that had given Doby the cold courage to do what he'd done. It must have been, Baldry figured, but he didn't know for sure.

And that frightened him most of all.

Wednesday

CHAPTER 38

ON THE MORNING after the Arcadia fire, I kick up out of the dark like an exhausted diver, oxygen-starved and delirious, fighting to escape something I can neither remember nor make out below. When I open my eyes, the faint light of dawn has drawn a horizontal line above my blackout curtains. Confused to have surfaced in my bed, barely buoyant enough to float, I find myself immersed in the scents of Nadine Sullivan.

Turning left, I see her once-familiar form beneath the covers, her shoulder-length blonde hair laying across the sheet. At first, I fear I'm still dreaming, but then her breathing reassures me that she's real. Better still, it tells me that after a difficult night, our coupling has left her feeling enough peace to sleep through my own rough return to consciousness.

I lie in the dark and watch the pale line grow lighter, trying to shake a formless dread, hoping to get another hour of sleep. But a bloom of light through my eyelids makes me glance at my bedside table, where my iPhone lies illuminated. The caller is Mason Morgan, Bienville's chief of police. I'd like to answer, but I don't want to wake Nadine, and without my prosthetic on I can't quickly exit the bedroom.

"You can get that," she groans from behind me.

"Sorry." I grab the phone. "What's up, Chief?"

Morgan's deep bass has a paternal quality and cadence, one not so different from Doc's. "Trouble, I'm afraid. The mayor asked me to call you, as a member of the task force."

"Where's Doc now?"

"Inbound from D.C., minutes from landing. I appreciate you getting him that plane. Forty-eight hours without him, and Sheriff Tarlton would be running this show."

"What's the bad news?"

"Somebody burned down the Daughters of Egypt last night."

I'm not sure what he's talking about, but adrenaline kicks my heartbeat right up the scale. "And Daughters of Egypt is . . . ?"

"A Black church. Nearly two centuries old. Out by the river, north end of the county."

The implications fill my head with white noise. "Anybody hurt?"

"Two deacons killed."

"Shit." Acid floods my stomach. I try to rub my eyes clear with my left hand. "Jesus, Mason."

"Burned it to the cement blocks. Organ gone. PA system. Every pew and hymnal. And two deacons, one old, one young. It's a tragedy for that congregation."

"A reprisal attack for yesterday's fires?"

"What else?"

I close my eyes and let this escalation sink into me. "How did it start?"

"Molotov cocktails. Basically napalm. Jellied gasoline in bourbon bottles. Cheap bourbon."

Surely a reprisal then. Likely carried out on impulse by drunk rednecks. "Who were the victims? Would I know them?"

"Kemontrae Woods and Duncan Gardner."

The second name hits me like a sucker punch. "Duncan Gardner belonged to the Black Dot Club, didn't he? The guys who saved John Lewis back in '65?"

"That's him. You knew him?"

"Interviewed him twice when I was writing my book on Henry Sexton."

"They didn't come any better than Duncan. Any braver, that's for sure."

"I'm really sorry, Chief. Do you have any forensics on the Arcadia or Tranquility fires yet?"

Nadine gets out of bed and pads into the bathroom. She doesn't bother covering up for the trip, and I can't pull my eyes away from her.

After a hesitant silence, the chief says, "I do, but I've been instructed not to share it yet. Given your background, I'm inclined to stretch a point, but . . . don't sell me out on this, Penn."

"I'm the last person you have to worry about."

"I believe you. I've just been burned recently. Give me a second." I hear paper shuffling. "Okay. The state fire marshal arrived this morning, just as the Arcadia fire was burning out. He suited up and walked through, searching for obvious signs of arson. He found them."

"No reason to hide arson if you're burning something as an act of protest. That supports the courthouse note being real. What did he find?"

"Spent flares, just like Marshall McEwan's caller predicted. *Military* flares. Here we go . . . used by the air force in planes like the A-10 Warthog."

My mind clicks into analytical mode, something that was once my daily labor. "Defensive flares? Like the ones used in conjunction with chaff?"

"Exactly. They burn at extremely high temperature, far hotter than standard flares. Over two thousand degrees Fahrenheit."

"Magnesium?"

I hear him checking the papers. "That's right. They come in a kind of cassette box, made of metal. They call it a bucket. They're triggered electrically, and fire from the box like fireworks."

"Was the Tranquility fire started the same way?"

Morgan doesn't answer right away, so I wait. In the end, he says, "I didn't say anything in response to that question. Which ought to tell you what you need to know."

A cold blade of premonition rakes through my chest. "So, bottom line, this was a high-tech operation, and whoever did it has specialized knowledge. Maybe a military background."

"That's what the FBI's starting with, as a profile."

"Do they have a team in town yet?"

"Two agents drove up from the New Orleans field office a couple of hours ago. They have an arson specialist flying over from Atlanta later today."

"What about the BATF?"

"Those flares got their attention. They'll be here in force by ten-thirty. We may even get some air force OSI as well. I'm going to have men shuttling feds from the airport all goddamn day."

"That's good. We need help on this, if only to keep Tarlton in check." I hear Nadine flush the commode. "Anything else you think I need to know?"

"Not at this time. I want to thank you for getting Ray Ransom and that newspaper photographer to shoot pictures of that fire crowd. I had so much on my mind I was late getting started on that."

"Anything turn up?"

"Not yet. I've got two officers trying to organize the photos now. There's close to a thousand shots. I want to ID everybody."

"Good. I probably won't be attending the task force meetings in person, but call me day or night if I can help you."

"I'll do it. I might want some advice on handling the press. This is going to be a nonstop nightmare."

"Here's my advice. When people want to interview you, don't do it live. Ask them to email you the questions. You're too busy to take time away from the case, especially to go on TV."

"I'll do that," he says in a relieved voice.

As Chief Morgan speaks, I scroll text messages from the past few hours. Several are from Doc Berry. The first reads:

I'll be at your house by seven-forty-five. Bringing Ray with me. He'll pick me up at the airport. Heard about Daughters of Egypt and the deacons. A storm's coming, Penn. Get ready.

"Penn?" says Chief Morgan. "Did I lose you? Hello?"

"I'm here."

"Listen to this. The governor just went on Paul Gallo's radio show and said he would be encouraging the attorney general to seek the death penalty for the Arcadia fire. He said that arson was domestic terrorism resulting in murder, and it won't be tolerated."

The death penalty. "Did he say the same thing about the arsonists who burned the Daughters of Egypt Church?"

"I don't believe he did, no."

"Uh-huh. It's all about the base for those guys. Look, Mason, I have one question for you. What about Sheriff Tarlton? Can you work with him on this thing or not?"

I can feel Chief Morgan straining to remain diplomatic, but in the end he fails. "Buck Tarlton's dangerous. I think that son of a bitch is the biggest liability we've got in this crisis. Just like the governor, he's far more likely to escalate this mess than try to defuse it."

"Agreed. I just wanted to hear you say it. We're going to have to figure a way to cut the sheriff's legs from under him."

"Glad to hear that from you. Give me a call if I can help."

"Again, Chief, I'm sorry about those deacons."

"Yeah. I'm out."

After I click off, Nadine walks around and sits beside me on the bed. She lays a hand on my chest and rubs softly.

"I'd kiss you," she says, "but I have morning breath. I didn't know if we're back to using each other's toothbrushes in a pinch."

This would normally bring a laugh, but after Chief Morgan's call I have none in me.

"Bad news from the chief?"

I tell her about the burned church, and the deacons.

Nadine closes her eyes and shakes her head, then rolls gently over me and lies face down on her side of the bed.

"Do you really have to go in this morning?" I ask, laying my hand on the small of her back.

She turns so that I can see her eyes. "I wish I didn't. But my usual help's sick. Which means I've got like five minutes to get out to my car."

"It's only five till six," I protest.

"I have a coffee bar, Penn. I've got cranky old dudes waiting at my door every morning. They don't buy many books, but they do drink some coffee."

"Cranky old dudes like me?"

She snorts laughter into the mattress. "No. *Really* old. Did I hear something about a task force?"

"Doc's putting one together."

"And you agreed to serve?"

I sigh heavily, thinking about the burned church. "So much for my plan to pull back from this mess after Mission Hill."

She squeezes my upper arm. For the first time since waking, a rush of images from the small hours of the night flashes through my mind. As casually as possible, I slide my hand beneath her torso, but she smacks me on the shoulder, then rolls over and hunts for her clothes on the floor. I offer to make coffee, but she declines, knowing mine will be terrible and that it will take too long for me to get my leg on and moving.

Once Nadine has her pants on, she stands over me, looking down into my eyes as she buttons her top. "We said a lot last night," she says softly. "We have a lot to process. But I'm thinking good stuff. Your cancer worries me, obviously, but I'm not scared. We're going to fight every step of the way. You think about the baby for a while, then talk to me about it when you're ready."

"I will. I mean, I am."

I see a glow of something like pleasure in her eyes.

Before I can stop myself, I voice my darker thoughts. "It's just really hard to accept that, even if we do the best we can fighting my illness, I'm not likely to live past this baby's seventh or eighth birthday."

Nadine shuts her eyes against what appears to be physical pain. "New rule. You don't get to say shit like that. I'm aware of the situation, and I understand. It's not great, but the alternative is worse. For all of us. So . . . end of discussion. Okay?"

"Okay."

Some color comes back into her cheeks. "Why don't you come by the store later for breakfast?"

"Doc and Ray are coming over for coffee. Our old campaign ritual."

Her eyes brighten. "Doc's back?"

"Any minute." I reach up and cup her left breast, and this time she allows it. "You sure you don't have a little time before you go?"

She gives me a chiding laugh. "Nope. I'll get a break around ten, but I need to run home for some things."

"I'm closer to Constant Reader than your house is. Get them here."

My invitation clearly pleases her. "We'll see. You're liable to be with the FBI by then." She kisses me on the cheek, then walks to the door, pauses, and looks back. "Hey . . . I've got a confession."

I wonder if she's chosen this moment so she won't have to stick around for the fallout from whatever she's about to admit. "What is it?"

"I couldn't sleep last night. And doodling around on your desk, I found your pages in that drawer. The longhand pages."

Now I understand. "Did you read them?"

"I didn't, actually. But when I looked in Peggy's satchel for something to read, I wound up with some chapters you'd written and given to her, apparently."

"Oh, yeah. My first attempts on the lynching project."

She nods, her face freighted with somber sincerity. "I could tell how deeply those old hangings have their hooks in you. Anyway, I went on and read some of Peggy's work about the same characters. She'd shown me a little herself, in the bookstore. I read most of the night, really. I couldn't stop. I know you don't want to start digging through your mom's satchel. It seems daunting. But given how deeply you're already into it . . . I think you need to."

"I read the duel chapter last night. She left me a note and told me to start there. I was impressed."

"Penn, what your mother did over the last year of her life . . . it's staggering, really. She culled through slave narratives that had been tampered with by both the Mississippi government and D.C. bureaucrats. She tracked down relatives, Black and white, and traveled to see them multiple times, until they decided to trust her. She discovered the kinds of things historians rarely do. It's a triumph. Annie deserves a lot of credit, too. Mostly for what she did as Peggy got sicker."

"Dad always said Mom was the smartest person in our family."

"I'd say Tom Cage knew his wife. I finally stopped because the light was starting to wake you. I found a couple of more letters she wrote to you, by the way. I think Peggy felt conflicted about this project, and she worked through her feelings by writing to you, assuming you'd read her letters someday."

"Really?"

"She discovered some pretty explosive stuff about those mass lynchings. For one thing, the death toll wasn't forty or fifty slaves, as Winthrop Jordan suggested in his book, but more than two hundred."

I raise myself onto my elbows. "*What?*"

Nadine nods. "Between September 1861 and the Union occupation of Natchez and Bienville in '63, the Vigilance Committee hanged two hundred and eight enslaved people."

"I had no idea."

"The number was recorded by a female abolitionist who came to Natchez in 1863 to document slave life during the war. The question of why they killed so many is a historical mystery."

"Wow. Maybe it's time I reopened that project."

"Your theory is that there never was any slave rebellion, right? Only a white panic, similar to the one triggered by the George Floyd demonstrations in 2020?"

"That's what I've theorized, yeah. After the relatively little research I've done."

"Well, your mother came up with a different solution. A much darker one."

"What was it?"

Nadine looks reluctant to answer without my doing the reading myself, but in the end she says, "Peggy believed that one or more wealthy Natchez planters used those lynchings as a campaign of terror to keep slaves working in the cotton fields as the war began looking dangerous for the Confederacy. By then, large numbers were refusing to work, or running away altogether. The continual lynchings kept them frightened enough to work, which brought in two more seasons of cotton and saved the fortunes of many a planter. Even so, by the end of this period, major planters were having to bribe their slaves to get them to go into the fields at picking time. I'm talking about huge bribes. Shares of the crop."

The ruthless genius of this plan has the cold ring of truth. "Annie told me yesterday that Mom suspected the hangings might have been secretly pushed by some of Natchez's wealthiest citizens, who were still respected decades after the war. In fact, she mentioned Charles Dufort's ancestor."

Nadine nods, a provocative glint in her eye.

"But Mom didn't find any proof, Annie said. Only a sort of oral tradition among the older Black families that might implicate some white families with otherwise good reputations."

"Peggy knew she wasn't likely to live long enough to find proof, if it even exists. She mentions the 'brain fog' she suffered from that drug she was taking, Revlimid. The one made from thalidomide. She also mentions severe headaches, which she always minimized to her doctors. She said once you're dying of one disease, you don't want to borrow trouble by revealing the symptoms of what might be another."

"God, that makes me sad."

"I'm sorry. I'd like to keep reading, if you don't mind."

"Sure. Take the satchel with you. Just guard it well."

Nadine smiles. "Annie's made copies of most of it. But still . . . precious cargo." She goes to my desk and lifts the leather satchel over her shoulder, then moves back into the doorway. "Hey . . . what about Peggy's burial?"

"It'll likely just be Annie and me, with Andrew McKinney to help me fill in the grave. That's what Mom wanted, I think. But it's got to be today. If you're not embalmed, you have to be in the ground within twenty-four hours."

"Hm. Okay. Well . . . if you're sure."

"Actually, there is something you could do for me—and Mom—if you're really going to go through that satchel. It's an idea I had last night. A legal theory."

"What is it?"

"A legal theory. I'll call you about it later."

"Okay. Don't push Doc too hard today. We can't afford to have him drop dead from a brain bleed."

"Are you kidding? I'll be the one trying to hold him back."

She smiles, blows me a kiss, then vanishes down the stairs.

LYING ALONE IN the bed, I'd like to revisit a rush of memories from last night, but what comes instead is a grainy image of old Duncan Gardner burning to death in his own church, a young man dying beside him, and the realization that I'll be burying my mother later today. Recalling my talk with Chief Morgan about the military flares, I can't see any prospect of good news in the immediate future.

I wonder whether Annie slept at all, or if she sat up all night with Mom's body.

Levering myself up on my elbows, I cry out as an arc of pain flashes out from my broken rib. I pull on some warm-ups from a nearby drawer, then begin the painful process of putting on my prosthetic leg. As I finally jam my stump down into its socket, I realize that I owe someone for the strength to shut out my frustration and simply get on with the business of the day. And it's not God or any higher power.

It's Nadine Sullivan.

BY SEVEN THIRTY I've showered, eaten, swallowed one of my mother's oxycodone tablets from her hospice box, and lined out a legal query that could have enormous impact on the redneck bastard who has been a thorn in our family's side for too long. By seven forty I've brewed six K-cups' worth of Community Dark Roast and dumped them into an old-fashioned thermal carafe like hotel room service used to send up to my parents when I was a kid. This I place on a tray holding the carafe, along with three large mugs, cream, and sugar, then carry the tray up to the second-floor terrace where I sat so long last night. The cream and sugar I brought in case Ray Ransom still likes flirting with diabetes in the mornings. Feeling edgy, I fill my own mug to get a quick caffeine charge. Then I sit back and look out over the bluff and river to see how last night's tragedy has changed the town.

Out past the sagging tents of the protesters in Confederate Memorial Park, the mile-wide tide of water sliding past Bienville on its way to Baton Rouge and New Orleans is flowing reddish brown today. On normal days, Doc likes to watch the morning people jog, power-walk, and exercise their dogs along the Mark Twain Trail, just across Battery Row. I prefer the river, with its variety of marine traffic, from kayaks to three-quarter-mile-long barge strings. Today the trail is sparsely populated, and while the bluff itself looks scrubbed clean in the sun, I feel a pregnant heaviness in the air, like the tension before a tropical storm rolls up from the Gulf of Mexico. I also detect the acidic bite of old smoke on the breeze.

With more than my customary dread, I pick up my iPhone and scroll through Twitter, Facebook, and Instagram. The Arcadia fire story has spread with unprecedented speed. The Bastard Sons note might have initially leaked on a right-wing site, but with the help of a cinematic video loop of the mansion collapsing into a vortex of flame, YouTube views already are in the millions and climbing. Yesterday the Bastard Sons of the Confederacy did not exist as a media entity; this morning they're rapidly overtaking Black Lives Matter as the most famous minority protest group on earth.

Commentary below the retweets is running about three to one in labeling the culprits terrorists, but a significant fraction refer to them as heroes or even "freedom fighters." Several Black commentators are cautiously supporting at least the motive of the perpetrators. Twitter might not be the real world, but as I stare at the video loop while the "Like" and "Retweet" counters beneath it spin like slot machine wheels, acid floods my stomach once more. I watched that fire myself, yet it's difficult to accept that the quiet town I'm sitting in has become ground zero for the global media detonation I'm witnessing on my phone.

My inside staircase creaks, then groans under the combined weight of Doc Berry and Ray Ransom. Reaching out for the carafe, I pour coffee into their mugs, then blank my mind in preparation for our discussion. After years of working in multiple professions, I've learned that the best tools available to me in any crisis are those I was born with—perception and instinct. But to use them effectively, you have to give them room to breathe.

"Yo, yo, *yo!*" calls Ray from the landing. "Where you at, Penn?"

Doc Berry's warm bass directs him to my bedroom, then the terrace. "Just like the campaign, Rayfield. Up and out, up and out. I smell the coffee already."

CHAPTER 39

BOBBY WHITE SAT in the command chair of his Flowood, Mississippi, radio studio, looking anything but in control. His first two appearances during the morning drive-time hour—Mark Levin and Mike Gallagher—had gone well. They'd been three-minute guest spots during which Bobby gave his views on the inadvisability—and the futility—of destroying historic landmarks, no matter how unpleasant or offensive some people might find them. He'd also pointed out that such acts tended to be the hallmark of small-minded, authoritarian regimes when carried out by governments, and terrorism when carried out by private citizens.

Bobby's third appearance, however, had quicky devolved into an altogether different experience—one that hurled him years back in time. Figuring he needed to raise his head in front of at least one far-right audience, he'd agreed to cohost Hogan Shanahan's show, which ran on Revelation Radio and claimed nine million weekly listeners. That was three million fewer than Bobby's own show, and six million fewer than Hannity. But it was the makeup of those listeners that drove Bobby's choice. Hard conservative, lily-white, and evangelical, Shanahan's listeners were considered a "load-bearing wall" of the Trump cult, and many had been die-hard fans of Rush Limbaugh until his passing in 2021.

Two seconds after Hogan Shanahan's producer opened up the phone lines in Jacksonville, Florida, the calls began hitting in relentless waves of outrage that after half an hour showed no sign of abating. The Tranquility and Arcadia fires, with their claim of Black responsibility, had triggered white—and white-hot—anger throughout the nation. Numberless listeners queued endlessly for a chance to vent their fury over the airwaves. The engineer had been running a seven-second delay, but he increased it to nine, so constant was the use of the N-word. On a normal day, Shanahan received almost no calls from Black listeners, but the "Bastard Sons" arsons had surprisingly prompted more than a few African Americans to tune in and find out how the right wing was reacting to having their precious antebellum symbols destroyed. When Shanahan's producer put a couple of Black callers through, Bobby engaged them about what the existence and even the celebration of such mansions meant to them. But no matter how delicately he tried to handle the subject, the callers came off sounding like they were defending the arsonists of the previous night. This drove Shanahan's white audience past all reason.

Long ago, Bobby had coined a term for the radio audience that powered shows like Hogan Shanahan's, and it wasn't the one Corey had suggested— *The Unsilent Minority*. Bobby called them *The Darkness*. Bobby had first felt the power of the Darkness two decades earlier, during an eerily cool Florida summer when he'd taken a bus down for a baseball camp in the Panhandle. One night after midnight, a friend of his uncle had asked if he'd like to "take a turn at the helm" of his show, the way he might ask his nephew if he wanted to "steer a real boat" out in the Gulf. A big baseball fan, the uncle had heard Bobby go on a rant about politics, and he'd been intrigued enough to give the young pitcher a turn at the mic.

The result had been instructive to all parties. For Bobby, putting on those cans, gripping the mic, and then waiting while the uncle's friend opened up the phone lines had been like watching someone turn the spigot on a spillway in a dam. There was no way he could have been prepared for the rush of black water that came blasting through. And while he'd somehow managed to hold himself erect and function—in fact, he had braced himself sufficiently to sub on the show for nearly a week—he'd also learned that putting oneself in that position was like transforming yourself into a lightning rod for some of the most toxic hatred in the nation. With every caller you had a choice: agree and act as a switch that routed their rage toward some Other—or push back and become a sort of modern-day sin-eater by defending the Other, thus absorbing some of the rage being channeled into you. Bobby had tried both strategies, but no matter which choice he made, he felt the Darkness suffusing the air around him, like the dark energy that physicists theorized was out there filling the void between matter and energy that made up the wholeness of the universe. No matter how immeasurable that vacuum might be, Bobby had touched the Darkness enough times to know that human hatred might well fill it. For it lived out there day and night, feeding upon itself, generating fear and pain and violence, always probing for a point of ingress into human affairs.

Unlike Bobby, Corey regularly engaged with the Darkness in his role as call screener, but that was profoundly different than talking to them on the air, when they knew their voices were being beamed all over the nation. Within the Darkness hid nebbishes who became bullying egomaniacs when a spotlight hit them. Paper-hangers ready to become dictators. The things they believed about race, religion, science, and politics defied all reason. They lapped up conspiracy theories that Cubby Broccoli would have laughed out of a James Bond script meeting. But it was their aggrieved fury that left Bobby feeling that America had become a nation of madmen ready to snap any second—an army of cranks in red AARP caps with Glocks hidden in their fanny packs. It was from among them that the cowards who threw Molotov cocktails in the dead of night were spawned. If later today Donny Kilmer put a bullet through Kendrick Washington's brain, these "thousand points of dark" would wax in power, convinced that God and fate had joined hands to further their fever dream, a thousand-year American Reich.

As the Darkness fulminated in his headphones this morning, Bobby flashed back to the early days of his satellite radio career, when he'd been trying to build an audience, and had occasionally taken calls like the ones now buffeting his eardrums. While Hogan Shanahan fended off one overwrought caller, he fought a wild compulsion to short-circuit their anger loop by shouting the most confusing non sequitur he could come up with.

I'm losing it, Bobby thought. *I've got to call a halt to this shit. Today is too important.*

He glanced across the ten yards that separated him from Corey's engineer/producer console. If Corey's deer-in-the-headlights look was any indicator of his own state of mind, he would be lucky to get off the air without making some kind of idiotic gaffe.

"Thank you, Doris Ann Edwards," said Hogan Shanahan, from his Jacksonville studio. "Now, Bobby, we have Charlie from Mississippi waiting to talk to you. He says he's been waiting months for this chance, but now he feels tongue-tied. Go ahead, Charlie, you're live on *Hogan Shanahan's Word*!"

Three seconds after the caller began speaking, Bobby knew he was in trouble. The voice in his headset tugged at his ear exactly the way it had twenty years earlier, when he awakened on Buchanan Avenue in Oxford, Mississippi, and his highest aspiration was to cut his 8:00 a.m. class. Even though the speaker's first unctuous words were *"My God, I can't believe I'm really talking to you!"* Bobby knew he was speaking to Charlot Dufort.

He wondered what kind of bullshit question Charlot had given Shanahan's call screener to get through, but Charlot had always been smart that way. In any case, Charlot wasn't about to waste his time singing with the choir. After Bobby thanked him, his old lover launched into a torrent of words that for some reason sounded like someone talking to himself in the bathtub:

"You know, Bobby, I realize those *mansions* that got burned were owned by private citizens—good loyal Americans, I'm sure—but when you consider the fact that those palaces were built by *enslaved* people who never received *one penny* for their work, and were then used to run these cotton empires that wouldn't have existed without the *generational servitude* of people who couldn't even hope that their *babies* would know freedom—well. You have to ask yourself if these arsonists don't have just a teensy-weensy little *point. Don't* we? Or am I crazy? Tell me, Bobby, because *I know you know*, if anybody does."

Corey was staring a hole through him. It had taken Corey a few seconds to catch on, but by the time Charlot descended into parody, he'd got it. Bobby made a slicing motion across his throat, hoping Corey would simply cut the connection and blame a technical glitch, but Corey looked bumfuzzled. He rolled his hand in the air, indicating that Bobby should go with the flow and handle Charlot as best he could.

"Well, Charlie, I appreciate you calling in. I sure recognize that Mississippi accent. Now, as to your question, you're right that what used to be called the 'peculiar institution' of slavery was a traumatic experience for enormous numbers of human beings. By 1860 there were nearly four million slaves in America. But today we're not talking about 1860—a year during which, I'll remind listeners, the practice was quite legal. We're talking about 2023. Further, we're talking about *crimes* committed in 2023, the crime being arson, a serious felony . . ." Bobby trailed off, realizing he was avoiding Charlot's point, which might make him angry enough to say something truly dangerous on the air. "But as to your point, Charlie . . . let's consider a historical analogy. In liberal California you have quite a few Spanish missions that survive to the present day. Now, historians know those missions were run by Catholic priests and friars who committed terrible, systematic offenses against the native Indians of that region. I'm talking about slavery, sex abuse, forced conversion. However, nobody's running around burning those missions to the ground. No one's even advocating that. Not even the descendants of the coastal Indians who suffered in those very structures. In a rational society, Charlie, we preserve such buildings and present them with historical context, so that people can make up their own minds about them."

"Bobby, I swear . . . you *do* make a good analogy," Charlot said. "But *might that be* because less than one percent of Native Americans survived the genocide carried out against them by European invaders? Whereas today African Americans make up almost fifteen percent of our population—"

The space around Bobby closed in so fast it was like someone had clapped their hands over his ears. He looked at Corey, who this time flipped his fingers across his throat, and Bobby understood then that someone in Hogan Shanahan's studio had killed the connection. This was unexpected, for Shanahan knew Bobby had the chops to handle any sort of caller, at least when his brain was firing on all cylinders. *Maybe this time*, Bobby worried, *Hogan heard something in my voice that made him doubt.* Maybe Charlot playing his little game had triggered something at such a deep level that his customary cool had deserted him.

Bobby sagged with relief as Shanahan went to commercial.

Corey got up, walked over, looked down at him with concern. "What the hell is Charlot playing at? He pulls that shit the morning after he asks you for money?"

"He must be high. He never recovered from being born rich. *He's furious at being brought so low that he has to beg.*"

Corey moved behind Bobby's chair and began rubbing his shoulders. "I wish we could bail on the rest of the half hour."

"No shit."

Bobby's headphones clicked, and then Shanahan's perpetually exuberant voice said, "Sorry about that, Bobby. We do our best, but now and then a yahoo gets through. You cool? You sounded a little seasick there for a couple of seconds."

"No problem. He just took me by surprise. My mind's on that golf tournament. Corey and I cut it close on the scheduling. I probably should have done a remote from Bienville rather than drive back to my studio."

"Tell you what, I'll cut you loose five minutes early to give you a head start into traffic."

Bobby looked up at Corey, who had lifted a spare pair of headphones to his ears. Corey nodded.

"I appreciate that, Hog. I've got some money riding on my game today."

"Who's your partner?"

"Eric McKinnon."

"Oh, hell, he's a magician. You guys are bound to win. Whoa—Back in five. Good luck today!"

Corey set down the headphones and went back to his console.

In his headphones, Shanahan began pushing a "big-time" study indicating that "libtard philosophy" and pedophilia might result from a common set of genes.

Charlot's decompensating, Bobby thought. *The question is, how much of a threat does he pose to the relationship between Charles and me? What would he do if he knew his father was providing the lifeblood of my campaign?*

When his cell phone rang, Bobby half expected to see Charlot's name on the caller ID screen. To his surprise he saw *Dixie Donnelly* glowing on the desk. A little reluctantly, he pressed the button to open the connection, then held the phone to his ear.

"Bobby White," he said.

"Good mornin', hon," came the Ava Gardner drawl he recalled from the Belle Rose card room. "Birdie wear you out last night?"

"I've still got a few sets of pushups left in me. What's up, Dixie?"

"Genuine news, I'm afraid. Don't know if it's good or bad, but I knew you'd want to know."

Bobby felt himself tense against the unknown. Glancing to his left, he saw Corey slipping his computer into its neoprene case. "Go ahead, Dix."

"Sheriff Tarlton just made an arrest in the arson case."

An electric thrill went through him. The odds that Buck Tarlton had already tracked down the actual arsonists were almost zero, but any escalation would likely inure to Bobby's benefit. "Well? You gonna keep me on pins and needles? Who's the lucky suspect?"

"Kendrick Washington."

Bobby froze. He felt as though he'd been turned to stone. *Kendrick Washington arrested?* He wished he were alone in the studio, but Corey stood only fifteen feet away, scrolling through something on his iPad.

Forcing his voice to remain calm, Bobby said, "On what grounds?"

"I'm not sure. They're still searching the house he lives in, but he's apparently made remarks to tourists about the antebellum homes being like Nazi concentration camps, and he's spent quite a bit of time with another rapper who suggested burning some of those mansions during the George Floyd demonstrations."

"What about physical evidence?"

"No idea. I haven't heard about any yet."

Bobby fought the urge to scream "Fuck!" at the top of his voice. "Is this something that's happening right now, or is it a fait accompli?"

"It's done, Bobby. Washington's a resident of the county jail."

"You know what this is, right?"

Dixie laughed deep in her throat. "Buck Tarlton getting his face on television?"

"Nothing but. God*damn*."

"I can tell this is a bad thing, but I'm not sure why."

"Don't worry about it. This just isn't the way I would have wanted it to go. Does Tarlton realize Kendrick has like thirty-five million followers on social media?"

"Forty-one and growing, last time I checked."

"Tarlton's going to be buried alive in criticism."

"By the Left! You think Buck gives a shit? He's like Tommy Tuberville. So long as his face is on TV and the MAGAs love him, he's happy as a pig in shit."

"Okay. I appreciate you calling, Dixie. Please keep me apprised."

"I'll do it, baby. And let me know if you need a personal report."

Bobby laughed with seeming good humor, but it took everything he had.

As he set down the phone, he felt that the momentum of fate had turned against him. For the first time in months, the flow of events had veered away from the path he'd foreseen, leaving him unable to do anything but react. One thing was sure: unless someone else intervened to free Kendrick Washington, the rapper and nascent civil rights leader wouldn't be standing on the bluff in front of thousands of people to be shot by Donny Kilmer. He would be safely ensconced in jail with no idea that he'd evaded the terminal event of life.

Bobby couldn't afford to let anyone—especially someone as sharp as Dixie Donnelly—know how much Washington's freedom on this day meant to him. For once he was assassinated, the FBI would backtrack relentlessly, and they would soon come to the white man who had been furious to learn the young rapper had been jailed. In a perfect world he could have simply picked up the phone, called Buck Tarlton, and asked him to let Washington go. But those days were long gone. Now everybody wanted their fifteen minutes.

"Bobby?" Corey called with concern. "Everything okay?"

"Yeah," he lied, wondering whether he could arrange to bail the kid out anonymously.

"We need to hit the road. You've got that Golf Channel thing."

Bobby waved his hand dismissively. "Get the Rover running, please."

Sensing his displeasure, Corey shouldered his bag and made for the studio exit door. After Bobby heard the hiss of it closing, he took two steps to his left, picked up an award he'd been given by the National Association of Broadcasters, weighed it in his hand. Holding it by one crystal spike, he hurled the trophy across the studio, where it smashed into the glass door of an audio iso-rack. Crystal fragments exploded onto the carpet, turning the floor into a minefield for anyone not wearing shoes.

"Buck fucking Tarlton," he muttered, as he gathered his things for the ride back to the country club. In his mind, the cinematic image of a crowd of thousands stampeding along the Bienville bluff while an automatic rifle chattered above them faded into a scene of pastoral hell: himself riding down a manicured golf course with some marginally intelligent golfer, talking about club choice.

"You country-ass camera-hogging son of a *bitch*!"

CHAPTER 40

DOC BERRY COMES through my terrace door first, followed by Ray Ransom, his lifelong friend. Doc wears a business suit, as he always did when he practiced medicine, plus a golf hat to hide the white bandage covering his skull, while Ray sports an Under Armour T-shirt that outlines a torso no one would guess belongs to a man over seventy. The bags under Doc's eyes look like old leather luggage. Ray, on the other hand, is living testament to the saying, "Black don't crack." His coffee-colored skin practically glows in the sun, while Doc is only three quarters as dark, light enough that he could visibly burn in the sun.

Doc embraces me tightly. "Thanks for that plane ride, boy."

"Worth it to get the captain of our ship back."

Doc ignores his usual chair and sits with his back to the balcony. Picking up his coffee mug, he takes a swallow, makes a sour face, then sits back and begins reading a long text message on his cell phone. Ray takes the chair to my left with the grace of a deer, alighting without even a faint scratch of metal on stone.

"Damn it!" Doc says, taking another quick sip from his coffee. "We've got a new problem. Right down on the bluff."

I glance down through the stainless steel terrace rail but see no sign of trouble.

"Under those trees," Doc snaps, frowning like I'm an intern who can't read an EKG. "Down at the memorial fountain. Last night somebody spray-painted 'BLM' and 'Fuck the Police' all over it in red, then painted black over the names of the Confederate dead."

"That's gonna make some white folks crazy," Ray remarks.

"Already has. There's eight Sons of Confederate Veterans down at the fountain right now, forming up."

"For what?" I ask, just making out about eight legs clad in boots and woolen gray trousers.

"Half are cleaning off the paint, the other half are standing guard. Some have flintlock muskets, others AR-15s. And they're all wearing Confederate uniforms."

Ray lowers his bullet-shaped bald head into his hands, turns it from side to side. "You're about to have a jurisdiction problem. Chief Morgan's gonna want those yokels to stand down, but Sheriff Tarlton's liable to pose for pictures and thank them for their service."

"The Supreme Court's on Tarlton's side," I remind them.

"Naturally," Doc mutters. "But that cuts both ways. After what happened at Daughters of Egypt, the deacons of nearly all the Black congregations are organizing defense teams to spend nights in their churches. Armed to the teeth, I'm sure."

This actually reassures me, though I worry that most of those churches are in the county, under Tarlton's authority. "There's no way Chief Morgan and Sheriff Tarlton are going to set aside their differences for the common good in these cases."

"Tarlton don't *see* no 'common' good," Ray says, turning to Doc. "And you've got to get your damn aldermen in line. No time for their petty bullshit during this crisis, Doc."

Doc sighs, looking worn out before we even start. "It's times like this I miss my practice. Heart disease and diabetes follow rules. Being mayor of this town's like being cruise director on a ship, not its captain."

My years as mayor of Natchez come flooding back with painful clarity. "Wait till you learn your hardest lesson."

Doc looks up from his phone without moving his head. "What's that?"

"In a crisis, sometimes your allies become your worst liabilities."

"Why you think I'm talking to you two and not my board?"

Ray laughs. "If they knew we were your brain trust, they'd start a recall today."

Doc isn't laughing. "Let me tell you my worst fear. Ever since we got Elijah and Robert elected, I've heard whispers from certain quarters about dissolving the city government. You know the pitch: we have redundant boards—county and city—redundant law enforcement, redundant fire protection, even trash pickup. Why not halve our expenses by dissolving the city and simply operating under county administration? Of course, the cost savings is just a cover. They want to get rid of the Black-led city police, city board, and on down the line. And using that local and private statute drafted by the Stennis Institute decades back, they could do it."

"*Not* while we control the board," Ray reminds him.

"And with Sophie Dufort representing Ward 6," I chime in, "it's generally four-to-two on most issues. Even when she votes with the whites, it's three to three, and you break every tie. They can't possibly dissolve the city with that setup."

"What if I'd been killed yesterday in Washington?" Doc asks bluntly.

This suggestion silences both Ray and myself.

"In times of emergency," Doc goes on, "when civil order breaks down, the 'high sheriff' and the governor wield extraordinary powers." He glances pointedly at me. "I think that might be worth my city attorney looking into, don't you?"

"I'll do it," I promise, thinking that having Annie do it would be faster. "Tell me this, though. The Confederate Memorial Fountain vandalism said 'Black Lives Matter'? Nothing about the Bastard Sons of the Confederacy?"

Doc nods. "Maybe the fire triggered a copycat group? We're bound to get some. Can you imagine antebellum homes burning all over Tenisaw County?"

"All over the state," Ray says. "After what happened to the deacons, we could be facing that by tonight. I'm hearing rumors we're gonna have people from both sides caravanning in to get a piece of this fight. Gang-bangers from Houston, militiamen from Texas and Louisiana."

"God, spare us that," Doc prays softly.

"Earl Bell at the Southern Poverty Law Center can't find anything on any Bastard Sons," I inform them. "But he doesn't think they mean to stop. Neither do I."

Ray snorts. "'Bastard Sons,' my ass. Nobody Black would pick that name for their group."

Doc cuts his eyes at his old friend. "Your formal education left a little to be desired, Rayfield."

"So did the educations of most Black folks I know."

"Ray's got a point," I concede. "It's possible that some white group from outside came in because Mississippi is a target-rich environment."

Doc considers this. "There's no point speculating on false-flag operations without evidence. Let's deal in practicalities."

"What's your first move after breakfast?"

"Publicly name my task force members. I'm also scheduling a unity rally for midday today. Announcements are going out over the radio as we speak. First a silent parade from Nadine Sullivan's bookstore to old Diamond Hill. I'm going to call every pastor in town, white and Black, and ask them to march beside me. Then . . . I'm going to ask Bobby White to join me onstage in a plea for restraint—even racial harmony—as we try to get to the bottom of these arsons."

Ray gapes at his mentor. "Bobby White? Doc . . . you might need to rethink that. Bobby's popular, but Black folks know he's a conservative radio host. They don't care about hearing what he's got to say about politics. Black folks, I mean."

"I know what you meant. But if I can't have a civil, meaningful conversation with a white man who holds different beliefs than I do after what's happened, how can I ask the community to hold their anger in check?"

Ray doesn't argue, but he looks far from reassured.

"Flying down from D.C.," Doc goes on, "I gave fifteen minutes to listing the white people I most respect in this town. After I studied it, I realized that not one would have the impact Bobby White will if he comes through the way I think he can."

Ray shakes his head but remains silent.

Doc swallows a sip of coffee. "Face it, Rayfield. Bobby White could be president of the United States one day. Governor at the very least. And while he may prove me a fool, I've got a feeling there's a lot more to him than people think."

Ray looks to me and raises his eyebrows.

"I'm not sure how I feel about Bobby politically," I confess. "But you told me yourself about the reaction he got at Mission Hill before the shooting started."

"That was kids reacting to his TikTok stuff!"

Doc gingerly probes the bandage on his skull. "He also ferried two Black kids to the hospital along with Penn's daughter, which surely saved their lives. Then there's his youth here in Bienville. He played public school baseball rather than pitch for any of the old seg academies that would have killed to have him. Along with Spider Jackson, he carried a half-dozen brothers to the state championship in 2000, and those guys still love him." Doc looks at me. "Penn?"

"One way or another, we've got to build a bridge between Black and white if we're going to prevent a war on this bluff. And you don't set an example by lining up nothing but your friends. You compromise with the other side."

Doc nods with satisfaction. "The only other choice I'm considering is Kendrick Washington. That boy's become a kind of superstar in the few days since Mission Hill. But as dramatic as his action was, I'm not sure he's ready to address five thousand people from a podium in dead silence."

Ray appears to settle into resigned silence. But then he says, "A hundred bucks says Robert E. Lee White won't appear beside you on that stage."

"I'll take that action," I tell him, knowing Bobby's fondness for living on the edge.

"I'm also going to set a curfew," Doc adds. "Safest way to counter these church burnings. Nine p.m. until five thirty a.m."

Ray's face falls. "You're gonna get serious pushback on a curfew, mainly from our people. Folks'll claim you're infringing their freedoms. Especially the political pastors. They'll scream you're selling out to the Man."

Doc groans in frustration. "God grant me patience."

Ray smiles like Doc is one of P. T. Barnum's original suckers. "Those triflin' sons of bitches will stand up and call you a racist in your own boardroom, and you know it."

"Then I'll have a private word and explain it's directed at the damn militias."

"Bad idea," I chime in. "Don't say the curfew is directed at any specific group. It's a general safety measure, strictly for the public good."

Doc nods wearily. "I hear you. And I sure hate to shut down the families standing vigil for the Mission Hill victims. Maybe we can make some sort of exception for them."

"Tough to slice that baby."

The mayor pushes back his chair, stands, then slowly turns and lays his hands on the balcony rail.

"Be careful over there," I warn. "You could have a dizzy spell."

He waves away my concern. "Chief Morgan says half the antebellum homeowners have told him they'll be patrolling their estates with rifles tonight, or else paying professionals to do it."

"Why half?" Ransom asks. "Are the others staying calm?"

"Hell, no. The other half called Sheriff Tarlton. He's telling them to hire gunmen like it's the Johnson County Range War. *Militia* guys." Doc gives an exhausted sigh. "Penn, you worked some big white supremacist cases in Houston. What do you think the odds are that the FBI gets to the bottom of this before the whole county goes to war?"

"After what happened at Daughters of Egypt? We've got no time cushion at all."

Doc leans back on the rail and fixes me with a direct gaze. "You gonna be at the task force meeting this morning?"

"Watching from the back."

Doc looks put out. "I know it'll be a goat rope, but it has to be done. Maybe we can convene a smaller group later. Behind closed doors."

"What's the feeling on the street?" I ask hesitantly. "The Black street. Things were bad enough after Mission Hill, which you could argue was a reckless accident. But the killings of those deacons was plain murder."

"There's a hunger for both justice and revenge," Doc says. "Neither of which the state will be interested in providing."

"But there's more fear than anything else," Ray adds.

"Of what?"

"The white backlash. The most dangerous thing in America."

"The whitelash, I call it," Doc says. "This is an old town, demographically speaking. And our people have long memories. What they know better than anything is what happens when white people get scared. Daughters of Egypt is a perfect example."

My thoughts fly back to 1861, when the Vigilance Committee ran riot over five counties. Not one white person was attacked, not one house burned, yet at least seventy Black men died by lynching, and if Nadine is right, maybe as many as two hundred. Ray is peering at me as though he can hear my thoughts, and I wonder if he's thinking of Doby, his ancestor who supposedly martyred himself to save the lives of his friends.

"I remember 1966 in this town," Doc says, watching three women power-walk along the bluff fence in brightly colored yoga pants. "The National Guard commander put antiaircraft guns in sandbagged emplacements on five street corners. Some right beside the courthouse. Then he brought the Klan leaders and the Black leaders down to watch the gunners demonstrate them. Same thing in Natchez in '65."

"I remember," says Ray. "I was fifteen. Scared the shit out of me."

"Fifty-eight years on," Doc says, "and we're liable to see the same thing by this afternoon. You know, I'd welcome the Guard if they were federalized. But with the governor in control, he'll just use them to please his base."

"Lining up soldiers to intimidate peaceful marchers is a recipe for tragedy," Ray says. "And you *know* that's what he's going to do."

"What about the white street?" Doc asks, giving me a probing stare.

"I hardly talked to anybody yet. But all it takes is the extreme one or two percent to trigger a riot. The destruction of those mansions will push the MAGA and militia types right over the edge. And a lot of mainstream whites will see this as Blacks going far beyond any legitimate grievance."

"You're kidding," Ray says. "After Mission Hill? And Memphis?"

"And slavery and Jim Crow," Doc adds wearily. "Penn's right."

My next words come out sounding more pompous and lawyerly than I intended, but I know I'm right. "The destruction of private property is a psychological trigger in any capitalist nation. Homes and businesses are symbols of civil order. Trespassing alone is a felony under certain circumstances. And attacks like the two yesterday? The targeted burning of buildings with symbolic historic resonance—"

"For the white half of town," Ray clarifies.

"Granted. But escalation can happen fast. We've all heard the saying, 'When the looting starts, the shooting starts.'"

"Last night wasn't looting!" Ray almost shouts.

"To whites it was worse. Listen . . . even my father, who would have voted for Obama if he hadn't died when he did, considered the wanton destruction of private property a red line that no government should allow its citizens to cross."

Doc listens with solemn attention. "In a different time, I agreed with Tom. But when police officers regularly kill unarmed citizens because of their race—during routine traffic stops—we have to rethink that attitude. You can't compare the loss of property to the loss of human lives."

"Not in the Black mind," I say carefully. "But only a minuscule percentage of whites will say destruction like what we saw last night constitutes justified protest. That's even a trip wire for the president."

"Who I'm desperately hoping to hear from," Doc reminds me.

Knowing that federal help is unlikely, we sit in bereft silence as the people on the bluff move slowly along the fence at its edge.

"The Daughters of Egypt killings have taken us to the brink of decision," Doc says. "The Black community, I mean. From this point forward, is our response nonviolent? Or do we protect our families by any means necessary?"

"You know where I stand," Ray says with passion. "With Malcolm and Ta-Nehisi. I don't even call it violence when it's in self-defense. I call it intelligence."

I glance at Doc. "You still with Dr. King?"

Doc gives me a pained look. "It's the old descending spiral into darkness. You can murder the liar, but not the lie. On the other hand, in 1956, after they firebombed his house, Martin applied at the sheriff's department for a permit to carry a concealed weapon."

"Denied, of course," Ray tells me. "But he kept guns in his crib after that. Dr. King wasn't no fool. But I still have one hope in this."

"Enlighten us, Rayfield," Doc pleads.

"The arsonist who burned Arcadia didn't mean to kill that homeless guy last night. Or to orphan that little girl. We know that because Tranquility was empty, too. They thought they could score a huge PR impact without casualties. They failed. That's why I don't think they're ex-military, even with the flares. If they were, they'd know that once you start this kind of trouble, innocent people are going to die."

Doc gives Ray a strange look, almost like a confession.

"Maybe they do know that," I suggest, "but they just don't care."

"Then why choose empty mansions?" Ray argues. "When so many have rich white people living in them?" He takes a sip of coffee and wipes his mouth with the back of his big hand. "You want to hear a war story? This ain't one I tell my boys."

Sensing that his friend is about to share a long-held secret, Doc pulls out his chair, takes his seat again, and waits.

"I hadn't been in 'Nam long when this happened," Ray begins, staring blankly at the table. "Just long enough to make myself a place in my company, earn a nickname."

"Which was?" I ask.

He hesitates, then says, "Inky."

I can't help but laugh. "You're shitting me. *Inky* Ransom?"

The old convict turns up his hands, revealing his grayish palms. "My sergeant said I could make myself invisible at night, so . . . Inky." A distant glaze comes into his eyes. "Man, when I think about that place, I *smell* it."

Doc nods, his eyes lost in the middle distance.

"Some of that funk I knew, being a Mississippi boy. Dead fish. Agent Orange—which was just like the herbicide sprayed on the cotton fields back home in them days. But the rest—pot smoke, Cosmoline, slope food, trench foot, diesel mixed with shit—made me sick as dog snot. I learned to tolerate that *stank*, but I never got used to it. And I've never forgotten it."

"For me it was the wounds," Doc says. "In my first three weeks, I saw American boys gutted by Stone Age booby traps, riddled with high-caliber rifle rounds, dismembered by mines and artillery shells, even skinned alive. I learned to run toward the screams, not away, but I never lost the feeling of revulsion in the pit of my belly."

"You just had to live with it," Ray says. "But in April of '68, something else happened. Something different. And it changed everything."

"Martin?" Doc says.

Ray gives a curt nod. "The rumor he'd been shot flashed through 'Nam faster than any news I could remember. Nobody wanted to believe it. Not the brothers, anyway. But we knew in our bones he'd been a dead man walking for a long time—just like us. Only instead of a VC sniper, it was a Missouri cracker who fired the bullet."

Ray's reverie deepens before our eyes. "We knew it was true when them damn rebel flags came out. All of a sudden, the Southern Cross was hanging everywhere, even on tents in the field. We were like, 'Where the fuck that *come* from, buddy? Your footlocker? Your pack?' We thought, 'What army these guys be fighting for, carrying that shit around?' There was a *massive* rebel flag flying over a command post. We had to threaten armed revolt to get it taken down."

Doc shakes his head.

"Needless to say, the brothers didn't take the news well. Didn't matter where you were—supply dump, kitchen, graves registration, or walking point in the field like me—that rage we lived with every day started boiling over. Small things at first: not policing up trash, shit like that. But before half a day passed, Black troops were pretending not to hear orders from white officers. You could feel insubordination like static electricity in the air. The officers started getting nervous, and most were too jumpy to call us out for any of it.

"I saw it in our lieutenant, a ninety-day-wonder who'd cost us two men a week 'cause he had a hard-on for promotion. Lieutenant Boyd Henderson from Cullman, Alabama. Roll fuckin' Tide. Bucking to prove to the captain he deserved another bar on his shoulder. Ol' Boyd barely spoke to his 'nigra' troops, as he called us. When he did, it was only to ride us. He gave us all the shit jobs, then bitched about us to whatever brass came around. He hadn't got his mind around the fact that Vietnam was a new world—except maybe in the rear, where the brass could act like it was still 1950 and get away with it."

"That shit didn't fly in the field," Doc recalls.

"Anyway," Ray goes on, "G company only functioned because of Leroy Simms, a lifer sergeant from Louisiana who'd enlisted after Korea. He'd climbed as high as the army would let him. Sergeant Simms took a shine to me right off. He'd 'educated' several lieutenants like Henderson in his time. He used patience and diplomacy, and he'd managed to pull his men through every leadership change with minimum casualties. But Boyd Henderson was different. He'd got a Black private named Willie Biggs killed for no reason. Sent him into a minefield. Kid didn't make it ten steps before a Russian mine blew off one leg at the knee and shredded the other to the hip."

My stump tingles at the thought of violent amputation.

"Sergeant Simms called in medevac, but Biggie bled out through his femorals before the Huey landed. Right that second, any of us would have put a bullet in the lieutenant's chest. Sergeant Simms settled us down by persuading Henderson to give up his fantasy of checking the tree line. But two days later, when the word came in about Martin . . . the last bit of string ran out.

"Brothers stopped rereading letters from home, stopped thinking about the strip of shacks outside Firebase Gloria where they could buy pussy, or the debts they had to pay before they could start gambling again. They stopped jonesing for the hash at Mamasan's. Man, they even stopped counting down to their DEROS. They wanted payback, and Boyd Henderson was *absolutely* the most convenient target."

Doc has gone still.

"We all knew killing the lieutenant could mean a firing squad, but most were past caring. When word went around that Henderson meant to send us up a mountain on a probing patrol the next day—in a sector MACV believed held uniformed NVA in regimental strength—a collective decision got made. Only Sergeant Simms was kept out of it."

Nausea unsettles my stomach.

"During my watch, I found out they meant to frag Henderson in the latrine after his five a.m. shit. Simple to rig. Problem was, it'd be obvious that enlisted had murdered an officer. That would mean a CID investigation or worse—pressure on everybody until somebody cracked. Now, no brother in that situation was gonna rat out anybody. We'd already got word that a couple of officers had been fragged that day, farther south. With any luck, all the white officers who died after Dr. King's death would be written off as 'coordinated sapper activity'—something the army could bury in a standard press briefing."

"Did you help them do it?" Doc asks with obvious disapproval.

Ray shakes his head. "They asked me to plant the grenade, since I could move the quietest. I hated Henderson as much as anybody, but . . . I couldn't bring myself to kill him in cold blood."

Doc sags in relief.

"When I refused, the guy who'd asked me to do it accused me of being a Mississippi slave. That cut me to the *bone*, man. With the history I got? Shit. I wanted to tell him about Doby, then beat him down. But in the end, I just cussed him and went back to standing watch."

"Did they frag the lieutenant?" Doc asks.

Ray closes his eyes again. "Sergeant Simms got up early, and he sensed right away something was wrong. He made the rounds, trying to suss out what was happening, but nobody talked." Ransom grimaces. "Until he came to me. I couldn't hold it in. Maybe it was all that church when my grandma was alive, but I told him what was going down. Man, a look come over Simms's face like . . . fifty years later I don't know what I saw in those eyes. But he took off for the latrines to stop whoever got the job of planting that grenade."

"Don't tell me," Doc says, like a man who's heard too many stories with tragic endings.

Ray nods with desolation. "Either Simms triggered the grenade trying to get it loose, or Henderson opened the door to the shitter just as Sarge got close. Simms died on the spot, and Henderson died en route to a chest cutter on a hospital ship."

Doc Berry sits with his eyes blank, breathing with measured effort.

"Nobody in our unit was the same after that. Their try for payback had killed the man best able to keep us alive in that hellhole. That's the lesson of revenge, right there."

"You're talking about the Arcadia arsonist," I say softly.

Ray nods. "I hope I am. Last night, whoever set that fire learned the same lesson we did with Sergeant Simms. If we're lucky . . . a man who didn't mean to kill anybody is doing some hard soul-searching today."

"I think that might be misplaced optimism, Ray."

The old convict leans toward me, his imposing physicality seeming to change the gravity around me. "Listen, Penn. Even in prison, I saw men— badass criminals—suffer that kind of regret. And sometimes it changed them. That's what we gotta hope for today. 'Cause without it . . . this town is *fucked*."

Doc seems to be breathing with exaggerated effort. "I hope you're right, Rayfield. But we can't count on that. Our arsonist could be a stone-cold terrorist. A fanatical extremist trying to provoke a second civil war. White or Black. And we have to prepare accordingly."

"How the hell we s'pose to do that?" Ray challenges, the arresting intensity still in his face.

"I learned one thing being mayor during Hurricane Katrina," I tell them. "During major crises, people look for a strong leader. They don't want a bunch of kumbaya bullshit. Doc, you need to drop your Marcus Welby manner and march into your board meetings like General Patton this week. Same thing dealing with Sheriff Tarlton, outside agencies, the governor, everybody. You've got to be the Man."

"*Preach*," Ray urges, his eyes shining. "You're in the spotlight now, Doc. You gotta leave zero doubt that you're the man for this moment."

Doc Berry gingerly touches his bandage above his left ear. Moving like a man who feels too old for yet another war, he stands, straightens his tie, then pulls his wrinkled shirt flat. "I want to speak to those Confederate men at the fountain."

I look at Ray, who's staring at his cell phone as though it has just announced the death of someone close to him.

"Mother*fucker*," he curses. "Sheriff Tarlton arrested Kendrick Washington about forty minutes ago. Suspicion of arson."

"On what evidence?" Doc asks angrily.

"Don't know yet. But I'll bet it was for things Kendrick said about the antebellum homes during his walking tours."

"What's Buck Tarlton thinking?" asks Doc. "Kendrick's the hero of

Mission Hill. He's got *millions* of social media followers! The whole nation's going to be enraged."

"Maybe a *third* of the nation," I remind him. "That's why Tarlton went after Kendrick. To knock down a Black hero and fire up his right-wing base. Kendrick has a military background, right? Tarlton will point to the military flares used in the firebombs. Plus any quotes people remember him making on his tours, about the antebellum mansions being like concentration camps. Also that song he sang yesterday."

"God*damn* it," Ray mutters. "Tarlton means to railroad that boy!"

"Not without evidence he won't," Doc declares.

"They'll *plant* the evidence!" Ray snaps. "Ask Penn."

I nod. "Happens every day. And Tarlton's not above it."

The three of us stare helplessly at each other. Something is going to have to be done about Kendrick, and I find myself hoping I'm not drafted to do it.

Then my iPhone rings. The caller is Nadine.

I press the answer button and put the phone to my ear. "I'm in the middle of something. Can I—"

"*Penn, can you hear me?*" she shouts. "*I'm at the jail.*"

"The jail?" I get to my feet. "What's going on?"

"They arrested Kendrick Washington for the fires!"

"We just heard! I'm with Doc now."

"Kendrick wants you to represent him!"

I close my eyes and brace myself for what's sure to follow. "I'm surprised he even knows I'm a lawyer."

"He didn't. But he knows now. He spends a lot of his breaks in my café. He used his one phone call to contact me, and he asked me to defend him."

"Smart move."

"I told him he needs you."

"*Not* smart. I retired a lot longer ago than you did."

"Bullshit. You won a record-breaking case a couple weeks ago. You're exactly what he needs in this supercharged atmosphere."

I open my eyes and rub them in frustration. "Nadine—"

"Kendrick's *innocent*, Penn!"

Doc and Ray are staring at me in puzzlement. Doc looks like he might be a little ahead of Ray in working out what's happening. I click my phone to speaker.

"Based on what?" I ask. "Him telling you so?"

"You know how well I can read people. I've known Kendrick for a couple of years now. If he did this, he'd be shouting it from the rooftops!"

I can't dispute her gift of perception, and Doc is nodding in agreement. "Ray Ransom's here with Doc and me. Let me talk to them and call you back."

"Do it quick. Buck Tarlton wants to hang Arcadia and Tranquility around this kid's neck. And he is freaking out."

"Kendrick's no kid, is he? Didn't he serve in Iraq?"

"No, Afghanistan. And he's only twenty-seven, which looks pretty damn young to me. Penn, he's just . . . naïve about the forces arrayed against him. And these goddamn deputies down here . . . it's all Velcro and body armor, like some kind of movie set. I'm getting a real militia vibe, I kid you not."

"That, I believe. I'll call you back."

"It's game on, ain't it?" Ray says as I click off.

"Kendrick wants me to represent him, based on Nadine's recommendation."

The gleam of a smile lights Doc's eyes. "Pro bono time, my friend."

I look to Ray. "Tell me about Kendrick."

"He got concussed by an IED near Kabul," Doc interjects. "Probably has some brain damage. PTSD for sure. Maybe some undiagnosed psychiatric sequelae. He doesn't like going to the VA in Jackson. I don't think he even owns a car. But he saved dozens of lives at Mission Hill, he's taking college classes in history, and his heart is in the right goddamned place. There's no way he's behind these arsons. That boy's a political prisoner."

"Damn right," Ray agrees. "Boy goes his own way. Does some overly theatrical stuff with the tourists, maybe. But Kendrick is solid."

"Christ," I curse, feeling my resistance crumbling.

"That boy went through my program," Ray declares. "I'd stake my house on his character. Tarlton's trying to score political points, that's all."

"Nadine agrees."

Ray folds his arms in exaggerated fashion, like a rapper at the end of a song.

Doc points a stiff forefinger at me. "Go get that boy out of jail, Penn. Play white savior for ten minutes. You know how to step those rednecks back. But do it quick, because this is only a sideshow. We've got to find the sons of bitches who really set those fires, before they hit their next target."

"Amen," says Ray, bouncing to his feet with his dark eyes flashing. "Let's get to work. I told the deacons I'd make sure they all have fresh ammo before tonight."

Doc sighs. "Rayfield . . ."

Ray throws up his hands, then heads into the house.

Before Doc and I can follow, I get a text from Annie, and my expression as I read it stops Doc from leaving me alone. "Everything okay?" he asks.

"I'm trying to bury my mother early this afternoon. She didn't want to be embalmed, so we have to get her in the ground today. The county board has a grudge against me from the Covid fight, and they're trying to cause delay."

Doc frowns with disgust. "No-class sonsofbitches."

"What do I do? I've got no influence over there. You don't either."

The mayor looks out over the park, then snaps his fingers. "I'll tell you who to call. Judge Shelby."

The only Judge Shelby I know of is a retired state supreme court justice, but he's eighty-five if he's a day. My impression is that he spends most of his time fishing and playing bridge. "Judge Clay Shelby? Are you sure?"

"Penn, Clay Shelby knows everybody in this county, and I mean *everybody*." Doc chuckles deep in his chest. "He can still throw a lot of weight. There's not a soul on the county board with the stones to say no to Clay. And he *loved* your mama."

"Really?"

"Trust me. Now let's move. Kendrick's waiting on you."

I follow Doc as he carefully makes his way through the terrace door and down the stairs. "You want to get back together around ten and make some notes for your unity speech?" I ask casually, thinking back to our campaign routine.

"Not this time," Doc answers gently. "Today I'm going to speak extemporaneously."

I do my best to mask my anxiety. More than a few times during Doc's mayoral campaign, I found myself trying to follow a meandering course that almost invariably led into the weeds of some policy issue, or worse, into a literary metaphor drawn from some juvenile classic that left people of voting age more puzzled than inspired. But I can see that Doc means to write his own words today.

As I lock the door, I feel an urge to go back inside and pocket a couple of oxy from Mom's box. But I suppress the urge. If I really need one, I can swing back by and get it later.

"I never knew you had a tattoo," I comment as we prepare to part ways. "Ray said a nurse in D.C. remembered you by it."

Doc smiles with a look of wistfulness. "That's right. It's on my left shoulder blade. A golden teddy bear beneath a Maltese cross."

"A *what*?"

"That was my unit emblem. First Medical Battalion, First Infantry Regiment. The Big Red One."

A strange feeling comes over me. "A golden teddy bear? I'd like to see that sometime."

"Why?"

"Didn't you hear I came face-to-face with a bear this past Friday?"

"Of course. I read the story in the newspaper."

"Well, that rattled me. It felt like a premonition of death. Related to . . . you know. My underlying illness."

One of the few to know of my long private battle, Doc shakes his head. "No. The 'golden bear' of our unit was a Louisiana black bear, just like the one you saw. Also the same species Teddy Roosevelt refused to kill because it was tied to a tree. That bear was our good luck charm through some of the worst shit in Vietnam. Your encounter was a good omen. Trust me."

"I wish I could. But about a week ago . . . I rolled over in bed and snapped a rib."

Doc's freezes, his features severe. "Well, then. That means your period of grace is over. But that's got nothing to do with any bear you saw. Your dispensation was bound to end sometime, Penn. So . . . you need a bone marrow biopsy, a PET scan, and a full blood workup. Make the appointments today, or I will."

"Doc—"

He shakes his head and lays his hand on my shoulder. "Don't even try, son. Go get Kendrick out of jail. Then we'll start making plans. Sounds like it's going to be a two-front war from now on. But with any luck, that bear you met's escaped all the hunters they sent after him and is roaming free upriver."

Doc squeezes my shoulder, then turns and walks toward the street corner with a slow, deliberate gait. Every person he passes, Black or white, raises their hand in respectful greeting. That's more than I can say for my term of administration over Natchez.

Doc's earlier quip about me playing white savior echoes in my ears. While it may not be politically correct, that's exactly what the situation calls for. I need to walk into Sheriff Tarlton's headquarters with enough understated outrage that he'll see not Penn Cage, but Gregory Peck in *To Kill a Mockingbird*. After I get the kid who wears the slave chains out of jail, I can go back to playing myself.

CHAPTER 41

WEARING AN AUSTRALIAN bush hat against the rain, Bobby White sat on an iron bench before a group of small headstones decorated with bright Confederate flags and tried to contain his fury. Crouching opposite him was Donny Kilmer, the skinny hillbilly from the Barlow militia. Donny wore a camo boonie hat and a green poncho bearing a logo that read BROUSSARD DRILLING CO., and he looked up at Bobby the way a high school quarterback might look at Peyton Manning. Behind Kilmer, four metal Southern Crosses of Honor had been staked into the earth. Bobby had chosen the site well, because their whole conversation felt imbued with a kind of sacred hush. Donny never once raised his voice to the level of everyday conversation, and he behaved as though they were speaking prior to a church service or funeral.

"Sorry about the rain," Bobby said.

"Don't mean nothin' to me. You got any more specific information on where Washington's going to speak?"

"Doesn't matter now. Sheriff Tarlton just pulled Kendrick off the street a little while ago. Arrested him for arson."

Donny's head snapped up. "Are you fuckin' kiddin' me?"

Bobby spat on the wet grass. "Do I sound like I'm kidding?"

"Course not. I'm sorry, sir. That pimp bastard oughta be sellin' used cars, not wearing a badge and carrying a gun."

Bobby chuckled bitterly. "Tarlton would trip over his own dick walking point. He also threw some drug charges. It's a world-class fuck-up, Donny."

"Why the hell did he do it? He got any evidence against Washington?"

"None I know of. Tarlton's a show pony, Donny. He just had to do something to get himself on TV."

Kilmer blew out a rush of air and cursed. "You don't reckon Kendrick started them fires for real, do you?"

"No. And it doesn't matter. We're going forward anyway. With the mission, I mean."

"We are? Who's my target, then?"

"The mayor of Bienville. Doc Berry."

Donny Kilmer looked both surprised and confused.

"Does that sit okay with you?" Bobby asked. He'd given a lot of thought to this move, but in the end he'd decided there were too many variables to delay. Who could know how long Washington would be stuck in Tarlton's jail? More worrisome still, who could know how long Donny Kilmer could keep his mouth shut about his new "partnership" with Bobby White? The kid seemed solid enough, but you couldn't know. Doc Berry was obviously inferior to Kendrick as a target in every way, but that wouldn't detract from Bobby's heroism in stopping the mass-shooting of Blacks. In fact, saving a beloved mayor like Doc would be far more palatable to whites than saving a chain-wearing radical like Kendrick Washington.

"Sure," Donny said. "I mean, orders are orders. But . . . all that old guy ever talks about is togetherness, Black and white. I can think of a lot better targets than him."

"Can you?" This was what happened when amateurs tried to use their brains. "There's a lot more to all this than you know, Donny. Wheels within wheels."

The kid bit his bottom lip, then nodded like a good soldier.

"The fact is, without Doc around, the board will be tied three to three, Black against white. And that sets things up for the white leaders in the city to retake control."

"Okay, I see. Well, if ol' Doc's gotta die to put us back in charge, I'll make it happen. When you want it done? And how?"

"Doc's announced some kind of unity parade at noon today, down-town, then a speech in the old Black business section at one p.m. Diamond Hill. You know that area?"

"Pretty well," Donny said uncertainly. "Whole thing's ringed with half-empty buildings. There's at least two church steeples, plus one water tower within rifle range, depending on where Doc's gonna set up. That is, if a long shot's what you want?"

"Absolutely. And while Doc's no Kendrick Washington, given the pub-licity around these arsons, there'll be a lot of cameras on him."

Donny nodded thoughtfully. "You want a heart shot or a head shot?"

"I don't want a bunch of kids seeing what a high-velocity round does to a human skull."

Donny smiled. "Heart shot it is."

"Now listen up, son. This is critical. You need to make sure I know where you are at all times. I'm going to be on the scene, keeping people away from your position until you fire. The only reason you break radio silence today is to keep me apprised of your position. Got it?"

"Understood."

"I've got a question for you, Donny."

"Shoot."

"You've knocked Doc down. The audience is going insane, people running everywhere. What do you do next?"

"Hell, I told you last night, pretty much. I been thinkin' about this for years. At that point, my mission's accomplished, and the best I can hope for is to maximize the casualties. Right? Depending on whether they have counter-snipers there, I might be able to take out a couple of hundred skinnies before they get me. You figure the FBI will be covering his speech? At Diamond Hill?"

Bobby's pulse had quickened at Donny's answer. "The Bureau almost certainly has teams covering the bluff by now, just like they do at the Super Bowl. On the south end of Battery Row, they'll likely man the roof of the Planters' Hotel. On the north end . . . I'd choose top of the Donnelly Oil Building. When Doc announced his speech at Diamond Hill, that location became important. If there's a team covering him today, you're liable to spot them before you take your shot. Now . . . you might feel tempted to neutralize them before you shoot. Human instinct, right? Self-protection. But I need you to hold fire until you take out your primary target. You shoot anyone else first, Doc could duck, or bolt, or someone nearby could dive in front of him and take the bullet."

"Mayors don't have Secret Service protection or anything, do they?"

"No, but a lot of people in this town love that old man. Doc's saved a lot of lives. There's folks who'd take a bullet for him."

"Like Kendrick Washington?"

"Perfect example. He'll be in jail, of course. But that doesn't mean someone else won't dive in front of him if you hesitate for any reason. Penn Cage, for example."

"Seriously?"

"Oh, yeah. He's just like his old man was. Born hero."

A strange smile touched Donny's lips. "I got it. You want me to take out the primary target knowing that a counter-sniper's gonna hit me as soon as his spotter can acquire me."

Bobby hesitated, then nodded. "It's the only way to guarantee a kill."

Donny took a long, deep breath, then exhaled slowly. "I got no problem with that. Like I told you in the bunker . . . I been preppin' for something like this a long time. It ain't for everybody. But I'm good with it."

"I've been in that spot myself," Bobby said, still fixated on how young Donny looked despite being in his fourth decade of life. "And I came out of it alive. After your kill, you're free to knock those Bureau bastards right out of their perches. Defend yourself to the best of your ability. That's every soldier's right."

Donny smiled more broadly. When a faint ray of sun touched his eyes, they looked Easter egg blue. Like the eyes of a baby.

"Got it," he said. "Those Feebies won't know what hit 'em. And after that, I'll just flip my selector to full auto and open up on the crowd."

This was the answer Bobby had been praying for. It was as though Donny already knew his script, even though it hadn't been written down anywhere. Bobby studied the youthful face, wondering how such reckless indifference could exist so peacefully behind it. "That's probably the best plan."

Bobby was tired of the rain, but he wanted to be sure his lost puppy would not only be in proper position, but be amped for action in a short time frame. So he laid it on thick. "Donny . . . I've seen your destiny, son. By two p.m. today, you're going to be on every TV set and smartphone in the world."

The militiaman's eyes went wide. "You think?"

"I know."

"How?"

"How much history do you know, Donny?"

"Umm . . . not much."

"But you know the Civil War."

"A little, sure."

"Well, all you need to know is that the fate of the whole United States was decided on July 3, 1863, in two places. One was in Gettysburg, Pennsylvania."

"Where I lost one of my cousins. Blown into red mist by a double-canister shot near the Stone Wall at the end of Pickett's Charge."

"Shot Barlow told me. That's something to be proud of. But an even more important hinge point happened just four miles from where we're sitting now. Vicksburg. Yankees celebrate July Fourth as the official surrender, but Pemberton actually broke and asked the Union for terms on the third."

"I knew that."

"On that day, the Confederacy was cut in half. Mortally wounded. Doomed. And one of the main reasons was a so-called colored man whose name nobody ever learned, because General Grant never bothered to write it down."

"What colored man?"

"An ex-slave who showed Grant a place to get forty thousand Union soldiers across the river, twenty miles above where Grant had thought he was gonna have to do it. That became the biggest amphibious movement of troops until D-Day, eighty-one years later."

Donny Kilmer whistled. "Damn."

"Damn straight. There's a whole lot going on behind these events, Donny. Wheels within wheels, like I said. But bottom line . . . today you're going to get a chance to pay those bastards back for Vicksburg. And if you do your duty, you can take this country back with a handful of clips."

Donny Kilmer had stopped breathing. His quivering hands told Bobby he could barely contain his excitement. Bobby hoped this wouldn't affect the kid's shooting ability. He thought about the target pistol in his ankle holster, the one he used at competitive shooting events. It already held the bullets that within a few hours would be lodged in Donny Kilmer's body. Maybe even his brain.

"You good?" Bobby asked, reaching out and squeezing the kid's knee.

Donny ducked his head, and rainwater spilled out of the boonie hat. "Yessir. I just still wish that Kendrick Washington was my target. He thinks he's a goddamn movie star."

He is a star, Bobby thought. "That bugs you, huh?"

"Aw, hell, I don't know. To tell you the truth, he looks pretty cool in them slave chains. And since this is what I'm gonna be remembered for, for all time, I'd rather be known for killin' a big buck wearing fifty pounds of chain than some old doctor wearing glasses. It'd look *so* much cooler on TV. And YouTube? The whole thing would be, you know . . . *fire*."

Bobby looked back at the kid as he might at an unpredictable insect. "We can't choose our destinies, Donny. Not in war."

"I reckon not."

"You're being offered a sacred chance. A chance to reverse history. To turn the clock back for the white race. For high civilization. And if you keep yourself alive today, you'll get another chance at Kendrick. I promise you that."

Bobby broke a twig off a nearby bush and dug out the number **82 in some mud where the grass was thin. "You live through today," he said again, "and I'll explain to you how that number there is ruling your destiny, and mine too."

The mild blue eyes blinked once. "Seriously?"

"You bet your ass, soldier. There's numbers behind everything. Codes, some made by man, others by nature. And a few . . . from a higher power."

Donny blinked in surprise. "No shit?"

"No shit."

The former derrickman shook his head. "I'll be damned. Eighty-two, huh?" The kid's lips slowly flattened into a smile that told Bobby he figured he'd be dead before sundown. "You can't tell me now?"

"Sorry, Donny. There's a way with these things."

Donny stared at the number in the mud as though it held the key to his future, which, ironically, it did. Then he panned his eyes across the beautiful graveyard. How odd to sit alone with him, Bobby thought, knowing that he would put a fatal bullet through the kid's heart or brain in a few hours.

Donny seemed fine with whatever lay ahead. "Shit," he said. "I better get downtown if I'm gonna set me up a good hide before the nigs start crowding into Diamond Hill."

Bobby glanced at his watch. "You'll be fine. Tell me something, Donny. What is it that makes you want to kill the colored like you do? I'm just curious. Did they do something to your family or something, way back?"

"Nah. Not directly. I'm just sick of their bitchin', and wantin' special treatment all the time. Goddamn reparations? Come on. The truth is, slavery wasn't that bad. My family sure never owned no slaves. But if a white man lost everything in them days, he was done for. His family could starve. A slave was gonna get took care of, be fed and housed to work. You see? Hell, you're a historian, you know how it was. But now they act like we owe 'em billions of dollars to make up for whatever shit they went through. Well, everybody's been through some shit, okay? Am I right? It's time they got the fuck over it. Hell, slavery's all through the Bible, and God don't condemn it."

Bobby wondered how people like Donny missed the essential reality of slavery. To be owned in perpetuity by a man who could sell your children on a whim, fuck your wife and daughters, even whip or dismember you for punishment, was clearly beyond their ability to grasp. But today wasn't the day to enlighten him. Wearing a paternal smile, Bobby nodded as though in full agreement. "The Greeks and Romans kept slaves as well, Donny. Hell, Ulysses Grant himself owned one slave before the Emancipation Proclamation."

Donny's head whipped up, his eyes shocked. "No shit?"

"No shit. His wife had the use of four of her father's slaves, as well. History is history, and life is hard. A war of attrition between the races and their faiths. Don't ever doubt it. I was just curious about your motivation."

They parted in silence, and as Bobby walked back through the tombstones, rain rattling on his hat brim, he thought about some old grief-shriveled Daughter of the Confederacy working night and day to weave the lies of the Lost Cause into the textbooks of the nation. How would she have felt to know that her patriotic labor might one day lead to the itchy and misguided trigger finger of Donny Kilmer raining death and hell down on innocent Black families? One day, Bobby imagined, he would likely write about that.

Possibly from his Presidential Library.

CHAPTER 42

NADINE WAS RIGHT about the militarized feel of the sheriff's department, but all that flees from my mind as I sit down to face the young defendant who awaits behind a wire-reinforced glass screen. I've dealt with kids like him as both prosecutor and defense attorney, but over the past decade I convinced myself that I'd left that kind of ordeal behind forever. Finding myself back in this seat brings on a weariness so heavy, I hesitate to ask the questions that must be asked in this situation.

Kendrick Washington is twenty-seven years old and about my height, but he's seen a lot more of the world than I had by his age. During the drive over, Nadine informed me that he'd lost his mother during childbirth, and as a boy lost his father to an accident on a pulpwood truck. His grandmother stepped in to raise him, and when she died, his aunt and uncle took over to get him through high school. His uncle pushed him toward the military as the best means to "make a man of him." As a young infantryman, he served in combat in the Afghan War.

Under the jail's fluorescent fixture, Kendrick has lighter skin than I recall from the street, with a sprinkling of dark freckles on either side of a strong, narrow nose. His eyes are brown and deep, his hair a medium Afro. Taken together, his features remind me of a young Huey Newton. Tarlton's men arrested him in a purple T-shirt, and his muscles bulge and ripple under the thin fabric.

"You Mr. Cage?" he asks.

"Call me Penn. I've seen you around Bienville, of course, giving your tours."

"Call me Kendrick. What you think about my chains?"

It's hard to imagine a more arresting sight in a Mississippi town, at least one that doesn't involve blood. "I'm not sure about them as everyday wear. But on the tours or in concert, they work."

He rolls his head in an unusual sort of nod. "Gotta be edgy to hold people's attention. Those old ladies in hoop skirts put people to sleep nowadays."

"I imagine you're right."

"I wasn't the first to wear them. A guy down in Natchez started it. A former marine named Jeremy Houston. He's older than me. First time I saw him down at the old Forks of the Road slave market, I knew that was the future of tourism 'round here. I'll tell you a secret, though. My chains are *real*. Found 'em myself one afternoon. Like destiny. Dug up a spiked collar, too."

"Don't tell me where. And don't let any of the Park Service people hear that."

Kendrick chuckles softly. "I didn't realize you were the writer when Nadine first mentioned you. A lot of people on my tours want to see the locations from your books. Especially Europeans. Dr. Harris over at the NAPAC museum told me about you working with Henry Sexton on those civil rights cold cases . . ."

My mind wanders as he speaks of what feels like ancient history. During the ride over, I called Judge Clayton Shelby, who was deeply offended that anyone would act as an impediment to my mother's burial, especially out of political spite. He told me to make my plans as if everything had already been authorized, and not to give it a second thought. I can't help but worry that he's overestimating his influence, but I have no better alternative than to trust him.

". . . and Dr. Harris said you and Henry done some stand-up shit."

"Thank you, Kendrick. Now—"

"See, I first wanted Nadine to represent me. But she told me you know more about criminal law than anybody between Houston and Atlanta."

"She exaggerated there. I did work as an assistant DA in Houston, and I handled some big cases. But I'm retired now."

"You don't look that old. I mean, you know, considering."

"Thanks."

"So what you doing here, if you're retired?"

"I'm here to help you, if I can."

He looks puzzled a bit longer. Then he smiles in a way I read as male camaraderie. "Oh, I get it, bruh. You here 'cause Nadine asked you. I can't blame you for that. She's good people." His eyebrows arch. "Fine, too, huh?"

"Tell me why she's good people."

"Let me count the *ways*. She practically reserves a table for me in her café. I used that bookstore like an office for my first year, and she never once kicked me out."

"I see. Well, you couldn't have a better ally. Now, I'd like to ask you a couple of questions. Whatever you tell me will remain private. Under the seal of privilege."

He smiles broadly. "Like on the cop shows, word? Let's do it."

I pause for several seconds, to give my first question more weight. "Did you set the Arcadia mansion fire?"

"*Hell*, no. Tell you the truth, though, I wish I had."

"Do you have an alibi for last night?"

"No. Just sleeping at my crib. I was wiped out. I helped a guy clear a vacant lot with nothing but sling blades. His weed-whacker crapped out. After that, I smoked up and crashed for about nine hours."

"I see." I decide to wait to deal with the possession charge, since it's merely an excuse to keep him in jail. "What about Tranquility in Natchez?"

Kendrick laughs. "Shit, I barely knew that place existed! But if it was one of them plantation houses like they told me, I wish I'd burned it, too."

I lean back in my chair. "Tell me why."

Kendrick looks incredulous. "'Cause I know what them places really are, man. Used to I didn't. I thought they were just rich people's cribs. But now I know they were work camps, like they had over in Nazi Germany. Concentration camps. Except the Nazis worked you till you died. In America the masters gave you the minimum to keep you alive, 'cause it cost too much to replace you. And they wanted you to have kids, to sell off along the way, then replace you when you got old. For free."

"Where did you learn the history of antebellum homes?"

"Different places. I came late to it, man. Didn't know shit before I left this town. A dude in my unit told me some stuff. After I got back, a Yankee lady at the VA library turned me on to some books. Malcolm, Richard Wright, James Baldwin. Ta-Nehisi. Zora Neale. Then I read slave narratives down at the NAPAC museum. True ones. See, the Mississippi narratives got edited by white folks before they were ever published. That's proven *fact*. Ask Nadine. They got slaves in there saying how kind and wonderful their enslavers were, except for a few bad apples. You read the unedited stories, though, you'll hear the truth. Now I've met historians and writers from all over, touring the slave market sites. Lots from Europe. They know more about what happened right here than anybody who lives in this town."

"I'm sure they do. And you believe those plantation houses should be destroyed? Even though they're part of history?"

Kendrick barks out a scornful laugh. "Man, you say 'history' like it's something *good*. White folks talk about 'heritage' like it's holy. Shit. If your heritage is slavery and genocide, your heritage is *evil*, yo? And them big white houses are monuments to all that. They ain't *Downton Abbey*, Mississippi style."

I think about Andrew McKinney and our quest to turn Pencarrow into a redemptive site for education. "And you believe there's nothing to be learned from them?"

Kendrick sits back and gives this some thought. "Not if you're gonna worship the damn places, like they do here. Man, I've had old ladies curse me for even mentioning slavery on a tour. All they want to know is whether the furniture is 'original to the house' or 'of the period.' Bitches couldn't care less how many people died building those places for nothing. Maybe they oughta leave a couple standing in every state. But if they do, they oughta pile up the shoes of everybody enslaved there, like they did in Auschwitz. But they can't, see? They ain't got no shoes to pile up! There's nothing left. Because after the war, the Confederates were still in charge down here! Slaves didn't own nothing decent enough to last. Not even the shacks they lived in. All that's left is *us*. The descendants, man." Kendrick sits shaking his head, unable to further illuminate his sense of loss. "So I say *burn those motherfuckers down*."

Washington is certainly an articulate advocate, but he'll make a terrible defendant if he's indicted for arson. I imagine the sheriff and the district attorney are trying to figure a way to get him in front of network cameras to spout off like this. Five minutes of that would be like gasoline vapor sprayed over an open flame of the present crisis. One thing is clear to me, though, and it would be to any honest jury member: if Kendrick Washington had burned Tranquility and Arcadia as acts of protest, he'd have posted a video of himself doing it online, then waited in his chains to inform the police and the media that he'd done it.

"You know something else?" he says. "The white folks who say 'You can't erase history just because you don't like it'? Most don't realize they never *even knew* the real history. That's what the true historians have taught me. White folks here were brought up believing a bullshit fantasy, like a movie. That Lost Cause bullshit. That's half the problem."

"It's about ninety percent of the problem. Tell me about the marijuana, Kendrick. Was that weed yours?"

His eyes dart left, right, then focus on mine. "Sure, man. I been smoking since I got back from the war."

"I was hoping they'd planted it on you."

He laughs. "Shit, they didn't have to. I *need* that weed, bruh. It's the only thing keeps my head straight after what happened to me over there."

"What did happen?"

"Roadside bomb. IED fucked my head up, man. I got after-effects, on top of PTSD. They call it something fancy up at the VA, but the bottom line is, I can't keep calm. That's where the weed helps. Smooths me out. Old Ray Ransom tries to help me with his mind trip stuff, but nothing works like herb, man."

"You can't get medical marijuana?"

"Not till a few months ago. Legislature finally got their shit together on distribution. Till then I had to rely on a buddy to bring it down from Colorado. Drives a big rig."

This is bad news indeed. Mississippi is one of the states where DAs still throw the book at certain offenders for the wrong kind of possession. "Let's switch gears for a second. Millions of people around the world see you as a hero after the Mission Hill shooting. You're breaking all kinds of social media records. And rightly so. I was there, and I saw what you did. You must have known those deputies might kill you when you confronted them, but you still went ahead."

Kendrick shrugs. "I'd been in spots like that before. Of course I was holding a gun then. Still, I knew if I didn't do something out on that bluff, a lot more than me would go down. Teenagers, mostly. So I stepped into the gap."

"One story reported that you anticipated the first volley of fire. I heard you saved two young women before you even confronted the deputies. How did you do that?"

He pooches out his lips and slowly shakes his head. "It's something you feel, like rain about to sweep over you. There's kind of a panic that takes over a unit sometimes, in iffy situations. It's a hunger to just *do* something. See, it's easier to shoot than *not* to shoot and have to deal with something complicated. Because shooting is simple. Or it *feels* simple, when you're in the suck. When you've got your finger on a trigger. That's how those deputies were, man. Amped up."

In less than ten minutes, I've learned what I needed to know. "Well, I have good news and bad news, Kendrick."

"Bad first. Always."

"The drug charge is serious. There are inmates in Parchman who've been there for years on simple possession charges."

"Oh, I know. Buried alive, man."

"Second, I'm not here to defend you on the drug charge. I know a woman who can do that job better than I could have in my prime. Her name is Doris Avery. Ever heard of her?"

He shakes his head. "I heard of *Quentin* Avery. Seen videos. Had that big white hair like Don King? Talk like Morgan Freeman?"

This characterization brings Quentin back to life for a few pleasing moments. "Quentin was Doris's husband. He was one of the best who ever lived, but he's dead now. For your problem, Doris is just as good."

"Is she Black?"

"Why?"

Washington rolls his eyes. "Sometimes it's good to have a white lawyer arguing your case in this state. Gotta play the game the way the Man set it up."

"Doris is Black, and about my age. She's the go-to civil rights lawyer in Mississippi. My daughter works for her now."

"Why would she defend me? I ain't got no bread. I can barely make rent."

"After what you did at Mission Hill, lawyers are going to line up to defend you for free. But I recommend Doris. If she won't take your case pro bono, I have a foundation that sometimes gets involved in cases like yours."

"You a rich liberal like George Clooney or something?"

"I'm sometimes seen that way. But the real answer's not so simple. I'm in a war with guys like the ones who'd love to frame you for this. That's why I came today. And one thing I've learned is to pick my battles. After last night, I think this one's worth fighting."

Kendrick chews his bottom lip. "Yeah. I played ball with Kemontrae and his brother, back in the day. Can't believe they burned that boy."

"I'm sorry. Listen . . . I do have one piece of advice for you. It just struck me as we were talking."

"Drop it on me."

"Whoever burned Tranquility and Arcadia is going to strike again. Probably soon. And if you're in jail when that happens . . . the DA would have a lot tougher time selling you as the arsonist."

A broad smile breaks out on Kendrick's face, like a sunrise. "Yo, I *like* that."

"Are you making it okay in this jail?"

He shrugs as though my question is inconsequential. "It's jail, cuz."

"Can you last a night or two in here without getting hurt or killed?"

"Oh, hell yeah. Them deputies ride my ass, but I got homeys in here. This ain't nothing compared to the army. Just one problem."

"What's that?"

"With Doc MIA, I been getting hundreds of requests to speak to the community. People seem to think I'm some kind of civil rights leader. Or about to become one."

"That role's waiting for you, to be sure. And God knows you can't make any kind of speech from jail. So . . . this is the first fork in our road. What does your gut tell you?"

Kendrick opens and closes his right hand, flexing his tautly muscled forearm. "I haven't done much public speaking in my life. Just singing, you know?"

I nod but don't comment.

"I know one thing. The longer I sit in this jail, the more followers I'll get, and the more the anticipation will grow. And if those firebugs burn another mansion while I'm in here, that all but puts me in the clear. Right? So I speak tomorrow instead of today. What's the difference?"

"Not much," I answer honestly. "Not in my view."

"Aiight then. We got a plan."

I stand and look down at him through the glass. "Let me make arrangements for Doris to represent you, and then we'll see if she agrees to you staying in here for a couple of days, if necessary. She might not like the idea."

"Screw that. *I* like it. I stay in here, I'll bet Lester Holt'll be down with cameras before you know it. Or Reverend Al."

"There's risk, obviously."

Kendrick throws up his hands. "There's risk to climbing a stepladder. Make you quadriplegic in half a second."

Washington crosses his arms over his chest in a gesture that reminds me of the Wakanda salute from *Black Panther*. His closed fists are large and scarred and reassure me that he can take care of himself behind bars. "You done good, Mr. Penn. Now, please tell Nadine *I'm* good, and thank her for everything."

"I'll tell her. Stay safe in here. Don't talk to anybody."

Above his smile, the eyes of a combat vet tell me that no one will have an easy time putting something over on him.

"I know the rules, chief. Later."

CHAPTER 43

I'D NEARLY REACHED the door to the lobby of the sheriff's department when a deputy pulled me aside and told me "the boss" wanted a word. This ritual I know well, especially in the South. When the political stakes are high, sheriffs like Buck Tarlton always want a look at the opposition. Especially if their opponent has a history as a prosecutor. At some level they see you as a defector, a traitor even, and they want to understand you. Or they think they do. What they really want is to gauge the level of danger you represent. Because you know from experience what's in their bag of tricks.

I've seen a lot of photos of Buck Tarlton in the newspaper lately, and I did open battle with him in court over the city's Covid restrictions back in 2020, albeit through his lawyers. He's a smoother version of Joe Iverson, his predecessor, a small-town law-enforcement professional of moderate education and experience. But after twenty seconds in his office today, alarm bells are ringing in my subconscious. As Sheriff Tarlton works to complete some paperwork, I realize that something about him reminds me of Forrest Knox, the latter-day leader of the Double Eagle group, the Klan offshoot I battled after Hurricane Katrina, which Knox ran from his high position in the Louisiana State Police. Like Knox, Tarlton radiates a sense of animal threat, well controlled but always there, deep in the eyes.

The threat feels remote in this moment, even haughty, a primal arrogance like that of an apex predator. But where Forrest Knox had the look of a lawman from a 1950s western—Sterling Hayden, maybe—Buck Tarlton has a professional sheen that an FBI recruiter would take to. That's rare in Mississippi towns, and probably why I initially misjudged him. At last he stands and extends his hand over his desk, then speaks in a rich baritone that would sound fitting coming from a country music legend.

"Morning, counselor. Or mayor, or whatever people call you now. Please sit."

I take in the starched brown shirt, gleaming badge, and expensive Stetson on a hat rack in the corner. Shaking his hand, I feel the strength of the young rodeo rider enshrined in photos on the wall behind him. Along with those images, I notice a diploma from Louisiana Tech and several awards for pistol shooting.

"You here to spring Malcolm X?" he asks with a good-natured smile. "Bail's liable to be half a million bucks, easy. Maybe even a million."

I sit in the small leatherette chair that faces his desk. "Bail him out? I may leave the man in here a week just to keep the buzz building. Either way, I think he's going to be with you for a while."

The sheriff's eyes narrow, his first sign of surprise. "Really?"

"You'll have to ask his counsel."

Tarlton sits back in his chair and steeples his fingers. "You're not his lawyer?"

"I am at this moment. But I think Doris Avery may be taking over his case."

"Ohhh, boy."

"She's the A-team, Sheriff."

His baleful glare tells me what he thinks of Doris Avery, and probably Quentin as well. "Kendrick Washington didn't burn Arcadia," I tell him. "Tranquility, either. If you spent five minutes talking to him, you'd already know that."

The sheriff concedes this with a tight smile. "It's not my job to determine guilt. That's up to the district attorney."

"Sure. Come on, Sheriff. This was a political arrest. You're throwing red meat to your base. Or the governor's."

Tarlton doesn't waste time denying it.

"Did you find any paraphernalia associated with arson at that kid's residence?"

"Sorry. Confidential."

"Military flares?"

Tarlton turns deep red. "Who the hell have you been talking to?"

"The wind. But I am a member of the mayor's task force."

This comes as no surprise to the sheriff. "It was either Doc Berry or the police chief. That's highly sensitive intelligence they're leaking."

"Well, they're both Black and one's gay. Had to be one of 'em, right?"

"Oh, go to hell. It was one of them because the need-to-know list is small, and I know their politics and known associates."

I let that comment lie between us for a while. "'Known associates' is a term you use with criminal suspects, Sheriff. Not elected officials."

Tarlton also takes his time before responding. "If they're leaking sensitive information, they could join that class pretty quick."

"Like you leaking the Bastard Sons note to the conservative media?" I shoot back.

His mouth stays open a moment too long. After a quick check of his cell phone, Tarlton leans back in his leather chair and crosses his Lucchese boots on the desk blotter. "I heard Bobby White was the original source of that leak."

"Doesn't matter now. Old news. How about we quit playing games?"

A small smile. "I know about you, Cage."

"What do you know?"

"About your career in Houston. You were a hell of a prosecutor. You sent twelve people to death row. You shot a guy who tried to snatch your kid. I respect that. So I'm going to talk straight to you. Last night, the Black Lives Matter assholes finally showed the world who they really are. They're not followers of MLK. They're domestic terrorists."

"The arsons weren't claimed by Black Lives Matter."

Tarlton gives me a patronizing smile. "Oh, they're all the same bunch. And they're not gonna be happy till every white man in this country is working his ass off to pay reparations to a bunch of people who were never slaves or even the sons or daughters of slaves. They don't care about America. They want to burn the whole place down. But I got news for them. They picked the wrong county to start their little war."

I'd had enough similar discussions since 2016 to know that arguing with his "logic" is pointless.

"I also read your book on Henry Sexton and your father," Tarlton says, a smug look on his face. "You left some gaps in your narrative. Especially in the section about you and Walt Garrity going against the Knox family. Seems to me some questions remain around the death of Forrest Knox. Snake, too."

I can't argue with this. "I ran over Snake Knox with a pickup truck. He was firing a rifle at me at the time. That's self-defense."

"So you say." Tarlton is acting as though the case was never reviewed by a district attorney.

"As did other witnesses," I point out. "This is old news, Sheriff. Are you really gonna try to dredge that up and make something out of it?"

"Depends on whether you make a nuisance of yourself or not. But I want you to know it's simmering up here." He taps his head in front of his ear, and strangely enough, the gesture doesn't look comical.

"The other thing I want you to remember is this. Bienville ain't Natchez."

"You've got me there. We haven't had a church-burning in Natchez since the sixties, if then."

Whatever humor was in Tarlton's face leaves it. "In my view, Natchez folks are soft. Always have been. Comes from all that old money. They surrendered twice during the Civil War, and after the occupation they treated the Yankees like goddamn liberators. Up in Vicksburg, people were eating rats."

"Bienville's not Vicksburg either. They didn't eat rats here."

"No. But we fought back a lot harder than Natchez did. And the Poker Club screwed those carpetbaggers twelve ways from Sunday until they left in 1877."

"Are we seriously arguing about the Civil War? If so, you might want to know that I'm descended from a Louisiana cavalryman and a South Carolina infantryman. Both wore gray."

"I'm damn relieved to hear that."

I consider telling Tarlton about the newly discovered Black branch of my family tree, then decide it's probably not the best time.

The sheriff slides his boots off the desk and sits up straight. "I have a feeling you'd like to tell me something."

As I sensed, his instincts are sharp. "Sheriff . . . there's a hurricane headed our way. And hurricanes are not political opportunities. I hope you and your friend the governor realize that."

This time his smile carries a strange sense of pleasure. "You were mayor of Natchez, Cage. You know the score. *All* disasters are political opportunities. Nine-eleven made Rudy Giuliani, for a while anyway. And Haley Barbour came out of Katrina bigger than he ever was before."

"Our present governor didn't come out of the pandemic looking too good. You'd better do a gut check before you throw in with him on this."

Tarlton weighs my warning. "I'll take that under advisement. But let's be clear. If those bastards burn another antebellum home in my county, they're gonna get stomped like ants at a church picnic. And let me give *you* some advice. The time's coming when you're gonna have to choose a side. No matter what liberal games you've been playing these past years, you're a white man. And those Blacks don't really *want* you on their side. Not really. One day you're going to figure that out. Best not wait until it's too late."

There it is. The ancient tribal appeal. The unshakable belief that in the end, even putative progressives will side with their own blood and kin.

"Sheriff, your base might like the *idea* of civil war. But a lot of folks thought storming the Capitol was a good idea, too, and they're sitting in federal prison. We need to do everything we can to keep this thing tamped down. Reined in. Whatever your metaphor. Sane and nonviolent is the point. If we don't, you and the governor are likely to find out the limits of state authority."

This time I gigged him like a frog. "What the fuck does that mean?"

he snaps, looking almost apoplectic. "It's *federal* authority that's limited! Don't you know about states' rights?"

"With all respect, Buck, I know more about that doctrine than you ever will. Have you ever heard of Operation Garden Plot?"

"Can't say I have, no."

"It was developed after the Watts and Detroit riots in '65, as a means to quell civil disorder. Garden Plot provided for the use of federal troops— regular army troops—to put down riots in this country."

"That's bullshit. You can't use regular troops against American citizens. Not inside the U.S. It violates the Posse Comitatus Act."

"You'd better get out your Google machine. Garden Plot was activated after the Rodney King riots in '93 to maintain order in Los Angeles. It forms the basis of the Insurrection Act now, but the power is still there. The irony is, under a president like Trump it could be used to quash racial unrest. But under a Democratic president, it could stop governors like ours from using the National Guard to repress Mississippi's Black citizens. If you two play this like I think you're planning to—using the Guard against peaceful protesters to gin up your base—you're liable to end up with the Tenth Mountain Division on your front steps. And then it truly won't be your county anymore."

Tarlton processes this with the ruthless acumen of a casino pit boss. He's gotten his look at the opposition, and he doesn't like it.

I get up and walk to the door.

"Cage!" he barks, his veneer of civility worn through. "You know enough law to know a high sheriff possesses extraordinary powers during a breakdown of civil order. I'm giving you fair warning: if you get in my way, I'll come down on you without mercy."

With my hand on the knob, I turn back, and when I speak there's almost no humanity in my voice. "Sheriff, four days ago, your deputies shot my daughter. They also killed a woman I cared for a great deal. If you *lean* in my direction . . . I'll personally engineer a federal takeover of the Tenisaw County Sheriff's Department. And if you doubt my ability, check the record in 1998, when I went up against an assistant FBI director."

Tarlton stares back at me like a predator that's misjudged its prey. Slowly, he draws his pistol and lays it on the desk, watching me with naked aggression. It always comes down to this: deep down, men like Forrest Knox and Buck Tarlton are killers. They work to mask it, but in the end, they always reveal themselves.

"Don't let anything happen to Kendrick Washington while he's in your custody," I warn him. "You'll never dig out from under the lawsuits."

After a long final look, Tarlton takes out his cell phone and waves me out of his office as though dismissing a menial laborer.

"One more thing?" I ask.

As though against his will, the sheriff looks up once more.

"As for Kendrick? You better tell your DA to get his game shoes on. Because Doris Avery comes to play."

CHAPTER 44

NO ONE WAS less surprised than Bobby White that he and his partner were leading the Bienville Pro-Am. Bobby had been paired with a young pro named Eric McKinnon, a wunderkind from Kentucky who thus far had lived up to his billing. Even so, everyone knew it was Bobby's superb play that was making the difference. The PGA pros differed only by small degrees in skill and scores, but a few of the amateurs were hacks. A few of the ex-ballplayers were scratch golfers, but Bobby had a 2 handicap, and his superb play to this point had pushed him and McKinnon to a three-stroke lead.

Making up their foursome were a Florida pro named Kelly something-or-other and Birdie Blake. This grouping had not happened by chance. When Bobby walked out to meet his caddy for the morning round, he'd found Birdie behind the wheel of a shining cart with a gamine smile and a big water bottle in her hand. She quietly informed him that she'd bribed Wyatt Cash, the tournament organizer, to let her use a cart to ease the pain of the ankle she'd "sprained" at last night's dance, even though all the other players would be walking. She'd also arranged to be paired with a hot young golfer from Arizona, and finally, for them to be placed just behind Bobby and McKinnon in the tee-off order, so that she and Bobby could share the cart—if Bobby was willing to be ragged for it all day. The payment? Posing for two minutes in one of Cash's Prime Shot Camo Dri-Fit shirts. When Bobby expressed surprise, Birdie told him the bargain would be worth it to avoid "getting stuck with some second-rate ballplayers who'll ogle my ass all day." Bobby laughed and gave her a discreetly sexual hug, which triggered a kiss that let him know her water bottle was already filled with chilled vodka.

A nice crowd had gathered at the sixth tee to watch him drive the ball, but Bobby was used to it. He always drew a crowd when he golfed. Even pros liked to watch a one-armed man who could outdo most fully able amateurs. The buzz of anticipation from the spectators reminded him of his high school pitching days, before the Taliban AK-47 blew his golden arm into unsalvageable fragments. He rocked his club in his warm-up swing, feeling the weight of the head, visualizing how he would strike the ball.

Going into his backswing, he felt the world slow down, the way it always had on the pitcher's mound two decades ago. In every stroke he felt the relentless journey that had led him here. A lot of people had forgotten that he'd been a major-league prospect at seventeen, and few had ever known he'd been ambidextrous since childhood. That gift had saved his life on the day he lost his arm. After shaking himself out of the initial shock, he'd drawn his pistol with his left hand and killed the man who shot him, then killed one more before he passed out from blood loss. Once he got back stateside, he'd rehabbed the surviving arm with fanatical discipline in an effort to learn to pitch with it and get back to baseball. That dream had proved a bridge too far, but he'd developed enough skill that he could outshoot most cops he knew and outplay most golfers he encountered short of the professional level.

When Bobby reversed his backswing, his arm fired down through its arc like the lever of a catapult, and the Titleist flew straight and true for nearly three hundred yards. The spectators gasped, as they always did, and Bobby felt the familiar, delicious pleasure of inspiring awe in a crowd. As the sound faded, he heard Birdie Blake croon, "*Sweet Betsy in the morning, what a honey!*"

Birdie had a quick tongue and no fear of using it.

Bobby waved to the crowd, and as they dispersed he gave Birdie a wink. She threw him a theatrical wave before heading back to her cart. As he turned back to his own, he saw his assistant give him a knowing look. Caddying was another skill that fell within Corey Evers's diverse list of duties. Corey was a single-digit handicapper himself, and very quick at reading unfamiliar courses. Belle Rose, of course—while the "new" country club in Bobby's childhood hometown—had been built ten years earlier, and they both knew the course well.

"If Birdie keeps drinking," Corey said softly, "you'll be fighting her off before the ninth hole."

"That's good," Bobby said with a chuckle. "Exactly the look we need. No doubt about who I'll be dancing with at the gala tonight. Hope the band's worth a shit."

Corey groaned. "Are you really going to that?"

"Part of the gig, Cor. Besides, Birdie's fun. She's kind of a B-team Dorothy Parker."

"You're kidding. I thought her writers gave her those lines."

"They might. She stole an actual Parker line earlier. Probably figured I wouldn't know."

"What line?"

"Beauty's only skin deep, but—"

"Ugly goes clean to the bone," Corey finished. "Who was she talking about?"

"Dixie Donnelly."

Corey gave a grunt of surprise. "Dixie looks pretty damn good for her age. As trophy wives are wont to do. And her husband could buy most Hollywood sugar daddies ten times over."

Corey waited for a media truck to cross in front of them, then started up the fairway toward Eric McKinnon, who had struck out with his caddy immediately after his drive. Bobby let his gaze roam across the horizon as he followed.

Bienville Poker Club investors had built Belle Rose and the white flight development that surrounded it. They'd chosen an Old South design theme, but with more of a Louisiana than a Mississippi feel. Every house was based on a classic A. Hays Town residence, while the expansive clubhouse had been inspired by Belle Rose itself, Charles Dufort's 1851 suburban villa. Belle Rose looked more like Destrehan or Oak Alley than the Greek Revival mansions typical of the Natchez District.

"I wonder if the club can keep the PGA designation," Bobby thought aloud. "The tourney's been pretty impressive so far."

"With that new billion-dollar paper mill sitting out by the river, they just might," Corey replied. "If the Chinese keep supporting it."

"Azure Dragon cost *two* billion," Bobby said, craning his neck to see if anyone was nearby. "Goddamn chinks taking over the country."

"Easy, buddy."

"Hey, fighting China is my brand."

"Yeah, but 'chinks' doesn't fly these days, not even in Mississippi."

Bobby lowered his head and scowled.

"You sound like your father," Corey said. "Keep your head in the game."

Bobby made a good second shot, landing his ball left of a water hazard thirty yards short of the green. He could easily make par, and he was starting to feel impatient. Walking to his left, he wondered whether he and Birdie might really be able to ride together for the duration of the round. It wasn't the usual custom, but this was basically a party day for the pros. Still, he didn't want to look too eager. Best if the crowd and the other players perceived Birdie as pursuing him.

A few minutes later, he chipped to within six feet of the hole, then waited his turn at the edge of the green.

"You're killing it today," Corey said from his right shoulder. "It's too bad you can't finish the round. You and Eric could win this thing."

"I can't let Doc Berry down," Bobby said, wondering what Corey would do if he knew his real plans for the midday speech. "By the way, Dixie told me Charles may ride over from the mansion to speak with me at some point during the round."

"*During* the round? How the hell are you supposed to manage that?"

Bobby shrugged. "Maybe we'll squeeze in ten minutes at the turn. I'll leave that to them. Hey, do you think Penn Cage will be at that gala tonight? After losing that leg . . ."

"Nah, he's a liberal, remember? This isn't his crowd. Also, he's burying his mother today."

"Really? She just died yesterday."

Corey shrugged. "I heard a county supervisor bitching about it at the buffet before you teed off. Some kind of small-town bullshit."

Bobby watched Tim McGraw sink a fifteen-foot putt with surprising ease. He whistled in admiration, then froze. A striking figure standing on the far side of the green had caught his attention. He wore a straw hat and blue-tinted Persol sunglasses, like Steve McQueen in *The Thomas Crown Affair*. But even this cover couldn't hide the pale skin among the surrounding tans, or the unhealthy pink splotches around the spectator's mouth. He looked like a medical patient who might lose his footing at any moment. The people nearest him had given him a couple of feet of buffer space, which suggested BO, and as Bobby stared, he recognized the distinctive build and bone structure of Charlot Dufort.

"What's up?" Corey asked.

Bobby leaned closer. "Look across the green. I think our friend spent his hotel money on a new disguise."

"Shit," Corey breathed. "How the hell did he get in here?"

"Bought a ticket like everybody else, I guess."

"High," Corey decided. "Gotta be."

The blue sunglasses couldn't hide the fact that Charlot's eyes were laser focused on Bobby.

Bobby broke eye contact and walked onto the green. Approaching his ball, he bet himself that he wouldn't let distraction cause him to miss the six-foot putt. With calm deliberation he went through his usual pre-stroke ritual, then drew back the club head and made his shot. The ball rolled two inches left and died. A collective "Awww" escaped the deflating crowd. Then Bobby heard Birdie Blake say, "Well, that fucking *sucks*."

He glanced at the actress, who was glaring at a matron who'd taken umbrage at her choice of words. Birdie put her hands on her shapely hips, then flipped the woman off and stalked back to her cart, drinking from her "water" bottle as she went.

Bobby decided to follow, and as he did, he saw the crowd streaming around Charlot, while the lawyer stood rooted to the earth, watching him. Bobby forced himself to turn away and quicken his pace. Birdie waved from behind the wheel. Before he reached the empty seat, though, someone tapped him on the shoulder and said, "Flash 80 just eagled the eighth. Better tighten up, Wolfman."

Whipping his head around, Bobby saw Tim McGraw look back and grin before walking on. The "Wolfman" nickname affectionately made fun of Bobby's work in radio, while "Flash 80" referred to Jerry Rice, the greatest NFL wide receiver of all time.

"You might want to rethink that gala tonight," Corey suggested in a whisper, having suddenly appeared beside him.

"I can't hide forever," Bobby muttered, while Birdie signed a program for an excited fan.

"Yeah, but the Belle Rose clubhouse is the kind of place where twenty people will film you on their iPhones if you get into something."

"Screw Charlot," Bobby said with real venom.

"I hope you won't. He looks barely this side of the grave today."

"He needs to transition to the next astral plane. And the sooner the better." Bobby clapped Corey on the shoulder. "Catch up when you can, okay? I'm going to ride with Birdie for a while. She's got vodka with her."

"Seriously?"

"This is supposed to be fun, damn it."

"I'm sure Charlot can snort a couple of lines with you in the bushes. Meth, anyway."

"Get this crate moving, baby," Bobby ordered with a grin. Then he pulled Corey close and hissed, "You watch that motherfucker today. He starts moving toward me, cut him off. Make him disappear. Especially if his father turns up. Charlot says the wrong thing within earshot of Charles, it could cost me the campaign."

Corey sighed and waved Birdie forward like a footman from a production of *Cinderella*. His list of duties had expanded yet again.

CHAPTER 45

JOHN LE CARRÉ wrote that a committee is an animal with four back legs. That's been my experience with mayor's task forces. Despite one's best intentions, they become bloated by bureaucrats no sane mayor would ever have included—sops to special interests, usually. With a few notable exceptions (such as my 2005 Hurricane Katrina task force in Natchez) I found that even the leanest task force is frequently sabotaged by members either pushing private agendas, grandstanding for cameras, or both. In a weak-mayor city government (the civil form shared by both Bienville and Natchez), that problem is only magnified. As Bienville's city attorney, which is merely an advisory position, I have even less direct power to steer any conclave than a mayor, and for this reason I've chosen to remain at the back of the meeting room during the inaugural gathering.

Bienville's most public meeting room shares its decor with a thousand others across America. Veneer furniture, a polished oak rail, fake hardwood floors, and white ceiling tiles stained by rain that seeps constantly from the two-century-old roof. A semi-professional video system has been set up to broadcast to the web and provide an archive.

In a misguided attempt to project transparency, Doc has opened this meeting to the public, and it's already crowded with nonessential personnel. The officials' table is dominated by the city board of aldermen, but the audience chairs are filled with everything from city employees to local pastors, political junkies, and journalists. Mixed with these, to my growing unease, are a handful of men dressed in Confederate military uniforms. Close inspection tells me they're not merely costumed agitators, but bona fide members of the Sons of Confederate Veterans. Their uniforms are reenactor quality, right down to the antique buttons and the canteens on their belts. Most disturbing, though, are the cold expressions in their squinting eyes, and their utter silence.

Just across the aisle from these men sit about a dozen people holding BLM signs. This lively group seems ready to engage their perceived opponents at the first opportunity. Beyond them, though, I see a sight that unsettles me more than all the rest. A Black woman of about forty, with the casual-but-put-together look of a college professor, sits with a framed poster resting on her lap. Her poster shows two familiar structures side by side: on the left stands Arcadia Mansion in all its majesty before the fire consumed it; on the right stands the chilling entrance to the Auschwitz concentration camp, with ARBEIT MACHT FREI in iron letters above the gate. No words adorn this poster, and their very absence seems to scream: *NO EXPLANATION REQUIRED.*

The faces at the front table are depressingly familiar after two years of serving as Bienville's attorney, and three out of the six alderpersons remind me of the ones I worked with during two terms as mayor of Natchez. Each wears a mask of comity, and each hides an agenda meant to serve the few to the detriment of the many. A couple serve themselves alone. That tired dynamic wore me out long ago, and it's only my loyalty to Doc that has kept me in my post until now.

I've come not to take part in the discussions, but to assess the possibility of Doc's worry: an attempt to take over or dissolve the city board. Doc has fixated on this idea over the past year, but the only time a board member ever raised the issue was in terms of consolidating redundant functions for financial savings, not unwinding the city itself.

Studying the board at the table today, I simply don't see how they could manage it. After the last election, Bienville wound up with three white alderpersons and three Black ones. Our white male alderman is an old-line Poker Club stooge, bought and paid for. Our white female mayor pro tempore, Vivian Paine, is in her early fifties, and gives a great Chamber of Commerce impression of cheerful moderation. But I've learned over time that her final refrain on almost every issue is "personal responsibility," and effectively, she functions as a hard-core Republican who occasionally reposts MAGA and QAnon conspiracy theories to her Facebook page. Our other white female, thank God, is Sophie Dufort, who sits at the table with striking composure, seeming to give each speaker her undivided attention.

On the Black side of the table, things are a little more interesting. We have two new progressives, both men. Robert Gaines and Elijah Keyes wouldn't vote to dissolve a Black-run board if you held a pistol to their heads, especially if it meant turning over power to the county. The third Black alderperson is Cicely Waite, an old-time malcontent whom I've always believed served herself over her people. Several courthouse wags recall Cicely leaving her office with brown paper bags filled with stacks of bills, or FedEx envelopes lined with season tickets or complimentary resort reservations. Yet even so, I can't see Cicely giving the Poker Club the satisfaction of removing the only source of real Black power in Tenisaw County.

The final vote in any tie, of course, rests with Doc Berry himself. So as long as Doc is mayor, he's sweating a non-issue. I'm not naïve enough to ignore the fact that someone may have tried to assassinate Doc while he was

in Washington; that is, in fact, why I'm here. But even had someone succeeded in killing Doc, I can't see the African American members standing
for blackmail or extortion without pushing back hard.

As for the meeting itself, Doc has already held a full minute of silence
for last night's victims. After this he listed the major agencies working
the fires, from the state fire marshal to the FBI and BATF, as well as the
Highway Patrol, the U.S. Air Force, and Homeland Security. He hasn't
yet been given definitive word on deployment of the National Guard, but
he assumes the governor will deploy troops "in an effort to safeguard the
city's remaining antebellum mansions, which must reasonably be assumed
to be future targets."

As the meeting slogs onward, Doc opens the floor to questions, and a
disturbing picture of local events begins to emerge. Panic buying of guns
has started all over the southern half of the state. There's been widespread
hiring of armed security guards, and the local animal shelter has run out
of dogs. People are frantically searching antebellum homes for pre-laid ex-
plosives. According to the school board president, many fights have broken
out, both at his schools and at nearby fast food restaurants. Major athletic
events have already been canceled, with coaches citing racial tension as
the cause. On the positive side, special prayer services are being held in all
churches around the city, and community leaders of both races are making
appeals for brotherhood and patience. But nobody in the audience seems
much impressed by this announcement.

My phone vibrates with a text. Looking down, I find a message from a
local pilot I know: *Flying east of town. Just saw military convoy headed into
Bienville. Gotta be the National Guard. Has the governor announced that?
I guess things are about to get serious.*

Without delay I forward this message to Doc, out of long habit making
no eye contact with him. No doubt the GOP governor will do all he can
to make Doc appear to be out of the loop on crisis control in the wake of
the fires. As I watch our mayor read and absorb my text, the door opens
behind me, and I turn to find a Black pastor named Willie Doucy striding
into the room like an African prince.

Doucy was Doc's bitterest foe during the election, mounting a vicious
homophobic campaign against him, one centered in the private homes of
elderly Blacks throughout the city. In the end, he failed, but his hatred of
Doc is legendary, and if he's here, it's only to cause all the damage he can.

As Pastor Doucy moves by me, Nadine slides through the door behind
him. Backing up to her, I say, "What brings you to this circus?"

"I'm president of the Downtown Merchants Association. At the last minute Doc asked me to serve on the task force."

"You have my sympathies. This is a pointless exercise, and it's about to go south for Doc. He needs to wind it up."

"Look at that sign," Nadine says, disbelief shining in her eyes.

In the audience, one of the men dressed as a Confederate sergeant has held up a sign that reads: IT'S HISTORY, SNOWFLAKE! GET OVER IT!

Nadine zooms her phone and snaps a picture. "Text Doc. Warn him Pastor Doucy's winding up for something."

As quickly as I can, I type: *Willie Doucy's here for blood. Informal meeting tonight at Pencarrow? Only the people who matter. I'll get Annie to bring food from Jackson. If you agree, send me the names of people you want or don't want. Shut this circus down! It's not going to end well for you.*

Thankfully, Doc stands almost immediately and announces he's been called away to consult with investigators working the fires. He promises regular updates, thanks everyone for making their concerns known. Moving quickly to beat the crowd, Nadine and I push through the door as Pastor Doucy's voice rises in accusatory thunder. It's nothing Doc hasn't dealt with before. I only wish he could be spared it. But that kind of bullshit comes with the office.

As Nadine and I stand hand in hand beside her car, my phone pings again. The message is from Annie. It reads:

I don't know who you called, but the county president's secretary just delivered a signed and notarized permit for us to bury Gram at Pencarrow today. She apologized for the delay and said to call if we need any further help. So unless you call me back, I'm arranging the burial for three p.m.

I type back: *Three sounds fine. If you ever run into a Judge Clay Shelby, thank him for this.*

Annie responds:

I've met Judge Shelby! He's super nice. He and Gram ate lunch together sometimes.

"What's going on?" Nadine asks.

"Mom's burial is set for three p.m. And I owe Clay Shelby a favor."

"Oh, Clay's a real gentleman. He was friends with Shelby Foote." She gives me an empathetic smile. "Are you sure you don't want me to be there when you bury her? I can get someone to watch the store."

"I'd rather you work on that little legal project I mentioned."

"Which is?"

My phone pings again. This time the message is from Chief Mason Morgan. It reads: *HUGE development! Come by the station. Can't risk texting this. Quick as you can.*

After showing Nadine the text, I kiss her lightly on the lips, hug her tight, then make my way as fast as I can to my Audi. "I'll call you from the car!" I holler over my shoulder.

She waves goodbye and gets into her own vehicle.

THANKS TO BIENVILLE'S new board of aldermen, one year ago the city police force moved its HQ from a dilapidated single-story 1970s office building on the north end of town to a three-story Victorian house that for more than seventy years served as the sheriff's department. This historic structure had stood empty for nearly twenty years after the sheriff's department moved into the brutalist pile that now serves as Buck Tarlton's paramilitary power base and profit-making jail. In the interest of giving the municipal police a home suited to its role in a town renowned for preserving its history, the newly constituted city board voted to transform the old Victorian into a modern police station.

Chief Morgan's office is on the second floor, and to reach it, visitors must pass a chillingly morbid exhibit known as "The Hangman's Door." While more than a few old law-enforcement buildings in America contain trapdoors once used to facilitate the hanging of condemned prisoners, the BPD's new Victorian home features a unique execution system. Built in the 1890s to fit into one of the stairwells in the old building, it appears to be a normal door. But once opened, it reveals a hangman's noose, perfectly tied and ready for its next victim. Below the noose waits a wide trapdoor of dull green steel that slams open at the press of a button, like the jaws of some great beast. I've seen many a grown man scramble backward when surprised by a demonstration, and more than half the women who see the trapdoor operate shriek in terror. I doubt I'd show it to a child, but teenagers are said to love it, the way they love horror movies. They ask to see the mechanism worked again and again.

A few seconds after I pass the Hangman's Door, Chief Morgan gets up and comes out to shake my hand. He's a big man, round of head and body, but in the way great defensive linemen are round—jolly, maybe, but capable of hitting you with the force of a small truck. His hand enfolds mine like a great paw, and with a shiver I recall last Friday's encounter with the bear. But Chief Morgan's eyes twinkle with good humor, and I sense he has good news for me.

"How's that task force meeting going?" he asks with a wink.

"Chinese fire drill, Mason."

He grins. "As expected."

"What's happened? It's not like you to call me over here."

"You're not gonna believe it, baby. Half an hour ago, two of my men discovered a firebomb in Attica."

My mouth falls open. "The antebellum home? Governor John Quitman's place in Bienville?"

Morgan nods, his eyes bright with triumph. "The device was designed to be controlled by a timer. It was set to go off at nine p.m. tonight."

"Holy God, Mason." I'm much more familiar with Monmouth, Quitman's home in Natchez, and one of the most popular tourist destinations in the city."

"Amen, brother. Talk about a stroke of luck."

"Did this device incorporate military flares?"

"You're damn right it did. Exact type used on Tranquility and Arcadia."

A rush of excitement goes through me. "Can I see it?"

"If you've got the balls. I'm told that if one molecule of oxygen reaches the interior of those M206 flares, they detonate instantly. Anybody in the immediate vicinity will burn to death. Any survivors will be permanently blind."

"Shit. So our perp—or perps—obviously have some skills."

"I'm thinking they really might be active-duty military, Penn, or at the least, veterans with expertise."

"Where's the bomb now?"

"Henry?" he calls over his shoulder. "Bring that little firecracker in here. Detective Radford was about to run it over to our firing range and store it underground."

Detective Henry Radford is one of the few high-ranking white officers to survive the elevation of Chief Morgan. A heavyset man with a black patch over his left eye, Radford worked his way up from rookie deputy to his present rank on the basis of dogged persistence and thoroughness on homicide cases. He slips into the chief's office as though the cardboard box he's carrying contains his daughter's wedding crystal.

"Henry, show the city attorney what our K-9 found."

Detective Radford obeys with a grudging look. The old detective makes me think of Wilford Brimley with an eye patch. As he pulls back one flap of the box top, I peer inside from an angle. I can't make out the whole device, but I do see an inch-thick tube marked with numbers and a handwritten notation in red. A bomb this size could be hidden almost anywhere with little chance of being discovered.

"It makes me think of the archaic term for a bomb," I tell them. "An *infernal machine*."

"No shit," says Chief Morgan. "A little piece of hell."

"You say your dog led you to this?"

"Damn right," Morgan confesses. "Thing was hidden in a large-size cereal box in the pantry. Frosted Flakes. I doubt we'd have found it without the K-9. That won't be in my public comment, of course."

"I appreciate it, Detective. Now how about you get that thing as far away from us as you can?"

"Happy to, counselor," Radford says gruffly.

As the detective vacates the office, Chief Morgan says, "You've probably guessed by now why I asked you over."

"To scare the shit out of me?"

The chief grins. "That's just a bonus. I want to know what you think we should do with it. Or rather, what I'm required to do with it?"

There's no mystery about Morgan's motive here. "You mean, do you have to turn it over to Sheriff Tarlton?"

A faint smile touches his lips.

"Chief . . . as far as I'm concerned, given the safety issues, the prudent course of action would be for you to contact the BATF and have them take possession at the location of your choosing. I'd have a couple of photographers there to memorialize the fact that it was your department that discovered the device. And I'd lose no time leaking the photo to Marshall McEwan so that it can go right up on the *Watchman*'s online edition."

Morgan's smile has grown wider. "I'd like to send a photographer to memorialize Sheriff Tarlton having a goddamn hissy fit when he finds out my department will be getting the credit for sparing the city a further disaster."

"You know, John Quitman was what they call a Confederate fire-eater—strongly pro-slavery. But he was larger than life in all ways. He was the only American to rule Mexico from the National Palace. The first line of the 'Marines' Hymn'—*From the halls of Montezuma to the shores of Tripoli*—refers to Quitman's division in the Mexican War. He wanted to create a feudal empire where the Confederacy ruled over South American slave colonies. Hell, he was ousted from the governor's office for plotting with Venezuela to help it conquer Cuba. Then, two years later, he was recruited by President Franklin Pierce to do the same thing for the U.S. The only thing that stopped that expedition was that Cuba would have been admitted to the Union as a slave territory."

"So you're saying Attica was a fitting target if the Bastard Sons really are Black? With a historical grudge?"

"Exactly. Only the Dufort place is the exception to that theory, so far, but even Dufort owned a lot of slaves." This new information intrigues me. As little as I know about my ancestors, I know that Captain Robert Pencarrow was very close to Quitman, despite being his political opposite. "That all you need me for, Chief?"

"For now. I appreciate your prompt attention, counselor."

Turning to go, I pause at the door and look back. "Mason, does that hanging shaft ever give you the damn willies, the way it does me?"

The chief laughs. "Not really. I like to think it has some deterrent effect, especially on these gang kids. Their eyes nearly bug out when it hits them how that trapdoor was used back in the day."

"Is there any danger?" I ask. "I mean, could somebody with mental problems use it to commit suicide? I was wondering the other day about potential liability."

"No, no. The rope in there's real enough, but it's been pre-cut above the noose. There's only thread holding it together, maintaining the illusion. You couldn't hang a housecat from that noose."

"And the trapdoor? That's a hell of a drop, all the way to the basement."

"There's a coded box in there that controls power to the actuator. Very few people know it. Don't worry, Penn. The city's not gonna be paying out millions in damages 'cause I let some fool hang himself in that shaft."

"Glad to hear it. And thanks for the heads-up on the firebomb."

"It's pretty damn sobering, when you think about it. If we hadn't found that thing, by eleven tonight, Attica would have burned to the ground, and we'd be right back on the national news."

"And that much closer to a race war."

"Probably in the middle of one."

"Are you going to handle security for Doc's unity march today?"

"Oh, yeah. Overtime's gonna kill us, but I don't think we have a choice."

"Agreed."

Morgan gives me a salute, and I go on my way. But as I climb into my car on the street, my cell phone rings. It's Annie's boss, Doris Avery.

"What's happening, Doris?"

"I've been thinking about your plan to leave Kendrick in the Tenisaw County jail until another antebellum home is burned. Normally that would be a sound strategy, but these are unprecedented circumstances. I don't trust Buck Tarlton or his men not to do something stupid. And Kendrick has become too important to the Movement to risk his life like that. The man has forty million followers on global social media, and the number keeps growing. I've never seen anything like it."

I start to play devil's advocate, but one obvious fact hits me: since the bomb planted at Attica was operated by a timer—and Kendrick was only arrested an hour and a half ago—he could easily have planted it. The fact that he might have been incarcerated when it was discovered means nothing. Another mansion would have to burn before my plan to exonerate him could work, and days might pass before that happens.

"Even though being a political prisoner would likely double those numbers, I think you're right," I tell Doris. "I'll make arrangements."

"The kid doesn't have any money for bail. Neither does the family."

"Woohoo." *This is going to get expensive.* "I'll take care of it."

Doris chuckles softly. "Thank God for that Dunphy judgment, huh?"

"It's gonna be spent before I ever get it. If I do get it."

"Welcome back to the bar, counselor."

CHAPTER 46

"IF YOU NEED to pee, you have two minutes," Dixie Donnelly said to Bobby, who'd just birdied the ninth hole, leaving his team one stroke ahead of Jerry Rice and his partner.

"I'm fine. Is Dufort here?"

Dixie pointed discreetly at a temporary elevated camera shelter that had been constructed near the eighteenth hole, in the shadow of the clubhouse. "Big Daddy's waiting for you in there, Ben Quick."

Bobby glanced at his watch. He had no real desire to speak to the old man this morning, but it struck him that he might turn such a visit to his advantage, in terms of future security. "You're confusing your characters, Dix. Big Daddy's from Tennessee Williams, *Cat on a Hot Tin Roof.* Burl Ives in the movie. It's Will Varner in *The Long Hot Summer*, which is Orson Welles, channeling Faulkner. But I'm definitely Ben Quick in this melodrama, and Jody Varner's being a pain in my ass."

"I saw Charlot earlier," Dixie said. "I'll talk to security. I don't want a scene with the PGA here."

Bobby was glad to hear that. "Let's do this."

Dixie laughed. "Oh, you're going in alone, honey bunch. Charles doesn't want me in there. Never mixes business with pleasure."

Bobby pinched Dixie's side, then set out toward the clubhouse. Before he could even begin gathering his thoughts, though, he sensed someone arrowing toward him through the crowd on his right, the way a cornerback moves toward a wideout running a post. It was Charlot, and while he wasn't running, he was moving fast enough to catch Bobby before he reached the camera shelter, where, unbeknownst to him, his father was waiting. Bobby wasn't sure how to avoid a confrontation. He didn't have the luxury of time to employ deceit, and just then his cell phone rang.

"I've got a problem," Bobby told Corey.

"I'm ten yards behind you. Just keep going, but work your way left. I'll cut him off and peel him away."

"Jesus, Cor, you're a godsend."

"Tell me something I don't know. Later."

Bobby smiled and waved at a couple in front of him—the woman was holding out a white cap for his autograph—then he slid left and kept moving toward the clubhouse. Ten seconds later he heard a squawk and some minor commotion behind him, but he didn't turn. He made straight for the elevated media trailer. As he climbed the rickety steps, he activated an iPhone app that would record audio until he switched it off.

BOBBY FOUND CHARLES Dufort sitting in a cushioned chair beside a large, high-tech TV camera with the NBC Sports logo emblazoned on it. The old man looked surprisingly youthful in navy slacks and a cream polo shirt with the Saudi Arabian LIV golf tour logo on its breast. Surprisingly handsome, too. Charlot's looks hadn't come down solely through his mother, who had been a beauty almost comparable to the first Mrs. Dufort—Sophie's mother. *How odd*, Bobby thought, noting that Charlot—probably thanks to drug and alcohol abuse—looked ten years older than his true age, while Charles looked ten years younger than his.

"Morning, Bobby," Dufort said without moving to get up, though he did offer his hand.

"Morning, Charles." The old man's grip was surprisingly soft.

"I see you and Eric McKinnon are staying just ahead of Rice and his partner."

"Luck."

Dufort snorted. "I don't believe in luck. Keep it up. Teach 'em a lesson."

"We'll try."

The old man fixed him with an unblinking gaze and spoke with precision. "I know you don't have much time, and I don't need much. But I feel like we'd better make sure we're on the same page through these next few days. A lot of tension in town. And I don't like telephones."

"I agree one hundred percent. You want to go first?"

"Happy to. I've got your money committed. The first of it, anyway. A hundred million. And more to come—a lot more—once you get your name on the ballot in all fifty states."

"That's great, Charles. Damn, you work fast."

"That I do. How we coming on those signatures?"

"We'll have the commitments in time for our Friday announcement deadline. Only thing that could interfere down the road is a couple of red states trying to make it illegal to accept electronic signatures for nominations. But even if they succeed, we'll still have time to get them our physical signatures. An inconvenience at most."

Dufort pursed his lips and nodded. "All right. Now what about this 'special project' you hinted about yesterday? Sounded dangerous, and you were pretty vague."

Here was the opportunity. If he were specific enough with Dufort about the Donny Kilmer assassination plan now, then he would come directly under the umbrella of the billionaire's self-protection, which would be considerable. There was nobody better to be stuck in a boat with when some district attorney came gunning for you.

"Intentionally so," Bobby said. "The less you know, the better. Just be prepared around midday today for the shit to hit the fan. Racially speaking. If it happens, it'll happen at Diamond Hill."

Dufort looked surprised. "The mayor's unity rally? In the old Black business section?"

"Yes. If everything breaks the right way, we'll have between one and fifty casualties, and I'll be a national hero on the order of the Lone Ranger."

The billionaire's face shone with interest. "Is that so? Well. How can you handle that and play in the pro-am as well?"

"I'm going to have to withdraw before the eighteenth hole. I already cleared it with the board. Doc Berry asked me to speak for unity at the rally, and I couldn't turn him down, right? Nobody blames me for that."

"I see. And where's Doc at the end of this little project of yours?"

Bobby hesitated only a moment. "Casualty number one, I'm afraid. I'd prefer it to be Kendrick Washington, but—"

"That young coon who wears the chains?"

"That's him. But Buck Tarlton arrested him this morning. For burning Tranquility and Arcadia."

"*What?* Is he guilty?"

"I seriously doubt it, Charles."

Dufort raked his hand over his chin and shook his head. "Buck Tarlton is one vain and prideful son of a bitch. He's got no patience to do things right, so instead he just grabbed some low-hanging fruit."

"That's about it." Bobby looked at his watch. "But I'm afraid we've got bigger problems. One in particular."

"Such as?"

"Your second son."

The old man blinked and went still.

"You probably know Charlot's deep in debt to Tommy Russo and some other operators. Last night he showed up at my hunting cabin, essentially trying to blackmail me into paying off what I can for him."

"I hope you kicked him out on his ass."

"I was gentle. Got him a hotel for the night. But I'm afraid he's even worse today. He's out here on the grounds, which means he's risking his life to try to confront me again. Last night he made some threats."

"Surely the boy has nothing on you!"

"I think he'd say anything to try to squeeze money out of me. There's also the jealousy factor. If he were to learn that you're funding my run for the White House, for example, he'd say anything to try to destroy our relationship."

Dufort dismissed this idea with a brusque wave. "Don't worry about that. I wouldn't believe a damn word the boy said. I know what drives him."

"I'm glad to hear it."

"Charles," Bobby said hesitantly, "you should also be aware that Charlot didn't only threaten me. He threatened you as well. I think he means to come to you sometime today and try to blackmail you."

"With what?"

"He wasn't explicit. But he made it sound like prison-level offenses. Felonies. He says your maids know more than he does, if that helps you."

Dufort drew back his head and blinked in surprise. "That boy . . . does he not watch *Game of Thrones*? Does he not know he's a goddamn Lannister?"

"Is he?" Bobby asked. "He never pays his debts."

Dufort laughed deep in his chest. "Maybe he's not my son after all!"

"I'm sorry, Charles. The clock's ticking. They're expecting me to drive on ten in three minutes."

"Just a second. I have one major concern, Robert. It's a potential deal breaker."

Bobby took a deep breath and sighed. "Let's get it handled, then."

"Oppo research. I need to know your weakness. The media's going to dismantle your life with an electron microscope, so I might as well hear it now. Is whatever they're going to find survivable?"

"Well . . . Charlot *does* actually have one thing on me. It's from long ago. Our school days, actually. Almost junior high."

"Well, that can't be too damaging, can it?"

"There's a corpse involved. Female."

The old eyes narrowed to slits. "Oh. I see. Who made it?"

"Not me. But my cousin did. By accident. The one who blew Charlot's trust fund in that internet music scheme? Martyn?"

Recognition dawned in Dufort's eyes. "Right, right. His mother's your aunt. Lives in Montcornet now. Married that bloodless Brit, Harold Black."

"Exactly. You have a good memory."

Dufort waved his hand, but Bobby could see he wasn't immune to flattery. "Anyway, it involves a young slut who hung around the ball fields when we were kids. Had a limp. Poor self-image, really promiscuous. I sort of recruited her to help Martyn pop his cherry. He was three years older than the rest of us, after all, and still a virgin. He begged me nonstop, so I gave in. You know how it was back then."

"Oh, hell, yeah. So what happened?"

"Well, this girl—Price was her name, Angie Price—she went out to Montcornet to do the deed, and the thing went sideways. She died. Martyn called me in tears, a full-blown panic. He was desperate for help, and . . . well, Charles . . . he's *family*. I didn't feel like I had any choice."

Charles Dufort smacked his right fist into his left palm. "You see? You're goddamn right you didn't. *You* behaved like a Lannister. Family first, everything else second."

"Not everyone agrees with that code, Charles."

"To hell with them! That story'll never see the light of day. Not through Charlot, anyway. I'll make sure. And your cousin, well . . . you two are in a MAD situation, right? So he's no worry."

"Right. No worries there."

The old man was nodding as though he'd already buried this potential problem for good. "I'm glad you were frank with me, son. If you'd told me there was nothing to find, I'd have been worried. We've all tried to bury mistakes. Like old Robert Penn Warren said: *There's always something.*"

"Yes, sir. But I'll tell you this. I've always planned on going as high as I could get. And a good soldier knows he might have to backtrack anytime, so he doesn't lay mines in his own footsteps. Now, if that's all . . . I need to get moving."

The old man got to his feet and shook Bobby's hand again, this time more firmly. "You won't see me again today. I'm not going to have my son begging for money in front of these people."

Bobby turned and walked to the door, but there he paused. "One thing, Charles. The root of Charlot's threat to us is his debts. You could pay those without difficulty. Given our plans, might it not be easier and quieter to do that? At least in the short run?"

Charles Dufort's face looked as hard as the face of a cliff. "Careful, Bobby. I don't like people prying into my personal affairs. But since you and I are partners, I'll allow it this once." The old man looked at the floor. "I can't tell you the number of times I've tried to save that boy. Funded rehab, paid off criminals, warned off . . . *degenerates*. I'm through now. Done. Finished. Charlot's going to have to live the consequences of his behavior, as we all do eventually."

Do we? Bobby asked himself. "And if it costs him his life?"

Dufort looked up, his eyes skeptical. "That's an extreme, I think. It won't. A little pain, perhaps. Make a man of him, in the end. Finally."

Dufort sniffed and gave Bobby a little fist pump.

"Good luck today. Teach that lawn jockey a lesson out there."

Is he talking about Jerry freaking Rice? Bobby wondered. *The GOAT in the history of the NFL?* "Will do, Charles."

Bobby shut the door to the camera shelter. Standing at the head of the rickety aluminum steps, he looked out over the crowd and switched off his recording app. He saw no sign of Corey or Charlot, but neither did he see Eric McKinnon waiting for him at the tenth tee. Confused, he made his way down the aluminum steps to the close-cut grass. Just then his phone pinged again, and he saw another text from Corey. It read:

> *I lied about tee-off. You still have five minutes. Walk through the club-house and meet me in the parking lot.*

At that point Bobby wasn't about to disobey an order from Corey. He began jogging through the dense crowd.

EMERGING FROM THE front door of the clubhouse, Bobby found Corey waiting nervously at the bottom of the broad tile steps.

"What's the matter?" he asked.

Corey shook his head. "I need to show you something."

Bobby followed him through the expensive sedans and SUVs filling the parking lot. As they approached the area where their Range Rover was parked, Corey took him by the arm and slowed him down.

"Look up by our front fender."

Bobby did. What he saw was a straw hat, tangled hair, and blue sunglasses that sent a chill racing along his arms. "What the hell is he *doing*?"

"Waiting for you. I thought I'd handled him earlier—persuaded him to leave—but he didn't go. I think he's passed out."

"Jesus. He's out of control!"

"Obviously. What do you want to do?"

"I'd like to call Tommy Russo. Let him handle it as he sees fit."

Corey looked down, then up into Bobby's eyes. "Do you really mean that?"

"No. I'm just . . . I'm tired of feeling threatened."

"Yeah. Does his father have a clue how bad it is?"

"More than a clue. I think the old man's resigned to whatever happens."

"Seriously?"

"Cor, look—"

"Don't tell me. You want me to get him out of here quietly. Right?"

Bobby could hardly bring himself to ask it.

Corey's sigh revealed the extent of his fatigue. "What is your plan, Bobby? This isn't going to resolve itself. Are you going to front Charlot the money to keep Russo off him?"

"I don't know. It seems like a pointless stopgap, given his father's position."

"But what's the alternative?"

Bobby shrugged and turned toward bright laughter from a couple of club cougars who'd just parked nearby. One winked at him, then giggled again and sashayed off with her friend. When he turned back to Corey, he realized that the sound had wakened Charlot from his sun-scorched nap. He got awkwardly to his feet, blinking in the light, then caught sight of Bobby and Corey standing thirty feet away.

Desperate hope filled his eyes, then morphed into rage.

"*Go*," Bobby said, pushing Corey forward as he backed toward the clubhouse. "Handle it. We can't let this get any worse."

"I've got it. Get out of here!"

"*Bobby?*" Charlot called. "Wait! *I need to talk to you!*"

Bobby quickened his pace. He heard Corey's voice rising as he struggled to deal with Charlot's panic.

"I know about your deal!" Charlot shouted. "Twelve million *a year*? What the fuck, Bobby? Why won't you help me? You wouldn't even feel it!"

Bobby began to jog. One way or another, this had to end.

CHAPTER 47

SNAKE CREEK CURLED through Bienville like the reptile it was named for, but it predated the town by thousands of years. The creek had meant life to the Indians who'd settled along it in the 1500s, for it brought deer and bear and the now-vanished panther to these parts. In 2018 an archaeologist named Buck Ferris had discovered a Snake Creek settlement nearer the Mississippi River that dated to 3500 BCE, and he was murdered for it. Since then, a paper mill had gone up near that site, while state and private monies had funded a massive excavation and world-class visitor's center nearby, neither of which had been completed.

Broad, shallow, and slow moving on most days, Snake Creek meandered through hardwood forest and gravel-crusted sandbars, but during rains it swelled to a depth of ten to fifteen feet, rushing toward the Mississippi River like a locomotive, carrying whole trees torn from its sandy banks. To look down from one of the seven bridges that crossed it in Tenisaw County was to look into a maelstrom you knew you could not survive.

The site that Charlot Dufort suggested to Corey Evers for their private conversation was known as the Snake Creek II site, an open stretch of ground with low ceremonial mounds at each end and bounded by woods on all sides, with the creek and its sandy bed cutting through the trees to the north, twenty-five feet below the level of the field.

Corey parked the Range Rover in a gravel turnaround. Then he and Charlot got out and started along a grassy path that paralleled the boundary of the north woods. They didn't speak much at first. During the drive, the distraught attorney had cycled repeatedly between anger and despair. He was deeply offended that Bobby hadn't taken the time to speak to him, and instead had sent Corey to do his dirty work. But Corey also heard grief in the spurned paramour's voice; Charlot was deeply wounded by the certainty that Bobby no longer cared for him as he once had.

When they'd walked about two hundred yards, Charlot spoke in an exhausted voice. "Why is Bobby making this so *hard*? He's like my fucking father. I *know* he's got the money to help me, okay? He got twelve *million* for that new contract! He's got a bigger audience than almost anybody but Hannity."

"Bobby's going to get you some money," Corey assured him. "The problem is, that's just a stopgap. If you lose your law license, you're going to keep needing more. This is going to take some planning."

"*Going* to get me some money?" Charlot cried, red-faced. "If I don't have it by this afternoon, I'll be dead in a gully by dark. My law license is irrelevant!"

"That's not going to happen, Charlot. Bobby already told Russo he's going to cover you, and to leave you alone until he did."

"Russo talks out of both sides of his mouth. I went by my house this morning, just through the neighborhood. Russo had guys there again, parked in my driveway."

Corey felt a chill. "Have you spoken to your father since last night?"

"That's my business. I'll tell you when I know what we need to know."

Charlot folded his arms together as if he were cold. The man radiated fear like a bad smell. Without another word, he set out along the path again.

Corey cursed and followed. He was glad they'd decided to take two vehicles to the golf tournament after returning from Flowood. If Bobby hadn't had the Toyota Tundra he kept at the camp for landscape and maintenance work, he'd have had to hitch a ride to town to appear with Doc at Diamond Hill.

As he and Charlot moved through the lengthening grass, Corey's sense of their surroundings changed. He sensed they were nearing water. He flashed back to his days in Afghanistan, in army intelligence, where he'd first met Bobby. "Bobby's going to cover you in the short run," he insisted, scanning the ring of woods around the field. "But you've got to give him some space. He's got a lot of eyes on him now."

Corey kept scanning the tree lines. Four hundred yards away, back toward the turnaround where he'd parked, he saw two figures moving. He squinted. His eyes were good enough to pick out an old man and a dog moving against the trees.

"What is it?" Charlot asked. "What do you see?"

"Old guy walking his dog. We don't need to be seen together. Does that path lead down to the creek?"

"They all do, eventually. It's a deer path."

Corey stepped sideways into the trees, picking his way between scarlet briars and tendrils of poison ivy. The land dropped quickly, the path switching back upon itself again and again as it led toward the creek bed.

"Watch the ground," Charlot warned. "Snakes moving this time of year."

"You know the woods around here?" Corey asked, trying to make small talk.

"Like I know the Tenisaw County courthouse. I hunted these creeks for arrowheads and dinosaur bones from the time I was five. My father used to bring me, believe it or not. Also to the gravel pits south of here."

Corey heard a hitch in Charlot's voice, and he regretted the question.

"After a big rain," Charlot went on, "all you have to do is look down in this creek bed and you'll find an arrowhead or spearpoint, if you know what you're looking for."

The deer path hit flat, rich earth. Corey felt relief as the trees closed around him. He could smell the creek from here. He followed the scent of decay, feeling the ground turn sandy under his feet. Then the woods ended, and he was looking out over a hundred feet of white river sand at the opposite bank. Snake Creek itself was a shallow course, with scarcely ten inches of water in most places, except for a few deep pools at the base of steep cutbanks.

Charlot caught up to him, panting heavily.

"I need to sit down," he groaned. "Not a kid anymore."

He stumped past Corey and plopped down on a driftwood log polished silver by floods. Corey stood a few feet away, wanting to get the meeting done. While Charlot caught his breath, Corey looked at the mirrorlike surface of a long pool that separated them from the steep bank rising above their heads. Brown fish moved languidly through the water, as if they knew they had no chance of escape. Only another rain could save them.

"I used to love this place," Charlot said. "Me and my buddies used to build long mudslides after rains, from the highest banks. You'd be going so fast when you hit the water, it'd knock the breath out of you."

"Sounds fun."

Charlot nodded. "Better than Disney World. All those guys . . . workaholics and couch potatoes now. A couple are dead."

Corey winced. "Tell me something. What's the real likelihood that your father will come through for you?"

Charlot shrugged. "I don't know. He disowned me years ago, and he's wished me dead to my face."

"I'm sorry. I mean that."

"Yeah, well. That and two bits will buy you . . . hey, look."

Charlot bent with a groan and lifted a small, flat piece of rock from the gravel between his dress shoes. The stone was dark and thin, with a sharp edge.

"See these beveled marks?" he said, holding the stone by its base.

"Is that an arrowhead?"

"Yep. Classic Tenisaw style. Boy, I had dozens of these when I was a kid. The day after I came out, my dad tossed them into his catfish pond. I never found them again. Son of a bitch."

"That's something," Corey said, trying to figure a way to calm the man down.

"How weird is that?" Charlot asked softly. "I just mentioned my dad . . . and there it was."

"When did you come out?" Charlot asked, looking genuine.

"Right after I graduated from high school."

"Wow . . . Bobby was supposed to do it with me, but he chickened out, of course. But I never said a word to anyone." Charlot shrugged. "It made me hate him a little, though."

Corey didn't risk commenting on that.

"You're not out down here, are you?" Charlot asked. "I mean, just you as an individual."

Corey shook his head. "Can't risk it. Not with Bobby's career."

"What do you guys do about people like me? People from the past who show up out of nowhere?"

Corey smiled. "The people I ran with back in the day don't show up in Mississippi. Most wouldn't be caught dead here."

"Still. You guys are really walking a tightrope."

"With fire below us," Corey agreed. "And no net."

Charlot looked up, and his eyes had a fresh light in them. "What the hell is Bobby thinking? All this talk of a third-party run for the White House? The scrutiny will be unbelievable, and constant. What are *you* thinking? There's no way you two can stay in the closet. And as a Republican? Exposure would destroy him. They wouldn't even give the Log Cabin Republicans a *table* at the convention in Texas."

"It's an issue," Corey conceded.

"And not the only one."

"What do you mean?"

"Nothing," Charlot said, waving his hand.

"Don't do that," Corey said, feeling manipulated. "What is it you're trying to get me to ask you?"

"I just wonder how well you know Bobby. Because I thought I knew him pretty well . . . and then I found out I didn't. I got quite a few surprises over the years, where he's concerned."

Corey hated to take the bait. But he felt he had no choice. "All right, tell me."

Charlot scratched some dark sand off the arrowhead. "You know about the girl, right?"

Before Corey could say no, his phone vibrated with a text. It was from Bobby. He noticed then that he had only one bar of reception.

The message read: *Everything okay?*

Corey didn't reply. He didn't want Charlot asking if he was in contact with Bobby.

Charlot stood up from the log so swiftly that Corey took a step back.

"I need that money today, Corey," Charlot said sharply. "By close of business, okay? You have to make it happen for me. And I need a big chunk of it in cash. All Bobby can get in cash. I need two hundred thousand, minimum."

"Two hundred! Last night you said one."

"I didn't know about Bobby's contract then. Two hundred's nothing to him. I told you, they were waiting at my house!"

Corey pocketed his phone and held up his hands, palms outward. "Take it easy. We're on your side, man."

"Bullshit you're on my side! You don't even *know* me. You're here to protect your lover, no other reason. You don't give a shit whether I live or die."

Corey felt a wave of panic in his chest. "That's not true. Look in my eyes, Charlot. I do care."

Charlot shook his head violently. "You guys don't understand what's going on. You don't grasp the threat. Maybe you can't when it's somebody else in danger. But you're about to grasp it. You just wait. You'll feel it."

"Charlot—"

"*Shut up!* Look at this, Corey."

Charlot thrust out his cell phone like a weapon. It showed a full-screen photo, but sun flare made the image hard to see. Corey squinted, and Charlot turned the phone slightly. "See it now?"

A wave of nausea rolled through Corey's stomach. On Charlot Dufort's cell phone, Bobby sat naked on the foot of the cabin bed, massaging Corey's foot.

"You feel it now, don't you?" Charlot said. "I've got twenty more like this one, and a *lot* more explicit." With his thumb he dragged right to left, and more photos revealing simple domestic intimacy flicked past in train. Charlot stopped at an image of Bobby and Corey kissing naked in the bedroom of the cabin. Just that single image hitting the TMZ website would trigger the equivalent of a nuclear explosion for a conservative radio star.

"You bastard," Corey said, working it out. "You were already outside the cabin when Bobby arrived last night. Then you humped out to the gate and pretended you'd just gotten there."

"Obviously. I've handled enough divorce cases that I know how the PIs do it."

"Charlot, for God's sake. If you care about Bobby at all—"

"Care about him? I still *love* him, you supercilious prick. Now, you call him and tell him to get me that two hundred grand, today."

"He can't do that. He's playing in that pro-am. You just saw him there. I'm going to have to handle this."

"*I don't care I don't care I DON'T CARE!*" Charlot screamed. "Get him over here NOW!"

Corey had no intention of doing that. But even as his mind gauged his chances of knocking Charlot's phone into the nearby pool, Charlot took a small pistol from his pocket and pointed it at Corey's stomach. It was a derringer, two-shot type. Most "gambler's guns" like that carried .22 Magnum rounds, Corey knew. Big enough to kill a bull alligator if you hit the brain.

"What the hell are you doing with that?" Corey asked with all the calm he could muster.

"My last protection against Russo's goons."

"Well, you don't need it now."

"Bullshit, I don't. You were about to jump me."

Corey shook his head. "It's those pictures, Charlot. You have no right to those photos. And I can't let you leave here with that phone."

"You can't stop me."

Corey wasn't sure whether he could or not, but he was going to have to try.

"Watch this," Charlot said. Taking his forefinger from the derringer's trigger guard, he touched the screen of his phone a couple of times.

"That's ringing Trident Media, Corey. They own the Hogan Shanahan show—the one I called into this morning to talk to Bobby. I *should* call my father, actually. God, would he lose his mind over these pics! That's how I knew Bobby was planning to run for office, you know. I sneaked into Belle Rose this morning. I heard Dad talking on the phone, asking some fascist fat cat about Bobby. They're thinking of giving him a war chest. *Hundreds of millions of dollars.* And he won't give me *two million*?" Bright pink moons bloomed on Charlot's cheeks. "Can you *imagine*? Being willing to watch your own son hurt or killed because he's gay? But giving a hundred times that to an outsider because you *can't see that he's gay*? It's insane!"

Corey was edging forward . . .

"Get back! I can text these photos with one touch!" Charlot shouted. "You call Bobby and tell him to get the fucking money. *Now*. Screw that stupid golf tournament!"

Staring at the cell phone in Charlot's hand, Corey felt a hot flash go through him. With one press of a button, Charlot could destroy Bobby's future, his whole life as a public figure—at least as a conservative.

"Okay!" Corey yelled. "Kill that connection first!"

It was too late. Someone had already answered.

"Charlot, *hang up*!"

Dufort's finger floated over the screen. Desperate to prevent disaster, Corey flung out his right foot and kicked the lawyer in the stomach. Charlot folded double, but somehow he managed to cling to both pistol and phone. Corey leaped forward and grabbed the wrist of his derringer hand, but he missed the one holding the phone.

"Drop the phone!" Corey screamed.

Charlot fought with surprising strength, but Corey managed to stay atop him. He squeezed the gun wrist with all his strength, and Charlot cried out, but still he refused to let go. Filled with panic, Corey jerked up the thick wrist, then slammed it down on the gravel beneath them. This time the gun came loose. As his eyes tracked it, he saw Charlot reach for his cell phone screen. With no other option, Corey hugged him close and rolled right.

They splashed into the pool together, no more than three feet of water, but enough to cover them both. Charlot was on top when they hit, but Corey rolled him like a crocodile rolling prey, then raised his head and sucked in a lungful of air. Charlot fought with the power of desperation, and Corey, feeling his terror, started to release him. But something stopped him. The phone might not be a threat any longer, but Charlot himself had proved he was. He was a living bomb, and every second he walked free in the world increased the odds that Bobby's future would be destroyed.

Charlot bellowed under the water, his muffled expressions of panic chilling Corey's heart. But Corey didn't let go; he tightened his grip instead. For even if Bobby gave Charlot enough money to buy a reprieve, he couldn't live on it forever. And what were the odds that Charlot would ever get clean? Addictions to gambling and drugs fed off each other; even if you made headway with one addiction, the other pushed you right back into the flame.

Something heavy and alive brushed Corey's side, and his skin crawled. He was terrified of poisonous snakes, and Mississippi was filled with them. Charlot's struggles had weakened to spasmodic kicks and jerks. Corey risked raising his head and sucking in more precious air. Ten seconds later, Charlot Dufort went still.

CHAPTER 48

WHEN DOC BEGAN his unity parade at Nadine's bookstore, he had only three hundred people behind him, massed under a gentle rain. By my count about twenty of those were white. But as they marched through the center of town, softly singing hymns, silent whites stood on second-floor balconies, hundreds of them, staring down in fear or fury.

After covering four blocks in an easterly direction, moving away from the river, Doc turned north, into the Blacker section, and by the time he'd reversed direction again and terminated his walk at Diamond Hill, where a huge crowd awaited him, there were nearly two thousand people in his wake. As he strode through the old Black business district toward a hastily erected outdoor stage, the crowd behind him stretched for blocks. By this time, perhaps fifty of his followers were white. This number disturbed me, since Doc had won the election by taking more than 90 percent of the vote.

A light but steady rain continued falling, but rather than function as a deterrent, it seemed to magnify the resolve of those attending his speech. I was standing backstage next to Kendrick Washington—whom I only succeeded in bailing out a half hour ago—when Annie remarked on this, and Kendrick said, "It's like when Prince played the Super Bowl. The half-time producer said, 'It's raining, Prince! Are you sure you're all right?' And Prince said, 'Can you make it rain *harder*?' Then he went out and blew up the place by playing 'Purple Rain.' That's what today's gonna be for Doc."

"I hope you're right," Ray Ransom said anxiously, holding a poncho over his bald dome like a soldier who'd got all the rain he ever wanted in Vietnam.

Kendrick nodded with confidence. "Doc's coming into his own today. He's gonna change some hearts. I feel it."

"I hope so," Annie said softly. Then she leaned close to me and whispered, "Did you write his speech?"

I shook my head.

"That's a good thing," Kendrick declared. "Not that you didn't help get the man elected. But with what we got going on now, Doc needs to speak from the heart. He'll be *aiight*. You'll see."

"Dad?" Annie says in a stunned voice. "What's *he* doing here?"

Without warning, Bobby White steps through the opening between two buildings behind us, walks past us without a word, and takes up a position behind the small dais from which Doc intends to speak.

"I'm about to win a bet." I cut my eyes at Ray. "Bobby must have pulled out of the pro-am to speak here."

"That blows my mind. What is Doc thinking?"

Kendrick shakes his head with obvious misgivings.

In his tailored chinos and dark blue jacket, Bobby looks as trim and impressive as he does on TV. From whence does such confidence spring? His prodigious athletic gifts? Surviving combat? BDE? I'll probably never know. Bobby may not know himself. He just seems to go with the flow.

It seems odd that he didn't pause to say hello, but maybe he's nervous about speaking in front of an all-Black crowd. Especially with national news cameras covering the event. Pondering this question, I realize Bobby is watching Kendrick from the corner of his eye. He seems preoccupied with our new young celebrity, in fact. Maybe more than preoccupied. He can't seem to take his eyes off him.

White-haired Pastor Aaron Baldwin walks cautiously between us and makes his way to the dais. As he shuffles to the podium, I look out into the tilted square known as Diamond Hill. For some reason never adequately explained to me, these two blocks at the juncture of the old white and Black sections of Bienville were bisected by narrow alleys laid on opposite diagonals. The collapse of some poorly built buildings along the side alleys in the 1930s resulted in an open, diamond-shaped space relative to the linear squares of the other city blocks. For this reason—and because these blocks sit on the first high ground at the western edge of Bienville proper—they became known as Diamond Hill. And since this neighborhood marked the northernmost boundary of acceptable white residence in the mid-nineteenth century—other than outlying plantations—Diamond Hill became the heart of Black commerce for the city, a place where even whites occasionally traded. The area still thrived during my childhood in the 1960s and '70s, but by the mid-eighties it began to fail, like so many Black business districts in America at that time.

In recent years—thanks to the combined efforts of white and Black boosters—some of the old buildings have been repurposed, and a few beloved old businesses have been revived. World Famous Barbecue, in particular, does a booming trade every day but Sunday, when it closes due to its co-owners' strict religious principles.

Aaron Baldwin isn't the kind of pastor who loves the sound of his own voice: he takes less than a minute to open the event with a prayer. As Doc walks to the lectern amid somber applause, I find myself anxious about what he'll say. As much as I love and respect the man, I listened to too many campaign speeches that wandered into the weeds. But Doc's rumpled jacket is well known to all, and viewed from behind—his big gauze bandage now replaced by two large Band-Aids—the circlet of kinky white hair rings his scalp like a pauper's crown.

"I don't intend to keep you long in this rain," he begins. "I'm an old man, and I don't like getting wet. I don't need an introduction, since I brought a lot of you into this world, and I've treated most of the rest for the ills and afflictions of this life. I come before you today for one reason: to ask a favor. But before I do, I want to tell you what I see . . ."

TWENTY YARDS BEHIND Doc, Bobby White looked out over the sea of faces to whom he'd had no intention of speaking today. But now he wasn't sure. Three minutes earlier, Donny Kilmer had practically snatched him into an alley that fed onto Pine Street and ruined his day for the second time. Sensing instantly that something was wrong, Bobby followed him thirty yards up the trashed cut-through and took refuge with him behind a green dumpster.

"What the hell are you doing here?" Bobby asked. "Why aren't you in position?"

Donny answered in a fierce whisper. "Because there's too many niggers in that square! Wait till you get up there. You'll see. Even the side streets are filled. The water tower had lawn chairs set up under it two hours ago! People were eating barbecue. Same with the churches. There wasn't any way for me to get access to the bell towers."

"Shit. What about the abandoned buildings that face the diamond?"

Donny shook his head. "The problem is, I'm *white*. Anywhere I go, I have a hundred Black eyes on me. Maybe a thousand. What I need is a goddamn tripod and some cameras. CNN is out here filming. I might get away with pretending to be a cameraman looking to shoot down on the crowd. But I don't have that, and the mayor's about to speak."

Bobby thought as fast as he could. "Do you still have your burner phone?"

"Yeah. Hell, yeah. But I tried to text you about fifteen minutes ago, and you must not have gotten it."

Bobby checked his burner and shook his head, a sinking sense of worry in his gut. "Where's your rifle?"

"Stowed in this dumpster right here. It's in a backpack, with the stock taken off."

"Jesus. Okay, I'll assess the space when I get up there. I'll try to direct you to a point of access. Probably to one of the churches."

Donny nodded, but he didn't look optimistic.

"Don't shoot from anywhere I don't direct you to. Got it?"

Kilmer's eyes shifted left and right so fast that Bobby wondered if he was on drugs. "If the mayor's that important of a target," Donny said, "why don't I just walk up and blow his shit away with my pistol? No way anybody can stop that."

Bobby blinked in disbelief. Obviously, the suicidal offer wasn't even worth considering. Even after such a desperate act, Kilmer would have a fairly high chance of survival, and sooner or later that would lead to him talking to the authorities. Besides, Donny couldn't know that the real objective of his mission wasn't the death of Doc Berry, but Bobby's heroic execution of a mass shooter. If the kid used a pistol from close range, there would *be* no mass shooting. Not one of sufficient scale. Worse, Bobby would have no way of predicting exactly when and from where the kid would fire. You couldn't stage the kind of scene Bobby needed without that information.

"If you're not in position in ten minutes, then abort," Bobby said. "We clear?"

"That's not long."

"He won't be speaking long. If we don't get him here, we'll get him later today. Watch your phone."

Bobby walked fast back to Pine Street, then turned toward Diamond Hill. Before long, he spied Penn Cage standing backstage near his daughter, Ray Ransom, and—

Bobby's chest thudded as though from the impact of a nearby mortar round.

Kendrick Washington was standing next to the Cages.

His prime target—the biggest internet sensation in history—was no longer in jail.

"Son of a *bitch*," Bobby cursed. "Penn must have sprung him."

He wondered if Doc planned to ask Kendrick to the podium to speak, or even just to show him off. Clearly the kid was the better target, for Bobby's ultimate purpose, anyway. But how could he re-prioritize Donny Kilmer? Via text message, obviously, if the phones would link. *But what if they continue to malfunction? Can I risk a live voice call?* Bobby checked his watch and wondered whether Donny was still searching for a shooting perch, or whether he'd already aborted the mission. "Goddamn it," he thought, cursing the flow of fate.

MY EYES ARE on Doc Berry's back when Bobby White appears at my left side. "I heard Kendrick Washington was in Tarlton's jail," he whispers.

"Was that just a rumor?"

"No. Tarlton arrested him, purely for theatrics. I wanted to leave him inside as protection if another house burned, but Doris Avery was worried they might try to kill him in jail, so I bailed him out. Barely got him arraigned in time for him to be processed and get here."

Bobby nods. "Is he going to speak today? Because he's a lot more suited to addressing this demographic than I am."

"Doc doesn't think so, apparently. So far as I know, you're closing this thing out, not Kendrick."

"Damn it. I think I may actually be nervous."

I find myself chuckling. "I doubt that."

Bobby gives me a smile like I'm right, but the truth is, he does look a little rattled as he walks away. It's not an expression I've ever seen on him before.

"WHEN I WAS a boy," Doc Berry says, turning his head to take in buildings that line the blocks surrounding Diamond Hill, "this neighborhood was filled with life. Every building had a *bid'ness* in it, and every owner *tended* to their business. Like their lives depended on it. Because they *did*. Those folks had just come off the plantations and sharecropping farms. They knew they had to work hard to get ahead and stay there. I look around this old diamond, and I remember every single mom-and-pop shop."

Doc raises his right hand and points at a line of partly occupied buildings, most in need of paint and repair, but others starting to look respectable. "Starting on the left there, going clockwise, you had the One-Minute Man grocery store, where they had pickled eggs and hog-head cheese right on the counter."

The older members of the audience laugh in fond memory.

"Then you had the High-Top Liquor Store, with the brown-bag crowd leaning against that wall like they was holding it up. Next came Pressley's Tailor Shop: 'Dress Like a King.' Then old Mr. West's Well-Heeled Sole Repair. 'No Holes in My Soles!' He's still kickin', believe it or not. And right through that alley past him, you could see the Prince Hall Mason Lodge, before it burned. Then you had Royal Cigars and dry goods, the Open Air Car Wash, and Pug's Mechanic Shop. What next? Ah . . ."

"Hubie Gray's Car Lot!" a man shouted from the front row of chairs.

"That's right!" Doc said with a grin. "Hubie would sell anything twice, and three times was better! Finally, at the point of the diamond up there, you had the true heart of Diamond Hill: R.L. Cooley's Tire Shop. But I'm gonna come back to that."

Doc takes a moment to gather himself, or perhaps to get control of his voice, which had cracked at the mention of R.L. Cooley. "Past Cooley's on my right, you had Klassic Kutz Barbershop, where you got your hair conked in the days before the Movement took hold, and Malcolm wore the natural. Then Red's Pool Hall . . . best left to memory. Beside Red's, of course, you had the World Famous Mississippi Pit Barbecue, which now truly lives up to its name, under management of the grandson of the founder, Oscar 'O.D.' Davis."

A huge cheer goes up for the newly successful Bienville eatery, which draws curious and loyal customers from Jackson, New Orleans, and even Memphis.

Doc points over the heads of the crowd. "Over there stood Professor Hamm's drugstore, where a high school football player with jock itch could cure it with homemade solution that'd burn the hide off a water buffalo—take it from me. You had to stand in front of a box fan to apply that stuff!"

Yelps of remembered agony burst from the male members of the audience.

"Next came Mama Lou's Hollywood Dress Shop. Made a woman feel twenty pounds lighter and look ten years younger. Then her half sister Janelle's salon next door. Next was Quincy's newsstand, where they'd gladly place a bet on the contest of your choice. Astro Radio and TV Repair, long gone, but I used to tinker around in the back. Then there was the Diamond Hill Record Shop, where *Miss* Shirelle Dee recorded 'Come to Me' in 1963 and put this place on the map with Stax and Motown for about a minute. Finally, at the entrance of the block, there was Ruby Mae's Soul Café. If it was still there, I'd pay fifty dollars right now for a plate of her fried chicken with mac and cheese."

More than a thousand people simultaneously release a groan of nostalgic hunger. "Yes, Lord!" comes a cry.

Doc leans forward over the podium. "I've resurrected old Diamond Hill today because my subject is R.L. Cooley."

A hush descends on the audience.

"Whatever I've accomplished in this life, I owe to Mr. R.L. His grandfather was born enslaved south of town, near Natchez, and as a boy, R.L. hisself plowed behind a mule as a sharecropper. But the first chance he got, he went to work at a white gas station and learned everything about the trade. He learned about motors, brakes, and tires. But he learned about *bid'ness*, too. He learned you got to buy cheap and sell for more. But you've also got to take care of your customers. So R.L. found a source of tires over in Shreveport that didn't mind selling to a Black man, and he went into business right across this old diamond, putting tires on anything that rolled. Y'all remember how busy that place was in the day?"

"Yes, indeed!" shout at least fifty voices.

"Cooley's tire men were like NASCAR pit crews. Wasn't nobody cheaper or faster finding a leak and fixing it, or doing an alignment. Tractor-trailer drivers from all over the South made a point of coming through Bienville just to have Cooley's crew service their rigs. I know, because my big brother Jackie worked there as a high school senior in 1966, before he got drafted."

Doc pauses to straighten his jacket.

"Because of R.L.'s savvy, by 1966 he'd cut into a lot of the white market around here. And some folks didn't like that. Competitors, mostly. Some of those men were Klukkers, or close to the Klan. And they sent him a message. Told R.L. he'd better up his prices to a fair level or get out of business."

Doc waits to make sure the crowd is with him. "But that wasn't the real problem. The *real* problem was, Cooley had always been generous to the Movement. He supported Medgar's NAACP work until Delay Beckwith killed him in '63. And R.L. always had a little extra for the other groups that come through trying to change things. I can't tell you how many starving young brothers he sent down to World Famous with enough money for a sandwich and a Co'-Cola. R.L. sent Stokely Carmichael down there. He sent Bob Moses down there. Why, R.L. sent Congressman John Lewis down there for a sandwich when he was just another young troublemaker!"

A low rumble rises from the crowd, and I sense both love and resentment within it.

"You know who else worked at Cooley's? A feisty Black stock car racer named Mason Gardner. He did all he could to help the Movement, too, and he died last night in a burning house of God, at the hands of men whose hearts are filled with hatred."

Screams of anger and grief burst from the audience, as though Doc had reached into them physically and yanked out some poisonous growth.

"You know what it cost R.L. to do that kind of thing for as long as he did?" he asks. "In the open like he did? Yes, you do. We all know."

Annie squeezes my hand. The square of Diamond Hill has fallen so silent that all I hear is a truck's horn sounding miles away.

"One night, just after closing time," Doc says softly, "a group of white men pulled up over there and tossed a firebomb through the office door.

They killed R.L. and a seventeen-year-old boy named Vernel Gates. My brother's best friend."

"Oh, Lord," moans an elderly woman.

"R.L. died instantly, they said. But as a physician, I can tell you . . . no man who burns to death dies *instantly*. Young Vernel lived a day and a half before succumbing to his injuries. That could easily have been my big brother Jackie instead. I thank God it wasn't. But later on . . . I realized that it *was*. Wasn't it? Just like R.L. Cooley was a second father to me. And to a lot of y'all out there. I know he was."

Something has begun spinning in my chest, like a heavy electric motor spooling up. I don't think I've ever heard Doc speak with such direct emotion. He has reached into the souls of the people out there, and they want to be reached today. A feedback loop has been closed, a thrumming connection that could make this audience far more powerful than the sum of its parts. Powerful enough to knock down buildings. I only hope Doc can somehow bring them back down after lifting them to such a pitch of feeling.

"My point," Doc goes on, "is that I've never forgotten that night. Because I was thirteen years old, and my brother was working at the coolest place in town. And I hung around there so much that Mr. R.L. started giving me nickels to run errands for him. Man, you don't *know* how proud I was to be one of Cooley's boys! Prouder than when I put on my first army uniform. Prouder than when I put on my white coat after graduating from medical school."

These intimate revelations infuse Doc with charismatic energy. "My first medical office was one block off this square when I opened it, and it still was when I closed it to run for mayor. But I always considered myself to be part of Diamond Hill."

A ripple of applause runs through the people facing us.

"You know I trained some under Dr. Tom Cage down in Natchez. He'd been a combat medic like me, only in Korea. I saw down there what it meant to help hometown folks in need. Really help them. That's why I moved back up here to do whatever good I could for my own folks."

Doc starts to go on, but the scrape of fifteen hundred chairs on concrete drowns him out, and the entire crowd comes to its feet.

"Lord, no, y'all . . . please sit down."

Nobody does. Only the elderly and disabled in wheelchairs remain seated. These grieving, angry people have found their lightning rod, and their leader.

SIXTY-FIVE YARDS FROM the stage, Donny Kilmer climbed to the top of a six-step concrete stair unit that ended at a locked door. Three minutes earlier he'd stolen a large DSLR camera from a journalist set up near the western perimeter of Diamond Hill. This gave him the talisman of free movement he'd lacked before, and as soon as he turned and leaned against the wall with his backpack, he could clear the steps with his pistol, assemble his AR, and open fire. He didn't have much elevation, but *man*, did he have proximity. At this range his bullets would impact with maximum energy, creating devastatingly fatal wounds in every case. Casualties would easily be in the hundreds . . .

All he needed now was weapons-hot clearance.

CHAPTER 49

I JUMP WHEN Bobby White takes hold of my arm and leans toward my ear again. "Penn, I think I saw one of Barlow's militiamen out in the crowd. Near the edge. I'm going out there to make sure they're not up to no good."

"You're supposed to speak! Let me call Chief Morgan."

"He'll never find him quick enough. If Doc calls me up, go out there and stall. Or send Kendrick up. I'll head straight for the stage. If we make it to that point, we'll know Doc's okay."

I don't know if Bobby's plan is sound, but if his past record is any guide, I should trust his instincts above anybody else's here today. "I'll do it. But what can you do without a weapon?"

Bobby's eyes are still tracking something in the crowd. "You ought to know by now—I *am* a weapon. But I'm not unarmed." He slides his left pant leg up far enough for me to see a black nylon ankle holster.

"Okay. What if Barlow *is* set up on Doc out there?"

"I'll kill or cripple the motherfucker." Bobby slaps me on the shoulder. "See you soon."

"WHY AM I talking about R.L. Cooley today?" Doc asks the crowd. "Because I want you to know something. I want you to know that *I know what anger feels like*. You hear me? *I know what grief is.* Some people ask me why I rarely attend my patients' funerals. Well, I'll tell you now: it's not because I don't mourn. It's because a human being can only stand so much grief. And to do what I did for a living, a man's got to pace himself. Mourning old R.L. damn near broke me as a boy. So, when you think about Deacon Gardner dying last night . . . *I know what you're feeling.* I treated Duncan for years. And while he lived a long life, he still died before his time. And he died *hard*, the same way R.L. did. There's no excuse for that! There wasn't in 1966, and there damn sure isn't now."

The rage in the crowd is palpable, and Doc is driving it. As I watch him come into his own, as Kendrick predicted he would, I search the sea of people for any signs of white faces. But I don't even see Bobby White, much less any Barlow militiamen. Taking to my cell phone, I step away from Annie and call Chief Morgan.

"What is it, Penn?" he asks.

"Bobby White told me he thinks he saw a Barlow militia guy out in the crowd. He just saw one, but he's worried about more."

"Jesus. Like an assassination?"

"Yep. Bobby went out into the crowd to try to find him. And he's wearing an ankle holster."

"I can't believe this."

"Should we get Doc off the stage?"

"I doubt he'd go unless you tell him what's going on right there by the microphone."

I look at my watch. "He can't have much left to say. Just look for white men out there and immobilize them. If I hear any commotion, I'll run out and tackle Doc. Cover him up."

"Good man. Out."

Without drawing attention to myself, I hang up and move as close as I dare to the back of the dais. I'd have to be standing on the stage to get any closer to Doc. With that thought, I mount the dais, edge forward, and wait about fifteen feet behind him. If I have to tackle him, we may both go off the front lip, but at least we'll be out of the direct line of fire.

DOC PUSHES ON, his instincts pitch perfect, leading this crowd exactly where he wants them to go. I stand rooted to the stage, watching for the slightest movement on the rooflines or in windows, listening for the faintest sound of commotion in the audience.

"All that said," Doc says in a tone of conclusion, "I've come to ask you folks a favor. Because we don't know who's burning these so-called antebellum homes. And until we do, none of us really knows what's going on in this town. *Our* town. Yet because we live in such a divided time in America, some people have decided to believe that Black folks are burning those places. These Bastard Sons of the Confederacy, or whoever. Well, I never heard of any damn Bastard Sons, and *neither have you*. I think it's all *bullshit*!"

A riotous cheer rises from the assemblage.

"I think somebody *white* is burning those houses to start up a second civil war down here. And what I've come here today to beg you *not* to do—is fall into their trap. It's an old trap, brothers and sisters! They want to stir you up and make you do something they can use to prove to the world you're everything they claim you are. They want to make you loot a store, or flip a police car, set a convenience store on fire. They want to point at you and say, '*Look at those animals! They've got no respect for property. They don't value human life the way we do.*' Folks, I know you're too smart to let yourselves be used like that."

Doc holds up both hands as if to stem the dark tide of anger threatening to turn the crowd into a mob. "It's so easy to give in to rage. I feel that temptation myself. If somebody would have come to me on the night R.L. was murdered and asked me to burn down a white man's house, I'd have done it! But if we had, Klukkers would have torched the whole north end of Bienville, just like they did in Tulsa. And I'm telling you . . . if you give them what they want today, there'll be more Black churches burning, and that'll be the *least* of the damage. We'll have more National Guard in here, more state police, and white militia convoying in from miles away to start up riots. That's not the way to handle this."

"*THEN WHAT IS?*" shouts a bass-voiced man.

"That's the question!" Doc answers, nodding. "And I don't have all the answers. All I can tell you is, I'm no tool of the white man. We've got a Black-run city government here, and I'm working with federal agencies to get to the bottom of these arsons. I won't pretend the state's being helpful. You know who runs the statehouse in Jackson. But the FBI is with us, and the ATF, and the air force security people. I even got a call from former president Obama this morning."

A hush of awe falls over the audience, and Doc pauses as if deciding how much to tell. "We spoke a good ten minutes, but the main message he told me to pass on to you is this: *You are not alone. The eyes of the world are on you, and on Mississippi . . .*"

AT THE EDGE of the crowd on the west side of Diamond Hill, Bobby White felt his burner phone vibrate. The caller could only be Donny Kilmer, but sixteen minutes had passed since they'd stood together in the alley. The kid should have aborted and gotten the hell away from Diamond Hill long before now.

Looking down at his phone, Bobby read words that tightened his sphincter to the limit: *Couldn't find good elevation, but I'm on low steps on the east of the diamond. Can easily make shot from here. Just give me the go.*

Jesus fuck! Bobby thought, standing on tiptoe and scanning the edge of the human sea that separated him from the buildings lining the east side of the diamond. He couldn't see a white face anywhere, and even if he did, he'd be unlikely to make it even halfway through the chairs and panicked people once Donny started shooting. The kid might kill a hundred people, even two hundred, before Bobby got a clear shot at him. That was too many. Not least because one of Morgan's city cops might well take Donny down before that—and all to take down kindly old Mayor Berry, when Kendrick himself was now standing less than thirty feet behind him. Then the whole thing would have been for nothing. Worse, if he opened fire before Bobby could retarget his aim, then Bobby wouldn't get a fraction of the payoff that he would if Kendrick were the first victim whose image flashed around the world. An even more unthinkable, if one of Morgan's cops knocked Donny down but didn't kill him, the whole underlying truth might come out once Donny started talking—

NEGATIVE! Bobby typed. *ABORT! ABORT! DO NOT FIRE!*

Getting no reply as Doc's voice rolled on, he followed with:

> *WILL EXECUTE LATER TODAY. PRIME TARGET NOW AVAILABLE AGAIN. GET CLEAR REPEAT GET CLEAR. ABORT.*

Bobby needed to get back to the stage, but he couldn't afford to until he knew Donny wasn't going to disobey and open fire. Sweat poured from the skin beneath his jacket. To his horror, it struck him that he was going to have to think of something to say to the people massed in these chairs, and whatever he came up with was going to be broadcast to the entire world over CNN. What the hell could he tell them that wouldn't sound empty or patronizing, or like he hadn't just made it up on the spot?

Staring in fury at the blank screen of the burner phone, Bobby realized he had no choice but to trust in fate. With a silent curse he began working his way back through the people jamming the sidewalk on the west side of the diamond, pushing toward the stage 150 yards away—

If Donny opens up now . . . God help us all.

"LADIES AND GENTLEMEN," Doc goes on, sensing the mood of his audience, "nothing would have been easier for me today than to come up here and whip you into a frenzy. I know there are voices out there pushing you toward violence. But *that's not what a real leader does.* You know the word 'antebellum' literally means 'before the war' in Latin? Now we have people using those whitewashed old palaces to push us toward war. Well, I've seen war up close. I carried a rifle in Vietnam. And take it from me: *You don't want no part of war.* I've seen young men die in ways you can't imagine. Women and babies, too. Kendrick Washington has seen the same, and you saw what he did at Mission Hill last week. He begged for restraint. He saved lives. That wise young brother stands just behind me today. Yes, there he is."

A cheer worthy of an SEC championship crowd rises from the people. The thrumming in my chest has reached a near frantic pitch, and I'm ready to make a scene if I have to, to pull Doc out of the line of fire. But then my old friend signals that he's reached the end.

"You are not foolish to show patience," Doc declared. "Showing restraint can be a sign of the greatest strength, not weakness. Mahatma Gandhi knew that. He proved it beyond doubt, by defeating the greatest empire of his age.

"Now, before I go, I'm going to ask you to listen to someone you didn't expect to hear from today. He's from our town, but he grew up on the *other side*. You know his name from the baseball fields of twenty years ago, and if you don't, then from the radio or TV. Ladies and gentlemen, please give just a few moments of your time to Mr. Bobby White."

A stunned silence greets this request, but Bobby doesn't hesitate. He climbs onto the stage from the front left side, surprising Doc, then walks to the podium with the somber assurance of an accomplished vocalist asked to sing a hymn at a funeral. He and Doc embrace beside the lectern, and then Doc walks backstage once more. I don't start breathing again until Doc passes behind the remnant of a brick wall that shades and protects the rear of the dais.

Now Bobby faces the crowd alone. He stands in silence for about twenty seconds, letting the people get a good look at him as the light rain increases. But no one gets up to leave. They look at the tall white man facing them, taking in the steel in his gaze, and the missing arm, which most know he left in Afghanistan.

Then Bobby begins to speak.

"Like Mayor Berry," he begins, his voice deep and deceptively powerful, "I have seen young soldiers die before their allotted time. They were the best men I ever knew. But the Bible's threescore and ten might as well have been a thousand years to them. Some were white. Others Black. Some were light brown. Heck, I served with a guy who identified as *Blackanese*, and I didn't even know what that was at the time. Nor did I care. All I cared was . . . *did the man do his duty?* Did he stand in the line and cover his brother when the bullets started flying? And I'm here to tell you, he did. They *all* did. I'll tell you this, too. We all bleed red, folks. *We all bleed red*. I'll tell you something else Doc knows. At night, *all blood looks black*. There's a lesson there, folks. A simple one. We are all of us brothers and sisters. We are all God's children."

"Amen!" shouts an older woman. "Yes, Jesus!" cries another.

I see heads nodding in the crowd, but my main initial emotion is relief to find Doc standing beside me, out of the line of a sniper's fire, except for a few windows that would allow a direct frontal shot through the brick arch behind the dais. As unobtrusively as possible, I interpose myself between Doc and those windows.

"We live in challenging times," Bobby goes on. "A difficult, divided era, as Doc told you. A lot of older people say they don't even recognize America anymore. But I think you older folks standing out in this rain do. Because you know what a lot of older white folks never realized: America was *always* divided. That's right. It's just that y'all couldn't afford to be honest about it. You couldn't risk telling the white boss that you knew exactly how bad he was screwing you. How short your end of the stick was. But *you knew*."

I see the whites of widened eyes in the front rows.

"Of course you did!" Bobby goes on. "And the damned truth is, things ain't changed much, have they? Not in Mississippi. Not up north, either. So, what am I doing up here talking to you? Well . . . Doc asked me to say a few words. And I don't like to waste a chance at accomplishing some good. So what I'll say is, *Not everybody on my side of town thinks the way you're afraid they do.* Some people over on the white side know things ain't right, and *they ain't never been right*!"

I can't recall having heard a more shocked silence.

AT THE PODIUM, Bobby felt as though he'd plugged his fingers into a 220-volt socket. He held up his only hand and reached out as though trying to take hold of a thorn bush. "The problem is that nobody's sure how to *fix* it," he told them. "Everybody's struggling just to get by. But one thing's sure: none of us—Black or white—is going to help his cause by going out in the street and tearing into each other over these fires. I'm talking to everybody now. As far as what happened to Deacon Gardner and young Kemontrae Woods, well . . . that kind of cowardly crime has always been with us. Those killers will be brought to justice. But not by any mob. If the police or the sheriff can't solve it, the FBI will. But as for the fires . . . whoever brought that evil upon us will be uncovered in the end. They will suffer the Lord's wrath, and the Lord's justice. No, I'm not fool enough to believe in miracles in this age. But I believe in the grace of God. So I'm going to leave you with a well-known verse from Matthew . . ."

AS ANNIE, DOC, and I stare in wonder, Bobby draws himself fully erect, then speaks with a power that the most gifted pastors in the crowd would be hard-pressed to match. "*Blessed are the merciful, for they shall obtain mercy. Blessed are the pure in heart: for they shall see God. And blessed are the peacemakers: for they shall be called the children of God.*"

Bobby raises his voice with breathtaking power, and I can tell by the expressions on the faces in the front row that those people will later swear they felt the holy spirit flowing through them as he spoke. "*Blessed are they which are persecuted for righteousness' sake: for theirs is the kingdom of heaven. Blessed are ye when men shall revile you, and persecute you, and shall say all manner of evil against you falsely for my sake.*"

Bobby falls silent, as though he has finished. But then, in a final flourish, he turns and with his solitary arm salutes both Kendrick Washington and Doc Ezra Berry. Then he repeats his third line, which has become his chorus: "*Blessed are the peacemakers!*"

And with that he leaves the podium.

"My God," Annie breathes, as Bobby walks toward us with glazed eyes. "He took over that crowd in three minutes!"

I can't deny it.

"I think half these people would vote for him for governor," she goes on, her voice filled with awe. "Maybe even president. I really do."

"He knows how to reach an audience."

As Bobby walks down the steps toward us, Doc Berry embraces him with obvious affection.

"He still scares me, though," Annie whispers. "Maybe more than before. Nobody should have that kind of power."

"I know," I murmur. "He scares me, too."

SIXTY-FIVE YARDS FROM the dais, Donny Kilmer stared at the screen of his burner phone in mute fury. He figured that in thirty seconds he could have cleared the steps with his pistol, attached the stock of his AR, killed Doc Berry, and taken out at least a hundred targets in the audience before anyone even got a shot off at him. And the only thing stopping him, the all-caps text message on the piece-of-shit cash phone in his shaking hand—

ABORT! DO NOT FIRE!

He was damn near angry enough to take a shot at Bobby White himself, but for the other critical words contained in the text:

WILL EXECUTE LATER TODAY. PRIME TARGET NOW AVAILABLE AGAIN. GET CLEAR REPEAT GET CLEAR.

Donny dropped the stolen camera into his backpack and descended the steps into the throngs of stinking Black people. As he walked away, he held his breath and imagined himself spinning in a circle with his trigger fully depressed. *Soon*, he told himself. *Soon . . .*

CHAPTER 50

THE CHARGED ATMOSPHERE after Doc and Bobby leave the Diamond Hill stage has a near-magical quality, after the sickening anxiety of the past few minutes. Breaking their embrace at last, Doc walks to my right shoulder, his eyes glowing with pride.

"I knew I was right to ask Bobby to speak. That was the capper. He really touched some people."

"It was *you* who touched the people," Kendrick says from behind him. "Just like I said you would."

Doc gives him a paternal smile of appreciation. "I can only hope, son. It's going to be a long day, either way."

As Doc accepts the good wishes of two elderly ladies escorting Pastor Baldwin, I whisper to Kendrick: "What did you think of Bobby White?"

The young vet looks deeply unsettled as he gazes back at me. "I don't know exactly. I ain't got him figured out. He reminds me of an officer I knew in the service."

"A good officer?"

"Depends on your definition. Grunts who never met him would have charged machine guns for him."

"I know what you mean. We'd better get him figured out quick, because I think he's way ahead of the rest of us."

"How did it go?" asks a female voice.

Nadine's bright eyes and blonde hair appear out of the massed bodies. "I caught some of it on CNN, but I couldn't get away from the store in time to make it down here."

"Doc did great," I tell her.

"He absolutely did," Annie says.

"And Bobby White?" Nadine asks. "Turd in the punch bowl?"

"Uhhh," Annie gives her a pointed look. "He effing killed it, actually."

Nadine looks surprised. "Did he *really*? Wow."

I nod to my left, where Bobby stands surrounded by laughing Black men who played baseball with or against him during high school. As I watch him engage them like a born raconteur, Doc appears at my elbow with Ray Ransom.

"Penn, we're going over to World Famous for some barbecue. Pop Davis insists we'll bring in a bumper lunch crowd. I'm going to invite Bobby, and

I'd like you and Nadine and Annie there as well. At my table. I feel really good about today."

"You should, Doc. And we're happy to come."

The mayor leans in close. "We'll probably pull a crowd in behind us, and I'd like to pick up as much of the tab as possible. Can you help me with that?"

I can't help but grin. "Doc, for once, I think this sounds like a damn good use for that Dunphy judgment money. We shall kill the fatted hog today. We'll buy every damned pig O.L. has buried in that pit of his."

"Now you're talking!" Ray cries with a grin. "And cold beer to wash it down!"

"All you can drink, brother."

His aged yellow eyes lit by happiness, Doc walks over to Bobby and invites him to the World Famous Mississippi Pit Barbecue. Bobby accepts without hesitation. When Doc returns, he says, "I've got to run home and check on David before I come over. He's not doing well."

Doc has lived with David Latour, an interior designer from New Orleans, for more than four years now, and he looks genuinely concerned. I remember Latour having a difficult time with Covid. "I wondered why he wasn't here."

"David's always had COPD, and now it looks like he may have long Covid. He was triple-vaccinated, but . . . you know how it is."

"Man, I'm sorry."

"I'm just going to give him a steroid shot. Won't take me fifteen minutes."

"I'll drive you," Ray offers.

"It's only five blocks. No, I want you to get things set up over at Pop's. Tell him about the bill, get the big center table, and make sure that baseball crowd doesn't hassle Bobby too much."

Ray shakes his head with frustration. "Okay, but take my truck. You'll be too long on foot."

Doc nods and accepts Ray's keys. "I'll see you guys in twenty minutes."

After Doc makes his exit, the crowd begins to dissipate from the concrete diamond, and those who heard our lunch plans begin moving toward the repointed red-brick front of World Famous. Ray manages to get out ahead of the crowd, but by the time Nadine and Annie and I squeeze our way into the restaurant, the only empty seats left are at the table reserved for Doc's party. There's a chair for Bobby, but he gives up any hope of reaching it and settles for drinking beer with the guys verbally replaying every game in which they batted against him.

Nadine sits at my left, at what's known as "the VIP table" in this restaurant, a round chunk of red oak that could seat half the Arthurian knights in a pinch. Her right hand rests on my left knee, squeezing every couple of minutes to let me know she's paying attention. Kendrick sits at my right, Annie beside him, while Ray and his wife, Lashanna, fill the next two seats. Lashanna is a big handsome woman twenty years Ray's junior, whom he married shortly after his decades-long stint in Parchman. More than once I've heard him joke about needing a "sturdy girl" to help him make up for lost time, and Lashanna Ransom looks more than capable of handling him.

The other two chairs await Doc and Bobby, the men of the hour. Before ten minutes pass, co-owner O.L. Davis, a thirty-year-old who played offensive tackle for two seasons at Mississippi State, emerges from his kitchen with steaming racks of ribs on metal trays, already slathered in his renowned wet sauce. He bangs the trays down at mid-table, and no one in our group is shy about serving themselves. Within a minute, we're covered in dark orange sauce and grease.

"What you think, Penn?" Ray asks, a chunky curved rib in his big right hand. "You think our speakers done some good today?"

"You were the one predicting disaster this morning. Saying the curfew would never hold. What do you think now?"

"I'm a hard sell, man. You learn that in prison. But I believe they swayed some folks. Doc was *preachin'*. Talkin' 'bout the old times like that? And R.L. Cooley? That was smart, man."

"I told you he'd bring it today," Kendrick reminds us. "I felt it building, like a hurricane."

"Where was *that* Doc during the campaign?" Ray asks.

"Doc don't care about politics," Kendrick explains. "He cares about *people*."

"You're right," Annie agrees. "That's Doc, all the way."

"Bobby spoke second?" Nadine asks. "I assumed he would introduce Doc."

Ray shakes his head. "Bobby closed it like a born headliner. Spoke from the heart, and even finished with scripture. He made these folks *believe*, man. I never saw that coming. You, Penn?"

"I definitely didn't. Religion can bridge some big gaps, I guess."

"*Praise Jesus*," Ray's wife avers, with conviction. "I know that's right."

"Yo, yo, *yo*," booms a voice so deep it can only belong to O.L. Davis. The patrons fall silent as one.

"Doc called five minutes ago and told me that since Bobby White's in the house, Pop needs to tell you why that meat in your mouth tastes better than the meat you buy at the sto'. If y'all agree that it does taste better."

A huge whoop goes up from the crowd.

"Well, then! Doc said since Mr. Bobby could be the next president, he needs to know this story. So y'all listen up!"

O.L. moves his huge bulk aside, and the man who replaces him, while somewhat smaller, must still weigh in at about 280. To my surprise, the voice of O.D. "Pop" Davis, who played tackle for Grambling, is pitched higher than his son's. But Pop is a natural storyteller, and despite his seemingly dry subject, he owns his crowd from the first sentence.

"I bet y'all don't know that ninety-nine percent of the cattlemen in Mississippi don't eat their own meat. They buy it down at the grocery for ten times what it cost 'em to raise it. And the pork they raise, they buy back from the Chinese owners of U.S. companies. Any cow you buy from the grocery—even one that grew up right across the fence from you in Tenisaw County—he done rode six or seven eighteen-wheelers all the way from Mississippi up to a feed lot in the Midwest—bypassing acres of corn in the Mississippi and Arkansas deltas—to get put in a pen with fifty thousand other cows from all over the country. *There*, he's force-fed Iowa corn, pumped full of antibiotics, then slaughtered and chopped up and packaged in plastic to get sent back down to within a mile of where he was born—all so they can charge you ten dollars a pound and tell you that's good for America! *That's* the gospel of corporate religion!"

The crowd has grown a little glassy-eyed, and they're still hungry, but enough of them know O.D. Davis to wait for the rest of it.

"Now *me*? I wants to eat meat raised on the same grass I was! I want to buy from my neighbor, pay him a fair price, and eat a healthy animal that lived a decent life in the open. And I'm gonna tell you a secret 'bout a hog. Just because a hog *will* eat anything, don't mean he *should*. That hog you're eatin' now tastes like heaven because every drop of water he ever drank came from the same branch of the Snake Creek me and my brothers skinny-dipped in as boys!"

A cry of mock disgust reverberates through the restaurant.

"That hog ate the grass my grandkids run and play on now. That hog ain't carrying no microbes from Idaho or any other damn place. He's Mississippi down to the bone and blood! Same as you! He ain't got no Chinese bird flu, or suspect antibiotics. He didn't *need* no antibiotics! He damn sure ain't been up to Arkansas in no eighteen-wheeler!"

Another appreciative whoop bursts from the crowd.

"But to get you that divine meat—the best this side of the Iberian peninsula—I damn near have to break the law! I gotta get me a *special dispensation*. Costs me time and money I can't afford, and miles on my trucks. But it tastes better than the meat at Peter Luger's steak house in Brooklyn, New York! Now, this system ain't *right*. It ain't *fair*. But that's how the fat boys who run this state like it. That's how the fat boys in Washington like it. They like lobbyists buying 'em season tickets to football games, flying 'em to trade shows and luxury hunts. Well, I say *to hell with them fat boys*!"

"Straight to hell!" yells a big man at the bar.

"That piece of heaven in your mouth is tellin' you, 'Help the *people* of Mississippi!' And I'm saying to Mister Bobby White . . . brother, it's time to get yourself elected to where you can do something about this bullshit and *help a hardworkin' nigga OUT*!"

Thunderous applause nearly raises the roof.

Bobby White laughs until his face is red, and his old ball-playing buddies pass him a giant mug of beer. He's raising it to his lips when two sharp cracks like Black Cat firecrackers pop off outside.

There's a glitch-in-the-matrix feeling, and the restaurant goes quiet, waiting. In the tense silence, I recall the sense of impending disaster I felt as I waited behind the dais, praying for Doc to finish his speech. Yet no more concussions sound from the street. The longer we wait, the more likely it seems that what we heard really was firecrackers, or a backfiring motor. In any case, gunfire is a regular occurrence in this part of town, and thus not something people freak out over. But as most patrons return to their ribs and beer, I see Ray's brows slowly knitting themselves.

"Doc's been gone too long," he says. "He shoulda been back by now." Ray looks at his watch. "Ten minutes ago, really."

"O.L. told us Doc just called, baby," says Lashanna.

Ray shakes his head. "Yeah . . . no. That's been a while. He really wanted to be here for this. Something's wrong."

I get to my feet. "My car's not far. I'll take you to check on him."

Ray starts to stand, but before he reaches his feet, five more pops in quick succession sound from outside, these much louder than before. Even I can tell they were gunshots. Heavier in caliber than the first two pops, the concussions seize the attention of everyone in the room.

"No," Ray says in a desolate voice. "No, no, *no*—"

CHAPTER 51

FROM THE PANICKED mob crushing through the door of World Famous Barbecue, Ray Ransom takes off on foot in the direction of Doc's house, leaving me to limp along as best I can. But his fear is contagious, and I push myself hard. Within seconds Bobby passes me at a full sprint, and he gains rapidly on Ray, then passes him. Nadine and Annie catch up quickly to me and do their best to help me run without falling, but we're far behind the leaders.

Because of the still-green foliage and the angle of the street, I soon lose sight of Bobby and Ray. At first there seems no plan except to cover the distance to Doc's house on foot. But then I hear a man scream *"No, goddamn it!"* followed by a shouted warning in the exaggerated military bellow of frightened cops everywhere. I have no idea what's happening ahead, but my guess is that any cop facing an angry Ray Ransom is going to experience panic. The yells seem to be coming from a mixed commercial area two blocks up from Doc's house. Before we reach it, a sheriff's department cruiser roars up from behind and blows past us, then cuts into the block by jumping a curb and sidewalk.

"This isn't good," I pant. "Annie—"

"Don't even think about telling me not to come!"

Shit . . . After another thirty seconds' struggle, we follow the path of the cruiser, which leads us into a small parking area between a pawnshop and a crumbling old building that looks like it's being used for storage. The opening is partly blocked by Ray's old burnt orange pickup, which he lent to Doc for his trip home. The old Ford looks like Doc must have driven it in at an angle, then abandoned it without any effort to properly park.

The space beyond the truck is hyperlit by red flashes from the cruiser and the white glow of a spotlight. Centered in that spot is Doc Berry, mayor of Bienville. He's lying atop a blond boy of about eighteen who looks vaguely familiar, and Doc has multiple gunshots stitched across his back and side. Both man and boy are clothed, but Doc is no longer wearing his suit. He's wearing old gray warm-ups like an actor on the set of *The White Shadow*.

Two sheriff's deputies stand to the side of the bodies, speaking quietly while Ray Ransom stares down at what remains of his friend. Moving closer, I see the boy's throat is a mass of red gore, and Doc's hand appears to be buried in it.

"What the hell happened here?" I hear myself ask.

"They killed him," Ray says. "That motherfucker right there shot Doc."

A deputy I've never seen before whirls toward Ray and barks, "I told you to get back!"

I realize now that I only judged this man to be a deputy because of his posture and the pistol in a holster on his left hip. He's actually not wearing a uniform. It's just that he stands exactly like the uniformed deputy. He's also wearing a Stetson, like most of Tarlton's deputies do.

"Who are you?" I ask.

The man turns his smoldering gaze to me, as if to walk forward and shove me back. "Sir, you need to leave this area immediately. This is a crime scene."

"I know what it is. I'm a former prosecutor. Now, you identify yourself."

The dark eyes blaze with anger. "Buddy, you don't tell me what to do. You get the fuck *back*!"

A wave of indignation swells in my chest, and I step toward the stranger, ready to tear him a new one, when I feel a lightly restraining hand on my shoulder.

"Hey, hey, easy now," says a man I didn't see until now.

It's Bobby White. He moves between me and the armed man.

"Penn's just trying to find out what happened," he says. "Let's all cool down, Deputy LeJay. Things are bad enough already."

"I don't know this guy!" says the deputy. "And I want him out of my face."

"Boy, you're digging a deeper hole every second," I tell him. "I'm the Bienville city attorney. You'd better tell me what happened here, and quick."

"That's it!" he snaps. "This motherfucker's under arrest."

"No, he's not," says Bobby White. "You need to take a breath and calm down, Kenny. And if you don't believe me, I'll get Sheriff Tarlton on the phone to set you straight."

Bobby's tone is so quietly commanding that I don't even question what a radio talk show host is doing ordering a deputy around. A natural power hierarchy has manifested itself, the way it sometimes does in war zones. By primal osmosis, the Stetson-wearing stranger is picking up that Robert E. Lee White is not someone you mess with—at least not without knowing more than he knows now. The uniformed Tenisaw County deputy certainly knows the direction of the wind, and he walks the hothead around the pawnshop to cool him off.

"Tarlton better get his ass down here, Bobby," I say. "This scene's going to go to hell in about two minutes."

"I know it, brother."

"He'd better call those damn National Guard troops up here. What the fuck happened?"

Bobby shakes his head helplessly. "You look at this scene and tell me. I haven't figured it out yet. But it looks bad."

"Ray?" I call out to my left. "Any ideas?"

Ray Ransom is sobbing softly, his face a wreck. "I can't . . . I don't know."

"What did the deputy say?"

Bobby shrugs at Ray's silence. "The stranger's an Amite County officer temporarily deputized to work as auxiliary manpower for today's march. Name's Kenneth LeJay. I just made a call to verify that. The guy told me Doc was strangling that kid when he got here."

"That's bullshit!" snaps Ray. "You know it is."

Bobby shrugs again. "LeJay claims he ordered Doc to get away from the kid—gave him specific instructions to lie flat and spread-eagled—and Doc refused to comply. Refused even to acknowledge his authority."

I hold up my hand. "After meeting that asshole, I know how Doc felt."

"Yeah."

"But even if all that's true, the deputy thought his next move was to shoot an unarmed man of seventy-four? What the hell, Bobby?"

Bobby shrugs again. "What do you want me to say? The guy claims Doc was assaulting the kid. He said it looked . . . you know, *personal*."

A chill goes through me. "Jesus. The kid's not more than eighteen, if that."

Bobby nods as though this self-evident truth is immaterial, or perhaps material in some way that we'd rather not think about.

"Impossible," I say softly. "Not in the context of where we just were. Doc knew we expected him back at World Famous right away. He *wanted* to be back there. There's no way, man."

Bobby holds up his sole hand. "I hear you. I get it. I'm just trying to figure this out. I'm open to alternate scenarios."

Another cruiser squeals in behind us, and this time I see from the markings that it's Sheriff Buck Tarlton's car. By the time Tarlton climbs out and moves toward us, his deputy is marching the plainclothes man back around the corner of the pawnshop.

"Somebody tell me what I'm looking at," Tarlton says, his right hand gripping the brim of his hat. "Because I don't believe my eyes."

"One of your men shot the mayor!" Ray cries, stepping forward in all his intimidating bulk. "You can believe *that*!"

Tarlton licks his lips and motions for Ray to step back. "I'm going to find out what happened, Ray. Please give me some room to do that."

"Is that guy an Amite County deputy?" I ask, pointing at the deputy who shot Doc.

Tarlton grimaces. "He is. Given the crowd I expected today, I augmented my team by deputizing about twenty officers from neighboring counties. This one's from Liberty."

"Klan country," Ray grumbles. "From *way* back. Goddamn it."

Tarlton's eyes flash. "Keep that talk to yourself. I wasn't going to have another Mission Hill."

"You've got something worse now," I tell him.

As one, all of us in our tight circle look back toward the street. Somehow we've sensed the approach of a large group of angry humans, just in time to see them turn the corner and start flooding into the space between the buildings. Some I recognize from the restaurant, but others look like denizens of the neighborhood. If they see Doc lying dead from a deputy's bullets . . . God only knows what they'll do. Without wanting to shield Tarlton in any way, I move quickly toward the street and block the path of the man in front, who turns out to be Pop Davis, the owner of World Famous Barbecue.

"Pop, I'm going to ask you to stay back for just a minute. There's a bad situation here, and we don't need too many people seeing it until we understand it better."

"Is Doc all right?" he asks, his eyes filled with worry. "That's all we want to know."

I don't answer right away, and Pop can see from my expression that I don't have good news. With a slow shake of his head, he signals for his delegation to remain behind him, then pushes past me and walks around the storage building.

"Oh, naw," he says. "Oh, *hell* naw! Lord, Lord . . . what happened up in here? What y'all done to my man? To my *doctor*? What y'all *done* to him?"

When I see tears stream down the quivering face of Pop Davis, the tough Grambling football player, wetness fills my own eyes. For the first time, the reality that my friend Doc Berry is gone breaks past my instinctive defenses.

"Pop?" says the sheriff with surprising gentleness. "I'm going to have to ask you to go back to your restaurant. We've got a lot of work to do here. A lot of questions to answer."

"Sheriff, you ain't got but one question to answer. What the hell's wrong with your department? Last week y'all shot thirty kids. Now you done kilt the best man in the county! You kilt a *peacemaker*, man. Ax *him*," he says, pointing to Bobby White. "He knows. Oh, Jesus. Ohhh, sweet Jesus, no . . ."

Pop turns away and half staggers out of the space between the buildings, returning to his people, who have no idea how to respond to the unthinkable.

I quickly return to Tarlton and speak as urgently as I can, trying to break through his stubbornness. "Sheriff, you've got two choices. Flood this space with backup—I mean state troopers and National Guard—or photograph the scene and get the fuck out of here. Honestly, I'd suggest option two. I don't think fifty men could secure this scene in the present circumstance."

Buck Tarlton rolls his head on his big shoulders and surveys the interior of the block. "Take it easy, Cage. I know how to do my job. We've got the men to handle this."

"You are *dreaming*, bud. There's more guns in the surrounding four blocks than in your whole damn headquarters. And if you think these folks are intimidated by the fact that you're law enforcement, you're a fool. When word gets out that some backwoods deputy shot Doc Berry, this town's going to *explode*."

As we stare at each other, Tarlton's eyes flicker with indecision. Then he looks left, where Bobby White stands listening to our exchange. I have a feeling Tarlton's waiting for guidance, but as he waits, a new sound comes to us—sirens. Only these, I know, belong to city police cars.

"There's your next problem," I say. "You're about to be in the middle of a jurisdictional dispute that'll take the state attorney general to settle. I don't like you, Buck, but I'm going to give you my best advice: choose discretion and get out of here before you're buried in shit and drowning in blood."

Tarlton wants to tell me go to hell, but before he can, Bobby White steps close to him. "Buck, that's good advice. This ain't the hill you want to die on. You hear me? I wouldn't, anyway."

The sheriff looks from one to the other of us, the veins in his temples straining. After a few miserable seconds, he jerks his head and signals his deputies to follow him back to the cruisers.

"Hey, Sheriff?" I call after him.

"What?"

"Don't let that deputy go back to Liberty. The shooter, I mean. LeJay. He's got a lot of questions to answer. And the chief of police is going to need to ask them."

"Screw that," mutters the Amite deputy from about ten yards away. "I did my job. I'm getting out of this crazy town."

"Shut up!" Tarlton snaps. "You'll do what I tell you."

"Screw you, too! I answer to *my* sheriff, not you."

Tarlton takes a couple of steps toward the young deputy. "Boy, you'll soon find there's not a cunt-hair's difference between me and Sheriff Coy Johnson. Now get in my deputy's cruiser. Y'all follow me back to the station."

After a few defiant seconds, the deputy obeys.

Tarlton's cruisers nearly crash into the municipal squad cars as they come wheeling into the interior of the block, but after some confusion, Chief Morgan parks and gets out of the lead car, followed by a plainclothes Black detective.

"What in God's name happened here, Penn?" Morgan asks.

"We can't make it out, Chief. Doc left World Famous to go check on his partner, and within twenty-five minutes, we heard gunshots. First, two shots. But at the time we weren't sure they were shots. Then a couple minutes' delay. Then four or five more shots. That time we were sure."

"Five shots," Bobby clarifies. "And it looks to me like every one hit Doc."

"What about this white teenager?"

"Could I come closer?" Nadine asks from a distance. "I think I recognize him."

"Come on up, Ms. Sullivan," Chief Morgan says.

Nadine slowly makes her way toward the two corpses. After looking away in horror for a few seconds, she turns and bends over the boy.

"I know him," she says in a strangled voice. "Penn, this is the boy who was playing that Arcade Fire song when Arcadia was burning. The one I shamed into silence. He's a senior at the Catholic School."

"What's his name?" asks the chief.

"Lance Seaver. His father is Paul Seaver. Lives in Tupelo now. His mother is—"

"Linda," I finish. "Linda Seaver. Lord. What the hell is going on?"

Nadine turns up her palms.

The police detective squats beside the bodies. Very slowly, I make my way over to a point where I can look sideways into Doc's face. His dead eyes are wide, but I can tell nothing from his stare or his position, other than that he must have turned and been trying to speak to the deputy when he was shot. But my rational faculties are far from objective at this moment.

"Any ideas?" I ask the detective.

"Not really. This isn't the kind of thing we usually see."

"Meaning?"

He looks at me as if I'm an idiot. "Seriously?"

I hold up my hands. "I just don't think that's what we're looking at. Not on this day."

"Do you know something I need to know?"

"Only that Doc left World Famous in a hurry, and he intended to come right back and join us. I was with his party."

"Okay. Now, maybe you'd better get back with the civilians."

Knowing this may be the last time I ever see my old friend, I touch Doc's hand and think of the nights decades ago that he ate at our family's dinner table as a third-year medical student. Seeing him and my father in the same mental frame warms me for a few moments. From pure instinct, I slide the right side of Doc's sweatshirt up past a bullet wound, high enough to expose his shoulder blade.

"Hey!" says the detective. "What are you doing?"

"Confirming ID," I lie. "Checking for a tattoo."

Sure enough, there it is: inked into Doc's yellowish skin is a faded Louisiana black bear walking on all fours in profile, the emblem of his medical unit in Vietnam. Sadly, the "good luck charm" he told me about didn't shield him today.

"What is that?" asks the detective.

"He was a medic in 'Nam. I hope you guys will be investigating this, and not Tarlton's department."

The detective shrugs. "We usually handle homicides within the city limits. But I was surprised to see Tarlton pull away from this one."

"Bobby and I did what we could to persuade him to leave."

"I appreciate that. I think."

Ray Ransom is sitting on the ground with his back against the pawnshop wall, staring at Doc's body. Looking left, I see four men and a woman, all Black, all in their late forties, watching from the sidewalk of the next block nearer the river. One is holding a blue Fender jazz bass. Fighting the pain in my stump, I walk over and crouch beside Doc's most loyal friend.

"Ray? You all right? I mean—"

"Nope. I'm not."

"I don't know what to make of this, man. Do you?"

"Nope. But it's not what they think."

"I believe you. But what is it?"

"Don't know. I keep thinking about them first two shots. And the delay. I think maybe this kid was in some kind of jam, and Doc tried to help him. Then he got shot for his trouble."

"Okay. I can see that. But what kind of jam?"

Ray shrugs, offers nothing.

"And this white kid being on this side of town? Up in here? What about that?"

Ray shrugs again. "Don't know. Looking for drugs, maybe? Pussy?"

As we stare helplessly at Doc and Lance Seaver, Pop Davis appears again, but this time he has an old man in tow. He escorts the newcomer up to the chief as though bringing a critical witness, and his manner is firm enough to draw both Ray and me toward them.

"Tell the chief what happened, Mr. Williams," Pop says.

I can't tell whether the rheumy-eyed old man is white or Black from his skin color or features, and it doesn't matter. He licks his lips and says, "I was sitting on my porch swing 'bout thirty minutes ago, and a passin' truck stopped in front of my house. Turned out it was my old doctor, Ezra Berry. Doc ax how my hip been doing, and I ax him how the city job was going. He told me he'd had a good day today. A blessed day. Then while we were talking, I heard a handgun go off. Two shots. Sounded close, and Doc heard 'em too. He climbed back in his truck to go check 'em out. That didn't surprise me none, since he'd been a medic in the war. And we hear gunshots all the time 'round here these days. Nothing out of the ordinary. I waited a bit, but Doc never came back, so I went inside to take my pain pill. Didn't think no more about it till Pop here knocked on my door. What's happened? Pop won't tell me nothin'."

"You should have been a detective," I tell Ray, as we walk away to let the chief answer. "Or a fortune teller."

Ray shakes his head, his eyes still shining with tears. "I just knew my friend." He turns in a slow circle, like a lost sailor searching for a star. "Man, it's like they've shut off the lights on the whole town. This place is doomed, Penn. There's no stopping it now."

"Come on, Ray. That's not what Doc wanted."

"I know. But I know the people, too. This will break 'em. Doc was like R.L. Cooley to these folks. But even more than that. He's like a saint. And all because of one trigger-happy redneck."

"What are you going to do now?"

"No idea."

"I'm going to go back to the restaurant and pay the bill. Then I'll talk to the board and try to get some sense of what's going to happen in the city. We can't let this thing spin out of control. Without Doc, the friction between city and county will be almost intolerable."

"Almost? To hell with this county, Penn. Think of those kids at Mission Hill. Think of that French woman you knew. Your own child! Fuck this city, man. I'm done with 'em."

"You're like R.L. Cooley yourself, Ray. More than you know. You've got a lot of influence in this town."

He shakes his head with bitter resolve. "Don't be looking to me to play Doc's role. I ain't no saint. I've seen too much shit like this in my life."

"I know you have. Look . . . I'm going to take Annie and Nadine back to the town house. You've got my number. Call me if you need me. Day or night."

Ray nods, but he doesn't look like he has any intent to call.

I turn and walk back to Annie and Nadine, who are both sobbing softly by a police car. "Let's go home. We'll stop off and pay the bill on the way."

"Can you make it?" Nadine asks. "You're limping badly."

"Hurts like hell. But what does that matter today?"

As we step into the street, I see that a crowd of close to five hundred people has filled the space between the houses on either side. They're nearly all Black. A line of about ten city policemen is all that stands between them and the interior of the block where Doc's body lies, and it's probably only Pop Davis keeping them where they are. Then I see Kendrick Washington talking to those in front, with both hands raised about chest high. He looks like a man holding back a river. Unable to stop myself, I walk up behind him.

"Can I do anything to help?"

"I don't think so."

"You're doing a good thing here."

"It's all I know to do. I don't want to see what's back there. I can't."

"You call us if you need anything. You come stay at my place on the bluff if you need to."

"I might do that."

With that, I leave Kendrick to his work.

As we make our way down the street, I realize that I vastly underestimated the size of the crowd. Word of Doc's death has made its way through Bienville at light speed, and the galvanic effect is tangible in the air. People stream past us like pilgrims nearing the site of a crucifixion. Ray is right: there's no telling what will follow this tragic event, but no threat of force is going to stop it. Sometime in the next few minutes, or hours, a tidal wave of grief—and perhaps rage—is going to roll over this town.

"Hey," I say to myself. "I meant to say goodbye to Bobby White."

"He left before we did," Annie explains. "His cell phone rang and he started talking, then he walked around the pawnshop to the next street. He waved at me like he was leaving for good. Or maybe so I'd tell you he was leaving. I wasn't really thinking about it at the time."

I wonder where he might have gone. "I just wanted to thank him. He did what he could to calm that asshole down back there."

"Which asshole?" Annie asks. "There were so many."

"The one who shot Doc. He was trying to play badass, and Bobby talked to him like a goddamn yardman."

Nadine nods. "I haven't been around Bobby much, but he seems military in a way that most vets I know don't quite measure up to."

"He's a natural leader. Born to command. It took me a while to understand it, but that's his thing. When he talks, other men listen."

"Women, too, I'm guessing," Nadine says.

"I imagine so."

"I feel sick," Annie intones. "And I'm worried about Kendrick. Those damn deputies are going to try to frame him for those fires. I know it."

"Kendrick's no babe in the woods. He can take care of himself."

"He wasn't doing too good a job before we got him out of jail."

"That's true. I told him he could stay with us tonight."

Annie nods thanks. "I just hope he will. Because it's going to get bad tonight."

As we slowly progress toward Diamond Hill, I say, "You understand now why I tried to talk you into leaving town after Gram died?"

"Yes. And I'm glad we didn't. Because if we had, I'd feel much worse than I do right now."

Nadine smiles sadly and squeezes my arm. She probably recognizes her younger self in Annie. "I can't believe Doc's gone. He was so happy back in the restaurant."

I think back to the joyous light in Doc's eyes after Bobby spoke, and his excitement about the impending celebration in his old friend's eatery. The feeling of hope had been like a tonic after all our recent stress, a validation of Doc's optimism.

"Are you guys sure you want to spend tonight on the bluff?" Nadine asks. "That doesn't seem like the safest place to be tonight."

"I'm staying there," Annie says sharply. "Marchers are going to need water, food, maybe internet access. It's going to get crazy. I don't trust the governor as far as I can throw him. Or the National Guard."

Annie's right, of course. But I'm not sure what we can do to protect

Black marchers from the National Guard or the Mississippi State Police, other than get ourselves hurt. But I suppose I'd feel different if I were twenty-nine. As we struggle up the last block to Diamond Hill, an image of Shot Barlow rises in my mind. The deputy who killed Doc is just a younger, blond version of Barlow. Barlow and his whole damn crew. God only knows how they'll take the news of Doc's death. They'll probably have a celebratory bonfire in Confederate Memorial Park, if they can fight their way into it.

Walking back into World Famous to pay the bill, I find myself glad that Annie insisted I bring my AR-15 back to Bienville after Mom died. Because she didn't want it in the house with her, it's now in the trunk of my Audi, which means it's within reach if things go the way I think they might this afternoon. Whites may be angry that someone has taken it upon themselves to burn the tangible symbols of their feudal history, but today a white man wearing a badge killed the elected leader of the city, and the spiritual leader of the Black community. Doc Berry was Bienville's personal incarnation of Dr. Martin Luther King, and now he's gone. I shudder to think of the damage that an enraged former Black Panther and Vietnam vet like Ray Ransom might be capable of in his grief. But if I multiply that by five or ten thousand . . . Yeats's "blood-dimmed tide" seems a lot closer than it did last night.

CHAPTER 52

EIGHTY YARDS FROM Doc Berry's cooling body, a sixteen-year-old girl named Ebony Swan crouched in the dirtiest gas-station bathroom in the city, her cell phone mashed against her ear, tears and snot covering her face.

"Jamaal gon' kill me!" she wailed. "He gon' come back to Mama's house and shoot me. Or send that Damien to do it."

"Get yourself together!" snapped her cousin Dontrelle. "Tell me again why Jamaal shot that white boy."

"I told you what's been goin' on last week, but you wasn't payin' attention."

"Girl, I *tol'* you, I was at *work.*"

"Okay, okay. Lance been selling X at the school for Jamaal."

"The white school?"

"What other school he go to? Jesus."

"I'm just tryin' to get it straight. 'Cause you in trouble, ho."

"I know that! Anyhow, he started out just gettin' X for a few friends, but Jamaal pushed him till he started moving real money's worth. Some of them white ballers eat that Vicodin like candy. All Jamaal's suppliers get it from their grannies and aunties, pay them old ladies a couple dollars a pill to beg it from their doctors. Anyway, Lance got scared 'cause somebody tol' the principal over there what was up, and they been watchin' him. So Lance told Jamaal he need to stop selling, or at least chill for a while. But Jamaal said, 'No, I need my money every *week.*'"

"Damn dealers don't care."

"Jamaal *also* said Lance was two hundred dollars behind, which I don't know nothin' 'bout. Anyway, Jamaal was throwed off when he showed up today—I mean all the way to the left—and they got to arguing. I tried to stop it, but Jamaal hit Lance, and then Lance hit him back. Too hard, I guess, 'cause Jamaal took out his pistol and smacked Lance with it."

"Oh, shit."

"Next thing I knew, they was fightin' for real. Then Jamaal yelled and the gun went off."

"Just one time?"

"Two times. But he hit Lance in the neck. Oh, Dontrelle, there was so much blood . . . and so *fast.* It just sprayed out his neck! Lance was trying to talk and couldn't, and girl, I just *ran.*"

"You stayed and watched, you said."

"Yeah, *after* I got 'round that old pawnshop. I was by that trash fence, where them old tires are piled up. I looked back to see what Jamaal was doin'. He was cold, girl. He went through Lance's pockets like a damn thief, and then he looked around—for me, I know—but then he took off. I was about to leave when this old truck come bangin' up over the curb, and out jumped Dr. Berry."

"*Mayor* Berry?"

"That's who I said! I guess he heard the shots and saw Jamaal runnin'. Or maybe he saw the gun, I don't know. But he jumped down on his knees and started workin' on Lance, tryin' to save him. He had one hand in Lance's neck, and he was tryin' to call 911 with the other. It was terrible! Then in the middle of that, this damn cop runs up on him with his gun out and starts screaming at him."

"Screaming at the mayor?"

"That's right. But Mayor Berry didn't pay him no mind. He was trying to save Lance."

"Doc Berry didn't say nothing to the cop?"

"He yelled like, 'Leave me alone, man! I'm tryin' to save this boy's life!' I *tol'* you, D, I got it all on my phone."

"You filmed it all?"

"Just like that girl who filmed George Floyd! That's what I was thinking when that cop was waving his gun. 'Cause the mayor, he was wearing like, a hoodie almost. A warm-up suit like the old heads wear when they ballin' in the park."

"Oh, I know them kind. But you didn't film Jamaal, right? 'Cause if you did, you good as dead right now."

"I'm not stupid, am I?"

"You're close to it, filming that cop like that. But why he shot the mayor?"

"'Cause he's Black! Why you think? A Black man yellin' at a white cop, '*Get away from me, boy, I'm workin' here*'? What you think gon' happen?"

"Did Doc tell that cop he was the mayor?"

"Sho' did! But it was like that cop never seen him before. Never heard of no Black mayor or something. I don't know. It was *crazy*, D. You gotta help me!"

"I can't do nothin'! Not now anyway. I'm at work. What happened next?"

Ebony wiped her face on her sleeve. "After he shot Doc, that cop got on his radio and called for backup, I guess. But next thing I saw was old Ray

Ransom tearin' round that corner on foot lookin' like he gon' kill some-body. I took off then. I ain't filmin' Ray Ransom killin' no white cop. He spent most all his life up in Parchman Farm. Mr. Ray don't play."

"That's a fact. And this wasn't a city cop? No uniform?"

"No! Sheriff's department. Country-ass. You know the kind."

"You know I do. Just like the sheriff's brother, right? Like that bunch that snakes BJs from their CIs twice a week. Motherfuckers."

"That's exactly what he looked like."

Ebony's panting filled the stinking restroom. She sobbed softly for a few seconds, then said, "D, what I'm gon' *do*?"

"First, you're gonna delete that video. Right now. Then you gotta get out of town. Just for a while, till I can get word to Jamaal you ain't gon' say shit to nobody. You can't, 'cause you didn't *see* nothin'. You hear me?"

"Yes, ma'am."

"*Nothing*, Ebony. Not the mayor, none of that. That's your only chance. 'Cause if Jamaal King start thinking you might have filmed him shootin' that white boy . . ."

"How can I get out of town, D? I ain't got no cash. Ain't got no ride. Nothing."

"Where you at now?"

"In the bathroom at Piney's gas station."

"Oh, that's *nasty*."

"I'm scared to go out on the street!"

"I'm thinking . . . Lord, you skipped school for this shit?"

"Well, Lance cut advanced biology, and he wanted to see me. So I ghosted. Caught a ride with Zeeny. I didn't know what was gonna happen! But I can't go back to school now. I need somewhere to *go*, D."

"Don't be asking to crash with me. I got my own troubles."

"D, *please*."

Her cousin fretted in silence for a few seconds. "The mayor's dead? For real?"

"For real, D. Layin' right on top of Lance."

"Sweet Jesus. This town's gonna go crazy tonight."

"Gonna be some Rodney King shit."

"Who's Rodney King?" asked Dontrelle.

Ebony shook her head helplessly. "Just help me, D."

"I'm thinking, girl . . . I'm thinkin'."

"Think faster."

CHAPTER 53

RAY RANSOM SAT on a fifty-five-gallon fuel drum in the back of what some people called the Old Rec Center behind Pastor Aaron Baldwin's church. Ray used this mildewed space to minister to "his boys," a catch-all term for the men he'd spent the seven years since his release from prison trying to help through the exigencies of life in small-town Mississippi. He'd stopped counting the young men who had shown up at his program only to leave after one or two visits, or those who'd come in the hope of working him to their advantage, foolishly thinking they had the street smarts to manipulate a man who'd walked the lightless paths he had. More than a few were already dead. Ray had reached the point where he focused only on his successes, and that meant any man still walking the streets without drugs in his blood, a gun in his waistband, or a monitor on his ankle while he awaited trial for a fourth offense or beyond. This group included more than a hundred people, boys as young as thirteen and men as old as sixty-nine.

This afternoon, though, only three young men in their late twenties and thirties occupied the Rec Center, sitting cross-legged on the tile floor where every year they repainted basketball key lines so the little kids could learn league ball. The three looked up at their mentor with puzzled faces, for they sensed something different in him—a profound anger that almost seethed from his eyes and skin.

"What's going on, Ray?" asked Cedric Wilson. "Is it true what they sayin' 'bout Doc?"

Ray nodded once. "It's true. Doc's gone."

"Cops killed him?"

Ray nodded again. "Out-of-town deputy. Shot him five times."

"Shit, bruh. That ain't right."

"And I'm hearing the sheriff may let the shooter go," Ray added. "I ain't confirmed that yet, but it wouldn't surprise me none. I don't know what to believe. That fake cowboy got all the power in this county."

"So what we doin' here?" asked Gloster "Easy" Easley. "Everybody be down on the bluff marchin', they say. I'm getting texts every minute. Shouldn't we get down there? Get heard? Ain't that what you always sayin'?"

Ray didn't answer at first. Then he said, "That ain't for us. Marchin' and singin'. Not after what they done to Doc. And not after last night, after they burned Daughters of Egypt. I knew Duncan Gardner, man. I went to school with his brother."

"I knew Kemontrae," said Easy. "He never hurt nobody, man. Never had a bad word for anybody."

"What *are* we doin' here?" asked Cedric. "Us three, I mean. How come you called us?"

"'Cause you're all over twenty-five," Ray said quietly. "And you all served in the military. You ain't boys no more."

The three looked at each other, searching for clues to Ray's intent.

"I've told a lot of stories in this building," Ray went on. "Y'all heard me tell some real shit, trying to scare boys straight. It's worth telling some hard truths to try to save kids from wasting their lives on that penal farm. But in the seven years I been doin' this, there's some shit I never told."

"How come?" asked Easy.

"Because some shit is just too hard. Some things about this world, if you knew how hopeless it is, you'd quit trying to move forward. You'd see there ain't no *use*. System ain't gonna let you do better, even if you try. Some ways, the system's built to keep a man from moving up, even if he bends his whole mind and body to it. You hear me?"

Two of the young men shrugged. "That ain't no news."

"You talkin' 'bout Doc?" asked Stoney Whitmore, a slim young former marine roped with muscle and whipcord, who hardly ever spoke.

Ray nodded. "A little bit, I am. See, Doc was a healer. A peacemaker. He did damn near everything right. He was a medic in the war. And he treated people—our people—for *fifty years* when he got out. A lot of 'em for free. You can't add up all the people Doc helped for nothing. After that, he ran for mayor to try to do even more. Not for vanity, or glory, but to *do more*. With this town coming down around his head, he tried to keep the peace. And what did they do in return? They shot him down."

"How come they shot him?" asked Cedric. "I heard they shot some white boy with him."

"I heard Jamaal shot that white boy," said Easy. "Or Damien, maybe."

"God*damn*it!" Ray barked. "Stop listening to bullshit and open your *minds*! A *cop* shot Doc. A cop from Liberty, Mississippi. Klan country! It may take a couple days, but it's gonna come out they murdered Doc. You'll see. But I'm here to tell you . . . I ain't waitin' for that shit. Not this time."

Stoney leaned forward. "What you mean, Ray?"

The old con slid off the oil drum and rose to his full six feet four. "Y'all might remember me sayin' that after I got out of Vietnam, I lived in Los

Angeles for a while. With the Panthers. I knew some good men out there. Young men just like y'all. The names don't mean nothin' to y'all, but some folks still remember. I knew Huey Newton, and Eldridge, Bobby Seale. I knew Plez Bolden and John Savage. I knew good sisters out there, too. I saw 'em try to make things better. And I watched the police and the FBI break every damn law you can think of to jail and kill 'em. And those cops succeeded, for the most part. Man, I've seen white cops terrorize a god-damn *free children's breakfast*."

Ray began pacing before the three young men. Despite his age he moved with the purposeful silence of a leopard. "I barely got out of Oak-land alive myself. When I did, I went to New Orleans before I came back home. And within two months, the damn NOPD had a *tank* down in the projects firing on the Panthers doing social programs in there. If the main population of the Desire projects hadn't shielded us, we'd have all been killed that day."

"When was this?" asked Cedric.

"Nineteen seventy." Ray knew these young men had no idea what he was talking about. "A month ago that seemed like another world. Now it seems like yesterday. Go up on the Bienville bluff and look at them federal guns, you'll see ain't nothing changed. *Nothing*."

"What you sayin', Ray?" Easy asked.

Ransom shrugged, but his voice grew softer as he spoke, and the young men leaned forward to hear. "I'm sayin' I'm tired. I'm tired of bein' tired. I'm wore *out*. You hear me?"

The chosen trio looked at each other. This was not the Ray Ransom they were accustomed to.

"I did my time in this town as a boy," Ray went on. "Goin' to the col-ored school and gettin' called nigger by skinny-legged old white men. I did my tour in 'Nam and made it back alive. But when I tried to move some-where better, they run me right back here. And here . . . well, coming home led me to thirty-two years on Parchman Farm. All for fightin' back against two white cops who wanted to beat my ass down for kicks."

Easy looked at Cedric with saucer eyes.

"Thirty-two years behind them walls," Ray muttered. "No Shawshank escape from that pen, boys. No movie bullshit. Just the bottom of the worst prison in the worst state in this white man's union."

Stoney looked at the floor and sighed. They all had friends behind those walls. Too many.

"You know," Ray went on, "in California I met a man just like me. He was from Morgan City, Louisiana, right down the road. Star quarterback in high school. Decorated war hero in 'Nam. He went out to Cali after the war, like me. Rose up in the Panther ranks, ran security for the top men. His name was Elmer, but he took the name 'Geronimo.' *Geronimo Pratt.* I loved that man. He was so good at his work, the FBI had to find a way to neutralize him. So you know what they did? The police and the FBI framed him for killing a white lady. He was four hundred miles away at the time, but that didn't matter. No. They jailed Geronimo for twenty-five years. A goddamn war hero. In the end, Johnnie Cochran got his conviction thrown out, but most of his life was wasted by then. Just like mine. But you know what he did with the rest of his?"

"What?"

"Worked for human rights. Till he died. *Activist*, they call him. Geronimo ended up being godfather to Tupac. I shit you not."

"I heard of him!" said Easy. "You *knew* him?"

Ray hunkered down on his heels. "You boys listen now. Geronimo was a better man than me. He was like Doc. But I ain't no Geronimo. I ain't no Doc Berry, either. I've turned my other cheek too many times. I'm *done* waiting for change. I can't watch this show no more. I've tried to walk the peaceful road. Tried hard. But in the end . . . it's no good. I'm no doctor. Ain't no pastor, neither. I'm a soldier. That's my only gift. And I reckon I've always been one."

"Say it plain, Ray," said Cedric.

"I believe them folks on the other side, the ones who killed Doc and Mason and Kemontrae . . . they want a fight this time. And if they want a fight . . . then I'm gonna give 'em one."

An electric charge flashed through the old rec room. Two of the young vets got up and began bouncing on the balls of their feet, as though about to take the basketball court for a game.

Ray stood and flexed his big shoulders. "Imma hit those motherfuckers *back*."

"Oh, shit," marveled Stoney Whitmore, his eyes bulging.

Ray rolled his head around on his corded neck. "Imma *hurt* somebody."

The male odor of surging testosterone filled the small space.

"Oh, Jesus," Easy muttered. "Tell us what to do, Ray."

"You ready to take orders?" Ray demanded.

"*Past* ready."

"I won't have no bullshit backtalk!"

"No, sir!"

"No goddamn *questions*—"

"No, sir!"

"Just like the army. You hear me?"

"*Yes, SUH!*"

"Are you *ready*?"

"*Born ready!*"

Ray went still and stared at his three disciples with smoldering eyes. "Let's show these cracker bastards what war is. Let's tear this mother-fucker *down*."

CHAPTER 54

EBONY SWAN MOVED through the streets of Bienville like a flying shadow. The text messages had started a half hour after she left Lance dead in the pawnshop lot near Diamond Hill. The first had come from Jamaal himself, pretending to be checking to make sure she was all right. Ebony hadn't dared answer. Once she acknowledged seeing his words, Jamaal would somehow pull her into his deadly embrace. He was like that talking snake in the *Jungle Book* movie that always scared her as a little girl, the one with the oily voice. She'd known grown-up men with that same voice, and she'd learned too young what they wanted. Even Jamaal's *texts* felt the way his voice did—physically pulling at her, even from miles away and out of sight.

The problem was, she had nowhere to run. She'd already spent the past six weeks moving from couch to couch, crashing with friends, still going to school, hoping to avoid being reported to the state authorities. Her mother was so far down into the dope that she'd likely never come up again, but Ebony was hell-bent on avoiding foster care. The problem was, she'd already become a burden to her friends, because she had so little money. Now if she showed up looking for shelter, she'd bring the lethal danger of Jamaal King and his paranoia with her. How could she lay that problem on the few girls who'd done all they could to give her a safe place to sleep?

Dontrelle Flowers had been her rock, but even D had advised her to get out of town. And where could she go without money? Ebony had a cousin in Jackson, but Latriece had worse problems than she did. A learning-disabled child and a crackhead baby-daddy. Ebony's only immediate hope had been to fetch the twenty-dollar bill she'd stashed at Dontrelle's place the previous day. She'd stashed it so she wouldn't have it on her when she and Lance met Jamaal, in case Jamaal told her to empty her pockets. Since Dontrelle was still at work, and D's mama sat with a sick white lady in the evenings, Ebony figured she could slip into their room, retrieve the bill from its hiding place—an old moth-eaten nurses' dictionary—and be right back on the street without anybody knowing she'd been there.

The visit wouldn't be without risk. Jamaal knew she sometimes stayed with Dontrelle, as well as with Keisha, Brandy, and Tamika. A couple of times she'd even crashed in the big Victorian on Hinton Avenue where

Lance had lived with his mother. Ebony had never slept in such a soft, safe place as that, not since she was a tiny thing at her grandmother's house in the Delta. But she'd never see the inside of that room again now. Because Lance was dead. Stone cold. Shot in the throat by Jamaal. And for *what*? A couple hundred dollars Lance supposedly held back for some reason?

Dontrelle and her mama rented a place on B Street: two rooms with a hot plate, a microwave, and access to a communal bathroom. There was a Walmart futon in D's room, and that's where Ebony slept when she crashed. The owner had six girls living in the one house, all paying for separate rooms, all sharing one bathroom. It stood on a corner, mostly exposed, and even the idea of approaching it frightened Ebony. But what choice did she have? The best idea she'd come up with was to hang back in the bushes on Pearl Street, which opened onto B, and watch who came and went long enough to get a sense of normalcy or danger. That's what she was doing now. Standing in the bushes catty-corner from the house, breathing hard and waiting.

I feel like an antelope trying to get up to a damn waterhole, she thought. *Goddamn hyenas prowling and crocodiles hovering in the water. I ought to send somebody in there for that twenty . . . but who? I can't trust nobody not to steal it and tell me it wasn't there. And I just thought like a quadruple negative. Mrs. Taylor would kill me for that. . . .*

Her mind was running like this when Damien Hodges opened the door of Dontrelle's rooming house, leaned out, and looked up and down the street. She knew it was Damien because when the sun hit his face, his electric green eyes sent an icy chill down her spine. As she shivered in the bushes, he spat on the sidewalk, then pulled back inside and closed the door.

Ebony had stopped breathing.

Damien was part of Jamaal's crew, and in some ways worse than Jamaal himself. He'd hurt people she knew. Damien handled the rough jobs for Jamaal. He collected money. He doled out punishment for violations of respect. Worst of all . . .

He killed people.

Damien had killed one boy of fifteen this past March, while he sat in a car outside his mother's house, for reasons nobody was ever sure of. Now he was waiting for Ebony to turn up where she was known to sleep on occasion. Jamaal had likely spread his crew among the places she'd been crashing. There was literally nowhere she could go. Even texting a friend would be a risk to them both.

I'm shaking, she realized, hugging herself in the thick leaves that concealed her. *It's not supposed to be this way.* Tears began to sting her eyes. *Not when you're sixteen. I ain't done nothing but try to get by. And they want to kill me. Just because I saw what Jamaal did.*

As she stood there wondering where to go, or who she might possibly turn to, another thought struck Ebony: *That's not the only thing I saw.*

CHAPTER 55

BOBBY WHITE PASSED the BIENVILLE CITY LIMITS sign going eighty in the Tundra, headed for his cabin on Canaan Plantation, where Corey sat working on the state ballots they had yet to nail down. After Corey's panicked call, it had taken Bobby nearly a minute of driving through town to calm himself, but he was nearly ready to make the two calls he needed to make.

Corey's take about Charlot echoed in his head. *I can't say much on the phone. He threatened you, though. Threatened his father, too. He knows about your latest satellite contract, and he's enraged. Coming apart, I'd say. Worse, he shot pictures last night before we even knew he was there. Intimate stuff. He nearly sent them to someone right in front of me. I had to get physical to stop him. I managed to short out his phone with water, but I nearly killed him, Bobby. I left him in that water close to two minutes. If I hadn't dragged him out and used my army training, he'd be gone now. I'm close to losing it, man. For a couple of minutes I thought he was dead. Seriously. Just get here, man. We have a lot to do, and we have to get him the money you promised last night. We have about six hours to do it. We're safe until then, no longer.*

Bobby tried to imagine Corey getting violent. Charlot must have really pushed him to trigger that kind of reaction in Corey. An existential threat could do a lot to people, and of course it was Bobby that Corey had been protecting . . .

Turning onto Highway 61, Bobby picked up his burner phone and dialed the only number it had ever called: Donny Kilmer.

"It's me," Donny answered, sounding out of breath.

"Don't say anything beyond answering my questions."

"Understood."

"Did you have anything to do with what happened to the mayor?"

"Absolutely not."

Bobby repeated the question, and this time Kilmer said, "I aborted as instructed." For some reason he believed the kid.

"Listen," Bobby said. "Your primary target is now out of jail. With Doc gone, a window is almost certain to open later today. I'm thinking the bluff will be the likely target area. Go somewhere safe, but no more than ten minutes from the bluff. And get as high as you can."

"Understood."

"Stay ready." Bobby clicked off, then picked up his encrypted phone and called Charles Dufort's residence. The call was answered by Ruby Brooks, the family maid. "This is Robert White. I need to speak to Mr. Dufort. It's urgent."

"Right away, Mr. White. I believe he's waiting for your call."

Ruby set the phone down with a soft clatter.

That's the way it's done, he thought with satisfaction. *Old school*. He imagined the day he'd be sitting in the Oval Office, an impenetrable ring of security around him, incalculable power at his fingertips.

He kept the Tundra on eighty as he waited for Dufort to pick up the phone.

CHARLES DUFORT SAT behind his study desk, an old tinted portrait of Charlot in his hands, shot when he'd been a sophomore in high school, when even Philippe was still alive. In the photo, Philippe stood behind his half brother, his right hand on the boy's shoulder. It was hard to imagine a handsomer young man than Charlot had been at that age. Beneath this photo, in the desk, sat a clear Lexan box filled with Indian arrowheads and spearpoints. For some reason, the portrait and the spearpoints were the only things blunting the unsettling thoughts Bobby White's call had planted in his head.

The murder of Doc Berry was bad enough—not the fact of his death, but that it had been carried out without warning, and by someone neither of them knew. Worse, Bobby seemed convinced that Charlot was coming apart, or at least losing control of his anger and fear. In that state he might be capable of anything, and Charles had no idea what the boy might really know about the family's past. His deepest fear at this moment was the army of federal agents and techs combing the still-smoking ruins of Tranquility down in Natchez. Again and again, he saw a nightmare image of superheated air blowing the top off a clay cistern that had lain closed for more than half a century, exposing contents that could put Charles into prison for the final years of his life. For this reason he'd instructed Amadu to drop a half dozen bags of lime down the old hole and fill it with water. If anyone questioned them about the flooded cistern, they could claim the firemen had accidentally filled it while fighting the blaze.

"Daddy?" Sophie said, marching smartly through the half-open study door. "From what I hear, Doc was found dead in . . . awkward circumstances."

Charles speared her with his gaze. "Awkward how?"

A soft knock sounded, then Ruby leaned through the door.

"I'm sorry, but that Donnelly woman is at the front door asking to see you."

Sophie closed her eyes and scowled. "What in God's name does that slut want?"

"No idea," said her father.

"Don't tell me you're"—Sophie looked down at the bearskin rug with distaste—"doing whatever you can still do with her?"

"Give me some credit." Dufort glanced over at Ruby. "Did she say what it's about?"

"Only that you'll want to hear it."

Charles gave an imperious wave of his hand. "Bring her in."

Ruby disappeared to fulfill her orders.

"Do you want me to leave?" Sophie asked.

"No need. "

Half a minute later, Dixie Donnelly pushed through the door and walked right up to Dufort's desk. Bright as a spring bouquet, she appeared to be dressed for the golf tournament. Glancing over her shoulder, she gave Sophie a brief nod, then looked back at the paterfamilias.

"Mayor Ezra Berry was just shot by an Amite County deputy. Downtown, near Diamond Hill. He's dead as a hammer."

"I'm aware," Charles said.

"Did you know he was shot while lying on top of a high school boy? Nobody's sure why, but the deputy is suggesting it may have been some kind of homosexual liaison."

Dufort squinted back at her with skepticism. "I always knew Doc was queer, but that doesn't sound like him."

"Is the boy all right?" Sophie asked.

"The boy's dead, too. Lance Seaver?"

"Oh, God," Sophie breathed. "I know the mother. Who killed the boy? Not Doc?"

"Nobody knows."

"That's *crazy*. Did this happen in a house or what?"

"No, behind some buildings. Not long after Doc's speech."

Sophie was shaking her head. "This is *nuts*."

"Maybe," said Dixie. "But that's the state of play in downtown Bienville as of a few minutes ago. And there's a crowd of you-know-what building down on the bluff, like a tornado moving over a bean field."

Dixie's language made Sophie wrinkle her face as though at a bad smell.

"How big a crowd?" asked Charles. "Hundreds? Thousands?"

"It'll be thousands before you know it."

"Goddamn it."

"You could have called and told us this," Sophie pointed out.

Dixie pursed her lips, clearly debating whether or not to speak sharply to Sophie. At length she turned back to Charles. "Obviously, something's going to have to be done. And I knew you'd want a say."

"What can he do about it?" Sophie asked. "Daddy has no official position."

The big-haired trophy wife of Blake Donnelly didn't bother to answer. Everybody in Bienville knew the Poker Club made most of the important decisions in town, and more than a few understood that Dixie carried Blake's vote now. But even Blake's power paled in the face of what Dufort could make happen by lifting a telephone.

Charles held up a restraining hand. "Who's managing the situation right now? Buck Tarlton?"

"Chief Morgan seems to be handling the shooting," Dixie told him, "but the deputy who actually shot Doc went back to Tarlton's headquarters after the incident. His boss is Sheriff Coy Johnson in Amite County. He was only deputized as extra security for Doc's rally. We're headed toward a serious jurisdictional dispute."

The old man sat thinking in silence.

Dixie's cell phone rang, but she ignored it.

"Who's torching these goddamned houses, Dixie?" Dufort finally asked. "Is it really some Black group? Or rednecks like the Barlow militia? I need to know."

Dixie gave him a pointed look. "It's Black radicals, Charles. That fist with a chain on it pretty much says it all. It's BLM bullshit, just next level."

"Dear God," breathed Sophie, but everyone in the study could almost hear the translation: *You can't be that dumb . . .*

"*Not* Shotwell Barlow's knotheads?" Dufort pressed.

"I don't think Shot would go that far," Dixie said with surprising cynicism. "They may own assault rifles by the dozen, but the fridges in that bunker are filled with Schaefer and Bud, not insulin and antibiotics."

Charles barked a laugh. "You don't think they're ready for the apocalypse?"

She snorted. "'Ready' is a flexible word."

Dixie's phone pinged, and this time she took it out of her flower-print skirt and read a text message. "Bluff crowd's over eighteen hundred now," she said. "Mostly male, one hundred percent Black, and growing fast. Let's see whether Shot and his boys want a piece of *that*."

Dufort slapped the desktop with enough authority to bring both women to attention. "I want Bobby White to handle this."

"Bobby *White*?" Sophie echoed. "What the hell can Bobby do about this? He's got less official power than either of you."

Dufort looked at Dixie. "Consider this an audition."

"For what?" Sophie interjected.

Charles smiled to himself. "You understand what I'm saying, Mrs. Donnelly?"

Dixie grinned back at him. "Oh, I surely do. But what about Sheriff Tarlton?"

Charles gave a wicked grin. "That's what makes this an audition." He waved his age-spotted hand. "He'll have to handle egos from Tarlton up to the governor. Somebody get me Bobby White on an encrypted phone."

Ruby knocked and leaned in again. "I've got the governor's chief of staff for you, Mr. D."

Dufort chuckled softly. "Looks like somebody's thinking the same way I am. Ruby, tell that peacock I'm managing a crisis down here, and I'll speak with him as soon as I can."

"Done."

The door closed. Dixie said, "I need to get back to the club. This tournament's running me ragged. I'll get Bobby on the line with you as soon as I leave. I may listen in, if you don't mind."

Sophie stared after her as she pranced toward the study door, but Charles said, "You'll get to your car quicker if you cut through the rosarium." When she turned, he pointed to the grand French doors to his left, which opened onto his private garden.

Dixie followed his gesture and pulled the doors shut after her with a superior smile. Once she'd vanished, Sophie grimaced and said, "What the hell are you up to with that Botoxed social climber? And what's her connection to Bobby White?"

Dufort answered without shame or apology. "You know, sometimes women born poor develop a quickness that those born to wealth and privilege never match."

Sophie already regretted engaging with him on this level. She turned and walked out of the study without looking back, certain at least that her father would watch her every step of the way. But she was wrong. Dufort's uneasy mind was already back on the federal officers and technicians of various agencies tromping over the damp grounds of Tranquility. He turned the portrait of Philippe and Charlot face down on his desk, then lighted a rare cigarette and waited for Dixie to connect him to Bobby White.

Sophie had grown harder as she aged, he reflected, and for that Charles was thankful. But some lessons in power she had yet to learn. The kind Philippe had been born knowing, and that Charlot had never been able to master. Doc Berry had probably had the same learning deficit Charlot did in this area. After all, they had shared the same fundamental weakness.

And Southern politics was a hard school.

CHAPTER 56

DESPITE BEING CALLED to the Bienville Police Headquarters by Chief Morgan himself, Marshall McEwan had been held outside the building by a ring of deputies under the command of Buck Tarlton, who was on site in some sort of RV trailer equipped as a mobile tactical command post. Marshall had thrice demanded to see the sheriff, but so far he'd been refused, and he was getting the distinct impression that he'd become a pawn in what was rapidly shaping up to be an urban siege. Chief Morgan had urged him by phone to be patient, to hover by the front entrance and wait for a diversion sufficient to give him the ten seconds he'd need to sprint across the street, up the steps, and inside.

After about ten minutes, Morgan texted him to be ready. He'd got word something big was about to break. Less than a minute later, Buck Tarlton charged out of the RV, screaming for his cruiser. Rather than wait to unravel whatever lay behind this event, Marshall marched across High Street, right past astonished deputies staring at their commander, and allowed himself to be jerked inside by two city cops who shoved the deputies guarding the main doors out of the way.

He found Chief Morgan inside, grinning inexplicably.

"What the hell happened to Tarlton? He left out of here like a bat out of hell."

"Somebody set Tarlton's house on fire! Blew it up, apparently."

"*What?*"

Morgan shrugged. "We're in a different world today, Mr. McEwan. This may be what civil war feels like."

"What about Deputy LeJay? Did Sheriff Tarlton really let LeJay go under his own recognizance? After he shot Doc?"

"He did indeed. I had a feeling he might, so I set up a roadblock on the two highways leading south out of town. We arrested him at one of those. Tarlton was trying to get him clear of town before his headquarters got surrounded by media or angry Black folks."

"Will you take me to see him?"

"Why?"

"I'd like to interview him."

"I'm not sure that's our first order of business."

"Maybe not. But it should be. Proof of life. If you don't get images outside this station that prove Kenneth LeJay is alive and being treated well, you're going to get two different county SWAT teams crashing through your doors and windows."

Morgan eventually nodded, accepting this. "LeJay's not in our main jail. I've got him in a second-floor holding cell, between my office and the Hangman's Door. It's only a historical relic, but convenient for this."

"Let's go, then. The faster we get images out, the safer everyone in here will be. An iPhone video will be good enough for the internet."

Chief Morgan signaled a couple of men to literally hold the fort, then led Marshall toward a narrow staircase.

"Who's guarding him?" Marshall asked.

"One of my detectives. Henry Radford."

"The old white guy with the eye patch?"

"That's Henry."

"Good thinking. Better optics."

Morgan grunted. "Safer, is what I was thinking. My Black cops know LeJay shot Doc. They might not kill him in cold blood, but they'll sure kick the shit out of him, given half a chance."

SHERIFF BUCK TARLTON stood in Fox Run Drive and watched the shattered remains of his house burn. The destruction had been well along by the time he arrived. Most of what he'd accumulated during his life thus far had turned to ash and ruin before his eyes. He'd just watched a treasured marksmanship trophy melt off the mantel in what an hour ago had been his private study.

Along with the fire department, his men had set up barricades to keep his neighbors from pushing forward to gawp, but he could hear them back there like a herd of spooked antelope. Thankfully, his wife and children hadn't been home during the attack. He'd told Darla to take the kids to her mother's and wait to hear from him, regardless of any calls she might receive from friends. The rain of texts and emails had quickly become a flood, and now she was in a panic. Buck, on the other hand, had shut all that out of his mind. Because this was something he had never once contemplated as a man—and certainly not as the supreme law-enforcement officer of Tenisaw County.

Someone had declared war on him.

The digital brain of his expensive security system had already been melted by the fire. Luckily, he still had a visual record of the attack in the Cloud, accessible through his cell phone. Due to his wife's absent-mindedness (Darla almost never armed the goddamn system during the day), Buck had not been alerted in time to prevent the attack, but now he could watch it in high-res color, like a goddamn football game.

At 2:27 p.m., three helmeted men dressed from head to toe in camouflage had ridden up on old dirt bikes—two Yamahas and a Suzuki—then climbed off and walked straight into his open carport. Two carried hammers. There they'd kicked down the pantry door and entered the split-level house. In short order, they located four primary points where propane was used—the downstairs heating system, the Viking cooktop in the kitchen, the outdoor kitchen oven, and the pool heater—then used the hammers to knock off the fittings linking the supply system to those appliances. Then they'd left the house and waited in the backyard while the interior filled with pooled explosive gas.

Buck wondered why no one in the neighborhood had thought to wonder what three men on trail bikes were doing messing around his house in the middle of the day. But in truth, you saw unusual activity in this neighborhood all the time. Most people probably assumed it was local kids playing a game, or even some of his officers doing maintenance on his orders. No one could have imagined it would be what it actually was: a brazen attack. But twenty minutes after the dirt bikes pulled up, the neighbors were left in no doubt, because at that point the visitors rode their motorcycles to opposite ends of the house and tossed lighted Molotov cocktails through the windows. They were fishtailing away when Buck Tarlton's suburban showpiece exploded into what looked like the climax of a Michael Bay movie.

"Buck?" his brother Wade said hesitantly, as they stood side by side in the biting smoke. "How you want to proceed?"

Sheriff Tarlton put his hands on his hips and made a slow turn, taking in the crowd at the barricade fifty meters up the street. A lot of neighborhood men had clearly been called away from work to come home and witness the spectacle.

"I'll tell you what this is," Buck said, feeling the deputies nearest him move closer. "This is a goddamn attack on the State of Mississippi."

"Absolutely," said his brother.

"It's terrorism, is what it is."

"Damn straight. So . . . what are we gonna do about it?"

Working hard to keep his anger in check, Buck took a tin of Copenhagen out of his pocket and stuffed a pinch behind his bottom lip. His office gave him a lot of power in Tenisaw County—especially during a state of emergency—and the temptation to unleash it was strong.

"First we're going to deploy our Caiman," he said. "As a show of force.

I want that armored bastard rolling down Battery Row within the hour, and I don't give a shit what the National Guard has to say about it. I want *our* MRAP patrolling our damn streets, and our men driving it. I want the sons of bitches who did this to know we mean business."

"Done," Wade said, taking out his phone to send a text.

"Second, I want my chopper to pick me up here. Right in the circle down there. From now on, my primary command post will be airborne. We're going to a combat footing."

Wade nodded with almost sexual satisfaction. He could feel raw power flowing between them, like a spring tide. "What about those flags that were on the dirt bikes? You want us to bring in Shot Barlow for questioning?"

The flags, Tarlton thought in frustration. That was the thing he didn't get. Two of the dirt bikes had been flying banners during the attack, but the symbols made no sense. The canton displayed a familiar white cross of stars on a field of blue, while the field showed thick red and white stripes—which was the regimental standard (and now the militia flag) of the Tenisaw Rifles.

"I'll call Barlow," Buck said. "No way his men had anything to do with this."

"But who else would have access to those flags?"

"God knows," Buck said, thinking hard. "But it wasn't militiamen under all that camo. There's not a white man in this county would challenge me like this. What we've got here is something we ain't seen in these parts since the sixties. Something I remember Daddy and his brothers talking about. I can smell it, Wade. I been smellin' it since they burned that first goddamn antebellum home in Natchez."

"What's that?"

"Niggers on the rampage."

"Oh, yeah."

Buck's Stetson dipped in emphasis. "Hard to credit in this day and age. But I guess Mission Hill stirred 'em up like a nest of hornets. They prob'ly been ginning themselves up night and day ever since it happened. Now look what it's come to. Not even a gated white neighborhood is safe."

Wade nodded slowly, then looked around at the other deputies. "Looks like the goddamn Taliban just left out of here," said one. "They coulda killed kids doing something like this."

"That's a fact," Buck said. "And there's only one way to handle this kind of terroristic activity. *Overwhelming force.*"

"Shock and awe," said one of the badged men.

"Break some fuckin' heads," Wade agreed. "We should start up on that goddamn bluff."

"I want every Black prisoner in the jail lookin' at those dirt bikes within the hour," Buck said. "I want every CI on our list lookin' at 'em. And I want every country-ass spade riding a horse down the county roads lookin' at 'em. And when we find the sons of bitches that rode those bikes . . . we won't be arresting anybody."

Wade went still. "What're we gon' do?"

Buck sniffed the stinking air. "We're gonna make an example. The way they used to around here when the colored got out of line. Back when this country knew what it was about. We're gonna set things back to rights. Because the citizens aren't going to tolerate this kind of anarchy. No, sir. They—will—*not*. Now, get me my helicopter."

"On the way, Buck."

Tarlton nodded with growing assurance. "I'm gonna make some phone calls. I need to speak to the Sovereign Sheriffs Association. I want every white man and woman from New York City to Los Angeles to see what was done here today. Hell, I want every Cuban in Miami to see it. Know why? Because your Latin respects property. He's got material aspirations, good Catholic upbringing. Not like the thugs who did this. So, let's get our drones up and remind people what happens when you let these Black punks get too damn big for their britches. I want the FLIR cams up at dark. Then we'll see what shakes out."

"We'll get 'em up." Wade was the best drone pilot in the TCSD, but only Roy Jackson was certified to fly them. Wade turned, caught Jackson's eye, then spun his finger in the air.

Roy Jackson ran for his four-by-four.

"Uh, Sheriff?" said another deputy.

"What is it?"

"I've got Sheriff Coy Johnson from Amite County on my phone. He says he's been callin' and you haven't picked up."

"You tell Coy what I'm dealing with here, and I'll get back to him soon as I'm able."

"But Sheriff—"

He drew his hand across his throat with a violence that left no doubt in his subordinate's mind. The deputy spoke into his phone, yanked it away from his ear, then apologized and pocketed the device.

"What did he say?"

The deputy shook his head. "Says if his deputy ain't out of the Bienville police station within an hour, he's bringing half his department over here to bust him out."

If his house hadn't been burning, Buck would have laughed. Sheriff Coy Johnson was just crazy enough to try it.

Something in the house cracked like lightning splitting a tree.

"*Where's my goddamn chopper?*" Buck bellowed.

"On the way!" Wade assured him.

Buck felt like pulling his pistol and emptying it into the flames, but he repressed the urge. Before long, he could empty it into the sons of bitches who'd blown up the house in the first place. The way he figured, they had to be the same bastards who'd been burning the antebellum homes. He laid his right hand on the checked grip and squeezed. If he didn't get a lead on them soon, he'd call Coy back, then go downtown and make that Black cop Morgan pay for the arrogance he'd displayed by arresting a fellow law-enforcement officer. Especially one employed by the state. There was a certain order to things, and Morgan had clearly forgotten that. Buck couldn't stand a man who didn't know his place.

When his phone pinged for what must have been the three hundredth time, he took it from his pocket, looked down at the screen, and cursed with poisonous rage. The text was from Dixie Donnelly, the new queen of the Poker Club. It read: *You're wanted in the conference room at Donnelly Oil. Expect to see Bobby White here. Sorry about your house, but don't waste time grieving it. The governor's calling, and we need a plan.*

"What's the matter, Buck?" Wade asked. "Who's that from?"

"The queen bitch of the county. For the moment, anyway."

Dixie was a familiar curse, but Bobby White was something else. A different kind of threat. Problem was, Buck couldn't figure which kind. The last thing he wanted to do was walk up into Donnelly Oil with his tail tucked.

"Wade, can we land the chopper on top of the Donnelly building?"

"Ahh . . . they don't have an actual helipad up there. But we could sure set you down on the roof, even if you have to jump the last two feet off the skid."

"Let's do it. I need to make an entrance."

Wade Tarlton whooped like a cowboy in a 1950s western.

RAY RANSOM PULLED the lowboy flatbed trailer into a long row of NO PARKING spaces along the wrought-iron fence that lined downtown's Hewson Park. The combination of cap, blue bandanna, and oversize sunglasses he wore would prevent even someone who knew him from recognizing him behind the wheel. As the air brakes hissed, Cedric Wilson, Easy Easley, and Stoney Whitmore leaped out of the passenger door with heavy leather gloves on their hands.

Ray had planned to wait in the grease-and-mildew stink of the cab, but he didn't want the boys to feel like he wasn't sharing the risks, and there was always a chance that someone might question them. With a groan, he set the parking brake, then climbed out and trotted over to the small side gate in the park fence.

Their target waited thirty yards past the long rank of iron spearpoints, on a five-foot pedestal of granite in the deep shade of elm trees. Reginald Hewson stood with one hand on his left hip and the other on the boxy little cotton gin depicted before him. The pudgy slaveholder looked mighty proud of himself, Ray thought. He'd invented a strain of cotton that had made him and others filthy rich, but not a damn cent more for the people who picked it. In fact, they'd never made one cent after their arrival in America.

Ray looked back toward the city truck. Cedric and Easy were dragging a heavy chain to the marble statue. Forty yards of chain was a hell of a burden, but the boys looked happy to be hauling it. Happy to be doing anything that made them feel like men. Burning Sheriff Tarlton's house had lit them up like white phosphorus.

Once they reached the statue, Ray began looping the chain around the sculpted figure. He fixed it tightly around Hewson's neck, to get the most leverage possible, then began turning it around the torso before anchoring it between the stubby legs. He only hoped it would hold when the truck began to drive away.

"How much does this statue weigh?" Cedric asked.

"I'm not sure," Ray admitted. "At least ten thousand pounds."

"Whoa! Will that truck really pull it down?"

Ray laughed and pointed at the D7 bulldozer parked on the lowboy. "The tractor that hauls that can pull this statue down like a toothpick. I just hope the fence don't come with it. Fence never did nobody no harm, and I'd hate somebody to steal it for salvage."

"Shit, let's do it," said Stoney. "'Fore we draw a crowd."

The screech that erupted when Ray let out the clutch and popped the slack out of the chain probably carried for a mile through the city. He didn't feel the statue go when it toppled, but he heard Stoney whoop and slap the window behind him. A second later the wrought-iron fence came away from the sidewalk and began trailing them up the street.

"Goddamn," Ray muttered, giving the wheel a wrench.

A loud boom overtook him, and he felt the truck break free from a load. Looking in his rearview, he saw Reginald Hewson's head and body wedged beneath a pickup truck on the other side of the street from the park, like a hit-and-run victim, which he was. Ray thought of the people who'd been fighting since the last election to keep the Black community from moving the granite incarnation that preserved the memory of the son of a bitch that statue had been carved to honor.

"Good luck puttin' Reggie back on his pedestal," Ray murmured, already thinking of his next target.

CHAPTER 57

EVEN IN THE wake of Doc's death, I could not have predicted the speed of the city's descent into chaos. The burning of the Daughters of Egypt Church—and the deaths of her two deacons—had hit the Black community hard, but the reaction had been largely internalized. The shooting of the mayor was different. Within an hour of my paying the barbecue bill at World Famous, a crowd of more than twenty-five hundred people had materialized on the bluff below the terrace of my town house—exactly the result . . . Doc had pleaded to prevent at Diamond Hill.

From what I could gather, this movement had been completely spontaneous. It began with Pop's small delegation on MLK Street but grew swiftly as it moved westward toward the river, gathering force like a wave surging toward shore. By the time the crowd reached Battery Row, the National Guard had been warned, but they didn't have the manpower to prevent the occupation of the bluff from Front Street on the south end of the bluff to the amphitheater on the north. Not without firing into an unarmed mass of men, women, and children, which not even the governor was willing to order.

Not yet, at least.

Past Battery Row, near the fence, Confederate Memorial Park is packed so tightly with Black people on blankets that it reminds me of the third Mississippi Blues Festival in Leland, Mississippi, back in 1980. Since my terrace is hardly more than a second-floor patio that extends partly over the broad sidewalk beside the Row, I have little separation from the crowd. I feel like I did in the days when I filmed football games from the roof of the concession stand for Annie's high school coach, back when she was cheerleading. When I commented on this, Annie snapped her fingers, then instantly set about tearing down the Ring doorbell cameras that form the security system of my town house and remounting them to create a multicamera livestream of the events on the bluff, which she's arranged to have accessible from both Kendrick's and the Bienville *Watchman*'s websites.

"Dad, look," she says, joining me at the terrace rail. "Since I got that deputy's name—Kenneth LeJay, the one who shot Doc—I've had a friend sifting through his social media, looking for connections to Bienville. LeJay may be from Liberty, Mississippi, but he's all over Facebook with

Sheriff Tarlton's deputies. Also with Barlow's militia nuts. There are tons of pics of them doing weekend tactical training at commercial facilities, hanging out at gun shows, all kinds of stuff. I've found at least two shots that show LeJay at Black Oak Plantation."

"Seriously?"

"Check this out."

Squinting at her small phone screen, I see the face that cursed me near Doc's body glaring over the scope of a .50-caliber Barrett rifle, while behind him Shot Barlow grins and gives a thumbs-up.

"No wonder Tarlton's trying to blame Doc for the shooting. He knows this stuff is out there. He's trying to get ahead of it."

Fifteen minutes ago, Buck Tarlton spoke to reporters in the lobby of the sheriff's department, and all but stated as fact that Mayor Berry brought his death upon himself by sexually assaulting a high school boy and refusing repeated orders to stop. The effect of this slander will be good for Tarlton: many whites will latch onto that narrative to reassure themselves that Doc's murder makes sense within an order they understand.

"Check this one," Annie says, holding her phone closer to my face. "Recognize that guy?"

In the next photo I see Deputy LeJay gripped under the tanned, ropy arm of Wade Tarlton, the sheriff's brother and Bienville's iteration of Bo Hopkins. Wade's grin is even wider, and his eyes glint at the person shooting the photo.

"I know him."

"I just blasted a collection of these to all of Kendrick's followers, plus the newspaper, thanks to Marshall McEwan. Since Kendrick's arrest this morning, his social numbers are literally ticking up by the millions. He's a global phenomenon, like a freaking Korean singer or a soccer star."

A chill of foreboding goes through me. "Annie . . . I get it, okay? This is big stuff. But the faster we escalate this, the more out of control the situation will get. And the effects aren't going to be digital. We're physically in the middle of it. You get that, right?"

She looks puzzled by my concern. "Of course."

It's not that she wants a riot, I realize. She merely feels that whatever sins Tarlton and his ilk have committed must be exposed and dealt with— fearlessly. And I can see her point. But when I look out over Battery Row, all I see is families and their children within easy reach of state guns. They are here because of emotion—justified by centuries of mistreatment, no doubt—but no justification will protect even one of them if order breaks down on this bluff tonight. Especially in the dark.

Annie's phone pings, and she checks a text. "I've got to run, Dad. Ken-drick's calling me down to the park."

"Please be careful, Annie."

"I will. Look. Are you okay? You're white as a ghost."

"Just anemic," I lie. If I hadn't swallowed some of my mother's hospice oxycodone after my attempted run down to where Doc died, I wouldn't be able to stand now.

Looking far more than worried, she squeezes my shoulder, then turns and takes off.

"I love you, Boo!" I shout, but she's already vanished into my bedroom on her way back downstairs. Were the terrace but a few feet closer to the ground, she'd probably have leaped over the rail.

After a brief delay, I see her squirt out from beneath the terrace and dart into Battery Row, where she would rapidly vanish were it not for the track of her light hair through the almost wholly Black crowd.

With Annie's disappearance, I feel remarkably alone. Nadine is at her bookstore. To distract herself from her pain over Doc, she has chosen to focus on Mom's research, especially where it touches on the Barlow and Dufort families. Without her I'm forced to face the fact that Doc's death has left me rudderless. Only with him gone do I finally understand how his quiet strength and lifelong example of service did more to unite the disparate elements of this town than I ever knew. My father used to tell me that none of us is irreplaceable. But in Doc's case . . . I'm not so sure. Without his presence, who can I turn to for rational help? Who has the power to do anything meaningful in the face of what might now become open conflict? Unless our racially divided city board can overcome its long-standing tribal divisions, all power now will lie in the hands of the county and the state. One look at Mississippi as a whole will tell you how that's likely to work out.

Down on the Row, two armored personnel carriers drone slowly up and down the avenue, reinforcing the long skirmish line of men and women wearing desert camo and carrying M4s. As I try to make out individual faces behind the riot masks, it strikes me again that the people in the park behind the troopers are the direct descendants of Mississippi slaves, and they're standing in unarmed protest under the guns of mostly white sol-diers. I've watched Kendrick Washington move along that line of troops for the past half hour, trying to engage them in conversation. The protest-ers on the bluff treat Kendrick with reverence, but the National Guard troops do their best to hold the stoic silence of British royal guards.

The wet taste of Mississippi heat sits heavy in my mouth. What are the thousands of grieving people stretched along the bluff with their children thinking? What do they expect to happen this afternoon? Are they waiting for something? Help? Or do they mean to try to help themselves? If so, how? Or are they merely revealing their pain for the world to see? To whoever is watching through the eyes of the cameras slung beneath the bellies of the two media helicopters now hovering over the Mississippi River?

The governor and his advisers are surely trying to answer the same questions before they react in any decisive way. But with the afternoon passing, they don't have much time. I suspect more National Guardsmen are being deployed here at this moment, and more state police as well. The automatic response of white authority to Black unrest is always more firepower.

"Dad?" Annie calls from the door behind me.

I can tell from her voice that I don't want to hear whatever she's come back to tell me. My phone pings with a text message, but I don't look down.

"I just got a text that Beauvoir is burning. On the coast."

Beauvoir.

Almost nothing she could have said would have surprised—or possibly relieved—me more. "Jefferson Davis's postwar home? In Biloxi?"

"That's what I heard. And I just checked the *Sun Sentinel*. Their website confirms it. There was some sort of explosion, and now the whole place is burning. There were tourists inside when it happened. Four injuries reported so far."

As terrible as this attack might be, the fact that it occurred 160 miles to the southeast gives me hope that the "Bastard Sons of the Confederacy" attacks might not be targeted solely at Bienville and Natchez. Of course, there's always a chance that the Beauvoir fire is simply a copycat event. But if the incendiary device turns out to be an M206 flare, I can rest easier on that score.

"Dad, I need to tell you something," Annie says, as though confessing some minor sin. "I reached out to Kelly yesterday, through an email he gave me before he left last time. I should have told you before now. I know you'll probably be mad, but . . . he's always told me not to hesitate if we really need him. And the truth is, we do. I've had a really bad feeling since . . . well, since Arcadia burned."

"You're not alone. I wish Daniel could be here, too. But he can't help us with this. He's light-years from here."

"The Middle East is only one day by jet."

"He's not in the Middle East." I give her an apologetic smile. "Has he responded to you?"

"Not yet."

"It's not just the distance. It's what he's doing."

She looks seriously concerned. "What's he doing? I mean, I know what he does. What's special about this deployment?"

"I can't tell you that. He almost didn't tell me, and I'm probably the only person who knows. Other than his employer."

"Who's his employer? A military contractor, right?"

"Not exactly." I look back over Battery Row at the massed crowd and the Guard troops. "He's working for the biggest military contractor in the world."

Annie shrugs. "So? Who's that? Aegis? Amentum?"

"I didn't say *private* contractor."

She looks blankly back at me for a couple of seconds, then her eyes widen.

I nod. "He's in Ukraine. Or maybe Belarus. And he can't just come and go as he pleases."

"Jesus. Okay."

"That's another reason I wanted us to get out of town. I almost reached out to him last night myself, but . . . then Ray kind of stepped into his place."

"Can anyone really step into Kelly's place?"

I hear myself chuckle. "Not really. Maybe Bobby White, if I'm honest, but I really don't know Bobby very well. He did what Kelly would have done at Mission Hill, though. He saved your life."

"I know. But I still have a funny feeling about him. I can't explain it."

"Bobby's not our new Kelly. If anyone takes that role, it'll be Ray."

My daughter steps forward, takes hold of my hands with her bandaged one, and looks into my eyes. "So what are we going to do?"

"Boo, we have no power to change this situation."

"You're still the city attorney."

I laugh dryly. "I serve at the pleasure of the mayor. And we no longer have one."

"There's a mayor pro tempore, surely?"

"She's a MAGA Republican. One step from QAnon."

"Not Vivian Paine—"

I nod.

"Goddamn it!"

As my phone pings to announce the text message for a second time, Annie sighs, then shrugs. "Maybe the shock of Doc's death will inspire her to act sanely?"

I look down at my phone. The text is from Robert Gaines, one of Bienville's new progressive aldermen. It reads: *There's a special-called city council meeting starting. I was specifically told NOT to inform you about it. But we're in trouble here, man. We're looking at the end of this city. Come if you can.*

I hold up my screen so Annie can read the message. "How does that make you feel?"

As her mouth falls open, a series of pops like gunfire echoes across Battery Row from the terrace. The reports don't sound like pistol shots; neither do they have the supersonic crack of rifle fire. But in the first ten seconds, at least forty of them reverberate against the buildings facing the Mississippi River.

"Look!" Annie cries. "By the Confederate fountain!"

Half crouching, I can just make out the figures of the Sons of Confederate Veterans who yesterday took it upon themselves to "guard" the vandalized fountain. From here it looks like two are covered with bright red blood. My heart thumps with panic, but then almost as quickly I see three or four Black teenagers sprinting through the bluff crowd carrying what appear to be paintball guns. They're moving along the fence as though acting in a movie, firing steadily from the compressed-gas-powered weapons.

"It's paintball!" I shout at Annie, over the growing roar of the crowd. "It's a prank!"

"Dad, look. Oh, no—"

As I gape in horror, three of the reenactors raise their assault rifles and unleash a volley of fire at the boys by the fence. The supersonic cracks of the AR-15s are deafening, and they trigger instantaneous panic. All along the bluff people hit the ground, while the Black teenagers begin leaping the cyclone fence to try to escape.

Most of them make it, but a couple of the smaller ones, blocked by National Guard troops, tear off in the direction of Battery Row. As they do, one gets tackled by a deputy from Buck Tarlton's sheriff's department.

"Stay here!" I order Annie, turning and limping into my bedroom.

"Fuck that!" she retorts, doing her best to help me to the stairway inside the town house.

CHAPTER 58

BY THE TIME we make it across the Row, we've picked up Nadine, who was returning from her bookstore. The gunfire has stopped for the moment, but that's no guarantee it won't start again. While I was tempted to retrieve my AR from the Audi's trunk, I decided to carry only my pistol, and in the time it took us to get to Confederate Memorial Park, a standoff has taken shape about forty feet from the fountain. The main participants have chosen as their dividing line the railroad tracks that have run along the bluff for 150 years.

On the city side of the tracks stands the big Tarlton deputy who tackled the Black kid, who looks about thirteen with his sticklike wrists in cuffs and a paintball rifle at his feet. Despite their size differential, the deputy keeps his huge right arm clenched around the struggling boy's chest. Beside these two stand five Sons of Confederate Veterans, armed with flintlocks and AR-15s. On and around the tracks stand about thirty National Guard troops, mostly male, but with several women mixed among them. They look unbelievably young to my eyes, younger even than Annie.

On the bluff side of the tracks stand at least a hundred Black protesters, and they clearly mean to prevent Tarlton's deputy from taking his juvenile prisoner anywhere. Standing at their head is Reverend Aaron Baldwin, the widely respected pastor who introduced Doc at Diamond Hill today. Among all the Black faces, I also see Professor Egan and his wife, the couple that Barlow's thug assaulted at the Tranquility fire. They must have been among the marchers when the kids started firing paintball rounds. Behind this initial rank, however, stand at least twenty-five hundred more Black citizens of Bienville.

"Y'all get the hell out of the way!" Tarlton's deputy shouts, angrily waving his pistol at Reverend Baldwin and the marchers. "This boy's under arrest!"

"For what?" I ask. "I'm the city attorney of Bienville. What's the charge?"

"Reckless endangerment!"

"Are you going to arrest these men for firing AR-15s in the city limits?"

"We were defending ourselves!" shouts one of the gray-clad Sons.

"With live .223 ammo? Against teens shooting paintball rounds?"

"We didn't know they were paintball rounds! It was red paint. I thought Joe'd been shot through the heart at first!"

"But he hadn't," says Reverend Baldwin. "And you opened fire with assault rifles in the middle of a crowd of hundreds. We're lucky we didn't have a repeat of Mission Hill here today! We still can't be sure no one was hit. We haven't found the other boys yet."

As the two sides face off against each other—half armed with M4 assault rifles, the other half only with concealed small arms—an armored military jeep pulls up Battery Row and stops behind the Black protesters in the street. Riding in it is Major General Claiborne Pike, commander of the National Guard troops. General Pike climbs out with all the pompous authority I associate with military martinets, and marches into the midst of the confrontation.

"Are you in charge of this riot?" he asks Reverend Baldwin in a note of challenge.

"Nobody's in charge of us," says a second man, who I note is also wearing a pastor's collar. "And this is no riot. This is a spontaneous demonstration against the murder of our mayor, Ezra Berry, MD."

General Pike shakes his head. "Well, you're about to disperse. I just got a call from the governor, and he gave me clear orders. Everyone gathered on this bluff is to return to their homes without delay. The governor's about to declare martial law. There will be no further demonstrations on this bluff. No marches, no vigils, no nothing."

Reverend Baldwin (whom I have always known to be a gentle man of restraint) looks at the Guard commander with deep sadness in his eyes. "General, we're not going anywhere."

Surprised to be met with defiance by a white-haired old man, the commander draws himself up and places his hands on his hips. "I've been instructed that if anyone refuses to leave, I should use whatever force is necessary to accomplish my orders. Further, if anyone fires a weapon at my troops or at an officer of the law, I'm authorized to fire live ammunition in return. Do you understand that, Reverend?"

Reverend Baldwin looks back at his people, some of whom clearly remember the slaughter of Mission Hill. "I heard what you said. But we mean no harm to anybody. And I want this boy here released by this deputy immediately. He was just part of a prank—an ill-advised one, granted—but he should not go to jail for that."

"We'll see what Judge Hinson says about that," says the deputy with a laugh.

"Damn right!" says one of the Confederate Sons. "These young thugs are a menace to the community."

"We wasn't doin' nothin' wrong!" the boy protests. "Just acting out Isaac Simpson's raid, like Dr. Egan told us about."

"Wait a second," I cut in. "Who's Isaac Simpson?"

"A figment of their imagination!" barks the reenactor. "Simpson was just some mule driver that never did a damn thing but haul cotton."

"That's bullshit," Nadine argues. "Several military scholars believe Isaac Simpson actually led the Union raid and spiked the seacoast cannon up here on the night Admiral Porter's fleet ran the guns at Vicksburg. He was an escaped slave, like Romulus Pencarrow."

"That's all CRT bullshit!"

"I beg to differ. U.S. Grant himself credited his Bruinsburg crossing below Vicksburg to an 'unknown colored man,' and without him the whole siege gamble might have failed."

"U.S. *Grant*," muttered the rebel descendant. He spat in contempt near Nadine's sandaled feet.

As we stand in tense silence, a car comes racing up to the park entrance, and the screech of brakes announces its stop. From behind the wheel climbs Alderman Robert Gaines. "What the hell's going on down here?" he shouts.

"The governor's ordered the Guard to clear the bluff of all protesters," I inform him. "He's authorized the use of all necessary force if they refuse to go."

"Oh, *hell*, no," he says, marching up to General Pike. "I'm Alderman Robert Gaines. These people are American citizens, and they ain't going *nowhere*. Not today. The sheriff has killed our children and our mayor. And *now* you want to say we got no right to peacefully protest? Man, you're crazy."

"I've got my orders," the general says. "Direct from the governor."

Gaines scowls at the officer. "I don't care if they're direct from the Almighty! We no longer recognize the authority of the governor! In fact, we may secede from this goddamn state before the sun goes down tonight!"

A cheer goes up from the group behind Gaines. But General Pike means business, and the potential for disaster is great. I don't know how many troops Pike has stretched out along Battery Row, but he's definitely outnumbered. The only way he can possibly even the odds and control this crowd is with the automatic rifles his troops carry. And I shudder to think how many pistols or even longer guns might be concealed in the larger crowd behind us. Enough to put up one hell of a fight if anyone fires into it. And my peripheral vision tells me more marchers are arriving every second. There might be as many as three thousand up here by now.

"Don't make me use force," the general almost pleads with Reverend Baldwin. "I don't want anybody hurt. But my orders are clear, and I will obey them."

Turning away, he takes out a radio and speaks quietly into it. I have a feeling that we will shortly be facing a lot more troops.

As I try to think of a way out of this predicament, the *whup-whup-whup* of an approaching helicopter starts drowning out our voices. At first I assume it's one of the media choppers, but when the craft keeps descending toward Battery Row, I realize our new arrival is the worst possible addition to this volatile mix.

It's Sheriff Buck Tarlton.

When the chopper's skids hit pavement, Tarlton jumps out of the wide door of the Bell 206B with his hand over his Stetson and marches right up to General Pike like he's John Wayne.

"What the hell's going on here, General?"

The Guard commander gives a brief summary of events, laying most of the blame on the Black teens, and stressing Baldwin's assertion that the Black crowd is refusing to go anywhere.

"They'll move soon enough," Tarlton asserts. "General, I'm in command of this county. If we let this go on, the crowd will grow to five thousand in another hour. The governor's right. It's time to nip this thing in the bud. Give them a countdown, and if they don't start moving, fire a volley over their heads. Anybody who doesn't vacate the bluff at that point is asking to be shot."

"What the hell?" Annie whispers in my ear. "Can they do that?"

"In a state of emergency."

"You've got enough troops and weapons," Tarlton goes on, "and I've got plenty more on the way."

"You can't let them do this!" Annie insists.

"I don't have the authority to stop them."

As General Pike ponders his next move, about forty more National Guardsmen deploy along Battery Row, spaced five yards apart. Their line is two deep now, making about a hundred troops facing the crowd of three thousand. With every trooper carrying multiple thirty-round magazines, the odds are more than even.

Gaines leans toward me and murmurs, "What the living hell do we do now?"

"We have no legal recourse, Robert. Don't do anything to provoke them. Because Tarlton looks crazed to me."

"Somebody just burned down his house. I think he's lost his shit."

"*What?*"

"That's what I heard. Burned it to the ground, just like Arcadia. There's no telling what he might do out here."

I start at the sound of General Pike's voice being transmitted at high volume from a PA speaker mounted on his jeep. Much louder than a conventional bullhorn, it gives him the power to reach even the back of the crowd, which presses up against the light cyclone fence at the bluff's edge.

"Ladies and gentlemen!" he announces. "I have been ordered by your governor to disperse this crowd. Very shortly, I'm going to begin a countdown from twenty. By the time I reach zero, I want to see everyone moving toward the Planters Hotel on Battery Row. If I do not see that, these troopers will fire a volley of live bullets over your heads. I do *not* want to give that order. But if you force me to, I will. And if you don't move then . . . my troops will have no choice but to fire directly upon you."

Initially, the sound of three thousand people mumbling in fear and resentment is not so different from that of an SEC football crowd reacting to a bad call by a referee. But the undercurrent of fear cannot be denied.

"Don't do this, General," I plead, stepping forward. "There's got to be another way. Let the pastor convince them to move."

"He says he won't!"

"Reverend Baldwin?" I prod.

The old man shakes his head with an expression of infinite sadness. "There comes a time where you have to stop backing up, Penn. For us, today is that day. We've let them do so damn much to us. If we let them kill Doc, and we keep backing up . . . then not even our children will be able to stand tall in their lifetimes. I sure won't live to see them do it. I'm telling you, brother. Today . . . if they want to move us, they're gonna have to kill us."

Reverend Baldwin means it. And the Guard troops within earshot know he does. As I stare in wonder, a Black sergeant standing a few yards from the commander says, "General, we can't fire on these people. Not even a volley in the air. We might kill somebody across the river."

General Pike's face reddens. "We've got *orders*, Sergeant! *You've* got orders!"

"Yeah? The goddamn Nazis had orders, too."

To my amazement, the sergeant raises his M4 above his head, walks out in front of the line of troops on Battery Row, then drops his weapon to the sidewalk.

"That's desertion!" shouts Sheriff Tarlton.

"I ain't killing no Americans," declares the sergeant. "And you get out of my goddamn face, Sheriff. You've got your own work to do, and from what I've heard, you ain't been doin' it."

Tarlton takes two steps toward the man as though to strike him, but the trooper doesn't flinch. In fact, he bows up like he's ready to knock the sheriff to the ground if necessary. This stops Tarlton in his tracks.

As we all witness this strange confrontation, two Black men burst from the bluff crowd carrying what appear to be assault rifles, and before anyone can react, they dive for cover behind the low gray marble monument to Bienville's World War II dead. Seconds later, they pop up in kneeling positions, covering the Guardsmen standing exposed on Battery Row with what appear to be heavily modified AR-15s.

"Goddamn it!" General Pike curses. "This is why we got the orders we did! This is no peaceful assembly!"

"You men back there!" Gaines shouts. "Put down those weapons! You're not helping anybody!"

"General," I implore, "if only ten percent of that crowd is carrying handguns, you've got three hundred weapons out there. Do you really want a full-on battle out here with those odds? Live on television?"

"If they fire on us, I have no choice."

"Don't start your countdown! Find another way to handle this."

General Pike shakes his head, then speaks into his PA radio transmitter again. "I'm addressing the two men behind that monument! The ones with the assault rifles. If you don't surrender in ten seconds, we will engage and kill you. You've forced our hand. I am counting . . . NOW."

The general doesn't count out loud, but he's looking at his watch awful hard. After what I judge to be ten seconds have passed, he shakes his head, then raises his hand.

To my horror, the supersonic crack of rifle bullets reverberates across Confederate Memorial Park, and an explosion of red mist and brain matter erupts from behind the WWII monument. One man flies backward far enough onto the turf that I can see him lying as still as the marble stone itself. The back of his skull is gone, and I can only assume his partner is dead as well.

Annie and Nadine scream in terror, and I shove them to the ground.

The look on Buck Tarlton's face is one of supreme pleasure.

"*Don't do anything else, General!*" I shout, but Pike is no longer paying attention. Rumbles of anger and shrieks of terror erupt from the crowd. *"Order your troops to stand down, damn it!"*

Tarlton is speaking into his collar radio, and I sense uniformed troops moving at the periphery of my vision. More Tarlton deputies, likely, converging from different points of the city and county. I'm sure that whoever has a gun in the crowd is getting it out now, if only for self-defense. *And if that many people are drawing guns, someone's going to discharge a round by accident . . .*

I feel the gut-level dread I've experienced when things go terribly wrong and you know there's no way to avert the disaster that's about to befall everyone around you. This is the kind of nightmare moment that Kendrick Washington somehow salvaged at Mission Hill—

"You have twenty seconds to clear this ground!" General Pike bellows over the PA.

The crowd begins to surge back and forth like a sea of flesh. Yet the final result doesn't move the mass in any particular direction. This time the general counts out loud: ". . . *nineteen, eighteen, seventeen, sixteen, fifteen . . .*"

"General!" snaps the sergeant who threw down his rifle. "If you do this, you'll go down in history like that stupid sergeant who fired his .45 on the students at Kent State!"

Pike doesn't even acknowledge his sergeant. But the Black NCO's words are not without effect. Out on the Row, I see three, no four, Black troopers lay down their rifles and kneel in the line. They appear to be praying. I feel a rush of emotion similar to that I felt when Kendrick raised his hands and walked out to confront Tarlton's deputies at Mission Hill—

"Pick up those rifles!" shouts an officer somewhere along the line.

His command has the opposite effect. Fifty yards away from me, a blond Caucasian girl of twenty kneels and sets her M4 on the concrete avenue.

"GET THAT GODDAMN RIFLE UP!" shouts the officer.

"I'm not shooting Americans!" the girl yells back. "I didn't sign up for this!"

Her response nearly brings tears to my eyes, but it's not enough. At least seventy troopers still stand with their rifles trained on the crowd. If they even fire a volley above the heads of that group, they'll start a stampede that could break down the fence and end with hundreds falling to their deaths.

". . . *seven . . .*" General Pike yells, the pitch of his voice rising. "*six . . . five . . . four . . . three—*"

Somewhere in that huge crowd, a pistol goes off.

A woman screams, and the crowd begins to come apart at the edges, spinning off women and children like some malfunctioning carnival ride.

"*TWO!*" shouts Pike. "*ONE . . .*

"*FIRE!*"

Seventy M4s fire as one, hurling a storm of lead over the heads of the assembled protesters, across the Mississippi River, and into Louisiana.

"*VACATE THE BLUFF!*" General Pike cries through his horn. "*This is your last chance! Move toward the Planters Hotel. You have ten seconds to begin.*"

It's hopeless to expect a mob to behave rationally. Half the crowd appear to have panicked at the shots, while the other seem committed to holding their ground. Hundreds of people have hit the earth in search of cover, while others trample their fellow marchers in their effort to escape the target zone.

". . . *six . . . five . . .*" General Pike counts over the PA, his voice softer this time, freighted with mortal dread, almost resigned to slaughter. ". . . *four . . . three . . .*"

An engine suddenly roars to my left.

Looking south, I see a large black vehicle not unlike a UPS delivery truck juddering up the railroad tracks. At first I'm not sure what I'm looking at, but then Sheriff Tarlton yells, "That's Bienville Police SWAT! Chief Morgan! He's too late. General, finish your countdown. This crowd's not going anywhere."

But General Pike has fallen silent. The black van appears to be moving up the tracks at close to sixty miles an hour, and the man behind the wheel clearly means to get where he's going before anything worse can happen.

"Goddamn it, Pike!" Tarlton screams. "I'll finish this if you won't!"

While the sheriff curses and talks to his men over their radio net, the big SWAT van squeals to a stop, throwing up divots of earth, gravel, and a cloud of dust. It's still rocking on its shocks when a side door opens and eight cops wearing full-body armor and carrying MP7 submachine guns launch themselves through it like they mean to seize the closest hilltop. But they're not focused on the crowd. In less than five seconds, this unit covers the troopers and deputies lining the Row. They may be vastly outnumbered, but trained shooters with MP7s could take out that line of Guardsmen in a matter of seconds, whereas the Guardsmen and deputies can't risk shooting back toward their commanders.

"What's going on here, Penn?" asks Chief Morgan, pulling off his helmet and goggles.

"You're interfering with orders from the governor!" General Pike tells Morgan. "I'm placing you under arrest!"

"To my knowledge," Morgan says coldly, "the governor has not yet declared martial law. You're not thinking clearly, General. And if the governor *does* order you to murder peacefully protesting American civilians—in the wake of a political assassination—then he's not, either, and he'll soon find himself out of a job."

Pike's face has gone as red as a boiled lobster. He starts to respond, but Morgan doesn't give him the chance.

"Here's what's going to happen, General. You're going to order your troops back to your tactical ops center. Sheriff Tarlton's going to take his chopper back to his office, and his men with him. And this crowd—which is too damn big to move anywhere—is going to stay *right here*. And before you gentlemen argue the point, take a look at those media choppers over the river. Everything you've done and probably said has been broadcast around the country, and maybe the world. Frankly, I'll be surprised if you're still employed in an hour."

"General Pike?" Sheriff Tarlton says. "Chief Morgan will soon have no authority whatsoever, *if* he still has any now. The City of Bienville has been dissolved as a municipal entity. As of today, I have the only law-enforcement authority in this county."

I turn to Robert Gaines. "Is that true?"

"Not yet! Vivian Paine was calling a vote on the issue when I left to come here. They can't dissolve the city without me present."

Tarlton grinds his teeth in fury.

In the brittle silence that follows, I hear the sudden pounding of running feet, then a ripple of excitement moving through the crowd. Then, as though Moses himself has been reincarnated, bodies from both sides of the standoff part at the skirmish line of railroad tracks. What appears in the gap where they stood is the only thing that could have parted them:

Kendrick Washington.

The young hero of Mission Hill is panting as though he sprinted all the way from Doc's corpse, and his eyes take in the essence of the scene without needing to be told a word. Before anyone can speak, Kendrick lunges to his right, grabs the handcuffed Black boy, and yanks him away from Tarlton's deputy. Sheriff Tarlton jerks his pistol, and while he's aiming it at Kendrick, the words, "Let go, you goddamn nigger!" fly from the big deputy's mouth.

Kendrick pays the word no more mind than he does the gun. And despite the deputy's size, three seconds of struggle result in the Black teen winding up in Kendrick's rippling arms, not those of the TCSD deputy. Kendrick hugs the boy like a father protecting his son.

"You surrender that damn prisoner," Tarlton says in a cold voice, menacing Kendrick with his pistol.

"I'm taking this boy home to his mama," Kendrick says with conviction. "You're gonna have to shoot me in the back to stop me, Sheriff."

Annie is squeezing my left leg so hard I feel shocks of pain.

"Everybody calm down," I say evenly. "You've all got cameras on you. You, too, Buck. Everything's going out to the whole world, okay? Right now. If you ever want to be governor, you'd better think about that."

The TV-handsome sheriff smirks. "I *don't give a shit*, Cage. I've got the law on my side. You know I do. And the people of Mississippi know it, too."

"We was just playin' history!" the boy protests from the relative safety of Kendrick's arms. "Blue versus gray!"

Tarlton jerks his gun at Washington's chest. "Your choice, homey," he says with relish. "Chain-wearing fool."

The young teen has tears streaming down his face, and shiny mucus running from his nose. Kendrick leans down and whispers something in his ear, but afterward the boy looks more frightened than before. I know in the marrow of my bones that Kendrick is about to turn and take him, and I know with equal certainty that Tarlton will execute Kendrick without remorse.

After one resigned breath, Kendrick starts his turn, but in that moment Chief Morgan leans into Tarlton's space with his MP7.

"Buck?" he says quietly. "You holster that weapon and get back to your office. You do *not* want a gunfight with my men today. Not after Doc. Think about that. *Your rented deputy killed Doctor Ezra Berry today*. He murdered a goddamn hero. You pass my warning on to Sheriff Johnson in Amite County as well. *Today is not the day*."

To my everlasting amazement, Buck Tarlton blinks and stands silent, processing Morgan's words and the tone of biblical conviction in which he spoke them. In this seemingly soundless lacuna of time, from the heart of an arsenal of weapons, a woman's voice says, "Oh my *God*" with the clarity of an invocation in church. Then close to a thousand people sigh as one. As I turn left, toward the river, a boom like cannon fire hammers the bluff and compresses my chest, driving the air from my lungs.

"What the goddamn hell was that?" General Pike cries.

A mile or so across the Mississippi, a tower of flame a hundred feet high has reached for the heavens.

"Oil well!" Chief Morgan replies. "Just like in Kuwait."

"We gotta clear this bluff!" Pike insists.

"You've got to get your ass back to a safe distance and let these people be!" Morgan insists. He whirls on Tarlton. "You, too, Buck, before somebody out here decides to pay you back for Doc."

Something in the honed edge of Chief Morgan's voice does the trick. Probably the truth. Without further protest, Sheriff Tarlton quietly orders his men to return to their HQ.

As Tarlton walks away from the gleaming tracks, General Pike looks around in apparent confusion. Then he too seems to deflate, like a boxer whose adrenal glands have sputtered out. Using visual signals, he orders his troops back to their TOC at the south end of the Row.

This is far from the climax of this drama, I know, but for now, it will do. Hundreds of people could have died in less than a minute. Now, at least, an uneasy peace reigns on the bluff.

"Who were those two men with AR-15s?" I whisper to Alderman Gaines. "Behind the monument. The ones the snipers shot?"

"I don't know," Gaines replies. "I hate that they paid with their lives, but if they hadn't . . . I think the first bullets would have gone into the crowd."

"Somebody was going to die up here today. It turned out to be them."

Nadine takes hold of my hand and pulls herself to her feet. Then Annie does the same. "Let's get back to the town house," Nadine says. "By law, you've got to bury your mother today."

"Who killed those two guys behind the WWII monument?" Annie asks.

I shrug. "National Guard overwatch snipers, probably. Could have been FBI, though. Maybe even state police."

"They shot them in cold blood."

"That's what snipers do. Kelly's done his share of work like that over the years. Bobby White, too, I'm sure."

"Jesus," Annie says with a shiver. "I feel sick."

"Real violence always makes you feel that. That's why TV and movies are bullshit. No matter how gory they make it, they can't get close to reality. They can't trigger that primal revulsion you're feeling now."

"Oh, God."

"What is it?"

"Nadine's right. We're supposed to bury Gram in an hour."

At last the truth of Nadine's words register. "We can do that." I put my arm around Annie as we walk. "Let's calm down for a few minutes. Then we'll ride out to Pencarrow and lay her to rest."

"Okay. I guess the world keeps turning, right?"

"It sure does," Nadine breathes, holding her cell phone out in front of us. "Beauvoir's gone."

Her words hit us like a blast of polar air. My eyes aren't what they once were, but even on Nadine's tiny screen I can see that where the house Jefferson Davis lived out his final years after the Civil War—entertaining visitors like Oscar Wilde and Sam Clemens on the Gulf of Mexico—now only brick pilings, scorched wood, and a massive column of smoke remain. It's a chilling sight, but on the other hand, all we need now to sleep a little easier in Bienville tonight is another note signed by the Bastard Sons of the Confederacy. Then at least we'll know that Bienville and Natchez are not their only targets.

"Oh, hell," I curse, realizing that Robert Gaines is no longer in sight. "I forgot my text from Gaines. Vivian Paine's trying to dissolve the city. I need to get over there and see if there's anything I can do to stop her. If she succeeds, then Chief Morgan and every cop on his force will be out of work by the end of business today."

"And the Black community will have no one to protect them," Annie says.

I take a long look at the column of flame across the Mississippi River. "I'll be back as soon as I can," I tell her, an image of Ray Ransom rising in my mind.

CHAPTER 59

EBONY SWAN STOOD outside the storybook house of Lance Seaver and tried to summon the nerve to knock. Three cars were parked on the street out front—expensive cars—which meant Mrs. Seaver almost certainly wasn't alone. And why would she be? Her son had just been killed. The house had probably seen a parade of sympathetic friends and relations ever since the news broke. You saw the same thing on the Black side of town, though once you got far enough down MLK Street there was a certain fatalism about death that sometimes resulted in mothers who'd lost their children sitting alone for too long.

Ebony felt mixed emotions about mothers like Linda Seaver. On one hand, she wanted to hate them for their sense of entitlement. But on the other, she'd been around St. Joseph's Preparatory School enough to see how those women doted on their kids. They took turns carpooling to distant academic events, planned special pregame suppers, and painted huge signs for sports tournaments, while the fathers spent endless hours working as assistant coaches or hamburger cooks at the concession stand, cutting grass, or driving the bus to the games, and doing all this thankless work with broad smiles. Those people were far from perfect, Ebony knew—Lance's mother had some substance abuse issues of her own—but when she thought of her mother lying like a zombie on the mattress in her stinking crib, using her only waking brain cells to try to figure out how to get her next hit . . . it filled her with shame and rage. Even when clean, her mother hadn't given a damn about fulfilling any of the requests that the Early College Academy had made about parental involvement. And yet . . .

Ebony knew on some level that her mother's plight was somehow related to the hereditary privilege of all the Karens and their husbands, going all the way back to slavery and Reconstruction and Jim Crow . . . She wasn't sure of the damned historical sequence, or the logic, but she *knew*. That's why the white school boards didn't want anybody teaching "critical race theory" in Mississippi, or any damn where else. That's why the goddamn governor and speaker of the house and the local school board stuck their noses up in all that. They didn't care if anybody got a good education, especially Black bodies; they just wanted to make sure kids *didn't* learn about certain things. The way their parents hadn't learned. They wanted the whitewashed version of history taught to their kids—and all kids—now and for all time.

Ebony could have rung the doorbell, but for some reason the prospect frightened her. She knocked instead, first softly, then louder. She immediately regretted it, wanting to bolt across the manicured lawn, but in the end she stood her ground.

She had nowhere else to go.

The door opened to reveal two white women who stood staring at her in astonishment. On the right was Mrs. Seaver, who wore a black dress and looked like she'd been given some kind of strong sedative, the kind a doctor administered with a syringe. On the left stood a heavyset woman wearing a dark blue skirt and a black blouse.

The heavyset woman frowned. "Can we help you? This is not a good time, hon. Are you selling something for the school?"

"Um . . . no, ma'am. I'm a friend of Lance's. I mean, I was."

Mrs. Seaver's face changed. At least a little light came into the dead eyes. "Oh, I see."

"You should wait for the wake," said the other woman. "Or I'm sure the school will have something. A memorial. This is just close friends and family right now."

Ebony nodded. "I came to see Mrs. Seaver, actually. I need to tell her something."

The stranger took a step forward. "What's that?"

"Oh, Nita, take it easy," Linda Seaver said. "She's a friend of Lance's. You go top up everybody's coffee. I'll be there in a minute."

Nita Daniels looked put out, but she knew how to follow orders. A few seconds later, Ebony was alone with Lance's mother.

"What did you want to tell me?" Linda asked, her eyes animated by the memory of good manners.

Ebony didn't know where to begin. She didn't know much about Linda Seaver beyond what Lance had told her. The woman hadn't reacted well to her husband leaving her some years ago. After he'd relocated to Jackson and begun seeing younger women, Linda had become reliant on anxiety meds, dieted all the time, and was always trying some new OTC appetite suppressant. Lance said she ought to just drop the benzos and take speed, to save herself the hassle.

"So, you're a friend of Lance's?" The scrubbed face still wore some artificial cheer.

"Um, yes, ma'am. A good friend."

"You go to St. Joseph's?"

"Uh . . . no, ma'am. I go to the Early College Academy. At the public school."

Confusion now. "Oh. I see. Well . . . how do you know Lance?"

"From a party."

"Ah. I see." But she clearly didn't.

"We got some of the same friends," Ebony said, feeling stupid.

"I'm sure. Well, I'm not sure how I—"

"I need you to see something!" Ebony said in an urgent whisper. "I know what happened to Lance."

Mrs. Seaver blinked in surprise. "I know what happened, too. It was terrible."

"No, I mean, I know who did it. And *why* they did it."

Linda Seaver was awake now. She blinked again, suddenly focused. Ebony's words had broken through.

"Jamaal said Lance owed him two hundred dollars. I didn't know nothing about that, but that's why they got into it. That's why Jamaal shot him."

"Linda, what in the world is going on?"

It was Nita Daniels again, poking her nose into her friend's business. She stood in the spacious foyer, another woman standing behind her, this one in a black pantsuit. Damn these nosy bitches—

"Y'all go back in the kitchen," Linda said. "I'm visiting with . . . Lance's friend—"

"Ebony. Ebony Swan."

"I'm talking to Ebony. I'll be right back with you."

The two women frowned as though at an unpleasant smell, but after quietly conferring, they vacated the foyer.

Mrs. Seaver walked outside and shut the door behind her. She looked fragile, but there was strength in her, too. Ebony could feel it. She hoped the woman was strong enough to handle what she had to tell her. If she was still standing after identifying her son's body today, she probably was.

"I don't understand what you said before," Linda said. "I don't know any . . . Jamaal? What two hundred dollars are you talking about? Are you saying Lance owed you money?"

Ebony shook her head hard. "No, ma'am. Jamaal said Lance owed *him* that money. Jamaal is a plug."

"A plug?"

"A drug dealer. A real bad guy. And Lance got mixed up with him somehow."

Mrs. Seaver drew back her head in disbelief. "How would Lance know someone like that?"

Ebony wondered if Mrs. Seaver could really be so naïve, or whether this was automatic denial of something she actually knew to be true. "The thing is," Ebony said, "Lance got himself trapped up because he'd fooled around a little bit with some stuff at parties. Nothing bad, you know, just like Molly or Xanax, you know."

Bewilderment had come into Mrs. Seaver's face. "I'm confused. Are you saying . . . Lance was taking drugs?"

Ebony nodded. "Yes, ma'am. Lots of people do."

"At St. Joseph's?"

"Yes'm. Especially the white ballplayers. The girls take Adderall to lose weight, but those jocks like it all. Pain pills, Molly, everything. And Lance had . . . well, he knew Jamaal from when he was younger, from ballin' in the street and stuff, so Jamaal just ended up being somebody those guys came to for that. That's how Lance got crossed up. Jamaal was okay when he was a kid, but now he's B-A-D. And all this happened right before the mayor showed up, see? The mayor heard the shots and was trying to save Lance, but this white deputy wouldn't let him, and that's how it all went so bad—"

Ebony had lost her. She realized it too late. She always spoke too fast when she was stressed, and people tended to zone out, or turn to someone else and start a new conversation. But in this case, she'd relayed too much painful information too quickly, and Linda had simply rejected it. Of course she had. Because to accept it would mean accepting that her life, and her son's life, was nothing like she'd imagined it to be—

"I can't listen to this," Mrs. Seaver said in a dreamy voice. "I'm sure you mean well, but those are lies, my girl. I don't know what you hope to gain by telling them to me. I suppose you're leading up to some kind of request for money. Well . . . I'm sorry. I know my son." She wiped mascara on her sleeve. "I *knew* him. And he was no drug addict. He certainly didn't *sell* drugs. Why would he? He didn't need money."

The answer to that question would probably fill a chapter in a psychology textbook, Ebony thought. But she'd never get a chance to explain it to Lance's mother. She wondered what Linda Seaver would say if she knew that the safest the desperate Black girl standing before her had felt in years was on the four nights she'd slept curled in the twin bed upstairs with her son.

"No, ma'am," Ebony said in a tone of apology. "I didn't mean nothing bad about Lance. Lance was the best boy I ever knew. Who ever talked to me, anyway. I just happened to be there when this terrible thing happened today. And I thought you should know. I thought maybe you could help me. Because the guy that shot Lance . . . he's trying to get me now. He thinks I'm gonna tell the police what he did. But I'm telling you instead."

She felt Linda Seaver trying to stay with her, trying to find it in herself to deal with what she was hearing. "Can I AirDrop something to your phone?" Ebony asked quickly. "It's a video of Lance."

"Of my Lance?" Linda echoed.

Who else's? Ebony thought irritably. But she reminded herself that this woman had just lost her son.

Linda had taken an iPhone from somewhere in the folds of her dress. Ebony found Mrs. Seaver's iPhone via Bluetooth, then called up the video she'd shot, took a breath, and hit SEND. While she was at it, she dropped her contact information into Mrs. Seaver's phone as well.

When she looked up, she saw Nita Daniels staring at her from a small window to the left of the door. The sour-faced woman pointed at her and said something harsh to someone out of sight.

"That's going to be hard to watch," Ebony said in a warning tone. "You should be alone when you do. Don't let those neighbor women see it. I sent you my phone number, too. I'm going to go now, but I'll stay close by. I've got nowhere to go, and I don't know what else to do."

Mrs. Seaver looked more confused than ever. It was as though a wave of whatever drug she was taking had just hit her brain.

"Why won't you talk to the police, child?" she asked.

Ebony shook her head. "I can't trust no police. And this video shows a cop killing the mayor."

"Dr. Berry?" Linda said dully.

Ebony nodded. "I've got friends who are informants for the sheriff's department, where if you agree to tell on other people, they don't send you to jail for a bust. Them deputies make these girls give 'em oral sex and stuff, to stay out of jail. Young girls, I'm talking about."

A look of revulsion distorted Linda's face. "That's awful."

"I ain't going to no police. But I have to stay away from Jamaal somehow. Or he'll do me like he did Lance."

This time, when the front door opened, Nita was griping as she came through it. Ebony reached out and squeezed Linda's arm to give her encouragement, then backed up and raced around the corner, into the space between the big houses.

CHAPTER 60

COREY WAS DRIVING Bobby east on Highway 462 toward the Belle Rose Country Club when the call he'd predicted came over their encrypted phone. Bobby was still processing what he'd seen behind the pawnshop near Diamond Hill, but no matter what lay behind that fatal interaction, he knew Doc's death would send the Black community into unquenchable rage. Before they translated that rage into action, though, they would crave guidance, and not just from Pastor Baldwin.

"Go," he said, answering with the push of a button, then putting the call on speaker.

"I hear an echo," said the now-familiar Ava Gardner drawl. "Am I on speaker?"

"I'm in the Rover."

"This isn't a call for Bluetooth," Dixie told him.

Bobby held his forefinger to his lips, and Corey nodded. "I'm alone, Dix. And you've got a big problem. That sheriff of yours has got a rogue department. Mission Hill was bad enough, but Doc was worse, and what just happened on the bluff was borderline insane."

"We know, hon. That's why I'm calling."

Corey gave him an "I-told-you-so" grimace.

"To dig you and your club out of the shit you've buried yourselves in?" Bobby asked.

"Exactly."

This admission surprised Bobby. "What's the situation downtown now?"

"Three thousand angry Black people on the bluff, and more on the way. Unless the National Guard uses Tiananmen Square tactics, they won't be able to do a thing about it. Worse yet, there are already news choppers over the river, and somebody just blew up an oil well on the Louisiana side. The optics are epically bad."

"And you think *I* can do something about that?"

"After the speech you gave in Diamond Hill today . . . you might. But what I think isn't material. Someone a lot higher up the totem pole than I am wants to talk to you."

Bobby motioned for Corey to pull onto the shoulder. "I'm listening."

As the Rover's tires ground on gravel, Charles Dufort's surprisingly powerful baritone said, "You know who this is, Bobby boy?"

Bobby shifted in his seat. "What can I do for you, sir?"

"I'd like you to handle the situation brewing downtown."

Corey firmly shook his head, but Bobby already felt something within him rising to the bait.

"We've got a potential riot down there," Dufort went on, "and I think you're the best man on the ground to solve it. Consider it an audition."

Bobby felt the metaphorical hook set in his gills. "Sir, given my lack of official authority, I'm not sure what I can do."

"You can go down to Donnelly Oil with Dixie and her crew and apply your skills, training, and instincts. Dixie will get you situated as regards lines of authority. If any white man can get this thing tamped down, it's you. As bad as this situation looks now, it could be your ticket. I don't know how—I leave that to you. But Bienville's your hometown, boy. This should be tailor-made for you."

"I suppose that's true."

"Think about our partnership, son. Nobody picks a general to lead an invasion if he's never won a battle."

Corey was still shaking his head.

Bobby closed his eyes and thought quickly. "Sir, when you called we were in the middle of working out the ballot numbers on the last seven states for Thursday's announcement. The most stubborn blue states. I have three minutes before I lose my window with my people. Could I call you back after that?"

"I'll expect to hear your voice in five minutes."

"Dix, could you stay on the line just a second?"

"How can I help, hon?" Dixie asked after Dufort hung up.

"I've got a couple of questions for you, but I need to speak to someone else before I give Charles the answer he wants. Stay on this line and wait for me."

"I wish I knew who you call for counsel in moments like this."

"You can read my tell-all in twenty years."

"Baby boy," Dixie drawled, "wouldn't you rather be downtown shaping events rather than watching them unfold on your phone?"

"I'll be back before you know it. Out."

Bobby disconnected and put his hand to his jaw, feeling his whole being engage with the chance being laid before him. A big tractor-trailer roared past, its vacuum sucking the Rover toward it, rocking the vehicle on its shocks.

"What do you think?" Bobby asked, turning to Corey. "Tell me straight."

Corey looked down the road. "Going down there would be potentially the most disastrous mistake of your life. It could destroy everything we've done so far."

Bobby shrugged. "No guts, no glory."

Corey turned to him, naked fear in his eyes. "You want to be cavalier? Think about your life up to now. Every move you've made has been determined by a near pathological dedication to avoiding risk. Keeping the deepest parts of yourself secret from the world." Corey let that sink in. "True?"

"True enough."

"Even so . . . we both know you harbor a rogue impulse to break out sometimes, to do the craziest thing imaginable—to walk out on a tightrope in front of millions and risk everything to dance on the wire. And you know what? I get that. Okay? After living as you have—as *we* have—it wouldn't be human not to feel that compulsion. But Bobby . . . these people? These Poker Club people? They're not like you. Or me. They're wealthy, sure, but they are *small town*. They are small-minded, and I fear small-*souled* as well."

"You can't be choosy when you're looking for the kind of money I am."

"I'm not sure I agree. You can make some distinctions."

"Tell me what you mean."

"Well . . . these people are racist in a way that you're not."

"How so?"

"You're more elitist than racist, for one thing. You believe in Jefferson's 'natural aristocracy,' and I don't think you really consider skin color when you determine who belongs in it. No matter what you claim. Remember how much you loved hanging out with Quincy Jones in L.A.? Or Byron Allen?"

Bobby looked at his lover with resignation. "You do know me, don't you?"

"More than that, I actually care about you. And I'm terrified that if you try to take over the management of this . . . this *justified protest*, you're setting yourself up for destruction. I'm not even sure we shouldn't transfer Friday's announcement to Atlanta or even Washington. Just get clear of this mess as fast as we can. Why taint yourself?"

Bobby wasn't sure what he felt, but he didn't like it. He appreciated that Corey knew him so well, yet it infuriated him that his lover felt entitled to fault him for taking on a challenge commensurate with his ability to accomplish the impossible. In this moment, Corey felt like an anchor chained around his neck.

"I can't run away, Corey. Don't you get that?"

"Why not? Any sane politician would."

Bobby shook his head. "*This is my hometown.* That means I have no choice. We're making the announcement from here, no matter what happens between now and then."

"I can see you're upset. But will you allow me to point out just one fact?"

"Sure. Go on."

"Setting aside the Mission Hill shootings by Sheriff Tarlton's department, all this started with the burning of the antebellum mansions in Bienville and Natchez. Right?"

Bobby nodded, frustration building like steam in his chest.

Corey held up his hands for patience. "We still have no idea who started those fires, or what their motives are. The burning of Beauvoir could be a good sign, but we don't know that."

Bobby forced himself to nod.

"What if—on the cusp of launching this run you've been dreaming about so long—the arsonists are caught, and they turn out to be white? A false-flag attack, as so many people have suggested?"

"Who would it be, Cor? The Poker Club itself? Or Barlow's Lost Cause militia boys?"

Corey turned up his palms. "Does it matter? The Proud Boys, the Oath Keepers, or the Confederate Cornholers. The problem is, that could be the reality. The whole thing explodes overnight, leaving you covered in shit. The obvious downside. Now the upside . . . well, that's the thing. I don't see one."

"Other than Charles Dufort's money, which has brought us to the high ground we now occupy."

"Aren't you forgetting what Tio Carrera said? If you're truly the golden boy, the money will come to you. Don't worry about it."

"He said we had to get the first hundred million."

"Well. This might be a good time to show Dufort that his money doesn't buy your soul."

Bobby stared at the Rover's LCD while traffic zoomed past on the same highway he'd driven up and down as a resentful teenager. Now the richest people in the city of his youth were begging for his help. Sure, the stakes were high. Not even national anymore. They were global. That was the league people thought of him in now. World leaders would be speaking his name tonight, tomorrow, and especially Friday night. How was he supposed to walk away from that?

"What do you want me to do?" he asked, as if he didn't know.

Corey sighed heavily. "Go back to the cabin. Pack your shit. We'll drive back to Jackson without a backward glance. Leave this nightmare to the people stuck with it by choice or birth and plan our announcement from a fitting venue. At this point, we have even bigger potential sources of funding than Charles Dufort. We don't have to announce Friday."

"Bullshit we don't. We're committed."

"Imagine launching just a little later," Corey suggested, "without all this racial bullshit hanging over our heads. If you're determined to work with the plutonium of 2024 presidential politics, then let's build a nuclear reactor, not an implosion bomb."

Bobby had to give Corey credit. He'd always had clear vision when it came to risk, and that had paid off in spades over the years. But today . . . it wasn't what he wanted to hear. Bobby instinctively understood that a third-party run—in this day and age—required a speed and agility that even Corey had not fully grasped, at least outside the digital world. And while other men or groups might have the money and will to try, they would not do it under the circumstances that Dufort would—with virtually no strings attached. None Bobby couldn't live with, anyway. The super PAC Dufort had funded wouldn't shy away from any move necessary for victory. Further . . . Corey didn't know it, but Bobby already intended to spend the late afternoon and evening on the bluff. He might as well spend it in the comfort of the Donnelly building's penthouse.

"I think there is an upside," Bobby said softly. "One you don't see."

Corey raised one eyebrow.

Bobby nodded. "Last night I talked to a kid at the Barlow bunker. Early thirties. Shot Barlow was worried about him planning some kind of mass-casualty attack. And I think he might be right. I think the chaos after Doc's death is going to put an unprecedented crowd of Black people on the Bienville bluff."

Corey's face tightened in worry. "What are you saying, Bobby?"

"You know what really drives presidential politics? At bottom? Not issues. It's heroes and villains. A few days ago, an unknown tour guide named Kendrick Washington displayed some spontaneous heroism at a rap concert, in a violent situation, and now he has more than forty million social media followers. How many years did it take me to build up nine million radio listeners?"

"What the hell are you saying? You want to, what . . . stalk this nut until he makes some kind of move, then save the day?"

"On camera," Bobby finished. "That may be exactly what I'm saying. And with my background . . . I'm the guy to do it. You know I am."

Corey was shaking his head with a mixture of awe and dread. Perhaps even revulsion. "Christ, Bobby. Do you realize how dangerous that would be? What if he straps a bomb to himself?"

Bobby shook his head. "Not the type. He might go down in a hail of bullets, but he's no suicide bomber."

"You don't know that!"

Bobby smiled. "But I do. That's where my sixth sense is dead-on. I proved that a dozen times overseas. A hundred. In tunnels and rooms so dark and twisted you could barely see, even with NVDs."

Corey reached over his laptop and pressed the dash in frustration. "At least I'm starting to see why you've been acting the way you have. Ever since you saw Kendrick Washington blow up online, you've sensed you might be able to do the same. And the fact that these fires are happening in your hometown—"

"Puts me in a perfect position to exploit them. And Doc's death, regrettable as it is—"

"Creates the highly unstable conditions you were praying for. No wonder you've been compulsively checking his social media."

Bobby shrugged and started to explain further, but Corey held up his right hand. "You might as well call them back and tell them you're in."

"Cor—"

"Don't apologize. You'll hate me for it later."

Bobby looked down the seemingly endless line of asphalt and thought of where they'd been, and of where he might be going. Picking up the encrypted phone, he called Dixie's cell back.

"Hel*lo*-oh," she said in a singsong voice. "Should I fix you a drink?"

"Dix," Bobby said in a conclusive tone, "from the first time you and I discussed any of this, I've sensed a personal motive on your part. I need to understand that before I put more skin in this game."

There was only awkward silence. Then Dixie said, "Can you be more specific?"

"Sure. Given the stakes, will you tell me why you're personally fucking around with who runs this little burg right now? Think before you answer, Dix. You only get points for truth today."

This time the silence lasted so long that Bobby wondered if they'd lost cellular reception. Then the deep female voice rose out of a well of silence.

"I didn't come from money, hon. Nor did I come from the bluest end of the gene pool. But I had one claim to fame: one of my ancestors was Reginald Hewson. Do you know who he was?"

"The guy Hewson Park is named after?"

"That's right."

"The man whose statue depicts him looking down at a box on a table?"

"That box is an Eli Whitney cotton gin, circa 1803."

Bobby found himself smiling. "I majored in history, Dix. Hewson invented the Bienville-Siamese variety of cotton. Made himself and others millions of dollars. That's 1840s millions. Real money."

"You're goddamn right," she said with brittle pride. "But those uppity sons of whores newly elected to the city board have decided to not only rename Hewson Park, but also to remove my ancestor's statue. And because it's not of a Civil War soldier, and it's on city property, nothing can stop them."

"Except the Poker Club?" Bobby finished. "And a decades-old Mississippi statute, courtesy of the Stennis Institute?"

"You got it, baby boy. That board is getting both barrels by the end of this week."

Corey shook his head in disbelief, but Bobby grinned. Corey had always had a disdain for people who let personal animosity affect critical decisions. Most of the time, Bobby did, too. But he could appreciate a thoroughgoing effort to punish a personal slight. "Remind me again why they want to remove his statue?"

"Reginald owned five hundred and forty-three slaves. Every one bought and paid for with money he'd earned by the sweat of his brow and the caliber of his intellect."

"And you don't have any problem with that?" Bobby pushed, baiting her.

"Darlin', *history is history*, as the TikTok candidate says. If God himself can't change it, then neither can the city board of Bienville, Mississippi. Certainly not *three black-ass aldermen* just one generation off welfare."

"Now, Dix, let's don't bring race into this."

"It's nothing *but* race, Bobby. All race, all the time. I'm sick to hell of it. So you'd better figure out exactly where you stand. Because that's gonna be the prime factor determining how many votes you pull from the fifty million free for the taking after the precipitous fall of Big Daddy Trump."

"I know exactly where I stand, Dix. And those fifty million will be fine. They can come to me or not. But I appreciate you being honest about what's going on with the board."

"Well, that ain't all of it—not near—or my associates wouldn't have let me proceed. It's about power. It's about the new public school, critical race theory, and showing the rest of the country what a few motivated people can accomplish in the political arena. But . . . I wanted you to know the whole truth."

Corey was rubbing his face like a man too depressed to respond to what he'd heard.

"Buck Tarlton's still a problem," Bobby said. "He thinks he's in charge. And the law says he is during an emergency. My instinct is to counsel restraint in dealing with the Blacks. Tarlton won't listen to that."

"That's why we need you down here."

"Who's down there with you?"

"Pretty much the same crew from our previous meeting."

"What about the governor? He controls the National Guard. To accomplish anything, I'll have to have input into what the Guard is doing."

"Charles will make sure you do."

Corey's eyes went wide.

"Whatever happens today will play out on national TV," Dixie said. "The governor is deeply concerned with projecting a strong image nationally. He's got the idea that he could be the VP pick in 2024. It drives everything he does. Just make sure you can sell your strategy as helping him in that cause. Understood?"

Corey shook his head violently.

"Hendrick's and tonic," Bobby said.

"What's that, hon?"

"My drink. Hendrick's and tonic."

"I'll have it waiting. Oh, I forgot one thing."

"What's that?"

"My daughter Jenna Kay was already flying in on our plane, hoping to see Faith Hill and Tim McGraw. She's staying in the penthouse apartment. She's an anchor for the Fox affiliate in Lexington, Kentucky, and, well . . . I didn't know we were going to have a goddamned riot and need you down there."

Corey mimed choking himself to death.

"No journalists, Dix. Not even your daughter."

"Jenna Kay knows what makes the mare go, Bobby. No worries on that score."

Jesus, he thought. "Just keep her out of whatever room I'm running things from."

"Ten-four, baby doll," Dixie said. "Now Charles is waiting, and we went over our five minutes."

"You'd better find some Vaseline for Buck Tarlton. Or else some Xanax."

"I can handle Buck, hon. You just get down here."

Bobby clicked off and turned to Corey, whose face betrayed unfeigned despair.

"Why am I even looking at the ballot numbers?" Corey asked the windshield. "When you could blow your whole campaign to hell this evening? On national TV?"

"Let's run by the cabin," Bobby said. "I want to grab a few things before I head down to the Donnelly building."

Corey's jaw flexed. "Sure." As he put the Rover through a U-turn, Corey said, "So Dixie's daughter was already flying in on the company jet. God, she's shameless. Pimping her own daughter to the man on the come."

Bobby laughed. "That's what Southern mamas do, Cor."

"If only she knew the truth."

Bobby turned and looked into his lover's eyes. "You're pretty good at reading people, but sometimes you miss big with women. I doubt there's anything about me that Dixie Donnelly doesn't already understand on some level. And the first time she's alone with you and me for two minutes, she'll get it."

Corey looked shocked by this prediction. "Well, then—"

"She won't *care*," Bobby finished. "Don't you see? That's the thing about mamas like Dixie. Same with the evangelical Republicans and their 'family values.' Or their positions on the deficit or communism. *It's all a lie.* A cover. At bottom, it's about money and power. The *end always justifies the means*. Dixie's daughter's the same, I'll bet. She'd marry a gay man to be First Lady, then divorce him four or five years down the road."

"I can't believe you're doing this," Corey said with desolation.

CHAPTER 61

BY THE TIME I reached the Bienville City Council chamber, Robert Gaines had returned, and all six members of the board of aldermen had risen to enter executive session in the side conference room dedicated to that purpose. Once they go through that door, their deliberations are no longer a matter of public record. In truth, most critical city business gets done in this room long before any public votes are taken, a regrettable practice that fosters neither transparency nor the good functioning of democracy.

There aren't more than a dozen people in the normally crowded audience seats, but a reporter for the Bienville *Watchman* is badgering Vivian Paine, the mayor pro tem, a well-tended real estate broker who wears too much makeup and smiles when she'd like to kill you. The video technician seems to be working hard to make sure he recorded whatever took place just prior to the last motion at this special-called meeting. As the three Caucasian board members file through the conference room door—the second in line being Sophie Dufort—I manage to catch up and plant my prosthetic foot in front of Alderwoman Paine, who is doing her best to brush off the reporter.

"I didn't get notice of this meeting, Vivian," I tell her, as though my omission must simply have been an oversight.

Sophie Dufort appears in the door and looks worriedly back at us.

"No, you didn't," Paine replies, a false note of regret in her voice. "As you know, Penn, the city attorney serves at the pleasure of the mayor, and while you were always Mayor Berry's choice, you were never mine. As mayor pro tem, I'll feel better seeking more politically balanced counsel going forward."

"I see. And who's the lucky lawyer today? I don't see one."

Another carefully curated smile. "I don't particularly see the need for legal counsel today."

"What business is before the board?"

"That's confidential."

I glance toward the conference room door, but Sophie offers me nothing.

"No, it's not," says Elijah Keyes, one of the Black progressives queuing behind Paine. "Penn, they're moving to try to consolidate the city with the county, under the Stennis local and private legislation act drafted during the 1970s. In effect, they're moving to dissolve the City of Bienville as a legal entity."

Exactly what Doc Berry feared for weeks, and a danger I foolishly discounted. Of course, I couldn't really imagine that Doc would be dead and his tie-breaking vote neutralized. "I'd say you need more than legal counsel to vote on that, Vivian. You'll need a thorough review by the state AG. There may even be constitutional issues."

Another strobe-bright smile. "I've already spoken to the AG, and he's in full agreement that the statute as promulgated and studied by the Stennis Institute is solid. As for the nuts-and-bolts details, County Attorney Stevens has given us a more than adequate analysis of the statute, as well as the steps we need to take to guarantee its lawful implementation."

Glancing over my shoulder, I catch sight of Alan Stevens, the fortyish attorney who represents the county board. Stevens is the archetypal small-town Mississippi lawyer: Ole Miss, Rotary Club member, casual golfer, avid deer hunter, Sunday School teacher, dues-paying member of Ducks Unlimited—

"So thanks *ever so much* for rushing down here," Vivian gushes, "but we won't be needing your advice today. Or, for that matter, going forward. You take care now, Penn."

In other words, translated from the Southern parlance, *Go fuck yourself.* In more specific terms, I realize, the mayor pro tem just fired me. As Paine turns to go, I catch hold of her arm. "Doc is barely even cold, and this is what you do? He may have been murdered, Vivian."

"I've certainly heard nothing to that effect from Sheriff Tarlton."

"What about the chief of police?"

This time her smile betrays the dark malice beneath. "Chief Morgan may not have a municipal portfolio much longer. Now, I really need to get inside. May I?" She removes her arm from my grip with exaggerated effort.

As the two Black male board members move past—the second being Robert Gaines, who texted me the warning—I see only weariness and anger in their eyes. *This,* they say silently, *is how it's always been. Why would we ever think it could be different?* The last to go by me is Cicely Waite, a woman I've never much cared for, and whose moral fiber I always doubted, especially when it came to lining her own nest. But today, I feel that if any of these three have the intestinal fortitude to dig in and resist the weight of the white power structure, it is she. Cicely came up in the hard school of 1970s Mississippi politics, which means she can get down in the dirt and scrap with the meanest dog in the yard.

"Don't let them do it, Cicely," I say softly into the ear beneath her copper-colored wig.

"I'm afraid this bout's been fixed," she mutters. "But I ain't knocked out yet."

"Robert?" I call before the door closes. "I need to ask you something. Just one minute."

I hear a scuffling sound, muffled angry words beyond the door. Then Gaines comes back through, his jaw set in anger at whoever attempted to stop him. Straightening his coat on his shoulders, he follows me toward the entrance, where we'll be out of earshot of any who hover by the conference room door.

"You know Chief Morgan arrested Deputy LeJay, right?"

"Jesus," Gaines breathes. "I admire his balls, but he may not have a job by close of business."

"Why would anyone think they have a chance of getting you guys to dissolve the city?" I ask. "Even with Mayor Berry dead, progressives are four-against-two, right? Even if somebody buys off Cicely, it's three-to-three."

A bitter chuckle escapes Gaines's lips. "That's the old world you talkin' 'bout. And Cicely ain't the problem. That old woman's got her back up over this. I thought she was gonna bitch-slap Vivian Paine a few minutes ago."

I'm impressed. "Then . . . who?"

Gaines looks over at the conference room door, where Sophie Dufort is standing as though waiting for someone. Turning my back to the door, I motion for Robert to continue, but quietly.

In a near whisper, he says, "They're pressuring us all, but especially Elijah Keyes. I don't know all the details . . . but it's a family thing. His niece is going before a judge somewhere. Elijah's hung tough so far, but . . . he's close to caving. I swore I wouldn't say anything, but they're about to destroy this town. I can't believe this shit is *legal*, man. John Stennis is still screwing the Black man, thirty years after his death. Are we really gonna let this bullshit go down this way?"

"Who's pressuring Keyes? The Poker Club?"

Gaines shrugs. "Who knows, these days? The people with the money and connections."

"Are the same people pressuring you as well?"

"Oh, hell yeah. I've got a ninety-six-thousand-dollar bank loan, and if I don't vote to merge—or dissolve, or whatever they call it—they're gonna call it in full."

"But your vote is solid?" I press.

Gaines takes another long breath. "If they call that loan, I'll lose my business. That's hard to explain to my wife and child."

Looking over my shoulder, I see Sophie still waiting. "Listen to me, Robert. If they call your loan, I'll pay it for you."

Gaines blinks in disbelief. "Are you shittin' me, man?"

"No. You heard about the Dunphy verdict?"

"Yeah, sure."

"If it comes to it, I'll use some of that to pay your loan."

Gaines looks as though he might sag against me in relief.

"What else can you tell me about the pressure on Keyes?"

"It's Alabama, that's all I know. South Alabama." Gaines chews on his bottom lip. "Possible vehicular homicide case. Keyes's niece hit somebody. Alcohol involved. Lots of discretion in charging and sentencing."

"Damn it."

"Yep."

"Listen, you sit by Elijah when you get in there. Tell him if I have to go to Alabama and hire detectives to investigate a judge or DA, I'll do it."

Gaines leans back to assess my sincerity. "Are you for real, Penn? This is the man's family in jeopardy."

"I'll do it for Doc. He tried to warn me, and I didn't take him seriously. Now he's gone. I let him down, Robert. I owe him."

Gaines nods like a man accustomed to bearing the cross of guilt. "I hear you, brother."

"Alderman Gaines!" calls Vivian Paine. "You're holding up the vote!"

Gaines throws up a hand in anger, then flips his mayor pro tem the bird.

"And tell Cicely to hold the line," I add. "That cranky old crow just might be the one to save us."

Robert closes his eyes as though trying to suppress some internal pain. When he opens them again, he says, "I'm forty-three, Penn. All my life I've heard the old heads talk about 1966, the night of the big riot. I don't know how bad it really got, but I've never felt what I felt out there when those snipers shot those guys. The old folks are scared, but they're fed up, too. After Doc? And these young brothers? They got guns, man. And they ain't scared of dyin'. If I was you, I'd get off that bluff tonight. I'm not sure I'm gonna stay myself. Maybe I should . . . but what can one man do when the levee breaks?"

"I hope we don't have to find out."

Gaines shakes his head one last time, then backs across the floor and finally turns to the conference room door.

I'm already going through the exit when someone catches hold of my shoulder. Turning, I find Sophie Dufort looking angrily into my face.

"What is it?" I ask.

"What the hell does Chief Morgan think he's doing?"

"You mean by arresting the man who murdered the mayor?"

She leans in close and hisses, "You know damn well what I mean. He's forcing a direct conflict between city and county authority while civil unrest brews on the bluff. I can't imagine anything more dangerous."

In moments like this I find it hard to believe that this woman and I slept together for nearly a year of our lives. "I'd say letting a potential murderer go without charging him meets that standard. Have you jumped on Buck Tarlton's ass for that yet?"

"Like it or not, Tarlton has the legal authority in this situation. You know that better than any of us."

"You sound pretty well-informed."

"Alan Stevens made it painfully clear to us before the meeting."

"Stevens serves the county, not the city. Whereas you guys—"

"No longer have a city attorney," she finishes.

"Ms. Dufort?" Vivian Paine calls from the door. "We can't wait any longer."

"That bourgeois *bitch*," Sophie hisses, then turns and marches over to the conference room.

Outside the administration building, I text Annie that I'll get back home as quickly as I can. Then I get into my Audi and head for Bienville Police Headquarters.

BIENVILLE POLICE HEADQUARTERS is a hive of anxiety and activity. Chief Morgan gives Marshall McEwan and me an interrogation room for privacy. Then he joins us, because it turns out he has some questions of his own. The first is what will happen to him and his men if the city board actually dissolve the city at that special meeting.

"First of all, Vivian Paine just fired me," I tell him. "So I have no official standing anymore. But if they really vote to merge with the county, then Tarlton can fire you and all your men tonight. If they go to 'will and pleasure,' that is, which they almost certainly will."

There's only silence at first. Then Morgan speaks with a chilling fatalism. "My men aren't leaving this building tonight. Not after what happened to Doc. They're not giving up Deputy LeJay to walk free."

Marshall is staring at me with his hands turned up.

"What if the sheriff demands you release LeJay?" I ask. "What if he threatens to storm the station to free him?"

Chief Morgan's answer is slow in coming, but it finally arrives. "I think that's what they call a FAAFO situation."

"What's that mean?"

"Ask your daughter when you get home."

"'Fuck around and find out,'" Marshall translates.

I don't know whether there's such a thing as an existential chuckle, but if so, Chief Morgan gives us one now. "You guys know there's a crowd building outside?"

"I didn't see many people when I got here."

"It's happening fast. We've got a half dozen Tenisaw County deputies out front, plus about fifty white folks of the redneck persuasion out back. Tarlton's about to turn this place into the Alamo. I think he lost his shit when they burned his house. Anyway, two thirds of my men are still down on the bluff."

Chief Morgan looks into Marshall's eyes. "I hope you're planning on sticking around a while. We'll stand a lot better chance of getting through the next twenty-four hours with a white newspaper publisher in here. Preferably broadcasting live."

I can see Marshall calculating where his presence will be most valuable. "I'll stick," he says finally, and then he gives me a hard look. "If you'll do all you can to stop that vote."

"I'm working on it. That's all I can tell you."

"You know," Marshall reflects, "if the Tenisaw County Board takes out the Black city government tonight, this'll be held up as a victory by the whole right wing in America. Fox News will canonize them."

"Not just a victory. A road map. An example of what you can do by manipulating the law to seize and hold power."

"No, sir," Chief Morgan says. "That ain't happening. Not while I wear this badge."

"That badge may be meaningless by sundown," Marshall points out.

Chief Morgan's face hardens into stone. "Wait till you see 'em try to take it off me."

As the chief gets up to tend to his main business, I ask him to wait just a minute. "Guys, while we three are in here face-to-face, let me ask a simple question. How exactly did we get here? Unless I'm mistaken, it began with two arsons."

"You could say it began with Mission Hill," Chief Morgan points out.

"True. But as bad as that was, it was more recklessness than anything else. The arsons were fully intentional. Yet now we find ourselves in the midst of some kind of power grab. So what the hell is actually going on? Who's burning these goddamn mansions? And why? We have no clue, correct? Yet they burned another house today, one of the most famous in the South."

Marshall holds up his forefinger like a professor. "What you're really asking is, are the arsonists white or Black? Because if they're Black, then these are actual retaliatory strikes for past injustice. But if they're white . . . then it's far more complicated. It's one hundred percent political, an attempt to stir white anger over perceived Black terrorism."

"Exactly. So, which is it?"

Chief Morgan snorts with something like self-contempt. "I don't have a clue. They could burn two more houses tomorrow and we still probably won't have a clue. Unless we catch somebody in the act."

"What would it cost," I ask, "to put cameras on every antebellum home here and in Natchez by dark tonight? Not that much, surely."

"No," says Marshall, "but some of the bombs are almost certainly already in place. K-9s won't necessarily find them all. They could have been there for weeks, for all we know."

"Besides," says Chief Morgan, "I'm not sure the arsons are the center of the trouble now. We're dealing with general unrest and rage, not only over the shooting of the kids at Mission Hill, but the dead deacons and the likely murder of Mayor Berry. Maybe *this* is what the arsons were meant to trigger."

"Why are they trying so hard to shut down the Black city board?" Marshall asks. "Could their main goal be to shut down your department, and thus any real investigations into those cases?"

"Any of these theories could be true," I think aloud. "But let me ask a truly crazy question. We've got a guy in town who may be running for president. He may be announcing his candidacy from here in two days."

"What are you wondering?" asks Marshall.

"Is it possible that someone has done this—the arsons of the mansions, I mean—to sabotage his campaign?"

"Are you serious?"

"Think about it. He's running as a third-party candidate. No one's ever succeeded doing that, but all the pundits say that if anyone ever had a real chance, it's Bobby White. Now, look at the Poker Club. They're political, right? Huge Republican donors, at both the state and national level. Who's to say they wouldn't pull something like this? Kill two birds with one stone?"

"What do you mean?" asks Chief Morgan.

"I mean, on one hand they make the local Blacks look like anarchists, and take a shot at getting control of the city back. And on the other, they take Bobby White's big announcement week and make it look like he comes from a racist hellhole."

"They blow up his campaign." Marshall thinks about it, then shrugs as if it might just make sense. "It's not impossible. Given what I know about the Poker Club. They don't give a shit about legality. Or democracy."

"I hope you're right," Morgan says, "and that we can prove it. Because that beats the shit out of the Bastard Sons being an actual Black terrorist group and us being in the middle of a race war."

"We may get the race war no matter who burned the houses," Marshall observes, holding up his phone. "Brace yourselves. One of my reporters just texted me that three white motorcyclists were shot at the Kudzu Country Store south of town."

"God*damn* it!" curses Chief Morgan. "That's county jurisdiction."

Before I can react there's a sharp knock at the door, then Detective Henry Radford pokes his round head into the room. "Two men and a woman blown to pieces south of town. Security footage shows two Black male perps with AR-15s. There's no audio, so we don't know what happened. The vics were on motorcycles, but they looked more like tourists than anything else. They had MAGA stickers on their bikes."

Marshall lets out a long sigh. We stare at each other in silence for about half a minute. Then the chief tells us he has to check the "siege force" and see to his men.

As soon as he shuts the door, I grip Marshall's wrist and look him in the eye. "You see how fast this situation is spiraling downward? And don't kid yourself. Buck Tarlton's crazy enough to storm this station with a SWAT team to break LeJay out, and Sheriff Johnson's twice as crazy as he is. They were ready to open fire on a crowd of defenseless women and children just an hour ago. You could die in here, Marshall."

The publisher pockets his cell phone and sits up straight. "I covered Iraq and nearly died there, but I made it out. This is my hometown, and it may be about to disappear. I've got no choice."

"That's not true."

"If my dad were alive today, he'd be right here with me. He published the *Watchman* for fifty-one years, through the worst of the Klan times."

"Your father's up on Cemetery Road, buddy. With your brother."

"He's watching me now."

What do you do with a man like this? Doesn't he know it's the twenty-first century? "Do you have any leverage over the Poker Club?"

A tinge of suspicion enters his eyes. "What makes you ask that?"

"Not asking wasn't a choice."

He looks far from comfortable. "I had some influence at one time, thanks to some things I discovered a few years ago. But the power dynamic in that group has changed. They used to be primarily about money. Now they've turned political."

"No way to get them to pull back any pressure on this vote?"

"I don't know. I'll think about it." Something in the publisher's eyes has changed.

"What is it?" I ask.

"Can I ask you a personal question?"

"Sure."

"You know I used to be with Nadine Sullivan. Right?"

"Yeah. Sure." I try to keep my face impassive.

"We were together when I was investigating the Poker Club. But I always knew she was with someone else before me. In a relationship that didn't work out. She never told me who it was."

I nod slowly, as though ignorant of his intent.

"Was that you?" he asks finally, his eyes settling on mine.

I've never seen any reason to hide this part of my history, and at this point I can no longer justify doing so. "It was, yes. And I never asked Nadine to keep that secret from you. I was going through a lot back then, and I'm something of a hermit, but keeping it from you was her choice, not mine."

Marshall seems to be working this out in his own way, in silence. "It's all right," he says finally. "I get it. She's a private person." The phone in his pocket pings again, but he ignores it. "Are you two back together now?"

"We've spent the last couple of days together. After years apart."

He looks at his Apple Watch to read a text. "I'd better get moving." Marshall reaches out and shakes my hand. "Let's hope there's no more bloodshed between now and the next time we meet."

"Look, Marshall—"

"Hey, don't worry about that stuff. I'd rather know than not. And I'd rather it be you than somebody else." He waves as he backs through the door.

"We never had that drink," I tell him, reminding him of the burning of Arcadia. "How about my terrace tonight, at midnight?"

He laughs. "Don't jinx it."

And then he's gone.

It's time for me to follow suit. I have to bury my mother.

CHAPTER 62

EBONY KNEW SHE could never find safety alone. Not with both drug gangsters and sheriff's deputies hunting her. *Maybe the thing to do*, she thought for the hundredth time, *is just post the damn video somewhere anyone can see it.*

If she sent it to only a few friends, she would be putting their lives in danger. But what if she simply posted the thing to Instagram? Facebook, even? If several hundred people saw it at once? Or several *thousand*? At that point the little movie would spread so fast it would be beyond anyone's control. And then the town of Bienville—or at least the Black half—would explode. Surely then she could appeal to somebody for help? One of the popular pastors, maybe. Pastor Baldwin, maybe. Ask for sanctuary in his church, like they did in Gothic romances.

But, said a tiny voice, *sooner or later the DA will ask you to get up on a witness stand and repeat what you saw. Everything from Jamaal shooting Lance to that deputy shooting Mayor Berry. And everybody will know way ahead of time that you're going to be doing that. Jamaal will know. You'd have to survive until you testify. And then afterward. Who's gonna take care of you all that time? Not Mama. That's for damn sure. And not Dontrelle or her mama—*

The only possible solution that had come to Ebony was a white man named Marshall McEwan, the publisher of the Bienville *Watchman*. Her Early College Academy class had taken a field trip to the newspaper offices last year. Mr. McEwan had stood in the newsroom—a very informal and chaotic place—and talked to them about the importance of journalism to America. He was a handsome man, and he'd been on TV before he moved back to Bienville to take care of his sick father. What stood out in Ebony's mind was how much Mr. McEwan had seemed to care about doing the right thing. He was worried that newspapers as a whole would disappear and be replaced by the internet. But most of all he worried that Americans no longer cared about facts, and didn't have enough knowledge to tell facts from lies anyway. He talked about "silos" a lot, which she didn't quite understand. But she also remembered that the publisher's father had fought against the Ku Klukkers back when he ran the paper. If she was going to find help, the McEwan family sounded like the most likely place.

But first she would have to find a way to call him.

LINDA SEAVER HAD searched her son's room for half an hour and found nothing. Now she sat on Lance's unmade bed and tried to tell herself that the Black girl at her door had been a hallucination. She'd first told herself that the kid was lying, but after two more Xanax washed down with wine, she'd begun to question whether "Ebony Swan" had been there at all. Maybe she was some sort of grief projection, or guilt projection, or something. After all Linda had done to raise her baby right, the idea that Lance would go in the alley to get with something like that . . . Linda simply couldn't abide the thought. She knew the world was different than when she'd been in school, but not *that* different. Not in Mississippi. Ebony Swan wasn't even one of the small Black contingent at St. Joseph's.

Early College Academy . . . at the *public* school. *My God.*

The thing was, the video on her phone made it plain that *someone* had contacted her about Lance's death. She'd gone twenty-two minutes now without watching it again, and mercifully the Xanax was kicking in enough to blunt the visceral horror of watching her son choke on his own blood. The first couple of times, sitting in the close air of the bedroom, the video had triggered a sensation like one of the unhinged nightmares she'd experienced during the period leading up to her divorce.

She'd fretted outside her son's door for a good five minutes before coming in to search. And then only after pacing all over the house telling herself she had nothing to worry about. But eventually her doubts had got the better of her, and she'd told Nita Daniels she needed some alone time to rest. After Nita left, she'd finally come in and started going through Lance's things.

That was a tough boundary to cross, because of some unpleasant history between them. Years ago, when Lance was just starting to use a computer, she'd installed a special security program that a friend had told her about, one that let her track her son's movements on the internet. All the concerned parents had been using similar programs at the time. Linda had tried this one for a couple of months, then forgotten it. When she remembered it two years later, and checked it, she'd been horrified. Some of the pornography sites Lance visited had shaken her badly—some because of their explicitness, but others because of their violence. She'd been too afraid to confront him about his habit, but it changed the way she looked at him, and perhaps even the way she treated him. Worse, she could not get the images out of her mind. For about six weeks, she'd found herself searching for similar images on her cell phone, and she even went through a sort of fever where she masturbated several times a week. When this urge finally subsided, she felt she'd come to terms with the situation. Then Lance had discovered the tracking program on his machine.

This caused a breach from which they'd never really recovered.

Though he smiled at her each day, and pretended things were fine, Lance never trusted her again. This was why she knew, deep down, that Ebony Swan was real. And that the girl's tale of Lance selling drugs might be true. While searching his desk, she'd thought she smelled marijuana in one of the drawers but hadn't discovered any. To be honest, she wasn't sure she remembered exactly what pot smelled like. What she did know was that she'd happily take her son back as a lifelong pothead . . . if she could only have him alive.

Linda got up and went to the door, then looked back into a space in which every object was now redundant. Some things she could not even bear to look at, because they dated to when Lance was a little boy. With a stabbing pain in her throat, she backed out and pulled the door shut.

She was walking down the hall when she noticed Lance's gym bag on the built-in hall shelf. Just a blue Nike bag, one he'd gotten back in ninth grade when he ran track. She picked it up to put in his room, so she wouldn't have to think about it anymore, but then she froze.

The rattle of pills was a sound she knew well, and it was unmistakable.

Unzipping the bag, she expected to find an orange prescription bottle, but all she saw was a pair of socks, a deodorant stick, and a can of Axe body spray. She squeezed the socks but found nothing hidden in them. Then she held the bag against the wall and pressed against it in several places, figuring there might be a secret pocket or something. Again, she found nothing. Frustrated, she shook the bag.

There!

This time she took out the deodorant stick and shook it, but it made no sound. Last came the body spray. When she shook the can, the rattle was immediate. It took her about twenty seconds to figure out how to open the can, which was not genuine, but rather some cheap receptacle sold to teenagers to hide things. In the barrel she found two one-hundred-dollar bills and fourteen large orange Xanax tablets that she'd heard a friend call *Xanbars*. As she counted the pills, an image of Ebony Swan's frightened face rose in her mind.

Jamaal said Lance owed him two hundred dollars. I don't know anything about that. . . .

As Linda stared at the bills, tears began to fall into the Nike bag.

It's all true, she realized. *Everything that girl said.*

And the video . . . it made sense now. Dr. Ezra Berry *had* been trying to save her baby. That goddamned deputy had shot the mayor while he was trying to save a boy's life. *Her* boy . . .

It was so awful, Linda couldn't bear to think of it. And yet . . . if she told anyone the truth, and she revealed how she'd found out . . . *everything* would come out. Not just about the girl. The drugs, too. *And* the girl. And the only thing anyone would ever remember about her precious baby was that.

Drugs and a colored girl.

Before she could second-guess her maternal instinct, Linda took out her cell phone and called up the video Ebony had sent her. She stood there with her thumb hovering over the DELETE button, but she couldn't bring herself to press it. Not yet. That video was probably the final image of her son alive on earth. She dropped the pill bottle and covered her eyes with her left hand, and the sob that came from her throat sounded as though it had been ripped out with a hook.

CHAPTER 63

BOBBY WHITE HAD never seen the top-floor suite of the Donnelly Oil Building, and he found it more impressive than expected. He'd assumed he would find the dark paneling and heavy furniture suited to a Mississippi oil company built in the 1970s, by a man now in his eighties. What greeted him instead was a twenty-first-century conference room renovated by a second wife who had not only design sense, but also political aspirations and an unlimited budget. The five present members of the Poker Club sat around an enormous Brazilian mahogany table, while Sheriff Buck Tarlton stood at a lectern in front of three large LCD monitors and two whiteboards that slid out from behind mahogany screens. The monitors displayed live news feeds of the action on the bluff one block away—some of which they could have seen by simply walking out to the spacious terrace seven floors above the ground. One whiteboard was covered with a diagram of the city's board of aldermen, coded with political affiliations, race, and several other items noted beside each name. The other was blank.

Tenisaw County's red-faced sheriff had momentarily terrified the group by landing his chopper on the roof, but Bobby knew amateur theatrics when he saw them. He'd kept his head down and listened as if he were actually interested in Buck Tarlton's plan to "counter Black unrest" in the wake of Mayor Berry's "unfortunate death." Bobby sat quietly at the farthest end of the table from Tarlton, trying to give the man space. He felt like a relief pitcher ordered to the mound in a game rapidly sliding out of control, and the Poker Club members had welcomed him that way upon arrival. Claude Buckman, Junior, the banker, had given him an unusually warm handshake. Tommy Russo, the casino owner, had squeezed his arm and let out a sigh of relief, while Wyatt Cash had slapped his back like an old teammate. Arthur Pine, the club's longtime consigliere, had simply given him a knowing look, but that was enough. It signaled a critical transfer of responsibility. Buck Tarlton, on the other hand, looked exactly like a failing pitcher about to be yanked from the mound in front of millions. Hapless. Frustrated. Put-upon. Furious.

"What history tells us," Tarlton was saying, "is that you have to get on top of these things *quick*. Once you lose the initiative, you never get it back. You have to react aggressively right from the beginning, to even the smallest displays of defiance, so the crowd knows who's boss. This is primal psychology when it comes down to it. And General Pike has some sense of that, thank goodness. Despite his last failure of nerve during that standoff earlier."

Dixie Donnelly looked back at Bobby and rolled her eyes.

"Where's General Pike now?" Claude Buckman asked.

"In his mobile command post," Tarlton said. "They've set up on the bluff side of the intersection of Battery Row and State Street."

Three-way intersection terminating at the bluff, Bobby noted.

"What kind of 'aggressive steps' are you talking about?" Arthur Pine asked in a worried tone. "Forty-five minutes ago, you and General Pike came within seconds of setting this state back fifty years in the public mind."

Tarlton's effort to restrain his temper showed as he leaned over the lectern. "Well, Lawyer Pine, I've had the city Wi-Fi switched off down in the bluff area. In recent years radicals who organize these types of demonstrations have tended to exploit the internet and social media to coordinate their movements. So we put a stop to that right away."

"Is that legal?" asked Buckman.

"Probably," said Pine. "Under the state of emergency. Wireless internet is a city-provided service for tourists, but if the sheriff deems it a threat to public order, I suppose he can terminate it. Like shutting off water or power to the house of a drug dealer."

"Speaking of water, we're shutting off the public fountains and spigots over the entire bluff. If this crowd has nothing to drink, they're going to get tired of this misbehavior mighty quick."

Everyone around the table shared uncomfortable looks.

"There are children in that crowd," Wyatt Cash pointed out. "Infants, even. I'm not sure we want to be seen depriving them of water. Or sanitation, which I assume would also be affected."

Tarlton shrugged. "Whatever danger exists down there, they're responsible for it. This is hardball, folks. These sons of bitches burned my house!"

More shared looks, even less confidence. "You don't know that," Pine said mildly. "Do you have any evidence?"

Tarlton's cheeks darkened from red to purple. "I've got security film!"

"Of masked men on motorcycles."

"Wearing Barlow militia colors," Bobby cut in.

"I'll have more within the hour," Tarlton said through gritted teeth. "I need to get back on duty. There's a lot of moving parts to this situation."

The Poker Club members looked uneasily at each other.

Tarlton hitched up his belt and took a deep breath. He was clearly unused to being the focus of scrutiny. Bobby had seen the same attitude in military officers accustomed to instant obedience.

"Now that Deputy LeJay is in Bienville Police custody," said Buckman, "and Marshall McEwan is livestreaming coverage from inside the station, the protesters know that you released LeJay almost immediately after he killed Mayor Berry."

"Not a good look," said Wyatt Cash. "I wish you'd have consulted us before you did that."

Tarlton's face tightened, and Bobby could tell he was ready to tell these civilians to go to hell. But he couldn't, of course. They had put him in office, and they could remove him almost as easily.

"Bobby? Are you with us?" Claude Buckman, the banker, was speaking to him.

"Sir?"

"What do you think about the situation with Deputy LeJay?"

Bobby shifted in his seat, but he finally looked Tarlton in the eye and refused him quarter. "Sheriff, I can't imagine you would have released LeJay unless he held something over you. You're no fool. You're in the middle of the fallout over Mission Hill. You know a federal investigation's coming. I'm assuming you tried to hold LeJay, and he told you to fuck off. He walked out meaning to drive straight home to Amite County. Now, why would you let him do that?"

Buck Tarlton shifted his weight from foot to foot like a four-year-old caught in a lie. "The only power I had over Kenneth LeJay was that I deputized him for auxiliary service this morning. His superior officer is Coy Johnson. And Sheriff Johnson ordered Ken to get back to the barn in Liberty."

"You could have arrested him," Bobby pointed out.

Tarlton's eyes bugged. "Arrest a man I deputized, and who carried out a justified shooting?"

"He shot an unarmed seventy-four-year-old physician," Tommy Russo clarified. "A doctor attempting to save a boy's life. You're going to have a hell of a time selling that as justified."

"They're canonizing Doc Berry online as we speak," said Arthur Pine. "After you basically blamed the mayor for his own death—implying it was some sort of homosexual rape, or child abuse—Kendrick Washington has been interviewing people about their memories of Doc, then blasting them out on the internet, where he has *millions* of followers. Penn Cage's daughter is filming the clips. I saw her in a few frames."

Tarlton shook his head in barely contained rage. "I should have shot that uppity son of a bitch at Mission Hill!"

"I hate to say it," said Russo, "but we'd all be better off if you had."

"I'll get another chance soon enough. That pothead will be down at the police station with his slave chains on before you can say Louis Farrakhan. He'll be calling for LeJay's execution."

Everyone in the room except Bobby sat up with a jerk. Bobby felt only the sense of deceleration that he always did when engaging with a crisis.

In a neutral voice, Arthur Pine said, "Bobby, I'd like to hear your thoughts on this jurisdictional standoff. Also how to handle the situation brewing on the bluff."

"Listen," Tarlton said sharply. "Y'all can talk till you're blue in the face up in this tower. I don't have time to listen to a *radio host* give amateur assessments on a real-world crisis. He's got no authority in this county, and no law-enforcement experience. He served in Afghanistan? So what. So did thirteen deputies on my force. I need to get back to my men."

As Tarlton moved to leave the podium, Claude Buckman said softly, "Stay just a minute more, Buck. If you don't mind."

The banker's words might as well have been a papal edict. Tarlton remained at the podium. He even looked at Bobby to see whether he should vacate it.

Bobby decided to speak from his seat. "Could somebody bring up a Google Earth view of the bluff on one of those monitors?"

Dixie Donnelly leaned over a small laptop computer and made it happen. The first thing that became obvious was the great brown river dominating the screen. Dixie had oriented the image so that the river bisected it horizontally—Louisiana above, Mississippi below—making it appear to flow east to west, while the westernmost blocks of downtown Bienville— the bluff area and the nearest streets—occupied the lower two thirds of the big screen.

"Thank you," Bobby said, keeping his voice even. "We're all familiar with the geography. Let's look at where we stand from a strategic perspective. We have eight proper blocks facing Battery Row at the bluff. That's roughly a thousand meters. Across Battery Row we have public green space. At its widest points it's less than a hundred meters wide, at its narrowest, only twenty feet deep. For all its length, that land ends in a cyclone fence and a two-hundred-foot drop to the riverbank—which is mostly trees or anti-erosion rock. Riprap. That's a confined, inherently dangerous environment. Nevertheless, it will hold a crowd of considerable size."

"How many people?" asked Wyatt Cash. "Five thousand?"

"Ten," said Sheriff Tarlton.

"It could easily hold twenty thousand," Bobby told them. "Even thirty. Thankfully, we don't have twenty thousand Black people in Tenisaw County. But that could change by tomorrow, if you handle this wrong."

This prospect clearly rattled the group.

Tommy Russo said, "I've seen talk on social media about people driving in here from all over to get into this scrap. From New Orleans gang-bangers to militia groups from Shreveport and Beaumont, all headed here in convoys."

"Christ," said Dixie. "That's the *last* thing we need."

"What would you suggest to prevent that eventuality, Bobby?" Buckman asked.

"Restraint. That should be the order of the night."

Tarlton blew hard and rolled his eyes.

"Could you elaborate?" the banker asked, sounding more than a little skeptical.

"Don't think about first steps," Bobby advised. "Think about where you want this thing to end up."

His audience shrugged as if unable to visualize a positive outcome to the present crisis. Bobby looked from face to face and spoke with authority.

"You want tonight to end with the whole world seeing this crowd as a bunch of crazed looters. Anarchists. A mob. You want the Fox News audience to see Tenisaw County's leaders—and the Bienville city worthies, of course—as models of good-faith negotiation. Hell, you want the MSNBC audience to see that. You want to be viewed as having bent over backward to hear these people's concerns and resolve their issues. But all to no avail. You know why? *Because they can't be reasoned with.*"

"How do we accomplish that?" asked Buckman. "I mean without triggering some sort of slaughter?"

"Easy," Sheriff Tarlton interjected. "These jungle bunnies are spoiling for a fight. Just give 'em what they want."

"They're more grief-stricken than angry," Bobby said. "They believe their mayor was murdered by the state. They believe white leadership will deny that fact and do all they can to protect the guilty."

"The very road Buck has started us down," Buckman said. "No offense, Sheriff. But you need to listen to this."

Tarlton ground his teeth again.

"I'm not sure yet how to handle the issue of Deputy LeJay," Bobby confessed. "That's like a bottle of nitroglycerin left in the sun. But as for the bluff crowd and potential riot . . . I'll tell you how special ops would handle it."

"Enlighten us," said Sheriff Tarlton.

"First, confine the crowd between Battery Row and the fence for the length of the middle six blocks. We do that using natural choke points where the park narrows. Second, the National Guard and state police should use Battery Row for their main troop lines and vehicles, making it easy to keep pedestrians off the pavement. That's a clear line everyone can understand: no pedestrians on pavement. Keep 'em on the grass."

Buckman looked at Tarlton to be sure he was noting this.

"Third, stop jamming cell service on the bluff." Bobby looked hard at Tarlton. "It's illegal for state and local authorities to do it, and if you think the FBI isn't already here investigating you for Mission Hill, you're crazy. They *know* you're jamming the cell service, which means you're already subject to federal charges. So stop. Let these protesters put out whatever they want. Same for Wi-Fi. For the time being, anyway."

"I don't understand your tactics, Bobby," Russo said. "How does any of this help us?"

"What you want," Bobby said, "is viral footage of Black rioters looting this bluff and attacking National Guardsmen who are simply doing their duty. Preferably *white* Guardsmen. You want that flashing around the world nonstop, at the speed of light."

His answer silenced the room. After about twenty seconds, Sheriff Tarlton said, "I'm confused."

Bobby finally stood and walked to the lectern. "If I may, Sheriff."

Tarlton got out of his way and took an empty seat at the table.

Bobby half turned to the Google Earth display. "Within an hour, we'll have five or six thousand protesters up here. By dark that could be seventy-five hundred. We control the lights, the internet, potable water, public sanitation. *Across* Battery Row, we have several commercial structures. The most visible—and most filled with food, drink, and other consumer merchandise—is Cotton Rowe, the indoor shopping center housed in the old cotton brokerage building. One block up from the town houses where Penn Cage lives."

"Why would they loot that shopping center?" asked Pine. "They can't even reach it if the Guard keeps blocking the Row."

Bobby nodded patiently. "Beginning now, we start denying water to everyone on the bluff. But not by switching it off. We need somebody to go out there and covertly rupture a supply pipe. We need a massive leak, but one that can be blamed on the crowd. Sheriff, can you get that done?"

Tarlton nodded. "I'm pretty sure we can do that. Hell, I can blame it on that bear that's runnin' loose."

A few laughs echoed through the room.

"Once everyone's aware of the leak, you can shut off the water. But keep it flowing deeper in town. We express regret, then announce that anyone suffering from thirst or exhaustion can leave the confined area at either end, using gates we'll establish at State Street or Madison. The catch is, once anyone leaves, they won't be re-admitted. We announce that up front. This should empty the space of children over time. But while we're encouraging people to leave voluntarily, we'll leave a gap in our fencing on the *south* end of Battery Row, where it's darkest. We'll get a steady stream of newcomers—mostly troublemakers—sneaking in from that side."

A few people around the table looked puzzled. But Tommy Russo seemed to have an instinct for where Bobby was going.

"Once the crowd gets thirsty and tired enough," Bobby told them, "something's going to go wrong. We can't predict what, so we'll have to play close attention and be ready. But once it happens, General Pike will move his boundary line one block deeper into the city. He'll tell the media he doesn't want to risk anyone being driven over the edge of the bluff in a panic. At that point, the crowd will wash up against those locked commercial buildings like a storm surge."

Now the group had it.

"First they'll open the hose pipes for water. But their second move will be to loot those stores of food and anything drinkable. There's plenty of alcohol in the bars in Cotton Rowe, by the way. If we're lucky, the crowd'll loot some retail merchandise as well, but that's not critical. Just good optics. Either way, we'll have live footage of a Black crowd that assembled in the name of protest but ended up looting a bunch of bars and stores—*like they always do*. You with me?"

"I love it," said Dixie. "It's perfect."

"So obvious we won't even have to say anything," Buckman said with relish.

"I see one problem," said Arthur Pine. "This crowd *did* assemble out of a desire to protest. They *are* grief-stricken. What if they *don't* loot the stores?"

Bobby took in every face around the table. "We're going to make sure they do."

"How?" asked Wyatt Cash.

Bobby turned to Sheriff Tarlton. "I'm guessing you know a lot of convicts, Sheriff. Local and state? Jailhouse trusties?"

Tarlton could sense that his particular expertise was needed, and he liked that. "That's a fact."

"I'm thinking you know the type that's willing to do damn near anything for a price? Informant types, I'm talking about?"

"No shortage of lowlifes in my world."

"I'm guessing guys like that wouldn't have any moral objection to picking up a park bench and smashing down a door with it?"

Tarlton was grinning. "That'd be the *least* criminal thing they've ever done, the skells I'm thinking of."

"We don't need more than two men for that job. If the looting doesn't begin spontaneously, they'll be the trigger. There's a metal bench right by the entrance to Cotton Rowe."

"That seems like a weakness in an otherwise sound strategy," Arthur Pine noted. "If those guys were ever to talk, I mean. And if all this happens on camera, we have to assume they will eventually be located. Just like the January 6 rioters."

Tommy Russo leaned forward. "They can't be located."

When no one made any comment, the casino owner shrugged. "I'll say it, if nobody else will." He looked at Sheriff Tarlton. "That's a risk we can't afford to take. I assume you'll choose those two accordingly?"

Tarlton looked around the table, but no one other than Bobby met his gaze. The sheriff got to his feet. "Anybody have anything else before I go?"

Nobody seemed to.

"One last thing, Sheriff," Bobby said. "Make sure that while we implement this strategy, the National Guard, the state police, and your department go out of their way to discipline any white troublemakers who make it onto the bluff. I'm talking about Barlow's militia, the Sons of Confederate Veterans, even drunk teenagers. Somebody sucker-punches a Black protester? Crack their head. Somebody throws a rock or a bottle? Arrest them. The network cameras will capture all that, and we'll get an exponential positive effect. Got it?"

Tarlton clearly didn't relish this idea, but he saw which way the wind was blowing. "Will do. Who's going to brief General Pike?"

"The governor," Dixie said. "Once we're all on the same page, he'll let Pike know he needs to take his marching orders from up here."

"Any questions, Sheriff?" Claude Buckman asked.

"What about Chief Morgan holding Deputy LeJay in the police station? He keeps that up, Sheriff Johnson's really might bring half his department from Amite County to bust him out."

"*That* cannot happen," Bobby said firmly. "The governor must make sure Sheriff Johnson knows that."

"Noted," Buckman said. "But Buck raises an important point."

"The city board is moving toward dissolution, correct?" Bobby asked. "If they dissolve the city, then Chief Morgan loses all authority to hold LeJay. The problem resolves itself."

"Last I heard," Dixie said uncomfortably, "they're in executive session and it's getting ugly in there. Cicely Waite's causing some unexpected problems."

"That's a damn late conversion," Pine remarked.

The banker gave his attorney a pained look. "Just assume you'll have city police to contend with tonight, Buck, one way or another. But take your cues from Bobby. Restraint. Right?"

Tarlton sighed as though the matter might be beyond his control. "Since Mission Hill, there's a lot of bad blood between those cops and my men. After Doc's death . . . it's going to be worse."

"Until you take back legal control of the city," Bobby said, "there's only one way to handle this—with kid gloves. Are we clear?"

Tarlton nodded without a word.

"Well, that's a blessing," Buckman said. "Again, I'm sorry about your house. You're insured, right?"

Tarlton muttered something and made for the door. He lifted his hand in farewell just before he exited, but there was no eye contact, and it left an awkward feeling around the table. The atmosphere eased a little after he was gone, but not much. It was Russo who voiced a common concern.

"Who the fuck would have the nerve to blow up the sheriff's house?"

Dixie shook her heavily sprayed head. "Nobody but radicals, Tommy. Black radicals. The damned Bastard Sons, whoever they are."

Arthur Pine was nodding. "I have to agree. I can't even imagine any other suspects."

"Bobby?" said Buckman. "What do you think?"

"I don't much care, honestly. In all candor, I'm afraid Deputy LeJay murdered Doc Berry on someone's order. I'm not sure it was premeditated . . . but there's no way that was a righteous shooting. I was against dissolving the city before, but I've changed my mind. You'd better get it done, and fast. Because if you don't, you could have cops killing cops by suppertime, and it'll dwarf whatever happens on the bluff. You won't be the good guys."

Buckman glared at Dixie, who got the message and immediately began texting on her phone. "We'll do it, Bobby. Thanks for coming up to consult on such short notice. I don't want our town coming off as some sort of repressive, police-state reincarnation of 1950s Mississippi. We'll leave that to Texas and Florida. When people hear 'Bienville,' I want them to think of the first thirty minutes of *Gone with the Wind* and our two-billion-dollar paper mill."

"They will," Bobby assured him. "I can't afford to have voters think of it any other way."

"Lucky for us," said Dixie, taking a sip from her sweating cocktail glass. She got up and smiled like a paid hostess, but Bobby saw a glint meant just for him. "What's your pleasure, Bobby? There's a bar in the next room. Let me fix you something."

"Hendrick's and tonic."

Tommy Russo walked over and shook Bobby's hand. "You want to walk out on the terrace and see that crowd for real? It's so close you can smell it, man. Like being at a college football game."

"Alcorn versus Jackson State," cracked Wyatt Cash.

"Probably better if the choppers don't film me standing out there."

Russo thought about this, then gave a conspiratorial wink.

Bobby started to follow Dixie into the next room, but Russo caught him gently by the arm and spoke in his ear. "I don't know if Tarlton said anything to you, but he's following up on that Charlot Dufort thing."

A squirt of adrenaline perked Bobby up. "He told me he has some security video of your assistant dropping Dufort off downtown last night. But that's nothing to worry about, I'm sure."

Russo gave him a suggestive look. "I think Buck may have something else on your boy, though. I only mention it because I'm looking out for you. Nobody gives a shit if Charlot Dufort is dead or alive. Except maybe me, who he stiffed for real money. Tarlton sure doesn't care. For him, the whole thing only has one value—potential leverage over you. So be careful."

"I hear you, Tommy. Thanks."

"Any time, brother. And I like your plan."

Bobby followed Dixie into the next room, which turned out to be a kitchen that also served the luxury apartment beyond the conference room.

"You impressed the hell out of them in there," Dixie said, handing him a glass. "I know this group's small-time compared to—"

"Tell me about Elijah Keyes," Bobby cut in. "The Black alderman.

What kind of pressure are you guys applying to make him vote to dissolve the city? Must be pretty serious to make him even consider that."

Dixie smiled to herself. "I thought you didn't want to know this kind of thing."

"I do now."

Dixie took a big sip of bourbon and swayed as though dancing. "Elijah has a sister in Dothan, Alabama. Her daughter got drunk and hit a pedestrian with her Hyundai. Could be anything from manslaughter to vehicular homicide. Real prison time. Sad situation."

"And you know the judge."

"The DA. He went to law school with Avery Sumner, one of our retired circuit judges. One of our members, Avery is."

Bobby shook his head. "Let me guess. Ole Miss? Alabama?"

"Neither. Yale."

"Wonders never cease."

This is how it's always worked down here, Bobby thought. *Everywhere, really, if you're on the inside of things.* Since he knew a certain subject would eventually come up, he decided to broach it himself. "I thought you said your daughter was flying in tonight."

Dixie let her pride show. "Oh, she did." Dixie lifted a graceful hand and motioned toward the apartment door. "Jenna Kay's right through there, freshening up. I didn't want to interrupt the meeting."

"I'll speak to her in a bit. But let's keep her out of the war room."

"No rush, sweetie. She's got work to catch up on."

Dixie moved closer to him, close enough that he could smell the bourbon on her breath. "Jenna's a looker, Bobby. But with class. And smart like her mama." She squeezed his wrist. "Tell me your biggest worry about tonight. While it's just us. What's the biggest risk?"

"Mass-casualty event. One runaway truck could kill dozens. One semiautomatic rifle could kill hundreds. One IED could turn Confederate Park into a slaughterhouse, and we still don't know who's setting those damned fires."

His brief answers wiped the smile from her face. "Well, then. Let's just hope the Bastard Sons really are Black."

"The biggest liability is that police station," Bobby went on. "Tarlton lost his mind over his house being burned. He *wants* to storm that station. And I'm not sure he'll listen to anyone telling him not to. Not even the governor."

Dixie had gone still. "Can you keep a secret?"

"Get real, Dix. What is it?"

Her eyes twinkled. "I've got a connection inside the police station."

Bobby felt a fillip of excitement. "A mole?"

Dixie held up her right forefinger and wiggled it back and forth. "Let's just leave it at that for now. See which way this thing rolls. But we're not as blind as everyone thinks."

"Good girl. Keep me apprised."

"Don't worry, sweetie. You're the horse I'm betting on."

CHAPTER 64

ONCE WE MADE it back to the town house, Annie and I decided to invite Nadine out to the burial with us. Neither of us felt right leaving her in town with things so unsettled. To our surprise, we all felt hungry after the confrontation on the bluff, so we stopped off at Constant Reader, Nadine's bookstore, to get some sandwiches to eat on the way out to Pencarrow.

Annie and I wait in the front of the store while Nadine gets the food and drinks from a refrigerator in back. The interior of Constant Reader is one of the most welcoming and intimate public spaces in all of Bienville. For a writer it's akin to Eden, a place you'd like to sit and write your next novel while being ferried coffee and muffins from its exquisite little café. My favorite spot is the large round banquette Nadine uses for author events, elevated two steps above the main floor. The walls above and behind it are covered with signed photographs of Southern authors and musicians who have appeared here, or whom Nadine befriended while she lived in North Carolina.

Some are old friends, others merely acquaintances, while others I only wish I'd met before they died. Rick Bragg and Pat Conroy hang side by side, with Eudora and Faulkner beneath. Above them hang Donna Tartt and Jesmyn Ward, along with Jimmy Buffett, Angie Thomas, Truman Capote, Larry Brown, and Michael Farris Smith. Blues legends Sam Chatmon and Son Thomas are here, wearing sober suits, while to my left is a brilliant tinted photo of the young Jerry Lee Lewis and Elvis standing backstage somewhere in their 1950s duds. The *Louisiana Hayride*, maybe?

"Is it really going to be just us out there?" I ask, feeling guilty that Annie made all the arrangements for Mom's burial.

"I don't know for sure," Annie replies. "I wouldn't be surprised to see a few of her closest friends find their way out there. Would you be okay with that?"

"I am if you are."

Nadine comes through the double doors at the back of the store and holds a large paper bag high. "Muffulettas," she says. "You guys okay with that? I made the olive salad myself."

"Sounds great," Annie says. "Let's get going."

OUTSIDE, ANNIE ASKS to drive, but for some reason I insist on taking the wheel. The idea of eating in the passenger seat while we roll toward my mother's open grave feels strange. Somehow, driving makes it seem less awkward. Nadine insists that Annie sit beside me, supposedly since she's the taller of the two (by an inch or two, at most).

"So, Annie," Nadine says, as I point the Audi toward the south edge of town. "We've got your dad captive for twenty minutes. I've been trying to get him to read your grandmother's work. He's resisted pretty hard, but he's got to read Romulus's personal statement, right?"

"Oh, God. You should read it *tonight*, Dad."

"I'll take a look, I promise. So long as we don't have any more firebombs. Or Kent State reenactments."

"More like Jackson State," Nadine corrects me. "But before you do, you need to get caught up on what happened after Captain Pencarrow died. You read the chapter about the duel, but not what happened after. How about Annie and I tell you now, while you can't run away?"

"Perfect," Annie says.

"Yeah, perfect," I mutter.

"You'll thank us later," Annie says.

"What's this personal statement you keep bringing up?"

"It's a sort of an oral history record taken down by a grandson of Romulus Pencarrow in 1934."

"Like a WPA interview?"

Nadine shakes her head vehemently. "No. Romulus actually did a WPA interview in 1932, and it's fairly well known. But he did a lot of self-censoring of that story when he told it, and of course it was edited and distorted by both Mississippi and D.C. officials before it ever saw print."

"So what are you referring to?"

"A first-person account, completely unedited. As close as you can get to unfiltered truth. Filled with things Romulus felt he had to hide all his life. He was in his nineties when he dictated it to his grandson, who persuaded him that his story should be preserved for posterity. And all of it, in one way or another, leads to you eventually being born."

A faint tingle goes through my chest. "This is the Romulus who swam out to the Union gunboat?"

"Yes. But before you read any of that, you need to understand the basics of the public story—by that, I mean what your mother's family grew up believing. Because the real story behind that one is . . . pretty hard to process."

"That's some buildup."

In the rearview mirror, I see Nadine give a solemn nod. "At the core . . . it transcends almost anything I've read in terms of personal sacrifice."

"Well," I say, taking a bite from the quarter of muffuletta that Annie holds up to my mouth, "you've only got a few minutes."

Nadine begins her tale like a litigating partner laying out a brief for a junior associate, and like Martine Boucher, she's an efficient storyteller.

"Ground zero: you grew up believing you were descended from an unmarried Acadian refugee woman named Helen Soileau who lived on Pencarrow Plantation. Your male ancestor, you've always believed, was Duncan Pencarrow, the white son of Captain Robert Pencarrow. Correct?"

"Right. Illegitimate from the beginning. Are you about to tell me different?"

"Yes. But please keep one thing in mind. I'm giving you the barest pencil sketch of these people. Your mother captured them in remarkable depth, and all this involves the complex issues surrounding a prewar cotton plantation. But for now . . . let's just focus on the relationships."

I open my mouth, signaling Annie to give me another bite. "Curtain's up. Go."

Nadine grimaces, resentful at being hurried. "Robert Pencarrow was the younger son of James Pencarrow, a hard, sober Scot and the founder of the plantation you now own. While Robert was off in Florida fighting the Seminole Wars, his elder brother—James Junior—died of fever, as did his mother, a Scottish girl from a rich Natchez family, who'd educated her slaves to read scripture. The patriarch survived the fever, but much diminished. James Senior was kept upstairs in the mansion, with powers of ownership but little else. Got it?"

"I think so."

"The fortunes of the plantation had flagged in Robert's absence, so his father effectively demanded that he marry another Natchez girl to save their financial fortunes. Against his personal desires, Robert agreed. He then fathered two sets of children by two different mothers, one white, the other Black."

"I read Mom's story of the duel last night, remember? So some of this I got from that."

"Good. But it gets more complicated. The first two Pencarrow children—the fully white ones—were the captain's legal heirs, Duncan and Evelyn. The third and fourth were fathered on the woman Robert really loved, an enslaved woman named Calliope. Calliope was two years younger than Robert, and they'd been raised together since childhood.

Calliope's surviving children were Romulus—the now-famous Black soldier and scout—and his younger sister Niobe. Niobe was by all accounts the favorite of the four in her father's eyes. Blessed, golden, beautiful—magical even. The four children were born in four successive years and were effectively raised together in a place where the normal Southern rules didn't apply."

"What do you mean?"

"Like all large plantations, Pencarrow was a world unto itself. Life there reflected the personality of the man who ran it, which was now Captain Robert. In his case, the rules about enslaved women were different, meaning that they could come and go without fear of being molested by any white man who happened to take a fancy to them."

My mind is swirling with what I remember of Mom's duel story in my exhausted state. "Okay, go on."

"Their childhood was unique, I'd say, given the era. The captain's half-Black children were educated better than the other slaves, who'd been taught to read only the Bible, if they chose. And since they got extra rations for doing so, you can imagine a crowded slave school. A Reverend Henry Calvert taught these classes, as he had done with Mrs. Pencarrow when she was alive, as well as running the Gothic chapel she'd built back by what's now your catfish pond."

That hewn-stone chapel still stands, a building of such beauty that it draws students and tourists from across the country.

"After Mrs. Pencarrow died, Calvert stayed on for several years, only leaving late in the war. By the way, it was Calvert who ended up being the white ancestor of Deborah Fannin, who started your mother on this whole long quest. But by a different slave woman."

"Father Calvert slept with an enslaved woman?"

"More than one, from what I can tell so far."

"Well, well. Things never change, do they?"

Nadine gives me an unsettling look. "The important thing is the relationship between the children. Three out of the four loved each other. But the white daughter, Evelyn, guarded her mother's ghost with jealous rage. She hated Calliope because her father had truly loved her and not his wife. And Evelyn hated Niobe even more, for being the captain's favorite. In the end, this would cause unimaginable misery."

This surprises me not at all, given my experience with human nature.

"Niobe was at the root of the duel with the Barlows that you read about."

"I remember," I reply, trying to keep my mouth closed as I chew my sandwich. "Romulus killed the overseer in the act of rape, his white brother claimed he'd done it—to protect him—but the dead overseer had been a friend of the Barlows, and the fallout eventually led to the duel, which Captain Pencarrow barely won."

Nadine smiles. "You get a star from teacher."

"Tell me this: Did you find out anything else about the mass lynchings since we spoke this morning?"

"Let's not get sidetracked, okay? But Peggy did uncover some information about Jupiter, the mystery slave who escaped being hanged during the lynchings. I'll tell you this much: Jupiter did something so ruthless during those lynchings that it earned him Romulus's anger for life, and even I haven't yet come to the part of the story where that gets resolved—if it ever does."

"All right. Let's move chronologically from now, if you can."

Nadine gathers herself like the veteran courtroom attorney she is. "What matters for us is the Pencarrow household. In spite of what people feared early on, it took quite a while for the war to get to southern Mississippi. Local planters or their sons raised regiments and rode off with plumes and family muskets, but around here, things pretty much went on as before."

"So who remained in the Pencarrow household?"

"The old patriarch, stubbornly clinging to life on the upper floor. Captain Pencarrow himself, but by '61 he was deathly ill and sinking steadily from National Hotel disease, as portrayed in the duel story. Calliope effectively ran the plantation, along with Cadmus, the butler. Cadmus had considerable business acumen, as he would prove after gaining his freedom and taking up residence in town with his own slaves."

"He seems to have had a lot in common with William Johnson, the Barber of Natchez."

"Yes and no. You'll get to that in Romulus's record."

I roll my hand forward, urging her on.

"In 1861 the Pencarrow children covered the span from Duncan, twenty, to Evelyn, nineteen, to Romulus, eighteen, to Niobe, the baby at seventeen."

"How old was Captain Pencarrow at this time?"

"He probably looked like an old man, but he was only forty-three. Calliope was forty-one."

"Okay."

"From what your mother divined, some of the final discussions between Pencarrow and Calliope before his death involved the fate of the plantation's slaves. The captain was anxious to free his mistress and their children, but Calliope was related to at least thirty people on the place, and she wanted them *all* emancipated. The problem was, the State of Mississippi had gone to great lengths in the final pre-war years to make manumission as difficult as possible. They didn't want a lot of free Blacks running loose. So where a few years earlier, a planter could simply have freed his slaves in his will, that was no longer possible. You had to physically travel to a free state with those slaves and manumit them on that ground. As ill as Captain Pencarrow was, that simply wasn't practical. A slave could be freed by special act of the Mississippi legislature, and Pencarrow wrote several letters in that cause for Calliope, but no one came through for him. War paranoia had taken over."

A chilling possibility strikes me. "Don't tell me that when Pencarrow died . . ."

Nadine nods, her face a shade paler than before. "His white children inherited his Black ones."

His white children inherited his Black ones. The horror contained in that statement is difficult to quantify. Remembering the characterization of Evelyn from the duel story, a chill of foreboding goes through me.

"The captain didn't last two weeks after he killed Frank Barlow," Nadine goes on. "He died a couple of days after Christmas, 1861."

"Why hadn't he freed his children in an earlier period, when it was simpler?"

"Because *he didn't actually own them.* His father did. And the old Scot didn't hold with giving away 'valuable property that couldn't take care of itself.'"

"What a guy."

"Exemplary Christian of the period," Nadine says under her breath. "And he outlived his son by quite some time. Anyway, given what I told you about Evelyn Pencarrow's emotional issues, you can imagine how terrifying it must have been for the other children when their father finally passed. The enslaved children were thrown onto the mercy of a sister who hated them. And once Pencarrow was dead, Evelyn began a campaign to take over the plantation from what she viewed as her weaker brother."

"Was Duncan weaker than his sister?"

"In most ways, yes. But Duncan genuinely loved his Black siblings. He always had. He treated them as if they were white, and loved playing public pranks with them growing up. He rode through the streets of stuffy old Natchez in a carriage sitting like a suitor beside Niobe, who was dressed as a white heiress, with Romulus driving them."

I can't help but smile. "That's the kind of thing you don't think about happening back then ... but surely must have. Kids being kids."

"In Natchez, anyway. Everyone for miles around always claimed the Natchez planters 'spoiled' their slaves, especially the house servants. Now, as the war got going farther north, planters around here grew contraband cotton to keep food in their mouths and cash flowing into their bank accounts. Evelyn worked relentlessly to make herself queen of this operation. She tried to shame her brother into raising a regiment and going off to fight, but Duncan refused to leave home. He was no true Confederate. But even with him there, Evelyn lost no opportunity to harass Calliope and her children. Duncan soon realized that if those two were going to survive the war, he'd have to get them away from her somehow."

"Romulus found his escape by swimming out to that gunboat. Right?"

"Not before doing all he could to ensure the safety of his mother and sister."

"How did he do that?"

"With help. Duncan and Romulus had promised their father they would safeguard Calliope and Niobe. By mid-1862, the war was heating up down here. By April, the battles of Shiloh and Corinth were over, which is basically north Mississippi. Three weeks later, Admiral Farragut captured New Orleans. He took Baton Rouge on May 8, and Natchez four days later. The Union didn't occupy the city at that time, but Yankee conquest was obviously coming. As a fighting-age white man, Duncan realized he'd have to leave soon or else be branded a turncoat. Worse yet, as the months went on, Evelyn blackmailed him. Told him that if he didn't go north and fight, she would expose Romulus as the killer of Overseer Book."

"God, she was cold."

Nadine nodded. "Evelyn was corresponding with a Mississippi officer named Nathaniel Harris about her brother. Harris had begun in the Warren Rifles, but after Antietam he was promoted to Lieutenant-Colonel. Evelyn was hell-bent on Duncan finding glory or an early grave."

"And revenge on Niobe," Annie added.

"So what did Duncan and Romulus do?"

"They enlisted the help of Cadmus, the butler, and Father Calvert to get Calliope, Niobe, and a few other endangered people to safety in the North."

"Why them?"

"Cadmus apparently had contacts in the Underground Railroad, which had ceased most of its activities by then, but he'd gotten people out before. And Father Calvert had the signs and symbols of authority required to help them create a legal cover that could protect refugees while traveling."

"Who were the other endangered people you mentioned?"

Nadine gives me an enigmatic smile. "The woman you've always believed you were descended from."

"The Creole woman, Helen Soileau?"

"Yes. She'd arrived in Bienville an impoverished war widow, close to starving, and Duncan had brought her home like a lost kitten. He grew to love her, in his way, and she'd delivered a child. But your mother long ago stopped believing that Duncan Pencarrow ever fathered that child. She thinks Duncan was homosexual, and that Soileau was likely pregnant when she showed up in Bienville."

I lean toward Annie and swallow the last bite of muffuletta, then look back at Nadine in the rearview. "So *this* is where the link with my old origin story breaks?"

"Yes. And your mother was fine with it."

"Well, hell." I look at my watch again. "You've got ten minutes left. Let's hear the rest."

"Not the rest. Just the setup. You're going to read Romulus's words for yourself."

"The rest of the prologue, then."

"Ultimately, it took most of a year to set up the escape. The arrangement that Duncan and Romulus made worked this way: Cadmus arranged for a contraband cotton boat going upriver to stop south of Natchez and pick up the Pencarrow refugees in a wagon at an old Underground Railroad dock. From there, they'd be given safe, though expensive, passage north."

"In the middle of the river war?"

"Contraband cotton was a cargo exploited by both sides throughout the war. It was too profitable to stop. The real challenge was the overland passage, where that wagon could run into anybody on the road. Slave catchers, Natchez Trace outlaws, quasi-military raiders, or patrols paid by either side. Even legitimate troops. They needed the most bulletproof cover they could get. And that's where Father Calvert came in."

"What did he come up with?"

"A pretty good plan. He had a personal incentive, after all."

She has me hooked. "Go on."

"To be truly safe, Niobe had to travel as a white woman, which physically she had no trouble doing. The simplest way to support this fiction was for her to travel under Helen Soileau's legal papers."

The simplicity of this hits me like a cool breath of wind. "But what would persuade Helen Soileau to let her do that? How would Helen travel herself?"

"As Duncan Pencarrow's wife."

"Whoa. For real, or just as a cover story?"

"Duncan legally married Helen Soileau one day before the escape wagon left the plantation. The trick was, she did it under the name of Elodie, a sister of hers who had died as a child. This marriage legitimized the baby she'd had while at Pencarrow, which probably meant the world to her. So, through this simple exchange of papers, facilitated by a little quasi-legal, ecclesiastical forgery, Niobe became white—"

"And that wagon became the means of a wealthy Southern planter protecting his white wife and mistress from the encroaching Yankees, while he departed to join the Confederate forces fighting in Virginia?"

"Exactly. Not something anyone guarding the road would question, so long as he could pocket a bribe in the process. The fact that this wife and mistress were sisters would hardly have turned a head in those circles."

"How did Calliope travel?"

"As Niobe's mammy, of course."

"Holy shit. That's genius. Anybody else with them?"

"One strong male slave named Hector, implicitly trusted by Romulus. They gave Hector a pistol, a bag of money, and the promise of freedom when he reached his destination."

I nod, deeply impressed. "Are you going to tell me Father Calvert's personal incentive?"

"Not yet."

"All right. Where did the evil Evelyn Pencarrow fit into all this? She just stood by and let it happen?"

"So far as Duncan and Romulus knew, she did. After all, it meant finally getting rid of the women she hated, once and for all."

This doesn't quite satisfy me, but my mind is already casting out ahead, trying to see the fates of all concerned. "All I know from my general knowledge of our family background is that Helen Soileau wound up in Quitman Parish, Louisiana, not the North. But I don't know how or when she got there. During the war? Or years afterward? Did that little wagon reach the contraband cotton boat safely and head upriver?"

Nadine sits in pensive silence for a few seconds. "Do you think it did? They had to cover twelve miles, much of it in the dark."

"Well . . . did Romulus and Duncan escort them?"

"No. Everyone left Pencarrow on the same afternoon. Romulus planned to hike west to camp beside the Mississippi, where he'd heard Farragut had gunboats moving between Natchez and New Carthage, just south of Vicksburg. Duncan planned to travel by rail to Virginia, to the bivouac of the Nineteenth Mississippi Infantry Regiment of Colonel Nathaniel Harris. This was shortly before the Battle of Chancellorsville, which would become Duncan's baptism of fire. Duncan and Romulus watched the wagon set off on the river road south, Hector at the reins, and then they departed by different paths."

"Hmm." I accept a plastic cup from Annie and take a long swallow of unsweetened tea. "The more I think about that wagon moving alone on that road, the more success seems like wishful thinking."

Nadine shrugs. "Maybe. But people trusted to thinner threads during the Civil War and survived. Even thrived."

Triggered by so many enticing details, my curiosity swells as I stare into Nadine's eyes in the rearview. "But not usually."

"Calliope was no fool, Penn. If she left in that wagon, she believed it represented their best chance of escape."

"Maybe it was," I allow. "But . . . this group didn't thrive. Did they?"

Nadine sighs, and I sense Annie's gaze upon me. "That depends on how far into the future you look. If you peer forward all the way to Peggy, and then to you, it turned out well. On a shorter time scale . . . their road led straight into hell. A darker hell than you've probably ever imagined. And I say that knowing your history."

As I consider possible outcomes, an unlooked-for epiphany pulls me up short. "Wait a minute. I think I missed the main revelation of this part of the story. *Which* woman in that wagon became my ancestor? Helen Soileau, the Acadian girl who showed up out of nowhere? Or Niobe, the slave who *traveled as Helen Soileau* on that night?"

An inscrutable look takes possession of Nadine's face, hiding whatever she's truly feeling. "Now you're earning your reputation."

"I'm tired of guessing! Tell me!"

Annie shakes her head with a faint smile, recognizing my impatience. "I wish Gram could tell you this story. But Nadine's doing great."

Nadine shifts on the back seat. "You, Penn Cage, are not the direct descendant of Helen Soileau, but of Niobe Pencarrow."

An electric hum has begun in my brain. "Seriously? By what father? For most of our lives, we believed our male ancestor was Niobe's white brother, Duncan."

Nadine shrugs. "As I read this story, I first suspected the father might be the priest, Henry Calvert. He had ready access to all the female slaves on Pencarrow."

"But?"

Nadine starts to continue, then shakes her head. "I'm not going to go any further, Penn. You need to read this part yourself."

Even in my anemic state, I feel myself color in frustration. "Annie already told me we're related by blood to the Barlow family! Can't you just close that loop for me? Was Niobe involved with one of the Barlow ancestors at the time? Was she raped by a Barlow? Something like that?"

Nadine steadily shakes her head. "You won't believe it without reading it in context. That's all I'm going to say. It's almost unbearable, really. The good thing—the thing you should focus on now—is that you, Penn Cage, are directly descended from Captain Robert Pencarrow and Calliope herself. And those two, if you haven't figured it out yet, are some powerful genes to have come from. So . . ." Nadine intertwines her fingers and folds her hands before her. "I think it's probably time we start thinking about Peggy. There was a lot more to her life than this final year of research."

Nadine's refusal to continue frustrates me to the point of anger, but as usual, she's absolutely right.

"I'm not trying to play games with you," she says. "I just think it's best that Romulus carry on the story from here. Maybe after the task force meeting tonight, you can read his dictated record."

"Does Romulus come back into Niobe's story?"

"Oh, yes. In a tragic way. I'll tell you this much, since you know a bit about what he did for Grant's forces during the Vicksburg campaign. After the Yankees broke the siege, in July of '63, Romulus expected to be enlisted as a full-fledged member of the Union army. But he wasn't. As an escaped slave, he was only a civilian scout, technically contraband of war. So, at the suggestion of white officers he'd fought under, he traveled south to Natchez to await the formation of the Fifty-eighth U.S. Colored Infantry, which was being created at the time. And that's how he wound up in a place we know as—"

"The Devil's Punchbowl," I finish with another chill of foreboding. "Human contraband camp."

Nadine nods solemnly, her eyes glinting. "You're hooked now, aren't you?"

There's no denying it.

"Thank God," Annie says.

We've come to the gate of Pencarrow at last. Rolling down my window to punch in the entrance code, I drive through, onto the three-quarter-mile asphalt drive that curves around to the mansion in the distance, standing beyond its reflecting pond. Four hundred yards ahead of us stands the Duel Oak, 110 feet tall, while beneath it waits Dr. Andrew McKinney, a slim, six-foot-tall, bespectacled Black man of twenty-nine. Andrew's leaning on a shovel, pondering what is like a deep hole in the ground. The Clemson-educated historian started life on the north side of Natchez as the child of some of the first Black schoolteachers to work in the white school system there. Now he's a rising star of historic preservation, and he's devoted nearly every hour of the past year to turning Pencarrow Plantation into a transformative site for visitors to learn the true story of slavery in the antebellum South.

"We're only five minutes late," Annie remarks. "Not bad, considering."

"I'm glad not to find a crowd waiting," I say softly.

As I pull through the gate, my iPhone rings. The number is Marshall McEwan's.

"Please don't give me more bad news," I answer.

In a breathless voice the publisher says: "Penn, there's apparently a video of Doc's shooting. It might prove he was murdered. A sixteen-year-old girl named Ebony Swan shot it on her cell phone, and she still has it. Tarlton's deputies have been chasing her all over town. So has some drug dealer who was on the scene before Doc was killed. He was apparently involved in the crime. This girl's got no car, no cash, no credit cards, nothing. She's hiding with her phone shut off. She needs to be picked up, and fast."

I look over at Annie and sigh. "Marshall, I just got out to Pencarrow. We're about to bury my mother. You're going to have to send one of Chief Morgan's people to pick her up."

"Ebony doesn't trust cops. Not even Black ones."

"Great." Annie is giving me a questioning look. "Then send a reporter."

"I've got none to spare. And listen, Ebony knows who you are, because she had to read one of your books in school. She's willing to trust you. There's an abandoned hospital near the Magnolia Heights subdivision—Tenisaw Memorial. It's separated from the neighborhood by a thick screen of forest. She can make it to that parking lot."

Despite being taken aback by McEwan's request, I feel I have to do what I can to bring about justice for Doc's murder. "I know the place, Marshall.

But the soonest I could make it is . . . ninety minutes. There has to be someone else."

"I haven't come up with anyone else I trust."

An interesting notion strikes me. "What about Sophie Dufort?"

"*What?*"

"Seriously. What could draw less attention than a woman picking up a teenage girl?"

"Shit . . . all right. I'll give Sophie a try. But this could be critical evidence, Penn."

"I trust her, Marshall. For this job, anyway."

"Okay, thanks. Later."

I hang up and pull the Audi over beside the Duel Oak, where Andrew stands with a solemn smile of welcome on his face.

"Dad, what was that about?" Annie asks.

"Yeah," says Nadine. "What job are you giving to Sophie Dufort?"

"I'll explain in a minute. Andrew's waiting. Let's do what we came to do."

CHAPTER 65

CHARLOT DUFORT SAT in a rusty metal chair on the porch of a shot-gun shack that had to be a hundred years old, and maybe twice that. In the other chair (there was only room for two on the porch) sat Pearl Brooks, mother of Ruby, the current Dufort family housekeeper. Pearl was ninety-five years old, but she still managed to get around on her walker, and she had a neighbor who rolled her oxygen machine outside in the mornings, then back inside at night. For company Pearl had her old spaniel, Sam, who lay at her feet like he might never get up again.

Charlot himself had felt that way only an hour ago, after Bobby's present lover pulled him from the pool as near as you could be to dead without being so. Finding himself unable to kill another man that way, Corey Evers had used his army training to express the water from Charlot's lungs, then perform CPR until he restarted his breathing. Having gone without air for maybe two minutes, Charlot wondered how many brain cells he'd lost. To his surprise, he felt more like himself now than he had in a long while. And he was glad it was Corey who had made the decision for resurrection. Bobby, he was sure—the Bobby of today—would have let him die.

The view from Pearl's shack was comforting. Still-thick foliage in the woods, barely any red or even yellow among the leaves, what looked like a wagon-rutted road leading into the trees, and a little of Blue-Tail Bayou showing off to the right, where Pearl had a weathered fishing dock she no longer used.

Charlot couldn't help but chuckle at the irony of Corey Evers driving him to the northwestern corner of the county in order to dump him in isolation, when in fact he had driven Charlot to within three miles of the home of one of the women who had raised him. Ruby Brooks had been working for Charles Dufort for nineteen years by the time Charlot was born, but her mother, Pearl, had been with the family since 1943 (having begun work at fifteen), and she stayed another fifteen after Charlot was born. She and Ruby had divided their labor between the old planta-tion houses back then—mostly Tranquility and Belle Rose—but Charlot had been raised by them both, and Pearl had only retired after Charlot's mother was killed in a freak sailboat accident on Lake Bruin (*Bear Lake*, according to *Encyclopaedia Britannica*—Charlot had looked it up as a grief-stricken boy).

He had not liked bears since.

Looking back on his childhood, Charlot believed he wouldn't have made it from fifteen to twenty had Pearl and Ruby not been there to protect him. Today he and Pearl had been sitting together for half an hour, hardly speaking a word, but they didn't need to. He studied the face that felt as close as family, and reflected that Pearl looked just as she had for the past decade, like Cicely Tyson made up to be old in *The Autobiography of Miss Jane Pittman*. More wrinkles on her face than you could count in a week. Like so many maids of her generation, Pearl took snuff, and had since she was thirteen. Even now, she would open her snuff box, take a pinch between her thumb and forefinger, and gently sniff it into her nostrils, enjoying her hit of nicotine as much as Charlot ever had a hit of cocaine. Charlot smiled as she replaced the transparent plastic cannula that ran from the humming oxygen machine that stood like a cheap R2-D2 on the faded boards beside her.

"You in trouble, ain't you baby?" Pearl said at last.

"Not in the best shape I've ever been in," Charlot replied.

"What you need? A place to stay?"

Charlot had never begged physical refuge from his old maid, but this time he actually considered it. "No, Pearlie," he said finally. "I need money. But more than you've got. More than you've ever seen, in fact. I've dug myself a pretty deep hole."

"Gamblin', I'm guessin'?"

"You know me."

"Lord, men and their cards. Lose your house in one evenin' if you don't watch 'em. My husband's brother lost his work truck in one game across the river one time."

"It's easier than you think."

Pearl lowered her right hand and gave droopy-eared Sam a long stroke. "Your daddy ain't gon' bail you out this time?"

"He's written me off, honey. For real this time. Been a long time since he's covered any of my debts. That's how I got in such a deep hole."

"Ruby told me she's worried about you. Sophie, too."

"They can't help me, though." Charlot lifted his right leg and braced his foot against the post. "You know, I didn't head out here on purpose. A man drove me out here to make sure I stayed lost for a few hours."

"What?"

"That's right. But you know, I can't help but wonder if fate didn't send me out to you."

"Fate," the old woman said dismissively. "Anything sent you out here, it was God. You know that."

"Well, maybe. But what I've been wondering about these last few days—can't get it off my mind in fact—is those old cisterns. The ones I found down under the house when I was nine. The 'Yankee bones' Daddy told us about."

"Yankee bones," Pearl muttered. "Yeah. There might be a few Yankee bones under there. Just enough to make up one soldier . . . maybe. But the rest? You don't want to know where them bones came from, and neither do I."

Charlot took a deep breath, then decided to push the old woman. "That's the thing, Pearl. I do want to know. I think it might be important."

"Important how?"

"Well . . . if I knew about some of those bones, I might be able to get Daddy to get me out of this hole. And if I don't—get out of this hole, I mean—you might not see me again. 'Cause the men I owe money to . . . they're not too charitable when it comes to waiting."

"Not many people is," Pearl said. "Boy, don't you axe me about them bones. Not unless you want to hear a rough tale."

A ripple of excitement went through Bobby's chest. "I don't have a choice, Pearl."

"Well, then." Pearl pulled on the cannula and took another hit of snuff, then replaced it and began to speak in a new tone, one that let him know she was speaking of a time long past.

"I must've been about forty when this happened. My mama Ida was, oh, sixty-seven. Ruby was fifteen, I 'member that. Anyhow . . . late one night, the phone rang, and then Mrs. Lily, old Mr. Charles's first wife, come shook me awake and said we was needed."

"Who was?"

"Me and Mama. My husband, too, Jubal. He was working as groundsman at Tranquility back then."

"I remember Jubal. He gave me candy sometimes."

Pearl smiled. "Y'all was a pair for a while. He used to let you ride his lap on that ol' riding mower."

"What year was this?"

"Nineteen sixty-eight. The year Dr. King got shot. And Bobby Kennedy. Charles Evers had come down to Fayette to take Medgar's place. He wasn't mayor yet, but he was runnin' some businesses up there, and not all on the up-and-up, you know. The kind you go to now."

"Okay."

"Anyhow, Mrs. Lily told us we wasn't needed at the house, but somewhere else. Turned out to be Room 305 at the Holiday Inn in Natchez. She told us to bring all our cleaning supplies. Formula 409 and Mr. Clean and such. Peroxide, too, she said. I remember that. Our own rags and brushes and towels, even. So we piled into the old station wagon and Jubal drove us over there. Well, Lord, when we finally got into that room, wasn't nobody there. But the second we walked in, I could smell the blood." Pearl wrinkled her lips in disgust. "It was like *hog-killin' time*, baby. It smelled 'xactly like somebody had killed a hog up in there.

"Well, 'bout that time Mr. Charles's father showed up and told us to clean the place from floor to ceiling. Wasn't none of us saying nothing. But then Mama just asked outright what had happened up in there. Old Mr. Charles said his son had got attacked by some men he was playing bourré with, and knives had come out. At least two got stabbed, he said, but they didn't want no po-lice involved, 'cause they was all drunk, and all at fault. Well, I sensed right then he was lying. Maybe he'd been lied to himself, I don't know. But we spent five or six hours cleaning that room. And before we was done, I was sure that blood hadn't come from no knife fight over a card game. When I was down on the floor, I found two or three little items likely to spill out of a woman's purse if she was rushed—or worse, fighting to protect herself. And when we cleaned the sheets . . . I could see people had been having relations in that bed."

Pearl shook her head at the memory. "Finally, when I come to the place with the most blood, which was like a *puddle* in that old carpet—I still remember the sucking sound it made on my shoes—I knew nobody who'd lost that much blood was still breathing. Now, I don't know what old Mr. Charles done about that puddle. He prob'ly paid off the manager or something. But anyway, we gathered up all them linens and towels and took 'em back to Tranquility. Then Jubal built a big fire out back and we burnt it all. And while we was doin' this, Ruby come outside to see what the commotion was, being middle of the night. We tried to make light of it, you understand, but then Ruby caught sight of that blood, and she *knowed* something was wrong."

"Did you ever find out whose blood it was?"

Pearl sighed heavily. "I believe I did. I think the Lord steered me to the truth. That night haunted me, baby. I knew young Mr. Charles had a temper, and I also knew—don't ask me how—that he sometimes fooled with prostitutes and such. He liked slummin', as they call it, or used to anyway. And around that time—a few weeks later—I heard a young girl had dis-

appeared from Jefferson County. That's Fayette, you know, and she never
had turned up. Not her dead body, and not living with relatives in California or Chicago or something like that. I had already told Jubal it didn't
set right with me, none of it, but Jubal axe me was I crazy. He said, 'All the
food on our table and all the gas in our car come from the Dufort family.
We'd be crazy to stir up trouble for them. That's white folk's bid'ness, and
we oughta stay right out of it.'"

"What did you say?"

"I said, 'If a Black girl got kilt in the middle of it, it ain't jus' white folks'
business, is it?' But Jubal was scared. We were gonna have to let it go if
we meant to keep our jobs. And Jubal might have been scared of worse, I
don't know. He knew things I didn't know about. 'Bout the Klan and the
deacons, like that. Life was mighty tense back then, and any nigger seen to
be makin' trouble could have a short life span. You know what I mean?"

"I do."

"If they could kill the likes of Dr. King and the Kennedy boys, what
you think they couldn't do to some maids and a yardman down in Mississippi?"

Charlot reached out and laid his hand on the old woman's knee. "I'm
sorry you had to go through that, Pearl."

"I am too, baby. And things ain't changed as much as folks thought
they had, either. Last night somebody burned my church."

A chill raced over Charlot's skin. "Daughters of Egypt?"

"That's right. Burned it to the ground, jus' like in the old days. I
swear . . . I don't know what this world's coming to. Seem like we goin'
backwards now."

Charlot wondered what worthless sons of bitches thought they were
accomplishing something by torching a church attended by a bunch of old
Black people. He might not know their names, but he knew their type.
He'd grown up with more than a few of them.

"I'm sorry, Pearl. What else did you find out about that missing girl?"

"Well. About ten years ago I was at the doctor's office, and I found myself sittin' next to this woman from Fayette. Cloretta Williams. I didn't
know her, cep' in passin'. But we got to talking, and we axed about each
other's chil'ren, like you do in those situations. Well, she tol' me about
two of hers, and I told her about mine. But then time dragged on, and she
got this look of sadness, and then she told me about her daughter Shondra. Shondra had disappeared when she was sixteen, and never came back.
Turns out this was the girl I'd heard about back in 1968, not long after
they hauled us out to clean up room 305. I asked if maybe Shondra hadn't

run off and got married or something, but Cloretta said no. Their family had been having trouble back then. The father of them babies had run off, and whenever he did come around, he beat her. The kids, too. Anyway, Shondra had started livin' with some other girls in a similar situation. Long and short of it was, the mama knew her baby had been seein' men for money. At sixteen. Terrible to think about, but that's how it was back then. Maybe nowadays, too, I don't know."

Charlot had focused all of his being on his old maid. "You think Daddy killed Shondra Williams?"

Pearl lowered her face into her hands and shook her head slowly. When she finally raised it, Charlot saw tears in her eyes. "Lord help me, but . . . I think he did. I think he kilt her, and then him and Amadu put her down in the cistern with them so-called Yankee bones."

Charlot shivered in the heat. "Jesus, Pearl."

"I think when you found them bones that time, it scared the hell out of your daddy. And he was lucky he had that old war story to fall back on."

"But you never did anything about it? Never talked to a cop or anything?"

Pearl looked at him hard then, and in her eyes he saw plain fear. "I didn't. Jubal was dead by the time I met Shondra's mother. There wasn't nobody I could have asked who I could trust not to talk. I thought about going down to look in that cistern myself a few times, but . . . with that Amadu hovering around all the time, I just couldn't find the nerve to do it. I worried I'd wind up dead down there myself."

"I'm glad you didn't try."

"Don't you try it, either! If they got any sense, they long ago moved whatever they put down there. But with all this DNA like you see on TV, there's no telling what the police might be able to prove nowadays."

"Is Shondra's mother still alive?"

"Cloretta? She's in about the same shape as me. Heavier than I am, but still in her own place. Just about blind, though."

Charlot thought about all the Black women whose lives had intertwined so tightly with those of the local white families.

Pearl spat off the porch. "I just wish to God Ruby wasn't still working for young Mr. Charles. And with that Amadu still up in there? Makes me think anything could happen. Any time. You just don't know what they might get up to in there. All them Duforts got tempers—the men, I'm talkin' 'bout. You never was like that, boy. Philippe, now, he had a temper. But far as I know, he died in that plane crash before it got him into any mischief."

"Do you think Daddy ever did anything else like that? Or was Shondra the only one?"

Pearl stared into the middle distance, plumbing her memory. "I can't say, baby. But I'd be surprised if she was the only one. Like I said, that temper. And he got into some bid'ness situations where men cheated each other. With mighty big sums, too. I wouldn't want to go down in that cistern and start countin' bones. Need a doctor do it, somebody who knows how to add 'em up."

"The human body has two hundred and six bones, Pearl."

She shut her eyes tight. "Now, see? That's something I don't want to know! 'Cause now I feel obligated to get down there and try to figure out how many be down there." She slapped Charlot's thigh. "You shouldn't have tol' me that, boy."

"I'm sorry."

Charlot's phone rang, and he hesitated before looking at it. But the caller was his sister. "Sophie?" he said. "Is everything okay?"

"Apparently so. You're not going to believe this, but Daddy wants you to come home."

A wave of heat went over Charlot's face. "What?"

"He said he's going to pay off your debts."

Charlot found himself unable to speak.

"Are you there?" Sophie asked. "Charlot?"

"I'm here. I just can't believe that. Do you believe it?"

"He seems sincere. I don't know what changed his mind. There's a lot of craziness going on right now. Maybe he's thinking about his legacy, I don't know. But he says home is the only safe place for you. Ruby's fixing up your old room as we speak."

Charlot reached out and squeezed Pearl's arm. "I . . . all right. I can't really believe it, but I have no choice but to see whether he means it."

"Then you'll come straight home from wherever you are?"

"Yes. But I'm in a good place." He smiled at Pearl. "You'd approve."

"Don't test me."

"I'm at Pearl's house."

Sophie was silent for a few seconds. "I can't believe it," she said finally. "I'm coming to get you. Tell her I can't wait to see her."

"I will. Where are you now?"

"Trying to help a brave young girl."

"Well . . . good. I'll see you when you get here."

"What's happened?" Pearl asked. "Was that Sophie?"

Charlot nodded, then explained the reason she'd called. Contrary to his expectations, though, his ancient housekeeper showed no signs of happiness, or even relief. "What is it?" he asked. "You don't trust Daddy?"

"You know I don't."

"Not even about this? Saving my life?"

The old woman shook her head without speaking. Then she turned to him and said, "How many times he helped you before?"

"A few," he said defensively.

"Maybe, but he always gives up on you. And then he blames you for it. I don't know. I think you ought to stay out here wit' me. See how sincere he is before you go home. Let him pay out some hard cash first."

"Pearl . . . I don't want to be ungrateful. Sophie thinks it's all right."

"My girl Sophie don't know him like I do. What if he sees on your face that you know what I told you?"

"He won't! But you've known what you have all these years and he's never done anything to hurt you."

"You don't know that. I don't, either. But anyway . . . that's different."

"How?"

"'Cause I'm just an old colored maid, fool! He knows I can't afford to say nothing. But you? Your daddy knows sometimes there's nothing you won't do, if you think you in the right."

She was right about that, he knew. But he still had to go home. He had no other way to get the money he needed. But more than that, perhaps, he wanted to know whether his father had really decided to save him. Whether letting his second son sink was something Charles Dufort simply couldn't do.

"Sophie's coming out to get me, Pearl. But I sure thank you for letting me visit with you like this."

"You know you're always welcome, boy. I got a sofa and a queen bed, paid for myself."

"One night I will stay with you. Anytime you need me, instead of the other way around."

"I just hope you know what you're doing."

"I do, too, Pearl. I do, too."

CHAPTER 66

WE'D PLANNED TO bury my mother at 3:30 p.m., Annie and Nadine and me, with Andrew McKinney helping us to fill the grave. But thanks to Judge Clayton Shelby, my image fell short of the mark. A black van from the funeral home had delivered Mom's remains to Pencarrow, leaving the simple oak casket at the bottom of the hole dug this morning by a kindly neighbor with a backhoe. The four of us were waiting awkwardly for the clock to strike the hour, possibly out of superstition, or a human desire for order, when my cell phone rang. Looking down, I saw with surprise that the caller was Bobby White.

"I'd better take this," I said, showing Annie my screen.

"Hey, Bobby," I said. "What's going on? Please tell me no one else has been shot."

"Not that I know of, but it sounds like we nearly had our own Amritsar massacre down on the bluff."

I'm betting Bobby White is the only American presidential candidate besides Nikki Haley who could even explain the reference, and she has an unfair advantage. "We nearly did. I was there, and it was close."

"Well, I'm calling in the hopes of preventing a repeat. With Doc gone, that leaves a massive leadership vacuum in the Black community. I know there are some Black leaders who'll try to rush in and fill that—Willie Doucy, for example—and I fear that could only make things worse."

"What are you thinking?"

"I'm thinking it might be time for that kid to step up—the one who prevented further violence at Mission Hill."

"Kendrick Washington?"

"Right. Somebody told me you might be his lawyer, or your daughter might. I'm just trying to do what I can to get someone whose head and heart are in the right place in a leadership position up on that bluff. Because a leaderless mob of thousands—or worse, one led by a corrupt actor—is a recipe for hundreds of deaths up there, given the circumstances."

Annie, Nadine, and Andrew are watching me anxiously. "I agree, Bobby. But I'm not his lawyer anymore. Technically, he's represented by Doris Avery. That means my daughter should be able to help you, if anyone can. We're about to bury my mother at Pencarrow, but I'll have her call you as soon as we're done. How does that sound?"

"It's the only thing I've heard since Doc's death that's given me any hope."

"Do you know anything more about the shooter? Is he still in custody at Tarlton's station?"

"I don't know. But I expect only the worst from Tarlton. I hear the man about lost his mind when they burned his house."

"I hear you. Well, I'm ready to help you do anything you can to try to keep a lid on things."

"Thanks. We'll talk later. And my condolences on your mother's passing. She was a great lady."

"Thanks. Goodbye, Bobby."

As I start to explain the call to Annie, a convoy of seven vehicles—led by Judge Shelby's funereal black Lincoln—turns through the gate and slowly rolls toward the Duel Oak. As it turns out, four of these cars are from Bienville, and three from Natchez. They contain about thirty people who, during various periods, have been close to my mother, and who want to pay their last respects in spite of any wishes she had to the contrary. The men wear Sunday suits, the women black dresses. Among them is a doctor's wife who was ordained a Presbyterian minister later in life. She asks whether Annie or I would object to her saying a prayer, and we tell her we're fine with whatever she'd like to say. While the remainder of the crowd forms a somber circle around the grave, Annie whispers that as soon as the prayer is done, she'll hurry back to the house and boil some frozen shrimp and make garlic cheese grits for the guests.

"It might not be the most appropriate repast," she says, "but it'll remind everybody of Gram. She taught me how to make them."

For the Natchez mourners who've chosen to attend, Pencarrow wasn't an easy drive. The plantation lies nearly forty miles north of the city, and part of Highway 61 along that stretch feels like it hasn't been resurfaced since Bob Dylan sang with Pete Seeger in Greenwood in 1963. Among those who've braved the washboard asphalt to witness her interment is Melba Price, one of Dad's old nurses, who "sat with" Mom during part of her final year of life. I also see elderly doctors' wives—all widows now—some of Mom's former teaching colleagues, and a couple of women who were our neighbors back in the early 1960s.

Judge Clayton Shelby looks like a Yankee's image of an old Southern gentleman—Hal Holbrook with a little more mass—handsome and white-haired, straight-backed, clad in a light-gray seersucker suit, with a blue bow tie, linen shirt, and polished wing-tips. Despite his advanced age, he walks with a surefooted gait, and his blue eyes shine with clarity.

Judge Shelby shakes my hand, brushing off my effusive thanks for his intervention with the county board, then leans close and says, "I heard we had quite a skirmish on the bluff today. I saw one of our town drunks on television calling it the Second Fort Sumter."

"Christ," I whisper. "If even one of those Confederate Sons had aimed two degrees lower, every paintball-shooting kid on that bluff could have been killed in seconds."

The judge nods. "God looks after little children and fools."

He gives my arm a squeeze and takes up a sentry-like position at the head of Mom's grave, next to the female minister. I've asked a few people about the judge since getting his help with the burial, and everyone gives a different answer. Shelby's judicial career was long and in some ways legendary. The hobbies people listed included fishing, hunting, gardening, bridge, dog breeding, and even painting. Yet the common thread among all accounts—the one word nearly everyone used—was integrity.

When the shuffling ceases in the little circle of hastily gathered humanity, Judge Shelby looks at me, and I nod. At this point, without even mentioning her intent, Melba Price steps forward and begins singing "Amazing Grace" without accompaniment. She has a deep, rich alto, and the ancient melody entwines us all, linking us in shared mourning of unexpected resonance.

After a final repetition of the first verse, Melba falls silent, and the minister begins praying. She's reciting from memory, it seems, but before I can place the words, a fusillade of automatic gunfire destroys the peace of our impromptu service.

I know instantly—from the direction of the sound—that my nominal neighbor, Shotwell Barlow, has decided to use this solemn occasion to escalate the feud that has festered between our families for more than a century and a half. The crack of supersonic rounds rends the air, triggering a rush of chemicals in my brain and body, but I force myself to remain still.

The minister stops speaking for a few seconds, but being a Mississippi native, she quickly assumes that she must be hearing boisterous target practice on a neighboring property. Raising her voice, she continues her prayer in the face of the man-made thunderclaps bursting from the direction of River Road.

Among the anxious faces around the grave, one pair of eyes finds mine and fixes me in their gaze. Judge Shelby looks inquisitive, but even as my temper flares like a welding torch, I shake my head, indicating that he should ignore the gunfire. Despite my gesture, the judge slides smoothly through the crowd and makes his way around to me.

Leaning up to my ear, he whispers, "Who the hell's staging a war during a funeral? Is that coming from the Barlow place?"

"Has to be. Black Oak's the only land over there."

"Barlow knows your mother's being buried now?"

"Oh, yeah."

The cannonlike report of a heavy-caliber weapon booms over the broad lawn, then echoes through the woods in waves. Several of the oldest mourners shudder in terror, and one man in a wheelchair looks distraught. Looking closer, I recognize him as a World War II bomber pilot, a jeweler whose business my father always went out of his way to patronize. As I close my eyes and pray the firing will stop, two more stunning reports hit me with physical force.

"That sounds like a goddamn Barrett rifle," mutters Judge Shelby. "Fifty-caliber. There's no excuse for that. They're not going to give Peggy a moment's peace."

"No, sir. I think it's time I take a ride over there."

Judge Shelby grips my upper arm and holds me fast. "That's what they want, son. There's nothing you can do. It's Barlow's property."

The judge is right, but it's all I can do to contain my fury.

"Penn," he says, "I don't think we should leave these folks out here exposed to falling rounds. We don't know where those fools are aiming."

The old man is right. As quietly as we can—and with the help of the bomber pilot, who has recovered himself—we usher the guests back to their cars, while Annie prepares to lead those who want to stay to the house for food and fellowship. The gunfire crackles almost continuously during this geriatric evacuation. As I move back to the unfilled grave, where Andrew McKinney stands waiting, Judge Shelby walks up behind me.

"Low-bred sons of bitches," he says.

My anger burns so hot that I hesitate even to speak. The judge pats me on the back and sighs in commiseration.

"You don't know the half of it, Judge," Andrew says quietly.

"What do you mean, son?"

"Those Barlows have been giving us hell most of this year. Harassing us night and day. Hardly a week goes by without some trouble."

Shelby gives me a questioning look. "That right, Penn?"

Andrew senses that I'd rather not get into our recent troubles, so he pulls back a green tarp, exposing two long shovels and one shorter sharpshooter. As the distant gunfire continues, the three of us pick them up and begin filling the grave.

"Let's just focus on the work, Judge," I say, my throat tight.

As a teenager, I spent two summers digging sewer ditches on a mostly Black crew, and I got to be a dab hand with a "canal rake." But that skill vanished with my right foot, leaving me a clumsy digging partner. Andrew is my height, six feet one, but he weighs about 145, a good fifty pounds less than I. And while he knows his way around a university library—and is a genius with a hammer and chisel on wood—he's not much of a hand with a shovel. Judge Shelby works with surprising efficiency for his age, but the small shovel left to him doesn't move much dirt. The combination makes for slow going.

As I spade my blade into the soft pile, I flash back to previous burials where I've done the same thing. My wife's. Our family maid's. Henry Sexton's. My father's. Walt Garrity's—

"Why are we burying Peggy here?" asks the judge. "Didn't she have her tombstone all picked out and waiting by Tom's at the Natchez Cemetery?"

Shelby must know she did. I don't answer right away, because I don't really want to get into the reason right now.

"I thought Peggy's people were from Louisiana," he presses.

"She thought so, too," I tell him. "But things change."

He looks intrigued. "Sounds like a story worth hearing to me. I got to know Peggy pretty well during her last year, and I know she was researching her family history. But she kept most of it to herself."

Another fusillade of gunfire shatters the twenty seconds of silence I had already taken for granted.

"That damned Barlow has some nerve," says the judge. "Your mother's funeral, for God's sake. Does this have to do with that duel back during the war?"

"I think it probably does."

Judge Shelby's eyes don't leave mine. "It's gonna take some time to fill this grave. Why not catch me up on this feud?"

I sigh and relent. "The modern phase started with a case of adverse possession, Judge. Or an attempted case."

"Boundary dispute? No surprise there. I've seen more men shot over land disputes than over their wives' honor."

"I've been learning some law since I got here," says Andrew. "Adverse possession seems to me like a method by which one landowner legally steals land from his neighbor."

Judge Shelby laughs. "That's pretty accurate. What's your understanding of it?"

"Well, first the thieving neighbor moves a fence to take in some of his neighbor's property. Then he puts up posted signs. Then he publicly treats the land like it's his own. If he gets by with that for seven years—in Mississippi—the land becomes his, and the original owner can't do a thing about it."

"You get an A. But Penn hasn't owned this land long enough for Barlow to do that."

"No," I agree. "But I bought the place just as the deadline was approaching for Barlow to take ownership of seven-odd acres he'd cadged off a previous owner—some nice ground bordering a creek to the south of here."

"And you stopped him?"

I heave a shovelful of moist earth into the hole. "Soon as I bought the place, I naturally paid a surveyor to mark my corners. He let me know right away that Shot had moved his fence. If I'd waited three days longer to do my survey, that land would have been Barlow's. The bastard was salivating over his great coup—until I notified him that he'd be moving his fence, or I'd have a crew out there moving it for him."

Judge Shelby cackles with relish. "I'll bet that went over well."

Andrew lets out a peculiar-sounding laugh.

"Do you know the Barlows well?" I ask. "Shot comes from a long line of low-bred sons of bitches, as you put it. During the antebellum days, that plantation over there was one of the most brutal in the entire Natchez District."

"Bar none," Andrew adds. "The more I've learned about Black Oak, the more horrific stuff I find. You know they had what historians call a sex farm over there for a while? They bred children for work and sale as fast as they could, and even raped the men. They called that 'buckbreaking.'"

Judge Shelby grimaces. "I'd rather have gone to my grave not knowing that."

"Ditto," I echo. "Anyhow, they've been harassing us since I won that case. Andrew's taken the brunt of it, I'm sorry to say."

I see the judge measure the young man from the corner of his eye.

"What kinds of things have they done?"

"It's been sort of a cold war. A game for Barlow and his chucklehead militia."

"They started by vandalizing a gate sign I'd worked on for weeks," Andrew answers. "It read, MYTH-FREE ZONE. Then it said, 'If you believe any of the following statements, you cannot understand this site or the world you live in.' Below that, it enumerated the main tenets of the Lost Cause myth of the Confederacy."

"Peggy showed me a picture of a sign like that near the house. New?"

"Third one. The first two were blasted with buckshot and covered in chicken blood. Just like they do with the Emmett Till sign up at the Tallahatchie."

Judge Shelby looks at me. "You couldn't prove Barlow's crew had done that?"

"Sheriff Tarlton wasn't interested in trying. Wrote it off as vandalism. That's when I found out where I stood with the local law."

"You said 'cold war' earlier. What else have they done?"

I shrug and plunge my shovel blade back into the dirt pile. "Gunfire day and night. They've run packs of dogs through here at night to chase our deer. Messed with our electronic gate a dozen times so it won't open. We finally had to run a hundred-yard wire to get the control box far enough inside our boundary that they'd leave it alone."

"They also sneaked in here and put invasive fish species in two of the ponds," Andrew says.

"Goddamn," says the judge. "That's truly malicious. Not to mention trespassing."

"Oh, that's nothing," says Andrew. "They've flown drones over here and dropped poison to kill trees and flowers. But how do you prove that without spending all day sitting around with a video camera? We don't have time for that."

"It's just a pain in the ass," I summarize, grunting as I dig up moister, heavier earth. "Each individual act is relatively trivial. Plus, they've got a former sheriff in their ranks, and I've seen Tarlton and his brother driving out there for target practice. A couple of times I've nearly sold this damned place just to be done with it. But Andrew's doing important work. Bottom line, Barlows have lived on that land since before Mississippi was a state, so we put up with it the way we do mosquitoes and kudzu."

"Is that the extent of it?" asks Judge Shelby. "I feel like Andrew here's holding back."

Andrew looks away, toward the gate.

"I can't believe these idiots haven't messed with you personally," Shelby goes on. "A young Black man living out here on his own?"

"There is more," I answer for Andrew. "But it's typical redneck crap. Tailgating, cutting him off on the road. 'Spilling' roofing nails on the

driveway by our gate. Throwing trash on our shoulder all the time. If this
was New York, I could get them fined or even jailed. But here . . . forget it."

Judge Shelby's eyes remain on Andrew. As he stares, something in the
young man's face changes. "Spit it out," the old man says.

Andrew shifts under the gaze of those cool blue eyes. "It hasn't all been
trivial stuff."

The judge encourages him with a nod.

"Some in that militia are worse than others," Andrew says quietly.
"There's a skinny dude over there, wears a Ted Nugent T-shirt all the
time. He must not ever shower, I swear. Name's Donny. Anyway, I was
filling the truck at Omar's one morning, and I went inside to use the
bathroom."

Omar's is the gas station at the head of River Road, where it meets
Highway 61. I feel myself tensing against whatever Andrew is about to
reveal.

"That Ted Nugent freak walked in while I was peeing, and he just
stood behind me, watching. When I turned to see what he was doing, he
punched me in the kidneys, then slammed me up against the urinal. Got
piss all over my pants."

Heat rises to my face.

"And?" prompts the judge.

Andrew has stiffened, his shovel hanging awkwardly from one hand.
"He put a chokehold on me. Then he told me to go back to wherever I
came from. Said if I didn't, I'd better check under my car every day. And if
I kept trying to turn Pencarrow into a 'museum for niggers,' it might just
burn down one night."

"Damn it, Andrew," I snap. "Why haven't you told me that before?"

His eyes meet mine with defiance. "Because I knew you'd pull the plug
on this whole project. And like you said . . . the work's important."

My cheeks burn with shame and anger.

Judge Shelby sniffs and looks toward the gate in the distance. Andrew's
story has offended something deep within him. And it clearly disappoints
him that I've tolerated this treatment rather than fight it. In truth, I've
disappointed myself.

"A lot of Black folks were maimed and killed across that road," Andrew
says. "I'm not even counting the lynchings in 1861. One slave was roasted
alive for repeatedly running away. Five generations back, but that Barlow
blood still holds true."

I sure as hell hope not, I say silently, remembering that I may be related
to him.

A half dozen rifle shots crack off between us and the river.

I stop filling the grave and lean on my shovel. "Judge . . . I believe I am going to take a ride over there. Have a little chat with Shot Barlow. Why don't you guys go join Annie and the others for food?"

"Penn," says Judge Shelby, "it's not worth it. Especially today. Those guys have serious weapons over there, and they're bound to be intoxicated. Given the present circumstances, that's almost a guarantee of violence."

"God looks after little children and fools, right?"

"And you're neither." Shelby studies my midsection, then my ankles. "You're not carrying, are you?"

"No, sir." I turn to Andrew. "Can you finish up here?"

"Sure. But . . . I'll come with you if you want. Maybe even the odds a little?"

"I respect and appreciate your offer, Andrew. But it's not a good idea. We don't need any extra melanin in this discussion. I want to keep it bloodless."

"Understood. I'll cover Mrs. Peggy up. I'm sure the judge will help me."

"No, I can't do that," says the judge. "If Penn's going, I'm going."

Seeing something he recognizes in Judge Shelby's face, Andrew says, "Let me get the Mule for you guys. I parked it over behind the pine trees, to carry the shovels back to the shed afterward."

"Thanks, Andrew."

He loosens his tie and walks toward the stand of pines to crank the four-wheel-drive work vehicle.

"I can see you're upset," Judge Shelby says. "And I don't blame you. But there's other ways to handle this kind of thing."

"Such as?"

Even a man of Judge Shelby's background and influence recognizes that one has few options against someone who cares nothing about the law—so long as he's on his own property. "Penn, with that bum leg, you can't even run away if they start shooting. And in the end, this is just about petty harassment. Isn't it?"

I look back with all affect stripped from my face. "You heard Andrew."

He nods slowly. "Is that the real reason you're going over there?"

"I don't know."

Andrew cranks the Mule with a muffled rumble.

As I try to think of an answer that will satisfy the judge, the simple truth comes to me. Pointing at the open grave, which is about two-thirds full, I say, "That's my mama down there in that box. And she deserved better than this. That's my reason."

The old man nods with moist eyes. "That's a fact, son. And if you're dead set on going over there ..."

"Judge, you don't have—"

I fall silent when he opens his jacket, revealing a pistol in a shoulder holster. "What the hell are you doing with that?" I ask.

"I've gone unarmed most of my life, Penn. But I knew that judge up in Wisconsin who was murdered last year. I used to fly up there and fish with him. That forced me to recognize a reality. Every so often, men I sent to the pen for murder finally get out, men who've been threatening revenge for years. Men like Shot Barlow, more times than not. I don't always know when that happens, so ever since my friend was murdered, I carry a pistol. I hate having to do it, but only a fool refuses to defend himself from real danger."

The green Mule noses out from behind the pine trees and starts our way. Soon the brakes squeal, and Andrew stops so that the driver's door is beside me. The young historian peers over at the main mansion of Pencarrow, its far side clad in a giant exoskeleton of red scaffolding. Andrew has given thousands of hours to that building over the past year.

"You're not doing this just because of what that Donny punk did to me, are you?" he asks.

"Not only because of that, no."

"Good. Then here's the truth. Everything those bastards have done has been like a lash across my back. The only reason I've kept on is because of the enslaved people murdered out here. Especially on that side of the road. But I don't want you guys getting killed on account of me."

"I really wish you'd told me they roughed you up, Andrew."

He shrugs. "Was I right that you would have shut the project down?"

"Probably."

"Then I did the right thing."

"Let's go if we're going!" Judge Shelby snaps. "I want to get back for some of that shrimp and grits before it's gone."

As Andrew chuckles, I take his place behind the wheel of the Mule. The judge walks around the vehicle, climbs into the passenger seat, and reaches up for the "Oh shit!" handle.

"What do you want me to tell Annie?" Andrew asks.

"As little as possible. If we're not back in twenty minutes, we might be dead. But don't tell her that. Just call Chief Morgan."

"The city cops don't have jurisdiction out here! You know that."

"It's still better than calling Sheriff Tarlton. Maybe Chief Morgan will think of something he can do—even if it's just retrieving bodies before Barlow's crew can drop us in a hole and cover us with lye."

The judge's laugh sounds forced.

I take one last look at the Duel Oak, where in 1861 Robert Pencarrow defended his family against the ancestor of the man trying to provoke me today. I hope I'm not playing the fool by giving him a chance at revenge.

"Well?" says Judge Shelby. "What are you waiting for?"

I jam the Mule into gear and hit the gas pedal.

CHAPTER 67

THE ELECTRONIC SECURITY gate of Pencarrow Plantation stands two hundred yards from my mother's grave under the Duel Oak. The wrought-iron gate of Black Oak Plantation is about a third of a mile down River Road. The geography is tortuous, given that the founders of both plantations sought to site their homes within view of the Mississippi River, to monitor the comings and goings of the steamboats that would bear their cotton to market. I push the Mule as hard as I dare with an old man in the passenger seat.

"What are you planning to do once we get there?" Judge Shelby asks.

"I won't know till I'm looking Barlow in the face."

"Leap before you look, huh?"

"Not quite."

From beyond the trees ahead comes the staccato clatter of two or three shooters emptying semiautomatic pistols in rapid sequences of double taps. The judge reacts as he might to birds tweeting, which is to say not at all. But the certainty of confronting heavily armed men at our destination hits me a little harder than it did back on my own land.

"You don't seem too bothered by that gunfire," I comment.

"I served in the JAG corps in Korea. Except for a couple of close calls, I was mostly away from the action. Unlike your father. But I heard my share of heavy ordnance going off, day and night."

"I see."

"I think Barlow's problem with you goes all the way back to that duel. That's classic blood-feud stuff, whether in Sicily, the hollows of Kentucky, or the muddy banks of the Mississippi."

"Even a hundred and sixty years after the fact?"

"The past is never dead, Penn. Not even past. That's the theme of most of your books, isn't it?"

"I'm not sure I believe that anymore. The past only has the power we give it. In truth, the present devours the past like a school of piranhas, every second without cease. There's only the ever-vanishing *now*."

"I'll have to give that some thought. How dangerous you figure Barlow's militia is? Are they just a bunch of weekend warriors? Toy soldiers?"

"They do some serious training on weekends. Out of town at these

camps run by military vets. Some are just good ol' boys, of course. Gun
bros, cosplay commandos, preppers. A few LARPers."

"What the hell's a LARPer?"

"Live-action role play gamer. Some of their combat events last for days.
But they're ultimately amateurs. Fetishists. Wannabes."

Judge Shelby shakes his head. "Sounds like a clown convention. Doesn't
mean they can't kill us, though."

"Barlow wouldn't tolerate clowns in his ranks. He may be half-crazy,
but he's serious. At least a couple of his guys are vets. Hell, there was a
retired Navy SEAL in that crowd that stormed the Capitol on January 6."

"Well, what the hell are we doing, then? A couple of lawyers with one
gun between us?"

"Take it easy. I'm not going over there to play Rambo."

"I hope you're not expecting me to fill that role."

"Nope. In fact, your presence ought to keep things from escalating to
violence. You have a lot of respect in this county."

Judge Shelby snorts. "I've got enemies, too, Penn. And from what I
know of Shot Barlow, pissed off is his default mode."

Another forty yards of asphalt pass beneath our wheels.

I turn to Clayton Shelby, my gaze as forthright as I can make it. "I made
this bed, Judge. Think about what Andrew went through in that restroom.
He was scared shitless, and he'll never forget that. But he hung tough so he
can finish his job here. Barlow and his crew need to learn there's a cost for
pulling that kind of crap." A phrase from my friend Daniel Kelly rises in
my brain. "A measure of deterrence that lives in the brain, day and night."

"You think you're the man to dish that out?"

"Maybe," I tell him, recalling a conversation about legal theory that I
had with Annie yesterday. "I have an idea about that. A legal idea. My
daughter actually came upon it before I did."

The old judge turns and studies me from the corners of his eyes. "Well,
now I'm interested."

"You'll hear it soon enough."

I pull through Pencarrow's main gate and turn onto River Road. Now
all the land to our right belongs to Barlow. You can't see much of his place
from here, thanks to a dense screen of trees that follows his fence line.

"Let me ask you a question," I say over the engine noise. "Have you ever
done that 23andMe stuff? Ancestry.com? Anything like that?"

The old man turns to me, one eyebrow raised. "Don't tell me you've got
a paternity suit cooking?"

I laugh out loud. "Hell, no. About a year ago, Mom took a DNA test because of a woman who came down from Minnesota doing genealogy research. A biracial woman named Deborah Fannin. She was descended from an enslaved woman on Pencarrow. She had a rich husband, and he bought the plantation for her."

"I remember that. Met the husband once. They thought she'd really shake up society here, but the locals turned out to be harder to shock than she expected."

"That's her. Well, Deborah's theory was that her white ancestor was the man who built Pencarrow Plantation into what it became, a decorated soldier named Robert Pencarrow."

"The man who won the duel."

Someone on the far side of the trees rips off a thirty-round magazine on full auto. The judge doesn't blink.

"Right. Well, Fannin turned out to be wrong about her theory, but that's getting into the weeds, and we're going to be facing the Barlow boys in about a minute."

"So cut to the chase. What's the big mystery? Your mama's DNA test?"

The last stone in my dam of resistance crumbles away. "That's right. What if I told you that Mom discovered—at eighty-four years old—that she was part African American?"

Judge Shelby glances at me, then looks back at the road. "I already know about that. She confided in me a couple of months ago, asked my opinion. Peggy didn't have much African blood. I mean, she had some color, but . . . hell, you're white as Beaver Cleaver. How Black was she?"

"Three point six percent."

"Right, I remember now. Hell, that's nothing in this corner of Mississippi. And you? Half of that?"

"Yeah."

"So what does this have to do with anything?"

"Nothing, now. By the old one-drop rule, it would mean we're Black."

Judge Shelby nearly doubles over with laughter. "Boy, that little fragment of DNA doesn't mean squat."

"I know that. And even Mom reacted to that news differently than I expected. She became obsessed with discovering her family's true past. She was sure she'd been lied to by her side of the family. Our history had always been known and documented on both sides—all the way back to the Revolution on Dad's side, before the Civil War on Mom's—and every known ancestor was white as Ivory Snow."

"So somebody back in the mists of time lied. That's probably the most common lie in this part of the country."

"Well . . . the most likely math led straight back to the Civil War."

"So? You know how many families south of the Mason-Dixon Line have a you-know-what in the woodpile? *Beaucoup*, counselor!"

"Okay, but that wasn't the only result from that test. There was never any great genetic bounty on my mother's side of the family. I always thought we were descended from an illegitimate arm of the Pencarrow family, where it had intersected with a poor Creole woman. The most notable Pencarrow other than the captain was his half-Black son, who's famous for swimming out to a Yankee gunboat in the river and fighting as a scout for Grant during the Vicksburg campaign."

"Was he your real ancestor?"

An imposing arch of black iron comes into view on our right, crowned with the words BLACK OAK PLANTATION, EST. 1821. It towers above the iron gate beneath. Beyond the gate, gently rolling meadows obscure all sign of human habitation on the Barlow plantation.

"Hell, I hope he was," I answer as we turn into the drive. "Because the alternatives ain't good. I didn't want to say this in front of Andrew, but according to Mom, we're also related to the Barlow family."

The judge whips his head in my direction. "You've got to be kidding."

"I haven't confirmed it yet, but Annie tells me Mom was convinced of it."

"Peggy Cage related to Shotwell Barlow? That's hard to imagine."

Rifle shots crack over the pasture again, reverberating in long waves over the rolling slopes.

"That gate looks like it's locked," Judge Shelby says with obvious relief. "You don't know the code, do you?"

I stop the Kawasaki on the gravel with a screech of brakes. "In a manner of speaking. Same company installed both our controllers."

Taking a screwdriver from the glovebox, I scan the gate and nearby trees for new security cameras, then climb through the fence and duck down to the control box that operates the heavy gate barring the drive. After popping off the metal lid, it's easy to trigger the OPEN command from the internal circuit board.

With a gnashing of gears, a chain begins rolling, and the two halves of the gate slowly swing inward. Once the road is clear, I lock the gate in the open position, then jog back to the Mule. My heartbeat is still accelerating as I climb back behind the wheel.

"Didn't see that," says Judge Shelby. "I was watching that cardinal over there."

"Clearly. What do you smell, Judge?"

The old man turns his nose into the wind. "Gunpowder. Some type of solvent. And . . . cordite?"

"Yep."

"So they're firing black-powder weapons along with the modern stuff. They must be shooting along Barlow's fence line." He points east along River Road. "To be as loud as possible on your place."

I put the Mule back into gear and drive through the gate, then turn right and start over the grass along the fence. As the meadowland falls gently away to our left, I catch sight of the two Barlow oil wells deep within the property, big pumpjacks moving steadily up and down like birds dipping their beaks into a puddle.

"How much money you figure Barlow earns off those wells?" I ask.

Shelby shrugs. "Landowner's share. And those aren't big producers. It's not Natchez money, but enough to keep Barlow in beer and bullets."

Thirty seconds later, we top a slope and see three pickup trucks parked fifty yards away. One is the red dually with the Confederate flags flying from its cab and the chrome testicles hanging from its trailer hitch. Despite a tremor of fear in my chest, I don't slow down. Five men stand near the opened tailgates of the trucks, and when I'm within fifteen yards of them, I stop the Mule.

A small arsenal leans against the tailgates, ranging from AK-47s and tricked-out AR-15s to flintlock muskets. A hundred yards along the fence, man-shaped targets have been set up against a hastily erected earthen berm. An orange Kubota tractor with a dozer blade is parked to the left of the berm.

Shot Barlow is the only man I recognize from this distance. Eight years my senior, he stands about five nine, but solid as a stump. He has a thick black beard, reddish-brown skin colored by decades of perpetual burn, and thickly corded arms with scarred, callused hands. He wears a button-down work shirt in the unique camouflage pattern made by Prime Shot Outfitters, whose owner (a member of the Poker Club) is rumored to be a financial backer of his militia group. I hoped some of the more affluent supporters might be present today, as potential moderating influences. But the closest thing is Joe Iverson, former sheriff of Tenisaw County. The other three look like they could be Barlow cousins: graying hair, goatees, baseball caps marked with logos. Two look a little softer than the others—their beards scarcely cover their double chins—but a stringy one standing behind Barlow shares a certain hardness with him. I remember his eyes from the truck bed yesterday morning: the gaunt, merciless face that doomed Union troops might have seen sighting down a musket barrel at the Rappahannock River in 1862.

"If this goes sideways," I say softly, "I'm going to pin the bastards against the truck. Feel free to shoot anybody you feel like."

"Damn it, Penn—"

I kill the engine, and there's only the ticking silence.

"Well, *hell*," Shot Barlow says in a voice slurred with whiskey. He walks toward us with a smile. "If it ain't the man from Black Lives Matter."

"Not exactly," I reply, keeping my seat in the Mule, and surveying the other men, who are clearly watching their leader for cues. They're like a pack of dogs, or maybe dogs bred with wolves.

"Judge *Clayton Shelby*?" says Barlow, stopping about seven yards from us. "What are you doing here with my libtard neighbor?"

"I'm a friend of Mr. Cage's," the judge answers mildly. "Also a guest at his mother's funeral."

"So what the hell you doing over here? Other than trespassing?"

"Gate was open," I tell him.

"That's a lie," Barlow says flatly.

"Ask the judge."

"Screw the judge, Cage. I'm talking to you."

Clay Shelby is clearly not accustomed to being spoken to or about in this way, but he keeps his composure. "Mr. Barlow, in all honesty, I'd prefer not to be here. But you've made yourself impossible to ignore. We've got a lot of elderly folks over at Penn's house. Grieving people. One's a World War II veteran. It upsets those folks to have prayers and hymns interrupted by a Barrett rifle, even if they don't know what one is."

There's no Barrett in sight. Barlow's probably amazed that the judge would recognize the weapon by its report. "This is my property, Judge. What we do over here's none of your damn business."

"That's one point of view. Not a very neighborly one, though."

Barlow looks back at his cronies. "Cage and I aren't exactly *neighbors* in that sense of the word."

A ripple of obligatory laughter follows.

"The Christian sense, you mean?"

A couple of members of Barlow's posse scowl, and it's then that I see the face of Ted Nugent leering from the T-shirt covering the scraggly guy's torso. I can't help but think of this punk pummeling Andrew's kidneys while jamming him against a gas station urinal.

Modulating my voice to the tone of a friendly minister making a call on a parishioner, I say, "We came over to ask you to rethink your position on that principle. If you could just lay off your target practice for a couple of hours, out of respect. Remember the golden rule? Do unto others . . . ?"

My politeness discombobulates this group. Barlow looks at his crew, then back at me. "Why the fuck would I rethink anything for you, Cage? I've never liked you, and I didn't care for your mama, either. She come from a dirt farm, like my people, but she spent her whole life puttin' on airs, like the damn Queen of Sheba."

My face burns with rising blood. "That's a lie."

Barlow laughs, knowing he got to me. "So why don't you just *get the fuck off my place*," he goes on, "before we *run* you off?"

I feel like Judge Shelby is wondering why we don't do just that.

"In fact," Barlow says, taking another step forward, "tell me why we shouldn't teach you a damn lesson right here and now about coming where you ain't wanted. Ain't a court in the land that'd convict us for giving you an ass-whippin' under these circumstances."

"Because it's not wise to throw stones when you live in a glass house."

Barlow pulls himself erect and makes an exaggerated show of looking around his land. "I don't see no glass house, counselor. Or mayor, or whatever the hell you are these days."

"Because you're not looking through the right lens." My voice remains friendly, but I'll not spare him anything today. "Let me tell you what I mean. Since yesterday, I've learned a lot more about your family than I used to know. For example, your ancestors spread a lot of seed back in their day. And I'm not talking about agriculture. I'm talking about—"

"I know what you're talking about." His yellow teeth gleam in the black beard. "Ain't no secret we like pussy out here. Always have, and we ain't changing for no 'Me Too' sob sisters."

Another chorus of laugher, right on cue.

"I'm glad to hear you admit that, Shot. Because from what I understand—apart from not being too particular about getting consent— your forefathers weren't exactly careful about where they spread that seed. Rich girls and poor, white and Black, slave and free."

Barlow flips me the bird. "It's all pink on the inside, in case you don't know."

I turn to Judge Shelby, who's staring at me as he might at a horse that's veered off a solid trail into quicksand.

"What the hell you gettin' at?" Barlow demands. "I ain't heard nothing *like* a point yet."

"My point is, sex is one of those hobbies that has consequences. Not all of them welcome."

He squints back at me, trying to pierce my armor of civility and divine my true intent. "I don't follow. You talking about VD or something?"

"No, sir. I'm talking about children. I'm talking about *heirs*. And potential heirs."

The militia leader's eyes narrow. He senses a point coming now. "I'm listenin'."

"Does the name Deborah Fannin ring a bell?"

After a couple of seconds, he nods. "Uh-huh. High-yella woman came down from Minnesota and paid for a bunch of DNA tests for the colored down here? Married to a white man. Lived on Pencarrow over there for a few months?"

"That's her. Well, I've had a friend doing research into Mrs. Fannin's findings." An image of Nadine flashes in my mind, and it brings me surprising comfort. "She's a lawyer, too, by the way. And after going through the results of Fannin's work, plus the research my mother did, she's already identified about two hundred and twenty likely blood descendants of your Barlow ancestors here."

I'm making these numbers up, but after discovering a comparable case, I figure I'm being conservative, given the Barlows' known proclivities. Shot Barlow stands blinking like a man who fears he might be suffering a retinal detachment.

"I'm talking about mixed-race children," I go on. "And there could easily be fifty or a hundred more. We're talking about a hundred and sixty-two years of procreation, so . . . you know—the math isn't on your side."

I don't think I've ever seen Shot Barlow paralyzed by fear. But I do now.

"What are you trying to say, Cage?" he asks in the most challenging tone he can muster. "Are you screwing with me? Or are you saying this legal bullshit is real?"

"Neighbor, I'm telling you that if any of your ancestors died intestate— that means without a will—or if they died *with* a will that did not specifically exclude all those other heirs—then you're looking at a lawsuit that will ultimately divide this plantation of yours among every descendant who can prove blood relation to you through DNA."

All the color has left his face.

"What you got here?" I ask him, though I know the answer well. "Four hundred acres? Even figuring just two hundred unacknowledged heirs, that'll split this place up into . . . maybe two-acre parcels for each claimant—including you, of course. Enough space for a little truck garden."

Several mouths behind Shot Barlow have gone slack. The founder of the Tenisaw Rifles has not moved, but I can see him going through what Hunter S. Thompson used to call an "agonizing reappraisal." The man appears to physically shrink before my eyes.

"But they *could* get a lot smaller than that," I tell him. "If there're more descendants out there. And that includes your mineral rights, of course. Can't forget those. Your oil royalty checks would . . . well, you know what'll happen."

Shotwell Barlow takes a step toward us, then another. "Are you trying to tell me the government would take my family's land and divide it up between a bunch of nappy-headed welfare queens and drug addicts?"

I shrug. "I'm not sure what they'll do, Shot. But I know you picked the wrong day to disrespect my mother. You hear me? Yeah . . . you hear. I'll see you in the funny papers, buddy."

Before I can start the Mule's engine, Barlow clenches his right hand into a fist and halves the distance between himself and the Mule's grille. But something stops him there. He's only half-crazy, not completely gone. Shot Barlow has lived long enough to know that the kind of threat I revealed cannot be neutralized by violence—at least not impulsive violence.

Starting the engine, I'm about to back away when a new voice says, "You think you're so damn big, comin' over here talkin' that legal shit, don't you?"

It's the kid in the Ted Nugent T-shirt.

The one with the sharpshooter's eyes.

Only he's not a kid, I realize. He's more like thirty-five, but with the eternal teenager vibe I've seen in so many wiry rednecks. He moves forward with an eerily fluid motion, ignoring the man who believes himself to be the leader of this group.

"Shot?" says Judge Shelby, in a voice edged with primal anxiety. "I don't like the look in your boy's eye. Tell him to take his hand off that pistol."

Looking down, I see what the judge noticed long before I did. Ted Nugent's right hand is gripping the butt of a heavy black automatic in a holster on his right hip. His blondish hair, light blue eyes, and pasty skin seem to have taken on a luminous sheen under the heightened tension, and he twitches and scowls like a baby gangster spoiling for a scrap.

I shift on the Mule's seat, wishing I had my AR-15 tucked under it.

"Donny?" says Shot Barlow. "Take it easy now. We're gonna let these bastards go home for now. Okay?"

"Nosir," Donny answers. "Not that easy. Not today. These motherfuckers think they can come over here and boss us, just like they do in courtrooms and banks and job sites . . . but this is our territory right here."

He's still moving forward, which has put him far enough past his master that he no longer has eye contact with Barlow. From this distance, I see his chin quivering with rage. The whites of his eyes look like those of a dog bent on attack.

"*Donny Kilmer!*" Barlow snaps, clearly worried himself. "Get back by the truck!"

But Donny isn't listening. Only a yard away from the Mule now, he draws his pistol and points it at my face. My blood pressure plummets so fast I feel faint. Staring into the black maw of the barrel, I realize death is much closer than I thought, even when I'm already carrying terminal cancer cells in my blood.

"Don't feel so high and mighty now, do you?" Donny says. "You 'bout to shit your diapers, ain't you, boss?"

We've stepped from the twenty-first century into a John Ford western. But I feel more like Jimmy Stewart than John Wayne. My mind is blank with fear. I have no idea how to get us out of the path of this angry moron, and I'm as surprised as he when the barrel of a second pistol enters my frame of vision from the right.

It's Judge Shelby's gun, drawn from the holster beneath his jacket.

"Shotwell?" the judge says softly. "Tell this boy to holster his weapon and back off, or this is going to end badly. For all of us. And there's no need for that."

"Donny?" Barlow says, his voice and eyes pleading. "The judge there's an old Southern gentleman. Comes from good people. I want you to save it for another day. You know what I'm talking about. You hear me?"

Donny's eyes flick from the judge's pistol to his face. "I don't think so, Cap'n. I don't think this wall-eyed old bastard could hit the broad side of a Buick. Not before I take 'em both down. You've seen me shoot."

Even as my heart thuds against my sternum, Judge Shelby moves his pistol an inch to the right and fires.

As my body jerks away from the blast, the chrome testicles hanging from the rear of the big dually truck explode into gleaming shards of shrapnel, leaving behind what looks like plastic vas deferens after a castration. Joe Iverson, who'd been standing only a foot away from them, shrieks in pain and terror, rolling on the ground with blood staining his pant leg. The judge fires twice more, knocking the shattered testicles across the grass like the Sundance Kid auditioning for a job. Another man shrieks and grabs his side, which is now peppered with blood. Even Donny Kilmer is so stunned by the judge's skill and speed that he doesn't resist when Shot Barlow lunges forward, pushes his gun down, then jerks it from his hand.

"Y'all get the hell out of here!" Barlow bellows. "Before somebody gets killed!"

I don't need any more prompting than that to get the Mule going. Twisting my head to look back, I see the kid in the Nugent T-shirt contorting his body as if to check his ass for shrapnel. Recalling his assault on Andrew in the restroom, I can't help but hope those chrome balls peppered him good.

AS JUDGE SHELBY and I roll back through Black Oak's gate, he finally says, "I didn't like doing that. I didn't like being put in that position."

"I'm sorry, Judge."

"Are you? I hope it's the stupidest thing you do all year. Because we could both have been killed. Easily."

"I know that. Jesus, those truck nuts blew up like a grenade!"

A muffled snort of laughter escapes the old man's nose. "I figured they would. They're basically chromed rubber." The Mule jounces over the cattle grate, then rolls onto the asphalt, carrying us back toward Pencarrow. "You know," Shelby goes on, "I always thought you were a pretty good lawyer. But I see now I was mistaken."

"Why do you say that?"

"Because a good lawyer doesn't reveal his case months before he files it. And you know that. Shit, boy, that Barlow's not likely to ever let you *near* a courtroom, after what you told him today. You just brought his darkest nightmare to life. The government seizing his ancestral property and dividing it up between a bunch of Blacks? Hell, you're liable to wake up with that Donny Kilmer cutting your throat one night, on Barlow's order."

"I don't think so."

"Then you're not thinking!"

"Judge—"

"Don't say anything else, goddamn it. Just get us back to Pencarrow and find me some whiskey. I haven't fired a bullet that close to a living man since Korea."

Turning, I look at the old jurist beside me, white-haired and bent forward at the upper spine. I wouldn't have believed that he would do what he did back there . . . and yet when the moment came, he didn't hesitate.

"I appreciate you doing it, though. I really do. I'm worried Joe Iverson might sue you, though."

Judge Shelby waves his hand to dismiss my thanks, but as I study his profile, I detect what looks like either pride or exhilaration on his face. "Fuck Joe Iverson and the horse he rode in on. He was a corrupt sheriff, and I can prove it."

I shake my head in wonder at this man I hardly knew of only yesterday.

"Eyes on the road, boy," he orders. "I did that for your mother. And you'll never convince me Peggy was related to that no-count son of a bitch back there. That's like saying Audrey Hepburn was related to Fatty Arbuckle. Now get us home. I'm ready for some shrimp."

CHAPTER 68

FOR THE PAST half hour, Sophie Dufort had sat in the old ER parking lot of Tenisaw Memorial Hospital without seeing any sign of Ebony Swan. Her SUV, an all-electric BMW iX, looked like a vehicle from the future compared to the vacant hospital, which was a monument to the worst 1970s architecture: white stucco boxes of varying sizes connected by breezeways and elevated pedways. Over the years, the stucco had become coated in various shades of mold, and since the hospital had been abandoned a couple of years ago, the process had accelerated to the point that parts of it looked like a set from a horror movie.

The trees to Sophie's left didn't look much more inviting, a dense strip of woods that could hide a great deal of mischief in their undergrowth. On their far side lay the neighborhood Ebony Swan had called Marshall McEwan from—Magnolia Heights—but if the girl had truly been there, she should have made it to the parking lot long before now. Unless someone had spotted her or staked out the trees between there and Sophie's vehicle.

Five minutes ago, Sophie had received a call from Ruby, their maid. In a tone more suited to a lifelong friend than a servant, Ruby had told her that her father had decided to pay off her brother's debts (or at least a percentage sufficient to keep his debtors from killing him while they worked out a solution to the underlying problem). It might mean another stint in rehab, or some other option, but right now Charles wanted his son home, to be sure that no lethal misunderstandings occurred, due to some mob collector not getting the word.

Sophie had literally broken down in the parking lot, so relieved was she to hear Ruby's news. When she asked why her father hadn't called her himself, Ruby answered, "You know that old man's not going to give you the satisfaction of admitting you beat him. Let's just thank God Charlot can sleep safe tonight."

As soon as she'd collected herself, Sophie called Charlot's cell phone, and was stunned to find him sheltering at the shack of Pearl Brooks, Ruby's mother. It struck her as odd that Ruby would be ignorant of this, but there would be time later to sort these things out. After Charlot agreed to come home (insisting there was no rush), Sophie had decided to give the Swan girl five more minutes.

Since then, she'd picked up what news she could by watching CNN on her phone and scrolling through social media. In a town as small as Bienville, Facebook often provided the most accurate local information, and much more quickly than TV news. It was on Facebook that she'd first seen the Hewson statue lying broken in the street, the sheriff's smoldering house, and photos of an oil well burning across the Mississippi River. Another post let her know that the Azure Dragon paper mill was being evacuated due to a bomb threat, one specific enough to be taken seriously by the Chinese owners, which was saying something.

Sophie shut down her browser and called Marshall McEwan at the Bienville police station.

"Have you got the girl?" Marshall answered in a quiet voice.

"I don't, Marshall. I'm sorry. She never showed up. Listen, I have a family emergency, and I have to leave. That's no exaggeration. Also, the city board may meet again soon, and that could end in dissolution. But for me this emergency is of a different magnitude. You're going to have to find somebody else to pick up Ebony Swan."

"Sophie, I don't *have* anybody else. She won't trust the police."

"I'm sorry. I'm here, but she's not. Can you reach her by phone?"

"No! I told her to keep her phone switched off. Tarlton and his men could nail her just from that signal."

"I'll give her five more minutes, Marshall. But find somebody to relieve me, because I'm pulling out of here then."

"All right. Thanks for calling, at least."

Sophie clicked off and forced herself not to start the engine. Only in the silence of the car did she realize she was close to hyperventilating. Sophie had brought along a small automatic pistol her father had given her when she left for college, but even with that, she didn't have the nerve to go into those shadowy woods—not even for a witness to Doc's potential murder. Ebony Swan had made enemies who were too dangerous to ignore. Bienville's drug dealers killed at least one or two people per month. And if Buck Tarlton's department meant to silence Ebony for some reason, then they were probably more dangerous than the dealers.

Were the town not in its present state of chaos, and her brother not at risk of being murdered, she would have agreed to wait another hour. But she couldn't afford it. Her vote would be critical in the next board meeting. And like the Black progressive members, Sophie was being pressured to vote against her conscience. The difference was, the Black members' families were being threatened in order to pressure them, whereas the pressure on Sophie was coming from *within* her family.

She nearly jumped out of her skin when a young Black man popped up at her passenger window. Pulling back against the driver's door, she watched him jam a slim-jim tool between her passenger window and doorframe, hack the lock, then yank open the door and climb into the seat beside her. The intruder appeared to be in his early twenties, very muscular with a layer of stubble on his cheeks. But the most arresting thing about him was his electric green eyes, which chilled her to the marrow as they moved slowly up her still-shapely legs to her breasts, and finally to her face.

"What you doin' out here, lady?" he asked in a playful voice.

"Who are you?"

"Damien. What you doin' at this old hospital?"

"I'm . . . making a phone call."

"Yeah? You look to me like you's waitin' for somebody."

"Maybe I am."

"You got a wedding ring on. Big ol' diamond, too. You hookin' up wid somebody on the side?"

"Maybe I am."

"Well, shit. You ain't gotta wait for that. I can give you whatever you need right now."

"You're not half my age."

Damien laughed. "Shit, you still look fine. I seen you around town, running in them tight yoga clothes, that long black hair runnin' down your back. I don't know how old you are, but that body don't look no more than thirty."

Sophie almost laughed, but before she grasped what he was doing, Damien had cupped his hand over her right breast and given it a rough squeeze.

"Got you a damned good titty job, too. I bet I can't even see the scars."

Sophie felt queasy, as if she were being dragged up the highest incline on a roller coaster. Despite Damien's "small talk," she knew this young man was part of the drug gang hunting Ebony Swan. She thought about telling him she had a gun, but then she decided that might be the fastest way to get herself shot.

"You see a Black girl anywhere around this lot?" Damien asked. "High school age? Kinda chunky?"

"I haven't seen anybody out here. That's why I'm here. Privacy."

Damien gave her a knowing smile.

"I want you to leave me alone," she said firmly. "I need to get home."

The young man didn't move anything but his eyes, which traveled over her skin like fingers. "You want me to give you a little rub?"

Sophie stiffened on the leather seat, fear working deep within her. "I asked you to get out of my car."

Damien laughed at her discomfort. "This ain't no car, baby. It's a SUV. And it look like one of them all-electrics. 'Cep' it's a Beemer, not a Tesla. You spent some money on this bitch."

"*Please* do what I asked."

Damien shifted so that he faced her squarely. His left hand went to his crotch, and he adjusted what appeared to be a fast-growing erection. She watched his hands, because she expected them to reach for her next. His gaze was already focused on her crotch.

"You don't want to get me upset," he said. "'Cause then I might stop asking permission for what I want. You hear me?"

Sophie knew then what to do.

Burying her fear so deep that even a functional MRI scanner would miss it, she leaned close to the young man and said, "Listen to me, you green-eyed punk. My family has a man who takes care of us. He drives my father's car. If you do anything to hurt me, he'll make you pay for it. With interest. You understand? And if I don't come home from this . . . he'll hunt you down and tear you to pieces."

Damien laughed louder than he had to this point, with open contempt. "That right, *Karen*? You gon' sic your *yardman* on me?"

He reached behind his back and drew a black semiautomatic pistol from the waistband of his pants. "I got something for him."

"He's no yardman," Sophie said, working hard to look unimpressed. "He's a chauffeur. And when he finds you, he won't kill you right away. He'll . . . do things first. You might know his name. He's originally from Africa."

"Yeah?" Damien ran his right hand over the dull metal of the pistol with sexual suggestiveness. He looked like he might be considering smacking her with the heavy butt. "What his name, this big bad yardman?"

"Amadu."

Damien's hand ceased moving, and his eyes locked onto Sophie's. "You talkin' 'bout the Amadu who drive the big Rolls for that old man?"

"That's right."

"That old man your daddy?"

"That's right. Charles Dufort."

Damien looked at her for a few more seconds, then scanned the parking lot as though Amadu might pull up at any moment. "Aiight then," he said in a newly constricted voice. "I was just foolin', you know. Imma . . .

prob'ly head out now. You keep your eyes open. This ain't no safe place. Lotta crackheads hit the pipe in them old buildings. Girls get raped up in there."

Sophie nodded, almost shaking with relief.

"And you're gonna tell Amadu I treated you right. Right?"

Sophie waited, making him suffer. "If you go now."

As the young man left the vehicle and walked toward the line of trees, she wondered why she'd been so certain that Amadu was the name that would insure her safety. She'd never seen her father's driver commit lethal violence. She had, however, heard the story of how Amadu was hired. During a trip to the rice farms of Sierra Leone to compare agricultural processes (Sophie's grandfather had owned a rice farm in South Louisiana), Amadu and his father had been hired to escort the Dufort men through the troubled nation. When four bush gangsters attempted to rob them on the road, Amadu and his father had killed two and crippled the other with machetes. Amadu's father turned down the subsequent offer of employment in America, but he'd encouraged his son to accept. In the chaos of colonial disintegration, in a country where domestic slavery had survived into the twentieth century, he saw little opportunity for advancement for a son whose skills had evolved in the dark margins at the edge of legitimate society. America offered physical safety under the protection of a wealthy patron.

For a few years after his arrival in the U.S., Amadu had worked as a foreman on the Dufort rice farm in Louisiana's Acadia Parish. But that wasn't all he did for his employer. After he took the position of butler and driver at Tranquility, Sophie—while snooping around the house—had come upon a box of grainy photographs on the driver's bed. Among the images inside were two in which a young Amadu wore leopard skins and held a leopard claw in his right hand. When Sophie worked up the nerve to question Ruby about them, the maid told her that Amadu's father and grandfather had once belonged to a secret society that used brutal violence to resist British and Dutch colonialism. Amadu himself had never been initiated, since independence had finally been achieved, but he had been partly trained, and in America he had used some of the trappings of the group to frighten anyone who posed a threat to his new employer—her father.

Sophie *had* seen the chauffeur act with silent and effective dispatch whenever they were approached by panhandlers or gas station muggers in towns like Baton Rouge and Jackson. She also knew that her father possessed secrets, and that Amadu was privy to many. But beyond this, her sense of Amadu as a kind of invisible protector was purely instinctual. Yet her instinct had proved accurate. A murderous American gangbanger in his twenties had given her a wide berth rather than risk the anger of a white-haired driver whom he believed had once roamed West Africa with the feared Leopard Men.

Sophie started her engine and scanned the parking lot.

She'd given Ebony all the time she could, and Charlot was waiting for her near the southern edge of the county. Poor Charlot. If she but closed her eyes, she could see herself at twenty-two, holding the baby boy her father's new wife had brought home from the hospital. Sophie had wanted to hate the child, but she couldn't find that emotion when she held him. He'd been a beautiful being from the moment he entered the world, and as he grew, she came to love him. It had always been that way between Sophie and her half brother, who had suffered so much under the tyranny of their common father.

Looking at her rearview mirror, Sophie watched the ominous trees fall slowly behind her as she drove out of the parking lot. She only prayed that nothing would happen to young Ebony Swan before she could get through the net closing around her. A sixteen-year-old girl from Bucktown had no Leopard Men to protect her. If she did, she wouldn't have sought help from a mild-mannered newspaper publisher. But Ebony Swan was not Sophie's problem. She wasn't family, anyway.

"Hang tight, baby Char," she whispered. "Sophie's coming."

CHAPTER 69

EBONY STOOD UNDER the darkening sky outside the house on Hinton Avenue and waited for Mrs. Seaver to come to the door. She had her doubts about Lance's mother, but the woman had admitted she was struggling with the whole thing and promised that she wanted to help if she could. She'd said what made her call was a feeling that if Lance had known Ebony was in danger, he would have wanted her to help. Ebony knew that much was true. About Lance, anyway.

It wasn't like Ebony had any choice. When she'd tried to reach the hospital parking lot to meet Sophie Dufort, she'd found every route blocked, either by Jamaal's enforcers or the sheriff's patrol cars. With no other option, she'd carefully made her way back to the Seaver house.

This time Lance's mother looked a little better than she had during that first meeting. Not like she'd slept, exactly, but maybe that she'd gotten some distance between herself and the trauma of all she'd seen that day. Or maybe she'd taken some different medicine. Ebony couldn't afford to worry about it.

"Hello again," Mrs. Seaver said. "Come on in."

Ebony followed her into the foyer, heard the door close solidly behind her. That sound gave her the first feeling of security she'd felt for hours.

"I've thought about everything you told me," Mrs. Seaver said. "About the drug dealer, and also your worries about the police. And the sheriff's department."

Ebony nodded but said nothing.

"I know you need a safe place to sleep," she went on. "And you can stay here for a night or two, if you need to. But what's really needed is a long-term solution to your home problem."

Oh, Jesus, Ebony thought. "You didn't call Child Protective Services, did you?"

"No, no," Mrs. Seaver said quickly. "I told you I wouldn't. But I did call a friend of mine."

Adrenaline flushed through Ebony's body. "Who?"

"Someone who knows about the things that scared you about the police. Things like sexual abuse. Somebody who can put you in touch with the right people."

"Like a shrink or something?"

"Kind of. I can tell you're terrified, Ebony. Everything's going to be all right. Come in the den with me. You're going to relax after talking to Kara for two minutes."

"Who's Kara?"

"My friend. I used to be related to her by marriage. Distantly, anyway. That doesn't matter. She's a great person, and great with kids."

As Mrs. Seaver led her through a gleaming kitchen that smelled of casseroles, Ebony told herself not to be paranoid, that in this world you could trust people to act in good faith. A TV was playing under a cabinet. On it the handsome man Ebony had arranged to meet in the parking lot was talking in front of a jail cell. Behind the cell bars stood the white deputy who had shot Doc Berry. He scowled into the camera, and his knuckles looked bloodless, he clinched the bars so tight. But the man in front of him was definitely Mr. McEwan, the publisher of the Bienville *Watchman*.

"I want everyone out there to know that Deputy LeJay is being treated according to proper legal procedure, and all his rights are being observed. Once he's completely booked and processed, the deputy will be interrogated as to his exact role in the death of Mayor Berry—"

"The den's right through here, honey."

With great effort Ebony allowed herself to be led into the den, where she found a woman of about thirty sitting on a sofa. She had dark hair, dark eyes, and olive-colored skin. Ebony didn't know if she was Italian or Latina, but she was something. And something about her set off an alarm in Ebony's head.

"Ebony, this is Kara Mascagni," Mrs. Seaver said. "She's related to my ex-husband."

Maybe it's the way she sits, Ebony thought. Which wasn't like a woman at all, but like a jock of some kind. A softball player, maybe. Tense. Like she was pretending to be a socialite, like Mrs. Seaver, when in fact she was something else.

"Why don't you sit down," Kara Mascagni suggested. "Tell me what happened and what you most need to feel safe right now."

Mrs. Seaver motioned her toward an upholstered chair, but Ebony didn't move. She couldn't. The alarm bell set off by Kara Mascagni had doubled in volume. She nearly had it . . . and then she knew.

Kara Mascagni worked for the sheriff's department.

Ebony had seen her wearing her tan-and-brown uniform, her gold badge and her hair pulled back tight and a big pistol on her butch-ass hip. She had some kind of special title, but she was still a deputy. Shontae Reece had tried to report a problem with her supervising officer when she was working as a CI, and this was who they had sent her to. But Kara Mascagni had not helped Shontae. In fact . . .

"Wait now, honey," Mrs. Seaver said, as Ebony backed toward the foyer.

Kara Mascagni got awkwardly to her feet.

Ebony wanted to run, but she wasn't quite in control of her movements. She was afraid she had peed on herself. And then she knew why. Kara Mascagni had taken out a small pistol and aimed it at her.

"Kara!" Mrs. Seaver cried. "What the hell are you doing?!"

"This girl is a drug dealer, Linda. Go in the other room. Backup's on the way, but I want to be sure you're safe."

Ebony bolted.

After what she'd seen happen to Lance and the mayor, she expected a bullet in the back, but none came. Three seconds later she was through the front door and running through the neighborhood. She startled a white man walking a small ugly dog, and then the wail of a siren reached between the houses, grasping for her. She had never felt so Black as she did running from that siren through that white neighborhood. She ran like her great-uncle had once told her to run at her junior high track meet: . . . *like you got hellhounds on your trail!*

Because this time she really did.

CHAPTER 70

BOBBY WHITE STEPPED onto the seventh-floor terrace of the Donnelly Oil penthouse and took a deep breath of wind blowing off the river. Above the water, down by the bridges, the sky was quickly turning to orange and yellow flame, with a purple curtain waiting to descend. For the first time in weeks, he'd felt the rhythms of fate stutter, and it gave him pause. The failure of his plan at Diamond Hill had inconvenienced him, but he'd felt confident that he would get another chance—likely before nightfall. But since then he'd waited in vain for Kendrick to step higher up out of the mass of humanity and embrace his destiny.

Bobby had seen online posts revealing that the young social media star was moving among the mass of marchers on the bluff, but so far no announcement of any large-scale speech had been made. Surely at some point the young man must become consumed with a vision of himself standing before the crowd below, like Jesus on the Mount or Martin on the Mall. And if not, surely someone close to him would suggest it. *Nature abhors a vacuum*, Bobby thought. *As true in politics as in science. Maybe someone close to Kendrick is discouraging him. Pastor Willie Doucy, or some other jealous Black leader who's been waiting for his chance to supplant Doc Berry—*

Bobby fought the urge to walk to the rail and look down at the people filling Confederate Memorial Park. Instead he focused on one column of flame near the southwestern edge of the Louisiana horizon. There was nothing quite like the distinctive V of a burning oil well. The sight annoyed him more than anything else. It represented a significant escalation by the Blacks, of course. But right now all it meant was a distraction that would drive the men of the Poker Club mad with anger and anxiety—things he didn't want to deal with right now.

What he needed from them was what Donny Kilmer possessed in apparently limitless reserves—patience. All Donny needed was a target, and he was content to wait for it. At this moment he was holed up in a room at the Planters' Hotel up Battery Row, cleaning his rifle, eating room service, and waiting for a targeting call on his burner phone. But the spoiled businessmen of the Poker Club wanted what they were accustomed to—instant results.

Bobby heard the near-silent slide of the expensive glass door behind him, cursed the thought of dealing with any more manipulative million-aires. Then he heard the scrape of bootheels on terrazzo, and he knew this was something else.

Turning, he saw the rangy figure of Wade Tarlton moving toward him, Wyatt Cash at his side. Wade Tarlton was a skinnier but harder-looking version of his brother, the sheriff. He'd likely not test as well on any written exam, but his eyes held a glint of canny intelligence that his brother's lacked. He was probably a good poker player.

"Does Buck know you're up here?" Bobby asked.

"Nope," said Wade Tarlton.

"So what are you doing here?"

"We got a problem, and I figure you need to know about it."

"Why hasn't Sheriff Woody told me about it?"

Wade Tarlton laughed at the *Toy Story* reference. "Buck figures he's in competition with you."

"Yes, he does. Well, what's this new problem?"

"There's a video out there of Deputy LeJay shooting Doc Berry."

Bobby gave the chief deputy his full attention. "What kind of video? Security cam or something?"

"Cell phone. There was a Black girl with that white kid when he got shot. Turns out the Seaver kid was selling dope into the Catholic school for a local dealer—one Jamaal King. It was King who shot the Seaver kid, over money. The girl bolted while they fought, but she stayed within sight and filmed it on her phone. Doc heard the shot, then tore up in there in Ransom's truck and tried to save the boy. LeJay shot Doc while he was rendering aid."

This scenario instantly made sense to Bobby. "You saw all this on video?"

"No. The girl showed up at the Seaver boy's mama's house. Told her the whole story."

"So you don't have the video?"

"Nope."

Bobby sighed. "Why not?"

"The mama erased it. Didn't want anybody finding out her baby sold drugs."

"I see. Does the video still exist anywhere? Do we even know?"

"The Black girl has the only copy we know about."

A fillip of fear went through Bobby. "But she hasn't posted it any-where?"

"Not so far. Something's holding her back. She's probably more afraid of Jamaal than us. Probably wants to talk her way out of trouble with him. Can't do that if she makes herself the center of attention."

"Where is she now?"

"In the wind."

Bobby leaned against the stone wall that bordered the terrace and sighed.

"That's why I brought Wade up," Wyatt said. "I knew this was bad."

Before Bobby could give the implications much thought, he realized that Dixie Donnelly had stepped out onto the terrace. She stood quietly near the door, waiting for him to notice her. When he did, she made no move toward him.

"Exactly what does the video show?" he asked Tarlton.

"We don't exactly know. All we got is the boy's mother's description, and she was half-stoned on sedatives. Her son's murder wasn't on the film, though it shows his body. But it does show a verbal exchange between Deputy LeJay and Doc Berry, and then the shooting. Mrs. Seaver was fuzzy on what was said, or even if it was completely understandable. There's apparently music playing during this exchange, and it covers up some of the talk. She says Doc was dismissive of LeJay and ignored his commands."

"But . . . ?"

Wade nodded. "*But* she's also pretty sure Doc identified himself as a doctor. Whether he gave his name or not, she isn't sure."

"Shit. Did he identify himself as the mayor?"

"She's fifty-fifty on that. She does say Doc made a reaching movement before he was shot. Like down toward his own belly. But more like he was reaching for a phone than a gun."

Bobby closed his eyes and absorbed the blow for what it was, then opened them and looked at Cash. "This isn't just bad," he said. He took a step toward the chief deputy and spoke to him the way he would to a soldier under his command. "You're going to find that girl, Wade. And you're going to make sure that video is never seen by another pair of eyes."

"Working on it now, sir."

"Do you know who she is?"

"One Ebony Swan. Mother's a junkie, father long gone. I've got pictures of her circulating, and we got a female deputy who was just in the same room with her. Kara Mascagni. She got her gun out, but there was a witness present and Kara hesitated. The Swan girl bolted."

Bobby shook his head. "How are you explaining the hunt for her?"

"In theory, to give her protection. Jamaal King's crew is hunting her too."

Some good news at last. "Perfect. Well, then . . . this story pretty much writes itself."

Wade nodded.

"But where does it end?" asked Wyatt Cash. "I mean . . . you know."

Bobby turned to the entrepreneur. This man had earned millions of dollars by selling computer-designed camouflage patterns and a line of outdoor vehicles built in China. Was he ready to do whatever was required to move forward rather than back? Maybe. After all, it was Cash who had brought Ebony Swan to his attention.

"What's the best ending?" Bobby asked. "From our point of view?"

Cash's mouth worked through several expressions as he considered the options. "Well . . . I suppose the *safest* thing would be for the video to dis-appear and . . . the drug dealer to find the girl?"

After a few seconds, Bobby nodded slowly. "I think you're probably right."

"How old is the girl?" Cash asked.

"Sixteen," Wade Tarlton answered.

Cash shook his head. "Damn. That's a shame."

Bobby considered asking his new law-enforcement buddy for more information about his brother, but the truth was, despite what had just passed between them, he didn't yet know the man. Not really. And he didn't want anyone named Tarlton knowing he felt vulnerable to any sort of pressure that wasn't mutual. Bobby reached out and shook the chief deputy's hand.

"Good luck, Wade. You be safe tonight."

"Will do."

"I'll remember you."

Wade Tarlton nodded. "Remember this, sir. My brother wants to be governor. I just want to be sheriff."

Bobby smiled, sensing he'd found a useful ally. "Noted."

When Cash led the chief deputy back through the door, Bobby caught enough of a look passing between him and Dixie Donnelly to let him know they were far from strangers. Bobby held his ground, processing what Tarlton had told him, waiting for Dixie to come to him, which she did, and quickly.

"Your boy Buck Tarlton is a pain in my ass."

"Mine, too," she said. "Wade'll pick up the slack. Forget them for now. Let's talk about the police station."

"I'm listening."

"We have three problems there. But it might be that one could solve the others."

"Lay it out for me."

"First, Deputy LeJay presents a problem for the Poker Club and for me personally."

Bobby laughed softly. "I've had that feeling for a while. But when I asked you before if LeJay murdered Doc, you said no."

Dixie's eyes went flint-hard. "Some things I won't say in front of Charles Dufort." After making some private judgment, she went further. "Kenneth is my cousin, Bobby. And he knows too much about too many things. This seems like a good place for his story to come to an end."

So Doc's killer is Dixie's cousin. Bobby nodded slowly. "I'll think about it. But not yet."

"The mole I have in there—"

"I said I'd think about it. Tell me about Marshall McEwan."

"Marshall is an existential threat to the Poker Club. He knows about certain critical dealings in 2018. The club basically sold a seat in the U.S. Senate to the Chinese. Two important votes, anyway. We had the power to appoint one of our members to a vacant seat. And in exchange for that we got—"

"The paper mill," Bobby finished. "Azure Dragon."

"In exchange for certain guarantees from us—promises to make certain improvements in the town. Marshall kept silent about what he knew. But things have gotten . . . unstable lately."

"Because you guys are pushing to take back control of the board?"

"Maybe. About an hour ago, Marshall started pushing back against us on that."

"How so?"

"He said if we don't let the Blacks vote their conscience, he'll go public over the Azure Dragon thing."

Bobby winced. He knew Marshall McEwan well enough to know he wouldn't make idle threats. His father had been a hard-ass, at least in the sphere of moral courage. He'd faced down the KKK more than once, and on some dark roads.

"You see the situation?" Dixie said.

"What's the third problem? The one that can solve others?"

"Sheriff Tarlton and Sheriff Johnson mean to get LeJay out of that police station one way or another, even if they have to bust him out with their SWAT teams. I'm not sure we can stop them. I thought we'd have control of the city by now, which would render Chief Morgan and his force powerless. But so far they've resisted the pressure we've put on them. And it's considerable."

"I'm still listening."

"Given that Kenneth killed Doc Berry, the idea that two or three Black cops lost their tempers and killed him in revenge would be easy to sell."

Bobby knew exactly where she was going. "And Marshall?"

She ran her tongue around inside her mouth. "I'm thinking about it."

"But your mole is ready and willing to take out LeJay?"

"He wouldn't be worth his weekly check if he weren't."

"Does anybody else in the club know you're talking to me about this?"

"Not yet. But it's what they all want. LeJay dead. Marshall, too."

"It's too soon, Dixie. Too soon and too risky."

"Bobby—"

He looked hard into her eyes. "You just tell the governor to make sure Buck Tarlton knows that storming that station will end with him in prison."

"That's another problem. The governor's unwilling to make that threat. In fact, he seems quite open to Buck and Johnson storming the BPD headquarters."

"Why the *hell* would he take that position?"

"I think Buck has convinced the governor that the Poker Club means to run you against him in the next election."

"These local politics are driving me batshit! It's like junior high all over again."

"You think national politics is any different? Maybe you shouldn't be running for president."

"I'll speak to the governor myself," Bobby said.

Dixie looked uncertain. "All right. But I'm going to be frank with you. Buckman and the others are starting to lose their patience with your plan."

Bobby chuckled with bitter irony. "You and Charles brought me in here for my expertise. And before this crisis ends, you'll see that crowd do exactly what I predicted it would. You just make sure Buck Tarlton lines up those jailhouse trusties like I asked him to."

Dixie clucked her tongue. "I think that's already done."

She started to leave him, but then she turned back. "Bobby, you know—"

"I answer to Charles Dufort, Dixie. Not you. And not the Poker Club. And here's my final word on killing Marshall McEwan: *Don't even think about it.* As for your cousin . . . we'll see. Meanwhile, I want you to do something for me."

"What's that?"

"Find Kendrick Washington. I want to know where he is and where he'll be for the rest of this night. What are his plans? Where's he sleeping? Any speeches in his near future?"

Dixie gave him a curious look. "I'll get on it."

As she turned back toward the door, she caught sight of the distant flames across the river. "Holy hell! What's burning over there now?"

"Another oil well. And I'd just as soon you not mention it inside until you have to. Those old bastards are upset enough."

"But . . . Bobby, I think that's one of ours. And I'm pretty sure Claude Buckman's father was in it with Blake."

"I'm sure he was," Bobby said. "But I need some peace to think before they come out here rending their garments. The true stakes of this game make a couple of oil wells look like Monopoly money."

"What are you doing out here anyway? Making calls?"

"*Thinking*, Dixie. Okay? And I need a damned drink. How about you get your daughter to fix me one?"

Dixie smiled at this prospect. "Now you're talking." She walked back to the door and turned. "Comin' up, hon."

Behind her the big glass door slid open, and Tommy Russo stepped through it, his face troubled. "We've got more problems, Bobby. It's basically a siege down at police headquarters now. Sheriff Tarlton just told Buckman that if Deputy LeJay hasn't been released by nightfall, he and Sheriff Johnson are going to storm the police station and take him."

"God*damn* it." Bobby turned and saw the sun sinking rapidly toward the horizon beyond the bridges. "Get me the governor on a video link."

CHAPTER 71

DESPITE THE TRAUMATIC day for all in city government, our night task force meeting at Pencarrow felt like exactly what everyone needed. Annie and Andrew brought slabs of salmon from Whole Foods in Jackson and grilled it on boards on the big barbecue Andrew kept set up behind the big house for the informal construction crews he sometimes gathered to help with his restoration work. We planned to eat on the long worktable that lines the interior of Pencarrow's main parlor, using benches gathered from all over the site as seating. We're a sizable group, and still growing, but nothing like the babel of this morning's chaotic task force meeting.

For actual elected officials, we have four of the six sitting aldermen, including the new progressives Robert Gaines and Elijah Keyes, with their partners and spouses, plus Sophie Dufort, who came alone. To my surprise, even old Cicely Waite showed up with her necessarily reticent husband. She must have seen the surprise on my face, for her first words to me were: "The enemy of my enemy is my friend. Ain't that what they say?"

"Indeed, Cicely. Glad to have you here."

Elijah Keyes hesitated when I met him at Pencarrow's front door, and he made a brief but somber declaration: "Normally I don't enter these antebellum structures, which I believe are accursed. But I understand the one-of-a-kind work that Brother McKinney is doing out here, so tonight I'm making an exception. As I have for the Whitney Plantation."

"I'm glad to hear that, Robert. And we're glad to have you."

Before they moved deeper into the house, both Gaines and Keyes gave me inquisitive looks. They knew I'd spent part of the afternoon trying to counter the illegal pressure being applied against them—some from Mississippi, some from Alabama, where Keyes's niece faces possible charges of vehicular homicide. I've recruited Judge Shelby to assist me in this effort, but even with Clay's help, we're making only limited progress. If we succeed, it will be thanks to the judge's lifelong connections.

Ray Ransom arrives next, along with his wife, but he isn't saying much tonight. Losing Doc has shaken him to the core. More than this, the big man radiates a seething anger that I fear nothing short of violent revenge will remedy. Needless to say, I worry that some of the attacks around town this afternoon could easily have been Ray's work.

We have to make do without Chief Morgan, who won't risk leaving headquarters or his "special prisoner," Deputy Kenneth LeJay. That means we also lack Marshall McEwan, who's stayed downtown to help Chief Morgan hold the fort—literally. But Judge Shelby is here, and I felt like I was greeting an old friend when he arrived. I even asked Bobby White to stop by, but he apologized and said he was committed to the PGA tournament at Belle Rose, and any break he got he would have to devote to his presidential campaign. The face I miss most is that of Kendrick Washington, who has decided to remain downtown on the bluff, believing that his presence helps to ensure constant coverage by national media—perhaps the best protection the crowd above the river could have.

While sheriffs Tarlton and Johnson failed to follow through on their threat to storm the Bienville Police Headquarters by nightfall if Deputy LeJay had not yet been released, everyone senses that such an assault could still happen—especially if those officials get the blessing of the governor.

While Annie and Andrew lay out paper plates and flatware on the table, most guests take a quick walking tour of the mansion. My funding of this restoration has generated a lot of curiosity over the past year, as has Andrew's reputation, and his hiring of various Black craftsmen from around the state. Everyone marvels at the work being done inside the house. Andrew has kept a detailed photographic record, which is on display in Captain Pencarrow's study, and it's impressive by any standard. Among his most interesting exhibits is a set of artifacts excavated by a class of HBCU college interns over the past summer, who worked a dig near the "quarters" area of Pencarrow, where large groups of the enslaved lived before emancipation. The students uncovered everything from cooking utensils to nearly complete sets of tools used in various trades of the era.

But what captures the guests' attention with almost magical power is a sculpted bust that Andrew himself carved out of wood salvaged from the slave quarters, using only hammer and chisel, which tonight is displayed in what was once Captain Pencarrow's private library. Titled *Calliope*, it was inspired by a painted locket Andrew discovered hidden in the bookshelves. That locket now hangs around the neck of the bust of the person it was created to immortalize, an enslaved woman of medium skin tone and striking beauty. But far more than beauty, Calliope projects an unconquerable strength, and also wisdom. Even the locket painting captured that. But what existed only in miniature has been brought to full flower in Andrew's life-size bust, and everyone marvels at what the young man has wrought with his gifted hands.

Standing beside a tower of rusty painter's scaffolding, his face glowing with pride, Andrew says, "I consider Calliope to be the soul of Pencarrow. Eventually, I think, everyone in America is going to know her history. After they do, we will all have a better grasp of the confounding complexity of life that existed in places like this. It's not an easy truth, but it's one I believe we have to think about."

I feel Andrew's gaze on me when he says this, and I wonder just how deeply my mother took him into her confidence during her research. Across the room, Sophie Dufort listens with something like rapture on her face. In her own way she is as striking as Calliope, except that she bears the color and features of what was, during Calliope's lifetime, the master class. And Sophie's ancestors owned many slaves. I've seen the records.

"You've got to read the rest of Romulus's story," Nadine whispers in my ear. "In his own voice. I feel like I know Calliope now, at least partly. I know her children. I know something of the nightmare she was trapped in, and the solace she found here before that."

"I'll get to it," I promise. "History isn't exactly my priority right now. The present is making some pretty serious demands on my time."

"Whoever's burning those mansions is thinking about history. And that face you're looking at right there . . . it isn't separate from you, Penn. It's part of you. This space we're in is where Calliope lived and breathed and moved. A reality that we'll never understand played out between these walls. What does a woman feel who is owned by a man (or rather his father), but for whom she also feels love and gratitude? Do we call that rape? In every case? Can we ever call it love? People will say no. But I've already uncovered cases of similar relationships that defy any simplistic characterizations."

Nadine's remark reminds me of the Port Gibson planter Richard Archer, who when dying begged his wife to let a formerly enslaved woman named Patty, with whom he had been intimately involved, return to nurse him, now that he was impotent. This Patty did, despite having been long freed by then, and being in no way bound to do so. Surely some human connection short of coercion existed between these two. But barring some lucky discovery of letters or a diary, we shall never be able to plumb its nature . . .

"I mean," Nadine goes on, "how different was Calliope's relationship with Captain Pencarrow, really, from some of the marriages that existed in so-called 'free' society at the time? She literally ran this place."

A strange chill goes through me. "How about easing up a little, okay?"

"Sorry. I just can't stop thinking about what I've learned from Romulus's testament, and from Peggy's writing. It's . . . terrible. Yet it's the fabric out of which the present was made. Your present. So it's confusing as hell, at bottom. It seems to me that no matter how obscene the circumstances people find themselves in, they try to find a way to have some semblance of normal life. Even if it's technically and legally impossible."

"Why don't you have another beer? Or better yet, find some whiskey."

Nadine pinches my side, hard, but she doesn't leave. "Have you ever noticed that Sophie Dufort almost never smiles?"

I suppose she's noticed me looking at Sophie, but my reason is simple. I'm thinking about Ebony Swan not showing up for the hospital parking lot rendezvous, and wondering if Sophie knows anything more about the fate of the high school girl. "You don't care for Sophie, do you?"

Nadine doesn't answer, as Andrew goes on expounding upon Calliope's unique role in the life of Pencarrow Plantation.

"When I was sixteen," Nadine whispers, "Sophie Dufort was the most beautiful woman in Bienville, bar none, even though she must have been forty. But she never smiled. She was obviously miserable. The thing was, I couldn't tell whether she was miserable because someone had done something terrible to her, or because she'd done something terrible to somebody else."

Sophie's dark gaze has moved onto me once more. "Which do you think it was?"

"I'd bet on both."

"Usually it is both."

"She strikes me like a ghost in search of redemption." Nadine takes the skin of my lower back between her thumb and forefinger and twists until I flinch.

"Jesus—"

"And I think maybe she sees you as her redemption. The kind of guy she never really got. Except for those six months you slept with her, of course."

"Beauty's overrated," I say wisely, and truthfully, my eyes not on Sophie but the bust of Calliope. "Yeats knew that. Beauty draws all manner of obsession and pain down upon itself."

"Good answer," Nadine whispers. "I'll get that whiskey now."

As she slips away, a round of applause breaks out for whatever Andrew said in conclusion (and I obviously missed).

As Alderman Robert Gaines leaves the library, he signals me to follow him. His urgency doesn't go unnoticed, and as I pursue him, I realize Elijah Keyes and Cicely Waite are trailing behind me. Gaines slips through a side door, out into the light of the security lamps behind the mansion proper. From here along the entire west side, Pencarrow is covered with a massive cage of scaffolding.

Ahead of me, Gaines walks as though carrying a heavy burden on his shoulders. Reaching up, he stops and closes his fists around a steel bar of scaffolding, then gives it a hard shake as though testing it. A couple of seconds later, Elijah and Cicely catch up and stand facing me.

"What's up, guys?"

It's Gaines who answers. "We need to know if you've made any progress neutralizing the pressure on us. Because they're ratcheting it up. There's going to be another vote on the Stennis statute in the morning. You can count on that. And unless you've found a way to torpedo the extortion coming our way . . ."

"Judge Shelby and I have tried several angles of attack," I tell them. "So far we've yet to succeed. But Shelby has got a lot of connections, and he's pushing them hard. It's tough to manage corruption from a distance, especially when you're dealing with paranoid attorneys who are breaking the law."

"I told you!" says Keyes. "They can't help us!"

"Damn it," curses Gaines.

"*But*," I push on, "while I can't be specific, there is someone in town who has real leverage over the Poker Club. And this evening he pushed back against them, hard. In fact, he's demanded that they lay off you guys, or he'll drop the hammer on them."

"What kind of hammer?" asks Cicely, her eyes narrowed in suspicion.

"A ball-peen hammer. Federal felony charges. Damn near treason. National in scope."

All three officials look intrigued, and clearly want to know more—which I cannot tell them. Before we can continue, though, Reverend Aaron Baldwin steps from the shadows to join us.

"I hope I'm not interrupting," he says gently.

"Never, Rev," says Alderman Gaines.

Pastor Baldwin radiates an almost Christlike self-possession that people sometimes mistake as weakness if they're not paying attention. But I've seen the old man move congregations like a summer wind, without even raising his voice.

"Another problem," says Gaines. "Vivian Paine is going to try to enact strict curfews tomorrow. She doesn't give a damn about safety. She wants to use curfews to clear the bluff."

"Hang on," I say, thinking aloud. "Is clearing the bluff really that bad an idea? I mean, if you want to identify the greatest potential for disaster, it's the bluff. The paintball clash today showed us that. Remove those marchers, and our chances of a mass-casualty event drop by ninety percent, easy."

"Not the point," Reverend Baldwin says. "This is about honoring the dead and wounded at Mission Hill. The martyrs. Even Pastor Doucy agrees, which makes this that rare case where you could say yes to us both."

Cicely Waite chuckles. "That *is* a rare situation."

Pastor Baldwin says, "I'm no lawyer, but what if the people who want to stand vigil simply do it in defiance of the curfew order? You know, stand and pray, like civil disobedience? On religious grounds. Chief Morgan could refuse to arrest them for expressing their religion."

Gaines and Keyes consider this as a practical solution.

"Speaking as your ex–city attorney," I interject, "that could come back and bite you on the ass, quick. If you somehow keep control of the board, the other side could use the same grounds to defy whatever orders you issue going forward."

"The way they did with Doc's Covid orders," Keyes mutters.

A flood of bitter memories returns.

"Daddy?" Annie calls from the kitchen door. "Are you and the aldermen out here? It's time to eat!"

"Anything else that can't wait?" I ask.

"All I know," says Reverend Baldwin, "is this is a different town without Doc. Somebody needs to step into his shoes, and fast. Who's gonna do that? It's got to be one of you three."

While the aldermen stare uncomfortably at each other, I say, "Nothing personal, but . . . Kendrick Washington has generated more social media interest in a shorter time than most international football stars. I'd really hoped to talk to him tonight, because he might be capable of taking control of this crisis in a way that has nothing to do with official authority."

"He's just a kid," Cicely says dismissively.

"Is he? He's young, but it's young people who change the world, Cicely. Neither Martin Luther King nor Malcolm lived to forty."

She grunts unhappily, but she doesn't argue.

"Whatever spark Kendrick has, I felt it at Mission Hill when I was on that killing ground with him. Indefinable maybe, but also unquenchable. Just like Bobby White. They were both heroes that day."

"You may be right," Elijah Keyes says. "I've watched the people react to Kendrick. They act like he's Gandhi or something. Let's get some food. I want to think about this."

"Good idea."

Elijah Keyes pokes me in the chest. "Whatever we decide, brother, you gotta get the pressure off us. Or we won't be able to vote but one way tomorrow. You hear me?"

I nod soberly, but without much confidence that I can get him what he needs.

As I turn to head back into the house, my phone rings. The caller is Chief Morgan. "What's happening, Mason?" I ask, clicking to speaker and signaling the others to wait.

"If we don't surrender Deputy LeJay within the hour, SWAT teams from two counties are going to bust up in here and take him out. Tarlton's and Coy Johnson's. They claim they have the permission of the governor."

"They can't! Your prisoner's been duly charged by the district attorney."

"They claim the sheriff's authority supersedes mine at all times, especially during time of emergency. Even with the city intact, which it might not be by tomorrow morning."

"Goddamn it, Mason. I'm sorry."

"Look, my men are in no mood to back down after what happened to Doc. But nor are they anxious to die facing heavy-caliber military weapons that they have no means to resist."

"Chief . . . nobody wants you guys fighting a war you can't win down there."

"I'll tell you this, Penn. I've been around this LeJay bastard for a while now. He's not some good ol' boy caught up in a bind. He's a killer. Back shooter, if you ask me. I'm certain he murdered Doc, and I think he did it on somebody's order."

"Do you have any more information on him?"

"A few minutes ago, I found out Deputy LeJay turns out to be the first cousin of Dixie Donnelly, newly minted member of the Bienville Poker Club."

"No shit?"

"Makes you wonder, doesn't it? Who's really calling the shots down in that tower? She's the one trying so hard to get the city dissolved."

"Noted, Mason. We'll do what we can from our end to stop any assault. But you guys hunker down and get ready, just in case."

"Preachin' to the choir, buddy. Figure fifty minutes."

WE BEGIN OUR supper with a blessing by Pastor Baldwin, who mentions how reluctant he was to leave his flock under the guns of the National Guard and state police. Only Kendrick Washington's promise to keep watch on "the faithful" convinced the old man to take an hour away from the bluff.

It's plain from the table conversation that Doc's murder has profoundly wounded the community. Everyone present shared a personal bond with him, and many grieve openly. The paintball-versus-AR-15 battle that followed his death pushed the town's collective fear to a new level, and the burning of Beauvoir—while shocking enough to make news around the world—only provided a limited amount of relief.

As our guests rush through dinner, knowing that the standoff downtown may soon approach its denouement, my cell phone pings with yet another text, as do two or three others at the table. Mine's from Chief Morgan, who tells me that Sheriff Tarlton just informed him via bullhorn that he has twenty-five minutes to send Deputy LeJay out of the station. Tarlton still claims he has the explicit permission of the governor to remove LeJay by force.

Alderman Gaines clearly received a similar message, and he quicky relates it to the assembled group. Normally, at this point everyone would dump their plates into the big barrel in the kitchen and break into smaller groups to express their private concerns. This is the way business gets done in small towns. But tonight Andrew sets up a small flat-screen TV on top of a big cabinet at the end of the worktable, and everyone stares with bated breath at the CNN feed, knowing that the fate of our town may hang on what happens next on that screen.

Most of the images are from helicopters or drones, aerials of the narrow streets surrounding police headquarters. Every couple of minutes CNN cuts away to show Confederate Memorial Park on the bluff— where an estimated crowd of five thousand has clearly gotten word of imminent action to the north. Police headquarters is only six blocks from the north end of the park, where the amphitheater sits on green space where the long-promised civil rights monument has yet to be built. (Now and then I hear rumors that Charles Dufort has offered to fund the monument from his own pocket, but this has yet to happen. That might be because Dufort's family, though they were known to have resisted secession and supported Lincoln, also owned more than five hundred human beings. With no one else offering, though, something like that might just happen.)

It's clear that the bluff crowd would like to move toward Chief Morgan's police station in support, but containment barriers have clearly been placed to prevent that.

Most people around our table are putting on a show of calm, but I see fear etched into their faces, and nearly everyone paces out invisible circles on the floor if they get up to refresh their drinks or run to the bathroom. Doc Berry has never been missed more acutely than tonight, in this room, on the verge of war between our city's law-enforcement agencies.

"I know how this would have ended in '66," says Reverend Baldwin. "I think we're about to see how much Mississippi has changed since then. If at all."

Ray Ransom snorts with pessimism. "Speaking as a Parchman alumni, Rev . . . don't get your hopes up."

CHAPTER 72

THREE BLOCKS WEST of the bluff in downtown Bienville, and three blocks north, sheriffs Tarlton and Johnson had deployed their armored SWAT vehicles to opposite ends of the block where the Bienville police HQ stood. Individual officers waited beside key windows and doors in the restored Victorian manse, ready to smash them with special hammers or blow them out with shaped charges of C-4.

Tarlton and Johnson crouched in the tactical command center across Jefferson Street, watching the clock tick down toward the deadline.

"That was damn good thinking, working the governor like that," Johnson said. "He about shit himself when you told him the Poker Club was going to run Bobby White as a write-in if he doesn't withdraw from the race."

Buck Tarlton laughed. "I wasn't lying. They meant to, until White pissed on their offer. Bobby wants the White House, and nothing less. The governor's just too paranoid to see that."

Coy Johnson raked his hand over his chin, and his face hardened. "One thing, Buck. If we storm that station, we're gonna be killin' cops."

"Black cops," Tarlton clarified.

"Still. That ain't gonna play well with a lot of folks. Even folks on our side. Back the blue, right?"

Tarlton's face reddened. "What the *hell* have you been bitchin' about all day if you weren't ready to go in hard? LeJay is your damned deputy! And he caused all this shit!"

Sheriff Johnson grimaced. "I—to tell you the truth, I didn't think Morgan had it in him to defy the governor. I figured he'd cave and send LeJay out."

"Well, he ain't going to. Doc getting killed hit these Blacks hard, man. He was like Martin Luther King to them. But things have gone too far for us to back out now. You understand?"

Johnson nodded. "I'm ready."

"Make sure your men are. I don't want anybody pullin' fire at the last second."

"Don't worry about that. Hell"—Sheriff Johnson ducked his head and looked around as though his words might be picked up by some nearby phone or camera—"half the guys in my unit are sons or grandsons of Klansmen."

Buck Tarlton chuckled dryly. "Well, that's more like it."

BOBBY LAY STRETCHED along a Roche Bobois sofa in the corporate apartment attached to the Donnelly Oil penthouse, his shoulders propped against the low back cushions. He was enjoying a break from the meddlesome millionaires of the private club, taking care of texts and emails he'd been ignoring for days.

Cringing at the sound of a light knock at the door, he found himself surprised when a tall, muscular young woman in her early thirties stepped in wearing yoga pants and a plain gray sweatshirt. She wore little or no makeup, and her light brown hair hung to her mid-chest, but her bone structure and large gray eyes were so striking that her beauty was of a type directly opposite of what he'd imagined in a Fox-affiliate news anchor—a type of which he'd met dozens while doing book tours on the road. In each hand she carried a crystal highball glass with a lime crushed over the edge.

"Are you Jenna Kay Donnelly?"

She smiled and nodded, then bent at the waist and passed him his gin and tonic.

"Sorry I hijacked your sofa. Your mother offered."

"Oh, no problem. I'm glad to have some company at last."

Dixie's daughter had a pleasingly low and unaffected voice for a newscaster, and almost no Southern accent.

Bobby pulled up his legs in case she wanted to sit on the sofa rather than the desk chair, and it turned out she did. She settled with her left hip against his feet, as though they had known each other for years.

"I don't generally do waitress work, but you've been a busy boy, and it is an honor to serve the man who took out Abu Nasir."

Bobby smiled. "I appreciate that. I needed something to cut the tension."

Jenna Kay nodded. "Things are getting tense up here today."

"I need to speak to the governor pretty soon. You don't have him in your pocket, do you?" Bobby tilted his head toward a bag on the end table. "Or maybe your purse?"

"No, sorry. Though I don't imagine it would be much of a challenge to get his attention."

"For you? Hell, no."

As she laughed, her mother opened the door and leaned in, smiling at the sight that greeted her. Then she scowled at the memory of her errand.

"I'm afraid the governor's refusing to talk to you right now, Bobby. I think somebody's been sabotaging his opinion of you."

Bobby groaned in frustration. "Well, isn't that special? How about you tell the *guv* that his next call will be coming from Brett Favre, and that Brett's call will be streamed live on the internet."

Jenna Kay's snort of laughter told Bobby she was more than familiar with the scandals in her native state.

"Dix," Bobby added, "it strikes me that you might see a rogue operation by our toxic twin sheriffs as a blessing in disguise, if it results in the loss of certain individuals in that station. I want to be sure you understand that's not the case."

"Oh, I know who's in charge tonight. I'm not bucking you on this. I only hope you don't regret it later."

"Let's see how this siege situation breaks. There'll be time to pivot later if changes become necessary."

"I'm not as confident of that as you are. Let me see if I can get you a line into the guv's mansion. You two need anything in the meantime?"

"Goodbye, Mom," Jenna called without looking.

Dixie pursed her lips and pulled the door shut after her.

"I like the way you handle my mother. Not many people can resist her, much less control her."

"She's not so bad."

"That's because she likes you." Jenna's eyes suddenly locked onto the muted TV mounted on a stand in the corner. "Hey, do you mind if I turn up the sound?"

Bobby glanced at the screen. On a makeshift stage in a dense crowd of Black people, Bobby saw a young girl wearing a white bandage across the left half of her face and skull. "Not at all. Who's that?"

"Octoroon. Or plain Octa, now. The rapper who was wounded by shrapnel at Mission Hill. And unless I'm wrong.... I think she's performing a hundred yards down Battery Row from us right now. Holy shit."

"Seriously? I didn't hear anything about this."

Octa marched from one end of the little stage to the other, catlike and challenging in her movements, a pair of large sunglasses joining the bandaged and unbandaged halves of her face.

"Me, either," Jenna said. "This'll be huge news, especially with that bandage on her face. I think she just started reconstructive surgery a couple of days ago."

"Do you know that song she's singing?"

"Sure. 'One-Drop Rules.' It's one of her hits."

"How old is it?"

"Ahhh, maybe a year."

"How old are you, Jenna?"

"Thirty-four."

"One-Drop Rules" ended with screams of approbation, and then the young singer began speaking to the crowd.

"You know," Octa said, "yesterday it hit me that I could've died back at Mission Hill, just like so many friends and fans who did, and aren't with us any longer. Right down this river they died, for no reason than a bunch of reckless cops didn't think before they pulled their triggers. Thirty-something shots in five seconds. More than twenty people dead, most of 'em kids. And now? They got us penned up here above the river, without water, while army tanks besiege our brothers and sisters in the city police, who are only doing their duty trying to hold on to the dirty cop who murdered Mayor Berry!"

The fans began booing loudly.

As Octa went on, Bobby noticed a Black cop in her late forties guarding the front right corner of the stage. He'd known Shirley Danvers since he was a kid. A police sergeant and mother of four, Shirley appeared to have been assigned to protect Octa during her appearance.

"I wanna thank Soul Sister Shirley here," Octa went on, "who with her crew is providing security for me and my entourage. I also wanna thank Dr. Dwight Ford, who flew me up from New Orleans in his chopper, same as he did the day of Mission Hill. And thanks for treating my mama before this show! 'Cause *Lawd*, she be stressed over this bullshit!"

The crowd laughed, even Jenna.

"Right now I'm gonna do a special song . . . an old song for y'all, one that fits this occasion to a T." In a surprisingly low register, Octa began an a cappella version of "Freedom Song," which Bobby knew from the Roberta Flack version in the 1970s, the song having played a role in the civil rights movement he'd studied so deeply in grad school.

"*Ohhhh, freedom. Ohhhh, freedom. Ohhhh, freedom, over me. And before I'll be a slave, I'll be buried in my grave. And go home . . . to my Lord . . . and be free.*"

Jenna checks an app on her smartphone and shakes her head. "This is being picked up all over the country. Much more of this, and Bienville will overtake Memphis as the center of the media universe . . . at least for tonight."

There was a quick knock, then Dixie threw open the door and swept in carrying a MacBook Pro, which she set on Bobby's lap with Zoom already running.

"Guv changed his mind," she said with a laugh. "Here he is, with his chaperone."

In one floating box Bobby saw the governor's chief of staff. The other square showed the governor himself, wearing a pink button-down shirt.

"Thanks, Dix. I'll take it from here."

Jenna's mother glanced at her as though she expected her daughter to follow her out, but Bobby blocked the computer's camera, then looked at Jenna and raised his finger to his lips. She smiled, then shooed Dixie out of the room.

After unmuting his audio link, Bobby sat straighter on the leather couch, squaring up before the monitor that showed the governor and his chief of staff in their Jackson offices. While he did, Jenna turned the sound on the television down to near silence.

"Governor, this is Bobby White speaking."

The governor threw out his hands and made a cartoon gesture of surprise. "I see you, Bobby. How's it goin' down there? Looks pretty bad on TV."

"Things were fine until you okayed Sheriff Tarlton to storm the goddamn police station. You do appreciate the potential optics of that, right?"

"Ahhh . . . far from ideal, obviously. But we've got a municipal chief of police defying state authority during a time of emergency. Sheriff Tarlton assures me drastic measures are called for, before the situation gets even worse."

"What *you* have," Bobby said firmly, "is two predominantly white sheriff's departments about to storm a police station manned almost exclusively by Black officers. They're doing that in order to break a *legally charged* murder suspect out of jail. In other words, Governor, in exactly about ten minutes, you're going to have cops shooting cops on your direct orders. How do you think that's going to play on the national news? Or at RNC headquarters?"

The governor beckoned to someone for a glass of water, which he swallowed audibly onscreen.

"I'll tell you this, Guv," Bobby said in a hard voice. "Nobody who gives that order is ever going to be vice president of a Rotary Club, much less the United States."

The governor blanched visibly onscreen.

"Forgive me, Bobby," said the chief of staff. "But as of this moment you're a radio talk-show host and private attorney. On the other side of this equation the governor has two duly sworn sheriffs. How are we supposed to justify taking your recommendation over theirs? You people have got chaos in Tenisaw County, and we have to do something about it."

"A common misconception," Bobby said. "That you always have to do something in a crisis. The instructors at SFOD and DEVGRU will tell you the opposite is often true. Sometimes it's best to do nothing. It's often the hardest thing, but also the wisest."

The governor nodded, then cut his eyes at his chief of staff.

"Finally," Bobby concluded, "let me give you one assurance, Governor. Take this as gospel. I have *zero intention* of running for your job next year, or any other. I have no desire to be governor of my home state, now or ever. I'm either going to be president of the United States or a radio host. Am I clear?"

The governor was looking at his chief again, and Bobby saw critical understanding pass between them.

"Clock's ticking," Bobby said. "And we are all about to look very, very bad to the rest of the nation."

"What if Sheriff Tarlton refuses to stand down?" the governor asked. "This close to the deadline?"

"Tarlton works for you, sir. He doesn't have the balls to defy your order. Be firm, and all this craziness will vanish like a puff of smoke."

The governor's grateful nod was almost desperate. "We'll get back to you."

Bobby hit MUTE again and set aside the computer.

"Looks like you're the one with the governor in your purse," Jenna quipped.

Bobby sensed a tiny dig in her comment, but he didn't analyze it too closely. It hadn't felt malicious, only probing.

Jenna turned the TV sound back up, and Octa's pure voice filled the room again as she worked her way to the end of "Freedom Song" like a small boat cutting its way to the shore of a dark stream. Even the visual of her holding a massive crowd entranced in silence with only her voice resurrected for Bobby the black-and-white documentary footage he'd viewed alone in the back rooms of the Ole Miss library.

"I'm singing from the heart of Mississippi!" she cried. "One of the former slave capitals of this country. The state that made the great Ms. Nina Simone sing 'Mississippi *Goddam*'! Don't tell me to *go slow* no more! I don't have the time."

"So you came in here to watch the TV?" Bobby asked.

Jenna smiled. "No. I figure we have about three minutes max before they drag you back out there to try to manage the insanity. Tomorrow I'm supposed to fly to Kiawah Island to be in a wedding, so I figure we ought to get on with what we both know this is."

Bobby found himself intrigued. "Which is?"

"One of the most selective auditions I've ever taken part in."

"Auditions? For what?"

"First Lady, right?"

Her directness took Bobby aback. "First Lady of . . . ?"

"Don't play with me. The United States."

"Ahh."

"There's just one problem I see," Jenna said with real curiosity.

"What's that?"

"I'm a woman. And my exquisitely refined instincts in these matters tell me that you're not much interested in those."

Bobby stared back at her in stunned silence. "And yet . . ." he said finally.

She nodded with an inscrutable smile. "And yet the job remains. Correct?"

Bobby took a long swallow from his gin and regarded her in silence.

SHERIFF TARLTON SAT impatiently in his mobile tactical operations center, counting down to breach, when the governor's face filled the video comm screen again.

"Buck, are you there?" he asked. "I'm having all kinds of trouble trying to reach you in that damned tactical op center."

Tarlton hesitated, glanced at his watch, then reluctantly opened the link. "Well, you've got me now, sir. Here in the TOC. With Sheriff Johnson," he lied.

"Buck, I'm afraid I'm going to have to ask you—well, order you, really—to stand down. At least for now."

Tarlton's face and neck began to sweat. "Will you repeat that, Governor?"

"We're going to give Chief Morgan a little more time to come to the proper decision on this LeJay matter. The death of Mayor Berry has been particularly hard on the Black community. Now we have Black police officers guarding the deputy legally charged with killing him. However frivolous that charge might be, we don't want to be seen to be ignoring the Black community on this."

"Sir, you can't be serious! Our men are about to breach. I'm not sure we can even get word to them in time. If we go in halfway, due to miscommunication, we could take serious casualties."

"Well, get them out of there! I'm ordering you to stand down. Let me be clear as crystal about that. Acknowledge."

Anger simmered like acid in Tarlton's gut. "Who got to you, Governor? Somebody's feeding you a line of bullshit!"

"I'd rather be wrong with zero casualties than right with a dozen, Buck. And all of them cops? Didn't Mission Hill teach you anything?"

Tarlton killed the link. "God*damn* it!" he shouted, looking around the op center. Only one man was in the trailer with him, and it wasn't Sheriff Coy Johnson. It was his comms officer, and as soon as Tarlton's gaze landed on him, the man said, "I didn't hear nothing, Sheriff. Not a damn thing. You do what you need to."

"Buck, this is Coy," came a voice over the radio. "I've got eight minutes till breach on the clock. Everything set to go?"

Tarlton closed his eyes. "Ten-four. Look . . . Morgan's clowns won't be able to stop us. They haven't done half the training we have. Their budget's a joke."

"I'm with you. No contest. Hey—I'm getting a call on my cell. It's from the governor's office."

"Don't answer! They're liable to start losing their nerve. You know these politicians. We can't let them order us to stand down. As soon as we have LeJay with us, we'll be heroes. If we let 'em stand us down, things just spiral down from there."

"Have you spoken to the governor since I left the TOC?"

"Just once, and he's pissing his diapers about casualties. He's scared of the PR, Coy. But he's got no idea how bad it could get if LeJay starts talking in there."

"What do you mean? What does Kenny LeJay know that can hurt anybody? Everybody knows he shot the mayor, but that was justifiable."

Tarlton started to give his old friend the full story, but they were on the police radio, and before he could begin, his mind filled with the image of his house burning on Fox Run Road.

"Just do what I'm doing, Coy. Look at this whole situation and ask yourself what your daddy woulda done."

"Which is what?"

"He sure wouldn't have pulled any Mike Pence bullshit. It's up to us to hold the line, boy."

There was silence on the net. Then Coy Johnson said, "You know what? Fuck Mason Morgan. He shoulda left my deputy alone. Fuck the governor, too. Fat-ass frat boy."

Buck Tarlton smiled with ineffable satisfaction. After years of waiting, he was finally about to go into real action, and not against punk drug dealers, but against the storm troopers of the Deep State.

THE GUESTS SEATED around the long worktable in Pencarrow's parlor hardly speak as Octa the rapper sings the old spiritual with the pious intensity of a soloist in a country saltbox church, and their silence holds for her final verse.

"There'll be no more weepin', no more weepin'. No more weepin' over me. And before I'll be a slave, I'll be buried in my grave. And go home to my Lord . . . and be free."

Several among us join in her final line: *"Yes, go home to my Lord . . . and be free."*

Octa falls silent at last, and the young girl begins speaking again about the dead and wounded of Mission Hill, and of Memphis. Some around our table have been profoundly moved by Octa's performance. A few weep openly, and to my surprise, one with the unexpected gleam of tears in her eyes is Cicely Waite.

"That little girl reminds me of Odetta," says the old politician. "Way back in the day. Some of these young sisters have got it goin' on, I tell you. That girl knows where she come from."

"Right now," Octa says from center stage, "I want to bring my new brother up to the stage. My *best* brother. The hero of Mission Hill: *Kendrick Washington!*"

The crowd erupts in a roar that's probably shaking the bluff.

Kendrick hops up onto the stage wearing a royal purple tank top rather than the slave chains this crowd probably expects, but they're clearly inspired by the sight of him.

"Yo, everybody!" he begins. "I got an announcement to make. Now that Mayor Berry has passed, I'm gonna tell you he had just seen his partner, Mr. David Latour, before being drawn to the sound of gunfire to help a young white man. There, while rendering aid, he got shot by Deputy Kenneth LeJay, who right now sits in the jail six blocks from here, legally charged with *murder*, while two white sheriffs threaten to break *into* the jail and take him out—making a travesty of the rule of law in these United States."

The crowd roars with anger and indignation.

"Before Doc headed back for World Famous Barbecue, he told Mr. David that, because his unity speech had gone so well at Diamond Hill, he intended to make another one tomorrow, at the amphitheater on the bluff. But now Doc will never give that speech, or any other. So Mr. Latour asked me would I give it for him—which I humbly intend to do tomorrow, from Confederate Memorial Park at two p.m. I can never truly take Doc's place, but I'm gonna do my best tomorrow to take on his burden. My subject will be these recent fires and violence, and the proper response to them. Should it be nonviolence, as Martin Luther King would have counseled? Or should we listen to Malcolm X, who believed freedom has to be seized *by any means necessary*, and without delay?"

A furious cheer erupts, making clear the immediate preference of this audience.

"Thank you, Miss Octa," Kendrick says, "for sharing this platform for a minute. Now I'm gonna go back to work on my speech."

"Not yet, K." Octa takes hold of his hand. "I've been asked if you'll sing us a verse and a chorus of the song you did at Mission Hill before you saved all those lives at the shooting. 'Southern Man.' Oh, yeaaaah! Give it up! *'Southern man, when will you pay them back?'* Seems we've got hold of a USB of your backing track we can play, if you'll do it for us."

Kendrick ducks his head, then reaches out and takes hold of a mic someone offers him as the slow hip-hop beat swells. A minor chord comes up behind the drums, and he begins to sing. As he does, in his warm baritone, my cell phone pings, and a message from Bobby White pops up on my screen.

Penn! Tarlton and Johnson still have their men and vehicles in assault position. All my instincts say there's a lot of danger downtown. I'm pushing every political button I can, but whatever stroke you have in Jackson, you'd better use it to pressure the governor. Or we're going to watch the bloody demise of democracy in Bienville, MS. Copy?

BACK IN THE Donnelly tower penthouse, Bobby had been distracted from his suitor's piercingly direct comment about his sexuality by the only thing that could have done it: the promise that Kendrick Washington was finally going to put himself into the crosshairs of Donny Kilmer's rifle, and under the exact circumstances Bobby required to fulfill his plan. Now

Bobby was texting Donny a much calmer message than the one he'd sent Penn Cage.

In case you didn't hear, Primary will be exposed tomorrow in perfect position two p.m., almost exactly where expected. Will contact you tonight w details and GPS pin. For now, go home and get all the rest you can. Acknowledge.

"WELL," JENNA KAY said, "don't you look like the cat that ate the canary?"

Before Bobby could reply, a return text pinged up. *Understood.* He smiled with almost physical satisfaction.

"You look like you just got the best news you've gotten in years," Jenna said, watching him closely from the corner of her eye.

"I might have," Bobby said cryptically.

Jenna shifted on the sofa and crossed her long legs before her. "Well . . . I figure we still have about a minute before they bust in here to get you, so I'm going to go ahead and go through with the audition."

"You certainly have my attention."

"As for my external qualifications, you see what you get. I've never had complaints, and when it comes to physical beauty, I work in a *shallow-ass*, superficial, highly judgmental industry—take my word."

"You clearly pass that test, in anybody's book."

"As for deeper assets, well . . . I know when to open my mouth and when to keep it shut. I'm fluent in both French and Spanish, and I have some rudimentary Mandarin. I can sing a high C, and dance well enough to get you through a State Department ball with style. Those might seem like the social virtues of the 1950s, but I still count them."

"As do I. Excellent First Lady material."

Jenna giggled in her throat. "Hmmm . . . what else? I can tell a decent joke, and lots of indecent ones as well. I've made both Judd Apatow and Steve Martin laugh—*with* me, not at me."

"Together or separately?"

"Separately."

Bobby put some pompousness into his voice. "And why do you want this job, young lady?"

Another soft laugh. "Honestly? I think of all the women I know—I mean smart ones—whose deepest ambition is to become an *influencer*. I mean . . . what the fuck does that really mean? I don't know. But I know this: no woman's job carries more influence than First Lady, if you handle it right. I mean, what was Jackie O? She influenced the whole world. Right? People *still* talk about her."

"I can't deny that."

Jenna Kay shrugged. "I can also fish, ski, hunt, canoe, and skydive. I killed a cottonmouth moccasin when I was seven, and I skinned my first deer when I was thirteen."

"Southern girl, for sure. Give me a confession. Small lie you tell or told."

She laughed, having fun with their odd ritual. "My CV says I'm vegan, but my fridge is filled with barbecue pork from the Korean place up the street from my condo."

"Favorite band?"

"I tell people Drive-By Truckers, but that's been a lie since Jason Isbell left. If I'm down, I listen to the Cure, but . . . my actual favorite is the Carpenters."

Bobby's mouth fell open. "Are you serious?"

"Damn straight! Gimme some Karen Carpenter singing Burt Bacharach, and I'm set."

"I can't believe that! Did you know John Lennon loved her voice?"

"No, but I believe it. Let's not lose our thread, though. Sexually I'm very fluid, but also very discreet. I'm into what I suspect you like, and if there's any incompatibility, well . . . I have an extensive toy collection."

"Did you say ex*tensive* or ex*pensive*?"

"It's both."

Bobby laughed appreciatively. "What are your negatives?"

"Limited. My *mother* can be a pain in the ass. Very controlling. But you seem to have that problem under control already."

Bobby laughed outright. "For now, maybe."

On the television, Kendrick Washington ended a shortened version of his Neil Young rewrite with his fists held high above his head, and then Octa returned to center stage.

"*Thank you, Kendrick!* Now I'm gonna ask HBCU Professor Egan's wife to accompany me on another old song, done in a new way. You're bound to know one version or the other, depending on what color you are. Just give it a minute, and then open your mind and heart to it."

Dr. David Egan, the white professor assaulted by the big Barlow goon at the Tranquility fire, helped his wife onto the stage, where she began picking out a familiar melody on a cheap synthesizer. Bobby recognized the tune because it was Rodgers and Hammerstein, from what he thought of as one of the whitest musical films in the world, *The Sound of Music*. As the notes tinkled along Battery Row, and through the condo, Jenna Kay

Donnelly began singing the well-known words in a beautifully controlled soprano.

"You really can sing," Bobby said with amazement. Jenna sounded as though she had near perfect pitch. But Octa's song choice seemed jarring, considering recent events. "I notice you skipped the kittens and mittens and went straight for the strudel and noodles."

She laughed, then nodded at the TV. "Listen."

Onstage, Octa had begun singing the same song. But it wasn't . . . the same song. Instead, she was rapping an alternative version with truly lacerating lyrics about Black rage and white greed.

"Holy fuck," Bobby breathed. "*That's* gonna push some people's buttons. What kind of cultural appropriation do you call that?"

"The best kind?" Jenna commented. "This version was written by Lauryn Hill. It's called 'Black Rage.'"

"How the hell have you survived at a Fox News affiliate?"

Jenna smiled to herself. "By the skin of my teeth."

"You wouldn't last a week at their main studios."

The anchor belly-laughed. "We may find out soon."

"How's that?"

"Turns out they're hiring a sprinkling of something they don't have right now, in the wake of the Dominion lawsuit and the Tucker firing."

"What's that? Actual journalists?"

"Precisely. Preferably ones that don't fit the old Stepford anchor mold."

"Well, you're a damn good start."

"Thanks, Bobby. Now . . . I have an idea. How about we trade foot massages? Before they come in here to pull you back to the fight?"

"Sounds good to me."

They had barely gotten their shoes off when the door burst open and four members of the Poker Club came through together. Wyatt Cash, Arthur Pine, Tommy Russo, and behind them Claude Buckman, all looking worried and angry.

"You've gotta do something, Bobby!" Russo demanded.

"About what?"

"Tarlton and Johnson aren't getting the message. They're still acting like they may assault police headquarters. We're down to four minutes."

Bobby grunted and started to roll off the couch, but Jenna subtly held him in place with her right hand.

"We're losing control of the whole narrative," said Arthur Pine. "And wasn't that your primary strategy?"

Bobby acknowledged the point with a low groan.

"That little Octa girl is taking over the global media airwaves while we stand here! And she's just getting started."

"She's down there defiling Rodgers and Hammerstein!" Claude Buckman barked. "As sacred a musical as there is!"

"I hate to interrupt the pussyfooting," he went on from behind Wyatt Cash. "And I can't say I blame you. But we can't have cops shooting cops in downtown Bienville. Do you think Tarlton's capable of that level of insanity?"

Bobby removed Jenna's hand from his hip and sat up. "Not before they burned his house down. But he's lost face now. And he's one of those guys who always regretted he never had a war. You know?"

No one answered. They'd all shared the same guilt.

"Look at that damned Egan woman!" Buckman bellowed, pointing at the TV, where the professor's wife was still backing Octa on "Black Rage." "And to 'My Favorite Things.' She's a goddamn race traitor!"

"She's harmless," Pine said. "That's actually a good look for the city. We need some diversity going out to the world tonight."

Buckman and Russo shook their heads in disgust.

"Okay," Bobby sighed, looking thoughtful at his watch. "I'm coming."

CHAPTER 73

AMITE COUNTY SHERIFF Coy Johnson was standing on Jefferson Street, watching the clock tick down the final minutes to breach, when an M167 antiaircraft-gun platform towed by a National Guard truck turned into the block and moved into firing position. The rotary cannon mounted on that turret fired three thousand rounds per minute, and nothing in the arsenals of Amite or Tenisaw Counties could stand against it. Not even the armored MRAP could take sustained bursts from a gun of that caliber and rate of fire.

"Buck, are you seeing this?" Sheriff Johnson said into his radio collar.

"What?"

"Pike just rolled one of his antiaircraft-gun platforms into Jefferson Street. And right now they've got their goddamn Vulcan trained on my SWAT van."

"That's all for show, Coy. They're not about to fire on state law-enforcement vehicles."

At that moment Sheriff Johnson saw the first line of National Guard troops march into the street. "Uh . . . I don't know, Buck. This looks pretty damn serious to me."

"Don't pay 'em any mind. I watched Pike back down from a bunch of street thugs today. You think he'll go against our SWAT teams? His troops are goddamn weekend warriors, not real soldiers."

Sheriff Johnson's cell phone rang then, and while he would usually have ignored it, something made him pick up. "Sheriff Johnson. Who'm I talking to?"

"This is Bobby White, Sheriff."

Johnson swallowed in surprise. "What do you want?"

"To keep your men alive and you out of jail."

"How's that?"

"The governor already ordered Sheriff Tarlton to stand down. I think Buck means to disregard that order. If you two assault that headquarters now, you're going to Parchman. Both of you. And if you or your men kill any cops while doing it, you'll likely get the death penalty."

Beads of sweat broke out on Johnson's face. "That's bullshit. They're holding my deputy in there without any—"

"Wake up, Coy. Your deputy was charged by a duly elected district attorney. And you know it."

"A goddamn RINO lawyer!"

"This is still America, Sheriff. A vote is a vote. You'd better get your mind right and get out of the line of fire of that gun system. Because General Pike got embarrassed today. He killed two men in cold blood. He's going to try to make up for that by following the letter of the law. Whereas your asshole buddy Buck Tarlton is trying to make up for his house getting burned by taking it out on the closest Black folks."

"Coy, can you hear me?" Tarlton asked anxiously. "We breach in three minutes!"

Something shifted deep in Coy Johnson's gut. "Buck . . . I've got Sergeant Bobby White on the phone, and he's telling me to stand down."

"So what? Bobby White's nothing but a goddamn *DJ*!"

"He's more'n that, and you know it. The people who run this town listen to him. The goddamn governor listens to him."

"But he's got no legal authority. *We* have that, Coy, just like in Old England. Sovereign sheriffs, damn it. *High* sheriffs! You went to the convention. You know the history. Every sheriff in the state—hell, the country—is watching to see how we handle this. Don't fail them now."

"Buck."

"We breach on the count. Are you ready?"

"Jesus, man."

"I heard all that," Bobby White said. "Don't be a fool, Coy."

Johnson shut his eyes and exhaled with resignation. "You're too late, Sergeant. That nigra chief shouldn't have arrested my deputy. This is happening."

"Damn straight," Tarlton snapped. "See you inside, Coy."

"I hope you two are as drunk as you sound, gentlemen," Bobby said. "Because depleted-uranium slugs are hell on earth."

IN THE GRAND parlor of Pencarrow, those attending the night task force meeting stare in disbelief as the National Guard commander establishes blocking positions with troops and antiaircraft guns at each end of Jefferson Street, where Bienville Police HQ occupies the block. Annie has set up her notebook computer next to the television, so that we can simultaneously follow events on the bluff through a livestream feed of the Ring security cameras from my town house.

Cicely Waite turns her head and looks at me with unfamiliar intimacy.

"Penn, you don't think the Guard would actually fire on those county vehicles, do you?"

"They might. That standoff at midday didn't go well for Pike. The national media have chewed him to pieces over killing those two men with sniper fire."

Judge Shelby takes a step closer to the monitor. "You're only half-right, Penn. Everything depends on the governor now. I know General Pike. If the governor orders him to prevent an assault, he'll use whatever equipment the job requires."

"Even that Vulcan minigun?" Ray Ransom asks, his voice skeptical. "On a city street?"

"You bet your ass," says Alderman Gaines. "Just like he was going to fire on us on the bluff earlier today. Caliber ain't gonna make no difference."

"You're right," says the judge. "Not with Pike."

"It ain't just the caliber," Ray almost whispers. "That gun fires like the wrath of God."

"If they stand by and *don't* stop an assault," I think aloud, "then we're going to see cops killing cops inside that police station."

"White cops killing Black cops," Gaines clarifies. "If it goes that far . . . I don't know what happens next."

"I do," I say softly. "I wrote the CIA a paper on it after 9/11. And there's no coming back from that."

As we stare in fearful anticipation, the lights of the SWAT vans at both ends of the block switch on, and two armored county vehicles begin rolling toward the center of the block. There's not going to be anything sneaky about this assault.

"Last chance, Chief Morgan!" Sheriff Tarlton shouts over his bullhorn. "Send out Deputy LeJay, or we're coming in to get him!"

Chief Morgan offers no response.

The door to the station remains closed.

"Reverend Baldwin," Ray says quietly. "This might be a good time for a prayer."

The white-haired old pastor shakes his head. "Let's bow our heads, brothers and sisters."

The guests bow their heads, but no one takes their eyes from the television.

IN THE COMMAND center of the Donnelly Oil Building, everyone was retaking their seats when Wyatt Cash said, "Claude, you're not going to believe this. I've got Clint Echols lined up on Zoom. It took half the damn day, because he's out on the Gulf of Mexico fishing."

Clint Echols is the Tenisaw County district attorney, and it was he who charged Deputy Kenneth LeJay with second-degree murder, allowing Chief Morgan to use the full power of his department to secure and defend him as a prisoner.

"Clint Echols?" the banker nearly spat. "That bastard put us in this position! Doesn't he know who he works for, for God's sake?"

"Why don't we find out?" Tommy Russo asked. "This may be our only chance to get him to withdraw the charges. We could head off this battle right away if he orders Chief Morgan to release LeJay."

"Get him on the screen!"

Two seconds later, the rugged, sunburned face of a seventy-year-old Bienville attorney filled one of the displays. Clint Echols looked tired, dirty, and put-upon.

"Talk fast, gentlemen," he growled. "I could lose reception any second."

"This is Claude Buckman, Clint. What the hell were you thinking when you charged Ken LeJay for our Black police chief? We've got a jurisdictional nightmare up here! City versus county. You need to drop all charges against LeJay, and I mean yesterday."

Echols sniffed and looked skeptical. "Is the man innocent?"

Buckman was taken aback by the question. "Hell, I don't know. The point is, this is what we need done. Same as what happened with Mission Hill. You did the right thing there, so what's different about this?"

"My point, Claude, is did this Amite County deputy murder Doc Berry? Because if he did, he's going nowhere but to trial."

Buckman glanced over at Arthur Pine as if he were talking to a crazy man. His eyebrows alone screamed: *What the hell?*

Pine addressed the screen: "Clint, I have a feeling you might have been a personal friend of the mayor's. Am I right?"

"Not really. But I'll tell you a quick story. Then I'm going back to my berth. Back in 2005, when Hurricane Katrina blew through Tenisaw County, my daughter Cindy was nine months pregnant. The baby was breech, or backward, whatever they call it when the feet are where the head's supposed to be. Trees were down all over, roads closed. They weren't even putting up rescue helicopters. Cindy was stuck out in the country, and she went into labor. We couldn't move her. Well, son, I pulled every string in the book to get help, called in every favor I could. But nobody would come. We were desperate. My wife was having a breakdown. Then my maid suggested I call Doc Berry. Well, let me tell you something. It took about an hour, but we sent a four-wheeler in his direction—through that damned storm, in the middle of the night—and Doc mounted up and rode seven miles through rain and hail to get to our house. He delivered that baby by *lantern light*. Like it was 1850. Thanks to him, today my granddaughter's a freshman at Mississippi State, and not lying under a marble stone in the cemetery. So you listen to me, Claude. Any man who shot Doc Berry is going to sit in jail until I get to the truth of what happened. And if I find out there's something crooked behind his death . . . by God, somebody will *die of old age in Parchman* before they ever walk free again. You hear me? That's all I've got to say on the matter."

"Now, Clint, just hang on a second," the banker tried, but the red-faced lawyer had teared up, and he shook his head angrily.

"In case you don't remember, Claude, I also served twelve years in the Army Reserves. And I've got only the highest respect for the service Doc did in Vietnam. So, if you boys don't like my position, take your shot at me next election. But you'd better come loaded for bear. Signing off."

The display went dark, leaving only images of armored vehicles on the empty streets outside Chief Morgan's police station on the other screens. Claude Buckman and Arthur Pine sat with their mouths hanging open, while Dixie Donnelly looked downright afraid.

"I didn't hear much wiggle room in that," Bobby said, trying to keep the pleasure out of his voice. "I'd say we're about to see a little skirmish, gentlemen."

AS THOUGH ON cinematic cue, the SWAT vehicles on Jefferson Street begin to accelerate as Reverend Baldwin ends his prayer. For an instant our screens white out, and everyone groans, thinking we've lost our connection. But we haven't. What we witnessed was the detonation of shaped charges on the police headquarters' windows and doors.

"*They breached!*" cries Ray Ransom. "That was C-4. It's on!"

"God help us," intones Judge Shelby.

Nadine clutches my arm and pulls me against her. "Do you think—"

The antiaircraft cannon on the M167 produces a distinctive ripping sound that a soldier I know described as "a fart from the ass of God" (or Satan, depending on where you are when it opens up). But the visual looks like a battle sequence from *Star Wars*. Thousands of tracer rounds merge into a single beam of deathlight as the engine compartment of the MRAP explodes into millions of pieces of shrapnel on Jefferson Street. People around the table scream as the fuel tank detonates in a conflagration of yellow and orange.

The uranium slugs hammer the MRAP onto its side and roll it like a toddler kicking a Tonka through a sandbox. The instant it stops, its rear hatch opens and four men wearing body armor tumble out like drunken football fans. They look like they have no idea where they're going, or even where they are. But I may be wrong, because not one moves *toward* the antiaircraft gun when he flees.

"My *God*," Sophie whispers.

As we stare in awe and disbelief, the turret of the M167 rotates with terrifying speed and precision. Its minigun is now trained on the rear of the Tenisaw County SWAT vehicle. If they fire from that angle—even for three or four seconds—something like two hundred bullets, each weighing as much as a handful of pennies, will chew Tarlton's SWAT team inside into ground beef and bone.

"*Get out, you stupid shitbirds!*" Ray shouts. "*Run for your lives!*"

As if they somehow heard Ray's order, the big rear door of the SWAT van opens and the team within leaps and scatters, scrambling for cover. Only then do I realize that the chatter in the background is small-arms fire—AR-15s and M4s as opposed to a six-barrel 20 mm AA cannon being fired at fifty rounds per second.

"There's fighting inside the station," I say softly. "You hear that? It's too late to stop this."

"The governor will stop it," Judge Shelby says hopefully. "The instant Pike fired that ack-ack, he revealed which side he's on. He'll force Tarlton and Johnson to stand down. Let's just hope we don't lose too many people first. Jesus, Lord. It reminds me of Randall Jarrell's poem. About the ball-turret gunner."

DOWN ON JEFFERSON Street, Sheriff Johnson burst into the TCSD tactical op center and tried to shake his counterpart into sanity or sobriety or both.

"Pull your team back, goddamn it!" Johnson shouted. "That gun'll kill every man in your van if they open up again!"

Buck Tarlton's face had gone slack. Johnson wasn't even sure he was capable of processing words at this point. Clearly Tarlton was in shock after seeing the M167 engage the Amite County MRAP. He was incapable of making any decision—certainly not a competent one.

"*Gimme that goddamn radio!*" Johnson bellowed, snatching the walkie-talkie out of Tarlton's hand. "This is Sheriff Coy Johnson, addressing all SWAT officers from Amite and Tenisaw Counties. Stand down immediately! Repeat, *stand down*! The National Guard is firing on us, which means the governor himself gave that order. *STAND DOWN!*"

Chaos erupted over the radio net, new voices drowned by the crackle of gunfire. Sheriff Johnson repeated his order, his eyes glued to the video being livestreamed onto a laptop in the TOC. The M167 was still aimed at the Tenisaw County SWAT van.

"*Do not fire on Bienville police!*" Sheriff Johnson ordered. "Acknowledge! *DO NOT FIRE ON FELLOW COPS.* Get out of that station ASAP! Leave Deputy LeJay in BPD custody! Is that clear? Please confirm, for God's sake!"

If anyone tried to confirm, their reply was drowned out by someone else trying to do the same.

AROUND THE WORKTABLE in Pencarrow, people have begun to process the possibility that the National Guard just acted to enforce rather than undermine the rule of law in Mississippi. Still, everyone sits in raw terror that the M167 will open fire again.

"What's happening in the station?" Sophie asks anxiously.

Before anyone can answer, five or six deputies burst from the front door of the great Victorian building.

"They're standing down!" Judge Shelby says hopefully. "Look!"

"Ray?" I ask.

"You don't run like that if you're still assaulting. I'd say somebody gave the order to abort. The governor, I guess."

"He had no choice," Judge Shelby says. "If he hadn't, it would have been the end of the rule of law in this state."

"Hell," Alderman Gaines cuts in, "we're past that point already, aren't we? Nationally, I mean."

"Not like this," says Ray. "Cops against the army in the streets?"

"Thank God," Nadine says softly.

"I know, right?" Annie murmurs.

Cicely Waite turns and squeezes my daughter's hand. "I can't believe you girls lived to see this. I thought we'd gotten past it in my time. But I fear this country may have its greatest challenge still ahead."

"Lord, I hope not," says Lashanna Ransom.

Everyone starts when Andrew McKinney steps into the room and pops the cork on a bottle of champagne. White foam spews from the bottle and runs down his dark arm.

"I'm not celebrating, exactly," he informs us, "since people might have been hurt during that exchange. But by God, we just saw something I feared we might not see for decades to come. The state authorities just backed up the rule of law against racist cops in the state of Mississippi. I don't want to give them too much credit. I'm sure they had political motives. But this will mean a lot when the world sees it. It will do our state—and our cause—a lot of good."

"Hear, hear!" echoed Judge Shelby, getting to his feet and holding out his Styrofoam cup.

As Andrew pours champagne for those with empty glasses, the news switches to an aerial view of the Bienville bluff rather than the city police station. It suddenly hits me that for some reason the bluff crowd has surged—or been allowed to surge—across Battery Row, which formerly served as the National Guard's primary defense line. But now the sea of humanity is washing against the line of retail stores and other buildings along the Row, including my town house.

"Oh, no," I breathe, as the CNN camera zooms in on the entrance to Cotton Rowe shopping center, where about thirty marchers appear to be fighting hand to hand against National Guard troops.

"What the hell's happening?" Ray cries, jumping to his feet.

The premier retail and dining space on Bienville's bluff, Cotton Rowe is housed in a large antebellum cotton brokerage building. While some protesters are only sharing water from a hose on the side of the building, two muscular men wearing wifebeater shirts have seized a metal park bench and begun trying to smash open the transparent security doors at the main entrance of the shopping center.

"If they break down those doors, it's looting," I think aloud. "That's exactly what the state police want. What the governor wants."

"When the looting starts, the shooting starts," Ray says in a fatalistic voice.

"Somebody has to stop them!" cries Reverend Baldwin, rubbing his eyes. "Who can we call?"

I gently take hold of his wrist. "You can't stop them, Rev. It's a mob now."

"Kendrick stopped worse at Mission Hill!"

"That was different. That was mostly kids, and it was just a concert. These people are enraged, grieving. They want payback."

"It's *two guys*," Ray argues, his eyes blazing.

Reverend Baldwin takes out his cell phone. Of course he knows almost everyone down on that bluff. If he reaches the right person, he might in fact possess the power to stop those men from breaking down the doors—or at least to inspire strong churchmen to attempt to stop them.

"Who should I call, Ray?" he asks.

"I wish to God I was down there, Rev, but I'm not."

"What about Kendrick?" Annie suggests.

"That's right, Annie," Reverend Baldwin says, but then he slaps his own forehead. "I'm not sure where I put his number. Somebody get that young man on the phone for me. *Please*. Hurry!"

Annie speed-dials Kendrick, but I can see from her expression as she presses her phone to her ear that he's not answering.

On TV, the rioters have yet to shatter the security doors, and we watch with morbid fascination as they keep trying. Several cops and Guardsmen approach and try to stop them, but a semicircle of male marchers take up defensive positions and work as blockers while the pair continues to slam the bench against what must be polycarbonate doors.

"There's Kendrick!" cries Annie. "He's there! He's trying!"

Sure enough, Kendrick has somehow gotten past the defensive perimeter and begun arguing with the men trying to smash the doors. But they lose no time pummeling him to the ground with fists and elbows, then go back to their work.

When Kendrick struggles up again, Annie screams. "Dad, we have to help him!"

"There's nothing we can do from here. That's why he didn't come tonight. He wanted to try to prevent this kind of thing from happening."

Annie sobs as Kendrick struggles to his feet, then gets battered to the concrete once more. Nadine turns away from the television.

Catching hold of Annie, I pull her against me and shield her eyes. Eventually she relents and stops struggling.

"Why are those guys doing that?" Andrew asks the heavens. "Don't they know how bad it looks? It's just what the bastards want!"

"They've gone most of the day without food and water," I answer. "And I don't think that was an accident. Now they've had what they need put within their reach. They're not going to stop."

Kendrick Washington has hardly moved in the past half minute, and I'm starting to worry that he's seriously injured. But as I stare, a huge young man in the realm of three hundred pounds charges into the fray, bends, and scoops Kendrick into his arms like a child.

"*Oh*, yeah!" Ray cries. "Get him out, Frosty!"

Annie whips her head off my chest, her eyes filled with hope. "Oh, thank God!"

"Who's that?" I ask.

"Kendrick's cousin! Frosty Givens. He's a rapper slash music producer."

Ray chuckles low in his big chest. "Frosty's a banger, man. He used to play left tackle for Bienville High, and he can knock a truck over with his forearm if you make him mad."

It quickly becomes apparent that the authorities have been waiting for just this kind of action by the crowd. The number of National Guard troops quickly doubles, and the Row becomes an arena for hand-to-hand combat. Clouds of tear gas swirl across the bluff, and the hollow, gut-wrenching *boom* of more gas rounds being fired is almost continuous. Mississippi state police wearing riot gear are making mass arrests along the Row, and quite a few of those arrested appear to be teenagers, both male and female.

"Oh, no," says Nadine. "Look."

A zoom shot shows a Black girl with a bloodied face being dragged along the sidewalk by her hair.

"Kendrick's still trying to stop them from breaking down the door!" Annie cries.

"Frosty'll get him out," Ray assures her.

As Frosty breaks free and turns to carry Kendrick away, one man helping to swing the park bench sucker-punches the back of his neck. Frosty staggers, then tries to ignore the blow and go on. Maddened by his resilience, the attacker leaps on Frosty's enormous back and drags him down.

Rolling Kendrick onto the sidewalk, Frosty struggles back to his feet. His assailant charges once more, windmilling wiry arms. Like an afterthought, Frosty throws out his right forearm and drops his attacker to the concrete. Another man leaps into his way as if to continue the fight, but one good look into the gangbanger's eyes dissuades him. As the would-be fighter retreats, however, the men wielding the bench finally achieve their goal, and one of the shopping center's entrance doors crumples inward.

"Oh, no," says Reverend Baldwin.

"Frosty got him away!" Annie cries, as CNN cuts to a wider shot again. "He was carrying Kendrick when they cut away."

"He'll be okay," I assure her.

"This is bad," Nadine says. "Oh, no. Look!"

On the commercial side of the Row, about two dozen young marchers have been lined up by the state police. Some of the officers—and what looks like some Tarlton deputies—are physically abusing their detainees, violently enough that marchers from the river side of the Row are shouting in protest, trying to draw the attention of reporters, or even of the helicopters aloft over the river. Deputies are shoving the teenagers around, striking anyone who protests, and being alarmingly free with their batons. Nearly every frame shows blood on dark skin.

As I watch with a terrible sense of foreboding, Sergeant Shirley Danvers sweeps across Battery Row with a half dozen Bienville city cops behind her, to try to stop the needless brutality. As they pass through the National Guard line, I'm stunned to see them meet resistance. At first I blame this on the fog of battle, but it soon becomes clear that the Guardsmen are also fighting municipal cops farther down the Row, where an officer blocks one of Morgan's officers with a Plexiglas shield. Staring in disbelief, I realize that somewhere, someone has given the order for American soldiers to resist American city cops. A prediction I published long ago is coming true before my eyes, but in a way I never expected.

As we all stare at the chaos unfolding on our screen, it strikes me that confusion might be the only good thing about it. Chaos on American streets is never good, but it beats nightmare close-ups that fulfill our worst fears. But even as I think this, Judge Shelby's carefully modulated voice reaches my ears.

"Penn, look," he says. "I fear we just lost the PR war."

Following the line of his outstretched finger, I see a frozen image of indelible power. A white female National Guard soldier about Annie's age stands in Battery Row with a mixture of bravery and fear on her helmeted face. The camera caught her in the act of holding up a Plexiglas shield against a big Black Bienville cop swinging his baton down toward her head. Behind her, a second city cop—also male and Black—appears to be charging to assist his comrade in this unequal struggle. To any white person older than fifty, every pixel of this image screams the end of the America they once knew and loved.

"Combined with those punks breaking down that door," Reverend Baldwin says, "that picture could set the Movement back fifty years."

"And it's bullshit!" snaps Andrew McKinney. "A complete misrepresentation. Out of the frame, the white Guardsmen are beating those Black kids with batons!"

"Just pray the helicopters and drones caught all that," I say softly. "Damn it."

But I know from experience that nothing can compete with a viscerally provocative photograph. Witness the fact that CNN has left the image of the two cops attacking the female Guardsman frozen on their screen. And in the blank space at the bottom, the words

MISSISSIPPI, 2023.

"They'll be studying that photo in schoolbooks a hundred years from now," Nadine says with prophetic certainty. "Goddamn it!"

"The GOP will raise ten million dollars off it by tomorrow," Alderman Gaines says bitterly. "Maybe twenty."

"They'll make it the cover of the history book in Arkansas," mutters Alderman Keyes.

"I can't watch any more," Nadine says.

She goes into the kitchen and begins washing dishes, and after looking into Annie's swollen red eyes for a second too long, I follow.

"BOBBY, YOU'RE A goddamn *genius*!" Tommy Russo shouted, slapping him on the back.

The Poker Club had gathered on the terrace at Donnelly Oil as the final act unfolded at street level, and this time even Jenna Kay had allowed herself to be dragged along with them. Screams of anger and confusion echoed up from below, but high above Bienville, ice tinkled audibly in the glasses that held their beverages of choice.

"I second that!" said Claude Buckman. "By God, Bobby, you predicted it this afternoon, and it happened *exactly* as you said it would."

"You can thank DEVGRU and the CIA for that. They model ops like this day and night."

"Don't hide your light under a bushel!" Dixie told him. "Buck Tarlton went down into the streets and got his tail feathers shot off with a laser beam, while you sat up here and ran this thing like a chess match."

"You make Trump's people look like a third-string softball team," Arthur Pine said.

Bobby didn't reply. On his left, Jenna brushed close enough to murmur, "I can tell you're sick of this. You need anything?"

"To be elsewhere."

"Heard and understood."

Bobby hoped she hadn't read his reply as a come-on.

Claude Buckman held up his highball glass. "I'll confess I had moments of doubt today. That bastardization of 'My Favorite Things' *really* pissed me off."

"Damn right," Pine agreed.

"But what a curtain call! We ended this show with global coverage of the Mississippi National Guard enforcing the rule of law. Then street thugs looting stores like animals. And finally, Black cops beating down a white girl who probably joined the National Guard to pay her college tuition. Smells like *victory* to me, folks!"

"Only one job left," Dixie said.

"What's that?" Buckman asked.

"Tomorrow we dissolve the city, fire Chief Morgan, and send LeJay back to Amite County a free man."

"Thank you, John Stennis," said Pine, the former city attorney.

"Governor Bilbo would be proud," Bobby muttered.

"What's that?" Pine asked.

Bobby shook his head and walked slowly back into the penthouse, wondering whether Wade Tarlton or his men had run down the Black girl with the video of Doc's shooting. He felt Jenna Kay Donnelly trailing him like magnetic dust that had somehow taken on female form. Again he thought of Corey—who was almost surely watching all this on television back at the Canaan cabin—but the image held no traction in his head. Almost nothing would.

"You look exhausted," Jenna said from across the room.

"Lots going on, I guess."

"Tell me what you need. I'll make it happen. Or tell me to fuck off. I can make that happen, too."

"You've been a surprise, Jenna. What do you feel like doing?"

She laughed with a note of cruelty. "Singing 'Black Rage' to Mr. Buckman out there, to the tune of 'My Favorite Things.' My Julie Andrews impression is almost perfect."

Bobby smiled for the first time in hours. "I'll give you a thousand bucks to do that."

CHAPTER 74

CHARLOT DUFORT HADN'T felt so clean for weeks. After a long, steaming shower, he'd dressed in some clothes he'd found in the back of his old closet. The only pants that would fit were warm-ups with an elastic waist, but an extra-large polo with long sleeves fit him all right. He was sitting in his father's chair at the head of the table in the formal dining room off the kitchen. Ruby had cooked his favorite meal—"Ruby-fried chicken" with mashed potatoes and gravy, and Le Sueur peas. Ruby herself sat in the chair to his right, her black uniform and the rich meal combining to send him thirty years back in time.

"How is it, baby?" she asked with maternal sincerity.

"Oh, my God," Charlot marveled, savoring the gravy even as he answered. "It's divine, Ruby." Charlot had nearly finished his second plate. "Don't you see how much I've eaten?"

"I haven't paid attention. I just like having you back here. It feels like it used to. Back in the old days."

"Does it?" Charlot's eyes were misty with recollection. "I can't believe Daddy invited me back. I can't believe he's going to pay my debts. I can't believe . . . any of it. Can you?"

Ruby's smile had diminished, but she said, "You're his son, boy. He wasn't gonna let you wind up dead in a ditch, no matter how hard you tried."

Charlot blushed. "I know I'm a screw-up, Ruby."

She squeezed his right forearm with surprising strength. "It's just sad. I remember back when you used to win all the prizes at the private school. One teacher thought you were a genius. Smarter than Philippe by miles. And that teacher had taught him twenty years earlier."

"Long time ago," Charlot said. "I'm nervous about confronting Daddy."

Ruby dismissed his concern with a wave of her hand. "You know he'll come on rough at first. But give him time. He'll come around."

The door behind Charlot opened, and Amadu came in wearing his black suit. "Mr. Charles is in the study. He's ready to see him now."

"You want me to stick around?" Ruby asked softly. "Make sure you're okay?"

"No, no," Charlot said. "If he's letting you go home tonight, go get yourself some rest. Or visit a friend. You need some alone time."

Ruby looked like she truly hated to leave. "All right, then. I guess I will. But you stand up for yourself when the time comes."

"I will," Charlot said, getting to his feet to hug the woman who had virtually raised him.

"Follow me, boy," Amadu said. "You know he don't like bein' kept waiting."

"Oh, I know."

As Charlot disengaged, Ruby gave him a last firm squeeze, as though she never wanted to let him go again. In the end he had to pull himself free, and as he turned he thought he saw the glint of tears in her eyes.

CHARLOT TOOK A seat in the chair facing his father's enormous desk, a seat he had dreaded all his life. His eyes immediately went to the old state championship tennis trophy that his brother Philippe had won back in the seventies. It still occupied pride of place on his father's desk, as it had for the past fifty years.

"You get washed and fed?" his father asked.

"Ruby took care of me."

"Well, she misses you. Always talks about you. Says you were her prettiest baby."

Charlot knew this had never given his father any pleasure.

"I want to show you something," the old man said. He lifted a small Lexan box off his desk beside the trophy. Charlot's heart skipped when he saw it, and he was unwilling to believe his eyes for several seconds.

"Recognize this?" asked his father. "Come on. Come get it."

Charlot got up and crossed the bearskin rug to the cherry desk. As soon as he took the four-by-eight-inch case in his hands, he recognized its weight, and its contents. At least thirty prime examples of spearpoints and arrowheads lay within, artifacts he'd collected after long expeditions up the local creeks with his father, prior to the age of thirteen. The colors ranged from pale white to orange and even onyx. The sight brought Charlot both joy and pain.

"You told me you threw this into the catfish pond," he said, omitting that Charles had said this on the night of the day Charlot had come out at eighteen.

"I wouldn't do that to you after all the work we put in finding those."

"But . . . Daddy, I must have dived into that pond twenty or thirty times hunting this box over the years. Hoping to find even just one arrowhead."

"I know you did." Charles's eyes were bright. "That's one of the few things you ever did that gave me real pride. You went down into that hole *over* and *over* again—a couple of times in the dead of winter—never mind that you weren't finding anything. You kept up the work! And that's all that matters in the end."

Charlot shook his head with infinite sadness. "No, it's not, Daddy."

"What do you mean?"

"If you had just told me you really hadn't thrown them away . . . it would have meant so much to me. The world, really. You have no idea."

"Now, son, don't make too much of it. It's just some old Indian junk."

Charlot shook his head with greater force. "No. It's more than that. It says so much about our whole relationship."

"Oh, Christ. Here it comes again."

"All my life . . . ever since I told you the truth about me . . . I've gotten nothing but judgment, the harshest kind, from you. But now I know how hypocritical that judgment was. You're more flawed than I've ever been. You had no right to judge me or anybody else."

"And how do you figure that?"

For a few seconds Charlot heeded the voices of Pearl and Ruby in his head, telling him to suppress his anger. But he couldn't. "Because you're a murderer. You're also a racist, a rapist, and God knows what else."

The old man's face had gone blank with confusion. "What the hell are you talking about, boy?"

"I'm talking about Shondra Williams, the girl whose blood you used to paint the walls of room 305 at the Natchez Holiday Inn."

The old man blanched. "Where did you hear that name?"

"Whose bones are laying in the old main cistern under the floor of Tranquility?"

Dufort's blue-gray eyes narrowed slowly. He studied his second son like he might a pet dog he suspected of having rabies.

"Boy, I believe you've lost your mind."

"I wish that were true. But no. You judge me? I've done a lot of thinking since I learned about that girl. Shondra. I thought about your first wife, too, drowning in her bathtub. Then my mother, getting her neck broken in a sailing accident—"

"Thirty people saw your mother killed at the dock that day! Not one ever suggested anything improper."

"Because you're such a great sailor, right? That little boat gliding into the dock . . . all you had to do was flick your wrist a little, just the right way, and she tumbled forward between the bow and the dock. I still remember when she shot up out of the water, gasping for air. The prow hit her under the chin and crushed her neck against the dock. I *still* have nightmares about watching her die. Pia does, too."

His younger sister returned home so rarely that the mention of her name was like that of a stranger to the old man. But perhaps the context gave the real reason for her self-exile.

"How did you feel while she lay there turning blue?" Charlot asked. "Knowing you had done that? I saw the truth in Mama's eyes that day. The horror of knowing you'd done it to her and being unable to speak. But I'll bet you felt like the world's greatest magician, murdering her right in front of everyone, and no one the wiser. It's like some lost Hitchcock film."

"Get out of my office," Charles said with venom. "Get out of my *house*!"

Charlot raised his hand to point at his father. "I knew this was too good to be true. You don't give a damn whether I live or die."

"That's where you're wrong. I do care about that. You're my son."

"Only by blood. You'd cut my throat with a nail file if it would get your precious Philippe back."

Charles looked back as though about to agree, but he said nothing.

"Hell, you'd trade me for Bobby White in a minute," Charlot added.

"Amadu?" Charles called, looking back over his shoulder.

Because his father's driver had left the room by the small door behind his father's chair, Charlot's gaze went there. He didn't hear the door behind him open, or Amadu slip noiselessly across the floor in his sock feet, as the Leopard Men had taught him to do as a boy in Africa.

The thick muscles of Amadu's upper and lower arms locked Charlot's throat in the V of a chokehold, and Charlot's windpipe instantly closed.

His face felt like someone was pumping it full of hot water, and though he tried to gasp, nothing could move though his trachea. By the time he saw his father nod, the scene in front of him had begun going dark at the edges. Then moving shadows like helicopter blades interposed themselves between his retinas and the box of arrowheads on the desk. He couldn't read the expression on his father's face, but it looked like . . . relief? He wanted to ask *Why?* or maybe *Why this way?* But there wasn't enough oxygen left in his system to power the mechanism of speech, even if Amadu's arm had not rendered it impossible. In his ear, the old African's bass voice murmured, "*Sleep now, boy.*"

Then the darkness consumed the last of the light.

CHAPTER 75

ANNIE LAY IN the dark in the slave quarters known as the "big cabin" and listened to Andrew McKinney breathe with the steady rhythm of sleep. She'd promised her father to return to her Jackson apartment, but by the time she and Andrew finished cleaning up what the group had left undone, they were exhausted. After locking the big house, Andrew wanted to make sure he'd gotten all his valuables from the quarters, and while Annie waited in the car, she dozed off on the passenger seat. Roused by Andrew a few minutes later, she'd followed him inside and collapsed on the mattress with him. While they had been intimate a few summers ago, they now observed the boundaries of platonic friendship, and with remarkably little awkwardness. After a brief discussion, they'd agreed to get five hours' sleep before heading out early, in time for Annie to reach Doris's office by 8:00 a.m. After all, there was an off-duty cop manning Pencarrow's locked gate.

Andrew rolled onto his back and soon began snoring softly. In her mind, Annie replayed the conversations of the dinner table, reconsidering her snap judgments of people she'd just met, or had only heard at any length tonight. It had buoyed her spirit to see a group of like-minded people banding together with the goal of doing all they could to de-escalate the crisis threatening their hometown. What worried her was a quiet conversation she'd heard Judge Shelby having with Alderman Gaines, about a rumor of a local version of what had been going on nationally—a sinister effort to twist existing law to seize power from duly elected representatives of the people. The panic she'd sensed rising in Bienville was also new to her: the frenzied buying of weapons and ammunition, the hiring of armed guards by the rich, all the clichéd signs of apocalypse. She wondered how long it would take that panic to spread east to Jackson.

As sleep settled slowly over her, she shuddered the way she sometimes did when the cracking thunder of a summer storm broke over Mississippi. But the cracks that wakened her tonight, on the ledge of sleep, came too fast for thunder, she realized: a series of dull concussions had rippled through the slave quarters almost as fast as a woven string of Black Cat firecrackers at Christmas.

"Andrew!" she cried, scrambling into her jeans beside the bed.

"Huh?" he grunted. "What was that?"

"I don't know! Get up!"

As they froze with their heads cocked like startled deer, a deep *whoooosh* sucked at the windows of the quarters. In the next room a windowpane shattered.

"Oh, no!" Andrew shouted, rolling off the mattress with a thud and darting to the window.

Annie followed. By the time she reached the glass, she saw the windows of the plantation house sixty yards away lit from within as though by a bonfire.

"Oh, God," she breathed. "Call 911!"

As Andrew dialed emergency services, Annie speed-dialed her father's phone. It took him five rings to answer, but he did.

"Annie? Is everything okay? You didn't have car trouble, did you?"

"Dad, we're still at Pencarrow. The house is on fire!"

"I told you to go straight home!"

"It's too late! We're safe in the quarters, but the main house is burning! The mansion. I mean like Arcadia did. Some kind of bomb or something went off—I heard it. The whole interior looks like it's on fire."

"I'll call 911. Don't go near that fire, and tell Andrew the same. Consider the house lost already."

As Annie tried to make out more clearly what was happening outside, she heard the door of the slave quarters slam. Whirling, she realized Andrew was no longer in the room. Through the window, she saw the silhouette of his body, clad only in underwear and a T-shirt, racing across open grass toward the big house. She screamed for him to stop, but he charged straight through the mansion's front door.

"Andrew just ran into the house! The *main* house! He's probably trying to put out the fire. Or to save something."

"Don't go after him! Don't get any closer than a hundred feet. You can yell for him, but do *not* go into that house." My mind has filled with nightmare memories from an earlier era of my life. "I did that the day I saved Ruby Flowers, and I nearly died."

"But Dad—"

"*Swear it!*"

"I won't go in, I swear. But I've got to go out there. I think he called 911, but please call them yourself. They'll listen to you."

"I will. Annie—"

"Wait, he's outside again. Thank God! *Andrew!*"

The figure that emerged from the basement, dragging what looked like a mantelpiece, ignored her. Andrew dropped the heavy carved board, then bolted to the side of the house and began ascending the construction scaffolding with the speed of a Filipino worker scaling bamboo.

"Christ, he's going up the scaffolding now. What is he thinking?"

"He's probably trying to turn on the top-floor sink taps. Soak the building in water from the inside if he can. Damn it! That's a brave man. But it's not worth it."

Annie's throat tightened down so hard she could barely speak, and tears came to her eyes. "Daddy, what can I do?"

"Get out there, stand clear, and if he comes out again . . . tackle him. He's probably out of his head, he's worked so hard on that place. He doesn't fully appreciate the risk."

"Okay, that's what I'll do. I'm going now. Hurry, Dad!"

Annie ended the call and raced outside in her bare feet, just as Andrew had done. But she stayed far enough back so as to see Andrew if he burst out of the house at any point on this side. She knew she could tackle him, if she focused. He weighed about 145, only twenty pounds more than she. And she'd been a hell of a defensive player in high school basketball. She could bring him down to save his life. She would cripple him if she had to.

Standing alone in the dark, overwhelmed by the speed of the flames and destruction, she began to shudder uncontrollably. She felt like she was no longer on her father's land, safe and protected. She didn't even feel she was in America anymore. Or rather that the America she'd grown up in no longer existed, replaced in a matter of days by a nation sliding into war.

She heard the rattle of iron and steel from the dark, and then Andrew leaped from the back side of the scaffolding and ran toward her.

"Thank God!" she cried, feeling a crushing weight leave her chest.

Andrew appeared to have a heavy sack slung over his shoulder. Darting out in front of him as he ran, she held up both hands and blocked his path.

"Move!" he shouted, dropping the sack and spilling a set of nineteenth-century books at her feet. "I'm fine. I got the water running in there. I've just got to go back in one more time."

"For *what*?"

"Calliope! My bust. I should have got it that first trip. But there was fire on the lower stairs."

"You can't! Calliope's in the library. That's too deep in."

"No, I looked down from the upper landing. I can get in through the side window. Come on, I'm going. She's the best thing I've ever done—the soul of this house. I'm not letting her burn with the rest of it."

Annie barely managed to keep pace as Andrew raced around the great building. "Daddy said don't let you back in!"

"If he were here, he'd be going in with me. You know he would!"

Annie cursed in frustration. Andrew knew her father well. He already stank of smoke and some sort of accelerant, though, and soot smudged his face and arms, which were streaked with sweat.

He pulled up short by the library window, whose sill was a good four and a half feet off the ground. Snatching up a red Natchez brick from the ground, he leaned back and smashed the window, then jerked his face away, hoping no flame would blast through to meet the fresh river of oxygen.

None did.

"Crouch down on all fours, so I can step on your back."

Annie reluctantly obeyed.

Andrew ripped off his shirt and wrapped it around his right hand, then used the pad to rake broken glass from the sill. As he did, Annie caught sight of headlights moving by the gate, five hundred yards away. She hoped it was a fire engine, but more likely it was the cop her father had paid to stand guard. As Andrew lifted himself through the window, she caught his arm and said into his ear: "Is Calliope worth your life? It's only a sculpture."

"She's only twenty feet away," he said, not looking back.

"Andrew—"

"I have to!"

Tearing himself free, he leaped through the window onto the floor. As she got to her feet, Annie had never felt so helpless, at least not since she'd been kidnapped as a girl of fourteen. She wished to God Daniel Kelly were here now, not only to stop Andrew risking his life, but also to protect them from whatever monster was setting these fires. But Kelly wasn't here. He was being paid to protect someone else, far overseas.

Every passing second Annie prayed to hear sirens, but only the roar of consuming flame bellowed from the house, which until this night had stood for 207 years. As she waited, she felt her limbs going weak, but then she heard Andrew shout, "I've got her!" above the roar. "I'm coming!" She could almost feel him moving back toward the window.

Then something colossally heavy gave way above them.

A deep crash sounded in the library, like a dud bomb plummeting through several floors of the house. She thought of the scaffolding the painters had been using on the walls of the library for the past week. What could have shattered—?

Bathtub, she realized. Andrew had probably flooded the upstairs tub on purpose, and it had proved too heavy for the fire-weakened floor . . .

A faint voice wailed in pain. Then it called her name: *"Annie! Get back from the window! Get away. There's fire falling from above."*

A flood of tears poured from her eyes, but she raised up on tiptoe and tried to peer through the window into the inferno. Her promise to her father was like a chain binding her to the safety of open space, but when no further answer came, she knew she could not obey. She gritted her teeth and summoned all the adrenaline in her body, all the pain and anger from Mission Hill, all her love for Andrew and his selfless dedication, and prepared to go in after him.

Far behind her, a man shouted her name. The off-duty cop who'd been posted on the gate. "*Get away from there, Miss Cage!*" he yelled. "*That whole wall could go any second. I'm a volunteer fireman! I know!*"

Officer Gabriel Davis was charging her way. Before he could get close enough to stop her, Annie laid her bandaged hand on the sill, scrabbled up the bricks with her bare feet, and rolled over the sill into hell.

CHAPTER 76

I'M STANDING IN the waiting room of Bienville General Hospital's emergency department, and it's taking all my willpower not to bull-rush the entry door and find Annie's treatment room. The reception nurse just assured me that the doctor will be coming to get me in a couple of minutes, and Nadine has a tight grip on my arm, doing her best to restrain me.

I hardly remember the second half of the drive from my Bienville town house, other than the blur of taillights as I blasted past them. It was then that I'd called the cop I'd paid to guard the Pencarrow gate and learned that Annie had gone into the house after Andrew after all. I think my heart stopped beating for a couple of seconds as I processed that, and it was only Gabriel Davis telling me that Annie had just heaved Andrew's unconscious body through the library window and leaped out herself that started it beating with regularity again. I do remember repeating a mantra of sorts for much of the drive.

"*I know who did this . . . I know who did this.*"

"Who?" Nadine asked.

"Shot Barlow and his militia."

"How do you know?"

I nod, my teeth clenched in fury. "He had the motive. Nobody else does. Not even the Bastard Sons of the Confederacy. Not this house. If it's Black activists setting these fires, Pencarrow is the last house they'd target. We're busting our asses to make it an accurate representation of the slaveholding South—with all the darkness intact. And Andrew sleeps out there, for God's sake! Everybody knows that."

"Maybe Black activists don't see those efforts the same way you do. Or Andrew, for that matter."

"Some probably don't. But this would be going too far. No Black commentator has even written an op-ed accusing us of anything negative yet. There are twenty or thirty better targets in this county alone. But Shot Barlow had a direct and recent motive."

"What motive?"

"The historical feud alone would be enough for that bastard. The other arsons just gave him a way to do it without being suspected."

The image I can't shake is that of Judge Shelby humiliating the redneck in the Ted Nugent shirt—the one who assaulted Andrew in the restroom of Omar's gas station. In truth, the old judge emasculated the wiry son of a bitch, first by showing no fear of him, and second, by blasting the truck nuts of the big red dually as though they were nothing but a novelty best used for target practice.

I'm sure my reticence about this afternoon's burial confrontation frustrates Nadine, but right now I can barely keep from smashing my fist through the window beside me. Part of me is furious at Annie and Andrew for staying at the house after promising to go back to Jackson. But my real anger I reserve for myself, for not doing a better job of searching Pencarrow when I took a brief rest there this afternoon, and for not hiring more security, like the other homeowners I'd considered paranoid only this afternoon.

"Where's Mr. Cage?" asks a male voice behind the glass partition.

"In the waiting room," answers the receptionist.

I take a step toward the entrance door, and Nadine grips my arm tighter. Then the door opens and a white-coated doctor of about forty motions for me to follow him into the treatment area. Once we're inside, he introduces himself as Dr. William Berg, a Jackson ER physician who sometimes covers shifts in Bienville and Vicksburg. As it turns out, he treated Nadine's mother a couple of times when she had to come into the ER late at night before she died.

"How are they doing, Doc?" I ask, straining not to ask only about my daughter. As much as I care about Andrew—and that's a lot—my fear for my only child is devouring me from the inside.

"Andrew McKinney is severely burned," he informs me. "They're about to load him into an ambulance to evacuate him to UMC."

"Is he conscious?"

Berg shakes his head. "He's out, from the painkillers."

"Prognosis?"

"He'll live, I believe. But he's going to have a long recovery. Months. He'll be scarred for life."

I shake my head, recalling Andrew's joyful smiles and passionate defense of his work during months of criticism by ignorant outsiders.

I swallow hard. "And my daughter?"

"Ann has got second-degree burns on both hands, and first-degree burns on the soles of her feet and knees. But other than that—and the effects of smoke inhalation—she's all right."

"Hands, knees, and feet?"

"When she got into the house, she found McKinney unconscious on the floor. An upstairs bathtub had crashed through and buried him under scaffolding. That scaffolding must have been hot as the hinges of hell, but she took hold of it anyway, and somehow lifted it off his back and dragged him outside. The bandage on her left hand—for the gunshot wound—gave her a little protection, but Christ . . . that girl saved his life, no question."

Tears well in my eyes. Dr. Berg reaches out and squeezes my shoulder.

"What's her outlook?" I ask.

"She's going to have a lot of pain while those burns heal, but we can handle her here, no problem. No need to send her to Jackson."

"Will she need to stay overnight?"

"Not if someone can watch her closely tonight. To administer meds and listen to her breathing."

"I've got her covered," Nadine says. "I'll sit by her bed all night."

I wipe my eyes and force myself to breathe slowly as the realization that Annie is basically all right sinks in. As it does, though, I realize that Andrew may never fully recover, and my heart goes out to his parents, who must be on their way by now.

"Listen, Doc," I say only half coherently. "The McKinneys are not affluent people. If I'm not here when they get here, or I'm distracted with the police, you tell them no effort will be spared. You hear me? Money's no object. Not even a consideration. Make sure they know that."

Dr. Berg smiles and nods assent. "Take it easy, Mr. Cage. I think you should sit down. When was the last time you had a physical?"

"Ah, it's been a while. But I'm not the patient."

"Still, I'm going to have a nurse take your blood pressure. Then you can go in and see your daughter. They're getting her vitals now."

Nadine looks grateful for this intervention.

"I'm fine," I protest, trying not to hyperventilate. "I just need to see my daughter."

"Well . . . beyond the physical, she's a little traumatized. Seeing that young man hurt like that . . . she's probably going to need to talk to somebody about it."

"I'll find her someone. I can relate to her situation."

"How's that?"

"I pulled somebody out of a fire like that about twenty years ago. Closer to twenty-five now, I guess."

"Where was this?"

"My parents' house. Somebody set fire to it, and I went in to get our elderly maid out."

"I see. Well . . . two heroes in one family."

I shake my head. "We do what we have to, right? Can we see her now?"

"She's in Treatment 4. Wait for the nurse by the door. And please sit while you're waiting. Your skin is almost utterly translucent, Mr. Cage. I think you may have severe anemia."

I'm not the fucking patient! I want to scream. But I don't. Berg is just trying to do his job, which includes saving people like me from myself.

After searching the numbers on the doors, I start toward number 4, but stumble taking my first step. Dr. Berg grabs my arm and steadies me.

"I want you to sit down until a tech pokes you for a CBC. Then you can see your daughter. I know you don't like that, but I'm going to insist. Nadine concurs. As soon as you get your land legs back, you can go in."

"I'm good," I assure him, pulling up my right pant leg to reveal the socket of my prosthetic. "It's just my leg. This still gives me trouble sometimes. Even after years, I sometimes forget I don't have my real foot."

Berg smiles in recognition. "I see it all the time in this state. Diabetes capital of the nation. Here you go."

I nod thanks as he helps me settle into the chair beside the treatment room door. From a few feet away, Nadine smiles with satisfaction, and this moment more than any other tells me that we are once again a couple and she means to take care of the father of her child. "Am I that pale?" I ask, holding my hand up to the light.

"Honestly? You look like you stepped out of an Anne Rice novel."

"Wonderful."

MY DAUGHTER COULD win Academy Awards for putting on a brave face. She spent much of her childhood perfecting the art, and tonight's no different. All her concern is for Andrew McKinney. Looking at her with both hands bandaged and her eyebrows singed off, I simultaneously want to burst with pride and eviscerate the bastards who did this to her.

"Dad, I'm sorry," she begins. "I know I promised I wouldn't go in. But I couldn't leave him in there. You wouldn't have, either."

"Forget about it. It's done. Thank God you did it. I couldn't have borne it if he'd died in there. It's a miracle you got yourself out, they tell me."

She nods into her pillow. "It was close, I think."

"You're a tough girl."

"I got that from Gram."

"I know you did."

A little cinder of fear burns through her façade. "I feel like they're not telling me the truth about Andrew's condition."

"He's in bad shape. But he's likely going to make it."

"His parents are going to lose their minds. They didn't want him to come back to Mississippi. Not that South Carolina's any better."

"I know. I'll speak to them."

"They may not want to hear from you. It was you and Pencarrow that brought him back here."

I wave my hand. "I know. And I regret it now. But the work was important to him. That was what he wanted to be doing. He told me that every time I saw him."

"I think his mama knows that."

"Good."

"I saved his Calliope bust first. Threw it right out the window, because that's what he'd gone in after. Dr. Berg said they put it beside his treatment bed. Can you keep it while he's being treated in Jackson? I don't think his folks will want it around, and somebody up there might steal it."

"Will do. I know a lot more about Calliope now."

"You do?"

Nadine nods beside me. "I told him a little more of the story. But he's still got a lot to learn."

"So you know we're related to her. At least in a small way. Still, direct blood descent."

"You can watch over that bust yourself. Dr. Berg says you can come home with us tonight, so long as somebody watches you."

"Thank God. But I want to go to Jackson to see Andrew as soon as I can. Tomorrow, if possible."

"I'm going to be pretty busy after this fire, but we'll find somebody to take you over there. As soon as the doctors clear you."

"What are you going to be doing?"

I start to answer, but the lump in my throat won't let me speak.

Annie's face fills with worry. "Dad, don't do anything crazy. I know you. If you kill Mr. Barlow, it won't make Andrew one bit better. You know that. And you're not in any shape for a fight. You look like you can hardly stand. If you're going to go after anybody, swear to me you'll reach out to Kelly. Don't do anything without him."

"I shouldn't have told Barlow I would break up his land with a lawsuit."

Annie looks at Nadine. "Don't let him try to handle this alone. Make him try to call Daniel Kelly."

"My plan is to get him into bed. I already had the doctor stick him for a blood count."

Annie manages a smile. "Promise me you won't go back over there to-night. To Black Oak."

"I won't. Not without law enforcement, anyway."

I lay my hand on her lower leg. "Nadine will help you get your stuff together. You want to rest here a while?"

"No." She looks at Nadine. "Would you mind staying with me at the town house?"

Nadine colors as she smiles. "That won't be a problem."

Annie laughs softly. "I think my pain shot just kicked in for real. So I'll confess something. I always saw you as a role model. You came off like a bohemian bookstore owner, but then I found out you'd been a big-time courtroom lawyer in North Carolina. And now . . . I'm a lawyer, too. Life's weird."

Nadine stands, shaking her head, fresh color in her cheeks. "Tell me what you need to get going."

EMERGING FROM TREATMENT 4, I find two men engaged in muf-fled, angry conversation between the nurses' station and the treatment rooms. I recognize Ray Ransom first, because he's six three, with that dis-tinctive bald head and huge shoulders. The second man is Sheriff Buck Tarlton. The starched uniform and Stetson would be sufficient, even with Ray's head blocking his face. Tarlton looks up as I approach and gives me a civil nod that one might interpret as an olive branch. But I'm not buy-ing it.

"Sorry to hear about your little girl, Penn."

Ray turns in my direction and gives me an informal salute, which is how he sometimes greets me. "I hear the McKinney boy's in bad shape."

"Dr. Berg says so."

At that moment the doctor marches up and says, "Penn, could I speak to you for a moment?"

"Yes, just one second. Listen, I want either the FBI or the municipal police working the Pencarrow arson."

"Impossible," Tarlton declares, folding his arms across his western khaki outfit. "The city police have no jurisdiction in the case." He drops his previous civility. "No joint task forces, none of that bullshit. It's a straight-up county case."

Everyone watches Tarlton in silence. It's plain that he loves authority. But my temper is running hot. I step right into his personal space. "You're right about jurisdiction, Buck. That fire belongs to *you*. And I'm making a formal accusation right now against your buddy Shot Barlow and his moron militia for burning my house. I want you to quit wasting time here, and get out there and question him. Tonight. Question his whole band of cosplay commandos. Search the whole place for evidence—the prepper bunkers, all of it—before they can destroy it. I know you know your way around out there."

"Hold on!" Tarlton says. "We're going to run a thorough, methodical investigation—"

"That'll be a change for your department."

The sheriff holds out both hands. "Do you have any evidence against Barlow that would constitute probable cause?"

"You've got a year's worth of harassment complaints we've filed for all the shit they've done to my property. I found out today that they assaulted Andrew McKinney in a gas station restroom a few weeks back. Now, on the day we bury my mother, they fire off a thousand rounds to disrupt the service. Judge Clay Shelby went over there with me and showed them the error of their ways. They probably kept drinking all afternoon and evening, and the news of that Natchez fire gave them the push they needed to go for revenge tonight. Think about it. Morgan found the bomb planted at Attica by the Bastard Sons, the one meant to go off tonight. And Beauvoir burned in the afternoon. That's two houses, just like yesterday. So Pencarrow is an outlier. It's got nothing to do with the Bastard Sons' target list."

Tarlton is shaking his head as I finish. "That's all conjecture. And Mr. Barlow already informed me that Judge Shelby fired a weapon at one of his guests today. He hurt some people with shrapnel wounds."

"Did those people file charges?"

"Barlow said they would have, but they hated to do it on the day you were burying your mother."

"Bullshit! I'm wasting my time talking to you."

Tarlton follows as I walk away in disgust. "Cage, listen. I can relate to how you feel. They burned my goddamn house earlier today! I was damn lucky my family wasn't in there when the gas blew. But don't you go off half-cocked and do something illegal. If you do, you could wake up in a cell yourself tomorrow, or worse."

I stop and turn. "Worse how?"

"Trespassing on the property of an armed militia group? That's begging for a violent response. That's how those guys roll."

As we face off near the nurses' station, Dr. Berg catches my shoulder and gently turns me to face him. "Penn, your hemoglobin is 6.5. You get much lower than that, we're talking a value inconsistent with life. You badly need some red cells."

As a teenager, I worked in my father's lab enough to know what such a low number means. Absorbing this news, I sense Nadine standing behind me and to my left.

"Why do I suspect this isn't a surprise?" Berg asks in a near whisper. "Do you have some kind of hematologic cancer?"

"Possibly," I concede.

Berg gives me a knowing look. "You know, I've read a couple of your novels, and I'd like to read a couple more, maybe find out what happened to some of the characters."

"You and me both."

"I think we should admit you now and transfuse you as soon as we can hang a bag of blood."

"I'm all for that," Nadine says from behind me.

"I can't do it, guys," I say with as much deliberation as I can muster. "Not tonight. Maybe tomorrow."

"Penn, your heart could stop," Dr. Berg says in a flat voice. "And with your marrow as depressed as it appears to be, any kind of infection could take you down. Bring on sepsis."

"I get that, okay? And if you'd asked me this afternoon, I'd have been happy to get topped up with some A-positive. But now? We're in the midst of a crisis. One that just became very personal."

I start when Nadine takes hold of my shoulders from behind. "Please, Penn. I know Annie would want you to as well."

"I'm going to get the blood, I promise. Just not tonight."

Berg slowly shakes his head, then shares a look of empathy with Nadine.

"I need some air," I tell them. "I need to make a couple of calls."

"You could go out on the helipad," Berg suggests, gesturing toward a broad pair of doors on the wall to my right. "You're not supposed to, but five or ten minutes out there is fine. No inbound flights at this time."

"Don't jinx it," Sheriff Tarlton warns from several yards away. "This night's far from over."

Berg looks back at me. "If you hear rotors, get back through these doors ASAP."

I nod and hit the big red button that opens the doors.

OUTSIDE, A SOFT breeze hits me, filling me with gratitude. Trying to shut out all I know about blood chemistry, I walk to the center of the circular concrete pad with the huge "H" painted at its center. I wish I were a smoker. My hands feel like useless appendages that crave action but have no immediate task, and my mind races so fast I can't make sense of the images flaring behind my eyes. All I can think about are the things I failed to do to protect my daughter and my employee from a lethal threat. How close they came to dying. How helpless the city cop I paid to stand guard at my gate was as a source of real protection.

All I see when I think of the Pencarrow fire is Shot Barlow and his retrograde militia gathered around their trucks with everything from flintlocks to AKs and sniper rifles, firing celebratory shots into the sky. Hell, they probably sat in trees in his pasture and watched the whole thing burn through rifle scopes, laughing at Andrew's desperate effort to salvage what he could from the place.

Picturing this, I take out my cell phone and search for the email address Daniel Kelly told me to use if I ever needed to reach him overseas. I'm the only person outside the government who knows he's in Ukraine. And while he might not be able to leave there, he would never forgive me for not calling when I really need him.

"Hey, Penn," says a low voice behind me. "You holding it together?"

It's Ray Ransom.

"Barely," I tell him, turning and squeezing his big muscular hand.

"Annie's gonna be all right, man. She's a tough girl."

A wave of heat and tears comes to my face. "Yeah."

He steps close enough to speak low and still be understood in the wind blowing over the helipad. "You really think Shot Barlow burned your place?"

"I damn sure do. The sheriff's right: I can't prove it yet. But I know it in my gut."

Ransom turns in a circle, surveying the dark trees that surround three sides of the helipad. "You're thinking about going out there, aren't you?"

"Between you and me? Yeah."

"To confront that sonofabitch?"

I shrug. "I want to know what's going on out there. I'll lay odds they're celebrating. And if they are, I want to know."

"Confrontation would be a bad idea tonight. I know how it is to want to even the score. With him in particular. You know I'm descended from a slave born on that place. But if you go out there tonight, alone, you'll be screwed. It's Barlow's property, man. The law's on his side."

I go back to scrolling through old emails on my phone.

"That said," Ray continues, "under certain circumstances, going out there might not be the worst idea imaginable."

I look up. "What do you mean?"

"Together we might learn a lot. More than the sheriff, who ain't gonna do shit. Chief Morgan's under siege in his own police station. You and me could at least find out who's out there and what they're up to. Of course, celebrating by itself doesn't mean they burned the place. Those guys who celebrated in 'Nam after Dr. King got shot didn't kill him."

"We?" I echoed.

Ray shrugged. "As far as I'm concerned, if Shot Barlow dies of fuckin' Ebola tomorrow, I'm good. You want to take a look out there tonight? I can make sure you don't get caught."

Ray is, in effect, offering to be my Kelly for the night. "You're a felon, man. You don't need to get tagged for felony trespass out there."

He gives me a sober nod. "I walked point for two years without getting caught or shot by the VC. I can damn sure scope out some Mississippi woods without getting caught."

"All due respect, the Vietnamese didn't have night-vision gear. Barlow's little tribe of psychos has all the fancy toys."

"But they won't be expecting company. Not from the direction we'd come in from. I can't tell you it's zero risk, but I'm ready. You want to do it or not?"

Blood transfusion? Or night reconnaissance on the land of my blood enemy? I don't even have to think about it. I shove my iPhone back into my pocket. "Let me get Annie situated at home first. I'm gonna have to sneak out. They want to admit me to the damn hospital."

Ray gives me a knowing look. "Text me when you're ready, bro. I'll pick you up outside your town house in my old truck. Sooner the better."

"What should I bring? A pistol?"

He nods. "And that AR carbine of yours, if you still have it. I can't own firearms in my name. Worst case, we'll say we followed some feral hogs onto Barlow's place. Thrill of the hunt."

"Good thinking."

"You got any night optics on that rifle?"

"A cheap digital night scope. For feral hogs, like you said."

"How cheap?"

"Six hundred bucks." Quality night-vision scopes commonly top thirty-five hundred dollars.

"Good enough." Ray purses his lips as he considers what else we might need. "Bring some dark makeup to color that Pillsbury face of yours. A flashlight would light you up like a road sign."

"I might have a balaclava mask somewhere, but I'll never find it."

"Too damn hot for those. I'll grab some of my wife's makeup. But bring a roll of white adhesive tape. You got any?"

"White? Yeah."

"That'll do us."

I hold out my hand. "I appreciate this, Ray."

He holds up a warning hand, as though I've risked jinxing our expedition. "Thank me after we get out clean."

CHAPTER 77

RAY RANSOM AND I stand at the southern boundary of Black Oak Plantation, the Mississippi River behind us, a fenced wall of hardwood forest in front. Ray has darkened my face, neck, and hands with two tubes of his wife's makeup, which prompted me to express hope that I wouldn't get caught for a mug shot while wearing blackface. Ray said that if I were caught by the Barlow militia out here, I'd be lucky to have that kind of problem.

I wanted to swing through the gate at Pencarrow to check the fire damage before trying this reconnaissance, but Ray refused even to turn his truck onto River Road. There will still be firemen and deputies there, not to mention the possibility of feds from the FBI and BATF. If anything happens while we're on Black Oak, he doesn't want those agencies having a memory of us being in the neighborhood. For this reason, we'll have to cross two hundred acres of Barlow land on foot to reach the bunker compound area that Judge Shelby and I visited earlier today.

"Have you been out here before?" I ask.

"Coupla times," Ray says. "Mostly I've stalked it on Google Earth. Late at night, I'll go over this place meter by meter, looking where the woods and meadows are, trying to see what this place was like when Doby was alive here. I've got old maps of the place, ordered off the internet. Plantation drawings and shit. Also, what records there are from people who were enslaved here, or whose ancestors were. This place was bleak, man. Worst in this corner of the state. Everybody knew that, even then. And no one did shit about it."

"I hear you."

My SIG Sauer pistol is jammed into the small of my back, while Ray carries my newly cleaned AR-15, mounted with the entry-level night scope I bought when feral hogs started overrunning the property Annie and I lived on when she was in high school. Ray turns and faces me, his back to the trees. The moon is already down. I can barely make out anything of his features.

"I know it feels dark," he says. "But that'll change soon."

"Doesn't feel like it."

"Trust an old point man. There's light everywhere. Deep in the woods. The jungle. Even underground. I've lain in a tunnel like a coffin and thought I was dying. But eventually, I saw light. There's things that glow down there, man. Creatures. Organic shit. So out here, above ground, within a few minutes you'll be seeing fine. The trick is not hurting yourself trying to go too fast, 'cause you're so jacked up. We can't have you breaking the only ankle you got left. I don't want to have to hump you out of this motherfucker on my back. I'm strong, but I can't do that no more. Now, I'm going to be ahead, setting the pace. And I'll be hard to see. So you watch these little strips of white tape I put on my heels. If I get too far ahead, call out quiet. I'll hear you and adjust. Got it?"

"Got it. Let's move. We've got a lot of ground to cover."

Ray slings my rifle over his shoulder. "Every so often I'll stop and use the night scope to make sure we're not being observed. With luck, any militia guards will be over by River Road, turned toward your place and Barlow's main gate."

"They will. Motherfuckers."

Ray slaps each heel, then slips through the barbed-wire fence and sets off across the dark ground.

Gritting my teeth against pain in my stump, I do likewise and begin to follow. It's rough going at the start, and the farther we go, the more my stump begins to lever in its socket, which could cause me tremendous pain by tomorrow, if not sooner. I brought along a couple of extra liner socks, though likely not enough to make the round-trip journey in comfort. But comfort isn't the point tonight. I'm here to find out whether Shot Barlow and not the Bastard Sons—whoever they really are—set fire to Pencarrow and put my daughter's life at risk.

Most of the ground is dry, though now and then we come to low places that suck at our feet. Ray does a good job avoiding holes and fallen limbs, and as he promised, my eyes eventually adapt to a remarkable degree. Soon it's a matter of simply tracking the tape strips on his heels, marching on autopilot.

As we walk, my mind drifts across the land to Pencarrow, which rationally I know no longer stands, but which, because I haven't seen it gone, still rises majestically in my mind. With this image comes my memory of Deborah Fannin first moving to Bienville and buying the place with her husband to restore as she did her genealogy work. Then her quest became my mother's, and after Fannin moved back north, Mom asked me to buy the place from her. I think of all the time she spent out there doing research. Early on, after I hired Andrew, she slept nights out there in a construction trailer, writing, I now understand. In the later stages of her illness, she would set up at a card table under the Duel Oak, where we buried her this afternoon, and write with slow, steady patience. Now, thanks to the oral "prologue" Nadine gave me today, I have some idea of the journey she was on, the truth she was trying to pin down. The almost unimaginably complex story of four Pencarrow children—two white and two Black—and the hidden life of Calliope and Captain Pencarrow.

Crossing the dark meadow behind Ray Ransom, I think also of Andrew McKinney, who now lies in a burn unit at UMC. Andrew took his irrepressible energy and hard-won education and poured it into that plantation with the dream of making it something that could change people's perception of history, and of what kind of redemption might be possible in the present. When I think of all of that vanishing in a few minutes of explosive destruction, there's only a screaming bitterness within me, throwing off sparks of rage and a hunger to punish. Beneath that burnt-rubber stink is a strange numbness, like neural fallout from a physical injury, as though the Pencarrow fire somehow arced into me from miles away and seared something vital, leaving only the smoldering certainty that whoever set that fire was among the men I threatened earlier today. As I track Ray's broad shoulders ahead, my eyes make out an orange glow in the sky.

"What's that?" I ask, feeling like I'm going to insist on a rest stop soon. The ache in my thighs is almost paralyzing, and the stinging pain at the end of my stump tells me the skin has surely ruptured. "Is that the remains of the fire?"

"Too bright," my guide responds.

"Then what?"

"Don't know. Let's keep moving. We're almost to River Road."

As we top the next ridge, I see a massive bonfire sited low between two gently sloped hills. It burns with a wild, pagan intensity, hurling geysers of sparks into the black sky. A crowd of maybe thirty men surges around the flames, laughing and horsing around as snatches of country music roll toward us up the hill. Forty yards from the flames, a line of pickup trucks waits like moored boats. I feel as though we've stumbled onto a scene of triumph, of Vikings celebrating a successful raid on the English coast. The obscenity of it offends me at a level far beneath conscious thought.

We've crossed the Black Oak land with amazing rapidity, far faster than I would have believed possible. This thanks to the sure-footed speed and navigation of Ray Ransom, a man over seventy years old. My own land lies less than half a mile away, just across River Road.

"What do you think?" I ask.

"I think we've seen what we need to see."

"Not yet. I need to get closer."

Ray looks at me like I'm crazy. "Why?"

"Look at those trucks parked over there. I want a photo of those license plates."

"Bullshit. You know who belongs to this outfit. That's no big mystery."

"We don't know who else might be here. And if they burned Pencarrow, whoever's here *tonight* makes a difference."

"Jesus. Okay. But once we cross this ridge, we're vulnerable to anybody with better equipment than we got. Which is likely all these motherfuckers. Or at least their sentries."

"Let's go, Inky. I'll follow you."

Ray's army nickname goes past him without any reaction, but his eyes betray serious doubt about my suggestion. "You want to see the plates, right? That's it?"

"Yep."

"We're gonna stay on this side of the ridge."

Belly crawling along the back side of the crest, Ray works as far right as he dares toward River Road. I keep my eyes on the two strips of tape on his heels and follow. When he stops, we're no more than eighty yards from the trucks.

"We can read most of those plates through the scope now," he says, sighting down the hill at a line of tailgates. "I can call them out, you write them down in your phone or whatever."

"That's not the same as photos."

"No, it ain't. And staying free ain't the same as going to jail."

"I mean that scope shoots digital photos. Let me shoot the plates, and I'll record each one."

"Deal. Just keep your movements to a minimum, okay?"

I scrabble forward and take the rifle from Ray. It's been a while since I operated the night scope and its integrated camera, but the procedure comes back quickly. One by one, I move down the line of F-250s, Rams, and even an old Hummer. The resolution on the scope-cam leaves something to be desired, but I can make out the plates well enough to get them run. As I come to the end of the line, a new vehicle enters the long shallow bowl of grass and makes its way toward the near end of the line of vehicles. It's not a truck, but an SUV, and something about its silhouette draws my attention away from the main line.

The new ride is boxy, sleek, and urban, even European looking. *A Range Rover*, I realize. It's like spotting a stockbroker walking across Shot Barlow's field wearing Zegna instead of camo. Watching through the scope, I see the driver climb out of the silver vehicle and make his way in a wide arc around the knot of men at the bonfire, as if toward some prearranged meeting place. This guy hasn't come to join the revelers. As he walks, moving with a sure but slightly unbalanced gate, I realize with a disorienting rush that I'm looking at Bobby White.

His silhouette unites with a second one, and the height differential quickly tells me that the second man is Shot Barlow. On the night my plantation house burned to the ground, Bobby White, nationally syndicated radio personality, has made a pilgrimage to speak to the fascist militia chief, the jefe, the Big Boss Man.

As the two stand talking, I press Record on the night-scope.

"Ray?" I say.

"Yeah?"

"That's Bobby fucking White."

"Who? The guy who just pulled up?"

"Yeah."

"Bobby White the radio guy? Here for the PGA thing?"

"Yeah."

"Huh. So?"

"So he's making a third-party run for president! And he's out here with these nutjobs."

"Well . . . white folks' bullshit, man. Can't say I'm surprised. Racists come in every kind of package."

"That's my point."

"Take a picture of him then."

"Already did. If that son of a bitch had something to do with burning Arcadia and Pencarrow . . . I'm about ready to walk down there and confront him."

Ray grabs my right arm and holds tight. "Don't even think that shit."

"Why not?"

"Oh, I don't know. How about this? If they *did* burn your place, and you walk down there and catch them together, it'll take 'em exactly one phone call to find out you were down at the ER yelling about coming out here and that the police chief and sheriff warned you against it. At the very least you'll have an 'accident.' At worst, they'll shoot us both and claim you started the scrap. And not even a judge will doubt it. You've got one option, Penn. Shoot these plates, get the hell out, and fight another day. Now, about face, soldier. I'm here to save you from yourself."

I know he's right, but the disconnect of seeing Bobby White walk into this world has knocked me through a looking glass. I couldn't have imagined it yesterday.

"Snap out of it!" Ray hisses, jerking my arm.

"Okay, goddamn it."

After a couple of uncertain seconds, Ray releases his grip.

My next coherent thought is the realization that I'm on the far side of the ridge, walking down toward Bobby White with so much adrenaline flowing through me that I no longer feel the pain in my stump. I hold my AR-15 outward to keep the scope before my eye, tracking White as he and Barlow move purposefully toward what might be a bunker entrance at the periphery of the bonfire's glow. Pausing a moment, I engage the scope camera and record three or four more seconds of White and Barlow walking together, then vanishing below my line of sight.

"*Freeze, asshole!*" barks a voice from the dark to my right.

I stop.

"Drop the rifle!"

I do.

"Identify yourself," demands the voice.

Utterly at a loss, I speak the first name that might sound plausible out here. "Jimmy Bowlin," I mutter, naming a local poacher I used to have a lot of trouble with.

"*What?* What the fuck you doin' out here, Jimmy? Don't you know Shot'll tear you a new asshole being on his land during something like this?"

I figure I have thirty seconds before this sentry realizes I'm not Jimmy Bowlin. And I can't even see him.

"I was out here checking out that Pencarrow fire, man. I just saw your bonfire. Figured I'd check it out, too."

"Curiosity killed the fuckin' cat, boy. Jeez, you got no sense. You need to make a beeline for River Road. If you don't, I gotta turn you in."

"I hear you, man. I'm goin' now."

"Hold up a sec. Why you got your face blacked like that? I seen you poachin' before, and you don't go to that trouble. Too damn lazy."

To this I have no answer.

"All right, Jimbo, you're coming with me. Down to the bonfire. Come on."

"Okay, okay. No problem."

"You packin' anything else, Jimmy?"

"Nothing but the rifle. I just came out to see that house fire."

"You're lying. I can hear it in your voice. Lie down on the ground. Spread eagle. I'm gonna search you."

"Aw, hell, brother. Come on."

"Do it!"

As carefully as I can, I bend my knees and start to get down, but the pain in my stump combines with some problem in my right knee, and I have to snap back erect or crash to the ground.

"I said *down*, damn it!"

The sentry smacks my right side hard with his fist, and pain blanks out everything but the crack of bones. He must have broken at least two ribs, which drives the air from my lungs as I drop to the ground, hugging myself in agony.

"I didn't hit you that hard, you pussy." He grabs at the pistol in my waistband. But before he can jerk it out, I hear a dull impact like a bat hitting a watermelon, and he collapses across my back. Another arc of pain drives a grunt of agony from my lungs.

"I shouldn't have brought you out here," Ray says. "You are *not of sound mind*." He rolls the sentry off my back. "Come on. We gotta tie this redneck up and get back out the way we came, double quick."

"I can't move yet, Ray. He fucked me up."

"He didn't hit you that hard, did he? Jesus."

I've barely managed to suck in enough air to stay conscious, so sharp is the pain. "I've got a bone problem. Nobody knows about it. I may have to lie here a couple of minutes."

"We ain't got a couple minutes. What kind of bone problem? Like arthritis?"

"No," I wheeze. "Cancer."

This is the one English word that still commands silence. Ray crouches beside me and lays his hand on my upper back. "Tell me what to do, bro."

"I don't know. Never had this happen before. But you're right, we've gotta get clear. Or we won't live long enough for me to die of cancer."

"Jesus, Penn. I had no idea."

"Why don't we just make a beeline across River Road, like this guy suggested?"

"Because we got no vehicle on this side. And if these yahoos figure out something's wrong, they'll run us down in about two minutes. They live for that kind of shit. No, the long way's the only way we get back safe."

"Great."

"Well, ain't this helpful?" Ray says, removing some cable restraints from the guy's tactical belt. After cuffing the sentry's hands behind him, Ransom pulls a 5.11 Tactical mask printed with shark's teeth off the guy's neck, balls it tight, then stuffs it into his mouth. "Time to move, Penn."

"Hold on. I need to add a sock to my prosthetic."

Rolling onto my ass with a groan, I remove my stump from the prosthetic socket, take a thick sock pad from my pocket, and pull it tight up around what remains of my lower leg. Then I force the tip of my stump into the socket and reach up to Ray.

"Pull me up, man."

He does, and I use my full weight to reseat the stump in the socket with a tighter fit than before. The pain in my side nearly paralyzes me, but remaining here is not an option. "I'm good. Let's move."

"I'm gonna go faster than I did walking in," Ray warns me. "Lemme know if I push you too hard. But they're gonna get on our asses pretty quick. If they do, I may slide into the woods a little. Let's hope the rattlers are bedded down good, 'cause we're liable to step on one in this dark."

"Oh, boy. Let's go."

THE PAIN I suffered between the hill where the sentry knocked me down and the place where Ray had parked his truck is something I hope never to repeat. We only stopped twice for me to rest and breathe, and I'm proud of that. But as we approach Ray's pickup, which he parked about twenty yards deep in the trees, to make it invisible to road traffic, someone rises up out of its bed and aims a pistol with a weapon light at us.

"You boys stop right where you are," says a strangely familiar voice. "I don't want to shoot you, but I will."

"Get that gun off us!" Ray demands, easing the barrel of my AR-15 a little higher.

"Don't do it, Ray," says the voice. "I'll put one through your eye."

The speaker sounds confident of fulfilling his threat.

"Who the fuck is that?" asks Ray.

"Bobby White," I tell him. "Isn't it?"

Soft laughter comes from the truck bed. "Can you see me past this gun light? Or did you recognize my voice?"

"I recognize your voice. The confidence in it."

Bobby laughs again. "What the hell were you doing out on Black Oak, Penn? Attempting suicide?"

"Trying to find out whether Barlow and his punks burned my house."

"And?"

"Oh, I know they did it. What I want to know now is, did you help them? Or did you order them to do it?"

Bobby lowers his pistol. "Come on, man. Are you crazy?"

"You went down in that bunker with Shot Barlow. What the hell do you expect me to think?"

"You're not thinking! I used to work for Shot Barlow when I was a boy. Tough-ass work, too. He's pestered me for months to come out and see what he's been building out there, and also to make a personal appearance for his little militia. With these recent arsons, and his place so close to mine, I figured I'd take him up on it, see if I could pick up if they were involved in any way."

This isn't the answer I expected. "So you talked to some of his whack-jobs tonight?"

"A couple."

Bobby's expression tells me the experience taught him some things. "And what vibe did you get? Could they have set the early fires?"

"Hard to say. My gut says Shot didn't order it. But a couple of fanatics in that bunker are on a pretty loose chain. I wouldn't put it past them."

"I can't see Barlow burning Tranquility and Arcadia, not even for a false-flag operation. Aren't those old antebellum homes the temples of his faith?"

Bobby settles into a new stillness. "I think he'd trade a handful of those mansions for national TV coverage. To stir up a fight. And if that's what he wanted, he's sure got it. Round-the-clock marches, media helicopters over the river, collateral violence. Bienville's coming apart on live TV."

I look out at the road and through the trees for signs of pursuit. I see no lights, at least. "I find it hard to believe that you'd take the political risk of coming out here just to play Good Samaritan detective."

Bobby snorts and looks back toward the road. "Like your late friend Doc, I don't consider every move through a political lens before I make it."

"Bullshit you don't. You're as natural a politician as any I've met. There's more to you being here than trying to figure out who burned Pencarrow."

"If there is, you won't find out tonight. You guys need to get the hell out of here."

"How did you know where to find us?" Ray asks.

Bobby chuckles. "As soon as the alarm went up and they started hunting you, I used my brain instead of my feet. We're seven miles outside town. Anybody who came to recon Black Oak—or target it—had to drive here first. That meant they had to leave vehicles on one of the roads bordering the place. All I had to do was keep my brights on and look for a reflection in the woods. Took me about six minutes to find your truck."

Ray shakes his head. "How 'bout you come work for our side, Mr. White? Old Man Cage here ain't up for it anymore."

Bobby flips easily over the side of the truck bed and lands in front of

Ray. His face is flushed with pleasure, and his eyes gleam in the dark. He looks like this is all a big game to him.

"Seriously," Bobby says. "You guys get moving, okay? I never saw you."

Ray nods and walks past him to the driver's door.

"Thanks, Bobby," I tell him.

"No sweat." He takes a step closer. "You sure you're okay, Penn? Most of whatever G.I. Joe combat makeup you were wearing has worn off. You're white as kindergarten paste."

"Honestly . . . I think I broke a couple ribs out there."

"No shit? Your cancer?"

"Yeah."

"Get your ass to a doctor. Stop playing at shit you got no business doing anymore. Leave it to the young bucks like me."

"Will you really help bust local guys like Barlow if you find out they're behind the arsons?"

"You're goddamn right I will. This is my hometown, and I'm running for president. Anybody shits in the waterhole around here, they're gonna have to deal with my professional side. And they will not enjoy it."

"You mean Bobby White the radio host? The attorney? What?"

He shakes his head with ominous deliberation. "The SFOD sergeant."

"You remind me of a buddy of mine."

"I'll bet I know which one."

"Yeah?"

"Daniel Kelly, SFOD-1."

"How the hell . . . ?"

Bobby smiles. "I read your book. The one about fighting the Double Eagles. Now get moving, old man. Next time you try shit like this, bring Kelly with you. Where is he, anyway?"

"Straight up?"

Bobby nods.

"Killing Russians in the Ukraine."

He smiles in the darkness. "Glad to hear it. See you tomorrow. And tell Annie hello from me."

"I'll do it."

He claps me on the shoulder, then vanishes into the trees.

CHAPTER 78

WHEN SOPHIE GOT home to Belle Rose after the post-tourney event at the club, she found her father sitting at the kitchen counter eating Blue Bell french vanilla ice cream out of the carton. The television was playing Fox News with the sound turned low.

"Where's Charlot?" she asked.

Charles took another bite and let it melt in his mouth, then swallowed. "I heard the vote to dissolve the city failed to pass."

She didn't want to engage with him about politics, but she wanted to know where her brother was. "That's right."

"Those two young aldermen are proving more resilient to pressure than those Poker Club pricks predicted."

Sophie said nothing.

"And you voted against."

"That's right. We're still a democracy, last time I checked."

"That's easy to say when someone else pays your bills."

"I'm not doing this tonight. Where's Charlot, Daddy?"

"Gone."

A hollow ache entered her abdomen. "I thought you told him he could stay here."

"Oh, I did. But you know your brother. Once I removed the acute pressure, he couldn't contain himself. Had to go celebrate."

"I don't believe that."

"Not my problem. Amadu heard an engine outside, then the front door closing, and he was gone. He'll probably call you from the casino in a few hours, sobbing about how he's in trouble again. Or else he's with one of his perverted friends, pursuing unnatural activities."

"Christ, Daddy. What did you do to relieve the pressure? Did you pay the debt or not?"

"Oh, there's more than one major debtor. But I wired Tommy Russo a quarter million dollars to keep him happy while we sort out the rest of it. He's owed close to another six hundred, best I can figure. Then there are the national debtors, the digital sites . . ."

Sophie sighed heavily. There was no denying that when Charlot fucked up, he did it in style. But it was hard to believe he wouldn't stay around even one night to demonstrate some gratitude. Or at least to fake some.

"I'm going to my room," she said. "I'm exhausted."

"Did you hear the latest news?"

She tensed. "What's happened?"

"Another antebellum home burned."

"You mean Beauvoir?"

"That's old news. No, Pencarrow. It exploded about two hours ago."

The blood drained from Sophie's face. "You can't mean it! I ate supper there tonight."

"Did you? You're back to fancying Penn Cage?"

"Oh, fuck off. Was anyone hurt?"

"The Black professor restoring the house was airlifted to Jackson with severe burns. Cage's daughter got superficial burns, I heard. Look, I'm not your secretary."

Sophie stalked out of the kitchen, her hands shaking like those of a young soldier fleeing a battlefield.

AS BOBBY WHITE walked into Charles Dufort's study, the driver called Amadu pulled the door shut behind him, leaving him shuttered alone with the old man. Sensing the driver standing post just outside, Bobby approached Dufort with confidence but kept his feet rather than take the proffered chair that faced the big desk.

"It's late to be called out here," he said. "What's got you stirred up?"

"I don't sleep much anymore. Did I take you away from something important? Nice piece of ass, maybe?"

"Depends on your point of view. I was out at Shot Barlow's place. Pencarrow Plantation just burned."

The old man's face remained unmoved. "I'm well aware. Did Barlow do it?"

"I don't know. One of his flaky followers might have."

Dufort leaned forward over his desk. "Did they burn the other houses, too, Bobby? Did that white trash burn Tranquility?"

"I don't think so. But I caught Penn Cage and Ray Ransom out there poking around on Black Oak."

Dufort's face tightened. "That's not good."

"They couldn't have seen anything important, other than me."

"Be careful with Penn Cage. He's a Boy Scout. Always has been."

"Not quite. He killed some of those Double Eagles about ten years back, one with his bare hands. And he ran Snake Knox down with a pickup truck. Broke him to pieces."

Dufort nodded. "I knew Brody Royal pretty well. Cage or Henry Sexton killed him with a Wehrmacht flamethrower. In his own house. I think that's where Tarantino got the idea for that movie of his."

Bobby chuckled at the idea of Charles Dufort sitting up watching *Once Upon a Time . . . in Hollywood*. He could see the old perv pulling his pud to *Jackie Brown*. "So what am I doing here, Charles?"

"I need you to do something for me."

"What's that?"

"Kill my son."

Bobby felt a tingle all across his skin. "Did I hear you right?"

"You know things have been moving in this direction for some time. Well, now we're there."

"I don't know any such thing."

Dufort looked at Bobby like he would indulge him for a few minutes if necessary. "I gave a lot of thought to what you told me today at the country club. The threats that Charlot presents to me, and also to you. And tonight I spoke to my son at length, something I haven't done in a long while. Not only about his financial difficulties, but also his legal ones, which are considerable. The truth is, even if I were to throw him another lifeline, he's not going to change. He'll be a threat to us both from now until I die. Same with you, I assume?"

Bobby sighed. "I can't disagree."

"The obvious corollary is that Charlot can only be a problem until *he* dies. After that, we're both safe from him forever."

Bobby said nothing.

"It's a hard thing to face," Dufort went on. "But there's no turning away from it. Not if you're really going to run for president."

It finally sank in that this rich old bastard was seriously discussing the murder of his son. Charles Dufort had to be the coldest ally Bobby had ever worked with, and that was saying something.

"I'm running," Bobby asserted.

"Well, then. This offers us a unique opportunity to establish unbreakable trust. Between ourselves, I mean."

Bobby felt like a chipmunk being angled into a corner by a wise old rattlesnake. "How so?"

"We agree on the best course of action. And this truth that we've recognized . . . you need to handle it."

"Why me?"

Dufort leaned back in his chair. "I'm his father, for God's sake. Much too close to commit that kind of violence against him. It must surely be

"Join me in the rosarium," he ordered Bobby.

Bobby followed Dufort out into the fragrant night. They walked a complex grid of paths, with Dufort occasionally reaching out to touch silken petals or pull a cutworm off a stem. "Eating the world," he muttered once. "While we sleep." Soon they came to a brick utility building with a slate-shingled roof.

"Amadu?" Dufort said.

The driver opened the green-painted door with a key, then dug a small black flashlight from his pocket and shone it inside.

Dufort motioned for Bobby to look through the door.

With growing dread, Bobby did.

Charlot lay across two stacks of sacks containing garden chemicals Bobby had never heard of. His eyes and mouth were open, and in the powerful LED beam Bobby saw scarlet petechiae in his eyes, and in the skin over his orbits.

Strangled.

Charlot's neck looked slightly swollen, but Bobby saw no bruising. *He was dead the whole time we were talking . . . during that whole sick discussion.* Bobby remembered a sadistic instructor from his Delta training. This was exactly the kind of shit that asshole would have pulled—

"He looks dead," Bobby observed.

"Gone," Amadu replied. "Happier in the next world."

For a moment Bobby considered breaking the driver's neck. He'd undoubtedly been the one who stole Charlot's life from him. But killing Amadu would have been misplaced vengeance. It was the father who deserved Old Testament justice. Only if Bobby killed Charles Dufort . . . he'd be shutting down his campaign bank.

"What was the point of that charade back there?"

"I learned something I needed to know," Dufort replied. "Something I couldn't learn any other way."

"Which was?"

"There's a limit to how far you'll go."

"I need sleep, Charles. Tomorrow's a big day."

"Yes, it is. What's Bobby going to do tomorrow, Amadu?"

"Kill some country niggers, ha-ha!" The driver grinned, the first time Bobby had ever seen any display of emotion from him.

Repelled, Bobby turned and marched out toward the back lawn, but Charles told him that going back through the house would take only half the time. Reversing course, Bobby soon reached the French doors that opened to the study. Dufort was calling out something from the garden, but he ignored the old man. He walked past the desk, straight to the door that led to the long hallway.

Rapid footsteps sounded on the floor behind him. It was Amadu. "Mr. Charles say wait!" he bellowed.

"Screw Mr. Charles!"

Amadu crossed the study with surprising speed. He seemed about to try to restrain Bobby, so Bobby spun and assumed a close-quarters-combat stance.

"I'll fuck you up, old man," he warned. "And I might do worse."

The stumpy driver tensed, then lunged. Bobby reacted with the speed and skill that had carried him through multiple missions overseas, seizing Amadu's right wrist and using his momentum against him, slamming the driver headfirst into the door frame with enough force to knock him unconscious. When Amadu struggled in vain to rise, Bobby raised one foot to stomp the back of his neck, which could have severed his cervical spine.

"*Don't!*" Charles Dufort shouted from the rosarium door.

After a couple of tempting seconds, Bobby lowered his foot to the hardwood floor. "I guess I learned something tonight, too, didn't I?"

"What's that?" Dufort asked.

"You care about this old servant more than your own son."

Bobby walked out and slammed the door behind him.

IN THE LONG, shadowy corridor that bisected much of the great house, Bobby paused and took a couple of breaths. Who could imagine that a run for the presidency would begin with the murder of an old lover, one he'd had to keep secret from the world from the beginning? He hoped Charlot had died without realizing that his father had ordered his death. But part of him knew different.

Bobby strode toward the large foyer that would give him escape from this nightmare mansion. As he did, a tall figure appeared at the other end of the hall. He thought at first that it might be Charlot's ghost, but then he saw the distinctively feminine outline, and he realized it was Sophie.

As she glided toward him in the dim light, he realized she wore a floor-length silk robe in a Japanese print, like something you might see Grace Kelly wearing in a fifties film. He wondered if Sophie knew Charlot's fate, but quickly decided that she couldn't possibly. She'd be a wreck if she did. Whatever her flaws, lack of empathy wasn't one. Sophie had always loved her half brother, and even Charlot had told him she'd always been good about helping him when he was down.

"What are you doing here?" she asked softly, slowing her progress over the waxed hardwood floor.

"I had to see your father about something."

They stopped once they were about two feet apart, facing each other in the near dark. He marveled at her beauty from such close proximity. Having recently been physically near a young woman as attractive as Jenna Kay Donnelly, it struck him forcefully now that Sophie Dufort belonged to that elite sorority of women who seemed immune to the passage of time. The lines of her face remained what they'd been at forty, and at forty they hadn't been much different than at twenty. Even her worst enemies would admit that she had some of the finest bone structure they'd ever seen. Her skin and muscle tone also retained their youthful integrity. Charlot would likely have been much the same, had he not worked so diligently at destroying himself.

"It's pretty late for business," Sophie observed.

"Not your father's business."

He heard disdain in her near-silent chuckle. "And just what is that?"

Bobby shook his head. "Too tiresome to discuss."

"I'm interested."

"Sorry."

Sophie looked past him for a few seconds. "You don't happen to know where Charlot is, do you?"

With great effort Bobby held his facial muscles in check. "I don't."

"Daddy told me he went out to celebrate his debts being paid off. Or partly paid, anyway."

"That sounds like Charlot."

Sophie nodded with infinite sadness. "Did you ever really love him, Bobby?"

The blunt question jolted him, and he was afraid he'd showed it. "Of course I did."

She shook her head. "You know what I mean."

"We were best friends for a long time."

"Oh, Bobby . . . Does Daddy know the two of you were lovers? Somehow I suspect he doesn't."

Bobby stood there trying to come up with the right thing to say, but his brain offered nothing. He had no idea that Sophie had known about them. He wondered how long, but he dared not ask. So much remained unspoken between them, and had for so long. Most of it twenty years or more, when they'd slept together in the pool house, him a sexually confused eighteen-year-old and her an exhausted woman of forty, fighting drug withdrawal and depression.

"You're mistaken," he said finally. "Charlot must have been having some fun with you and given you the wrong impression."

Sophie looked amused by his feeble attempt. "Is that so?"

While his mind searched for a more substantive defense, she raised her hand and opened the top of her robe, revealing one full breast. His eyes went to the dark nipple, which quickly became erect in the cool air of the hallway. He stood frozen, strangely afraid that her father would suddenly appear.

"Kiss it, Bobby," she whispered. "I need the release."

"Sophie, what the hell's going on?"

"It won't take long. Seriously. I need it. I've got to blank everything out. Just for a while. Suck it . . ."

"What happened tonight? Something's got you upset."

"I'm always upset." She took hold of his hand and slid it into her robe, guided the fingers to her inner thigh, then upward. He tensed when he felt her pubic hair.

"I'd better go," he said, trying to pull his hand away, but she held it there. With her other hand, she found his penis and checked its tumescence.

"What's the matter? No latent desire to nail your friend's big sister?"

He stood in awkward embarrassment, unable to believe the situation.

"Nice size," she went on, pulling gently. "I'd forgotten. But not much use in its present state."

Bobby blinked but said nothing. The situation confused him. Despite his primary sexual orientation, the equipment had always worked regardless of whom he lay down with—something not true for many gay friends he knew.

Sophie pulled harder, stroking him with expert patience. "I'm serious," she murmured. "It's bound to be better than self-abuse."

An image of Corey Evers flickered through Bobby's brain, then vanished. "I think we'd better talk, Sophie. But not here."

She slid the robe back over her breast, covering it once more. "My rooms are at the other end of the house. As far as I can get from the paterfamilias. Follow me."

With a last squeeze of his dormant cock, she released him, then turned and started down toward the foyer.

Bobby couldn't think of anything to do but follow.

CHAPTER 79

NADINE WAS REREADING the conclusion of Romulus's personal narrative when she heard Penn pull into the garage and clatter through the pantry door. Only then, in a sudden lightheaded rush, did she realize that her heart had been running between ninety and a hundred beats per minute for the duration of his absence. She sat on the sofa with two fingers in the hollow of her neck, feeling the deceleration in her carotid, praying Penn had done nothing on Black Oak that would send him to a jail cell by morning.

When he left the town house—after having assured himself that Nadine truly had Annie covered for the night if necessary—she'd gone out to the truck to beg Ray to protect Penn from himself. Ransom had promised that he would, but since he'd spent most of his life in the state penitentiary, he might not be the best person to counsel impulse control under stress.

She expected Penn to slip quietly into the house, being hyperconscious of disturbing Annie. Instead, he swept in like a man bent on waking everyone within. What he'd seen at Black Oak had proved worse than he'd expected.

"A fucking bonfire!" he cried. "Like a celebration after a football game!"

Nadine wasn't sure how to respond. "That doesn't mean they burned Pencarrow. Even if they're glad it happened."

His eyes widened in disbelief. "Oh, they're more than glad. They took their chance and got their revenge. I don't think they even give a shit who knows it—so long as nobody can prove it."

There was a current in Penn's voice she'd never heard before. Hysteria. Through all the years she'd known him—which, admittedly, didn't encompass those he'd spent in violent contention with the Double Eagle group—he'd always held his extreme emotions in check. Even when tested, his slow-burning reactions kept him focused and rational. But now she heard a man who might be driven to a self-destructive act of vengeance by the slightest provocation.

"Penn, exactly what did you see out there?" she asked, trying to gentle him with her tone from the couch.

At last he turned squarely to her and looked down into her eyes. "Bobby White, for one thing."

Her mouth fell open. "Bobby White the radio host?"

A single nod beneath blazing eyes.

"That's . . . *nuts*. Why would Bobby risk being seen with those guys? That could kill his campaign."

"He claims he went out there to try to figure out whether the Barlows were behind the burning. At least of Pencarrow. He apparently used to work for Barlow when he was a boy, and you can imagine that Barlow's militia guys worship him."

"What was he doing exactly?"

Penn shrugged. "He walked from his Range Rover to the entrance of a bunker, then disappeared."

"A *bunker*?" she echoed.

"They've built a goddamn end-of-days compound out there."

"I didn't know they were that far gone. The Tenisaw Rifles, or whatever. I thought it was just rednecks playing dress-up."

"They're serious about their dress-up."

Nadine tried to get her mind around the cultures of the Barlow militia and Bobby White merging at any point. White was deeply conservative, of course, but he'd always managed to steer clear of the QAnon or even Trump strains of extremism and paranoia. "Was Bobby still there when you left?"

"He could *still* be there, for all I know. We had to get out of there in a hurry."

"Why?"

Penn looked away. "A sentry walked up on us. On *me*."

A flicker of panic went through her. "Shit. Did he identify you?"

"I don't think so. Ray had my face painted pretty dark. We wiped it off during the drive back, in case of a traffic stop."

"Any physical altercation result between you and the sentry? Enough to generate assault-and-battery charges in the morning?"

Penn kept his eyes lowered, clearly not wanting to get into it. "If *I* make the charges. I think the guy broke two of my ribs."

"Jesus."

"My bone density must be down to nothing. I'm afraid even to look at my stump. Feels like it's been bleeding for a while. I haven't covered that much ground in a long time." He limped to the refrigerator and poured a glass of tea, then looked back at her. "Ray knocked the sentry out, blind-sided him. I think we're okay on ID."

Nadine exhaled in relief.

"I shot some decent video through my night scope. Bobby talking to Shot Barlow, walking with him."

"Holy shit. That could really damage his campaign prospects."

"Maybe. Who knows in this current climate?"

Like a restless animal waking from a tranquilizer dart, Penn began to pace again, groaning with nearly every step. "Anyway, I can't sit around on this all night. I need to make some calls. The Bureau first, maybe John Kaiser. He's retired, but he knows a lot of people. Then there's BATF, and Earl Bell at the Southern Poverty Law Center. I mean, they blew up my goddamn house! That's terrorism, no question."

Nadine nodded slowly. "I'm not sure that's true, legally speaking. We should certainly look into it. But as for tonight . . . Penn, you're exhausted."

"Yes and no. I'm tired, but I can't bear to do nothing."

She stood and went to him, hoping to pull him down to the sofa and rub his legs, anything to settle his nerves. But Penn avoided her as though without intent, walking in circles and carrying on an unintelligible conversation with himself.

"Penn . . . please come sit with me. I don't know that I've ever seen you like this."

"I've never felt this impotent," he replied. "In the past, what, fourteen hours, Doc has been murdered, Andrew has been burned so badly he could die, and Annie's got severe burns over her gunshot wound. I mean . . . I have to do *something*."

The hollowness of his eyes gave Nadine the sense of peering through brittle windows into a building that might collapse inward at any moment. The more he spoke, the more she realized that his voice had entered a higher-than-normal register.

"How about I make you a gin and tonic?" she suggested.

"Don't need it."

"I think you do. In fact, I'd feel better if you drank one."

He laughed then, the note of hysteria returning. "You're gonna have one?"

"I would if I weren't pregnant. I think I'll make two for you, though. Why don't you turn on the TV and see what they're covering?"

"You know what it's going to be. Those goddamn viral images from the looting on Battery Row. Those literally wiped away everything else that happened in the public mind. The white mind, anyway. And you know that torpedoed our chances of getting help from Washington. In the short run, anyway."

"I'll bet they're running Octa leading her protest song."

Penn dropped beside her on the sofa and clicked through CNN, MSNBC, Fox, and the rest. Sure enough, several reports were already running, and for the first time Penn saw a video image—what looked like a drone shot—of Pencarrow burning.

"My God," he said, feeling hollow. "Look at that!"

Nadine already regretted telling him to look.

"You know," Penn murmured. "By noon tomorrow this town may not even exist anymore as a legal entity. Unless Judge Shelby can back some of those crooked Alabama politicians off our guys' relatives."

"I've got faith in Clay," she said with sincerity.

Penn nodded, his eyes on the screen. "He's a tough old piece of bark, I'll grant you."

Like a clairvoyant, or maybe just an old lover with good instincts, Nadine could already see how this would go. The slanted news stories, watched one after another as he panned through the channels, would drive Penn to an ever-higher pitch of agitation. Then he'd start calling people out of bed, maybe even making demands that they would remember in the morning. She didn't need to let that vicious cycle get started. But how to stop it? A single G&T wouldn't do it. Not even a double. Then she remembered finding a certain cardboard box in the upstairs bathroom. Annie had brought it up from Edelweiss earlier today.

To keep Penn contained, she popped the release on his prosthetic and helped him pull his stump out of the socket. To her horror, she saw that his inner sock liner was indeed soaked in blood.

"Jesus Christ," he grunted as his flesh pulled free from the vacuum.

"Oh, no," she sighed. "I'm going to have to clean this up. But I'm going to make those drinks first."

A faint smile touched his lips. "Thanks for keeping your priorities straight."

"Does it hurt bad?"

"Bad enough."

"I'm going to get some painkillers from your mom's hospice box."

Despite the oxy already in his system, Penn wasn't about to turn down a top-up. "Sounds like the perfect garnish for my drink."

Nadine's laughter feels forced. "Have you thought any more about your hemoglobin?" she asked, her eyes on the bloody mess covering his bruised skin and traumatized suture lines.

"Not really. I got pretty short of breath out at Black Oak, to be honest."

"Damn it, Penn. You're getting that transfusion tomorrow."

"I know. The problem is, the procedure will eat up most of a day. In this town, anyway."

"It's your life!"

"I know." He squeezed her wrist and promised, "I'll do it."

"I did some reading about myeloma on Google tonight. There are some drugs we need to get you on, and quick. High-dose steroids, for one. Things are a lot different than they were back in the nineties, when you were diagnosed."

"I know. I'm going to do what I need to do."

After closing her eyes and sighing in relief, Nadine went into the kitchen, opened two Fever Tree tonics, and quickly poured them over ice in crystal highball glasses. Into that she sloshed the Hendrick's, then made a quick run to the upstairs bathroom.

There, under the sink, she found the box that held the remains of the hospice meds Peggy had been prescribed during her final days. There were fentanyl patches, morphine capsules, and also liquid Xanax, which could be administered by dropper or brush to patients who could no longer swallow. Nadine was tempted to bring the Xanax as well. She was no nurse, but she'd lived enough in the real world to understand basic Xanax dosages. She read the bottle, then pocketed the dropper and floated back downstairs like a nurse on a night ward dispensing sedatives.

She helped Penn swallow an oxycodone tab with the G&T, then offered him enough liquid alprazolam to knock out a bear cub. To her surprise, he turned down the anxiolytic and focused on his drink while she laved his abraded skin with warm rags. Ten minutes later, he passed out with his eyes glued to the television and his thumb on his iPhone screen. Nadine drew the phone from his hand and explained to his friend from the Southern Poverty Law Center that he'd simply collapsed from exhaustion, and from the stress of losing Pencarrow. Earl Bell said he understood completely.

"May I ask who this is?" Bell added.

"I'm Nadine Sullivan."

"Well, Ms. Sullivan, I'm glad to know someone's there to watch over him. Penn sounds pretty frazzled."

"Yes."

"I—just a minute, you said Nadine Sullivan?"

"Yes."

"You're not the lawyer who freed Aaron Moses from death row in North Carolina? That pro bono case?"

Nadine's face colored at the flash of pride that went through her. "I used to be. I run a bookstore down here in Mississippi now."

"Oh, I know that. I mean, I'd heard it at some point. Well . . . Penn's a lucky man to have you taking care of him. How's he making it on that leg?"

"Not so great, honestly. Mr. Bell?"

"Earl, please."

"Do you think Bobby White could be involved with an extremist militia group like the Tenisaw Rifles?"

"Bobby White?" The lawyer sighed. "Nadine, before tonight, I would have said no. But over the past few years, I've lost my capacity to be surprised. Racism is a deeply ingrained tendency, and I've seen people I never would have suspected revealed to be rabidly atavistic once you peel away their masks."

"But Bobby White has so much to lose."

"True. But he's far smarter and more capable than Trump or any of the other pretenders. And he has a true mass audience. All he needs to do is pivot right to hoover up millions of disaffected Trump voters. This mess with the burning mansions could be his moment. His excuse. The fear and fury in the white community over these fires is like nothing I've ever seen. It's confirmation of every worst assessment of Black radical motives. The ultimate vindication of years of demonization."

"Which is why I don't believe the people behind this are really Black," Nadine said. "It's a suicidally destructive move for them, politically speaking."

"Unless," Bell said cryptically.

"Unless what?"

"Unless this is a full-on transition to a new strategy. Like Malcolm X endorsing violence in self-defense: progress 'by any means necessary.'"

"You mean—"

"I mean I've watched a protest poster made in Bienville go viral tonight. On the left it shows the Arcadia mansion before the fire, like a promo shot for *Gone with the Wind*, and on the right—"

"The gate of Auschwitz II?" Nadine finished.

"You've seen it?"

"I saw it in person, at the meeting where they revealed it."

"That's the power of the targets these Bastard Sons of the Confederacy have chosen. To white people, those mansions represent—at worst—some uncomfortable history. Easily written off as part of a 'dead' past. But to Black people, especially those who've done their research, those plantations are death camps. Not just work camps. Because the joke was the same. 'Work Shall Make You Free.' The only way any Jew was getting free of Auschwitz was up the chimney. Same with the enslaved in the fields run by the owners of those mansions. The only freedom was death. Even their children would be owned in perpetuity. In only two days, these fires have pushed that parallel to the forefront of a national conversation. And it's not going to stop anytime soon, no matter how upset white people get. I have more than a few Black friends who might have taken a step like this to achieve that. I have quite a few who refuse to condemn those arsons now."

"Even with the deaths that have resulted?"

"Even then."

A deep chill went through her. "I hear you. Well . . . I need to get Penn ready for bed. This is going to be a long week."

"For the whole country, I fear. But especially you guys. Mississippi hasn't got much in the way of leadership. Not in statewide office, anyway. Keep your heads down."

"We will, Earl."

"Good night, Nadine."

She murmured good night and clicked END. Then she leaned forward over her knees and began to breathe deeply. When her heartbeat finally slowed, she got up and went to hang the wet rags in the bathroom, weeping as she walked.

Penn never stirred.

Returning to the den, she dabbed his darkly bruised stump dry, then decided that rather than try to move him, she would make herself a bed on the nearby Eames recliner. As she laid out a comforter, she realized that Penn had not only not stirred, but hadn't even changed position. Worried about his heart in such an anemic state, she laid her finger into the crook of his neck to make sure it was beating regularly.

It seemed to be.

After a long look at the recliner, she decided to go back to Annie's room and sleep beside her in the double bed, which offered the best chance of a decent night's rest. Tomorrow would be another traumatic day, one fraught with risk. She thought of Doc Berry and his selfless efforts to bring the community together. Now he was gone. Who would replace him? And what could they do to mitigate the present crisis? While men like Doc worked to solve problems, men like the governor lived solely to exploit them. They cared nothing for the consequences to their constituents, only for the power granted them by their rabid base.

Lying beside Annie in the dark, she snapped awake in the midst of a twisted dream, like something from a children's book: a little Black boy stood with his fist jammed into a hole in a dike, while above him brown river water washed over the top. As the water swirled around his knees, she recalled the historian John Barry's description of the Black sharecroppers who in 1927 were forced at gunpoint to try to reinforce shuddering Delta levees as the swollen Mississippi bored under them, bringing biblical apocalypse to the South. In a shivering sweat, Nadine checked Annie's pulse and temperature, then rolled over and slowly went back to sleep.

CHAPTER 80

COREY EVERS STOOD sweating in the azalea bushes on the west side of Belle Rose, his eyes glued to Sophie Dufort's breasts and shoulders as she sat astride Bobby and ground her pubis against him with slow, relentless persistence. Having flattened her palms on his chest, she used them as points of leverage to flex her core muscles, which resulted in her body moving with obvious power from the waist down, while her upper body remained fixed, her wide eyes focused on Bobby's face below.

The emotional disconnect triggered by the vision before him was simply too overwhelming to process, so Corey focused on details. For some reason, the couple was facing the foot of the bed, which gave Corey a complete frontal view of Sophie while denying him any view of Bobby (save the top of his head and his shoulders). But that was enough. The stump of the right arm below the ripped shoulder muscles was so familiar to Corey that the sight in this visual context sickened him.

He wondered whether this was the first time Bobby had ever made love with Sophie Dufort. Bobby had spent a lot of time in this house as a teenager. It wasn't hard to imagine a summer night when the two might have collided in a fog of alcohol, and she'd decided to scratch a carnal itch (or temporarily fill her emotional emptiness) with a handsome young athlete. He couldn't remember everything Bobby had ever told him about Sophie, but sexual precociousness and promiscuity had always been main themes. Still, even if they had been together before, why restart things now, when it carried so much risk?

That's not how Bobby sees it, he realized. *He's not fucking her in* spite *of the risk. This is an audition.*

Standing in the humid air, the *cheeeeeep* of crickets nearly deafening, Corey remembered his day up to that point. Playing watchdog at the pro-am tourney that morning . . . diverting Charlot from the parking lot ambush . . . driving him out to Snake Creek Indian Village . . . actually *fighting* him down in the sandy creek bed, wrestling underwater in the deep hole, nearly drowning him. And finally, the last-second decision to spare Charlot's life. (Had it even been a decision, or merely instinctive panic? For some desperate fraction of a minute Corey had actually believed him dead.)

Corey had come so close to killing Charlot. And why? To protect

Bobby, of course. To save his goddamn *campaign*. Earlier today Corey had done his best to persuade Bobby to steer clear of both the Poker Club and Dufort, arguing that they could find new sources of funding that involved no complications from the past. But Bobby had ignored him. As he had more and more lately. Now that his ambition had shifted into high gear, Bobby would do nothing that might slow his ascending arc. And what were the next points on that arc?

The shedding of the last threats to his goal.

The filling of those gaps that, up to now, had been tolerable, but would soon be a drag on his rocket-powered campaign. And the most glaring gap of all? According to Tio Carrera: "*No Jackie O!*" While Sophie might not be a Jacqueline Bouvier by modern measuring methods, her chief deficit was her age. In almost every other way, she fit the bill. Beauty, intellect, patrician lineage, charm, and even grace when required. If Bobby handled her debut properly, her age might even prove a positive with female voters. With Sophie Dufort at his side, Bobby would come across as a man who followed his heart rather than a calculating politico in search of a trophy wife. Viewed through the right lens, Sophie's age simply transformed her from Jacqueline Bouvier into Jackie Onassis, which might shade Bobby into the territory of an American Macron.

I wonder if she speaks French, Corey thought bitterly. *Of course she does! Her mother lived half her childhood in France.*

Corey recalled his final, heartrending conversation with Charlot Dufort as he drove the desperate man deep into the southeastern corner of Tenisaw County, which Google Earth had shown was the emptiest part. Almost everything they said to each other had confirmed the impression that Corey and Charlot were mirrors of each other, the only difference being that Charlot no longer served Bobby's ends, while Corey did. (Charlot had actually used the phrase "personal assistant with benefits," which had lodged like a poisoned dart in Corey's heart.) Pulling into the weeds beside an overgrown gravel road, Corey had removed the SIM card from Charlot's dead iPhone, then inserted it into his own. After checking to be sure it had no reception, he'd passed his phone to Charlot. That way, he maintained possession of the incriminating sexual photographs while giving Charlot the means to eventually call someone for rescue (if there was anyone left who might come for him). Charlot's face had shown genuine gratitude as Corey pulled the door shut, then turned and drove back the way they had come. Corey had actually said "Good luck" through the window as he pulled away, then "God help you" as Charlot shrank to nothing in the rearview mirror.

Driving into Bienville to buy himself a new iPhone, Corey had realized just how many hours it might be before he saw Bobby again. But there was nothing unusual about that. Every day of his life was designed around Bobby's needs and wishes—

A muted scream interrupted his thoughts.

Twenty feet inside the swirling antique window glass, Sophie's face had darkened with blood, and reddish blotches bloomed on her skin. The marks stood out like islands on a map of the area from her long throat to the space between her breasts. She was working toward climax—by her usual pattern, it seemed.

But Bobby had other plans.

Horror constricted Corey's throat as Bobby's muscular left arm rose and his talented hand gripped Sophie's hair, then pulled her violently to the left, onto her back. Releasing her hair, Bobby braced himself on his solitary hand and mounted her with almost balletic grace. Corey heard a muted cry as he reentered her and began thrusting with a relentlessly powerful rhythm. If he touched the window, he knew (or even the wall), he would feel the impacts as Bobby drove himself into her. But that wasn't what had upset Corey most. It was *the way Bobby turned her* that had made him go numb. Two or three times in his life, Corey had let his hair grow past his shoulders, and during those times Bobby had flipped him in exactly the same way during sex . . .

Without knowing why, Corey raised his cell phone and filmed Bobby hammering her against the mattress. After twenty seconds, he stopped recording and shot a couple of stills. Then he waited for Sophie to show her face again. When she screamed—this time louder, and with obvious pleasure—he knew it wouldn't be long until he took his final photograph.

After Bobby rolled off her, she propped herself on her elbow and looked down into his face. She wasn't smiling. She was clearly thinking. Corey could not know her thoughts with certainty, but something told him Sophie Dufort was peering into a future that, until tonight, had never even entered her mind.

She was looking at a life as Jackie O.

Not a fantasy.

Real life.

As the *First Lady* . . .

For one wild instant Corey thought of rapping on the glass, if only to see them jump up in panic. But he wasn't that small. *You're not*, he told himself. *You're smaller than that. You don't even exist anymore. You're simply unwanted baggage. Soon-to-be-lost luggage. Tomorrow, or the next day, or maybe next week, Bobby will open the hatch on his shiny new rocket, shove you out into the frozen vacuum of space, and tug his new copilot/navigator inside. Only this one will be female, his own Valentina Tereshkova, only much more suitable for the TV masses than the one now serving in the Russian Duma.*

With tears welling in his eyes, Corey turned and walked silently out of Charles Dufort's azaleas, knowing that whatever happened tomorrow . . .

He would never see Bobby again except on a screen of some kind.

CHAPTER 81

AT 4:00 A.M. on the night Pencarrow burned, I open my eyes and find myself lying on my town house sofa beneath a comforter my mother crocheted decades ago. My cracked or broken ribs make every breath painful, but I feel strangely calm, and quite aware of all that took place earlier tonight. While my eyes adjust to the dim light, I see a note laying on the ottoman before the sofa. In Nadine's handwriting, it reads:

> Sleeping in Annie's bed. She's doing well. There's cold brew coffee in the fridge (yes, from my store). If you need something to do, the pages in the manila folder under this note contain Romulus Pencarrow's interview with his grandson. Read it, Penn. Your life will never be the same. (You can pick up where we left off on page 7.) And please, don't leave the house until we talk. Don't talk to state or local law enforcement without me present (your lawyer). Things are going to get dangerous out there today.

Raising my eyes from her note, I make out the manila envelope laying on the ottoman. Marked with a white label and what looks like Annie's handwriting, it reads: ROMULUS TRANSCRIPT: COPY 2. God bless my daughter and her talent for organization. She must have been of enormous help to my mother during the last few months of her life.

As I try to rise from the sofa, my left leg buckles from fatigue, and I nearly crash to the floor. The pain in my stump is shattering, and only the ottoman spares me a hard fall in front of the sofa. I'll be paying for my trek across Black Oak for days.

Gasping with each arc of agony, I make my way to the refrigerator to get a coffee. Nadine's homemade cold brew, which has been known to bring me back from the dead, or close to it, anyway. Tonight, without added Vicodin, it's unlikely to do the job. I'd happily accept some of my mother's end-of-life fentanyl, but I'd never make it up the stairs to get it.

I feel an impulse to turn on the television and check the cable channels for coverage of the fires, but I stop myself. I don't want to flood my body with cortisol quite yet. As Nadine predicted before I passed out, it is going to be a long day.

After the caffeine jolts my heart into a steady rhythm, I stagger back to the sofa and open the envelope, recalling as I do the summary Nadine gave me during the drive out to Mom's burial yesterday afternoon. What sticks most clearly in my mind was my mother's account of half-white Romulus's brutal killing of the overseer caught raping his sister Niobe. Also, the night departure of the little group that hoped to escape terrible fates in the wartime South. As I recall, Romulus fled west to the river to try to reach a Yankee gunboat, while his white brother, Duncan, boarded a train north to join Confederate troops in Virginia. Most vulnerable of all were those aboard the wagon driven by Hector, a strong and trusted slave. Behind him rode Romulus's quadroon sister, Niobe, his mulatto mother, Calliope, and the Creole woman Helen Soileau, whose identification papers—along with those forged by the plantation priest—had made the journey possible. I remember Nadine refusing to tell me whether or not the little wagon had reached the cotton boat that had been paid to take them north to safety.

The first page of the transcript begins with the speakers identifying themselves. *My name is Romulus Pencarrow. I was born on Pencarrow Plantation in southwest Mississippi in 1843. Yesterday I turned ninety-three years old in Gary, Indiana. I retired as a die maker for the Hoffman Tool Company in 1911, but I worked from my own shop till I was eighty-seven years old.* The next speaker stated: *My name is Jadon Anderson. I'm a sophomore at Wilberforce University in Ohio. I'm recording my grandfather's words for posterity, not for any school project, and I here promise to keep them private until after his death.*

From this point forward, the interview progresses with only parenthetical initials to mark who is speaking, though even these aren't strictly necessary. The distinctive voice and obvious depth of historical knowledge would have made it plain without any identifiers. Turning to page 7, I find a pencil-marked arrow that Nadine must have left to bring me back into her tale at the point where Romulus had completed his service as a scout to Grant during the Vicksburg campaign and traveled to Natchez to await the formation of the U.S. Fifty-eighth Colored Infantry.

Taking another sip of cold coffee, I lean back on the sofa and descend into the narrative of a man I am somehow related to by blood, though the concept seems more unbelievable to me the further that I read.

[RP] See, I'd known I was technically "contraband of war," as they called all escaped slaves back then. But I figured that, because of my service, they would take me into the regular army, into one of the units I'd been serving as a scout. But the army don't work that way. The army has rules,

*and they mostly stick to them, at least at the command level. So I talked
to a couple of officers I trusted, and they told me to take a good horse
down to Natchez and wait for the 58th Infantry to form up. That seemed
like the best plan, so I lost no time doing it.*

*That's how I came to find myself in the first contraband camp they
had down there, in the summer of 1863. I've read where people call it the
Devil's Punchbowl Camp, but it wasn't actually inside the Punchbowl.
It was just north of town, between the home of Mr. Andrew Brown and
his sawmill, which the army plundered to build the initial barracks. It
was a hellhole, though. Or it turned into one quick. The truth is, so many
slaves were escaping around that time, Natchez got flooded with them.
This was happening all over the South, near every federal army camp.
The Union Army didn't have the resources to feed and house all those
people, so these contraband camp cities grew up everywhere.*

*The one I was in started with about four thousand people in it.
Legally, you could come and go, but movement was discouraged by the
authorities. There wasn't enough food, and almost no sanitation, so
disease set in pretty quick. There was dysentery, TB, all the usual army
illnesses. By late in the summer, two thousand former slaves had died,
and more were dropping every day. So I got myself out of there and found
a place to stay up on the bluff, in a little place owned by Cadmus Nelson,
Captain Pencarrow's old butler.*

*In spite of my father's will, Cadmus had somehow got his freedom
even before the surrender, and he set himself up in a house with three
slaves of his own, which he beat the same as any white man did.
After emancipation, he started paying the slaves and working as a
moneylender, even though he was registered with the town as a negro
barber. Cadmus let me stable my horse at his place, and didn't charge
me anything to stay, other than me occasionally introducing him to
Yankee officers I knew to be involved in the contraband cotton trade. See,
everybody back then was working some kind of angle on the war, if they
could. Seems like that's the way wars have always been conducted, and
the Civil War was no different. Cadmus worked the system to make ends
meet, and Yankee officers did the same, sometimes for their own benefit,
and sometimes on the orders of their superiors. We'd done the same on
the plantation in 'sixty-one and 'sixty-two, growing cotton to run the
blockade to England.*

[JA] *What did you do in Natchez while you waited for the 58th to be
organized?*

[RP] Well . . . I worked wage labor where I could, to keep food and drink in
my belly. Gambled a little, for the same reason. And I did what I could
to help the folks in the contraband camp. I knew quite a few people in
there. Former Pencarrow slaves, and folks from other Tenisaw County
plantations. As a teamster, I knew slaves from nearly every big place
between Vicksburg and St. Francisville, Louisiana. That's why I'd been
valuable as a scout. I didn't just know the land, but the people too, and
on both sides of the river. Even General Grant was amazed to find out
I'd seen Mr. Jefferson Davis many a time in the flesh, on Hurricane
Plantation.

[JA] Did you ever speak to Jefferson Davis?

[RP] Oh, no. But I stood less than a stone's throw from him, heard him talk
plain as you and me talking now. He was just a man, like anybody else.

[JA] Please go on.

[RP] Well, it was in the contraband camp that my life changed forever. I
guess that's what I'm here to talk about today. Things were getting worse
in there as the summer dragged, with the heat. The army had sent in a
bunch of shovels and told the slaves to just bury their dead where they
fell. About the middle of September, I went in there to help cover some,
and it was that evening I stumbled on Hector, the slave I'd sent with
Mama and Niobe on the wagon. Hector had TB by then, and he was
dying, but he called out my name as I passed, like a child calling for his
mama.

I couldn't imagine what he was doing there, when I thought he was
way up north watching over my people. Well, it turns out everything old
Cadmus had done to get that wagon north was a lie. Evelyn wasn't going
to help Mama and Niobe get away to freedom. She wanted them dead,
or worse. She always had. And what they got was worse.

[JA] Do you mean all of it? Even the false identification papers made by
Father Henry Calvert weren't real?

[RP] No. Father Calvert had done his best to help them get away. He loved
Niobe, and Mama too, I think. But Cadmus hadn't made any deal with
Underground Railroad people to get them on a cotton boat. He'd sold
them South through a slave trader, to a plantation owner who'd coveted
Mama ever since seeing her years before, during a visit to Pencarrow.
Evelyn had remembered that, and she'd got Cadmus to use that man to
take her revenge. His name was Richard Darbonne, and he owned Seven
Oaks, one of the big places down by St. Francisville.

[JA] Hector hadn't been sold with them?

[RP] No, he had. But he managed to escape later. When the Yankees first took the places along the river in West Feliciana Parish. I was furious when I first saw him, sick as he was. I felt like he'd betrayed my trust. But he didn't have any choice. He told me that wagon didn't make it three miles south of Pencarrow before the slave traders showed and took it over. They took his gun and his money, and all the papers. Then two men took the white lady—the real white lady, Helen Soileau, and her baby—and ferried them south to New Orleans. They'd been sold to a cathouse for cash money. Another part of Evelyn's revenge. Then the trader's crew separated Mama and Niobe. Mama they took to Mr. Charles Dufort, who'd had his eye on her since the first time he saw her. I think he also wanted her because he'd known he couldn't have her, long as the captain was alive.

[JA] And Niobe? Where did they take her?

[RP] They took Niobe to Mr. Shot Barlow's place, Black Oak, right across the road from home. But Barlow didn't keep her there. He'd sat out the war to that point, but by now General Grant was in the Mississippi Delta, trying to find a way to get his army past the big guns at Vicksburg. Yazoo Pass, they call it. They was trying to widen existing bayous and rivers to get little steamboats through. They tried about four different routes that winter before they give up. Lake Providence was one. None of them worked. One reason was because Rebels like Barlow would come in the night and wreck or undo what the bluecoats had done during the day.

Barlow took twenty men out in February or March to harry the Union forces, and he stayed about a month. But the next time he and his men went out, they didn't intend to suffer. Oh, no. They took six young slave girls along, to cook for the men and give 'em "comfort" when they wanted it. Niobe was one of them. He took Hector too, to work. Those lazy bastards would lay up during the day, drinking and violating those girls, then go out at night and chop down trees over the Union canals.

[JA] I can't even think about that, it's so terrible. And where was Calliope during this time? At Charles Dufort's mansion?

[RP] Yes, indeed. Tranquility in Natchez. Her hell was more comfortable, but it was still hell. He dressed her in the finest clothes from New Orleans, even Paris. But she never gave him any pleasure. Not willingly. But it was Niobe who suffered the most. After she'd been up in the Delta about a week, she led Hector and them other girls in an escape after the men left one night. They were loose most of the next day, trying to reach the Union lines. They eventually come up on some bluecoats walking across a flooded field. The bluecoats swore they'd help them. But that afternoon they stopped to rest, made a fire. Then they raped them girls *one after the other. They was still doing that when Barlow and his men come out of the trees and killed 'em all. Barlow had been tracking Niobe since the night before.*

[JA] *My God.*

[RP] *She never trusted Northerners any more than Southerners after that.*

[JA] *Did Niobe wind up at Seven Oaks Plantation in the end, though?*

[RP] *She did. After Grant gave up on the canals, Barlow took the girls home, and he gave Niobe back to Evelyn, like he promised. Calliope had already been sold down to Seven Oaks by then. Evelyn had the slave traders load Niobe up with Hector and take 'em down the river to Seven Oaks. Which meant that everything Duncan and I had done to try to save them had got them just fifty miles south of where they started, onto a place a hundred times worse than they'd lived all their lives.*

[JA] *And all because of your white half-sister? Or was Cadmus involved, too? Was he just following orders? Or had he wanted some sort of revenge himself?*

[RP] *I didn't know—not then. But I meant to find out. See, it was only my belief that Mama and Niobe were safe that had let me live and fight like I had during the past year. After I found out they never had been, I came up out of that camp ready to cut Cadmus's throat and shoot Evelyn through the heart.*

[JA] *What was Evelyn's situation then?*

[RP] *Oh, she was running Pencarrow, same as she had been since we left. Only she had her a Yankee officer sweetheart paying court and protecting her in her business dealings as well. She was no fool. She was like that Scarlett O'Hara in that big book,* Gone with the Wind. *Make the best of any situation. But cold as a damn winter frost on the river. A devil deep down, I'm telling you. Whatever the worst of white folks is, it lived in her.*

[JA] *So, what did you do?*

[RP] *After Hector died, I buried him. Then I went up that bluff and confronted Cadmus in his own house. First time I ever saw that old man scared to death. He knew I wasn't the boy who'd left the plantation. I'd had a year of war, and death was nothing to me. He knew I'd take his life like pulling a weed. He told me Evelyn had done it all. Planned it all. He said she hated us, even Duncan for not joining a regiment early in the war and putting the plantation at risk because of it. He said she held a lot over him, including his freedom, because she had more than one will written by the captain, and some other secret papers. Most of all, he said he'd had no way to actually get Mama and Niobe to freedom. He* told himself they'd be safer down at Seven Oaks than they would have been under Evelyn's power, and so he just did what she wanted. That way he protected himself and gave Duncan and me something we could believe when we left.

[JA] Did you believe him?

[RP] I don't know. I didn't kill him.

[JA] What did you do?

[RP] I took fifteen hundred dollars from him, to buy Mama and Niobe back, if I could get myself a chance. I got my horse fed. Then I went and visited a Yankee officer I trusted more than the rest. He wrote me out a safe passage to a plantation just south of Seven Oaks, about fifty miles south of Natchez. Stated that I was on business of the Union Army in the Gulf District, and I was not to be interfered with. Most troops on the road would understand that someone dressed in civilian clothes, with them kind of papers, was working the cotton trade for the federals. Then I got a night's sleep.

[JA] What did you mean to do, Grandpa?

[RP] Fetch Mama and Niobe back from Seven Oaks, one way or another.

[JA] Was it still a functioning cotton plantation?

[RP] Best I could find out from Natchez, Seven Oaks had been liberated a few months before by the Union. But it was still operating under what they called the federal leasing system. Something General Butler started down in St. Bernard and Plaquemines, and then General Banks expanded. The politicians talked it up a lot, but basically it was just slavery by another name. Workers signed a contract for ten dollars a month, and for that they worked ten hours a day every day but Sunday. They couldn't leave the plantation, and while their former owners couldn't beat them anymore, Union military personnel could. So you basically had army overseers running these old slave plantations in Louisiana.

[JA] But the former owners still owned the land? Confederate planters?

[RP] They did if they declared support for the Union. It was part of Lincoln's "ten-percent Reconstruction plan." And Mr. Richard Darbonne had been one of the first to do that, of course. To get all his land and slaves back two years before the war even ended. Just white men taking care of each other, regardless of what side they was on, like usual. The way of the world, Jadon.

[JA] Had Hector told you anything about the condition your mother and sister were in?

[RP] All he knew was that they were both alive when he got loose from there. But he said Mr. Darbonne had used Mama bad. That's all he would say. "That man treat her bad, Romulus. The way they do at Black Oak." He told me Niobe had taken up with a white man who worked Seven Oaks, and that he might be watching over her. I hoped she had, because without protection, a place like that broke people down fast.

[JA] All right. What happened on your trip?

[RP] It was only fifty miles down to St. Francisville by the Woodville Road, and then following the rail spur. But I planned for two days there, and two back. There was still Confederate cavalry operating in that area, raiding for harassment and profit both, living off the land. Then there was jayhawkers preying on the population, same as everywhere up and down the river. Plus, even with my papers, I was still a contraband slave traveling on his own, subject to any kind of devilment by a white man. Especially a sheriff or deputy. So when I made that trip, my Sharps carbine and Colt 1860 weren't just for show. I knew I might have to use them.

[JA] Where did you get weapons like that?

[RP] Off dead men. A lot of troops died in the run-up to Vicksburg, and my first commanding officer told me to arm myself as best I could. So I had. I also took a spare horse along, to bring somebody back on. One of Cadmus's mounts. He didn't argue a peep, either. I wanted to take two, but that would have slowed me down too much, and made me a target for every outlaw on the road. I figured that if I found Mama and Niobe, I could buy or steal a wagon and get them back to Natchez somehow. Or else put Niobe up behind me.

[JA] How did your trip go?

[RP] Good weather. Bad luck.

[JA] Do you feel like continuing? Or do you need a rest?

[RP] I better tell it now. Or I may never tell it again.

[JA] Take your time, Grandpa.

[RP] I'm old, boy. I get sentimental sometimes. Don't mean nothing.

[JA] Yes, sir. I understand.

[RP] Ain't no way you understand. But maybe after I tell you this, you will. Maybe.

[JA] Yes, sir. That's why I'm here.

[RP] Truth is, I ran into trouble pretty quick on the road. Confederates had been raiding around there, so the federals had troops out, challenging everybody. My papers got me through, but I could see I wouldn't have an easy passage. I got into a misunderstanding when I was waiting to ford the Homochitto River, and I had to pull my pistol. But I didn't shoot *anybody. After that, I moved off the main road, and I made a cold camp after I'd covered about thirty-two miles.*

[JA] Did you commonly cover that much land in a day's ride?

[RP] Depended on the terrain. And the mount. But I'd been riding since I was four, and a horse was like part of me then. I did fifty miles in a day once during the Vicksburg campaign, carrying a message for Admiral Porter.

[JA] What happened next?

[RP] First bad luck. I got ambushed in camp the next morning, by a couple of half-starved rebel outlaws. I shot them both, but then a woman traveling with them squirted out from behind a tree and gigged me with a little knife she had. Just a flesh wound, but it almost killed me a week later with the fever and pus.

[JA] What happened to the woman?

[RP] What you think happened, boy? I left here there, having defended myself.

[JA] All right. I see.

[RP] I got back on the high road, passed through Woodville, then rode parallel to the railroad spur that terminated at St. Francisville. It was good riding through that cut, which was a mercy, because my knife wound was starting to throb. Just after dinner, I was closing on Seven Oaks. Passing the next nearest plantation, I could see how things was running down there, under this new lease system. Plantations seemed more like military prison camps than anything else I'd seen. Military guards, military overseers. Freed slaves working the fields looked worse off than the slaves at Pencarrow had it during the war, much less before. Getting lashed by federal troops.

[JA] How did you get access to Seven Oaks?

[RP] Brazened it out, as a New York captain I knew used to say. First, I stashed my horse in an old barn in the woods near the plantation. Then I rode up to the gate and told the guard I needed to speak to Mr. Richard Darbonne himself for two reasons. One, a Yankee officer I represented had a prime buyer for his cotton. And two, a couple of his former slaves were wanted for questioning in a crime that had happened just before the war in Bienville. The death of an overseer. I figured if they asked for details, I'd give them the facts of my own case, killing Overseer Book.

[JA] Did it work?

[RP] It got me onto the place. Luckily Mr. Darbonne was in New Orleans, and not due back till next day. They said I could put up in one of the slave quarters, long as I found my own food and liquor, or paid cash

money for what they had. That suited me fine. I set up in the quarters like I meant to stay overnight. Then I tended my knife wound as best I could and went looking for Mama and Niobe.

[JA] *Did you find them?*

[RP] *I found Niobe. Mama was dead by then.*

[JA] *Oh, no. How did she die?*

[RP] *Resisting that damn Darbonne. He'd bought her to have her, just like I feared. Just like Hector had told me. But Mama couldn't submit to that. Not after the life she'd had. She didn't have it in her. So she fought.*

[JA] *Do you know how long she survived?*

[RP] *A few weeks. Niobe told me she basically starved to death. On purpose.*

[JA] *My Lord.*

[RP] *No, sir. Wasn't no God watching over that place, boy. God, if there is one, left that place to rot. And my mama died there. If she'd lived a few more weeks, she'd have seen the Yankees liberate Seven Oaks for real. But like I told you, that didn't change much for the Black folk there. Because most of those who escaped got sent right back. It might have saved Mama, though. Because it seems the federal authorities did step in to punish some cruelty in individual cases. At least the history books say they did. What I saw on the ground was the same thing I'd seen growing up beside Black Oak. Hell on earth, and white men holding the whip.*

[JA] *What condition was your sister in?*

[RP] *Niobe was physically all right. It took me till dark to find her, because she wasn't living on the plantation. I finally tracked her to a little house in the country, where she was living with a carpenter who used to work on Seven Oaks.*

[JA] *A white carpenter?*

[RP] *Right.*

[JA] *Are you saying she was living as a white woman?*

[RP] *She was.*

[JA] *Can you tell me more about her situation?*

[RP] *She was five months pregnant. Showing. She was getting ready to leave that part of the state.*

[JA] *Who was the father? The carpenter?*

[RP] *Be patient, boy. I'm trying to tell you. It's complicated. See, as soon as the slave traders took their wagon, Mama understood what had happened. I imagine she must have regretted not killing Evelyn in the cradle when she was a child. But who can see the future? Still, I didn't understand how bad it really had been until I found Niobe. This time with the Barlows was part of the special revenge that Evelyn had arranged for her. All the while that General Grant tried different schemes to bypass the big guns at Vicksburg, Niobe was stuck with Barlow and his men. They'd slip quietly around Lake Providence and sabotage Union canal work during the day, chopping trees across the waterways and such, then at night go back to their camp and rape those slave girls. After a few hours' sleep, they'd go back to pestering the Yankees. Niobe somehow survived five or six weeks of that . . . but that's how and where she got pregnant. Most likely by Barlow, according to Hector. Said he was mighty possessive of her.*

[JA] *I can't believe a woman would do that to her own blood.*

[RP] *Believe it, boy. Learn from it. I don't know to this day what Barlow and Dufort paid or traded Evelyn to have those weeks with Mama and Niobe. I guess I never will. But they got what they wanted. Revenge on the captain through the women he loved. And Evelyn savored every minute of it, like some starving spider. Anyway, by the time they were both settled at Seven Oaks, Niobe realized what they were in for. She watched Mama going down fast, so she did what people do, which is try to figure a way to make the best of her situation. She managed to survive until the Yankees took the place, and by then this carpenter had taken to her. She knew by then she was pregnant, but the carpenter didn't seem to mind. The day after the Federals escorted Darbonne off the place—before he declared for the Union—the carpenter paid an overseer buddy to go in and get the papers Niobe had carried in the wagon. The ones identifying her as Helen Soileau. Darbonne had them in his private office. Once they had those, the carpenter packed her up and simply took her off the place, not too far away, but somewhere he figured Darbonne wouldn't look. Besides, he figured Mr. Darbonne would have his hands full dealing with the Union army for a while. Of course, it turned out that Darbonne settled his business quickly, and that meant that Niobe and her carpenter weren't safe close by anymore.*

[JA] *Did you offer to bring Niobe back to Natchez?*

[RP] *Of course I did. That's what I'd come to do, wasn't it? And I assumed she'd jump at the chance.*

[JA] *But she didn't?*

[RP] *No, sir. She couldn't see the point in going to Natchez as a contraband slave. She'd been living as a white woman for some time by then, and I think she felt safer than she ever had in her life. More important, she felt her child would be safe. There in that little shack, living with a white man and pretending to be his wife. It hurt me bad to see that. I spent most of that night trying to persuade her to come back with me. I swore I'd protect her, told her I had the connections to protect her. I promised I'd take her north myself, on the railroad—even though I doubted I could. But none of it mattered. That was when she told me about her escape from Barlow's camp, and what them Yankee deserters done to her. I couldn't deny that soon as we got to Natchez, she'd be expected to report to the contraband camp near the Devil's Punchbowl. And things had got bad enough there that word had reached even Seven Oaks. More than half the camp population was dead of disease by then.*

[JA] *No mother would want to deliver a child into that.*

[RP] *No. I was figuring I could put her up at Cadmus's house and get by with it. But she wouldn't hear of that. She told me that if she ever saw Cadmus again, she'd cut his throat. It was then I found out Cadmus had been part of Evelyn's plans from the start. According to Niobe, Mama had always been suspicious that Cadmus had been working for himself alone, against everyone else, even other slaves. She even believed that people he'd claimed to have helped to the Underground Railroad, he'd actually sold south to places like Seven Oaks, or west to Texas, and pocketed the money. All in the quest of building up a stake to pay for his life after freedom. I don't know if that's true, but he sure set up with his own slaves as soon as he could, didn't he?*

[JA] *How did that night with Niobe end?*

[RP] *She refused to leave. She didn't want to be rescued. That night, looking right in my face, she turned her back on her whole life, on everything she'd ever been, to become white. I couldn't believe it then. Even now, sometimes, I find it hard. I'd risked my life to save her when that overseer raped her. And Duncan risked his life to save me for killing the overseer. Then our father killed Frank Barlow in the duel that grew out of all that mess. Yet in one night Niobe turned away from all that and walked out of her life. She erased everything she ever was, and some of what we had been, just to feel a little safer. She was like a snake eating its own tail, a black snake, and when she was finished eating, she'd flipped inside out . . . and she was white.*

[JA] *How long did she live like that?*

[RP] *Forever! When they found out late that night that I'd brought a spare mount, Niobe asked straight out if she could have it. I got her the horse and gave her half of Cadmus's money. Her eyes nearly bugged out. They pulled up stakes the next morning, and went to Quitman Parish in North Louisiana, where the carpenter was from. It was still in Confederate hands, but they just brazened it out. They'd married on the road, and his people simply took her in. To them she was Helen Soileau, and that was that. The Creole origin explained her little touch of color, and she'd always had white girl's hair. The child was born white as the carpenter's people.*

[JA] And who was the father again? I'm just making sure.

[RP] I didn't know then. But I do now. The father was that damned Barlow, Shot Barlow. I'd been half hoping it was the priest, the one who'd written the attestation claiming the father was Duncan Pencarrow. He'd always fancied Niobe, and he'd fiddled with a couple of the girls along the way. But no.

[JA] So Reverend Calvert wasn't helping out of Christian kindness when he assisted the escape. He was covering the betrayal of his vows. As well as any crimes that resulted from his involvement with slave women.

[RP] The way of the world, son. Mama probably used what she knew to get what she needed from him.

[JA] Did you ever see Niobe again?

[RP] I did. Many years later. Even though she begged me never to try. I don't really want to talk about that now. Maybe tomorrow.

[JA] Of course. Is there anything else you want to say about that trip?

[RP] I'm not sure. There's more. It's sinful, if you believe in sin. But it's what happened. And maybe you ought to know about it.

[JA] I'm listening.

[RP] As I told you, I nearly died from that knife wound over the next week. It festered up bad. Before I left Seven Oaks, though, I studied on staying one day and having me a reckoning with Mr. Richard Darbonne. But my wound was plaguing me, and I discovered somebody'd already stolen the sundries I'd left in the quarters. Sticking around didn't seem like the best idea. I didn't even try to find Mama's grave. I rode out at the crack of dawn and made Natchez in two days, burning up with fever.

[JA] Grandpa? Is this where you want to stop?

[RP] I better tell you about Cadmus. I went to his place to recover, if I could. And I didn't breathe a word about how bad it had been. I kept my pistol in my bed, and I paid a tough little tavern wench to stay with me, fetch me my own food and drink and throw his away. I feared Cadmus

might poison me out of fear, which, looking back, he should have done.
Because after I recovered, after we got word that the 58th was going to be
official, and I got my name enlisted on the roll, I waited for Mr. Cadmus
Nelson on the road from the Natchez racetrack where he liked to gamble
now and again.

[JA] *Nelson was Cadmus's surname?*

[RP] *That's right. I talked to him on the shoulder of that road, in the falling*
dark. And I made him tell me all he'd done to "get by," as he called
it, while living on Pencarrow, and then at his house in town. If you
want to talk about sin, you could study the life of that man. He was as
thoroughly corrupted as any soul could be. I left that road knowing he'd
shortened the lives of many, many people, including my father as well as
my mother.

[JA] *Was he alive when you left him?*

[RP] *I left him as Niobe would have, if she could. As Mama would have.*

[JA] *I see.*

[RP] *And I wasn't finished, either. When I rode back to Natchez to wait*
to take up my post in the 58th, my belly burned with hunger for the
only reckoning that still mattered to me. My sister Evelyn. That cursed
woman was alive and richer than ever, wearing spangles to Yankee
balls paid for with black market cotton money, while Mama lay in
her grave.

After reading that line, I drop the page onto the ottoman and get carefully to my feet. The pain is, if anything, worse than before, but compared to the horrors I just read about, it's nothing. I can see a few more pages left in Romulus's account, but I need to stop and process what I've only begun to absorb. This afternoon, Nadine revealed that my actual ancestor was Niobe. But only now do I see the credible way that this connection could have existed without the knowledge of almost anyone living. My mother's true ancestry, and mine, remained secret for the very reason that our ancestor did everything humanly possible to keep it so. Niobe did that to protect not us, but herself and the child who had still been inside her when she made her fateful decision. And by making the choice she did, she made her survival and comfort in Louisiana a much higher-percentage shot than she would ever have had as a woman of color.

On the other hand . . . in a single stroke Niobe silenced herself forever, and erased every molecule of her previous existence, at least whatever existed outside her own mind and heart. After all, it was the voice of Romulus that brought me her story—or only the barest beginning of it—not the voice of Niobe herself. Niobe sentenced herself to a living lie of whiteness, in a white world, with an ostensibly white child. Moreover, she did this in one of the most conservative states in the Union, a place where the KKK waxed and waned in power across the decades—years that Niobe ultimately lived through while concealing a deadly secret. How did she carry off such a deception, and so masterfully, that no one in her lifetime uncovered the truth? Did her child ever know its true origin? I wonder. Did any generation that followed even suspect it? Or did they effectively "become white" for all time?

I suppose I'm the living answer to that question.

CHAPTER 82

HALF A MILE south of the Bienville boat ramp, Ray Ransom and his three soldiers guided a stolen ski boat along the Mississippi riverbank and watched the mountainous silhouette of the Matheson Lumber yard grow closer in the darkness. Within a few feet of the water, stacks of chemically treated lumber had been piled twenty feet high under the bluish glow of security lamps.

As the boat reached the first stack, Ray steered to within a foot of shore, so that Easy could toss a plastic container near the base of the woodpile. As soon as it landed, gasoline began to leak from the open spigot. They repeated this process all the way down the line, then circled the boat and made one more pass. This time they lighted handfuls of kerosene-soaked kindling and tossed them into the wet puddles of gas. The vapor instantly exploded into flame, and before they'd completed their second pass, the whole western edge of the storage lot was burning like a California forest fire.

Ray pulled back on the throttle and watched their handiwork with a deep sense of satisfaction. He and his crew were wearing ski masks to hide their identities, but Ray saw no security cameras down here, and the heat of the flames was cooking his face. Ripping the mask from his head, he lit a Salem from his pocket and stood smoking for another thirty seconds while the boys clapped him on the back and marveled at the results of their work.

"Time to book," Ray said, tossing his butt into the muddy water with a sizzle.

As he gunned the throttle and curved away from the conflagration, he thought about Paul Matheson, one of the better men in the Poker Club, whose father and grandfather had built their lumber business over generations. The father—like Charles Dufort—and been a real son of a bitch in his day, but he was dead now. This blow would hurt the son, of course, but most of all it would infuriate the Poker Club and terrify white Bienville. If the storage lot had not been downstream from the city proper, it might have required evacuation of the whole area. As it was, it would simply cast a pall for miles downstream, and serve as a sort of flag of distress.

The only problem with this attack remained unknown to Ray Ransom. There *was* one security camera covering this part of the lot: placed there by Paul Matheson to keep tabs on one of his workers. That camera had recorded much of the group's actions as they piloted the boat through their amateur naval assault—as well as every detail of Ray's face as he smoked his cigarette.

By morning he would be a fugitive.

EBONY WISHED SHE had a cigarette. She had never felt true exhaustion until this night, and she hadn't smoked since noon. She'd lost her pack of Virginia Slims during the shooting, and doing without had given her a pounding headache. As she half stumbled down the dark tunnel of North Maple Street, she wondered if this was how animals felt all the time, being hunted by both humans and their own kind. If so, she felt nothing but empathy. She was now prey for both a drug gang and the law. Jamaal's crew knew everyone to whom she might turn for help, and the sheriff's department ruled the streets. In trying to evade both, she had run until she could run no more. She'd never been an athlete anyway. Now she had walked near to what must be her limit. Ten minutes ago she'd sat on a cement block that was part of a curb, then awakened after she slid off, sound asleep. Her only option now was to find somewhere safe to pass out until dawn.

After fleeing the white neighborhood where Lance's mother lived, Ebony had unconsciously made her way toward the river. Even as isolated as she was, she knew that most of Bienville's Black population was down on the bluff, protesting the murder she'd seen with her own eyes earlier in the day. How could it be that something that motivated thousands to rise up and demand justice also made her life close to worthless? *Maybe the thing to do*, she thought for the hundredth time, *really is just post the damn video somewhere anyone can see it. But you know where that road ends . . .*

A trial.

With me on the stand speaking against Jamaal.

A roaring engine sent Ebony flying into a black clump of shrubs in the nearest yard. She didn't bother trying to land softly, but fell hard into the branches at the base. Thank God the owner had put down some mulch. Ebony kept her face pressed into the crushed bark as the car rolled past on Maple, and only moved when she sensed it had reached the end of the block. Then she raised her head and leaned out far enough to see the dark light-bar of a sheriff's department cruiser as the vehicle turned left.

"To hell with this," she groaned.

She knew she was close to the bluff. She could smell the river. Still half-obscured by the bushes, she took her bearings as best she could. The next block didn't look residential. It took a few seconds, but she finally recognized the back of a warehouse, and that told her that the next building over was the newspaper. The Bienville *Watchman*. This realization took her back to the handsome face she'd seen on the television in Lance's mother's house. The newspaper publisher, Mr. McEwan, who'd left a TV career in Washington to move home and take care of his sick father.

She couldn't just walk into the newspaper building, though. Not at this hour. What were the odds that the publisher would even be there at this hour? Of course, with all that was going on, he might be. Still, the instant someone recognized her—a secretary or even a maintenance man—they might call either law enforcement or even someone who'd rat to Jamaal. She needed a way to speak to Mr. McEwan alone.

Maybe watching the parking lot for a while was her best hope. She could see it from here, and if the publisher appeared, she could call out and run for it.

She just needed cover while she waited, and she'd found that, if by accident.

This block was the northernmost part of Bienville's main downtown grid. Beyond the north water tower lay what the white folks called the Garden District. Ebony wasn't sure why. Compared to the government housing where she'd grown up, even this little stand of shrubs on Maple Street was a garden. Looking up at the massive water tower to the west of her, she decided she'd walked as far as she could. There were no dogs barking, no bright lights, no humans in sight.

With the last of her strength, she drew her upper body back between what she now saw were three dense bushes and sat with her butt in the soft mulch and her eyes on the newspaper lot. As she slipped into a kind of stupor, she remembered the crushed bark scent from her grandmother's house. Yet it wasn't her grandmother that the fertile smell reminded her of, but her grandfather, Gideon Swan, who had died on the day she turned two years old.

It gladdened Ebony's heart to know that her mind had been alert and alive and happy enough at the age of two to imprint something that would last another fourteen years, and still impart a feeling of goodness and security. She wondered whether her mother still remembered anything like that through the smothering haze of drugs in her brain. The dark parking lot across the street wavered in her field of view. Ebony rubbed her eyes and blinked, but it did little good. *If I sit here another minute*, she thought, *I'll pass out*. Letting caution slip from her shoulders, she struggled to her feet and began walking toward the rear parking lot of the newspaper building.

An indeterminate amount of time later, she staggered past a rusted green dumpster and stopped before a brown steel exit door with a metal bar across it. A heavy stink emanated from the dumpster, like a dead possum or something. Ignoring it, she raised her hand and knocked hard on the door.

No one answered.

She was raising her hand to knock again when a vehicle swung into the lot and parked next to a car across the lot. Ebony tried not to look, but she couldn't help it. Her eyes took in LED lights and curb feelers near the front tires. Then two terrifying things happened at once. As she peered around the dumpster to see who was driving the car, the whole steel container shifted against her, as though flicked by a giant. Then the driver got out of the car, and she saw that it was Damien, Jamaal's emerald-eyed hit man.

Whirling in terror, Ebony banged hard on the security door, hard enough to break her knuckles. Still no one came. Then she heard the lightning patter of Damien's shoes sprinting toward her, and in that sound she perceived death.

But the instant Damien rounded the dumpster, his predatory eyes triumphant, something exploded from the square opening of the steel box, a massive monster of hair and claws, knocking Damien a half-dozen yards across the parking lot. Then the monster roared and began advancing toward the fallen gangbanger.

Ebony stared in horror, then backpedaled away, eyes wide, taking in the pure terror on Damien's face as the thing advanced upon him. Whirling, she raced back the way she had come. Adrenaline powered her legs for about a hundred yards, but they gave out near the bushes where she'd fallen in the mulch before.

Enervated by fear, she let herself fall among the branches, face down in the fragrant bark. With that scent the memory of her grandfather returned, and with it a story he'd once told her of Teddy Roosevelt and the Mississippi Delta bear that had inspired the "teddy bear" that had comforted so many children since. Even as this thought passed through her mind, she heard a male scream—more a shriek, really—truncated into utter silence. Though she had feared and hated the cruel Damien, she shut her mind against his likely end.

The final thought that flickered through her mind before she slipped into unconsciousness was, *I had people who loved me once. If Jamaal's crew or the sheriff's thugs or even that bear find me here, at least I'll take this smell with me to heaven . . .*

Thursday

CHAPTER 83

IN THE FIRST light of dawn, the muddy Mississippi ran gray under steely clouds sweeping eastward from Louisiana and Texas. From the high Natchez bridges, the water had a dull gleam, but up close it was dull as runoff in a flooded street. The river was high for October; a fishing cork tossed into the river at Bienville at 3:00 p.m. the previous day could have drifted under the Natchez bridges by eleven. But Charlot Dufort's body had endured a troubled journey over those forty miles, colliding with logs, hanging up in tree branches, being bumped by barges, battered by an enormous gar, and partly ingested by a seven-hundred-pound alligator in the slip-off slope of the Rodney Island bend. It passed the saloon at Natchez Under the Hill at 5:40 a.m., as faint light limned the sky and the drone of big rigs made the silver cantilevered bridges moan. The peripheral current carried the lifeless body steadily in toward shore, and five minutes later the legless corpse drifted against the johnboat of an eighty-year-old fisherman named Joe Landry.

Landry had spent his life on the river, so he recognized the bump of something soft. From the weight, he figured a dead blue catfish or alligator gar. Flicking on a small flashlight, he shone the white beam into dead eyes that looked more than a little familiar.

Joe's heartbeat barely accelerated. He'd discovered his share of corpses over the years, mostly green workers who'd fallen off barges or towboats, but occasionally a suicide who'd leaped from the bridge. Once he'd discovered a fraternity boy who'd jumped from a yacht on a bet that he could swim to shore and beat his buddies to the saloon. Clearly this body had been in the river long enough to become acquainted with its wildlife, yet its face was somehow handsome even in death. Like a corpse on *Barnaby Jones* or *Mannix*.

Without much hope, Joe leaned over, then grunted and reached under the hips to grope the pockets of the legless trousers still belted to the waist. To his surprise, he felt a wallet. Carefully removing the soggy leather, he extracted the Mississippi driver's license and glanced not at the name but the address, which showed the city of residence as Bienville, Mississippi.

"You made it a fair piece last night," Joe muttered. Only then did he look at the name, on the off chance that he might really know the dead man. This time his pulse picked up.

"I'll be goddamned," he said.

Joe not only recognized the dead man; he knew the father. Charles F. Dufort was the richest man in Tenisaw County to the north, and maybe the whole state. A blue-blood planter descendant and lawyer who'd grown wealthier still by working smart during the Wilcox oil boom of the sixties and seventies. Unlike the typical oilman, who would accumulate a pile, then risk all on an ever-bigger scheme, Dufort had husbanded his production and was sitting pretty when the bust came in '84. From what Joe had heard, the son—also a lawyer—had inherited none of his father's self-restraint. Charles Dufort the Fourth—Charlot to his friends—had a gambler's constitution, which had got him deep into debt with the casino boys. The kind of debt a law degree couldn't get you out of. Joe had also heard the boy was queer, which was common on this part of the river. With a shake of his head, Landry took out his cell phone and dialed the sheriff of Tenisaw County, whom he'd known since he was a boy. While he waited for an answer, he checked the cloud cover in the growing light.

"Rain's gonna stick," he grumbled, sniffing the breeze. "Weatherman's wrong again."

"Buck Tarlton," said the sheriff. "I don't recognize this number. Who's this?"

"Joe Landry. Got a corpse in the river down here at the Natchez landing. Bienville fella."

"Hey, Joe. Who is it?"

"Charles Dufort's boy. Charlot."

"No shit?" Tarlton's voice tensed a little. "Natchez, huh? You got the body in your possession?"

Landry looked down at the gray swollen face, which looked as alone and abandoned as any he had seen in a long time. "He's floating right here beside my johnboat. I'll lash him on and tow him to the ramp at Under-the-Hill."

"Don't lose him. I'll be down there soon as I can. Cover him with a tarp or something. I don't want any rubberneckers. Have you informed the Adams County sheriff?"

"Not yet. You were my first call."

"I'll call Sheriff Marsh. When he gets there, tell him you called me first because you knew I know the family."

"I know the drill."

"Good man. See you soon."

"Better get a move on, Sheriff. Rain's a-comin'."

"Out the door in five minutes. I owe you one, Joe."

Landry smiled. "That's the way I like it."

SHORTLY AFTER SUNRISE on Thursday, Wyatt Cash stood with Tim Warden, the Belle Rose Country Club golf pro, on a thirty-foot ridge above the fourth fairway and stared out over the green expanse in disbelief. The owner of Prime Shot Outfitters shook his head and stared through the morning mist with disgust. For as far as he could see, the perfectly manicured fairway had been mutilated by deep ruts dozens of yards long. In some places the tears in the earth stretched for hundreds of yards. A heavy vehicle of some kind, perhaps more than one, had spun out in several places, creating angled rips in the ground that would be impossible to repair in any reasonable time frame.

"How far does this go?" Cash asked.

"Eight more holes," Warden answered.

"Shit! Can they play on that?"

"Unplayable," Warden said flatly.

"Oh, man."

"If it was just two or three holes, we might be able to use our working green and finish out the tournament. But there's no way, Wyatt. Four greens have massive 'BLM' letters carved into them with tire ruts. There's no way we can cover all that up before a media drone or chopper gets up and gets a shot of it. And there's no way to carry out repairs for even minimal tournament standards in time to begin play on schedule. I don't want to be the one to say it . . . but we're fucked. The tournament's over."

Cash felt like weeping. He'd devoted three years of his life to bringing a PGA tournament to Bienville, and his company had sponsored several of the players. He would never be able to repeat this advertising opportunity. "How could this happen?" he asked. "Did you guys not get any kind of alert or alarm or anything?"

Warden shook his head. "Does it matter?"

"I'm just trying to understand it."

"What's to understand? The jigs finally did what they wanted. They shut us down."

"Jesus. Tim. The local Black community wouldn't do this. They know what kind of money this tourney's bringing to the town."

Warden scowled. "But the goddamn malcontents have been bitching for years about our membership list, our policies and fees. They've tried to shut us down before, legally."

"That was under our old rules."

"Walk down to Number Five and look at that BLM ripped into the ground. Then you decide who did this." Warden stuck up his middle finger, then spat on the ground and started back toward their maintenance cart. "Tournament's over, boss. We'd best start making calls."

CHAPTER 84

NADINE TIPTOED DOWN the stairs at 6:00 a.m. and poured herself some cold-brew coffee. She tried to be quiet, but I came awake on the sofa and called out softly to her. She looked over the counter at me.

"Annie woke up and took a pain pill. She's dozing now."

"Good."

"Have you looked online at coverage of the fire?"

"No."

Nadine padded around to the sofa and gave me a sip from her mug. After I'd swallowed, she said, "Somebody took drone photos and posted them on Facebook. There's nothing left of the main house but one chimney."

I shook my head, knowing it must be true but not quite able to accept it. "I've been thinking about riding out there for a look."

"Really? I'd like to go, too."

"What about Annie?"

"Oh, she'll insist on coming."

"In her condition?"

"You won't keep her in that bed, Penn. She's planning on going over to UMC to visit Andrew today. You'd better just accept that."

I sat up and pulled on my jeans, then worked my stump into my prosthetic. "Then let's load her up. I want to see the crime scene before I talk to anyone else today."

Nadine's gaze fell on the pages of Romulus's oral remembrance of his trip to find Niobe. "Did you read any of that last night?"

"Most of it. Through Niobe's decision not to be rescued by her brother. To pass for white. You were right. I don't think I've fully absorbed it yet."

Nadine's eyes deepened. "I know what you mean. You're descended from her, Penn. From Niobe." Nadine laid her left hand on her abdomen. "And now I'm *carrying* part of her."

I blinked as the reality of this hit me. "Jesus. But there's still so much missing. We know nothing of what was in Niobe's mind. Or the history that followed. That's what I can't stop thinking about. But I'm hitting pause for now. We have to live in the present today. Let's get moving."

She leaned down and kissed my forehead. "I'll get Annie ready."

IT TAKES ABOUT twenty minutes to drive from downtown Bienville
to the Pencarrow gate, if you obey the speed limit, mostly because the sole
access road narrows to a single car-width as you approach the bluff's edge
from the south end of town. Annie has stretched out in the passenger seat,
her bandaged hands on her lap, while Nadine sits crossways in the back.
We smell the fire half a mile from the entrance turn, and as we approach
the gate, I find a stern-looking Tenisaw County deputy guarding it with
nearly black sunglasses.

"You need to turn that car around," he says, as I pull up and brake. "You
can't go in."

"This is my property, Officer."

This throws him a little. "Sheriff Tarlton says nobody gets in without
his permission. Nobody means nobody."

I hit my remote and open the gate behind him. "You'd better call Buck,
then, because I'm going in. Tell him Penn Cage is inspecting the fire damage on his property."

As the flustered deputy makes his call, I drive past him into what is
now a four-hundred-acre crime scene. Making the long circuit through
the trees, past the Duel Oak and the reflecting pond, I see that not even
the chimney is standing anymore. Its upper half collapsed since those
drone photographs hit Facebook. The only thing still silhouetted against
the trees is some of the scaffolding Andrew must have scampered up to
turn on the second-floor water taps.

"I can't believe it," Annie murmurs from the passenger seat. "All the
work we put into this place. Even Gram. But Andrew especially. It feels so
personal. It's a violation."

"It *was* personal," I tell her. "This wasn't any Bastard Sons of the Confederacy. This was Shot Barlow's bunch."

"You don't know that," Nadine says cautiously.

"They had a goddamn bonfire to celebrate. Didn't I tell you last night?"

"*What?*" Annie asks, her eyes wide.

I nod. "Ray and I sneaked out here last night and saw it. What's more, I
saw Bobby White out there meeting with Barlow."

Annie looks incredulous. "What the fuck?"

"I haven't figured it out yet. But I will before this day is out."

I pull the Audi up to the little concrete pad beside the slave quarters
and stop. "Can you walk from here?" I ask Annie. "Or do you want me to
pull right up to the wreckage of the big house?"

"Closer, please, if you can manage."

This time I park within ten feet of the fallen chimney.

"You guys go ahead," Annie says. "I'll come after my pain pill kicks in a little more."

"I'll stay with you," Nadine offers. "Go on, Penn."

As I walk through the smoking ruin of Pencarrow, the burnt-carbon stink hurls me back to 1998, when a man named Ray Presley burned my parents' house—my childhood home—and with it the library my dad had spent the first sixty-six years of his life building. The loss of Pencarrow isn't nearly that personal for me, for the plantation contained little in the way of sentimental possessions. But I spent a fair amount of time helping Andrew restore the place, and my mother spent months here writing and doing research. Having finally read some of Romulus's story, in his own words, I feel I have some sense of what this place really was, of who worked and loved and hated and slept within these vanished walls, and the impenetrably complex life they must have lived before the war.

Hearing stones shift behind me, I whirl, but it's only Nadine and Annie, standing and talking near the collapsed chimney. I wonder whether Annie has read the transcript of Romulus's oral testament, then realize that she must have. There's no way she assisted my mother for the months she did without exploring the fruits of her research. Looking back, I remember Annie traveling to the Midwest with Mom more than once by air. She probably met Romulus's Black descendants in person.

Confronted by the harsh fact of how little remains of the 207-year-old house, I find myself glad it was the carved bust of Calliope that Annie saved, rather than some relic of the early nineteenth century. Captain Pencarrow's original locket, with its small painting of the real Calliope, remained attached to the sculpture with brads, and as Andrew said at last night's dinner, he considered Calliope to be the soul of the house. Romulus's harrowing tale had done nothing to change my mind about that.

"Dad!" Annie cries. "Come look at this!"

She sounds alarmed or excited, I can't tell which. I hurry through the mess, taking care to avoid upturned nails, and by the time I reach Annie and Nadine, they've set a small metal strongbox on the still-warm bricks of the fireplace hearth. Orange-brown water leaks from one rusted corner of the box.

"Where'd you find that?"

"Right here, in with the chimney bricks. Nadine kicked a little pile, and there it was."

"That water's not a good sign," Nadine observes.

Annie holds up her bandaged hands. "See if y'all can get it open."

Nadine crouches and fiddles with the latch, which appears stuck. Then she digs a fingernail under it and promptly breaks the nail.

Looking down and digging for a few seconds, I find the rusted poker that always sat on this hearth. Its point is still strong, and with it I manage to prize open the lid of the box.

"*Holy . . .*" Annie breathes, looking at the soaked mess of paper inside.

"Be careful," I warn Nadine, who's already reaching in.

"I will. This looks like a couple of envelopes and folded notepaper on top. But I think there's some sort of bound book underneath. Maybe more than one."

With dexterous hands, she carefully picks through the contents, doing as little damage as possible. A leather-bound diary about an inch thick waits at the bottom, as well as what appears to be two thinner journals, but whether used for accounting or for more personal entries, it's impossible to tell.

After Nadine dumps the water, she replaces the faded paper in the box. On the top piece I make out the image of what appears to be a smoking locomotive and the word *confederate*. A little chill runs along my neck.

"That's Confederate money. A hundred-dollar bill."

"Seriously?" Annie says. "So we may have found another piece of the family puzzle?"

I shrug. "Maybe. I wish to God Mom could have been here when y'all found that."

"We should talk to Mimi at the Historic Natchez Foundation," Annie says. "She'll know what do to. We're bringing this with us, right?"

I nod. "We're sure not leaving it for Sheriff Tarlton or the state fire marshal."

"We're going to have to dry this out somehow," Nadine says. "I have some dehumidifiers at my store, from when my pipes broke."

My daughter gives me an urgent look. "Let's get it back to town before anybody gets out here to see us with it."

"Don't worry. Nobody's taking that box from us."

Nadine touches my arm and points across the reflecting pond to the drive near the gate. A sheriff's-department cruiser is making its way around toward the house, and not at a leisurely pace. "Twenty bucks says that's Buck Tarlton," she says.

My chest tightens with anger. "Take the strongbox to the car. I'll deal with that asshole. He's just the man I want to see."

"Don't provoke him," Nadine warns. "You're not exactly on firm legal ground, considering where you were last night."

I roll my eyes, but that's not good enough for her.

"If I see you arguing," she says, "I'm coming over to shut you up. In fact, I'm going to settle Annie in the car and then stand with you while you talk to him. As your lawyer."

"Fine. Just get that box into the trunk."

"When his car passes behind those cypress trees," Annie suggests. "Hurry!"

CHAPTER 85

BOBBY WHITE AWAKENED in Sophie Dufort's bed in a state that for him was close to shock. Sophie herself was in the next room taking a shower; he could hear water hitting the Italian marble tile. He was grateful for her temporary absence, for he needed to get a grip on himself and his situation.

His tactical position was perfect. Kendrick Washington had already confirmed on social media that he intended to speak on the bluff at 2:00 p.m. in Confederate Memorial Park. That meant that Bobby only had to prevent widespread disaster up there for a few more hours, and then he could fulfill his plan.

Strategically, however, his position had gotten more complicated.

In order to maintain his public-facing sexual cover, Bobby had been sleeping with women for most of his life—the higher their profile, the better. But the depressing truth was that sex with those women was a performance from start to finish, an acting job during which he pretended to be something he was not, to have appetites he did not, and in fact impersonated the best iteration of the thing he was not, which was a heterosexual male. For this reason, Bobby had honed his skills and stamina the same way he had after losing his arm, when he'd become a superb golfer and champion pistol shot. This, combined with his generous natural endowment, was usually enough to give those women an experience memorable enough to recount to their friends before much time passed.

But last night with Sophie had been no performance.

The sister of his first real lover, she had known he was gay (or whatever the hell he was) before she even removed her clothes. Yet she'd pressed forward with her intention as though mutual satisfaction were quite possible, regardless of that fact. Shortly after she began her ministrations, reality had proved her prescient. For during their revelatory coupling, *Bobby had remained himself.* This was unique in his experience, at least in the years since high school. Having sex with a woman like Birdie Blake was work, with some perfunctory pleasure tacked onto the end. But making love with Sophie was a kind of double exploration, of both her and himself.

Sophie Dufort had slept with many men, and was an accomplished lover in the carnal sense. She'd made it plain from the start that there was nothing she would not do. Better still—to Bobby's way of thinking—she had a technique that surpassed all others, since it applied to almost any act. When Sophie did something that caused pleasure, she let her partner know—without words, yet without doubt—that she would not cease doing it until some pinnacle had been reached, no matter how long that might take.

Hearing the shower stop, Bobby checked his phone, something he'd been putting off since last night, when he sent Corey a text saying that he was strategizing with Charles Dufort and would be unable to get away until very late. Now, checking his messages, he saw that he'd lucked out almost beyond belief. Corey's reply informed him that a problem had cropped up in Georgia, where the Republican legislature was trying to make electronic signing of nomination petitions illegal. To respond, Corey had booked a 6:00 a.m. Delta flight out of Baton Rouge, so as to be at the capitol as early as possible. There he would meet with their Atlanta allies and try to get the GOP effort stopped. This meant that Bobby would have most of the morning free from the burden of lying to Corey while he set himself up to kill Donny after the kid opened up on Kendrick and the bluff crowd.

When the bathroom door opened, Bobby stood to give Sophie a kiss, but he instantly saw she did not want one. Her face was flushed, tears streamed from her eyes, and her hands—which she was holding out in front of her—were shaking badly. She'd tied a robe around her, but she was still sopping wet from her shower.

"What's the matter, Soph? What's happened?"

She shook her head like someone going into shock. "I got a call from someone I know at the medical examiner's office. Sheriff Tarlton brought Charlot in this morning."

Bobby instantly slipped back into acting mode. "*In?* In where? To jail?"

"No. The morgue. He apparently washed up at the Natchez landing this morning. Bobby . . . Charlot's *dead*."

Bobby blinked and shook his head as though in disbelief. "Are they positive it was him?"

"They found his wallet on him. His driver's license was in it."

"Oh, Jesus. I'm sorry."

"Tommy Russo," Sophie said. "It had to be him. His casino's right on the river. Some of those goons killed my brother and dumped him over the side like garbage."

Bobby was glad her initial suspicion had run in this direction, but he suspected it wouldn't stay there long. Sooner or later she would remember yesterday's sequence of events, and if she was as smart as he suspected . . . a little bell would ring.

"Will you come here?" he said, beckoning her with his hand.

She hesitated, but in the end she came to him, and he enfolded her with his one arm and held her tight. She sobbed against his chest, and he petted her dark hair. As he did, it struck him how different the future looked after a night with her. No question about it: he could handle four years with Sophie Dufort as his wife. He wouldn't even have to lie, except to the public, which he had always done with ease. Only now he would have another partner in deception—not a gay man like Corey, or an amoral opportunist like Jenna Kay Donnelly, but a beautiful woman whose very presence in his life and bed would confirm he was what the voters wanted—a red-blooded cis male.

"I'm so, so sorry, Sophie," he murmured. "Just let it out. The pain, I mean. We'll find out what happened."

"If Tommy Russo killed him—or ordered it done—I'll kill that wop bastard myself, I swear to God."

"No, you won't. Too much risk." He drew back and kissed her forehead. "I'll do it for you."

She blinked in surprise, and her eyes shone with something like awe. "You really mean that? You'd do that for me?"

Bobby shrugged. "I loved Charlot, too."

"But . . . you'd *kill* Russo?"

"That used to be my job, you know. Not a big deal. If Russo murdered Charlot, he deserves it."

She laid her cheek against his chest. "I can't believe last night."

"Me, either," he said, thinking back to certain things she'd done.

"Did you really enjoy it?"

"I did."

She breathed steadily against him, and the moist heat of her respiration brought blood into his skin. "I tried to watch for signs you were faking," she whispered.

"I wasn't."

"I didn't think so. Look . . . whenever you want me, just call. I'll do whatever you want. No questions asked."

"I will."

She hugged him tighter. They stood there embracing, neither wanting to separate and reenter the world as it had existed before.

"I'm sore," she said softly.

"I'm sorry."

"No, I like it." After a time, she lowered her right hand and gently groped him with curiosity. "Did you wake up hard?"

"Mm-hm."

"You need to pee?"

"It can wait."

She dug her pointed chin into his chest as she looked up into his eyes. "Can you hold me up with one arm?"

"Absolutely."

Opening her robe, Sophie clasped both hands around his neck and hiked herself up onto him. She weighed 140 pounds, but thanks to genetics and ceaseless swimming, every one was in the proper place. With her anchoring arm quivering from strain, she reached down and guided Bobby into her with the other. As she settled against him, he walked her toward the nearby wall, where he could pin her and use his strength to give her what she craved, which was escape from grief. Soon for her the world would disappear, and she would cling to him as to a raft in a raging sea.

Bobby gave all of himself he could spare, but much of his mind had already spun out into the future, when he would step into a blizzard of bullets burning down from the water tower on the bluff and blow Donny Kilmer off his Erector-set perch. After that . . . there would be no stopping his ascent to 1600 Pennsylvania Avenue . . .

The American throne.

CHAPTER 86

FOUR MILES FROM Bienville's northern city-limit sign, a seventy-three-year-old former beauty queen named Loveta Corbin Black slept the sleep of the damned in an Italianate palace with a French name, Mont-cornet. Back in the late 1930s, Montcornet had been one of the favorite homes of tourists on pilgrimage to Bienville, but the place had slowly deteriorated over the decades, and after a brief renaissance during the eighties, when a desperate Loveta had married Harold Black, the older banker who'd inherited the house from his mother, it went down fast. For the past seven years, it almost seemed to be sinking into the over-grown land around it.

As she did every night, Loveta had drunk vodka until nearly 3:00 a.m. But last night, the icy fluid had been spiked with lorazepam from her bot-tle of sleeping pills. Only she didn't know that. She sprawled across the bed in her second-floor master suite while the television played a morning soap, still snoring, more deeply asleep than usual at this hour. On the floor beside the bed lay an open suitcase, half-packed with old family photos and mementos from her youth. A candid sorority pic from Spring Hill College in Mobile lay on top. The handsome boy smiling beside her wore a scarlet sweater that blared, ROLL, TIDE!

Loveta's labored breathing provided the only competition for the hum and rattle of the overhead ceiling fan, until a cell phone rang in the hall-way AC closet, closing a circuit with a metal cassette designed for the belly of an A-10 fighter aircraft. In less than two seconds, eight magne-sium flares ejected from the cassette like cannon shells, blasting through the closet door and igniting everything they touched, including a heavy faded tapestry of a Southern hunt scene adorning the wall opposite the closet.

Loveta rolled over in bed but did not wake. By the time the first Black tentacles of smoke feathered over her face, there was no possibility of es-cape. A younger, more sober woman might have awakened and tried to leap from the second-floor window, but Loveta was too far gone. The fire consumed the old wooden palace like a ravenous monster, and finally the roar of the flames stirred her from her slumber.

Unalloyed horror jolted her like cardiac paddles. Her surgically lifted eyes went wide, filled by the living nightmare of a medieval witch's death. By then the flames had cut off all possibility of escape, and the last blessing in a mostly wasted life was that she died of smoke inhalation a few seconds before the flames reached her marmoreal skin.

CHAPTER 87

SIX HUNDRED YARDS from Confederate Memorial Park, Donny Kilmer climbed the ladder pegs on the southwest leg of the Bienville municipal water tower. It stood 165 feet from foot to crown—taller than the average oil-drilling mast in these parts—and the footings were sunk into one of the taller city blocks at the edge of the Garden District, which, thanks to the erosion-prone loess soil, put them maybe twenty-five feet above street level. This gave the stored water plenty of height to build up hydrostatic pressure, which made for damn good showers. It also gave any man on the utility walkway that encircled the tower's steel reservoir a God's-eye view of more than half the Bienville bluff to the south.

As he climbed, Donny noticed a column of dark smoke rising hundreds of feet into the sky to the north, but its source seemed to be in the forest. He wondered idly whether the "Bastard Sons of the Confederacy" had decided to strike again.

Today it made no difference to him.

Donny always felt close to the Lord when he climbed. He'd seen beautiful things from the monkey boards of oil derricks. Mostly the flat scrub landscape of East Texas, which could be pretty at certain times of day. But he'd also gazed out over the vast jungle of the Atchafalaya Swamp, and the endless serpent of the Mississippi cutting through sandbars as it found its way to the gulf. What he remembered most was working up by the crown blocks on the big offshore rigs, 250 feet over the waves. From there you could see to the edge of the world, where vast schools of menhaden rose to feed in the dawn, and rare Gulf of Mexico whales breached at sunset.

Donny shifted his right shoulder, then flexed against the heavy cable trailing to the ground. Compared to three hundred feet of cable, the H&K rifle in the soft case slung over his left shoulder weighed nothing. The stripper clips affixed to his belt were noticeable, but their heaviness reassured him. He had more than six hundred rounds on him, and with that he could pretty much control his own destiny, no matter how they tried to take him. Right now the biggest pain in his butt was literally in his butt—tiny chrome shrapnel from the TruckNutz that old judge had blasted at Barlow's yesterday. Not even a girl he screwed sometimes had been able to remove it with tweezers. What the hell? Soon it wouldn't matter at all.

The early sun flashed dully on his watchband, but he wasn't worried about being seen. The water tower was painted off-white, and he'd bought himself a mechanic's jumpsuit of the same color at Walmart only forty minutes ago. He'd also given his rifle and clips a quick coat of white matte latex from a spray can. Even if some pedestrian spotted him climbing the tower, they'd assume he was a city maintenance worker. Or maybe a man from one of the cellular companies that had festooned the old tower with antennas. An engineer might wonder what he was doing trailing a couple of hundred feet of cable to the ground, cable that ran right across High Street to the adjacent block. But the odds of that happening were slim to none, and Slim was out of town. Especially on a day like today, when all anybody white was thinking about was nigger trouble.

Nobody Black was going to question him.

Donny felt the euphoria of God's hand touching his shoulder, guiding him to his destiny. He'd known it for sure when Bobby White told him the mission target was Kendrick Washington again. The truth was, he'd always had a soft spot for old Doc Berry. Doc was as good as a colored man came. He'd helped a lot of poor folks, white and Black. Whereas the other one was nothing but a thug with a Jesus fantasy. He'd even talked publicly about Jesus *being* Black, which was the joke of all time. All you had to do was open any illustrated Bible to see what Jesus looked like. Look at the colored-glass windows in the churches, for God's sake. Kendrick Washington had to be cranked on meth all the time to believe the words coming out of his own mouth. But after today it wouldn't matter.

Today Donny Kilmer would let his rifle speak for him.

And Kendrick Washington would speak no more.

CHAPTER 88

I WAS LYING in a narcotic haze on the downstairs sofa of my town house when one of Natchez's most well-known citizens called me. Long before my political period, Tony Byrne served multiple terms as mayor of Natchez, during some of the city's most racially troubled times. Working with Medgar Evers's brother Charles, Tony managed to do a good job shepherding the city through its civil rights difficulties. Close to eighty now, the handsome businessman remains a renowned athlete who led the city's team to two successive Mississippi championships in the 1950s, and he's beloved by most everybody.

"What's happening, old friend?" I ask, more than a little surprised.

"Hard to say, Penn. I'm down at Natchez Under-the-Hill. I was doing my daily run, and I noticed the Tenisaw County sheriff down on the boat landing with Joe Landry. I also saw the Adams County coroner's van, which told me a corpse had probably washed up down there."

A premonitory chill goes through me.

"Naturally I turned down there, and I instantly recognized the body, even though the water had messed him up some. It was Charlot Dufort."

A blade of guilt or regret slices through the painkiller in my blood. "Oh, no. Oh, man."

"I'm afraid so. His bad habits finally caught up with him, one way or the other."

"Any sign of foul play?"

"Nothing obvious, but I wouldn't rule it out. Not with the rumors I've been hearing lately. And keeping my ears open, I got a feeling Tarlton is thinking homicide."

Trust an old politician like Tony to use his instincts. "What was Sheriff Tarlton doing down there? Why wasn't the Adams County sheriff handling it?"

"That's one reason I called. Things felt a little fishy to me, though I can't say exactly why. I've never been a fan of Tarlton's, though."

"That's two of us."

Even though Charlot's life was purportedly a wreck, I never figured him for a suicide. "Well, I appreciate you reaching out, Tony. I don't really have an official position anymore, but I'm still involved to a degree up in Bienville."

"I actually called you for a couple of reasons. First, I've got a group of concerned shop and bar owners down here, and they're pretty anxious about the political situation. Everybody's worried about civil unrest. You have any advice for them?"

"Well . . . I'd advise anybody with a business under the bluff or on top of it to close while it's still light and lock up tight. What's your feeling?"

"The same. I've spent my whole life in this town, and I've never felt the tension get this bad. Not even during the worst of the sixties."

"Really?"

"Well . . . when I was elected mayor in '68, there was a pretty bad riot, and I hadn't officially taken office. As I came back from the lake to try to handle it, I met 375 highway patrolmen the governor had sent down here to control things. I reached out to Charles Evers for help, but he was in California doing the Johnny Carson show. He told me not to talk to any of that bunch. I couldn't do a damn thing to ease the situation until he got back, so that was a tense couple of days. But this feels worse, somehow. Losing all those kids at Mission Hill wounded the Black community in a way I've never seen before. And the burning of the city's antebellum homes . . . that's really knocked the white community off balance. I'm afraid it's going to come down to guns in the streets before we're through. Am I crazy?"

"I wish I could say yes. But you know better."

"I sure feel bad about Charlot. He was a troubled soul, but smart as anybody I ever met. And his daddy is a sure 'nuff son of a *bitch*."

"Agreed on all points, my friend. Hey . . . you said you called me for a couple of reasons. What was the other?"

"Oh! We had another bear sighting. That made me think of you, because of your encounter last week."

A surreal sense of lightness makes me suddenly dizzy. "When was this, Tony? How close did it get?"

"Just a few minutes ago. We were preoccupied with the corpse, and there was a string of barges passing, so the bear got within about thirty feet of us before somebody up on the road hollered a warning. We all turned together, and Buck Tarlton panicked. He drew his service weapon and fired without waiting."

A rush of irrational anger flashes hot through my face. "Did that SOB kill the bear?"

"No. He may have hit it, but he definitely didn't put it down. Damn thing was too big. It ran into some thick saplings down in the riprap, then south along the bluff while Tarlton fired after it. I'm pretty certain he got away."

"Jesus. What was it doing before Tarlton fired?"

"Just watching us, it seemed to me. That's it. But he had blood on his snout, and paws too, I thought. A lot of it."

"Was he on four legs, or standing?"

"Standing. Just like a man."

Again the chill of recognition and hidden meaning. "Was it a juvenile bear? Or older?"

"Oh, older, I'd say. Fully mature. Looked scarred to me, and big. Reminded me of Faulkner's bear. Old Ben. Remember that story? They found fifty-two bullets in him after he was finally killed. That's the feeling this bear gave me."

"That sounds like the one that visited me, all right."

"Might have been. Joe Landry says he's seen a bear like that off and on for years down under the bluff over about a five-mile stretch. And that's pretty close to Edelweiss."

"And it appeared just when Charlot died."

"You think that means something?"

I'm a little reluctant to answer honestly, but I do. "I don't know, Tony. I got a mighty queer feeling when I was standing within two feet of that animal. Like it was trying to tell me something. And my mother died just a few days after that. Hell, I'm probably crazy."

"You never know, Horatio. There are more things under the sun than are dreamt of in your philosophy."

Our literate former mayor brings a smile to my mouth. "Thanks, Tony. Let me know if you hear anything else about the riot/protest situation. Or the bear."

"Will do, Penn. Us old mayors gotta stick together. Like old soldiers."

After hanging up, I force myself to my feet and hobble toward the kitchen for something to drink. Before I can make it, a text comes into my phone. I don't recognize the sender's number, but the heading says NOT JUNK! BOBBY WHITE & BIENVILLE.

Filled with a powerful sense of foreboding, I start to click the message, then stop myself. After last night, I have a strangely inexplicable aversion to communicating with Bobby White—at least until I know more than I do now about his deeper motives. My new caution was inspired by Annie, who spent some of her morning reviewing the motion alerts from the Ring cameras she'd repurposed last night to show us what was happening on Battery Row during our informal task force meeting. While waiting for my mother's painkillers to kick in, I decided to do something similar, by reviewing the motion alerts from the cams I'd used at Edelweiss to monitor Mom's and Annie's sickbeds when I didn't have a sitter or nurse. My hope, I suspect, was to discover that

Mom had regained consciousness at some point, even briefly, and managed to leave us some final goodbye, or testament to what she was feeling at the end.

On this score I was to be disappointed. But my instinct to search those recordings was more than validated, because one of the first things I found was a strange, even chilling conversation between Annie—who was more than half-sedated on opioids—and Bobby White, who had gone in to visit her on the night of the shooting, while I checked Mom's IV and vitals. Annie began the conversation, which went something like this:

Annie: I wanted to thank you . . . for saving my life. You're nothing like I thought you were.
Bobby: Happy to do it, Annie. You in much pain?
Annie: I thought you were some kind of QAnon crazy . . .
Bobby: (Laughter.)
Annie: Are you going to be president, Bobby?
Bobby: (More laughter.) Well, I don't know, hon. I'm sure running for it.
Annie: But why? Why do you want to be president? That job sucks.
Bobby: To tell you the truth, I don't want to be president.
Annie: Whaaat? Then why are you running?
Bobby: Well. Just because I don't want to be president, doesn't mean I don't have to be. Does it?
Annie: Wait . . . I don't—I don't understand.
Bobby: It's pretty simple, darlin'. I have to be president. On a certain day, at a certain time, a certain decision must fall to me. I probably shouldn't be telling you that, but . . . you sound pretty stoned.
Annie: (Snickering laughter.) I feel like I just ate a handful of gummy bears.
Bobby: If I'm not president when the hour of decision comes . . . then it could all be over.
Annie: What could?
Bobby: Everything. For people like us, anyway. But don't worry about that. It's all going to be fine.
Annie: Is it, though? Are you really going to win?
Bobby: I am. Go to sleep now. Let me find your daddy.
Annie: But how do you know for sure?
Bobby: Because. I'll do whatever is necessary to make it so. All right?
Annie: I'm glad somebody will. Ohh-kay. Night-night.

On the replay I watched Bobby exit the dim guest room without any awareness that a camera was filming him.

An eerie, tingling numbness circulated through me after hearing that exchange, which I listened to in full at least four more times. The one thing that remained constant through every listen was the utter sincerity with which Bobby was speaking to my half-conscious and barely coherent daughter.

He believed every word he was saying.

I obviously lack sufficient information to evaluate his words, but since it's clear that he's referring to some point in the future—beyond our next presidential election—it seems plain that Bobby White is in the grip of some sort of complex delusion.

And that seems like something the American public needs to know.

Looking down at my iPhone, I think again about Charlot Dufort being pulled from the brown water at Natchez Under-the-Hill, but I push away the thought and tap on the message I received a couple of minutes ago. I can't escape the feeling that somehow, the storm of recent violence has triggered a series of reactions in people who have been holding in secrets for days or even weeks. The text reads:

Penn,

I'm not ready for witness protection, so I'm contacting you.
Bobby White hopes to be the first gay president. The problem is, he's not telling anybody that. Personally, I'd LOVE to see a gay president. But it can't be Bobby White. Why? Because Bobby is a MONSTER. If you doubt that, scratch the surface. You'll see.

A Guilty Friend

As I read the last lines, yet another text message arrives, this one containing two web news headlines followed by long internet links in the familiar bright blue typeface:

Army General Paul Beckley Murdered in Mt. Olivet Cemetery

Black Mississippi Mayor Shot by White Sheriff's Deputy

I drop into a chair at the kitchen table. While both headlines mention violent deaths, they don't seem related in any obvious way. But for the first time since Tranquility burned and Bienville began sliding toward anarchy, I feel I have an ally out there, someone who might possess enough information to lead me to an explanation of our troubles—or toward one, anyway. With a shaking right hand, I press the first link and begin to read.

CHAPTER 89

I'VE BEEN SITTING on the bench outside the city council building for ten minutes, waiting to find out whether Bienville, a city founded in 1717, will survive one more day. I'm thankful for the dark cloud ceiling over the city, which at least protects me from the sun, if not the humidity. Despite my being outside the admin building, I've heard shouting in the private conference room reach such a pitch that I can make out phrases on the street. Considering the kind of pressure that the Black aldermen have been placed under—intense, personal, and illegal—I'm surprised they haven't resorted to physical retaliation.

Doc warned me that the county might be angling to destroy the Black city government, and I discounted his anxiety. Now he's dead, and his greatest fear is on the verge of coming to pass. Have I become so self-absorbed over the past weeks that I've missed critically important signs? Six days ago, when I encountered the black bear outside Edelweiss, my first thought was that it symbolized my impending death. Now, less than a week later, my mother is dead, Doc has been murdered, and the city I live in is about to vanish into history—on paper, at least. More important, the only center of Black political power in this county is about to be destroyed—power that thousands of people fought for decades to get. And not destroyed by votes, but by political gamesmanship, extortion, and the stroke of a pen. If they lose that power, it will take generations to regain—if they ever do.

The clip-clop of hooves comes from my right, and then a tired brown horse pulls a carriage filled with smiling tourists past. *Aaaand, here is the building where the city you're in is about to cease to exist!* As they roll on, I wonder who's behind the pressure on the aldermen. Likely the Poker Club—since their power runs all the way back to Reconstruction, when they formed as a sort of carpetbagger-resistance organization—but it could be anybody. Whoever it is, they're ruthless enough to use prison sentences of family members as threats. Considering this reality, I realize that the attack on Doc in the D.C. metro station might well have been a professional hit attempt. I could be far behind the curve of events, blind to an agenda that's plain to others. The trouble is, I can't see how gaining control of Bienville proper could help local whites in any material way that justifies that level of risk required to accomplish it. But then I had no problem with Barack Obama being president. The millions who still excuse or even support the January 6 insurrection experienced that event as a total inversion of their world—or at least the world they desired—and they're prepared to try to return the author of the subsequent treason to the Oval Office. I suppose anyone willing to go that far wouldn't hesitate to try to bring about a similar change on the local level, regardless of any legal niceties.

The scrape of wing-tip shoes coming up Commerce Street from my left doesn't sound that different than the horse did, though my mind might be playing tricks on me. I realize I must be dozing when a fuzzy image of Nadine lying beside me in bed resolves into Alan Stevens, the county attorney, taking a seat beside me on the bench. Stevens lives in a meticulously restored Victorian home a couple of blocks south, so the walk was nothing for him.

"You come back to find out whether we still have a city?" I ask.

"I promised I would." Stevens sighs and turns slowly to me. He looks like what he is: a young family man who probably didn't get enough sleep last night, thanks to being run ragged by the county worthies who employ him.

"Penn . . . whether they pass that act tonight or tomorrow, or next week, it's going to pass. This county hasn't got the money or the patience to operate redundant governments going forward. Two separate law-enforcement agencies, separate fire protection, or . . ."

I sit in silence until he peters out. "Is that what you tell yourself, Alan? That we're waiting at a special-called meeting on the day after our mayor was shot five times so that we can eliminate financial redundancies?"

This time his silence lasts longer. "Penn, I'm just a board attorney. The county has wanted to take this step for a long time. Mayor Berry was the chief obstacle. We both know why. The City of Bienville is the only real mechanism of Black authority in this county. If you're Black, you want Black aldermen in charge of hiring and firing civil servants, plus all those appointed positions. You want Black aldermen voting funds into your ward to fix drainage and handle garbage and every other thing. I understand, and I sympathize. I really do. But I work for Tenisaw County. The consolidation statute was drafted by John Stennis fifty years ago, and my understanding is that the Stennis Institute approved it. In the end, if a racially mixed board votes to dissolve *itself*—and the city along with it—there's nothing to be done about it. Certainly not by me. Doc Berry will roll over in his grave, but that's the end of it."

What can I say to this? It's the plea of every hapless public functionary from the Roman Empire to Nazi Germany. "Alan, tell me one thing. Why would a racially split board vote to dissolve the Black city government? In my mind, in Mississippi, that's an impossibility."

Stevens shrugs. "You may be right."

"So why do I feel like that's exactly what's about to happen in that room?"

The lawyer looks at the sidewalk, and for a moment I see discomfort, if not outright shame in his face. "Be honest with me, Alan. We may have political differences, but they're the old differences, like in our fathers' day. Liberal versus conservative, you know? Just talk to me. What's the county trying to do here? Why the sudden power grab?"

After a few seconds, he finds my eyes and turns up his hands. "Penn . . . I'm no politician. I like golfing and piddling around at the hunting camp. These people who run for office, even on the local level, they're not like me. Or you."

"I ran for mayor."

"Because you're a damn crusader! But these people have axes to grind. Some are serving special interests. Others just want the damn attention. To play the big man—or woman, these days. Hell, I think some of this is payback over the board trying to move that Reginald Hewson statue out of the park."

"You've got to be kidding. They'd destroy the city over something like that?"

Stevens laughs without humor. "Brother, *all* politics is local."

"Alan . . . Jesus. I can't believe America has lasted this long."

"Don't jinx it, brother. I'm right with you. The country's gone crazy. Hell, I voted for Trump the first time and then"—the lawyer lowers his voice—"Then I didn't. I don't like all this anger and violence. I stood with you on the Covid rules, didn't I? Even though I took a lot of heat for it. We saved lives."

"We did. You can be proud of that. But this play . . . Alan, your board is basically trying to disenfranchise the Black citizens of Tenisaw County."

Stevens does a good pantomime of skepticism. "Buddy . . . there's something going on in this country that I don't understand. I hear things I haven't heard since I was a kid, and people laughing about them. I don't like it, but I'm not like you, okay? I'm no hero. I just—"

"I'm no hero, Alan! God knows."

"Oh, bullshit. You'll charge a windmill in a minute. You've done it all your life. Your daddy was the same. But that's not me. My kids are still young, and I have to take care of them. My job is providing legal advice to the county board, not evangelizing about democracy and the intent of the founding fathers. No matter what my personal philosophy might be."

Stevens's mention of his young children makes me think of Nadine and the baby she's carrying. Should I be more like Alan? I wonder. No. Hell, no. He should commit himself to ensuring that his kids grow up in a better world, even if it means personal risk.

"Let's talk brass tacks for a second, Alan. If they dissolve the city, what will happen to the municipal police department?"

"They'll come under the command of the sheriff."

As I expected. "Will Tarlton have the last word on hiring and firing? Or will they be civil service?"

Stevens shifts his weight on the bench. "That'll be Tarlton's prerogative. If they go will-and-pleasure, that is. Which they will."

"So he could terminate every Black officer by close of business today?"

"You know how this movie goes." Alan shakes his head and looks up Commerce Street. "All I'd accomplish by trying to change the script is get myself fired."

Sitting out in front of the city council chamber, I wonder if this is the way democracy dies in America. A decent man who knows better—a lawyer—decides it's not his job to voice his personal beliefs about the running of his own state, then stands by while other men use the letter of the law to eviscerate its spirit. As I ponder this, Stevens gets to his feet and hikes up his pants as if about to walk away.

"You're not going to wait it out?" I ask.

"I promised my little girl I'd help her with her science project."

A wistful smile touches my mouth. "I remember those days."

"And now Annie's a lawyer. Trying to save the world." A shadow crosses Stevens's face. "Penn . . . I'm not sure I'd spend tonight up on that bluff, if I were you. Why don't y'all drive down to Natchez and stay at Edelweiss?"

"Annie would never go for it."

"No, I guess not. I get it."

"I feel like I'm waiting for a jury to come back in a murder trial."

Stevens doesn't answer, but in his eyes I clearly see the words: *You just might be.* He's reaching out to give my hand a farewell shake when a sustained burst of automatic gunfire erupts from the south end of Battery Row, three blocks west of us. No other sound hits the guts quite like that—so laceratingly real after the compressed version we hear on TV. I jump to my feet despite the pain in my stump, and several more bursts rend the air.

"What the hell, Alan?"

He shakes his head, his eyes wide with worry. "Sounded like ARs or M4s to me."

The prospect of a mass shooting triggers such panic now that I see people three blocks away racing toward what they must hope is safety. The deep sound of an engine roars between the buildings, followed by a more distant crackle of assault-rifle fire.

"Mass shooting?" I ask.

"If so, there's more than one shooter. Three or four, at least."

That's hundreds of rounds, I realize.

A hammer blow of an explosion reverberates along the bluff, and then a column of gray smoke jets into the air over the rooftops that face the bluff.

"I'm going over there," I tell him. Starting across Commerce Street, I take out my phone and speed-dial Chief Morgan.

"Are you sure?" Stevens calls. "You're not armed, are you?"

I look back, incredulous. "You're not coming?"

The county attorney wavers for a moment, then shakes his head. "I told you, buddy. Not what they pay me for."

I freeze in the street, my eyes locked onto his. Alan's a smart man, a good father, a man I once respected; but in his eyes now I see two unfamiliar emotions: defiance and shame. And before I turn away, he calls: "A veteran I know once told me a terrible truth."

"What's that?"

"It's better to be a living dog than a dead lion."

CHAPTER 90

"THEY GOT IT stopped!" Wyatt Cash cried, watching the live feed from Sheriff Tarlton's department drone.

"Have they?" Claude Buckman, Junior, asked. "I think they did."

"Whoever was in that MRAP rammed his ass!" Cash said from across the table. "Thank God we never pulled up those railroad tracks!"

Bobby White sat at the far end of the Donnelly Oil conference table, which faced the big LCD monitors lining the conference room wall, behind the podium where Sheriff Tarlton had briefed them yesterday. Apart from Buckman and Cash, the others at the table were Dixie Donnelly and Arthur Pine. Tommy Russo had absented himself to deal with security concerns at his casino, which occupied a vulnerable piece of real estate two hundred feet below the bluff. One of the TV screens was playing CNN, and the anchor was announcing they would have live footage of a possible vehicle attack from Mississippi momentarily.

"*Attempted* vehicle attack," Cash corrected. "Holy shit, that could've been bad. We dodged a bullet!"

"A missile, more like," Bobby said.

He had the personal history to be shaken by what he'd seen. As far as he could tell, a large pickup—it looked like an F-250—had pulled up to the National Guard barrier at the south end of Battery Row. After some argument with the soldiers posted there, it had rammed through and leaped the curb, its driver meaning to plow over the green space crowded from curb to fence with human beings of all ages.

As soon as he broke through, the barrier guards had opened fire on the rear of the big pickup, but the only thing that stopped unimpeded slaughter was a double line of railroad tracks that followed the bluff to what had once been Bienville's main station (now a restaurant and visitors' center). The truck's wheels had somehow gotten hung up in those tracks, and while the driver tried to wrench them free, a quick-thinking deputy sitting in his department's idling armored Caiman had floored his gas pedal and rammed the big Ford's left front fender, bringing it to a dead stop in a cloud of smoke.

"I've witnessed a successful attack like that in an open street," Bobby said. "That truck could have taken out a hundred people, easy. Even two or three hundred. We'd have had dead babies bouncing like basketballs live on CNN. What the hell is Tarlton doing? What is the Guard doing?"

"I think that was actually Tarlton's MRAP that stopped the pickup," Arthur Pine said. "I'm not a fan, but I'll give him that."

"I'll be *damned*," Cash said. "Guess that was money well spent after all. But *seriously*. We almost paid to pull up those railroad tracks six months ago!"

Dixie was watching Bobby closely. "What do you think?"

"I want to know who was driving that F-250. A local idiot? Or some PSP fool from Arkansas with a plan and lots of friends?"

"On it."

Dixie picked up her cell phone and left the table.

"Who the hell *are* these 'Poison Springs Provisionals' I keep hearing about?" Buckman asked. "Why did they elect themselves to come to Bienville to 'help the cause,' as they say?"

"Ouachita County, Arkansas, isn't that far from here," Cash explained. "They and Barlow's guys have trained together. Go to gun shows and shit. The PSP is a younger bunch, though. Crazier by a damn sight. Half of Barlow's crew still listens to George Strait, if that tells you anything, while the PSP are metalheads from the ranks up."

"Barlow has a nephew in the PSP," Bobby told them.

"That's right," said Cash. "I forgot that."

Dixie came back to the table and spoke loudly enough to take over the conversation. "Wade Tarlton says the driver was a local kid employed at the paper mill. High on meth. Seems Azure Dragon let him know they weren't renewing his work contract, and when the plant was evacuated today, he went out to his truck, tweaked, and came up here to 'remind them niggers of their place.' His words."

"Good," Bobby said. "That's the best case, given what we saw. We just need to make sure it's not repeated. The governor needs to get General Pike to realize what he'll likely be facing up here today."

"We'll be hearing from his chief of staff before long," Dixie said.

"The key today," Bobby said, "is keeping white troublemakers off the bluff. Our whole strategy is to give these protesters enough rope to hang themselves. Just like last night."

Claude Buckman nodded. "We're all on the same page, Bobby."

"It's Tarlton I'm worried about."

"Buck'll toe the line. He still wants the governor's seat one day. Christ, can we get some food sent up here? I could tear up some fried shrimp."

Arthur Pine seconded this with a hungry groan.

While they polled the room for orders, Bobby pretended to check his cell phone for messages.

"Bobby?" said Arthur Pine. "You look preoccupied. Everything okay?"

Bobby looked up, surprised to be surprised. He realized then that most of his mind was focused on the moment in the future that Kendrick Washington would stand before the crowd in Confederate Memorial Park and give a speech meant to have been given by Doc Berry. Unbeknownst to Kendrick, it would be the last he would ever give. And thanks to his sacrifice, Donny Kilmer and Bobby White would go down in history, one as a mass shooter, the other as the hero who stopped that shooter in the most dramatic fashion imaginable.

"You ought to check on Jenna Kay," Dixie Donnelly suggested, leaning down to his ear. "She's bored to tears in there."

Despite the surprising ease he felt around Jenna Kay, Bobby had forbidden her presence in the conference room. There was simply too much being said that could put her in the position of becoming the next Cassidy Hutchinson a year or two down the road. Dixie was somehow convinced that her journalist daughter could perform the impossible feat of witnessing news—possibly even crimes—and yet remain silent about them. And maybe she could, so long as the benefits of those crimes aligned with her personal interests. After all, wasn't that the prime creed of Trumpism? Hell, even Reagan Republicanism. But the moment those two lines began to diverge . . .

"I might just do that," he lied. "I want to check on the bluff situation first. See what kind of crowd the hero of Mission Hill's going to have for his speech."

The truth was, Bobby already knew the situation on the bluff. The National Guard had managed the crowd as he'd advised on the previous day, and the results today were pretty much the same. The crowd continued to grow slowly, even as exhausted mothers and children were released through the barriers at either end. Another "broken water main" accelerated this process, and the typically slow city response only aggravated the problem.

"Here we go again," said Wyatt Cash. "Check the CNN feed."

Bobby looked up. On the right-hand screen, above letters crediting the website of the Bienville *Watchman*, publisher Marshall McEwan stood in front of a jail cell holding Deputy Kenneth LeJay. Bobby remembered LeJay's face from the parking lot where they'd discovered Doc's corpse. LeJay's pale blue eyes, sparse blond mustache, and bland features marked him as a member of the class Bobby still thought of as white trash. Then

Chief Mason Morgan stepped in front of the camera. His bulldog head, deep-set eyes, and powerful voice gave a marked contrast to everything LeJay projected.

"As Marshall McEwan can attest," the chief said, "we are observing all proper procedures in our handling of murder suspect Deputy Kenneth LeJay. We are presently in contact with the district attorney as to appropriate next steps to take in this matter."

From somewhere, a massive roar of support from the African American marchers in the streets could be heard on CNN.

"That ain't good," Cash observed.

"No," Arthur Pine agreed. "It's going to make it a hell of a lot harder to resolve this jurisdictional standoff."

"Let's see how the city vote goes," Dixie said. "All they whine about is the rule of law. Let's see if they're willing to follow it when it goes against them."

"Mute that shit!" ordered Buckman. "Here's the governor's chief of staff!"

On another monitor, the young fox-faced functionary who both served and managed the state's chief executive took a sheet of paper from a hand that crossed the video screen in a blur.

"It looks like you guys have another problem about six blocks away from you! I hope you already know about it."

"Give it to us!" Bobby demanded, leaning forward in his chair.

"You've got a standoff in progress between your city police and the sheriff's department. Near the bluff, at a place called the Corner Bar."

Bobby snapped his fingers and yelled for someone to get Tarlton on the phone. Dixie was already dialing. "Do you know what started it?"

"Three Black families passed by on their way to join the protest. Some Arkansas militia skinheads heckled them from the door. The Blacks tried to ignore them, but it ended up in a brawl. City police responded to a 911 call, but the sheriff's department was already there. You've literally got cops and deputies aiming guns at each other. *Again*."

"God*damn* it!" Bobby shouted, feeling his blood pressure spike. "Give me Tarlton!"

It took a couple of minutes, but the sheriff's voice finally came into Bobby's left ear. A helicopter turbine whined, threatening to drown him out. Bobby immediately lit up Tarlton for losing control of his men.

"The Corner Bar is only one block from the cameras feeding CNN and MSNBC!" he shouted into the phone. "Right now those cameras have nothing to show but Black folks singing gospel songs. But one kid could get a drone over that intersection any second. And if you let the PSP break into the crowd on Battery Row, we'll have headlines like 'My Lai on the Mississippi.' You hear me, Sheriff? You know the reference?"

At first he got no response. Then Tarlton came through with a curt "Ten-four."

"Now, get your men to stand down at that bar. Treat the city police as if they still have all their powers until you hear from us. Clear?"

Tarlton didn't respond, but Bobby saw the governor's man nodding as he spoke. "The governor's with us on this, Sheriff. Button it down over there!"

After an excruciating silence, Bobby heard another "Ten-four. Out."

"It's killing him not to be running this show," Cash said.

"I want those Arkansas hillbillies run out of town," Buckman muttered.

The conference room door opened, and Tommy Russo hurried in. The casino owner looked rough but excited, his olive skin flushed and covered with perspiration. "It's nuts out there! I had to wait ten minutes for the cops to move enough people to get my car across Battery Row. On TV it looks like a bunch of church-singing and hand-holding, but that crowd is *pissed*."

"They have reason to be," Pine said. "Just thank God Kenneth LeJay wasn't Tarlton's deputy. Tacked onto Mission Hill—"

"It's still too much," Bobby said. "Penn Cage's daughter has already tied LeJay to Tarlton and Barlow ten different ways on social media. Barlow's Facebook page looks like a club for racist cops."

"We'll worry about that later," Buckman said, picking at his shrimp. "Where are we on the city board vote?"

While Buckman and the others veered into a discussion of local politics, Russo signaled Bobby to join him near the glass doors that led to the balcony.

"How you holding up, man? These backseat drivers getting you down?"

"The army's worse. Good-idea fairies."

"How about Charlot Dufort?" Russo whispered. "Heir to the richest bastard in the state, and he couldn't do any better than drowning in the river. You sure lucked out."

Bobby tensed. "What do you mean?"

"Only that you don't have to worry about buying him out of the hole now. His debt died with him. Unless you still want to pay it."

Bobby laughed. "In your dreams, Tommy. Charlot's a cautionary tale.

Best forgotten." Bobby pretended his phone had vibrated in his pocket. "I need to answer this."

Russo walked over to the catering table and prowled through the restaurant boxes. He scowled like a man who'd seen more cold seafood than he ever cared to. In the lull that followed, Bobby considered going out to the balcony and calling Sophie, but before he could, his phone lit up again. The caller ID read *TCSD*. Tenisaw County Sheriff's Department. "Who's this?" he asked.

"Listen to me, Bobby boy," said Buck Tarlton. This time there were no helicopter blades competing for bandwidth. "You've been giving me some pretty harsh treatment in there with your fat cat friends. You may have the governor in your back pocket, while I've got the media jamming a procto-scope up my ass. But you could find yourself getting the same treatment real soon, if you don't change your attitude."

"What are you talking about?"

"Your fag assistant, Corey Evers."

Fear knifed through Bobby's chest. "Still don't know what you're talking about."

"Turns out we've got another witness that puts Dufort and Evers to-gether on the day before his body was found. This time at the Snake Creek Indian Village."

Bobby's belly clenched.

"In case you don't remember from your youth, that creek runs right out to the Mississippi River, where Dufort's corpse was ultimately discovered."

"Who's this witness you're referring to?"

"Just tell your boy to stop by my office tomorrow morning to clear up some things. Mighty isolated out there, that Indian village. Lots of pri-vacy. Good place for skinny-dippin', if a man had a mind. Or two men. I don't go for that myself, not past the age of eleven or twelve. But you might be different, I don't know."

Bobby imagined himself taking Buck Tarlton apart piece by piece. At that moment nothing would have given him more satisfaction. "Sheriff—"

"So you start giving me some god*damned* respect in that room," Tarl-ton finished. "And have Evers at my office by ten. Out."

By the time Bobby clicked off, he was struggling to keep his face calm. Before anyone could buttonhole him with more pointless bullshit, he slid open the big glass door and walked out to the stainless steel terrace rail, took a deep breath, and looked north toward Vicksburg. How long ago had Ulysses Grant done essentially the same thing? Five hundred meters along this bluff—and four blocks back from its edge—stood the two-hundred-foot water tower where Donny Kilmer perched with his rifle like the hand of God. Bobby wondered where Kendrick Washington was at that moment. Probably studying a bunch of scrawled notes and realizing that giving a prepared speech to a crowd with high expectations was a lot harder than spontaneous heroism.

For a few moments Bobby wondered who among the crowd below would die in the interval between Donny assassinating Kendrick and Bobby shooting him off the tower. The kid had said he was going to flick his selector to full auto (he'd modified the weapon himself) and take out as many "colored" as he could before the FBI snipers got him. With the rate of fire on his AR, and the density of this crowd, that could easily be a hundred people, if Bobby didn't nail him with the first two or three shots. Maybe even two or three hundred. Bobby felt a little better knowing that most of the small children had been shepherded off the bluff by their mothers.

He turned and walked back toward the glass door, looked at the people gathered around the conference table, the flickering bank of TVs. Bobby jumped as Dixie Donnelly rapped on the glass from the inside. "*We need you,*" she mouthed.

"Love trouble?" Dixie asked with a pointed gaze, after he slid the door open.

"I just needed some space. What the hell's going on?"

"A hard-core group of PSP are refusing to vacate the Corner Bar. They've declared it their 'temporary HQ' for the 'Bienville Bluff Riot.' They literally posted that on the internet. And they're armed."

"Open-carry laws," said Wyatt Cash. "Nothing we can do."

"Where's Bobby White?" cried the chief of staff through the television link. "State police captain just told us there's a PSP-marked bus moving through Bienville toward the bluff. At least ten men inside, sitting forward. They're coming up Wall Street at a good clip, and they'll pass directly by the Corner Bar as they approach the Battery Row barrier."

"Oh my God!" Dixie cried, a phone pressed to her ear, and her voice filled with excitement. "They *did* it!"

"What?" Bobby asked.

"The council just voted four to two to dissolve the city! *The City of Bienville is no more!*"

Silence filled the room.

Then a cheer went up, a combined shout of joy and incredulity. To Bobby it sounded like dogs catching up to the ambulance one more time.

Claude Buckman heaved his bulk out of his chair. "Can we trigger some more looting or something? Seems like the perfect distraction."

Bobby stood firmly before the webcam transmitting his image to the governor's chief of staff. "No distraction is going to stop that bus. Those Arkansas crackpots are serious. I learned all about them when I was a boy."

While the chief of staff spoke fearfully into his cell phone, Bobby addressed Dixie and Wyatt Cash. "Get Shot Barlow on the phone. Maybe he can reach the PSP leader before those guys turn themselves into burnt toast. But tell Sheriff Tarlton and the Guard that if that bus tries to break through our barriers, they should blow it to hell and gone. They can use their antiaircraft cannon if they want. I don't care if they use a Javelin missile. These Arkansas hog-fuckers think every white man in Mississippi is on their side. Well, not today, people!

"Today we're calling the shots!"

Everyone in the room stared at Bobby as though he'd lost his mind.

"This is what you hired me for, isn't it?" he challenged them. "Well, strap your asses in, boots. The shit's about to get real."

In a soft voice Claude Buckman said, "We're not in Iraq, Bobby."

Bobby looked at the soft banker with contempt. "Put down your shrimp cocktail, Claude, and tell that to the people down on the street."

CHAPTER 91

I'M STARING AT the smashed wreck of a Ford F-250 when my daughter bursts out of the crowd behind me and grabs my shoulders, shaking me back to the present.

"What the actual fuck, Dad?" Annie asks, as Kendrick Washington emerges from the mass of bodies behind her.

The crowd here is 98 percent Black, leavened only by state and federal law-enforcement officers, plus a few well-known local liberals. It's formed a giant circle around what appears to be a surrealist sculpture of mechanical fornication: a military personnel carrier attempting to mount a tricked-out Ford F-250. Black smoke pours from the Ford's engine as firemen blast it with streams of white foam. The crowd hums with fearful excitement, everyone understanding that only an unlikely combination of bravery and luck prevented hundreds of deaths among them and their neighbors.

"It's a miracle!" Kendrick declares.

"Closest thing to it," I agree. "But this is a bad sign."

"At least the cops got the driver away before the crowd tore him to pieces."

"What have you guys been doing?" I ask him and Annie. "I saw you trying to get the Guard troops to talk to you."

"Not much success there," Kendrick reports. "But I figure if they see us as people, they'll have a harder time shooting us."

"I've mostly been interviewing people about Doc," Annie informs me. "But Kendrick gave an impromptu speech by the memorial fountain, and it went over so well that MSNBC ran forty-seven seconds during their news report. Here, check this out."

Glowing with excitement, she holds an iPad up to my face. "Kendrick's standing on the fountain with those armed Confederate Sons glaring at him."

The hero of Mission Hill speaks into Annie's iPhone camera with utter conviction. "Two nights ago, just outside my Mississippi hometown, two deacons were murdered in one of our most historic churches. That church was burned to the ground. Now our *mayor* has been murdered by the same sheriff's department behind the shootings at Mission Hill. And instead of appropriate action, we've got two sheriff's departments trying to break him out of jail. That jail, of course, is guarded by Black police."

The crowd groans around him.

"Another so-called antebellum home was burned today, but nobody knows who's behind those fires. *I say it was white men.* These arsons are being committed as an excuse to take over our local city government. Our new Black aldermen are being pressured to dissolve the city. Why? Because the county's afraid of what we'll uncover about Mission Hill. Now I hear we've got skinhead militia convoying in from all over the South. The crazies are coming. We need help, folks! SOS! SOS!"

Annie's eyes flash as though lighted from within. The neurochemical jolt of taking hold of the third rail of race politics has scrambled her faculties. I've spent my share of time at the center of media frenzies, and I know the euphoria they can generate.

"Kendrick, you did great there, but as bad as things seem right now, they could get a lot worse, and fast." I point at the two wrecked vehicles. "I don't want to say too much yet, but this stuff does not feel random. Somebody's pulling strings. What are you thinking about saying in your speech at two?"

He looks at Annie, then at the ground, and shakes his head. "I'm not sure. I don't want to just talk to my people here on the bluff. I want to move the people out in the country, the way Malcolm and Dr. King used to. The way Doc did at Diamond Hill. That was his job, but Doc's gone now. And these preachers we've got can't handle it. It's too big for them." He looks up into my eyes, honestly seeking my opinion. "What you think, Mr. Cage?"

"I think you're right. I'd find a quiet place and work hard over what I was going to say. There are network cameras in those helicopters, and you may not get a chance like this ever again. This crowd will listen to you, Kendrick. Maybe *only* you."

Gratitude shines from Annie's eyes. Before I can go on, my iPhone pings with a text. It's from Alderman Robert Gaines. A rush of acid rises through my esophagus as I read his words: *Penn, the City of Bienville has ceased to exist. Vote 4–2. Elijah caved. I hung tough. (You still owe me $96,000.) BTW, Sophie D voted to dissolve. Stay safe, brother. Thanks for trying. I won't forget.*

"Goddamn it," I murmur in disbelief. "God*damn* it!"

"What happened?" Annie asks, blank fear in her eyes.

I hold my phone where they can read Gaines's message. "The county rules it all now. Welcome to MAGA-land."

Kendrick closes his eyes like a boxer absorbing an organ-crushing blow. "What about the police?"

"Tarlton can fire Chief Morgan right now, and he almost certainly will. They'll have no authority to hold Deputy LeJay any longer."

"Mother*fuckers*," Kendrick curses. "This ain't right!"

"No, but it's legal. I need to get to the city council building. Anybody got a car? My stump is killing me."

"My cousin Frosty got a ride," Kendrick says.

"How close?"

Kendrick throws up his hand and gives a signal like a quarterback calling a favorite lineman onto the football field. Frosty instantly begins rushing toward us like an excited defensive tackle.

"I wouldn't mind hiring him for security myself."

Kendrick's furious face shows a momentary smile. "Sorry. He's taken."

INSIDE BIENVILLE POLICE Headquarters, Chief Mason Morgan and Marshall McEwan stared anxiously out of the second-floor window overlooking Jefferson Street. The station was ringed with sheriff's-department vehicles, ranging from cruisers and SUVs to SWAT vans and even the one surviving APC. Standing behind his command cruiser was Sheriff Buck Tarlton, while beside him stood Sheriff Coy Johnson, who also wore a straw Stetson today. His uniform was lighter in color than Tarlton's, and he was a head shorter, but he stood as rigidly as if he had equal authority.

"How's it feel, boys?" called a singsong voice from behind Marshall. It belonged to Kenneth LeJay, the man who'd shot Doc Berry to death. "Ready for payback for last night? They're about to storm this motherfucker for the second time. And this time they won't be stopping. This time the National Guard will be backing them up, not chewing their asses with a Vulcan gun. You guys don't have a *prayer*."

Marshall leaned closer to Chief Morgan. "Do you think he's right?"

"If the city vote goes the way I hear it might, then he will be." Both Morgan's and McEwan's phones pinged. When they checked their screens, they found two versions of the same message.

"Penn Cage says the aldermen just dissolved the city," Marshall intoned in a desolate voice.

Chief Morgan sagged as though he might collapse. "My source just confirmed. We're well and truly screwed now, brother."

"Hey, what's going on?" called Deputy LeJay. "You boys get some news?"

Chief Morgan sighed but gave him no answer.

The brittle sound of a human voice amplified by a bullhorn penetrated the old Victorian building. "You men in there, listen up! This is Sheriff Buck Tarlton. The City of Bienville has just been officially merged into the county. I am now your superior officer. As of this moment, you are all *relieved of duty*. Unemployed. You have *no legal authority*. You can re-apply for work at my office tomorrow morning, but until you do, and are rehired, *you are civilians*. I repeat, civilians! I order you to remove your badges and service weapons and leave them in the station armory. Once you vacate the building, my deputies will assume custody over any prisoners in your jail. If you do not comply, you will be charged appropriately under the state criminal code. That is all."

"What are you going to do?" Marshall asked the chief.

Morgan hiked up his pants and activated the radio mic on his collar. "I want everybody in the station on the first floor in thirty seconds, except those pulling guard duty."

The sound of heavy boots echoed through the building. Marshall could feel the floor shaking.

"Follow me," said Morgan.

Leading Marshall to the staircase, Morgan called back over his shoulder: "Henry! Come out here and keep an eye on this son of a bitch."

As they descended the staircase, Marshall looked back and saw the one-eyed detective, Henry Radford, walk out of his office and take a seat in a chair beside LeJay's holding cell. The last thing that registered in his mind was the so-called Hangman's Door behind which waited a fake noose and two-story drop to concrete.

Chief Morgan stopped on the landing and waited for his men to finish assembling below. His phone pinged once more, and he held up the screen so that Marshall could see it. The text was from Penn Cage. It read, *As your former city attorney, I believe the city of Bienville was just ILLE-GALLY dissolved by using a legal statute. The votes were EXTORTED, and that will be proved in time. Given the crisis facing the city, I believe you should continue to carry out your police duties to the fullest of your ability. If you don't wish to put your men's lives at risk, I understand. But you have my legal opinion. Godspeed and good luck, Chief Morgan.*

"Jesus," whispered Marshall. "We're truly in the shit now."

Chief Morgan stood straight, took a step forward, and laid his big, bearlike hands on the rail of the stairwell. The upturned faces were filled with doubt and anxiety, but also with hurt pride and longing for leadership. The one that made Marshall's heart clench belonged to Shirley Danvers, the sergeant unfairly damned by last night's viral news photograph.

"I ain't much on making speeches," Chief Morgan began. "Y'all know that."

Among the two dozen or so cops assembled below, a third covertly checked their cell phone screens. Clearly the news was going viral.

"Sheriff Tarlton's telling you the truth, as he sees it. A few minutes ago, the city board voted to merge with the county, which in this case would give all the power to the county and officially dissolve the city. It's technically legal, but I believe some board members were blackmailed into doing it. The Black ones, especially. Our former city attorney, Penn Cage, believes the same. I don't intend to take off this uniform or turn in my badge and gun, nor will I ask you to do those things. Neither will I ask you to stand here with me without clear authority, and continue to do your duty for the pittance you are paid. But I *hope* you will do that. This is that moment in the old westerns and war movies where the CO draws a line in the dirt and says 'Anybody who doesn't want to stand with us, step over this line. Nothing will be held against you.' Well, I mean that, boys—and ladies. I won't hold anything against you if you leave. Sheriff Tarlton and Sheriff Johnson could come through these windows with flash-bangs any second. After last night, they want payback. But they don't give a shit about justice. Especially for *our people*. They don't give a shit about Doc. Doc went to Vietnam and fought for them, patched up their fathers. But they won't do the same for him here. So make your decisions. If you're leaving, stow your gear and move out. If you're staying . . . let's form up for defense."

At first, no one moved on the station floor. Then slowly, three of the four white cops in the group made their way to the front door. A few Black officers shook their heads and muttered, but nobody said anything Marshall could understand. Everyone tensed as the main door opened to let the defectors out. Marshall felt his bladder turn to stone. It hit him then that last night's skirmish might be repeated any second, but with exponentially greater force.

It also hit him that he was unarmed. "Chief Morgan?" he said softly.

"Speak up, brother."

"Have you got a gun I can use? I know I'm not a police officer, but—"

"Hell, man, I ain't no police officer anymore myself. Didn't you hear Sheriff Tarlton?"

"So . . ."

"You ever carry a gun before?"

"I covered the war in Iraq for several months. I got caught in a pretty big shoot-out with an army buddy of mine. Paul Matheson. He lent me his M4. I did all right, but I got captured by Al Qaeda in the end."

Morgan grinned. "That's good enough for me, bud. Let's get to the armory."

CHAPTER 92

———

KENDRICK'S COUSIN FROSTY GIVENS drives a '73 Buick Riviera stuffed with enough audiophile-level amps to power eighteen speakers. They shake the buildings on both sides of the street as we pass. The rapper/music producer drops me in front of the city's administration building, where Sophie Dufort stands talking to a male reporter in his early twenties.

"Thanks, Frosty," I tell the big man, shaking his hand.

"Yo, Mayor. Have a good one. I gotta get back on Kendrick."

I struggle out on my bruised stump, take a seat on the bench I sat on for much of the past hour, and wait for the reporter to leave. I'd half hoped Robert Gaines would still be here, but he's probably too damned angry to stand in one place for more than a few seconds.

"Are you waiting for me?" Sophie asks.

Beyond her, I see the reporter climb into a Honda Accord and drive away.

I nod. "What bullshit reason did you give that kid for destroying the city that three years ago you told me you joined this board to save?"

Sophie purses her lips with something between disgust and disdain. "Don't give me that shit, Penn. This town is disintegrating around us. The mayor's dead, the chief of police is playing 'Remember the Alamo' at his station, and the bluff is about to erupt into open warfare. The county board is the only body capable of making the decisions necessary to bring things back under control."

"There it is, the white mantra. 'Control.'"

"The alternative, if you don't remember, is chaos."

"But who's really in control?" I ask. "The Poker Club? Your father?"

She waves her hand angrily. "Don't give me that Alan J. Pakula crap. The seventies are long behind us."

"Are they? You know all three Black aldermen had people trying to extort their votes—at least two successfully."

"Will they testify to that in court?"

"One almost certainly will."

Sophie shrugs. "I'll look forward to hearing that."

"The thing I want to know," I tell her, suddenly seeing her vote in a different light, "is what someone could have threatened you with to get *your* vote."

She turns toward the street traffic like someone looking for a taxi. Of course, Bienville has no taxis. Too small. We don't even have Uber.

"Don't be ridiculous," she says. "Nobody in this town has anything on me. If they did, they'd know better than to threaten me."

By phrasing her reply in this way, she narrowed the possibilities to exactly one. "It was your father, wasn't it? Had to be. No one but Charles could have made you do this. You've spent the past three years voting progressive on this board. You wouldn't have chosen to dissolve the city. You love it, in your own way."

She gives me a forced smile and holds her pointed chin high, but she can't manage a denial.

"What the hell does Charles have on you?" It strikes me that there are likely many answers to this, but surely she must have as much on him. "Never mind. But God . . . I don't know many fathers who would blackmail their daughters."

After a few moments, Sophie sits beside me on the bench. "Isn't it obvious? Even with Philippe dead nearly twenty years, and Mother gone even longer, I still have almost nothing to my name. If Daddy died tomorrow, I could still find myself disinherited. Unable to support myself, just like Charlot."

"I'm sorry about Charlot, by the way. I mean that."

She waves away my condolence, but looks on the verge of tears.

"Your father threatened you with poverty?" I ask. "Over *this* vote?"

She sighs heavily. "Don't ask me why. Because I don't know."

I grip the forward bench slat and start to heave myself to my feet, but Sophie catches my arm and holds me in place. "I want you to tell me something."

"If I can."

"When you and I drifted apart ten years ago, I never really knew why."

I close my eyes, wishing I hadn't come after all. "Are you sure you want to know?"

"Yes."

I might as well tell her. "Two reasons. The first happened when your father asked me to do that legal work for him. Something far too small for me to fool with, even back then. But I did it, as he knew I would, because I was sleeping with you at the time. Anyway, I discovered that through his construction company, he'd cheated the city out of a hundred and fifty grand. When I called him out on it, he lied. Right to my face. He must have known I wouldn't be able to let that go. Because weeks later, when I brought it up to him again, he showed me a forged letter—written on my letterhead—that made me look as guilty as he was. He'd done that for insurance, to protect himself from my guilty conscience. Now . . . I suppose Charles could have sent a burglar into my office to get that letterhead. But he didn't, did he?"

Sophie doesn't look at me. "No. I didn't know what he wanted it for, if that makes any difference."

"But you knew he didn't want me to know about it."

Again the hesitation. "Yes."

"You weren't a kid when you did that, Sophie. Why'd you take it for him?"

"It's hard to explain." She puts her sharp elbows on her knees, then drops her head between her knees and breathes deeply, her black hair trailing on the sidewalk. "You said there were two reasons," she reminds me.

"During that same period, I had to go out to one of Charles's other houses to meet some guy from his construction company. Your old maid lived out there then, Ruby Brooks's mother."

"Pearl?"

"Right. Well . . . Pearl seemed to think I was out there for a different reason."

"Such as?"

"To bring her money."

Sophie looks at me in surprise. "Money?"

"She'd apparently been receiving regular payments from your father for years, even though she was retired. Anyway, she told me—quite angrily—that she didn't want *one more dollar* from 'Young Master Charles.' Which seemed pretty unusual to me. I haven't met many people who turn down free money."

"Did she say why?"

"Not that day. She just kept saying, 'You tell Master Charles I don't want another dollar. I'll stay out here 'cause this is all I got, but he can keep his blood money. I don't want it.'"

Sophie lost a shade of color. "*Blood* money? Did you ever find out what she meant?"

"Partly. I couldn't shake the feeling it left me with, so I went back two days later. That time she told me more."

"Like?"

"A long time ago, when your father was about thirty, he was staying in the Holiday Inn in Natchez for some reason. Late one night, Pearl and her mother got called out of bed to go clean up whatever room he'd rented. What Pearl remembered was that the room was covered with blood. The walls, the bathroom, everything. And a puddle on the carpet. 'Like they'd kilt a hog in there,' she said."

Sophie stares at me with horror in her face. "Penn . . . what had happened?"

"She didn't know, or didn't want to tell me. But she was sure there was a girl involved. A Black girl from Fayette, she thought. Charles Evers's town. Back then, of course, Pearl didn't tell anybody that had happened. That was 'white folks bid'ness,' according to her husband. But over the years it haunted her more and more."

"And this . . . this thing changed your view of *me*?"

I shrug. "I hate to say it, but yes. I always sensed a sort of shadow in your family, Sophie. A darkness. Like with Philippe. He and I were friends for a while, but he had a sense of entitlement that always bothered me. A certainty that nothing bad could ever really touch him. And when he hit that woman with his car in college, drunk out of his mind, what happened to him? Nothing. Your father spread some money around, and it all went away. Anybody else would have gone to jail."

"That was Philippe, not me."

"But the same rules applied to you—or lack of them. I remember you and two girlfriends getting busted for pot down in Woodville during high school. This was the era when Black kids were being sentenced to long stretches in Parchman for simple possession. But not Sophie Dufort. You were out of there in two hours with an apology from the sheriff."

She looks at me as though asking whether she should have spat in the face of leniency and gone to prison. "Do you want to know why?"

"At this point . . . I don't think I do. It's too late for me to help."

Her eyes communicate profound sadness. "Did you ever tell anyone about the motel room? The blood?"

"Henry Sexton, the reporter. I doubt he had time to look into it, though. He was killed shortly afterward. Maybe you should do that. Look into it."

"Maybe I will. Hey . . . did you get a text about Bobby White today?"

Her question stuns me. "How did you know that?"

"I'll tell you how I know, if you tell me what the text said."

I consider this deal for a bit, but I decide against it. "I'm sorry, Soph. I can't do it."

"What do you think about Bobby? Surely you can answer that."

"Well, he saved my daughter's life at Mission Hill, so it's hard for me to be objective."

"Try."

"To tell you the truth . . . I'm not sure Bobby's sane."

She blinks in surprise. "Seriously?"

"Yes. I'm starting to think that what we've always called heroism doesn't mean that the person who fills that bill is better than the rest of us in any other way. Just be careful, if you spend time with him. Okay? Pay attention."

She nods thoughtfully. "I will."

A text from Annie comes in to my phone. It reads: *I'm still with Kendrick on the bluff, filming segments with different kinds of protesters, and bringing them water and medical supplies. Come back out if your leg's not hurting too bad. We'll figure a place to meet.*

Any idea where Nadine is? I reply.

Still drying the pages from the Pencarrow lockbox.

"I've got to go," I tell Sophie, though what I mean to do is find Ray Ransom, not fiddle with a dehumidifier or trail my daughter while she plays Mother Teresa to the marchers.

"What's going on?" Sophie asks.

"Nothing bad. That was my daughter. But bad things will happen soon, Soph, thanks to your vote. You can count on that."

She gives me a look of genuine sadness. "I'm so jealous of Annie."

"Why? Because she's a lawyer?"

"Oh . . . maybe a little. But no. More because she had a decent father."

Sophie's reply is raw with pain. "I believe you. I never really liked your father, but . . . I've come to believe Charles is probably much worse than I ever suspected."

Sophie nods and signals for me to look away while she wipes more tears from her eyes. "I'm going to miss Charlot so much."

"I know. He was one of a kind."

"For good or ill," she says with a laugh.

As I start to struggle to my feet, Sophie says, "I noticed you limping earlier. Do you need a ride to your car?"

"It's only a block away. But my leg is pretty messed up. I hate to ask you, after all I said earlier."

"It's all right. Sit tight here. I'll pick you up in sixty seconds."

As she turns away, I catch her hand, and she looks back at me. "Are you okay?" she asks, real concern in her eyes.

"Yeah. I just . . . does it seem weird to you that we used to sleep together?"

She looks back with deep sadness for several seconds, but then I see the ghost of a smile. "Not really. We all do the best we can, when we can. I don't think there's any more to it than that."

I squeeze her hand once more, then let her go.

CHAPTER 93

ANNIE HAD NEVER felt awkward being the lone white person in a group of Black people. In fact, through working for Doris Avery, she had become quite accustomed to it. But after all that had happened over the past two days, being on the Bienville bluff was different. With each step she took, each new face she passed, she sensed perceptions changing around her. Suspicion was part of it, but there was something more, and it was universal. Here, she was the Other. In the dense crowd, each new set of eyes picked up her white face, darkened with tension, and only softened after they recognized Kendrick beside her. Were she not with him, she knew she might not feel safe on this ground.

After her father left, Kendrick had led her through the crowd, moving steadily toward the fence at the bluff's edge, talking to people as he had been all day. But this time, he held her hand tight as they walked, and frequently pulled her arm and shoulder against his as though to protect her. The general mood of the people was hard to read. There was anger in it, and bitterness, but grief was the glue that held them all together beneath the steel-gray clouds that had lingered since the morning. It had been since Mission Hill.

As they moved along the cyclone safety fence, the breeze off the river giving a welcome break from the collective body heat of the thousands around them, another pillar of fire leaped into the sky over Tensas Parish across the river. The flaming column was silent at first, like a candle being lit in the dark. Then a deep boom rolled over the bluff like a thunderclap, with an accompanying shockwave that buffeted the air in Annie's lungs as it knocked her back. The bluff crowd emitted a collective gasp of awe and terror, and hundreds pressed against the fence to see the new curiosity. Annie's chest filled with fear that the fence might give way and she'd be driven over the edge.

"We need to get you away from here!" Kendrick said, dragging her back through the crowd. "Nobody's thinking straight."

"What the hell is going *on*?"

"Somebody's gone to war with the money in this town."

"The money? Who is that, really?"

"The money, girl. The Man. The Poker Club, the corporations, groups like that. Somebody's declared war on them. Payback for Doc, maybe."

"God . . . the whole thing makes me sick. Like vomit-up-my-lunch sick."

"You didn't eat any lunch, did you?"

"Not really. What do we do about Frosty?"

"He'll find us. I'll text him on the way."

Kendrick set off through the crowd at a faster clip. An old memory flashed through Annie's mind from her childhood, before her father lost his leg, when he'd walked with that kind of speed and purpose.

Kendrick cut northeast across the park, taking a long diagonal toward the Cages' town house. Annie clung to his hand, but even though she took long strides, she was essentially being pulled along. She looked left and right as they walked, trying to do Frosty's job for him. But if she was honest with herself, she had no way to pick a threat out of this crowd. As fast as they steamed past her, most of the young men registered like matching pieces of a set, and the women only slightly less so.

She didn't see the white man until it was too late.

The tanned face was dark and mostly concealed under a baseball cap, and it passed before she even realized something was wrong. Her first hint was a hitch in Kendrick's stride. Then he stumbled, caught himself, grabbed his side with both hands, and fell flat on his face. Annie screamed and looked behind her, but the baseball cap had already vanished. She had a momentary impression of a bald skull lighter than those around it, but then she was whirling again, back to Kendrick, who had been rolled over by kneeling members of the crowd. Dark blood had already soaked the lower left quarter of his T-shirt, and when a man slid the cotton up his stomach, she saw the ugly mouth of a knife wound in his side.

"They shanked him!" said the man leaning over him. "We need an ambulance!"

Annie felt faint as dark blood pulsed from Kendrick's wound. Wobbling on her feet, she realized that the slit looked just like the prison stabbings she'd become accustomed to while working for Doris Avery. As two men passed each other in the crowded prison yard, one would knife the other without even looking at his victim, using whatever homemade weapon he'd crafted for the killing. A dozen people around her had already called 911, but Annie called anyway, knowing from experience that her white voice might be the one that pushed the dispatcher to do the right thing without delay.

As she waited, helpless tears streaming down her face, she felt Kendrick grope for her hand with a childlike desire for reassurance. Without thought she lay her head flat against his chest and hugged him tight.

"I'm here," she told him. "The ambulance is coming. You're going to be fine."

But what she thought was, *Don't die. Please don't die . . .*

I'VE BEEN DRIVING the backroads of Tensas Parish, my eyes peeled for Ray Ransom's burnt orange pickup, when Annie calls me again. I figure she's going to plead with me to come back to the bluff with her and Kendrick, so I start to ignore the phone. Finding a way to keep Ray Ransom from putting himself back in prison seems far more important. But after five rings, something makes me pick up the call. I'm glad I did, because Annie sounds panicked.

"Hey, boo, take it easy! What's happened?"

"Kendrick's been stabbed!"

I sit up in my seat with a jerk. "By who?"

"I think it was a skinhead. PSP, maybe? I was right there, but I didn't see anything until it was too late. It happened in the crowd on the bluff."

"What's his condition?"

"They're stabilizing him now. There was a lot of blood, but I think he's going to be okay."

"Where are you? The ER?"

"Yes. Bienville General. He got the same doctor who worked on me and Andrew. Berg."

"Good. Are you going to be there awhile?"

"We should, but Kendrick keeps saying he needs to get back to the bluff. He's got that speech, remember?"

"He can't do that now! Can he?"

"I don't think so. But you know there's no stopping him from trying."

"That's probably why they stabbed him. Only way to keep him quiet."

"He claims he's going into that amphitheater to speak at five-thirty tonight, no matter what."

"We'll see about that. Have you heard anything from Ray?"

"Ray Ransom? No. But I'll tell you something crazy. It looked like Kuwait across the river when we left the bluff."

"I heard somebody blew up another oil well. When you're finished at the hospital, are y'all going back to the town house?"

"That's what I'll push for. Dad, have you seen the news from Tennessee?"

"No. What's happened now?"

"The State Police just carried out what they're calling a 'decapitation' raid at Shiloh Military Park. Some of the Tennessee marchers managed to sneak a heavy truck in and were threatening to pull down parts of the *Defeated Victory* monument with a winch. At least one leader was killed, and several more wounded. All Black, of course. It sounds like chaos up there, but it really makes me worry what the Mississippi State Police might do on the bluff tonight."

"You're right to worry. But focus on Kendrick now. Don't borrow trouble."

"Okay. Please come home as soon as you can!"

"I will. Be careful."

I'm thankful that I brought my AR-15 along in its soft case, plus sixty rounds of ammunition. With the situation deteriorating downtown, getting back to the bluff could take me through some very dangerous situations.

Without a clear idea of what to do next, I decide to try direct action. I call the cell number of Ray's wife, Lashanna Ransom. The LPN answers after about seven rings, which tells me that she almost didn't answer at all.

"Hello?" she says in a taut voice.

"Mrs. Ransom, this is Penn Cage. Please don't hang up. I know you're probably close to losing it right now, and I don't blame you. I'm calling because I'm worried that Ray's put himself into a bad situation. Really bad. He's upset about Doc's death, and I'm worried he's"—I decide not to mention the vandalism specifically—"taking risks that could send him back to prison. I can't imagine any kind of situation in which you would want that, so I've called to ask you to help me reach him—to help me try to talk some sense into him."

"He's not answering your calls?"

"No, ma'am. And that's a first. Is there anything you can do to help me reach him?"

The silence that follows my plea drags without relief. A couple of times I think I'm hearing a woman cry softly, but I'm not sure.

"Lashanna?" I say into the void.

"I can't," says a tiny voice I can barely associate with the big woman I remember from World Famous Barbecue and our "task force" party at Pencarrow.

"You can trust me, Lashanna. Look, I'm not just worried about Ray going back to prison, which would be bad enough. If he's got anything to do with the sheriff's house burning, or torching these oil wells, he could hurt himself. He could blow himself up."

"He won't do that," says the voice. "Ray knows what he's doing 'round stuff like that. But . . . I don't want him taken back to prison."

So it's prison that terrifies her. "Lashanna, that is a real possibility. That's why . . . I'm begging you, ma'am. Help me help your husband."

The silence in my phone is vast, and filled with fear. Finally she says, "They've already got him, if they want him. The sheriff's brother come by here with some pictures from a security camera at the Matheson Lumber Mill. It caught him and three boys setting some wood on fire last night, down on the river."

"Oh, no. Does Ray know this?"

"Not from me. If he did . . . he might get self-destructive in what he's doing."

"Lashanna—"

"I can't do it, Mr. Cage. You're a nice man, but I can't betray my husband. Thank you for calling, though."

And with that she is gone.

Staring over the muddy Louisiana crop rows, seeing a gray wall of rain in the distance, I wonder, *Where is Ray now? What's his next target? What about Black Oak Plantation? The ancestral land of the Barlow who caused the suicide of his ancestor, Doby? The present Shot Barlow owns two oil wells . . . and Ray could burn them. But those would be defended . . .*

There are simply too many potential targets.

If I'm to have any success finding Ray, I need to convince his wife to tell me what she knows. And if my legal career is any indicator, I'm likely to do better in person than on the phone. In my rearview mirror, the empty fields falling behind me look barren and hopeless. With an ache in my belly, and a scream of pain from my broken ribs, I gun the Audi, heading back east toward the great river.

It's time to get back to Mississippi, the true front line of this war.

CHAPTER 94

ONCE I GOT inside Lashanna Ransom's house, it took all of twelve minutes to break her resolve to stay silent. I don't take pride in that. A woman terrified that her husband will be returned to Parchman prison for the brief remainder of his life—or worse, be killed by police—isn't the most difficult of interrogation subjects. While the television ran continuous coverage of the racial violence in Memphis and Shiloh Military Park, I reassured her as best I could about Ray's odds of making it through the day and night. But in my own mind, I was far from at peace. Driving away from her house, I recalled what she said when I lied and told her that, worst case, Ray might have to do a couple of years in jail, if he were caught.

"He won't go back to prison," she said, breaking down. "He'll make them kill him first."

I wasted twenty minutes checking out two possible targets Lashanna had mentioned, one a warehouse owned by a group of investors that includes Wyatt Cash and Shot Barlow. But I saw no sign of any intruders there. The other was a fuel distribution company, and it too seemed deserted, as well as too close to a neighborhood to risk arson.

The third possible target on her list has brought me out Cemetery Road, past Bienville's famous graveyard, to a familiar spot where two pumping units stand about forty yards off the road, slowly pulling crude oil from rich sands beneath Bienville's high ground. As I turn into the dirt access road, my cell phone rings. The caller is Sophie Dufort. Braking to a stop, I answer.

"What do you need, Sophie?"

"I have a forensic question. You worked a lot of murder cases in Houston, right? As a prosecutor."

"Sure. But I'm pretty busy right this minute."

"Just one question. What does lime do to bodies?"

"Quicklime?"

"Uh . . . yeah. I think so."

A rush of memories comes flooding into my mind. "Actually, it doesn't do what most people think it does."

"Which is what?"

"Dissolve them. Bones, in particular."

"Really?"

"Yeah. I actually convicted a killer who thought he had destroyed a corpse by covering it with lime. That idea came from the long history in popular fiction. It dates back to the eighteenth century, at least. It's *lye* that will dissolve a body. Mexican drug cartels still use lye, in fact. All the time. But quicklime actually *preserves* bones. For a good while, anyway."

"Are you serious?"

Rolling slowly forward down two muddy ruts, I spy the ass-end of Ray Ransom's orange pickup truck peeking out of the underbrush to my right.

"Yes. Now I have to go. And take some advice from me. Don't come into town this evening if you can avoid it."

"I don't plan to. Thanks."

Before driving the length of the access road, I shift my AR-15 from the floor to the front seat. Then I drive through six-foot-tall weeds until I come to the turnaround that the operator parks in while he checks the well.

I see no sign of more vehicles. Nor do I see any people, not even in the shadows under the volunteer trees that grow thickly on the hill bordering the city cemetery. But just as I'm about to swing my wheel left and pull out again, I catch sight of a bright white go-cup on the dirt under the trees. It's classic white Styrofoam, and it looks too fresh to have been here more than a couple of hours.

Parking and locking my car, I get out and walk to the edge of the trees with my AR. (I'm not going to leave it here, where any kid could bust in and decide to play *Call of Duty* with live rounds.) Under the trees I see a small path that leads alongside the two-inch pipe that runs to what must be a nearby tank battery. Every well has at least one storage tank, for holding crude oil until it can be picked up by truck—usually once per month—and sold. As I follow the path, I unzip my gun case and take out the AR-15, checking that all is in order.

The operator's path rises gently for about a hundred feet, then begins falling again. The woods get deeper as I walk, but then I hit the stink of old crude, and soon I come into a clearing, where a black-walled tank the size of a small convenience store stands in the middle of an earthen fire berm about three feet high. Inside this firewall I see Ray Ransom's broad back and leg muscles flexing as he crouches by the side of the tank, his focus about a foot off the ground.

"Ray!" I call, not even hesitating.

He doesn't jump like a startled deer, but he goes still, which tells me that Lashanna must have called to warn him I might be coming.

"What are you doing, Ray?"

"What's it look like?" he asks, not changing position. "Opening this bull valve. Letting out some crude. With the valves on top of the tank open and venting, gas from the oil inside starts filling the air. Once I get a little lake of oil down here, I can walk away and toss in a cigarette. I'll feel a hot wind hit my back when it catches, and by the time I make my truck, the gas will go in a big WHOOSH! And sometime before I get to my house, I'll hear this tank go. That'll sound like a napalm bomb from a B-52 hitting the ground."

The voice coming from the crouching man has very little in common with the warm bass I'm accustomed to hearing from Doc's old friend. "Ray . . . you don't need to blow up this well. If you keep this up, you're going to bring down a response that will crush you and maybe everybody else on that bluff."

His hands go back to working at the valve. "Maybe that's what has to happen before anything changes. You think about that? It's how the Jews ran the British out of Palestine."

"We don't live in Palestine. Listen, Kendrick is going to speak at five-thirty tonight. Even though he got stabbed."

"I heard that rumor. What makes you think that young brother's gonna be preaching your sermon instead of mine?"

It hadn't occurred to me that Kendrick might have made a Damascene conversion to violent resistance, or that he might be in contact with Ray.

Ray stands erect, wipes his hands on his jeans, then turns to me. At the level of his lower calves, a thick, viscous stream of crude oil begins pouring onto the earth. Left alone, it will create a flammable lake within the deep berm in minutes.

"They killed Doc," he says, his eyes hard beneath the bill of his cap. "Murdered him. Now they've dissolved the city. Yeah, I got word. And next they'll kill Kendrick, to shut him up. Or they'll frame him for the antebellum fires and drop him in a hole in Parchman, the way they did me, and my friend Geronimo Pratt." Ray looks down at his hands. "You ever hear of Geronimo Pratt?"

"Of course. I've worked cases like Geronimo's throughout my career. I think you're forgetting my history, Ray."

He looks back at me in silence for a bit, but then he nods. "You're right. I should have known you'd know about Geronimo. You're a good man, Penn. You've done some good things for us. You fought our enemies. But in the end, brother . . . you're still white. And maybe that's something you can't truly see past, or see out of."

Ray's words upset me, but they're also strangely familiar. Somebody said those same things only days ago. *Who?* Bobby White? No . . . Sheriff Buck

Tarlton. The first time I met him in his office. *In the end, you're white*, he told me. *In the end, you're going to have to choose a side. And they don't want you on their side. Not really.*

"I'm not your enemy, Ray."

"Are you sure?" He gives me a sort of squinting smile, as though he's weighing up factors. "You see us as friends. And we are, up to a point. But where is that point? When you went to my house to talk to Lashanna, did you realize you'd never been there before today? Did you think about that?"

"I did," I answer truthfully. What I don't say is how shocked I was at how modestly Ray and his wife live. It's something people like me just don't think about. In the city of Bienville, Ray seems a larger-than-life figure, but in truth he's a convict who served most of his life in prison, and his wife is a licensed practical nurse. I probably pay Andrew McKinney more for restoring Pencarrow than Ray and his wife live on every year.

"You hit that first oil well yesterday, didn't you?" I guess. "You burned the Matheson lumberyard too, just like Tarlton says. You burned his house down and hit his shooting range as well. All these targets . . . you've declared war on the Poker Club."

His half smile is all the answer I need.

"Tell me the truth, Ray. Why are you doing this? As an SOS? To try to draw the attention of Washington, D.C.? I've told you, the president's not going to invoke the Insurrection Act to bring U.S. troops into conflict with U.S. domestic law enforcement. So be straight with yourself. Are you just reveling in the satisfaction of hitting back at the people you hate—the people who killed Doc? Who owns this well, anyway?"

"Claude Buckman, Junior. And his daddy. The big man at the Bienville Southern Bank."

"The head of the Poker Club. Is that all you're doing? Trying to hit those guys in their pocketbooks? You're willing to risk burning the north end of Bienville to do that?"

"What if I am? Those sons of bitches go through life thinking they're invincible. Untouchable."

"Those guys won't even *feel* losses like this! But it hurts the town bad. It hurts your cause as well. It's going to put you back in Parchman. Kendrick, too, if you draw him into this."

Anger and frustration twist Ray's mouth. "That's what I mean when I say you can't see past being white! This kind of action scares you way down deep. To a man raised like you, this is chaos—civil disorder. It's the world you know coming unraveled. But to me? It's just the *next phase*, brother.

It's where we're at. Where we've been for a while, but just didn't see it. Buckman and his kind have been at war with us forever. This is just me facing that and responding in kind. Actually, it ain't even what they call *proportional response*. Because Doc is *dead*. Now and forever."

"I know that."

"Well . . . maybe this response is what separates who's on which side. Shirts and skins, brother. Because the truth is, people on my side got nothing to lose. We the skins. We don't own shit. We got nothing they can take but our rights and our bodies. We're like the 'Cong that way, or the Taliban. But Buckman and the others? Blake Donnelly? They *own* things. Hell, Buckman alone owns four houses in different parts of the country! There's more than fifty oil wells in this county alone, and more across the river. There's over a hundred around Natchez, and Dufort's in a lot of those. They got *tons* of shit to lose! And don't even get me started on Old Man Dufort. That motherfucker owns houses in *Europe*!"

I flex my right arm, which has grown tight under the weight of my AR. "Come out of that pit, Ray. Come out from behind that fire wall. Let's talk for real."

He smiles strangely. "Man, we *been* talking for real. Maybe for the first time. What you doin' with that assault rifle?"

I look down at my AR-15 and shrug. "The bluff's spinning out of control. I figure it could be a free-fire zone by the time I get back."

"Are you pointing that gun at me?"

"Hell, no! Are you kidding?"

Before Ray can reply, I hear a creak of metal above me, and then two young Black men step up to the edge of the tank lid. Both wear do-rags, and one holds a semiautomatic pistol loosely in his right hand. Their eyes look far less friendly or charitable than Ray's.

"Yo, brah," says the one with the gun. "You need to get away from here and let us finish our business."

Why didn't I guess there were men up top? Ray told me the gas had to be vented in order for the oil in the tank to catch and blow. I drop the AR-15 and hold up my hands. "Don't do this, Ray."

"Oh, we're doin' it," says the guy above me. "We blowing this mother-fucker to the moon."

My heartbeat kicks into high gear. Trying not to show fear, I lower my left hand and look at my watch. "Give me an hour, Ray. Maybe an hour and fifteen minutes. Let Kendrick talk to the people waiting for him. Let's let the younger people guide us."

Ray seems not to hear me. He's watching the thick black oil fill the fire pit around him.

"Leave one of these guys here," I suggest. "But come with me to hear Kendrick speak. The crowd is massive. Everybody's waiting. If nothing changes after Kendrick talks—if we don't see a good sign—then you can call here and give the order to blow this well to hell and gone."

Ransom finally looks up at me, but I can't read anything behind his dark eyes. And in the two pairs of eyes fifteen feet above me, all I see is suspicion and hatred.

"You don't know what you're up against," Ray says. "Why you think they dissolved the city? They're gonna do things you haven't even imagined yet. Doc felt it coming. But you didn't. You told him don't worry. Now here we are. And worse is coming, mark my words. I'm just letting those devils know they're gonna pay for every soul they take."

My cell phone pings in my pocket. With a slow, careful motion, I withdraw it and find a message from Bobby White. It reads: *I heard Kendrick Washington got stabbed by a skinhead. Things are getting serious. We need KW to address the black community before things spin completely out of control. You and I should talk.*

After one glance at Ray, I reply, *Agreed. My town house, 10 minutes.*

"Reporting to your big-boss man?" Ray asks in a sarcastic voice.

"No, Ray, I'm trying to do what Doc would have wanted us both to do. Keep the peace."

Ray's dark features narrow in pain and grief. "Doc's gone, Penn. And nobody round here can replace him."

"That might be true. Just please listen to me. Wherever you go from here, keep your head down. They've got photos of you guys setting fire to the Matheson lumber mill. Lashanna told me not to tell you. but there's no point in lying now. Anytime they want, they can put out a felony APB on you. I don't know why they haven't yet, but rest assured, they do."

Ray Ransom looks back at me with something close to gratitude. Then he nods once and turns back to his potentially lethal work.

CHAPTER 95

I DON'T KNOW where Bobby White was when he texted me, but he was waiting at my house when I arrived. After an awkward few seconds where I manage not to shake hands with him, I lead him into the kitchen, and he chooses a Diet Mountain Dew from the refrigerator.

"So you made it home all right last night?" he asks.

"Mm-hm."

"You were limping pretty bad. And you sounded like you could hardly breathe."

"Barlow's sentry broke a couple of my ribs. My bone density's pretty low."

"Shit. I know even normal ribs can hurt bad."

"Did I tell you last night that I got some photos of you and Barlow together?"

Bobby chuckled. "No. You hoping to make some money from TMZ?"

I don't comment, and he asks nothing further about the pictures, which frankly amazes me. Still, there's no way he'll leave this house without asking me to delete them.

"Talk about damaging photos," he said. "How about that shot of the two Black cops attacking the National Guard girl? I think it's already been seen more than the Kent State photo from the seventies."

"Somebody'll get a Pulitzer off that, even though it misrepresents the hell out of what was really happening."

After pouring myself one of Nadine's cold-brew coffees, I clumsily lead Bobby upstairs to the terrace where Doc and Ray and I used to hold our campaign breakfasts. Bobby settles into a wrought-iron chair at an off angle, where he can turn and address me if he wishes, while his main gaze surveys the crowded bluff and Confederate Memorial Park below us.

"You've got a hell of a view of this National Guard exercise," he says with a chuckle. "Exercise in futility. But I guess that's all our governor knows to do in a crisis, right? Fire up his base."

"You seem calmer than you did in your text."

"I heard Kendrick means to address the bluff crowd at five-thirty in spite of his wound, which can only be a good thing. They're blasting it over social media like the Second Coming."

Bobby could have called and told me this, and saved himself a trip. Yet here he sits, cutting his eyes at me like a man waiting for a signal to commence combat.

"Somebody sent me an interesting text about you earlier today, Bobby. I'd like to know what you think about it."

"What does it say?"

Taking out my iPhone, I forward him the first message, the one about him being a monster. The following text—with links to the articles about the two killings—I keep to myself for the time being.

Bobby reads the message with no discernible reaction.

"No comment?"

"I've all but announced that I'm running for president," he replies. "I'm now one of the most famous people in the world. Some people love me, others hate me. And that's only going to get worse."

"I got the feeling this person knows you, Bobby."

He looks back at me with mild curiosity. "You haven't asked the obvious question."

"Which is?"

"Am I gay?"

I give this a few seconds, but then I decide to push ahead. "Are you?"

"Does it matter?"

"Not to me. But if you are, and you're lying about it . . . then yes, I'd say it matters. Given that you're running for president."

"What if I say yes on this terrace, but deny it later?"

Is he telling me he's gay? "Why would you do that?"

"Because America's not ready to elect a gay president."

"We might be, if he's the guy who took out Abu Nasir."

Bobby gives me a wistful smile. "If only, brother."

"Bobby . . . I'm going to ask you something personal. How many people have you killed?"

He looks genuinely surprised by the question. "That's my business, isn't it?"

"If they were all in the line of duty, I'd agree. But I'm not sure that's the case."

Bobby's mind must be moving at warp speed, but his face remains impassive. Is this the reaction of an innocent man? Wouldn't an innocent man laugh at the absurdity of my question? Or become indignant? To sit there coolly, unmoved as a robot, does not strike me as normal. On the other hand, what's the normal affect of a man who has killed people in war? And not from two hundred yards away with a rifle, but up close, with a knife or even his bare hands? Most men will never know what that feels like. If I were questioning my father about the Chinese he killed in Korea, how would he react? I have no idea. I never asked him, and he never volunteered any information.

"You've killed before," he says finally. "Outside the law, by any definition. You want to give me the lowdown on how it affected you?"

The last moments of some of the Knox family flash through my brain. "Not especially."

Bobby rolls his fingertips on his bulging right thigh, which is contained in navy golfing slacks that probably cost as much as a business suit. "I get the feeling you're not telling me everything you know. Or suspect."

"This has been a traumatic week. Going right back to Mission Hill. And there you were a hero, no question. You saved my daughter's life. So it's hard for me to see you as anything *but* a hero. That said, you're not like anybody I've ever known. And since Mission Hill, some pretty upsetting things have happened in this town."

"Who do you think I killed, Penn? Doc?"

"I didn't say that."

"The church deacons?"

"Didn't say that, either."

"Well, who's left? Is somebody else dead?"

I consider bringing up General Paul Beckley, because Bobby can't be expecting to hear that name from me. But if I reveal that knowledge, then he might easily guess—or know—the source of my information.

"Charlot Dufort is dead," I say flatly.

Bobby blinks a few times, then shakes his head. "I didn't know that. I really hate to hear it."

"Do you?"

"I was pretty close to Charlot at one time. We roomed together for a year in college."

"And Charlot was gay. How close were you two?"

Bobby's stare is hard and flat, the gaze of a machine gunner waiting to fire. "Are you asking whether I fucked him?"

"Did you?"

This isn't the kind of conversation I was expecting as I drove over here, but something about Bobby's manner makes me think I need to push him, regardless of risk.

"No," Bobby replies, dropping his hand on his knee. "Are we done, counselor?"

"Where were you last night?" I press. "Before you went visiting your militia buddies?"

Bobby looks back with casual defiance. "None of your business, Penn. You're not a cop. You're not even a mayor anymore."

"Hell, I'm not even the city attorney. I'm nobody. But I've got a queasy feeling about the way things have been going since you came back to town. And I think the fact that you saved Annie's life has given me a blind spot where you're concerned."

"Penn, I'm running for president. I don't give two shits what happens in this little burg."

"I don't believe you. I think what happens in your hometown means a lot to you. It would to any candidate. It's part of your myth. Right? Your origin story. You don't want anybody running around telling the world you're queer, either. Especially somebody who might actually know."

"You really bought into that text message, didn't you? You really believe I'm a *monster*? Surely you received harassment like that when you were mayor?"

"I got a few threats, sure. But nothing like that."

"Maybe you're just lucky."

Again I feel the impulse to mention the general murdered in the D.C. cemetery. But even as I consider it . . . it strikes me that, if I do, I might not walk out of this house alive again. An irrational conclusion, perhaps, but subjectively it feels as real as anything I've experienced in a while. Instead, I take a different tack, hoping to provoke Bobby into a response that might betray his true state of mind.

"If I hadn't discovered something else a bit unsettling this morning, I might not have interrogated you like this. But I was going back through the motion alerts on my Ring cameras from Edelweiss—I'd used them to monitor Mom and Annie in their sickbeds—and I came across a recording of you speaking to Annie while she was half-sedated on OxyContin."

For the first time I see surprise in Bobby's eyes.

"Didn't know there was a camera in there, did you? Well, anyway, I thought it was a pretty odd conversation, in that you tell her you don't want to run for president, but you have to. Like you have no choice."

Bobby nods slowly. "Mind if I hear that conversation?"

Picking up my iPhone, I access the digital file, hit PLAY, and lay it on the wrought-iron table. Bobby's face remains impassive as he listens to himself with Annie, and then the conversation fades to silence.

"Well?" I prompt. "Did that sound normal to you?"

"What do you mean?"

"What did you mean, you *have* to run for president? That some fateful hour is approaching and you have no choice but to be leading America if you're going to, hell, I don't know . . . save the world?"

Bobby glances over the rail at the mostly Black protesters down in Confederate Memorial Park. "I meant just what I told her, Penn. Just what you heard."

"Which is?"

"Are you familiar with the three-body problem?"

"Ahhh . . . Some iterations of it, I guess. In astronomy. Atomic structure. Sibling rivalry. I think it's being studied as regards nuclear weapons development in China. It has to do with leaps in levels of complexity between two and three independent actors."

"God, it's a nice change to talk to someone with a brain. Well . . . I'm running for president because of what I see as an existential imperative. We, as in the United States, are fast approaching a choke point in history. We've come to them before, and we will again. As a historian, I've noted that we've struck one every eighty-two years. But we've never faced one with a nuclear arsenal. I believe that if I'm not president in 2027, we may—in fact, will—cease to exist as a world power."

I try to hide my shock as he lays out this grandiose assertion. "I see. Well . . . what makes you think that, Bobby?"

"I've had a vision. A revelation, I suppose. Perhaps not much different than the encounter you had with your bear. Only this vision has been exactly the same every time, without variation, and it's becoming more and more frequent."

"What sort of vision?"

"An apocalyptic one. It takes place in an elevator, on a seemingly endless downward ride. It reminds me of a scene from the old movie *Fail Safe*, in which Larry Hagman—the Russian translator—is descending to an underground command post with the president—Henry Fonda. But in my vision, *I'm* the president, and we're minutes from making a decision that will decide the fate of the world."

"And when does this happen?"

"2027, I believe. I'm certain, in fact."

"So, during the next presidential term."

"Exactly."

"And you say these happen every . . . eighty-two years?"

"That's right."

His certainty about this particular number triggers a quiet alarm in my head. "For example?" I prompt him.

"The critical battles of our major wars. The existential turning points. Seventeen eighty-one, the Battle of Yorktown. Eighteen sixty-three, Gettysburg and Vicksburg—decided *on the same day*. And then of course 1945: Hiroshima."

The certainty in his voice is chilling. "Sooo . . . next comes 2027? What's the political situation then? The crisis, whatever?"

Bobby waves his hand. "I don't have time to get into the weeds on that. Suffice to say it's a three-body problem."

"Humor me."

Bobby takes a sip of his Mountain Dew. "Well, as I said, it's potentially apocalyptic. The venue is the Holy Land, of course. And this is a three-body problem in three different ways: political, religious, and racial."

"What are the countries?"

"Israel, Iran, China. The religions, obviously Judaism, Islam, and god-lessness. And the races: Semitic, Persian, and Asian."

"Sounds like a pretty complicated war you have brewing there."

Bobby nods. "We're well on our way toward it now, though we don't seem to know it."

"How so?"

"Simple. Israel under Netanyahu is leaning ever further to the right, almost to fascism in some ways. They're supposedly the most vigilant nation in the world. But I'm not so sure. It's easy to get complacent. Iran is pouring resources into Hamas and Hezbollah, and they mean business. Israel, of course, possesses more than four hundred nuclear weapons as of today. And China has announced its intention to double its nuclear arsenal, as well as to modernize it."

"But Iran has no bombs, as of yet."

"None you know of. In fact, their enrichment activities have for many years now been a cover. By 2027 they'll possess a considerable seaborne nuclear arsenal—in the form of nuclear drones, not subs—and they will put it into the field. This, Israel will not tolerate, since a single Iranian nuke could render the entire nation uninhabitable for a thousand years."

I can't find a flaw in any of Bobby's statements so far, other than a lack of proof of his assertions about Iran. "So what does this lead you to?"

"My vision. In 2027, Israel's leader will become convinced that Iran is fielding its nuclear arsenal. Israel will ask us to destroy that arsenal for them, using our submarines and ASW aircraft. If we refuse, Israel will attempt to do it alone. There our scenario becomes a true three-body problem. China—wishing to be seen as taking the moral high ground—announces that if we attack Iran, it will seize and hold Taiwan, arguing that Iran has just as much right to self-defense as the Israelis. At that point, the best predictions of our experts are that, if we fulfill the Israelis' wish, we will set ourselves on the road to global nuclear war. At the very least, the U.S. president will have to disappoint our closest ally and religious cousin in the Middle East—Israel—while at worst, we might actually have to attack Israel to prevent them initiating Armageddon out of paranoia."

It takes me about twenty seconds to organize his hypothetical in my head, but it survives a quick water test. "So you're saying that—when this happens—you need to be the guy making the decision about our nukes? You'll be the president willing to act against Israel, regardless of the consequences."

Bobby gives me a sober nod. "If I'm not in that elevator, it'll be like Mickey Rourke in the one at the end of *Angel Heart*—an endless descent into hell."

To my surprise, a wave of dread rises from some dark place in my memory. "Okay. Well . . . Bobby, if this is what you believe, why don't you just run for president on a foreign policy platform? God knows you've got some cred in that area."

He chuckles at my naïveté. "Just go on TikTok and CNN and start telling people they should vote for me because I can predict the future?"

I hear my own laughter on the terrace. "Okay. Probably not the best idea."

"Penn, to me the culture war crap that decides elections is the most absurd and useless waste of time I can imagine. But that seems to be all the voters care about. And for some reason, I'm a natural at it. So why not win this election on my home field, so to speak? Once I'm in the Oval, I can do what I need to do."

I find myself nodding at this. "How authentic is your culture war stuff, Bobby? Do you really believe what you've been putting out there?"

The expression that comes back to me is something like a smile, but one without the usual emotion of a smile powering it. "What do you want from me, Penn? *The World According to Bobby White*?"

"I might."

"Kill your cell phone, then. We'll have a frank conversation. Just two old Mississippi boys."

"Mississippi white boys," I say, switching off my iPhone. I'd like nothing better than to hear Bobby White unplugged, being truly honest about his politics, even if I can't record it. "There you go." I show him my blank screen. "No mics. Talk away."

"Toss it here."

I do, and his sole hand snatches it out of the air like an eagle's talon. After briefly checking the device, he tosses it back. "You'll reciprocate in kind? Be completely honest about your feelings on race, et cetera?"

"I'll try."

He looks skeptical. "I guess that'll have to be good enough." Bobby gets up and leans back against the terrace rail, facing me directly. "Fire away, Mayor."

"Are you really pro-choice on abortion, the way that ad portrayed you?"

The ghost of a real smile touches his lips. "That's the position I'll be supporting. Am I for abortion itself? Not for white women, no."

He sees his answer jars me. "The major industrialized nations of the world are in deep birth-rate depressions. China, Europe, the U.S. We need more babies—a lot more—and I'd prefer they be white ones. With good support networks. But since I can't pass a law banning abortion only for white women, the best I can do with that issue is use it to win the White House."

"You probably couldn't say anything more racist than that."

Bobby smiles strangely. "Oh, I could. Because here's the thing: I *am* racist. Most people are, at bottom. But let's not get hung up on that. We could be here all day. Pick another subject, and I'll still blow your mind."

He sounds like an adolescent anticipating an intense video game. "Okay. Ah . . . as president, how would you deal with our mass-incarceration problem?"

Bobby looks disappointed. "That's still race. But I'll answer. If elected, it's my intention to establish a new penalty for certain classes of felonies. I'll also use it on people currently serving sentences for violent crimes."

"The firing squad?" I ask, only half joking.

Bobby laughs. "Nothing that final. No, I'm talking about banishment."

"*Banishment?* You mean like deportation?"

"Exactly. Some Latin American governments have built ultramodern Supermax prisons that hold tens of thousands of inmates. I'm going to contract with those countries—probably some African ones as well—to house our violent prisoners there."

"You're serious?"

"Absolutely. The gangbangers of Chicago better start brushing up on their Spanish. And those who stay in U.S. prisons won't be spending their days playing basketball or pumping iron in the yard. Our prisons will become factories for unskilled labor. New rule number one: In Bobby White's America, *everybody works*."

"People will argue that's cruel and unusual punishment."

"And the present Supreme Court will laugh in their faces. Free citizens in America work. How can it be 'cruel and unusual' to make convicts do the same?"

"Have you said anything about these ideas on your radio show?"

"Of course not." Bobby grins. "I'm no fool." He makes a fist and flexes his arm. "Damn, it feels good to get this out!"

"When do you mean to tell the American public about your banishment plan?"

"The day after I'm elected, of course. My first hundred days are going to be pretty hectic."

"Any other radical policy changes in mind? That would stun the country, I mean?"

Another boyish grin lights his handsome face. "I mean to reinstate the draft. Two years for everybody, male or female. Even the gender-confused."

This sets me back several seconds. "You mean compulsory *national service*, right? Like the Peace Corps? Or the WPA under Roosevelt?"

"Nope. Army, navy, air force, marines. Coast guard."

"You're crazy, Bobby. The American people won't go for that."

"Think not? As of one month ago, according to Gallup, forty-nine percent of Americans support a return to the draft."

That statistic leaves me gobsmacked. "So why aren't you talking about this? Why aren't you putting these points in your TikTok videos?"

"Because if I did, I might not win the general election."

"Okay. But once you're in the Oval Office, you'll just . . . do whatever you want?"

"Why not? Five years ago my plans would have been impossible. But with the Supreme Court we have now, most of it's a lock."

This conversation is not going the way I expected. "Tell me more about your first hundred days."

"Energy self-sufficiency is priority one."

"Keep throwing money to the oil companies?"

"Nope. 'All Nuclear, All the Time.' That's my motto. I've already had experts divide the nation into energy zones. I'll begin construction of one hundred high-efficiency reactors during my first year in office. I don't have time to worry about what the goddamn Saudis are doing while I work on my main agenda."

"A *hundred* nuclear reactors?"

"One hundred and forty, actually. But we'll start with a hundred. We're sitting in zone seventy-four now."

The specifics of his plans give me an eerie sense of discomfort. "What about the Defense Department?"

"Russia and China have already fielded hypersonic missiles, so we have to do the same. But they're only a stopgap. My dream is the same as President Reagan's: space-based laser defense."

"Star Wars?"

"It's the only thing that can truly keep us safe from the Chinese."

"How are you going to pay for all this?"

"Easy. *Taxes.*"

Again he's taken me by surprise. "You're going to *raise* taxes?"

"No. I'm going to *collect* taxes. But there'll be a lot of new names on my collection list. It'll include churches, billionaires, and major corporations like Apple."

"You sound like a progressive Democrat."

"I sound like a president who means to *build* Star Wars, not just talk about it. Don't even get me started on AI and cybersecurity. Under my administration, the U.S. will be known as *Fortress America*. Hackers who violate it will experience the full wrath of the U.S. national security machine."

"What does that mean exactly?"

"Maybe we freeze your bank accounts. If you're out of our physical reach, we might have the NSA empty them. Last resort, you'll get a visit from a half dozen guys like me. Delta operators. Or DEVGRU."

"Jesus, Bobby."

Again the strangely lighthearted laughter. "These are only my first-term policies! Wait till you hear my dream list. I'm going to open the damned borders."

"*What?*"

"You heard me. But only to children. Adults need not apply."

"I don't understand."

"Remember what I told you about the birth rate? *We need kids.* We *don't* need more adults. I'm going to establish a robust nationwide foster care system. We'll raise those immigrants to eighteen, put them in our military for two years, and after they get out, they'll be Americans."

"If they manage not to get banished or put in your Supermax prison system."

"Well, obviously. Anyway . . . I think you've pretty much got the picture."

"I'm worried I'm the only one who has. These are basically fascist policies. Hitler building the Autobahn and making the trains run on time.

What I *don't* get is where all this came from. You've had your radio show for, what, six years now?"

"Nine, brother. Get with it."

"And in all that time, you've never advocated these extreme positions. But suddenly you have this secret Christmas list of fascist policies you want to sneak into the Oval Office to implement?"

"I'm not sneaking anywhere. The voters are going to carry me in on their shoulders, and my policies with me."

His confidence is almost overwhelming. Had he not accomplished what he has already, I might think he was a mental patient. "Then why don't you tell the American people what you really hope to do?"

He answers as if talking to a five-year-old. "Because . . . I *might— not—win—the—general—election*. People want these policies, Penn, but they can't come out and admit it, any more than I can. Or not enough of them can."

I very much doubt that he's right . . . but I can't be sure. "How the hell did you come up with this scheme?"

"Can't you guess? Trump. Surely that should be obvious by now."

"How so?"

The prospect of discussing his likely opponent in the upcoming election brings a look of distaste to Bobby's handsome face. With a screech of metal he rotates his chair so that he can gaze off the balcony at the families of the protesters in the park below. Before he looks back, I slide my hand down and switch on my iPhone, then quickly set it to *Do Not Disturb*. Unsure how to be most discreet, I switch off the ringer, but before I can turn on the recording memo function, I sense Bobby turning back to me. I barely manage to slide the device beneath my thigh before he does.

"In 2016," he says, "after Trump was elected, I realized that America had declined to the point that we were willing to put a complete idiot in the White House. A con man with almost no objective qualifications for the office. Trump had obviously racist beliefs, criminal tendencies, serious problems with women, repeated business failures, no ethics whatsoever, no conscience, no remorse. He even despised the military. Yet white America, in its panic, wrapped their arms around the guy and rode him all the way into Washington. Even the *evangelicals* went with him. And why? Because he personified all their secret hopes and fears and prejudices. He gave them permission to be their real selves. Their worst selves. In essence, he was a living 'Fuck you' to everyone who ever made a rube feel stupid, or small, less than the next guy. *He still is.* He's the white O.J. Simpson, Penn. His supporters know he's guilty—of all of it—but they don't give a shit. That's not the point for them. Anyway, the myth of my grade-school years was finally true: anybody *could* become president! Anybody with sufficient fame, and the willingness to say and do anything necessary to win, that is."

Bobby turns and scans the bluff once more, from habit probably, but I dare not try to switch on the recorder before he looks back at me.

"But the idea that we would hand the nuclear codes to a fool who couldn't find Ukraine on a map," he goes on, "who worshipped Vladimir Putin . . . I could hardly grasp it. Like you and everybody else, I had to struggle to bury that reality deep enough to allow me to function."

The rationality of Bobby's account leaves me more curious than ever to struggle to hear what lies at the bottom of his revealed ambition.

"But what put me *here*, you want to know? On the verge of being on ballots of all fifty states as a third-party candidate? It was something I never sought: the public revelation that I killed Abu Nasir. That single deed hurled me into the political stratosphere, and I'm still ascending. That's when I started to feel the current of destiny. And *that's* when my visions began."

"Bobby, with all respect, you're clearly a rational and intelligent man. An attorney, historian, soldier, author. Self-aware. What makes you think this vision of yours was real? *Is* real. Not a medical hallucination?"

He takes a very deep breath and lets it out slowly. "I don't like confessional conversation, Penn. But I'm going to tell you something. Between the ages of seven and thirteen, I worked summers with my grandfather. In the Delta mostly: Louisiana, Mississippi, and Arkansas."

"Farming?"

"Nope. He was a traveling preacher. Itinerant, some call it. He'd guest preach in country churches, other times he'd do tent revivals. But the thing is . . . it was all a con. A long con. *Fleece the rubes*. It took me a while to figure it out, but by the time I was nine, I was part of the game. He had me doing things that you only see up in the mountains of Appalachia, to draw in the marks. Fooling with fire and poisons, talking in tongues— hell, even handling live snakes—after I'd milked them, of course. Copperheads and rattlesnakes I'd scooped out of the roadside ditches myself."

"Jesus, Bobby."

"You said it. Anyway, there's a point to this. Most times, I was faking it right to the hilt, just like Granddad wanted."

"Hang on. Is this the grandfather who fought in the Battle of the Bulge?"

Bobby smiled. "The very one, bubba. Life's strange, ain't it? Later on he was murdered for screwing another man's wife. But at this point he still had a while to live."

"Please go on. I'm sorry."

"All I meant to tell you is that most times, I was fully aware I was conning these folks. Handling these iced-down, milked pit vipers, or talking in tongues using stuff I'd copied from weak-brains I'd seen in other churches across the South." Bobby falls silent, as though looking deep within himself. "*But*—every so often, I would feel something different as I played those people. Something I can only describe as a spirit would take hold of me, and I would say and do things I had no idea were even within me. I mean it, man."

I lean forward, genuinely held by his candor and intensity. "What kind of spirit?"

He shakes his head, obviously mystified himself. "Sometimes . . . Penn, I wouldn't milk the snakes before the show. Service, whatever. I'd stand on that altar at the age of ten with a live rattlesnake crawling over me, one with enough venom to put me under the ground if it gave me a full dose on a strike."

"Did you ever get bit?"

"Oh, hell, yeah. More than once. But never one of those times. When it was real. In my trance or whatever."

A light chill goes through me, and I shudder. "What else did you do like that?"

"The glossolalia."

"Speaking in tongues?"

Bobby nods. "Most times I was just making up bullshit, like a drunk scat singer on a good roll. But man . . . a couple times, I heard myself goin' on like some sort of sanctified being, knowing that every note that escaped my throat was working on the people in the pews, moving them to come forward, tears in their eyes, wailing with the power of some ancient magic."

"Jesus. What are you telling me, Bobby?"

"I'm telling you—from the heart of a very young con man—that when my visions come, I have that same feeling I did on those rare times back then. That something infinitely bigger than I am has ahold of me, and I'd be a fool to ignore it."

I sit back in my chair, feeling strangely enervated. Mom's stolen pain meds must have kicked in, because the agony in my bruised stump is gone. "You keep saying you're certain about the time of this future crisis. How can you be? Is somebody in the elevator holding a newspaper or something?"

Bobby laughs. "Newspaper? Hell, nobody reads newspapers anymore. In 2027 they'll barely exist."

"Then how?"

"There are three military officers in the elevator in my vision. One is the commander of the U.S. Space Force. The fourth time I experienced the vision, I realized that his insignia—the one on his cap, and also his breast—didn't match the one in real life. The real one—now—shows a Delta symbol over the globe, in a field of stars with Polaris in the distance. But in my vision, *this* guy is wearing one that shows the bow of a whaling boat with a harpoon lying in it, point forward. And in the distance, you see something like a satellite amid a sea of stars, like a fleeing whale."

I nod slowly, taking this in. "And what have you made of that?"

"Well, it took me quite a while to uncover anything at all. But I finally discovered that the harpoon insignia is a new design that's set to go into use in 2027. And only a few people know that, Penn. I mean, *very* few."

While I reflect on this, a National Guard truck rolls loudly along Battery Row, and it's a blessing because only seconds later the phone beneath my thigh vibrates. Glancing down while Bobby's attention is diverted, I see a text from Annie that contains a video file. The message reads *PRIVATE, URGENT, READ ALONE.*

This time the chill that goes through me is like what I feel when I have the flu. "Bobby, do you mind if I hit the head for a minute? I'm having some stomach problems from my pain meds."

He waves his head as if he couldn't care less. "Hell, no, do what you need to. I've got a lot of emails to return. You need any help standing up?"

"I think I can make it."

As I struggle to my feet, I notice him watching me with genuine concern.

"Did I freak you out with that story?" he asks.

"Southern Gothic for sure, bro."

He nods with a strange sort of pride. "My granddad was a weird son of a bitch. A lot of those old guys were. Charles Dufort's right up there with 'em, I'm starting to think."

I laugh knowingly. "I'm with you on that. I'll be right back."

CHAPTER 96

I'M SITTING ON the toilet off my upstairs bedroom, just two doors away from Bobby White, watching a video file sent by my daughter, whose covering text read:

> *Saw Bobby White's vehicle at the town house. Looks like you on terrace with him? You need to see this. Drone footage shot by Mississippi Free Press reporter last night during the "looting" that spawned the viral photos that hurt us so bad. Look at the pre-roll as the drone flies past the Donnelly Oil tower. Think about "The Fugitive" movie while you watch. You'll see what I mean. Sitting up there like Jerry Jones in his fucking skybox at a Cowboys game. WTF, Dad? I feel like we've been miles behind events all week long. Get back to me when you can.*

Rubbing my gritty eyes, I look down at my phone screen. In the pools of streetlights I see only the endless crowd beneath the buildings facing Battery Row and the river. From the camera's POV I realize the little aircraft must be over the Mississippi River, boring slowly in toward Bienville's bluff. As the drone moves closer to the Donnelly Oil Building, I discern several figures standing on its penthouse terrace. Soon I recognize faces: Wyatt Cash, the outdoor equipment millionaire; Tommy Russo, who owns the Sun King casino; Claude Buckman, Junior, the old banker's son. Even Dixie Donnelly, latest wife of Blake, king of the local oil magnates.

What did Annie tell me? "Think about *The Fugitive* . . ."

Staring at the little group, I realize there's another figure on the terrace, and maybe two. The drone lurches in midair, then continues on toward Confederate Memorial Park. But as it does, I see what appears to be a one-armed man standing behind Russo and Dixie Donnelly. His shoulder is what gives him away.

"Bobby White," I say softly.

My stomach rolls, and the back of my neck tingles with a sort of reverse premonition, as though I should have realized something long before now, when it's too late to use the knowledge. The thing is, I think, was he up there stage-managing every move right up to the viral photos of the attack on the female Guardsman? Or was he doing what he would later tell me he was doing at the Barlow bunker? Working to figure out who might be behind the burning of the antebellum mansions?

The strangest thing of all is that the man himself is sitting a few feet away on my terrace right now. I can simply go out and ask him. But if he is guilty . . . and if the "monster" text an unknown sender transmitted to me this morning is correct, then I'd be a fool to let him know I suspect him of any of it.

So what do I do?

As impossible as it would have seemed a few months ago, the chance that Bobby White could become president is quite real. The question is, what would he *really do* with that power, if he somehow attains it? The few things he confided in me during our last exchanges were terrifying enough. But what provokes me more than anything else is the racial nature of everything that's happened since Mission Hill. Where, I want to know, does Bobby really stand on the violently polarized state of our society as we head into the election that could lift him into the White House?

WALKING BACK ONTO the terrace, I take my seat and say, "Bobby, everything that's happened here since the Mission Hill shooting is race-related. The burning of the antebellum homes. The murder of Doc Berry. The paintball standoff on the bluff yesterday, which ended with the National Guard snipers killing those two Black guys behind the monument."

"So? You think all that has something to do with me?"

"I don't know. You're the unknown factor in all this. The black swan, no pun intended. I saw you at the Barlow bunker, and they're openly racist militia. The Poker Club is behind the attempt to dissolve the Black-controlled city government, and I'll bet any amount of money you're tight with those people. And ten minutes ago you told me straight-up that you're a racist. What am I supposed to think?"

"I don't care what you think. I just need your vote."

"My *vote*? Earlier you were talking like a cross between Hitler and Mussolini."

"Penn, be honest with yourself. Every policy I've proposed will make our country stronger. You may disagree with my methods, but you can't argue with the intent or the results."

"You're never going to see the results, unless you keep hiding your true agenda. No majority of Americans is going to vote for those policies."

His confident laughter makes me question my assertion. "They will, actually. Penn, to understand race in America you need to face some hard truths. And I'll tell you one. More than a few of the Greatest Generation were racist as hell. After fighting in the 99th Infantry Division at the Bulge—the Battle Babies, they called them—my grandfather literally liberated part of the Dachau concentration camp. But let me tell you . . . he hated him some Jews. All his life, an anti-Semite. And him a preacher."

"What's your point?"

"Racism is hardwired, brother. The only question is: What's it pointing at, in each person."

"You really believe that?"

"I know it. The GOP is in the process of destroying itself out of stupidity. And I'm about to gut the right wing and center of the Democratic Party. You may not know it until Election Day. But then you're going to learn the deepest truth of all about America. White America, anyway."

"Which is?"

"*Everything* in this country comes down to race. You want to know why?"

"Go for it."

"The Democrats keep warning everybody that if we're not careful, we're going to lose our democracy. The thing is, *white people don't really care about democracy. They never did.* We talk a good game, like any Americans who go to church and pretend they're Christians. But in the end, at bottom, we know our tribe ruled this country from day one. One person, one vote? That's rule by the rabble—by definition. Now, your average white person who grew up reciting the Pledge of Allegiance in school isn't going to go out in the street like these QAnon morons, or even extreme Trumpers, and advocate for a fascist takeover. But mark my words . . . if you offer most of your friends the Norman Rockwell America of Dwight Eisenhower—with women's rights airbrushed into the picture—then in the silence of the voting booth, *they'll take it.* In a heartbeat, my friend. Because this country we have now, and where it's going . . . they don't see a part in it for themselves. They don't *want* a part in it. They want an America somewhere between John Wayne's and Frank Capra's. And I don't know when you last saw those movies, but left or right, they were ninety-eight percent white."

Bobby falls silent, his expression a relaxed smile. Beyond him, maybe five thousand descendants of enslaved Africans mill across the bluff, waiting to hear from a twenty-seven-year-old Black man who wears chains during his day job. The whole situation is so surreal I can hardly grasp it.

"You may be right, Bobby. Only time will tell. But are you *really* a racist? I saw you hanging with those old Black baseball players yesterday. You loved it. What do you mean when you say you're racist?"

He shrugs as though the answer should be obvious. "I believe white people are intellectually superior to Blacks. Not by much, but measurably so. Though we've gotten so lazy, we've about squandered our advantage. Barack Obama is brilliant because he's half-white and was raised by a white mother. I also believe Asians are slightly superior to us. Standardized tests bear that out. It's not even controversial, really."

I find myself blinking in amazement at his frankness.

"Of course, the trendy thing now in science is to say that race is an artificial construct. Which is laughable. Because Blacks are the first to claim race is real wherever it involves Black superiority. Look at sports. Blacks will tell you Black people make the best NFL and NBA players. 'Just look at the leagues!' they say. 'Incontrovertible evidence!' And of course they're *right*. Black men *do* make the best NFL players. No scientist in the world can disprove that. Or prove that they aren't Black."

Bobby's guiltless laughter rolls out toward Confederate Memorial Park and the bored-looking National Guardsmen watching Black families eat po-boys from cardboard boxes by the bluff fence.

"But—as soon as you apply that same evidentiary test to a different field, Blacks scream about historical bias and prejudice, claiming unfair treatment to explain their obvious deficit. 'The test is unfair!' they moan, even if the test is all of human history."

"For example?"

Bobby holds up his forefinger. "How about physics? In my book, European Jews made the greatest physicists. Now, that's probably shifted some as time has passed, to races that share some traits of your nineteenth-century Jew—reverence for education, phenomenal work ethic—which are not traits you generally find in your African gene line, regardless of geographic location."

"Couldn't Blacks make a case that they've never had equal access to the fundamentals of the advanced sciences?"

Bobby laughs outright. "Whose fault is that? Who advanced those sciences in the first place? With the exception of the Arabs, who preserved mathematics during the Dark Ages, it was white men and Jews. Blacks aren't even in the conversation. And in another hundred years, they *still won't be*. It's not whether or not they can do the math. It's that historically they never even came close to it. Never. Not remotely."

I'm trying to come up with a counter-argument, but on this point I can't. Not without time to do some research.

"Penn, in all the annals of mankind, there has never been a technologically advanced Black state. Nor even a *philosophically* advanced one that transcended the primitive. That's why the specialty of Afrocentric history is cultural appropriation. Whenever I hear a Black professor or 'content creator' yelling about people stealing their culture, I want to laugh. Because Afrocentric historians are attempting the greatest cultural heist of all. They've claimed the achievements of Egypt as Black African. And now—hubris of all time—they even want to claim high Greek culture as African. You want to sue the Rolling Stones and the Beach Boys for ripping off Chuck Berry? I'm all for Chuck. But comparing that to flat-nosed Africans stealing credit for the pyramids and the tragedies of Euripides? *There's* your tragedy. Gimme a fuckin' break."

"I don't think I've heard you talk this way on your radio show, Bobby. Even though a percentage of your listeners would undoubtedly go crazy for it."

He chuckles quietly again. "I didn't figure you for one of my listeners." Bobby's smile fades as he shrugs. "There's no point belaboring the obvious. America's so-called reckoning on race? Let them have their little tantrum. Let them make *Black Panther* and a raft of sequels and wallow in their fantasy until the inevitable fate of all fantasies finally crashes down."

"Which is?"

"Truth. The inevitable antidote to fantasy."

"And what is the truth?"

This time Bobby hesitates before answering, but in the end he plunges on, unable to stop himself. "The awful, obvious truth is that Africa is the worst hellhole on this planet. You might argue that primitive Africa was less horrible, until you see the Hutu rape and slaughter nearly a million Tutsis with machetes. The *Black Panther* fantasy of a hidden Black nation of super-advanced technology and medicine? In a world where all evil was caused by white colonizers? That's the biggest load of crap ever conceived by the human mind. You don't get an advanced technological state without shaking hands with the devil. Can't happen. Human evil resides in the human heart, regardless of race. And while evil may date back to the Garden, its worst manifestations come from the dark side of technology itself. No fantasy in history ever shoved more reality under the rug than *Black Panther*."

"Weren't *Superman* or *Batman* just as fantastical? Or *Wonder Woman*?"

"No! Those first two stories are merely childish fantasies. *Superman* was the fantasy of a couple of skinny Jewish kids who dreamed of being strong and able to fly, and also to fit into American culture. But do you hear people screaming that Superman should be played only by a Jew? What a clown show this country has become. Batman was a kid who lost his parents, who resolves to fight crime though he has no superpowers. But *Black Panther*? That's full-on lust for a racially homogeneous nation-state that never existed and never will. It aspires to a super-*culture* that might exist, were it not for the evil machinations of white people. And that, my friend, is poison to the body politic."

"You've given this a lot of thought."

He waves his hand as if he couldn't care less. "Not really. It's just a relief to say these things out loud. But let's not waste time talking about comic book characters."

In that moment, something—perhaps Bobby's leaps from topic to topic—triggers me to toss out a piece of bait and see how he reacts. I could, of course, do something more direct, like show him the footage of him standing on the Donnelly Oil terrace last night, but all I really want to do is test the knowledge of my unknown texter from this morning.

"All right, Bobby," I say lightly, "tell me one thing. Who was General Paul Beckley to you?"

As I guessed, whatever reptilian mechanism that allows Bobby White to remain unmoved on the surface regardless of his internal emotional state apparently fell into dormancy during his rant. For at the word "Beckley," his eyes widen, and I sense something like the third, transparent eyelid possessed by crocodiles, falcons, and some other predators rise to protect the brain behind it. At the same time, he ceases breathing until he realizes he's likely betrayed his true reaction to my question.

"*Paul* Beckley?" he echoes, having still not regained his full composure.

"That's right."

"There was an army intel officer I served with in Afghanistan."

I nod but offer nothing more.

Bobby studies me in silence for a few seconds, trying to read what's behind *my* eyes. "He was murdered on Monday, I believe."

"Were you in Washington when that happened?"

"That was a travel day for us, I believe. We were in D.C. and New York to do TV shows. You remember me going up for that, don't you? The day after we had drinks at Edelweiss."

"I do."

"What brought on that question? Did your mysterious texter mention Paul Beckley?"

"I happened to read an article that mentioned both you and Beckley this morning. Came up in a Google search. Someone in D.C.—a blogger in the intel community—is trying to draw connections between Beckley's murder and some highly placed figures that he apparently meant to accuse of some shady doings in a book he was doing for HarperCollins. You were one of those figures, Bobby."

"Really. I hadn't seen Beckley for close to twenty years when I heard he'd died."

"He didn't *die*. Not in the passive sense that you're giving the word. He was apparently in excellent health. Someone murdered him. To keep him from talking about something."

"I understand. The thing is, that's got nothing to do with me. My only connection with Beckley was praying he had the quick reaction force in place on the night we hit Abu Nasir's hideout."

So here we are. Like Charles Dufort and me after I confronted him over his dinner table years ago. Bobby is lying to me. I know he's lying, and I'm pretty sure he knows that I know. Given his history and training, that's not a very safe position to be in. After a couple of moments, I double over in my chair, clenching my stomach.

"Jesus. My fucking stomach's going on me again. I could be longer this time. I think maybe you'd better go."

"No, I'm fine," he says mildly. "You told me about your cancer, remember? I'd better wait for you, make sure you're all right."

Right . . . "Okay."

Getting slowly to my feet, I stumble back into my bedroom, leaving the sliding door partly open behind me, to reassure him I'm not trying to make a run for it.

BOBBY WHITE SWITCHED on his cell phone and stared at the open terrace door, images of Paul Beckley's dying face flashing through his mind. He had no more doubt; the anonymous sender of the text Penn had received had to be Corey Evers. Until Penn mentioned Beckley, Bobby had figured there was some chance it might have been Sophie Dufort. But Sophie knew nothing about Paul Beckley. He supposed it was possible that she could have found the same article Penn read and tacked a mention onto her list of accusations. But that was doubtful. And why would she do it? Especially after he'd shared her bed last night? But whoever was responsible, their identity wouldn't change the outcome. If it was Corey, the fact that he'd contacted Penn with vague accusations rather than the FBI with hard evidence revealed that he was afraid to come at Bobby directly. Which made Penn the more immediate threat. And the only solution to the threat he posed was the one that had silenced Beckley.

Penn had to die.

Bobby hated to face that fact. He'd always liked the writer. Moreover, if the body count kept rising in this tiny town, someone at the FBI would make it his mission to solve the murders. Still . . . Bobby couldn't allow the threat to persist, not even for the brief hours before Kendrick's scheduled speech. He was alone with Penn now—so far as he knew, anyway—and the safest play was to kill him here, make it look accidental, and get the hell out.

Bobby was getting to his feet when the lawyer stepped back through the door holding his AR-15 in his hands.

"Don't make any quick moves," Penn said. "You may think I don't know how to use this, but I do. I've killed with it."

"What the fuck are you doing?" Bobby asked, as though Penn were behaving like a madman.

Penn raised the rifle until its barrel pointed at Bobby's sternum. "Protecting my life. Here's what's about to happen. I don't want to risk you even walking through my house to leave. I know what you can do. You're quite capable of climbing over that rail and dropping down to the sidewalk. It's about twelve feet, I think. Nothing for a Delta operator."

"Penn—"

"I don't want to hear it, Bobby. You wouldn't have left this house without finishing me off. I shouldn't have mentioned Beckley. But I had to try to penetrate that armor of yours. And I see that I did."

"I don't know what you're talking about."

"Spare us both, man. Hit it. Over the rail."

Bobby hesitated, but there was really no play out on the terrace with a table between them, thousands of people across the Row, and cameras everywhere. If he were closer, maybe. But Penn wouldn't let him any closer.

"Go on, Bobby. I'll shoot you if you don't."

"Based on what? An anonymous text message that offers no evidence of anything?"

"Instinct, brother. Nothing but."

WAITING FOR THE radio star to go over the rail and drop to the sidewalk, it strikes me that Bobby White is a truly reckless man. Had I merely recorded what he said during the last twenty minutes, then posted his remarks on the internet, his chance at the White House would surely have evaporated in a matter of hours.

Wouldn't it?

But then I remember Trump on the bus with Billy Bush. He survived that. Last night Bobby White made an appearance in the bunker of a declared white supremacist—a suicidal move for most politicians—but for Bobby, maybe it wasn't. As he scissors one leg up and over the rail, a new question strikes me with a chill: *What if, where Bobby White is concerned . . . the old rules simply don't apply?*

Just before he drops off the ledge, a beam of sunlight slices through the gray clouds and limns him with an almost beatific glow. Even in this crazy situation, he stands ramrod straight with his open look of optimism, as if all the future stretches before him like a broad, endless avenue. The twenty years' difference in our ages feels like an unbridgeable chasm. Which, of course, it is. Bobby White is in his vivid prime, while I and my worldview belong to a passing age . . .

"Take it easy, Penn," he says, holding up two fingers in a peace sign—or is he mimicking Churchill's V for Victory? "And don't get too worked up over this local racial friction. One way or another, we had to move past it as a town. This way's as good as any other."

"Even if it ends bloody?"

He nods with the hard-earned fatalism of a man who has seen blood spilled in battle, and spilled some himself. "It's blood that gives things a certain finality. It marks the epochs of history. Just be sure not to lose too much of your own."

As he drops to the sidewalk, it strikes me that Bobby didn't even ask me not to reveal the photos of him with Shot Barlow and the Tenisaw Rifles. Or the recording of him saying he doesn't want to run for president. Any other politician would have been scared shitless from the moment I mentioned having those things. But Bobby isn't. Whatever I decide to do, he's more than capable of rolling with the punches and ending up on his feet again. That's what life has taught him. To a man with his moral outlook and skill set, the old rules mean nothing.

BOBBY STOOD LIGHTLY on the sidewalk beside Battery Row, trying to figure out what had transformed Penn Cage from a bemused confidant into an armed adversary, when his cell phone began playing "Stayin' Alive" by the Bee Gees. He didn't even consider not answering.

"Mom? What's up? Dad still hanging in?"

"Oh, he's fine, considering. Am I interrupting anything important? You're not golfing with Peyton or Eli, are you?"

"No, no. They canceled. We can talk. What's going on?"

"Something's been bothering me all day. I didn't want to pester you, but the harder I try not to think about it, the louder it gets in my mind. You ever have that happen?"

Bobby sighed almost silently and looked around at the thousands of

Black marchers beyond the thin rank of National Guard troops standing in the Row.

"I do, Mom. What is it? What's bothering you?"

"Montcornet burning down. And Loveta burning up in it."

"Well, that's only natural. She was your sister."

"Do you remember I told you that when Harold died, it turned out he didn't have a pot to piss in? Loveta had been expecting a decent inheritance, if not a gold mine. But all he left was that damned house, and the insurance on it. And he only paid that because his father guilt-tripped him his whole life never to let anything happen to it."

Bobby looked impatiently at his watch. His mind was turning to Donny Kilmer. "I remember."

"Well, I forgot to tell you one thing, darling. I guess it just seemed like . . . *exaggeration* at the time. Overreaction. But for two weeks after Harold died, Loveta drank twice as much as usual, and that's saying something. She'd call me rambling in depression and anger, slurring her words. And more than once, she said, 'What am I gonna do, Frances? The only way I'll come out of this with enough money to eat and keep the AC running somewhere is burn this place down for the insurance.' And then she'd laugh. That weird Bette Davis laugh she got sometimes when she was drunk, remember? At the time, I laughed, too. But Bobby . . . I'm not laughing now. When I think of it, it gives me the chills."

Bobby had gone still. Black people streamed past both sides of him on the sidewalk, like dark river water around a pale rock. The entire world had shrunk to the signal coming into his ear.

"Robert . . . ? Are you there, hon?"

"I'm here," he said dully.

"You don't think . . . ? No. She wouldn't."

Bobby's internal radar had registered a whole new threat in the distance, an unknown shape of massive size, and it was coming in his direction. But he kept his voice calm. "No, Mama. Whoever's been burning these other mansions just had Montcornet on their list. I don't know why, and it doesn't matter."

"Are you sure? Do they still not have any idea who's behind those fires?"

"Not yet."

"Well . . . I just need to get out of this damned hospital for a while. I've got cabin fever. Loveta made such a mistake marrying that bloodless Englishman. He was too damned old, and I don't just mean physically. Existence in that house was living death. And now I worry about Martyn. They didn't have the best relationship, he and Loveta, but that boy was dependent on her, I swear. Though he didn't seem to know it. I don't know what he'll do without her."

"Martyn will be fine," Bobby said, still trying to get a sense of his new perception of what might really have happened to Montcornet—or had been happening all along. "He only lives about half in the real world anyway."

His mother laughed. "That's the Lord's truth! At least he'll get the insurance money, if there really is any. It'll be the first real money he ever had in his life. It's too bad Loveta missed out on it."

A casual listener would likely be surprised to learn that Frances White was discussing her just-deceased sister, but Frances had never been one for false piety or exaggerated emotion.

"Yeah," Bobby agreed, feeling even more heat in his face. "It's a shame."

"Have you *called* Martyn, Bobby? You really should. I know you boys are about as different as boys can be, but it would do him a *world* of good. I know it would."

"I spoke to him yesterday, actually. Just for a minute."

"Oh, Bobby," she said, astonished. "That makes me feel so much better."

Bobby looked across the river at the yellow-white column of flame in the distance. It made him think of the pillar of fire God had used to guide the Israelites across the desert. Staring into the distant light, he suddenly knew the truth. The shape out in the distance had come clear to him, and it was much closer than he'd suspected.

"I think I'll call Martyn back," he said softly. "Just to ask what he's been up to. I was in a rush yesterday."

"You do that, son! I'm going to run out to Target. Your father needs a few things. New underwear, and some of those damn compression socks . . ."

"All right, Mom. You be careful in traffic. You're preoccupied."

"Always, baby. Love you."

Then she was gone.

Bobby shut his eyes, but the afterimage of distant flame remained alive on his retina. *How could I not have seen it?* he wondered in disbelief. *My God, the simplicity of it. And the absurdity! A whole city standing on the precipice of war, and all because of something that had no relation to the issue that had triggered the conflict. All because his loser of a cousin—a poor, entitled white boy—felt the world owed him a golden parachute.*

CHAPTER 97

BOBBY WHITE SAT in the wing chair across from Charles Dufort's Brazilian rosewood desk at Belle Rose. He'd gone out of his way to come here, and taken a certain amount of risk in doing so. If his instinct about his cousin was correct, time was critical. Yet Dufort's status as his primary financier made Bobby want to test the old man's nerve and fortitude before they became too entangled, and before Bobby took his next likely step.

Dufort regarded him with avian attentiveness, which went with the old man's hawklike features. They'd shared a little small talk, but when Charles showed him a Lexan box containing Indian arrowheads and spearpoints that Charlot had collected as a boy, an awkward, guilty silence descended in the study. Dufort clearly wanted to find out what had brought Bobby to his home.

"It's simple and almost unbelievable," Bobby told him. "It turns out we had the wrong idea about the antebellum fires. Including the one that destroyed Tranquility."

Dufort's full attention focused like a beam of light. "How's that?"

"It wasn't any Black radical group, Charles. Or even one activist, like Kendrick Washington. The real arsonist is a white man. And if I'm right, his motive has nothing to do with politics."

Dufort absorbed this without showing emotion. "Are you positive?"

"Not a hundred percent. But close. The stupid son of a bitch was trying to get the insurance money on a house he inherited, and he used the other arsons to mask the only one he really cared about."

"You're kidding."

"Nope. It reminds me of that guy in the fifties who blew himself up on an airliner in order to get his wife his insurance money. No regard whatever for other human beings."

Even as Bobby said this, he knew that some people—knowing his plan for this afternoon—would place him in the same class of sociopaths.

"And how did you figure this out when the police and FBI can't?" Dufort asked.

"Because the idiot in question is my cousin. Martyn Black."

"My God. Loveta's boy?"

He nodded.

"Unbelievable. So what's your next move?"

"In my view, the present narrative must be preserved: antebellum homes are being burned by Black radicals. These protesters are anarchists attacking history itself. That's the narrative that works with the voters, and we don't want anything contradicting it."

Dufort shrugged in his seat. "Agreed."

Bobby focused on a golden tennis trophy he remembered from his high school days. Won by Dufort's elder son, Philippe, back in the seventies, it had sat here ever since, an eternal rebuke to Charlot, the son of his second wife. "I'd like to take whatever steps are necessary to preserve the present story."

The old man raised both hands a couple of inches off his lap. "You don't need to confirm that kind of thing with me. Or get my permission."

Bobby nodded, relieved. "I'm glad to hear that. That's why I came, honestly—to be sure this is the essence of our arrangement."

"Well, now you know. I write the checks, you do what your instincts tell you to. If I see you swerve too far off the road, I'll let you know. But other than that . . . you're the master of your fate."

Bobby stood and started to lean over the desk.

"No need to shake hands," Dufort told him. "Get about your business, Sergeant."

Bobby nodded curtly.

"Oh. Did you hear that the board dissolved the city?"

"I did. A neat trick. Was that what you wanted?"

"Badly enough to make sure Sophie cast the deciding vote."

This intrigued Bobby more than a little. "How did she feel about that?"

Dufort's next smile was a pure expression of Machiavellian satisfaction. "She didn't like it one bit. I also heard that Black boy got stabbed. Washington."

Bobby betrayed zero emotion. "That's right. Arkansas skinheads shanked him."

"It's all over the news. Is that a problem for us?"

"None at all. He's a tough soldier. He's going to speak at the amphitheater at five-thirty now."

"Why do you need him to speak?" Dufort asked.

"The less you know, remember? Let's just say he's starring in a little reality show I'm producing."

"Hmm. Will I be able to watch it live?"

"Keep your eyes on the national news."

Charles Dufort reached out and shifted the tennis trophy a little on his desk. "You know, I haven't had this much fun in twenty years. Don't ever let anyone tell you money can't buy happiness. It's like playing chess with living pieces."

"I imagine so," Bobby said. "I need to run, Charles. Enjoy the show later."

SOPHIE DUFORT WAITED in the long hallway outside her father's study. She'd seen Bobby's Range Rover parked out front, and she meant to speak to him before she confronted her father. Bobby emerged from the inner sanctum as few people did—with a self-satisfied smile on his handsome face. This alone roiled Sophie's stomach, after learning what she had recently. She'd shared a long history with Bobby White before sleeping with him last night—having known him as both toddler and adolescent, as well as college student and grown man.

"I didn't expect to see you," he said easily. "You look like the day hasn't gotten any better since this morning."

She swallowed some of her rage. "I assume you know about the city board vote? Bienville is no more. Not as a municipal entity, anyway."

Bobby nodded.

"Well . . . there's not much point in doing a postmortem. At least, not on the city." She touched herself low on the chest. "I'm so sick over Charlot. And the more I've thought about it, the less I blame Tommy Russo. The drugs, the gambling . . . those were just symptoms of a deeper problem. And the problem sits just beyond that door. You want to know who killed Charlot? You were just talking to him."

It took all of Bobby's talent to hold his composure. "What do you mean?"

"I mean Daddy always had it in his power to save Charlot, and he didn't. Worse, he created the hole in Charlot that led to the other problems. From the time he was a boy, Daddy beat him down mentally, emotionally. Even physically sometimes. I can't bear to think about it. And I'm going to confront him about it."

Bobby shifted on his feet. "Are you sure you want to do that?"

"Why not? I'm not scared of him. I mean . . . I actually am, or I wouldn't have voted to dissolve the city. But now that I've given him what he wanted, I'm not."

"I just meant, is it worth it? Won't he just ignore you? Or toy with you? Fight with you for the hell of it?"

Sophie took a deep breath, then closed her eyes and sighed. "You know him, all right. God, I wish . . . I wish he would just *die*."

Bobby looked back at her with a deep calm. "Are you serious?"

"I am. Will you do to him what you said you'd do to Tommy Russo?"

Bobby seemed to freeze where he stood. Only for a moment, but the reaction was irrevocable, undeniable. Then his muscles relaxed, and his eyes narrowed like those of a man who's been told something that makes no human sense. "I can't, Sophie. Charles is practically funding my campaign single-handedly. Through his super PAC."

She studied him in silence for a while. Then she looked back over her shoulder at the study door. Very softly she said, "If he died, I'd inherit at least half his estate. I could do everything he's doing for you, and more."

Her suggestion floated around Bobby's head like a fragrant haze, a cloud of possibility. But this hallway wasn't the place to ponder that.

"I need to get back downtown," he said.

"Mm-hm," she murmured, stepping closer to him. "After whatever's going to happen today happens . . . come find me. If you're not in jail. We have a lot to talk about."

"I'll try."

Sophie trailed her fingernail along his arm as she walked past him and opened the study door.

AS SHE MARCHED toward her father's desk, Sophie was glad she had run into Bobby. Before that, she'd been thinking of some pills she had in her bedroom, an old prescription that would blunt the edge of the pain raking her heart and brain. But then she thought of *Daddy*, sitting behind the same old polished door on the day his son's body washed up in the river. And what was he doing? Not mourning. No. He was plotting a Machiavellian fantasy with the son he'd always wanted but had not had since Philippe died in the plane crash. Not even then, really. Because Philippe had never possessed the strength or will of Bobby White. Maybe it took the white-trash genes abundant in the White family to produce a man with that kind of toughness.

Sophie drew herself erect before the desk. Charles looked up in surprise, and the expression deepened as he took in the fury in her eyes.

"What can I do for you, dear?"

"Answer a question. Do you really think you can make Bobby White president of the United States?"

Charles chuckled as though at some light humor. "Put it this way. I don't know who can stop me."

She blinked in surprise at his forthright answer. "With a third-party run?"

"You're well informed. Or are you simply repeating rumors?"

"You must be getting dementia. That's like flushing money down the world's biggest toilet."

Her father smiled. "Perhaps. But I have plenty to flush. As do my friends. But I wouldn't be so quick to adopt the conventional wisdom. People are tired of the two-party zoo we have now. Or perhaps one-party, I should say."

Her rage returned in all its power. "Today you threatened to take everything from me—all my inheritance—while you piss away money on an election fantasy. That hurts me, Daddy. But it doesn't compare to what you did to Charlot."

His gaze went to the Lexan box on his desk. "What I . . . ? What did I do to Charlot?"

"You let his life fall apart without even trying to help him. And then you tried to replace him with your fantasy ideal of a son, Bobby White."

"I did no such thing. Charlot squandered my repeated attempts to save him. Everyone who loved him did more than any reasonable person would to try to help him salvage his life." Dufort leaned forward. "Admit it, Sophie. Don't you feel just the tiniest bit of relief today? That you won't get that call at four a.m. from a county jail somewhere? Or a casino security guard?"

Sophie's scream was so loud and filled with rage that even her aged father clapped his hands over his ears like a little boy.

"You heartless *bastard*! You . . ." She could hardly remember what she'd come into the study for. Right now she wished Bobby were in here to slap the old man silly. "You think you're a damned *visionary*, don't you? You always have. Because you're rich. But this time you're really deluding yourself. You've gotten too old for this game."

Dufort looked mildly amused. "Why do you say that?"

"Because your new toy, your golden boy isn't what you think he is. You disowned your biological son for being gay. You threw Charlot onto the trash heap and drove him into poverty and depression because he was different from you. But Bobby White is *exactly like him*."

Her father looked momentarily discomfited. "What do you mean?"

"I mean your golden boy is queer! A fag! A homo! Or bisexual, whatever. I don't really know what he is. I fucked him last night and I don't even know!"

This was the first thing she'd said that had shocked him. She could see it in his face. But he recovered quickly.

"All those things you called Charlot all these years, Daddy? Bobby White's *the same*. No different. Do you hear me? He and Charlot were lovers in college! My God, the irony is *breathtaking*."

After a few seconds' silence, Dufort regained his composure. She could see the wheels turning behind his eyes, but she couldn't begin to guess his true thoughts.

"You couldn't be more wrong, Sophronia," he said finally. "Bobby and Charlot are as different as a hawk and a hummingbird."

"What do you mean?"

"Do you really think my disdain for Charlot's lifestyle sprang from some contemptibly provincial attitude about sex? Some vestigial puritanical *dogma*? Bobby White is an alpha male. Classic archetype. Charlot was a beta, at best. Lambda is more accurate. Charlot was *soft*, dear. Pretty as a woman, and women loved him. But he was weaker than any woman I ever knew."

"That doesn't change his nature! He was gay, Daddy. So what? He was a lawyer. But to your precious right-wing buddies, Bobby White became *unelectable* the first time he took it up the ass. Or he becomes so the first time he admits it. Or someone else proves it."

Her father shook his head as if Sophie were a little girl once more, hopelessly, angrily lost in the pages her physics teacher had assigned. "I don't like speaking this way with my daughter," he said in an almost prim voice.

"My *God*, Daddy. Do you not see how old I am? Don't you know the things I've done in my life?"

A look of distaste crossed his face. "Probably things not so different from those I've done. But that doesn't make them suitable for conversation."

"Oh, Lord help me," she almost moaned. "Would you fucking grow *up*?"

"Grow up?" he echoed, a harsher note coming into his voice. "All right. You want reality? You tell me Bobby White fucked a man? Here's my response. Put Bobby White in a prison, and he'll fuck men all night long. Put him in a convent, he'll fuck nuns. He's a carnivore, Sophie! An omnivore. A predator. I know his type *very* well. We're brothers under the skin, he and I."

The brutal honesty of his answer took Sophie aback. "He's not in a prison now. But he's been fucking men as long as I've known him."

Dufort shrugged. "Maybe to him the world is a prison."

This too caught her off guard, and temporarily silenced her.

"I'm quite familiar with the lifestyles of classical antiquity," Charles said. "Suetonius claimed Julius Caesar was 'every man's woman, and every woman's man.' Let's not even start on Alexander. And they conquered the world."

"But—"

"How much do you know about Gore Vidal?" Charles pressed on.

She blinked in momentary confusion. The conversation was moving too fast for her. "A bit. I know he was gay."

Her father raised his right hand and tilted it right and left. "Probably, in the end. But Gore *hated* being categorized. He too was omnivorous. He'd had sex with over a thousand people by the age of twenty-four—mostly men, but women, too—and he bragged about it. He was the literary Wilt Chamberlain. I met him several times, you know. He had a strong Mississippi connection. His grandfather was Senator Thomas Gore. But what Gore himself wanted in sex was *dominance*. He was a *top*, Sophie. He was all about the conquest."

"So you say," she said under her breath, as a book she'd read long ago started coming back to her. "I heard he was a starfucker."

Charles again wrinkled his lips with distaste. "That language doesn't suit you, dear."

"Oh, fuck your false propriety! I remember now. Gore Vidal screwed Rock Hudson, Tyrone Power, and ugly old Charles Laughton. Even Brad Davis from *Midnight Express*. And he was a bottom *then*. He was whatever he had to be to stay close to fame. So go to hell with your man-of-the-world act!"

Anger flashed in the old man's eyes for the first time. "All right," he said, getting to his feet. At six feet four inches tall, Charles towered over both the desk and her. "You want the bottom line on Bobby White? He doesn't go through life getting knocked off his feet by the unseen. If he means to run for president, he's already made peace with whatever he'll have to do to get there. He knows what he'll have to give up, and he's already dealt with it. He also knows his deficits, and he's acting to fill them. That's good enough for me. So—if you hoped to come in here and pop my balloon, you'll have to find another way to do it."

She looked down at the desk, tears of rage in her eyes. You couldn't beat the old son of a bitch. Her eyes lighted on one of her father's most prized possessions, the trophy her brother Philippe had won as a senior in high school: the state singles championship in tennis. "You know, Daddy . . . Charlot was good at things, too. He had talents. But you never encouraged him."

"Oh? What was his talent? Macramé?"

"He was an artist. A *real* artist. He could both draw and paint. He had musical aptitude as well. You know how gifted he was. But an artist wasn't good enough for the heir of Charles Dufort. You wanted him out on those god*damned* ball fields."

Dufort frowned and took his seat again. "Sophie, dear . . . I have some calls to make. I'd appreciate some privacy before dinner."

"Dinner?" She reached out and touched the golden racket in the hand of the slim male figure atop the trophy on the desk. It was all she could do not to snap it off. She recalled the final line of Housman's "To an Athlete Dying Young": '. . . The garland briefer than a girl's.' Leave it to a gay poet to see through the illusion of athletic glory, especially the masculine ideal of it.

"Both my brothers are dead," she said. "But you're not grieving. You're trying to replace them with a fantasy. Well, I'll be waiting for the day someone unmasks your alpha male candidate, which is inevitable."

Charles shrugged. "I don't think so."

She laughed then. "It'll be money that does it in the end, which is a delicious irony. Some old lover will reappear, some drunken one-night stand. A grubby waiter from New Orleans, or a pretty Muslim boy from Afghanistan. Someone who shot a Polaroid. They'll give it to TMZ for a pittance, not knowing you would have paid a thousand times the price to bury it. Wait till Bobby's on TV every night. It'll be a mercy killing by then. I could do it myself, if I felt like it."

At these words, the humanity drained from her father's face. "I'd think very hard before I did that," he said in a voice as dripping with menace as the hiss of a water moccasin.

Fear brought her alert. "Why is that?"

"Politics is a dangerous game, Sophronia." The old man grinned suddenly, his eyes glowing with some rapt vision of the future. "But give Bobby a vivacious First Lady and a towheaded son, and he'll be unstoppable. No rumor will kill his candidacy."

"You're beyond hope," she said in an exhausted voice.

Her father chuckled with a strange sound. "It's too bad you're not twenty years younger. You'd have given Jackie Kennedy a run for her money in the White House."

A single laugh escaped her perfect lips. "You think Bobby wouldn't take me if he could get me? You're betraying your ignorance in the sexual sphere, Daddy. But why should that surprise me?"

With a languid motion she reached out and flicked over the tennis trophy like a chess master tipping over an opponent's king.

Dufort gasped as though she had struck him.

Without a word Sophie turned and walked out of the study.

As she passed through the door, he had to admit to himself that she was about as perfectly preserved as any female her age could be. And he didn't find it difficult to believe that Bobby would accept a night in bed with her. But anything more? No. Bobby had already told him that parents had been throwing their daughters at him for years.

Charles slid open his top drawer and removed two sheets of paper. The first was a pen-and-ink portrait of himself, drawn by Charlot when he was in junior high school. The hand was untutored but clearly gifted, the likeness startling. Charles's patrician face radiated an idealized paternal presence—clearly a father as he would wish to be seen by his son. Sliding this aside, Charles exposed a second and similar portrait, a pencil drawing Charlot had made just two years later. Clearly done in haste, it neverthe-less captured the deeper essence of its subject. The avian eyes, hawklike nose, and strong jaw set in anger combined to produce a chilling portrait of insatiable hunger, a barely concealed rapaciousness, like fangs folded back in a viper's mouth. This was how Charlot had truly seen his father, or perhaps the creature that lived inside him. Charlot had surely seen that face last night, just before he died.

Dufort looked at the second portrait for as long as he could bear it. While he did, he thought of what his daughter had told him about Bobby White. If she could be believed, then Bobby had fucked both his elder daughter and his younger son. Charles asked himself whether he cared, and after a few moments he realized that he did not. Bobby White was an alpha predator, as he had argued to Sophie. All Charles cared about was making sure that, in achieving his ambition to reach the highest office in the land, Bobby did not also screw the patriarch of the Dufort family.

CHAPTER 98

"ONE MILITIA NUT with an assault rifle could take out five hundred people from up here before they got him," said Martyn Black. "Maybe a thousand. And if it's Black people setting those oil wells on fire, pretty soon the governor may send cops up here to do it."

At five stories, the Planters' Hotel had been the tallest in Bienville until 1937, when the Aurora was built four blocks deeper into town. And until the 1970s, when Blake Donnelly constructed his own monument on the bluff, the view of the Mississippi River from the roof of the bluff-facing hotel had been considered the best available for two hundred river miles. This afternoon, a white man in his forties and a Chinese woman in her twenties stood at the northwest corner of that roof and watched the crowd in the bluff park grow steadily in size and number.

Since the Chinese woman said nothing, Martyn continued speaking as though Lanying actually cared what he said.

"I wonder how many of those marchers will stay down there overnight?" He pointed at the sky, which was darkening to a steelier gray as the clouds above swelled with rain. "It may storm."

"Will the authorities allow anyone to stay?" Lanying asked finally. "In China the authorities would move in now, while it's still light. Press their advantage. They would drive everyone out. Straight to prison."

"The cops don't really have an advantage here. Because they can't fire anything but gas or nonlethal rounds. This is still America, at least for now."

"What about those snipers we met earlier?"

Three hours ago, a pair of men that Martyn had deduced must be an FBI sniper-spotter team had asked them politely to leave the roof. Martyn had guessed their vocation from their haircuts, their bearing, and the long gun cases they carried. Hell, half the hotel seemed to be filled with federal agents, from Bureau and BATF to more military types. The rest seemed to be national media folks. Thankfully, ten minutes ago the sniper team had packed up and yielded the roof back to whoever had the nerve to stand up here.

"They're here to protect the crowd," Martyn explained, "probably from the white supremo nutjobs I was talking about. Lone-wolf neo-Nazi types."

Martyn prided himself on his understanding of strategy. He earned a portion of his living playing video games professionally. But now he had left the virtual world behind. Beginning with Tranquility on Tuesday, he had burned every antebellum mansion but one that the law-enforcement agents of the city, state, and nation had assembled to investigate. The house he'd burned today, Montcornet, was the one he'd been raised in, and the woman who'd died there was his mother.

"I'm frightened," said Lanying.

Martyn put an arm around her and squeezed her close, but he sensed only revulsion in response. She was trying to hide it, but the effort was wasted. He'd first picked up the feeling after Arcadia, after they'd heard that a homeless man had died in the blaze. Something had changed in Lanying then, if not before. He could have been blind to it earlier. He'd been taking her for granted for a while, he knew, which was foolish. He was lucky to have her. If she weren't an illegal alien, she wouldn't be here at all.

Lanying had fled China in a container ship, after paying two years' salary to a snakehead for passage to New Orleans. Nearly everyone in the container had been arrested upon arrival in the port, but Lanying and two boys had somehow managed to break away during the chaotic arrests. Martyn met her a year later, while working a contract computer job in Metairie. His primary work was as IT manager for the City of Bienville, but this had made him an expert on a fairly antiquated bookkeeping program, so occasionally the city hired him out—or even loaned him out—to solve problems for other municipalities. On that particular job he had been paid his usual rate, but it had proven to be the jackpot of his life. For there he had met Lanying, who'd been working as a data-entry clerk for minimum wage. It hadn't taken him long to find out she knew more about computers than he did, so he lost no time getting her hired for occasional contract work at Bienville city hall.

Lanying had possessed a truly wretched set of false papers, and this had helped Martyn to make her dependent on him. First, he'd gotten her work at a decent wage. Then he'd promised to get her a better-quality ID, and even to pay a lawyer to look into applying for political asylum for her. He'd done neither of the latter two things yet, though he talked a good game. If anyone had gotten to know Lanying well—and no one had, by his design—they would have been puzzled to learn that she believed the American immigration system to be a secretly Byzantine maze of hidden connections that involved bribery and a complex system of favors, despite appearing to be fairly straightforward to someone doing research online.

What made all this hassle worthwhile was simple: Lanying was the most beautiful creature Martyn had ever seen. A tiny goddess, one he would never have been allowed to approach, much less touch, under any other circumstances. For a while things had been perfect, or as nearly perfect as the mortal world would allow. But now . . . he had let his greed, and his repressed anger, bring him close to ruin.

"Are you afraid, too?" Lanying asked.

"Why do you ask that?"

"Ever since your cousin called, you've been anxious. I know you've tried to hide it, but . . . do you think he suspects the truth?"

"No. There's no way. He called because he heard about the fire and that Mom might have been in it. She was his aunt. That's all."

Lanying shook her head, unconvinced. "Something about the rhythm of the call seemed strange."

"What do you mean?"

"Where the pauses were. The sound of your voice."

He cursed her phenomenal perception, and not for the first time.

"And Charlot Dufort dying in the river?" she pressed. "After you heard that, you got even more tense."

"That's totally unrelated. I knew him is all. Charlot owed loan sharks money. Lots of it. Look, I don't want to talk about this stuff. Everything's cool. We're fine. You're going to make me paranoid."

Lanying sighed but did not push him harder.

Martyn watched the people below walk around as though in search of a leader. Burning the mansions hadn't been his idea. It was his mother's. After Martyn's British stepfather died, she'd expected to inherit a considerable fortune. Not truly big money, of course, but at least a million in insurance, and another mil in assorted investments. But as it turned out, Harold Black, at the parched old age of ninety-three, had left behind nothing but brittle bones and the insurance on his family's ancestral home, Montcornet. For days afterward, his enraged wife had wandered the halls blind drunk, cursing the bloodless old man on whom she had wasted the "prime years" of her life. Just seventy-three when Harold died, Loveta had clung to him in the hope that he would at least provide for a more comfortable old age than the one he'd allowed himself. With this last dream shattered, it hadn't taken her long to begin mumbling about burning the old place down for the insurance money.

She'd sounded so serious, and developed such a fixation, that Martyn had had to sit her down and explain that arson was probably the most dangerous crime any American could commit, with the highest odds of being caught, short of robbing a bank on camera without a mask. The reason was simple: insurance companies didn't like paying out millions, and they had the funds to hire the best forensic investigators in the world. Finally, except in rare cases, the person who profited from the fire was always the prime suspect. It had taken Martyn more than a week of grinding her down to banish the thought from her mind—at least to the point that he didn't worry that she might try it while drunk.

Of course, by then he had gamed out at least three ways to burn the house and get away with it. There was no point remembering those, because in the end chance or fate had stepped in and offered him what it almost never offered anyone—

A chance to commit the perfect crime.

What man—what *gamer* with functioning testicles—could walk away from an opportunity like that? It was Mission Hill that had given him the idea. After all those Black kids had gotten shot by the white deputies (and after Kendrick Washington got famous for pulling his Black Jesus Walks on Water stunt), Martyn had watched the explosion of social media chatter that resulted. And it was then that he'd seen the Black rapper posting about burning antebellum mansions in revenge. After doing a little research, he'd discovered that similar things had been said locally during the George Floyd protests. Once he knew that, he'd seen the future laid out before him like a damned Yellow Brick Road.

How simple could it be? If a bunch of Black radicals got angry about the shooting of a bunch of Black kids—and burned down some antebellum homes in revenge—who the hell would ever suspect the *homeowner* of the *fourth* mansion targeted of being behind all the crimes? Especially if it was merely one in a line of six or seven? Carrying out such a plan would require only three things: first, the brains to burn buildings while not actually being present; second, the willingness to risk harm to others, even if one's intent was not to hurt anyone; and third, the nerve to act quickly and without fear. Martyn possessed all that, in spades. Better still, he had a brilliant and compliant (if not enthusiastic) accomplice.

But now—in her place—he found he had a guilt-ridden young woman who had not yet faced the fact that she believed he'd murdered his mother. The fact was . . . Martyn had. Because once he'd started planning the fire—an intent he'd shared with his mother, and which had filled her final days with the fierce joys of imminent revenge—he'd discovered that his stepfather had left not only the insurance on his home, but also a whole life policy on Loveta Corbin Black in the amount of three hundred thousand dollars.

That discovery had sealed his mother's fate.

"I'm cold," Lanying said, still looking down at the people moving along the metal fencing that the National Guard had set up at the edge of Battery Row.

"It's seventy-four degrees."

She shrugged.

It was true: she was shivering.

Martyn followed her gaze. When walkers below reached the intersection with State Street, where the makeshift gate was, the Guard troops would let them through two at a time, or more if there were small children. It all felt very alien to him, un-American, but he supposed it reminded her of home.

Six days ago, when he'd decided to go ahead with his plan, he could not have begun to imagine the chaos that would ultimately result. If he had known, he would certainly never have—

Stop it, he told himself. *Stop pretending to be better than you are. The truth is, after living a singularly unremarkable life—after years of feeling smarter than everyone around you—you finally got a chance to prove it. Now you're doing it. The smartest forensic investigators in America are spread across this county with their faces stuck in ashes and dirt, and getting nowhere. And you're standing on top of this hotel with an Asian goddess, one and a half million dollars richer than you were this morning—at least on paper. All the rest of it, the possible race war, is just collateral damage that no one could have expected you to foresee. Who knew Mississippi was still so fucked up that the rednecks can't tolerate a couple of burned mansions without torching churches in revenge? They're probably the same morons who keep defacing Emmett Till's memorial signs at Money, sixty-eight years after the kid was murdered. Genetic debris. Poor protoplasm. It's the only explanation. The state's about a quarter filled with hyper-religious white people who spent the pandemic as unvaccinated, ivermectin-guzzling cranks, owning the libs until the moment they panicked and shot up with fetal-tissue-developed monoclonal antibodies, or begged for the vaccine as a tech prepped the endotracheal tube—*

"I wish we'd stayed home," Lanying said. "I don't like seeing this. It's too much like what I left behind."

"Sorry," Martyn said from reflex.

But he wasn't. At some level, he'd wanted her to see the show on the street below. Because he was the one who had taken her furthest from this kind of reality. And he had promised to do more. *Maybe it's time I did,* he thought. *Or at least time to make a better show of trying.*

Besides, he loved staying at the hotel. It reminded him of New Orleans, with its wrought-iron balconies and French flourishes. And with Mont-cornet only a pile of ashes now, this would be the closest he'd likely get to the real thing—at least until he quit his job. And that he would have to wait a while to do, at least until a few months after he got the insurance money. He looked out over the river, at the distant column of fire under the darkening sky.

"Let's go back in," he said. "Let's get in bed."

As he turned, he looked down into the street at all the Black people moving cautiously under the eyes and guns of the National Guard troops. They looked lost. Demoralized. Like refugees in their own land. He saw Black soldiers among the ranks, and he wondered what they thought of these protesters. Did they feel kin to them? Or did they feel embarrassment? Even repulsion? As Martyn turned away, he thought of the supply sergeant from whom he'd bought the A-10 flares he'd used to start the fires. A gamer like himself, but . . . no real flair. A journeyman, really. But always in need of money, and a thrill-seeker.

At least they had that in common.

And God, this had been a thrill . . .

CHAPTER 99

I'VE JUST DROPPED Annie and Nadine off at her bookstore when Marshall McEwan rings my phone. After my confrontation with Bobby on my terrace, I knew he would see no option but to kill me. I first considered body armor and hiring security guards, but those things can't protect you from someone who really means to kill you, especially someone with the skills of Bobby White. Then I realized that the most effective measure I could take was to know where Bobby is at all times. To this end, I hired Gabriel Davis, the Natchez cop, to solve that problem. The veteran police officer picked up Bobby outside the Donnelly building, and he's stuck with him ever since. I can breathe easy for the time being, but tonight could be another matter. Rolling down toward the bluff, I answer Marshall's call using the car's speakerphone.

"Go ahead, Marshall."

"I got another contact from Ebony Swan."

A thrill of excitement shoots through me. "Seriously? Where does she say she is now?"

"Attica."

This gives me pause. "The antebellum home where Morgan's guys found the bomb yesterday? The one that fronts Sargent Street?"

"Right. Exactly."

Braking hard, I turn left on Wall Street and hit the gas. "That's a long hike from the Magnolia Heights neighborhood. Or the hospital parking lot."

"She got a ride there."

"You talked to her?"

"No, this was a text."

This gives me a sense of unease. "You had a text conversation with her?"

"No," Marshall says, sounding peeved. "She just sent me a block of text. I'll forward it to you if you want. I told her not to use her phone, remember? Not even to switch it on. She's trying to follow my advice, and at least she's still alive. Ebony also said she'd rather I come for her, since you didn't show up last time."

"That's bullshit. Sophie was there, and she stayed as long as she could."

"Well, anyway. Can you get her?"

"I'm on my way. I'll be there in five, six minutes."

"You can't bring her to the police station, Penn. Tarlton or Johnson could see her."

"I'll take her to my town house."

"Perfect. Call me when you've got her."

"Will do."

"Hey, we just made a very weird discovery down here, probably related to that bear you saw."

"What's that?"

"Our maintenance man found a human head in our back parking lot. A head and a few other remains, but not much."

"What?"

"Morgan's cops say it was a kid named Damien. He's muscle for that drug crew that's hunting Ebony. Looks like he staked out the wrong parking lot. We have a stinky dumpster out there, probably drew the bear in. Damien became the main course."

"Jesus."

"Poetic justice, I call it."

"Agreed."

"Go get that girl, Penn."

"Consider it done."

I turn left again on State Street, which will take me almost all the way to Attica. I'm not going to let this girl down a second time. Plus, if she has video of Doc's murder, I want to see it. As for the bear attack . . . against all my rational skepticism, I'm even more certain than before that the creature has appeared as an agent of whatever forces influence human affairs, whether karmic, random, or divine. I only hope no hunter gets him before he accomplishes his final task.

FOR MANY, THE name *Attica* conjures images of the state prison in New York, the onetime home of David Berkowitz, the Son of Sam; of Black Panther H. Rap Brown; and of Mark David Chapman, who murdered John Lennon. More people probably know it from Al Pacino screaming "*Attica! Attica!*" in *Dog Day Afternoon*. But in Bienville, Mississippi, Attica refers to a nearly perfect Greek Revival mansion set sixty yards back from Sargent Street, a suburban villa completed in 1836, and one of the few Greek Revival buildings that I must concede is beautiful.

Painted bright white, its twelve fluted Doric columns are twenty-four feet tall and stand twelve feet apart. The entire house is surrounded by a two-story portico, with a cupola on its red roof and a wrought-iron balcony set a few feet above its wide oak door. Ancient oaks stand like sentinels between the road and the house, and the perfectly manicured lawn beckons visitors to stop and tour this living ghost of another age.

An asphalt drive passes through its front gate and runs halfway to the house, where a concrete circular carriageway begins, the same one that carried General Ulysses Grant up to the front door in 1863 (though it would have been dirt then, or oyster shell). To my surprise, the gate stands open today. Odd, since Attica's Massachusetts owners are up north for the month.

Turning into the drive, I wonder how a sixteen-year-old Black girl settled on this place as a pickup point, but it must have been because of its isolation in the midst of town. For someone fleeing sheriff's deputies and a drug gang, Attica could appear to be an inviting sanctuary. *Where would she hide?* I wonder as I roll along the driveway. *Somewhere she could watch her potential rescuer approach, yet without being seen. Probably in the azalea bushes below the porch, or behind one of those big oak trees.*

Approaching the carriageway, my eyes take in the mansion's familiar white façade: the fluted columns, the cupola over the red roof, the balcony over the door. As I start to make the turn, my foot hits the brake and stops the car dead.

Acid has flooded my stomach, and my hands are going numb.

Despite the daylight hour, the big brass lamp beneath Attica's balcony is on, and hanging from its chain is a human being—strung from what appears to be six feet of rope. As an assistant DA in Houston, I worked hundreds of homicide cases, and also visited my share of suicide scenes. I know the difference between a dead woman hanged and one with life left in her. There's an angle to the hyperextended neck, the violently upturned jaw, that no film or television show ever captured, an obscene anatomical distortion utterly incompatible with life. The woman suspended beneath Attica's big porch lamp, her black hands bound behind her, looks just that way.

Before I even recognize the impulse, I find my AR-15 in my right hand. My eyes track across the lawn surrounding the house, searching for threats. Then it hit me: this is no trap designed to hurt *me*. The text from Ebony Swan's phone went out to Marshall McEwan. Whoever hanged this girl—if indeed the figure hanging from beneath that balcony is Ebony—wanted publicity for their obscene crime, not another victim.

Taking my foot off the brake, I accelerate around the carriageway, then stop before the concrete steps. Gun in hand, I get out and climb onto the portico, looking up all the way. I didn't know Ebony Swan, but it's clear to me that the body above belongs to a teenage girl. She looks heavy in her

jean-clad hips, a trait probably accentuated by the rapid postmortem settling of blood into her lower body. That also explains the extreme darkness
of her bound hands.

Clotted blood.

"No, no, no," I murmur pointlessly, as if my plea of denial could turn
back time. "Not this . . . not now."

My first instinct is to lift her up, which I manage for a few seconds,
but this does no permanent good. I can't free her from the lamp chain
like this. Easing her back down to the sound of creaking rope, I turn and
almost immediately see the aluminum stepladder that her killer or killers
must have used to hang her. It's lying in the flower bed, behind a line of
dull-green azaleas. With some difficulty, I retrieve the ladder and set it up
beneath the corpse. As I climb awkwardly upward, I realize that the only
way a single murderer could have killed Ebony like this was to have co-
erced her to participate in her own murder. To physically force her would
have required two or three men, and even to suspend a dead body would
require the same.

As carefully as possible, I work higher up the ladder, but as my face
comes even with Ebony's, I realize that to disturb this crime scene would
be an injustice to both the victim and her family. The best thing I can
do would be to remove my raincoat and cover her face with it, to prevent
passersby from violating the privacy of her victimhood.

Thankfully, her eyes are closed, but her face is a mask of pain, not peace.
Pressing two fingers into her distended neck, I confirm that she has no
pulse. She likely hasn't for some time. Her skin isn't cold, but it's cool and
clammy in the cloud-filtered sun.

"I'm sorry, Ebony," I say uselessly, working to unzip my raincoat and
remove it without falling. If I can cover her head, then tie the arms of
my coat around her neck or shoulders . . . it will give her some measure
of protection from gawkers out on the road. But as I twist to accomplish
this task, my prosthetic foot catches in the ladder, and I feel my center of
balance go. A split second later I'm clinging to the dead girl's legs for life,
trying to keep from breaking my neck as I fall.

I end by crashing onto the fallen ladder, feeling the aluminum scrape a
divot in my side as my weight bends one of the legs like a child's toy.

"God*damn* it!" I shout. "Motherfucker!"

The corpse above me sways like a human plumb bob, the horsehair rope
creaking in sickening accompaniment. Sliding my iPhone out of my pants
pocket, I call Marshall McEwan.

He answers immediately. Before I can croak out ten words, he asks me to start over. I realize then that I'm sobbing, weeping for a girl I never knew in life.

"She's dead, Marshall," I choke out.

"Who? Not Ebony!"

"They lynched her, man. She's hanging from the porch lamp chain out here!"

"Oh, no . . . oh, God. Has anybody else seen her?"

"I don't think so. But they will. I tried to cover her face, but I fell off the ladder. Can you get Chief Morgan out here with some men?"

"He's downstairs now. I'll get him the second we hang up. Are you physically okay?"

"Shit, I don't know. I already had broken ribs. Just get the cops out here. This is bad, man. This is the worst thing I've seen in a long time."

"I can't believe it. If Tarlton's men did this to her . . . I don't know how we hold this town together."

"I don't know if it deserves to *be* held together. If whoever did this was here now, I'd shoot him in the fucking face."

"Hang tight, Penn. Help's coming."

"*Goddamn it,*" I curse, looking back toward Sargent Street.

"What is it?"

"Two cars have stopped out by the gate. The drivers are out . . . they're aiming their phones at the house. Buddy, this lynching is going to go viral in about two minutes." I feel like puking. "In half an hour, Bienville, Mississippi, will be as notorious as Money and Philadelphia were in the fifties and sixties."

"You can't cover her face?"

"No! I bent up the ladder when I fell."

"Jesus God. Morgan's cops are going to lose their minds over this. I'd better warn the National Guard."

"You'd better warn everybody. I'm just sorry I wasn't here sooner. Maybe I could have saved her."

"Don't go there, man. Not your fault. Are you *sure* she's dead?"

"She'll never take another breath. Start making calls, Marshall. Get the cops here *now*. Or Tarlton and his men will take over the case. And that would be the final obscenity."

CHAPTER 100

LANYING STOOD ALONE on the balcony of Martyn Black's room at the Planters' Hotel and looked across the river into Louisiana. Two more columns of fire had appeared to the right of the first one, probably a mile or two away. The sight triggered nauseating fear within her, a sense that things were spinning out of control in a way that wasn't supposed to happen in America. The pace of movement in the bluff park below had picked up. On the ground it probably didn't seem so, but from her vantage point she could see swirls of humanity amid the larger crowd, like whirlpools in a lake. It reminded her of the video she'd seen of the Mission Hill crowd after the first shots rang out—only in slow motion.

She'd been in crowds like that before, at ground level, but what she remembered most clearly wasn't this early phase of excitement, but the aftermath: the exhaustion and shock after the police had come through with their gas and batons and the arrests were made. The dispirited taste of defeat, the dread of delayed punishment if they'd managed to capture your face on camera, which was more often than not.

Martyn was dozing on the bed inside, still hoping for sex, but Lanying had protested that she felt sick. She'd claimed to be coming out to the balcony to get some air, but in truth she just wanted to get as far as she could from him. She'd known for some time that he wasn't a good man. But what she had seen revealed this week terrified her. And now . . . to look down upon all that his greed and disregard had wrought . . . she couldn't take in the enormity of it. Martyn was like one of those people in California who, by carelessly setting a small fire, ended up burning a quarter million acres and a town.

Except, of course, he hadn't begun carelessly. He had planned those fires to the last detail. He hadn't meant for *this* to happen, of course. But it had. And the worst part was, she'd allowed herself to be drawn into the nightmare. She had helped him to plan, to prepare, even to carry it off. Lanying had been with him when he purchased the aviation flares on the Gulf Coast, near Keesler Air Force Base in Biloxi. The moral implications hadn't really penetrated until after the second mansion burned. Because during the planning, Martyn had talked only of burning empty mansions. Except his mother's, of course, which was the point of the whole plan. To burn his family home so his mother could collect the insurance.

Or so he'd claimed in the beginning.

Loveta Corbin Black had truly started it all. For a while even Lanying had feared the old lady would set fire to her house in a drunken rage. Lanying understood that anger, if it was true that old Mr. Black had promised to care for her into old age, and then had not. But even so . . . to destroy a house in which you had spent most of your life seemed deranged in some way. At least to Lanying.

Burning the other homes to cover the crime . . . that had simply seemed like another of Martyn's video games. A brilliant piece of strategy, sound in a logical sense, but never quite real. And the mansions that were his targets—colossal boxes of brick and plaster, big enough to house a dozen families, yet sitting empty for ten months out of the year—none of it made any sense to her.

The first fire, the Tranquility mansion in Natchez, had gone about as she'd expected. Not a huge spectacle, but one that had drawn a crowd fascinated by watching a relic burn. But the second target, Arcadia . . . had changed everything. The Arcadia fire had killed a homeless man and orphaned his daughter, and that had shaken Lanying out of whatever haze had enveloped her during this strange phase of her life. With that death, the truth of what Martyn had pulled her into suddenly became sickeningly real. The vague awareness that she'd let herself become dependent on a man who was using her finally crystallized into a certainty. She had let her fear of being deported back to China keep her with someone who wanted her only for sex and company. And now he had drawn her into something beyond comprehension.

If it hadn't happened so fast, she thought, she might have resisted more. But they had bought the flares on Monday, just two days after the Mission Hill massacre. By Tuesday afternoon the bombs were planted, and Tranquility was burning. The timing had been an accident, actually. Martyn had planned for both fires to begin after dark on Tuesday night. Something had triggered the flare bomb in Tranquility a few hours prematurely. But Arcadia had caught fire right on schedule. She could hardly believe Martyn had acted with such dispatch, yet some part of her hadn't really been surprised. It was as though the digital avatar he became while competing in his online video tournaments had become real in the world of matter and time. Her actions, too, had gone from theoretical to consequential. The speed of that flip had left her in shock.

She had never been attracted to Martyn, only drawn to him because he'd so plainly and frankly offered her security. More security than she'd known in New Orleans, at least. But during the past week, she had gone from passively tolerating his attentions to suffering attacks of nausea when he came near, or—God forbid—touched her. And this, she suspected, was because at some level she had begun to believe that he'd used the fire at Montcornet as a way to murder his mother.

He'd denied it a dozen times, even though she'd never quite accused him. But Martyn had gone into exhaustive and repetitive detail about how much care he'd taken to be sure that Loveta would be sober and downstairs when the flares ignited in the air conditioner closet outside the master bedroom upstairs. He couldn't have guessed that she would lie to him about where she *was* in the house. Could he? Why would she lie? She never had before, to his knowledge.

Lanying hadn't disputed any of this aloud. It wasn't the kind of situation that allowed for proof one way or another. But she'd heard his voice when he spoke of it, and she'd watched his eyes. It wasn't that he hated his mother. If he had, Lanying would have known it long before, and she'd have been unable to remain with him. The terrible truth was that he'd simply cared more about the money that her death could bring him than about the woman herself living in the world even a minute longer. And now she was dead.

Burned alive . . .

For Lanying, coming from the culture she had, such a thing was so profoundly obscene that she couldn't bear to think of it for long. She only knew she had to get away from him, whatever the consequences. She was only here tonight because some part of her hoped to find a way to leave while avoiding two things: prison and deportation.

Four floors below, a light patch darted through the dark crowd once more. It was the girl again. The blonde lawyer who'd spent the day slipping back and forth across Battery Row, moving among the throngs of Black people with a camera phone and bottles of water. Lanying had watched her for nearly an hour before asking Martyn who she was. Martyn had used his phone camera to zoom in on her face, then said, "That's the city attorney's daughter. Cage. Uhh . . . *Ann* Cage. She's a lawyer in Jackson. Clearly suffering from a white-savior complex."

Maybe so, Lanying had thought, and then she'd asked what kind of law the girl practiced. *But at least she's brave and committed to something, like I used to be.*

Now the blonde hair moved along the west barricade of Battery Row, pausing near this person or that, then moving on. Earlier in the day, Ann had paused to talk to many children in the crowd, but now most of the kids seemed to be gone, or out of sight. After reaching the orange-and-white barrier at Front Street, which led down to the river, she turned and moved back north toward her father's town house, which stood four blocks up Battery Row. Watching her go, Lanying remembered that Martyn had never answered her question about the law. Taking out her cell phone, she found a listing under a small Jackson firm headed by a black woman named Doris Avery. The first words under Avery's name were *civil rights law.*

When Ann Cage disappeared under the trees that lined Confederate Memorial Park, Lanying felt her spirit follow. Then she heard Martyn calling her irritably to bed. For the briefest instant she felt a compulsion to climb onto the iron balcony and let herself fall. Better that than to lie beneath her desperate sweating jailer for another ten minutes—

The impulse passed with a shudder, leaving her hollow and shaken.

"Come to *bed*," Martyn repeated. "I need you."

I can't live another day like this, she thought. *I can't . . .*

Martyn's cell phone rang: "Lovesong" by the Cure.

Lanying heard him sit up suddenly in bed.

"Bobby?" he said. "Is that you?"

A few seconds passed in fraught silence.

"I'm, uh . . . I'm actually down here on the bluff now . . . in the Planters' Hotel . . . Uh-huh . . . Yeah, sure, but . . ."

A jolt went through Lanying then, deeper than thought, powerful as an electric shock. Martyn would be naked. He'd been waiting to have her. All his concentration was on his cousin—she could feel it. For whatever reason, Bobby White had rattled him. He always did.

She took a deep breath, as though preparing to leap into the sea from a high cliff. Then she stepped through the balcony door and in her most annoying voice said, "What is it? Who was that?"

Perched naked on the edge of the unkempt bed, looking terrified, Martyn angrily waved her away. That was all she needed. Lanying obeyed, walking past him toward the bathroom, and then of course past the bathroom door. Once at the main door, she slid the chain to the right with her left hand, and quietly turned the knob with her right. Another breath and then . . .

She pulled open the door and stepped into the hall.

Finding it empty, she sprinted down to the elevators, pushed both buttons, then shot into the stairwell and flew down the steps, bouncing from walls to banister like a sparrow evading a hawk.

Twenty seconds later she stepped onto the sidewalk that ran along the east side of Battery Row. A young Black National Guardsman in uniform waved flirtatiously at her. Shaking in disbelief, she waved back.

Free at last . . .

SOPHIE WAS MAKING herself a cup of herbal tea in the kitchen of Belle Rose when Ruby walked in behind her. She'd spent the past hour in her bedroom, trying not to think about the way things had gone today. With one corrupt vote, she had nullified everything positive she'd done since getting elected to the board three years earlier. She might have secured her inheritance by doing so, but . . . even now there was no guarantee of that.

"You all right?" Ruby asked, her voice quavering with emotion.

"Not really. Has something happened?"

"I'm not sure how to answer that. I heard you in there hollering at your daddy. Heard some of what y'all said. And it made me so sad."

"I'm sorry, Ruby."

"It's not your fault. And I feel even worse over Charlot."

Sophie closed her eyes and fought back tears. She'd already cried too much over her brother.

"I need to tell you something," Ruby said. "Something Charlot told me to do, and I should have done it before now."

Sophie turned to her family's maid. "What are you talking about?"

"Last night that boy told me that for the next few days, he was gonna call or text my cell every six hours. So I'd know he was all right."

"What made him do that? He knew those casino men still meant to hurt him, I guess."

"I don't think that was it, Ms. Sophie."

"Then what?"

The maid's face had never before looked so troubled. Ruby lowered her voice to a near whisper: "I don't think Charlot trusted your father to do what he said he was gon' do. You know, pay off his debts. He was suspicious that Mr. Charles would invite him to stay here, after treating him so bad for so long. He feared he had some other reason besides paying off his debts."

"I did, too, to be honest."

"Well, Charlot never even called me the first time. After he disappeared, I mean. Last night I cooked him his favorite meal, and then your daddy sent me home. Told me to take a night off. Which ain't like him at all, as you know."

"No."

"I need to tell you something else, too. Something a lot worse."

Sophie hugged herself with inexplicable dread. "I'm listening."

"I cleaned up a little before I left out of here, and on my way out, I heard a scuffle of feet, and then Amadu yelling something. Turns out he was chasing Mr. Bobby White, who had come out here for some reason, before you got back."

"Bobby was here before I came back?"

Ruby nodded. "Anyhow, Amadu meant to stop him from leaving out of here in a rush, but Mr. White turned and done something I've never seen."

"Which was?"

"He cold-cocked Amadu like he was nothing but a child. I believe he meant to kill him until your father told him to stop."

"What? Why would he do that?"

The maid looked at the floor and shook her head. "I don't want to tell you."

"Ruby, you have to. Things have gone too far. We have to get to the truth under all this."

"Well . . . I saw that they'd all been out in the rose garden. So as soon as it was clear, I went out there and poked around."

"And . . . ?"

"And I found something I wish I never had."

Sophie winced against knowledge she did not yet have, but suddenly felt certain of. "Not Charlot?"

Ruby nodded slowly. "He was wedged up in that old garden shed out there, blue and cold."

"Was he alive?"

Ruby wiped her eyes. "No, baby. He'd was gone. Looked to me like somebody had choked the life out of him. Amadu, if I had to guess."

"Dear God." Sophie almost wailed. "Why?"

The maid shrugged. "I reckon only your daddy would know that. But probably to protect Mr. Charles somehow, or save him money."

"I feel sick. Do you think Bobby was involved? In the killing, I mean?"

"I don't think so. I think he saw or was shown what was done, and he went crazy with rage. That's why he meant to kill Amadu. I think Bobby always cared a great deal for Charlot. Loved him, even."

"I do too." Sophie cupped her hands around her tea for warmth, but did not drink. "Do you think Daddy is really capable of ordering the murder of his son?"

Ruby took a seat at the kitchen counter. "Two nights ago, when Tranquility burned, we rode over there to see, remember?"

"Of course."

"And Penn Cage come round and talked to your daddy."

"I remember."

"Well, after he left, I heard Mr. Charles tell Amadu that as soon as everybody left out of there, whether it was that night or the next day, he should dump a half dozen sacks of lime down in the old cistern. The one that used to sit right under the house."

Sophie froze. "The one Charlot got spanked so bad for playing in that time?"

Ruby nodded. "I think Charlot went down there more than once. Might even have taken a friend down there, playing army or something. Or just to show off them 'Yankee bones.'"

"Oh, God, Ruby, what are you trying to tell me?"

"Why would Mr. Charles want to put lime down there now? Especially after that fire? 'Less he was trying to hide something from them state investigators."

"Oh, God."

"I think my mama may know something about it, too. But I hate even thinking about it."

Sophie took a scalding sip of tea. Perspiration broke out on the back of her neck. "Earlier today Penn Cage told me Pearl said something to him a few years ago about a murder at a Natchez hotel. Back in the sixties. My family called your mother and father to help clean it up. Maybe your grandmother, even."

Ruby solemnly shook her head. "I asked Charlot what I should do if he didn't call me for a while. He said, 'Nothing. If that happens . . . don't worry about it.'" She shook her head. "That baby just wanted somebody to know he was gone, I guess."

Sophie wiped her eyes again.

"But then he told me that if he stopped calling, I should tell you," Ruby went on. "He said that was information you might need someday. Because the same thing might happen to you."

Sophie raised her hands to her face and covered her eyes.

"What we gon' do, Ms. Sophie?" Ruby asked.

"I don't know. I think . . . maybe we should call Pearl."

The maid's eyes widened. "My mama Pearl?"

Sophie dropped her hand. "Yes."

"Why you think that?"

"The same reason you do, I'm guessing."

The seventy-year-old maid blinked twice, then took out her cell phone and looked at it. "I think you're right."

"What's your reason?" Sophie asked.

Ruby looked up, her eyes hard. "'Cause Mama knows Mr. Charles down to the bone. And she might be old . . . but Mama don't play."

CHAPTER 101

SINCE THE MURDER of Doc Berry, Ray Ransom had declared war on white Bienville, specifically the Poker Club. His weapons had been elemental—fire and water. Nothing destroyed property faster than flood and flame. And nothing made wealthy white men pay attention like financial losses. Most of his targets had been insured, of course, but the sheer chaos created by his attacks would create an unbearable sense of anxiety in men accustomed to controlling every part of their world.

Ray was driving down the levee road in Louisiana when the photo of Ebony Swan hanging from the light fixture in front of Attica showed up on one of his boys' cell phones. When Easy Easley held it over the seat so Ray could see, Ray closed his eyes, then braked and pulled onto the grassy shoulder, his hands shaking.

"You boys see that?" he asked. "Take a good look. That's what they used to do to us back in the day. Now they feel threatened . . . and they're doin' it again."

"I know that girl's mama, Ray," Easy said. "The downers 'bout got her in the ground. I've seen her huff acetone when she got nothing else."

"But her little girl's gonna get there first."

The truck swayed as a big tractor-trailer roared past on the flat road, headed toward Texas.

"What we gon' do now, Ray?" asked Cedric. "Stick to the plan?"

"Nope. Gloves comin' off now. Time for some proportional response."

The three young men looked at one another. They'd thought the gloves *were* off. "What you mean?" asked Stoney Whitmore. "We gon' hang somebody?"

Ray shook his head. "We're gonna focus. From now on, fires only. By tonight, this county and parish are gonna look like Kuwait in '91. They gonna see the fires all the way from *space*. If they can see 'em from space, they'll see 'em in Washington, D.C."

"Aiight then," said Easy. "Let's get on with it."

Ray said a quiet prayer for Ebony Swan, but as he did, the anger in him began to build. It had been there so long—born during his childhood, growing during Vietnam, easing a little in Los Angeles, when he'd found himself doing good work with the Panthers. But then it returned when the government began breaking laws to stop them helping people. Then his homecoming. First New Orleans, where the police brought their tank down to Desire to stop them. The people had saved them that time, the poorest of the poor, the denizens of the projects. Then had come his true homecoming: Bienville, where no one but his own welcomed him back.

Last came Parchman.

There he'd felt the full weight of the apartheid state on his shoulders— crushing his spine, constricting his heart, poisoning his mind. Twisting his soul, in the end. But Ray took everything they dropped on him. That was the thing that made him different, that had allowed him to survive. Ray could take anything. Everybody knew it. On a football field. In a rice paddy. In a tin-roofed concrete box in the Mississippi Delta. Ray Ransom could take it.

But now it was time to give back.

All of it.

Anybody that would string up a little girl like that had it coming. Doc had done his best to steer Ray toward nonviolence, to keep his temper in check. But Doc was gone now, one more gentle soul cut down before his time.

All of it . . .

Ray stuck his head out the window and looked back to make sure the road was clear. As he pulled onto the asphalt, Easy said, "What'd you say, Ray?"

"Nothin'."

"Sounded like you said 'All of it.'"

"Maybe I did. Listen . . . you boys ever seen a grain elevator go off?"

"What you mean? Like explode?"

"Yeah. Deadliest ever to happen was in Westwego, Louisiana, a hundred and seventy miles south of here. Around Christmas of '77."

"What they blow it up with?" asked Easy.

"Nothing. It's the dust," Ray explained. "You don't need a bomb. Grain dust trapped in the air is five or six times as powerful as gunpowder."

"Damn!" Cedric exclaimed. "You're not thinking about the big-ass elevator down on the river?"

"That's exactly what I'm thinking."

"How we gonna survive setting it off?"

Ray looked over the seat with a strange smile. "I got a bag of old fireworks from the last Fourth of July party. All we need is a couple of Roman candles."

Easy shook his head in wonder.

"You boys with me on this?"

"Shit," said Stoney. "You the CO, man. We follow orders. At least we know what we fightin' for this time. Just point us up a hill. We'll go."

"You're the man, Ray."

"No, I ain't. I knew some back in the day, though. Real men. I'm just all that's left 'round here." He turned around and looked into the young faces in the back seat. "But we gon' do what we can. While we can. And how it ends don't matter. That's what I learned from Charlie in 'Nam. We ain't fightin' for ourselves. We fightin' for those comin' behind us."

"Like that girl," said Cedric in his bass voice. "Ebony."

Ray nodded. "Now you learnin', son."

ANNIE AND NADINE stood in the open door of the guest bedroom on the ground floor of Penn's town house, staring at Kendrick Washington, who lay motionless on the bed, breathing with a deep, regular rhythm.

"I feel so guilty," Annie said. "Are you sure it's not dangerous? Liquid Xanax? Hospice stuff?"

Nadine shrugged. "He's young and strong. He'll be fine. Didn't you say Kendrick checked himself out of the hospital against doctor's orders?"

"Absolutely. He was practically hysterical. Kept yelling that he had to get back to the bluff for his speech, even while they were probing the knife wound."

Nadine smiled and squeezed Annie's shoulder. "You can wake him up in time, if you really want to risk him going back out into that crowd."

"I don't," Annie said in a grave voice. "But that's not my decision to make. Is it?"

"I don't know."

"What do you think, though? Tell me."

Nadine laughed softly, then reached out for the doorknob. "I think Kendrick's pretty hot."

Annie blushed and burst into suppressed laughter as Nadine pulled the door shut.

They were coming up the hall when a steady knocking started at the main door. Annie darted forward, then looked back at Nadine. "Who could that be? Are we expecting anybody?"

Nadine shook her head. "Not that I know of. But with that crowd out there, it could be anybody. Be careful."

Annie closed the distance to the door, then leaned forward and looked through the peephole with her right eye. On the other side of the door stood a Chinese girl who appeared to be no more than five feet tall.

"What the . . . ?" she whispered.

"Who is it?" Nadine asked, standing a few feet behind her. "I'm going to get your father's pistol."

"No, no need," Annie said, holding up her right hand. "It's a Chinese girl. Or woman, I guess."

The visitor knocked again, harder this time.

"Get behind the arch there," Annie said, pointing to the den.

"You don't know me!" said a female voice with a Chinese accent. "I need to see Miss Ann Cage. I need a lawyer."

Annie and Nadine shared a look of incredulity.

"Are you alone?" Annie asked.

"Yes! And I'm in danger. People are hunting me! Please. Is Miss Ann Cage inside? I saw her earlier, helping people in the crowd. I need a civil rights lawyer. Immigration, too."

Nadine shrugged and signaled that Annie should open the door. Blowing out a rush of air, Annie turned the knob and opened it to the length of the security chain.

"I'm Ann Cage," she said through the crack. "But I'm afraid I'm not taking clients right now. I've got all I can handle on my plate."

"*Please*," the girl pleaded, her eyes wet. "I have nowhere else to go!"

"Why do you need a lawyer?"

"I've committed crimes. Serious crimes. Not intentionally. But a man I was with . . . I think I may be a, what do you call it . . . accessory?"

"Who's hunting you? The immigration authorities? ICE?"

"No, no. The man I mentioned."

"Who is he?"

The girl looked deeply conflicted. "A man who's done very bad things. I'm afraid I helped him. More than I should have."

"What did he do?" Annie asked. "What did *you* do?"

The dark-haired girl took a deep breath, then looked into Annie's eyes and shook her head with the resolve of a martyr walking to her death. "We set the fires. The fires that burned the slave mansions."

Annie's eyes popped wide. "You what?"

The girl nodded. "Every fire. Except the one at the house called Pencarrow."

Annie's ears were ringing. "You—wait, tell me one thing. What did you use to start those fires?"

"Military flares. Model M206. He bought them from a soldier he knows on the Gulf Coast. Another gamer. Keesler Air Force Base."

Annie's heart lurched. "You'd better come inside."

"Thank you. Oh, thank you."

Annie unhooked the chain, then caught hold of the girl's arm and pulled her into the house. Before she shut the door, she looked up and down Main to see whether anyone had watched her enter.

"I don't think anyone saw me," said the girl. "My name is Lanying, by the way."

"Does *anyone* know you're here? Or that you were coming?"

"No one. I didn't know myself until I ran for my life."

Before Annie could speak again, Lanying caught sight of Nadine watching her from the den. She nearly jumped out of her skin.

"It's all right!" Annie assured her. "Nadine's my friend, and she's a lawyer as well. She won't tell anybody about you."

"I won't," Nadine promised. "And I'm on my way out." She looked at Annie. "I need to run by my store and check those journal pages from the chimney box. See how they're drying in the dehumidifiers."

"I'm going to sit down with Lanying and find out her story."

The Chinese woman backed against the wall like a skittish animal as Nadine passed, but Nadine's eyes were wide with shock and staring at Annie as if to say: *This is the craziest shit I've ever heard!*

"Hey," Annie said softly, holding out her hand until Lanying clasped it. "You just hired your lawyer."

CHAPTER 102

BOBBY WHITE LEANED against the hotel room desk and stared at his cousin Martyn, who sat hunched at a little marble-topped table before the glass doors leading to the balcony. Martyn had wept off and on as he related his story, and it was all Bobby could do not to slap his snotty face to bring him back to his senses. But he didn't. He let Martyn tell it the way he wanted, even though the risk of being in this room increased with every passing minute.

"Bobby?" Martyn prompted finally.

Bobby realized then that his cousin had fallen silent.

"What should I do?"

"Martyn, you are a world-class fuck-up."

"I know. I know I am."

"You've always *been* a fuck-up. The thing is, except for Angie Price, your mistakes have been relatively inconsequential."

Martyn nodded almost gratefully. "I've tried to keep myself together, Bobby. Between the ditches, you know. Psychologically speaking."

"Be that as it may, this time you dropped the reins."

"I should have seen it coming. Maybe I even did. I knew Lanying was getting antsy. But when you called . . . I dropped my guard, just for a little bit."

"Forget it. We're going to find her. But we have more immediate problems."

"Such as?"

"It can never be known that you were behind these fires. *Never*, you understand?"

"Totally, man. And it won't be. Not from me. Lanying is the problem."

"Leave that girl to me. Now listen. This isn't a video game. Do you get that? This is the real world."

"I do, believe it or not. What do you want me to do? Just tell me."

Bobby was relieved to hear his cousin sound so submissive. Martyn was older than he, and he'd always had an unpredictable arrogance about certain things. "What was your plan? If Lanying hadn't ghosted you today?"

"Hit some more houses, of course. Make sure Montcornet wasn't the last one in line, which would eventually draw all the attention to me."

"How many more?"

"At least one. Right? Preferably two or three. Every attack increases the risk, of course."

Bobby nodded as if in admiration. "Then that's what you're going to do. Stick to your plan."

Martyn's eyes filled with relief. "Okay, cool. No problem."

"But—you're going to hit the next house tonight."

Martyn's mouth fell open. "*Tonight?*"

"Are all the flares pre-planted, like the one the police found at Attica? Or can you hit a mansion at will?"

Martyn took his time with this. "I can hit one with a drone device."

"Do you have to rig it? Or is it ready to go?"

"I've got one ready. I was going to use it on a Louisiana mansion, down on the River Road, near St. Francisville."

"Perfect. I want you to hit a house near the bluff with that one instead—within the next hour, if possible."

Eyes narrowed in skepticism, Martyn said, "Which house, Bobby? There are a couple right on Battery Row."

"Neither of those. I want this fire close enough to be visible from the bluff—and the news choppers, obviously—but not so close that it forces an evacuation. Let me think about it. Meanwhile, let's talk about Lanying."

Martyn looked at the floor. "All right."

"You must have some idea of where she would run."

Martyn shook his head.

"*Think*, Martyn! She must have given you some clue. People don't make these kinds of moves on a whim. Especially computer engineers. Something triggered her."

"It was the Montcornet fire! Mama's death, I'm telling you. Lanying thinks I did it on purpose."

Bobby stared hard at his cousin, but he made no accusation. "Go back over everything she said to you in the last twenty-four hours."

"I will."

"*Now.* I'll think about the target house."

"Okay, okay." Martyn rubbed his eyes and looked out onto the balcony.

Bobby knew he was picturing his lover standing there only an hour ago. Placing himself between Martyn and the exit door, Bobby visualized the buildings that lined the first three streets running parallel to the face of the bluff. Thankfully, it took less than thirty seconds for the obvious target to come to him. The visibility requirement made the choice.

Built in 1799, McFadyen's Tavern looked much like a famous old Natchez building once known as Connelly's Tavern, but now called the

House on Ellicott's Hill. That building had two claims to fame, one proved false long ago. Historians recorded that the first American flag to fly over the Natchez Territory—in 1797—had been raised over it, and this was true. Second, some authorities held that Aaron Burr, after being arrested near Natchez on the orders of President Thomas Jefferson, had planned his successful legal defense to treason in the tavern. The problem was, later research had established that the real Connelly's Tavern had stood a block away from Ellicott's Hill.

Work by a Bienville-born historian had recently proved that on at least two occasions—even as he carried on a romance with a very young woman from Natchez—the fifty-year-old Burr had met with his attorney in McFadyen's Tavern in Bienville. Thanks to its position on a high hill, McFadyen's had been visible from many parts of town during the nineteenth and early twentieth centuries, and still clearly was from the bluff. The building had been lovingly preserved in the 1930s, right down to the bullet holes in its long bar—proof that lethal brawls from earlier eras had not been confined to the riverfront beneath the bluff.

"McFadyen's Tavern," Bobby said. "Could you hit that and be sure to get away clean?"

Martyn's eyes lit up. "Absolutely! In fact, that's about the best target you could have picked, from that point of view."

"Why?"

Martyn grinned like a little boy. "Because I can see it from my office window. I can fly the drone from my desk! All I need is a launch site that won't be suspicious if anyone observes the takeoff."

"Can you think of one?"

"Sure, yeah. Probably ... Fleming Park, that little green square off Pearl Street? Anybody who sees a drone take off from there will assume it's a recreational or news drone."

"Is this some fancy six-rotor contraption?"

"Hell, no. A standard quad-rotor commercial DJI, made in China. I could launch it from my office window, actually."

A flash of worry went through Bobby. "That's a toy!"

"Not when it's carrying M206 flares. Plus incendiary magnesium flakes."

"Sounds like you did your work right."

"I always do. You know that. But ..."

"What?"

"Does McFadyen's Tavern make sense as a *political* target? Doesn't it predate the Civil War era? I mean, were any slaves involved in building it?"

Bobby gave the question ten seconds' thought. "If I remember correctly, Callum McFadyen owned seven or eight slaves at the time he settled here and built that tavern."

Martyn shook his head in amazement. "You've gotta be the only baseball player in the world who knows that kind of shit."

Bobby frowned with regret. "If I were still a baseball player, I wouldn't know it." *So I guess I'll have to settle for being president—*

"Shit!" Martyn cried.

"What is it?" Bobby asked, coming up off the edge of the desk.

"I just remembered something Lanying asked me. It might be important."

"Tell me."

"Earlier today, she noticed a white girl running through the crowd, filming people, giving them water, giving treats to the kids."

"The Cage girl?" Bobby asked. "Penn's daughter?"

Martyn nodded. "Ann Cage, right. Lanying asked me who she was. Wanted to know what kind of law she practiced."

Bobby nodded slowly, his instinct hardening into conviction. "Civil rights law. With Quentin Avery's widow."

Martyn nodded again. "Doris Avery. She's big time, Bobby."

"Oh, I know. Her husband was a giant." He began pacing out the space between the flat-screen TV and the two beds. "Cage's town house is right down Battery Row from here. Did Lanying know that?"

"I'm pretty sure I told her at some point."

"Jesus, Martyn! She's probably there now, telling her goddamn story like it's the movie of the week."

Martyn shook his head. "I don't know. She's not quick to trust anybody."

"She trusted *you*."

Martyn put up his hands in surrender. "Granted. Should I try to call her again?"

"No! Have you been trying?"

"Four or five times at first, but not since. Until you called, I was super paranoid. I was trying to figure a way to leave the country without being stopped."

"Jesus, man. Get your shit together. I gave you your mission."

"I know. I'm going to get right on it."

"But there's one thing you have to do first."

Existential fear entered Bobby's eyes. "What's that?"

"I need all the flares you have left."

Martyn stared at his cousin for twenty seconds, trying to work out Bobby's intent. "All of them?"

"You can keep enough to hit one more house after McFadyen's. That would be ideal. But I need the rest."

"What for?"

"We're going to frame somebody for the fires."

"Who?"

"Don't worry about it. Better you don't know in advance. You can find out on the late news tonight. In case you haven't noticed, there's a war starting outside. A real one."

Martyn got up off the bed. "Come on, Bobby. You're no fun. Tell me!"

"Sorry. Now, close those suitcases and get ready to move. This hotel's crawling with law enforcement. Give me ten minutes after I walk out, then leave."

"Are you going to meet me to pick up the flares?"

"Are you brain-damaged? Hell, no. Where are they? Montcornet? Or your house?"

Martyn hesitated. "My house. Buried in ammo boxes."

"Okay. I'm going to send a couple guys to pick them up."

Martyn started to protest, but Bobby silenced him with a wave of his hand. "Two guys. They may look scary, but they won't touch you. They're protecting you now. They'll take the flares and go. Then you hit Mc-Fadyen's. Don't wait. Don't try to double-check with me. Just burn it. You understand?"

"Affirmative. But . . . Bobby, I'm scared."

"You should be. You put yourself and a lot of other people at risk."

"I know, but . . . it's not that. It's *you*, man. I feel like I let you down, and I know you don't tolerate that."

Bobby still found it difficult to believe Martyn was three years older than he. Taking a deep breath, he sighed, then stepped forward and hugged his cousin. Martyn resisted for a few seconds, then sagged against him and sobbed.

"You don't have to worry," Bobby assured him. "We're blood. And we've had mutual assured destruction ever since we laid Angie to rest in those woods. Right?"

Martyn nodded into his shoulder.

"All right, then. Let me go. The world's going to change tonight. And the sooner you get your job done, the sooner you can forget all this."

CHAPTER 103

ANNIE WAS SERVING tea to Lanying and Judge Clayton Shelby, whom she had called to consult on Lanying's case, when someone turned the knob of the pantry door. They were sitting at the kitchen table, and Lanying was finishing an anxious summary of her actions over the past two weeks. The elderly judge had listened patiently, attentively, and Annie noticed that he did not communicate reproach, not even when the young woman described obviously criminal acts. Shelby had actually been her third choice for backup. Annie's first call after Nadine left her alone with Lanying had been to her boss, Doris Avery, but Doris hadn't answered. Her second was to her father, but even he had not picked up, which was very unusual. Recalling how impressed she had been with Judge Shelby when she spoke to him after her grandmother's funeral, she had decided to call him.

After Lanying fell silent, the first words out of Judge Shelby's mouth were, "Young lady, I'm afraid you're in serious legal jeopardy. But your real problem is political. You're in possession of explosive knowledge—which could buy you a lot of leniency with the federal authorities—but that same knowledge could put you behind the bars of a state prison for life. And I'm afraid that's where state authorities will want to put you, unless you play the game the way they want you to."

Before Annie could ask Judge Shelby to clarify this, the knob of the pantry door turned. Because that door was inside the garage, Annie assumed it meant her father was returning. Nevertheless, when she got up, she obeyed Judge Shelby's signal and waited for him to stand behind the panel with his pistol drawn. Then she opened the door to the length of its security chain.

A black boot crashed through the gap, knocking Annie back through the pantry. Then a heavyset man with dark hair bulled through after the boot and bowled Annie off her feet. Sensing someone behind the door, the black-bearded intruder smashed the wood against the pantry wall, then began hammering Judge Shelby with it. The judge's pistol went off, but the man kept hurling his weight against the door. When he finally pulled the cracked panel away, Shelby collapsed to the floor, unconscious. Annie got out a half second's scream, but a meaty hand clapped over her mouth and dragged her into the kitchen.

Lanying shrieked and tried to bolt from behind the little table, but two more men burst through the open door and caught her before she reached the den.

"Bobby was right!" bellowed Shot Barlow, releasing Annie and shoving her into the arms of one of the younger men. "This little Chink bitch has been hiding in plain sight! Hell, she ain't no bigger'n a minute."

"Let's get 'em out," said one of the other men. "While we can still get a vehicle up here. It's gettin' crowded out there. Cops are gonna close off the streets, and that's Judge Clayton Shelby we just beat the shit out of."

The judge groaned from the floor, and hope surged in Annie's chest. She'd worried he might be dead.

"Clay Shelby again!" spat Barlow. "That old *Mayberry R.F.D.* mother-fucker? No, no. Buck will make sure we get out clean." Barlow eyed Annie with a strange light in his eyes. "Besides, there ain't no more city cops. Not real ones. Just jungle bunnies playing dress-up. No, I want to look at this little honey for a minute. She's acted so goddamn high and mighty all these years, since she was a teenager. Too good to be my neighbor, I guess."

"I never lived on Pencarrow," Annie said defiantly.

Barlow's eyes filled with delight at her display of resistance. "Now, that's a lie for sure. You lived out there with that Black boy redoing the place, didn't you? Goddamn right you did," Barlow nodded with enthusiasm. "Yeah, we know what you done out there. Donny even taped you a couple of times, howling in that construction trailer. Goddamn pussy traitor's what you are. Not another Princess Di, like you think."

Annie felt her face go bright red.

"So you want to try to take my land, huh? You and your daddy? Give it to a bunch of Black bastard children? Well, that ain't never gonna happen. You know why?"

"Let's deliver these bitches where we're s'posed to," said the man holding Lanying, whose eyes looked like those of a panicked puppy being held down by a vet. "Mr. White seemed pretty damned anxious about this Chinese girl."

"Calm down, son, it's all good." Barlow moved like an old man anticipating a dance with a pretty young girl. "We got the little bitch now. *Both* of 'em. And I'll tell you what we're gonna do before we go, boys. We're gonna give Princess here the same treatment the Frenchies gave the sluts who humped the Germans during the occupation. We're gonna give her a *shave and a haircut!*"

MARTYN BLACK'S OFFICE was on the third floor of the city administration building on the south side of Bienville, four blocks off the bluff.

His target, McFadyen's Tavern, stood six blocks to the north and three back from the bluff. Peering through a narrow crack in his curtains, Martyn had a direct line of sight to the upper floor and distinctive shed roof around the white building's central gable. A quick Google search told him that the tavern had been under renovation by one of Bienville's garden clubs for the past two years, which made it likely to be empty and poorly secured.

The admin building was virtually empty at the end of the business day, especially with the chaos and danger on the nearby bluff. For this reason, Martyn had decided to launch his drone from his office window rather than risk leaving it unattended in a park for even ten minutes. The odds that anyone would witness it taking off from his third-floor window were minuscule. The more urgent risk now was rain, which looked like it could let go from the threatening sky at any moment.

Martyn had powered up the drone in the open trunk of his car below, then oriented it to the satellites that would guide it to its destination. Checking the controller software on his iPad Mini, he satisfied himself that he could rely on an uneventful flight. The device itself—a DJI Phantom 3—now sat on his desk near the window like what it was, a hybrid of hobbyist's toy and deadly weapon. Available in Best Buys, Walmarts, and big-box stores across the nation, the Phantom was still a device of considerable sophistication. Piloted by an expert, it could do remarkable things. After deciding to burn his mother's house as part of a series of arsons, Martyn had made the drone his first choice. It made sense because the prime consideration in such crimes was to be nowhere in the vicinity when the fires started. But Martyn's early research had revealed that most antebellum mansions in the area had metal roofs, which militated against a light drone-delivered incendiary device. Even with the military flares he'd procured—which burned at three thousand degrees Fahrenheit—he could be much more assured of success by physically planting the flares inside the mansions in advance. The risks had been high, but he'd succeeded beyond his wildest dreams.

The problem was that after the Arcadia fire, widespread searches of local mansions had begun. And not by amateurs, but by professionals like the BATF and the FBI. A police dog had uncovered the flares he'd planted at Attica, preventing one of the two fires he'd planned for the second day's attacks. Part of him had wanted to go back and hit Attica with the drone-delivered flare, but that was teenage thinking. Now he had a real mission.

Looking down at his project, he recalled the white-knuckle nightmare of separating a single M206 flare from the heavy cassette normally deployed as a defensive measure in the A-10 attack aircraft. That cassette weighed forty-one kilograms: more than forty times the weight that could be carried by the DJI. Martyn had had to surgically remove a single flare from the unit, which required handling material that would burst into searing flame if it touched even one molecule of oxygen. He'd been tempted to get stoned before attempting that operation, but in the end, he'd performed it during forty minutes of nerve-stripping tension.

Once he'd secured the flare, he'd constructed a simple, reliable device with a built-in weight cushion that allowed for slight human miscalculation, and also for some variation in atmospheric conditions. The DJI could comfortably lift, carry, and deliver three pounds of weight above that of its own components. The M206 flare weighed 195 grams. The USB power bank that would detonate the flare weighed 180 grams. Together these two components weighed less than a pound. After realizing that, Martyn had forced himself to remove another M206 and add it to the drone, despite the additional risk of immolating himself.

Even after adding the second flare, he had 330 grams of excess carrying capacity shy of the two-pound limit he'd assigned himself. He exploited this with brilliant efficiency, by carving a magnesium fire-starter block of the type commonly carried by campers into thin shavings and binding them around the flares in a Ziploc bag. When these M206 flares ignited, they would blast the burning magnesium outward, filling whatever space the drone occupied with fire that almost could not be extinguished. Martyn had no doubt that his device would set McFadyen's Tavern aflame. The difficult part would be forcing himself to leave his office before watching the beauty of his handiwork unfold in the world.

That, he thought. *And sweating out the hours or days it could take for Bobby to track down Lanying. And yet, Bobby might well be right about Lanying taking refuge with Penn Cage's family. And if that is the case . . . he'll already be taking steps to remove the risk of Lanying telling what she knows.*

Martyn wasn't sure how Bobby would go about that, but he didn't need to know. Bobby White was a survivor. If it came to a choice between his own future and someone else's . . .

Standing in the U of his computer desk, Martyn pulled down both joysticks on his controller and engaged the props on the Phantom. His office filled with the thrumming whir of a hundred hornets going mad under the ground. Satisfied that its guidance system was locked to the proper satellites, he leaned over the back of his desk and raised his office window. Then he spread the curtains, checked the street below—empty, cleared by fear of rain—and lifted the iPad controller off his desk. With a few touches of his fingertips, gentle manipulation of the joystick, the drone lifted off his desk and moved through the window as if guided by its own intelligence.

Once clear of the building, it climbed two hundred feet and began tracking across the city toward McFadyen's Tavern—seven hundred yards away. Martyn fought the urge to fly VFR from the window, and instead closed his curtains, sat, and resigned himself to piloting the reminder of the mission through the eye of the DJI's camera. It would be just like Desert Storm—a TV-guided JDAM bomb boring in against its target until it blinded itself in the fiery orgasm of mission success.

SHOT BARLOW DREW a tactical knife from a scabbard at his belt and held it up to Annie's cheek. She tried to jerk away, but the redneck holding her was far too strong to escape. For some reason, as Barlow came closer with the knife, Annie found herself thinking back to the story of his ancestor, to the duel under the oak tree where they'd buried Peggy, where Captain Robert Pencarrow had unexpectedly shot this man's rapacious forebear through the heart.

"Be *still* now, baby girl," Barlow crooned, touching her cheek with the blade's cold edge. It gleamed like a mirror, reflecting her wide eye. "I don't wanna slip and cut your pretty throat. I might have a use for that later. This baby's sharp, see, but cuttin' hair's an art. Shaving's even trickier. Which you'll find out *directly*."

He grabbed a hank of auburn hair over Annie's shoulder, pulled it taut, then dug the blade in at an angle, sawing hard. Her scalp burned, but she held her silence, knowing he'd only enjoy it more if she betrayed her distress.

Lanying sobbed on the floor as Barlow cut.

After Barlow managed to shear off about four inches of hair, the militia leader grabbed another hank and started again. "God*damn*, that's tough," he grunted, his sunburned forearms flexing. "I wonder if it's any softer down low."

"I bet that brother who wears the chains could tell us," said the younger man holding Annie.

Barlow's teeth dug into his bottom lip while he sawed. "Oh, hell, yeah. If we're lucky, maybe he'll turn up and we can have a conversation about it. Tell him he's number two in the train now, behind the one hanging in the burn unit at UMC."

Tears squeezed from Annie's eyes at the thought of Andrew McKinney.

"That's the one we got on tape," said the warm voice in her ear. "Once you go black, you never go back. That's what they say, ain't it?"

"That's a myth," said Barlow. "I get some every New Year's for luck, but it ain't no better'n white stuff."

The slow creak of the pantry door hinges had an oddly domestic sound, and it triggered terror in Annie, who feared above all that her father would walk into the kitchen and be killed in a futile effort to defend her. But the man who walked through the pantry was not her father. It was his blond UPS delivery driver. She was praying the young man would not be hurt when she registered wrinkles at the corners of his eyes and a Florida tan. Then—like a bolt of revelation—she understood she was not looking at the UPS driver.

The newcomer was Daniel Kelly.

Never in her life had Annie experienced a rush of relief like the one that flooded through her in that moment.

"Well, look at this little soiree," Kelly said, absorbing the scene with apparent equanimity.

"Who the fuck are you?" asked Barlow.

Kelly's eyes had already taken in the absence of firearms. "Mister . . . I'm this girl's fairy godmother. But I'm a little jet-lagged today. Just flew in from a combat zone. So I'm gonna give you boys twenty seconds to get the hell out of here with your balls still attached."

Barlow looked at his men with incredulity. "And if we stay instead?"

Kelly's answering tone was as mild as that of a priest greeting worshippers at a church door. "You won't like it. And you might not live through it. You've got ten seconds now."

Barlow's next laugh still contained a note of incredulity, but perhaps the first hints of awareness had begun to dawn. His bearded mouth fell open as Kelly's hands dropped. Years of expensive tactical training had prepared neither him nor his men for what the former Delta operator unleashed next. When Kelly moved, the kitchen itself seemed to spin. Somehow his foot appeared in the same visual frame as Barlow's eyes, and Annie shuddered from the sympathetic impact transmitted through the militia leader's burly arms. A second later Barlow was down, groaning gibberish like a man with a cracked skull.

His younger accomplices bolted for the door, but Kelly snatched them back like a father wrestling toddlers. Then he began hammering their heads against countertops and cabinets. The banging brought Annie's gorge to her throat, and the blood spray was worse. Flattening herself against the counter, she scooted left, then left again, and finally crouched over Lanying, who was cowering in the corner. It felt as though a tornado had spun up at the center of the kitchen, like they once had in the TV commercials of her childhood. "*Stronger than dirt!*"

Then, almost as suddenly, silence reigned again.

Kelly's blond head turned slowly as he surveyed the results of his work. Then he shook out his long hair and focused on Annie, his blue-gray eyes and easy smile as familiar as ever. "You okay, boo?"

His voice was a unique blend of Florida, Texas, and California that she'd always loved. "I . . . I don't know. I think so."

"The new 'do looks good," he told her, reaching out and petting the butchered tresses at her neck and ear. "Cyndi Lauper circa 1988. *Asymmetric*, baby!"

Annie threw her arms around his neck and burst into tears.

FROM THE WINDOW of Martyn Black's office in the city admin building, his drone bomb appeared to crash through the third-floor window of McFadyen's Tavern without sound. Martyn doubted whether many people heard it even on the street immediately below the target. By this time the rumbling engines of police and military vehicles on Battery Row were drowning out most ambient noise, while the marchers—ten thousand strong—had begun to sing gospel songs or chant in different levels of unison. When the screen on Martyn's iPad controller went blank due to the destruction of the drone's camera, he set the unit on his desk, then opened the curtains of his office window and looked north.

At first he saw nothing unusual over the rooftops. A fillip of fear went through him, a worry that the flare might not have detonated or, even if it had, had not found sufficient flammable material to ignite a fire that would not quickly burn out.

As the minutes ticked past, though, an orange glow ate through the roof of McFadyen's Tavern atop its hill, and then yellow flame shot skyward, glowing bright against the dark clouds. Martyn thought of the preceding fires, most of which he'd watched in person—all but the one at Montcornet. (He and Lanying had even driven down to Natchez to catch the end of the Tranquility fire, which had gone off prematurely.) Martyn felt the satisfaction he always did when his work fulfilled whatever challenge he'd set himself. But today it meant more, because Bobby had assigned him this mission. Soon his cousin would be able to look up from almost anywhere downtown and see fire blazing above one of the oldest landmarks in the city.

But . . . what to do now?

Martyn had given the remainder of his flares to Bobby's skinheads. The PSP, or whatever they called themselves. He'd been glad to get clear of those fascists with his heart still pumping. What he most wanted now was to go home and lie in the bathtub with Lanying, to chew a couple of gummies and sip some Don Q Gold rum. Of course, he was never going to get to do that again.

Not with her.

Sitting back in the protective U of his desk, he rubbed his eyes, which stung from the tears that had plagued him since Lanying bolted from the hotel room. He was still doing this when his door opened and the two skinheads who had helped dig up his ammo boxes walked in and quietly shut the door behind them.

"Remember us?" said the taller one.

"Sure. What's going on?"

"We forgot to give you something."

The man reached into his jeans pocket and brought out a small brown prescription bottle. He twisted off the white cap, then shook four tiny oval tablets on Martyn's desk. They were orange and scored halfway across.

"Bobby wants you to have these."

"What is it?" Martyn asked suspiciously. "They look like Xanax."

"They do," said the skinhead.

The shorter guy laughed. "Yeah."

Martyn noticed the taller man was wearing surgical gloves on both hands. The other man was not. *He doesn't want to touch the pills*, Martyn realized. It took an act of will, but Martyn looked up into their eyes, which held not a trace of human warmth. Peering into the vacuous orbs, Martyn suddenly understood that he would not leave this room alive. The orange pills seemed to be the suggested exit route, but he had no doubt that these men would drop him right out of the window if he refused to swallow them.

"What are they, really?" he asked, fearing the answer would be "cyanide" and praying it would be "fentanyl."

"Chinese bootleg shit," said the taller freak. "You know what that usually means."

"Fentanyl?"

"If you're lucky," said the shorter man.

Martyn closed his eyes and thought of Lanying. With terrible self-awareness, he finally let himself see that in so many ways, she had been his prisoner while they were together. But that didn't alter the fact that he loved her.

It didn't—

"Hey!" said the skinhead. "Don't drift off, okay? We ain't got all night."

As badly as he wanted not to, Martyn saw the face of Angie Price appear before him, first laughing, then gasping with bulging eyes as he tried to choke the laughter out of her. He saw Bobby shaking his head in the dusk, cussing as they covered Angie with dirt in the thick trees near the rear of Montcornet Plantation. And now . . . now Bobby wanted even Martyn gone as well.

Covered over with dirt.

His tears returned.

"Oh my fuckin' *Lord*," said the shorter freak.

"I just realized something," Martyn said, surprising himself.

"What's that?"

"I'm going to die on the same day as my mother."

He closed his eyes, then swept all four pills off his desktop and popped them under his tongue.

Seventeen seconds later he ceased breathing.

CHAPTER 104

THE LYNCHING OF Ebony Swan hit me harder than Martine's death, harder than Doc's—perhaps even harder than my mother's. Even now, driving away from the Magnolia Heights subdivision in the humming silence of my Audi, tears run steadily down my face. Why such intensity? Maybe because Doc Berry was over seventy and my mother nearly ninety, while Ebony was only two months shy of seventeen. Seeing that girl hanging motionless from the lamp-hook at Attica was like discovering Annie in the same position.

Waiting for Chief Morgan and his men, I lay groaning beneath the twisted ladder, probing my brittle bones where they'd struck the concrete, and I was still sobbing in impotent fury when a squad car pulled up and disgorged the chief, a detective, three patrol officers, and one forensic technician. I did my best to concentrate while Morgan questioned me, but all I could really hold in my head was a memory of the day I was diagnosed with terminal cancer—in my mid-thirties.

Perhaps that's how we most truly relate to death, by seeing ourselves in the deceased. On that day—driving back to Mississippi from seeing Sam Walton's doctor in Little Rock—only my knowledge of history gave me some relief. I kept thinking of the young British boys—a whole generation—condemned to crouch beneath the parapets of stinking trenches and wait for the whistle and the cry of "OVER THE TOP!" that would send them into the jaws of expertly laid machine guns—into the maw of agonizing death. Hunkered in the mud with seconds to live, trapped in a system that made no sense, cut off from home and family, clinging to talismans sent from loved ones, missing their mothers above all, knowing they'd likely never see them again. How much luckier was I to know I would live at least a few months, or even years? So what if I'd spend them under a mortal shadow, with no hope of a cure? Spend them I would. In the lucky decades that followed, from time to time I would notice men and women who had accomplished great things during their youth but died too young. Despite what others would have seen as my bad luck, I outlived many of my heroes, some by many years.

They live within me still, this secret population of souls who accomplished so much in youth that it makes one feel utterly inadequate. Their ages are branded next to their names in my mind, eternal reminders of potential and fulfillment. *John Lennon* (40), *Elvis* (42), *Van Gogh* (37), *Raphael* (37), *Jane Austen* (41), *Flannery O'Connor* (39), *Oscar Wilde* (46). Then there are those whose lives were snuffed out so young that we're left to wonder what beauty they might have wrought had they passed on a more conventional time frame. *Buddy Holly* (22), *Jean-Michel Basquiat* (27, born the year I was), *Otis Redding* (26), *Jim Croce* (30), *Gram Parsons* (26), *Robert Johnson* (27), *Jimi Hendrix* (27). Last of all, the two great what-ifs of 20th century America: the Kennedy brothers, shot into oblivion at 46 and 42 respectively. As I lay on the polished stone porch of Attica, it struck me that, had Robert F. Kennedy, Sr., lived to be president, the teenage Ebony Swan might not have died hanging from the lamp hook of an antebellum plantation house in Mississippi fifty-five years later.

I was useless at the crime scene until my phone rang and the caller turned out to be Linda Seaver, the mother of Ebony's murdered boyfriend. Like a hundred other mothers from Sacred Heart, Linda had received a texted photo of Ebony's suspended body, and the horrific sight had triggered some sort of religious conversion in her. She'd become convinced that her duty was to bring her son's killer to justice, whatever might happen to Lance's good name in the process. Ebony's video file was too large for Linda to email to me using her phone, so I left Attica to retrieve it in person. As I moved to go, Mason Morgan told his tech to document everything down to the smallest detail, then turned to me and helped me to my feet.

"Ebony didn't die by hanging, Penn."

"How, then?"

"She's got a bullet in her lower back."

I quickly process this. "Can he be sure they didn't just shoot her while she was hanging there?"

"Not a hundred percent. But she has no petechiae in the conjunctiva, not even a trace."

"That's not always present with hangings. In fact, it's often missing."

"Tech says that with complete body suspension and a higher BMI, they're much more likely to have it. And Ebony's a little heavy for her age, God forgive me. He thinks somebody shot her in the back while she was running away."

I shake my head in despair. "Goddamn it, Mason."

"Yeah. But it's better than thinking about somebody hanging this poor baby while she was wide awake and terrified. You know?"

"No question about it."

While I look into the chief's round face, his professional composure comes apart. His chin begins to quiver, and he breathes like a little boy after getting hit in the chest with a baseball. "I don't know 'bout this world no more, Penn," he says in his bass voice. "I just don't *know*."

"Me either. This is off the chain, Mason. I can't imagine who would do this."

I step forward and hug the chief like I would my father. The man's mass and strength make me think of the bear that confronted me last Friday. If physical strength were enough to defeat evil, Mason Morgan could crush it with the arms that now enfold me. But it's not. After several seconds, I pull back and look into his hooded brown eyes. The yellow sclera are shot with blood, and his orbits bruised from stress and lack of sleep.

"What I'm s'posed to do?" he asks. "This poor girl ain't even got no people to bury her. Her mama's a stone addict."

I shake my head helplessly, but then I hear Doc's voice in my ears. "The Dunphy judgment," I say softly.

"The what?"

"That case I won against Triton Chemical. Doc said I should spend the money to help people. We'll let Joe Dunphy bury Ebony. He'd have done it himself, if the cancer hadn't got him."

Morgan nods. "That'll be a blessing. But people gonna take this hard, Penn. They gonna be angry. They gonna want payback."

"I know exactly how they feel. We need help, Mason. Federal help."

"We need something, brother."

A few hopeless seconds later, we shake hands and part without comfort.

After driving to Linda Seaver's house and retrieving Ebony's video via AirDrop, I set out to deliver it to Marshall McEwan at the police station. Marshall has remained because Chief Morgan believes a famous white journalist is the best deterrent against any further assault by the sheriff's department. But two blocks from the station, I realize I have no chance of getting inside. Sheriff Tarlton and Sheriff Johnson have ringed the place like the Alamo once more, and they would like nothing more than an excuse to search and detain me. Instead, I pull over and load a special app that allows the transmission of large video files by email. Then I sent the file to Marshall and headed back toward my town house on the bluff.

The most tragic thing about Ebony's video is that she died over it. In our brave new world of cell phone recordings memorializing police abuse, this one is the apotheosis of the form: fifty-seven excruciating seconds of what will appear to Black viewers (and any fair-minded white person who knows Doc was a physician) to be Dr. Ezra Berry desperately trying to save the life of a white teenager without medical equipment—mostly by pressing on an artery in his wounded neck—while a furiously angry white deputy points a gun at him, screams, and then executes him.

But—

What many whites will see is a Black adult male in sweat clothes kneeling aggressively over a white teenager, throttling him while ignoring direct commands from a white deputy (who isn't wearing a uniform but has a badge on his belt) and shouting angrily at the deputy to get the hell away from him.

What will ultimately divide the millions who watch this—and likely any jury—is a single movement. Just prior to being shot, Doc reaches down between himself and Lance Seaver with his right hand in a rapid motion. I'm convinced he was looking for his cell phone (which was found between his thigh and Seaver's belly, still connected to a 911 operator). But anyone could easily convince himself that Doc might have been reaching for a handgun. And Deputy LeJay—who's neither a Bienville native nor a resident—has already claimed that he had no idea he was dealing with either the mayor or a physician.

When my phone rings, I answer without looking.

"I've watched it three times," Marshall says. "It won't make things any better. It'll make them worse."

"Agreed."

"That girl *died* for this footage, Penn."

"I know. The only cause for hope I see is that Deputy LeJay appears to be talking during the encounter—but not to Doc. Did you notice? I mean he's shouting at Doc, but he also seems to be speaking in a normal voice in between."

"I think he was on a Bluetooth call," Marshall says.

"Me, too. He was talking to somebody else when he fired."

"You can't hear him though. That band playing next door drowned out everything but the shouting."

"With time we can find out what he was saying. And maybe who he was talking to."

"We don't have that time. Those lynching photos are flashing through the city at light speed. Hell, they're going around the world. One of my reporters has already seen them on the BBC."

"I believe it."

"'Mississippi Burning Redux' was the headline."

"That's the thing. It's the terrible fulfillment of every stereotype about Mississippi since the Civil War. Ebony is the new Emmett Till. But I don't get the why of it. She was shot, not hanged. So why did the killers string her up like that? And then send a text to you? They wanted the publicity. They wanted it to look as bad as it could. Which means they *want* the attention."

"You don't think it's retaliation for the burning of the mansions?"

"Hell, no. That's not proportional response. They want war. And they want national coverage."

"You're right. Well . . . I'm going to keep at Deputy LeJay. I think this son of a bitch murdered Doc, and he knows who hired him."

"You think he'll talk?"

"I don't know. Dead kids make me want to throw away the rules."

"I hear you. I'm nearly home. Call me if I can help."

"Will do. Goddamn it."

Three blocks from the bluff, traffic has stopped moving. The downtown streets have become a chaotic parking lot, packed from curb to curb with the vehicles of people who've traveled for hours to join the combat they believe will begin tonight on the Bienville bluff. The pickup truck ahead of me has a Texas flag painted on the tailgate, while the Oldsmobile 442 beside it has an Orleans Parish license plate. It'll be a miracle if the occupants of these two vehicles don't shoot each other before they reach the bluff.

Looking along the left side of the street, I see no space large enough to park my car, not without leaving its tail sticking into the street. I decide to give it five minutes, to see if law enforcement does anything about the chaos. *After all*, I think, *how much can happen in five minutes?*

Ironically, it's Buck Tarlton's deputies who make it possible for me to reach my house without abandoning my car. They come through the stalled traffic on foot like storm troopers, forcing people to back out and drive in the opposite direction of the bluff and the river. Anyone who gives them backtalk they arrest on the spot. I show them my driver's license—which proves my address and gets me to the barricade at Main Street and Battery Row. The National Guard troops manning the barrier hassle me a little, but ultimately let me through to my garage door, which is only a few yards from the corner.

After the garage closes fully behind me, I climb out of the Audi with a grunt of pain and go to the pantry door, which opens as I get to it. Annie stands there with red, swollen eyes, but also with a smile so broad that her face seems to shine. Something about her looks jarringly different.

"Did something happen to your hair?" I ask, realizing that about half of it appears to be gone.

"I'll tell you in a minute. I've got a surprise for you."

"What . . . ?"

Daniel Kelly steps into the doorway and grins. His long blond hair and blue-gray eyes register like the features of a long-lost brother after years apart. "I made it after all," he says.

"*Duuude*," is all I can manage as relief floods through me.

"And just in time," Annie adds. "Shot Barlow paid us a little visit. Kelly had to teach him some manners."

"What do you mean?"

"He's tied up in the back bedroom," Kelly explains.

"Along with two of his punk-ass militia guys," Annie adds. "They weren't ready for the real deal."

"You look like hell, Penn," Kelly says, pulling me inside. "Get in here and let me pour you a beer."

"I'd rather have a gin and tonic."

"I'm easy."

As I step forward, Annie blocks my way. "I have one more surprise, Dad. It's a big one."

I'm suddenly certain that my daughter knows nothing about the death of Ebony Swan. This seems impossible, since she's always connected to the metaverse or whatever they call it now. But there's no way she would be acting so . . . *normal* if she knew. Not even after Kelly's arrival.

"Bigger than Daniel showing up? You're scaring me, Boo."

"You need to meet somebody."

Now my defenses go up in earnest.

Annie backs out of the doorway, allowing me to walk through the pantry and into the kitchen. There, at the table where I usually eat breakfast, sits a small Asian woman that I judge to be Chinese. She looks up at me with obvious trepidation, but she also has a certain self-possession that at least keeps her sitting calmly in her chair.

"Who's this?" I ask.

"This is Lanying. She's one of the Bastard Sons of the Confederacy."

A hot wave of confusion passes over my face. "She's . . . *what*?"

Annie shakes her head in wonder. "It turns out there are only two of them, and one's a woman."

I can scarcely get my head around this concept.

"I mean it, Dad. Lanying is one of the arsonists who've been setting the fires. Tranquility? Arcadia? Even Beauvoir. All except Pencarrow. I think the Barlows did our house."

"You're kidding, right? About this girl, I mean."

"Nope. Her boyfriend is the real arsonist. The instigator. Lanying's an accessory. But get ready for a bombshell: the guy did it for the *insurance*. No other reason. He wanted the insurance on his mother's house, and he burned the others as a cover. To misdirect the cops. Is that pathetic or what? And I'm Lanying's lawyer."

I can't take my eyes off the young woman at my table. "Is her boyfriend Chinese, too?"

"Nope," Annie says with undisguised pleasure. "Her boyfriend is *white*."

I feel like the earth just shifted beneath me.

"Which house was it? The real target?"

Lanying speaks at last. "Montcornet."

"My God. The arsonist is Martyn Black? The city IT guy?"

"Yes, sir. And I believe Martyn intentionally murdered his mother as part of the crime. I had no idea he meant to do it, but I believe he did."

"Is that not *sick*?" Annie asks, her eyes bright and expectant. "I mean, this will blow everybody's reality *inside-out*. There're just a few legal issues we need to work out before we can tell anybody the truth."

"Uhhh, you think? Look . . . Annie, there's something you need to know. Did you switch off your phone or something?"

She nods. "I switched off everything to listen to Lanying's story. I know that's hard to believe, but what's happened? What did I miss?"

"Do you know a girl named Ebony Swan? She's sixteen years old. Black."

Annie's face tightens as she thinks about the name. "I don't think so. She's not one of the Mission Hill victims, is she?"

I shake my head.

"Well? What happened to her?"

With dread in my heart, I tell her. As Annie absorbs my news, Kelly lays his hand on her shoulder and squeezes silently. Standing there in shock, Annie switches on her phone and finds the lynching photographs, which are long past going viral. These she studies in silence for a few seconds, and then she begins to cry.

"Why?" she asks in a hoarse voice.

"We don't know."

"That's not what I meant. I mean . . . one hour ago, somebody came here to hurt me. Probably to kill me, in the end. But I'm alive. Not only alive, but unhurt. Whereas this girl . . . is dead. Because she tried to do the right thing. The rich white girl's alive, and the Black girl's dead."

"You're right," I agree. "There's no escaping that. And the reason's simple. You have a functioning family. We have resources. You have a father who spends part of every hour thinking about your safety. We have friends like Daniel, a guy who can get on a jet in Ukraine and fly here on a moment's notice. Ebony Swan . . . had nobody. Chief Morgan told me she doesn't even have anyone to bury her."

Annie covers her eyes with her left hand. "This is so fucked up. Don't tell me any more."

"I can hardly think about it myself. I think we should call Jill Collen Jefferson. Get her on this right away." Jill Jefferson is a young Black, Mississippi-raised, Harvard-trained lawyer who specializes in modern-day lynchings in her home state.

"Agreed. God, Kendrick's going to lose his mind over this."

"Where is he, by the way?"

"Sleeping in the back room. Resting for his speech. He still plans to take the stage at five-thirty p.m."

Christ, the pressure never lets up.

"Judge Shelby's doing the same upstairs," Kelly says. "He took a serious beating from the Barlows before I got here. He probably needs some X-rays."

I sigh heavily. "And Nadine?"

Annie gives me an encouraging look. "She was at the bookstore when everything went down, thank God."

"That's one blessing. Well . . . I guess we'd better get to work on this Lanying problem. We don't have much time."

Annie reaches out and squeezes my hand. "It's the only thing that could unravel this mess before it blows apart."

"I brought video of Doc's shooting, but it's not going to save us in the next half hour. Let's assemble the troops."

"The troops?" Annie echoes. "What do you mean?"

"You, me, Nadine, Judge Shelby. If you can get Doris on the phone, that's five lawyers. If we can't solve this problem *tout suite*, we should be disbarred."

CHAPTER 105

"THEY MURDERED HIM!" Annie declares, standing in front of the wide-screen television in my town house den, which just showed five bullets slamming into Doc Berry's back and side, driving him down onto Lance Seaver. She turns back to the rest of us, all lawyers: Nadine, myself, and Judge Shelby, who sits hunched at the kitchen table with three Ziploc bags of ice resting on his battered arms. "There's no way that's a righteous shooting," she says. "Right? That's cold-blooded murder."

"It looks bad," I agree. "But it's not that black-and-white. People will have different opinions."

"Based on what color they are," Nadine says.

"We need better audio, and we need it fast."

"What's that music overriding the spoken words?" asks Judge Shelby. "I couldn't make out some of what Doc said. And the deputy seemed to be talking throughout the encounter. I couldn't understand anything he said below the level of a shout."

I'm surprised the judge can make out anything on the tape, so swollen are the orbits of his eyes and the left side of his head.

"The music is Marvin Gaye's 'Mercy Mercy Me,'" Nadine explains. "There was a band rehearsing in the building next door. Doc had planned another unity event, and he wanted that song played. The band was rehearsing for him. Isn't that crazy?"

"I think LeJay is speaking on a Bluetooth earpiece," I tell the judge. "While the confrontation is going on. And that's pretty damned suspicious."

"I feel sick," Annie moans, rubbing her cheek with both hands.

Judge Shelby gently pats her shoulder. "There's no defensible reason for what that deputy did. It's obvious Doc was trying to save that boy's life."

"Given what we know about Doc," I say, hating myself, "someone who didn't know he was a physician might not agree."

"What do you mean, *what we know*?" Annie asks, her face coloring.

I don't need to answer this question. All I have to do is wait.

"Jesus," my daughter says. "Didn't the old man in that neighborhood say Doc responded to shots? That's what took him to that parking lot. Not some kind of *tryst*."

I hold up my hands defensively. "I know. But they used his sexuality against him in the campaign, and they'll do it now. Tarlton started before Doc had been dead five minutes."

"So what do we do with this video?" Nadine asks. "It's explosive, and it could trigger a riot by itself, given how that crowd outside felt about Doc. But if you throw this video out there on top of the photos of Ebony hanging at Attica, we'll be in a shooting war before we can count to ten."

Annie is nodding. "I think when we find out who that deputy was talking to—and what was said—we're going to find out they murdered him."

"As important as this video is," I say, "I think we need to focus on Lanying's situation. Because what she knows about the arsons is the only thing that could defuse some of the anger in that crowd. If we can let the protesters know that all those fires were set by a white man trying to swindle an insurance company, we might save some lives."

"Granted," Annie concedes. "But we have to find a way to do that without dooming Lanying to life in prison. Which we have yet to figure out how to do."

"Is she still asleep upstairs?" Judge Shelby asks.

I start to answer, but my phone pings with a text. The screen reads *CHIEF MORGAN*. Touching it, I see the words: *I've got bad news. Too bad to text. Call me.*

"Jesus," I mutter, wanting to go into another room to make the call, but too afraid of the pain in my stump to get up unless I absolutely have to.

"What is it?" Annie asks, her eyebrows raised.

"I don't know. You guys stay on the Lanying dilemma. I'll join you in a minute."

As they resume talking among themselves, I call Chief Morgan back and wait. As soon as he picks up, he says, "Deputy LeJay is dead."

My stomach muscles clench, and my ribs drive a spear of pain right through the narcotic meant to blunt it. "How, Mason?"

"Somebody came in here while I was at the Ebony Swan scene and hanged him in that shaft we have. The Hangman's Door."

I fight the urge to exclaim, *I thought that was a fake rope!*

"It looks like retaliation for the Ebony Swan killing," he goes on. "Tit for tat. Like a lynching from 1920, except people are going to think it was Black cops hanging a helpless white man. Nobody's gonna believe it was anything else."

"*Was* it retaliation?"

"Hell, no! At least I don't think so."

"What does Marshall say about it? Is he about to post this on the *Watchman*'s website?"

"No chance of that."

"Thank God." But then I realize I don't know what would stop him. Marshall doesn't work for the Bienville Chamber of Commerce. "Why not?"

"Because he's in a coma at UM Med Center."

A wave of nausea rolls through me. "But . . . I spoke to him just, what, a half hour ago? About Ebony."

"I know. But he's messed up now, Penn. I think he tried to stop whoever went after LeJay, and got into a scrap with him—or them, whoever. In any case, somebody threw him down the shaft. Looked like he tried to grab the rope on the way down. He's got friction burns on his hands. But in the end he couldn't hang on. He probably fell fifteen or twenty feet and took a hell of a blow to the head. They don't know if he'll walk again, or even talk. Neurosurgeons are trying to figure out how to operate on him now. I'm sorry, brother."

"Dad?" Annie asks. "You look like you're about to faint."

I hold up my hand for patience, but she refuses to look away. I feel as though someone walked up behind me with a club and hit me over the ear. Everyone at the table has fallen silent, and their eyes are heavy upon me. I know what this news will do to Nadine. Though I'm seated, I feel myself wobbling, the dizziness making me sway as it did when I stood in the ER treatment room with the corpse of my murdered fiancée in 2005.

"I also called to tell you I'm giving the order to abandon this station," says the chief. "There's nothing left to protect down here, and the bluff situation's deteriorating rapidly. Ebony's lynching has got everybody really stirred up, and I'm worried what the state police or the Guard might do if the crowd gives them any kind of excuse."

"Okay, Mason. Understood. Just . . . keep doing what I told you earlier. Act as if all your power remains intact. I'll fight the dissolution all the way to the Supreme Court. I've got Judge Shelby with me, and I believe he will, too."

Clayton Shelby nods, his bruised old blue eyes filled with conviction.

"I'm glad to hear it. I've had about enough of these bastards. But tell me one thing: Do you have any idea what Kendrick Washington is going to say when he goes out on the bluff to speak?"

"I don't. And right now, there's still a chance he might not. He won't if I can talk him out of it. But you know how that's likely to go."

"Yeah. Well, you just make sure your daughter has a father in the morning. Life's gotten pretty cheap in this town."

"I can't believe it, Mason."

"I sure miss Doc right now."

"That's why they killed him, buddy. So he wouldn't be here to guide us through this. You be careful, too. If you have to make any kind of strategic retreat, my town house is right here."

"What is it, Dad?" Annie asks. "Who's dead?"

I get slowly to my feet. The pain in my stump and ribs registers, but it no longer matters. "Somebody hanged Deputy LeJay in that old shaft at the police station. Mason doesn't know who did it."

"Oh, my God," Nadine whispers, and shakes her head slowly.

"That's not the worst of it, I'm afraid. Not for us."

"What is?" asks the judge.

Reaching out, I take hold of Nadine's hand and squeeze tight. "Whoever killed LeJay pushed or dropped Marshall down the shaft. He's in a coma at UMC, being prepped for brain surgery."

She tries to jerk her hand away, but I hang on tight. "*No*," she says. "Don't say that, Penn."

"Chief Morgan just told me. They're going to try to save him, but it's bad."

Nadine sits blinking as I did seconds ago, and then her eyes begin to shine with tears. She spent at least two years in an intimate relationship with Marshall McEwan, and even considered marrying him. She probably knew him better than anyone else on earth.

"I'm so sorry," Annie says, her voice cracking as she lays her hands on Nadine's shoulders. "Do they know who did it?"

"No idea. You know Tarlton will blame the Black cops, though. He'll say Marshall tried to stop them from killing LeJay, and was attacked for his trouble."

While I watch helplessly, Annie kneels and hugs Nadine, and Nadine doesn't pull away. In fact, she squeezes my daughter in what must be a painfully tight embrace. Clay Shelby watches me with the eyes of a man who has witnessed and endured great loss over many years. I'm giving him a grateful nod when the town house rocks on its foundations, the way it does when straight-line winds race over Louisiana from Texas and smash into the bluff with enough force to snatch Edelweiss right off the rim.

"What the hell was that?" Judge Shelby asks. "Earthquake?"

Annie breaks away from Nadine and races upstairs to look out from the terrace. We who remain stare at each other in shock. Then Annie calls from the landing: "Looks like a tanker truck blew up on the Mississippi end of the bridge! Y'all better come see!"

"Go without me," says the judge.

Everyone else gets up as Daniel Kelly glides past us from outside (where he's been casually guarding the house) and trots up the stairs. As Nadine helps me to the staircase, I realize I'm going to need stronger pain meds to get me through this night.

"I'm sorry about Marshall," I murmur, gripping her arms as she helps me up the steps.

"I can't believe it," she whispers. "Are you *sure*?"

"Yes. Marshall has been with LeJay pretty much the whole time. And even though I didn't know him that well, I think Marshall would have done all in his power to try to prevent a murder—even of someone he didn't like."

"You're right. Oh, God, Penn. What are we doing on this bluff?"

"I'm not sure. And I'm not sure we should stay much longer."

She nods. "Except—"

"What?"

"You were right about Lanying. We have to find a way to reveal what she knows."

"We will."

"Not in time! Not if Kendrick's speaking at five thirty."

"Hell, he isn't even awake yet. Hang on." We've reached the top of the stairs. "I need a second."

"That's partly my fault, I'm afraid," Nadine says, as I try to adjust my stump in the socket.

"What do you mean?"

"Remember when I sedated you with your mom's meds?"

"Uh-huh."

"Annie did the same with Kendrick. He came in talking crazy . . . and I told her what I'd done with you. She thought it was the best idea she'd heard in a while."

"Christ, you women are ruthless."

I meant it lightly, but her face squeezes into a perfect portrait of pain and grief. "You are *not* going to take any insane risks tonight. We've only just got back together, and I'm going to have a baby. You're not going to play hero, you're not going to tempt fate. I'm afraid Marshall did both, and now . . . dear Lord. You hear me?"

"I do."

"All right, then."

"HOW MANY PEOPLE are in that mob down there?" Claude Buckman, Junior, asked the people lined up beside and behind him. "Seventy-five hundred?"

"Easy," said Tommy Russo. "Closer to ten thousand, I'd say."

"Ten thousand plus," Bobby White corrected. "Maybe even twelve."

The banker's face reddened. "What the *hell*, Bobby? Those are Blake Donnelly's wells burning across the river! I own a piece of most of them."

The towers of fire burning five miles distant were hard to ignore. Whoever had blown the oil wells had a good grasp of political theater.

"Are we just supposed to sit here while this . . . this *rabble* destroys a life's work? This is a hundred times worse than looting! This is goddamn *anarchy*!"

"Damn right," muttered Blake Donnelly, who had made his way out onto the terrace on his walker. "My patience is gone. What the hell do we have a National Guard for, if not to stop this kind of communist behavior?"

"And what about *that*?" Buckman asked, pointing back to his left, where McFadyen's Tavern burned steadily against the darkening sky. "That building has stood since 1799! Now it's going up in flames, right under our noses. What the *fuck*, Bobby? Talk to me."

"I know it looks bad," Bobby admitted. "But it could be worse. A lot worse."

"I don't see how!"

"Do you see any blood down there? Corpses?"

This gave the banker a moment's pause. "Maybe that's the problem. Maybe if the police cracked a few heads, this shit wouldn't be out of hand."

"That's ten thousand people," Bobby repeated. "You don't get anywhere cracking a few heads."

"Oh, I don't know," said Sheriff Tarlton, who had just emerged on the terrace. He'd spent the past hour besieging the police station and overflying the protest in his chopper. "Tear gas and batons can go a long way, even with a big crowd. Not to mention beanbag rounds and rubber bullets."

"Yeah," Bobby said sarcastically. "If anybody's feeling tempted by that kind of talk, think about Mission Hill for ten seconds. That's where that strategy takes you."

"Look down there!" Buckman cried. "That's Pastor Willie Doucy leading those jungle chants! And Cicely Waite! I haven't seen Cicely march for anything in fifteen years. Doesn't want to break a heel on her thousand-dollar shoes!"

"It's the lynching," Bobby explained. "The Swan girl. She's the new Emmett Till. Nothing's going to stop this crowd from expressing their anger. But how bad it gets depends on how you respond."

"And you still counsel prudence? Caution? *Restraint?*"

Bobby pointed out over the river, where three news helicopters hovered, shooting constantly. "Those are national news cameras. So, yes. If this crowd pushes, you bend. People get tired of beating against a soft target. Wears them out. But if you push back, they'll escalate."

"Let 'em!" barked Sheriff Tarlton. "Any blood that results is on them."

Bobby was finding it difficult to focus on the argument. What filled most of his mind was his inability to reach Shot Barlow by phone. He'd ordered the militia leader to check out Penn Cage's town house—as carefully as possible—to determine whether a young Chinese woman might be hiding inside. Barlow had promised to do so, then promptly dropped off the radar.

Bobby wondered if he should have taken Buckman into his confidence—at least partly. There were so many moving parts to this thing. Wade Tarlton was working the frame on Kendrick, for the Bastard Sons fires, and the timing was going to be tricky. Wade had Martyn's flares, and they'd dug the hole behind Kendrick's apartment to "discover" them after getting a tip from a "reliable informant." Buck Tarlton knew about all this, but he was acting like he didn't care. The wannabe-cowboy within was driving him toward some theatrical response on the bluff, where everybody could see him play the big man.

"My real question," Buckman said, "is do we let that Washington kid speak or not?"

Bobby tensed at the suggestion that they would try to prevent Kendrick from giving his planned address.

"How can we stop him?" Arthur Pine asked. "It's a free country."

Buckman made a sour face. "You know that's bullshit. Declare a state of emergency. Say there's a bomb threat. No matter *what* we do, I'd like to see this bluff cleared. The governor doesn't want to listen to that thug mouth off for an hour on national TV. And neither do I."

"I can clear the bluff," Tarlton promised. "And I'll tell you something else. If we let Washington get up in front of these people—and he orders them to cross Battery Row and kill every cop in their way—there won't be anything we can do to stop them. It'll be too late."

Bobby started to argue, but thankfully Dixie Donnelly came to his aid. "Why would Washington do that? He's a peacenik! Nonviolent. He wants to be the next Martin Luther King."

"Are you so sure about that, Dix?" Wyatt Cash asked. "A lot's happened since Mission Hill. That kid got stabbed today. And Ebony Swan got lynched. He may have had a change of heart."

"Like Malcolm X," said Pine. "He may have flipped from 'turn the other cheek' to 'by any means necessary.'"

Just give it forty-five minutes, Bobby thought. *Let the kid walk out and start his speech. Five minutes after that, the world will be a different place. Donny Kilmer will rise up on that water tower and write this town into the history books—*

"Just tell me this," Tarlton said. "If we hold off, and they bust across Battery Row and start trouble like yesterday—looting or whatnot—can I give my men the go-ahead without worrying about getting second-guessed the whole way?"

"You can indeed," Buckman declared. "If that happens . . . you show them who runs this city."

The banker glanced at Bobby, almost daring him to challenge the order, but Bobby's mind was still on Donny Kilmer. Only minutes ago, Bobby had issued the kid an order of his own via text on his burner phone. He'd kept it intentionally vague, but Kilmer's reply had made it clear that he understood. Bobby's order read: *First shot remains Primary. Second shot PCage. 3rd ACage. After that: free fire zone. Acknowledge.*

This was the best Bobby could do in terms of silencing Penn and his new suspicions. The former mayor had put a tail on Bobby—an off-duty cop—and while Bobby could easily have killed the man, he didn't want to do anything that might sabotage the larger-than-life action sequence he had planned for the bluff in less than an hour.

"One thing," said Tommy Russo. "I keep hearing bout hundreds of cars in convoys headed here to join the fight. Gangbangers from Baton Rouge and New Orleans, militia groups coming in from North Louisiana and Texas. I've seen chopper footage of the convoys on TV. Are we doing anything about that?"

Tarlton nodded. "We've got roadblocks set up on the highways coming in from the south. The north, too, to stop the Delta gangbangers from coming down. Lots of homeboys up there."

"What about the bridges?" Russo asked.

Tarlton smiled. "Those we'll leave open. No reason to stop good red-blooded Americans from doing a little vacation travel from Texas and North Louisiana."

A half dozen mouths opened to laugh, but then a flash of light shot upriver from the Mississippi side. The flash came from the south. It was silent, but the shock wave that followed shook the bluff itself, and the Donnelly building with it. Out in Confederate Memorial Park, ten thousand people gasped as one.

"What the hell was that?" cried Buckman. "That was no oil well!"

"I think somebody just blew one of the bridges," Tarlton said in disbelief. "Look down there! My God."

Slowly, as the reality came home to them, the grieving crowd down on the bluff began to cheer.

BY THE TIME Nadine helps me onto the balcony of my town house, the bluff crowd is roaring as though waiting for Beyoncé to take the stage after her warmup act. In the distance I see the familiar pillars of fire and smoke that mark the burning oil wells across the river. Near-biblical in scale, they appear to be holding up the clouds over Tensas Parish. But looking south, toward the source of a cacophony of horns and grinding engines, I see new columns of black smoke rising above the east end of the Mississippi River bridges.

"That's *two* tanker trucks," Annie says, shielding her eyes with the flat of her hand. "One on each bridge. You don't think it's like . . . another vehicle attack? Like the guy with the truck who tried to drive down Battery Row?"

I stare at the rising flames against the unusual blue-gray color of the river. "No. I think somebody just purposely blocked the bridges."

"But why?"

"To stop the militia units from Texas and Louisiana from getting into the city," Kelly informs us.

Nadine whistles long and low. "Wow. That's . . ."

"Strategy," Kelly finishes. "We're witnessing the start of a war."

"The whole house shook when that blast hit," Nadine says. "I don't see how the people who blew up those trucks even survived."

I only pray they did, thinking of Ray Ransom.

Annie looks at me with the obvious question in her eyes. "But who would do that? Who could pull that off?"

"Somebody we know, maybe," I say softly. "Somebody who's tired of nonviolent resistance."

Kelly cuts his eyes at me.

"You may meet him soon," I tell him. "A Vietnam vet I know. He was really close to Doc."

"Oh, my God," Annie says. "Ray?"

I shrug. "Don't say that too loud."

"Oh, man. I can't even—"

Annie's in midsentence when yet another explosion sends a hammering shock wave across the river from the Louisiana side. But this is no oil well or tanker truck. A mile downriver from the bridges, the crown of the Vauxhall Grain Elevator just blasted into the sky like a SpaceX rocket detonating on the launch pad. A mushroom cloud of flame and smoke billows skyward, and this time the crowd falls into an almost reverent silence.

"War," Kelly says again. "Civil war. I don't think I really believed it was possible until now."

I flex my stump, trying to hold my balance as I go lightheaded with dizziness. "Guys, we need to figure a way through this Lanying problem, and then get the hell off this bluff."

Annie's face has gone white. "Dad, Kendrick *has* to speak. This whole crowd is waiting for him. Ten thousand people. And he's the only one who might be able to keep the lid on things."

"Is that what he means to do? I've been worried that he might feel so angry that he'll issue a call to arms."

"The skinheads already stabbed that boy," Judge Shelby reminds us. "He'd be crazy to walk out in front of that crowd. He'll be so exposed that a nine-year-old could take him down with a .22 rifle."

"That crowd wouldn't hurt him!" Annie argues.

"Most wouldn't," I agree, my eyes locked on the raging inferno across the river. "But we have no idea who's out on that bluff. Nor can we be certain who the threat is. Hell, Malcolm X was killed by Black men."

"I wouldn't recommend him going in front of this crowd," Kelly tells her. "We don't have even a semblance of control."

Every face below us is turned southward, toward the bridges and the grain elevator, staring in awe at the destruction someone has wrought. But those people are also waiting for something more. They want to *do* something. Only yesterday they had their elected leader stolen from them by violence. Less than an hour ago, as they protested peacefully, they saw proof that one of their own children had been lynched—murdered and hung from the gallery of an antebellum mansion. The sense of impending battle in the air is as tangible as the charge before an electrical storm. The only thing holding their fury in abeyance, I feel sure, is the expectation that Kendrick will address them soon. This realization brings me instantly to another.

The people stretched from Confederate Memorial Park to the head of Front Street near Fort Langlois constitute a potential army. Kendrick might have it within his power to restrain their anger, if he devotes all his passion to that end. But what if Annie is wrong? What if he sends these people across Battery Row with vengeance in their hearts and justice on their minds? They would sweep over the assembled forces of the state like a tidal wave, taking casualties, yes, but in the end winning the field as surely as the tide takes every beach.

"Dad?" Annie says in a strange voice. "You need to see this."

A chill goes through me as she holds an iPad Mini up to my face. Filling its screen is another airborne drone shot of the terrace at Donnelly Oil. Amid a small crowd of people wearing polo shirts and golf clothes, I see the handsome face that only hours ago told me tales of a Gothic childhood in the scorching deltas of Arkansas, Louisiana, and Mississippi. As we watch, Bobby turns into direct sunlight shining almost horizontally from the southwest.

"Still up there," Annie says. "Like a master of the universe. I'll bet he's been up there all afternoon, moving chess pieces. Black and white. Making fools of us all."

Of course I've known Bobby has been in and out of the Donnelly building today, thanks to the surveillance of Gabriel Davis, my off-duty Natchez cop. But somehow I didn't imagine him standing on the penthouse terrace like some Olympian demigod meddling in human affairs.

"What do you think he's doing up there?" Annie asks.

"I don't know. I think he's mentally disturbed. That's why he's always given you the willies. But I also think he has a legitimate chance to win the presidency. Which scares the shit out of me."

Walking to the corner of my terrace, I grip the guardrail, then lean out to the left. I can clearly see the upper face of the Donnelly Oil Building set back from the Row to the north of my town house. The penthouse balcony looks empty now, but it strikes me that with a laser pointer I could easily hit somebody standing at that rail from here. *Or with the AR-15 locked in my closet in that bedroom . . .*

"I need to talk to Bobby again," I say under my breath, but Annie hears me.

"Why?" she asks, pulling me carefully back within the safety of the rail. "Dad. Kendrick's supposed to speak in thirty minutes. He needs to be able to tell that crowd what Lanying knows."

I shake my head. "I don't see how we can make that happen. Not within the rules of our profession."

"We have to find a way. In thirty minutes, everybody in the world needs to know who Martyn Black is, and that he set those fires."

"You're right. But I . . ."

"Dad? Are you okay? What is it?"

"I just realized something that I've known since I was in junior high, but didn't remember until now."

"What?"

"Martyn's mother and Bobby White's mother are sisters."

"What?"

I marvel at my own stupidity. Maybe it's the painkillers. "Martyn and Bobby are first cousins."

"Are you . . . are you saying Bobby is really behind the arsons?"

"No. Not necessarily. I'm just saying that he and Martyn are cousins. Which is pretty damned suspicious."

"It's more than that."

As I stare into my daughter's eyes, the rain finally begins to fall.

"The thing is, I can't imagine why Bobby would want to burn those houses. How does it help him? And Lanying never said a word about Bobby being involved. Just Martyn and the insurance. Right?"

"I think it's time we wake Lanying up," Annie says.

CHAPTER 106

"SO WHAT DO you think?" I ask Judge Shelby, who's sitting at the head of my dining table, his face and forearms bruised almost beyond belief with dark hematomas.

Lanying has told her story twice: first to Annie and Judge Shelby, now to them again plus myself, Nadine, and Doris Avery, who is listening via speakerphone on Annie's cell. Even when questioned closely by five attorneys, the young Chinese woman's details have remained consistent. I've worked with dishonest witnesses and defendants in my time, and I feel confident that Lanying's story—at least the part she's told us—is true. And so far, Bobby White has not appeared in it.

"I don't see a way out," Judge Shelby declares. "Not given the constraints we're dealing with, including the one our client has placed upon us."

Shelby is referring to Lanying's demand that she not be deported to China under any circumstance—or even be put at risk of that.

"I second that opinion," Doris says via speakerphone.

"Why, exactly?" asks Annie. "I agree, I just want to know y'all's reasoning."

Judge Shelby tilts his head like an entomologist mulling over some interesting specimen. "Her problem is more political than legal. She's obviously committed both state and federal offenses—terrorism being the worst on the federal side, and murder and probably terrorism under state statutes. The problem is, given the civil unrest on the streets of Bienville, I think the DOJ would fall over itself to offer her immunity to tell what she knows. I'm sure we all know U.S. attorneys we could call and cut a deal with right now."

Annie nods excitedly. "If she can prove a white man set those fires, then the spark that triggered all this racial insanity will be revealed to be illusory. As crazy as it seems, this *all* resulted from a misunderstanding of events."

"More from a deliberate deception," Nadine clarifies. "Conceived by Martyn Black, according to our client."

"If only that were the extent of it," says Judge Shelby. "The real problem is that the powers that be in Mississippi government are exactly like the Poker Club, Barlow's militia, or the average terrified white voter of Tenisaw County. They've bought into and acted on the narrative that Black radicals started those fires. I can promise you that every white politician from the governor on down *loves* that those arsons have distracted the media from the Mission Hill shootings. But if it turns out that a lone white man torched those mansions out of simple greed . . . well, all the old political embarrassments come roaring right back."

"But the state can't keep Lanying quiet," Annie argues. "I mean, they can't *gag* her."

"Don't be so sure," Doris cuts in from her cell. "That depends on your client."

"Please elaborate, Ms. Avery," says the judge.

As Doris answers, my attention wanders to the TV screen across the room. It's running the CNN feed from a helicopter flying over the Mississippi River about a half mile from my front door. Beside the TV, Annie also set up a twenty-seven-inch computer monitor that's displaying the feeds from my Ring doorbell cameras, which she pointed at the bluff and routed to Kendrick's social media sites. All the images show what appears to be a tense truce between the line of National Guard and state police officers on Battery Row, and the ten-thousand-odd people penned into the green space between the Row and the bluff fence. In my mind I hear the haunting high harmonic and subversive groove that begins "For What It's Worth" by Buffalo Springfield.

"It doesn't matter if the attorney general offers Lanying immunity for any and all crimes right back to original sin," Doris concludes. "When that homeless man burned to death in Arcadia—and when the arsonist's mother died today—Lanying committed two murders under state law. And the state isn't about to offer her immunity to tell what she knows. In fact, given what I know of Mississippi prosecutors, they're liable to offer her some kind of crazy under-the-table deal to keep her mouth shut."

"In exchange for what?" I ask.

"Who knows? But *that's* our real problem. The feds would like Lanying to hold a news conference in five minutes, while the state would prefer she be struck dumb by a thunderbolt. And both have the power to jail her for a very long time."

Through all this legal debate, Lanying has sat in self-effacing silence. Watching her, I think about Shot Barlow and his thugs tied up in my back room. Before we sat down here, I couldn't resist walking back there to have a look. The hatred burning in Barlow's eyes was something to behold, but I couldn't stop myself from laughing. Not once has that bastard ever pictured himself spending the race war he's lusted after for so long hog-tied in a lawyer's apartment with half his face the color of an eggplant.

"What about jurisdiction?" I ask. "If we call the FBI and ask if she can turn herself in to them—"

"Forget that," Doris advises. "They'll hand her straight to ICE. She's an alien. ICE has jurisdiction over her. In fact, even if the local sheriff arrested her and your county DA charged her, ICE could come in and take her. If they end up in a dispute, ICE will win in the end."

"Which means deportation?"

"Almost surely. Look, we do *not* want this girl in the custody of the state. Capital murder's only the beginning. They can charge her with terrorism under the new 2019 law, or if they get authorization from the legislature—which in Mississippi is as red as Santa Claus's suit."

"Damn it!" Annie curses.

"Hold on," I cut in. "Look at the TV. Something's changed down the Row."

CNN has somehow got a camera feed from one of the Row buildings facing the river, probably the Planters' Hotel. It shows an unbroken line of people—mostly young men—standing in massed ranks that press right up against the orange-and-white barriers lining the curb of Battery Row, where the National Guard troops stand in ranks before a dozen or so armored vehicles. The grim faces and stances of the protesters radiate a general tenor of anger, and I feel certain that they have not had food or water for several hours.

Chief Morgan is out there with his recently fired municipal police officers, strung along Battery Row like a skirmish line separating the true civilians from the armored soldiers. What must Morgan be thinking as he stands in that uncertain borderland? Staring at the sullen faces behind him, I feel a sudden premonition of disaster. The energy is far more negative than positive, like an energy vacuum calling something into existence.

As we watch the screen, a woman starts singing "We Shall Overcome," but the song dies before it even gets going. Deep in the crowd, a boom box begins pounding out a hip-hop beat, but whoever is pushing that gets shouted down as well. Then, from somewhere within the sea of dark faces, Pastor Willie Doucy steps out and begins to chant something. I cringe when I see him, for I sense that his dark moment has come. The afternoon belonged to Pastor Aaron Baldwin, a man I've more than once compared to Gandhi. But Reverend Willie Doucy is his opposite in every way. He lives for power and control—coveting it, acquiring it, wielding it—and he used all he had to try to prevent Doc Berry from winning the mayor's office. One of his prime tactics was going into the homes of Black families and telling them Ezra Berry was a sodomite who had broken the sacred laws of God. To see him on the bluff now, beginning a chant of "Justice now!," feels so wrong that I can't put it into words. From Aaron Baldwin's mouth, those words would have sounded like a prayer, a plea, an entreaty for divine intercession. From Willie Doucy, they sound like a call to arms, an insult, an imprecation. I understand the desire to deal out pain for pain after Doc's loss, as Ray Ransom may be doing at this moment, but even Ray hates Willie Doucy.

The crowd surges against the barriers, like a storm tide hammering a dock. Reverend Doucy stands with a Bible in his left hand and his right fist raised, shouting at the top of his lungs. Surrounding him are younger men wearing black suits, and they look as angry as he. Whenever I'd see those young men during Doc's campaign, I always thought of the men in the Audubon Ballroom crowd who assassinated Malcolm X. I had no factual basis for making that connection, but I always felt it.

"They're going to knock down those barriers," Judge Shelby says.

"Yep. And the blood's going to hit the fan again."

"I've only got a couple more minutes," Doris Avery says from Annie's cell. "May I ask a question?"

"Speak, Doris."

"Why is Lanying so reluctant to return to China? Is she a dissident?"

For the first time in quite a while, Lanying speaks. "I protested often there. I was jailed three times. I don't know if I qualify as a political dissident."

"But you're not a criminal?" Doris asks. "Please be honest."

"I committed no crimes there other than unauthorized protests."

"We're not going to be getting an answer in enough time to make any difference tonight. I think you all need to focus on your personal safety and that of your client. Every person I've talked to says that bluff is going to be a war zone tonight. I've experienced exactly one riot in my life, and I'll never go near another."

"Which riot?" Judge Shelby asks.

"L.A. in '92. I was—"

Doris's voice disappears into the boom of gunfire. Two deep concussions, then another.

"Shotgun," Judge Avery says, coming to his feet.

"Tear gas rounds?"

"Let's hope so."

As one, we turn back to the screens against the wall. Sure enough, Battery Row now looks like a street in Ukraine. Thick clouds of smoke drift across the avenue, while uniformed troops run back and forth with raised batons, swinging at dark figures that bloom out of the haze, then vanish as quickly as they appeared. A wide shot from a helicopter reveals single marchers and pairs sprinting across the Row between the crowd and the commercial buildings facing it.

"It's finally coming apart," I murmur. "We need to lock the house down."

Six or seven more booms shake the walls. Then the door slams and Kelly comes in, his usually twinkling eyes now devoid of humor.

"Things are about to get ugly," he says. "Let's take inventory of the weapons we've got up here. I've got some stuff in cases in an SUV outside, but I wasn't sure we weren't going to evacuate."

He looks hopeful.

"We can't evacuate," Annie tells him. "Not yet, anyway. Kendrick's still going to speak."

"I've got an AR in my car trunk," I tell him. "We'd better get that."

Kelly is about to retrieve my rifle and his cases when Kendrick staggers into the dining room, his right hand on his wounded side. He stares at the screens as though he's just come out of a coma, which may be how he feels, depending on how big a dose of my mother's drugs Annie gave him.

"Riot's starting," I tell him, and point at the TV. "I don't think you're going to be speaking tonight, buddy."

Kendrick looks like he doesn't understand a word I said.

"Hey, man," Kelly says, moving toward him. "Are you okay?"

"Some guys just busted into the back of the house," he says. "They're trying to get that Barlow out."

Kelly bolts down the hall so fast that I hear gunfire from his pistol before I can even call after him. Male screams reverberate up the hall, followed by more gunshots.

"Hit the floor, everybody!" I shout. "Now! On the ground."

After a couple of seconds, Kendrick turns and staggers back down the hall as though to help Kelly repel the intruders.

"Don't go, Kendrick!" Annie shouts, but he disappears anyway.

Muffled sounds of close-quarters combat come from the rear of the ground floor, and the stink of gunpowder floats up the hallway. Then everything goes silent. I think we're afraid to find out what might have happened just yards away from us. But after about a minute, Kelly calls, "Nobody fire! Friendlies coming up the hall!"

Then my old friend drags the scheduled speaker out of the smoke and dimness of the hallway. Kendrick's face is bruised and bloody, and one shoulder sags, but his eyes glow with life. Kelly props him against a wall, then pulls a chair beneath him.

"Is he all right?" Annie asks.

"He'll make it," Kelly replies. "He's not a bad fighter for a pacifist."

"Oh, my God, your *side*!" Annie exclaims.

Sure enough, Kendrick's knife wound has begun hemorrhaging again. His T-shirt is wet with blood, and the stain appears to be growing.

"I'll take him to the bathroom," Kelly says. "See how bad he needs a doctor."

"What happened back there?" I call.

"You've got one dead tango on the floor. The rest left wounded, and Barlow himself got away before I reached the back."

Damn it, I curse silently.

As they move down the hall, I hear Judge Shelby say, "Penn? Come see this."

Through some combination of brute force, tear gas, and the possibly divine intercession of Reverend Aaron Baldwin—who pleaded with the crowd through a bullhorn—the vast majority of protesters has remained on the bluff side of Battery Row. CNN is reporting approximately two hundred arrests, and while they continue to run old footage of merchandise being carried out of Cotton Rowe (mostly cases of liquor), the bluff itself seems to have returned to a state of uneasy peace.

Doris Avery has left us to our own devices, which results in myself, Judge Shelby, and Annie reconvening around the table to find a new angle on the Lanying problem, while Nadine reruns Ebony's video of Doc's shooting on an iPad she's set up on the table. Kelly is treating Kendrick's wound in the bathroom, and when I went back to check on him, the young activist made it clear he has no intention of letting anything stop him from making his scheduled speech, which he's already posted will take place in the amphitheater on the north end of the bluff, and not Confederate Memorial Park, which is obviously too small.

"You know what we need?" Nadine says suddenly. "A *lip reader*. We need to know everything Doc said to the deputy, right? But even more important, we need to know what Deputy LeJay was saying. If he was on a Bluetooth call and someone gave him an instruction to fire—or if he acknowledged an order and then fired—that's capital murder. For both the deputy and the person on the phone."

"If it really happened that way," I say, "then whoever was on the other end of that phone had a motive to murder Deputy LeJay. To keep him quiet. That would go a long way toward getting Chief Morgan and his men off the hook."

"My money's on Buck Tarlton," says Annie. "He's the one who brought LeJay in from Amite County. He knows the guy from his weekend militia training. And he's the one who released LeJay almost immediately."

"The thing is," I think aloud, "Doc's shooting doesn't feel premeditated to me. It actually couldn't have been, in the classical sense. Doc's trip to see his partner was spur of the moment. He didn't even know he was leaving the restaurant until one minute before he did. If anything, it's like Deputy LeJay already meant to kill Doc, found himself in a convenient situation, and took advantage of it."

"They could have been tapping his phone," says Annie. "Or following him."

"This is all speculation until we know who LeJay was talking to," says Nadine. "How long are we going to sit on this tape? Linda Seaver gave it to you for a reason, Penn. We have to find out what it means, then let the world see it."

"At *last*," says a deep male voice from behind us. "Somebody got their head screwed on straight. But you've still got the order wrong."

We all whirl to see Kendrick step in from the hallway.

How much did he hear? I wonder.

"Have y'all lost your minds or what?" he asks. "I heard you talking about trying to find a *lip reader*? Man, you can't wait for that. I'm going out there to speak in ten minutes. I ain't waiting for no damn lip reader. You should have put that footage out the minute you got it. The internet would've told you in five minutes what they're saying."

Nadine nods. "He's right."

"What about the risk?" Judge Shelby asks. "Provoking another riot?"

Kendrick shrugs. "If people riot, maybe it's because that's what we need. After what they done to Ebony, I don't see how this day could have ended any other way, to tell you the truth."

I sense Judge Shelby trying to find appropriate words to explain why we should wait at least long enough to be sure of the implications of the video before releasing it to the world. We all want justice for Doc, but not all of us are resigned to the inevitability of large-scale violence.

"Where's Kelly?" I ask.

"Outside, keeping us all safe and sound." Kendrick's voice is freighted with resentment.

"How long would it take us to find a lip reader?" I ask. "In Bienville."

"Twenty minutes," says Nadine. "Maybe less. I have several deaf customers at my bookstore. Let me make a call."

"There's no *time* for that!" Kendrick insists. "Besides, y'all are missing the whole point. *It ain't your decision to make.* That video isn't yours. Not unless Ebony gave it to you herself. Did she?"

"Lance Seaver's mother gave it to me," I tell him. "Ebony gave it to her, when she went to Mrs. Seaver for help."

Kendrick snorts, then shakes his head with exasperation. "That sounds about like Ebony, going to the nice white lady for help. Thinking some Karen gon' get her out of trouble. But Karen didn't, did she?"

I turn up my hands. "She tried, but . . . not in the right way. And her name is Linda."

Kendrick's smile betrays only sarcasm. "So now you have the video, Mr. Cage. But it *belonged* to Ebony. Ebony shot it. Ebony died to protect it. And now that she's gone, it belongs to those people out on the bluff. So who's going to give it to them?" He looks expectantly at me. "You?"

Kendrick takes a step toward me, but old Judge Shelby interposes himself between us. "Son, please listen. Surely you can see that it might be better to know the full implications of that tape before showing it to ten thousand grieving people. Or ten million."

"I'm not your son, old man," Kendrick replies, and for a moment I worry he's going to shove the eighty-six-year-old judge out of his way.

"Kendrick!" Annie says sharply. "Take it easy."

He whirls on her, his eyes filled with anger. I can't quite read the look in his eyes, but it's enough to push Annie back a step. Has she just learned a hard lesson? That there's a dividing wall between her and Kendrick that she might never be able to truly breach? While she stares at him in confusion, he turns back to me with deep resolve in his face.

"Don't make me take it from you, Mr. Cage."

This is the selfless young man who at Mission Hill walked unarmed into the guns of Buck Tarlton's deputies. Yet before I even think consciously, my mind goes to the SIG Sauer 365 in my bedroom. *Why am I thinking about that?* Kendrick is right: the video isn't mine. And one way or another, it's going to get out into the world—in hours, if not minutes.

With a sigh of resignation, I punch in my password and hand him my cell phone. Kendrick takes the iPhone and begins the process of posting the video to his social media accounts. He's perceptive enough to know that asking Annie to do it for him—as she has with most of his other recent posts—would be a mistake. But he made his choice knowing that.

Annie gets up and walks back toward her bedroom.

Kendrick hands my phone back to me and looks down the hall after her. Then he says, "Let's talk about what really matters now."

Nadine, Judge Shelby, and I share a puzzled look.

"I want the name," Kendrick says.

"Name?" I echo. "What name?"

Kendrick points at Lanying, who sits so quietly in her chair that it's almost as if she's not here. Kendrick rolls his eyes, then holds up his wrist-watch. "The white boy who burned the mansions. I want his name."

Shit.

He laughs softly. "Y'all got so caught up in your lawyer talk you didn't pay attention to what was right outside this room. *Me.*"

"Kendrick, this isn't like the video," I tell him.

"You damn right it's not! It's *worse.*"

"You don't understand."

"*You* don't! You're sitting here with knowledge that might save lives—dozens of lives, or even hundreds, depending on what happens up here tonight—and you want to hold it back to protect this girl here who *helped commit the crimes.*"

"Kendrick—"

"Man, I heard y'all arguing it out! All the ethical bullshit. And I don't *care.* You put all that on one side of the scale with this girl, and on the other side you put Doc Berry and Ebony and the ten thousand people on that bluff. *You* might have a hard time figuring out which side weighs the most . . . but I don't."

I look to Nadine, who offers me nothing. Judge Shelby could write a masterpiece of legal scholarship on why our republic rests upon the sacrosanct rights of the accused, including and especially attorney-client privilege, but in this moment that seems somehow superfluous.

"The name," Kendrick repeats. "I need the firebug's name."

"Do you intend to reveal it tonight?" I ask.

"I don't know, Mr. Cage. But I might."

I take a deep breath and sigh. "I can't give it to you, Kendrick. I can't stop you from telling the crowd that a white man set those fires. In fact, I'd like to tell them that. But I can't do it myself."

"Annie will tell me," he says with certainty.

Nadine's laugh is a single bark. "Not in a million years."

Kendrick studies her for a few seconds, then nods slowly and looks at Lanying. "Is that girl even American?"

I shake my head.

"Jesus, y'all. What the fuck, huh?"

"Kendrick," I say softly, "if I were you, I wouldn't go out there tonight. I've got a bad feeling. The town's full of militia nuts. Barlow just escaped from here. You've already been stabbed, and now you want to tempt fate a second time?"

He waves his hand in dismissal of danger.

The sound of a door slamming makes me think Kelly is returning, but I'm only half-right. It's Kelly leading Ray Ransom, who dwarfs him. Ray's bald head and big shoulders dominate the room, and I can see that Kelly likes him already.

"Busy day?" I comment, and Ransom gives me a sly smile.

"I just came to check on the headliner," he answers, looking at Kendrick. "You still planning on speaking at the amphitheater?"

Annie appears at the near end of the hall, but she says nothing.

"Yes indeed, Mr. Ray," Kendrick says. "Got a little something to say."

"You calling for peace or revolution?"

"Don't know yet."

Ray nods thoughtfully.

I step closer to Ray. "I was just telling Kendrick he ought to think twice before going out in front of a crowd he nearly got killed in once before."

Ray looks at me for a few seconds, then turns and addresses Kendrick. "Young brother . . . listen to an old head just a minute. I know the people want to hear you represent. They're desperate for leadership. And you got a bright future, boy. *Bright.* You've got guts, I know. You got my respect. But you can't pretend it's safe out there. And there's not much any of us can do to protect you."

I'm surprised and grateful that Ray is willing to go so far in the cause of making the young man see reality.

"People said the same thing to Martin," Kendrick replies. "And Malcolm. They knew they were being targeted. But they didn't hide in their houses. What did Martin say? 'I may not get there with you . . .'"

You're not Martin, I want to tell him. *You're not Malcolm, either. Not yet.* But who am I to make that judgment? Kendrick is young, but he's done at least one great thing already. Who knows what else he might be capable of? And who else can possibly salve the pain of the thousands waiting out there in the rain? If anyone can challenge the height of Kendrick's ambitions, it's Ray Ransom. But Ray leaves the words unsaid.

"Hey, Ray," Kendrick says, a fresh note of energy in his voice.

"Yeah?"

"You know who burned all those antebellum homes?"

"No. Wait . . . are you saying you do know?"

"I do now. All these folks know, too. It was some white man, lookin' for insurance money."

Ray's eyes narrow, but then he laughs deep in his chest. "Shit, you had me goin' for a second."

"I'm not shittin' you, bro. Ask your friend here."

Ray's eyes darken as he senses the friction between Kendrick and me. "What's he talking about, Penn?"

"A white man did burn the mansions, Ray. All but Pencarrow. I can't give you his name, though. Because of attorney-client privilege."

"Are you representing the motherfucker?"

"In a way. Annie is, and she asked my advice."

After staring back at me for several seconds, Ray slowly begins to nod. "I knew it. Bastard Sons of the Confederacy, my *ass*. Doc knew it, too! Some white boy made up that bullshit."

"I need the name," Kendrick says again. "The guy who set the fires."

Ray shrugs. "You heard the man. He can't give it to you."

"I need it for my speech!"

"No, you don't. Look, I don't follow every rule, okay? And Penn don't, either. But some rules you don't break. That's one."

Kendrick looks perplexed. "What am I supposed to do?"

Ray steps toward him. "Make 'em believe, young brother. That's what. You want to be Martin or Malcolm? *Make 'em believe*."

Kendrick curses and looks at his watch. "It's time to go."

Ray grins at Kelly. "You ready to escort this young man across the street?"

"Happy to oblige, Sergeant."

"Then let's do it."

ONE BLOCK FROM the town house, Bobby White walked out of the Donnelly building and into the rainy street. In his right hand was the burner phone he reserved for contact with Donny Kilmer. One minute ago, he'd risked his second text of the day.

Are u still in position?

As he made his way toward his Range Rover, the reply came back:

Affirmative. Looks like ZULU DAWN down there!

Bobby smiled to himself. He could picture Shot Barlow and his ragtag militia gathered around a TV in their survival bunker, watching eighteen hundred British soldiers fight off an assault by twenty thousand African tribesmen at Isandlwana, cheering like a football game. The Zulu slaughtered the British in the end, of course, but Donny Kilmer probably liked to fantasize about how it would have gone had he been perched above that battlefield with his AR-15 and a couple of thousand rounds.

Without turning, Bobby felt his tail pick him up. The Black man in plainclothes looked close to fifty, and he walked like a cop. Penn Cage had to be paying the guy. After pulling the rifle on his balcony, Penn must have figured he was a target himself, or soon would be—which was true. Bobby would have to lose the tail before he played out his scene with Donny on the tower. That would take about five minutes. If he couldn't lose the old guy in that time, he'd have to kill him.

Closing himself into the Range Rover, Bobby looked toward the barrier at Battery Row. Just around that corner stood Cage's town house. For all he knew, Martyn's Chinese girlfriend was sitting inside. He could pull down there and simply knock on the door. But something told him not to. Because Shot Barlow had surely visited the house already. And whatever had happened there—or was still happening—Bobby did not need on his résumé.

He could find a way through whatever complications arose from a Barlow screw-up. Even if Lanying publicly accused Martyn of setting the antebellum fires, the M206 flares would damn Kendrick, both under the law and in the court of public opinion. Creativity would supply a way of tying Martyn to the young civil rights activist. All Bobby could do now was pray Buck Tarlton didn't do something stupid and stop Kendrick from going before the crowd. Because shortly after he took the stage, Donny Kilmer would rain fire down upon this throng, and the world would never be the same. After some unknown number had perished and ascended to heaven . . . Bobby White would enter Valhalla in the collective mind of the American public.

The American *electorate*, he reminded himself.

Bobby made a tight U-turn in the middle of Second Street, then headed north. First he'd lose the cop, then return to Battery Row to find the best vantage point from which to fire on Donny after he opened up on the crowd. *What a spectacle this is going to be*, he thought. *Michael Bay meets JFK. We're going to create a new genre: Assassination Porn.*

CHAPTER 107

KENDRICK'S ANNOUNCEMENT THAT he would reveal the identity of the Bastard Sons of the Confederacy arsonists at 5:30 p.m. stunned me, but it sent near-visible arcs of electric excitement and anticipation through the largest crowd to assemble on the bluff since the beginning of the Bienville crisis. The ominous sky and waves of rain seemed not to bother the thousands waiting in and around the amphitheater, but the loss of the Confederate symbols in Confederate Memorial Park—the seacoast guns in particular, which had provided such trenchant visual contrast for him during his past public remarks—seemed to weigh heavily upon Kendrick. But the bluff is considerably wider at the amphitheater than at the park, and the move will allow thousands more people to hear him directly.

The scene backstage is close to bedlam, but it would be worse had not the congregation of Reverend Aaron Baldwin stepped in to put together a sort of production village similar to those on Hollywood sets. Immediately behind the canvas shell that backs the amphitheater stage stand two walled canopy tents, each with a catering table and a few chairs inside. Beyond the tents wait two large recreational vehicles. One is the mobile command post brought by Chief Morgan, who enlisted a half dozen of his officers to assist with Kendrick's close security. To my surprise and relief, they're still wearing their duty uniforms and sidearms. The mobile command post isn't actually mobile at this moment, since it was towed here by a truck and parked, but it's providing valuable resources like access to law-enforcement radio channels and the internet.

Twenty feet closer to the bluff fence stands a silver Airstream RV capable of moving itself. This trailer belongs to one of Reverend Baldwin's more affluent church members, and it's inside this Airstream—under the watchful care of Nadine Sullivan—that Lanying waits in a state of extreme anxiety. I feel abject failure when I think of her. Well before we made the move here from my town house, it became obvious that our efforts to gain any legal immunity to state charges against her would be futile. If I'm honest with myself, about the only thing likely to keep Lanying out of the Mississippi State Penitentiary will be flight to a nonextradition country. And if Kendrick reveals her name in a few minutes (an impossibility, I believe, since to my knowledge he does not possess it), he will make her a target for any number of people with extreme political agendas.

Annie is standing with Kendrick and Reverend Baldwin behind the rear stage steps. Kendrick has forgone his slave chains and torn military fatigues in favor of a black suit, starched white shirt, and skinny black tie ferried to my house from the north side by Frosty's mother. He did this to cover the bulletproof vest that Kelly and Ray convinced him to wear for his speech, and it makes him look more like the leader of a choir than a combat veteran or runaway slave. I figured this result would make him unhappy, but Kendrick is smart enough to know what effect this look is likely to have on an older Black crowd.

As I stand taking in the buildup, like the final backstage rituals before a stadium-size political rally, Ray Ransom suddenly appears beside me.

"Kendrick's pretty upset that you won't tell him who set those fires. Are you going to represent the arsonist in court or something?"

"No."

"Then—"

"Let's not even discuss it, Ray. No one's going to reveal the name."

He nods reluctantly. "Aiight, then."

"Tell me this. Two days ago, Kendrick was walking around like the patron saint of nonviolent resisters. Gandhi meets Thoreau. But today . . . it occurs to me that he could send this entire crowd across Battery Row like an invasion army. And I have no idea which gospel he intends to preach tonight. Martin's or Malcolm's."

"Me, either."

"And what if he does? Have you thought about that?"

Ray bristles beside me. "Didn't old Thomas Jefferson say a little revolution now and then wasn't a bad thing?"

"Don't be so naïve. You can't fight the government with small arms. Not even with Barrett rifles and black-market mortars. The government has Reaper UAVs, A-10s, Abrams tanks, and Spectre gunships. If Kendrick sends ten thousand people into town to wreak havoc . . . all he'll accomplish is to bring down hell on them."

"So what does the government do to monsters who lynch sixteen-year-old girls?"

"Executes them. If it finds them and proves its case."

Ray shakes his head at me, then drifts back toward Kendrick and Frosty.

My phone pings with a text, and the news that Officer Gabriel Davis's message brings is most unwelcome. It reads: *I lost Bobby White in his Range Rover downtown. Trying to reacquire, but no luck so far. Will update u ASAP.*

So Bobby is no longer watching the show from the Donnelly tower balcony.

The only thing countering my anxiety over the impending speech and its attendant risk is the lift I got upon discovering that Daniel Kelly has returned. His rescue of Annie and Lanying from Barlow's crew was dramatic, but in my experience, all in a day's work for my old friend. It means more to know that he'll be nearby when whatever happens next starts to happen.

Unlike Annie and Lanying, Judge Shelby did not come through the Barlow encounter unscathed, but even he insisted upon accompanying us across Battery Row to hear whatever Kendrick intends to say. "It's not often we get to be witnesses to history in the making," Shelby told me, rubbing a swelling bruise that now covers the left side of his face. "I brought the good bourbon from your house. You just find me a damned lawn chair."

Kelly has already developed an easy camaraderie with both Ray Ransom and Chief Morgan, as well as Frosty Givens, the good-natured three-hundred-pound "hip-hop producer" who showed up to act as unofficial security for Kendrick. While Kelly and the other men circulate in the area between the stage and the RVs, reinforcing the security provided by Bienville's defrocked city policemen, I crouch beside Judge Shelby's lawn chair, near the Airstream.

"How much do you know about Bobby White?" I ask.

The old lawyer takes a sip of bourbon. "More than you'd think, I imagine. Why?"

"Because I think he's had a big hand in stage-managing half of what's gone on over the past three days."

A faint smile touches Shelby's lips. "Wouldn't surprise me. More disturbing is the quiet rumor I'm hearing of an alliance with Charles Dufort. Charles has the money to make Bobby White's most hubristic fever dreams a reality."

"Okay. But why the hell are they messing around in this local nightmare?"

"Because our recent insanity has national implications. Don't be disingenuous, Penn."

"Why risk it? Depending on how this shakes out, it could turn into a disaster for either side."

Judge Shelby lowers his voice as though speaking in a sidebar conference in court. "If Bobby's out here tonight, he's got a plan. He sees a play, an upside, that outweighs whatever risk there might be for him. And so far, I'd say he's got things running his way."

"Well, I don't see his play. All I see is a rising body count."

The judge's eyes narrow. "Do you suspect Bobby of being involved in that girl's lynching?"

I give the old man a frank look. "I wouldn't rule it out."

Shelby smiles like he might at a first-year law student. "Don't underestimate Sergeant Bobby White. Or his new banker. You'd do so at your peril."

"I think I've been doing that for a while."

Before Judge Shelby can speak again, Kendrick Washington mounts the steps leading to the amphitheater stage, and Annie follows him. She gives him a long embrace on the top step, but the crowd has caught sight of their new messiah, and the low hum of an expectant audience quickly builds to a roar.

SIX HUNDRED METERS from Confederate Memorial Park, and 165 feet above the ground, Donny Kilmer lay prone on the narrow service platform that surrounded Bienville's North Water Tower. His specially modified HK417 G28 rifle had been trained on the lectern at the center of the amphitheater stage for the past two minutes.

Sergeant White had told Donny to expect his target to speak near the Confederate Memorial Fountain, and perhaps even to climb onto one of the old seacoast guns near the bluff fence in the park. But it had become obvious more than an hour ago that Kendrick Washington meant to speak from the amphitheater stage. The shot distance was now 150 yards closer, which was great. But the angle from the water tower to the stage lectern had become more acute, right at the border of the tricky zone. The canvas arch stretched over metallic framing that protected the stage from rain came far enough forward that it almost obscured Donny's line of sight to the podium. Still . . . he was confident he could make the shot.

He'd trained for a moment like this for years, and he'd done it with *this rifle*. His certainty after all the months since January 6 (when he'd watched that goat rope of an insurrection on TV) that he now had it in his power to alter the course of history had pushed him into a state of high arousal. His usual coolness deserted him. His pulse pounded, his face and ears felt hot, key muscles twitched, and his penis had grown painfully hard. He had to resist a compulsion to jam his hand beneath his waistband and rub one out for relief. But in the time that would take him, anything might happen.

The specter that had been growing in his mind was Bobby's warning that the FBI would have a counter-sniper covering this event from the roof of the Donnelly Oil Building, and possibly from other perches as well. The Donnelly tower looked out over nearly all the north end of the bluff. The military called that kind of coverage "overwatch" with good reason, and they'd been doing it at events like the Super Bowl since 9/11. Of course, that meant today's speech was like the Super Bowl of the Bienville crisis. And Donny Kilmer was one of the key players on the field.

Only nobody knew that yet.

Soon they would.

Donny had confirmed the presence of one counter-sniper half an hour ago, when the agent set up. To Donny's surprise, the man didn't have a spotter with him. Or maybe he did, and the spotter was close by but somewhere Donny couldn't see him. Connected by radio, like him and Bobby White through the burner. As he lay there, unnaturally and uncomfortably still, his mind became a stew of speculation and second guesses. Bobby had instructed him to shoot Kendrick Washington first, despite any temptation to take out the counter-sniper as a prophylactic measure. Only by doing that could he guarantee a fatal hit, or any hit at all. Donny knew this was probably true. Kendrick Washington's combat instincts were sound; he'd proved that at Mission Hill. So as soon as Donny fired the HK—even with its flash suppressor—Kendrick would know what he was hearing. And he wouldn't wait to be hit by a second bullet.

If I shoot the nigger first, Donny thought, *how long will I have to shift my aim and kill that counter-sniper before he blows my shit away? He hasn't seen me yet . . . if he had, I'd be dead already. Since I can open fire on the crowd anytime I choose, he's probably pre-cleared to take me out. And he's got to be quick at target acquisition, or he wouldn't have the gig. But now I'm supposed to shoot Penn Cage and his daughter with shots two and three . . .*

"Goddamn it," Donny muttered, knowing his nerves were betraying him. That's what happened when you waited years to fulfill your dream. To take his mind off the negative possibilities, he focused on practicalities.

He had thirty-three loaded clips with him, twenty rounds per transparent magazine, now painted white and stacked within reach, against the cool metal of the tower reservoir. Nearly a million gallons of water pressed against the curved steel that touched him along his right side and thigh, cooling both him and his 660 rounds of match-grade ammunition. Donny could likely empty those clips in twelve to fifteen minutes, real world. The result? The dead and wounded on the ground would trigger a panic incomparable to anything except the Las Vegas shooting of 2017.

With luck, it would take cops on the ground two to five minutes to pin-point his location, and even longer to engage. Once they did, he could drop a helicopter on them to ratchet up the panic. Of course, that would mean shutting one of the windows that the world would be watching him work through. Better to wait till the last minute for that—

Donny stopped breathing. A third helicopter had joined the other two.

The third bird was no media platform. Painted matte black from nose rig to tail rotor, it flew much lower than the news choppers over the con-crete triangle below, with no regard for the man scheduled to speak. When it got low enough, the crowd began looking up in anger, then booing and waving their arms, and Donny saw the FBI legend painted on it in yel-low. He also saw a FLIR pod mounted below the chopper's nose. For him that pod was like the eye of God. A FLIR pod scanning the roofs of these buildings would register body heat against those cold structures like neon signs against a night sky. That FLIR pod could see *him*.

It might be picking him off the water tower right now.

Donny felt his face go cold as the blood drained from his hard-on. If he waited where he was for the "Fire" code order from Bobby White—*Arcadia*—he might never get a chance to fire even one round. With the slow purpose of a snake in winter, he edged backward on his belly until the cool curve of the tank lay between him and the FBI chopper. For the time being he was safe. The problem was, he could no longer see or shoot at the lectern on the amphitheater stage.

AFTER SPEAKING BRIEFLY with Reverend Baldwin and Annie at the rear curtain, Kendrick Washington bows his head, gathers himself, then walks out to the lectern and looks out over the sea of Black faces. From my position by the steps I can see white faces in the crowd, most of them young, but also some middle-aged and older. Still, the audience is easily 95 percent Black.

"Thank you for coming," Kendrick says in a surprisingly low voice. "I'm surprised they let me get up here to talk at all, the people who run this town. But since I got stabbed today, and after all the threats I've got since, maybe they're hoping something else will happen to me out here. If it does, don't let that stop you. Don't go back home and sit in fear. Find Mr. Penn Cage and make him tell you who started these fires we been having around here. Then you look up at those helicopters, find reporters with cameras, and tell them what they ought to know already. That's who I'm talking to today, besides you. Those helicopters and reporters. And through them I'm talking to America. I'm a Black man who served his country, but I'm talking to you from a town that's been sealed off from the rest of America by white law enforcement, after its elected leader was assassinated—and after its Black city government dissolved itself under the threat of extortion . . ."

As Kendrick finds his voice, I peer over the mass of people, searching for signs of danger or disruption. I can't escape the feeling that since the sheriff and the governor and the Poker Club and Bobby White have decided to let this event go forward, they've figured some way to exploit it to their benefit. Nothing else can explain this. They have all the power. Who decided upon restraint? And is this seeming peace only the prologue to some imminent disaster?

Looking along the front row of the audience, I see mostly local Black officials and city worthies, then Father Willie Doucy, who has seated himself about as far from Aaron Baldwin as he can get, but still in the row where he will be seen by all cameras. Two helicopters hover above, just high enough that their turbines won't overpower the portable PA system set up by the church. The noise is annoying, but the cameras in those choppers are probably the only thing allowing this event to continue.

I see more white faces near the far edges of the crowd, as Kendrick must have when he walked up to the lectern. Some are topped by Stetsons, the blue-gray hats indicating state police, the brown indicating Buck Tarlton's deputies. But I haven't seen or heard anything like a disturbance yet. The crowd is listening to Kendrick the way a congregation attends a preacher from whom they expect an illuminating arc and revelatory climax. Looking over at Annie, I see her watching Kendrick's back with obvious admiration. His words or delivery seem to have caused her to abandon her usual analytical posture and enter a pure state of identification. That's the mark of a truly charismatic leader, and for the first time, I wonder if Kendrick might have a future that stretches far beyond this town.

And yet . . .

I also sense danger. Somewhere in this crowd lurk Shotwell Barlow and at least some of his men, and their minds are bent on revenge.

"I'm here to talk to you today about a case of mistaken identity," Kendrick informs the audience. "Or maybe misplaced credit. There's a long history of that between Black folks and white folks in this country. Usually when a white man takes credit for some good thing a Black man managed to do. But more times it happens the other way—when a Black man gets blamed for something bad a white man actually did. Most of y'all know I work as a tour guide up here sometimes. I don't have much formal education, but I know some stories. Some have been written down in books, others in letters. But others were just passed down father to son, mother to daughter.

"One of my favorites tells about April 17, 1863, when the gunboats of a Union admiral named David Porter had to somehow get south of the big cannons at Vicksburg before he could join up with General Grant's army in Louisiana and ferry them across the river so they could march up here and lay siege to Vicksburg. Now, Bienville wasn't near as dangerous to those ironclads as the fortress at Vicksburg. The river ran straight and fast past here back then, just like today, but the rebels *did* have two big guns on the heights. Confederate copies of what they call Rodman guns. Rifled cannon capable of 'plunging fire.' Some could throw a shell three miles. That's what Doc's notes here say. Plunging fire can sink an ironclad, which is what Porter had. But—as the history books will tell you—on the historic night Admiral Porter ran his boats past here, the guns at Bienville were silent. The *books* say that's because a white Union officer from Rhode Island led a party of men up here on the night of the sixteenth and spiked the guns before Porter made his run. 'Spiking' a cannon is when you take a special tool, or a ramrod, and hammer it down into the touch-hole where they light off the shell. You can't fire the gun after that's been done. And the *books* say he was led by a white Southerner from Bienville named Philippe Dufort, who sympathized with the Union, despite coming from a family of slave owners. But the story *I* know—the *true* story—is that that Yankee officer was led up this bluff in the dark by a formerly enslaved man named Isaac Simpson from Bienville, Mississippi. Isaac was a teamster—a mule driver—who knew the face of this bluff like the back of his hand in the dark. Isaac had run away from his master months before and joined the Union army as a scout. Now, *his* name ain't in the history books, any more than the name of the so-called 'colored man' who showed General Grant the best place to cross the river—at Bruinsburg instead of Rodney—and saved Grant twenty miles of marching with forty thousand men on the biggest amphibious operation in the world until D-Day. The name in the history books belongs to that white boy from Rhode Island. But I'm told that Isaac's name may be in there before too long. So how 'bout y'all give me a big hand for Brother Isaac Simpson? He's one reason you don't live in the Confederate States of America today!"

The crowd applauds wildly, and many leap to their feet. As the energy rises, a ripple of heat passes over my face, and a formless fear comes to pulsing life in my belly.

A MERE SIXTY meters from the water tower, Bobby White sat behind the tinted windows of his Range Rover, using his laptop to monitor the feed from the sheriff's-department drone flying high above the news helicopters. On the cell phone clipped to his dash mount, CNN streamed Kendrick Washington's remarks live. Bobby stared at the feed with a furrowed brow. After the change of venue, he'd fought the urge to contact Donny to be sure he understood the new geometry, and that he was in position. Every communication from this point forward entailed more risk, and the kid knew what to do. It was Kendrick who was slowing things down, taking his time getting to his big reveal. *Maybe he's starting to like the cameras*, Bobby thought. Bobby knew what that felt like . . . the pull of those big lenses on you, like divine eyes.

It was time to put an end to Kendrick's foreplay.

Bobby lifted the radio to his lips to give the go code, then depressed the button. "*Arcadia*," he whispered. "*Arcadia*."

He braced for the sound of the rifle shot.

Nothing happened.

He blinked in disbelief as Kendrick droned on about naval maneuvers during the Vicksburg Campaign of 1863.

"Today," Kendrick went on, "a hundred and sixty years later, we got us a different case of mistaken identity. But it's the *other* kind of mistake. Where a white man has done somethin' bad—*real* bad—but tries to lay it on the Black man. This past Tuesday, somebody set fire to an antebellum slave mansion down in Natchez, called Tranquility. Later that night, they done the same to Arcadia, right here in Bienville. And since then, they've been burnin' mansions every day. And not just houses. *People* died in those fires. Now . . . the arsonist who *set* those fires left notes claiming it was done as some kind of protest by a radical Black group. The Bastard Sons of the Confederacy. He wanted to create a picture of crazy Black terrorists in white folks' minds. He even slandered Tupac to do it! And *man*, did he succeed! He succeeded beyond his wildest *dreams*. 'Cause white folks were primed and ready to believe that very thing."

Bobby's iPhone rang. Not taking his eyes from the screen, he pressed the button to speak to Shot Barlow, whom he hadn't heard from in more than two hours.

"Where the fuck have you been?"

"Tied up in Penn Cage's house, goddamn it! You were right. They have that Chinese girl, and I think she knows everything about the fires."

Bobby jerked up in his seat. "Why do you say that?"

"There's no time to explain. All that matters is that Cage took the girl with him when he left here, and he's backstage at that speech now. One of my guys is up there. They've got her in an Airstream trailer backstage. I'm guessing they're gonna bring that little bitch out and let her tell that crowd what she knows."

"Jesus!"

"I don't know what you can do about it—maybe stop the whole show with a bomb threat—but you need to know one thing: Cage has some kind of special forces buddy in town, and he's dangerous. I kid you not, Bobby."

Bobby White disconnected and called Buck Tarlton, who was waiting in his office.

"Yeah," said the sheriff.

"The situation has changed."

"No shit. I've been watching the speech. That boy sure likes hearing himself talk."

"I want you to go out and start your press conference. Right now. Hold up the flares and *weld* them to Kendrick Washington. Bury him, Buck. Say that if anybody white was involved in the Bastard Sons fires, it was as part of a conspiracy with Washington. Because if this goes any other way . . ."

"I know. What's changed?"

"The Chinese girl your man told us about. Martyn's girlfriend. She's still in town, apparently, and she may come out tonight and speak."

"What can we do about her?"

Bobby already knew the answer. "I think she's about to share someone else's fate."

"Sounds good to me. The last flight of Madame Butterfly?"

"You just start muddying the waters now. Say that at least one of your men has already been in contact with a material witness, and that the story is far more complex than Kendrick Washington is portraying it to be."

"I know how to play that angle. You do what you need to do."

"Ten-four. Out."

Bobby disconnected from the sheriff. Despite his sensation that the world had reversed its rotation, he felt his nerves settling. That's what battle experience did for you. He studied Kendrick onscreen, watching for signs that he was about to bring someone else onstage with him. As he watched, barely breathing, the walkie-talkie on the Rover's console clicked twice more.

"We got a problem," said Donny Kilmer in frustration. "This fuckin' Bureau helicopter's giving me fits. I'm not sure I can wait."

"I gave you the go order a while ago."

"I didn't hear it!"

"Just as well. I've got another target for you. Make her shot four."

"Jesus, Sergeant. You should have come up here as a spotter for me."

"Yeah, well. You can handle it."

CHAPTER 108

SPECIAL AGENT BILL Davenport methodically glassed the crowd both inside and outside the amphitheater at the north end of Battery Row. He focused at the edges more than the center, where the number of white faces was greatest. He supposed there could be Black men in that audience who posed a threat to Washington, as in the case of Malcolm X in 1965, but today command had assessed that the threat would come from white supremacists.

Contrary to what Donny Kilmer believed, Agent Davenport did have a spotter. Keith Dibley had been working beside him for three years. They'd covered everything from presidential speeches to a World Series together. But Dibley wasn't at his shoulder today. He wasn't even on the Donnelly roof. He was in the Bureau chopper overhead—which had arrived twenty minutes late. Those twenty minutes might cost them the day if anyone down there meant Kendrick Washington harm.

"What do you see?" Davenport asked the lav mic at his lips.

"Looks like the Saturday crowd at an Atlanta Hawks game," Dibley replied. "Whole lotta Black folks."

"Big surprise."

"See any threats?"

"Not yet." Even as he said it, Davenport doubted his assessment. Even with the FLIR screen, searching for a hostile actor down in that crowd was like trying to find a coral snake in a twisting carpet of scarlet king snakes. You couldn't do it. Not in time to save a primary target.

Davenport muted his mic and speed-dialed Dibley on his cell phone, knowing his partner could listen in private on the Bluetooth earbud in his left ear.

"We got some REMFs running this show today," he complained. "You ought to be up here with me."

"Agreed."

"There are more firing lines into that amphitheater than it seemed like from the diagram. I'm worried about long guns from odd places. I've been going over every elevated position that offers concealment, working my way outward. But I feel like I've got some blind spots."

"How far out have you got? Glassed that water tower out there yet?"

"Much as I could see. That's a good five hundred meters, though. And no escape for the shooter. That's a minimal threat, I'd say."

"We'll swing out and take a look anyway. Murphy's law. Moving now."

The crowd cheered in gratitude as the FBI helo lifted higher into the gray sky and flitted off toward the North Bienville Water Tower.

"Thanks, buddy. And glass anything else that looks like it's off-angle from me on our way."

"I'll do it on the way back," Dibley replied. "I see what looks like heat residue on the maintenance rail of that tower. Faint, but . . . I think it's real. Doesn't look right."

"Bird sat up there a while maybe? Buzzard or something? Big enough to leave a trace?"

"Hang on . . . yeah, I don't like this."

"You see any movement?"

"I'm not sure. Could be my eyes playing tricks. We're pushing in now . . . I'll know in a few seconds. Turn your rifle this way."

"I hate to while Washington's still talking."

"Do it. That Tenisaw militia probably has guys who could make a five-hundred-meter shot. I know that fuckin' PSP does."

"Somebody who'd fire with no escape?"

"That's exactly the kind of flake these militias breed. You know that."

Davenport trusted his friend, but he didn't turn his rifle.

FROM HIS EYRIE atop the water tower, Donny watched the FBI chopper bore in toward him. Destiny had arrived, and his choices had shrunk to three. Two offered him continued life, while the third—which he had been ordered to make—would almost surely kill him.

Keeping his rifle trained on Kendrick Washington, Donny watched the approaching helo from the corner of his left eye. While he did, he thought about a literal "rule of thumb" that the Viet Cong had used after years of dealing with the American Huey. If a Vietnamese infantryman held up his thumb, and a chopper overhead appeared equal in size to, or larger than, that thumb, then it could be brought down with rifle fire. Keeping both hands firmly on his weapon, Donny extended his left thumb far enough out to gauge the size of the chopper, which he now recognized as a Bell JetRanger. It wasn't quite close enough for a definite kill shot, but in a few seconds it would be. *Three targets . . .*

If he fired on the chopper first, he'd have to traverse his gun about forty degrees, reacquire Kendrick Washington, and fire with lethal effect—all before Washington dove for cover. How fast would the combat vet react to a rifle fired five hundred meters away? Maybe not instantly. But if a helicopter started spinning in the sky, its desperate pilot trying to autorotate to a safe landing? Washington would be long gone. He'd lunge backstage or be tackled by the entourage that had escorted him there. *No*, Donny realized, *if I'm going down in the goddamn history books . . . I gotta take the shot that counts.*

If he shot Washington first, then he'd have to execute the same move in reverse: blast the chopper with a dozen rounds, then turn to the Donnelly building roof and take out the counter-sniper who would likely already be firing at him. *That's a tough row to hoe*, Donny thought, seeing the sequence in his mind's eye, like a movie trailer. He didn't much like the footage, which looked like a suicide mission. Drawing a quick but deep breath, he took his aim off Kendrick Washington's face and transferred it to the nose of the approaching JetRanger. Christ, it was getting big fast . . .

Bobby would have a stroke if he didn't shoot Kendrick Washington with his first bullet. But White wasn't up here. He was down on the street in his air-conditioned Range Rover—a hundred-thousand-dollar ride. Why the hell should he get to choose the target sequence?

As the final fluid seconds slid into eternity, Donny wondered what America would remember after this day. The death of Kendrick Washington, who'd been completely unknown until the Mission Hill massacre? Or would that be merely a footnote to mass slaughter? *Yeah*, he realized. Mass casualties would fill every channel in permanent rotation—panic porn—and send the country around the final bend into Crazy Town. The thing was, unlike Kendrick Washington or the FBI snipers, this crowd had no way of escaping his rifle. They were penned on that bluff top like a bunch of felons in a prison yard. They wouldn't know which way to jump. They'd be trampling each other to death, and he'd be cutting them down like summer wheat with a scythe. Maybe he could afford to try the other targets first. Maybe he'd give Bobby White that. Then he'd switch the HK to full auto and go to work.

His heart swelling with blood, Donny forced himself to look away from both the Donnelly tower and the approaching JetRanger and turn his rifle on the man standing at the lectern like Malcolm X reincarnated . . .

I DIDN'T HEAR the bullet that knocked down Kendrick until nearly a second after he was lying on his back. I did the math later to be sure I wasn't crazy. The sound of the shot traveled eleven hundred feet per second, while the bullet made the five-hundred-meter trip from the water tower at more than twenty-six hundred feet per second. Kendrick's security detail was on him within three seconds, but by that time the assassin on the tower had shifted fire to the FBI chopper, and five seconds later the aircraft was spinning out of control. As the crowd in front of the stage disintegrated in terror, I heard one more shot, then the shooter switched to full automatic and began spraying bullets into the sea of people.

Instantly I was back at Mission Hill, watching with visceral horror as unprepared humans went into blind panic. Only this time Annie was screaming beside me, and I had to hold her back to stop her from running to Kendrick, but Kelly and his cousin were already dragging him back toward us. Shoving Annie toward the Airstream, I followed in a crouch as the gunfire continued behind me.

"Into that tent!" Kelly shouted. "Let me check him!"

"You a doctor?" asked Frosty Givens.

"Delta Force," Kelly barked, using a term that's no longer accurate but one he knew would register with the young man. "I know gunshot wounds. I'm trained to treat them."

As Frosty yielded to the force of Kelly's will, the supersonic crack of a rifle bullet hammered my eardrum and blasted a divot from the ground at Annie's feet. Less than a second later another round cleaved the distance between our heads. Whoever was firing that rifle was targeting us! Seizing Annie's arm, I hurled her into the tent after Kelly. Before I could follow, for three exposed seconds I froze in grief on the bluff, staring into the glassy eyes of Judge Clayton Shelby, who had been shot through the sternum by whoever was raining death down from above. His bourbon glass lay empty on the grass beneath his lawn chair, and I caught the sugary scent as I broke forward and followed Kelly and Frosty under one of the walled canopy tents, then swept the food off the catering table so that they could deposit him there. Kelly unbuttoned Kendrick's coat, then his white shirt, which showed blood but far less than I'd expected.

"He's wearing a vest!" I remember. "Thank God."

"No plates in it, though," Kelly says. "He refused them. It's a pistol vest. Wound'll be a lot worse because of that."

It finally hits me that Kendrick is unconscious. "Did the round puncture the armor?"

The screaming outside almost drowns out the gunfire.

Kelly has bent over the wound with a small penlight. "Don't know. It drove the fabric into him. What we've got here is broken ribs, a terrible bruise, and probably hydrostatic shock. The impact wasn't far from his heart, so there's no telling how bad this is. Could have ruptured a major vessel internally. Hell, a baseball going fast enough can stop a heart. This is like getting hit by the force of a Mack truck across a quarter inch of your body."

"So he needs a hospital."

"He needs a trauma team, but we'll have hell getting an ambulance up in here."

"No hospital!" yells Frosty. "Not in this town. He'd never get out alive."

"He's got to have it," Kelly insists. "He needs X-rays, and he needs a real surgeon."

Kendrick jerks up from the waist, lifts his torso, and gasps for air. Blinking like an exhausted man trying to stay awake, he croaks, "*No hospital.* Frosty's right. Get me out of here, man. Before somebody finishes the job."

"He's right," says Frosty, who pulls some sort of machine pistol from his oversize pants pocket. "That motherfucker still shootin'. We're sittin' ducks up here. We gotta blow."

"We'll never get off this bluff in a vehicle," Ray Ransom says, entering the tent from the back. As the flap closes, I see a screen of Black city cops protecting the tent with their guns drawn. "Not unless we run over people. Take us twenty minutes to clear the Row, at least."

"What if this was just the start of a larger attack?" I ask.

"Come on, man," Frosty says. "Let's get him in a ride."

"No hospital!" Kendrick groans again. "I mean it."

"If he needs a trauma team, that means UMC in Jackson," I tell them. "And trying to get him out by road means Tarlton's guys or the state police could stop him anywhere. I know a doctor with a helicopter."

"Dr. Ford!" exclaims Frosty. "Hell, yeah!"

"He landed me right on the bluff Tuesday afternoon. And he's still in town. His chopper's small, not really suited for medevac." I look at Kelly. "You think Kendrick would survive us strapping him into a seat and a fifteen-minute flight to Jackson?"

"Sounds like his best option to me."

I take out my cell phone and call Dwight Ford. To my amazement, he answers almost immediately.

"Dwight, you texted me that if you could help, you'd do it. What's the chance of you landing on the bluff at the amphitheater and medevacking a kid to Jackson?"

"Kendrick Washington? I saw it on my phone."

"Yep. I won't kid you. You might get arrested. But I'll represent you for free, and you won't spend a night in jail."

"I can try it, Penn. But the soonest I can get there is a half hour."

"Half an hour! You flew me from Natchez to Vicksburg in forty-five minutes."

"I'm not home now, but I'm turning back."

"Jesus, Dwight. Keep going, I'll call you back."

"Half an hour's too long," Kelly says as I hang up. "Not because of the wound, necessarily, but because the locals aren't going to give us that time."

Looking toward Battery Row, I see three sheriff's cruisers crawling through the crowd in our direction.

"Goddamn it!"

"Get me *out* of here!" Kendrick groans. "I ain't going back to that jail."

"What about the river?" Ray asks.

We all whip our heads toward him.

"What do you mean?" asks Kelly.

"There's a boat down there. A ski boat. Big one. I used it last night."

"How does that help us?"

"Nobody will expect us to run that way. We can get to that boat in two, three minutes. It's hidden between Matheson Lumber and the casino."

Hidden tells me he probably stole it.

"It can get us to the main Bienville landing," Ray says, "or all the way to Vicksburg or Natchez if you want."

Daniel Kelly isn't a slow thinker. "None of those. I landed my Cessna out at Penn's place. Pencarrow. How far upriver is that?"

"Three miles," I tell him. "By water. If somebody meets us with a vehicle where I tell them to, we can cut around Black Oak Plantation and have Kendrick at your plane in . . . shit, fifteen minutes? Twenty at the most."

Kelly nods. "That's the plan. I can assess his wound better in the boat, and if it's worse than it looks now, we can divert to a city landing."

"How do we stop people from following us? The media. Tarlton's deputies. The PSP. We don't know who the biggest threat is."

This takes Kelly all of ten seconds to solve.

"Whichever of Chief Morgan's cops is closest in size to Kendrick, get him in here now. We'll switch their clothes. Morgan's guys can haul the double out under a sheet, shove him in the back of an official car, and start fighting through the crowd like they're trying to reach the hospital. We'll hang here three or four minutes, then head down the bluff in that Airstream. Some of Morgan's men can go out to Pencarrow by road to beef up security. We'll kill all the birds with one stone."

Frosty is nodding with admiration. "Damn, brah, you *thinkin'*."

"That's the plan," Kendrick croaks. "Make it happen."

"One second." I hold up my hand and look at Kelly. "Wouldn't

Dr. Ford's helicopter be a better medevac delivery than your plane? It could set Kendrick right on the UMC helipad. I can route him out to my place now."

"A Robinson R44, you said?"

I nod.

"He'll travel a lot better in the belly of my plane. Plus I can outrun the local sheriff's chopper if they get onto us. I'll arrange to have a LifeFlight chopper waiting at the Jackson airport when I land."

"Okay. Let's move."

DONNY KILMER HAD never felt such exultation as the moment he knocked the FBI helicopter out of the sky. First, he'd struck his primary target within inches of his heart, on a rifle rated at twenty-inch accuracy at six hundred meters. Then he'd punched a hole in the center of the cocky old judge's chest while he sat drinking in his lawn chair. Bobby White would be pissed about that, but Penn Cage and his daughter had already been moving, and Donny still felt the sting of humiliation from the previous day when the judge blasted the truck nuts with his pistol and hit Joe Iverson in the back with some chrome shrapnel. Knocking down the JetRanger had been child's play after that. Still, the thrill was ten times what he'd felt after shooting Kendrick Washington. The flaming plunge and subsequent crash into High Street was like a scene from a John Woo movie.

But his exultation was short-lived. About four seconds into it, the sniper atop Donnelly Oil blew a hole in the reservoir inches above his back, and the resulting spurt of water expanded so fast that it hit his side like a power drill, driving him away from the metal wall, toward open space. Donny's perch was no longer tenable. He scrambled back along the rail, but the sniper fired again, and again, tracing his path, trying for a kill shot.

Enraged, Donny steeled his nerves and lay still, then sighted in on the agent on the roof. He saw the man aiming at him, then a muzzle flash. He felt something in him drop away. *Fear.* He pulled his trigger as another bullet punched through the reservoir over his head. Not a half second later, he saw the sniper's skull explode into chunks of gore.

Water drilled into his back again, but this time he grabbed the steel rail and pulled himself to his knees. Now he could move. With a flick of his forefinger he switched the rifle to auto and aimed down into the bluff-top crowd, which was now panicking in the open sea of the amphitheater. The six-pound trigger unleashed a torrent of rounds on a target so densely packed that every bullet impacted flesh.

He'd emptied the first magazine and begun firing the second when another bullet hammered the tank only inches from his shoulder. Another shooter had acquired him, obviously, but he couldn't take time to try to figure out who—not with such a target-rich scene unfolding on the ground below. After this clip ran dry, he would start looking for targets of opportunity, like the backstage RVs, which were probably packed with cowering VIPs.

The next incoming bullet struck as Donny's firing pin hit an empty chamber. This one hit closer than the first, but as it did, he realized he'd heard no supersonic crack. *A pistol round?* Was it possible? Whoever was shooting wasn't some panicked cop. They knew what they were doing. He'd either have to pick them out of the chaos below, or hope his vest stopped the next round.

It didn't.

Donny was loading his third magazine when a bullet plowed through his left upper arm, cracking and possibly snapping the bone. A bright splash of blood painted the metal behind him. He knew then that his aim was fucked. He wouldn't even be able to spray the distant crowd with accuracy. Not with that wound. And if he stayed where he was much longer, the shooter below was likely to put one through his eye socket.

Screaming in fury, Donny dropped his rifle off the tower, then scooted along the rail until he could no longer be seen from the bluff. The shooter below would be watching the ladder, expecting a panicked descent, but Donny had no intention of using it. With a flush of pride he reached out for the handle he'd rigged before settling into his firing position, something that would have the news anchors comparing him to Houdini before an hour passed.

As he prepared to leap from the tower, he looked back toward the amphitheater, then down along the street below. Without his scope it looked far away. He wondered who'd managed to put the bullet in him from that distance. Then he saw the running figure in the street below, one arm upraised, a long-barreled pistol in its hand.

And he knew.

BOBBY WAS POSITIVE he'd hit Donny, as he'd planned to all along, but he didn't know how badly. Unlike the kid, Bobby had no scope. He was firing a target pistol, one of those that had led him into the national championships during the period after he'd first returned from Afghanistan. Learning to pitch a baseball at major-league level with his solitary arm had proved beyond him, but golfing and shooting pistols had not. He'd become a champion at both—which had made this week, and especially today, possible. And he could easily explain having had one of his pistols in his vehicle, especially during a potential riot.

Bobby was shooting less than a hundred meters, a distance from which he was highly proficient, but he was shooting under combat conditions and at a very high angle against a moving target. His first two rounds had missed, while his target murdered unarmed townspeople at a high rate. But his third shot had painted the tower with a huge scarlet flower, which meant he'd likely hit a significant blood vessel.

When Donny scooted far enough around the tower to vanish from sight, Bobby had bolted for the base of the tower, knowing that every move he made from that point forward was likely being filmed by at least one of the surviving helicopters in the sky. But even as he moved to shut down the possibility of exposure, he held his nerve and confidence.

He could explain everything—how he'd parked near the end of Battery Row to listen to Kendrick's speech but stayed in his vehicle so as not to provoke any Black people who might not like his politics. How, after noticing some white thugs hassling Black people on the edges of the crowd, he'd left his vehicle and warned them away. In a couple of cases, he'd made a point to get physical with guys to get them to stop, something witnessed by quite a few Black folks who'd expressed gratitude. Most important, they would remember his actions later, and could testify to them in front of a grand jury, if necessary.

As Bobby climbed the hill to the base of the water tower, he looked up at the ladder on the northwest leg. It was empty. He focused on the narrow catwalk that surrounded the tower. Again, he saw no sign marking Donny Kilmer's position. His heart began pounding as he climbed the rest of the way up the hill, and he looked up again as more of the catwalk became visible.

Still . . . no sign of Kilmer.

Fear began eating at him. *Did the crazy son of a bitch fall from the ladder while I was running? No. That'd be like a wounded raccoon falling from a tree trunk. You never see that. I guess I'll find out when I get up the fucking ladder . . .*

Bobby didn't want to have to climb. In fact, he had no real way to do it. To prevent litigation, the ladder didn't even touch the ground. It began its upward journey twenty feet *above* the ground. He wasn't sure how Donny had covered that first twenty feet of space, but a former oil-field derrick man probably didn't have any trouble with an obstacle like that.

As this thought went through his head, Bobby felt something let go in his gut. This time, when he looked up, he didn't focus on the perforated steel platform, but the narrow rail above it. And there, on the back side of the tower from the Battery Row area, he saw something that in all his planning he had not imagined—a thin metal cable stretching down and across the street, deep into the trees on the next block. From the ground it looked like an electrical line.

All Bobby's instincts told him it was anything but.

In those seconds he realized that Donny Kilmer was more of a thinker than Bobby had thought—and more of a survivor, too. By now Donny almost certainly knew who had shot him on the tower. In fact, he might be sighting down on Bobby from the next block with that damned designated marksman variant of the HK417—

You clever little motherfucker, Bobby muttered.

Sprinting to the edge of the hill, he started sliding hell-for-leather down to the street. At this point he had no choice but to find Donny and kill him. Any other outcome would end his career, and probably his life. For Donny Kilmer could sign Bobby's name under every death on the Bienville bluff in the public mind, if he chose to, condemning him as a public monster. Donny could also blow out his brains from any reasonable distance, a fate that might be preferable to being publicly branded for what he now knew himself to be, at least by conventional moral judgment.

In the distance he saw terrified people stampeding past his Range Rover. Looking back up at the thin cable stretching down from the tower, he raised his cell phone to his ear and called Buck Tarlton.

"It's me," said the sheriff.

"Meet me at the base of the north water tower. *Right now.* And bring an army."

"That could be tough right now, considering."

"We're going to nail that mass shooter, Buck. Sound good?"

"Uh, ten-four. Cavalry's coming."

WE WAITED ANXIOUSLY inside the Airstream while Chief Morgan's men played out the charade Kelly had scripted in the canopy tent. After Tarlton's cruisers followed our decoy vehicle, rolling away from the bluff as fast as our police driver dared move through the crowd, we huddled in the tight cubicle of the RV's central area—Ray and Annie and Nadine and Lanying and me—while Kendrick lay in a semi-fetal position on the double mattress in back with Kelly constantly checking his vitals and his three-hundred-pound cousin standing guard in the tiny aisle.

"What about the crowd?" Kendrick asked at one point. "How many people shot?"

Kelly looked past Frosty Givens at me. The darkness in his eyes had less to do with Kendrick than what we both knew we would eventually learn about what happened in the amphitheater. At minimum, there would be dozens, perhaps even hundreds, of casualties. But even as we shared this moment of dread, our minds reached toward the future.

"It's time to get down to that boat," Kelly says suddenly. "Before anybody gets too curious. Who can drive this RV?"

"I got it," Ray declares, moving to the front.

"What if somebody films us driving down there?" I ask. "Tarlton's guys could review the media footage and see us board the boat."

"We just have to risk that," Kelly says. "I'll have Kendrick in the air in half an hour. Lanying can come, too. I can take more than that in the Caravan."

"Hang on," I tell him, holding up my hand. Then I walk forward and speak to Ray in a whisper. "Call one of your boys and blow that oil well. The one by the cemetery."

Ray looks up from the driver's seat, his eyes wide.

"You blow that thing, every chopper will fly straight to it like moths to a flame."

After a few seconds, he nods and brings out his cell phone.

I walk back to Nadine, who leans toward me and asks, "Am I going with y'all in this thing? Didn't you say we'll need another vehicle out at Pencarrow?"

"Kelly needs his rented SUV. He's got two heavy Pelican suitcases in there from his deployment. Critical gear, I'm sure. Also, I left my rifle in my trunk, so it wouldn't be in the house with the Barlows. So get that stuff, please, but don't go back into the house."

She sighs heavily, then gives me a gentle hug. "I wish you weren't going out on that damned river."

"It's safer than being up here tonight. Hey, please bring that box of Mom's leftover hospice drugs. The fentanyl patches, everything. Kelly might be able to use some on Kendrick."

"I will." She shakes her head against my chest. "I feel like the house is safe, but I still feel a kind of premonition."

"Of what?"

"It's the river. You never finished Romulus's narrative. After surviving the Civil War, he damn near died on the Mississippi. Right at the end. And now you're going out there in this weather . . . I just don't like it."

For some reason her superstitious explanation brings a smile to my face. I hug her to reassure her. "I'm going to be fine. You can tell me the ending of Romulus's story when you get out to Pencarrow. We'll wave to Kelly and Kendrick as they fly off into the sunset."

"Don't joke about it, Penn."

I wipe the smile from my face. "We'll be fine. Seriously. I know how to handle a boat on that river. You know that."

"Let's move!" Kelly calls.

"Give it just a minute," I say, holding up my hand again.

"Not long now," Ray warns.

The first thing I hear is a deep *WHOOSH* from the north. A few seconds later, a gentle wind rocks the Airstream—followed by a concussive *BOOM* reverberates across the bluff, as if the biggest transformer in the world just blew out a few miles away.

"Should I ask?" Kelly calls from the back.

Nadine pushes open the door and steps lightly to the ground. "Please be careful, guys. Watch for snags."

"If you move fast, you can meet us at the ramp below the bluff just south of Black Oak."

She nods. "I'll be there. Call me before then, though."

"I will."

"Hey!" says Annie, running up to me with her cell phone. "This is a zoom photo shot from one of the news choppers. That's the water tower shooter. Doesn't he look familiar?"

Without a second's delay I recognize Donny Kilmer, the Ted Nugent superfan. Staring at the grainy image, with a sick rush I suddenly understand why Judge Shelby was one of the first victims to be shot.

"I know that crazy punk! He's part of Barlow's militia crew."

"That's not all. Somebody's reporting a rumor that the guy on the ground that stopped the shooter in the midst of his massacre was no cop. Some people are saying it might have been Bobby White."

"*What?* What are the odds of that?"

"He was a Delta Force operator," Ray reminds me.

"Still . . . the odds that he'd be first to pick the guy out . . . and have a gun capable of engaging at distance? This is fucked up, Ray. This isn't what it seems to be. Let's get the hell out of here."

"With you, bro. Let's hit the river."

CHAPTER 109

"THEY CALL IT a Geronimo line," said Sheriff Tarlton. "You see 'em more in Texas and out in the gulf than you do around this area. Derrick men use them to bail on a rig if they get a big blowout, or some other emergency."

Buck Tarlton and Bobby stood alone in a child's tree house, hardly more than a large box with a partial roof, built about twelve feet up in an oak tree that stood two hundred feet from the Bienville water tower. This was the termination point of the cable Donny Kilmer had stretched from the high rail as his escape route. Inside the tree house they'd found a simple wooden chair seat much like those on commercial zip-line tour rigs. This seat connected to a vertical steel bar and a pulley handle with a bicycle-type hand brake attached to the cable, so that the rider could regulate his downward speed as he escaped what was usually a burning oil derrick.

"That little bastard is sharper than I gave him credit for," Bobby averred, studying how the cable and pulley handle had been rigged. "Gave himself a way out, didn't he? I figured it was a suicide mission."

Tarlton shook his head. "Man, it must take some balls to leap off that tower with nothing to ride but this skimpy seat."

"Donny Kilmer doesn't experience fear the same way we do."

"I reckon not. Where you figure he's gone now?"

"No telling. Not far, is all I hope. And from the signs . . . I may get my wish."

There was a lot of blood inside the tree house. It looked to Bobby like Donny had been forced to sit for a bit before continuing his escape—maybe to bandage his wound, or maybe because he'd been too weak to go on without rest. In any case, there were more than twenty deputies searching the immediate neighborhood, and so far none had seen hide nor hair of Kilmer. Nor had they found more bloodstains.

Bobby looked over the wall of the tree house, toward the Victorian house whose backyard it had been built in. Tarlton had ordered his men to establish a perimeter forty feet from the tree, so that no one would hear their conversation. After yesterday's exchanges, Bobby didn't blame him. But Tarlton had so far pretended that nothing awkward had occurred between them.

"All right," the sheriff said. "You wanted to run this show . . . well, fine.

I'm listening. We're in some pretty deep shit here. What do you want to do now?"

As if they were both young boys, Bobby bent and sat on the plywood floor, then leaned back against the wall of the confined space. Taken aback, Tarlton decided he had little choice but to do the same. As if FBI agents might not come charging up the ladder at any moment . . .

"I hope to hell Kendrick Washington's dead by now," Bobby said. "But if he isn't, you need to find him and arrest him."

"Sure. But what if he's in a hospital ER?"

"Handcuff him to the bed. He's the arsonist behind the Bastard Sons fires, now and forever."

"Okay. I hear you. And I think he was refusing to be taken to a hospital. But either way, he's already lawyered up with the Cages, or Doris Avery."

Bobby shrugged. "Can't be helped. The key is for him not to live out this day. If we're lucky, Donny took care of that for us."

"That game Chief Morgan played with the squad car sure screwed us."

Bobby shook his head. "You had your drone up, right? That's the key. Go back and review the footage. With a little luck, you'll see them move him. It'll be after that little switch Morgan pulled."

Tarlton was relieved to have a lead worth following. "All right. I'll get to it."

"We still don't have that Chinese girl."

"All I can do is have my people watch for her while they trail the others."

"We've got to come up with a mechanism to keep her silent."

"Bullet's the best mechanism I know for that."

"Agreed."

Buck rolled onto his knees to crawl through the square exit hatch, but at the last minute he turned and looked back at Bobby. "What about Donny Kilmer?"

Bobby looked puzzled. "What about him?"

Tarlton pointed at the splashes of blood around the interior of the tree house. "He's still out there somewhere. And I'm guessing he's not too well disposed toward you at this point. If I was you, I'd keep my head down for a while."

Bobby flicked his hand as though at a bull gnat. "I *hope* he comes for me, Buck, looking for revenge. If he does, I become the hero who nailed the Water Tower Shooter."

Tarlton's eyes narrowed. "Is that what they're calling him?"

"It'll be something like that. Or even more colorful, if I'm lucky."

"I guess. I wouldn't want that skinny psycho after me."

"One of the many differences between us, Sheriff. Now go find out where they took Kendrick."

"Will do."

Tarlton climbed down the ladder and left Bobby alone with Donny's blood. Bobby tried to feel what Kilmer must have felt as he came flying into this little box with blood streaming from his wounds. Betrayed, surely. Bobby had viewed Donny as a sort of flawed robot, a traumatized automaton with corrupted code. And perhaps he was. But his successful escape from the high tower raised the possibility that he was more—certainly more of a threat—and Bobby needed to silence him before anyone else became aware of the depth and nature of their involvement.

"Where are you, Donny boy?" Bobby half sang. "Where do you go to lick your wounds?"

Even as he spoke, he had the feeling that home for Donny Kilmer was the bunker complex at Black Oak Plantation. Where else did a lifetime loser like that have to go? If he had anywhere else, he wouldn't have wound up as part of Barlow's crew in the first place.

"Black Oak," Bobby said with something close to certainty. "A mile from my cabin. Outstanding."

CHAPTER 110

PILOTING A FIBERGLASS-HULL boat on the Mississippi River can be dangerous, as Nadine warned. Even in good light, heavy tree trunks floating beneath the surface can hole you and take you down the way they did full-size steamboats in the nineteenth century. I pilot us away from the trees at the shore myself, but once we're in the main channel, Kelly asks me to come back to the transom lounge seat where he's stretched Kendrick out to thoroughly check his wound.

Annie and Lanying sit forward in the bay, while at my suggestion Frosty has kept his three hundred pounds amidships for stability. Ray takes the wheel of the twenty-nine-foot Bowrider, and I trust that the man who drove this stolen boat after setting fire to a wood treatment plant last night can safely carry us the three miles upstream to the ramp half a mile below Pencarrow.

"It's like someone hit him just right of the sternum with a sledgehammer," Kelly says, palpating the tissue around Kendrick's wound. "The whole area's crushed inward, like the bone is pulped." He leans over Kendrick's face. "Be glad you're a muscled-up young Black man. Bone density to spare. If Penn or I had taken that impact, we'd be dead as sparrows."

"I don't know about that," Kendrick groans. "I feel like a dog that got hit by a truck."

"Luckiest dog in the city!" calls his cousin.

"If that bullet had hit *left* of the sternum," says Kelly, "your heart would have taken the full brunt of the impact, and it wouldn't have stood it. And I'm not saying you're all right. Your aorta could be torn inside, like Penn's was after he got T-boned fifteen years ago. You could need a stent right now to keep it from coming apart. I'm telling you, it's worth a trip to the hospital."

"They can't implant stents at the Bienville hospital," I tell him. "We'd have to get him to UMC in Jackson, or down to McComb. They've got interventional cardiology there."

"That's what my plane's for."

"You still think the plane is better than the chopper? Dwight Ford is sitting in his R44 with the rotor turning. He can land at Pencarrow in fifteen minutes."

"Keep him on standby where he is," Kelly says.

"Just get me to Penn's place," Kendrick pleads. "Get me out of this damn bouncy boat! After that, I don't care what kind of ride you put me in."

Kelly is examining Kendrick's stab wound, which has begun leaking blood. "I can't even take your blood pressure," he mutters. "You need a surgeon, stat."

Kendrick winces, but the light in his eyes is resolute. "Every bit of that nightmare was on CNN, right? They gotta have seen it in D.C."

"They saw it," I agree. "The whole world is seeing it by now. God only knows what's happening in Bienville."

"I didn't even get to tell them about Lanying," Kendrick says. "Did I? I can't remember."

"It don't matter, cuz," Frosty says, shifting the trim of the boat as he moves closer to the stern. "Whole world's gonna want to get to the bottom of our shit now. I mean, Rev. Al's gonna be *hollerin'* about that shit on his show."

A painful smile animates Kendrick's face, but then it vanishes, and I know he's thinking what we all are at some level. A lot of people probably died in the wake of the shots that began with the one that hit him. There are probably wounded still lying on the bluff now, awaiting evacuation, or dying in ambulances on the way to the hospital.

"Joy Reid, too," Frosty goes on. "Joy gon' do a whole show on you, man!"

Kelly casually reaches out to take Kendrick's brachial pulse again.

"I'm betting Buck Tarlton is calling this some kind of gang hit by now," I say bitterly.

"Aw, bullshit," says Frosty. "Come on."

"You watch," Kendrick says. "They'll be saying I assassinated Tupac before ten tonight."

"How far do we have to go?" Kelly asks, looking more than a little concerned about Kendrick's artery.

I scan the banks as the sun begins to sink behind us. "Two, three minutes to the ramp."

"Nadine's meeting us there?"

I nod. "With Chief Morgan, if he gets there fast enough. By the way, he said your ruse worked perfectly. Tarlton's men boxed in the car a mile before it reached the hospital and tried to arrest Kendrick for the flares they supposedly found buried by his rented place. They lost their minds when they figured out it wasn't him."

I expect a hearty laugh and maybe a grin of satisfaction from Kelly, but he only nods. It's clear something has him worried, and I'm guessing it's Kendrick's prognosis. Without a word I look up into his eyes, and what I see there does not inspire confidence.

FIVE HUNDRED MILES from Mississippi, Corey Evers accepted a gin
and tonic from the bartender in Cat Cora's at Hartsfield-Jackson Airport
in Atlanta. He had a table in the corner of the restaurant proper, but he
wanted to check the news, which was running on a television over the bar.

"Have you heard?" said an older businessman sitting on a stool beside
him. "*Again*. This country's gone batshit crazy."

"What?" Corey asked.

"Another goddamn mass shooting."

"Where?" Corey asked, though he was certain he already knew the answer.

"Some little nothing of a town on the Mississippi River. Close to Vicksburg. All-Black crowd. Shot them from a water tower. Kind of like the Las
Vegas thing."

The bartender flipped the channel to CNN. On the screen above,
Corey saw a drone shot of the Bienville bluff. As the camera descended, he
made out at least fifty figures lying motionless in the city's amphitheater.
Digitally blurred circles covered the faces and wounds of the dead, but
there was no disguising the horror of the scene.

The anchor's voice suddenly burst from the TV. "Apparently, were it
not for someone in the crowd firing on the shooter on the water tower,
dozens or even hundreds more could have died. At this point the Good
Samaritan has not been identified, but the sheriff's department, the city
police, the FBI, and even the National Guard are doing their best to find
him. He's been described as a white male in his early forties. The FBI was
already in Bienville because of racial tensions in the city."

"Change the channel!" someone down the bar barked irritably. "I don't
want to see that shit. Everything's race, race, race!"

Corey turned and made his way back to his table. How long would it be
until the anchor reported that the "Good Samaritan" who had likely saved
hundreds of lives was Bobby White, the potential presidential candidate
who was known to be a competitive pistol shooter, as well as the hero who
killed terrorist leader Abu Nasir in 2008?

"Fifty dead," Corey whispered, thanking God he'd gotten the hell
out of Bienville when he did. *But you didn't do it in time, did you?* he
thought. *You didn't text Penn Cage in time. You should have gone straight
to the FBI—*

"Oh, my God," said a woman sitting at the table next to his. "They're
saying the man who shot the mass shooter off that water tower was Bobby
White."

"Who?" asked the woman sitting across from her.

"The radio host! The one running for president. The third-party guy!"

"Ohhh, the TikTok guy! Wow. That's crazy."

"He's already got my vote," said the first woman. "He hunted down that Taliban bastard back in 2007. Or was it 2008? Hell, I can't keep track of time anymore. But he's exactly what we need in the White House. Not these old guys who can't remember their grandkids' birthdays."

Without warning, a chill went through Corey that brought him to his feet. He started to walk out of the restaurant without paying, but then he forced himself not to overreact. *Be methodical*, he thought, recalling Bobby's tactical advice on another occasion. *You've got time to do this right. First, verify your assumptions . . .*

A FORMER DELTA operator named Zeke Calhoun walked into Cat Cora's like anyone else—reading his cell phone—but he was not checking his email or scrolling Instagram. He was zeroing in on Corey Evers's cell phone, which he'd been tracking ever since he left South Carolina.

For the past few hours, Evers appeared to have been moving from restaurant to restaurant, probably staying in each until the waitstaff asked him to leave. Zeke had not yet decided how he would kill Evers, but he wanted to get eyes on the man. Sometimes simply seeing a target in the flesh steered him toward a particular method. Since Evers could in theory board any aircraft at any time (if he was already holding a ticket, or multiple tickets, which Bobby had said might be a possibility), Zeke knew he needed to act fast.

The signal seemed to be coming from the interior corner table, which abutted the partition that separated the dining area from the kitchen. But that table was occupied, and not by a handsome man of forty. A Middle Eastern couple was seated there, the woman with an infant on her lap.

Zeke rotated slowly in place, trying to verify the position of the transmitter. The two tables nearest the corner were also occupied: one by an elderly Black couple, the other by two women in their fifties who were heavy into the cocktails.

No question. The signal was coming from the corner table, or somewhere very near it. Zeke knew he was increasing his risk, but he didn't have time to screw around.

"Excuse me," he said, stepping up to the Middle Eastern couple's table and checking every inch of its surface with his eyes. "I was sitting at this table before you came, and I think I may have left my cell phone here."

"You're holding your cell phone." said the man, who looked quite put upon, but also wary of Zeke's obvious muscularity and fitness.

"My work phone, I should have said. I carry two phones. Tax reasons. Do you mind if I check the floor beneath you?"

"Sir, we very much—"

Zeke knelt and checked the floor. *No cell phone . . .*

While the husband continued to protest, Zeke twisted his neck and looked up at the underside of the table. There, taped securely in place with red duct tape, was what appeared to be a recently purchased iPhone.

"Son of a *bitch.*"

The husband was raising a ruckus now. A waiter was approaching to see what the problem was.

"Thank you," Zeke said to the couple. "*Shukran lak.*"

He rapidly made his way out to the crowded concourse. He hated to tell Bobby what he'd found, but Corey Evers—whom Bobby had informed him was a former army intel officer—was now clearly aware that he was a target.

Zeke was going to have to up his game.

And his fee.

COREY SLID INTO an empty seat halfway down the length of the crowded Greyhound bus. He'd never boarded a commercial bus at an airport, but he found it surprisingly easy. His new shirt itched at the neck and underarms, but so did the new underwear and pants. Only the shoes, which were Skechers, felt comfortable. The new phone was a typical burner, but at least it was a smartphone.

"Mind if I sit down?" asked a woman of about forty-five, who looked too well dressed to be leaving the airport on a Greyhound. She lowered her voice. "There aren't many open places, and you look like a nice young man."

"I am," Corey assured her. "Please sit down."

Looking around at his fellow passengers, Corey realized she meant nice *white* man.

"Isn't it terrible?" she asked, as she settled herself on the aisle seat next to him. "That Mississippi shooting? They're up to fifty-eight dead now, and twice that many wounded."

"It's awful," Corey said. "I don't know if these things are ever going to end."

"You won't believe what I just saw on Twitter. They're saying the guy who knocked down the shooter was Bobby White, the radio host who's running for president. Can you believe that?"

Corey shook his head as though he could not, in fact, believe it. "That's amazing, if true."

"Well, he's got my vote. Have you seen him on TV? He is *hot*, honey. A real man. Old school, you know? But not *old*."

Corey forced a smile, then began playing Wordle on his new phone.

"Here he is!" said the woman, holding up her iPhone. "See what I mean? That's what a president ought to look like."

Corey couldn't bear to look.

"Oh, hey," said his new neighbor. "You've still got a price tag on your shirt."

"Really?" Corey said, looking down at the printed tag marked SALE in red. "How embarrassing. I spilled a glass of pinot noir on my last one. I had to buy this just to get through the rest of the day."

"Your wife's going to love that," said the woman, plucking off the tag with a quick jerk.

"Oh, I don't have to worry about that," Corey said with a smile. "No wife, no kids."

His seatmate smiled more broadly. "Really? Well, I just find that hard to believe. I'm Tracy, by the way."

That's the South for you, Corey thought. *That's what Bobby would have whispered in my ear just now—*

"Do you think Bobby White has a real chance to win?" Tracy asked. "I mean, running third party and all?"

Corey thought about the question. "I don't know," he said finally. "I don't really know much about politics."

CHAPTER 111

KELLY'S WORRY ABOUT an ambush on the overgrown ramp below Black Oak and the other river properties atop the bluff north of town turned out to be unfounded. Nadine met us there with a church van borrowed from Reverend Baldwin, and we lay Kendrick out on the second bench seat for the ride up to Pencarrow. Kelly freaked a little when he realized she hadn't brought his rented SUV, but recovered when he saw that she'd transferred his two Pelican cases to the van. Before we even started up the hill, something told me to call Dwight Ford and ask him to fly to Pencarrow—just in case we ran into any kind of difficulties with Kelly's plane.

I was soon glad I'd listened to my instinct. The plantation's electronic gate was closed—and it operated as usual—so we weren't prepared for what we found when we reached the back meadow where Kelly had landed his Cessna Caravan: a scorched prop lying on the grass ten yards from the fuselage, and deformed engine fragments scattered around the plane like parts at a scrap metal sale.

We left Nadine, Annie, and Lanying hunkered down between the van seats as we examined the debris, not wanting anyone who might be observing us to realize Lanying was within their grasp, or that they might use Annie or Nadine for leverage.

"Some of Barlow's guys must have seen me land," Kelly says, as he and I walk around the plane. The operator has his pistol out, and he keeps scanning the tree lines on both sides of the meadow. The shadows under those trees are deepening, so it's hard to tell whether anyone might be watching us from there.

Ray Ransom trots up, having seen the damage from the van. "What the fuck, man? Who did this?"

"Probably Barlow's people," Kelly answers. "The question is, was this part of their usual fuck-with-Penn-Cage-and-his-friends campaign, or did they know we were coming?"

"How could they know?" I ask. "We weren't sure ourselves until we got in the boat and you checked Kendrick again."

Kelly nods after a few seconds. "I guess so."

"Thank God for Dwight Ford and his chopper," I say, taking out my cell phone and punching in his number.

Kelly watches me with disheartening pessimism. "No answer?"

I press it to my ear again. "I don't seem to have any reception. I'm showing bars but getting nothing. What the hell?"

"Keep trying. But we can't count on medevac until he touches down. For now . . . Kendrick is seriously hurt. It might not be as bad as I think, but it might be worse. He could be bleeding to death internally." Kelly focuses on me. "Do you remember anything about your torn aorta?"

"Medically?"

"The aorta has three layers. If the inner layer tears, and blood gets between two of them, the pressure starts dissecting the layers apart. That could happen over twenty-four hours or twenty-four minutes. But once the process starts, without a surgeon, Kendrick's a walking dead man."

"Then let's get him to a hospital," Ray says. "Damn the risks. We'll take him by road."

Kelly looks over the long field once more. In the distance, I see Chief Morgan's squad car racing across the grass. "Pray that chopper can make it in. I've got a feeling the roads aren't an option any longer."

We're nearly back to the van when Chief Morgan's car skids to a stop over the grass. He climbs out and says, "There are two Tenisaw County sheriff's cruisers parked at your gate. Worse, I've seen some of those PSP guys rolling back and forth in an old GMC Jimmy."

Kelly doesn't look surprised, but I can't quite believe it. In one minute we've gone from doing everything we can to avoid attracting attention to desperately needing all the attention we can get.

"It's time to call the FBI," I tell them. "Regardless of Lanying's position, or any charges against Kendrick for the flares or whatever." I look at Ray. "Or even any charges against you. We're up against it now."

Chief Morgan shakes his head. "We're not calling anybody, Penn. They're jamming the cellular frequencies. I tried to call the rest of my men when I saw Tarlton's cars at the gate. I couldn't reach anybody."

"They can't do that. Not legally, I mean."

Kelly chuckles bitterly. "Bro . . . adjust your perception. They're not concerned with legality. They're here to kill us."

Ray and I stand looking at him, and each other, with a paralyzing sense of unreality.

"What buildings are left on this property?" Kelly asks. "We probably don't have much time to prepare a defense."

"We've got to get the women out of here," I tell them. "When Dr. Ford lands, we'll put Lanying and Annie and Nadine aboard. If Dwight okays the weight, we'll drape Kendrick across them in the back."

"What if the chopper can't take them all?" Ray asks.

"Annie will insist on giving up her seat to Kendrick."

"Nadine won't let her do that," Ray says, squeezing my arm. "No way, nohow."

"We're burning time," Kelly says in a tense voice, his eyes on the darkening sky. "We don't know whether your friend will make it in or not. Also, there's real risk in trying to escape that way. Small arms can easily bring down a helicopter. Especially a little piston chopper like the R44. *Buildings*, Penn. Tell me what's here."

At Kelly's words, a caustic fear begins settling into my gut. Not for myself, but for my daughter. "The only building of any size and strength is the old quarters, where Captain Pencarrow's enslaved wife and children lived. It's brick, two-story. Originally it was six rooms, but now it's subdivided into . . . nine?"

"Any other buildings near it?"

"There's the Gothic chapel we passed coming this way. But that's just a single room. And far from the quarters."

"Built like a brick shithouse, though," Ray says. "Not bad for a last stand."

"A single room's too vulnerable," Kelly declares. "We'll use the slave quarters. How many men do you have with you, Chief?"

"Behind Penn's gate?" Morgan squints. "Seven."

Kelly nods. "That's twelve men, including Frosty but discounting Kendrick. Call it eleven since Penn's next to useless. Plus Nadine, Annie, and Lanying. I know Annie can fire a pistol. What about Nadine?"

I shrug. "She carries when she takes her payroll to the bank. I don't know whether she can shoot it or not."

"Let's hope she can. Because when the PSP come down that road . . . it's going to get ugly fast."

"What about trying to talk our way out?" I ask. "If Tarlton's here . . ."

Kelly looks at me with something like pity. "Penn. They're here to shut us up. There's only one way to be sure they do that."

"You really think they've come to kill us all?"

Before anyone else can speak, the rattle of an assault rifle rolls across the field from the direction of the river. There's a brief silence, and then another rifle starts up to our left, probably from the road.

"What the hell?" I cry. "What are they shooting at?"

"If I had to guess," says Kelly, "your friend Dr. Ford."

Yet another rifle begins firing, and it's suddenly impossible to tell how many guns have joined the fray.

"God*damn* it!" I shout, feeling helpless.

Ray shakes his head and curses. "Kelly's right," he says bitterly. "They're here to kill us. Like I told you at that cemetery well. It's war now."

CHAPTER 112

"FIRST RULE OF war," said Bobby White. "Every plan goes to hell in the first five minutes."

"Who said that?" asked Shotwell Barlow.

"Helmuth von Moltke. A little more formally, of course."

They were gathered around a small table in what Shotwell Barlow called the "command bunker" of his end-of-the-world militia complex on Black Oak Plantation. Bobby White, Sheriff Buck Tarlton, his brother Wade, and Barlow himself. Half of Barlow's face was now a deep black bruise, and his left eye was swollen nearly shut from his encounter with Penn Cage's special forces buddy. Everyone was sweating, and the rattling air blower that competed with Bobby's voice did little to alleviate the claustrophobic heat. Bobby was thinking that most post-apocalyptic fantasies went easy on the harsh realities.

Space in the bunker was so tight that their chair backs touched the metal walls, which, like the rest of the bunker, were plastered with Confederate memorabilia. The most prominent relics were the battle standards of various Mississippi regiments raised by private citizens in 1861. Bobby noted that, of them all, it was Barlow's Tenisaw Rifles, along with the Eleventh Mississippi, that featured a Christian cross in the canton, with the more familiar St. Andrew's cross forming the field.

"We did well last night," Bobby went on. "But today we lost the initiative. Then we lost control of events. There were too many variables in play. Now it's down to damage control. Time to lock down our narrative and silence conflicting voices. Agreed?"

The three men nodded back at him.

"The only thing that even makes this possible is the presence of the Poison Springs Provisionals." Bobby focused on Shot Barlow. "I know that puts you in a tough position. You have a relationship with that unit. And what I'm planning to do is brutal—no question. But I need to know if you can live with it. Because if you breathe one word to Baldur Pussett, we'll be fighting those bastards for our lives. And we might lose."

Barlow looked far from happy, but he nodded. "I can see there ain't no other way."

"Good man. Has he done what I asked? How many did he bring out here on that bus?"

"Sixteen. The rest are still in town. And they're pissed."

"If he'd brought forty, we'd have no control out here."

"I know. It'll be all right."

Command and control were Bobby's greatest concerns, and he was skeptical of Barlow's assurances. "One thing. I want their cell phones before they go in. All of them. Even Pussett's. I don't want them videoing their assault or posting any goddamn atrocity porn, live or later. As Gil Scott-Heron said, 'The revolution will not be televised.'"

"Gil who?" asked Barlow.

"Nobody. Don't worry about it."

Bobby shifted his focus to Sheriff Tarlton. "Tell me about our drone feed. How long can you keep that camera in the air?"

"Sixty minutes, with two minutes lost every twenty or so to change out batteries."

"This should be resolved well before then. Will the drone feed keep working with the cellular jamming?"

Buck Tarlton swelled with pride. "Affirmative. That's a tough thing to pull off, but we've drilled our system for crisis situations, and it works."

"Outstanding." Bobby bumped his fist on the desk. "So tell me about those buildings on Cage's property," he said, his attention back on Barlow.

"There's not much to speak of, now that the main house is gone. A stone chapel they could make a stand in, but it's small—only one room, with a couple of stained-glass windows. Not many places to fire from."

"And that leaves the old slave quarters?"

"Pretty much. There's a barn over there, but we could burn that in two minutes. The slave quarters is solid brick, though. It's a house, really, built for Captain Pencarrow's Black mistress and kids. The real workers lived in rows of shacks farther back. Anyway, it's two stories, with shutters heavy enough to give them some protection."

"Let's assume they'll rally there. And that Cage's special forces buddy will lead the defense."

Barlow's mouth twisted with anger, but something else also. "I'm glad we're not storming that place against that asshole," he confessed. "I'll bet he can shoot like Carlos fuckin' Hathcock."

Bobby grinned. "That'll be Mr. Pussett's problem."

The other faces all showed relief.

"Let's talk about Donny Kilmer for a second," Bobby said. "Anybody sees him out here, they shoot him on sight." He focused on Barlow. "You understand the imperative there, Shot?"

"I do. First time I ever told you about Donny, I said I was worried he'd do something like he done today. Remember? And he knows way too much about my group to ever let him get in front of media cameras."

Bobby tried not to show how relieved he was to get Barlow's support on this point. "I'd like to get the credit for taking Donny out," he admitted. "But the priority now is shutting his mouth. So it's open season. If we kill him out here, we'll dump his body on my land and say he tracked me down, looking for revenge for me shooting him on the water tower."

Sheriff Tarlton nodded. "I'll tell my men."

"Excellent. Any questions?"

"Yeah," said Barlow. "This parley you want to have with Cage before Pussett's men go in. What's the point of that?"

Bobby looked back with a steady gaze. "If we can get this done without slaughtering everybody over there, I'm at least open to the possibility. It's a low-percentage play, but I think Penn Cage has changed over the past few years. He's a pragmatist now. He's also seriously ill. And he knows his little girl's at risk."

"You can't trust that motherfucker, no matter what he tells you," Barlow asserted. "There's only one way to keep guys like him quiet. Same for his little girl. We ought to just accept that now. The sooner we do, the sooner all this will be behind us."

Bobby glanced at Wade Tarlton, who shrugged as though willing to try it either way. Buck Tarlton, though, leaned forward and spoke with profound worry in his voice. "My department's been under a hell of a lot of scrutiny since Mission Hill. After Doc's death, and that fucking video— and now the shit that went down on that bluff this afternoon?—it'll be a hundred times worse. If we can shut these arson cases without another big body count, I'm all for it."

Bobby tried to gauge how far the sheriff would go to keep them all safe from federal interference. "Understood, Sheriff. And agreed. So . . . time's burning. Let's go see Baldur Pussett."

CHAPTER 113

THANK GOD FOR OXYCODONE, I say silently.

Humping my prosthetic up the slope from the reflecting pond in the low ground before the ruins of Pencarrow, aiming for the Duel Oak, I hear Daniel Kelly in my mind. He's warning me not to waste what remains of my life talking to Buck Tarlton, or any other emissary of Bobby White.

"They're not here to negotiate, damn it," he insisted back at the slave quarters where Annie, Nadine, Kendrick, Frosty, and Lanying now wait, guarded by a handful of Chief Morgan's recently fired city cops. "They just want to get you close enough to take you off the board first—without any strain."

"You really believe they'll shoot me in cold blood?" I asked him. "An attorney and former mayor? Under a white flag?"

"I don't know why you refuse to believe it. Ego, I guess. I don't want you going up to that tree alone. And I'm not going with you. Nobody sane is."

In the end I convinced Kelly by appealing to his practical sense. "I'm a one-legged man," I told him. "An average shot at best, who hasn't fired more than a couple of rounds in three years. My value as an infantry rifleman is negligible. My value as a negotiator, however, is high. So let me do what I do best."

In the end Kelly relented, but he was right about no one coming with me. I wouldn't have let anyone walk beside me here anyway. The chance of this being a suicidal gesture is all too real. But as the Tenisaw County Sheriff's Department cruiser noses through the Pencarrow gate and rolls the two hundred yards across my line of sight to the big oak shading my mother's grave, I feel like I'm right to take the small chance that Bobby White will offer us a way out of this—one that doesn't involve the death of my daughter.

One hundred twenty yards down the slope behind me, Kelly and Ray wait with rifles that will be trained on me and whoever arrives in Tarlton's cruiser. This gives me a little comfort, but their presence is less likely to prevent my death than the ballistic vest I'm wearing beneath my shirt—protection lent to me by former police chief Mason Morgan. Kelly and Ray have the Mule with them, the little utility four-by-four that Judge Shelby and I used to visit Black Oak yesterday afternoon. Now, I recall with a stab of grief, Judge Shelby himself will have to be laid to rest in a couple of days.

I wish I'd driven the Mule up here, but if this "negotiation" ends with me lying dead in the road, I'd hate for Kelly and Ray to lose their ride back to the slave quarters. Climbing the last thirty yards to the asphalt drive, I recall the other thing I told Kelly about our besiegers' psychology, and which may have convinced him in the end: "I don't think Bobby wants to kill us if he doesn't have to. Why not? Because bottom line, we're white, affluent, and I'm moderately famous. And this is my land. Killing me— much less my daughter—will be hard for Tarlton to explain later. Bobby, too. In a court of law, or even in the court of public opinion. Nadine also comes from an old Bienville family, by the way, on her mother's side."

"You're forgetting how much things have changed in the past couple of years," Kelly argued. "Guys like Tarlton and Barlow even turn on their own now. To Barlow you're some kind of Marxist lib race traitor."

"But not to Bobby. And especially not to Tarlton. He's transactional. He wants to make a deal, I guarantee it."

"And you?" Ray asked from behind Kelly. "Is there a deal you'll make today? Because the price will be selling out Kendrick Washington. You can count on that."

"Let's find out," I told them. "But whatever I decide, I'm begging you guys to go along with it. At least until we get clear of here with the women alive. After that, all bets are off."

Kelly understood me then. And I believe Ray did, too.

Buck Tarlton's gleaming cruiser stops beneath the Duel Oak, and the sheriff gets out wearing his familiar Stetson. When the passenger door opens, I expect to see Bobby White climb out with his half-amused smile, but instead I get Wade Tarlton, who always has the look of the second heavy in an old western to me. Craggy face, ropy limbs, cruel eyes.

"We both know why I'm here," Buck says, as I come level with him.

"Actually, I'm confused. Why don't you spell it out?"

"To apprehend two fugitives and secure the safety of a material witness."

"You have a name on that witness?"

"She's a Chinese illegal."

"Hang on, goddamn it," Wade Tarlton says, pushing up to me. "Hands on the car."

After I assume the position, Wade gives me a vigorous search just short of a cavity probe, covering every millimeter of my body, then sliding his hand deep into my crack to be sure I'm not concealing a recording device of any type. The sheriff stands silent during this process, only speaking again after his brother gives him a curt nod.

"I tell you what," I say to Buck as I straighten up. "How about we cut through the bullshit and do what we need to do? I want to walk out of here with everyone alive. What do you need to let us do that, Buck? And don't tell me it has anything to do with Lanying, unless you're going to admit you want her dead. Because her story will nullify the entire narrative you guys have been selling since Arcadia burned."

A glint in Buck's eyes tells me the sheriff is concealing some sort of surprise. "Actually, that Chinese girl can walk out here safer than any of you. All she has to do is state for the record that she saw her boyfriend meet Kendrick Washington on at least two occasions about getting those flares and burning antebellum homes—both here and in Natchez. She does that, she's free and clear. No state charges."

The simplicity of this request—and the enormity of his promise—both surprises and worries me. I hadn't quite realized how easily a simple fabrication by Lanying could give Bobby and Tarlton the outcome they want and need.

"FYI," Buck goes on, "I have a deputy who'll testify that Lanying approached him yesterday afternoon with a story of her boyfriend doing exactly that."

I temporize while the full implications of the sheriff's pitch come to me. "Do you think that girl will implicate an innocent Black kid in order to spare herself the trouble of a trial?"

Wade Tarlton grins. "Damn near any woman I ever knew would do that in order to keep from spending her life in prison. And I've learned a little about this girl in the past couple of hours. She'll do anything to keep from getting deported back to China."

Buck nods to reinforce this. "Let us put it to her, Penn. After she's presented with the alternatives, she'll tell her version of the truth. You don't really have anything to do with it, so you won't have to feel bad about it."

Buck Tarlton—or whoever came up with this offer—is no fool. I'd hate to put these two scenarios to Lanying and have to trust her to choose the moral high ground. Fear is a corrosive motivator. I learned that again and again as an ADA in Texas.

"What about you, Penn?" Buck asks. "Which alternative will you choose? You don't have much time to decide, frankly."

"What choice are we talking about?"

"Do you give up the fugitives and the witness, or do you force me and my men to come in and get them?"

"Hold up a second. We were talking about Lanying and Kendrick. Now it sounds like you're talking about Ray Ransom."

Buck sniffs and looks down at the pond. "I told you this day would come."

"What day's that?"

"That you'd have to choose sides. You're white, buddy. That's the bottom line here. You've spent this week trying to fight their battles for them. You and your little girl. And where has it gotten you? You want to die for Ray Ransom?"

"No. But he's my friend. And he already spent too many years in prison."

"He burned my fucking house down! He torched God knows how many oil wells! He nearly destroyed our fucking bridges. We've got footage of him doing it on state security cams. He's out of control!"

"Well, Kendrick didn't do a bit of that, and you're ready to send him to Parchman for life. How fucked up is that? Don't pretend you give a shit about what's right and wrong."

Buck looks at the ground and takes a few seconds to get himself back under control. Then he raises his head, his eyes filled with urgency. "This is a bad day for Bienville, I tell you. That goddamn Donny Kilmer fucked up the city but good. I don't care if all his victims were Black, it's still a goddamn shame, and a stain on the state."

"I don't know why you're surprised. He's exactly the type to slaughter innocent people. That's your buddy Barlow's business, isn't it?"

"Let's not get sidetracked here," Buck says. "I'm going to make you a different offer, on my own hook. It's just occurred to me, but it seems fair, in the biblical sort of way. Sort of a King Solomon solution."

"Splitting the baby?"

Buck nods. "Just like that. If you really want Kendrick to walk free, then let Ray take the weight for him. For the fires. Ray's over seventy now, and God knows he likes torching shit. He's got the Black Panther history. And he already spent most of his life in Parchman. He can finish his days there and keep Kendrick out of jail forever. How's that sound to you, Penn? Because I think it's the way out for all of us."

To my amazement, I feel like Buck Tarlton, the most mediocre mind among us, may have stumbled upon the only plan that might actually result in both life for all and something at least in the same neighborhood as justice. The truth is . . . to save lives, Ray might take a deal like that. He's almost certainly going back to Parchman anyway, for the Matheson lumber yard fire.

"What about you guys finding the air force flares at Kendrick's place?"

"Ray can say he buried them there. To throw us off."

God, Buck looks pleased with himself. Wade doesn't look as certain about this idea, but he hasn't argued against it.

"Think about your daughter, Penn," Buck says softly. "Nadine, too. Jesus, man. Say yes and let's get the hell back to town. I'm tired. We still got that bluff scene to deal with. It's a slaughterhouse up there."

I can't afford to say no to his offer. Not under the present circumstances. It's just as true that Tarlton—and Bobby White—know that. So the tone of my response is everything.

"Don't drag this out, Cage," Wade Tarlton presses, sounding anxious.

"Any answer but yes is going to get bloody quick," his brother adds.

"On both sides. You boys can rely on that."

"Not for my people," says Buck Tarlton. "You say no, it'll be the PSP coming through that gate. And they're psychos, man. They'll give no quarter. My guys won't show up until they're finished with you. The girls, too. And in every news report, we'll be the Seventh Cavalry, arriving ten minutes too late to save the homesteaders."

The vivid horror of this scenario actually loosens my bowels. Bobby would have hit on this scenario quickly—a solution that keeps him utterly clean, and that can also be sold effortlessly not only to the public, but to the FBI. All he and Tarlton would have to do (other than execute my family and loved ones) is wipe out the PSP during the "attempted rescue" before they leave Pencarrow, to silence any contradictory narrative.

"Let me talk to Ray," I suggest. "How long can you give me?"

Buck shakes his head. "Sorry. No can do. You'll have to decide, and right now."

"How can I decide for Ray? He's the one who'll have to do the time."

"He'll do it," Buck avers. "Once he thinks about it. Ray's an old con. He knows the rules, and he likes helping young bucks out. Given a choice between himself and Kendrick, he'll take the rap. Because if Ray doesn't confess, Kendrick is absolutely going down for the fires. We filmed ourselves digging up those flares at his place. So let's not waste time we don't have."

I can almost see the hand of Bobby White pulling Tarlton's strings. The time pressure must be great indeed if they won't give me ten minutes to close a deal that could spare them from committing mass murder.

"All right," I concede, like a man giving up something precious. "You're right. Given that choice, I believe Ray will take the martyr's road."

Buck looks back at me for about ten seconds, skepticism in his eyes. "You mean it? You're gonna make this happen?"

"Ray confesses to the fires, everybody else walks away clean. That's the deal. Right?"

Buck looks over at his brother. Wade shrugs with uncertainty, like he's wondering why Buck would even ask his opinion. And then I realize that Buck isn't. He's asking *Bobby's* opinion. What confirms it is Bobby's voice, which comes from somewhere to my left—probably the walkie-talkie on Wade's belt.

"Negative," he says. "That's not gonna work. It was a good idea, Sheriff, and Ray would probably take the deal. And live with it. Penn would too, I believe. But he's not himself anymore. He's got cancer. Bad. He might not be around to make his daughter toe the line. And without him there . . . she won't."

The disappointment in Buck's face is palpable. I wish I were actually negotiating with the sheriff, but he's only an errand boy. It's all he's ever been.

"Wade?" Bobby says.

"Yessir."

"Arcadia."

Surprise lights the chief deputy's eyes. He gives me a funny smile, then draws his pistol from the holster at his side and shoots me low in the belly.

"*FUCK, I KNEW IT!*" Kelly cried, watching Penn fall.

Lying along a broad tree branch at the pond's edge, the former Delta operator focused his right eye on Wade Tarlton's face in his reticle . . .

And squeezed the trigger.

The rifle bucked against his shoulder.

Wade Tarlton's forehead imploded under the impact of Kelly's bullet, transfixing his brother, who stood close enough to be painted scarlet by the result. Buck gaped at the stunned face, while the uniformed body hung in the air as though suspended by wires, then collapsed like a dropped marionette.

Buck's brainstem told him to run, but his bladder was emptying down his leg while his stomach tried to disgorge what remained of his hurried lunch. At some point during this physiological chaos, he grasped that another bullet might be headed his way, and he bolted.

ALL I CAN see is branches and sky.

Pain arcs through my chest and side, driving out everything else. Men were shouting in the distance until a flat crack reverberated across the land, ending in a rain of blood and bone fragments. A volley of bullets erupts from the direction of the gate . . . then another comes upslope from the pond—

Kelly, I remember. *Kelly and Ray . . .*

Someone is whimpering close by me.

The sheriff's boots scrape on the pavement. One door of the cruiser slams shut, then the engine roars as the car leaves me exposed on the ground. In the midst of crackling rifle fire, I try to roll over to get clear of the road, but something slams into my pelvic wing, like a jackhammer trying to drill through my body—

Everything else goes black.

"THEY SHOT HIM *again*!" Ray shouted.

"You spot the muzzle flash yet?" Kelly cried, pumping four more rounds into the woods beyond the sheriff's cruiser.

"Hell, no!"

"I'm going up there to get him!" Kelly yelled, steadily laying rounds into the trees across the drive.

"Bullshit!" Ray countered, climbing into the Mule, while above him the army veteran fired with steady discipline. "You're the better shot. *I'll* get him."

"They want us to come for him. Stay as low as you can. Drive blind!"

"Just find that fucking muzzle flash!"

WHOEVER SHOT ME in the hip is still shooting. A heavy bullet slams into the earth only inches from my right shoulder. Then someone from my side responds with counterfire. Kelly or Ray, it must be. The sniper isn't close. He's shooting from at least the distance of the road, and maybe farther than that.

I hear the roar of an engine coming upslope from the pond . . . The nearer it gets, the higher grows the rate of sniper fire. *That's covering fire*, I realize. *Suppressive fire.* As the engine gets close, the hammer blows of bullets slamming into steel assault my ears. Then the Mule interposes itself between me and the trees on the north side of the drive. Looking left, I see Ray Ransom crawling toward me on his belly. When he stops, his face is inches from mine, his eyes filled with anxiety.

"How bad you hit, Penn?"

"I'm fucked up. I don't know how bad. Can you look?"

Ray vanishes for a second, and I feel him pull up my blood-wet shirt. "You're messed up all right, I can't lie." He rolls onto his back and strips off his shirt. "Bow up, brother. I'm jamming my T-shirt into that hole."

He balls up the cloth, then stuffs it into whatever new space has been created in my body. The pressure and pain drive the wind from my lungs in an explosive grunt.

"I'm gonna pick you up now," Ray warns me, panting. "Gotta get you into that Mule. You ready?"

"Just do it, man."

"Here we *go*—"

I scream from the moment Ray flexes until he slides me into the open cabin, while Kelly sends a hail of bullets into the woods. It suddenly strikes me that the sniper's fire has decreased. *Kelly must be homing in on the shooter*—

I scream again as Ray wrenches the wheel and starts us back down the bumpy slope toward the pond.

"Hang on, brother!" he cries, putting his big right arm across my chest like a father protecting his child. "I'll get you there."

"Where?"

"A better place than here!"

CHAPTER 114

BOBBY WHITE LOOKED down at the video feed from Buck Tarlton's drone and shook his head. The sheriff's cruiser was squealing away from his dead brother's corpse as if he expected a swarm of zombies to appear and devour him. In contrast to this, Ray Ransom was working his way up the slope from the reflecting pond to rescue Penn Cage from the road, under deliberate and highly effective covering fire from Daniel Kelly, who remained downslope in the trees.

"Give me your PSP man," Bobby said.

Shot Barlow held his iPhone across the table. On it, the neo-Nazi Baldur Pussett waited in silence, linked to the bunker by the FaceTime app created in ultra-liberal Silicon Valley. With his shoulder-length blond hair and pale blue eyes, he looked like an extra from the *Vikings* TV series.

"Send in your men," Bobby ordered. "*Fast.* Don't give them time to regroup or even recover. Hit them hard and crush them. No quarter. No survivors."

Pussett's eyes seemed to drill through the computer screen when he spoke. "Let's get something straight. You just passed command to me. It's my men going in there, and I just saw what at least some of what you called 'soft' opposition can do with a rifle. I've got a scout in there who says they've already fortified that old slave quarters. So I'll take my men in my way, at my own speed. I shouldn't have let you limit my strength like you did, given that we're gonna hit a fortified position. I'm tempted to call for my guys in town, but that'd take a half hour you say we don't have. I said we'd go, so we'll go. But from here out, you can kiss my ass. If you want to send me more men, I'm happy to take them in with us. Otherwise, *fuck off.*"

The computer screen went blank.

Bobby stared at the screen, wondering whether the sadistic militiaman had the tactical skill to take the quarters from a band of city cops being led by a veteran counterterror operator.

"What do you think?" he asked. "Can that fucking alien do the job?"

"Baldur will get it done," Shot Barlow assured him. "Only thing is, it'll be ugly when we finally get down there. I hate to think about it, with those girls in there."

"That'll only reinforce our narrative, Shot."

"Well . . . okay, then. We gonna stay in here and watch?"

Bobby nodded. "If things go right, we shouldn't have to move from this spot until it's over."

Barlow looked back without speaking. Then he said, "I guess I'll make some coffee."

"I'll take some."

After the militia leader stood, he said, "Who's gonna kill that crazy son of a bitch when this is over?"

"That'll be me," Bobby said quietly. "I'm looking forward to it."

CHAPTER 115

"WE'VE GOT TO make some fast decisions," Kelly says. "They're going to be coming, and soon. I want us ready in three minutes."

We've gathered in the largest room on the ground floor of Pencarrow's former slave quarters, sixteen of us, all told. I'm lying beside Kendrick on a double mattress dragged from the bedroom where Annie and Andrew napped the other night, before the fire. It's already soaked with blood from my wounded hip.

The emotions on the faces of those standing around me run the gamut from bravery to panic, and even despair. Lanying is whimpering like a child, begging to be set free, not realizing that there's nowhere safe to run. Chief Morgan and his former officers seem generally resolute, but also anxious, and a couple look fearful. Kendrick's cousin Frosty Givens has a bellicose scowl, and he's swinging his machine pistol around as though he can't wait to use it. Kendrick seems unable to take in much beyond the pain of his chest wound, but he's still able to move all right.

It's the girls who concern me most. Nadine looks surprisingly calm, but I can tell she is deeply afraid. Annie's eyes seem twice as wide as usual, as though she developed hyperthyroidism only minutes ago. She's listening closely to every spoken word, but most of all to Kelly, whose instincts she trusts more than mine during times of physical danger—and rightfully so.

"It won't be Tarlton's men coming," Kelly goes on. "It'll be those Poison Springs Provisionals. They mean to let them loose in here, then blame the PSP for our deaths. They'll finish off the PSP, then claim they came out to serve warrants or rescue us but arrived too late. I hate to say it out loud, but you need to know. This is basically the Alamo. Don't expect mercy. Kill anybody who gets close. But for God's sake, wait till you have a decent shot. You cops, use fire discipline. You know what that means."

A couple of the older policemen nod.

"On the positive side? We've got a lot of veterans in this room, some highly trained. We've blocked the doors as best we can with your squad cars, and that'll help a lot. It'll stop groups of assaulters from rushing in, anyway. I have a couple of toys from my recent deployment, as well, which will give those freaks some surprises as they move in."

"Enough to make a difference?" asks one of Morgan's cops.

"We'll find out," Kelly says. "On that note—anybody who saw my Pelican cases upstairs, don't get tempted. If I go up there needing a grenade, it better be there. Understood?"

Most of the cops nod.

"Okay. I want Kendrick and Penn upstairs in a corner room. That's for the wounded. A couple of you guys run that mattress up there when we deploy. I want the women up there, too—armed. Clear?"

The cops keep nodding. They seem comforted by Kelly's strong leadership.

"If you see men in uniform among the attackers—local deputies, say— don't get confused. Don't hesitate to shoot, not even if you recognize them. If they're working with the PSP, they're here to kill you. If they're on their own, they're here to kill you. Is anybody confused about that?"

I crane my neck to be sure I see everyone's reaction. Nobody appears to be confused about loyalties.

"What do you want us to do exactly?" asks a young patrolman. "Man the windows?"

"That's exactly it. Split up as you think best, but be sure you cover all sides of this building—and both floors. All lines of fire. We should have just enough men to do it. Knock out a couple of shutter slats for a firing slit and get ready. There are trees on three sides of this house, which is both good and bad for us. Don't expose yourselves until the enemy does. Wait for clean shots."

"Where are you going to be?" asks Chief Morgan.

"Outside."

"*What?*" comes a chorus of voices.

"I'm going out to even the odds a little before they get here."

"That sounds like a suicide mission," says the chief.

"No. It's what I was trained for."

"Even special forces work in teams."

Kelly shrugs as if this is of little consequence. "I don't have a team tonight."

"You've got a partner," says Ray Ransom.

Kelly looks dubiously at Ray. I'm sure he sees a man older than seventy and little more, despite Ray's obvious physical fitness. "Mr. Ransom—"

"I walked point in Vietnam for two years and lived through it. I know how to handle myself in the field. I can help you."

"Well—"

"And I got no problem wasting those fuckers," Ray presses.

Chief Morgan holds up his hand. "Two of my men are the sniper-spotter team for our joint SWAT with the county. They might do you even more good than Ray."

As Kelly ponders his choices, his eyes suddenly brighten. "That big explosion we heard on the bluff, before we drove down to the river. The diversion." He looks at Ray. "That was you?"

Ray nods warily.

"What was that? An oil well?"

"Sort of. A tank battery for a pair of wells."

A slow smile spreads over Kelly's face. "What if I told you there are two oil wells pumping across that road on Black Oak Plantation right now?"

Ray takes it in. "I get you."

"I saw them from my plane as I landed earlier. You blow one of those, we'll have a distress signal a hundred feet high."

"They'd see that from town!" Chief Morgan says. "The FBI would be out here in minutes. After losing that chopper today? I'll bet they have fifty agents in Bienville by now."

"Let me get going, then," Ray says. "Before those militia bastards box me in."

"A lot of them are already coming this way," Kelly tells him. "And Tarlton's deputies beyond them. Maybe Barlow's guys are back on Black Oak by now. The odds are against you. Way against."

Ray gives him a cynical grin. "They ain't that great in here, either, chief. I'll swing out through Penn's woods before I cross River Road."

Ray is already moving to the back door. "My ancestors worked Black Oak, brother. As *slaves*. I know that land, and I know this place, too. I'll make it. You guys just hold out here as long as you can."

"Shouldn't he take somebody with him?" Morgan suggests. "To cover him while he runs?"

"Can't spare the gun," Kelly decides. "He makes it or he doesn't."

A young cop walks to the back door and hands Ray a pistol. Ransom smiles in thanks, then looks once at the semicircle of people facing him, waves, and forces his way through the tight space between the building and the squad car Chief Morgan drove up to the back steps to block the door as best he could.

I feel certain I will never see Ray alive again.

"Sniper-spotter team with me," Kelly says.

Two uniformed cops in their late twenties move toward him.

"Any questions?"

No one asks anything.

"I have one," I tell him. "Should we maybe send Lanying through the back woods with somebody? Try to get her away from here? She clearly won't be any help with the defense, but she'd survive to testify later. And if we get a chance to negotiate with anybody after this, we can tell them she's already gone. Maybe that'll lessen their desire to risk their own to hit us."

Kelly gives me an indulgent smile. "I thought about that. But remember my plane? Somebody's already been back there, and they still could be. Second, we'd have to lose a shooter for the errand. I don't think we can afford that for such a risky play."

"Annie and I could try to get her out," Nadine says, surprising me. "Annie knows the ground. Probably a lot better than the attackers."

"I'm all for that," I say firmly.

"No way," Annie says. "I'm not leaving my dad, and I'm not leaving you guys here to fight without us."

"Annie—" I start, but she holds up her hand.

"Not leaving," she insists. "No way. That's flat."

Nadine watches her for a few seconds, then shakes her head. "We shouldn't risk being caught out there by the PSP anyway."

Kelly's silent eyes reflect the wisdom of this statement, but Annie simply shrugs and focuses on me.

"*Please* be stingy with your ammo," Kelly concludes. "Fear will make you spray bullets, but this is a whites-of-the-eyes kind of situation. *Don't* forget that."

"We really gonna wait for them to get that close?" asks Frosty Givens.

"You'd better. The longer you wait, the more you'll kill."

Frosty jerks a shoulder as big as a ham upward in some sort of club dance move. "Aiight, then. *Bring it on, bitches.*"

"Before you take the wounded upstairs," Kelly says, "everyone check their cell phones. Does anybody have service?"

Everyone's phones come out, and people hold them up at every possible angle. One cop sprints to the second floor to try to connect to a tower. But no one succeeds in acquiring a usable signal.

"The cell service out here is sketchy at the best of times," Annie explains. "So it's probably easy for them to jam it."

Kelly nods and starts to say something, but before he can, the crack of a rifle sounds outside—the report so loud and vivid it feels like it's in the room with us. The echo is long, but then several more shots crackle across the land.

"Let the games begin," Kelly concludes. "Get the wounded upstairs."

While the sniper-spotter team awaits him by the door, Kelly walks over to Annie and pulls her into a fierce hug. She's crying against him, but he forces her away, then takes a pistol from a Velcro holster on his leg and places it in her hand.

"No," she says, pushing it away. "You need that."

He shakes his head. "I'm not leaving until you take it and swear to me you'll use it."

My daughter tries to argue, but she's crying too much to manage it. At last she simply nods and kisses Kelly on the cheek. He smiles and marches quickly to me on the mattress, then reaches down and shakes my hand. His familiar blue eyes are like water poured over my wounds.

"I love you, brother," he says. "Here's hoping we meet on the other side."

CHAPTER 116

RAY RANSOM RACED across River Road, ducked between two strands of barbed wire, then broke into open ground between some trees and pumped his legs like Usain Bolt in the final ten meters of an Olympic run. He was on Black Oak Plantation now. He hadn't run like this since Vietnam. As the favored point man of his CO, Ray had killed more men than he wanted to remember. The act had almost always triggered guilt in him—and shame. But tonight was different. Tonight he was running over land that his ancestors had trod as slaves, and he had a mission. He knew where Barlow's wells were, and he knew how to blow them to hell and gone. But more than this, Doby, his fearless ancestor, had sweated and bled into this dirt for nineteen years before he chose to drown himself rather than doom his friends to the lynch rope. If Barlow's men rose up now between Ray and his objective . . . he would kill them just as Doby would have . . .

With savage joy.

A HALF MILE from Ray Ransom, twelve feet under the earth, Bobby White and Shot Barlow sat watching Baldur Pussett and his men approach the slave quarters through the trees that surrounded it on three sides. The drone camera was about five hundred feet in the air, and Bobby could see the militiamen moving cautiously, even though most were still a good sixty yards from the house.

Ten seconds later, Bobby saw their caution justified.

From somewhere beneath the thickest part of the canopy, snipers began firing at the PSP men with shocking accuracy. At first he thought he must be seeing four or five shooters working, but quickly enough he realized it was only two. He felt a desperate desire to release a Hellfire missile on those snipers, but he had to face the humiliating reality that the drone feeding him the images was no air force UAV, but a cheap Chinese-made toy.

"God*damn* it," he snapped, getting to his feet in the cramped bunker room. "Whoever's behind those rifles is chewing Pussett and his men to pieces. The assault already stalled."

"No," Barlow said. "They're still advancing. It's gonna be a scrap, that's all. Those cops ain't gonna die easy."

"It's not the cops," Bobby said, sure he was right. "It's that Kelly guy."

Bobby put one hand on the ladder that led to the surface.

"Where the hell you going?" Barlow asked him.

"You know what they say. If you want something done right . . ."

Shot Barlow shook his head slowly. "I wouldn't go down there yet. Pussett doesn't like you much. Give him a chance. He'll wear 'em down. We just have to be patient."

Bobby didn't respond at first. He'd been getting a steady stream of texts from Dixie Donnelly and Wyatt Cash on his burner phone. The FBI had been pouring special agents into Bienville since the shooting, and the governor's people were getting nervous about the whole situation.

"I don't know if we have that kind of time."

Shotwell Barlow turned up his callused hands. "Well. Either we go down there and help Pussett, or we wait it out here the way we said."

"You have your guys ready for the final phase?" Bobby asked.

Barlow nodded. "They know what they have to do. But you're gonna deal with Baldur, right?"

"If Kelly doesn't deal with him first."

CHAPTER 117

SOPHIE HAD MEANT to confront her father in his study, but in the end she waited until he went into the kitchen to raid the carton of Blue Bell. He seemed too powerful to attack in his study, which somehow embodied the financial and political power he'd amassed during his long life. But seated at the kitchen counter, digging his big stainless spoon into the french vanilla, he looked as mortal as any elderly man, albeit stronger and better preserved.

"Did you hear about the mass shooting on the bluff?" Charles asked. "I guess it was only a matter of time until Mississippi got one."

"We just had Mission Hill, didn't we?"

"That was different. Anyway. It sounds like our boy Bobby White got to play hero again."

"How so?" she asked, genuinely curious.

"Someone just identified him from news footage. He's the guy who chased the shooter off the water tower by firing a pistol. The FBI found blood splashes on the ladder, so it looks like Bobby hit him at least once, and pretty good, too. If he hadn't, that sniper might have killed another couple of hundred people. Maybe more."

"What's the death toll now?"

"More than forty killed for sure, maybe as many as seventy-five. Countless wounded."

"Are you proud of yourself?"

Her father froze with the spoon half out of his mouth. Then he lowered it and set it on the marble countertop. "What do you mean?"

"I think you knew about this attack ahead of time. Not only that. Every bit of what's been going on. The arsons, Doc Berry, that poor Black girl who got lynched—"

"Are you insane?"

"That's you, Daddy. Master of the universe. I just can't believe it took me this long to see it. Pearl knew, long ago. I only wish she'd told me sometime before this week. I think Charlot understood, too, at some level. He knew about those bones in the 'broken' cistern at Tranquility. He knew they weren't Yankee bones. Not most of them, anyway. What a load of shit."

"I'm sorry, Sophie. But I don't know what you're talking about."

"Is that why you killed him?"

"Who?"

"Charlot."

The blue-gray eyes narrowed. "Charlot?"

"You killed him last night, didn't you? Or Amadu did. That's why you invited him back here to stay. To get him into a vulnerable position, where nobody would have any idea what was happening. But you forgot something, Daddy."

"What?"

"Our maids loved that boy. They knew he was weak in some ways, but they saw you abuse him all those years. They knew whose fault his problems really were. And last night Charlot told Ruby that if he didn't call her every few hours, she should assume something bad had happened to him. At your hands."

Her father dismissed this with a flick of his big hand. "Oh, for Christ's sake. That boy was a drama queen from the age of three."

"So? You've been a killer since you were a boy. God only knows what evil you've done in your life. I don't even want to know. It won't matter after tonight anyway."

Sophie reached into her pocket and took out the .32-caliber automatic she'd owned since college. Her father stared at the pistol as though he recognized it.

"You gave me this when I left for Tulane," she reminded him. "Did you ever imagine I would use it on you?"

"Of course I remember it. I was trying to be sure you were as safe as you could be. Especially in New Orleans."

"Don't act like you don't know what I'm about to do."

Charles blinked in genuine confusion. "What are you talking about?"

"I'm going to punish you for killing my brother."

Dufort tried to look as if he were struggling to take her seriously. "Now who's the drama queen? Why would I have paid Tommy Russo a quarter of a million dollars to make sure Charlot was safe if I was about to kill him?"

"To give yourself an alibi, of course. A quarter million is *nothing* to you. One Wilcox oil well. But I see you now, Daddy. And you're not walking away this time."

Charles Dufort slid off the stool and stood straight and tall. "And how are you going to explain a dead father with a bullet in him?"

Sophie smiled strangely. "I spent a good bit of time thinking about that. At first I thought I might say we were cleaning my gun and it went off.

Given our social and financial status, the sheriff's unlikely to take it past that. *'I'm so sorry about your daddy, Ms. Sophie, just let me know if there's anything I can do.'* I mean, once I inherit your money, everybody around here will be kissing my ass just like they kiss yours. Right up to the governor and our esteemed senators.

"But then I thought about the cistern," she went on. "I could drop you right down there with Shondra, and whoever else you and Amadu have put down there over the years. Business rivals . . . God knows who. But with Charlot knowing about that like he did, and Tranquility having burned, which means all kinds of forensic investigators around . . . best to leave that alone."

Dufort shook his finger at her. "You've lost your mind, girl. Too much of that dope back in the seventies and eighties."

"Then I remembered the blueberry farm," Sophie went on. "There's a big ol' cypress swamp out behind the fields. If I took you out there and left you, there wouldn't be anything left of you in a week. And with the town falling apart around us, nobody's going to waste much of that week hunting for you."

The matter-of-fact tone in her voice was starting to give Charles pause. "Sophie, that's enough. I know you're upset about Charlot—I am as well— but you've really gone around the bend with these accusations. If anybody murdered your brother, it was Thomas Russo."

"Why would Tommy kill Charlot if you were going to pay off his debts? Businessmen like Russo don't take unnecessary risks. But let's not get sidetracked. See, the thing is . . . in order to inherit your money, I need your body to be found. Your death recorded. It's not good for me if you just disappear. But I think I've got it worked out now. I'm going to give Amadu a supporting role. Because he *so* richly deserves it."

"Amadu?" Her father looked perplexed.

"And don't worry about me being bored after you're gone. I foresee a lot of excitement. Bobby and I have worked out a nice little arrangement. We're going to take a stab at running the world. The country, anyway. With my lefty-lib leanings I can counter his fascist tendencies. We'll have divided government, right there in the White House."

"Do you really think Bobby is any different than I am? Hell, he's worse."

"I'm not blind, Daddy. Nor am I a fool. But he's not worse than you. You're in a class by yourself."

"Put the gun down, Ms. Sophie," Amadu said in his deep bass voice.

Sophie looked calmly to her left, where the driver had appeared in the door holding a large black handgun. "Are you going to shoot me, Amadu?"

"If I have to, missy."

"You've been wanting to for a while, haven't you?"

He shook his head. "No, ma'am."

"Oh, you can be honest. I never liked you, and you never liked me. Except in one way, of course. You haven't taken your eyes off my ass since I was thirteen. But your name did get me out of a jam yesterday. I thank you for that."

Amadu cut his eyes at his employer. "I don't know what you're talking about, Ms. Sophie."

"Doesn't matter. When you killed my brother, you lost all credit with me."

"Put the gun down. Please."

"Do it, honey," her father said. "Or I'll have to tell him to take it from you."

"Look at me, Daddy. I know what you are now. Do you understand?"

"I don't, actually." But his eyes told her that he did.

"This is the end of the line for the great Charles F. Dufort. No male heir left. And I'm too old to crank one out. That's probably a good thing."

"What do you think you're going to do?" Charles asked. "Seriously. Shoot me and then . . . what?"

"I told you, Daddy, your golden boy Bobby White tried to recruit me last night. And the more I've thought about his pitch, the more I like it."

"You can't be serious. Bobby wouldn't waste that spot on you."

"Thanks for your vote of confidence." Her smile carried a great deal of pain. "But don't be so sure. Bobby's good at telling people what they want to hear. Especially people like you. Also, he's not a bad lay for a gay man. I'm pretty sure I could take four years of what he's got."

"You're disgusting. Trying to blame Amadu for looking at you? You pranced around Natchez like a Bourbon Street hooker from the day you turned twelve. It's nobody's fault but yours if men tried to get a taste."

Sophie straightened her gun arm. "Make your peace, Daddy. You're about to pay for Charlot, but not his death. You're going to pay for his life of misery—in full. Get out while you can, Amadu. If you stay, this won't end the way you think."

Charles focused on his faithful servant. "She's not going to give us any choice, old friend." He looked back at Sophie. "I'll give you one last chance."

"I don't need it."

The old man's face sagged with genuine confusion. "All right, then. I hate this, darling."

She locked her aim on her father's chest.

Dufort nodded at Amadu, but instead of a pistol shot, Sophie heard the sound of sharp steel cleaving meat. It made her shudder as she turned.

Amadu clawed at his left shoulder and side, trying to reach the source of his pain. When he spun and jerked in vain, she saw what it was he could not reach: two big kitchen knives protruding from his back. Driven by expert hands, they'd entered at about kidney level, though one blade might have struck his heart, judging by the angle of its handle. The driver roared with anger, desperately clawed for the knives once more, then collapsed on the floor in a puddle of blood. Behind him, in the doorway, stood Ruby and Pearl, staring down without the slightest gleam of pity in their eyes. After a few moments, they looked up at their employer.

Pearl said, "You was gonna have him kill your daughter, too, Master Charles. My *God*, you're sick. Time to put you down, boy. Like a mad dog."

The fear and comprehension in Dufort's eyes defied all explanation.

"Get out of here!" he barked. "All of you! All your lives you've lived by my leave, off my money. Now you want to turn on me? Steal my fortune? My land? That's it, isn't it? Well, you won't get it!"

Sophie raised her gun higher, noticing how it shook in her hand.

"Finish it, baby," said Pearl. "Or give the gun to me. It really ought to be me. For Shondra. I owe that poor girl. Her mama, too."

At last Charles dropped all pretense and roared at her: "*Go to hell, you ungrateful, dried-up old—*"

Sophie fired three times.

She only hit him twice, but twice was enough. The holes in her father's midsection stayed small for a second, but then his shirtfront bloomed bright red and sagged from his belly. He looked down in confusion, catching at the fabric with his hands, trying to pull it away to examine his wounds. But his strength was draining too fast for him to do himself any good. Sophie felt nothing as he fell face down onto the terrazzo tiles.

Pearl crossed the floor and hugged her tight. "You all right, girl?"

"I don't know."

"You done good. Showed what you're made of. This won't bring your brother back . . . Shondra, neither. But you prob'ly saved some people we'll never know."

Sophie shook her head in dazed relief. "God, I hope so."

CHAPTER 118

BEING FORCED TO listen to the gun battle outside the slave quarters while trapped in a small room upstairs is the stuff of nightmares for all who share our fate. With his cousin's help, Kendrick has levered himself up on the mattress beside me so that his back leans against the inner wall of the little room. He told me he actually feels better while sitting up than lying on the mattress beside me, that his breathing is easier. But every time one of the assault rifles lets off a burst, he shudders, and whenever Frosty fires his pistol through the window, he jumps.

I lie on my back, stuck to the mattress by my own clotting blood. The pistol round that hit my abdomen resulted in a terribly painful wound, but the vest spared me its worst effects. The upper left wing of my pelvis, however, has been partly shattered by the sniper's bullet. And while the projectile didn't tear an artery, the bleeding has slowed but will not stop. If it weren't for the fentanyl patches I copped from my mother's hospice box and smacked onto Kendrick and myself, I don't think either of us would be able to do much beyond shiver in pain.

Just as downstairs, the lion's share of my fear focuses on Annie and Nadine. The archetypal nightmare of our situation is twofold: first, the shattering noise of battle engenders profound fear for our friends outside and below, whom we cannot help or even see; but worse is the near certainty—almost admitted by Kelly earlier—that they will eventually be overrun and the invaders will penetrate the house, visiting unimaginable cruelties upon us. Despite putting on a convincing show of courage while Lanying cowers in a corner, Annie and Nadine have been suffering the same terrifying projections into what seems an inevitable future. Worst of all, I can't banish the conviction that when Kelly forced the gift of his pistol into Annie's hands before leaving the slave quarters—and made her promise to use it—he was offering her a last-ditch escape from what was once called a "fate worse than death."

"How long can this go on?" Nadine asks, covering her ears like a toddler. "I can't stand it much longer."

"Don't listen," I advise her.

"How can we ignore it?"

"Don't try to make sense of it. You can't. It's like listening to a baseball game from outside a stadium, with no commentary. You can hear the bat hit the ball, but you don't know who's swinging it. It'll drive you insane."

Nadine shakes her head in a way that tells me she believes even intelligent men are idiots most of the time.

"I'll tell you one thing," Frosty says from the window. "That Kelly done knocked down more than a few of them dyed-blond motherfuckers out here. He don't play."

Nadine seems unimpressed by this revelation, but Annie nods steadily. She knows better than any of us how deadly Daniel can be when he removes all constraint from the warrior that dwells within him.

"Holy Jesus," Frosty says in a tone of wonder. "I just . . . I think I just saw a bear."

In spite of my steadily leaking wounds, a wave of heat passes over my face. "A bear? Where? Help me up. Let me see."

"He's already gone. He was standing at the edge of the woods, just like a man. On two legs! Anyway, if we move you now, you won't make it. It's gonna take a ambulance crew to get you outta here, Mayor."

"Tell me about the bear!"

"What you mean? It was a bear. Covered head to toe with hair."

"What color?"

"Black."

"What color was his nose?"

Frosty looks confused, but then he closes his eyes and tries to remember. "Yellow, I think. Yeah."

"What did he do?"

"He just stood there, like he wanted me to come down there and talk to him or something. But then he dropped down and backed into the trees again. Them guns must be scaring him."

Another intense exchange of rifle fire rattles the quarters. Nadine closes her eyes. Hoping to distract her, I say, "Tell me about the river."

She blinks in confusion. "What?"

"Back on the bluff, you told me you were scared for me to go on the river. Because of Romulus. Something about the end of his story. Tell me now."

"Are you serious?"

"It's better than listening to what's out there."

"Tell him," Annie says. "I can't sit here waiting for Kelly to get killed."

Nadine draws her legs up beneath her in the corner, then looks over at Kendrick, who is staring at her with glassy eyes. His breathing is labored, but not much worse than mine, to be honest. Frosty stands to one side of the window, watching the action below and jerking like a man sitting three feet from the boxing ring during a heavyweight fight.

"Well," Nadine says, trying to think of where to start. "You read Romulus's story up to where Niobe refused to return to Natchez with him. Refused to be rescued from that Louisiana plantation. Remember?"

"I do. She married the white carpenter and moved to his home parish in Louisiana. Where my mother was from. And she was passing for white already by then."

Nadine nods. "Well, after that, Romulus went back to Natchez and joined the Fifty-eighth Colored Infantry Regiment, when they went active a couple of weeks later. His war service is well known. What isn't is that about a year after what happened to Calliope and Niobe, he sneaked back out to Pencarrow to confront his half sister, Evelyn, whom he blamed for Calliope's death."

"Calliope," I repeat, my mind filling with an image of the startlingly alive bust that Andrew McKinney sculpted from the locket he found in Captain Pencarrow's library. The bust he called "the soul of Pencarrow."

"Did Romulus go out there to kill her?" I ask, recalling that my distant ancestor had finished off Cadmus the butler after confronting him near the old Natchez racetrack.

"I don't know. Even in the part of the narrative you read, he was quite open about hating Evelyn. Wanting revenge. He may well have gone out there to kill her. But I think as much as that, he wanted to understand how she could do what she did to her own sister. He understood Evelyn's hatred of his mother, who had displaced her own. But Niobe was her blood, and Evelyn had sold her not just into slavery, but into hell."

"That was her goal all along," I muse. "That's what I got from Romulus's narrative. In Evelyn's eyes, Niobe was a living rebuke of her family's honor. Her father had loved a female slave more than his saintly white wife, and Niobe was the proof. Worse, Pencarrow loved his mulatto daughter more than lily-white Evelyn. Evelyn didn't just want Niobe dead. She wanted her to suffer every minute that she walked the earth. That's why she gave them to Barlow and Dufort first."

"I think you're right. Evelyn had a sugar daddy by then, a Yankee officer who made sure that she and her plantation weren't preyed upon by anyone but him. When he was away, Romulus rode out and confronted Evelyn in her father's study. And a hardened a soldier as he'd become by then, he still wasn't prepared for what happened. Evelyn was sitting behind her father's desk working on her accounts when Romulus came in. And no more than three minutes into the conversation, she took a pistol from the drawer and shot him in the chest. Romulus barely escaped with his life. A Bienville barber removed the ball from his pectoral muscle, but he lived in fear from then until the end of the war, that Evelyn would somehow use her Yankee officer to punish or even kill him."

None of us speaks for several seconds, and then I remember what prompted me to begin this conversation. "I still don't get the thing about the river."

"Oh," Nadine says, but I can see that she too has become preoccupied by the sounds of life-and-death struggle outside. The gunfire has lessened considerably, but I still hear the crack of supersonic bullets every five or ten seconds.

"The river?" I prompt her again.

She nods and starts to answer, but before she can, a *WHOOSH!* like the breath of a giant rattles the windows of the slave quarters.

"What the *hell*?" Annie cries. "What was that?"

"Shock wave," grunts Kendrick. "Almost like a fuel-air explosive."

My heart begins pounding with excitement. "That was Ray!"

"Ray blew the Black Oak well?" Nadine asks, her eyes shining with hope.

I nod. "Nothing else would make that sound."

"We've got our smoke signal?" she asks excitedly. "The FBI will see that from town?"

"Not yet. Not that." I think back to what Ray told me when I confronted him at the Buckman well. "That sound was vented gas. The tank itself needs to blow. But that should follow any second now. No more than a couple of minutes, anyway."

The hope in Nadine's eyes sputters out. Even a few moments' reprieve from her worst fears has made the prospect of facing two more minutes of men trying to shoot their way in here difficult to endure.

"The *river*," I say again, repeating my new mantra of distraction. "Tell me the rest of it."

"Tell him," Annie says. "That well's going to blow. It will. Finish the story."

"The *river*," Nadine says, by sheer force of will. "After the war ended, Romulus decided to move to the North, as fast as he could get there. So in April—twelve days after Lincoln was assassinated—he used cash to buy a ticket on the *Sultana*, a steamboat headed upriver to St. Louis. By the time he boarded at Vicksburg, where the boilers were being serviced, the boat's capacity had been oversold five times over. A vessel built to carry three hundred seventy-six passengers left the next day with more than twenty-one hundred souls aboard. Most were Union soldiers who'd been captured and held in prison camps in Alabama and Georgia. Andersonville. They were desperate to get home and didn't care how they got there."

"*Sultana*," I think aloud. "I remember that name. But I can't remember why. Maybe from grade school?"

"They don't teach this in school," Kendrick croaks beside me.

He's more alert than I thought.

"Most of the men on *Sultana* were white," Nadine goes on, "but Romulus saw another former slave he recognized on board, working on the crew."

"Who?" I ask.

"Jupiter. The mysterious man who'd tried to help gin up the slave rebellions at Natchez and Bienville back in 1861. The ones that resulted in the lynchings."

"I remember! Romulus and Doby believed Jupiter had murdered the simple boy who'd overheard them discussing a possible revolt. To keep him quiet. Eli was the boy's name. Right?"

Nadine nods. "Doby had vowed to kill Jupiter if they ever found him again. Well, four years later, Romulus did. And he meant to drown him. But the river took care of that for him."

"How?"

"Seven miles north of Memphis, around three a.m., one of *Sultana*'s boilers exploded. The boat went down in an hours-long firestorm that became the greatest maritime disaster in U.S. history."

"Bigger than the *Titanic*?" Frosty asks from the window, his voice skeptical.

"More lives lost," Nadine says. "Three hundred more, at least."

"How many died?" Annie asks, though I'm sure she must have a general idea, from the research she did for my mother.

"About eighteen hundred on *Sultana*," Nadine replies, "drowned or burned alive. Just over fifteen hundred on *Titanic*."

"*Day-um*," Frosty marvels. "I wonder why it's not more famous?"

"Because of Lincoln's assassination," Kendrick explains.

"That's right," says Nadine. "As harrowing as the survivors' stories were, the capture of John Wilkes Booth the previous day drove them off the front pages."

"But Romulus survived," I say. "He was a strong swimmer, right? He'd escaped slavery by swimming out to that Union gunboat."

"That's not how he survived. I can't believe you didn't read those last pages."

"Tell me!"

"The boiler explosion had broken one of his arms and one leg, but it didn't throw Romulus into the water. A lot of men who went in early got dragged down by those who couldn't swim. But once the boat started going down, he had no choice. The water was icy spring runoff, flooded three miles wide. Romulus didn't have a chance, really. He was just floating, close to drowning, when an emaciated Union soldier kicked up with a long wooden box. It was a coffin."

"A coffin?" Annie echoes.

Nadine nods. "The Yankee rolled the coffin, and the corpse floated out and down the river. Then he somehow got Romulus into the box. The coffin was mostly filled with water, but it kept his nose above the surface. Romulus wrote that he remembered looking at the moon, then nothing. When he came awake again, the Yankee soldier was gone. A few minutes later, the lights of Memphis appeared, and a fisherman pulled him into a rowboat."

"Did he ever see the Yankee soldier again?" I ask.

Nadine shakes her head. "He almost certainly drowned. They figure Romulus was in the water for about three hours."

"That's one hell of a story," says Frosty. "That Romulus was a badass brother."

The words have hardly left the big man's mouth when a concussion that dwarfs the previous explosion rocks the quarters.

"*That's it!*" I cry in triumph. "Ray did it! Those flames will be a hundred feet high within a minute. Just like the wells across the river today."

"Thank *God*," Nadine breathes. "Thank God!"

Elation fills the room like a breeze of nitrous oxide. The sporadic gunfire now seems like falling action prior to a rescue rather than an ominous prelude to a final assault. The average interval between shots has stretched to fifteen or twenty seconds, or even longer. I'm not counting.

But even as I feel a glimmer of hope, a harsh crack of automatic rifle fire penetrates our room, sounding much closer than the most recent exchanges. I see my worry reflected on Annie's face, and Kendrick's, too. Then the walkie-talkie Kelly left me crackles at my waist, and his voice enters the room like that of some unquiet ghost. The strong, casual tone that always buoys his words is gone, replaced by a reedy groan, as if each phrase costs him oxygen he cannot spare.

"*Penn, it's Daniel . . . Listen . . . a minute ago I had good news for you . . . but I'm down now. Can't really move.*"

Annie's face crumples.

"*What about my men?*" Chief Morgan cuts in from his radio.

"*They went down about a minute ago, Chief. Sorry . . . they did good.*"

"Daniel, it's me. Fall back to us," I plead. "We'll make a last stand together, right here."

First there's only static in reply. Then Kelly says, "*Can't do it, bud . . . you know I would if I could. Listen, now . . . the PSP's shot to shit. We took care of that . . . but Barlow's men will be coming. Or the sheriff's deputies. Maybe both. I think it was one of them who got me . . . anyway. Fuck . . . I'm calling to say that if anybody in there can run for it . . . now's the time. I know you can't move, but . . . if you want to get Annie and Lanying out, send them now. Same with Nadine . . . Annie won't want to leave you, but you need to make her go. Tell her Daniel said go, and get Nadine to push her . . . Chief Morgan's guys can lead them out.*"

"Understood, bubba. Will do."

Annie shakes her head fiercely.

"*One weird thing . . . my mind might be playing tricks on me, but I thought I heard Black Hawk helicopters flying north to south a minute ago. Coupla miles away maybe . . . I couldn't see them . . . trees too thick. But I've ridden enough of them to know the sound of those blades and engines. Nothing like 'em.*"

"Could that have been the FBI?"

"*No. The Bureau flies Bell 407s . . . the only FBI unit that uses Black Hawks is the Hostage Rescue Team, and they wouldn't be down here . . . all fantasies aside. Sounded about a thousand feet up . . . hell, I'm probably out of it. You get those girls moving. We can talk each other through the last act of this Alamo remake once they're out.*"

"Understood. I'll get back to you."

"*Hey, hey—there's four grenades left in my Pelicans. M67s, five-second delay. Pile those fuckers up by the window and drop them when Barlow's guys go for the front door.*"

"Ten-four, buddy. I'll give 'em hell."

Kelly says no more, and I know he won't until I reach out to him. He's given me my charge—get the women to safety while there's any chance.

"Chief!" I call. "This is Penn. Can you come up for one second?"

Morgan doesn't reply over the radio, but seconds later I hear his heavy shoes on the staircase. Then he's pushing into the room, a uniformed Black man in his early fifties with the terrible weight of dead and wounded men in his eyes.

"Chief, you heard Kelly. Anybody who can still run should make a break for the woods. I didn't want to risk anybody outside hearing this, but I'm telling you to go while you can. You don't have to stay till the end."

"I've got three men left shooting, Mr. Cage. The rest are dead or wounded. If I leave, I'll be leaving my wounded to the mercy of whoever's still out there."

"I hadn't thought of that. I was going to ask you to take these women out."

He nods in understanding. "I wish I could. But I'll tell you this. I don't know about you, but I'd rather be shot in the chest making a last stand than in the back running for my life."

Annie is nodding. "I'm not leaving, Dad. Forget it. Maybe those choppers Daniel heard are coming."

Chief Morgan shakes his head. "I'm not looking for help there. But with Ray blowing that well like he did . . . you have to believe there's a chance."

"I do," I lie, knowing that time is vanishing like water through a hole in a barrel.

"Frosty," Kendrick says from against the wall. "Help me up, brah."

The big man moves quickly from the window to the mattress and starts lifting his cousin to his feet.

Chief Morgan climbs onto the mattress to help them, planting his black shoes in the sticky slick of blood I've left around us.

"What are you doing, Kendrick?" I ask.

"Me and Frosty are gonna try to get Lanying out. If she wants to go, that is."

Lanying pops up from the corner like a jack-in-the-box. She's been so quiet for the past few minutes that I forgot she was even there.

"You guys get me up, too," I order them. "Please."

"Dad, you can't walk anywhere," Annie protests.

"No, but I'm not going out of this world sitting down. Get me up, Chief. Frosty?"

Kendrick leans against the wall while the police chief and the ex-gangbanger lift me out of a puddle of my own blood. Gritting my teeth, I thank the heavens for fentanyl once more.

"Do you want to try to make the woods?" I ask Lanying.

She nods intensely. "Please, yes. *Please.*"

Kendrick nods as if he's been pondering this move for a while. "I won't make a dollar's worth of difference in a last stand here, but if we can get her to the trees, maybe she can make it out. That way, at least her story gets out. Right? The truth about those goddamn fires gets out."

"Yes," Chief Morgan agrees, surprising me with his passion.

"What about that bear I saw?" Frosty asks anxiously. "He down there somewhere. And he might be hungry."

"That bear's your good luck spirit," I tell him. "Doc Berry told me that yesterday. It's the same bear I saw on the street last week, Frosty. He's the sign you should go. He's showing you the way!"

"Well, shit," Frosty says uncertainly. "Aiight, then, I guess."

Chief Morgan says, "Kelly and my boys cut those PSP bastards to pieces before they got taken down. I don't trust that back meadow where the plane was, but if you break to the west right now—toward Highway 61— you might make the tree line. We can give you covering fire when you go."

"Thanks, Chief," Kendrick says, stepping carefully off the mattress and testing his legs.

"*Word*, chief," Frosty adds, making a fist in solidarity. "You *old school*."

"I can walk," Kendrick says, "if my damn chest will hold together. *Jesus*. How far is Highway 61 through those woods?"

Testing my left leg on the floor, I'm surprised to find my pelvis holding together and keeping me erect. "Half a mile," I tell him. "Maybe three quarters. It'll be tough going in there—bushes and briars all the way—but maybe that's good. Hard for anybody to track you."

"Let's go," Kendrick says, starting toward the door. "The longer we wait, the less chance we got."

Frosty slaps my left shoulder. "Give 'em hell, homes. It was good knowin' ya." Then the big man follows his cousin.

"Thanks for all you've done, Chief," I say to Morgan's back.

He pauses and turns in the open door. "It's my job. Or it was until today. I'll be back, Penn."

I salute him, and then he's gone.

Annie and Nadine and I look at one another as their feet trudge down the stairs, Kendrick's slower and without rhythm. In my daughter's face I see hope, but in Nadine's only fear that in less than a minute both Kendrick and his cousin will lie dead behind the quarters, and we'll be almost defenseless.

"I want you both to go with them," I say with all the force and conviction I can muster. "Get down there now and break for it."

Annie's voice is so calm and collected when she answers that it dismisses my plea altogether. "Dad, you know I'm not leaving. Daniel knows it, too. He just had to try."

I take hold of Nadine's arms and squeeze. "You've got to go. You know why. For that baby."

Annie blinks and looks from me to Nadine. "What baby?"

"Nadine's pregnant," I tell her. "You've got to get her out of here, Annie. And you've got to go with her."

"Oh, my God," Annie says softly. "You can't be."

Nadine nods that she is, and I recognize the instant that Annie believes her.

"I'm not going to make it, y'all," I tell them. "I wish things were different. But you two *have to*. You're all that's left of our family. You're the future. Now go!"

The two women look at each other for several seconds, and then, in the same moment, they shake their heads.

"I don't think Kendrick and Frosty are going to make it," Annie confides. "The best chance is right here, as scary as it seems."

Nadine nods in agreement, then steps forward and hugs me tight. When she draws back and looks into my eyes, she silently tells me what I guess I've known since we barricaded ourselves in this place: *Annie won't go without you unless someone knocks her unconscious and carries her, and Kelly was the only one who could have managed that. I'm not leaving without her, or you—*

Something crashes near the back door, and then a burst of gunfire breaks out behind the quarters. It sounds to me like pistols up close rather than rifles. Somebody screams, and then I hear Frosty yell, "Run, K, *RUN!*"

Annie flies from the room, and I know she must be racing to a back window. In her absence, Nadine comes to me and pulls me into her arms, then stands on tiptoe and speaks hotly in my ear. "I always loved you. You hear me? From the time we were together, I never stopped. We missed our chance, but that doesn't change anything. Okay?"

Pulling back, I look into her frightened eyes, then kiss her and crush her in an embrace. We're still standing that way when Annie walks back into the room, her eyes wide in shock.

"What happened?" I ask in full dread.

"They made it. They reached the trees. Lanying first, by twenty yards."

"Frosty, too?"

"I think he got hit in the back, but he made it. That guy weighs three hundred pounds. Morgan's cops shot a couple of people outside the back door. This is *insane*."

"It's war, Annie. The worst thing there is."

CHAPTER 119

KENDRICK AND FROSTY crashed through the undergrowth as fast as they could go, but Lanying was still ahead of them. They'd given up trying to be stealthy. Frosty had a bullet high in his back—taken during the frantic sprint for the tree line—and the stabbing pain in Kendrick's chest made any extraneous movement too costly. Besides, the gunfire behind them still sounded like a medium-intensity firefight in a combat zone. No one was going to hear a couple of squirters staggering through Bambi country.

Lanying had a different view.

After her seeming paralysis in the slave quarters, the Chinese girl moved through the woods with ghostly speed and almost no sound. Her natural survival instincts would have impressed an army ranger. Whenever she paused and looked back at her escorts, Kendrick motioned her forward. He didn't want her to die merely because he and Frosty couldn't keep up. Besides, after basic training and two combat tours, he knew his own body. He could stand a lot of punishment, but this time something deep within him was broken. Whatever it was, wasn't going to hold for much longer. Lanying could have gotten much farther ahead already, but she seemed to sense that she wasn't yet clear of danger. If they encountered more men with guns, she would need Kendrick to stop them from taking her.

Kendrick checked the borrowed Glock as he staggered through a thicket of thorns between two pines. The long green spikes drew blood from both arms, but he bulled through them, and Frosty followed, cursing mightily. Penn had said they had a half mile of woods to get through before they'd reach Highway 61. The whole area was likely crawling with sheriff's deputies and militiamen. The only thing that gave Kendrick comfort was the knowledge that, if they could somehow cross 61 without being taken, they'd be moving downhill into the bottomland along the Mississippi River. And there, on that narrow flood-prone plain, nine out of ten houses would hold Black families.

Help and comfort . . .

Kendrick wasn't sure when he realized someone was behind them. One minute he'd been focused on his pain; the next all his instinct had zeroed in on a fresh set of sounds behind him. Behind and to the right. Someone moving through the woods with a similar level of stealth to the girl.

Maybe even more. Like an echo of Kendrick's own movements, but . . . there would be no echoes in this forest. Foliage killed reverberation.

Someone—or some*thing*—was tracking them.

Could it be the bear? he wondered. *Or did someone out of sight see us go into the woods?* He thought back to the moment they'd crashed into the undergrowth beneath the trees. *Have they followed us from the beginning?* He didn't think so. Also, the closer he listened, the more he had the sense that the person hunting them was out to the right, somewhere between them and River Road. Could someone have anticipated their escape attempt and moved in from the side to cut them off? It didn't seem likely, or even possible. Not unless they had some kind of intelligence that was impossible out here. It would take ISR like they'd had in Afghanistan and Iraq. An overhead platform. A drone.

Sheriff Tarlton has a drone, Kendrick reminded himself. *They had it up at Mission Hill.* Why couldn't it be above them now? It could have transmitted their sprint from the slave quarters to anyone on the other end of the digital feed—

Up ahead, Lanying had paused to wait for them. This time, instead of motioning her forward, Kendrick beckoned her back. The girl looked terrified, but she did as he asked. When she got within earshot, he bent nearly double and leaned against a tree to catch his breath. She knelt beside him, her ear near his face.

"Someone's behind us," he told her.

The almond eyes went wide.

"Out that way," Kendrick said, flinging his hand toward River Road.

Tears welled instantly.

"It's no good trying to outrun them," he said, the pain making him want to scream. "Not me and Frosty." Kendrick looked from her face to that of his cousin, who was wheezing so badly that Kendrick wondered if he could make another hundred yards. "You've got two choices: stick here and fight it out . . . or go on as fast as you can while we hold them off. You book it. Haul ass. You understand?"

Lanying nodded.

"If we weren't wounded, I'd say stick here and fight with us. But I can't do much, and I'm guessing you don't know anything about guns."

Lanying shook her head.

"Then your best bet is to get the hell out of here. I've watched you move. You're greasy, girl. So if you have the guts, this is it. Run like the devil. Understand?"

She nodded. "Thank you, Sergeant. For trying."

Kendrick pointed ahead into the trees. "Get on, girl!"

With that she was gone.

"Adios, baby," Frosty said beside him. "Damn, she can go!"

As Lanying vanished, Kendrick found himself listening for the footsteps that had dogged them to this point. At first he heard nothing. Then a rush of leafy sounds over a rapid drumbeat came to him. The drumbeat he felt through the earth—

Panic hit him when he realized their pursuer was no longer concerned with them but racing after Lanying. *He watched me send her on*, Kendrick realized. *He's here to get her. To silence her. She's the priority—*

"Goddamn you!" he shouted. "Come back here, motherfucker! Come out of those trees and fight it out!"

No one answered.

Kendrick heard a distant crash of something heavy moving through foliage. Then nothing.

"Let's go," he said to Frosty.

With a grunt of pain, Kendrick straightened up and began moving forward again. They had no prayer of catching Lanying, unless something terrible happened, and then it would be pointless, of course. But they had their guns, and Highway 61 still seemed like the most logical destination.

A muted *pop* sounded in the trees directly in front of them.

One shot.

A hundred meters through the trees, maybe.

"No," he said.

But beside him Frosty shook his big round head. "That li'l bitch be dead, cuz. I feel it."

Kendrick felt it, too. Their pursuer had carried out a flanking movement and then charged in and killed her.

Kendrick had failed in his duty. But he was still a soldier. He had to confirm what had happened, so that later he could report it to whoever survived. He started forward again.

"Yo, we still goin' that way?" Frosty asked.

Kendrick looked back at his cousin, whose face was almost a cartoon of cautiousness. "We can't evade whoever that is out there. Not in these woods. It's going to end in a fight either way. Let's go for the highway. Just stay ready."

Frosty shook his head at the apparent absurdity of Kendrick's words. "Cuz, we got the frying pan behind us and the fire up ahead. Or the other way around, I ain't sure which."

"Rock and a hard place for sure." Kendrick grunted against a hot arc of pain. "But we're gonna make it."

Frosty sighed, then summoned a boy's grin. "Shit, I hope so. This more walkin' than I done in *years*." He bent at the waist and took a couple of deep breaths, then straightened up again as though ready to jog a few miles. "You the leader out here. Lead on."

Kendrick listened to the low hum of an engine far ahead beyond the trees. *Highway 61*, he realized. "You hear that motor?"

"I hear it, baby. Let's move!"

Kendrick tensed against his pain and started forward again, toward the place where Lanying had likely met her death. They made it twenty more yards before two shots blasted out of the dimness ahead.

Even as he hit the ground, Kendrick heard the bullets thud into his cousin's chest. Frosty gasped like he'd been sucker-punched, then sank to his knees and fell onto his face. Kendrick heard one long exhalation, but Frosty didn't move again.

Rage flooded through him. He wanted to empty his pistol into the shadows ahead, but he knew from experience that would be the stupidest thing he could do.

"You *mother-FUCKER*!" Kendrick screamed. "*Come out! I'll kill your ass!*"

"Not today, Kendrick," called a taunting voice from the undergrowth.

The use of his first name stunned Kendrick. Freaked him a little, anyway. Maybe Lanying hadn't been the killer's main target after all. Maybe he'd come for them both—

"*Stand up, Kendrick*," called the voice.

"FUCK YOU, MOTHERFUCKER!"

Kendrick crabbed sideways and yanked Frosty's pistol from his hand. Now he had two guns, at least—

"*Stand up or I'll kill you where you lie*," commanded the voice.

A chill raced up Kendrick's back. It sounded like the owner of that voice was high in a tree, looking down on him through a scope reticle.

"*I don't have time to fool around*."

Something about the voice was familiar, Kendrick realized. He'd definitely heard it before. Maybe not in person, though. It was like the voice of somebody on a TV show. The news, maybe . . .

"Don't move," said Bobby White, aiming a pistol down at him from ten feet away. "I've got a message for you, Kendrick. Words of wisdom from Gil Scott-Heron."

Kendrick blinked up in confusion at the tall white man who had suddenly stepped from behind a big tree. "What the fuck . . . ?"

Bobby smiled. "The revolution will not be televised."

"Wait," Kendrick said, not yet resigned to his fate. "Tell me one thing before you fire."

Bobby looked mildly curious. "What's that?"

"Did you kill Ebony Swan?"

White's mouth held still for a second, but then it widened in the eeriest of smiles. "I gave the order to kill her if they caught her. But in the end it was Jamaal King that ordered that. His guys found her sleeping in some bushes downtown, and they decided to use the circumstances to lay the blame on white supremacists. Worked great for me, because it helped guarantee your speech would be carried on TV around the world."

Tears of guilt came into Kendrick's eyes. "Damn, you're cold, man."

Bobby steadied his pistol. "Adios, soldier."

Kendrick jerked when the shot came, but to his amazement he was not the recipient of the bullet. Bobby White spun in place, nearly fell, then recovered and fired in the opposite direction. Kendrick saw blood running from the stump of White's left shoulder, where the arm had been amputated years before. It struck Kendrick then that whoever was out there had purposely shot the man in his stump.

Bobby had dropped into a defensive crouch, but it did him no good. The concealed shooter put three rounds into the tree beside him—only inches away—and unlike the first bullet, each carried the supersonic crack of rifle fire.

"Drop your gun, Sergeant White," said a boyish voice with the accent that Kendrick always called *country-ass.* "Drop it, or the next one goes through your cervical spine."

At this threat, White straightened up and dropped his pistol onto the carpet of leaves at his feet.

A second later, a skinny white guy stepped out of the foliage to Kendrick's right. He held a pistol in his left hand and a tricked-out assault rifle in his right. An HK maybe, Kendrick guessed. He'd seen them in Afghanistan, usually in the hands of special forces.

"Hey, Donny," Bobby White said. "You fucking shot me, man."

"You shot me first, motherfucker."

Bobby smiled strangely. "True enough."

"We got business to finish."

Bobby nodded. "I guess we do."

Whoever Donny was, he turned his baby blue eyes toward Kendrick and said, "You get on away from here, soldier."

This order stunned Bobby White. "You're going to let him go?"

"Not my decision," Donny answered. "The Lord spared him."

"What?"

"I shot him in the chest, and he's still walking."

A wave of heat and childlike terror went through Kendrick as he realized that this scrawny gunman had been the assassin on the water tower. God only knew how many innocent people he'd killed and wounded today—

"He's like a criminal who gets hanged and the rope breaks," Donny explained. "He's got the mark on him." Donny focused his baby blue eyes on Kendrick. "You've still got things to do on this earth, apparently. God's not finished with you yet."

In that moment Kendrick realized that the pain of his wounds had left him. *There must be so much adrenaline surging through me that my brain is shorting out—*

"Go on," Donny said. "Me and this fella here have something to settle. And you don't want no part of it."

Despite his fear, Kendrick slowly got to his feet and backed through the trees. As the two white men became obscured by leaves and branches, he heard the skinny guy say, "God is finished with *you*, though, Bobby. He sent me to let you know."

Kendrick turned and started running as hard as he could.

BOBBY KNEW HE was as close to death as he'd ever been. The mild blue eyes of Donny Kilmer had looked down on hundreds of panicked people earlier this day, while a finger connected to the same brain depressed a trigger that sent a rain of hot lead streaming down into the living bodies of men, women, and children. The blood now running down Bobby's side was testament to Donny's willingness to inflict pain. To survive this encounter would require all the guile, instinct, and reflexes Bobby possessed.

"What is it you want to know?" he asked.

"Why you think I want to know something?" Donny asked in a defensive tone.

"Because I'm still alive. You could have killed me with your first shot."

The kid nodded. "That's true. What I want to know is, did you plan to kill me all along? Was I your patsy? Your goddamn Lee Harvey Oswald? You wanted to be Jack Ruby, I guess? But better lookin'?"

"You know I didn't want any of that," Bobby said, thinking the kid had got pretty close to the truth. "You were supposed to be shot by FBI counter-snipers. You knew that going in. I pretty much told you that when we met at the cemetery."

Donny thought about it. "I guess you did. But every soldier has a right to try to save himself in the end, don't he?"

Bobby almost smiled at the idea of Donny Kilmer seeing himself as a soldier. "That Geronimo-line rig you set up was pretty sweet."

A faint smile widened Donny's lips. "Just oil-field experience."

Bobby nodded with admiration. "Still."

Donny stood there with his modified assault rifle in his right hand and the pistol in his left. Bobby didn't have a chance of reaching his own gun or getting close enough to hurt the kid before he was shot.

"So," he said. "You going to kill me or what?"

Donny was clearly considering it. But before he could say or do anything, the analog radio on Bobby's belt crackled.

"This is Bravo Actual," said Buck Tarlton. "Bravo Two, I've got word the Bureau has formed up a line of SUVs in town and may be headed this way. You need to get back here and help us finish this ASAP. Acknowledge."

Relief flooded through Bobby like a blast of cocaine. Fate had thrown him a lifeline. He looked at Donny with what he hoped would appear to be fraternal respect. "You heard that. They're down at the slave quarters, launching another assault. They need help. Sounds like the Federal Bureau of Integration is coming, and fast. If you're really a soldier, Donny, you'll come down there with me and help finish it. We can settle our differences afterward."

Bobby could see conflict behind the blue eyes. But some part of him knew the outcome was foreordained. A loser like Donny Kilmer simply couldn't walk away from a chance to play a role in events that felt bigger than the life he'd known up to that point.

"Fuck it, okay," Donny said. "Get movin'."

Bobby did nothing to betray his triumph. "I'm going to pick up my pistol now. Don't do anything crazy."

"Follow your own advice. I'll be marching right behind you, with two guns on your back."

Bobby smiled. "I'm keenly aware, soldier."

He bent at the knee and fished his pistol off the ground with his thumb and forefinger. "How about you help bandage my shoulder before we go? I can't manage it with one arm. You can use my belt."

"Fuck your damn shoulder. You make it or you don't. Let's go."

Bobby nodded as though he'd been greedy to ask for such an indulgence. Then he turned and started walking away from Donny Kilmer.

The trick, he said to himself, *is not giving the slightest physical tell that your body is about to defy the normal rules of motion.* He'd learned this during some of the most boring afternoons and evenings of his life, on firebases out in the Afghan provinces, practicing krav maga disarms and takedowns with his fellow Rangers until they convinced themselves they could all be hired as Hollywood fight choreographers after the war. Bobby's feet moved lightly over the ground, so that his ears wouldn't miss the moment when Donny took his first following step. For that would pinpoint his position, even to a man looking away from him—

The rustle finally came, and Bobby's right arm flew back like an uncoiling whip, even as his legs, hips, and upper body continued their forward momentum as though engaged in nothing but a casual stroll. He was pulling the trigger before his hand popped to full extension, and he emptied his clip in less than three seconds.

He knew before he turned that Donny was down, because he wasn't dead himself. Buck Tarlton's voice crackled from the walkie-walkie again, more urgent now—even panicked—but Bobby ignored it. He walked back and looked down at Donny Kilmer, who lay on his side, panting like a wounded deer.

The kid had at least three bullets in him, stitched across his narrow chest. Bobby figured Kilmer would look up, maybe ask him something, but he only stared straight ahead with glassy eyes.

"Soldier, my ass," Bobby said.

Someone would have to move the corpse over to Canaan to sell the story that Donny had come looking for revenge against the citizen-hero who'd shot him off the water tower during his killing spree. But that would have to wait. Bobby bent and popped the slide on Donny's web belt, then yanked it out of the pant loops with some difficulty. Kilmer shuddered as though he wanted to resist, but he was nearly dead. Bobby started to tie off his stump, but considering what Tarlton had said about the FBI, he decided to try to stem the bleeding while on the run. Turning away from Donny Kilmer, he trotted swiftly through the deepening shadows under the trees, back toward Pencarrow.

CHAPTER 120

THE LULL THAT followed the departure of Kendrick, Frosty, and Lanying made us all wonder if we made a terrible mistake in not trying to get out when they did. Five minutes lengthened to ten, then twelve, with only sporadic rifle fire directed at the slave quarters' windows—and that from some considerable distance, it seemed. We take no more casualties during this strange lacuna of time—not even Chief Morgan or his men—but the cell jamming continues, and the occasional gunshots remind us that we cannot leave the safety of these brick walls without risking death.

A low, bone-rattling rumble announces the final phase of our siege. A heavy engine seems to vibrate the earth and the walls of the slave quarters as it approaches, though it seems to be advancing at no more than a walker's pace. *What has Bobby White brought to end this battle?* I wonder. *A bulldozer to ram the building and smash it into rubble?* Unable to endure the suspense of grinding gears and bellowing pistons, I get Nadine to help me crawl to the window. There I pull myself up onto a chair she's dragged to the left of it, then peek out through a hole created by three blown-out shutter slats.

What I see looks like a *Twilight Zone* parody of the climax of *Kelly's Heroes*, when Clint Eastwood, Donald Sutherland, Don Rickles, and Telly Savalas walk up to a German Tiger tank commander to persuade him to rob a bank during World War II. But instead of that motley crew, I see Bobby White, Sheriff Buck Tarlton, Shot Barlow, and the blond psycho Baldur Pussett walking behind a blue GMC pickup from the 1980s. Someone has tied a stained white T-shirt to its radio aerial.

Bobby White hasn't come through the earlier action unscathed. His left shoulder is covered with blood, and the stump of his right arm appears to be tied off with a web belt. Shot Barlow looks like an extra who wandered into the scene from a horror film on the next lot. Half his face is a blue-black bruise, and one eye is swollen shut. I suspect he got these adornments from Kelly at my house. Flanking these four principals—about twenty yards behind them—are three uniformed deputies from Tenisaw County.

"What are they doing?" Nadine whispers from beside me.

"I don't know . . . it looks like they want to parley. Get away from the window."

The film comparison struck me because you could flip a coin to decide which man in this crew is the young Eastwood. Buck Tarlton, with his TV looks, would no doubt claim it, but it's Bobby who has the brooding power and ruthlessness that gave the actor his career. A young Sutherland could have doubled for Baldur Pussett, if he lifted weights for a year and wore white-blond shoulder locks. And if bullet-headed Rickles went without shaving for a month, he could have played Shot Barlow. Each man carries at least one gun, and they follow the truck until it stops thirty-five yards from the front of the slave quarters. *They're not here to rob a bank*, Kelly told me earlier. *They're here to kill us.*

"Annie?" I whisper, recalling Daniel's last radio transmission. "Bring me the grenades from Kelly's Pelican cases."

"Are you kidding?"

"Please do it now."

"Why?"

The driver's door of the GMC opens, and the driver—a PSP militia skinhead—climbs out with an M4 assault rifle at his side. Only his rifle is mounted with a grenade launcher below the barrel. One shot through this window would take us all out.

"We need all the time we can get," I tell her. "And I need my AR-15, *now*. Whatever this is, we have to stretch it out and hope help is coming. This may be a cover for something. They may storm the back of this building. Someone else may be moving up from the sides right now. I only see three deputies. You know Tarlton has plenty more. Nadine, please go to the staircase and tell Chief Morgan to watch the rear."

I hear Annie digging cautiously in Kelly's hard-shell gear cases. "The grenades are round like baseballs," I tell her.

"No shit," she says. "Explosive baseballs."

"Penn, this is Bobby!" shouts the candidate's powerful voice. "I know you can hear me, so let's not fool around. I want you to come down and talk to me."

I look back at Annie, who's shaking her head that I shouldn't go. She's holding the grenades now, but she appears to be rooted to the floor. As I beckon her toward me, I wonder if those guys have a sniper covering the window from somewhere, waiting to fill it with fire the instant I answer.

"You tell that PSP son of a bitch to drop that grenade launcher! If he doesn't, I'm going to put a round through his chest." Spinning my hand fast at Annie, I mouth, *"My rifle!"*

"Nobody's going to shoot you, Penn," Bobby drawls, as if the idea is ludicrous. "We've got a serious time issue now. We need to get on with this."

"Why would I come down? You almost killed me up on the driveway an hour ago."

"To negotiate!" comes the reply.

I shake my head, incredulous. "The last time we tried that, you put a bullet through my pelvic wing."

"That wasn't personal. I just didn't think you or Annie would stick to any deal. But you're still alive. So let's get to it. I'm ready to give you your deal, if you convince me you and Annie can live with it."

"What deal?"

"The one Tarlton pitched you, and you took. Ray confesses to the fires—all the fires—and does the time instead of Kendrick."

This makes me wonder if Kendrick is dead.

Hearing a floorboard depress, I turn and see Nadine coming back into the room. She gives me a thumbs-up, then shuts the door behind her and walks over to the outer wall.

"What about Lanying?" I ask, not wanting to give Bobby the question he likely expects.

"She's no longer a factor."

Shit. "Is she dead?"

"Afraid so."

Looking back to my right, I see Annie's face crumple. But it's not Lanying she's thinking of. A wave of dizziness makes me sway on the chair. I must have lost more blood than I thought. Nadine takes hold of my shoulders and braces me against the wall to my left.

"Is Kendrick dead?" I call. "Is that why you're suddenly willing to accept Ray as your sacrifice?"

"When I last saw him, he was alive."

Annie fiercely shakes her head, unwilling to believe it without proof.

"You're going to have to prove that to me," I call.

"How? In all honesty, I was going to kill him, but Donny Kilmer stepped out of the trees and shot me. *He* let Kendrick go. Donny claims God is sparing Kendrick for some future purpose. He was crazy as a shithouse rat. But Kendrick's out there somewhere, if his earlier wound hasn't killed him."

Bobby's answer has the crazy ring of truth to my ears, but I know it won't satisfy Annie.

"It was Donny who first shot Kendrick, by the way. He was the Water Tower Shooter, which is what they've christened him on the internet."

"Was, was, was," I echo. "Donny Kilmer's dead?"

"As a hammer. Life's cheap today, brother. And if you want to avoid the same fate for your loved ones, you're going to have to trust me."

"But I don't!"

"Nor I you, okay?" Bobby counters. "So let's make this transactional. The people behind me need a Black arsonist to take the rap for those fires. Does it matter who 'those people' are? It's white Bienville. White America, really."

Letting go of my shoulders, Nadine finally retrieves my AR-15 from the floor beside the mattress and puts it in my right hand, so that I can use it as a crutch to hold myself up.

"And what do you need, Bobby?" I call.

"A clean slate. Credit for taking out Donny Kilmer. A story that covers this fucking battle today and keeps me in the race."

"You're crazy."

"Not at all. You guys have so many fugitives out here, this story writes itself. Sheriff Tarlton's presence puts it all under color of law, and the excesses can be blamed—"

"On Baldur Pussett and the PSP," I say softly.

"Elsewhere," Bobby finishes. "How does that sound?"

Again Kelly's words and wisdom come back to me. "Like an empty sales pitch! You're here to kill us! I don't know why you're playing this game except to cover some other gambit."

"Goddamn, you're paranoid. The deal's the same as before. Only the context has changed."

"That skinhead just raised his rifle about halfway up," Nadine whispers.

A chill of fear races up my back. Easing up my AR, I lean right and peer through one of the broken shutter slats. Sure enough, the PSP thug seems to be preparing to fire a grenade through our window.

"What's the sudden time pressure?" I call, making sure my AR is ready to fire.

"Doesn't concern you!" Bobby replies. "There's plenty of time for us to storm that house and kill you all. But the bloodless alternative is better."

"Elaborate on the context change."

"I've talked to Ray Ransom. He'll do the prison time to spare Kendrick having to. He's good with it. And I figure if Ray can live with it, you can, too."

"When did you talk to Ray?"

"Five minutes ago."

"Bullshit!"

"No bullshit! If you can't see me now, find a way to look out. Nobody's going to shoot you."

"Don't do it," Nadine whispers.

Pulling back a little from the bullet-pocked shutters, I shout, "I see you."

Bobby nods at Baldur Pussett, who walks up to the back of the truck, drops the tailgate with a bang, then drags something out. As he does, the skinhead with the grenade launcher raises his rifle a little higher. I hear a groan, then I see Ray Ransom being hauled to his feet by the muscle-bound militia leader. Ray's left side is soaked with blood, but he seems to be standing under his own power, and his eyes blaze with hatred. Baldur Pussett draws a .45 from a leather holster and points it at Ray's belly.

"Tell him, Ray," Bobby says. "Make Penn believe in this deal."

As Ray begins speaking, I realize he's no more than a talking marionette for Bobby White. As street- and prison-savvy as Ray is, he knows the only reason he's still alive is to convince us to let down our defenses and come out to be executed.

"What game is Bobby playing?" Annie asks. "Even if we agree to this, we'd never let Ray die in prison for something he didn't do."

I look over at her. "It's all to get me downstairs. He doesn't want to storm the house. Maybe Kelly and those cops slaughtering the PSP screwed up his cover story somehow, I don't know. But this is all to get me down there. After they kill me, they figure killing the rest of you will be easy."

The coldness of my assessment drains the blood from Annie's face, and I hear something like a quiet sob. "Do you think Kendrick is dead?" she asks.

"I can't say, boo. I hope not."

"We have to drag this out as long as we can. But Bobby's going to force the time issue. Go see what else Kelly has in those cases. We'll be fighting for our lives in about a minute."

Now she's whimpering for real. "What are we going to do?"

Making eye contact with Nadine, I ask, "Would you be willing to stand still while I brace my rifle on your shoulder?"

"For what?" she asks warily.

"I may need to fire it in a second."

Annie closes her eyes and goes back to the Pelican cases, while Nadine stands a few feet back from the window and crouches enough to brace her palms on her knees. As carefully as I can, I step out from the wall, turn to the window, and lay my rifle over Nadine's right shoulder. "Remember, cover your ears when I tell you."

She nods once.

It's time to test Bobby's sincerity. Shouting through the shutters, I call, "It doesn't matter what Ray says with a gun pointed at his belly! If you'll really honor this deal, we'll take it. But nobody trusts you, Bobby, any more than you trusted me up on the road. We're at a stalemate. You've got to give me something. You've got to convince me you'll leave us in peace."

Even from this hole in the window I can see frustration twist Bobby's features. "How the hell do I do that?"

I consider for a few seconds. "Easy. Have Ray write and sign a confession now. Hell, record him confessing on your cell phone camera. But then you take all these men and go. Leave Ray here. Let tonight pass, and he'll turn himself in to Tarlton in the morning. Downtown."

Silence greets my proposal.

"Is there a problem?"

"Can't do that, Penn," Bobby replies. "The sheriff needs a perp. ASAP. Bienville's out of control *now*. It's the top of every newscast on every network. Ray has to be in a cell tonight."

Dripping with disgust, Baldur Pussett's voice fills the silence that follows Bobby's demand. "This is some chickenshit right here. Let's just storm that slave house and kill 'em all. Crow here can *spall 'em all* out with one round from that M203."

"You can't choose your family, Bobby," I call, unable to resist the temptation to jab him. "But you can choose your friends."

A cold smile touches his mouth. "You want me to give you something? All right."

I jerk back from the window as the rifle hanging in his hand comes up, but instead of shooting at me, Bobby turns and fires twice into Baldur Pussett's chest.

The looks of shock on the big militiaman's face freezes as he dies, while the suddenness of Bobby's act temporarily paralyzes the man beside him, the one called Crow. I assumed Bobby would kill him too, but all four men in front of the truck seem uncertain what to do next.

"*Cover your ears!*" I snap as "Crow" whirls toward Tarlton with his M4, but aims it at Bobby.

Bobby tries to aim around Tarlton as I squeeze my trigger, and a single round tears through the PSP man's left pectoral muscle, his chest, and exits the other side. He hangs in the air for a moment, then falls heavily. I fire twice more, and my second round smashes the tube beneath the M4's rifle barrel.

"*Good shooting, Penn!*" Bobby calls, with something like laughter in his voice.

I pray Annie wasn't watching, but looking to my right, I see that she was through another blown-out place in the shutters. She shakes her head with visceral revulsion, then looks down at the floor as though she might lose her stomach.

"*What happened?*" Nadine whispers. "I couldn't see."

"Bobby just murdered Baldur Pussett. No warning. Nothing. I took out the other PSP guy."

"To save Bobby White?"

"Bobby's the only one with the power to save *us*. Give me what Annie didn't. The damned grenades."

"Okay!" Bobby shouts. "You wanted something? I just gave it to you!"

Nadine slides back to the cases, then brings me one spherical M67 grenade. It feels light, about a pound, and roughly the size of a baseball. I stuff it into my right front pocket, then carefully look back out the window.

Baldur Pussett's corpse lies on the ground with his .45 pistol beside it. Everyone but Bobby is staring at what remains of the white supremacist leader. To my surprise, Shot Barlow seems a little uncomfortable, and Buck Tarlton looks like he'd give all the money he has to be anywhere else. But Bobby is staring straight at the shutters that conceal my silhouette, as though he can see right through the wood.

"You didn't give me anything," I call to him. "Killing Pussett was always part of your cover for killing us."

It's impossible to escape the math. One minute ago, five principals stood out there threatening us. Now there are only three. All my instinct tells me that if Bobby were removed from that number, there would indeed be a deal to be made. One that could get us back to town alive. But with Bobby in the mix, all the momentum pushes the other way—

The sound of a floorboard creaking behind me makes me think Nadine has gotten to her feet, but when I turn I see that the door has opened and a dark-haired young woman in a brown deputy's uniform is standing in the opening with a semiautomatic pistol in one hand and a bloody tactical knife in the other. The pistol is pointed at me. I suppose the knife got her past Morgan's men, but here she stands, murder in her eyes.

Behind her stands a male deputy, about a foot taller than she. Glancing down to my right, I see my AR-15 leaning against the wall. A minute ago it was in my hand. Now it's too far away to do any good.

"This is Kara Mascagni!" the deputy shouts at the open window. "We're up here, Bobby! We've got 'em! *We didn't even have to shoot!*"

Peering down through the slats, I see Buck Tarlton nodding excitedly and speaking to Bobby, but I can't make out what he's saying.

"What do you want me to do?" Mascagni shouts through the window.

There's a pregnant silence. Then Bobby throws up his only hand as though in disgust and calls, *"Finish it!"*

Mascagni's eyes bulge a little at this order, and she hesitates.

I can't reach my rifle, but I can reach Annie. Stretching out my right arm, I fold her into my chest, holding her head down so she can't see the end coming. I want to find Nadine's eyes, but instead I look down and kiss the top of Annie's head. "Everything's all right, boo. I love you—"

The gunshot bursts like a crack of lightning.

CHAPTER 121

TWO SHOTS SHATTERED the sacred silence of the room, but I'm still standing, still clinching Annie to my chest. Looking up, I see Nadine aiming a smoking pistol at my chest. On the floor between us lies Deputy Kara Mascagni, her lower face a wreck of blood, teeth, and splintered jawbone.

The male deputy stares transfixed, as though he can't believe what's happened, but then he raises his gun toward Nadine. A fire of rage blazes in my chest. Shoving Annie aside, I grab my rifle from the wall and turn it on the deputy. He shoots Nadine before I can fire, but I put three rounds into him before he can fire again, and my bullets hammer him back through the door, dead on his feet before he falls.

Nadine slides down the wall to my right, leaving a bright red streak above her left shoulder as she sinks. Her eyes are so dazed that I'm not sure she knows who or where she is. Annie scrambles across the room and crouches to attend her, but I go back to the window, trying to see what Bobby is doing.

"Mascagni!" Buck Tarlton calls. "Report!"

This moment will decide our fates.

I can't impersonate a female deputy, nor could Annie fool Tarlton for more than a few seconds. Through holes in the slats I see the three men outside beginning to suspect something's gone wrong. I'm almost certain this will push them to the hard option.

Bobby barks something at Tarlton, and the sheriff raises a radio to his lips. Panic starts my heart pounding. In a moment they will come. Maybe dozens at once. As Annie removes the pistol from Nadine's hand, I throw open the shutters, expose myself to Bobby, and call out to him, trying to get and hold eye contact.

"They're dead, Bobby! Both of them. They tried to kill my kid!"

I see the shock hit Buck Tarlton, but Bobby doesn't look surprised. He knows anything can happen when bullets start flying.

Looking down, I see Chief Morgan's squad car parked before the concrete steps that lead to the front door. Below the steps runs the light well dug around what my mother used to call the "potato bunk," but which was in fact a shallow basement used to keep certain stores during the nineteenth century. Looking down at the geometry of all this, I see a chance— one desperate chance—to work the math equation that came to me a few moments ago.

"Don't storm this place, Bobby!" I shout. "I'm coming down!"

"What for?" he hollers back. "It's too late to deal now!"

"You said that's what you wanted. You don't give a shit about those deputies. Give me sixty seconds' conversation. My little girl's up here, man! I'll do anything to save her. You know that!"

"But will *she* do anything to live? I don't think so."

"She will! She's never seen shit like this up close. Give me two minutes to get down there. I'm wounded pretty bad."

"Get down here, then. Come out with your hands up and high. One bullshit move and you die, Penn. No goodbyes."

"I can't make it any farther than the front steps. I'm shot twice."

"Get moving, then!"

BOBBY KNELT BEHIND the truck with Tarlton and Shot Barlow, while Ray Ransom sat with his back against a tire on the left side of the vehicle, wheezing as he breathed. His wound had kept him quiet, and so far had even stopped him from trying to escape. Bobby was glad of it.

"You're going to talk to Cage?" Barlow asked. "Why take the risk?"

"The risk is leaving him up there and having to assault the place. He just killed two deputies. You want to storm that building when he might have grenades up there? Kelly used three during the firefight with the PSP."

Barlow acknowledged this with a shift of his head.

"You get any more word on that Bureau convoy?" Bobby asked.

Tarlton nodded. "They formed up but didn't leave. They're parked up on the bluff with dozens of agents milling around the vehicles and drivers in place, but nobody's rolling."

"Good for us." Bobby leaned around the bumper and checked Ray Ransom. The old ex-convict looked oblivious to his surroundings. Pulling back to Barlow and Tarlton, Bobby whispered, "Close enough to talk is close enough to kill. And once Penn's dead, it's over."

"You sure?" Tarlton asked.

Bobby nodded. "Cops on the first floor could have shot any of us during that talk. They didn't. They're firing defensively. That's all. I'm telling you . . . there's only one leg holding up this stool. Get ready to lock our story down."

I WOULD HAVE liked to say a meaningful goodbye to Nadine, but she isn't really coherent, and I must exploit even the barest chance of saving her life along with Annie's. Steeling myself against the pain in my pelvic wing, I force myself to march to the door, then grab the rail at the head of the narrow staircase before I fall. This staircase was once walked every day by Romulus, Calliope, and Niobe, before the man who owned them died and their family was blown apart by a blood relation who hated them beyond measure. Annie has followed me, as I knew she would, but before she can plead with me not to go down, I grab her right wrist and lean close to her. "I need you to do something for me, boo. Maybe the hardest thing you'll ever do. And there's no time to argue. I'm your father, and you must do what I ask of you now."

"Daddy, he'll kill you if you go down there. He's a monster."

"I know he is. But listen . . . all right? *We—have—no—choice.*"

"But we do! There's something you don't know. I got Lanying to make a statement about the fires earlier today. It's on my phone. That'll be worth something to Bobby White. Use it to bargain."

"Bobby doesn't care about that! He'll have your phone ten seconds after he kills us."

Panic has driven Annie close to hysteria. Her eyes are mostly white as she grips my arms to plead with me. "Tell him you've got a cell signal, that you're about to transmit the statement out to the world."

"He'll know I'm lying." Yet even as I deny her suggestion, a better one like it comes to me.

"Then I don't know. Daddy, I don't know, I don't *know*! But if you go down there, he's going to kill you. I know that for sure. You can't do it."

I look at my wristwatch—Dad's Korean-era Hamilton that Mom wore while he was in prison, and that she placed on my wrist seventy-two hours before she died. I'm wasting my two minutes arguing with my daughter instead of getting her to do what she must do to save herself—

"I won't be alone," I tell her, speaking as calmly as I can. "Ray is down there."

"Ray's shot to shit!"

As I try to marshal my words, an image of the bear Frosty described appears in my mind. As crazy as it seems, I feel certain it's the same bear I encountered on the Bienville bluff six days ago. The one that left me feeling he'd come to forewarn me of my impending death.

"Ray's tough," I tell her. "If he can help me, he'll find a way. Now you listen to me. I need you to *stop talking*. I need you to do something risky as hell—but it's our only chance at a future. Do you hear me?" I shake her once. "Do you understand?"

Annie nods, her eyes finally locking in on mine.

"We're going to kill Bobby White."

Her mouth falls open, but then, God bless her, she nods once. "How?"

Taking the baseball-size grenade from my pocket, I hold it out to her. "With this."

Her eyes widen.

"Take it," I tell her, placing it in her hand.

"Me?"

"It has to be you. They'll search me when I go down, if they even risk getting that close."

"What do you want me to do with this? Throw it?"

"No. Drop it out the window. Straight down."

"When?"

"When I get Bobby up onto the steps. Preferably when he's right beside me."

Annie is shaking her head. "I don't understand."

"I think you do. The steps down there go over the light well like a bridge."

"Light well?"

"The moat. Some people call it a dry moat."

"Okay. I know the thing you mean."

"Those steps are concrete. Once Bobby is close to me, I want you to pull this pin right here and drop the grenade down between us."

"*What?*" Her eyes fill with terror.

"Listen, boo! I'll know it's coming, but *he won't*. I'll throw myself off those steps and roll under them. Bobby can't react that fast. Nobody can who doesn't know ahead of time what's about to happen."

Annie's shaking her head still harder. "Dad, that's *crazy* . . . I'll kill you if I do that."

"You could," I admit. "But you *won't*."

"I can't do it. I can't!"

"I'm going down there either way. And once I'm on those steps, you're my only chance. Don't second-guess yourself. Don't hesitate."

"Daddy, please . . . think of another way."

"There's not one. Look, we don't know how much time I have left anyway. With luck, this chance gets us a future. This gets you children. It gives that baby in Nadine's belly a father. It gets me grandchildren. If we just wait and pray to be rescued, then . . . there's none of that."

My mention of children breaks through. Raising my hand, I lightly brush a strand of hair from her eyes. "Think of your grandmother. She wouldn't hesitate. Would she?"

Annie shakes her head like a little girl. She knows I'm right.

"Don't say another word, boo. There's no time. Just listen to what I tell you now. The timing is everything. Everything."

"How do I count?"

"Just like grade school. *One-Mississippi, two-Mississippi, THREE.* Toss it down on three. Not three-Mississippi. *ON* three. Okay?"

"On three. Got it."

Pulling the walkie-talkie off my belt, I stuff it into her front pocket. "I haven't spoken to Kelly since that last transmission. He's probably gone. But in the thirty or forty seconds it takes me to get down these steps, try to call him. You're like his own child, Annie. You know that. Tell him you need him now like you never have before. Tell him to save you."

Annie is sobbing, her eyes shot with blood and terror. "He's shot, too. *Please* don't go. Please don't leave me alone."

Gripping her upper arms, I see an image of myself removing my father's watch and buckling it onto her wrist before I go. But if I do that . . . she'll know the truth. She'll see me lying dead and she won't be able to do what she must. With a last kiss on her forehead, I whisper, "I love you, boo. Mama did, too. You were her angel. Now, make me proud."

With that I turn my back and hobble down the steps.

ANNIE STOOD TWO feet back from the window, staring at Nadine and listening to her father struggle down the steps. With a shaking hand she depressed the long side button on the walkie-talkie and spoke into it.

"Daniel? This is Annie. Are you there? It's me."

Nothing but static came back to her.

"Kelly . . . ? I need you to wake up. Okay? It's bad up here. It's basically down to me and my dad, and he's bleeding out. He's going to try something desperate."

When Annie released the key, she heard something different. A grunt of pain, maybe? "*Daniel?*" she cried. "Say something! For God's sake!"

"Annie?"

Hope surged through her. It was his voice.

"Get up!" she cried. "Get up, damn it! You said if I ever needed you, you'd be there. Get to the edge of the woods. Just let the sons of bitches see you! They're scared to death of you. Just seeing you could change everything. *Can you hear me?*"

She heard what sounded like something falling.

Then nothing.

As she listened with all her concentration, she realized she no longer heard her father struggling down the steps like Long John Silver in the movies.

She keyed the walkie-talkie again. "I have to go," she said in despair. "Daddy needs me. I hope you're not in too much pain."

She let the radio fall to the bloodstained floor.

BY THE TIME I pull the front door inward, I don't have to think about faking physical incapacity. I'm lucky I made it down the stairs without falling. Over the roof of Chief Morgan's squad car I see Bobby, Buck Tarlton, and Shot Barlow watching me from thirty yards away. They look stunned by my condition, but I can't be sure, because their faces are wavering as though through heat waves over a highway. I know Ray must be out there somewhere, but I can't see him.

With the last of my strength and balance, I throw up my hands so that Bobby can see they're empty, but then I collapse against the doorframe. I sit wheezing and praying that Bobby will not simply shoot me from the farthest clear angle he gets. If Kelly and Chief Morgan hadn't blocked the doors of the quarters with police cruisers, he could shoot me from beside the pickup.

"Bobby?" I call. "I can't see you. I'd stand, but I'm too messed up. Can you come a little closer?"

"I can hear you fine from here."

"I'm shot, man. But listen . . . we've got something you need."

"Yeah? What's that?"

"Your buddy Donny Kilmer made a video telling the world that you colluded with him to assassinate Kendrick. That you were part of that mass shooting from the start. If you want to control the narrative after this shit, you're going to need that."

I had no idea I was going to lead with those words until I heard them leave my mouth, the way I was sometimes given a gift in the courtrooms of Harris County in Houston during an inspired cross. But once I knew it was Donny Kilmer who'd been firing from that water tower—and Bobby White who'd shot him off it—some part of me understood that the whole thing had been a Bobby White Special from the beginning. Coincidence to that degree would be well-nigh impossible.

At first Bobby says nothing in reply.

That was my last cast . . .

Either he takes the bait or he doesn't.

TWELVE VERTICAL FEET above her father's head, Annie stood inside the shutters with the dull green sphere in her right hand. She stared down at Bobby White as he eased around the rear of the squad car, being careful to maintain his distance from her father. The grenade was heavier than a baseball. Maybe three times as heavy. She'd studied the pin mechanism, wondering if it would be too complicated for an untrained person to operate. But it was so simple, a first grader could figure it out.

"What are you doing?" Nadine asked from the floor by the wall.

Wounded in the shoulder, Nadine had nevertheless remained on the floor without moving, and Annie worried she was bleeding internally.

"What my dad told me to do."

"Which is what?"

"One-Mississippi, two-Mississippi . . . Is that how you learned to count in school?"

"I think so," Nadine croaked. "I mean, I remember counting like that when I was a kid."

"Do you think people in other parts of the country learn that same way? Or do they say, 'One-Alabama, two-Alabama,' like that?"

Nadine took a few seconds with that one. "I think people from all over use Mississippi. Because of the river, probably."

"Oh. Yeah."

Annie tensed. Down on the ground, Bobby White had taken three quick steps toward the trunk of the police cruiser . . .

I'M CLOSE TO passing out from blood loss when Bobby rises slowly into view on my right, behind the trunk of Chief Morgan's squad car. All I've been able to think about is how binary my choice would be if I really had a choice. The light well is about four feet deep, and runs directly under the steps I'm sitting on, like a four-foot-wide canal beneath a short bridge. If I throw myself off the steps and don't hit my head, then I have a good chance of rolling under the protective concrete before the grenade explodes.

Two seconds would be just about enough time.

In high school I ran sixty yards in six seconds, and I wasn't really fast. But therein lies my problem. A jock like Bobby White can really move. And Bobby was also a soldier. He *trained* with grenades. Even if he doesn't know one is coming, he's practiced reacting to the sight of them. Hell, he probably had Russian grenades used against him in Afghanistan. Real-world experience. If Annie summons the nerve to toss the thing down between us, he'll have the same two seconds I do to reach a nonlethal distance, which I'm guessing is about twenty feet. Bobby could definitely cover that—and more—in that interval of time.

"Hey, Penn," Bobby says, leaning out around the rear fender of the police cruiser. "Man, you look rough."

"I feel worse than I look."

He gives me what appears to be a look of empathy. "Hey . . . did I tell you I saw your bear?"

I blink and look back at him, trying to divine his purpose in asking such a thing in this situation. "No. Where'd you see him?"

"Out at my cabin. Late Tuesday night. He came right up to my deck. I did a kind of test. I set down my gun and closed my eyes . . . gave him a chance to kill me. But he didn't. He let me be, same as he did with you."

"I guess he's leaving us to work out who lives and who dies."

Bobby laughs softly. "Oh, there's no question about that."

"Kendrick's cousin saw a bear at the edge of those trees not long ago. You'd think the gunfire would frighten him off, but an old bear might not be intimidated."

Bobby's gaze drifts over the squad car, back toward Tarlton and Shot Barlow. "I was just thinking . . . about the irony, you know? Out of everybody on this place, you're the one I'd most prefer to have a conversation with. Right? Yet I'm here to kill you."

"You could cancel out that contradiction by keeping that last part in the theoretical realm."

Bobby laughs again. "Yeahhh . . . not really an option." He holds up his hand, which contains a small automatic pistol. "What about that video you mentioned? Donny Kilmer. He really make one implicating me?"

A painful, racking laugh tears through my chest. "Finally scared of something, Bobby?"

"Not exactly. But my plan worked pretty damned well, considering. If I can just keep Donny's mouth permanently shut. But if he's trying to talk from the grave . . ."

"What about your assistant, Corey? Was he down with this politics-as-mass-murder gambit?"

Bobby's face softens for a few seconds, but then he waves his hand in dismissal. If I do have a damning video, he figures it'll be in his possession a few seconds after I'm dead, which should be soon. And if Annie or the others have it, he's relying on their internet jamming to prevent its distribution.

"What are you thinking, Penn?" Bobby asks, his eyes filled with real curiosity. "Seriously. Right now. In this moment."

"Morbid curiosity?"

"Maybe." He slides around the cruiser's fender like a teenager rubbing a spot of wax off his car with his backside. "Are you thinking about your little girl? Your dad, maybe? Good old Tom Cage?" He slides a step farther along the car. "Or are you thinking about that conversation we had earlier? We're about to transition, boy. As a nation. We're at the *fork in the road*. Everybody's gotta pick their side. The funny thing is, what some people don't get—even smart people like you—is that for *this* war, you were born in your uniform."

Bobby's nearly at the cruiser's rear door. Now I need him to step away from the car, toward me—

"You know what I'm really thinking, Bobby? Honestly . . . I can't believe that what brought us to this pass was the greed of one spoiled millennial loser. A fucking video gamer trying to defraud his father's insurance company? That's what takes us to a race war?"

My answer brings a fully engaged smile to Bobby's face. His eyes shine with enjoyment. "As a historian, that's the *easiest* thing for me to accept. As polarized as this country is, it doesn't take much to light the fuse. Martyn was our Gavrilo Princip. Small-scale version."

"Who was our Archduke Ferdinand?"

"Doc Berry? The deacons in the burned church? Was it the antebellum homes themselves? Or will historians look back and say it was Ebony Swan, lynched at sixteen? The funny thing is, here on the ground, it doesn't really matter. The Second Civil War has basically started already."

"You sound happy about it. What's the upside for you, Bobby? Is chaos your path to securing the presidency? And ultimately to post-democratic rule?"

"You *see*?" Bobby says excitedly. "You get it! This evening's shooting didn't work out exactly the way I'd hoped, but I'll still come off the hero. Social media's already filled with clips of my bullet hitting Donny, and him fleeing the water tower."

With sudden energy Bobby pushes off the squad car, then spins and sits beside me on the steps. Were it not for the guns and blood, we might look like two dads shooting the shit after a day's work. His bloody left arm smears my right shoulder. "You think I can have a conversation like this with those idiots back there?"

"I'm surprised you'll sit next to me, Bobby. Take any risk you don't have to."

He pats my knee and laughs softly. "This is no risk for me."

"Why not?"

"You can't kill me, Penn. Not in any scenario."

In the realm of combat, Bobby thinks of me the way he would a child, or a senior citizen. "Are you so sure of yourself?"

More laughter. "Look at us, man! You lost your leg, I lost an arm. I came nearly all the way back in less than a year. But you never did half the rehab you should have done for that leg. Remember me dragging you across the field at Mission Hill? Hell, you can barely walk."

He's right, of course.

"Mentally, we're evenly matched. But given my special ops training...?"

Right again. But underestimating one's adversary is a dangerous mistake, especially when judging the will to fight and die—an error the American military has made more than once.

Today that fuse is truly lit, only Bobby doesn't know it.

The physical geometry is simple. Before us sits the parked squad car, behind us stands the slave quarters door. To my left is unimpeded space, a clear drop to the light well. That way offers life, or seems to. Nadine's baby. My daughter's eventual wedding. Grandchildren. But to my right sits Bobby White. And if he survives this day, those other things will never come to be. *And what other things would take their place?* I wonder. *What future stretches out before this strange and violent man beside me?*

"You didn't answer my question, Bobby."

"I don't even remember it. But listen . . . this war's been brewing since Appomattox. Like World War II after Versailles. You know that. And when it finally breaks into the open—nationwide, I mean—I'll play my role. I was born for this." He turns to me at last, his eyes trying to communicate his sense of destiny. "For that *scale*, you know? Not for sitting in a sterile studio with a microphone and a bunch of angry morons waiting on the phone lines. And when 2027 gets here—that moment of crisis in the elevator—I'll be there to make the right decision. To buy America another eighty-two years. All I have to do is get this scene cleaned up good, lose Lanying's body where it'll never be found, and blame the PSP. I just wish Donny Kilmer hadn't let that damn Kendrick—"

There's no warning when the moment comes.

No scrape of metal on wood from above, no faint sound of Annie murmuring: *One-Mississippi, two-Mississippi.* There's only a brief blur between Bobby and me, like what you see in Little League bleachers when you're not paying attention and the batter fouls a ball past your head.

Bobby's eyes register the blur as the grenade hits his left thigh—

He looks down, freezes, then grabs for the green sphere. But before he can hurl it away, I close my left hand over his, then drive my right arm beneath his shoulder and lock his arm against my chest. He roars like an embattled lion, then sinks his teeth into my neck. I scream in pain, but a shriek from above shreds my scream into background noise. Seconds dilate into eternity as four eyes lock onto the little sphere of death. In a final attempt to escape our fatal embrace, Bobby's last act is to drive his powerful legs to full extension, launching us rightward, toward the dry moat. Spinning in the air, I throw my arms out to break my fall, but there seems no need . . .

The impact never comes.

All the world is consumed in a yellow-white flash.

CHAPTER 122

BOBBY WHITE WAS still alive when Annie reached the bottom of the stairs. She'd seen him twist away from her father in midair, his remarkable athleticism giving him one last chance at life. But the grenade was simply too close. The detonation blew a searing blizzard of shrapnel into his back and left side, shredding him like a shotgun blast, driving him down onto the rim of the light well.

When Annie pulled open the slave quarters' door, she found him staring at the sky. He appeared to have some consciousness that she would be his last sight on the planet. Despite her terror over her father's fate, Annie hesitated, wanting Bobby to register her presence, or maybe the fact that she'd killed him. He didn't. But as she moved to step over him, his eyes refocused, and she felt the mind behind them take her in. Bobby White opened his mouth as though to speak . . . but no words emerged. In his eyes, the life force flickered and burned in bare comprehension of its own ending.

Annie couldn't wait for it to wink out.

All she could think of now was her father. The grenade blast had hurled Penn to the bottom of the dry moat that ran along the edge of the quarters where Calliope had once lived. Now he lay on his side, moaning in pain, the only sign that he still lived. She heard a sudden commotion beyond the squad car, then rifle shots, but she couldn't think how to defend herself against an unknown threat.

Looking up at last, she saw Daniel Kelly standing at the edge of the trees, shirtless, half his weight supported by a splint he'd fashioned from his assault rifle and a tree branch, then belted to his bloody left thigh. Kelly's right hand held a pistol aimed at Tarlton and the remaining deputies. Annie felt as though the outcome were still in doubt until Ray Ransom rose beside the pickup truck, a pistol in his own hand. By this time Shot Barlow lay dead on the dirt, his head a mass of gore. Annie had no knowledge of how that had occurred, but Ray had probably had something to do with it. When Kelly gave Ray a respectful wave, Annie dropped down into the light well and gently turned her father on his back.

"Who's there?" Penn croaked. "Bobby . . . ?"

Annie's face was scarcely a foot above her father's, and his eyes were wide open, yet he seemed unable to see her. "Daddy, it's me. Annie."

"Boo?" he cried, his voice hopeful. "I can't see you. Say something else."

"It's me! I'm right here!" She took his bloody right hand and held it in the warm hollow of her neck.

"I can barely hear you. Ears . . . roaring."

Looking down the length of her father's body, she saw that he too had been riddled with shrapnel. She let out a desolate sob, then choked it down.

"I'm right here," she told him. "Kelly's here, too. He's still alive . . . he's coming."

"Where's Bobby?" Penn asked in a fearful voice, jerking his head left and right.

"He's gone."

"Gone?"

"Dead. Finished. Over."

"Okay . . . okay. Thank God."

A shadow covered Penn's face, then Kelly eased down into the dry moat with a grunt of pain. Jamming a finger under Penn's jaw to check his pulse, he used his other hand to run the length of his friend's body, assessing his wounds.

"What do you think?" Annie whispered.

Kelly grimaced. "Almost no pulse. Gotta be bleeding internally."

"No!"

"I was hoping Bobby took the brunt of the blast, but Penn clearly absorbed a good bit."

"He can't see," she whispered.

"Hey, buddy?" Kelly said, waving his hand above Penn's eyes. "Can you see anything? The sun?"

"Shadow. Left side. Nothing on the right."

Kelly sighed. "Okay. Don't sweat it. That explosion rang your bell, that's all."

"Yeah . . ." Penn swallowed and tried to smile.

"Should I try CPR?" Annie asked.

"Please don't," Penn said. "Seriously. I don't need more broken ribs on top of this shit."

"What about the sheriff's helicopter? Can Tarlton medevac him out?"

"Maybe," Kelly said. "To be honest, I don't think . . ." The veteran operator opened his hand twice and splayed his fingers, which Annie translated as "ten minutes."

"Forget the chopper," Penn said. "If you guys move me, that's it. Let's just rest here, okay? Just a couple minutes."

Annie closed her eyes, expressing tears from the corners.

"Let me ask you something, Penn," Kelly said gently. "If for any reason you don't happen to make it . . . where do you want us to put you? By your mom under that oak tree? Or with Tom, back in Natchez?"

Annie couldn't believe Kelly had asked something so morbid. And yet, she realized, the question would probably be important soon. Given all that they'd learned from Peggy's research, her father might well choose to rest in the Pencarrow land beside his mother. But when he answered, his voice barely above a whisper, he said, "Put me in Mom's original grave . . . next to Dad. That's where I belong. Natchez is still my hometown."

Annie began crying openly. "Gram wrote that in her last letter."

"What?" Kelly asked. "What did Peggy write?"

"*I die in peace because you are your father's son.*"

Kelly nodded. "She had that right. Jesus. Two of a kind."

"I'm still here, goddamn it," Penn groaned. "But Mom was right. I'm cold as hell, by the way."

Kelly chuckled and squeezed his upper arm. "Can't help with that. But we're with you, bud."

Nearly bereft of hope, Annie rose and looked over the rim of the moat, unable to watch her father in such shape as he prepared to pass from the world. As her teary eyes found focus, she realized that she was looking into the eyes of a massive bear standing in the tree line about forty yards northeast of where she stood.

"My God," she breathed, in a combination of awe and terror.

"What is it?" Kelly asked from below.

"It's the bear again! The one Frosty saw earlier, I guess."

"Is it on all fours, or standing?" Penn asked.

"Standing, just like a person. It's staring right at us."

"How big is he?"

"Big as a Mini Cooper, and he looks as old as the hills."

"I knew it. Damn."

"You told Frosty it was a good luck symbol."

"I just wanted to keep Frosty's courage up. Doc told me the good-luck thing, but it didn't help him any. From the beginning I've believed that bear was a messenger of mortality. Mine, to be frank."

"That's superstitious bullshit," Kelly said.

"Maybe, bro. But maybe not. Hey, boo . . . ?"

"I'm here," Annie said, crouching once more and leaning close to her father's lips.

"You've had some bad luck, you know? You lost your mother so young."

Fresh tears poured from Annie's eyes. "It's all right. I can't even remember her, really."

"*I* remember. She loved you so much. I couldn't save her. Nobody could. Not even Papa. Same with Caitlin. But . . . you had some good luck, too, baby."

Annie sobbed openly. "I did. I know I did."

"You're so grown-up now, I can't even believe it."

"I don't feel much like it today."

Penn was still staring skyward, his eyes unfocused. He lifted his right hand, searching for something. "I have to ask a favor, Daniel."

"Oh, man," Kelly muttered. "Don't even." But then he took hold of his friend's bloody hand and squeezed tight. "Don't worry about Annie, brother. I've got her back. You know that."

Hearing this assurance, Penn seemed to settle in relief and resignation. His eyelids slowly closed. As Annie waited for what might be his last words, she slowly became sure that she'd already heard them. This happened much as it had in Edelweiss, when her grandmother had finally ceased breathing. Just as then, a stillness Annie had never witnessed in life slowly took possession of her father. She sensed that all she remembered of their lives together was moving further away, and all that would survive was now within her.

"Is he gone?" she whispered.

"Close." Kelly folded Penn's bloody hands over his chest. "I hate to rush things, but I gotta find a surgeon. Otherwise you'll be burying me beside him."

"We can't have that. I can't lose both of you, damn it!"

"What's that bear doing now?"

Annie rose and scanned the tree line. First she saw no sign of the animal. Then, about fifteen yards from his previous position, she saw the ursa major peering at her from deeper in the shadows. Still standing erect, the bear met her gaze with level intensity for several seconds, but then it looked skyward and froze.

"Can you give me a hand, babe?" Kelly asked, his voice tight with pain.

Annie was helping him out of the light well when two enormous helicopters descended out of the clouds, flared, then settled to earth eighty yards from the slave quarters.

"I guess the FBI finally decided to get off its ass," she said bitterly. "They're about ten minutes and a lifetime too late."

Kelly was shaking his head in wonder. "That's not the FBI. See that insignia? That's the goddamn Tenth Mountain Division! *Jesus.* You know what that means?"

"No. What?"

"Somebody invoked the Insurrection Act! I think the politicians in Washington finally figured out Tennessee isn't the real war zone."

"But . . . isn't it still too late?"

"Shit! Those medics are the best in the world at treating battlefield trauma. They've got plasma expanders, everything! You said you know CPR?"

She nodded, feeling her own heart kick. Glancing north again, she realized that the bear had vanished altogether—unless the black shadow she saw cantering low through the trees was its disappearing form.

"Get down there and start it on your father!" Kelly ordered.

The army vet yanked the walkie-talkie off his belt and tuned it to a new frequency. *"Black Hawk pilots, Tenth Mountain, Black Hawk pilots, this is Sergeant Daniel Kelly, First Special Forces Operational Detachment— Delta. Mayday! Mayday! We have urgent wounded. M67 grenade wounds, eighty meters south of you, the brick building. Mayday! Mayday! M67 wounds! We need your medics. I say again, this is Sergeant Daniel Kelly, Task Force Green. Please respond . . ."*

EPILOGUE

ELEVEN WEEKS HAVE passed since the mass shooting on the Bienville bluff and the pitched battle at Pencarrow. The Tenth Mountain Division remained in Tenisaw County for nine days, and during that period the National Guard was federalized over the objections of the governor and state legislature. Those objections became less vocal as subsequent investigations revealed extensive communications between the capitol, the governor's mansion, and the people in the Donnelly Oil tower penthouse leading up to and during the violence. Thankfully, the NSA possesses transcripts of many of those communications, which reveal not an attempt to minimize the violence, but rather a concerted effort to illegally take over the Black-controlled city government and to consolidate power afterward. NSA recordings—and text messages obtained through FOIA requests—have also implicated officials of the Tenisaw County Board of Supervisors in the attempt to illegally dissolve the City of Bienville.

These investigations were greatly facilitated by former city attorney and "Poker Club" member Arthur Pine, who—after securing a plea deal with the Tenisaw County district attorney—laid a great deal of the blame at the feet of Dixie Donnelly, a Republican fundraiser and the wife of multimillionaire Blake Donnelly.

Digital enhancement of the video shot by high school student Ebony Swan—and a review of relevant cell phone records—revealed that it was Dixie Donnelly on the phone with Deputy Kenneth LeJay while he confronted and shot Mayor Ezra Berry. Cellular records revealed that Donnelly had been in close contact with LeJay over the previous two days, as LeJay followed Mayor Berry everywhere he went. LeJay, who was Donnelly's first cousin, asked his cousin for a "go order" just prior to shooting Mayor Berry five times in the back.

Deputy LeJay himself died by hanging (from a jerry-rigged leather belt) in the Bienville Police Headquarters, but Marshall McEwan lived. After two brain surgeries, he remains in the Methodist Rehabilitation Center in Jackson, re-learning the basic life skills he'd lost to his head injury. His mind, thank God, remains intact. One of the first things Marshall did upon recovering from surgery (and waking from his coma) was to give a deposition stating that Detective Henry Radford, who had been assigned to guard Deputy LeJay, murdered the deputy during the conflict between city and county law enforcement in Bienville. It was Radford who pushed Marshall down the shaft as he tried to prevent the detective from committing this crime.

It was only after I read a detailed article in the *Atlanta Journal-Constitution* that I grasped the full scale of the tragedy that enveloped Bienville in the week after the Mission Hill Massacre. Simply listing the toll of dead and wounded took more space than most newspaper stories. Fifty-eight protesters perished after being shot from the water tower by Donny Kilmer. Of those, fifty-six were Black, many leading figures in the community. Kilmer also wounded 113 people, 109 of them Black.

Related deaths in Bienville included Mayor Ezra "Doc" Berry; high school student Ebony Swan; deacons Duncan Gardner and Kemontrae Woods; attorney Charles "Charlot" Dufort; oil speculator Charles F. Dufort; City of Bienville IT manager Martyn Black; and Amite County Deputy Kenneth LeJay. Casualties from the gun battle at Pencarrow included Tenisaw Rifles militia leader Shotwell Barlow, Arkansas militia leader Baldur Pussett, Tenisaw Rifles militia member Donny Kilmer, rapper Frosty Givens, Chinese refugee Lanying Yan, and Tenisaw County Deputy Kara Mascagni. Also killed at Pencarrow were seven officers of the Bienville Police Department, four deputies of the Tenisaw County Sheriff's Department, and eleven members of the Arkansas militia known as the Poison Springs Provisionals.

By any measure, the events of that final day constituted the opening battle in what amounts to a civil war. Since the arrival of the U.S. Army in Tenisaw County, the internet has largely divided itself between those who believe that the murders instigated by the right-wing faction that included billionaire Charles Dufort, presidential candidate Bobby White, and militia member Donny Kilmer were justified acts in a struggle for the soul of America; and those who believe that this faction represents the greatest threat to America itself—at least as a democracy with a government of, by, and for the people.

In twenty days I will enter University Hospital for what is commonly known as a stem cell transplant. My oncologist would have preferred that it be done sooner, but the gunshot and shrapnel wounds I suffered at Pencarrow damaged several bones, and with my disease those take a long time to heal. I'll be getting my transplant just two hours from home, a vast improvement over the era when I was first diagnosed and only a few centers in the nation even attempted them. Annie and Nadine are scheduling special meals, as well as loading movie and book files on an iPad, to keep me sane during the three to four weeks that I'll be isolated in the transplant unit. Nadine has also sent me a topless photo of her standing with her hands splayed over her stomach to remind me that I now have more than one child to live for, and also more than children.

Since Mission Hill, Annie and Doris have been buried in legal work, but while they've turned down most requests for representation, they made room for the case of Ray Ransom, who was filmed by security cameras at more than one industrial location that was subsequently destroyed by fire. If convicted, Ray will likely spend his final years in prison. After I paid his bail, Ray visited me in University Hospital, where he told me that, even if he's convicted, the blows he struck at those responsible for Doc's death were worth it. He's especially proud of blocking the bridges at Bienville with the oil tanker trucks, which authorities credited with preventing the arrival of two Texas militia convoys on the day of the final clash at Pencarrow. While I have great faith in Doris Avery and my daughter, I whispered to Ray that I would fund any effort he might make to reach a non-extradition country prior to trial. Whatever he did on that final day, Ray Ransom has unjustly spent too many years of his life in prison already.

Sheriffs Buck Tarlton and Coy Johnson have already been fired by the governor, in an attempt to scapegoat county-level officials for the political scheme in which the chief executive was a co-conspirator. While the governor remains in office, his chances of being named VP on any Republican presidential ticket have evaporated.

In the wake of Doc's murder, a special election has been scheduled for the office of mayor. It will be held two days before I enter the transplant unit. Mayor Pro Tem Vivian Paine has tossed her hat into the ring, as has freshman alderman Robert Gaines. I've thrown considerable support behind Gaines, knowing that Joe Dunphy would have vociferously approved this expenditure.

The most shocking surprise to come out of the ten days following the Mission Hill massacre was the revelation of Bobby White's true nature and activities. The military hero universally embraced by the American public turned out to be what the lover who knew him better than anyone else had declared him to be—a monster. Between the revelations of Corey Evers and those of a twenty-three-year-old dollar-store cashier named Britney Spillers (who emerged as Donny Kilmer's girlfriend), it became clear that Robert E. Lee White had not only murdered General Paul Beckley, but also conspired with Kilmer to plan assassination attempts on both Ezra Berry and Kendrick Washington, as well as the mass shooting on the bluff, so that Bobby might play the role of hero on a thousand cell phone cameras. What has haunted me from time to time in the weeks since Bobby's death is how fast some of his predictions began to come true. Within twenty-eight hours of him taking his last breath, Hamas—supported by Iran—breached the borders of Israel (supposedly the most vigilant state on earth) and began the most vicious and deadly massacre since the Holocaust. Bobby White would not have been the least surprised.

As for Kendrick Washington, the hero of Mission Hill, early on I heard a rumor that he might run for mayor, but Kendrick dispelled this notion when he visited me in the hospital. For now, he's continuing his heritage tours of Bienville—occasionally wearing his chains for special occasions— but he's considering several offers from production companies that want to make a streaming series based on his life.

ON THE DAY I was released from the hospital after treatment for my wounds, Annie and I paid a visit to Belle Rose, where Sophie Dufort has been living since the deaths of her father and brother. The death of the patriarch had been declared the result of a violent altercation between Charles Dufort and his driver, Amadu, over money. A half dozen contradictory rumors spread across town, but since the story of a financial dispute had been put forth by Sophie—and the subsequent violence between the two men attested to by both Pearl and Ruby Brooks—the D.A. accepted it. I'd heard that Sophie put Belle Rose on the market on the day her father was buried, and that she might be moving out of town once it sells. I wasn't sure what those facts implied about her state of mind, but I did know the news that we carried would send her into depression, if not outright fury. Annie had been busy while I was in the hospital, and she'd uncovered a great deal of information that my mother would have loved to know (and any Duforts would have preferred to remain buried until the end of time).

Sophie greeted us from the great desk in her father's study, and I couldn't help thinking how much she looked like Charles sitting behind it. She radiated power and self-possession, and of course, by then, thanks to the wealth she'd inherited, she did possess considerable influence.

At least for the time being.

"I'm so glad to see you out of the hospital," she said with a smile.

"Thanks. You probably won't be in a few minutes. We've got some news for you, and I doubt any of it will be welcome. But you need to know it. So that you'll understand what's likely coming at you."

Sophie took a deep breath and settled her hands on the desk. "All right. Let's hear it."

"It's best if Annie tells you. She's the one who uncovered most of it."

Sophie nodded for my daughter to begin.

"First," Annie began, "the whole Dufort family history is basically a historic deception. The story that your namesake sympathized with the Union and supported Lincoln for moral reasons? That's bullshit. He did that because he thought secession would destroy the sugar industry, which could wipe out his Louisiana holdings. We know now that the Charles Dufort of that era spent most of the war selling contraband cotton to the enemy, but not to help Lincoln or the Union army—and certainly not to help the South. He lived for profit and power, nothing else. He was buried up to his neck in corruption, and tied in heavily with Union General Benjamin Butler and Lorenzo Thomas. They protected his holdings from their own armies throughout the war. Of course, even President Lincoln wanted the Southern cotton economy functioning during the war, and so encouraged a certain amount of this trade. But your ancestor didn't give a damn about that. As best we can discover, he multiplied his net worth twenty-fold between 1861 and 1865. And how he did that . . ."

Sophie shifted slowly on her seat. Then, in an icy tone, she said, "And where did you get this information?"

"Partly from the journals and diaries of one of our ancestors, Evelyn Pencarrow. Ironically, the fire that destroyed the Pencarrow mansion uncovered those sources in an old lockbox. Evelyn was in business with your ancestor. She was in with Shot Barlow's people as well."

Sophie held up her hand for Annie to pause. Gathering herself as though for an argument, she said, "What's the point of this, Penn? It's ancient history."

"Not exactly. You'll understand in a minute. See, your father's namesake fancied one of our ancestors. A mixed-race woman named Calliope."

"I remember her bust from the dinner at Pencarrow."

"That's her. Well, after Robert Pencarrow died, his daughter Evelyn took her chance to get revenge on the Black—or mulatto, actually—woman who had displaced her mother. To that end, she sold Calliope and her daughter Niobe south to a slave owner at Seven Oaks Plantation in Louisiana. But before she delivered them, she gave Calliope to your ancestor for a month, to have his way with her, in exchange for something she badly wanted."

"I thought you said she did it for revenge."

"Not revenge alone. Evelyn was obsessed with clinging to what remained of her father's status and fortune. In exchange for some weeks with Calliope, she got your ancestor to handle all sales of *her* contraband cotton crop as well as his own. So rather than keeping only twenty-five percent of the value of her crop, she got close to one hundred percent—just as the Charles Dufort of that era did. Your ancestor got these terms through his connection with General Butler, and occasionally by trading under buying licenses signed by President Lincoln himself. The amounts were staggering. Anyway . . . by forcing Calliope into your ancestor's bed, *our* ancestor earned a great deal of money. She did something similar by renting Calliope's daughter, an enslaved girl named Niobe, to Shotwell Barlow's ancestor for about a month during the prelude to the siege of Vicksburg, an ordeal she nearly didn't survive. But I'm getting sidetracked. That's not why we've come today."

Sophie's exasperation was quite clear. "I'm still confused about why you have come."

"Did you ever know about the Second Creek lynchings at Natchez? And the Black Oak lynchings that happened afterward, near Bienville?"

"I heard a lecture about the Natchez lynchings once."

"Well, it turns out your family was at the center of that story, too."

"That's crazy. My family had nothing to do with those killings."

"On the contrary. We're now certain that the Charles Dufort of that era was the man who secretly pushed for the formation of the Vigilance Committee that carried out all the torture and hangings after the outbreak of war. Not only of the fifty or so slaves hanged in September of '61, but the more than two hundred hanged between '61 and '63, when Union forces finally occupied Bienville and Natchez."

"Why in God's name would he do that?"

"The simplest reason in the world. Greed. He knew a lot of slaves were thinking about fleeing the plantations—hundreds had bolted from the area already—and he was unwilling to sustain those losses. He first tried bribing his slaves with cash, but he soon discovered that enslaved workers didn't care much about money. Not even when he offered them half the value of the crop. So Dufort raised the stakes. If money wouldn't motivate them, he figured, fear would. So he started the rebellion panic, and the lynchings. That allowed him to plant and harvest his cotton even in wartime, which he could then sell on the black market for obscene amounts of money. Mass murder kept the money flowing, and your ancestor was fine with that. Your ancestor was basically a drug dealer, Sophie, only cotton then was worth more than any drug ever was, in relative terms."

She slid her chair back with a screech, her face pale with fury. "Why have you come here with this shit?"

"We'll get to that in a minute," Annie said. "But my research has also revealed that your ancestor's desire to rape Calliope was no isolated incident. He made pretty free with the women of color he owned, as well as some women enslaved by other planters. Some of those were *productive* couplings, Ms. Dufort. It also seems to have been a habit perpetuated by his offspring, through the Jim Crow era and onward. So far, I've discovered more than one hundred and eighty people of color who are almost certainly descended from your ancestors. And *that* has thrown a lot of doubt on the chain of inheritance going back up the line in your family tree."

"Maybe you've heard about the Barlow lawsuits?" I interjected. "By the time that's over, and they finish passing out plots to the rightful heirs and assigns, Shot Barlow's white heirs aren't likely to inherit more than two acres in their own names."

"Get out of my house."

"It all depends on how the wills were written," I tell her. "But that's quite a few wills, and Annie has already uncovered some irregularities."

My daughter smiles.

Sophie got up from her father's old desk and paced a circle around it. Then she stopped and looked down at us. "Why are you doing this, Penn? You're not doing it to *him*, you know. You're doing it to *me*. You want to take everything I might inherit after all these years of waiting?"

"It's really got nothing to do with you, Sophie."

Her face went scarlet. "It's got everything to do with me!"

I shook my head sadly.

Annie started to go on, but I stopped her by raising my hand. "I'm afraid the crimes weren't limited to the 1850s. Your father almost certainly committed murder in 1968, by killing a young Black girl named Shondra Williams. But I suspect you know that already. Since he's dead, that doesn't matter much in a legal sense. I know this is hard for you, Sophie."

"Do you?"

"Yes. But as the saying goes, we reap what we sow. The hell you're about to go through is courtesy of your father, not us."

"Get out, Penn. Please."

I figured we'd accomplished what we'd set out to, or at least most of it.

I raised my hand in farewell, not looking at Sophie as I turned. "We'll find our own way out."

"Have a *blessed* day," Annie told her.

WHILE PREPARING FOR my transplant, I've been living at Edelweiss, something I thought I would never do after the murder of my fiancée.

But I've come back to my town at last.

Natchez.

Despite the difficulty of the long staircase, I write on the third floor of the old chalet. I may be blind in one eye now, but I can still see fourteen miles of the Mississippi River from my window, and that makes the exertion worth it. I keep my desk at the center of the room, which is sparsely furnished. It contains my desk, an electric wheelchair, an iMac Pro, a bookshelf, and a long, handmade table that holds a few mementos of the people who meant the most to me, but who are now gone.

My mother left me several personal items, but what I've kept in this room is the cotton sack dating to the 1930s, which she probably used when she did her picking. Ten feet long and two feet wide, it'll hold a hundred pounds of bolls, and she began filling a smaller one like it when she was three. When I feel tired from writing, I remember that.

From the other side of my family I have an iron froe that Andrew McKinney dug up on the grounds of Pencarrow. Though I'll never know for sure, I like to think it's the one Romulus used to brain the rapacious overseer, Gilmer Book. Along with the froe, Andrew gifted me his most treasured artwork—the bust of Calliope, my maternal ancestor. Andrew once called this sculpture the soul of Pencarrow, and he's right. The house itself may be gone, but Calliope remains, and the house remains within her, in the very wood. I tried to persuade Andrew to keep the bust, but he refused, though he did accept the painted locket he'd used as his muse and model.

Calliope now sits on the table beneath my window, facing me at a slight off-angle, so I won't feel her gaze too heavily. Even so, I sometimes sense a certain pressure from her as I ponder history. I often think of Romulus and his desperate winter swim to the Union gunboat, and his near death after the sinking of *Sultana* four years later. I've read the testament he dictated to his grandson a hundred times, and something from the last couple of pages has never left me.

In 1936 Romulus's grandson asked him how he felt about how the world had changed for "colored people," and how he thought it was likely to change in the future. Romulus's answer sounded typical of the time, and did not surprise me. But then the grandson asked him—a man saved from drowning by a Union soldier bearing a coffin—how he felt about white people in general. Romulus's answer haunts me to this day.

"Oh, there's good white folks out there," he said. "And when you deal with 'em by themselves, they'll treat you just like a brother. In fact, I wouldn't be alive today without one or two. But when you deal with 'em in groups . . . things change. I don't know why that is, but they do."

"But you have no ill feelings against white people in general?" his grandson pressed.

"How can I answer that, boy? I'm more than half-white myself! Yet all my life I been nothing but Black. One drop, right? The truth is, all people are good *and* bad. There ain't many saints in this world, regardless of color. I've known white people good as anybody. Generous, kind, compassionate. There just ain't quite enough of 'em."

There just ain't quite enough of 'em.

I think about that a lot. I think about how Black people must feel when they take a DNA test and discover that they have a significant percentage of "white" blood—almost certainly the result of rape in their family's past. What gives me empathy for them is not my discovery that I have a percentage of "Black" blood, but that I'm partly descended from Shotwell Barlow of Black Oak Plantation. To know that my mother, Annie, and I are links in the chain of generations issuing from the "rape camp" set up by Barlow during his regiment's resistance to U. S. Grant's Yazoo Pass expedition is difficult to bear. I've tried telling myself that it's nurture, not nature, that most influences what we become. But then I think about Black Oak Plantation, where five generations after the Civil War, Barlow's heir and namesake remained a ruthlessly cruel son of a bitch until the moment Ray Ransom blew his brains out. Strong genes, apparently. I only wish I'd gotten to kill Barlow myself, for Niobe's sake. But as the descendant of Doby Freeman, who drowned himself to protect his friends from the noose, Ray deserved the honor more.

I also think about Romulus's testament when I get mail from readers asking why I keep "dragging up unpleasant history." They often ask—or rather demand—to know what the "point" is. Most of all they wonder when we will "get past" slavery. The truth is, they're already past it. They'd never even have thought about it unless forced to. What they really want to know is when *Black people* will be "past it." They'd prefer to have a date to look forward to, so they can stop worrying about it. I could give a glib answer, like "They'll get past it the day the Jews 'get past' the Holocaust."

But that won't help anybody.

The book I'm writing now is the one my mother asked me to set aside, the one about the wartime lynchings. (When I say "wartime" these days, I mean the Civil War, just like everybody else around here.) When I began, I believed there had been about fifty murders; now I suspect there were 211. What's hardest to accept is that the lessons I've learned while writing this book—predominantly about white panic and greed, and the violence that often results—are so readily applicable to the world we live in 160 years later. But there's no denying it.

So I study, and reflect, and I write what comes. I do so knowing that my blood is betraying me as I work; thanks to malignant plasma cells, sooner rather than later I will join the train of forebears who preceded Annie and me. But now she will not carry on alone. Nadine is carrying a son, something I've never had before. I intend to have as many years with him as I can get. I will fight as hard for life as my mother did, so that in more ways than his genes that boy—whom we have already named—will carry the legacy of Tom Cage into the future. The world needs more of those traits: courage, compassion, honesty, humility. I rest easier knowing that once I'm gone, Annie and Nadine will carry on preparing him for this painful world.

Nadine has asked whether I intend to retire after I finish "the lynching book." I told her that writers never really retire. As a bookstore owner, she knows that, but she probably hopes for an exception to the rule. The question is really more germane to my second career, which has never really had a name. I know I still have that second (or third or fourth) vocation, because a lot of people have come up to Edelweiss to talk to me over the past few weeks. White people. Black people. Desperate people, most of them. Victims, usually, or relatives of victims. All come searching for help. Some want legal help; others want a different kind. I don't practice law anymore. I haven't really practiced for nineteen years. As for the other things I sometimes do—with the help of Daniel Kelly, who is still recovering from the terrible wound he sustained in the Pencarrow battle—only time will tell, I suppose. I'm no longer able to take on the corrupt and brutal among us the way I once did the Double Eagles. But, thankfully, I've found that there's usually someone like Ray Ransom willing to step in and handle the physical challenges.

For now, though, I simply write, and think about my mother deciding that she had no way to penetrate the mind behind Calliope's eyes. I think about Calliope lying with a man whose father owned her, and producing the children who would ultimately produce me. I think about her starving herself to death rather than submitting to the master of Seven Oaks Plantation. I long to plumb the dark gulfs between her childhood and the relative safety of her years with Captain Pencarrow, and the hopeless hell where her life ended, but I have no way to do that. And yet . . . Calliope is not the impenetrable mystery at the heart of this story.

Niobe is.

I cannot tally the hours I've spent pondering the dilemmas she faced. Born in peace, she came of age during war. Born enslaved, she was tied by blood to her enslavers. Her white father loved her, yet he did not obtain her freedom from his father. Her white brother loved her, but her white sister did all she could to destroy her. (Evelyn's journals reveal the savage joy she took at Niobe's deprivation and defilement. She even asked Shot Barlow for details of the wartime rape camp. This made me wish many times that Romulus had succeeded in killing her on the afternoon she shot him.) Niobe watched her mother—a strong woman—sink by choice into the darkness of the grave. But the choice Niobe made for herself must have been harder still. Maybe not at first, when she was threatened from all sides. But in the end, surely. She broke the heart of a heroically strong man—her brother—by vanishing into the true heart of darkness, which for him was whiteness.

My mother wanted to find some hidden truth that would explain how the mixed-race children of Robert Pencarrow and the enslaved Calliope became the "white" family from which descended Peggy, Penn, and Annie Cage. But the awful reality is that, while Romulus's life has historical existence (tangible records and "secret" context provided by Romulus's testament to his descendants), Niobe's life has none. Niobe Pencarrow, the half-Black enslaved girl, disappeared into the whiteness of the Thorn family in Quitman Parish, Louisiana, in 1865, and from that blankness she never emerged. So far as I know, none of her descendants—until the present generation—ever learned the truth. Her old life only intersected with the world twice more that I know about.

I learned about those incidents from the papers that Nadine and Annie discovered in the strongbox hidden in the Pencarrow chimney. Once the contents finally dried sufficiently to be cataloged and examined—five days after Bobby White died—we found that one of the books inside was a handwritten diary kept by Evelyn Pencarrow. I won't dwell on the sins it contained (which were many), and I've gone on too long to detail the events here. I'll say only that in 1913, Niobe traveled to Mississippi and confronted the elderly Evelyn Pencarrow in order to gain some legal protection for her first child, a daughter named Phoebe—something she could use to defend Phoebe should anyone ever make the charge that she was not fully white. To gain what she needed—something Evelyn resisted giving—Niobe made a threat that could not be countered, and thus went home with her daughter safer than when they'd crossed the river.

Finally, Niobe was also threatened by the husband of the Creole woman whose name she had appropriated when fleeing Pencarrow—Helen Soileau. A criminal of the lowest order, Soileau traveled to Quitman Parish with blackmail on his mind. But he did not leave with any money from Niobe. In fact, my research suggests that he likely never left Quitman Parish at all. Like her mother, Niobe was a formidable woman.

I end this tale with Niobe because, while Romulus Pencarrow lived an almost legendary life, and has been celebrated for it, it's Niobe from whom my family descended. But when I try to follow the path backward from us to her, there simply isn't one. After 1865, the traumatized young woman who did more than anyone to ensure that one day Annie and I would exist ceased to exist herself, in her quest to be sure that her first child would survive. In my view, Niobe committed a form of suicide. Racial suicide, though scientists tell us that race does not exist. By so doing, she survived, if within the "she" that remained, her true identity lived on. Given the characters of two of her descendants—my mother and daughter—I choose to believe that it did.

You ask me when we will "get past" slavery?

Here is my answer: After Niobe tells us her story, and we acknowledge it as true . . .

Then we shall be free.

ACKNOWLEDGMENTS

───────

This novel was written under the most uniquely stressful circumstances of my career. Most trying was the experience of writing while undergoing chemotherapy. I mention this because so many people named below went above and beyond the call of duty to help make this book possible.

I want to particularly thank Dr. Jack Rodriguez, Heather Covington, Rachael Lambert, and all the staff at Natchez Oncology Clinic. My thanks also to Dr. Stephanie Elkins and all the doctors, nurses, and staff at the University of Mississippi Medical Center Bone Marrow Transplant Unit. Closer to home, I thank my father's younger colleagues, now in their prime (or close!) who stepped forward in time of need to help make this book possible: Drs. Lee England, Vikramaditya Dulam, Randy Tillman, and Akinremi Akinwale. Thanks also to my good friends Dr. Rod Givens, Dr. Aaron Smith, and Dr. Kellen Jex for their generous off-duty help. Finally, to all nurses and staff at Merit Health Natchez, as well as the first responders who helped in acute crises.

At William Morrow/HarperCollins: Thank you Liate Stehlik, Emily Krump, David Highfill, Tavia Kowalchuk, Danielle Bartlett, and everybody up and down the chain who made *Southern Man* possible! Thanks also to Dan Conaway at Writers House for helping to negotiate unpredictable times. Special thanks to Ed Stackler, who's been with me since he first discovered *Spandau Phoenix* in 1991. This one took a hell of a march to make it!

For all things Natchez—and history-related: Mimi Miller, Mayor Tony

Acknowledgments

Byrne, Sheriff Travis Patten, Deborah Cosey, Tony Fields, Mayor Darryl Grennell, Keshia Mitchell, and Denzel Fort (a bright, young talent gone too soon: may he rest in power).

For legal insight and so much more: Scott Slover, Jill Collen Jefferson (check out julianfreedom.org), Madeline Iles, Mark Iles, and Mike Mac-Innis.

For political insights and eclectic expertise: Sidney Blumenthal, Stuart Stevens, Michelle Barry, James McBride, Stanley Nelson, Jerry Mitchell, James Wiggins, Courtney and Terri Aldridge, James Schuchs, Sarah Carter Smith, Mark Brockway, Lantz Foster, and the published works of Robert Penn Warren (the GOAT).

Finally, for the incalculable hassle of keeping me going: Caroline Hungerford, Geoff Iles, Nancy Hungerford, Betsy Iles, and Jane Hargrove. For the chicken pot pies: Tracy Henry.

All mistakes are mine.